PENGUIN CLASSICS

PENGUIN ENGLISH POETS
GENERAL EDITOR: CHRISTOPHER RICKS

ALEXANDER POPE: THE ILIAD OF HOMER

ALEXANDER POPE was born in London in 1688. His family were Roman Catholics and in 1700 they moved to Binfield, in Windsor Forest, probably in conformity with anti-Catholic legislation. A precocious boy, he was briefly at one or two Catholic schools but mostly studied at home. When he was about twelve he had the first of several illnesses which left him with ruined health and finally a tubercular spine, though he continued his intensive reading and writing. In May 1709 Pope's *Pastorals* were published, which drew him some fame. A major work, *An Essay on Criticism*, a brilliant statement of neoclassical critical principles, appeared in 1711. In 1712 he published the first version of 'The Rape of the Lock'; this masterpiece of mock-heroic technique starts as a joke arising from a natural incident, but contains some very powerful, even tragic, poetry. A collection of his works, preserving all he thought worthy of his earlier poetry, was published in 1717. For ten years Pope worked on his translation of the *Iliad* (6 volumes, 1715–20) and for a further three (with assistants) on the *Odyssey* (5 volumes, 1725–6). The proceeds from his translations of Homer added considerably to Pope's financial independence, and from 1719 he lived in Twickenham, where he spent much of his time improving the garden he often refers to in his writing. He became embroiled in the literary in-fighting of the time, and in 1728 the first 'Dunciad' heralded his later career as the principal satirist of the age. Associated with the satirical passages in the 'Dunciad' are the 'Imitations of Horace', which contain some of Pope's most concentrated wit and virtuoso writing in conversational and other varied couplets. As well as being the major poet of the eighteenth century, Pope was also a very considerable critic and a brilliant letter writer. He died in 1744.

STEVEN SHANKMAN was educated at the University of Texas at Austin, Trinity College, Cambridge, and Stanford University. He has taught at Princeton, Columbia, and Harvard universities and is currently Professor of English and Classics at the University of Oregon (Eugene) and Director of the Oregon Humanities Center. He is the author of *Pope's Iliad: Homer in the Age of Passion* (1983) and *In Search of the Classic: Reconsidering the Greco-Roman Tradition, Homer to Valéry and Beyond* (1994).

The Iliad of Homer
Translated by Alexander Pope

EDITED BY STEVEN SHANKMAN

PENGUIN BOOKS

PENGUIN BOOKS

Published by the Penguin Group
Penguin Books Ltd, 27 Wrights Lane, London w8 5TZ, England
Penguin Books USA Inc., 375 Hudson Street, New York, New York 10014, USA
Penguin Books Australia Ltd, Ringwood, Victoria, Australia
Penguin Books Canada Ltd, 10 Alcorn Avenue, Toronto, Ontario, Canada M4V 3B2
Penguin Books (NZ) Ltd, 182–190 Wairau Road, Auckland 10, New Zealand

Penguin Books Ltd, Registered Offices: Harmondsworth, Middlesex, England

This edition first published 1996
1 3 5 7 9 10 8 6 4 2

Set in 9.5/11.5pt Monotype Ehrhardt
by Datix International Limited, Bungay, Suffolk
Printed in England by Clays Ltd, St Ives plc

For Melissa and Emily

Contents

The Iliad of Homer, translated by Alexander Pope

Acknowledgements

I am grateful to Howard Erskine-Hill, David Foxon, and Maynard Mack for taking the time to discuss with me the problems of editing Pope's *Iliad*. I very much appreciate their continued generosity in responding so fully to my detailed questions about editing Pope.

Christopher Ricks, the General Editor of this series, was a constant source of prudent, meticulous, and promptly offered advice.

I have benefited as well from the sympathetic ear and knowledgeable editorial skills of William Rossi. James Earl read an early draft of the Introduction and Note on the Style of Pope's *Iliad* and offered excellent criticisms. Richard Heinzkill and James Fox (now of the University of Michigan) of the Knight Library at the University of Oregon and Stephen Ferguson of Princeton's Firestone Library were very helpful, as were the staff of the Humanities Research Center at the University of Texas at Austin, of the Woodson Collection of the Rice University Library, and of the British Library. Particular thanks are due to Clifford Mead, Head of Special Collections at the Oregon State University Library. I am very grateful to him for allowing me to borrow the copy of the 1743 edition of Pope's *Iliad* that I used as the basis for this Penguin edition.

I would like to express my appreciation to the University of Oregon for enabling me to work on this edition with the help of a Summer Research Award, grants from the Stewart Fund, and financial support that allowed me to employ research assistance. The second grant from the Stewart Fund and grants from the Vice-Provost for Research and the English Department of the University of Oregon allowed me to employ the efficient and poetically sensitive services of Steven Shurtleff, who was an invaluable resource in many ways. He helped me to proofread, to compose the Glossary, to track down and translate many of the passages from Greek and Latin in Pope's notes, and to collate the 1743 edition with the first-edition folio and with many of the readings from the first duodecimo edition. I am grateful to Mary Jaeger, Nathaniel Kernell, and Mary Kuntz for generously giving me the time to consult with them about how best to translate some of the Latin quotations in Pope's commentary.

I should also thank the National Endowment for the Humanities for awarding me a Travel to Collections Grant so that I could work in the British Library.

Introduction

Why read Pope's *Iliad* today? Are there not available, for those who have denied themselves the pleasures of Greek, more accessible versions of the poem, recent translations that do not place such a formidable stylistic barrier between Homer and the contemporary reader?

First, Pope's *Iliad* is one of the greatest verse translations in the English language. Samuel Johnson was less restrained. He called Pope's *Iliad* 'the greatest version [translation] of poetry which the world has ever seen' and declared that 'its publication must therefore be considered as one of the great events in the annals of learning'.[1] More recently, George Steiner remarked: 'Informed literacy is far from allowing the fact – yet surely it is obvious – that Pope's *Iliad* is a masterpiece in its own right and an epic which, as far as English goes, comes second only to Milton.'[2] Pope's version should be tried because it offers – in many ways more successfully than any other version of the *Iliad* in English – an answerable style to Homer's stately, formal, and yet readable (perhaps it would be more accurate to say listenable) dactylic hexameter.

Second, any edition of Pope's poetry that does not include his *Iliad* gives an incomplete account of the poet's achievement. For Pope spent his formative years as a poet translating Homer, first the whole of the *Iliad*, then much of the *Odyssey*, as well as overseeing the work of his helpers Fenton and Broome. It was the success of the *Iliad* translation that made him the first English man of letters, who was not a professional dramatist, to be able to support himself on what he earned from his own writings. Pope, then, owed a good deal to Homer, and not merely his Twickenham villa that allowed him to live his *vita Horatii* on his English Sabine farm. For those years of living on a daily basis with Homer's verse would have an effect on much of his own

1. From the *Life of Pope* in *Lives of the English Poets*, ed. G. B. Hill, 3 vols. (Oxford: Clarendon Press, 1905), III, 119.
2. *The Times Literary Supplement*, 16 November 1982, p. 1259.

original poetry. Homer would provide him with themes, tropes, ideas about structure and ideas about style, and much else. Pope as a Homeric translator and commentator responded to Achilles' wrath with an empathy that you do not find in the often moralistic pronouncements of his predecessors in the fields of Homeric translation and commentary. It is perhaps therefore no coincidence that the poet who spent a decade or so of his life – from his early twenties to his early thirties – responding critically but empathetically to Achilles would derive much of the poetry of his later life from his own anger at perceived injustice.

This Edition

The first edition of Pope's *Iliad* was published in six volumes (both quarto and folio) between 1715 and 1720. The subsequent editions of Pope's *Iliad* published during Pope's lifetime are the following, as listed in R. H. Griffith, *Alexander Pope: A Bibliography*:[3]

  1720: Volumes I–VI, duodecimo. For Bernard Lintot.
  1720: 6 vols., duodecimo. Printed by Bowyer, for Lintot.
  1720–21: Vols. I–III, duodecimo. 'The Second Edition'.
  1721: Vols. IV–VI, duodecimo. 'The Second Edition'. Volumes
    III, IV, and VI were printed by J. Bettenham; Volume V by
    W. Hunter.[4]
  1732: 6 vols., duodecimo. 'The Third Edition'. Although Vol.
    III is dated 1731.
  1736: 6 vols. Woodfall for Lintot.
  1743: 6 vols. Henry Lintot.

I have used the 1743 edition, which contains Pope's final revisions, as the basis for this Penguin edition. I have collated the 1743 edition with the first-edition folio and I have also consulted the textual variants cited in the Twickenham Edition.[5]

Anyone who attempts to edit Pope's *Iliad* in the wake of the

---

3. (Austin: University of Texas Press, 1922–6), 2 vols., I, 91.

4. I obtained this information about which volumes were printed by Bettenham and which by Hunter from the British Library; this information is not given in Griffith.

5. *The Twickenham Edition of the Poems of Alexander Pope*, General Editor John Butt, 11 vols. (London and New Haven: Methuen & Co. Ltd and Yale University Press, 1938–68).

monumental Twickenham Edition owes an enormous debt to the accuracy and erudition of that edition, which is unfortunately (in late 1994) out of print. Such an editor is also obliged to make clear the ways in which his or her edition will differ from the Twickenham Edition, which is now rightly considered the standard edition of Pope's *Iliad*. My choice of the 1743 edition as the basis for this Penguin edition requires some explanation, since it has been common practice in editing to use a first edition as copy-text, as the Twickenham editors preferred, or even a manuscript, if it exists in the author's own hand. The rationale for printing a manuscript is that it is closest to the author's intentions. This is not the case for Pope, since we know that he worked closely with his printers and corrected proofs. These corrected proofs, judging from those which survive,[6] have authorial sanction and often differ from the manuscripts.

The rationale for printing a first edition is that it, similarly, accurately reflects the author's intentions and that errors will inevitably creep into later editions. It may be true, as Maynard Mack has argued in the introduction to the Twickenham Edition, that the revisions in the later editions of Pope's *Iliad* published during the translator's lifetime 'are in fact disappointingly limited, unsystematic, [and] desultory, especially after the first duodecimo edition of 1720. Even there one is obliged to wonder how many of the more trifling alterations such as *and* to *or*, *'em* to *them* (and vice versa), come from the compositor's hand rather than the author's.'[7] Mack goes on to remark, in regard to the minor alterations in the prose notes, that 'continuance of a reading from the duodecimo edition of 1720 through the duodecimo of 1743 proves little about its authority in a body of prose that it is plain the author never systematically corrected'. But the revisions – however unsystematic and minor – in both the poetic text and the prose sections were made and, in Mack's and in Samuel Johnson's opinion, they appear to be Pope's. As Johnson writes in his *Life of Pope*:

His declaration, that his care for his works ceased at their publication, was not strictly true. His parental attention never abandoned them; what he found was

---

6. See Robert M. Schmitz, 'The "Arsenal" Proof Sheets of Pope's *Iliad*: A Third Report', *Modern Language Notes* 74 (1959), 486–9. Here Schmitz argues (based on an advertisement in *The Post-Boy*, 25–28 June), that the publication date cited by Griffith for the folio of 10–15 June needs to be revised to 30 June (488). See also Norman Callan, 'Pope's *Iliad*: A New Document', *Review of English Studies*, N.S. IV (1953), 109–21.

7. *The Twickenham Edition of the Poems of Alexander Pope*, VII (ed. Mack *et al.*), xix.

amiss in the first edition, he silently corrected in those that followed. He appears to have revised the *Iliad*, and freed it from some of its imperfections.[8]

Despite Professor Mack's remarks about the limited extent of Pope's alterations and despite his reservations about how many of the more minor changes were the work of Pope himself, he generally incorporates these alterations into the Twickenham Edition, including the alterations introduced into the 1743 edition that I have used as the basis for this Penguin edition. Whereas the Twickenham Edition used the first edition quarto (published in six volumes between 1715 and 1720) as copy-text, I have relied upon the last edition printed in Pope's lifetime. I have done so for two reasons. First, the 1743 edition includes Pope's final revisions.[9] Second, the printing style of this edition – as with the first duodecimo printing of his *Iliad* in 1720 – reflects, with regard to accidentals, Pope's desire to modernize his text. More specifically, in the 1743 edition Pope, as in the earlier duodecimos, drops the systematic capitalization of all common nouns that characterizes the first edition (both quarto and folio).

As David Foxon has recently argued in *Pope and the Early Eighteenth-Century Book Trade*, Pope pioneered a more modern style of printing with regard to the use of (1) initial capital letters in common nouns, and (2) italics. It is the first that concerns us here, for the first edition of the *Iliad* uses italics only for proper nouns and not

---

8. *Lives of the English Poets*, ed. Hill, III, 221.

9. In a letter written in 1742, Pope says that he hopes Warburton will look over the Preface to the *Iliad* and the *Essay on Homer* (the latter, written by Thomas Parnell, is not included in this Penguin edition) and suggest what might be 'amended: there being a new Edition preparing, in which I would alter any Errors I can'. In a letter dated 4 June 1742, Pope again asks Warburton to help him correct the *Essay on Homer*. On 18 July 1742 Pope thanks Warburton for his help with these two prose pieces that introduce his *Iliad* and mentions, 'What I could correct, in the dissipated life I am forced to lead here, I have; & some there are which still want your help to be made as they should be' (*The Correspondence of Alexander Pope*, ed. George Sherburn, 5 vols. [Oxford: Clarendon Press, 1956], IV, 384, 400, 403). While Pope may not have systematically corrected proofs (as he did for at least some of the volumes of the first edition) of what was to be the last version of his *Iliad* published in his lifetime, he certainly indicates here that he intended to revise the work. In using this last edition, I am following the suggestion of David Foxon, *Pope and the Early Eighteenth-Century Book Trade* (Oxford: Clarendon Press, 1991), revised and edited by James McLaverty. Foxon argues against the orthodoxy of using the first editions of Pope's works as copy-texts and says that 'If we return to the old textual principle of following the last edition revised by the author, we can see that here it has considerable merit – though, of course, we would not follow it blindly into error' (226).

for emphasis, such as we find, for example, in the first edition of the *Essay on Criticism* (1711).[10] Beginning with the 1720 duodecimo edition, Pope in his *Iliad* abandoned the routine capitalization of the first letter of every noun. As one printer wrote, a 'prodigious number of Capitals . . . disfigures the page, by an abuse introduced, thro' want of taste, into English books more than any other'.[11] The practice of abandoning the routine capitalization of nouns is continued in the duodecimo reprintings of the *Iliad* as well as in the editions (including the first edition, 1725–6) of the *Odyssey*. This change from capitalizing every noun to a more modern style is, as Foxon writes, a 'clear-cut and systematic'[12] choice on the part of Pope and was initiated with the publication of the 1717 *Works*. The 1743 edition of the *Iliad* adheres to this modernizing practice and I have reproduced both the substantives and the style of the accidentals of that edition. On occasion, I have preferred the punctuation of the first edition folio,[13] which we know that Pope carefully proofread, to the 1743 duodecimo edition. While Pope announced his clear intention to revise his translation for the 1743 edition, it is doubtful that he systematically corrected proofs for that edition, and so it is possible – indeed, likely – that some of the alterations of particular accidentals do not have authorial sanction.

10. One does occasionally find, in the duodecimo edition that I have used as the basis of this Penguin text, italics used for emphasis – but only in the notes, and not in the poetic text. Foxon (233–4) observes that, in some of his trade editions, Pope made use of italics for emphasis, an aid to understanding that the readers of his luxury editions perhaps would not have required. At other times, however, the duodecimo puts into Roman type what the first edition had printed in italic, so that a clear pattern is not discernible.

11. Thomas Johnson, in 'The Booksellers Advertisement' prefaced to his Dutch pirated edition of Pope's *Iliad* (1718). It may be true that 'a prodigious number of Capitals' will disfigure the page of small octavos such as Thomas Johnson's pirated edition, but to my eye this is not necessarily true of the spacious pages of the first edition of Pope's *Iliad*, which contain only twenty (in the quarto) or twenty-two (in the folio) poetic lines per page. In a paperback such as this Penguin edition, in which the number of lines per page and the size of the printed letters more closely resemble the duodecimo reprints rather than the first edition, routine capitalization would indeed tend to disfigure the page. For a discussion of Thomas Johnson's pirated edition, see Reginald H. Griffith, 'A Piracy of Pope's *Iliad*', *Studies in Philology* 28 (1931), 737–41.

12. *Pope and the Early Eighteenth-Century Book Trade*, 184.

13. I have collated the 1743 edition with the first edition folio (the luxury trade edition) rather than quarto (the subscribers' edition), since the folio represents a further stage of revision. See Schmitz, 'The "Arsenal" Proof Sheets of Pope's *Iliad*'; and Foxon (154): 'One result of this revision between the quarto and folio was that the public and not the subscribers received the more polished text; the readers of the *Twickenham* are in the same plight as the subscribers.'

I have included a list of variant readings – which in most cases means earlier, unrevised readings – of the poetic text. For the variant readings of Pope's notes and the preface, the reader is directed to the Twickenham text. Variant readings for the preface can be found there in the critical apparatus at the foot of the page in Volume VII, pages 3–25; textual notes on Pope's notes can be found on pages 475–7 of Volume VII and pages 617–21 of Volume VIII. Even though I have taken a different path from the Twickenham Edition, I must make clear here my indebtedness to it. Specifically, I am indebted to the Twickenham editors for their listing of variant readings. I did not collate all the various texts myself, although I did check the veracity of all the alternative readings listed by the Twickenham editors.

While most of the volumes in this *English Poets* series have been modernized with regard to accidentals, the following edition has not been modernized beyond Pope's own attempts at modernization. The practice of more or less thorough modernization is easily justified in an edition of, for example, Swift's poems, since Swift, as Pat Rogers has observed, 'did not punctuate with the care of his friend Pope'.[14] But Pope did punctuate carefully. He was greatly concerned with the question of precisely how his works were to be printed, and this concern included a meticulous concern with accidentals. Given this attitude of meticulous care, it seemed appropriate to be as faithful as possible to Pope's preferences with regard to accidentals.

There is another argument to be made for choosing, for this edition, the duodecimo style of printing over the more ornate style of the first edition. As Foxon surmises, '[t]here is good evidence that Pope preferred' smaller pocket editions 'to his grand quartos and folios'.[15] Foxon points us to the following passage in a letter (14 [?] July 1741) written by Pope to Ralph Allen, in which the poet speaks slightingly of luxury editions of his work: 'I have done with expensive Editions for ever, which are only a Complement to a few curious people at the expence of the Publisher, & to the displeasure of the Many ... for the time to come, the World shall not pay, nor make Me pay, more for my Works than they are worth.'[16] This Penguin paperback edition is a

14. *Jonathan Swift: The Complete Poems* (Harmondsworth: Penguin, 1983).

15. *Pope and the Early Eighteenth-Century Book Trade*, 32.

16. *Correspondence*, IV, 350. Pope told Spence (26–28 August 1742), 'I was forced to print in little by other printers' beginning to do so from my folios' (*Observations, Anecdotes, and Characters of Books and Men*, ed. James M. Osborne, 2 vols. (Oxford:

direct descendant of the pocket editions ultimately favoured by Pope. It is therefore fitting that its style of printing be made to resemble that of the trade editions Pope came to prefer. Moreover, the duodecimo editions of Pope's *Iliad* were printed in the style that Pope associated with the printing of classical Latin texts,[17] since in these texts – distinguished by their typographical simplicity – common nouns are not capitalized.

In one significant way, however, the format of this edition differs from both the 1743 edition and the Twickenham Edition, because the notes in this edition are printed as endnotes, as they were in the first edition, rather than at the foot of the page, as they were in the later editions published during Pope's lifetime, including the 1743 edition. Pope's notes to his *Iliad* are often lengthy. This means that, when they were printed at the bottom of the page of the duodecimo editions, they sometimes crowded the poetic text to such an extent that many pages contained more notes than poetry. Pages 2–6 of the first volume of the duodecimo reprints of the poetic text of Pope's *Iliad* contain, for example, only two lines of poetry per page. The rest, to adapt a phrase from a poem by J. V. Cunningham, is gloss.[18] It is gloss that is, moreover, printed in reduced type. To place Pope's notes at the bottom of the page, as was done in the later editions published by the Lintots as well as in the deeply learned and indispensable Twickenham Edition, is to diminish the Longinian sense of spacious and uncluttered elevation that Pope saw in Homer and tried to simulate in English. It distracts the attention from the whole to parts, which Pope decries throughout his poetry. It threatens the integrity of the reading experience by constantly drawing attention to the commentary, which is of

---

Clarendon Press, 1966), I, 91). Is this a reference to the printing of the first duodecimo edition of the *Iliad*, which may have been an immediate response to the pirated pocket edition printed in Holland? Even if it is and Pope felt he was at first 'forced' to print smaller editions of his works, it is still possible that he came to prefer these editions, as the letter to Ralph Allen clearly suggests.

17. See *Pope and the Early Eighteenth-Century Book Trade*, 23–32 ('*An Essay on Criticism* and the Elzeviers') and Maynard Mack, *Alexander Pope: A Life* (New York and London: Norton, 1985), in which Mack remarks that Pope, in choosing the printing style of his *Iliad*, was 'no doubt influenced by Tonson's editions of the Latin classics, where in contrast to contemporary practice capital letters appear only at the opening of sentences and proper names, and italic letters do not appear at all' (267).

18. I am thinking of the concluding lines of Cunningham's poem *To the Reader*: 'Search in this gloss/No text inherent: The text was loss. The gain is gloss'. *The Exclusions of a Rhyme* (Chicago: Alan Swallow, 1960), 70.

only secondary importance to the poetry. Pope himself pokes fun at just this kind of pedantry when, in the *Dunciad*, he at times purposely overwhelms only a line or two of poetry with a whole page of pseudo-learned commentary. I have chosen to print Pope's 'Observations' as endnotes[19] so that they may be consulted after the poetry has been experienced. It is, moreover, in keeping with the convention of this *English Poets* series to print endnotes rather than footnotes.

I have retained the spelling and punctuation of the original, with some exceptions. The long 's' has been modernized. The placing of quotation marks has been modernized: they appear at the beginning and the end of each quoted section, while in the eighteenth-century editions they were placed at the beginning of each line. The Greek has been accented in accordance with modern convention and not eighteenth-century practice. The same is true of the Latin, which means that – in the case of Latin quotations – accents and long marks have been eliminated.

The substantive revisions of the poetic text in the later editions are quite minor. One of the most significant changes involves the opening lines of the poem. The first edition reads as follows:

> The Wrath of *Peleus*' Son, the direful Spring
> Of all the *Grecian* Woes, O Goddess, sing!

Beginning with the 1736 edition, the opening lines read:

> Achilles' wrath, to *Greece* the direful spring
> Of woes unnumber'd, heav'nly Goddess, sing![20]

I surmise that these changes reflect Pope's response to two events: John Dennis's criticism and Thomas Tickell's rival translation of the first book of the *Iliad*. In his 'Remarks Upon Mr. Pope's Translation of Homer' (1717),[21] Dennis had objected to Pope's inaccurately rendering Homer's μυρία ἄλγεα ('countless woes') as 'all the *Graecian* woes'.

---

19. As the notes were printed in the first edition (1697) of Dryden's *Aeneis*. Maynard Mack speculates that it was perhaps the placing of Ogilby's commentary on the same page as the poetic text of his translation that encouraged Pope to take a different path. Mack remarks that Ogilby's 'elegant column of verse (eight to twenty lines on a page) is surrounded like a tiny peninsula by a vast weedy sea of commentary rising against it from three sides: an offense to the eye that Pope was careful not to repeat in his Homer translations, where the commentary is placed at the back' (*Alexander Pope: A Life*, 45).

20. *Twickenham Edition*, VII, 82.

21. *The Critical Works of John Dennis*, ed. E. N. Hooker, 2 vols. (Baltimore: The Johns Hopkins Press, 1939–43), II, 127.

Addison's Oxford protégé Tickell begins his translation with the following lines:

> ACHILLES' fatal Wrath, whence Discord rose,
> That brought the Sons of *Greece* unnumber'd Woes,
> O Goddess sing.[22]

It looks as though Pope, who nervously awaited Tickell's rival version and undoubtedly read it with scrupulous care, took over Tickell's translation of Homer's μυρία ἄλγεα and transposed 'unnumber'd Woes' into 'woes unnumber'd'.[23]

The present edition makes available, for the first time in paperback, Pope's notes in their entirety. These notes should be of value to students of Homer and Pope as well as to anyone interested in the history of literary criticism. We are here presented with the opportunity of being able to listen to one poetic genius commenting at length on the work of another. The notes show Pope to be a superb critic, one of the most gifted and penetrating of the early eighteenth century. Pope considered it his obligation to be a literary critic of Homer, in the fullest and most humane sense of the word 'critic', rather than a specialized pedant. 'It is something strange,' as he says at the beginning of his observations on the first book, 'that of all the commentators upon *Homer*, there is hardly one whose principal design is to illustrate the poetical beauties of the author. They are voluminous in explaining those sciences which he made but subservient to his Poetry, and sparing only upon that art which constitutes his character. . . . The chief design of the following notes is to comment upon *Homer* as a poet.' In this same passage, in commenting upon what he considers to have been the interpretative excesses of some of his predecessors in the field of Homeric literary criticism, Pope at one point makes a pithy remark, worthy of Samuel Johnson, about the vanities of literary criticism that our own era would do well to heed: 'it is generally the fate of such people who will never say what was said before, to say what will never be said after them'. In Pope's notes we are treated to a recounting, in elegant English, of the entire tradition of learned commentary. We get the chance, as well, to view Homer's influence

---

22. London, 1715.

23. Samuel Johnson observed, in the *Life of Tickell*, that 'Pope seems to have . . . borrowed something' from Tickell's opening lines 'in the correction of his own' (*Lives of the English Poets*, ed. Hill, II, 309).

upon the Western epic tradition that he initiated, as Pope continually observes the ways in which poets such as Virgil, Statius, Lucan, Tasso, Ariosto, Spenser, and Milton have imitated particular passages from the *Iliad*.

Included in this edition, along with Pope's notes, are Pope's preface and the three informative indexes that were included in the editions published during Pope's lifetime. I have chosen not to include the *Essay on Homer*, which was written by Thomas Parnell. Pope revised Parnell's essay, but never to his satisfaction: 'Parnell wrote the essay on his [i.e. Homer's] life which is prefixed to the *Iliad*,' Pope told Spence in 1735. ''Tis still stiff, and was written much stiffer. As it is, I think verily it cost me more pain in the correcting than the writing of it would have done.'[24] The essay consists largely of speculation ('You know there is nothing certain about him,'[25] Pope mentioned to Spence about Homer); it is overly long; and it pales in comparison with the brilliant preface, written by Pope himself, that preceded it in the eighteenth-century editions. Those wishing to read the *Essay on Homer* can find it in the Twickenham Edition, VII, pp. 26–80.

I have provided translations of the citations of passages in Greek, Latin, Italian, and French that Pope includes in his notes. Unless otherwise indicated below, the translations of these passages are my own. Steven Shurtleff helped me to compose idiomatic translations of the Greek and Latin passages in Books VIII through XXIV. The passages from Quintilian, which Pope left untranslated, are cited from the Loeb Library edition, translated by H. E. Butler (Cambridge, Mass.: Harvard University Press, 1920). The translation of Valerius Flaccus is also from the Loeb edition (1934); the translator is J. H. Mozley. The translation from Strabo is taken from Horace Leonard Jones's Loeb rendition (1927) of *The Geography of Strabo*. Lucretius, Cicero, and Juvenal are cited from the Loeb editions (1966, 1969, 1967), translated respectively by W. H. D. Rouse, G. G. Ramsay, and H. Rackham. The passage from Horace's *Epistle* II, 2 is cited from the translation of H. Rushton Fairclough in the Loeb edition (1920). For Lucan, I have cited the translation of P. F. Widdows (Bloomington and Indianapolis: Indiana University Press, 1988). I have often slightly adapted the scholarly translations I have used. The translated passages from the *Aeneid*, cited by Pope only in the original Latin, are from

24. *Observations, Anecdotes, and Characters of Books and Men*, ed. Osborne, I, 84.
25. ibid., I, 83.

Dryden's version,[26] which Pope in the *Iliad* preface calls 'the most noble and spirited translation I know in any language'. Pope clearly had Dryden's *Aeneid* at his fingertips and at times Dryden's example directly influenced Pope's choice of language in his translation of the *Iliad*.[27] The reader should be aware that Dryden's translation is not a literal one. The translations from Tasso are cited from Edward Fairfax's poetic version of 1600; the spelling and punctuation have been modernized. Fairfax, like Dryden, does not render his author word for word. The passages cited from Dryden's *Aeneid* and Fairfax's version of Tasso's *Gerusalemme Liberata* sometimes correspond to slightly more of the original Latin and Italian than the specific lines cited by Pope.

The Twickenham editors performed the extremely useful and time-consuming task of identifying, with specificity, the passages from the critics and scholars cited by Pope in his notes. I have at times included these references, for which I am indebted to the editors of the Twickenham text.

26. Dryden's *Aeneid* will be cited from *The Works of Virgil in English 1697*, ed. William Frost and Vinton A. Dearing, Vols. 5, 6 (Berkeley, Calif.: University of California Press, 1987). The styling of that edition, however, is brought into line with this edition: Dryden's routine capitalization of substantives, for example, is dropped.

27. When Pope cites *Aeneid* IX, 434–7 in his note on *Iliad* VIII, 371, for example, he is clearly reading Virgil through Dryden, for he borrows phrases from Dryden's translation in order to translate Homer. Pope takes the phrase 'overcharg'd with rain' (*Iliad* VIII, 371) directly from Dryden (*Aeneid* IX, 584) as well as the rhyme with 'plain'.

Table of Dates

2 November Swift, according to Bishop Kennet, begins soliciting subscribers for Pope's *Iliad*.
26–29 December Selection from Book XIII of Pope's *Iliad* published in Steele's *Miscellany*.
March Publication of *Windsor-Forest*.

1714 *March* Enlarged version of *The Rape of the Lock* published. Pope signs a contract with Bernard Lintot to prepare a verse translation of the *Iliad*.
1 August Queen Anne dies; George I ascends the throne.

1715 *February* Publication of *The Temple of Fame*.
6 June Publication of translation of the *Iliad*, Vol. I (Books 1–4).
8 June Tonson publishes Thomas Tickell's rival translation, *The First Book of Homer's Iliad*.

1716 *22 March* Publication of Vol. II (Books 5–8) of the *Iliad*.
The Popes sell Binfield and move to Chiswick, near Lord Burlington.

1717 (?)*3 June* *Iliad*, Vol. III (Books 9–12). *Verses to the Memory of an Unfortunate Lady* and *Eloisa to Abelard* published in collected volume of Pope's works. A similarity may be noted between Pope's sympathetic view of Achilles' passionate character and the poet's depiction of the unfortunate lady and Eloisa. Death of Pope's father.

1718 *28 June* *Iliad*, Vol. IV (Books 13–16).

1719 Pope, having reaped the considerable profits from the success of the *Iliad* translation, moves to Twickenham with his mother.

1720 *12 May* *Iliad*, Vols. V (Books 17–21) and VI (Books 22–24). Gay writes, probably during this year, his poem *Welcome from Greece*, congratulating Pope on his finishing the *Iliad* translation; the poem was not published until 1776.

1721 Pope edits Parnell's *Poems*.

1725 *March* Publication of Pope's edition of Shakespeare, in six volumes.
April Translation of the *Odyssey*, Vols. I–III. The *Odyssey*

translation is a collaborative effort, executed with the help of Elijah Fenton and William Broome. While Pope apparently revised the work of his assistants, there was an attempt made to obscure just how much of the work was originally translated by Fenton and Broome. Broome translated Books 2, 6, 8, 11, 12, 16, 18, and 23; Fenton translated Books 1, 4, 19, and 22. Pope translated the remaining twelve, with help from Henry Layng (unbeknown to Fenton and Broome) on parts of Books 10 and 15.

1726   Swift visits Pope from London.
Lewis Theobald, in *Shakespeare Restored*, attacks Pope's edition of Shakespeare.
June   Publication of first volume of Joseph Spence's *Essay on Mr. Pope's Odyssey*.
October   Swift's *Gulliver's Travels* published.
Odyssey, Vols. IV–V, including *Postscript*, in which the translator laments the problems he faced in trying to render the more lowly or domestic elements of the poem with the requisite Augustan dignity.

1727   Vols. I and II of Pope–Swift *Miscellanies*. George I dies; George II ascends the throne.
August   Publication of second volume of Spence's *Essay on Mr. Pope's Odyssey*.

1728   *March*   In Vol. III of Pope–Swift *Miscellanies* is published *Peri Bathous or the Art of Sinking in Poetry*, an ironic pseudo-treatise on how *not* to achieve the kind of Longinian elevation that Pope had seriously struggled to attain in his years as a Homeric translator.
May   Publication of three-book version of *The Dunciad*, a mock-heroic poem (with Theobald as hero) dependent for its structure on the *Aeneid*, but possessing Iliadic fire rather than Virgilian pathos and, like the *Iliad*, a vital cultural critique.

1729   *April*   Publication of *The Dunciad Variorum*.

1730   *December*   Colley Cibber is appointed Poet Laureate.

1731   *December*   *Epistle to Burlington* published (to become the fourth of the *Moral Essays* in the 1735 *Works*).

1732   *August*   Pope–Swift *Miscellanies*, Vol. IV.
        4 December   John Gay dies.

1733   *January*   *Of the Use of Riches, an Epistle to the Right Honor-
        able Allen Lord Bathurst* published (later to become the third
        of the *Moral Essays*). Pope introduces his theory of the ruling
        passion, perhaps influenced by his early and long exposure to
        what he described as Achilles' 'prevailing Passion' of 'Anger'
        (Pope's commentary upon *Iliad* XX, 489ff.), an obsessive
        anger that at last relents in *Iliad* XXIV only under the most
        extraordinary circumstances of divine intervention.
        February   Pope's first Horatian imitation (*The First Satire of
        the Second Book of Horace, Imitated in a Dialogue between
        Alexander Pope of Twickenham . . . and his Learned Council . . .*)
        is published. It is remarkable for its colloquial ease and wit, as
        well as for its tone of anti-establishment Achillean outrage at
        injustice.
        February–May   Publication of *Essay on Man*, Epistles I–III.
        In Epistle III, Pope develops his theory of the ruling passion.
        7 June   Pope's mother dies at the age of 91.

1734   *January*   *Epistle to Cobham* published (to become the first of
        the *Moral Essays*), containing more of Pope's theory of the
        ruling passion; *Essay on Man*, Epistle IV.
        July   *The First Satire of the Second Book of Horace . . . To
        which is Added, The Second Satire of the Same Book* (which is
        the first edition of Pope's imitation of Horace's *Sermones* II, ii).
        December   *Sober Advice from Horace* (*Sermones* I, II), pub-
        lished anonymously, with notes in parody of Richard Bentley,
        the famous classical scholar who had belittled Pope's achieve-
        ment as a Homeric translator.

1735   *January*   *Epistle to Dr. Arbuthnot* published.
        February   *Of the Characters of Women: An Epistle to a Lady*
        published (to become the second of the *Moral Essays*).
        Arbuthnot dies.
        May   Curll publishes *Letters of Mr. Pope, and Several Emi-
        nent Persons.*

1737   J. P. de Crousaz, a professor of mathematics and philosophy in
        Lausanne (Switzerland), criticizes Pope's *Essay on Man* as
        Spinozist and deistic, and therefore anti-Christian.

Further Reading

Arnold, Matthew, *Last Words on Translating Homer* (1862). For a more recent scholarly edition, see *On Translating Homer* in *The Complete Prose Works of Matthew Arnold*, ed. R. H. Super, 11 vols. (Ann Arbor: University of Michigan Press, 1960–77), I (*On the Classical Tradition*), 97–216.

Berry, Reginald, *A Pope Chronology* (Boston: G. K. Hall & Co., 1988).

Brower, Reuben A., *Alexander Pope: The Poetry of Allusion* (Oxford: Clarendon Press, 1959). See especially Chapter 4 ('True Heroic Poetry').

—— *Mirror on Mirror: Translation, Imitation, Parody* (Cambridge, Mass.: Harvard University Press, 1974). See Chapters 4 ('Pope's *Iliad* for Twentieth-Century Readers') and 5 ('From the *Iliad* to the Novel via *The Rape of the Lock*').

Callan, Norman, 'Pope's *Iliad*: A New Document', *Review of English Studies*, N.S. IV (1953), 109–21. Discusses the so-called 'Arsenal' proofs, corrected in the poet's own hand, of the first two volumes of the first-edition folio of Pope's translation.

Carne-Ross, D. S., 'A Mistaken Ambition of Exactness', *Delos* 2 (1968), 171–95. Review of Richmond Lattimore's translation of the *Odyssey*.

Clark, H. W., 'In Praise of Pope's Notes', *College Literature* 3 (1976), 203–18.

Clarke, Howard, *Homer's Readers: A Historical Introduction to the Iliad and Odyssey* (Newark: University of Delaware Press, 1981). See especially pp. 135–40 on Pope's understanding of Achilles' character.

Connelly, Peter J., 'The Ideology of Pope's *Iliad*', *Comparative Literature* 40:4 (1988), 358–83.

—— 'Pope's *Iliad*: Ut Pictura Translatio', *Studies in English Literature* 21:3 (1981), 439–55.

Crossley, Robert, 'Pope's *Iliad*: The Commentary and the Translation', *Philological Quarterly* 56 (1977), 339–57.

Foxon, David, *Pope and the Early Eighteenth-Century Book Trade*, revised and edited by James McLaverty (Oxford: Clarendon Press, 1991). See particularly Chapters 2 ('Homer: Business and Aesthetics') and 4 ('Pope's Text: The Early Works').

Frost, William, '*The Rape of the Lock* and Pope's Homer', *Modern Language Quarterly* 8 (1947), 342–54.

Griffith, Reginald H., *Alexander Pope: A Bibliography*, 2 vols. (Austin: University of Texas Press, 1922–6). Presents detailed descriptions of the publication of Pope's works, including his *Iliad*.

—— 'A Piracy of Pope's *Iliad*', *Studies in Philology* 28 (1931), 737–41.

Herington, C. J., 'The New Homer', *The Yale Review* 64 (Summer, 1975), 568–79. Review of Robert Fitzgerald's translation of *Iliad*.

Hodgart, Matthew, 'The Subscription List for Pope's *Iliad*', in *The Dress of Words: Essays on Restoration and Eighteenth-Century Literature in Honor of Richmond P. Bond*, ed. R. B. White, Jr (University of Kansas Press, 1978), 25–34.

Johnson, Samuel, *Life of Pope* (1781). See Vol. III of *Lives of the English Poets*, ed. G. B. Hill, 3 vols. (Oxford: Clarendon Press, 1905). Includes a defence of Pope's *Iliad*, which Johnson considered 'the greatest version of poetry which the world has ever seen'.

Knight, Douglas M., 'The Development of Pope's *Iliad* Preface', *Modern Language Quarterly* 16 (1955), 237–46.

—— *Pope and the Heroic Tradition: A Critical Study of his* Iliad (New Haven: Yale University Press, 1951).

Levine, Joseph M., *The Battle of the Books: History and Literature in the Augustan Age* (Ithaca and London: Cornell University Press, 1991). Chapter 6 is devoted entirely to a discussion of Pope's *Iliad*.

Mack, Maynard, General Editor of Vols. VII–XI ('Translations of Homer') of *The Twickenham Edition of the Poems of Alexander Pope*, 11 vols. (London and New Haven: Methuen & Co. and Yale University Press, 1938–68). See the Introduction at the beginning of Vol. VII.

—— *Alexander Pope: A Life* (New York and London: Norton, 1985). See especially pp. 347–58.

Mason, H. A., *To Homer through Pope: An Introduction to Homer's* Iliad *and Pope's Translation* (London: Chatto & Windus, 1972).

Rogers, Pat, 'Pope and his Subscribers', *Publishing History* 3 (1978), 7–36.

Rosslyn, Felicity, *Alexander Pope: A Literary Life* (Houndshills, Basingstoke, Hampshire: Macmillan, 1990). See Chapter 3 ('Making it New').

—— (ed.), *Pope's* Iliad*: A Selection and Commentary* (Bristol: Bristol Classical Press, 1985).

Schmitz, Robert M., 'The "Arsenal" Proof Sheets of Pope's *Iliad*: A Third Report', *Modern Language Notes* 74 (1959), 486–9.

Shankman, Steven, 'Led by the Light of the Maeonian Star: Aristotle on Tragedy and *Odyssey* XVII: 415–44', *Classical Antiquity* 2:1 (1983), 108–16.

—— *Pope's Iliad: Homer in the Age of Passion* (Princeton: Princeton University Press, 1983). Places Pope's translation within the context of neoclassical literary theory and practice.

—— 'Through Pope to Homer, Through Homer to Pope', *Hellas* 4:2 (1993), 14–42. The first part shows how Pope's translation can help a modern reader better understand the ethical import of the *Iliad*; the second explores the pervasive influence on Pope's original poetry of his many years devoted to translating Homer.

Sherbo, Arthur, '"Scar'd Porkers" in Pope's *Iliad*', *Notes and Queries* 30 (228): 6 (December 1983), 502–4. On Pope's epic diction.

Sherburn, George, *The Early Career of Alexander Pope* (Oxford: Clarendon Press, 1934).

—— (ed.), *The Correspondence of Alexander Pope*, 5 vols. (Oxford: Clarendon Press, 1956).

Spence, Joseph, *An Essay on Mr. Pope's Odyssey*, 2 vols. (London, 1726–7).

Thomas, Claudia, 'Pope's *Iliad* and the Contemporary Context of his "Appeals to the Ladies"', *Eighteenth-Century Life* 14:2 (1990), 1–17.

Zimmermann, Hans-Joachim, *Alexander Popes Noten zu Homer: Eine Manuskript- und Quellenstudie* (Heidelberg: Carl Winter, 1966).

A Note on the Style of Pope's Iliad

While Homer can be plain and direct, he is also often very grand, and while Pope had difficulties in capturing Homer's plainness, he made it his business to try to bring across Homeric elevation into English. You will find plainness in twentieth-century translations of Homer, but you generally will not get the elevation, the feeling that you are reading an unquestionably big and important poem. Homer's verse would probably have sounded often exotic and very different from the conversational Greek of the period in which the poems were composed, for the poet was attempting to recreate the legendary Mycenean age in a language that was in many ways indebted to that earlier (by some three or four hundred years) period of glory in Hellenic civilization. In a translation, then, you might well want a diction that could simulate this sense of legendary remoteness from mundane life.

Let us hear the lines in the original Greek, followed by a literal translation:

> Μῆνιν ἄειδε, θεά, Πηληϊάδεω Ἀχιλῆος
> οὐλομένην, ἣ μυρί᾽ Ἀχαιοῖς ἄλγε᾽ ἔθηκε,
> πολλὰς δ᾽ ἰφθίμους ψυχὰς Ἄϊδι προΐαψεν
> ἡρώων, αὐτοὺς δὲ ἑλώρια τεῦχε κύνεσσιν
> οἰωνοῖσί τε πᾶσι, Διὸς δ᾽ ἐτελείετο βουλή,
> ἐξ οὗ δὴ τὰ πρῶτα διαστήτην ἐρίσαντε
> Ἀτρεΐδης τε ἄναξ ἀνδρῶν καὶ δῖος Ἀχιλλεύς.[1]

(The wrath of Achilles, son of Peleus – make this your
    song, Goddess –
That devastating wrath that brought so much grief to the
    Achaeans
And hurled to Hades many mighty souls
Of heroes, and turned their bodies into prey for dogs

---

1. Cited from the Oxford Classical Text, ed. David B. Munro and Thomas W. Allen, 2 vols. (Oxford: Oxford University Press, 1966), I, 1.

And all kinds of birds, and the decree of Zeus was being
  brought to its fulfilment;
Begin the song, then, Goddess, from that moment when
  the quarrel began
Between Atrides, king of men, and brilliant Achilles.)

Let us now listen to Pope. The opening of the poem reads:

Achilles' Wrath, to *Greece* the direful spring
Of woes unnumber'd, heav'nly Goddess, sing!
That Wrath which hurl'd to *Pluto*'s gloomy reign
The Souls of mighty Chiefs untimely slain;
Whose limbs unbury'd on the naked shore
Devouring dogs and hungry vultures tore:
Since great *Achilles* and *Atrides* strove,
Such was the sov'reign doom, and such the will of *Jove!*

These lines convince us that we are in the presence of a mighty
poem. For the unfailing regularity of Homer's dactylic hexameter Pope
substitutes the Miltonically proven iambic pentameter, and the rhym-
ing couplets reassure us that this is not ordinary conversation. Pope's
choice of the rhyming couplet might, to a modern ear, seem to cramp
Homer's elevation. This was not necessarily the case in the Restoration
and eighteenth century. To an Augustan ear, it was often difficult to
distinguish blank verse from prose, and therefore from the prosaic. As
Samuel Johnson remarked, 'blank verse is verse only to the eye'.[2]
Through his use of rhyme, Pope could exalt his poetry above the level
of ordinary conversation. For what the writer of a sublime epic such as
the *Iliad* wants to represent is nature, but nature – to quote Neander
in Dryden's *Essay of Dramatic Poesy* – 'wrought up to an higher
pitch'. 'Heroic rhyme', according to Neander, is nearest this kind of
'nature, as being the noblest kind of modern verse'.[3] Once this air of
distinction is conveyed, moreover, the poet is no longer forced to
depart so violently from idiomatic usage, as Pope believed Milton was
forced to do in *Paradise Lost* in order to distinguish his blank verse
from prose.[4] Pope had another reason for choosing to translate Homer

2. *Lives of the English Poets*, ed. G. B. Hill, I, 193.

3. *Of Dramatic Poesy and Other Critical Essays*, ed. George Watson, 2 vols. (London
and New York: Everyman), I, 86–7.

4. See Thomas Parnell's presentation of Pope's view of Milton's style, *Homer's Battle
of the Frogs and Mice with Remarks of Zoilus* (London, 1717); Spence's *Observations*,

into rhyming couplets: the couplet was the form of which he was a master. His genius as a poet cannot be separated from his genius as a master of the rhyming couplet. For Alexander Pope to have translated the *Iliad* into blank verse, or any other form apart from the heroic couplet, was not a realistic possibility.[5]

Since Pope firmly establishes his metrical norm, he is able to say what he wants by varying from it in subtle but telling ways as the occasion demands. Line 8 ('Such was the sov'reign doom, and such the will of *Jove*'), for example, is a stately Alexandrine that befits its Jovian content. At times, it is true, the necessity of rhyme causes Pope's style to become less than completely perspicuous. The metaphor of the 'direful spring/Of woes unnumber'd' in the first two lines – a metaphor that is not present in the original – was described by Samuel Johnson as 'harsh'.[6] Perhaps Pope created the metaphor in response to the necessity of having to find a word ('spring') to rhyme with 'sing' in line two. But the presence of this figure of speech can be justified, as can many of Pope's stylistic choices in these lines, in terms of what Pope – following Aristotle, Milton, and Addison – thought of as the traditional means of elevating poetic style.

'The Language of an heroic Poem,' Addison writes in *Spectator* No. 285 (26 January 1712), 'should be both Perspicuous and Sublime.' How you achieve sublimity is by following Aristotle's advice in *Poetics* XXII: there the poet is advised (1) to use bold metaphors; (2) to use 'Idioms of other Tongues', including 'placing the Adjective after the Substantive, with several other foreign Modes of Speech'; and (3) to lengthen phrases 'by the Addition of Words, which may either be inserted or omitted'. Pope's opening lines embody these stylistic principles. 'The direful spring/Of woes unnumber'd' is a bold metaphor; (2) the phrase 'woes unnumber'd' is a Latinate idiom in which the adjective is placed after the substantive, and 'to *Greece* the direful spring' is a transposition of words; (3) 'heav'nly Goddess', 'Pluto's gloomy reign', and 'mighty Chiefs' are all examples of 'the length'ning of a Phrase by the Addition of Words, which may either be inserted or

---

Anecdotes, and Characters of Books and Men, ed. James M. Osborne, 2 vols. (Oxford: Clarendon Press, 1966), I, 173; and Pope's postscript to the *Odyssey*, Twickenham Edition, 10:31.

5. For a more detailed discussion of Pope's use of the couplet, see Chapter 6 of my *Pope's Iliad: Homer in the Age of Passion* (Princeton: Princeton University Press, 1983).

6. *Idler* No. 77, Saturday, 6 October 1759.

omitted'. Those who object to Pope's translation because it contains such phrases should realize that they are objecting to the traditional means of elevating poetic style as stated by Aristotle in the *Poetics*, as achieved by Milton in *Paradise Lost*, and as restated by Addison in the papers of the *Spectator* in which he tries to account for the power of Milton's style.

Pope continues in the high heroic manner, exemplified in English epic by Milton (although in Pope's case graced in addition by pleasing rhyme), as he addresses the muse once again and then begins to open the plot:

> Declare, O Muse! in what ill-fated hour
> Sprung the fierce strife, from what offended pow'r?

This sounds like a great English epic. For did not Milton, following the example of Homer and Virgil, begin *Paradise Lost* by asking a question?

> Say first, for Heav'n hides nothing from thy view
> Nor the deep Tract of Hell, say first what cause
> Mov'd our Grand Parents in that happy State,
> Favour'd of Heav'n so highly, to fall off
> From their Creator, and transgress his Will
> For one restraint, Lords of the World besides?
> Who first seduc'd them to that foul revolt?   (I. 27–33)[7]

Yes, Milton did, as Pope reminds us in his *Observations* on the opening lines of the *Iliad*. Pope is, to a great extent, still speaking the language of that Miltonic epic world. The Augustan poet continues:

> *Latona*'s son a dire contagion spread,
> And heap'd the camp with mountains of the dead;
> The King of Men his rev'rend Priest defy'd,
> And, for the King's offence, the people dy'd.
>   For *Chryses* sought with costly gifts to gain
> His captive daughter from the victor's chain.
> Suppliant the venerable father stands,
> *Apollo*'s awful ensigns grace his hands:
> By these he begs; and lowly bending down,

7. *The Poetical Works of John Milton*, edited after the original texts by H. C. Beeching (London and New York: Oxford University Press, 1914), 182.

Extends the sceptre and the laurel crown.
He su'd to all, but chief implor'd for grace
The Brother-Kings, of *Atreus*' royal race.

Pope's verse is grand: note the Latinate 'extends', the transposition of words in the line 'Suppliant the venerable father stands', and the adjective 'awful' (i.e. awe-inspiring). His verse is also delicately sugges-tive: the shadowy significance of mortals in comparison with the awe-inspiring power of the divine is deftly hinted at in the near juxtaposition of the words 'awful' and 'grace' in the line '*Apollo*'s awful ensigns grace his hands'.

There is more to Homer, however, than elevation. While Homer's style is elevated, it is also very clear: his style is remarkable for its achievement – to quote Addison's terms (derived from Aristotle's *Poetics*) – of both sublimity and perspicuity. Aristotle (Chapter 22 of the *Poetics*) observes that the most excellent style should combine these two traits. Elevation is necessary to prevent a style from being too prosaic, but if you overemphasize this quality, your language will be merely enigmatic. Clarity is also necessary to the best style, but if a style is too colloquial it becomes prosaic. Not many poets have been able to achieve both of these qualities at once. Milton, for instance, is very sublime but often not very perspicuous. Pope was aware of this shortcoming of Milton's style. Homer was widely admired for his ability to span the stylistic scale. Dionysius of Halicarnassus describes the two major literary styles as the 'graceful' (ἡ γλαφυρά) and the 'austere' (τὸ σεμνόν). There is a third kind of style, Dionysius says, 'which is a mixture obtained by selecting the best qualities of the other two . . . The standard of excellence in this style was set by Homer, and there is no style that could be said to combine the other two qualities of charm and dignity more effectively.'[8]

Pope agreed with Dionysius. It was this middle ground that Pope believed had eluded many Homeric translators:

Nothing that belongs to *Homer* seems to have been more commonly mistaken than the just pitch of his style: Some of his translators have swell'd into fustian in a proud confidence of the *sublime*; others sunk into flatness in a cold and timorous notion of *simplicity*. Methinks I see these different followers of

8. *Dionysius of Halicarnassus: The Critical Essays in Two Volumes*, trans. Stephen Usher, Loeb Classical Library (Cambridge, Mass. and London: Harvard University Press and William Heinemann, 1974), I, 399.

Homer, some sweating and straining after him by violent leaps and bounds, (the certain signs of false mettle) others slowly and servilely creeping in his train, while the Poet himself is all the time proceeding with an unaffected and equal majesty before them.

Did Pope himself find the just pitch of Homer's style? I think he himself knew the answer: not exactly. In the postscript to his translation of the *Odyssey* Pope confesses that it was a good deal more difficult for him to translate those parts of the poem that dealt with the kind of 'common, or even domestic things'[9] that often bring a style to life than it was for him to transpose Homeric elevation into English. Pope's trusted friend Joseph Spence agreed.[10] Coleridge was on to something when, in the second chapter of the *Biographia Literaria*, he criticized Pope's *Iliad* for its poetic diction, although, as I have argued elsewhere,[11] I believe that Pope is taking the blame for qualities of style that had been suggested by Aristotle and realized by Milton. It must be said, however, that in the achievement of perspicuity, modern poetic translators such as the accomplished and deft Robert Fitzgerald or the muscular Robert Fagles are often superior to Pope.

There are those who have charged that, if Pope's *Iliad* is elevated, it is an elevation of a particularly artificial kind. 'A pretty poem, Mr Pope,' Richard Bentley said in the famous remark, 'but you must not call it Homer.'[12] Pope, it is true, composed his translation before August Wolf, in his *Prologomena ad Homerum* (1767), directed modern Homeric scholarship along the path that would result in Milman Parry's ground-breaking (if still controversial) work on the poet's oral-formulaic style. Pope did not conceive of Homer as a poet who composed orally. He was, however, aware that the poems had originally been sung and he wished to preserve the stylistic qualities – such as the repetition of stock epithets and even of entire passages – that we now associate with the unmannered simplicity of the oral-formulaic style. Pope saw such qualities as the mark of a writer who was above the stylistic fussiness of modern authors who incessantly vary their diction. Homer's genius, Pope believed, was 'too fiery to regard' what he called '*little exactnesses*'.[13]

---

9. Twickenham Edition, 10:387.
10. See *An Essay on Mr. Pope's Odyssey in Five Dialogues* (London, 1737).
11. See *Pope's Iliad: Homer in the Age of Passion*, 150–64.
12. Cited from the *Life of Pope* in *Lives of the English Poets*, III, 213.
13. See his note on *Iliad* III, 47ff.

In the *Rhetoric* (III, 12), Aristotle had distinguished between the more polished and detailed written style of oratory and the more spontaneous and inexact oral style, and he associated the oral style with Homer. 'The style of oratory addressed to public assemblies,' Aristotle writes, 'is really just like a rough sketch or outline' (σκιαγραφία), which E. M. Cope describes as 'a painting in outline and *chiaroscuro*, or light and shade, without colour, and intended to produce its effect only *at a distance* – herein lies the analogy to public speaking – consequently rough and unfinished, because *from the distance* all niceties and refinements would be entirely thrown away'.[14] Pope, in his remark that Homer is 'like those free Painters who (one would think) had made here and there a few very significant strokes, that give form and spirit to all the piece',[15] reproduces the terms of Aristotle's description of the oral style. Much of the allegedly prettified diction of Pope's translation – e.g. 'liquid road' in *Iliad* I, 409 for Homer's ὑγρὰ κέλευθα ('watery paths', l. 312) – can, paradoxically, be attributed to the English poet's attempt to preserve what he took to be Homer's bold negligence.

14. E. M. Cope, *The Rhetoric of Aristotle with a Commentary by Edward Meredith Cope*, ed. J. E. Sandys, 3 vols. (Cambridge: Cambridge University Press, 1877), III, 152. On the importance of Aristotle's distinction for Horace and in Latin literature generally, see Wesley Trimpi, 'The Meaning of Horace's *Ut Pictura Poesis*', *Journal of the Warburg and Courtauld Institutes*, 36 (1973), 1–34, and 'Horace's *Ut Pictura Poesis*: The Argument for Stylistic Decorum', *Traditio*, 34 (1978), 29–73.

15. Note on *Iliad* V, 116ff.

THE
ILIAD
OF
HOMER

VOLUME I

Te sequor, O Graiæ gentis Decus! inque tuis nunc
Fixa pedumi pono pressis vestigia signis:
Non ita certandi cupidus, quam propter amorem,
Quod te imitari aveo —

LUCRET.

PREFACE

Homer is universally allow'd to have had the greatest *Invention* of any writer whatever. The praise of judgment *Virgil* has justly contested with him, and others may have their pretensions as to particular excellencies; but his Invention remains yet unrival'd. Nor is it a wonder if he has ever been acknowledg'd the greatest of poets, who most excell'd in that which is the very foundation of poetry. It is the Invention that in different degrees distinguishes all great Genius's: The utmost stretch of human study, learning, and industry, which masters every thing besides, can never attain to this. It furnishes Art with all her materials, and without it, Judgment itself can at best but *steal wisely*: For Art is only like a prudent steward that lives on managing the riches of Nature. Whatever praises may be given to works of Judgment, there is not even a single beauty in them to which the Invention must not contribute. As in the most regular gardens, Art can only reduce the beauties of Nature to more regularity, and such a figure, which the common eye may better take in, and is therefore more entertain'd with. And perhaps the reason why common Criticks are inclin'd to prefer a judicious and methodical genius to a great and fruitful one, is, because they find it easier for themselves to pursue their observations through an uniform and bounded walk of Art, than to comprehend the vast and various extent of Nature.

Our author's work is a wild paradise, where if we cannot see all the beauties so distinctly as in an order'd Garden, it is only because the number of them is infinitely greater. 'Tis like a copious nursery which contains the seeds and first productions of every kind, out of which those who follow'd him have but selected some particular plants, each according to his fancy, to cultivate and beautify. If some things are too luxuriant, it is owing to the richness of the soil; and if others are not arriv'd to perfection or maturity, it is only because they are over-run and opprest by those of a stronger nature.

It is to the strength of this amazing invention we are to attribute that unequal'd fire and rapture, which is so forcible in *Homer*, that no man of a true poetical spirit is master of himself while he reads him. What he writes, is of the most animated nature imaginable; every thing moves, every thing lives, and is put in action. If a council be call'd, or a battle fought, you are not coldly inform'd of what was said or done as from a third person; the reader is hurry'd out of himself by the force of the Poet's imagination, and turns in one place to a hearer, in another to a spectator. The course of his verses resembles that of the army he describes,

Οἱ δ' ἄρ' ἴσαν, ὡς εἴ τε πυρὶ χθὼν πᾶσα νέμοιτο.

They pour along like a fire that sweeps the whole earth before it. 'Tis however remarkable that his fancy, which is every where vigorous, is not discover'd immediately at the beginning of his poem in its fullest splendor: It grows in the progress both upon himself and others, and becomes on fire like a chariot-wheel, by its own rapidity. Exact disposition, just thought, correct elocution, polish'd numbers, may have been found in a thousand; but this poetical fire, this *Vivida vis animi*, in a very few. Even in works where all those are imperfect or neglected, this can over-power criticism, and make us admire even while we disapprove. Nay, where this appears, tho' attended with absurdities, it brightens all the rubbish about it, 'till we see nothing but its own splendor. This *Fire* is discern'd in *Virgil*, but discern'd as through a glass, reflected from *Homer*, more shining than fierce, but every where equal and constant: In *Lucan* and *Statius*, it bursts out in sudden, short, and interrupted flashes: In *Milton* it glows like a furnace kept up to an uncommon ardor by the force of art: In *Shakespear*, it strikes before we are aware, like an accidental fire from heaven: But in *Homer*, and in him only, it burns every where clearly, and every where irresistibly.

I shall here endeavour to show, how this vast *Invention* exerts itself in a manner superior to that of any poet, through all the main constituent parts of his work, as it is the great and peculiar characteristic which distinguishes him from all other authors.

This strong and ruling faculty was like a powerful star, which in the violence of its course, drew all things within its *vortex*. It seem'd not enough to have taken in the whole circle of arts, and the whole compass of nature to supply his maxims and reflections; all the inward passions and affections of mankind, to furnish his characters; and all the outward forms and images of things for his descriptions; but wanting yet an ampler sphere to expatiate in, he open'd a new and boundless walk for his imagination, and created a world for himself in the invention of *Fable*. That which *Aristotle* calls the *Soul of poetry*, was first breath'd into it by *Homer*. I shall begin with considering him in this part, as it is naturally the first, and I speak of it both as it means the design of a poem, and as it is taken for fiction.

Fable may be divided into the *probable*, the *allegorical*, and the *marvelous*. The *probable fable* is the recital of such actions as though they did not happen, yet might, in the common course of nature: Or of such as though they did, become fables by the additional episodes and manner of telling them. Of this sort is the main story of an Epic poem, *the return of* Ulysses, *the settlement of the* Trojans *in* Italy, or the like. That of the *Iliad* is *the anger of* Achilles, the most short and single subject that ever was chosen by any Poet. Yet this he has supplied with a vaster variety of incidents and events, and crouded with a greater number of councils, speeches, battles, and episodes of all kinds, than are to be found even in those poems whose schemes are of the utmost latitude and irregularity. The action is hurry'd on with the most vehement spirit, and its whole duration employs not so much as fifty days. *Virgil*, for want of so warm a genius, aided himself by taking in a more extensive subject, as well as a greater length of time, and contracting the design of both *Homer*'s poems into one, which is yet but a fourth part as large as his. The other Epic Poets have us'd the same practice, but generally carry'd it so far as to superinduce a multiplicity of fables, destroy the unity of action, and lose their readers in an unreasonable length of time. Nor is it only in the main design that they have been unable to add to his invention, but they have follow'd him in every episode and part of story. If he has given a regular *catalogue* of an *army*, they all draw up their forces in the same order. If he has funeral games for *Patroclus*, *Virgil* has the same for *Anchises*, and *Statius* (rather than omit them) destroys the unity of his action for those of *Archemorus*. If *Ulysses* visit the shades, the *Æneas* of *Virgil* and *Scipio* of *Silius* are sent after him. If he be detain'd from his return by the allurements of *Calypso*, so is *Æneas* by *Dido*, and *Rinaldo* by *Armida*. If *Achilles* be absent from the army on the score of a quarrel through half the poem, *Rinaldo* must absent himself just as long, on the like account. If he gives his heroe a suit of celestial armour, *Virgil* and *Tasso* make the same present to theirs. *Virgil* has not only observ'd this close imitation of *Homer*, but where he had not led the way, supply'd the want from other *Greek* authors. Thus the story of *Sinon* and the taking of *Troy* was copied (says *Macrobius*) almost word for word from *Pisander*, as the Loves of *Dido* and *Æneas* are taken from those of *Medea* and *Jason* in *Apollonius*, and several others in the same manner.

To proceed to the *allegorical fable*: If we reflect upon those innumerable knowledges, those secrets of nature and physical philosophy which *Homer* is generally suppos'd to have wrapped up in his *allegories*, what a new and ample scene of wonder may this consideration afford us? How fertile will that imagination appear, which was able to clothe all the properties of elements, the qualifications of the mind, the virtues and vices, in forms and persons; and to introduce them into actions agreeable to the nature of the things they shadow'd? This is a field in which no succeeding poets could dispute with *Homer*; and whatever commendations have been allow'd them on this head, are by no means for their invention in having enlarg'd his circle, but for their judgment in having contracted it. For when the mode of learning chang'd in following ages, and science was deliver'd in a plainer manner; it then became as reasonable in the more modern poets to lay it aside, as it was in *Homer* to make use of it. And perhaps it was no unhappy circumstance for *Virgil*, that there was not in his time that demand upon him of so great an invention, as might be capable of furnishing all those allegorical parts of a poem.

The *marvelous fable* includes whatever is supernatural, and especially the machines of the Gods. He seems the first who brought them into a system of machinery for poetry, and such a one as makes its greatest importance and dignity. For we find those authors who have been offended at the literal notion of the Gods, constantly laying their accusation against *Homer* as the chief support of it. But whatever cause there might be to blame his *machines* in a philosophical or religious view, they are so perfect in the poetic that mankind have been ever since contented to follow them: None have been able to enlarge the sphere of poetry beyond the limits he has set: Every attempt of this nature has prov'd unsuccessful; and after all the various changes of times and religions, his Gods continue to this day the Gods of poetry.

We come now to the *characters* of his persons, and here we shall find no author has ever drawn so many, with so visible and surprizing a variety, or given us such lively and affecting impressions of them.

Every one has something so singularly his own, that no painter could have distinguish'd them more by their features, than the Poet has by their manners. Nothing can be more exact than the distinctions he has observ'd in the different degrees of virtues and vices. The single quality of *courage* is wonderfully diversify'd in the several characters of the *Iliad*. That of *Achilles* is furious and intractable; that of *Diomede* forward, yet listening to advice and subject to command: That of *Ajax* is heavy, and self-confiding; of *Hector*, active and vigilant: The courage of *Agamemnon* is inspirited by love of empire and ambition, that of *Menelaus* mix'd with softness and tenderness for his people: We find in *Idomeneus* a plain direct soldier, in *Sarpedon* a gallant and generous one. Nor is this judicious and astonishing diversity to be found only in the principal quality which constitutes the main of each character, but even in the underparts of it, to which he takes care to give a tincture of that principal one. For example, the main characters of *Ulysses* and *Nestor* consist in *wisdom*; and they are distinct in this, that the wisdom of one is *artificial* and *various*, of the other *natural*, *open*, and *regular*. But they have, besides, characters of *courage*; and this quality also takes a different turn in each from the difference of his prudence: For one in the war depends still upon *caution*, the other upon *experience*. It would be endless to produce instances of these kinds. The characters of *Virgil* are far from striking us in this open manner; they lie in a great degree hidden and undistinguish'd, and where they are mark'd most evidently, affect us not in proportion to those of *Homer*. His characters of valour are much alike; even that of *Turnus* seems no way peculiar but as it is in a superior degree; and we see nothing that differences the courage of *Mnestheus* from that of *Sergesthus*, *Cloanthus*, or the rest. In like manner it may be remark'd of *Statius*'s heroes, that an air of impetuosity runs thro' them all; the same horrid and savage courage appears in his *Capaneus*, *Tydeus*, *Hippomedon*, &c. They have a parity of character, which makes them seem brothers of one family. I believe when the reader is led into this track of reflection, if he will pursue it thro' the *Epic* and *Tragic* writers, he will be convinced how infinitely superior in this point the invention of *Homer* was to that of all others.

The *speeches* are to be consider'd as they flow from the characters, being perfect or defective as they agree or disagree with the manners of those who utter them. As there is more variety of characters in the *Iliad*, so there is of speeches, than in any other poem. *Every thing in it has manners* (as *Aristotle* expresses it) that is, every thing is acted or spoken. It is hardly credible in a work of such length, how small a number of lines are employ'd in narration. In *Virgil* the dramatic part is less in proportion to the narrative; and the speeches often consist of general reflections or thoughts, which might be equally just in any person's mouth upon the same occasion. As many of his persons have no apparent characters, so many of his speeches escape being apply'd and judg'd by the rule of propriety. We oftner think of the author himself when we read *Virgil*, than when we are engag'd in *Homer*: All which are the effects of a colder invention, that interests us less in the action describ'd: *Homer* makes us hearers, and *Virgil* leaves us readers.

If in the next place we take a view of the *sentiments*, the same presiding faculty is eminent in the sublimity and spirit of his thoughts. *Longinus* has given his opinion, that it was in this part *Homer* principally excell'd. What were alone sufficient to prove the grandeur and excellence of his sentiments in general, is that they have so remarkable a parity with those of the scripture: *Duport*, in his *Gnomologia Homerica*, has collected innumerable instances of this sort. And it is with justice an excellent modern writer allows, that if *Virgil* has not so many thoughts that are low and vulgar, he has not so many that are sublime and noble; and that the *Roman* author seldom rises into very astonishing sentiments where he is not fired by the *Iliad*.

If we observe his *descriptions*, *images*, and *similes*, we shall find the invention still predominant. To what else can we ascribe that vast comprehension of images of every sort, where we see each circumstance of art, and individual of nature summon'd together by the extent and fecundity of his imagination; to which all things, in their various views, presented themselves in an instant, and had their impressions taken off to perfection, at a heat? Nay, he not only gives us the full prospects of things, but several unexpected peculiarities and side-views, unobserv'd by any Painter but *Homer*. Nothing is so surprizing as the descriptions of his battles, which take up no less than half the *Iliad*, and are supply'd with so vast a variety of incidents, that no one bears a likeness to another; such different kinds of deaths, that no two heroes are wounded in the same manner; and such a profusion of noble ideas, that every battle rises above the last in greatness, horror, and confusion. It is certain there is not near that number of images and descriptions in any Epic Poet; tho' every one has assisted himself with a great quantity out of him: And it is evident of *Virgil* especially, that he has scarce any comparisons which are not drawn from his master.

If we descend from hence to the *expression*, we see the bright imagination of *Homer* shining out in the most enliven'd forms of it. We acknowledge him the father of poetical diction, the first who taught that *Language of the Gods* to men. His expression is like the colouring of some great masters, which discovers itself to be laid on boldly, and executed with rapidity. It is indeed the strongest and most glowing imaginable, and touch'd with the greatest spirit. *Aristotle* had reason to say, He was the only Poet who had found out *living words*; there are in him more daring figures and metaphors than in any good author whatever. An arrow is *impatient* to be on the wing, a weapon *thirsts* to drink the blood of an enemy, and the like. Yet his expression is never too big for the sense, but justly great in proportion to it. 'Tis the sentiment that swells and fills out the diction, which rises with it, and forms itself about it: And in the same degree that a *thought* is warmer, an *expression* will be brighter; as that is more strong, this will become more perspicuous: Like glass in the furnace, which grows to a greater magnitude and refines to a greater clearness, only as the *breath* within is more powerful, and the *heat* more intense.

To throw his language more out of prose, *Homer* seems to have affected the *compound-epithets*. This was a sort of composition peculiarly proper to poetry, not only as it heighten'd the *diction*, but as it assisted and fill'd the *numbers* with greater sound and pomp, and likewise conduced in some measure to thicken the *images*. On this last consideration I cannot but attribute these also to the fruitfulness of his invention, since (as he has manag'd them) they are a sort of supernumerary pictures of the persons or things to which they are join'd. We see the motion of *Hector*'s plumes in the epithet Κορυθαίολος, the landscape of mount *Neritus* in that of Εἰνοσίφυλλος, and so of others; which particular images could not have been insisted upon so long as to express them in a description (tho' but of a single line) without diverting the reader too much from the principal action or figure. As a metaphor is a short simile, one of these epithets is a short description.

Lastly, if we consider his *versification*, we shall be sensible what a share of praise is due to his invention in that. He was not satisfy'd with his language as he found it settled in any one part of *Greece*, but search'd thro' its differing *dialects* with this particular view, to beautify and perfect his numbers: He consider'd these as they had a greater mixture of vowels or consonants, and accordingly employ'd them as the verse requir'd either a greater smoothness or strength. What he most affected was the *Ionic*, which has a peculiar sweetness from its

never using contractions, and from its custom of resolving the diph-
thongs into two syllables; so as to make the words open themselves
with a more spreading and sonorous fluency. With this he mingled the
Attic contractions, the broader *Doric*, and the feebler *Æolic*, which
often rejects its aspirate, or takes off its accent; and compleated this
variety by altering some letters with the license of poetry. Thus his
measures, instead of being fetters to his sense, were always in readiness
to run along with the warmth of his rapture, and even to give a farther
representation of his notions, in the correspondence of their sounds to
what they signify'd. Out of all these he has deriv'd that harmony,
which makes us confess he had not only the richest head, but the finest
ear in the world. This is so great a truth, that whoever will but consult
the tune of his verses, even without understanding them (with the
same sort of diligence as we daily see practis'd in the case of *Italian
Operas*) will find more sweetness, variety, and majesty of sound, than
in any other language or poetry. The beauty of his numbers is allow'd
by the criticks to be copied but faintly by *Virgil* himself, tho' they are
so just to ascribe it to the nature of the *Latin* tongue: Indeed the *Greek*
has some advantages both from the natural *sound* of its *words*, and the
turn and *cadence* of its *Verse*, which agree with the genius of no other
language. *Virgil* was very sensible of this, and used the utmost diligence
in working up a more intractable language to whatsoever graces it was
capable of; and in particular never fail'd to bring the sound of his line
to a beautiful agreement with its sense. If the *Grecian* poet has not
been so frequently celebrated on this account as the *Roman*, the only
reason is, that fewer criticks have understood one language than the
other. *Dionysius* of *Halicarnassus* has pointed out many of our author's
beauties in this kind, in his treatise of the *Composition of Words*, and
others will be taken notice of in the course of my Notes. It suffices at
present to observe of his numbers, that they flow with so much ease, as
to make one imagine *Homer* had no other care than to transcribe as fast
as the *Muses* dictated: and at the same time with so much force and
inspiriting vigour, that they awaken and raise us like the sound of a
trumpet. They roll along as a plentiful river, always in motion, and
always full; while we are born away by a tide of verse, the most rapid,
and yet the most smooth imaginable.

Thus on whatever side we contemplate *Homer*, what principally
strikes us is his *invention*. It is that which forms the character of each
part of his work; and accordingly we find it to have made his fable
more *extensive* and *copious* than any other, his manners more *lively* and

strongly marked, his speeches more *affecting* and *transported*, his sentiments more *warm* and *sublime*, his images and descriptions more *full* and *animated*, his expression more *rais'd* and *daring*, and his numbers more *rapid* and *various*. I hope in what has been said of *Virgil*, with regard to any of these heads, I have no way derogated from his character. Nothing is more absurd or endless, than the common method of comparing eminent writers by an opposition of particular passages in them, and forming a judgment from thence of their merit upon the whole. We ought to have a certain knowledge of the principal character and distinguishing excellence of each: It is in *that* we are to consider him, and in proportion to his degree in *that* we are to admire him. No author or man ever excell'd all the world in more than one faculty, and as *Homer* has done this in *invention*, *Virgil* has in *judgment*. Not that we are to think *Homer* wanted judgment, because *Virgil* had it in a more eminent degree; or that *Virgil* wanted invention, because *Homer* possest a larger share of it: each of these great authors had more of both than perhaps any man besides, and are only said to have less in comparison with one another. *Homer* was the greater genius, *Virgil* the better artist. In one we most admire the *man*, in the other the *work*. *Homer* hurries and transports us with a commanding impetuosity, *Virgil* leads us with an attractive majesty: *Homer* scatters with a generous profusion, *Virgil* bestows with a careful magnificence: *Homer*, like the *Nile*, pours out his riches with a boundless overflow; *Virgil* like a river in its banks, with a gentle and constant stream. When we behold their battles, methinks the two Poets resemble the heroes they celebrate: *Homer*, boundless and irresistible as *Achilles*, bears all before him, and shines more and more as the tumult increases; *Virgil*, calmly daring like *Æneas*, appears undisturb'd in the midst of the action; disposes all about him, and conquers with tranquillity: And when we look upon their machines, *Homer* seems like his own *Jupiter* in his terrors, shaking *Olympus*, scattering the lightnings, and firing the heavens; *Virgil*, like the same power in his benevolence, counselling with the Gods, laying plans for empires, and regularly ordering his whole creation.

But after all, it is with great parts as with great virtues, they naturally border on some imperfection; and it is often hard to distinguish exactly where the virtue ends, or the fault begins. As prudence may sometimes sink to suspicion, so may a great judgment decline to coldness; and as magnanimity may run up to profusion or extravagance, so may a great invention to redundancy or wildness. If we look upon

Homer in this view, we shall perceive the chief *objections* against him to proceed from so noble a cause as the excess of this faculty.

Among these we may reckon some of his *marvellous fictions*, upon which so much criticism has been spent, as surpassing all the bounds of probability. Perhaps it may be with great and superior souls as with gigantick bodies, which exerting themselves with unusual strength, exceed what is commonly thought the due proportion of parts, to become miracles in the whole; and like the old heroes of that make, commit something near extravagance amidst a series of glorious and inimitable performances. Thus *Homer* has his *speaking horses*, and *Virgil* his *myrtles distilling blood*, where the latter has not so much as contrived the easy intervention of a Deity to save the probability.

It is owing to the same vast invention, that his *Similes* have been thought too exuberant and full of circumstances. The force of this faculty is seen in nothing more, than in its inability to confine itself to that single circumstance upon which the comparison is grounded: It runs out into embellishments of additional images, which however are so manag'd as not to overpower the main one. His similes are like pictures, where the principal figure has not only its proportion given agreeable to the original, but is also set off with occasional ornaments and prospects. The same will account for his manner of heaping a number of comparisons together in one breath, when his fancy suggested to him at once so many various and correspondent images. The reader will easily extend this observation to more objections of the same kind.

If there are others which seem rather to charge him with a defect or narrowness of genius, than an excess of it; those seeming defects will be found upon examination to proceed wholly from the nature of the times he liv'd in. Such are his *grosser representations* of the *Gods*, and the vicious and *imperfect manners* of his *Heroes*, which will be treated of in the following **Essay*: But I must here speak a word of the latter, as it is a point generally carry'd into extremes, both by the censurers and defenders of *Homer*. It must be a strange partiality to antiquity, to think with Madam *Dacier*, 'that † those times and manners are so much the more excellent, as they are more contrary to ours.' Who can be so prejudiced in their favour as to magnify the felicity of those ages, when

---

* *See the Articles of* Theology *and* Morality, *in the third Part of the* Essay [not included in this edition].

† *Preface to her* Homer.

a spirit of revenge and cruelty, join'd with the practice of Rapine and Robbery, reign'd thro' the world; when no mercy was shown but for the sake of lucre, when the greatest Princes were put to the sword, and their wives and daughters made slaves and concubines? On the other side, I would not be so delicate as those modern criticks, who are shock'd at the *servile offices* and *mean employments* in which we sometimes see the Heroes of *Homer* engag'd. There is a pleasure in taking a view of that simplicity in opposition to the luxury of succeeding ages, in beholding Monarchs without their guards, Princes tending their flocks, and Princesses drawing water from the springs. When we read *Homer*, we ought to reflect that we are reading the most ancient author in the heathen world; and those who consider him in this light, will double their pleasure in the perusal of him. Let them think they are growing acquainted with nations and people that are now no more; that they are stepping almost three thousand years back into the remotest antiquity, and entertaining themselves with a clear and surprizing vision of things no where else to be found, the only true mirror of that ancient world. By this means alone their greatest obstacles will vanish; and what usually creates their dislike, will become a satisfaction.

This consideration may farther serve to answer for the constant use of the same *epithets* to his Gods and Heroes, such as the *far-darting Phœbus*, the *blue-ey'd Pallas*, the *swift-footed Achilles*, &c. which some have censured as impertinent and tediously repeated. Those of the Gods depended upon the powers and offices then believ'd to belong to them, and had contracted a weight and veneration from the rites and solemn devotions in which they were us'd: They were a sort of attributes with which it was a matter of religion to salute them on all occasions, and which it was an irreverence to omit. As for the epithets of great men, Mons. *Boileau* is of opinion; that they were in the nature of *Surnames*, and repeated as such; for the *Greeks* having no names deriv'd from their fathers, were oblig'd to add some other distinction of each person; either naming his parents expressly, or his place of birth, profession, or the like: As *Alexander* the son of *Philip*, *Herodotus* of *Halicarnassus*, *Diogenes* the *Cynic*, &c. *Homer* therefore complying with the custom of his country, us'd such distinctive additions as better agreed with poetry. And indeed we have something parallel to these in modern times, such as the names of *Harold Harefoot*, *Edmund Ironside*, *Edward Long-shanks*, *Edward* the *black Prince*, &c. If yet this be thought to account better for the propriety than for the repetition, I shall add a farther conjecture. *Hesiod* dividing the world into its different ages, has plac'd a fourth age between the brazen and the iron one, of *Heroes distinct from other men, a divine race, who fought at* Thebes *and* Troy, *are called Demi-Gods, and live by the care of* Jupiter *in the islands of the blessed.** Now among the divine honours which were paid them, they might have this also in common with the Gods, not to be mention'd without the solemnity of an epithet, and such as might be acceptable to them by its celebrating their families, actions, or qualities.

What other cavils have been rais'd against *Homer* are such as hardly deserve a reply, but will yet be taken notice of as they occur in the course of the work. Many have been occasion'd by an injudicious endeavour to exalt *Virgil*; which is much the same, as if one should think to raise the superstructure by undermining the foundation: One would imagine by the whole course of their parallels, that these Criticks never so much as heard of *Homer*'s having written first; a consideration which whoever compares these two Poets, ought to have always in his eye. Some accuse him for the same things which they overlook or praise in the other; as when they prefer the fable and moral of the *Æneis* to those of the *Iliad*, for the same reasons which might set the *Odysses* above the *Æneis*: as that the Heroe is a wiser man; and the action of the one more beneficial to his country than that of the other: Or else they blame him for not doing what he never design'd; as because *Achilles* is not as good and perfect a prince as *Æneas*, when the very moral of his poem requir'd a contrary character: It is thus that *Rapin* judges in his comparison of *Homer* and *Virgil*. Others select those particular passages of *Homer* which are not so labour'd as some that *Virgil* drew out of them: This is the whole management of *Scaliger* in his *Poetices*. Others quarrel with what they take for low and mean expressions, sometimes thro' a false delicacy and refinement, oftner from an ignorance of the graces of the original; and then triumph in the aukwardness of their own translations. This is the conduct of *Perault* in his *Parallels*. Lastly, there are others, who pretending to a fairer proceeding, distinguish between the personal merit of *Homer*, and that of his *work*; but when they come to assign the causes of the great reputation of the *Iliad*, they found it upon the ignorance of his times, and the prejudice of those that followed: And in

* Hesiod, *lib.* 1. v. 155, &c.

pursuance of this principle, they make those accidents (such as the contention of the cities, &c.) to be the causes of his fame, which were in reality the consequences of his merit. The same might as well be said of *Virgil*, or any great author, whose general character will infallibly raise many casual additions to their reputation. This is the method of Mons. *de la Motte*; who yet confesses upon the whole, that in whatever age *Homer* had liv'd, he must have been the greatest poet of his nation, and that he may be said in this sense to be the master even of those who surpass'd him.

In all these objections we see nothing that contradicts his title to the honour of the chief *Invention*; and as long as this (which is indeed the characteristic of Poetry itself) remains unequal'd by his followers, he still continues superior to them. A cooler judgment may commit fewer faults, and be more approv'd in the eyes of *one sort* of Criticks: but that warmth of fancy will carry the loudest and most universal applauses, which holds the heart of a reader under the strongest enchantment. *Homer* not only appears the Inventor of Poetry, but excells all the inventors of other arts in this, that he has swallow'd up the honour of those who succeeded him. What he has done admitted no encrease, it only left room for contraction or regulation. He shew'd all the stretch of fancy at once; and if he has fail'd in some of his flights, it was but because he attempted every thing. A work of this kind seems like a mighty Tree which rises from the most vigorous seed, is improv'd with industry, flourishes, and produces the finest fruit; nature and art conspire to raise it; pleasure and profit join to make it valuable: and they who find the justest faults, have only said, that a few branches (which run luxuriant thro' a richness of nature) might be lopp'd into form to give it a more regular appearance.

Having now spoken of the beauties and defects of the original, it remains to treat of the translation, with the same view to the chief characteristic. As far as *that* is seen in the main parts of the Poem, such as the fable, manners, and sentiments, no translator can prejudice it but by wilful omissions or contractions. As it also breaks out in every particular image, description, and simile; whoever lessens or too much softens those, takes off from this chief character. It is the first grand duty of an interpreter to give his author entire and unmaim'd; and for the rest, the *diction* and *versification* only are his proper province; since these must be his own, but the others he is to take as he finds them.

It should then be consider'd what methods may afford some equiva-

lent in our language for the graces of these in the *Greek*. It is certain
no literal translation can be just to an excellent original in a superior
language: but it is a great mistake to imagine (as many have done) that
a rash paraphrase can make amends for this general defect; which is no
less in danger to lose the spirit of an ancient, by deviating into the
modern manners of expression. If there be sometimes a darkness, there
is often a light in antiquity, which nothing better preserves than a
version almost literal. I know no liberties one ought to take, but those
which are necessary for transfusing the spirit of the original, and
supporting the poetical style of the translation: And I will venture to
say, there have not been more men misled in former times by a servile
dull adherence to the letter, than have been deluded in ours by a
chimerical insolent hope of raising and improving their author. It is
not to be doubted that the *fire* of the Poem is what a translator should
principally regard, as it is most likely to expire in his managing:
However it is his safest way to be content with preserving this to his
utmost in the whole, without endeavouring to be more than he finds
his author is, in any particular place. 'Tis a great secret in writing to
know when to be plain, and when poetical and figurative; and it is
what *Homer* will teach us, if we will but follow modestly in his
footsteps. Where his diction is bold and lofty, let us raise ours as high
as we can; but where his is plain and humble, we ought not to be
deterr'd from imitating him by the fear of incurring the censure of a
meer *English* Critick. Nothing that belongs to *Homer* seems to have
been more commonly mistaken than the just pitch of his style: Some of
his translators having swell'd into fustian in a proud confidence of the
sublime; others sunk into flatness in a cold and timorous notion of
simplicity. Methinks I see these different followers of *Homer*, some
sweating and straining after him by violent leaps and bounds, (the
certain signs of false mettle) others slowly and servilely creeping in his
train, while the Poet himself is all the time proceeding with an
unaffected and equal majesty before them. However of the two ex-
treams one could sooner pardon frenzy than frigidity: No author is to
be envy'd for such commendations as he may gain by that character of
style, which his friends must agree together to call *simplicity*, and the
rest of the world will call *dulness*. There is a *graceful* and *dignify'd*
simplicity, as well as a bald and sordid one, which differ as much from
each other as the air of a plain man from that of a sloven: 'Tis one
thing to be tricked up, and another not to be dress'd at all. Simplicity
is the mean between ostentation and rusticity.

This pure and noble simplicity is no where in such perfection as in the *Scripture* and our Author. One may affirm, with all respect to the inspired writings, that the *divine Spirit* made use of no other words but what were intelligible and common to men at that time, and in that part of the world; and as *Homer* is the author nearest to those, his style must of course bear a greater resemblance to the sacred books than that of any other writer. This consideration (together with what has been observ'd of the parity of some of his thoughts) may methinks induce a translator on the one hand to give into several of those general phrases and manners of expression, which have attain'd a veneration even in our Language from being used in the *Old Testament*: as on the other, to avoid those which have been appropriated to the Divinity, and in a manner consign'd to mystery and religion.

For a farther preservation of this air of simplicity, a particular care should be taken to express with all plainness those *moral sentences* and *proverbial speeches* which are so numerous in this Poet. They have something venerable, and as I may say *oracular*, in that unadorn'd gravity and shortness with which they are deliver'd: a grace which would be utterly lost by endeavouring to give them what we call a more ingenious (that is a more modern) turn in the paraphrase.

Perhaps the mixture of some *Græcisms* and old words after the manner of *Milton*, if done without too much affectation, might not have an ill effect in a version of this particular work, which most of any other seems to require a venerable antique cast. But certainly the use of modern terms of war and government, such as *platoon*, *campagne*, *junto*, or the like (into which some of his translators have fallen) cannot be allowable; those only excepted, without which it is impossible to treat the subjects in any living language.

There are two peculiarities in *Homer*'s diction which are a sort of *marks* or *moles*, by which every common eye distinguishes him at first sight: Those who are not his greatest admirers look upon them as defects, and those who are seem pleased with them as beauties. I speak of his *compound epithets* and of his *repetitions*. Many of the former cannot be done literally into *English* without destroying the purity of our language. I believe such should be retain'd as slide easily of themselves into an *English-compound*, without violence to the ear or to the receiv'd rules of composition; as well as those which have receiv'd a sanction from the authority of our best Poets, and are become familiar thro' their use of them; such as the *cloud-compelling Jove*, *&c.* As for the rest, whenever any can be as fully and significantly exprest

in a single word as in a compounded one, the course to be taken is
obvious. Some that cannot be so turn'd as to preserve their full image
by one or two words, may have justice done them by circumlocution;
as the epithet εἰνοσίφυλλος to a mountain would appear little or
ridiculous translated literally *leaf-shaking*, but affords a majestic idea in
the *periphrasis: The lofty mountain shakes his waving woods.* Others
that admit of differing significations, may receive an advantage by a
judicious variation according to the occasions on which they are
introduc'd. For example, the epithet of *Apollo*, ἑκήβολος, or *far-shooting*,
is capable of two explications; one literal in respect of the darts and
bow, the ensigns of that God; the other allegorical with regard to the
rays of the sun: Therefore in such Places where *Apollo* is represented
as a God in person, I would use the former interpretation, and where
the effects of the sun are describ'd, I would make choice of the latter.
Upon the whole, it will be necessary to avoid that perpetual repetition
of the same epithets which we find in *Homer*, and which, tho' it might
be accommodated (as has been already shewn) to the ear of those
times, is by no means so to ours: But one may wait for opportunities of
placing them, where they derive an additional beauty from the occa-
sions on which they are employed; and in doing this properly, a
translator may at once shew his fancy and his judgment.

As for *Homer*'s *Repetitions*; we may divide them into three sorts; of
whole narrations and speeches, of single sentences, and of one verse or
hemistich. I hope it is not impossible to have such a regard to these, as
neither to lose so known a mark of the author on the one hand, nor to
offend the reader too much on the other. The repetition is not
ungraceful in those speeches where the dignity of the speaker renders
it a sort of insolence to alter his word; as in the messages from Gods to
men, or from higher powers to inferiors in concerns of state, or where
the ceremonial of religion seems to require it, in the solemn forms of
prayers, oaths, or the like. In other cases, I believe the best rule is to
be guided by the nearness, or distance, at which the repetitions are
plac'd in the original: When they follow too close one may vary the
expression, but it is a question whether a profess'd translator be
authorized to omit any: If they be tedious, the author is to answer
for it.

It only remains to speak of the *Versification*. *Homer* (as has been said)
is perpetually applying the sound to the sense, and varying it on every
new subject. This is indeed one of the most exquisite beauties of
poetry, and attainable by very few: I know only of *Homer* eminent for

it in the *Greek*, and *Virgil* in *Latin*. I am sensible it is what may sometimes happen by chance, when a writer is warm, and fully possest of his image: however it may be reasonably believed they design'd this, in whose verse it so manifestly appears in a superior degree to all others. Few readers have the ear to be judges of it; but those who have will see I have endeavour'd at this beauty.

Upon the whole, I must confess my self utterly incapable of doing justice to *Homer*. I attempt him in no other hope but that which one may entertain without much vanity, of giving a more tolerable copy of him than any entire translation in verse has yet done. We have only those of *Chapman*, *Hobbes*, and *Ogilby*. *Chapman* has taken the advantage of an immeasurable length of verse, notwithstanding which there is scarce any paraphrase more loose and rambling than his. He has frequent interpolations of four or six Lines, and I remember one in the thirteenth book of the *Odysses*, *v*. 312. where he has spun twenty verses out of two. He is often mistaken in so bold a manner, that one might think he deviated on purpose, if he did not in other places of his notes insist so much upon verbal trifles. He appears to have had a strong affectation of extracting new meanings out of his author, insomuch as to promise in his rhyming preface, a poem of the mysteries he had revealed in *Homer*: and perhaps he endeavoured to strain the obvious sense to this end. His expression is involved in fustian, a fault for which he was remarkable in his original writings, as in the tragedy of *Bussy d'Amboise*, &c. In a word, the nature of the man may account for his whole performance; for he appears from his preface and remarks to have been of an arrogant turn, and an enthusiast in poetry. His own boast of having finish'd half the *Iliad* in less than fifteen weeks, shews with what negligence his version was performed. But that which is to be allowed him, and which very much contributed to cover his defects, is a daring fiery spirit that animates his translation, which is something like what one might imagine *Homer* himself would have writ before he arriv'd at years of discretion.

Hobbes has given us a correct explanation of the sense in general, but for particulars and circumstances he continually lopps them, and often omits the most beautiful. As for its being esteem'd a close translation, I doubt not many have been led into that error by the shortness of it, which proceeds not from his following the original line by line, but from the contractions abovementioned. He sometimes omits whole similes and sentences, and is now and then guilty of mistakes, into which no writer of his learning could have fallen, but thro' carelessness. His Poetry, as well as *Ogilby*'s, is too mean for criticism.

It is a great loss to the poetical world that Mr. *Dryden* did not live to translate the *Iliad*. He has left us only the first book and a small part of the sixth; in which if he has in some places not truly interpreted the sense, or preserved the antiquities, it ought to be excused on account of the haste he was obliged to write in. He seems to have had too much regard to *Chapman*, whose words he sometimes copies, and has unhappily follow'd him in passages where he wanders from the original. However had he translated the whole work, I would no more have attempted *Homer* after him than *Virgil*, his version of whom (notwithstanding some human errors) is the most noble and spirited translation I know in any language. But the fate of great genius's is like that of great ministers, tho' they are confessedly the first in the commonwealth of letters, they must be envy'd and calumniated only for being at the head of it.

That which in my opinion ought to be the endeavour of any one who translates *Homer*, is above all things to keep alive that spirit and fire which makes his chief character: In particular places, where the sense can bear any doubt, to follow the strongest and most poetical, as most agreeing with that character; to copy him in all the variations of his style, and the different modulations of his numbers; to preserve in the more active or descriptive parts, a warmth and elevation; in the more sedate or narrative, a plainness and solemnity; in the speeches a fulness and perspicuity; in the sentences a shortness and gravity: Not to neglect even the little figures and turns on the words, nor sometimes the very cast of the periods; neither to omit or confound any rites or customs of antiquity: Perhaps too he ought to include the whole in a shorter compass, than has hitherto been done by any translator, who has tolerably preserved either the sense or poetry. What I would farther recommend to him, is to study his author rather from his own text, than from any commentaries, how learned soever, or whatever figure they may make in the estimation of the world, to consider him attentively in comparison with *Virgil* above all the ancients, and with *Milton* above all the moderns. Next these, the Archbishop of *Cambray*'s *Telemachus* may give him the truest idea of the spirit and turn of our author, and *Bossu*'s admirable treatise of the Epic poem the justest notion of his design and conduct. But after all, with whatever judgment and study a man may proceed, or with whatever happiness he may perform such a work, he must hope to please but a few; those only who have at once a taste of poetry, and competent learning. For to satisfy such as want either, is not in the nature of this undertaking;

since a meer modern wit can like nothing that is not *modern*, and a pedant nothing that is not *Greek*.

What I have done is submitted to the publick, from whose opinions I am prepared to learn; tho' I fear no judges so little as our best poets, who are most sensible of the weight of this task. As for the worst, whatever they shall please to say, they may give me some concern as they are unhappy Men, but none as they are malignant writers. I was guided in this translation by judgments very different from theirs, and by persons for whom they can have no kindness, if an old observation be true, that the strongest Antipathy in the world is that of fools to men of wit. Mr. *Addison* was the first whose advice determin'd me to undertake this task, who was pleas'd to write to me upon that occasion in such terms, as I cannot repeat without vanity. I was obliged to Sir *Richard Steele* for a very early recommendation of my undertaking to the publick. Dr. *Swift* promoted my interest with that warmth with which he always serves his friend. The humanity and frankness of Sir *Samuel Garth* are what I never knew wanting on any occasion. I must also acknowledge with infinite Pleasure, the many friendly offices, as well as sincere criticisms of Mr. *Congreve*, who had led me the way in translating some parts of *Homer*. I must add the Names of Mr. *Rowe* and Dr. *Parnell*, tho' I shall take a farther opportunity of doing justice to the last, whose good-nature (to give it a great panegyrick) is no less extensive than his learning. The favour of these gentlemen is not entirely undeserved by one who bears them so true an affection. But what can I say of the honour so many of the *Great* have done me, while the *first names* of the age appear as my subscribers, and the most distinguish'd patrons and ornaments of learning as my chief encouragers. Among these it is a particular pleasure to me to find, that my highest obligations are to such who have done most honour to the name of Poet: That his Grace the Duke of *Buckingham* was not displeas'd I should undertake the author to whom he has given (in his excellent *Essay*) so complete a Praise.

> *Read* Homer once, *and you can read no more;*
> *For all Books else appear so mean, so poor,*
> *Verse will seem Prose: but still persist to read,*
> *And* Homer *will be all the Books you need.*

That the Earl of *Halifax* was one of the first to favour me, of whom it is hard to say whether the advancement of the polite arts is more owing to his generosity or his example. That such a genius as my Lord

Bolingbroke, not more distinguished in the great scenes of business, than in all the useful and entertaining parts of learning, has not refus'd to be the critick of these sheets, and the patron of their writer. And that the noble author of the Tragedy of *Heroic Love*, has continu'd his partiality to me, from my writing Pastorals to my attempting the *Iliad*. I cannot deny my self the pride of confessing, that I have had the advantage not only of their advice for the conduct in general, but their correction of several particulars of this translation.

I could say a great deal of the Pleasure of being distinguish'd by the *Earl* of *Carnarvon*, but it is almost absurd to particularize any one generous action in a person whose whole life is a continued series of them. Mr. *Stanhope*, the present Secretary of State, will pardon my desire of having it known that he was pleas'd to promote this affair. The particular Zeal of Mr. *Harcourt* (the son of the late Lord Chancellor) gave me a proof how much I am honour'd in a share of his friendship. I must attribute to the same motive that of several others of my friends, to whom all acknowledgments are render'd unnecessary by the privileges of a familiar correspondence: And I am satisfy'd I can no way better oblige men of their turn, than by my silence.

In short, I have found more patrons than ever *Homer* wanted. He would have thought himself happy to have met the same favour at *Athens*, that has been shown me by its learned rival, the University of *Oxford*. And I can hardly envy him those pompous honours he receiv'd after death, when I reflect on the enjoyment of so many agreeable obligations, and easy friendships which make the satisfaction of life. This distinction is the more to be acknowledg'd, as it is shewn to one whose pen has never gratify'd the prejudices of particular *parties*, or the vanities of particular *men*. Whatever the success may prove, I shall never repent of an undertaking in which I have experienc'd the candour and friendship of so many persons of merit; and in which I hope to pass some of those years of youth that are generally lost in a circle of follies, after a manner neither wholly unuseful to others, nor disagreeable to my self.

THE
FIRST BOOK
OF THE
ILIAD

The ARGUMENT

The Contention of *Achilles* and *Agamemnon*

In the War of Troy, *the Greeks having sack'd some of the neighbouring towns, and taken from thence two beautiful captives,* Chruseïs *and* Briseïs, *allotted the first to* Agamemnon, *and the last to* Achilles. Chryses, *the father of* Chruseïs *and Priest of* Apollo, *comes to the* Grecian *Camp to ransome her; with which the action of the poem opens, in the tenth year of the siege. The priest being refus'd and insolently dismiss'd by* Agamemnon, *intreats for vengeance from his God, who inflicts a pestilence on the* Greeks. Achilles *calls a council, and encourages* Chalcas *to declare the cause of it, who attributes it to the refusal of* Chruseïs. *The King being obliged to send back his captive, enters into a furious contest with* Achilles, *which* Nestor *pacifies; however as he had the absolute command of the army, he seizes on* Briseïs *in revenge.* Achilles *in discontent withdraws himself and his forces from the rest of the* Greeks; *and complaining to* Thetis, *she supplicates* Jupiter *to render them sensible of the wrong done to her sex, by giving victory to the* Trojans. Jupiter *granting her suit incenses* Juno, *between whom the debate runs high, 'till they are reconciled by the address of* Vulcan.

The time *of two and twenty Days is taken up in this book; nine during the plague, one in the council and quarrel of the Princes, and twelve for* Jupiter'*s Stay with the* Æthiopians, *at whose Return* Thetis *prefers her petition. The scene lies in the* Grecian *camp, then changes to* Chrysa, *and lastly to* Olympus.

Achilles' Wrath, to *Greece* the direful spring
Of woes unnumber'd, heav'nly Goddess, sing!
That Wrath which hurl'd to *Pluto*'s gloomy reign
The Souls of mighty Chiefs untimely slain;

5 Whose limbs unbury'd on the naked shore
Devouring dogs and hungry vultures tore:
Since Great *Achilles* and *Atrides* strove,
Such was the sov'reign doom, and such the will of *Jove!*
    Declare, O Muse! in what ill-fated hour

10 Sprung the fierce strife, from what offended pow'r?
Latona's son a dire contagion spread,
And heap'd the camp with mountains of the dead;
The King of Men his rev'rend Priest defy'd,
And for the King's offence the people dy'd.

15   For *Chryses* sought with costly gifts to gain
His captive daughter from the victor's chain.
Suppliant the venerable father stands,
Apollo's awful ensigns grace his hands:
By these he begs; and lowly bending down,

20 Extends the sceptre and the laurel crown.
He su'd to all, but chief implor'd for grace
The Brother-Kings, of *Atreus*' royal race.
    Ye Kings and warriors! may your vows be crown'd,
And *Troy*'s proud walls lie level with the ground.

25 May *Jove* restore you, when your toils are o'er,
Safe to the pleasures of your native shore.
But oh! relieve a wretched parent's pain,
And give *Chruseïs* to these arms again;

If Mercy fail, yet let my presents move,
And dread avenging *Phœbus*, son of *Jove*.　　　30
　　The *Greeks* in shouts their joint assent declare,
The priest to rev'rence, and release the fair.
Not so *Atrides*: He, with kingly pride,
Repuls'd the sacred sire, and thus reply'd.
Hence on thy life, and fly these hostile plains,　　35
Nor ask, presumptuous, what the King detains;
Hence, with thy laurel crown, and golden rod,
Nor trust too far those ensigns of thy God.
Mine is thy daughter, Priest, and shall remain;
And pray'rs, and tears, and bribes shall plead in vain;　　40
'Till time shall rifle ev'ry youthful grace,
And age dismiss her from my cold embrace,
In daily labours of the loom employ'd,
Or doom'd to deck the bed she once enjoy'd.
Hence then; to *Argos* shall the maid retire,　　45
Far from her native soil, and weeping sire.
　　The trembling priest along the shore return'd,
And in the anguish of a father mourn'd.
Disconsolate, nor daring to complain,
Silent he wander'd by the sounding main:　　50
'Till, safe at distance, to his God he prays,
The God who darts around the world his rays.
　　O *Smintheus!* sprung from fair *Latona*'s line,
Thou guardian pow'r of *Cilla* the divine,
Thou source of light! whom *Tenedos* adores,　　55
And whose bright presence gilds thy *Chrysa*'s shores:
If e'er with wreaths I hung thy sacred fane,
Or fed the flames with fat of oxen slain;
God of the silver bow! thy shafts employ,
Avenge thy servant, and the *Greeks* destroy.　　60
　　Thus *Chryses* pray'd: the fav'ring Pow'r attends,
And from *Olympus*' lofty tops descends.
Bent was his bow, the *Grecian* hearts to wound;
Fierce as he mov'd, his silver shafts resound.
Breathing revenge, a sudden night he spread,　　65
And gloomy darkness roll'd around his head.
The fleet in view, he twang'd his deadly bow,
And hissing fly the feather'd fates below.

On mules and dogs th' infection first began,
70 And last, the vengeful arrows fix'd in man.
For nine long nights, thro' all the dusky air
The *Pyres* thick-flaming shot a dismal glare.
But ere the tenth revolving day was run,
Inspir'd by *Juno*, *Thetis*' god-like son
75 Conven'd to council all the *Grecian* train;
For much the Goddess mourn'd her Heroes slain.
    Th' Assembly seated, rising o'er the rest,
Achilles thus the King of men addrest.
Why leave we not the fatal *Trojan* shore,
80 And measure back the seas we crost before?
The plague destroying whom the sword would spare,
'Tis time to save the few remains of war.
But let some Prophet, or some sacred Sage,
Explore the cause of great *Apollo*'s Rage;
85 Or learn the wastful vengeance to remove,
By mystic dreams; for dreams descend from *Jove*.
If broken vows this heavy curse have laid,
Let altars smoke, and hecatombs be paid.
So Heav'n aton'd shall dying *Greece* restore,
90 And *Phœbus* dart his burning shafts no more.
    He said, and sate: when *Chalcas* thus reply'd;
Chalcas the wise, the *Grecian* priest and guide,
That sacred Seer, whose comprehensive view
The past, the present, and the future knew:
95 Uprising slow, the venerable Sage
Thus spoke the prudence and the fears of age.
    Belov'd of *Jove*, *Achilles!* wou'dst thou know
Why angry *Phœbus* bends his fatal bow?
First give thy faith, and plight a Prince's word
100 Of sure protection by thy pow'r and sword.
For I must speak what wisdom would conceal,
And truths, invidious to the Great, reveal.
Bold is the task, when subjects grown too wise,
Instruct a monarch where his error lies;
105 For tho' we deem the short-liv'd fury past,
'Tis sure, the mighty will revenge at last.
    To whom *Pelides*. From thy inmost soul
Speak what thou know'st, and speak without controul.

Ev'n by that God I swear, who rules the day,
To whom thy hands the Vows of *Greece* convey,   110
And whose blest oracles thy lips declare;
Long as *Achilles* breathes this vital air,
No daring *Greek* of all the num'rous band,
Against his Priest shall lift an impious hand:
Not ev'n the Chief by whom our hosts are led,   115
The King of Kings, shall touch that sacred Head.
    Encourag'd thus, the blameless man replies:
Nor vows unpaid, nor slighted sacrifice,
But he, our Chief, provok'd the raging pest,
Apollo's vengeance for his injur'd Priest.   120
Nor will the God's awaken'd fury cease,
But plagues shall spread, and fun'ral fires increase,
'Till the great King, without a ransom paid,
To her own *Chrysa* send the black-ey'd maid.
Perhaps, with added sacrifice and pray'r,   125
The Priest may pardon, and the God may spare.
    The Prophet spoke; when with a gloomy frown,
The monarch started from his shining throne;
Black choler fill'd his breast that boil'd with ire,
And from his eyeballs flash'd the living fire.   130
Augur accurst! denouncing mischief still,
Prophet of plagues, for ever boding ill!
Still must that tongue some wounding message bring,
And still thy priestly pride provoke thy King?
For this are *Phœbus*' Oracles explor'd,   135
To teach the *Greeks* to murmur at their Lord?
For this with falshoods is my honour stain'd;
Is Heav'n offended, and a Priest profan'd,
Because my Prize, my beauteous maid I hold,
And heav'nly charms prefer to proffer'd gold?   140
A maid, unmatch'd in manners as in face,
Skill'd in each art, and crown'd with ev'ry grace.
Not half so dear were *Clytemnestra*'s charms,
When first her blooming beauties blest my arms.
Yet if the Gods demand her, let her sail;   145
Our cares are only for the publick weal:
Let me be deem'd the hateful cause of all,
And suffer, rather than my people fall.

The prize, the beauteous prize I will resign,
150   So dearly valu'd, and so justly mine.
But since for common good I yield the fair,
My private loss let grateful *Greece* repair;
Nor unrewarded let your Prince complain,
That he alone has fought and bled in vain.

155   Insatiate King (*Achilles* thus replies)
Fond of the pow'r, but fonder of the prize!
Would'st thou the *Greeks* their lawful prey shou'd yield,
The due reward of many a well-fought field?
The spoils of cities raz'd, and warriours slain,
160   We share with justice, as with toil we gain:
But to resume whate'er thy av'rice craves,
(That trick of tyrants) may be born by slaves.
Yet if our Chief for plunder only fight,
The spoils of *Ilion* shall thy loss requite,
165   Whene'er, by *Jove*'s decree, our conqu'ring pow'rs
Shall humble to the dust her lofty tow'rs.

        Then thus the King. Shall I my prize resign
With tame content, and thou possess of thine?
Great as thou art, and like a God in fight,
170   Think not to rob me of a soldier's right.
At thy demand shall I restore the maid?
First let the just equivalent be paid;
Such as a King might ask; and let it be
A treasure worthy her, and worthy me.
175   Or grant me this, or with a monarch's claim
This hand shall seize some other captive dame.
The mighty *Ajax* shall his prize resign,
Ulysses' spoils, or ev'n thy own be mine.
The man who suffers, loudly may complain;
180   And rage he may, but he shall rage in vain.
But this when time requires – It now remains
We launch a bark to plow the watry plains,
And waft the sacrifice to *Chrysa*'s shores,
With chosen pilots, and with lab'ring oars.
185   Soon shall the fair the sable ship ascend,
And some deputed Prince the charge attend;
This *Creta*'s King, or *Ajax* shall fulfill,
Or wise *Ulysses* see perform'd our will;

Or, if our royal pleasure shall ordain,
Achilles' self conduct her o'er the Main;   190
Let fierce *Achilles*, dreadful in his rage,
The God propitiate, and the pest asswage.

At this, *Pelides* frowning stern, reply'd:
O tyrant, arm'd with insolence and pride!
Inglorious slave to int'rest, ever join'd   195
With fraud, unworthy of a royal mind.
What gen'rous *Greek*, obedient to thy word,
Shall form an ambush, or shall lift the sword?
What cause have I to war at thy decree?
The distant *Trojans* never injur'd me: 200
To *Pthia*'s realms no hostile troops they led,
Safe in her vales my warlike coursers fed;
Far hence remov'd, the hoarse-resounding main
And walls of rocks, secure my native reign,
Whose fruitful soil luxuriant harvests grace,   205
Rich in her fruits, and in her martial race.
Hither we sail'd, a voluntary throng,
T'avenge a private, not a publick wrong:
What else to *Troy* th' assembled nations draws,
But thine, ungrateful, and thy brother's cause?   210
Is this the pay our blood and toils deserve,
Disgrac'd and injur'd by the man we serve?
And dar'st thou threat to snatch my prize away,
Due to the deeds of many a dreadful day?
A prize as small, O tyrant! match'd with thine,   215
As thy own actions if compar'd to mine.
Thine in each conquest is the wealthy prey,
Tho' mine the sweat and danger of the day.
Some trivial present to my ships I bear,
Or barren praises pay the wounds of war.   220
But know, proud monarch, I'm thy slave no more;
My fleet shall waft me to *Thessalia*'s shore.
Left by *Achilles* on the *Trojan* plain,
What spoils, what conquests shall *Atrides* gain?

To this the King: Fly, mighty warriour! fly,   225
Thy aid we need not, and thy threats defy.
There want not chiefs in such a cause to fight,
And *Jove* himself shall guard a monarch's right.

Of all the Kings (the Gods distinguish'd care)
230 To pow'r superior none such hatred bear:
Strife and debate thy restless soul employ,
And wars and horrours are thy savage joy.
If thou hast strength, 'twas Heav'n that strength
          bestow'd,
For know, vain man! thy valour is from God.
235 Haste, launch thy vessels, fly with speed away,
Rule thy own realms with arbitrary sway:
I heed thee not, but prize at equal rate
Thy short-liv'd friendship, and thy groundless hate.
Go, threat thy earth-born *Myrmidons*; but here
240 'Tis mine to threaten, Prince, and thine to fear.
Know, if the God the beauteous dame demand,
My bark shall waft her to her native land;
But then prepare, imperious Prince! prepare,
Fierce as thou art, to yield thy captive fair:
245 Ev'n in thy tent I'll seize the blooming prize,
Thy lov'd *Briseïs* with the radiant eyes.
Hence shalt thou prove my might, and curse the hour,
Thou stood'st a rival of imperial pow'r;
And hence to all our host it shall be known,
250 That Kings are subject to the Gods alone.
     Achilles heard, with grief and rage opprest,
His heart swell'd high, and labour'd in his breast.
Distracting thoughts by turns his bosom rul'd,
Now fir'd by wrath, and now by reason cool'd:
255 That prompts his hand to draw the deadly sword,
Force thro' the *Greeks*, and pierce their haughty Lord;
This whispers soft, his vengeance to controul,
And calm the rising tempest of his soul.
Just as in anguish of suspence he stay'd,
260 While half unsheath'd appear'd the glitt'ring blade,
Minerva swift descended from above,
Sent by the *sister and the wife of *Jove*;
(For both the Princes claim'd her equal Care)
Behind she stood, and by the golden hair

* *Juno.*

Achilles seiz'd; to him alone confest;   265
A sable cloud conceal'd her from the rest.
He sees, and sudden to the Goddess cries,
Known by the flames that sparkle from her eyes.
　　Descends *Minerva*, in her guardian care,
A heav'nly witness of the wrongs I bear   270
From *Atreus*' Son? Then let those eyes that view
The daring crime, behold the vengeance too.
　　Forbear! (the progeny of *Jove* replies)
To calm thy fury I forsake the skies:
Let great *Achilles*, to the Gods resign'd,   275
To reason yield the empire o'er his mind.
By awful *Juno* this command is giv'n;
The King and you are both the care of Heav'n.
The force of keen reproaches let him feel,
But sheath, obedient, thy revenging steel.   280
For I pronounce (and trust a heav'nly pow'r)
Thy injur'd honour has its fated hour,
When the proud monarch shall thy arms implore,
And bribe thy friendship with a boundless store.
Then let revenge no longer bear the sway,   285
Command thy passions, and the Gods obey.
　　To her *Pelides*. With regardful ear
'Tis just, O Goddess! I thy dictates hear.
Hard as it is, my vengeance I suppress:
Those who revere the Gods, the Gods will bless.   290
He said, observant of the blue-ey'd maid;
Then in the sheath return'd the shining blade.
The Goddess swift to high *Olympus* flies,
And joins the sacred senate of the skies.
　　Nor yet the rage his boiling breast forsook,   295
Which thus redoubling on *Atrides* broke.
O monster, mix'd of insolence and fear,
Thou dog in forehead, but in heart a deer!
When wert thou known in ambush'd fights to dare,
Or nobly face the horrid front of war?   300
'Tis ours, the chance of fighting fields to try,
Thine to look on, and bid the Valiant die.
So much 'tis safer thro' the camp to go,
And rob a subject, than despoil a foe.

305 Scourge of thy people, violent and base!
Sent in *Jove*'s anger on a slavish race,
Who lost to sense of gen'rous freedom past,
Are tam'd to wrongs, or this had been thy last.
Now by this sacred sceptre, hear me swear,
310 Which never more shall leaves or blossoms bear,
Which sever'd from the trunk (as I from thee)
On the bare mountains left its parent tree;
This sceptre, form'd by temper'd steel to prove
An ensign of the delegates of *Jove*,
315 From whom the pow'r of laws and justice springs:
(Tremendous oath! inviolate to Kings)
By this I swear, when bleeding *Greece* again
Shall call *Achilles*, she shall call in vain.
When flush'd with slaughter, *Hector* comes, to spread
320 The purpled shore with mountains of the dead,
Then shalt thou mourn th' affront thy madness gave,
Forc'd to deplore, when impotent to save:
Then rage in bitterness of soul, to know
This act has made the bravest *Greek* thy foe.

325   He spoke; and furious, hurl'd against the ground
His Sceptre starr'd with golden studs around.
Then sternly silent sate. With like disdain,
The raging King return'd his frowns again.
    To calm their passion with the words of age,
330 Slow from his seat arose the *Pylian* sage;
Experienc'd *Nestor*, in persuasion skill'd,
Words, sweet as honey, from his lips distill'd:
Two generations now had past away,
Wise by his rules, and happy by his sway;
335 Two ages o'er his native realm he reign'd,
And now th' example of the third remain'd.
All view'd with awe the venerable man;
Who thus, with mild benevolence, began:
    What shame, what woe is this to *Greece*! what joy
340 To *Troy*'s proud monarch, and the friends of *Troy*!
That adverse Gods commit to stern debate
The best, the bravest of the *Grecian* state.
Young as ye are, this youthful heat restrain,
Nor think your *Nestor*'s years and wisdom vain.

A Godlike race of Heroes once I knew,   345
Such, as no more these aged eyes shall view!
Lives there a chief to match *Pirithous'* fame,
Dryas the bold, or *Ceneus'* deathless name;
Theseus, endu'd with more than mortal might,
Or *Polyphemus*, like the Gods in fight?   350
With these of old to toils of battel bred,
In early youth my hardy days I led;
Fir'd with the thirst which virtuous envy breeds,
And smit with love of honourable deeds.
Strongest of men, they pierc'd the mountain boar,   355
Rang'd the wild deserts red with monsters Gore,
And from their hills the shaggy *Centaurs* tore.
Yet these with soft, persuasive arts I sway'd;
When *Nestor* spoke, they listen'd and obey'd.
If, in my youth, ev'n these esteem'd me wise,   360
Do you, young warriors, hear my age advise.
Atrides, seize not on the beauteous slave;
That prize the *Greeks* by common suffrage gave:
Nor thou, *Achilles*, treat our prince with pride;
Let Kings be just, and sov'reign pow'r preside.   365
Thee, the first honours of the war adorn,
Like Gods in strength, and of a Goddess born;
Him awful majesty exalts above
The pow'rs of earth, and sceptred sons of *Jove*.
Let both unite with well-consenting mind,   370
So shall authority with strength be join'd.
Leave me, O King! to calm *Achilles'* rage;
Rule thou thy self, as more advanc'd in age.
Forbid it Gods! *Achilles* should be lost,
The pride of *Greece*, and bulwark of our host.   375
    This said, he ceas'd: The King of Men replies;
Thy years are awful, and thy words are wise.
But that imperious, that unconquer'd soul,
No laws can limit, no respect controul.
Before his pride must his superiors fall,   380
His Word the law, and he the Lord of all?
Him must our hosts, our chiefs, our self obey?
What King can bear a rival in his sway?

Grant that the Gods his matchless force have giv'n;
385   Has foul reproach a privilege from Heav'n?
        Here on the Monarch's speech *Achilles* broke,
And furious, thus, and interrupting spoke.
Tyrant, I well deserv'd thy galling chain,
To live thy slave, and still to serve in vain,
390   Should I submit to each unjust decree:
Command thy vassals, but command not me.
Seize on *Briseïs* , whom the *Grecians* doom'd
My prize of war, yet tamely see resum'd;
And seize secure; No more *Achilles* draws
395   His conqu'ring sword in any woman's cause.
The Gods command me to forgive the past;
But let this first invasion be the last:
For know, thy blood, when next thou dar'st invade,
Shall stream in vengeance on my reeking blade.
400   At this, they ceas'd; the stern debate expir'd:
The chiefs in sullen majesty retir'd.
        Achilles with *Patroclus* took his way,
Where near his tents his hollow vessels lay.
Mean time *Atrides* launch'd with num'rous oars
405   A well-rigg'd ship for *Chrysa*'s sacred shores:
High on the deck was fair *Chruseïs* plac'd,
And sage *Ulysses* with the conduct grac'd:
Safe in her Sides the hecatomb they stow'd,
Then swiftly sailing, cut the liquid road.
410   The host to expiate next the King prepares,
With pure lustrations, and with solemn pray'rs.
Wash'd by the briny wave, the pious train
Are cleans'd, and cast th' ablutions in the main.
Along the shore whole hecatombs were laid,
415   And bulls and goats to *Phœbus*' altars paid.
The sable fumes in curling spires arise,
And waft their grateful odours to the skies.
        The army thus in sacred rites engag'd,
Atrides still with deep resentment rag'd.
420   To wait his will two sacred heralds stood,
Talthybius and *Eurybates* the good.
Haste to the fierce *Achilles*' tent (he cries)
Thence bear *Briseïs* as our royal prize:

Submit he must; or if they will not part,
Ourself in arms shall tear her from his heart.   425
   Th' unwilling heralds act their Lord's Commands;
Pensive they walk along the barren sands:
Arriv'd, the Hero in his tent they find,
With gloomy aspect, on his arm reclin'd.
At awful distance long they silent stand,   430
Loth to advance, or speak their hard command;
Decent confusion! This the Godlike man
Perceiv'd, and thus with accent mild began.
   With leave and honour enter our abodes,
Ye sacred ministers of men and Gods!   435
I know your message; by constraint you came;
Not you, but your imperious lord I blame.
Patroclus haste, the fair *Briseïs* bring;
Conduct my captive to the haughty King.
But witness, heralds, and proclaim my vow,   440
Witness to Gods above, and men below!
But first, and loudest, to your Prince declare,
That lawless tyrant whose commands you bear;
Unmov'd as death *Achilles* shall remain,
Tho' prostrate *Greece* should bleed at ev'ry vein: 445
The raging Chief in frantick passion lost,
Blind to himself, and useless to his host,
Unskill'd to judge the future by the past,
In blood and slaughter shall repent at last.
   Patroclus now th' unwilling Beauty brought;   450
She, in soft sorrows, and in pensive thought,
Past silent, as the heralds held her hand,
And oft look'd back, slow-moving o'er the strand.
   Not so his loss the fierce *Achilles* bore;
But sad retiring to the sounding shore,   455
O'er the wild margin of the deep he hung,
That kindred deep, from whence his mother sprung:
There, bath'd in tears of anger and disdain,
Thus loud lamented to the stormy main.
   O parent Goddess! since in early bloom   460
Thy son must fall, by too severe a doom;
Sure, to so short a race of glory born,
Great *Jove* in justice should this span adorn:

Honour and fame at least the Thund'rer ow'd,
465 And ill he pays the promise of a God:
If yon proud monarch thus thy son defies,
Obscures my glories, and resumes my prize.
   Far in the deep recesses of the main,
Where aged *Ocean* holds his wat'ry reign,
470 The Goddess-mother heard. The waves divide;
And like a mist she rose above the tide;
Beheld him mourning on the naked shores,
And thus the sorrows of his soul explores.
Why grieves my son? Thy anguish let me share,
475 Reveal the cause, and trust a parent's care.
   He deeply sighing said: To tell my woe,
Is but to mention what too well you know.
From *Thebè* sacred to *Apollo*'s name,
(*Aëtion*'s realm) our conqu'ring army came,
480 With treasure loaded and triumphant spoils,
Whose just division crown'd the soldier's toils;
But bright *Chruseïs*, heav'nly prize! was led
By vote selected, to the Gen'ral's bed.
The priest of *Phœbus* sought by gifts to gain
485 His beauteous daughter from the victor's chain;
The fleet he reach'd, and lowly bending down,
Held forth the sceptre and the laurel crown,
Entreating all: but chief implor'd for grace
The brother kings of *Atreus*' royal race:
490 The gen'rous *Greeks* their joint consent declare,
The priest to rev'rence, and release the fair;
Not so *Atrides*: He, with wonted pride,
The sire insulted, and his gifts deny'd:
Th' insulted sire (his God's peculiar care)
495 To *Phœbus* pray'd, and *Phœbus* heard the pray'r:
A dreadful plague ensues; Th' avenging darts
Incessant fly, and pierce the *Grecian* hearts:
A prophet then, inspir'd by heav'n arose,
And points the crime, and thence derives the woes:
500 My self the first th' assembl'd chiefs incline
T'avert the vengeance of the pow'r divine;
Then rising in his wrath, the monarch storm'd;
Incens'd he threaten'd, and his threats perform'd:

The fair *Chruseïs* to her sire was sent,
With offer'd gifts to make the God relent;   505
But now he seiz'd *Briseïs*' heav'nly charms,
And of my valour's prize defrauds my arms,
Defrauds the votes of all the *Grecian* train;
And service, faith, and justice plead in vain.
But Goddess! thou, thy suppliant son attend,   510
To high *Olympus*' shining court ascend,
Urge all the ties to former service ow'd,
And sue for vengeance to the thund'ring God.
Oft hast thou triumph'd in the glorious boast,
That thou stood'st forth, of all th' æthereal host,   515
When bold rebellion shook the realms above,
Th' undaunted guard of cloud-compelling *Jove*.
When the bright partner of his awful reign,
The warlike maid, and monarch of the main,
The Traytor-Gods, by mad ambition driv'n,   520
Durst threat with chains th' omnipotence of heav'n.
Then call'd by thee, the monster *Titan* came,
(Whom Gods *Briareus*, Men *Ægeon* name)
Thro' wondring skies enormous stalk'd along;
Not *he that shakes the solid earth so strong: 525
With giant-pride at *Jove*'s high throne he stands,
And brandish'd round him all his hundred hands;
Th' affrighted Gods confess'd their awful lord,
They dropt the fetters, trembled and ador'd.
This, Goddess, this to his remembrance call,   530
Embrace his knees, at his tribunal fall;
Conjure him far to drive the *Grecian* train,
To hurl them headlong to their fleet and main,
To heap the shores with copious death, and bring
The *Greeks* to know the curse of such a King: 535
Let *Agamemnon* lift his haughty head
O'er all his wide dominion of the dead,
And mourn in blood, that e'er he durst disgrace
The boldest warriour of the *Grecian* race.

Unhappy son! (fair *Thetis* thus replies,   540
While tears celestial trickle from her eyes)

* *Neptune.*

Why have I born thee with a mother's throes,
To fates averse, and nurs'd for future woes?
So short a space the light of heav'n to view!
545   So short a space, and fill'd with sorrow too!
Oh might a parent's careful wish prevail,
Far, far from *Ilion* should thy vessels sail,
And thou, from camps remote, the danger shun,
Which now, alas! too nearly threats my son.
550   Yet (what I can) to move thy suit I'll go,
To great *Olympus* crown'd with fleecy snow.
Mean time, secure within thy ships from far
Behold the field, nor mingle in the war.
The sire of gods, and all th' ætherial Train,
555   On the warm limits of the farthest main,
Now mix with mortals, nor disdain to grace
The feasts of *Æthiopia*'s blameless race;
Twelve days the pow'rs indulge the genial rite,
Returning with the twelfth revolving light.
560   Then will I mount the brazen dome, and move
The high tribunal of immortal *Jove*.
    The Goddess spoke: The rowling waves unclose;
Then down the deep she plung'd from whence she rose,
And left him sorrowing on the lonely coast,
565   In wild resentment for the fair he lost.
    In *Chrysa*'s port now sage *Ulysses* rode;
Beneath the deck the destin'd victims stow'd:
The sails they furl'd, they lash'd the mast aside,
And dropt their anchors, and the pinnace ty'd.
570   Next on the shore their hecatomb they land,
Chruseïs last descending on the strand.
Her, thus returning from the furrow'd main,
Ulysses led to *Phœbus* sacred fane;
Where at his solemn altar, as the maid
575   He gave to *Chryses*, thus the hero said.
    Hail rev'rend priest! to *Phœbus*' awful dome
A suppliant I from great *Atrides* come:
Unransom'd here receive the spotless fair;
Accept the hecatomb the *Greeks* prepare;
580   And may thy God who scatters darts around,
Aton'd by sacrifice, desist to wound.

At this, the Sire embrac'd the maid again,
So sadly lost, so lately sought in vain.
Then near the altar of the darting King,
Dispos'd in rank their hecatomb they bring: 585
With water purify their hands, and take
The sacred off'ring of the salted cake;
While thus with arms devoutly rais'd in air,
And solemn voice, the priest directs his pray'r.

God of the silver bow, thy ear incline,   590
Whose power encircles *Cilla* the divine;
Whose sacred eye thy *Tenedos* surveys,
And gilds fair *Chrysa* with distinguish'd rays!
If, fir'd to vengeance at thy priest's request,
Thy direful darts inflict the raging pest;   595
Once more attend! avert the wastful woe,
And smile propitious, and unbend thy bow.

So *Chryses* pray'd, *Apollo* heard his pray'r:
And now the *Greeks* their hecatomb prepare;
Between their horns the salted barley threw,   600
And with their heads to heav'n the Victims slew:
The limbs they sever from th' inclosing hide;
The thighs, selected to the Gods, divide:
On these, in double cawls involv'd with art,
The choicest morsels lay from ev'ry part.   605
The Priest himself before his altar stands,
And burns the off'ring with his holy hands,
Pours the black wine, and sees the flames aspire;
The youth with instruments surround the fire:
The thighs thus sacrific'd, and entrails drest,   610
Th'assistants part, transfix, and roast the rest:
Then spread the tables, the repast prepare,
Each takes his seat, and each receives his share.
When now the rage of hunger was represt,
With pure libations they conclude the feast;   615
The youths with wine the copious goblets crown'd,
And pleas'd, dispense the flowing bowls around.
With hymns divine the joyous banquet ends,
The *Pæans* lengthen'd 'till the sun descends:
The *Greeks* restor'd the grateful notes prolong;   620
Apollo listens, and approves the song.

'Twas Night: the Chiefs beside their vessel lie,
'Till rosie morn had purpled o'er the sky:
Then launch, and hoise the mast; indulgent gales
625 Supply'd by *Phœbus*, fill the swelling sails;
The milk white canvas bellying as they blow,
The parted ocean foams and roars below:
Above the bounding billows swift they flew,
'Till now the *Grecian* camp appear'd in view.
630 Far on the beach they haul their bark to land,
(The crooked keel divides the yellow sand)
Then part, where stretch'd along the winding bay
The ships and tents in mingled prospect lay.

But raging still amidst his navy sate
635 The stern *Achilles*, stedfast in his hate;
Nor mix'd in combate, nor in council join'd;
But wasting cares lay heavy on his mind:
In his black thoughts revenge and slaughter roll,
And scenes of blood rise dreadful in his soul.
640 Twelve days were past, and now the dawning light
The Gods had summon'd to th' *Olympian* height.
Jove first ascending from the wat'ry bow'rs,
Leads the long order of ætherial pow'rs.
When like the morning mist, in early day,
645 Rose from the flood the daughter of the sea;
And to the seats divine her flight addrest.
There, far apart, and high above the rest,
The Thund'rer sate; where old *Olympus* shrouds
His hundred heads in Heav'n, and props the clouds.
650 Suppliant the Goddess stood: One hand she plac'd
Beneath his beard, and one his knees embrac'd.
If e'er, O father of the Gods! she said,
My words cou'd please thee, or my actions aid;
Some marks of honour on my son bestow,
655 And pay in glory what in life you owe.
Fame is at least by heav'nly promise due
To life so short, and now dishonour'd too.
Avenge this wrong, oh ever just and wise!
Let *Greece* be humbled, and the *Trojans* rise;
660 'Till the proud King, and all th' *Achaian* race
Shall heap with honours him they now disgrace.

Thus *Thetis* spoke, but *Jove* in silence held
The sacred counsels of his breast conceal'd.
Not so repuls'd, the Goddess closer prest,
Still grasp'd his knees, and urg'd the dear request.   665
O Sire of Gods and Men! thy suppliant hear,
Refuse, or grant; for what has *Jove* to fear?
Or oh! declare, of all the pow'rs above
Is wretched *Thetis* least the care of *Jove*?

     She said, and sighing thus the God replies,   670
Who rolls the thunder o'er the vaulted skies.
What hast thou ask'd? Ah why should *Jove* engage
In foreign contests, and domestic rage,
The Gods complaints, and *Juno*'s fierce alarms,
While I, too partial, aid the *Trojan* arms?   675
Go, lest the haughty partner of my sway
With jealous eyes thy close access survey;
But part in peace, secure thy pray'r is sped:
Witness the sacred honours of our head,
The nod that ratifies the will divine,   680
The faithful, fix'd, irrevocable sign;
This seals thy suit, and this fulfills thy vows –
He spoke, and awful, bends his sable brows;
Shakes his ambrosial curls, and gives the Nod;
The stamp of fate, and sanction of the God: 685
High Heav'n with trembling the dread signal took,
And all *Olympus* to the centre shook.

     Swift to the seas profound the Goddess flies,
Jove to his starry mansion in the skies.
The shining synod of th' immortals wait   690
The coming God, and from their thrones of state
Arising silent, wrapt in holy fear,
Before the Majesty of Heav'n appear.
Trembling they stand, while *Jove* assumes the throne,
All, but the God's imperious Queen alone: 695
Late had she view'd the silver-footed dame,
And all her passions kindled into flame.
Say, artful manager of heav'n (she cries)
Who now partakes the secrets of the skies?
Thy *Juno* knows not the decrees of fate,   700
In vain the partner of imperial state.

What fav'rite Goddess then those cares divides,
Which *Jove* in prudence from his consort hides?
To this the Thund'rer: Seek not thou to find
705 The sacred counsels of almighty mind:
Involv'd in darkness lies the great decree,
Nor can the depths of fate be pierc'd by thee.
What fits thy knowledge, thou the first shalt know;
The first of Gods above, and Men below:
710 But thou, nor they, shall search the thoughts that roll
Deep in the close recesses of my soul.

Full on the Sire the Goddess of the skies
Roll'd the large orbs of her majestic eyes,
And thus return'd. Austere *Saturnius*, say,
715 From whence this wrath, or who controuls thy sway?
Thy boundless will, for me, remains in force,
And all thy counsels take the destin'd course.
But 'tis for *Greece* I fear: For late was seen
In close consult, the silver-footed Queen.
720 *Jove* to his *Thetis* nothing could deny,
Nor was the signal vain that shook the sky.
What fatal favour has the Goddess won,
To grace her fierce, inexorable son?
Perhaps in *Grecian* blood to drench the plain,
725 And glut his vengeance with my people slain.

Then thus the God: Oh restless fate of pride,
That strives to learn what heav'n resolves to hide;
Vain is the search, presumptuous and abhorr'd,
Anxious to thee, and odious to thy Lord.
730 Let this suffice; th' immutable decree
No force can shake: What *is*, that *ought* to be.
Goddess submit, nor dare our Will withstand,
But dread the pow'r of this avenging hand;
Th' united Strength of all the Gods above
735 In vain resists th' omnipotence of *Jove*.

The Thund'rer spoke, nor durst the Queen reply;
A rev'rend horror silenc'd all the sky.
The feast disturb'd with sorrow *Vulcan* saw,
His mother menac'd, and the Gods in awe;
740 Peace at his heart, and pleasure his design,
Thus interpos'd the Architect divine.

The wretched quarrels of the mortal state
Are far unworthy, Gods! of your debate:
Let men their days in senseless strife employ,
We, in eternal peace, and constant joy. 745
Thou, Goddess-mother, with our sire comply,
Nor break the sacred union of the sky:
Lest, rouz'd to rage, he shake the blest abodes,
Launch the red lightning, and dethrone the gods.
If you submit, the Thund'rer stands appeas'd; 750
The gracious pow'r is willing to be pleas'd.
    Thus *Vulcan* spoke; and rising with a bound,
The double bowl with sparkling *Nectar* crown'd,
Which held to *Juno* in a chearful way,
Goddess (he cry'd) be patient and obey. 755
Dear as you are, if *Jove* his arm extend,
I can but grieve, unable to defend.
What God so daring in your aid to move,
Or lift his hand against the force of *Jove*?
Once in your cause I felt his matchless might, 760
Hurl'd headlong downward from th' etherial height;
Tost all the day in rapid circles round:
Nor 'till the Sun descended, touch'd the ground:
Breathless I fell, in giddy motion lost;
The *Sinthians* rais'd me on the *Lemnian* coast. 765
    He said, and to her hands the goblet heav'd,
Which, with a smile, the white arm'd Queen receiv'd.
Then to the rest he fill'd; and, in his turn,
Each to his lips apply'd the nectar'd urn.
Vulcan with aukward grace his office plies, 770
And unextinguish'd laughter shakes the skies.
    Thus the blest Gods the genial day prolong,
In feasts ambrosial, and celestial song.
Apollo tun'd the lyre; the *Muses* round
With voice alternate aid the silver sound. 775
Meantime the radiant Sun, to mortal Sight
Descending swift, roll'd down the rapid light.
Then to their starry domes the Gods depart,
The shining monuments of *Vulcan*'s art:
Jove on his couch reclin'd his awful head, 780
And *Juno* slumber'd on the golden bed.

OBSERVATIONS

ON THE

FIRST BOOK

The epigraph on the frontispiece of Volume I (Books 1–4) consists of the following lines:

> *Te sequor, O Graiæ gentis Decus! inque tuis nunc*
> *Fixa* [sic] *pedum pono pressis vestigia signis:*
> *Non ita certandi cupidus, quam propter amorem,*
> *Quod te imitari aveo –*   LUCRET.

[I follow you, O glory of the Grecian race, and on the marks you have made I firmly plant my own footsteps, not because I feel driven to rival your pre-eminence, but rather because I yearn to resemble you.]

It is something strange that of all the commentators upon *Homer*, there is hardly one whose principal design is to illustrate the poetical beauties of the author. They are voluminous in explaining those sciences which he made but subservient to his Poetry, and sparing only upon that art which constitutes his character. This has been occasion'd by the ostentation of men who had more reading than taste, and were fonder of shewing their variety of learning in all kinds, than their single understanding in Poetry. Hence it comes to pass that their remarks are rather philosophical, historical, geographical, allegorical, or in short rather any thing than critical and poetical. Even the Grammarians, tho' their whole business and use be only to render the words of an author intelligible, are strangely touch'd with the pride of doing something more than they ought. The grand ambition of one sort of scholars is to encrease the number of *various lections*; which they have done to such a degree of obscure diligence, that (as *Sir H. Savil* observ'd) we now begin to value the first Editions of books as most correct, because they have been least corrected. The prevailing passion of others is to discover *new meanings* in an author, whom they will cause to appear mysterious purely for the vanity of being thought to unravel him. These account it a disgrace to be of the opinion of those that preceded them; and it is generally the fate of such people who will never say what was said before, to say what will never be said after them. If they can but find a word that has once been strain'd by some dark writer to signify any thing different from its usual acceptation, it is frequent with them to apply it constantly to that uncommon meaning, whenever they meet it in a clear writer: For reading is so much dearer to them than sense, that they will discard it at any time to make way for a criticism. In other places where they cannot contest the truth of the common interpretation, they get themselves room for dissertation by imaginary *Amphibologies*, which they will have to be design'd by the Author. This Disposition of finding out different significations in one thing, may be the effect of either too much, or too little wit: For Men of a right understanding generally see at once all that an Author can reasonably mean, but others are apt to fancy two meanings for want of knowing one. Not to add, that there is a vast deal of difference between the learning of a Critick, and the puzzling of a Grammarian.

It is no easy task to make something out of a hundred pedants that is not pedantical; yet this he must do, who would give a tolerable abstract of the former expositors of *Homer*. The commentaries of *Eustathius* are indeed an immense treasury of the *Greek* learning; but as he seems to have amassed the substance of whatever others had written upon the author, so he is not free from some of the foregoing censures. There are those who have said, that a judicious abstract of him alone might furnish out sufficient illustrations upon *Homer*. It was resolv'd to take the trouble of reading thro' that voluminous work, and the reader may be assur'd, those remarks that any way concern the Poetry or art of the Poet, are much fewer than is imagin'd. The greater Part of these is already plunder'd by succeeding commentators, who have very little but what they owe to him: and I am oblig'd to say even of Madam *Dacier*, that she is either more beholden to him than she has confessed, or has read him less than she is willing to own. She has made a farther attempt than her predecessors to discover the beauties of the Poet; tho' we have often only her general praises and exclamations instead of reasons. But her remarks all together are the most judicious collection extant of the scatter'd observations of the ancients and moderns, as her preface is excellent, and her translation equally careful and elegant.

The chief design of the following notes is to comment upon *Homer* as a poet; whatever in them is extracted from others is constantly own'd; the remarks of the ancients are generally set at length, and the places cited: all those of *Eustathius* are collected which fall under this scheme: many which were not acknowledg'd by other commentators, are restor'd to the true owner; and the same justice is shown to those who refus'd it to others.

The plan of this poem is form'd upon anger and its ill effects, the plan of *Virgil*'s upon pious resignation and its rewards: and thus every passion or virtue may be the foundation of the scheme of an Epic poem. This distinction between two authors who have been so success-ful, seem'd necessary to be taken notice of, that they who would imitate either may not stumble at the very entrance, or so curb their Imaginations as to deprive us of noble morals told in a new variety of accidents. Imitation does not hinder Invention: We may observe the rules of nature, and write in the spirit of those who have best hit upon them, without taking the same track, beginning in the same manner, and following the main of their story almost step by step; as most of the modern writers of Epic poetry have done after one of these great poets.

1.] *Quintilian* [*Inst. Orat.* X. 1. 48] has told us, that from the beginning of *Homer*'s two poems the rules of all *Exordiums* were deriv'd. '*In paucissimis versibus utriusque operis ingressu, legem Prooemiorum non dico servavit, sed constituit.*' ['In the few lines with which he introduces both of his epics, has he not, I will not say observed, but actually established the law which should govern the composition of the exordium?'] Yet *Rapin* has been very free with this invocation, in his *Comparison between* Homer *and* Virgil; which is by no means the most judicious of his works. He cavils first at the Poet's insisting so much upon the effects of *Achilles*'s anger, That it was 'the cause of the woes of the *Greeks*', that it 'sent so many Heroes to the shades', that 'their bodies were left a prey to birds and beasts', the first of which he thinks had been sufficient. One may answer, that the woes of *Greece* might consist in several other things than in the death of her Heroes, which was therefore needful to be specify'd: As to the bodies, he might have reflected how great a curse the want of burial was accounted by the

Ancients, and how prejudicial it was esteem'd even to the souls of the deceas'd: We have a most particular example of the strength of this opinion from the conduct of *Sophocles* in his *Ajax*; who thought this very point sufficient to make the distress of the last act of that tragedy after the death of his Hero, purely to satisfy the audience that he obtain'd the rites of sepulture. Next he objects it as preposterous in *Homer* to desire the Muse to tell him the whole story, and at the same time to inform her solemnly in his own person that 'twas the *will of Jove* which brought it about. But is a Poet then to be imagin'd intirely ignorant of his Subject, tho' he invokes the Muse to relate the particulars? May not *Homer* be allow'd the knowledge of so plain a truth, as that the will of God is fulfill'd in all things? Nor does his manner of saying this infer that he *informs* the Muse of it, but only corresponds with the usual way of desiring information from another concerning any thing, and at the same time mentioning that little we know of it in general. What is there more in this passage? 'Sing, O Goddess, that wrath of *Achilles*, which prov'd so pernicious to the *Greeks*: We only know the Effects of it, that it sent innumerable brave men to the Shades, and that it was *Jove*'s will it should be so. But tell me, O Muse, what was the source of this destructive anger?' I can't comprehend what *Rapin* means by saying, it is hard to know where this *Invocation* ends, and that it is confounded with the *narration*, which so manifestly begins at Λητοῦς καὶ Διὸς υἱός. But upon the whole, methinks the *French* Criticks play double with us, when they sometimes represent the rules of Poetry to be form'd upon the practice of *Homer*, and at other times arraign their master as if he transgress'd them. *Horace* has said the *Exordium* of an Epic poem ought to be plain and modest, and instances *Homer*'s as such; and *Rapin* from this very Rule will be trying *Homer* and judging it otherwise (for he criticises also upon the beginning of the *Odysses*). But for a full answer we may bring the words of *Quintilian* [X.1.48] (whom *Rapin* himself allows to be the best of Criticks) concerning these propositions and invocations of our author. '*Benevolum auditorem invocatione dearum quas præsidere vatibus creditum est, intentum proposita rerum magnitudine, & docilem summa celeriter comprehensa, facit.*' ['By his invocation of the goddesses believed to preside over poetry, he wins the goodwill of his audience; by his statement of the greatness of his themes, he excites their attention and renders them receptive by the briefness of his summary.']

1.] *Μῆνιν ἄειδε θεὰ Πηληϊάδεω Ἀχιλῆος.*

Plutarch observes there is a defect in the measure of this first line (I suppose he means in the *Eta*'s of the Patronymick.) This he thinks the fiery vein of *Homer* making haste to his subject, past over with a bold neglect, being conscious of his own power and perfection in the greater parts; as some (says he) who make virtue their sole aim, pass by censure in smaller matters. But perhaps we may find no occasion to suppose this a neglect in him, if we consider that the word *Pelides*, had he made use of it without so many alterations as he has put it to in *Πηληϊάδεω*, would still have been true to the rules of measure. Make but a diphthong of the second *Eta* and the *Iota*, instead of their being two syllables (perhaps by the fault of transcribers) and the objection is gone. Or perhaps it might be design'd, that the verse in which he professes to sing of violent anger should run off in the rapidity of Dactyles. This art he is allow'd to have us'd in other places, and *Virgil* has been particularly celebrated for it.

8. *Will of Jove.*] *Plutarch* in his treatise of reading poets, interprets *Διὸς* in this place to signify *Fate*, not imagining it consistent with the goodness of the supreme being, or *Jupiter*, to contrive or practise any evil against men. *Eustathius* makes [*Will*] here to refer to the promise which *Jupiter* gave to *Thetis*, that he would honour her son by siding with *Troy* while he should be absent. But to reconcile these two opinions, perhaps the meaning may be that when *Fate* had decreed the destruction of *Troy*, *Jupiter* having the power of incidents to bring it to pass, fulfill'd that decree by providing means for it. So that the words may thus specify the time of Action, from the beginning of the poem, in which those incidents work'd, 'till the promise to *Thetis* was fulfil'd, and the destruction of *Troy* ascertain'd to the *Greeks* by the death of *Hector*. However it is certain that this Poet was not an absolute *Fatalist*, but still suppos'd the power of *Jove* superior: For in the sixteenth *Iliad* we see him designing to save *Sarpedon* tho' the Fates had decreed his death, if *Juno* had not interposed. Neither does he exclude *free-will* in Men; for as he attributes the destruction of the Heroes to the *will* of *Jove* in the beginning of the *Iliad*, so he attributes the Destruction of *Ulysses*'s friends to their *own folly* in the beginning of the *Odysses*,

Αὐτῶν γὰρ σφετέρῃσιν ἀτασθαλίῃσιν ὄλοντο.

9. *Declare, O Muse.*] It may be question'd whether the first period ends at Διὸς δ' ἐτελείετο βουλή, and the interrogation to the Muse begins with 'Εξ οὗ δὴ τὰ πρῶτα – Or whether the Period does not end 'till the words, δῖος Ἀχιλλεύς, with only a single interrogation at Τίς τ' ἄρ σφῶε θεῶν – ? I should be inclin'd to favour the former, and think it a double interrogative, as *Milton* seems to have done in his imitation of this place at the beginning of *Paradise Lost*.

> – *Say first what cause*
> *Mov'd our grand parents?* &c.   And just after,
> *Who first seduc'd them to that foul revolt?*

Besides that I think the proposition concludes more nobly with the sentence *Such was the Will of* Jove. But the latter being follow'd by most editions, and by all the translations I have seen in any language, the general acceptation is here comply'd with, only transposing the line to keep the sentence last: And the next verses are so turn'd as to include the double interrogation, and at the same time do justice to another interpretation of the words 'Εξ οὗ δὴ, *Ex quo tempore*; which marks the *date* of the quarrel from whence the Poem takes its rise. *Chapman* would have *Ex quo* understood of *Jupiter*, *from whom* the debate was suggested; but this clashes with the line immediately following, where he asks What God inspir'd the contention? and answers, It was *Apollo*.

11. Latona's *Son.*] Here the Author who first invok'd the Muse as the Goddess of Memory, vanishes from the Reader's view, and leaves her to relate the whole affair through the poem, whose presence from this time diffuses an air of majesty over the relation. And lest this should be lost to our thoughts in the continuation of the story, he sometimes refreshes them with a new invocation at proper intervals.   *Eustathius.*

20. *The sceptre and the laurel crown.*] There is something exceedingly venerable in this appearance of the Priest. He comes with the ensigns of the God he belong'd to; the laurel crown, now carry'd in his hand to show he was a suppliant; and a golden sceptre which the ancients gave in particular to *Apollo*, as they did a silver one to the moon, and other sorts to the Planets.   *Eustathius.*

23. *Ye Kings and warriors.*] The art of this speech is remarkable. *Chryses* considers the constitution of the *Greeks* before *Troy*, as made

up of troops partly from kingdoms and partly from Democracies:
Wherefore he begins with a distinction which comprehends all. After
this, as *Apollo*'s priest, he prays that they may obtain the two blessings
they had most in view, the conquest of *Troy*, and a safe Return. Then
as he names his petition, he offers an extraordinary ransom, and
concludes with bidding them fear the God if they refuse it; like one
who from his office seems to foresee their misery and exhorts them to
shun it. Thus he endeavours to work by the art of a general application,
by religion, by interest, and the insinuation of danger. This is the
substance of what *Eustathius* remarks on this place; and in pursuance
to his last observation, the epithet *Avenging* is added to this version,
that it may appear the Priest foretells the anger of his God.

33. *He with pride repuls'd.*] It has been remark'd in honour of *Homer*'s
judgment, and the care he took of his reader's morals, that where he
speaks of evil actions committed, or hard words given, he generally
characterises them as such by a previous expression. This passage is
given as one Instance of it, where he says the repulse of *Chryses* was a
proud injurious action in *Agamemnon*: And it may be remark'd that
before his Heroes fall on one another with hard language, in this book,
he still takes care to let us know they were under a distraction of anger.
Plutarch, *of reading Poets.*

41.   *'Till time shall rifle ev'ry youthful grace,*
       And age dismiss her from my cold embrace,
       In daily labours of the loom employ'd,
       Or doom'd to deck the bed she once enjoy'd.]

The *Greek* is ἀντιόωσαν, which signifies either *making* the bed, or
partaking it. *Eustathius* and Madam *Dacier* insist very much upon its
being taken in the former sense only, for fear of presenting a loose idea
to the reader, and of offending against the modesty of the *Muse* who is
suppos'd to relate the Poem. This observation may very well become a
Bishop and a Lady: But that *Agamemnon* was not studying here for
civility of expression, appears from the whole tenour of his speech; and
that he design'd *Chryseis* for more than a servant maid, may be seen
from some other things he says of her, as that he preferr'd her to his
Queen *Clytemnestra*, &c. The impudence of which confession Madam
Dacier herself has elsewhere animadverted upon. Mr. *Dryden*, in his
translation of this book, has been juster to the royal passion of

Agamemnon; tho' he has carry'd the point so much on the other side, as to make him promise a greater fondness for her in her old age than in her youth, which indeed is hardly credible.

> *Mine she shall be, 'till creeping age and time*
> *Her bloom have wither'd and destroy'd her prime;*
> *'Till then my nuptial bed she shall attend,*
> *And having first adorn'd it, late ascend.*
> *This for the night; by day the web and loom,*
> *And homely houshold-tasks shall be her doom.*

Nothing could have made Mr. *Dryden* capable of this mistake, but extreme haste in writing; which never ought to be imputed as a Fault to him, but to those who suffer'd so noble a genius to lie under the necessity of it.

47. *The trembling priest.*] We may take notice here, once for all, that *Homer* is frequently eloquent in his very silence. *Chryses* says not a word in answer to the Insults of *Agamemnon*, but walks pensive along the shore, and the melancholy flowing of the verse admirably expresses the condition of the mournful and deserted father.

> *Βῆ δ' ἀκέων παρὰ θῖνα πολυφλοίσβοιο θαλάσσης.*

61. *The fav'ring God attends.*] Upon this first prayer in the poem, *Eustathius* takes occasion to observe, that the poet is careful throughout his whole work to let no prayer ever fall entirely which has justice on its side; but he who prays, either kills his enemy, or has signs given him that he has been heard, or his friends return, or his undertaking succeeds, or some other visible good happens. So far instructive and useful to life has *Homer* made his fable.

67. *He bent his deadly bow.*] In the tenth year of the siege of *Troy*, a plague happen'd in the *Grecian* Camp, occasion'd perhaps by immoderate heats and gross exhalations. At the introduction of this accident *Homer* begins his Poem, and takes occasion from it to open the scene of action with a most beautiful allegory. He supposes that such afflictions are sent from Heaven for the punishment of our evil actions, and because the Sun was a principal Instrument of it, he says it was sent to punish *Agamemnon* for despising that God and injuring his Priest.

Eustathius.

69. *Mules and dogs*.] *Hippocrates* observes two things of plagues; that their cause is in the air, and that different animals are differently touch'd by them according to their nature or nourishment. This philosophy *Spondanus* refers to the plague here mention'd. First, the cause is in the air, by reason of the darts or beams of *Apollo*. Secondly, the mules and dogs are said to die sooner than the men; partly because they have by nature a quickness of smell which makes the infection sooner perceivable; and partly by the nourishment they take, their feeding on the earth with prone heads making the exhalation more easy to be suck'd in with it. Thus has *Hippocrates* so long after *Homer* writ, subscrib'd to his knowledge in the rise and progress of this distemper. There have been some who have refer'd this passage to a religious sense, making the death of the mules and dogs before the men to point out a kind method of providence in punishing, whereby it sends some previous afflictions to warn mankind so as to make them shun the greater evils by repentance. This Monsieur *Dacier* in his notes on *Aristotle*'s art of poetry calls a Remark perfectly fine, and agreeable to God's method of sending plagues on the *Ægyptians*, where first horses, asses, &c. were smitten, and afterwards the men themselves.

74. Thetis' *god-like son convenes a council*.] On the tenth day a council is held to enquire why the Gods were angry? *Plutarch* observes how justly he applies the characters of his persons to the incidents; not making *Agamemnon* but *Achilles* call this council, who of all the Kings was most capable of making observations upon the plague, and of foreseeing its duration, as having been bred by *Chiron* to the study of Physick. One may mention also a remark of *Eustathius* in pursuance to this, that *Juno*'s advising him in this case might allude to his knowledge of an evil temperament in the air, of which she was Goddess.

79. *Why leave we not the fatal* Trojan *shore*, &c.] The artifice of this speech (according to *Dionysius* of *Halicarnassus*, in his second discourse, περὶ ἐσχηματισμένων) is admirably carry'd on to open an accusation against *Agamemnon*, whom *Achilles* suspects to be the cause of all their miseries. He directs himself not to the assembly, but to *Agamemnon*; he names not only the plague but the war too, as having exhausted them all, which was evidently due to his Family. He leads the *Augurs* he would consult, by pointing at something lately done with respect to *Apollo*. And while he continues within the guard of civil expression, scattering his insinuations, he encourages those who may have more knowledge to speak out boldly, by letting them see there is a party made for their safety; which has its effect immediately in the following speech of *Chalcas*, whose demand of protection shows upon whom the offence is to be plac'd.

86. *By mystic dreams.*] It does not seem that by the word ὀνειροπόλος an interpreter of dreams is meant, for we have no hint of any preceding dream which wants to be interpreted. We may therefore more probably refer it to such who us'd (after performing proper rites) to lie down at some sacred place, and expect a dream from the Gods upon any particular subject which they desir'd. That this was a practice amongst them, appears from the temples of *Amphiaraus* in *Bœotia*, and *Podalirius* in *Apulia*, where the enquirer was oblig'd to sleep at the altar upon the skin of the beast he had sacrific'd in order to obtain an answer. It is in this manner that *Latinus* in *Virgil*'s seventh book goes to dream in the temple of *Faunus*, where we have a particular description of the whole custom. *Strabo, lib.* 16. has spoken concerning the Temple of *Jerusalem* as a place of this nature; 'where (says he) the people either dream'd for themselves, or procur'd some good dreamer to do it': By which it should seem he had read something concerning the visions of their Prophets, as that which *Samuel* had when he was order'd to sleep a third time before the ark, and upon doing so had an account of the destruction of *Eli*'s house: or that which happen'd to *Solomon* after having sacrific'd before the ark at *Gibeon*. The same author has also mention'd the Temple of *Serapis* in his seventeenth book as a place for receiving oracles by dreams.

97. *Belov'd of Jove*, Achilles!] These appellations of praise and honour with which the Heroes in *Homer* so frequently salute each other, were agreeable to the style of the ancient times, as appears from several of the like nature in the scripture. *Milton* has not been wanting to give his poem this cast of antiquity, throughout which our first parents almost always accost each other with some title that expresses a respect to the dignity of human nature.

> *Daughter of God and Man, immortal* Eve.
> Adam, *Earth's hallow'd mould of God inspir'd.*
> *Offspring of heav'n and earth, and all earth's Lord.* &c.

115. *Not ev'n the Chief.*] After *Achilles* had brought in *Chalcas* by his

dark doubts concerning *Agamemnon*, *Chalcas* who perceiv'd them, and was unwilling to be the first that nam'd the King, artfully demands a protection in such a manner, as confirms those doubts, and extorts from *Achilles* this warm and particular Expression. 'That he would protect him even against *Agamemnon*,' (who, as he says, is *now* the greatest man of *Greece*, to hint that at the expiration of the war he should be again reduc'd to be barely King of *Mycenæ*). This place *Plutarch* takes notice of as the first in which *Achilles* shews his contempt of sovereign authority.

117. *The blameless.*] The epithet ἀμύμων, or *blameless*, is frequent in *Homer*, but not always us'd with so much propriety as here. The reader may observe that care has not been wanting thro' this translation, to preserve those epithets which are peculiar to the author, whenever they receive any beauty from the circumstances about them: as this of *blameless* manifestly does in the present passage. It is not only apply'd to a priest, but to one who being conscious of the truth, prepares with an honest boldness to discover it.

131. *Augur accurst.*] This expression is not meerly thrown out by chance, but proves what *Chalcas* said of the King when he ask'd Protection, 'That he harbour'd anger in his Heart.' For it aims at the prediction *Chalcas* had given at *Aulis* nine years before, for the sacrificing his daughter *Iphigenia*.   *Spondanus*.

This, and the two following lines, are in a manner repetitions of the same thing thrice over. It is left to the reader to consider how far it may be allow'd, or rather praised for a beauty, when we consider with *Eustathius* that it is a most natural effect of anger to be full of words, and insisting on that which galls us. We may add, that these reiterated expressions might be suppos'd to be thrown out one after another, as *Agamemnon* is struck in the confusion of his passion, first by the remembrance of one prophecy, and then of another, which the same man had utter'd against him.

143. *Not half so dear were* Clytemnestra's *charms.*] *Agamemnon* having heard the charge which *Chalcas* drew up against him in two particulars, that he had affronted the Priest, and refus'd to restore his daughter; he offers one answer which gives softening colours to both, that he lov'd her as well as his Queen *Clytemnestra* for her perfections. Thus he would seem to satisfy the father by kindness to his daughter, to excuse

himself before the *Greeks* for what is past, and to make a merit of yielding her, and sacrificing his passion for their safety.

155. *Insatiate King.*] Here, where this passion of anger grows loud, it seems proper to prepare the reader, and prevent his mistake in the character of *Achilles*, which might shock him in several particulars following. We should know that the Poet rather study'd nature than perfection in the laying down his characters. He resolv'd to sing the consequences of anger; he consider'd what virtues and vices would conduce most to bring his Moral out of the Fable; and artfully dispos'd them in his chief persons after the manner in which we generally find them; making the fault which most peculiarly attends any good quality, to reside with it. Thus he has plac'd pride with magnanimity in *Agamemnon*, and craft with prudence in *Ulysses*. And thus we must take his *Achilles*, not as a mere heroick dispassion'd character, but as compounded of courage and anger; one who finds himself almost invincible, and assumes an uncontroul'd carriage upon the self-consciousness of his worth; whose high strain of honour will not suffer him to betray his friends, or fight against them, even when he thinks they have affronted him; but whose inexorable resentment will not let him hearken to any terms of accommodation. These are the lights and shades of his character, which *Homer* has heighten'd and darken'd in extremes; because on the one side valour is the darling quality of Epic Poetry, and on the other, anger the particular subject of this Poem. When characters thus mix'd are well conducted, tho' they be not morally beautiful quite through, they conduce more to the end, and are still poetically perfect.

Plutarch takes occasion from the observation of this conduct in *Homer*, to applaud his just imitation of nature and truth, in representing virtues and vices intermixed in his Heroes: contrary to the paradoxes and strange positions of the Stoicks, who held that no vice could consist with virtue, nor the least virtue with vice.

Plut. de aud. Poetis.

169. *Great as thou art, and like a God in fight.*] The words in the original are θεοείκελ' Ἀχιλλεῦ. *Ulysses* is soon after call'd Δῖος, and others in other places. The phrase of *divine* or *god-like* is not used by the Poet to signify perfection in men, but apply'd to considerable persons upon account of some particular qualification or advantage, which they were possess'd of far above the common standard of

mankind. Thus it is ascrib'd to *Achilles* upon account of his great valour, to *Ulysses* for his preheminence in wisdom, even to *Paris* for his exceeding beauty, and to *Clytemnestra* for several fair endowments.

172. *First let the just equivalent.*] The reasoning in point of right between *Achilles* and *Agamemnon* seems to be this. *Achilles* pleads that *Agamemnon* could not seize upon any other man's captive without a new distribution, it being an invasion of private property. On the other hand, as *Agamemnon*'s power was limited, how came it that all the *Grecian* Captains would submit to an illegal and arbitrary action? I think the legal pretence for his seizing *Briseïs* must have been founded upon that Law, whereby the Commander in chief had the power of taking what part of the prey he pleas'd for his own use: And he being obliged to restore what he had taken, it seem'd but just that he should have a second choice.

213 *And dar'st thou threat to snatch my prize away,*
     Due to the deeds of many a dreadful day?]

The anger of these two Princes was equally upon the account of women, but yet it is observable that they are conducted with a different Air. *Agamemnon* appears as a lover, *Achilles* as a warriour: The one speaks of *Chryseïs* as a beauty whom he valu'd equal to his wife, and whose merit was too considerable to be easily resign'd; the other treats *Briseïs* as a slave, whom he is concern'd to preserve in point of honour, and as a testimony of his glory. Hence it is that we never hear him mention her but as his *Spoil*, the *Reward of War*, the *Gift the* Græcians *gave him*, or the like expressions: and accordingly he yields her up, not in grief for a mistress whom he loses, but in sullenness for an injury that is done him. This observation is Madam *Dacier*'s, and will often appear just as we proceed farther. Nothing is finer than the Moral shewn us in this quarrel, of the blindness and partiality of mankind to their own faults: The *Græcians* make a war to recover a woman that was ravish'd, and are in danger to fail in the attempt by a dispute about another. *Agamemnon* while he is revenging a rape, commits one; and *Achilles* while he in the utmost fury himself, reproaches *Agamemnon* for his passionate temper.

225. *Fly, mighty warriour.*] *Achilles* having threaten'd to leave them in the former speech, and spoken of his warlike actions; the Poet here

puts an artful piece of spite in the mouth of *Agamemnon*, making him opprobriously brand his retreat as a flight, and lessen the appearance of his courage by calling it the love of contention and slaughter.

229. *Kings, the Gods distinguish'd care.*] In the original it is Διορεφεῖς, or *nurst by* Jove. *Homer* often uses to call his Kings by such Epithets as Διογενεῖς, *born of the Gods*, or Διοτρεφεῖς, *bred by the Gods*; by which he points out to themselves, the offices they were ordain'd for; and to their people, the reverence that should be pay'd them. These expressions are perfectly in the exalted style of the eastern nations, and correspondent to those places of holy scripture where they are call'd *Gods*, and *the Sons of the most High*.

261. Minerva *swift descended from above.*] *Homer* having by degrees rais'd *Achilles* to such a pitch of fury, as to make him capable of attempting *Agamemnon*'s life in the council, *Pallas* the Goddess of Wisdom descends, and being seen only by him, pulls him back in the very instant of execution. He parleys with her a while, as imagining she would advise him to proceed, but upon the promise of such a time wherein there should be a full reparation of his honour, he sheaths his sword in obedience to her. She ascends to Heaven, and he being left to himself, falls again upon his General with bitter expressions. The *allegory* here may be allow'd by every reader to be unforc'd: The prudence of *Achilles* checks him in the rashest moment of his anger, it works upon him unseen to others, but does not entirely prevail upon him to desist, 'till he remembers his own importance, and depends upon it that there will be a necessity of their courting him at any expence into the alliance again. Having persuaded himself by such reflections, he forbears to attack his general, but thinking that he sacrifices enough to prudence by this forbearance, lets the thought of it vanish from him; and no sooner is wisdom gone, but he falls into more violent reproaches for the gratification of his passion. All this is a most beautiful passage whose Moral is evident, and generally agreed on by the Commentators.

268. *Known by the flames that sparkled from her eyes.*] They who carry on this allegory after the most minute manner, refer this to the eyes of *Achilles*, as indeed we must, if we entirely destroy the bodily appearance of *Minerva*. But what Poet designing to have his Moral so open, would take pains to form it into a Fable? In the proper mythological sense, this passage should be referr'd to *Minerva*; according to an opinion of the ancients, who suppos'd that the Gods had a peculiar light in their eyes. That *Homer* was not ignorant of this opinion, appears from his use of it in other places, as when in the third *Iliad Helena* by this means discovers *Venus*: And that he meant it here is particularly asserted by *Heliodorus*, in the third book of his *Æthiopick* history. 'The Gods,' says he, 'are known in their apparitions to men by the fix'd glare of their eyes, or their gliding passage through air without moving the feet; these marks *Homer* has us'd from his Knowledge of the *Ægyptian* learning, applying one to *Pallas*, and the other to *Neptune*.' Madam *Dacier* has gone into the contrary opinion, and blames *Eustathius* and others without overthrowing these authorities, or assigning any other reason but that it was not proper for *Minerva*'s eyes to *sparkle*, when her speech was *mild*.

298. *Thou dog in forehead.*] It has been one of the objections against the manners of *Homer*'s Heroes, that they are abusive. Mons. *de la Motte* affirms in his discourse upon the *Iliad*, that great Men differ from the vulgar in their manner of expressing their passion; but certainly in violent passions (such as those of *Achilles* and *Agamemnon*) the Great are as subject as any others to these sallies; of which we have frequent Examples both from history and experience. *Plutarch*, taking notice of this line, gives it as a particular commendation of *Homer*, that 'he constantly affords us a fine lecture of morality in his reprehensions and praises, by referring them not to the goods of fortune or the body, but those of the mind, which are in our power, and for which we are blameable or praise-worthy. Thus,' says he, '*Agamemnon* is reproach'd for impudence and fear, *Ajax* for vain bragging, *Idomeneus* for the love of contention, and *Ulysses* does not reprove even *Thersites* but as a babbler, tho' he had so many personal deformities to object to him. In like manner also the appellations and epithets with which they accost one another, are generally founded on some distinguishing qualification of merit, as *Wise* Ulysses, Hector *equal to* Jove *in Wisdom*, Achilles *chief Glory of the* Greeks,' and the like.   Plutarch *of reading Poets.*

299. *In ambush'd fights to dare.*] *Homer* has magnify'd the *ambush* as the boldest manner of fight. They went upon those parties with a few men only, and generally the most daring of the army, on occasions of the greatest hazard, where they were therefore more expos'd than in a regular battle. Thus *Idomeneus* in the thirteenth book expressly tells

Meriones that the greatest courage appears in this way of service, each Man being in a manner singled out to the proof of it.   *Eustathius.*

309. *Now by this sacred sceptre.*] *Spondanus* in this place blames *Eustathius*, for saying that *Homer* makes *Achilles* in his passion swear by the first thing he meets with: and then assigns (as from himself) two causes which the other had mention'd so plainly before, that it is a wonder they could be overlook'd. The substance of the whole passage in *Eustathius* is, that if we consider the sceptre simply as wood, *Achilles* after the manner of the ancients takes in his transport the first thing to swear by; but that *Homer* himself has in the process of the description assign'd reasons why it is proper for the occasion, which may be seen by considering it symbolically. First, That as the wood being cut from the tree will never reunite and flourish, so neither should their amity ever flourish again, after they were divided by this contention. Secondly, that a Sceptre being the mark of power and symbol of justice, to swear by it might in effect be construed swearing by the God of Power, and by Justice itself; and accordingly it is spoken of by *Aristotle*, 3 *l. Polit.* as a usual solemn oath of Kings.

I cannot leave this passage without showing, in opposition to some Moderns who have criticiz'd upon it as tedious, that it has been esteem'd a beauty by the ancients and engaged them in its imitation. *Virgil* has almost transcrib'd it in his 12 *Æn.* for the sceptre of *Latinus*.

> *Ut sceptrum hoc (sceptrum dextra nam forte gerebat)*
> *Nunquam fronde levi fundet virgulta nec umbras;*
> *Cum semel in silvis imo de stirpe recisum,*
> *Matre caret, posuitque comas & brachia ferro:*
> *Olim arbos, nunc artificis manus ære decoro*
> *Inclusit, patribusque dedit gestare Latinis.*   [206–11]

> [Ev'n as this royal sceptre (for he bore
>   A sceptre in his hand) shall never more
>   Shoot out in branches, or renew the birth;
>   An orphan now, cut from the mother earth
>   By the keen axe, dishonour'd of its hair,
>   And cas'd in brass, for *Latian* kings to bear.]

But I cannot think this comes up to the spirit or propriety of *Homer*, notwithstanding the judgment of *Scaliger* who decides for *Virgil*, upon a trivial comparison of the wording in each, *l.* 5. *cap.* 3. *Poet.* It fails in a greater point than any he has mention'd, which is, that being there us'd on occasion of a peace, it has no emblematical reference to division, and yet describes the cutting of the wood and its incapacity to bloom and branch again, in as many words as *Homer*. It is borrow'd by *Valerius Flaccus* in his third book, where he makes *Jason* swear as a warrior by his spear,

> *Hanc ego magnanimi spolium Didymaonis hastam,*
> *Ut semel est avulsa jugis a matre perempta,*
> *Quæ neque jam frondes virides neque proferet umbras,*
> *Fida ministeria & duras obit horrida pugnas,*
> *Testor.*   [III. 707–11]

[By this spear, once the spoil of great-souled Didymaon, which will nevermore put forth green shade of foliage, since once it was torn from the rocks and bereft of its mother tree and now, a knotted shaft, gives trusty service in hard-fought encounters, by this spear I swear.]

And indeed, however he may here borrow some expressions from *Virgil* or fall below him in others, he has nevertheless kept to *Homer* in the emblem, by introducing the oath upon *Jason*'s grief for sailing to *Colchis* without *Hercules*, when he had separated himself from the body of the *Argonauts* to search after *Hylas*. To render the beauty of this passage more manifest, the allusion is inserted (but with the fewest words possible) in this translation.

324. *Thy rashness made the bravest* Greek *thy foe.*] If self-praise had not been agreeable to the haughty nature of *Achilles*, yet *Plutarch* has mention'd a case, and with respect to him, wherein it is allowable. He says that *Achilles* has at other times ascrib'd his success to *Jupiter*, but it is permitted to a man of merit and figure who is injuriously dealt with, to speak frankly of himself to those who are forgetful and unthankful. .

333. *Two generations.*] The Commentators make not *Nestor* to have liv'd three hundred years (according to *Ovid*'s opinion;) they take the word γενεά not to signify a century or age of the world; but a generation, or compass of time in which one set of men flourish, which in the common computation is thirty years; and accordingly it is here translated as much the more probable.

From what *Nestor* says in this speech, Madam *Dacier* computes the age he was of, at the end of the *Trojan* war. The fight of the *Lapithæ* and *Centaurs* fell out fifty-five or fifty-six years before the war of *Troy*: The quarrel of *Agamemnon* and *Achilles* happen'd in the tenth and last year of that war. It was then sixty-five or sixty-six years since *Nestor* fought against the *Centaurs*; he was capable at that time of giving counsel, so that one cannot imagine him to have been under twenty: From whence it will appear that he was now almost arriv'd to the conclusion of his third age, and about fourscore and five, or fourscore and six years of age.

339. *What shame.*] The quarrel having risen to its highest extravagance, *Nestor* the wisest and most aged *Greek* is raised to quiet the Princes, whose speech is therefore fram'd entirely with an opposite air to all which has been hitherto said, sedate and inoffensive. He begins with a soft affectionate complaint which he opposes to their threats and haughty language; he reconciles their attention in an awful manner, by putting them in mind that they hear one whom their fathers and the greatest Heroes had heard with deference. He sides with neither, that he might not anger any one, while he advises them to the proper methods of reconciliation; and he appears to side with both while he praises each, that they may be induc'd by the recollection of one another's worth to return to that amity which would bring success to the cause. It was not however consistent with the plan of the poem that they should be entirely appeased, for then the anger would be at an end which was propos'd as the subject of the Poem. *Homer* has not therefore made this speech to have its full success; and yet that the eloquence of his *Nestor* might not be thrown out of character by its proving unavailable, he takes care that the violence with which the dispute was manag'd should abate immediately upon his speaking; *Agamemnon* confesses that all he spoke was right, *Achilles* promises not to fight for *Briseïs* if she should be sent for, and the council dissolves.

It is to be observ'd that this character of authority and wisdom in *Nestor*, is every where admirably used by *Homer*, and made to exert itself thro' all the great emergencies of the poem. As he quiets the Princes here, he proposes that expedient which reduces the army into their order after the sedition in the second book. When the *Greeks* are in the utmost distresses, 'tis he who advises the building the fortification before the fleet, which is the chief means of preserving them. And it is by his persuasion that *Patroclus* puts on the armour of *Achilles*, which occasions the return of that Hero, and the conquest of *Troy*.

394. – *No more* Achilles *draws*
          His conqu'ring sword in any woman's cause.]

When *Achilles* promises not to contest for *Briseïs*, he expresses it in a sharp despising air, *I will not fight for the sake of a woman*: by which he glances at *Helena*, and casts an oblique reflection upon those commanders whom he is about to leave at the siege for her cause. One may observe how well it is fancy'd of the Poet, to make one woman the ground of a quarrel which breaks an alliance that was only form'd upon account of another: and how much the circumstance thus consider'd contributes to keep up the anger of *Achilles*, for carrying on the Poem beyond this dissolution of the council. For (as he himself argues with *Ulysses* in the 9th *Iliad*) it is as reasonable for him to retain his anger upon the account of *Briseïs*, as for the brothers with all *Greece* to carry on a war upon the score of *Helena*. I do not know that any commentator has taken notice of this sarcasm of *Achilles*, which I think a very obvious one.

413. *The ablutions.*] All our former *English* translations seem to have err'd in the sense of this line; the word λύματα being differently render'd by them, *offals*, or *entrails*, or *purgaments*, or *ordures*, a gross set of ideas of which *Homer* is not guilty. The word comes from λούω, *eluo*, the same verb from whence ἐπιλυμαίνοντο, which precedes in the line, is deriv'd. So that the sense appears to be as it is render'd here [*They* wash'd, *and threw away their* washings.] Perhaps this lustration might be used as a physical remedy in cleansing them from the infection of the plague; as *Pausanias* tells us it was by the *Arcadians*, from whence he says the plague was called λύμη by the *Greeks*.

430. *At awful distance silent.*] There was requir'd a very remarkable management to preserve all the characters which are concern'd in this nice conjuncture, wherein the heralds were to obey at their peril. *Agamemnon* was to be gratify'd by an insult on *Achilles*; and *Achilles* was to suffer so as might become his pride, and not have his violent temper provok'd. From all this the Poet has found the secret to extricate himself, by only taking care to make his heralds stand in sight, and silent. Thus they neither make *Agamemnon*'s majesty suffer by uttering their message submissively, nor occasion a rough treatment from *Achilles* by demanding *Briseïs* in the peremptory air he order'd; and at the same time *Achilles* is gratify'd with the opportunity of giving her up, as if he rather sent her than was forc'd to relinquish her. The art of this has been taken notice of by *Eustathius*.

451. *She, in soft sorrows.*] The behaviour of *Briseïs* in her departure is no less beautifully imagin'd than the former. A *French* or *Italian* Poet had lavish'd all his wit and passion in two long speeches on this occasion, which the heralds must have wept to hear; instead of which, *Homer* gives us a fine picture of nature. We see *Briseïs* passing unwillingly along, with a dejected air, melted in tenderness, and not able to utter a word: And in the lines immediately following, we have a *contraste* to this in the gloomy resentment of *Achilles*, who suddenly retires to the shore and vents his rage aloud to the seas. The variation of the numbers just in this place adds a great beauty to it, which has been endeavour'd at in the translation.

458. *There bath'd in tears.*] *Eustathius* observes on this place that it is no weakness in Heroes to weep, but the very effect of humanity and proof of a generous temper; for which he offers several instances, and takes notice that if *Sophocles* would not let *Ajax* weep, it is because he is drawn rather as a madman than a hero. But this general observation is not all we can offer in excuse for the tears of *Achilles*: His are tears of anger and disdain (as I have ventur'd to call them in the translation) of which a great and fiery temper is more susceptible than any other; and even in this case *Homer* has taken care to preserve the high character, by making him retire to vent his tears out of sight. And we may add to these an observation of which Madam *Dacier* is fond, the reason why *Agamemnon* parts not in tears from *Chryseïs*, and *Achilles* does from *Briseïs*: The one parts willingly from his mistress, and because he does it for his people's safety it becomes an honour to him: the other is parted unwillingly, and because his general takes her by force the action reflects a dishonour upon him.

464. *The Thund'rer ow'd.*] This alludes to a story which *Achilles* tells the embassadors of *Agamemnon*, *Il.* 9. That he had the choice of two fates: one less glorious at home, but blessed with a very long life; the other full of glory at *Troy*, but then he was never to return. The alternative being thus propos'd to him (not from *Jupiter* but *Thetis* who reveal'd the decree) he chose the latter, which he looks upon as his due, since he gives away length of life for it; and accordingly when he complains to his mother of the disgrace he lies under, it is in this manner he makes a demand of honour.

Mons. *de la Motte* very judiciously observes, that but for this fore-knowledge of the certainty of his death at *Troy*, *Achilles*'s character could have drawn but little esteem from the reader. A hero of a vicious mind, blest only with a superiority of strength, and invulnerable into the bargain, was not very proper to excite admiration; but *Homer* by this exquisite piece of art has made him the greatest of heroes, who is still pursuing glory in contempt of death, and even under that certainty generously devoting himself in every action.

478. *From* Thebæ.] *Homer*, who open'd his Poem with the action which immediately brought on *Achilles*'s anger, being now to give an account of the same thing again, takes his rise more backward in the story. Thus the reader is inform'd in what he should know, without having been delay'd from entering upon the promis'd subject. This is the first attempt which we see made towards the poetical method of narration, which differs from the historical in that it does not proceed always directly in the line of time, but sometimes relates things which have gone before when a more proper opportunity demands it to make the narration more informing or beautiful.

The foregoing remark is in regard only to the first six lines of this speech. What follows is a rehearsal of the preceding action of the poem, almost in the same words he had used in the opening it; and is one of those faults which has with most justice been objected to our Author. It is not to be deny'd but the account must be tedious, of what the reader had been just before inform'd; and especially when we are given to understand it was no way necessary, by what *Achilles* says at the beginning, that *Thetis knew the whole story already*. As to repeating the same lines, a practice usual with *Homer*, it is not so excusable in this place as in those where messages are deliver'd in the words they were receiv'd, or the like; it being unnatural to imagine, that the person whom the Poet introduces as actually speaking, should fall into the self-same words that are us'd in the narration by the Poet himself. Yet *Milton* was so great an admirer and imitator of our author, as not to have scrupled even this kind of repetition. The passage is at the end of his tenth Book, where *Adam* having declar'd he would prostrate himself before God in certain particular acts of humiliation, those acts are immediately after describ'd by the Poet in the same words.

514. *Oft hast thou triumph'd.*] The persuasive which *Achilles* is here

made to put into the mouth of *Thetis*, is most artfully contriv'd to suit the present exigency. You, says he, must intreat *Jupiter* to bring miseries on the *Greeks* who are protected by *Juno*, *Neptune*, and *Minerva*: Put him therefore in mind that those Deities were once his enemies, and adjure him by that service you did him when those very powers would have bound him, that he will now in his turn assist you against the endeavours they will oppose to my wishes. *Eustathius*.

As for the story itself, some have thought (with whom is Madam *Dacier*) that there was some imperfect tradition of the fall of the Angels for their rebellion, which the *Greeks* had receiv'd by commerce with *Ægypt*: and thus they account the rebellion of the Gods, the precipitation of *Vulcan* from Heaven; and *Jove*'s threatning the inferior Gods with *Tartarus* but as so many hints of scripture faintly imitated. But it seems not improbable that the wars of the Gods, described by the poets, allude to the confusion of the elements before they were brought into their natural order. It is almost generally agreed that by *Jupiter* is meant the *Æther*, and by *Juno* the *Air*. The ancient Philosophers suppos'd the *Æther* to be igneous, and by its kind influence upon the *Air* to be the cause of all vegetation: Therefore *Homer* says in the 14*th Iliad*, That upon *Jupiter*'s embracing his wife, the earth put forth its plants. Perhaps by *Thetis*'s assisting *Jupiter*, may be meant that the watry element subsiding and taking its natural place, put an end to this combat of the elements.

523. *Whom Gods* Briareus, *Men* Ægeon *name.*] This manner of making the Gods speak a language different from men (which is frequent in *Homer*) is a circumstance that as far as it widens the distinction between divine and human natures, so far might tend to heighten the reverence paid the Gods. But besides this, as the difference is thus told in Poetry, it is of use to the Poets themselves: For it appears like a kind of testimony of their inspiration, or their converse with the Gods, and thereby gives a majesty to their works.

557. *The Feasts of* Æthiopia's *blameless race.*] The *Æthiopians*, says *Diodorus, l.* 3. are said to be the inventors of pomps, sacrifices, solemn meetings, and other honours paid to the Gods. From hence arose their character of piety, which is here celebrated by *Homer*. Among these there was an annual feast at *Diospolis*, which *Eustathius* mentions, wherein they carry'd about the statues of *Jupiter* and the other Gods, for twelve days, according to their number: to which if we add the

ancient custom of setting meat before statues, it will appear a rite from which this fable might easily arise. But it would be a great mistake to imagine from this place, that *Homer* represents the Gods as eating and drinking upon earth: a gross notion he was never guilty of, as appears from these verses in the fifth book, v. 340.

> Ἰχώρ οἷός πέρ τε ῥέει μακάρεσσι θεοῖσιν·
> Οὐ γὰρ σῖτον ἔδουσ᾽, οὐ πίνουσ᾽ αἴθοπα οἶνον,
> Τοὔνεκ᾽ ἀναίμονές εἰσι, καὶ ἀθάνατοι καλέονται.

[For not the bread of man their life sustains,
Nor wine's inflaming juice supplies their veins.]

Macrobius would have it, that by *Jupiter* here is meant the *sun*, and that the number *twelve* hints at the twelve *signs*; but whatever may be said in a critical defence of this opinion, I believe the reader will be satisfy'd that *Homer* consider'd as a Poet would have his machinery understood upon that system of the Gods which is properly *Grœcian*.

One may take notice here, that it were to be wish'd some passage were found in any authentic author that might tell us the time of the year when the *Æthiopians* kept this festival at *Diospolis*: For from thence one might determine the precise season of the year wherein the actions of the *Iliad* are represented to have happen'd; and perhaps by that means farther explain the beauty and propriety of many passages in the Poem.

600. *The Sacrifice.*] If we consider this passage, it is not made to shine in poetry: All that can be done is to give it numbers, and endeavour to set the particulars in a distinct view. But if we take it in another light, and as a piece of learning, it is valuable for being the most exact account of the ancient sacrifices any where left us. There is first the purification, by washing of Hands. Secondly the offering up of prayers. Thirdly the *Mola*, or barley cakes thrown upon the victim. Fourthly the manner of killing it with the head turn'd upwards to the celestial Gods (as they turn'd it downwards when they offer'd to the infernals). Fifthly their selecting the thighs and fat for their Gods as the best of the sacrifice, and the disposing about them pieces cut from every part for a representation of the whole: (Hence the thighs, or μηρία, are frequently us'd in *Homer* and the *Greek* poets for the whole victim.) Sixthly the libation of wine. Seventhly consuming the thighs in the fire of the altar. Eighthly the sacrificers dressing and feasting on the rest, with joy and hymns to the Gods. Thus punctually have the ancient Poets, and in particular *Homer*, written with a care and respect to religion. One may question whether any country as much a stranger to christianity as we are to heathenism, might be so well inform'd by our Poets in the worship belonging to any profession of religion at present.

I am obliged to take notice how intirely Mr. *Dryden* has mistaken the sense of this passage, and the custom of antiquity; for in his translation, the cakes are thrown into the fire instead of being cast on the victim; the sacrificers are made to eat the thighs and whatever belong'd to the Gods; and no part of the victim is consum'd for a burnt-offering, so that in effect there is no sacrifice at all. Some of the Mistakes (particularly that of *turning the roast meat on the spits*, which was not known in *Homer*'s days) he was led into by *Chapman*'s translation.

681. *The faithful, fix'd, irrevocable sign.*] There are among men three things by which the efficacy of a promise may be made void; the design not to perform it, the want of power to bring it to pass, and the instability of our tempers, from all which *Homer* saw that the divinity must be exempted, and therefore he describes the *nod*, or ratification of *Jupiter*'s word, as *faithful* in opposition to *fraud*, *sure* of being perform'd in opposition to *weakness*, and *irrevocable* in opposition to our *repenting* of a promise.   *Eustathius.*

683. *He spoke, and awful bends.*] This description of the Majesty of *Jupiter* has something exceedingly grand and venerable. *Macrobius* reports, that *Phidias* having made his *Olympian Jupiter*, which past for one of the greatest miracles of art, he was ask'd from what pattern he fram'd so divine a figure, and answer'd, it was from that archetype which he found in these lines of *Homer*. The same Author has also taken notice of *Virgil*'s imitating it, *l*. 10. [113–15]

> *Dixerat, idque ratum Stygii per flumina fratris,*
> *Per pice torrentes atraque voragine ripas;*
> *Annuit, & totum nutu tremefecit Olympum.*

> [The *Thundr'r* said;
> And shook the sacred honours of his head;
> Attesting *Styx* th'inviolable flood,
> And the black regions of his brother god:
> Trembl'd the poles of heav'n; and earth confess'd the nod.]

Here indeed he has preserv'd the *nod* with its stupendous effect, the making the heavens tremble. But he has neglected the description of the eye-brows and the hair, those chief pieces of imagery from whence the artist took the idea of a countenance proper for the King of Gods and Men.

Thus far *Macrobius*, whom *Scaliger* answers in this manner; *Aut ludunt Phidiam, aut nos ludit Phidias: Etiam sine* Homero *puto illum scisse, Jovem non carere superciliis & cæsarie.* [Either they are mocking Phidias, or Phidias is mocking us. For I think that, without the help of Homer, he would have known that Jove lacked neither eye-brows nor hair.]

694. Jove *assumes the Throne.*] As *Homer* makes the first council of his men to be one continued scene of anger, whereby the *Græcian* chiefs became divided, so he makes the first meeting of the Gods to be spent in the same passion; whereby *Jupiter* is more fix'd to assist the *Trojans* and *Juno* more incens'd against them. Thus the design of the Poem goes on: the anger which began the book overspreads all existent beings by the latter end of it: Heaven and earth become engag'd in the subject, by which it rises to a great importance in the reader's eyes, and is hasten'd forward into the briskest scenes of action that can be fram'd upon that violent passion.

698. *Say, artful Manager.*] The Gods and Goddesses being describ'd with all the desires and pleasures, the passions and humours of mankind, the commentators have taken a licence from thence to draw not only moral observations, but also satyrical reflections out of this part of the Poet. These I am sorry to see fall so hard upon womankind, and all by *Juno*'s means. Sometimes she procures them a lesson for their curiosity and unquietness, and at other times for their loud and vexatious tempers. *Juno* deserves them on the one hand, *Jupiter* thunders them out on the other, and the learned gentlemen are very particular in enlarging with remarks on both sides. In her first speech they make the Poet describe the inquisitive temper of womankind in general, and their restlessness if they are not admitted into every secret. In his answer to this, they trace those methods of grave remonstrance by which it is proper for husbands to calm them. In her reply, they find it is the nature of women to be more obstinate for being yielded to: And in his second return to her, they see the last method to be used with them upon failure of the first, which is the exercise of sovereign authority.

Mr. *Dryden* has translated all this with the utmost severity upon the Ladies, and spirited the whole with satyrical additions of his own. But Madam *Dacier* (who has elsewhere animadverted upon the good Bishop of *Thessalonica*, for his sage admonitions against the fair sex) has not taken the least notice of this general defection from complaisance in all the commentators. She seems willing to give the whole passage a more important turn, and incline us to think that *Homer* design'd to represent the folly and danger of prying into the secrets of providence. 'Tis thrown into that air in this translation, not only as it is more noble and instructive in general, but as it is more respectful to the Ladies in particular; nor should we (any more than Madam *Dacier*) have mention'd what those old fellows have said, but to desire their protection against some modern criticks their disciples, who may arraign this proceeding.

713. *Roll'd the large orbs.*] The *Greek* is Βοῶπις πότνια Ἥρη, which is commonly translated *The venerable ox-ey'd* Juno. Madam *Dacier* very well observes that Βοῦ is only an augmentative particle, and signifies no more than *valde* [certainly]. It may be added, that the imagination of oxen having larger eyes than ordinary is ill grounded, and has no foundation in truth; their eyes are no larger in proportion than those of men, or of most other animals. But be it as it will, the design of the Poet which is only to express the largeness of her Eyes, is answer'd in the Paraphrase.

741. *Thus interpos'd the architect divine.*] This quarrel of the gods being come to its height, the Poet makes *Vulcan* interpose, who freely puts them in mind of pleasure, inoffensively advises *Juno*, illustrates his advice by an example of his own misfortune, turning the jest on himself to enliven the banquet; and concludes the part he is to support with serving *Nectar* about. *Homer* had here his *Minerva* or *Wisdom* to interpose again, and every other quality of the mind resided in Heaven under the appearance of some Deity: So that his introducing *Vulcan*, proceeded not from a want of choice, but an insight into nature. He knew that a friend to mirth often diverts or stops quarrels, especially when he contrives to submit himself to the laugh, and prevails on the angry to part in good humour, or in a disposition to friendship; when grave representations are sometimes reproaches, sometimes lengthen the debate by occasioning defences, and sometimes introduce new parties into the consequences of it.

760. *Once in your cause I felt his matchless might.*] They who search another vein of allegory for hidden knowledge in natural Philosophy, have consider'd *Jupiter* and *Juno* as *Heaven* and the *Air*, whose alliance is interrupted when the Air is troubled above, but restor'd again when it is clear'd by *Heat*, or *Vulcan* the God of Heat. Him they call a divine artificer, from the activity or general use of fire in working. They suppose him to be born in Heaven, where philosophers say that element has its proper place; and is thence deriv'd to the earth which is signify'd by the fall of *Vulcan*; that he fell in *Lemnos*, because that Island abounds with subterranean fires; and that he contracted a lameness or imperfection by the fall; the fire not being so pure and active below, but mix'd and terrestrial.   *Eustathius.*

767. *Which with a smile the white-arm'd Queen receiv'd.*] The Epithet λευκώλενος, or *white-arm'd*, is used by *Homer* several times before in this book. This was the first passage where it could be introduced with any ease or grace; because the action she is here describ'd in, of extending her arm to the cup, gives it an occasion of displaying its beauties, and in a manner demands the epithet.

771. *Laughter shakes the skies.*] *Vulcan* design'd to move laughter by taking upon him the office of *Hebe* and *Ganymede*, with his aukward limping carriage. But tho' he prevail'd, and *Homer* tells you the Gods did laugh, yet he takes care not to mention a word of his lameness. It would have been cruel in him, and wit out of season, to have enlarg'd with derision upon an imperfection which is out of one's power to remedy.

According to this good-natur'd opinion of *Eustathius*, Mr. *Dryden* has treated *Vulcan* a little barbarously. He makes his character perfectly comical, he is the jest of the board, and the Gods are very merry upon the imperfections of his figure. *Chapman* led him into this error in general, as well as into some indecencies of expression in particular, which will be seen upon comparing them.

For what concerns the laughter attributed here to the Gods, see the notes on *lib.* 5, v. 517.

778. *Then to their starry domes.*] The Astrologers assign twelve houses to the Planets, wherein they are said to have dominion. Now because *Homer* tells us *Vulcan* built a mansion for every God, the ancients write that he first gave occasion for this doctrine.

780. Jove *on his couch reclin'd his awful head.*] *Eustathius* makes a distinction between καθεύδειν and ὑπνοῦν; the words which are used at the end of this book and the beginning of the next, with regard to *Jupiter's* sleeping. He says καθεύδειν only means lying down in a disposition to sleep; which salves the contradiction that else would follow in the next book, where it is said *Jupiter* did not sleep. I only mention this to vindicate the translation which differs from Mr. *Dryden's.*

It has been remark'd by the scholiasts, that this is the only book of the twenty-four without any *simile*, a figure in which *Homer* abounds every where else. The like remark is made by Madam *Dacier* upon the first of the *Odysses*; and because the Poet has observ'd the same conduct in both works, it is concluded he thought a simplicity of style without the great figures was proper during the first information of the reader. This observation may be true, and admits of refin'd reasonings; but for my part I cannot think the book had been the worse, tho' he had thrown in as many *similes* as *Virgil* has in the first *Æneid.*

THE
SECOND BOOK
OF THE
ILIAD

The ARGUMENT

The Trial of the Army and Catalogue of the Forces

Jupiter *in pursuance of the request of* Thetis, *sends a deceitful Vision to* Agamemnon, *persuading him to lead the army to battle; in order to make the* Greeks *sensible of their want of* Achilles. *The General, who is deluded with the hopes of taking* Troy *without his assistance, but fears the army was discourag'd by his absence and the late plague, as well as by length of time, contrives to make trial of their disposition by a stratagem. He first communicates his design to the Princes in council, that he would propose a return to the soldiers, and that they should put a stop to them if the proposal was embrac'd. Then he assembles the whole host, and upon moving for a return to* Greece, *they unanimously agree to it and run to prepare the ships. They are detain'd by the Management of* Ulysses, *who chastises the insolence of* Thersites. *The Assembly is recall'd, several speeches made on the occasion, and at length the advice of* Nestor *follow'd, which was to make a general muster of the troops, and to divide them into their several nations, before they proceeded to battle. This gives occasion to the Poet to ennumerate all the forces of the* Greeks *and* Trojans, *in a large catalogue.*

The time *employ'd in this book consists not intirely of one Day. The* scene *lies in the* Græcian *camp and upon the* sea-shore; *toward the end it* removes to Troy.

Now pleasing sleep had seal'd each mortal eye,
Stretch'd in the tents the *Grecian* Leaders lie,
Th' immortals slumber'd on their thrones above;
All, but the ever-wakeful eyes of *Jove*.
5 To honour *Thetis'* son he bends his care,
And plunge the *Greeks* in all the woes of war:
Then bids an empty Phantome rise to sight,
And thus commands the *Vision* of the night.
   Fly hence, deluding *Dream*! and light as air,
10 To *Agamemnon*'s ample tent repair.
Bid him in arms draw forth th' embattel'd train,
Lead all his *Grecians* to the dusty plain.
Declare, ev'n now 'tis giv'n him to destroy
The lofty tow'rs of wide-extended *Troy*.
15 For now no more the Gods with Fate contend,
At *Juno*'s suit the heav'nly factions end.
Destruction hangs o'er yon' devoted wall,
And nodding *Ilion* waits th' impending fall.
   Swift as the word the vain Illusion fled,
20 Descends and hovers o'er *Atrides*' head;
Cloath'd in the figure of the *Pylian* Sage,
Renown'd for wisdom, and rever'd for age;
Around his temples spreads his golden wing,
And thus the flatt'ring dream deceives the King.
25   Canst thou, with all a Monarch's cares opprest,
Oh *Atreus*' son! canst thou indulge thy rest?
Ill fits a Chief who mighty nations guides,
Directs in council, and in war presides,

To whom its safety a whole people owes,
To waste long nights in indolent repose?   30
Monarch awake! 'tis *Jove*'s command I bear,
Thou, and thy glory, claim his heav'nly care.
In just array draw forth th' embattel'd train,
Lead all thy *Grecians* to the dusty plain;
Ev'n now, O King! 'tis giv'n thee to destroy   35
The lofty tow'rs of wide-extended *Troy*.
For now no more the Gods with fate contend,
At *Juno*'s suit the heav'nly factions end.
Destruction hangs o'er yon' devoted wall,
And nodding *Ilion* waits th' impending fall.   40
Awake, but waking this advice approve,
And trust the vision that descends from *Jove*.
    The Phantome said; then, vanish'd from his sight,
Resolves to air, and mixes with the night.
A thousand schemes the monarch's mind employ;   45
Elate in thought, he sacks untaken *Troy*:
Vain as he was, and to the future blind;
Nor saw what *Jove* and secret fate design'd,
What mighty toils to either host remain,
What scenes of grief and numbers of the slain!   50
Eager he rises, and in fancy hears
The voice celestial murm'ring in his ears.
First on his limbs a slender vest he drew,
Around him next the regal mantle threw,
Th' embroider'd sandals on his feet were ty'd;   55
The starry faulchion glitter'd at his side;
And last his arm the massy sceptre loads,
Unstain'd, immortal, and the gift of Gods.
    Now rosie morn ascends the court of *Jove*,
Lifts up her light, and opens day above.   60
The King dispatch'd his heralds with commands
To range the camp, and summon all the bands:
The gath'ring hosts the monarch's word obey;
While to the fleet *Atrides* bends his way.
In his black ship the *Pylian* Prince he found;   65
There calls a Senate of the Peers around.
Th' Assembly plac'd, the King of Men exprest
The counsels lab'ring in his artful breast.

Friends and Confed'rates! with attentive ear
70 Receive my words, and credit what you hear.
Late as I slumber'd in the shades of night,
A dream divine appear'd before my sight;
Whose visionary form like *Nestor* came,
The same in habit, and in mien the same.
75 The heav'nly Phantome hover'd o'er my head,
And, dost thou sleep, Oh *Atreus'* son? (he said)
Ill fits a Chief who mighty nations guides,
Directs in council and in war presides,
To whom its safety a whole people owes;
80 To waste long nights in indolent repose.
Monarch awake! 'tis *Jove*'s command I bear,
Thou and thy glory claim his heav'nly care.
In just array draw forth th' embattel'd train,
And lead the *Grecians* to the dusty plain;
85 Ev'n now, O King! 'tis giv'n thee to destroy
The lofty tow'rs of wide-extended *Troy*.
For now no more the Gods with fate contend,
At *Juno*'s suit the heav'nly factions end.
Destruction hangs o'er yon' devoted wall,
90 And nodding *Ilion* waits th' impending fall.
This hear observant; and the Gods obey!
The vision spoke, and past in air away.
Now, valiant chiefs! since heav'n itself alarms,
Unite, and rouze the sons of *Greece* to arms.
95 But first, with caution, try what yet they dare,
Worn with nine years of unsuccessful war?
To move the troops to measure back the main,
Be mine; and yours the province to detain.
He spoke, and sate; when *Nestor* rising said,
100 (*Nestor*, whom *Pylos'* sandy realms obey'd)
Princes of *Greece*, your faithful ears incline,
Nor doubt the vision of the pow'rs divine;
Sent by great *Jove* to him who rules the host,
Forbid it heav'n! this warning should be lost!
105 Then let us haste, obey the Gods alarms,
And join to rouze the sons of *Greece* to arms.
Thus spoke the sage: The Kings without delay
Dissolve the council, and their chief obey:

The sceptred rulers lead; the following host
Pour'd forth by thousands, darkens all the coast.   110
As from some rocky cleft the shepherd sees
Clust'ring in heaps on heaps the driving bees,
Rolling, and black'ning, swarms succeeding swarms,
With deeper murmurs and more hoarse alarms:
Dusky they spread, a close embody'd crowd,   115
And o'er the vale descends the living Cloud.
So, from the tents and ships, a length'ning train
Spreads all the beach, and wide o'ershades the plain:
Along the region runs a deaf'ning sound;
Beneath their footsteps groans the trembling ground.   120
Fame flies before, the messenger of *Jove*,
And shining soars, and claps her wings above.
Nine sacred heralds now proclaiming loud
The monarch's will, suspend the list'ning crowd.
Soon as the throngs in order rang'd appear,   125
And fainter murmurs dy'd upon the ear,
The King of Kings his awful figure rais'd;
High in his hand the golden sceptre blaz'd:
The golden sceptre, of celestial frame,
By *Vulcan* form'd, from *Jove* to *Hermes* came: 130
To *Pelops* He th' immortal gift resign'd;
Th' immortal gift great *Pelops* left behind,
In *Atreus*' hand, which not with *Atreus* ends,
To rich *Thyestes* next the prize descends;
And now the mark of *Agamemnon*'s reign,   135
Subjects all *Argos*, and controuls the main.

   On this bright sceptre now the King reclin'd,
And artful thus pronounc'd the speech design'd.
Ye Sons of *Mars*, partake your leader's care,
Heroes of *Greece*, and brothers of the war!   140
Of partial *Jove* with justice I complain,
And heav'nly oracles believ'd in vain.
A safe return was promis'd to our toils,
Renown'd, triumphant, and enrich'd with spoils.
Now shameful flight alone can save the host,   145
Our blood, our treasure, and our glory lost.
So *Jove* decrees, resistless Lord of all!
At whose command whole empires rise or fall:

He shakes the feeble props of human trust,
150   And towns and armies humbles to the dust.
What shame to *Greece* a fruitless war to wage,
Oh lasting shame in ev'ry future age!
Once great in arms, the common scorn we grow,
Repuls'd and baffled by a feeble foe.
155   So small their number, that if wars were ceas'd,
And *Greece* triumphant held a gen'ral feast,
All rank'd by tens; whole decads when they dine
Must want a *Trojan* slave to pour the wine.
But other forces have our hopes o'erthrown,
160   And *Troy* prevails by armies not her own.
Now nine long years of mighty *Jove* are run,
Since first the labours of this war begun:
Our cordage torn, decay'd our vessels lie,
And scarce ensure the wretched pow'r to fly.
165   Haste then, for ever leave the *Trojan* wall!
Our weeping wives, our tender children call:
Love, duty, safety, summon us away,
'Tis nature's voice, and nature we obey.
Our shatter'd barks may yet transport us o'er,
170   Safe and inglorious, to our native shore.
Fly, *Grecians* fly, your sails and oars employ,
And dream no more of heav'n-defended *Troy*.
    His deep design unknown, the hosts approve
Atrides' speech. The mighty numbers move.
175   So roll the billows to th' *Icarian* shore,
From East and South when winds begin to roar,
Burst their dark mansions in the clouds, and sweep
The whitening surface of the ruffled deep.
And as on corn when western gusts descend,
180   Before the blast the lofty harvests bend:
Thus o'er the field the moving host appears,
With nodding plumes and groves of waving spears.
The gath'ring murmur spreads, their trampling feet
Beat the loose sands, and thicken to the fleet.
185   With long-resounding cries they urge the train,
To fit the ships, and launch into the main.
They toil, they sweat, thick clouds of dust arise,
The doubling clamours echo to the skies.

Ev'n then the *Greeks* had left the hostile plain,
And fate decreed the fall of *Troy* in vain;   190
But *Jove*'s imperial Queen their flight survey'd,
And sighing thus bespoke the blue-ey'd Maid.
    Shall then the *Grecians* fly? Oh dire disgrace!
And leave unpunish'd this perfidious race?
Shall *Troy*, shall *Priam*, and th'adult'rous spouse,   195
In peace enjoy the fruits of broken vows?
And bravest chiefs, in *Helen*'s quarrel slain,
Lie unreveng'd on yon' detested plain?
No – let my *Greeks*, unmov'd by vain alarms,
Once more refulgent shine in brazen arms.   200
Haste, Goddess, haste! the flying host detain,
Nor let one sail be hoisted on the main.
    Pallas obeys, and from *Olympus*' height
Swift to the ships precipitates her flight;
Ulysses, first in publick cares, she found,   205
For prudent counsel like the Gods renown'd:
Oppress'd with gen'rous grief the Hero stood,
Nor drew his sable vessels to the flood.
And is it thus, divine *Laertes*' son!
Thus fly the *Greeks* (the martial maid begun)   210
Thus to their country bear their own disgrace,
And fame eternal leave to *Priam*'s race?
Shall beauteous *Helen* still remain unfreed,
Still unreveng'd a thousand heroes bleed?
Haste gen'rous *Ithacus*! prevent the shame,   215
Recall your armies, and your chiefs reclaim.
Your own resistless eloquence employ,
And to th'Immortals trust the fall of *Troy*.
    The voice divine confess'd the warlike maid,
Ulysses heard, nor uninspir'd obey'd.   220
Then meeting first *Atrides*, from his hand
Receiv'd th' imperial sceptre of command.
Thus grac'd, attention and respect to gain,
He runs, he flies, thro' all the *Grecian* train,
Each Prince of name, or chief in arms approv'd,   225
He fir'd with praise or with persuasion mov'd.
    Warriours like you, with strength and wisdom blest,
By brave examples should confirm the rest.

The monarch's will not yet reveal'd appears;
230   He tries our courage, but resents our fears.
Th' unwary *Greeks* his fury may provoke;
Not thus the King in secret council spoke.
Jove loves our chief, from *Jove* his honour springs,
Beware! for dreadful is the wrath of Kings.

235   But if a clam'rous vile Plebeian rose,
Him with reproof he check'd, or tam'd with blows.
Be still thou slave! and to thy betters yield;
Unknown alike in council and in field!
Ye Gods, what dastards would our host command?
240   Swept to the war, the lumber of a land.
Be silent, wretch, and think not here allow'd
That worst of tyrants, an usurping crowd.
To one sole Monarch *Jove* commits the sway;
His are the laws, and him let all obey.

245   With words like these the troops *Ulysses* rul'd,
The loudest silenc'd, and the fiercest cool'd.
Back to th' assembly roll the thronging train,
Desert the ships, and pour upon the plain.
Murm'ring they move, as when old *Ocean* roars,
250   And heaves huge surges to the trembling shores:
The groaning banks are burst with bellowing sound,
The rocks remurmur, and the deeps rebound.
At length the tumult sinks, the noises cease,
And a still silence lulls the camp to peace.

255   *Thersites* only clamour'd in the throng,
Loquacious, loud, and turbulent of Tongue:
Aw'd by no shame, by no respect controul'd,
In scandal busy, in reproaches bold:
With witty malice studious to defame,
260   Scorn all his joy, and laughter all his aim.
But chief he glory'd with licentious style
To lash the great, and monarchs to revile.
His figure such as might his soul proclaim;
One eye was blinking, and one leg was lame:
265   His mountain-shoulders half his breast o'erspread,
Thin hairs bestrew'd his long mis-shapen head.
Spleen to mankind his envious heart possest,
And much he hated all, but most the best.

Ulysses or *Achilles* still his theme;
But Royal scandal his delight supreme.   270
Long had he liv'd the scorn of ev'ry *Greek*,
Vext when he spoke, yet still they heard him speak.
Sharp was his voice; which in the shrillest tone,
Thus with injurious taunts attack'd the throne.

  Amidst the glories of so bright a reign,   275
What moves the great *Atrides* to complain?
'Tis thine whate'er the warrior's breast inflames,
The golden spoil, and thine the lovely dames.
With all the wealth our wars and blood bestow,
Thy tents are crowded, and thy chests o'erflow.   280
Thus at full ease in heaps of riches roll'd,
What grieves the Monarch? Is it thirst of gold?
Say shall we march with our unconquer'd pow'rs,
(The *Greeks* and I) to *Ilion*'s hostile tow'rs,
And bring the race of royal bastards here,   285
For *Troy* to ransom at a price too dear?
But safer plunder thy own host supplies;
Say, would'st thou seize some valiant leader's prize?
Or, if thy heart to gen'rous love be led,
Some captive fair, to bless thy kingly bed?   290
Whate'er our master craves, submit we must,
Plagu'd with his pride, or punish'd for his lust.
Oh women of *Achaia*! men no more!
Hence let us fly, and let him waste his store
In loves and pleasures on the *Phrygian* shore.   295
We may be wanted on some busy day,
When *Hector* comes: So great *Achilles* may:
From him he forc'd the prize we jointly gave,
From him, the fierce, the fearless, and the brave:
And durst he, as he ought, resent that wrong,   300
This mighty tyrant were no tyrant long.

  Fierce from his seat, at this, *Ulysses* springs,
In gen'rous vengeance of the King of Kings.
With indignation sparkling in his eyes,
He views the wretch, and sternly thus replies.   305
Peace, factious monster, born to vex the state,
With wrangling talents form'd for foul debate:

Curb that impetuous tongue, nor rashly vain
And singly mad, asperse the sov'reign reign.
310 Have we not known thee, slave! of all our host,
The man who acts thè least, upbraids the most?
Think not the *Greeks* to shameful flight to bring,
Nor let those lips profane the name of King.
For our return we trust the heav'nly pow'rs;
315 Be that their care; to fight like men be ours.
But grant the host with wealth the gen'ral load,
Except detraction, what hast thou bestow'd?
Suppose some Hero should his spoils resign,
Art thou that Hero, could those spoils be thine?
320 Gods! let me perish on this hateful shore,
And let these eyes behold my son no more;
If, on thy next offence, this hand forbear
To strip those arms thou ill deserv'st to wear,
Expel the council where our Princes meet,
325 And send thee scourg'd, and howling thro' the fleet.
    He said, and cow'ring as the dastard bends,
The weighty sceptre on his back descends:
On the round bunch the bloody tumours rise;
The tears spring starting from his haggard eyes:
330 Trembling he sate, and shrunk in abject fears,
From his vile visage wip'd the scalding tears.
While to his neighbour each express'd his thought;
Ye Gods! what wonders has *Ulysses* wrought?
What fruits his conduct and his courage yield?
335 Great in the council, glorious in the field.
Gen'rous he rises in the crown's defence,
To curb the factious tongue of insolence.
Such just examples on offenders shown,
Sedition silence, and assert the throne.
340   'Twas thus the gen'ral voice the Hero prais'd,
Who rising, high th' imperial sceptre rais'd:
The blue-ey'd *Pallas*, his celestial friend,
(In form a herald) bade the crowds attend.
Th' expecting crowds in still attention hung,
345 To hear the wisdom of his heav'nly tongue.
Then deeply thoughtful, pausing e're he spoke,
His silence thus the prudent Hero broke.

Unhappy monarch! whom the *Grecian* race
With shame deserting, heap with vile disgrace.
Not such at *Argos* was their gen'rous vow,   350
Once all their voice, but ah! forgotten now:
Ne'er to return, was then the common cry,
'Till *Troy*'s proud structures shou'd in ashes lie.
Behold them weeping for their native shore!
What cou'd their wives or helpless children more?   355
What heart but melts to leave the tender train,
And, one short month, endure the wintry main?
Few leagues remov'd, we wish our peaceful seat,
When the ship tosses, and the tempests beat:
Then well may this long stay provoke their tears,   360
The tedious length of nine revolving years.
Not for their grief the *Grecian* host I blame;
But vanquish'd! baffled! oh eternal shame!
Expect the time to *Troy*'s destruction giv'n,
And try the faith of *Calchas* and of heav'n.   365
What past at *Aulis*, *Greece* can witness bear,
And all who live to breathe this *Phrygian* air.
Beside a fountain's sacred brink we rais'd
Our verdant altars, and the victims blaz'd;
('Twas where the plane-tree spread its shades around)   370
The altars heav'd; and from the crumbling ground
A mighty dragon shot, of dire portent;
From *Jove* himself the dreadful sign was sent.
Strait to the tree his sanguine spires he roll'd,
And curl'd around in many a winding fold.   375
The topmost branch a mother-bird possest;
Eight callow infants fill'd the mossie nest;
Herself the ninth: The serpent as he hung,
Stretch'd his black jaws, and crash'd the crying young;
While hov'ring near, with miserable moan,   380
The drooping mother wail'd her children gone.
The mother last, as round the nest she flew,
Seiz'd by the beating wing, the monster slew:
Nor long surviv'd; to marble turn'd he stands
A lasting prodigy on *Aulis*' sands.   385
Such was the will of *Jove*; and hence we dare
Trust in his omen, and support the war.

For while around we gaz'd with wondring eyes,
And trembling sought the pow'rs with sacrifice,
390 Full of his god, the rev'rend *Calchas* cry'd,
Ye *Grecian* warriours! lay your fears aside.
This wondrous signal *Jove* himself displays,
Of long, long labours, but eternal praise.
As many birds as by the snake were slain,
395 So many years the toils of *Greece* remain;
But wait the tenth, for *Ilion*'s fall decreed:
Thus spoke the Prophet, thus the fates succeed.
Obey, ye *Grecians*! with submission wait,
Nor let your flight avert the *Trojan* fate.
400   He said: the shores with loud applauses sound,
The hollow ships each deaf'ning shout rebound.
Then *Nestor* thus – These vain debates forbear,
Ye talk like children, not like heroes dare.
Where now are all your high resolves at last?
405 Your leagues concluded, your engagements past?
Vow'd with libations and with victims then,
Now vanish'd like their smoke: the faith of men!
While useless words consume th' unactive hours,
No wonder *Troy* so long resists our pow'rs.
410 Rise, great *Atrides*! and with courage sway;
We march to war if thou direct the way.
But leave the few that dare resist thy laws,
The mean deserters of the *Grecian* cause,
To grudge the conquests mighty *Jove* prepares,
415 And view, with envy, our successful wars.
On that great day when first the martial train
Big with the fate of *Ilion*, plow'd the main;
Jove, on the right, a prosp'rous signal sent,
And thunder rolling shook the firmament.
420 Encourag'd hence, maintain the glorious strife,
'Till ev'ry soldier grasp a *Phrygian* wife,
'Till *Helen*'s woes at full reveng'd appear,
And *Troy*'s proud matrons render tear for tear.
Before that day, if any *Greek* invite
425 His country's troops to base, inglorious Flight,
Stand forth that *Greek*! and hoist his sail to fly;
And die the dastard first, who dreads to die.

But now, O Monarch! all thy Chiefs advise:
Nor what they offer, thou thy self despise.
Among those counsels, let not mine be vain;   430
In tribes and nations to divide thy train:
His sep'rate troops let ev'ry leader call,
Each strengthen each, and all encourage all.
What chief, or soldier, of the num'rous band,
Or bravely fights, or ill obeys command,   435
When thus distinct they war, shall soon be known,
And what the cause of *Ilion* not o'erthrown;
If fate resists, or if our Arms are slow,
If Gods above prevent, or Men below.

To him the King: How much thy years excel,   440
In arts of council, and in speaking well!
Oh would the Gods, in love to *Greece*, decree
But ten such sages as they grant in thee;
Such wisdom soon should *Priam*'s force destroy,
And soon should fall the haughty tow'rs of *Troy*!   445
But *Jove* forbids, who plunges those he hates
In fierce contention and in vain debates.
Now great *Achilles* from our aid withdraws,
By me provok'd; a captive maid the cause:
If e'er as friends we join, the *Trojan* wall   450
Must shake, and heavy will the vengeance fall!
But now, ye warriors, take a short repast;
And, well refresh'd, to bloody conflict haste.
His sharpen'd spear let ev'ry *Grecian* wield,
And ev'ry *Grecian* fix his brazen shield,   455
Let all excite the fiery steeds of war,
And all for combate fit the ratling car.
This day, this dreadful day, let each contend;
No rest, no respite, 'till the shades descend;
'Till darkness, or 'till death shall cover all: 460
Let the war bleed, and let the mighty fall!
'Till bath'd in sweat be ev'ry manly breast,
With the huge shield each brawny arm deprest,
Each aking nerve refuse the lance to throw,
And each spent courser at the chariot blow.   465
Who dares, inglorious, in his ships to stay,
Who dares to tremble on this signal day,

That wretch, too mean to fall by martial pow'r,
The birds shall mangle, and the dogs devour.
470   The monarch spoke: and strait a murmur rose,
Loud as the surges when the tempest blows,
That dash'd on broken rocks tumultuous roar,
And foam and thunder on the stony shore.
Strait to the tents the troops dispersing bend,
475   The fires are kindled, and the smokes ascend;
With hasty feasts they sacrifice, and pray
T'avert the dangers of the doubtful day.
A steer of five year's Age, large limb'd, and fed,
To *Jove*'s high altars *Agamemnon* led:
480   There bade the noblest of the *Grecian* Peers;
And *Nestor* first, as most advanc'd in years.
Next came *Idomeneus* and *Tydeus*' son,
Ajax the less, and *Ajax Telamon*;
Then wise *Ulysses* in his rank was plac'd;
485   And *Menelaüs* came unbid, the last.
The Chiefs surround the destin'd beast, and take
The sacred off'ring of the salted cake:
When thus the King prefers his solemn pray'r.
Oh thou! whose thunder rends the clouded air,
490   Who in the heav'n of heav'ns hast fix'd thy throne,
Supreme of Gods! unbounded, and alone!
Hear! and before the burning sun descends,
Before the night her gloomy veil extends,
Low in the dust be laid yon' hostile spires,
495   Be *Priam*'s palace sunk in *Grecian* fires,
In *Hector*'s breast be plung'd this shining sword,
And slaughter'd heroes groan around their Lord!
    Thus pray'd the chief: his unavailing pray'r
Great *Jove* refus'd, and tost in empty air:
500   The God averse, while yet the fumes arose,
Prepar'd new toils and doubled woes on woes.
Their pray'rs perform'd, the Chiefs the rite pursue,
The barley sprinkled, and the victim slew.
The limbs they sever from th' inclosing hyde,
505   The thighs, selected to the Gods, divide.
On these, in double cauls involv'd with art,
The choicest morsels lie from ev'ry part.

From the cleft wood the crackling flames aspire,
While the fat victim feeds the sacred fire.
The thighs thus sacrific'd and entrails drest,   510
Th'assistants part, transfix, and roast the rest;
Then spread the tables, the repast prepare,
Each takes his seat, and each receives his share.
Soon as the rage of hunger was supprest,
The gen'rous *Nestor* thus the Prince addrest.   515
   Now bid thy heralds sound the loud alarms,
And call the squadrons sheath'd in brazen arms:
Now seize th' occasion, now the troops survey,
And lead to war when heav'n directs the way.
   He said; the Monarch issu'd his commands;   520
Strait the loud heralds call the gath'ring bands.
The chiefs inclose their King; the hosts divide,
In tribes and nations rank'd on either side.
High in the midst the blue-ey'd Virgin flies;
From rank to rank she darts her ardent eyes: 525
The dreadful *Ægis*, *Jove*'s immortal shield,
Blaz'd on her arm, and lighten'd all the field:
Round the vast orb an hundred serpents roll'd,
Form'd the bright fringe, and seem'd to burn in gold.
With this each *Grecian*'s manly breast she warms,   530
Swells their bold hearts, and strings their nervous arms;
No more they sigh, inglorious to return,
But breathe revenge, and for the combate burn.
   As on some mountain, thro' the lofty grove
The crackling flames ascend and blaze above,   535
The fires expanding as the winds arise,
Shoot their long beams, and kindle half the skies:
So from the polish'd arms, and brazen shields,
A gleamy splendour flash'd along the fields.
Not less their number, than th' embody'd cranes,   540
Or milk-white swans in *Asius*' watry plains,
That o'er the windings of *Cayster*'s springs,
Stretch their long necks, and clap their rustling wings,
Now tow'r aloft, and course in airy rounds;
Now light with noise; with noise the field resounds.   545
Thus num'rous and confus'd, extending wide,
The legions crowd *Scamander*'s flow'ry side;

With rushing troops the plains are cover'd o'er,
And thund'ring footsteps shake the sounding shore:
550 Along the river's level meads they stand,
Thick as in spring the flow'rs adorn the land,
Or leaves the trees; or thick as insects play,
The wandring nation of a summer's day,
That drawn by milky steams, at ev'ning hours,
555 In gather'd swarms surround the rural bow'rs;
From pail to pail with busy murmur run
The gilded legions glitt'ring in the sun.
So throng'd, so close, the *Grecian* squadrons stood
In radiant arms, and thirst for *Trojan* blood.
560 Each leader now his scatter'd force conjoins
In close array, and forms the deep'ning lines.
Not with more ease, the skilful shepherd swain
Collects his flock from thousands on the plain.
The King of Kings, majestically tall,
565 Tow'rs o'er his armies, and outshines them all:
Like some proud Bull that round the pastures leads
His subject-herds, the Monarch of the meads.
Great as the Gods th' exalted Chief was seen,
His strength like *Neptune*, and like *Mars* his mien,
570 *Jove* o'er his eyes celestial glories spread,
And dawning conquest play'd around his head.
    Say, Virgins, seated round the throne divine,
All-knowing *Goddesses!* immortal Nine!
Since earth's wide regions, heav'n's unmeasur'd height,
575 And hell's abyss hide nothing from your sight,
(We, wretched mortals! lost in doubts below,
But guess by rumour, and but boast we know)
Oh say what Heroes, fir'd by thirst of fame,
Or urg'd by wrongs, to *Troy*'s destruction came?
580 To count them all, demands a thousand tongues,
A throat of brass, and adamantine lungs.
Daughters of *Jove* assist! inspir'd by you
The mighty labour dauntless I pursue:
What crowded armies, from what climes they bring,
585 Their names, their numbers, and their Chiefs I sing.

The hardy warriors whom *Bœotia* bred,
Peneleus, Leitus, Prothoënor led:
With these *Arcesilaus* and *Clonius* stand,
Equal in arms, and equal in command.
These head the troops that rocky *Aulis* yields,   590
And *Eteon*'s hills, and *Hyrie*'s watry fields,
And *Schœnos, Scolos, Grœa* near the main,
And *Mycalessia*'s ample piny plain.
Those who in *Peteon* or *Ilesion* dwell,
Or *Harma* where *Apollo*'s Prophet fell;   595
Heleon and *Hylè*, which the springs o'erflow;
And *Medeon* lofty, and *Ocalea* low;
Or in the meads of *Haliartus* stray,
Or *Thespia* sacred to the God of Day.
Onchestus, *Neptune*'s celebrated groves;   600
Copœ, and *Thisbè*, fam'd for silver doves,
For flocks *Erythrœ*, *Glissa* for the vine;
Platœa green, and *Nisa* the divine.
And they whom *Thebè*'s well-built walls inclose,
Where *Mydè, Eutresis, Coronè* rose;   605
And *Arnè* rich, with purple harvests crown'd;
And *Anthedon*, *Bœotia*'s utmost bound.
Full fifty ships they send, and each conveys
Twice sixty warriors thro' the foaming seas.

   To these succeed *Aspledon*'s martial train,   610
Who plow the spacious *Orchomenian* plain.
Two valiant brothers rule th' undaunted throng,
Iälmen and *Ascalaphus* the strong:
Sons of *Astyochè* the heav'nly fair,
Whose virgin charms subdu'd the God of War: 615
(In *Actor*'s court as she retir'd to rest,
The strength of *Mars* the blushing maid comprest)
Their troops in thirty sable vessels sweep
With equal oars, the hoarse-resounding deep.

   The *Phocians* next in forty barks repair,   620
Epistrophus and *Schedius* head the war.

From those rich regions where *Cephisus* leads
His silver current thro' the flow'ry meads;
From *Panopëa*, *Chrysa* the divine,
625   Where *Anemoria*'s stately turrets shine,
Where *Pytho*, *Daulis*, *Cyparissus* stood,
And fair *Lilæa* views the rising flood.
These rang'd in order on the floating tide,
Close, on the left, the bold *Bœotians* side.

630   Fierce *Ajax* led the *Locrian* squadrons on,
Ajax the less, *Oileus*' valiant son;
Skill'd to direct the flying dart aright;
Swift in pursuit, and active in the fight.
Him, as their Chief, the chosen troops attend,
635   Which *Bessa*, *Thronus*, and rich *Cynos* send:
Opus, *Calliarus*, and *Scarphe*'s bands;
And those who dwell where pleasing *Augia* stands,
And where *Boägrius* floats the lowly lands,
Or in fair *Tarphe*'s sylvan seats reside;
640   In forty vessels cut the yielding tide.

Eubœa next her martial sons prepares,
And sends the brave *Abantes* to the wars:
Breathing revenge, in arms they take their way
From *Chalcis*' walls, and strong *Eretria*;
645   Th' *Isteian* fields for gen'rous vines renown'd,
The fair *Carystos*, and the *Styrian* Ground;
Where *Dios* from her tow'rs o'erlooks the Plain,
And high *Cerinthus* views the neighb'ring main.
Down their broad shoulders falls a length of hair;
650   Their hands dismiss not the long lance in air;
But with portended spears in fighting fields,
Pierce the tough cors'lets and the brazen shields.
Twice twenty ships transport the warlike bands,
Which bold *Elphenor*, fierce in arms, commands.

655   Full fifty more from *Athens* stem the main,
Led by *Menestheus* thro' the liquid plain,
(*Athens* the fair, where great *Erectheus* sway'd,
That ow'd his nurture to the blue-ey'd maid,
But from the teeming furrow took his birth,
660   The mighty offspring of the foodful earth.

Him *Pallas* plac'd amidst her wealthy fane,
Ador'd with sacrifice and oxen slain;
Where as the years revolve her altars blaze,
And all the tribes resound the Goddess' praise.)
No Chief like thee, *Menestheus*! *Greece* could yield,   665
To marshal Armies in the dusty field,
Th' extended wings of battel to display,
Or close th' embody'd host in firm array.
Nestor alone, improv'd by length of days,
For martial conduct bore an equal praise.   670

    With these appear the *Salaminian* bands,
Whom the gigantic *Telamon* commands;
In twelve black ships to *Troy* they steer their course,
And with the great *Athenians* join their force.

    Next move to war the gen'rous *Argive* train,   675
From high *Trœzenè*, and *Maseta*'s plain,
And fair *Ægina* circled by the main:
Whom strong *Tyrinthè*'s lofty walls surround,
And *Epidaure* with viny harvests crown'd:
And where fair *Asinen* and *Hermion* show   680
Their cliffs above, and ample bay below.
These by the brave *Euryalus* were led,
Great *Sthenelus*, and greater *Diomed*,
But chief *Tydides* bore the sov'reign sway;
In fourscore barks they plow the watry way.   685

    The proud *Mycœnè* arms her martial pow'rs,
Cleonè, *Corinth*, with imperial tow'rs,
Fair *Arethyrea*, *Ornia*'s fruitful plain,
And *Ægion*, and *Adrastus*' ancient reign;
And those who dwell along the sandy shore,   690
And where *Pellenè* yields her fleecy store,
Where *Helicè* and *Hyperesia* lie,
And *Gonoëssa*'s spires salute the sky.
Great *Agamemnon* rules the num'rous band,
A hundred vessels in long order stand,   695
And crowded nations wait his dread command.
High on the deck the King of men appears,
And his refulgent arms in triumph wears;
Proud of his host, unrival'd in his reign,
In silent pomp he moves along the main.   700

His brother follows, and to vengeance warms
The hardy *Spartans*, exercis'd in arms:
Phares and *Brysia*'s valiant troops, and those
Whom *Lacedæmon*'s lofty hills inclose:
705 Or *Messè*'s tow'rs for silver doves renown'd,
Amyclæ, *Laäs*, *Augia*'s happy ground,
And those whom *Oetylos*' low walls contain,
And *Helos*, on the margin of the main.
These, o'er the bending ocean, *Helen*'s cause
710 In sixty ships with *Menelaüs* draws:
Eager and loud, from man to man he flies,
Revenge and fury flaming in his eyes;
While vainly fond, in fancy oft he hears
The fair one's grief, and sees her falling tears.

715   In ninety sail, from *Pylos*' sandy coast,
Nestor the sage conducts his chosen host:
From *Amphigenia*'s ever fruitful land;
Where *Æpy* high, and little *Pteleon* stand;
Where beauteous *Arenè* her structures shows,
720 And *Thryon*'s Walls *Alphëus*' streams inclose:
And *Dorion*, fam'd for *Thamyris*' disgrace,
Superiour once of all the tuneful race,
'Till vain of mortal's empty praise, he strove
To match the seed of cloud-compelling *Jove*!
725 Too daring bard! whose unsuccessful pride
Th' immortal *Muses* in their art defy'd.
Th' avenging *Muses* of the light of day
Depriv'd his eyes, and snatch'd his voice away;
No more his heav'nly voice was heard to sing,
730 His hand no more awak'd the silver string.

    Where under high *Cyllenè* crown'd with wood,
The shaded tomb of old *Æpytus* stood;
From *Ripè*, *Stratie*, *Tegea*'s bord'ring towns,
The *Phenean* fields, and *Orchomenian* downs,
735 Where the fat herds in plenteous pasture rove;
And *Stymphelus* with her surrounding grove,
Parrhasia, on her snowy cliffs reclin'd,
And high *Enispè* shook by wintry wind,
And fair *Mantinea*'s ever-pleasing site;
740 In sixty sail th' *Arcadian* bands unite.

Bold *Agapenor*, glorious at their head,
(*Ancæus'* son) the mighty squadron led.
Their ships, supply'd by *Agamemnon's* care,
Thro' roaring seas the wond'ring warriors bear;
The first to battel on th' appointed plain,   745
But new to all the dangers of the main.

   Those, where fair *Elis* and *Buprasium* join;
Whom *Hyrmin*, here, and *Myrsinus* confine,
And bounded there, where o'er the vallies rose
Th' *Olenian* rock; and where *Alisium* flows;   750
Beneath four chiefs (a num'rous army) came:
The strength and glory of th' *Epean* name.
In sep'rate squadrons these their train divide,
Each leads ten vessels thro' the yielding tide.
One was *Amphimachus*, and *Thalpius* one;   755
(*Eurytus'* this, and that *Teätus'* son)
Diores sprung from *Amarynceus'* line;
And great *Polyxenus*, of force divine.

   But those who view fair *Elis* o'er the seas
From the blest Islands of th' *Echinades*,   760
In forty vessels under *Meges* move,
Begot by *Phyleus*, the belov'd of *Jove*.
To strong *Dulichium* from his sire he fled,
And thence to *Troy* his hardy warriors led.

   Ulysses follow'd thro' the watry road,   765
A chief, in wisdom equal to a God.
With those whom *Cephalenia's* isle inclos'd,
Or till'd their fields along the coast oppos'd; Or where
Or where fair *Ithaca* o'erlooks the floods,
Where high *Neritos* shakes his waving woods,   770
Where *Ægilipa's* rugged sides are seen,
Crocylia rocky, and *Zacynthus* green.
These in twelve galleys with vermillion prores,
Beneath his conduct sought the *Phrygian* shores.

   Thoas came next, *Andræmon's* valiant son,   775
From *Pleuron's* walls and chalky *Calydon*,
And rough *Pylenè*, and th' *Olenian* steep,
And *Chalcis* beaten by the rolling deep.
He led the warriors from th' *Ætolian* shore,
For now the sons of *Oeneus* were no more!   780

The glories of the mighty race were fled!
Oeneus himself, and *Meleager* dead!
To *Thoas*' care now trust the martial train,
His forty vessels follow thro' the main.

785   Next eighty barks the *Cretan* king commands,
Of *Gnossus*, *Lyctus*, and *Gortyna*'s bands,
And those who dwell where *Rhytion*'s domes arise,
Or white *Lycastus* glitters to the skies,
Or where by *Phœstus* silver *Jardan* runs;

790   *Crete*'s hundred cities pour forth all her sons.
These march'd, *Idomeneus*, beneath thy care,
And *Merion*, dreadful as the God of war.
    Tlepolemus, the son of *Hercules*,
Led nine swift vessels thro' the foamy seas;

795   From *Rhodes* with everlasting sunshine bright,
Jalyssus, *Lindus*, and *Camirus* white.
His captive mother fierce *Alcides* bore
From *Ephyr*'s walls, and *Sellè*'s winding shore,
Where mighty towns in ruins spread the plain,

800   And saw their blooming warriours early slain.
The Hero, when to manly years he grew,
Alcides' uncle, old *Lycimnius*, slew;
For this, constrain'd to quit his native place,
And shun the vengeance of th' *Herculean* race,

805   A fleet he built, and with a num'rous train
Of willing exiles wander'd o'er the main;
Where many seas, and many suff'rings past,
On happy *Rhodes* the chief arriv'd at last:
There in three tribes divides his native band,

810   And rules them peaceful in a foreign land:
Encreas'd and prosper'd in their new abodes,
By mighty *Jove*, the sire of men and gods;
With joy they saw the growing empire rise,
And show'rs of wealth descending from the skies.

815   Three Ships with *Nireus* sought the *Trojan* shore,
Nireus, whom *Agläe* to *Charopus* bore,
Nireus, in faultless shape, and blooming grace,
The loveliest youth of all the *Grecian* race;
Pelides only match'd his early charms;

820   But few his troops, and small his strength in arms.

Next thirty galleys cleave the liquid plain,
Of those *Calydnæ*'s sea-girt isles contain;
With them the youth of *Nisyrus* repair,
Casus the strong, and *Crapathus* the fair;
Cos, where *Eurypylus* possest the sway,   825
'Till great *Alcides* made the realms obey:
These *Antiphus* and bold *Phidippus* bring,
Sprung from the God by *Thessalus* the King.

   Now, Muse, recount *Pelasgic Argos*' pow'rs,
From *Alos*, *Alopè*, and *Trechin*'s tow'rs;   830
From *Pthia*'s spacious vales; and *Hella*, blest
With female beauty far beyond the rest.
Full fifty ships beneath *Achilles*' care
Th' *Achaians*, *Myrmidons*, *Helleneans* bear;
Thessalians all, tho' various in their name,   835
The same their nation, and their chief the same.
But now inglorious, stretch'd along the shore,
They hear the brazen voice of war no more;
No more the foe they face in dire array;
Close in his fleet their angry leader lay: 840
Since fair *Briseïs* from his arms was torn,
The noblest spoil from sack'd *Lyrnessus* born,
Then, when the chief the *Theban* walls o'erthrew,
And the bold sons of great *Evenus* slew.
There mourn'd *Achilles*, plung'd in depth of care,   845
But soon to rise in slaughter, blood, and war.

   To these the youth of *Phylacè* succeed,
Itona, famous for her fleecy breed,
And grassy *Pteleon* deck'd with chearful greens,
The bow'rs of *Ceres*, and the sylvan scenes,   850
Sweet *Pyrrhasus*, with blooming flourets crown'd,
And *Antron*'s watry dens and cavern'd ground.
These own'd as chief *Protesilas* the brave,
Who now lay silent in the gloomy grave:
The first who boldly touch'd the *Trojan* shore,   855
And dy'd a *Phrygian* lance with *Grecian* gore:
There lies, far distant from his native plain;
Unfinish'd his proud palaces remain,
And his sad consort beats her breast in vain.

860 His troops in forty ships *Podarces* led,
     Iphiclus' son, and brother to the dead;
     Nor he unworthy to command the host;
     Yet still they mourn'd their ancient leader lost.
         The men who *Glaphyra*'s fair soil partake,
865 Where hills encircle *Bœbe*'s lowly lake,
     Where *Pheræ* hears the neighb'ring waters fall,
     Or proud *Iölcus* lifts her airy wall,
     In ten black ships embark'd for *Ilion*'s shore,
     With bold *Eumelus*, whom *Alcestè* bore:
870 All *Pelias*' race *Alcestè* far outshin'd,
     The grace and glory of the beauteous kind.
         The troops *Methonè*, or *Thaumacia* yields,
     Olyzon's rocks, or *Mœlibæa*'s fields,
     With *Philoctetes* sail'd, whose matchless art
875 From the tough bow directs the feather'd dart.
     Sev'n were his ships; each vessel fifty row,
     Skill'd in his science of the dart and bow.
     But he lay raging on the *Lemnian* ground,
     A pois'nous *Hydra* gave the burning wound;
880 There groan'd the chief in agonizing pain,
     Whom *Greece* at length shall wish, nor wish in vain.
     His forces *Medon* led from *Lemnos*' shore,
     Oileus' son whom beauteous *Rhena* bore.
         Th' *Oechalian* race, in those high tow'rs contain'd,
885 Where once *Eurytus* in proud triumph reign'd,
     Or where her humbler turrets *Trica* rears,
     Or where *Ithomè*, rough with rocks, appears;
     In thirty sail the sparkling waves divide,
     Which *Podalirius* and *Machaon* guide.
890 To these his skill their *Parent-God imparts,
     Divine professors of the healing arts.
         The bold *Ormenian* and *Asterian* bands
     In forty barks *Eurypilus* commands,
     Where *Titan* hides his hoary head in snow,
895 And where *Hyperia*'s silver fountains flow.
         Thy troops, *Argissa*, *Polyphætes* leads,
     And *Eleon*, shelter'd by *Olympus*' shades,

* *Æsculapius.*

Girtonè's warriours; and where *Orthè* lies,
And *Oloösson*'s chalky cliffs arise.
Sprung from *Pirithoüs* of immortal race,   900
The fruit of fair *Hippodamè*'s embrace,
(That day, when hurl'd from *Pelion*'s cloudy head,
To distant dens the shaggy *Centaurs* fled)
With *Polypætes* join'd in equal sway
Leonteus leads, and forty ships obey.   905

    In twenty sail the bold *Perrhebians* came
From *Cyphus*, *Guneus* was their leader's name.
With these the *Enians* join'd, and those who freeze
Where cold *Dodona* lifts her holy trees;
Or where the pleasing *Titaresius* glides,   910
And into *Peneus* rolls his easy tides;
Yet o'er the silver surface pure they flow,
The sacred stream unmix'd with streams below,
Sacred and awful! From the dark abodes
Styx pours them forth, the dreadful oath of Gods!   915

    Last under *Prothous* the *Magnesians* stood,
Prothous the swift, of old *Tenthredon*'s blood;
Who dwell where *Pelion*, crown'd with piny boughs,
Obscures the glade, and nods his shaggy brows;
Or where thro' flow'ry *Tempè Peneus* stray'd,   920
(The region stretch'd beneath his mighty shade)
In forty sable barks they stem'd the main;
Such were the chiefs, and such the *Grecian* Train.

    Say next O Muse! of all *Achaia* breeds,
Who bravest fought, or rein'd the noblest steeds?   925
Eumelus' mares were foremost in the chace,
As eagles fleet, and of *Pheretian* race;
Bred where *Pieria*'s fruitful fountains flow,
And train'd by him who bears the silver bow.
Fierce in the fight, their nostrils breath'd a flame,   930
Their height, their colour, and their age the same;
O'er fields of death they whirl the rapid car,
And break the ranks, and thunder thro' the war.
Ajax in arms the first renown acquir'd,
While stern *Achilles* in his wrath retir'd: 935
(His was the strength that mortal might exceeds,
And his, th' unrival'd race of heav'nly steeds)

But *Thetis*' son now shines in arms no more;
His troops, neglected on the sandy shore,
940 In empty air their sportive jav'lins throw,
Or whirl the disk, or bend an idle bow:
Unstain'd with blood his cover'd chariots stand;
Th' immortal coursers graze along the strand;
But the brave Chiefs th' inglorious life deplor'd,
945 And wand'ring o'er the camp, requir'd their Lord.
  Now, like a deluge, cov'ring all around,
The shining armies sweep along the ground;
Swift as a flood of fire, when storms arise,
Floats the wide field, and blazes to the skies.
950 Earth groan'd beneath them; as when angry *Jove*
Hurls down the forky light'ning from above,
On *Arimè* when he the thunder throws,
And fires *Typhæus* with redoubled blows,
Where *Typhon*, prest beneath the burning load,
955 Still feels the fury of th' avenging God.
  But various *Iris*, *Jove*'s commands to bear,
Speeds on the wings of winds thro' liquid air;
In *Priam*'s porch the *Trojan* chiefs she found,
The old consulting, and the youths around.
960 *Polites*' shape, the monarch's son, she chose,
Who from *Æsetes*' tomb observ'd the foes;
High on the mound; from whence in prospect lay
The fields, the tents, the navy, and the bay.
In this dissembled form, she hasts to bring
965 Th' unwelcome message to the *Phrygian* King.
  Cease to consult, the time for action calls,
War, horrid war, approaches to your walls!
Assembled armies oft' have I beheld;
But ne'er 'till now such numbers charg'd a field.
970 Thick as autumnal leaves, or driving sand,
The moving squadrons blacken all the strand.
Thou, Godlike *Hector*! all thy force employ,
Assemble all th' united bands of *Troy*;
In just array let ev'ry leader call
975 The foreign troops: This day demands them all.
  The voice divine the mighty chief alarms;
The council breaks, the warriours rush to arms.

The gates unfolding pour forth all their train,
Nations on nations fill the dusky plain,
Men, steeds, and chariots shake the trembling ground;　　980
The tumult thickens, and the skies resound.
Amidst the plain in sight of *Ilion* stands
A rising mount, the work of human hands,
(This for *Myrinne*'s tomb th' immortals know,
Tho' call'd *Bateïa* in the world below)　　985
Beneath their chiefs in martial order here,
Th' auxiliar troops and *Trojan* hosts appear.

　　The Godlike *Hector*, high above the rest,
Shakes his huge spear, and nods his plumy crest:
In throngs around his native bands repair,　　990
And groves of lances glitter in the air.

　　Divine *Æneas* brings the *Dardan* race,
Anchises' son, by *Venus*' stol'n embrace,
Born in the shades of *Ida*'s secret grove,
(A mortal mixing with the Queen of Love)　　995
Archilochus and *Achamas* divide
The warriour's Toils, and combate by his side.

　　Who fair *Zeleia*'s wealthy valleys till,
Fast by the foot of *Ida*'s sacred hill:
Or drink, *Æsepus*, of thy sable flood;　　1000
Were led by *Pandarus*, of royal blood.
To whom his art *Apollo* deign'd to show,
Grac'd with the present of his shafts and bow.

　　From rich *Apæsus* and *Adrestia*'s tow'rs,
High *Teree*'s summits, and *Pityea*'s bow'rs;　　1005
From these the congregated troops obey
Young *Amphius* and *Adrastus*' equal sway;
Old *Merops*' Sons; whom, skill'd in fates to come,
The Sire forewarn'd, and prophecy'd their doom:
Fate urg'd them on! the Sire forewarn'd in vain,　　1010
They rush'd to war, and perish'd on the plain.

　　From *Practius*' stream, *Percote*'s pasture lands,
And *Sestos* and *Abydos*' neighb'ring strands,
From great *Arisba*'s walls and *Sellè*'s coast,
Asius Hyrtacides conducts his host:　　1015
High on his car he shakes the flowing reins,
His fiery coursers thunder o'er the plains.

The fierce *Pelasgi* next, in war renown'd,
March from *Larissa*'s ever-fertile ground:
1020   In equal arms their brother-leaders shine,
Hippothous bold, and *Pyleus* the divine.

Next *Acamas* and *Pyrous* lead their hosts
In dread array, from *Thracia*'s wintry coasts;
Round the bleak realms where *Hellespontus* roars,
1025   And *Boreas* beats the hoarse-resounding shores.

With great *Euphemus* the *Ciconians* move,
Sprung from *Trezenian Ceüs*, lov'd by *Jove*.

Pyrechmes the *Pæonian* troops attend,
Skill'd in the fight their crooked bows to bend;
1030   From *Axius*' ample bed he leads them on,
Axius, that laves the distant *Amydon*,
Axius, that swells with all his neighb'ring rills,
And wide around the floated region fills.

The *Paphlagonians Pylæmenes* rules,
1035   Where rich *Henetia* breeds her savage mules,
Where *Erythinus*' rising clifts are seen,
Thy groves of box, *Cytorus*! ever green;
And where *Ægyalus* and *Cromna* lie,
And lofty *Sesamus* invades the sky;
1040   And where *Parthenius*, roll'd thro' banks of flow'rs,
Reflects her bord'ring palaces and bow'rs.

Here march'd in arms the *Halizonian* band,
Whom *Odius* and *Epistrophus* command,
From those far regions where the sun refines
1045   The ripening silver in *Alybean* mines.

There, mighty *Chromis* led the *Mysian* train,
And Augur *Ennomus*, inspir'd in vain,
For stern *Achilles* lopt his sacred head,
Roll'd down *Scamander* with the vulgar dead.

1050   *Phorcys* and brave *Ascanius* here unite
Th'*Ascanian Phrygians*, eager for the fight.

Of those who round *Mæonia*'s realms reside,
Or whom the vales in shade of *Tmolus* hide,
Mestles and *Antiphus* the charge partake;
1055   Born on the banks of *Gyges*' silent lake.
There, from the fields where wild *Mæander* flows,
High *Mycalè*, and *Latmos*' shady brows,

And proud *Miletus*, came the *Carian* throngs,
With mingled clamours, and with barb'rous tongues.
Amphimachus and *Naustes* guide the train,   1060
Naustes the bold, *Amphimachus* the vain,
Who trick'd with gold, and glitt'ring on his car,
Rode like a Woman to the field of war,
Fool that he was! by fierce *Achilles* slain,
The river swept him to the briny main: 1065
There whelm'd with waves the gaudy warriour lies;
The valiant victor seiz'd the golden prize.

    The forces last in fair array succeed,
Which blameless *Glaucus* and *Sarpedon* lead;
The warlike bands that distant *Lycia* yields,   1070
Where gulphy *Xanthus* foams along the fields.

OBSERVATIONS

ON THE

SECOND BOOK

1. *Now pleasing sleep,* &c.] *Aristotle* tells us in the twenty-sixth chapter of his art of poetry, that this place had been objected to by some criticks in those times. They thought it gave a very ill idea of the military Discipline of the *Greeks*, to represent a whole army unguarded, and all the Leaders asleep: They also pretended it was ridiculous to describe all the Gods sleeping besides *Jupiter*. To both these *Aristotle* answers, that nothing is more usual or allowable than that figure which puts *all* for the *greater part*. One may add with respect to the latter Criticism, that nothing could give a better image of the superiority of *Jupiter* to the other Gods (or of the supreme Being to all second causes) than the vigilancy here ascrib'd to him, over all things divine and human.

9. *Fly hence, deluding* Dream.] It appears from *Aristotle, Poet. cap.* 26. that *Homer* was accus'd of impiety, for making *Jupiter* the author of a lye in this passage. It seems there were anciently these words in his speech to the dream; Δίδομεν δὲ οἱ εὖχος ἀρέσθαι, *Let us give him great glory.* (Instead of which we have in the present copies, Τρώεσσι δὲ κήδε' ἐφῆπται [and evils are sure to befall the Trojans].) But *Hippias* found a way to bring off *Homer*, only by placing the accent on the last syllable but one, Διδόμεν, for Διδόμεναι, the infinitive for the imperative; which amounts to no more than he bade the dream to promise him great glory. But *Macrobius de Somnio Scip. l. I. c.* 7. takes off this imputation entirely, and will not allow there was any Lye in the Case. '*Agamemnon* (says he) was order'd by the dream to lead out *all* the forces of the *Greeks* (Πανσυδίη is the word) and promis'd the victory on that condition: Now *Achilles* and his forces not being summon'd to the assembly with the rest, that neglect absolv'd *Jupiter* from his promise.'

This remark Madam *Dacier* has inserted without mentioning its author. Mr. *Dacier* takes notice of a passage in the scripture exactly parallel to this, where God is represented making use of the malignity of his creatures to accomplish his judgments. 'Tis in 2 *Chron.* ch. 18. v. 19, 20, 21. *And the Lord said, Who will persuade* Ahab, *that he may go up and fall at* Ramoth Gilead? *And there came forth a spirit, and stood before the Lord, and said, I will persuade him. And the Lord said unto him, Wherewith? And he said, I will go forth, and I will be a lying spirit in the mouth of all his Prophets, And he said, Thou shalt persuade him and prevail also: Go forth and do so.* Vide *Dacier* upon *Aristotle*, cap. 26.

20. *Descends and hovers o'er* Atrides' *head*.] The whole action of the *dream* is beautifully natural, and agreeable to philosophy. It perches on his head, to intimate that part to be the seat of the soul: It is circumfused about him, to express that total possession of the senses which fancy has during our sleep. It takes the figure of the person who was dearest to *Agamemnon*; as whatever we think of most, when awake, is the common object of our dreams. And just at the instant of its vanishing, it leaves such an impression that the voice seems still to sound in his ear. No description can be more exact or lively.

Eustathius, Dacier.

33. *Draw forth th' embattel'd train,* &c.] The dream here repeats the message of *Jupiter* in the same terms that he receiv'd it. It is no less than the Father of Gods and men who gives the order, and to alter a word were presumption. *Homer* constantly makes his envoys observe this practice as a mark of decency and respect. Madam *Dacier* and others have applauded this in general, and ask'd by what authority an embassador could alter the terms of his commission, since he is not greater or wiser than the person who gave the charge? But this is not always the case in our author, who not only makes use of this conduct with respect to the orders of a higher power, but in regard to equals also; as when one Goddess desires another to represent such an affair, and she immediately takes the words from her mouth and repeats them, of which we have an instance in this book. Some objection too may be rais'd to this manner, when commissions are given in the utmost haste (in a battel or the like) upon sudden emergencies, where it seems not very natural to suppose a man has time to get so many words by heart as he is made to repeat exactly. In the present instance, the repetition is certainly graceful, tho' *Zenodotus* thought it not so the third time, when *Agamemnon* tells his dream to the council. I do not pretend to decide upon the point: For tho' the reverence of the repetition seem'd less needful in that place than when it was deliver'd immediately from *Jupiter*; yet (as *Eustathius* observes) it was necessary for the assembly to know the circumstances of this dream, that the truth of the relation might be unsuspected.

93. *Now valiant chiefs*, &c.] The best Commentary extant upon the first part of this book is in *Dionysius* of *Halicarnassus*, who has given us an admirable explication of this whole conduct of *Agamemnon* in his second treatise ἐσχηματισμένων. He says, 'This Prince had nothing so much at heart as to draw the *Greeks* to a battel, yet knew not how to proceed without *Achilles*, who had just retir'd from the army; and was apprehensive that the *Greeks* who were displeas'd at the departure of *Achilles*, might refuse obedience to his orders, should he absolutely command it. In this circumstance he proposes to the Princes in council to make a tryal of arming the *Grœcians*, and offers an expedient himself; which was that he should sound their dispositions by exhorting him to set sail for *Greece*, but that then the other Princes should be ready to dissuade and detain them. If any object to this stratagem, that *Agamemnon*'s whole scheme would be ruin'd if the army should take him at his word (which was very probable) it is to be answer'd, that his design lay deeper than they imagine, nor did he depend upon his speech only for detaining them. He had some cause to fear the *Greeks* had a pique against him which they had conceal'd, and whatever it was, he judg'd it absolutely necessary to know it before he proceeded to a battel. He therefore furnishes them with an occasion to manifest it, and at the same time provides against any ill effects it might have, by his secret orders to the Princes. It succeeds accordingly, and when the troops are running to embark, they are stopp'd by *Ulysses* and *Nestor*.' – One may farther observe that this whole stratagem is concerted in *Nestor*'s ship, as one whose wisdom and secrecy was most confided in. The story of the vision's appearing in his shape, could not but engage him in some degree: It look'd as if *Jupiter* himself added weight to his counsels by making use of that venerable appearance, and knew this to be the most powerful method of recommending them to *Agamemnon*. It was therefore but natural for *Nestor* to second the motion of the King, and by the help of his authority it prevail'd on the other Princes.

111. *As from some rocky cleft.*] This is the first simile in *Homer*, and we may observe in general that he excels all mankind in the number, variety, and beauty of his comparisons. There are scarce any in *Virgil* which are not translated from him, and therefore when he succeeds best in them he is to be commended but as an improver. *Scaliger* seems not to have thought of this when he compares the similes of these two authors (as indeed they are the places most obvious to comparison.) The present passage is an instance of it, to which he opposes the following verses in the first *Æneid* v. 434.

> *Qualis apes æstate nova per florea rura*
> *Exercet sub sole labor, cum gentis adultos*
> *Educunt fœtus, aut cum liquentia mella*
> *Stipant, & dulci distendunt nectare cellas:*
> *Aut onera accipiunt venientum, aut agmine facto*
> *Ignavum fucos pecus a præsepibus arcent;*
> *Fervet opus, redolentque thymo fragrantia mella.*

> [Such is their toyl, and such their buisy pains,
> As exercise the bees in flow'ry plains;
> When winter past, and summer scarce begun,
> Invites them forth to labour in the sun:
> Some lead their youth abroad, while some condense
> Their liquid store, and some in cells dispence.
> Some at the gate stand ready to receive
> The golden burthen, and their friends relieve.
> All with united force, combine to drive
> The lazy drones from the laborious hive;
> With envy stung, they view each other's deeds;
> The fragrant work with diligence proceeds.]

This he very much prefers to *Homer*'s, and in particular extols the harmony and sweetness of the versification above that of our Author; against which censure we need only appeal to the ears of the reader.

> Ἠΰτε ἔθνεα εἶσι μελισσάων ἀδινάων,
> Πέτρης ἐκ γλαφυρῆς αἰεὶ νέον ἐρχομενάων,
> Βοτρυδὸν δὲ πέτονται ἐπ᾽ ἄνθεσιν εἰαρινοῖσιν,
> Αἱ μέν τ᾽ ἔνθα ἅλις πεποτήαται, αἱ δέ τε ἔνθα, &c.

But *Scaliger* was unlucky in his choice of this particular comparison: There is a very fine one in the sixth *Æneid*, v. 707. that better agrees with *Homer*'s: And nothing is more evident than that the design of these two is very different: *Homer* intended to describe the *multitude* of *Greeks* pouring out of the Ships, *Virgil* the *diligence* and *labour* of the builders at *Carthage*. And *Macrobius* who observes this difference *Sat. l. 5. c. 11.* should also have found, that therefore the similes ought not to be compar'd together. The beauty of *Homer*'s is not inferior to *Virgil*'s, if we consider with what exactness it answers to its end. It consists of three particulars; the vast number of the troops is exprest in the swarms, their tumultuous manner of issuing out of the ships, and the perpetual egression which seem'd without end, are imaged in the bees pouring out of the rock, and lastly, their dispersion over all the shore, in their descending on the flowers in the vales. *Spondanus* was therefore mistaken when he thought the whole application of this comparison lay in the single word ἰλαδόν, *catervatim* [in masses], as *Chapman* has justly observ'd.

121. *Fame flies before.*] This assembling of the army is full of beauties: The lively description of their overspreading the field, the noble boldness of the figure when fame is represented in person shining at their head, the universal tumult succeeded by a solemn silence; and lastly the graceful rising of *Agamemnon*, all contribute to cast a majesty on this part. In the passage of the *sceptre*, *Homer* has found an artful and poetical manner of acquainting us with the high descent of *Agamemnon*, and celebrating the hereditary right of his family; as well as finely hinted the original of his power to be deriv'd from heaven, in saying the sceptre was first the gift of *Jupiter*. It is with reference to this that in the line where he first mentions it, he calls it Ἄφθιτον αἰεί, and accordingly it is translated in that place.

138. *And artful thus pronounc'd the speech design'd.*] The remarks of *Dionysius* upon this Speech I shall give the reader all together, tho' they lie scatter'd in his two discourses περὶ ἐσχηματισμένων, the second of which is in a great degree but a repetition of the precepts and examples of the first. This happen'd, I believe, from his having compos'd them at distinct times and upon different occasions.

'It is an exquisite piece of art, when you seem to aim at persuading one thing, and at the same time inforce the contrary. This kind of Rhetorick is of great use in all occasions of danger, and of this *Homer* has afforded a most powerful example in the oration of *Agamemnon*. 'Tis a method perfectly wonderful, and even carries in it an appearance of absurdity; for all that we generally esteem the faults of oratory, by this means become the virtues of it. Nothing is look'd upon as a greater error in a Rhetorician than to alledge such arguments as either are easily answer'd, or may be retorted upon himself, the former is a weak part, the latter a dangerous one; and *Agamemnon* here designedly deals in both. For it is plain that if a man must not use weak arguments, or such as may make against him, when he intends to persuade the thing he says; then on the other side, when he does not intend it, he must observe the contrary proceeding, and make what are the faults of oratory in general, the excellencies of that oration in particular, or otherwise he will contradict his own intention, and persuade the contrary to what he means. *Agamemnon* begins with an argument easily answer'd, by telling them that *Jupiter had promis'd to crown their arms with victory*. For if *Jupiter* had promis'd this, it was a reason for the stay in the camp. *But now* (says he) *Jove has deceiv'd us, and we must return with ignominy*. This is another of the same kind, for it shews what a disgrace it is to return. What follows is of the second sort, and may be turn'd against him. *Jove will have it so*: For which they have only *Agamemnon*'s word, but *Jove*'s own promise to the contrary. *That God has overthrown many cities, and will yet overturn many others*. This was a strong reason to stay, and put their confidence in him. *It is shameful to have it told to all posterity that so many thousand* Greeks, *after a war of so long continuance, at last return'd home baffled and unsuccessful*. All this might have been said by a profest adversary to the cause he pleads, and indeed is the same thing *Ulysses* says elsewhere in reproach of their flight. The conclusion evidently shews the intent of the speaker. *Haste then, let us fly*; φεύγωμεν, the word which of all others was most likely to prevail upon them to stay; the most open term of disgrace he could possibly have us'd: 'Tis the same which *Juno* makes use of to *Minerva*, *Minerva* to *Ulysses*, and *Ulysses* again to the troops, to dissuade their return; the same which *Agamemnon* himself had used to insult *Achilles*, and which *Homer* never employs but with the mark of cowardice and infamy.

The same Author farther observes, 'That this whole oration has the air of being spoken in a passion. It begins with a stroke of the greatest rashness and impatience. Jupiter *has been unjust, Heaven has deceiv'd us*. This renders all he shall say of the less authority, at the same time that it conceals his own artifice; for his anger seems to account for the incongruities he utters.' I could not suppress so fine a remark, tho' it falls out of the order of those which precede it.

Before I leave this article, I must take notice that this speech of *Agamemnon* is again put into his mouth in the ninth *Iliad*, and (according to *Dionysius*) for the same purpose, to detain the army at the siege after a defeat; tho' it seems unartful to put the same trick twice upon the *Greeks* by the same person, and in the same words too. We may indeed suppose the first feint to have remain'd undiscover'd, but at best it is a management in the Poet not very entertaining to the readers.

155. *So small their number*, &c.] This part has a low air in comparison with the rest of the speech. *Scaliger* calls it *tabernariam orationem* [shop talk]: But it is well observ'd by Madam *Dacier*, that the image *Agamemnon* here gives of the *Trojans*, does not only render their numbers contemptible in comparison of the *Greeks*, but their persons too: For it makes them appear but as a few vile slaves fit only to serve them with wine. To which we may add that it affords a prospect to his soldiers of their future state and triumph after the conquest of their enemies.

This passage gives me occasion to animadvert upon a computation of the number of the *Trojans*, which the learned *Angelus Politian* has offer'd at in his *Preface to* Homer. He thinks they were fifty thousand without the auxiliaries, from the conclusion of the eighth *Iliad*, where it is said there were a thousand funeral Fires of *Trojans*, and fifty men attending each of them. But that the auxiliaries are to be admitted into that number appears plainly from this place: *Agamemnon* expressly distinguishes the native *Trojans* from the aids, and reckons but one to ten *Græcians*, at which estimate there could not be above ten thousand *Trojans*.   *See the notes on the catalogue.*

163.   – *Decay'd our vessels lie,*
          And scarce ensure the wretched power to fly.

This, and some other passages, are here translated correspondent to the general air and sense of this speech, rather than just to the letter. The telling them in this place how much their shipping was decay'd, was a hint of their danger in returning, as Madam *Dacier* has remark'd.

175. *So roll the billows*, &c.] One may take notice that *Homer* in these two similitudes has judiciously made choice of the two most wavering and inconstant things in nature, to compare with the multitude; the *waves* and *ears* of *corn*. The first alludes to the noise and tumult of the people, in the breaking and rolling of the billows; the second to their taking the same course, like corn bending one way; and both to the easiness with which they are mov'd by every *breath*.

243. *To one sole Monarch.*] Those persons are under a mistake who would make this sentence a praise of absolute monarchy. *Homer* speaks it only with regard to a general of an army during the time of his commission. Nor is *Agamemnon* styl'd *King of Kings* in any other sense, than as the rest of the Princes had given him the supreme Authority over them in the siege. *Aristotle* defines a King, Στρατηγός γὰρ ἦν καὶ δικαστὴς ὁ βασιλεύς, καὶ τῶν πρὸς θεοὺς Κύριος; *Leader of the war*, *Judge of controversies*, and *President of the Ceremonies of the Gods*. That he had the principal care of religious rites appears from many places in *Homer*; and that his power was no where absolute but in war: for we find *Agamemnon* insulted in the council, but in the army threatning deserters with death. He was under an obligation to preserve the privileges of his country, pursuant to which Kings are called by our Author Δικασπόλους, and Θεμιστοπόλους, the dispensers or managers of Justice. And *Dionysius* of *Halicarnassus* acquaints us, that the old *Græcian* Kings, whether hereditary or elective, had a council of their chief men, as *Homer* and the most ancient Poets testify; nor was it (he adds) in those times as in ours, when Kings have a full liberty to do whatever they please. *Dion. Hal. lib.* 2. *Hist.*

255. Thersites *only.*] The ancients have ascrib'd to *Homer* the first sketch of *Satyric* or *Comic* Poetry, of which sort was his poem call'd *Margites*, as *Aristotle* reports. Tho' that piece be lost, this character of *Thersites* may give us a taste of his vein in that kind. But whether ludicrous descriptions ought to have place in the *Epic* poem, has been justly question'd: Neither *Virgil* nor any of the most approv'd Ancients have thought fit to admit them into their compositions of that nature; nor any of the best moderns except *Milton*, whose fondness for *Homer* might be the reason of it. However this is in its kind a very masterly part, and our Author has shewn great Judgment in the particulars he has chosen to compose the picture of a pernicious creature of wit; the chief of which are a desire of promoting laughter at any rate, and a contempt of his superiors. And he sums up the whole very strongly, by saying that *Thersites* hated *Achilles* and *Ulysses*; in which, as *Plutarch*

has remark'd in his treatise of envy and hatred, he makes it the utmost completion of an ill character to bear a malevolence to the best men. What is farther observable is, that *Thersites* is never heard of after this his first appearance: Such a scandalous character is to be taken no more notice of, than just to shew that 'tis despised. *Homer* has observ'd the same conduct with regard to the most *deform'd* and most *beautiful* person of his poem: For *Nireus* is thus mention'd once and no more throughout the *Iliad*. He places a worthless *beauty* and an ill-natur'd *wit* upon the same foot, and shews that the gifts of the body without those of the mind are not more despicable, than those of the mind itself without virtue.

275. *Amidst the glories.*] 'Tis remark'd by *Dionysius Halicarnass.* in his treatise of the *Examination of Writers*, that there could not be a better artifice thought on to recal the army to their obedience, than this of our Author. When they were offended at their General in favour of *Achilles*, nothing could more weaken *Achilles*'s interest than to make such a fellow as *Thersites* appear of his party, whose impertinence would give them a disgust of thinking or acting like him. There is no surer method to reduce generous spirits, than to make them see they are pursuing the same views with people of no merit, and such whom they cannot forbear despising themselves. Otherwise there is nothing in this speech but what might become the mouth of *Nestor* himself, if you except a word or two. And had *Nestor* spoken it, the army had certainly set sail for *Greece*; but because it was utter'd by a ridiculous fellow whom they are asham'd to follow, they are reduc'd, and satisfy'd to continue the siege.

284. *The* Greeks *and* I.] These boasts of himself are the few words which *Dionysius* objects to in the foregoing passage. I cannot but think the grave Commentators here very much mistaken, who imagine *Thersites* in earnest in these vaunts, and seriously reprove his insolence. They seem to me manifest strokes of Irony, which had render'd them so much the more improper in the mouth of *Nestor*, who was otherwise none of the least boasters himself. And consider'd as such they are equal to the rest of the speech, which has an infinite deal of spirit, humour, and satyr.

326. *He said, and cow'ring.*] The vile figure *Thersites* makes here is a good Piece of *grotesque*; the pleasure express'd by the soldiers at this action of *Ulysses* (notwithstanding they are disappointed by him of their hopes of returning) is agreeable to that generous temper, at once honest and thoughtless, which is commonly found in military men; to whom nothing is so odious as a dastard, and who have not naturally the greatest kindness for a wit.

348. *Unhappy Monarch!* &c.] *Quintilian* [*Inst. Orat.* X.1. 47–8] speaking of the various kinds of oratory which may be learn'd from *Homer*, mentions among the greatest instances the speeches in this book. *Nonne vel nonus liber quo missa ad Achillem legatio continetur, vel in primo inter duces illa contentio, vel dictæ in secundo sententiæ, omnes litium ac consiliorum explicat artes? Affectus quidem vel illos mites, vel hos concitatos, nemo erit tam indoctus, qui non sua in potestate hunc autorem habuisse fateatur.* [Do not the ninth book containing the embassy to Achilles, the first describing the quarrel between the chiefs, or the speeches delivered by the counsellors in the second, display all the rules of art to be followed in forensic or deliberative oratory? As regards the emotions, there can be no one so ill-educated as to deny that the poet was master of all, tender and vehement alike.] It is indeed hardly possible to find any where more refin'd turns of policy, or more artful touches of oratory. We have no sooner seen *Agamemnon* excel in one sort, but *Ulysses* is to shine no less in another directly opposite to it. When the stratagem of pretending to set sail, had met with too ready a consent from the people, his eloquence appears in all the forms of art. In his first Speech he had persuaded the captains with mildness, telling them the people's glory depended upon them, and readily giving a turn to the first design, which had like to have been so dangerous, by representing it only as a project of *Agamemnon* to discover the cowardly. In his second, he had commanded the soldiers with bravery, and made them know what part they sustain'd in the war. In his third, he had rebuk'd the seditious in the person of *Thersites*, by reproofs, threats, and actual chastisement. And now in this fourth, when all are gather'd together, he applies to them in topics which equally affect them all: He raises their Hearts by putting them in mind of the promises of heaven, and those prophecies of which as they had seen the truth in the nine Years delay, they might now expect the accomplishment in the tenth year's success: which is a full answer to what *Agamemnon* had said of *Jupiter*'s deceiving them.

Dionysius observes one singular piece of art, in *Ulysses*'s manner of applying himself to the people when he would insinuate any thing to

the Princes, and addressing to the Princes when he would blame the
people. He tells the soldiers, they must not all pretend to be rulers
there, let there be one King, one Lord; which is manifestly a precept
design'd for the leaders to take to themselves. In the same manner
Tiberius Rhetor remarks the beginning of his last oration to be a fine
Ethopopeia or oblique representation of the people, upon whom the
severity of the reproach is made to fall, while he seems to render the
King an object of their pity.

> *Unhappy Monarch! whom the* Græcian *race*
> *With shame deserting,* &c.

402. *Then* Nestor *thus.*] Nothing is more observable than *Homer*'s
conduct of this whole incident; by what judicious and well-imagined
degrees the army is restrain'd, and wrought up to the desires of the
General. We have given the detail of all the methods *Ulysses* proceeded
in: The activity of his character is now to be contrasted with the
gravity of *Nestor*'s, who covers and strengthens the other's arguments,
and constantly appears thro' the poem a weighty Closer of debates.
The *Greeks* had already seen their General give way to his authority, in
the dispute with *Achilles* in the former book, and could expect no less
than that their stay should be concluded on by *Agamemnon* as soon as
Nestor undertook that cause. For this was all they imagin'd his
discourse aim'd at; but we shall find it had a farther design, from
Dionysius of *Halicarnassus*. 'There are two things (says that excellent
critick) worthy of admiration in the speeches of *Ulysses* and *Nestor*,
which are the different designs they speak with, and the different
applauses they receive. *Ulysses* had the acclamations of the army, and
Nestor the praise of *Agamemnon*. One may enquire the reason, why he
extols the latter preferably to the former, when all that *Nestor* alledges
seems only a repetition of the same arguments which *Ulysses* had given
before him? It might be done in encouragement to the old man, in
whom it might raise a concern to find his speech not follow'd with so
general an applause as the other's. But we are to refer the speech of
Nestor to that part of oratory which seems only to confirm what
another has said, and yet superinduces and carries a farther point.
Ulysses and *Nestor* both compare the *Greeks* to children for their
unmanly desire to return home; they both reproach them with the
engagements and vows they had past, and were now about to break;
they both alledge the prosperous signs and omens receiv'd from

Heaven. Notwithstanding this, the end of their orations is very differ-ent. *Ulysses*'s business was to detain the *Græcians* when they were upon the point of flying; *Nestor* finding that work done to his hands, design'd to draw them instantly to battel. This was the utmost *Agamemnon* had aim'd at, which *Nestor*'s artifice brings to pass; for while they imagine by all he says that he is only persuading them to stay, they find themselves unawares put into order of battel, and led under their Princes to fight.'

Dion. Hal. περὶ ἐσχηματισμένων, *Part* 1 *and* 2.

We may next take notice of some particulars of this speech: Where he says they lose their time in *empty words*, he hints at the dispute between *Agamemnon* and *Achilles*: Where he speaks of those who *deserted the* Græcian *cause*, he glances at *Achilles* in particular. When he represents *Helen* in affliction and tears, he removes the odium from the person in whose cause they were to fight; and when he moves *Agamemnon* to advise with his council, artfully prepares for a reception of his own advice by that modest way of proposing it. As for the advice itself, to divide the army into bodies, each of which should be compos'd entirely of Men of the same country; nothing could be better judg'd both in regard to the present circumstance, and with an eye to the future carrying on of the war. For the first, its immediate effect was to take the whole army out of its tumult, break whatever cabals they might have form'd together by separating them into a new division, and cause every single mutineer to come instantly under the view of his own proper officer for correction. For the second, it was to be thought the army would be much strengthen'd by this unison: Those of different nations who had different aims, interests and friendships, could not assist each other with so much zeal or so well concur to the same end, as when friends aided friends, kinsmen their kinsmen, &c. when each commander had the glory of his own nation in view, and a greater emulation was excited between body and body; as not only warring for the honour of *Greece* in general, but for that of every distinct *State* in particular.

440. *How much thy years excel.*] Every one has observ'd how glorious an elogium of wisdom *Homer* has here given, where *Agamemnon* so far prefers it to valour, as to wish not for ten *Ajax's* or *Achilles's* but only for ten *Nestors*. For the rest of this speech, *Dionysius* has summ'd it up as follows. '*Agamemnon* being now convinc'd the *Greeks* were offended at him on account of the departure of *Achilles*, pacifies them by a

generous confession of his fault, but then asserts the character of a
supreme Ruler, and with the air of command threatens the disobedient.'
I cannot conclude this part of the speeches without remarking how
beautifully they rise above one another, and how they more and more
awaken the spirit of war in the *Græcians*. In this last there is a
wonderful fire and vivacity, when he prepares them for the glorious
toils they were to undergo by a warm and lively description of them.
The repetition of the words in that part has a beauty, which (as well as
many others of the same kind) has been lost by most translators.

> Εὖ μέν τις δόρυ θηξάσθω, εὖ δ' ἀσπίδα θέσθω,
> Εὖ δέ τις ἵπποισιν δεῖπνον δότω ὠκυπόδεσσιν,
> Εὖ δέ τις ἅρματος ἀμφὶς ἰδὼν –.

[His sharpen'd spear let every *Grecian* wield,
And ev'ry *Grecian* fix his brazen shield,
Let all excite the fiery steeds of war,
And all for combate fit the ratling car.]

I cannot but believe *Milton* had this passage in his eye in that of his
sixth book.

> *– Let each*
> *His adamantine coat gird well; and each*
> *Fit well his helm, gripe fast his orbed shield,* &c.

485. *And* Menelaus *came unbid.*] The criticks have enter'd into a warm
dispute, whether *Menelaus* was in the right or in the wrong, in coming
uninvited: Some maintaining it the part of an impertinent or a fool to
intrude upon another man's table; and others insisting upon the
privilege a brother or a kinsman may claim in this case. The *English*
reader had not been troubled with the translation of this word
Αὐτόματος, but that *Plato* and *Plutarch* have taken notice of the
passage. The verse following this in most editions, Ἥδεε γὰρ κατὰ
θυμόν [He knew in his heart], &c. being rejected as spurious by
Demetrius Phalereus, is omitted here upon his authority.

526. *The dreadful* Ægis, Jove's *immortal shield.*] *Homer* does not
expresly call it a shield in this place, but it is plain from several other
passages that it was so. In the fifth *Iliad*, this *Ægis* is describ'd with a
sublimity that is inexpressible. The figure of the *Gorgon*'s head upon it
is there specify'd, which will justify the mention of the serpents in the

translation here: The verses are remarkably sonorous in the original. The image of the Goddess of battels blazing with her immortal shield before the army, inspiring every Hero, and assisting to range the troops, is agreeable to the bold painting of our author. And the encouragement of a divine power seem'd no more than was requisite to change so totally the dispositions of the *Græcians*, as to make them now more ardent for the combate than they were before desirous of a return. This finishes the conquest of their inclinations, in a manner at once wonderfully poetical, and correspondent to the moral which is every where spread through *Homer*, that nothing is entirely brought about but by the divine assistance.

534. *As on some mountain*, &c.] The imagination of *Homer* was so vast and so lively, that whatsoever objects presented themselves before him impress'd their images so forcibly, that he pour'd them forth in comparisons equally simple and noble; without forgetting any circumstance which could instruct the reader, and make him see those objects in the same strong light wherein he saw them himself. And in this one of the principal beauties of Poetry consists. *Homer*, on the sight of the march of this numerous army, gives us five similes in a breath, but all entirely different. The first regards the splendour of their armour, as a fire, *&c.* The second the various movements of so many thousands before they can range themselves in battle-array, like the swans, *&c.* The third respects their number, As the leaves or flowers, *&c.* The fourth the ardour with which they run to the combate, like the legions of insects, *&c.* And the fifth the obedience and exact discipline of the troops, ranged without confusion under their leaders, as flocks under their shepherds. This fecundity and variety can never be enough admired.

Dacier.

541. *Or milk white swans on* Asius' *watry plains.*] *Scaliger*, who is seldom just to our author, yet confesses these verses to be *plenissima nectaris* [most full of nectar]. But he is greatly mistaken when he accuses this simile of impropriety, on the supposition that a number of birds flying without order are here compar'd to an army ranged in array of battel. On the contrary, *Homer* in this expresses the stir and tumult the troops were in, before they got into order, running together from the ships and tents: Νεῶν ἄπο, καὶ κλισιάων. But when they are placed in their ranks, he compares them to the flocks under their shepherds. This distinction will plainly appear from the detail of the five similes in the foregoing note.

Virgil has imitated this with great happiness in his seventh *Æneid*.

> *Ceu quondam nivei liquida inter nubila cycni*
> *Cum sese e pastu referunt, & longa canoros*
> *Dant per colla modos, sonat amnis & Asia longe*
> *Pulsa palus —*

[Like a long team of snowy swans on high,
Which clap their wings and cleave the liquid sky,
When homeward from their watry pastures born,
They sing, and *Asia*'s lakes their notes return.]

Mr. *Dryden* in this place has mistaken *Asius* for *Asia*, which *Virgil* took care to distinguish by making the first syllable of *Asius* long, as of *Asia* short. Tho' (if we believe Madam *Dacier*) he was himself in an error, both here and in the first *Georgic*.

> *— Quæ Asia circum*
> *Dulcibus in stagnis rimantur prata Caystri.*

[Such as rummage for food, around Asia's meadows, in the sweet marshes of Caystros.]

For she will not allow that Ἀσίῳ can be a Patronymic Adjective, but the Genitive of a proper Name, Ἀσίου, which being turn'd into *Ionic* is Ἀσίεω and by a *syncope* makes Ἀσίω. This puts me in mind of another Criticism upon the 290*th* verse of this book [Pope must mean the 290th verse of the Catalogue of Ships, which is l. 783 of this book.]: 'Tis observ'd that *Virgil* uses *Inarime* for *Arime*, as if he had read Εἰναρίμοις, instead of Εἰν Ἀρίμοις. *Scaliger* ridicules this trivial remark, and asks if it can be imagin'd that *Virgil* was ignorant of the name of a place so near him as *Baiæ*? It is indeed unlucky for good writers, that men who have learning should lay a stress upon such trifles, and that those who have none should think it learning to do so.

552. *Or thick as insects play.*] This simile translated literally runs thus; *As the numerous troops of flies about a shepherd's cottage in the spring, when the milk moistens the pails; such numbers of* Greeks *stood in the field against the* Trojans, *desiring their destruction.* The lowness of this image in comparison with those which precede it, will naturally shock a modern critick, and would scarce be forgiven in a poet of these times. The utmost a translator can do is to heighten the expression, so as to render the disparity less observable: which is endeavour'd here, and in

other places. If this be done successfully, the reader is so far from being offended at a low idea, that it raises his surprize to find it grown great in the poet's hands, of which we have frequent instances in *Virgil's Georgicks*. Here follows another of the same kind, in the simile of *Agamemnon* to a *Bull* just after he has been compar'd to *Jove*, *Mars*, and *Neptune*. This, *Eustathius* tells us, was blam'd by some criticks, and Mr. *Hobbes* has left it out in his translation. The liberty has been taken here to place the humbler simile first, reserving the noble one as a more magnificent close of the description: The bare turning the sentence removes the objection. *Milton*, who was a close imitator of our author, has often copy'd him in these humble comparisons. He has not scrupled to insert one in the midst of that pompous description of the rout of the rebel-angels in the sixth book, where the Son of God in all his dreadful Majesty is represented pouring his vengeance upon them:

> *– As a herd*
> *Of goats, or tim'rous flocks together throng'd,*
> *Drove them before him thunder-struck –.*

568. *Great as the Gods.*] *Homer* here describes the figure and port of *Agamemnon* with all imaginable grandeur, in making him appear cloath'd with the majesty of the greatest of the Gods; and when *Plutarch* (in his second oration of the fortune of *Alexander*) blamed the comparison of a man to three deities at once, that censure was not pass'd upon *Homer* as a Poet, but by *Plutarch* as a Priest. This character of majesty, in which *Agamemnon* excels all the other Heroes, is preserv'd in the different views of him throughout the *Iliad*. It is thus he appears on his Ship in the catalogue; thus he shines in the eyes of *Priam* in the third book; thus again in the beginning of the eleventh; and so in the rest.

572. *Say, Virgins.*] It is hard to conceive any address more solemn, any opening to a subject more noble and magnificent, than this invocation of *Homer* before his catalogue. That omnipresence he gives to the Muses, their post in the highest Heaven, their comprehensive survey thro' the whole extent of the creation, are circumstances greatly imagined. Nor is any thing more perfectly fine, or exquisitely moral, than the opposition of the extensive knowledge of the divinities on the one side, to the blindness and ignorance of mankind on the other. The

greatness and importance of his subject is highly rais'd by his exalted manner of declaring the difficulty of it, *Not tho' my lungs were brass,* &c. and by the air he gives, as if what follows were immediately inspir'd, and no less than the joint labour of all the Muses.

586. *The hardy warriours.*] The catalogue begins in this place, which I forbear to treat of at present: only I must acknowledge here that the translation has not been exactly punctual to the order in which *Homer* places his towns. However it has not trespass'd against geography; the transpositions I mention being no other than such minute ones, as *Strabo* confesses the author himself is not free from: Ὁ δὲ Ποιητὴς ἔνια μὲν χωρία λέγει συνεχῶς, ὥσπερ καὶ κεῖται· οἱ θ' Ὑρίην ἐμένοντο καὶ Αὐλίδα, etc. ἄλλοτε δ', οὐχ ὡς ἔστι τῇ τάξει, Σχοῖνόν τε Σκῶλόν τε, Θέσπειαν Γραῖάν τε ['The poet mentions some places in the order in which they are actually situated: "And these dwelt in Hyria and Aulis," etc.; but at other times not in their actual order: "Schoenus and Scolus, Thespeia and Græa".'] *lib.* 8. There is not to my remembrance any place throughout this catalogue omitted; a liberty which Mr. *Dryden* has made no difficulty to take and to confess, in his *Virgil.* But a more scrupulous care was owing to *Homer,* on account of that wonderful exactness and unequal'd diligence, which he has particularly shewn in this part of his work.

649. *Down their broad shoulders,* &c.] The *Greek* has it ὄπιθεν κομόωντες, *a tergo comantes* [wearing their hair long in back of their heads]. It was the custom of these people to shave the fore-part of their heads, which they did that their enemies might not take the advantage of seizing them by the hair: the hinder part they let grow, as a valiant race that would never turn their backs. Their manner of fighting was hand to hand, without quitting their javelins (in the way of our pike-men.) *Plutarch* tells us this in the Life of *Theseus,* and cites, to strengthen the authority of *Homer,* some verses of *Archilochus* to the same effect. *Eobanus Hessus* who translated *Homer* into *Latine* verse was therefore mistaken in his version of this passage.

> *Præcipue jaculatores, hastamque periti*
> *Vibrare, & longis contingere pectora telis.*

[Chiefly hurlers of the javelin, well-practised in brandishing the spear, and in reaching the breasts of the enemy with their long weapons.]

711. *Eager and loud from man to man he flies.*] The figure *Menelaus* makes in this place is remarkably distinguish'd from the rest, and sufficient to shew his concern in the war was personal, while the others acted only for interest or glory in general. No leader in all the list is represented thus eager and passionate; he is louder than them all in his exhortations; more active in running among the troops; and inspirited with the thoughts of revenge which he still encreases with the secret imagination of *Helen*'s repentance. This behaviour is finely imagined.

The epithet Βοήν ἀγαθός, which is apply'd in this and other places to *Menelaus*, and which literally signifies *loud-voiced*, is made by the Commentators to mean *valiant*, and translated *bello strenuus* [vigorous in war]. The reason given by *Eustathius* is, that a loud voice is a mark of strength, the usual effect of fear being to cut short the respiration. I own this seems to be forc'd, and rather believe it was one of those kind of sirnames given from some distinguishing quality of the person (as that of a loud voice might belong to *Menelaus*) which Mons. *Boileau* mentions in his ninth reflection upon *Longinus*; in the same manner as some of our Kings were called *Edward Long-shanks, William Rufus*, &c. But however it be, the epithet taken in the literal sense has a beauty in this verse from the circumstance *Menelaus* is described in, which determined the translator to use it.

746. *New to all the dangers of the main.*] The *Arcadians* being an inland people were unskill'd in navigation, for which reason *Agamemnon* furnish'd them with shipping. From hence, and from the last line of the description of the sceptre, where he is said to preside over *many islands*, *Thucydides* takes occasion to observe that the power of *Agamemnon* was superiour to the rest of the Princes of *Greece*, on account of his naval forces, which had render'd him master of the sea.

Thucyd. lib. 1.

815. *Three Ships with* Nireus.] This leader is no where mention'd but in these lines, and is an exception to the observation of *Macrobius*, that all the persons of the catalogue make their appearance afterwards in the poem. *Homer* himself gives us the reason, because *Nireus* had but a small share of worth and valour; his Quality only gave him a privilege to be nam'd among men. The poet has caused him to be remember'd no less than *Achilles* or *Ulysses*, but yet in no better manner than he deserv'd, whose only qualification was his Beauty: 'Tis by a bare Repetition of his name three times, which just leaves some Impression

of him on the mind of the reader. Many others, of as trivial memory as *Nireus*, have been preserv'd by Poets from Oblivion; but few Poets have ever done this favour to want of merit with so much judgment. *Demetrius Phalereus* περὶ Ἑρμηνείας, *sect.* 61. takes notice of this beautiful repetition, which in a just deference to so delicate a Critick is here preserv'd in the translation.

871. *The grace and glory of the beauteous kind.*] He gives *Alcestis* this elogy of the glory of her sex, for her conjugal piety, who dy'd to preserve the life of her husband *Admetus. Euripides* has a tragedy on this subject, which abounds in the most masterly strokes of tenderness: in particular the first act, which contains the description of her preparation for death, and her behaviour in it, can never be enough admired.

906. *In twenty ships the bold* Perrhæbians *came.*] I cannot tell whether it be worth observing that, except *Ogilby*, I have not met with one translator who has exactly preserv'd the number of the ships. *Chapman* puts eighteen under *Eumelus* instead of eleven. *Hobbes* but twenty under *Ascalaphus* and *Ialmen* instead of thirty, and but thirty under *Menelaus* instead of sixty. *Valterie* (the former *French* translator) has given *Agapenor* forty for sixty, and *Nestor* forty for ninety. Madam *Dacier* gives *Nestor* but eighty. I must confess this translation not to have been quite so exact as *Ogilby*'s, having cut off one from the number of *Eumelus*'s ships, and two from those of *Guneus: Eleven* and *two and twenty* would sound but oddly in *English* verse, and a poem contracts a littleness by insisting on such trivial niceties.

925. *Or rein'd the noblest steeds.*] This coupling together the men and horses seems odd enough, but *Homer* every where treats these noble animals with remarkable regard. We need not wonder at this enquiry, *which were the best horses?* from him, who makes his horses of heavenly extraction as well as his heroes; who makes his warriours address them with speeches and excite them by all those motives which affect a human breast; who describes them shedding tears of sorrow, and even capable of voice and prophecy: In most of which points *Virgil* has not scrupled to imitate him.

939. *His troops,* &c.] The image in these lines of the amusements of the *Myrmidons*, while *Achilles* detain'd them from the fight, has an exquisite propriety in it. Tho' they are not in action, their very diversions are military, and a kind of exercise of arms. The cover'd chariot and feeding horses, make a natural part of the picture; and nothing is finer than the manly concern of the captains, who as they are suppos'd more sensible of glory than the soldiers, take no share in their diversions, but wander sorrowfully round the camp, and lament their being kept from the battel. This difference betwixt the soldiers and the leaders (as *Dacier* observes) is a decorum of the highest beauty. *Milton* has admirably imitated this in the description he gives in his second book of the diversions of the angels during the absence of *Lucifer.*

> *Part on the plain, or in the air sublime,*
> *Upon the wing, or in swift race contend;*
> *Part curb their fiery steeds, or shun the goal*
> *With rapid wheels, or fronted brigades form.*

But how nobly and judiciously has he raised the image, in proportion to the nature of those more exalted beings, in that which follows.

> *Others with vast* Typhœan *rage more fell*
> *Rend up both rocks and hills, and ride the air*
> *In whirlwind; hell scarce holds the wild uproar.*

950. *As when angry* Jove.] The comparison preceding this, of a fire which runs thro' the corn and blazes to heaven, had exprest at once the dazling of their arms and the swiftness of their march. After which *Homer* having mention'd the sound of their feet, superadds another simile, which comprehends both the ideas of the brightness and the noise: for here (says *Eustathius*) the earth appears to *burn* and *groan* at the same time. Indeed the first of these similes is so full and so noble, that it scarce seem'd possible to be exceeded by any image drawn from nature. But *Homer* to raise it yet higher, has gone into the *marvellous,* given a prodigious and supernatural prospect, and brought down *Jupiter* himself, array'd in all his terrors, to discharge his lightnings and thunders on *Typhœus.* The Poet breaks out into this description with an air of enthusiasm, which greatly heightens the image in general, while it seems to transport him beyond the limits of an exact comparison. And this daring manner is particular to our author above all the ancients, and to *Milton* above all the moderns.

1012. *From* Practius' *stream,* Percote's *pasture lands.*] *Homer* does not expressly mention *Practius* as a River, but *Strabo, lib.* 13. tells us it is to be understood so in this passage. The appellative of pasture lands to *Percote* is justify'd in the 15*th Iliad*, v. 646 where *Melanippus* the son of *Hicetaon* is said to feed his oxen in that place.

1032. Axius, *that swells with all his neighb'ring rills.*] According to the common reading this verse should be translated, Axius *that diffuses his beautiful waters over the land*. But we are assured by *Strabo* that *Axius* was a muddy river, and that the ancients understood it thus, Axius *that receives into it several beautiful rivers*. The Criticism lies in the last word of the verse, Αἴη, which *Strabo* reads Αἴης, and interprets of the river *Æa*, whose waters were pour'd into *Axius*. However, *Homer* describes this river agreeable to the vulgar reading in *Il.* 21. v. 158. Ἀξιοῦ, ὃς κάλλιστον ὕδωρ ἐπὶ γαῖαν ἵησιν [of Axios, which diffuses its most beautiful water over the land]. This version takes in both.

OBSERVATIONS *on the* CATALOGUE

If we look upon this piece with an eye to ancient learning, it may be observ'd, that however fabulous the other parts of *Homer*'s poem may be, according to the nature of Epic poetry, this account of the people, princes, and countries is purely historical, founded on the real transactions of those times, and by far the most valuable piece of history and geography left us concerning the state of *Greece* in that early period. *Greece* was then divided into several dynasties, which our Author has enumerated under their respective princes; and his division was look'd upon so exact, that we are told of many controversies concerning the boundaries of *Græcian* cities which have been decided upon the authority of this piece. *Eustathius* has collected together the following instances. The city of *Calydon* was adjudg'd to the *Ætolians* notwithstanding the pretensions of *Æolia*, because *Homer* had rank'd it among the towns belonging to the former. *Sestos* was given to those of *Abydos*, upon the plea that he had said the *Abydonians* were possessors of *Sestos*, *Abydos*, and *Arisbe*. When the *Milesians* and people of *Priene* disputed their claim to *Mycale*, a verse of *Homer* carry'd it in favour of the *Milesians*. And the *Athenians* were put in possession of *Salamis* by another which was cited by *Solon*, or (as some think) interpolated by him for that purpose. Nay in so high estimation has this catalogue been held, that (as *Porphyry* has written) there have been laws in some nations for the youth to learn it by heart, and particularly *Cerdias* (whom *Cuperus de Apoth. Homer.* takes to be *Cercydas*, a Law-giver of the *Megalopolitans*) made it one to his countrymen.

But if we consider the catalogue purely as poetical, it will not want its beauties in that light. *Rapin*, who was none of the most superstitious admirers of our author, reckons it among those parts which had particularly charm'd him. We may observe first, what an air of probability is spread over the whole poem by the particularizing of every nation and people concern'd in this war. Secondly, what an entertaining scene he presents to us, of so many countries drawn in their liveliest and most natural colours, while we wander along with him amidst a beautiful variety of towns, havens, forests, vineyards, groves, mountains, and rivers, and are perpetually amus'd with his observations on the different soils, products, situations, or prospects. Thirdly, what a noble review he passes before us of so mighty an army, drawn out in order troop by troop; which had the number only been told in the gross, had never fill'd the reader with so great a notion of the importance of the action. Fourthly, the description of the differing arms and manner of fighting of the soldiers, and the various attitudes he has given to the commanders: Of the leaders, the greatest part are either the immediate sons of Gods, or the descendants of Gods; and how great an idea must we have of a war, to the waging of which so many Demi-gods and heroes are assembled? Fifthly, the several artful compliments he paid by this means to his own country in general, and many of his contemporaries in particular, by a celebration of the genealogies, ancient seats, and dominions of the great men of his time. Sixthly, the agreeable mixture of narrations from passages of history or fables, with which he amuses and relieves us at proper intervals. And lastly, the admirable judgment wherewith he introduces this whole catalogue, just at a time when the posture of affairs in the army render'd such a review of absolute necessity to the *Greeks*; and in a pause of action, while each was refreshing himself to prepare for the ensuing battels.

Macrobius in his *Saturnalia, lib.* 5. *cap.* 15. has given us a judicious piece of criticism, in the comparison betwixt the catalogues of *Homer* and of *Virgil*, in which he justly allows the preference to our Author for the following reasons. *Homer* (says he) has begun his description from the most noted promontory of *Greece* (he means that of *Aulis*, where was the narrowest Passage to *Eubœa*.) From thence with a regular progress he describes either the maritime or mediterranean towns as their situations are contiguous; he never passes with sudden leaps from place to place, omitting those which lie between; but proceeding like a traveller in the way he has begun, constantly returns to the place from whence he digress'd, 'till he finishes the whole circle he design'd. *Virgil*, on the contrary, has observ'd no order in the regions describ'd in his catalogue, *l.* 10. but is perpetually breaking from the course of the country in a loose and desultory manner. You have *Clusium* and *Cosæ* at the beginning, next *Populonia* and *Ilva*, then *Pisæ*, which lie at a vast distance in *Etruria*; and immediately after *Cerete*, *Pyrgi*, and *Graviscæ*, places adjacent to *Rome*: From hence he is snatch'd to *Liguria*, then to *Mantua*. The same negligence is observable in his enumeration of the aids that follow'd *Turnus* in *l.* 7. *Macrobius* next remarks, that all the persons who are nam'd by *Homer* in his catalogue, are afterwards introduc'd in his battels, and whenever any others are kill'd, he mentions only a multitude in general. Whereas *Virgil* (he continues) has spar'd himself the labour of that exactness; for not only several whom he mentions in the list are never heard of in the war, but others make a figure in the war, of whom we had no notice in the list. For example, he specifies a thousand men under *Massicus* who came from *Clusium*, *l.* 10. v. 167. *Turnus* soon afterwards is in the ship which had carry'd King *Osinius* from the same place, *l.* 10. v. 655. This *Osinius* was never nam'd before, nor is it probable a King should serve under *Massicus*. Nor indeed does either *Massicus* or *Osinius* ever make their appearance in the battels – He proceeds to instance several others, who tho' celebrated for heroes in the catalogue, have no farther notice taken of them throughout the poem. In the third place he animadverts upon the confusion of the same names in *Virgil*: As where *Corinæus* in the ninth book is kill'd by *Asylas*, v. 571. and *Corinæus* in the twelfth kills *Ebusus*, v. 298. *Numa* is slain by *Nisus*, *l.* 9. v. 554. and *Æneas* is afterwards in pursuit of *Numa*, *l.* 10. v. 562. *Æneas* kills *Camertes* in the tenth Book, v. 562. and *Juturna* assumes his shape in the twelfth, v. 224. He observes the same obscurity in his *Patronymics*. There is *Palinurus Iasides*, and *Iapix Iasides*, *Hippocoon Hyrtacides*, and *Asylas Hyrtacides*. On the contrary, the caution of *Homer* is remarkable, who having two of the name of

Ajax, is constantly careful to distinguish them by *Oïleus* or *Telamonius*, the *lesser* or the *greater Ajax*.

I know nothing to be alledg'd in defence of *Virgil*, in answer to this author, but the common excuse that his *Æneis* was left unfinish'd. And upon the whole, these are such trivial slips as great Wits may pass over, and little Criticks rejoice at.

But *Macrobius* has another remark which one may accuse of evident partiality on the side of *Homer*. He blames *Virgil* for having vary'd the expression in his catalogue to avoid the repetition of the same words, and prefers the bare and unadorn'd reiterations of *Homer*; who begins almost every article the same way, and ends perpetually, Μέλαιναι νῆες ἕποντο, &c. Perhaps the best reason to be given for this, had been the artless manner of the first times, when such repetitions were not thought ungraceful. This may appear from several of the like nature in the scripture: as in the twenty-sixth chapter of *Numbers*, where the tribes of *Israel* are enumerated in the plains of *Moab*, and each division recounted in the same words. So in the seventh chapter of the *Revelations*: *Of the tribe of* Gad *were sealed twelve thousand, &c.* But the words of *Macrobius* are, *Has copias fortasse putat aliquis divinæ illi simplicitati præferendas. Sed nescio quo modo Homerum repetitio illa unice decet, & est genio antiqui Poetæ digna.* [Perhaps someone thinks that these examples of *copia* ought to be preferred to that divine simplicity. But in some inexplicable manner, that repetition is especially fitting in Homer, and is worthy of the peculiar genius of the ancient poet.] This is exactly in the spirit, and almost in the cant of a true modern critick. The *Simplicitas*, the *Nescio quo modo*, the *Genio antiqui Poetæ digna*, are excellent general phrases for those who have no reasons. *Simplicity* is our word of disguise for a shameful unpoetical neglect of expression: The term of the *Je ne sçay quoy* is the very Support of all ignorant pretenders to delicacy; and to lift up our eyes, and talk of the *Genius of an ancient*, is at once the cheapest way of shewing our own taste, and the shortest way of criticizing the wit of others our contemporaries.

One may add to the foregoing comparison of these two authors, some reasons for the length of *Homer*'s, and the shortness of *Virgil*'s catalogues. As, that *Homer* might have a design to settle the geography of his country, there being no description of *Greece* before his days; which was not the case with *Virgil*. *Homer*'s concern was to compliment *Greece* at a time when it was divided into many distinct states, each of which might expect a place in his catalogue: But when all *Italy* was swallow'd up in the sole dominion of *Rome*, *Virgil* had only *Rome* to celebrate. *Homer* had a numerous army, and was to describe an important war with great and various events; whereas *Virgil*'s sphere was much more confined. The ships of the *Greeks* are computed at about one thousand two hundred, those of *Æneas* and his aids but at two and forty; and as the time of the action of both poems is the same, we may suppose the build of their ships, and the number of men they contain'd, to be much alike. So that if the army of *Homer* amounts to about a hundred thousand men, that of *Virgil* cannot be above four thousand. If any one be farther curious to know upon what this computation is founded, he may see it in the following passage of *Thucydides, lib.* 1. '*Homer*'s Fleet (says he) consisted of one thousand two hundred vessels: those of the *Bœotians* carry'd one hundred and twenty men in each, and those of *Philoctetes* fifty. By these I suppose *Homer* exprest the largest and the smallest size of ships, and therefore mentions no other sort. But he tells us of those who sail'd with *Philoctetes*, that they serv'd both as mariners and soldiers, in saying the rowers were all of them archers. From hence the whole number will be seen, if we estimate the ships at a medium between the greatest and the least.' That is to say, at eighty-five men to each vessel (which is the mean between fifty and a hundred and twenty) the total comes to a hundred and two thousand men. *Plutarch* was therefore in a mistake when he computed the men at a hundred and twenty thousand, which proceeded from his supposing a hundred and twenty in every ship; the contrary to which appears from the above mention'd ships of *Philoctetes* as well as from those of *Achilles*, which are said to carry but fifty Men a-piece, in the sixteenth *Iliad*, v. 207.

Besides *Virgil*'s imitation of this catalogue, there has scarce been any epic writer but has copy'd after it; which is at least a proof how beautiful this part has been ever esteem'd by the finest genius's in all ages. The catalogues in the ancient Poets are generally known, only I must take notice that the *Phocian* and *Bœotian* towns in the fourth *Thebaid* of *Statius* are translated from hence. Of the moderns, those who most excel, owe their beauty to the imitation of some single particular only of *Homer*. Thus the chief grace of *Tasso*'s catalogue consists in the description of the Heroes, without any thing remarkable on the side of the countries: Of the pieces of story he has interwoven, that of *Tancred*'s amour to *Clorinda* is ill placed, and evidently too long for the rest. *Spencer*'s enumeration of the *British* and *Irish rivers* in the eleventh canto of his fourth book, is one of the noblest in the world; if we consider his subject was more confined, and can excuse his not observing the order or course of the country; but his variety of description, and fruitfulness of imagination, are no where more admirable than in that part. *Milton*'s list of the fallen angels in his first book is an exact imitation of *Homer*, as far as regards the digressions of history and antiquities, and his manner of inserting them: In all else I believe it must be allow'd inferior. And indeed what *Macrobius* has said to cast *Virgil* below *Homer*, will fall much more strongly upon all the rest.

I had some cause to fear that this catalogue, which contributed so much to the success of the author, should ruin that of the translator. A meer heap of proper names, tho' but for a few lines together, could afford little entertainment to an *English* reader, who probably could not be appriz'd either of the necessity or beauty of this part of the poem. There were but two things to be done to give it a chance to please him; to render the versification very flowing and musical, and to make the whole appear as much a *landscape* or *piece of painting* as possible. For both of these I had the example of *Homer* in general; and *Virgil*, who found the necessity in another age to give more into description, seem'd to authorise the latter in particular. *Dionysius* of *Halicarnassus* in his discourse of the *Structure and Disposition of Words*, professes to admire nothing more than that harmonious exactness with which *Homer* has placed these words, and soften'd the syllables into each other, so as to derive Musick from a crowd of names which have in themselves no beauty or dignity. I would flatter my self that I have practis'd this not unsuccessfully in our language, which is more susceptible of all the variety and power of numbers than any of the modern, and second to none but the *Greek* and *Roman*. For the latter point, I have ventured to open the prospect a little, by the addition of a few epithets or short hints of description to some of the places mention'd; tho' seldom exceeding the compass of half a verse (the space to which my author himself generally confines these pictures in miniature.) But this has never been done without the best authorities from the ancients, which may be seen under the respective names in the geographical table following.*

The table itself I thought but necessary to annex to the map,† as my warrant for the situations assign'd in it to several of the towns. For

* Omitted in this edition.
† Also omitted in this edition.

in whatever maps I have seen to this purpose, many of the places are omitted, or else set down at random. *Sophianus* and *Gerbelius* have labour'd to settle the geography of old *Greece*, many of whose mistakes were rectify'd by *Laurenbergius*. These however deserv'd a greater commendation than those who succeeded them; and particularly *Sanson*'s Map prefix'd to *Du Pin*'s *Bibliothèque Historique* is miserably defective both in omissions and false placings; which I am obliged to mention, as it pretends to be design'd expressly for this catalogue of *Homer*. I am persuaded the greater part of my readers will have no curiosity this way, however they may allow me the endeavour of gratifying those few who have: The rest are at liberty to pass the two or three following leaves unread.

THE
THIRD BOOK
OF THE
ILIAD

The ARGUMENT

The Duel of *Menelaus* and *Paris*

The Armies being ready to engage, a single combate is agreed upon between
Menelaus *and* Paris (*by the intervention of* Hector) *for the determination
of the War.* Iris *is sent to call* Helena *to behold the fight. She leads her to
the walls of* Troy, *where* Priam *sate with his counsellors observing the
Græcian leaders on the plain below, to whom* Helen *gives an account of
the chief of them. The Kings on either part take the solemn oath for the
conditions of the combate. The duel ensues, wherein* Paris *being overcome is
snatch'd away in a Cloud by* Venus, *and transported to his apartment.
She then calls* Helen *from the walls, and brings the Lovers together.*
Agamemnon *on the part of the* Græcians, *demands the restoration of*
Helen, *and the performance of the articles.*

*The three and twentieth day still continues throughout this book. The
scene is sometimes in the* fields *before* Troy, *and sometimes in* Troy *itself.*

Thus by their leader's care each martial band
Moves into ranks, and stretches o'er the land.
With shouts the *Trojans* rushing from afar
Proclaim their motions, and provoke the war:
5   So when inclement winters vex the plain
With piercing frosts, or thick-descending rain,
To warmer seas the cranes embody'd fly,
With noise, and order, thro' the mid-way sky;
To pygmy nations wounds and death they bring,
10   And all the war descends upon the wing.
But silent, breathing rage, resolv'd, and skill'd
By mutual aids to fix a doubtful field,
Swift march the *Greeks*: the rapid dust around
Dark'ning arises from the labour'd ground.
15   Thus from his flaggy wings when *Notus* sheds
A night of vapours round the mountain-heads,
Swift-gliding mists the dusky fields invade,
To thieves more grateful than the midnight shade;
While scarce the swains their feeding flocks survey,
20   Lost and confus'd amidst the thicken'd day:
So wrapt in gath'ring dust, the *Grecian* train
A moving cloud, swept on, and hid the plain.
    Now front to front the hostile armies stand,
Eager of fight, and only wait command;
25   When, to the van, before the sons of fame
Whom *Troy* sent forth, the beauteous *Paris* came:
In form a God! the panther's speckled hyde
Flow'd o'er his armour with an easy pride,

His bended bow across his shoulders flung,
His sword beside him negligently hung,
Two pointed spears he shook with gallant grace,   30
And dar'd the bravest of the *Grecian* race.

    As thus with glorious air and proud disdain,
He boldly stalk'd, the foremost on the plain,
Him *Menelaüs*, lov'd of *Mars*, espies,   35
With Heart elated, and with joyful eyes:
So joys a lion if the branching deer
Or mountain goat, his bulky prize, appear;
Eager he seizes and devours the slain,
Prest by bold youths, and baying dogs in vain.   40
Thus fond of vengeance, with a furious bound,
In clanging arms he leaps upon the ground
From his high chariot: Him, approaching near,
The beauteous champion views with marks of fear,
Smit with a conscious sense, retires behind,   45
And shuns the fate he well deserv'd to find.
As when some shepherd from the rustling trees
Shot forth to view, a scaly serpent sees;
Trembling and pale, he starts with wild affright,
And all confus'd, precipitates his flight.   50
So from the King the shining warriour flies,
And plung'd amid the thickest *Trojans* lies.

    As god-like *Hector* sees the Prince retreat,
He thus upbraids him with a gen'rous heat.
Unhappy *Paris*! but to women brave,   55
So fairly form'd, and only to deceive!
Oh had'st thou dy'd when first thou saw'st the light,
Or dy'd at least before thy nuptial rite!
A better fate than vainly thus to boast,
And fly, the scandal of thy *Trojan* host.   60
Gods! how the scornful *Greeks* exult to see
Their fears of danger undeceiv'd in thee!
Thy figure promis'd with a martial air,
But ill thy soul supplies a form so fair.
In former days, in all thy gallant pride,   65
When thy tall ships triumphant stem'd the tide,
When *Greece* beheld thy painted canvas flow,
And crowds stood wond'ring at the passing show;

Say, was it thus, with such a baffled mien,
70   You met th' approaches of the *Spartan* Queen,
Thus from her realm convey'd the beauteous prize,
And *both her warlike Lords outshin'd in *Helen*'s eyes?
This deed, thy foes delight, thy own disgrace,
Thy father's grief, and ruin of thy race;
75   This deed recalls thee to the proffer'd fight;
Or hast thou injur'd whom thou dar'st not right?
Soon to thy cost the field wou'd make thee know
Thou keep'st the consort of a braver foe.
Thy graceful form instilling soft desire,
80   Thy curling tresses, and thy silver lyre,
Beauty and youth, in vain to these you trust,
When youth and beauty shall be laid in dust:
Troy yet may wake, and one avenging blow
Crush the dire author of his country's woe.

85   His silence here, with blushes, *Paris* breaks;
'Tis just, my brother, what your anger speaks:
But who like thee can boast a soul sedate,
So firmly proof to all the shocks of fate?
Thy force like steel a temper'd hardness shows,
90   Still edg'd to wound, and still untir'd with blows,
Like steel, uplifted by some strenuous swain,
With falling woods to strow the wasted plain.
Thy gifts I praise, nor thou despise the charms
With which a lover golden *Venus* arms;
95   Soft moving speech, and pleasing outward show,
No wish can gain 'em, but the gods bestow.
Yet, wou'd'st thou have the proffer'd combate stand,
The *Greeks* and *Trojans* seat on either hand;
Then let a mid-way space our hosts divide,
100   And, on that stage of war, the cause be try'd:
By *Paris* there the *Spartan* King be fought,
For beauteous *Helen* and the wealth she brought:
And who his rival can in arms subdue,
His be the fair, and his the treasure too.
105   Thus with a lasting league your toils may cease,
And *Troy* possess her fertile fields in peace;

* *Theseus* and *Menelaus*.

Thus may the *Greeks* review their native shore,
Much fam'd for gen'rous steeds, for beauty more.
    He said. The Challenge *Hector* heard with joy,
Then with his spear restrain'd the youth of *Troy*,   110
Held by the midst, athwart; and near the foe
Advanc'd with steps majestically slow.
While round his dauntless head the *Grecians* pour
Their stones and arrows in a mingled show'r.
    Then thus the Monarch great *Atrides* cry'd;   115
Forbear ye warriors! lay the darts aside:
A Parley *Hector* asks, a message bears;
We know him by the various plume he wears.
Aw'd by his high command the *Greeks* attend,
The tumult silence, and the fight suspend.   120
    While from the centre *Hector* rolls his eyes
On either host, and thus to both applies.
Hear, all ye *Trojans*, all ye *Grecian* bands!
What *Paris*, author of the war, demands.
Your shining swords within the sheath restrain,   125
And pitch your lances in the yielding plain.
Here, in the midst, in either army's sight,
He dares the *Spartan* King to single fight;
And wills, that *Helen* and the ravish'd spoil
That caus'd the contest, shall reward the toil.   130
Let these the brave triumphant victor grace,
And diff'ring nations part in leagues of peace.
    He spoke: in still suspense on either side
Each army stood: The *Spartan* Chief reply'd.
    Me too ye warriors hear, whose fatal right   135
A world engages in the toils of fight.
To me the labour of the field resign;
Me *Paris* injur'd; all the war be mine.
Fall he that must beneath his rival's arms,
And live the rest secure of future harms.   140
Two lambs, devoted by your country's rite,
To *Earth* a sable, to the *Sun* a white,
Prepare ye *Trojans*! while a third we bring
Select to *Jove*, th' inviolable King.
Let rev'rend *Priam* in the truce engage,   145
And add the sanction of consid'rate age;

His sons are faithless, headlong in debate,
And youth itself an empty wav'ring state:
Cool age advances venerably wise,
150   Turns on all hands its deep-discerning eyes;
Sees what befell, and what may yet befall;
Concludes from both, and best provides for all.

The nations hear, with rising hopes possest,
And peaceful prospects dawn in ev'ry breast.
155   Within the lines they drew their steeds around,
And from their chariots issu'd on the ground:
Next all unbuckling the rich mail they wore,
Lay'd their bright arms along the sable shore.
On either side the meeting hosts are seen,
160   With lances fix'd, and close the space between.
Two heralds now dispatch'd to *Troy*, invite
The *Phrygian* Monarch to the peaceful rite;
Talthybius hastens to the fleet, to bring
The Lamb for *Jove*, th' inviolable King.
165   Mean time, to beauteous *Helen*, from the skies
The various Goddess of the rain-bow flies:
(Like fair *Laodicè* in form and face,
The loveliest Nymph of *Priam*'s royal race)
Her in the palace, at her loom she found;
170   The golden web her own sad story crown'd.
The *Trojan* wars she weav'd (herself the prize)
And the dire triumphs of her fatal eyes.
To whom the Goddess of the painted bow;
Approach, and view the wond'rous scene below!
175   Each hardy *Greek* and valiant *Trojan* Knight,
So dreadful late, and furious for the fight,
Now rest their spears, or lean upon their shields;
Ceas'd is the war, and silent all the fields.
Paris alone and *Sparta*'s king advance,
180   In single fight to toss the beamy lance;
Each met in arms, the fate of combat tries,
Thy love the motive, and thy charms the prize.

This said, the many-colour'd maid inspires
Her husband's love, and wakes her former fires;
185   Her country, parents, all that once were dear,
Rush to her thought, and force a tender tear.

O'er her fair face a snowy veil she threw,
And, softly sighing, from the loom withdrew.
Her handmaids *Clymenè* and *Æthra* wait
Her silent footsteps to the *Scæan* gate.   190

 There sate the seniors of the *Trojan* race,
(Old *Priam*'s Chiefs, and most in *Priam*'s grace)
The King the first; *Thymætes* at his side;
Lampus and *Clytius*, long in council try'd;
Panthus, and *Hicetäon*, once the strong,   195
And next the wisest of the rev'rend Throng,
Antenor grave, and sage *Ucalegon*,
Lean'd on the walls, and bask'd before the sun.
Chiefs, who no more in bloody fights engage,
But wise thro' time, and narrative with age,   200
In summer-days like grasshoppers rejoice,
A bloodless race, that send a feeble voice.
These, when the *Spartan* Queen approach'd the tow'r,
In secret own'd resistless beauty's pow'r:
They cry'd, No wonder, such celestial charms   205
For nine long years have set the world in arms;
What winning graces! what majestick mien!
She moves a Goddess, and she looks a Queen!
Yet hence, oh heav'n! convey that fatal face,
And from destruction save the *Trojan* race.   210

 The good old *Priam* welcom'd her, and cry'd,
Approach my child, and grace thy father's side.
See on the plain thy *Grecian* spouse appears,
The friends and kindred of thy former years.
No crime of thine our present suff'rings draws,   215
Not thou, but heav'ns disposing will, the cause;
The Gods these armies and this force employ,
The hostile Gods conspire the fate of *Troy*.
But lift thy eyes, and say, What *Greek* is he
(Far as from hence these aged orbs can see)   220
Around whose brow such martial graces shine,
So tall, so awful, and almost divine?
Tho' some of larger stature tread the green,
None match his grandeur and exalted mien:
He seems a Monarch, and his country's pride.   225
Thus ceas'd the King, and thus the fair reply'd.

Before thy presence, Father, I appear
With conscious shame and reverential fear.
Ah! had I dy'd, e're to these walls I fled,
230   False to my country and my nuptial bed,
My brothers, friends, and daughter left behind,
False to them all, to *Paris* only kind!
For this I mourn, 'till grief or dire disease
Shall waste the form whose crime it was to please!
235   The King of Kings, *Atrides*, you survey,
Great in the war, and great in arts of sway.
My brother once, before my days of shame;
And oh! that still he bore a brother's Name!

With wonder *Priam* view'd the Godlike man,
240   Extoll'd the happy Prince, and thus began.
O blest *Atrides*! born to prosp'rous fate,
Successful Monarch of a mighty state!
How vast thy empire? Of yon' matchless train
What numbers lost, what numbers yet remain?
245   In *Phrygia* once were gallant armies known,
In ancient time, when *Otreus*' fill'd the throne,
When Godlike *Mygdon* led their troops of horse,
And I, to join them, rais'd the *Trojan* force:
Against the manlike *Amazons* we stood,
250   And *Sangar*'s stream ran purple with their blood.
But far inferior those, in martial grace
And strength of numbers, to this *Grecian* race.

This said, once more he view'd the warriour-train:
What's he, whose arms lie scatter'd on the plain?
255   Broad is his breast, his shoulders larger spread,
Tho' great *Atrides* overtops his head.
Nor yet appear his care and conduct small;
From rank to rank he moves, and orders all.
The stately ram thus measures o'er the ground,
260   And, master of the flocks, surveys them round.

Then *Helen* thus. Whom your discerning eyes
Have singled out, is *Ithacus* the wise:
A barren island boasts his glorious birth;
His fame for wisdom fills the spacious earth.
265   *Antenor* took the word, and thus began:
My self, O King! have seen that wondrous man;

When trusting *Jove* and hospitable laws,
To *Troy* he came, to plead the *Grecian* cause;
(Great *Menelaus* urg'd the same request)
My house was honour'd with each royal guest: 270
I knew their persons, and admir'd their parts,
Both brave in arms, and both approv'd in arts.
Erect, the *Spartan* most engag'd our view,
Ulysses seated, greater rev'rence drew.
When *Atreus*' son harangu'd the list'ning train,   275
Just was his sense, and his expression plain,
His words succinct, yet full, without a fault;
He spoke no more than just the thing he ought.
But when *Ulysses* rose, in thought profound,
His modest eyes he fix'd upon the ground,   280
As one unskill'd or dumb, he seem'd to stand,
Nor rais'd his head, nor stretch'd his sceptred hand;
But, when he speaks, what elocution flows!
Soft as the fleeces of descending snows
The copious accents fall, with easy art;   285
Melting they fall, and sink into the heart!
Wond'ring we hear, and fix'd in deep surprize
Our ears refute the censure of our eyes.
    The King then ask'd (as yet the camp he view'd)
What Chief is that, with giant strength endu'd,   290
Whose brawny shoulders, and whose swelling chest,
And lofty stature far exceed the rest?
Ajax the great (the beauteous Queen reply'd)
Himself a host: the *Grecian* strength and pride.
See! bold *Idomeneus* superior tow'rs   295
Amidst yon' circle of his *Cretan* pow'rs,
Great as a God! I saw him once before,
With *Menelaüs*, on the *Spartan* shore.
The rest I know, and could in order name;
All valiant chiefs, and men of mighty fame.   300
Yet two are wanting of the num'rous train,
Whom long my eyes have sought, but sought in vain:
Castor and *Pollux*, first in martial force,
One bold on foot, and one renown'd for horse.
My brothers these; the same our native shore,   305
One house contain'd us, as one mother bore.

Perhaps the Chiefs, from warlike toils at ease,
For distant *Troy* refus'd to sail the seas:
Perhaps their sword some nobler quarrel draws,
310   Asham'd to combate in their sister's cause.
 So spoke the fair, nor knew her brother's doom,
Wrapt in the cold embraces of the tomb;
Adorn'd with honours in their native shore,
Silent they slept, and heard of wars no more.
315   Meantime the heralds, thro' the crowded town,
Bring the rich wine and destin'd victims down.
Idæus' arms the golden goblets prest,
Who thus the venerable King addrest.
Arise, O father of the *Trojan* state!
320   The nations call, thy joyful people wait,
To seal the truce and end the dire debate.
Paris thy son, and *Sparta*'s King advance,
In measur'd lists to toss the weighty lance;
And who his rival shall in arms subdue,
325   His be the dame, and his the treasure too.
Thus with a lasting league our toils may cease,
And *Troy* possess her fertile fields in peace;
So shall the *Greeks* review their native shore,
Much fam'd for gen'rous steeds, for beauty more.
330   With grief he heard, and bade the chiefs prepare
To join his milk-white coursers to the car:
He mounts the seat, *Antenor* at his side;
The gentle steeds thro' *Scæa*'s gates they guide:
Next from the car descending on the plain,
335   Amid the *Grecian* host and *Trojan* train
Slow they proceed: The sage *Ulysses* then
Arose, and with him rose the King of Men.
On either side a sacred herald stands,
The wine they mix, and on each monarch's hands
340   Pour the full urn; then draws the *Grecian* Lord
His cutlace sheath'd beside his pondrous sword;
From the sign'd victims crops the curling hair,
The heralds part it, and the Princes share;
Then loudly thus before th' attentive bands
345   He calls the Gods, and spreads his lifted hands.

O first and greatest pow'r! whom all obey,
Who high on *Ida*'s holy mountain sway,
Eternal *Jove*! and you bright orb that roll
From east to west, and view from pole to pole!
Thou mother *Earth*! and all ye living *Floods*!   350
Infernal *Furies*, and *Tartarean* Gods,
Who rule the dead, and horrid woes prepare
For perjur'd Kings, and all who falsely swear!
Hear, and be witness. If, by *Paris* slain,
Great *Menelaüs* press the fatal plain;   355
The Dame and treasures let the *Trojan* keep,
And *Greece* returning plow the watry deep.
If by my brother's lance the *Trojan* bleed;
Be his the wealth and beauteous dame decreed:
Th' appointed fine let *Ilion* justly pay,   360
And ev'ry age record the signal day.
This if the *Phrygians* shall refuse to yield,
Arms must revenge, and *Mars* decide the field.

   With that, the Chief the tender victims slew,
And in the dust their bleeding bodies threw: 365
The vital spirit issu'd at the wound,
And left the members quiv'ring on the ground.
From the same urn they drink the mingled wine,
And add libations to the pow'rs divine.
While thus their pray'rs united mount the sky;   370
Hear mighty *Jove*! and hear ye Gods on high!
And may their blood, who first the league confound,
Shed like this wine, distain the thirsty ground;
May all their consorts serve promiscuous lust,
And all their race be scatter'd as the dust!   375
Thus either host their imprecations join'd,
Which *Jove* refus'd, and mingled with the wind.

   The rites now finish'd, rev'rend *Priam* rose,
And thus express'd a heart o'ercharg'd with woes.
Ye *Greeks* and *Trojans*, let the chiefs engage,   380
But spare the weakness of my feeble age:
In yonder walls that object let me shun,
Nor view the danger of so dear a son.
Whose arms shall conquer, and what Prince shall fall,
Heav'n only knows, for heav'n disposes all.   385

This said, the hoary King no longer stay'd,
But on his car the slaughter'd victims laid,
Then seiz'd the reins his gentle steeds to guide,
And drove to *Troy*, *Antenor* at his side.

390   Bold *Hector* and *Ulysses* now dispose
The lists of combate, and the ground inclose;
Next to decide by sacred lots prepare,
Who first shall launce his pointed spear in air.
The people pray with elevated hands,

395   And words like these are heard thro' all the bands.
Immortal *Jove*! high heav'n's superior lord,
On lofty *Ida*'s holy mount ador'd!
Whoe'er involv'd us in this dire debate,
Oh give that author of the war to fate,

400   And shades eternal! Let division cease,
And joyful nations join in leagues of peace.

      With eyes averted *Hector* hasts to turn
The lots of Fight, and shakes the brazen urn.
Then, *Paris*, thine leap'd forth, by fatal chance

405   Ordain'd the first to whirl the weighty lance.
Both armies sate, the combate to survey,
Beside each chief his azure armour lay,
And round the lists the gen'rous coursers neigh.
The beauteous warriour now arrays for fight,

410   In gilded arms magnificently bright:
The purple cuishes clasp his thighs around,
With flow'rs adorn'd, with silver buckles bound:
Lycaon's cors'let his fair body drest,
Brac'd in, and fitted to his softer breast;

415   A radiant baldric, o'er his shoulder ty'd,
Sustain'd the sword that glitter'd at his side:
His youthful face a polish'd helm o'erspread;
The waving horse-hair nodded on his head;
His figur'd shield, a shining orb, he takes,

420   And in his hand a pointed jav'lin shakes.
With equal speed, and fir'd by equal charms,
The *Spartan* hero sheaths his limbs in arms.
      Now round the lists th' admiring armies stand,
With jav'lins fix'd, the *Greek* and *Trojan* band.

Amidst the dreadful vale the Chiefs advance,   425
All pale with rage, and shake the threat'ning lance.
The *Trojan* first his shining jav'lin threw;
Full on *Atrides*' ringing shield it flew,
Nor pierc'd the brazen orb, but with a bound
Leap'd from the buckler blunted on the ground.   430
Atrides then his massy lance prepares,
In act to throw, but first prefers his pray'rs.
  Give me, great *Jove*! to punish lawless lust,
And lay the *Trojan* gasping in the dust:
Destroy th' aggressor, aid my righteous cause,   435
Avenge the breach of hospitable laws!
Let this example future times reclaim,
And guard from wrong fair friendship's holy name.
  He said, and pois'd in air the jav'lin sent,
Thro' *Paris*' shield the forceful weapon went,   440
His cors'let pierces, and his garment rends,
And glancing downward, near his flank descends.
The wary *Trojan*, bending from the blow,
Eludes the death, and disappoints his foe:
But fierce *Atrides* wav'd his sword and strook   445
Full on his casque; the crested helmet shook;
The brittle steel, unfaithful to his hand,
Broke short: the fragments glitter'd on the sand.
The raging warriour to the spacious skies
Rais'd his upbraiding voice, and angry eyes: 450
Then is it vain in *Jove* himself to trust?
And is it thus the Gods assist the just?
When crimes provoke us, heav'n success denies;
The dart falls harmless, and the faulchion flies.
Furious he said, and tow'rd the *Grecian* crew   455
(Seiz'd by the crest) th' unhappy warriour drew;
Struggling he follow'd, while th' embroider'd thong
That ty'd his helmet, dragg'd the chief along.
Then had his ruin crown'd *Atrides*' joy,
But *Venus* trembl'd for the Prince of *Troy*:   460
Unseen she came, and burst the golden band;
And left an empty helmet in his hand.
The casque, enrag'd, amidst the *Greeks* he threw;
The *Greeks* with smiles the polish'd trophy view.

465   Then, as once more he lifts the deadly dart,
In thirst of vengeance, at his rival's heart,
The Queen of Love her favour'd champion shrouds
(For Gods can all things) in a veil of clouds.
Rais'd from the field the panting youth she led,
470 And gently laid him on the bridal bed,
With pleasing sweets his fainting sense renews,
And all the dome perfumes with heav'nly dews.

    Meantime the brightest of the female kind,
The matchless *Helen* o'er the walls reclin'd:
475 To her, beset with *Trojan* beauties, came
In borrow'd form the *laughter-loving dame.
(She seem'd an ancient maid, well-skill'd to cull
The snowy fleece, and wind the twisted wool.)
The Goddess softly shook her silken vest,
480 That shed perfumes, and whisp'ring thus addrest.

    Haste, happy nymph! for thee thy *Paris* calls,
Safe from the fight, in yonder lofty walls,
Fair as a God! with odours round him spread
He lies, and waits thee on the well-known bed:
485 Not like a warriour parted from the foe,
But some gay dancer in the publick show.

    She spoke, and *Helen's* secret soul was mov'd;
She scorn'd the champion, but the man she lov'd.
Fair *Venus'* neck, her eyes that sparkled fire,
490 And breast, reveal'd the Queen of soft desire.
Struck with her presence, strait the lively red
Forsook her cheek; and, trembling, thus she said.
Then is it still thy pleasure to deceive?
And woman's frailty always to believe?
495 Say, to new nations must I cross the main,
Or carry wars to some soft *Asian* plain?
For whom must *Helen* break her second vow?
What other *Paris* is thy darling now?
Left to *Atrides*, (victor in the strife)
500 An odious conquest and a captive wife,
Hence let me sail: And if thy *Paris* bear
My absence ill, let *Venus* ease his care.

* Venus.

A hand-maid goddess at his side to wait,
Renounce the glories of thy heav'nly state,
Be fix'd for ever to the *Trojan* shore,   505
His spouse, or slave; and mount the skies no more.
For me, to lawless love no longer led,
I scorn the coward, and detest his bed;
Else should I merit everlasting shame,
And keen reproach, from ev'ry *Phrygian* dame: 510
Ill suits it now the joys of love to know,
Too deep my anguish, and too wild my woe.
   Then thus, incens'd, the *Paphian* Queen replies;
Obey the pow'r from whom thy glories rise:
Should *Venus* leave thee, ev'ry charm must fly,   515
Fade from thy cheek, and languish in thy eye.
Cease to provoke me, lest I make thee more
The world's aversion, than their love before;
Now the bright prize for which mankind engage,
Then, the sad victim of the publick rage.   520
   At this, the fairest of her sex obey'd,
And veil'd her blushes in a silken shade;
Unseen, and silent, from the train she moves,
Led by the Goddess of the Smiles and Loves.
   Arriv'd, and enter'd at the Palace gate,   525
The maids officious round their mistress wait;
Then all dispersing, various tasks attend;
The Queen and Goddess to the Prince ascend.
Full in her *Paris'* sight the Queen of Love
Had plac'd the beauteous progeny of *Jove*;   530
Where, as he view'd her charms, she turn'd away
Her glowing eyes, and thus began to say.
   Is this the Chief, who lost to sense of shame
Late fled the field, and yet survives his fame?
Oh hadst thou dy'd beneath the righteous sword   535
Of that brave man whom once I call'd my Lord!
The boaster *Paris* oft' desir'd the day
With *Sparta*'s King to meet in single fray:
Go now, once more thy rival's rage excite,
Provoke *Atrides* and renew the fight: 540
Yet *Helen* bids thee stay, lest thou unskill'd
Should'st fall an easy conquest on the field.

The Prince replies; Ah cease, divinely fair,
Nor add reproaches to the wounds I bear;
545 This day the foe prevail'd by *Pallas*' pow'r;
We yet may vanquish in a happier hour:
There want not gods to favour us above;
But let the business of our Life be Love:
These softer moments let delights employ,
550 And kind embraces snatch the hasty joy.
Not thus I lov'd thee, when from *Sparta*'s shore
My forc'd, my willing heav'nly prize I bore,
When first entranc'd in *Cranaë*'s isle I lay,
Mix'd with thy soul, and all dissolv'd away.
555 Thus having spoke, th' enamour'd *Phrygian* boy
Rush'd to the bed, impatient for the joy.
Him *Helen* follow'd slow with bashful charms,
And clasp'd the blooming Hero in her arms.
While these to love's delicious rapture yield,
560 The stern *Atrides* rages round the field:
So some fell lion whom the woods obey,
Roars thro' the desart, and demands his prey.
Paris he seeks, impatient to destroy,
But seeks in vain along the troops of *Troy*;
565 Ev'n those had yielded to a foe so brave
The recreant warriour, hateful as the grave.
Then speaking thus, the King of Kings arose;
Ye *Trojans*, *Dardans*, all our gen'rous foes!
Hear and attest! From heav'n with conquest crown'd,
570 Our brother's arms the just success have found:
Be therefore now the *Spartan* wealth restor'd,
Let *Argive Helen* own her lawful Lord,
Th' appointed fine let *Ilion* justly pay,
And Age to Age record this signal Day.
575 He ceas'd; his army's loud applauses rise,
And the long shout runs echoing thro' the skies.

OBSERVATIONS

ON THE

THIRD BOOK

Of all the books of the *Iliad*, there is scarce any more pleasing than the third. It may be divided into five parts, each of which has a beauty different from the other. The first contains what pass'd before the two armies, and the proposal of the combate between *Paris* and *Menelaus*: The attention and suspense of these mighty hosts, which were just upon the point of joining battel, and the lofty manner of offering and accepting this important and unexpected challenge, have something in them wonderfully pompous and of an amusing solemnity. The second part, which describes the behaviour of *Helena* in this juncture, her conference with the old King and his counsellors, with the review of the heroes from the battlements, is an episode entirely of another sort, which excels in the natural and pathetick. The third consists of the ceremonies of the oath on both sides and the preliminaries to the combate; with the beautiful retreat of *Priam*, who in the tenderness of a parent withdraws from the sight of the duel: These particulars detain the reader in expectation, and heighten his impatience for the fight itself. The fourth is the description of the duel: an exact piece of painting where we see every attitude, motion, and action of the combatants particularly and distinctly, and which concludes with a surprizing propriety, in the rescue of *Paris* by *Venus*. The machine of that goddess, which makes the fifth part, and whose end is to reconcile *Paris* and *Helena*, is admirable in every circumstance; The remonstrance she holds with the Goddess, the reluctance with which she obeys her, the reproaches she casts upon *Paris*, and the flattery and courtship with which he so soon wins her over to him. *Helen* (the main cause of this war) was not to be made an odious character; she is drawn by this great master with the finest strokes, as a frail, but not as an abandon'd creature. She has perpetual struggles of virtue on the one side, and softnesses which overcome them on the other. Our Author has been remarkably careful to tell us this; whenever he but slightly names her in the foregoing part of his work, she is represented at the same time as repentant; and it is thus we see her at large at her first appearance in the present book, which is one of the shortest of the whole *Iliad*, but in recompence has beauties almost in every line, and most of them so obvious that to acknowledge them we need only to read them.

3. *With shouts the* Trojans.] The book begins with a fine opposition of the noise of the *Trojan* army to the silence of the *Græcians*. It was but natural to imagine this, since the former was compos'd of many different nations, of various languages and strangers to each other; the latter were more united in their neighbourhood, and under leaders of the same Country. But as this observation seems particularly insisted upon by our Author (for he uses it again in the fourth book, v. 486) so he had a farther reason for it. *Plutarch*, in his treatise of reading the Poets, remarks upon this distinction, as a particular credit to the military discipline of the *Greeks*. And several ancient authors tell us, it was the manner of the *Barbarians* to encounter with shouts and outcries; as it continues to this day the custom of the Eastern nations. Perhaps these clamours were only to encourage their men, instead of martial instruments. I think Sir *Walter Raleigh* says, there never was a people but made use of some sort of musick in battle: *Homer* never mentions any in the *Greek* or *Trojan* armies, and it is scarce to be imagined he would omit a circumstance so poetical without some particular reason. The verb Σαλπίζω which the modern *Greeks* have since appropriated to the sound of a trumpet, is used indifferently in our Author for other Sounds, as for thunder in the 21*st Iliad*, v. 388. Ἀμφὶ δὲ σάλπιγξεν μέγας οὐρανός –. He once names the trumpet Σάλπιγξ in a *simile*, upon which *Eustathius* and *Didymus* observe, that the use of it was known in the poet's Time, but not in that of the *Trojan* War. And hence we may infer that *Homer* was particularly careful not to confound the manners of the times he wrote of, with those of the times he liv'd in.

7. *The cranes embody'd fly.*] If wit has been truly describ'd to be a similitude in ideas, and is more excellent as that similitude is more surprizing; there cannot be a truer kind of wit than what is shewn in apt comparisons, especially when composed of such subjects as having

the least relation to each other in general, have yet some particular that agrees exactly. Of this nature is the simile of the *cranes* to the *Trojan* army, where the fancy of *Homer* flew to the remotest part of the world for an image which no reader could have expected. But it is no less exact than surprizing. The likeness consists in two points, the *noise* and the *order*; the latter is so observable as to have given some of the ancients occasion to imagine the embatteling of an army was first learn'd from the close manner of flight of these birds. But this part of the simile not being directly express'd by the author, has been overlook'd by some of the commentators. It may be remark'd, that *Homer* has generally a wonderful closeness in all the particulars of his comparisons, notwithstanding he takes a liberty in his expression of them. He seems so secure of the main likeness, that he makes no scruple to play with the circumstances; sometimes by transposing the order of them, sometimes by superadding them, and sometimes (as in this place) by neglecting them in such a manner as to leave the reader to supply them himself. For the present comparison, it has been taken by *Virgil* in the tenth book [264–6], and apply'd to the clamours of soldiers in the same manner.

> – *Quales sub nubibus atris*
> *Strymoniæ dant signa grues, atque æthera tranant*
> *Cum sonitu, fugiuntque Notos clamore secundo.*

[Thus, at the signal giv'n, the cranes arise
Before the stormy south, and blacken all the skies.]

26. *The beauteous* Paris *came, In form a God.*] This is meant by the Epithet θεοειδής, as has been said in the note on the first book, v. 169. The Picture here given of *Paris*'s air and dress, is exactly correspondent to his character; you see him endeavouring to mix the fine Gentleman with the warriour; and this idea of him *Homer* takes care to keep up, by describing him not without the same regard when he is arming to encounter *Menelaus* afterwards in a close fight, as he shews here, where he is but preluding and flourishing in the gaiety of his heart. And when he tells us, in that place, that he was in danger of being strangled by the strap of his helmet, he takes notice that it was πολύκεστος, *embroider'd*.

37. *So joys a Lion if the branching deer, Or mountain goat.*] The old scholiasts refining on this simile will have it that *Paris* is compar'd to a goat on account of his incontinence, and to a stag for his cowardice: To this last they make an addition which is very ludicrous, that he is also liken'd to a deer for his *skill in musick*, and cite *Aristotle* to prove that animal delights in harmony, which opinion is alluded to by Mr. *Waller* in these lines,

> *Here love takes stand, and while she charms the ear*
> *Empties his quiver on the list'ning deer.*

But upon the whole, it is whimsical to imagine this comparison consists in any thing more, than the joy which *Menelaus* conceiv'd at the sight of his rival, in the hopes of destroying him. It is equally an injustice to *Paris*, to abuse him for understanding musick, and to represent his retreat as purely the effect of fear, which proceeded from his sense of guilt with respect to the particular person of *Menelaus*. He appear'd at the head of the army to challenge the boldest of the enemy: Nor is his character elsewhere in the *Iliad* by any means that of a coward. *Hector* at the end of the sixth book confesses, that no man could justly reproach him as such. Nor is he represented so by *Ovid* (who copy'd *Homer* very closely) in the end of his epistle to *Helen*. The moral of *Homer* is much finer: A brave mind, however blinded with passion, is sensible of remorse as soon as the injur'd object presents itself; and *Paris* never behaves himself ill in war, but when his spirits are depress'd by the consciousness of an injustice. This also will account for the seeming incongruity of *Homer* in this passage, who (as they would have us think) paints him a shameful coward, at the same time that he is perpetually calling him *the divine Paris*, and *Paris like a God*. What he says immediately afterwards in answer to *Hector*'s reproof, will make this yet more clear.

47. *As when a shepherd.*] This comparison of the serpent is finely imitated by *Virgil* in the second *Æneid* [379-82].

> *Improvisum aspris veluti qui sentibus anguem*
> *Pressit humi nitens, trepidusque; repente refugit*
> *Attollentem iras, & cærula colla tumentem:*
> *Haud secus Androgeus visu tremefactus abibat.*

> [As when some peasant in a bushy brake,
>   Has with unwary footing press'd a snake;
>   He starts aside, astonish'd, when he spies
>   His rising crest, blue neck, and rowling eyes;
>   So, from our arms, surpriz'd Androgeus flies.]

But it may be said to the praise of *Virgil*, that he has apply'd it upon an occasion where it has an additional beauty. *Paris* upon the sight of *Menelaus*'s approach, is compar'd to a traveller who sees a snake shoot on a sudden towards him. But the surprize and danger of *Androgeus* is more lively, being just in the reach of his enemies before he perceiv'd it; and the circumstance of the serpent's rouzing his crest, which brightens with anger, finely images the shining of their arms in the night-time, as they were just lifted up to destroy him. *Scaliger* criticizes on the needless repetition in the words παλίνορσος and ἀνεχώρησεν, which is avoided in the translation. But it must be observ'd in general, that *little exactnesses* are what we should not look for in *Homer*; the genius of his age was too incorrect, and his own too fiery, to regard them.

53. *As God-like* Hector.] This is the first place of the poem where *Hector* makes a figure, and here it seems proper to give an idea of his character, since if he is not the chief hero of the *Iliad*, he is at least the most amiable. There are several reasons which render *Hector* a favorite character with every Reader, some of which shall here be offer'd. The chief moral of *Homer* was to expose the ill effects of discord; the *Greeks* were to be shewn disunited, and to render that disunion the more probable, he has designedly given them *mixt* characters. The *Trojans*, on the other hand, were to be represented making all advantages of the others disagreement, which they could not do without a strict union among themselves. *Hector* therefore, who commanded them, must be endu'd with all such qualifications as tended to the preservation of it; as *Achilles* with such as promoted the contrary. The one stands in contraste to the other, an accomplish'd character of valour unruffled by rage and anger, and uniting his people by his prudence and example. *Hector* has also a foil to set him off in his own family; we are perpetually opposing in our own minds the incontinence of *Paris*, who exposes his country, to the temperance of *Hector* who protects it. And indeed it is this love of his country which appears his principal passion, and the motive of all his actions. He has no other blemish than that he fights in an unjust cause, which *Homer* has yet been careful to tell us he would not do, if his opinion were followed. But since he cannot prevail, the affection he bears to his parents and kindred, and his desire of defending them, incites him to do his utmost for their safety. We may add that *Homer* having so many *Greeks* to celebrate, makes them shine in their turns, and singly in their several

books, one succeeding in the absence of another: Whereas *Hector*
appears in every battel the life and soul of his party, and the constant
bulwark against every enemy: He stands against *Agamemnon*'s magna-
nimity, *Diomed*'s bravery, *Ajax*'s strength, and *Achilles*'s fury. There
is besides an accidental cause for our liking him, from reading the
writers of the *Augustan* age (especially *Virgil*) whose favorite he grew
more particularly from the time when the *Cæsars* fancy'd to derive
their pedigree from *Troy*.

55. *Unhappy* Paris, &c.] It may be observ'd in honour of *Homer*'s
judgment, that the words which *Hector* is made to speak here, very
strongly mark his character. They contain a warm reproach of coward-
ice and shew him to be touch'd with so high a sense of glory, as to
think life insupportable without it. His calling to mind the gallant
figure which *Paris* had made in his amours to *Helen*, and opposing it to
the image of his flight from her husband, is a sarcasm of the utmost
bitterness and vivacity. After he has named that action of the rape, the
cause of so many mischiefs, his insisting upon it in so many broken
periods, those disjointed shortnesses of speech,

> (Πατρί τε σῷ μέγα πῆμα, πόληῖ τε, παντί τε δήμῳ
> Δυσμενέσιν μὲν χάρμα, κατηφείην δὲ σοὶ αὐτῷ.)

That hasty manner of expression without the connexion of particles, is
(as *Eustathius* remarks) extremely natural to a man in anger, who
thinks he can never vent himself too soon. That contempt of outward
shew, of the gracefulness of person, and of the accomplishments of a
courtly life, is what corresponds very well with the warlike temper of
Hector; and these verses have therefore a beauty here which they want
in *Horace*, however admirably he has translated them, in the ode of
Nireus's *prophecy*.

> *Nequicquam Veneris præsidio ferox,*
> *Pectes cæsariem; grataque fœminis*
> *Imbelli cithara carmina divides,* &c.

> [Vainly confident that Venus
>   is your protector, you will comb
>   your hair, and you will sing – to the
>   accompaniment of the unwarlike lyre –
>   the kind of songs that women love to hear.–
>   I. xv. 13–1 5.]

72. *And both her warlike lords.*] The original is Νυὸν ἀνδρῶν αἰχμητάων. *The spouse of martial men.* I wonder why Madam *Dacier* chose to turn it *Alliée à tant de braves guerriers*, since it so naturally refers to *Theseus* and *Menelaus*, the former husbands of *Helena*.

80. *Thy curling tresses, and thy silver lyre.*] It is ingeniously remark'd by *Dacier*, that *Homer*, who celebrates the *Greeks* for their long hair [καρηκομόωντας Ἀχαιούς] and *Achilles* for his skill on the harp, makes *Hector* in this place object them both to *Paris*. The *Greeks* nourished their hair to appear more dreadful to the enemy, and *Paris* to please the eyes of women. *Achilles* sung to his harp the acts of Heroes, and *Paris* the amours of lovers. The same reason which makes *Hector* here displeas'd at them, made *Alexander* afterwards refuse to see this lyre of *Paris*, when offer'd to be shewn to him, as *Plutarch* relates the story in his oration of the fortune of *Alexander*.

83. *One avenging blow.*] It is in the *Greek*, *You had been clad in a Coat of Stone.* *Giphanius* would have it to mean stoned to death on the account of his adultery: But this does not appear to have been the punishment of that crime among the *Phrygians*. It seems rather to signify, destroy'd by the fury of the people for the war he had brought upon them; or perhaps may imply no more than being laid in his grave under a monument of stones; but the former being the stronger sense, is here followed.

86. *'Tis just, my brother.*] This speech is a farther opening of the true character of *Paris*. He is a master of civility, no less well-bred to his own sex than courtly to the other. The reproof of *Hector* was of a severe nature, yet he receives it as from a brother and a friend, with candour and modesty. This answer is remarkable for its fine address; he gives the hero a decent and agreeable reproof for having too rashly depreciated the gifts of nature. He allows the quality of courage its utmost due, but desires the same justice to those softer accomplishments, which he lets him know are no less the favour of heaven. Then he removes from himself the charge of want of valour, by proposing the single combat with the very man he had just declined to engage; which having shewn him void of any malevolence to his rival on the one hand, he now proves himself free from the imputation of cowardice on the other. *Homer* draws him (as we have seen) soft of speech, the

natural quality of an amorous temper; vainly gay in war as well as love; with a spirit that can be surprized and recollected, that can receive impressions of shame or apprehension on the one side, or of generosity and courage on the other; the usual disposition of easy and courteous minds, which are most subject to the rule of fancy and passion. Upon the whole, this is no worse than the picture of a *gentle Knight*, and one might fancy the heroes of the modern romance were form'd upon the model of *Paris*.

108. *Much fam'd for gen'rous steeds, for beauty more.*] The original is Ἄργος ἐς ἱππόβοτον, καὶ Ἀχαιΐδα καλλιγύναικα. Perhaps this line is translated too close to the letter, and the epithets might have been omitted. But there are some traits and particularities of this nature, which methinks preserve to the reader the air of *Homer*. At least the latter of these circumstances, that *Greece was eminent for beautiful women*, seems not improper to be mention'd by him who had rais'd a war on the account of a *Grecian beauty*.

109. *The challenge* Hector *heard with Joy.*] *Hector* stays not to reply to his brother, but runs away with the challenge immediately. He looks upon all the *Trojans* as disgrac'd by the late flight of *Paris*, and thinks not a moment is to be lost to regain the honour of his country. The activity he shews in all this affair wonderfully agrees with the spirit of a soldier.

123. *Hear all ye* Trojan, *all ye* Grecian *bands.*] It has been ask'd how the different nations could understand one another in these conferences, since we have no mention in *Homer* of any interpreter between them? He who was so very particular in the most minute points, can hardly be thought to have been negligent in this. Some reasons may be offer'd that they both spoke the same language; for the *Trojans* (as may be seen in *Dion. Halic. lib.* 1.) were of *Grecian* extraction originally. *Dardanus* the first of their Kings was born in *Arcadia*; and even their names were originally *Greek*, as *Hector, Anchises, Andromache, Astyanax, &c.* Of the last of these in particular, *Homer* gives us a derivation which is purely *Greek* in *Il.* 6. v. 403. But however it be, this is no more (as *Dacier* somewhere observes) than the just privilege of Poetry. *Æneas* and *Turnus* understand each other in *Virgil*, and the language of the Poet is suppos'd to be universally intelligible, not only between different countries, but between earth and heaven itself.

135. *Me too ye warriours hear*, &c.] We may observe what care *Homer* takes to give every one his proper character, and how this speech of *Menelaus* is adapted to the *Laconick*; which the better to comprehend, we may remember there are in *Homer* three speakers of different characters, agreeable to the three different kinds of eloquence. These we may compare with each other in one instance, supposing them all to use the same heads, and in the same order.

The materials of the speech are, The manifesting his grief for the war, with the hopes that it is in his power to end it; an acceptance of the propos'd challenge; an account of the ceremonies to be us'd in the league; and a proposal of a proper caution to secure it.

Now had *Nestor* these materials to work upon, he would probably have begun with a relation of all the troubles of the nine year's siege which he hop'd he might now bring to an end; he would court their benevolence and good wishes for his prosperity, with all the figures of amplification; while he accepted the challenge, he would have given an example to prove that the single combate was a wise, gallant, and gentle way of ending the war, practis'd by their fathers; in the description of the rites he would be exceeding particular; and when he chose to demand the sanction of *Priam* rather than of his sons, he would place in opposition on one side the son's action which began the war, and on the other the impressions of concern or repentance which it must by this time have made in the father's mind, whose wisdom he would undoubtedly extol as the effect of his age. All this he would have expatiated upon with connexions of the discourses in the most evident manner, and the most easy, gliding, undisobliging transitions. The effect would be, that the people would hear him with pleasure.

Had it been *Ulysses* who was to make the speech, he would have mention'd a few of their most affecting calamities in a pathetick air; then have undertaken the fight with testifying such a chearful joy, as should have won the hearts of the soldiers to follow him to the field without being desired. He would have been exceeding cautious in wording the conditions; and solemn, rather than particular, in speaking of the rites, which he would only insist on as an opportunity to exhort both sides to a fear of the Gods, and a strict regard of justice. He would have remonstrated the use of sending for *Priam*; and (because no caution could be too much) have demanded his sons to be bound with him. For a conclusion, he would have us'd some noble sentiment agreeable to a hero, and (it may be) have enforc'd it with some inspirited action. In all this you would have known that the discourse hung together, but its fire would not always suffer it to be seen in cooler transitions, which (when they are too nicely laid open) may conduct the reader, but never carry him away. The people would hear him with emotion.

These materials being given to *Menelaus*, he but just mentions their troubles, and his satisfaction in the prospect of ending them, shortens the proposals, says a sacrifice is necessary, requires *Priam*'s presence to confirm the conditions, refuses his sons with a resentment of that injury he suffer'd by them, and concludes with a reason for his choice from the praise of age, with a short gravity, and the air of an apothegm. This he puts in order without any more transition than what a single conjunction affords. And the effect of the discourse is, that the people are instructed by it in what is to be done.

141. *Two lambs devoted.*] The *Trojans* (says the old scholiast) were required to sacrifice two lambs; one male of a white colour, to the *Sun*, and one female, and black, to the *Earth*; as the *Sun* is father of light, and the *Earth* the mother and nurse of men. The *Greeks* were to offer a third to *Jupiter*, perhaps to *Jupiter Xenius* because the *Trojans* had broken the laws of hospitality: On which account we find *Menelaus* afterwards invoking him in the combate with *Paris*. That these were the powers to which they sacrific'd, appears by their being attested by name in the oath, v. 346, *etc.*

153. *The nations hear, with rising hopes possest.*] It seem'd no more than what the reader would reasonably expect, in the narration of this long war, that a period might have been put to it by the single danger of the parties chiefly concern'd, *Paris* and *Menelaus*. *Homer* has therefore taken care toward the beginning of his Poem to obviate that objection; and contriv'd such a method to render this combate of no effect, as should naturally make way for all the ensuing battels, without any future prospect of a determination but by the sword. It is farther worth observing, in what manner he has improved into Poetry the common history of this action, if (as one may imagine) it was the same with that we have in the second book of *Dictys Cretensis*. When Paris (says he) *being wounded by the spear of* Menelaus *fell to the ground, just as his adversary was rushing upon him with his sword, he was shot by an arrow from* Pandarus, *which prevented his revenge in the moment he was going to take it. Immediately on the sight of this perfidious action, the* Greeks *rose in a tumult; the* Trojans *rising at the same time, came on,* *and rescued* Paris *from his enemy. Homer* has with great art and invention mingled all this with the marvellous, and rais'd it in the air of fable. The *Goddess of Love* rescues her favourite; *Jupiter* debates whether or no the war shall end by the defeat of *Paris*; *Juno* is for the continuance of it; *Minerva* incites *Pandarus* to break the truce, who thereupon shoots at *Menelaus*. This heightens the grandeur of the action without destroying the verisimilitude, diversifies the poem, and exhibits a fine moral; that whatever seems in the world the effect of common causes, is really owing to the decree and disposition of the Gods.

165. *Mean while to beauteous* Helen, &c.] The following part, where we have the first sight of *Helena*, is what I cannot think inferior to any in the Poem. The reader has naturally an aversion to this pernicious beauty, and is apt enough to wonder at the *Greeks* for endeavouring to recover her at such an expence. But her amiable behaviour here, the secret wishes that rise in favour of her rightful Lord, her tenderness for her parents and relations, the relentings of her soul for the mischiefs her beauty had been the cause of, the confusion she appears in, the veiling her face and dropping a tear, are particulars so beautifully natural, as to make every reader no less than *Menelaus* himself, inclin'd to forgive her at least, if not to love her. We are afterwards confirm'd in this partiality by the sentiment of the old counsellors upon the sight of her, which one would think *Homer* put into their mouths with that very view: We excuse her no more than *Priam* does himself, and all those do who felt the calamities she occasion'd: And this regard for her is heighten'd by all she says herself; in which there is scarce a word that is not big with repentance and good-nature.

170. *The golden web her own sad story crown'd.*] This is a very agreeable fiction, to represent *Helena* weaving in a large veil, or piece of tapestry, the story of the *Trojan* war. One would think that *Homer* inherited this veil, and that his *Iliad* is only an explication of that admirable piece of art.   *Dacier.*

201. *Like grasshoppers.*] This is one of the justest and most natural images in the world, tho' there have been cricks of so little taste as to object to it as a mean one. The garrulity so common to old men, their delight in associating with each other, the feeble sound of their voices, the pleasure they take in a sun-shiny day, the effects of decay in their chillness, leanness, and scarcity of blood, are all circumstances exactly parallel'd in this comparison. To make it yet more proper to the old men of *Troy*, *Eustathius* has observ'd that *Homer* found a hint for this simile in the *Trojan* story, where *Tithon* was feign'd to have been transform'd into a grasshopper in his old age, perhaps on account of his being so exhausted by years as to have nothing left him but voice. *Spondanus* wonders that *Homer* should apply to grasshoppers ὄπα λειριόεσσαν, a *sweet voice*, whereas that of these animals is harsh and untuneful; and he is contented to come off with a very poor evasion of *Homero fingere quidlibet fas fuit*. But *Hesychius* rightly observes that λειριόεσσαν signifies ἁπαλός, *tener* or *gracilis*, as well as *suavis*. The sense is certainly much better, and the simile more truly preserv'd by this interpretation, which is here follow'd in translating it *feeble*. However it may be alledg'd in defence of the common versions, and of Madam *Dacier*'s (who has turn'd it *Harmonieuse*) that tho' *Virgil* gives the epithet *raucæ* to *Cicadæ*, yet the *Greek* poets frequently describe the grasshopper as a musical creature, particularly *Anacreon*, and *Theocritus Idyl*. 1. where a shepherd praises another's singing by telling him,

> Τέττιγος ἐπεὶ τύγε φέρτερον ἄδεις.

It is remarkable that Mr. *Hobbes* has omitted this beautiful Simile.

203. *These, when the* Spartan *Fair* [sic] *approach'd.*] Madam *Dacier* is of opinion there was never a greater panegyrick upon *beauty* than what *Homer* has found the art to give it in this place. An assembly of venerable old counsellors, who had suffer'd all the calamities of a tedious war, and were consulting upon the methods to put a conclusion to it, seeing the only cause of it approaching towards them, are struck with her charms, and cry out, *No wonder!* &c. Nevertheless they afterwards recollect themselves, and conclude to part with her for the publick safety. If *Homer* had carry'd these old mens admiration any farther, he had been guilty of outraging nature, and offending against probability. The old are capable of being touch'd with beauty by the eye; but age secures them from the tyranny of passion, and the effect is but transitory, for prudence soon regains its dominion over them. *Homer* always goes as far as he should, but constantly stops just where he ought.   *Dacier.*

The same writer compares to this the speech of *Holofernes*'s Soldiers on the sight of *Judith, ch.* 10. v. 18. But tho' there be a resemblance in the words, the beauty is no way parallel; the grace of this consisting in the age and character of those who speak it. There is something very gallant upon the beauty of *Helen* in one of *Lucian*'s dialogues. *Mercury* shews *Menippus* the skulls of several fine women; and when the philosopher is moralizing upon that of *Helen*: *Was it for this a thousand ships sail'd from* Greece, *so many brave men dy'd, and so many cities were destroy'd? My friend* (says *Mercury*) *'tis true; but what you behold is only her skull; you would have been of their opinion, and have done the very same thing, had you seen her* face.

211. *The good old* Priam.] The character of a benevolent old man is very well preserv'd in *Priam*'s behaviour to *Helena*. Upon the confusion he observes her in, he encourages her by attributing the misfortunes of the war to the Gods alone, and not to her fault. This sentiment is also very agreeable to the natural piety of old age; those who have had the longest experience of human accidents and events, being most inclin'd to ascribe the disposal of all things to the will of heaven. It is this piety that renders *Priam* a favourite of *Jupiter*, (as we find in the beginning of the fourth book) which for some time delays the destruction of *Troy*; while his soft nature and indulgence for his children makes him continue a war which ruins him. These are the two principal points of *Priam*'s character, tho' there are several lesser particularities, among which we may observe the curiosity and inquisitive humour of old age, which gives occasion to the following episode.

219. *And say, what chief* [sic] *is he?*] This view of the *Grecian* leaders from the walls of *Troy*, is justly look'd upon as an episode of great beauty, as well as a masterpiece of conduct in *Homer*; who by this means acquaints the readers with the figure and qualifications of each hero in a more lively and agreeable manner. Several great Poets have been engag'd by the beauty of this passage to an imitation of it. In the seventh book of *Statius*, *Phorbas* standing with *Antigone* on the tower of *Thebes*, shews her the Forces as they were drawn up, and describes their commanders who were neighbouring Princes of *Bœotia*. It is also imitated by *Tasso* in his third book, where *Erminia* from the walls of *Jerusalem* points out the chief warriors to the King; tho' the latter part is perhaps copied too closely and minutely; for he describes *Godfrey* to be of a port that bespeaks him a Prince, the next of somewhat a lower stature, a third renown'd for his wisdom, and then another is distinguish'd by the largeness of his chest and breadth of his

shoulders: Which are not only the very particulars, but in the very order of *Homer*'s.

But however this manner of introduction has been admir'd, there have not been wanting some exceptions to a particular or two. *Scaliger* asks, how it happens that *Priam*, after nine years siege, should be yet unacquainted with the faces of the *Grecian* leaders? This was an old cavil, as appears by the *scholia* that pass under the name of *Didymus*, where it is very well answer'd, that *Homer* has just before taken care to tell us the heroes had put off their armour on this occasion of the truce, which had conceal'd their persons 'till now. Others have objected to *Priam*'s not knowing *Ulysses*, who (as it appears afterwards) had been at *Troy* on an embassy. The answer is, that this might happen either from the dimness of *Priam*'s sight, or defect of his memory, or from the change of *Ulysses*'s features since that time.

227. *Before thy presence.*] *Helen* is so overwhelmed with grief and shame, that she is unable to give a direct Answer to *Priam* without first humbling herself before him, acknowledging her crime, and testifying her repentance. And she no sooner answers by naming *Agamemnon*, but her sorrows renew at the name; *He was once my brother! but I am now a wretch unworthy to call him so.*

236. *Great in the war, and great in arts of sway.*] This was the verse which *Alexander* the great prefer'd to all others in *Homer*, and which he propos'd as the pattern of his own actions, as including whatever can be desired in a Prince.   *Plut. Orat. de fort. Alex.* 1.

240. *Extoll'd the happy Prince.*] It was very natural for *Priam* on this occasion, to compare the declining condition of his kingdom with the flourishing state of *Agamemnon*'s, and to oppose his own misery (who had lost most of his sons and his bravest warriours) to the felicity of the other, in being yet master of so gallant an army. After this the humour of old age breaks out, in the narration of what armies he had formerly seen, and bore a part in the command of; as well as what feats of valour he had then performed. Besides which, this praise of the *Greeks* from the mouth of an enemy, was no small encomium of *Homer*'s countrymen.

258. *From rank to rank he moves.*] The vigilance and inspection of *Ulysses* were very proper marks to distinguish him, and agree with his character of a wise man no less, than the grandeur and majesty before described are conformable to that of *Agamemnon*, as the supreme ruler; whereas we find *Ajax* afterwards taken notice of only for his bulk, as a heavy Hero without parts or authority. This decorum is observable.

271. *I knew their persons*, &c.] In this view of the leaders of the army, it had been an oversight in *Homer* to have taken no notice of *Menelaus*, who was not only one of the principal of them, but was immediately to engage the observation of the reader in the single combate. On the other hand, it had been a high indecorum to have made *Helena* speak of him. He has therefore put his praises into the mouth of *Antenor*; which was also a more artful way than to have presented him to the eye of *Priam* in the same manner with the rest: It appears from hence, what a regard he has had both to decency and variety in the conduct of his poem.

This passage concerning the different eloquence of *Menelaus* and *Ulysses* is inexpressibly just and beautiful. The close, *Laconick* conciseness of the one, is finely opposed to the copious, vehement, and penetrating oratory of the other; which is so exquisitely describ'd in the simile of the snow, falling fast, and sinking deep. For it is in this the beauty of the comparison consists according to *Quintilian, l.* 12. *c.* 10. [64] *In Ulysse facundiam & magnitudinem junxit, cui orationem nivibus hybernis copia verborum atque impetu parem tribuit.* [He gives to the eloquence of Ulysses a mighty voice and a vehemence of oratory equal to the snows of winter in the abundance and the vigour of its words.] We may set in the same light with these the character of *Nestor*'s eloquence, which consisted in softness and persuasiveness, and is therefore (in contradistinction to this of *Ulysses*) compar'd to honey which drops gently and slowly: a manner of speech extremely natural to a benevolent old man, such as *Nestor* is represented. *Ausonius* has elegantly distinguish'd these three kinds of oratory in the following verses.

> *Dulcem* in *paucis* ut Plisthenidem,
> Et *torrentem* ceu Dulichii
>   *Ningida* dicta.
> Et *mellitæ* nectare vocis
> Dulcia fatu verba canentem
>   Nestora regem.

[Sweet in few words, like the son of Plisthenes (i.e. Menelaüs), and

forcefully eloquent like the words of the Dulichian (i.e. Odysseus) –
words that fall like snow. –
And like King Nestor singing words sweet – on account of the nectar
of his honeyed voice – in their utterance.]*

278. *He spoke no more than just the thing he ought.*] *Chapman*, in his
notes on this place and on the second book, has described *Menelaus* as
a character of ridicule and simplicity. He takes advantage from the
word λιγέως here made use of, to interpret that of the *shrillness* of his
voice, which was apply'd to the acuteness of his sense; He observes
that this sort of voice is a mark of a fool; that *Menelaus*'s coming to his
brother's feast uninvited in the second book has occasion'd a proverb
of folly; that the excuse *Homer* himself makes for it (because his
brother might forget to invite him thro' much business) is purely
ironical; that the epithet ἀρηΐφιλος, which is often apply'd to him,
should not be translated *warlike*, but one who had *an affectation of
loving war*. In short, that he was a weak Prince, play'd upon by others,
short in speech, and of a bad pronunciation, valiant only by fits, and
sometimes stumbling upon good matter in his speeches, as may
happen to the most slender capacity. This is one of the mysteries
which that translator boasts to have found in *Homer*. But as it is no
way consistent with the art of the Poet, to draw the person in whose
behalf he engages the world, in such a manner as no regard should be
conceiv'd for him; we must endeavour to rescue him from this
misrepresentation. First then, the present passage is taken by antiquity
in general to be apply'd not to his pronunciation, but his eloquence. So
Ausonius in the foregoing citation, and *Cicero de claris Oratoribus*
[*Brutus*, xiii. 50]: *Menelaum ipsum dulcem illum quidem tradit Homerus,
sed pauca loquentem.* [Homer relates that the famous Menelaus himself
was a pleasing speaker, but a laconic one.] And *Quintilian l.* 12. *c.* 10.
[64]. *Homerus, brevem cum animi jucunditate, & propriam* (*id enim est
non errare verbis*) & *carentem supervacuis, eloquentiam Menelao dedit*,
&c. [Homer assigns to Menelaus an eloquence, terse and pleasing,
exact (for that is what is meant by 'making no errours in words') and
devoid of all redundance.] Secondly, tho' his coming uninvited may
have occasion'd a jesting proverb, it may naturally be accounted for on
the principle of *brotherly love*, which so visibly characterises both him

---

* Pope has slightly misquoted the Latin.

and *Agamemnon* throughout the poem. Thirdly, ἀρηΐφιλος may import a love of war, but not an ungrounded affectation. Upon the whole, his character is by no means contemptible, tho' not of the most shining nature. He is called indeed in the 17th *Iliad* μαλθακός αἰχμητής, *a soft warriour*, or one whose strength is of the second rate, and so his brother thought him when he prefer'd nine before him to fight with *Hector* in the 7th book. But on the other hand, his courage gives him a considerable figure in conquering *Paris*, defending the body of *Patroclus*, rescuing *Ulysses*, wounding *Helenus*, killing *Euphorbus*, &c. He is full of resentment for his private injuries, which brings him to the war with a spirit of revenge in the second book, makes him blaspheme *Jupiter* in the third, when *Paris* escapes him, and curse the *Grecians* in the seventh when they hesitate to accept *Hector*'s challenge. But this also is qualify'd with a compassion for those who suffer in his cause, which he every where manifests upon proper occasions; and with an industry to gratify others, as when he obeys *Ajax* in the seventeenth book, and goes upon his errand to find *Antilochus*, with some other condescensions of the like nature. Thus his character is compos'd of qualities which give him no uneasy superiority over others while he wants their assistance, and mingled with such as make him amiable enough to obtain it.

280. *His modest eyes*, &c.] This behaviour of *Ulysses* is copy'd by *Ovid*, *Met.* 13.

> *Astitit, atque oculos parum tellure moratos*
> *Sustulit –.*

[He stood up and, after pausing and looking at the ground for a while, he lifted up his eyes.]

What follows in the *Greek* translated word for word runs thus: *He seem'd like a fool, you would have thought him in a rage, or a madman.* How oddly this would appear in our language, I appeal to those who have read *Ogilby*. The whole period means no more than to describe that behaviour which is commonly remarkable in a modest and sensible man, who speaks in publick: His diffidence and respect gives him at his first rising a sort of confusion, which is not indecent, and which serves but the more to heighten the surprize and esteem of those who hear him.

309. *Perhaps their swords.*] This is another stroke of *Helen*'s concern: The sense of her crime is perpetually afflicting her, and awakes upon every occasion. The lines that follow, wherein *Homer* gives us to understand that *Castor* and *Pollux* were now dead, are finely introduc'd and in the spirit of poetry; the muse is suppos'd to know every thing, past and to come, and to see things distant as well as present.

315. *Meantime the heralds*, &c.] It may not be unpleasing to the reader to compare the description of the ceremonies of the league in the following part, with that of *Virgil* in the twelfth book. The preparations, the procession of the Kings, and their congress, are much more solemn and poetical in the latter; the oath and adjurations are equally noble in both.

342. *The curling hair.*] We have here the whole ceremonial of the solemn oath, as it was observ'd anciently by the nations our Author describes. I must take this occasion of remarking that we might spare our selves the trouble of reading most books of *Grecian antiquities*, only by being well vers'd in *Homer*. They are generally bare transcriptions of him, but with this unnecessary addition, that after having quoted any thing in verse, they say the same over again in prose. The *Antiquitates Homericæ* of *Feithius* may serve as an instance of this. What my Lord *Bacon* observes of authors in general, is particularly applicable to these of Antiquities, that they write for ostentation not for instruction, and that their works are perpetual repetitions.

361. *And age to age record the signal day.*] ἥ τε καὶ ἐσσομένοισι μετ᾽ ἀνθρώποισι πέληται. This seems the natural sense of the line, and not as Madam *Dacier* renders it, *the tribute shall be paid to the posterity of the* Greeks *for ever*. I think she is single in that explication, the majority of the interpreters taking it to signify that the victory of the *Grecians* and this pecuniary acknowledgment *should be recorded to all Posterity*. If it means any more than this, at least it cannot come up to the sense Madam *Dacier* gives it; for a nation put under perpetual tribute is rather enslaved, than received to friendship and alliance, which are the terms of *Agamemnon*'s speech. It seems rather to be a fine, demanded as a recompence for the expences of the war, which being made over to the *Greeks*, should *remain to their posterity for ever*; that is to say, which they should never be molested for, or which should never be redemanded in any age as a case of injury. The phrase is the same we use at this day, when any purchase or grant is at once made over to a man *and his heirs for ever*. With this will agree the *Scholiast*'s note, which tells us the mulct was reported to have been half the goods then in the besieg'd city.

364. *The chief the tender victims slew.*] One of the grand objections which the ignorance of some moderns has rais'd against *Homer*, is what they call a defect in the manners of his heroes. They are shock'd to find his Kings employ'd in such offices as slaughtering of beasts, *&c.* But they forget that sacrificing was the most solemn act of religion, and that Kings of old in most nations were also Chief-priests. This, among other objections of the same kind, the reader may see answered in the Preface.

433. *Give me, great Jove.*] *Homer* puts a prayer in the mouth of *Menelaus*, but none in *Paris*'s: *Menelaus* is the person injur'd and innocent, and may therefore apply to God for justice; but *Paris*, who is the criminal, remains silent.   *Spondanus.*

447. *The brittle steel, unfaithful to his hand, Broke short* – This verse is cut to express the Thing it describes, the snapping short of the sword. 'Tis the observation of *Eustathius* on this line of the original, that we do not only see the action, but imagine we hear the sound of the breaking sword in that of the words. Τριχθά τε καὶ τετραχθὰ διατρυφὲν ἔκπεσε χειρός. And that *Homer* design'd it, may appear from his having twice put in the Θῆτα (which was a letter unnecessary) to cause this harshness in the verse. As this beauty could not be preserv'd in our language, it is endeavour'd in the translation to supply it with something parallel.

479. *The Goddess softly shook,* &c.] *Venus* having convey'd *Paris* in safety to his chamber, goes to *Helena*, who had been spectator of his defeat, in order to draw her to his love. The better to bring this about, she first takes upon her the most proper form in the world, that of a favourite servant-maid, and awakens her passion by representing to her the beautiful figure of his person. Next, assuming her own shape, she frightens her into a complyance, notwithstanding all the struggles of *shame*, *fear*, and *anger*, which break out in her speech to the goddess. This machine is allegorical, and means no more than the power of *love* triumphing over all the considerations of *honour*, *ease*, and *safety*. It has an excellent effect as to the poem, in preserving still in some degree our good opinion of *Helena*, whom we look upon with compassion, as constrain'd by a superior power, and whose speech tends to justify her in the eye of the reader.

487. *She spoke, and* Helen's *secret Soul was mov'd.*] Nothing is more fine than this; the first thought of *Paris*'s beauty overcomes (unawares to herself) the contempt she had that moment conceiv'd of him upon his overthrow. This motion is but natural, and before she perceives the Deity. When the affections of a woman have been thoroughly gained, tho' they may be alienated for a while, they soon return upon her. Homer *knew* (says Madam *Dacier*) *what a woman is capable of, who had once lov'd.*

507. *For me, to lawless love no longer led, I scorn the Coward.*] We have here another branch of the female character, which is, to be ruled in their attaches by *success*. *Helen* finding the victory belong'd to *Menelaus*, accuses herself secretly of having forsaken him for the other, and immediately entertains a high opinion of the man she had once despised. One may add, that the fair sex are generally admirers of courage, and naturally friends to great soldiers. *Paris* was no stranger to this disposition in them, and had formerly endeavour'd to give her that opinion of himself; as appears from her reproach of him afterwards.

515. *Should* Venus *leave thee, ev'ry charm must fly.*] This was the most dreadful of all threats, loss of beauty and of reputation. *Helen*, who had been proof to the personal appearance of the Goddess, and durst even reproach her with bitterness just before, yields to this, and obeys all the dictates of love.

531. *She turn'd away Her glowing Eyes.*] This interview of the two lovers, plac'd opposite to each other, and overlook'd by *Venus*, *Paris* gazing on *Helena*, she turning away her eyes shining at once with anger and love, are particulars finely drawn, and painted up to all the life of nature. *Eustathius* imagines she look'd aside in the consciousness of her own weakness, as apprehending that the beauty of *Paris* might cause her to relent. Her bursting out into passion and reproaches while she is in this state of Mind, is no ill picture of frailty; *Venus* (as Madam *Dacier* observes) does not leave her, and fondness will immediately succeed to these reproaches.

543. *Ah cease, divinely fair.*] This answer of *Paris* is the only one he could possibly have made with any success in his circumstance. There was no other method to reconcile her to him, but that which is generally most powerful with the sex, and which *Homer* (who was learned every way) here makes use of.

551. *Not thus I lov'd thee.*] However *Homer* may be admired for his conduct in this passage, I find a general outcry against Paris on this occasion. *Plutarch* has led the way in his treatise of reading Poets, by remarking it as a most heinous act of incontinence in him to go to bed to his Lady in the *day-time*. Among the commentators the most violent is the moral expositor *Spondanus*, who will not so much as allow him to say a civil thing to *Helen. Mollis, effœminatus, & spurcus ille adulter, nihil de libidine sua imminutum dicit, sed nunc magis ea corripi quam unquam alias, ne quidem cum primum ea ipsi dedit (Latini ita recte exprimunt* τὸ μίσγεσθαι *in re venerea) in Insula* Cranaë. *Cum alioqui homines primi concubitus soleant esse ardentiores.* [A soft, effeminate, and filthy adulterer, he says that none of his lust is diminished, but that he is captivated now more than at any other time – even more than when she first 'gave herself to him' (as the Latins decorously refer to sexual intercourse) on the island Cranaë. Since men's passions tend to be more fully aroused in their first sexual encounter.] I could not deny the reader the diversion of this remark, nor *Spondanus* the glory of his zeal, who was but two and twenty when it was written. Madam *Dacier* is also very severe upon *Paris*, but for a reason more natural to a Lady. She is of opinion that the passion of the lover would scarce have been so excessive as he here describes it, but for fear of losing his mistress immediately, as foreseeing the *Greeks* would demand her. One may answer to this lively remark, that *Paris* having nothing to say for himself, was obliged to testify an uncommon ardour for his Lady, at a time when compliments were to pass instead of reasons. I hope to be excus'd if (in revenge for her remark upon our sex) I observe upon the behaviour of *Helen* throughout this book, which gives a pretty natural picture of the manners of theirs. We see her first in Tears, repentant, cover'd with confusion at the sight of *Priam*, and secretly inclin'd to return to her former spouse. The disgrace of *Paris* increases her dislike of him; she rails, she reproaches, she wishes his death; and after all, is prevail'd upon by one kind compliment, and yields to his embraces. Methinks when this Lady's observation and mine are laid together, the best that can be made of them is to conclude, that since both the sexes have their frailties, it would be well for each to forgive the other.

It is worth looking backward, to observe the *allegory* here carry'd on with respect to *Helena*, who lives thro' this whole book in a whirl of passions, and is agitated by turns with sentiments of honour and love. The Goddesses made use of, to cast the appearance of fable over the story, are *Iris* and *Venus*. When *Helen* is call'd to the tower to behold her former friends, *Iris* the messenger of *Juno* (the Goddess of Honour) is sent for her; and when invited to the bedchamber of *Paris*, *Venus* is to beckon her out of the company. The forms they take to carry on these different affairs, are properly chosen: the one assuming the person of the daughter of *Antenor*, who press'd most for her being restor'd to *Menelaus*; the other the shape of an old maid, who was privy to the intrigue with *Paris* from the beginning. And in the consequences, as the one inspires the love of her former empire, friends and country; so the other instills the dread of being cast off by all if she forsook her second choice, and causes the return of her tenderness to *Paris*. But if she has a struggle for Honour, she is in a bondage of love; which gives the story its turn that way, and makes *Venus* oftner appear than *Iris*. There is in one place a lover to be protected, in another a love-quarrel to be made up, in both which the Goddess is kindly officious. She conveys *Paris* to *Troy* when he had escap'd the enemy; which may signify his love for his mistress, that hurry'd him away to justify himself before her. She softens and terrifies *Helen*, in order to make up the breach between them: And even when that affair is finished, we do not find the Poet dismisses her from the chamber, whatever privacies the lovers had a mind to: In which circumstance he seems to draw aside the veil of his Allegory, and to let the reader at last into the meaning of it, that the Goddess of Love has been all the while nothing more than the Passion of it.

553. *When first entranc'd in* Cranaë's *isle.*] It is in the Original Νήσῳ δ' ἐν Κραναῇ ἐμίγην φιλότητι, καὶ εὐνῇ. The true sense of which is express'd in the translation. I cannot but take notice of a small piece of *Pruderie* in Madam *Dacier*, who is exceeding careful of *Helen*'s character. She turns this passage as if *Paris* had only her *consent to be her husband* in this island. *Pausanius* explains this line in another manner, and tells us it was here that *Paris* had first the enjoyment of her, that in gratitude for his happiness he built a Temple of *Venus Migonitis*, the mingler or coupler, and that the neighbouring coast where it was erected was call'd *Migonian* from μιγῆναι, *a miscendo*.

Paus. Laconicis.

THE
FOURTH BOOK
OF THE
ILIAD

The ARGUMENT

The Breach of the Truce, and the first Battel

The Gods deliberate in council concerning the Trojan *war: They agree upon the continuation of it, and* Jupiter *sends down* Minerva *to break the Truce. She persuades* Pandarus *to aim an arrow at* Menelaus, *who is wounded, but cured by* Machaon. *In the mean time some of the Trojan troops attack the* Greeks. Agamemnon *is distinguished in all the parts of a good General; he reviews the troops, and exhorts the Leaders, some by praises and others by reproofs.* Nestor *is particularly celebrated for his military discipline. The battel joins, and great numbers are slain on both sides.*

The same day continues thro' this, as thro' the last book (as it does also thro' the two following, and almost to the end of the seventh book.) The scene is wholly in the field before Troy.

And now *Olympus*' shining gates unfold;
The Gods, with *Jove*, assume their Thrones of Gold:
Immortal *Hebè*, fresh with bloom divine,
The golden goblet crowns with purple wine:
5   While the full bowls flow round, the pow'rs employ
Their careful eyes on long-contended *Troy*.
   When *Jove*, dispos'd to tempt *Saturnia*'s spleen,
Thus wak'd the fury of his partial Queen.
Two pow'rs divine the son of *Atreus* aid,
10 Imperial *Juno*, and the martial maid;
But high in heav'n they sit, and gaze from far,
The tame spectators of his deeds of war.
Not thus fair *Venus* helps her favour'd knight,
The Queen of Pleasures shares the toils of fight,
15 Each danger wards, and constant in her care
Saves in the moment of the last despair.
Her act has rescu'd *Paris*' forfeit life,
Tho' great *Atrides* gain'd the glorious strife.
Then say ye pow'rs! what signal issue waits
20 To crown this deed, and finish all the Fates?
Shall heav'n by peace the bleeding kingdoms spare,
Or rowze the Furies, and awake the war?
Yet, would the Gods for human good provide,
Atrides soon might gain his beauteous bride,
25 Still *Priam*'s walls in peaceful honours grow,
And thro' his gates the crowding nations flow.
   Thus while he spoke, the Queen of Heav'n, enrag'd
And Queen of War, in a close consult engag'd.

Apart they sit, their deep designs employ,
And meditate the future woes of *Troy*.   30
Tho' secret anger swell'd *Minerva*'s breast,
The prudent Goddess yet her wrath supprest;
But *Juno*, impotent of passion, broke
Her sullen silence, and with fury spoke.

    Shall then, O tyrant of th' æthereal reign!   35
My schemes, my labours, and my hopes be vain?
Have I, for this, shook *Ilion* with alarms,
Assembled nations, set two worlds in arms?
To spread the war, I flew from shore to shore;
Th' immortal coursers scarce the labour bore.   40
At length, ripe vengeance o'er their heads impends,
But *Jove* himself the faithless race defends:
Loth as thou art to punish lawless lust,
Not all the Gods are partial and unjust.

    The Sire whose thunder shakes the cloudy skies,   45
Sighs from his inmost soul, and thus replies;
Oh lasting rancour! oh insatiate hate
To *Phrygia*'s Monarch, and the *Phrygian* state!
What high offence has fir'd the wife of *Jove*,
Can wretched mortals harm the pow'rs above?   50
That *Troy*, and *Troy*'s whole Race thou woud'st
      confound,
And yon' fair structures level with the ground?
Haste, leave the skies, fulfil thy stern desire,
Burst all her gates, and wrap her walls in fire!
Let *Priam* bleed! If yet thou thirst for more,   55
Bleed all his sons, and *Ilion* float with gore,
To boundless vengeance the wide realm be giv'n,
'Till vast destruction glut the Queen of Heav'n!
So let it be, and *Jove* his peace enjoy,
When heav'n no longer hears the name of *Troy*.   60
But should this arm prepare to wreak our hate
On thy lov'd realms whose guilt demands their fate,
Presume not thou the lifted bolt to stay,
Remember *Troy*, and give the vengeance way.
For know, of all the num'rous towns that rise   65
Beneath the rolling sun, and starry skies,

Which Gods have rais'd, or earth-born men enjoy;
None stands so dear to *Jove* as sacred *Troy*.
No Mortals merit more distinguish'd grace
70 Than god-like *Priam*, or than *Priam*'s race.
Still to our name their hecatombs expire,
And altars blaze with unextinguish'd fire.

At this the Goddess roll'd her radiant eyes,
Then on the Thund'rer fix'd them, and replies.
75 Three towns are *Juno*'s on the *Grecian* plains,
More dear than all th' extended earth contains,
Mycenæ, *Argos*, and the *Spartan* wall;
These thou may'st raze, nor I forbid their fall:
'Tis not in me the vengeance to remove;
80 The crime's sufficient that they share my love.
Of pow'r superior why should I complain?
Resent I may, but must resent in vain.
Yet some distinction *Juno* might require,
Sprung, with thy self, from one celestial Sire,
85 A Goddess born to share the realms above,
And styl'd the consort of the thund'ring *Jove*.
Nor thou a wife and sister's right deny;
Let both consent, and both by turns comply:
So shall the Gods our joint decrees obey,
90 And heav'n shall act as we direct the way.
See ready *Pallas* waits thy high commands,
To raise in arms the *Greek* and *Phrygian* Bands;
Their sudden friendship by her arts may cease,
And the proud *Trojans* first infringe the peace.

95 The Sire of men and Monarch of the sky
Th' advice approv'd, and bade *Minerva* fly,
Dissolve the league, and all her arts employ
To make the breach the faithless act of *Troy*.

Fir'd with the charge, she head-long urg'd her flight,
100 And shot like light'ning from *Olympus*' height.
As the red comet from *Saturnius* sent
To fright the nations with a dire portent,
(A fatal sign to armies on the plain,
Or trembling sailors on the wintry main)
105 With sweeping glories glides along in air,
And shakes the sparkles from its blazing hair:

Between both armies thus, in open sight,
Shot the bright Goddess in a trail of light.
With eyes erect the gazing hosts admire
The pow'r descending, and the heav'ns on fire!   110
The Gods (they cry'd) the Gods this signal sent,
And fate now labours with some vast event:
Jove seals the league, or bloodier scenes prepares;
Jove, the great arbiter of peace and wars!

    They said, while *Pallas* thro' the *Trojan* throng   115
(In shape a mortal) pass'd disguis'd along.
Like bold *Laödocus*, her course she bent,
Who from *Antenor* trac'd his high descent.
Amidst the ranks *Lycaön*'s son she found,
The warlike *Pandarus*, for strength renown'd;   120
Whose squadrons, led from black *Æsepus*' flood,
With flaming shields in martial circle stood.

    To him the Goddess: *Phrygian*! can'st thou hear
A well–tim'd counsel with a willing ear?
What praise were thine, cou'd'st thou direct thy dart,   125
Amidst his triumph, to the *Spartan*'s heart?
What gifts from *Troy*, from *Paris* wou'd'st thou gain,
Thy country's foe, the *Grecian* glory slain?
Then seize th'occasion, dare the mighty deed,
Aim at his breast, and may that aim succeed!   130
But first, to speed the shaft, address thy vow
To *Lycian Phœbus* with the silver bow,
And swear the firstlings of thy flock to pay
On *Zelia*'s altars, to the God of day.

    He heard, and madly at the motion pleas'd,   135
His polish'd bow with hasty rashness seiz'd.
'Twas form'd of horn, and smooth'd with artful toil;
A mountain goat resign'd the shining spoil,
Who pierc'd long since beneath his arrows bled;
The stately quarry on the cliffs lay dead,   140
And sixteen palms his brows large honours spread:
The workman join'd, and shap'd the bended horns,
And beaten gold each taper point adorns.
This, by the *Greeks* unseen, the warriour bends,
Screen'd by the shields of his surrounding friends.   145
There meditates the mark; and couching low,
Fits the sharp arrow to the well–strung bow.

One from a hundred feather'd deaths he chose,
Fated to wound, and cause of future woes.
150 Then offers vows with hecatombs to crown
Apollo's altars in his native town.
     Now with full force the yielding horn he bends,
Drawn to an arch, and joins the doubling ends;
Close to his breast he strains the nerve below,
155 'Till the barb'd point approach the circling bow;
Th' impatient weapon whizzes on the wing,
Sounds the tough horn, and twangs the quiv'ring string.
     But thee, Atrides! in that dang'rous hour
The Gods forget not, nor thy guardian pow'r.
160 Pallas assists, and (weaken'd in its force)
Diverts the weapon from its destin'd course;
So from her babe, when slumber seals his eye,
The watchful mother wafts th' envenom'd fly.
Just where his belt with golden buckles join'd,
165 Where linen folds the double corslet lin'd,
She turn'd the shaft, which hissing from above,
Pass'd the broad belt, and thro' the corslet drove;
The folds it pierc'd, the plaited linen tore,
And raz'd the skin and drew the purple gore.
170 As when some stately trappings are decreed
To grace a monarch on his bounding steed,
A nymph in Caria or Mæonia bred,
Stains the pure iv'ry with a lively red;
With equal lustre various colours vie,
175 The shining whiteness and the Tyrian dye:
So, great Atrides! show'd thy sacred blood,
As down thy snowy thigh distill'd the streaming flood.
With horrour seiz'd, the King of Men descry'd
The shaft infix'd, and saw the gushing tide:
180 Nor less the Spartan fear'd, before he found
The shining barb appear above the wound.
Then, with a sigh that heav'd his manly breast,
The royal brother thus his grief exprest,
And grasp'd his hand; while all the Greeks around
185 With answering sighs return'd the plaintive sound.
     Oh dear as life! did I for this agree
The solemn truce, a fatal truce to thee!

Wert thou expos'd to all the hostile train,
To fight for *Greece*, and conquer, to be slain?
The race of *Trojans* in thy ruin join,   190
And faith is scorn'd by all the perjur'd line.
Not thus our vows, confirm'd with wine and gore,
Those hands we plighted, and those oaths we swore,
Shall all be vain: When heav'n's revenge is slow,
Jove but prepares to strike the fiercer blow.   195
The day shall come, that great avenging day,
Which *Troy*'s proud glories in the dust shall lay,
When *Priam*'s pow'rs and *Priam*'s self shall fall,
And one prodigious ruin swallow all.
I see the God, already, from the pole   200
Bare his red arm, and bid the thunder roll;
I see th' eternal all his fury shed,
And shake his *Ægis* o'er their guilty head.
Such mighty woes on perjur'd princes wait;
But thou, alas! deserv'st a happier fate.   205
Still must I mourn the period of thy days,
And only mourn, without my share of praise?
Depriv'd of thee, the heartless *Greeks* no more
Shall dream of conquests on the hostile shore;
Troy seiz'd of *Helen*, and our glory lost,   210
Thy bones shall moulder on a foreign coast:
While some proud *Trojan* thus insulting cries,
(And spurns the dust where *Menelaüs* lies)
'Such are the trophies *Greece* from *Ilion* brings,
And such the conquests of her King of Kings!   215
Lo his proud vessels scatter'd o'er the main,
And unreveng'd, his mighty brother slain.'
Oh! e're that dire disgrace shall blast my fame,
O'erwhelm me, earth! and hide a monarch's shame.

He said: A leader's and a brother's fears   220
Possess his soul, which thus the *Spartan* chears:
Let not thy words the warmth of *Greece* abate;
The feeble dart is guiltless of my fate:
Stiff with the rich embroider'd work around,
My vary'd belt repell'd the flying wound.   225
To whom the King. My brother and my friend,
Thus, always thus, may heav'n thy life defend!

Now seek some skilful hand whose pow'rful art
May stanch th' effusion and extract the dart.
230 Herald, be swift, and bid *Machaön* bring
His speedy succour to the *Spartan* King;
Pierc'd with a winged Shaft (the deed of *Troy*)
The *Grecian*'s sorrow, and the *Dardan*'s joy.

With hasty zeal the swift *Talthybius* flies;
235 Thro' the thick files he darts his searching eyes,
And finds *Machaön*, where sublime he stands
In arms encircled with his native bands.
Then thus: *Machaön*, to the King repair,
His wounded brother claims thy timely care;
240 Pierc'd by some *Lycian* or *Dardanian* bow,
A grief to us, a triumph to the foe.

The heavy tidings griev'd the godlike man;
Swift to his succour thro' the ranks he ran:
The dauntless King yet standing firm he found,
245 And all the chiefs in deep concern around.
Where to the steely point the reed was join'd,
The shaft he drew, but left the head behind.
Strait the broad belt with gay embroid'ry grac'd
He loos'd; the corslet from his breast unbrac'd;
250 Then suck'd the blood, and sov'reign balm infus'd,
Which *Chiron* gave, and *Æsculapius* us'd.

While round the Prince the *Greeks* employ their care,
The *Trojans* rush tumultuous to the war;
Once more they glitter in refulgent arms,
255 Once more the fields are fill'd with dire alarms.
Nor had you seen the King of Men appear
Confus'd, unactive, or surpriz'd with fear;
But fond of glory, with severe delight,
His beating bosom claim'd the rising Fight.
260 No longer with his warlike steeds he stay'd,
Or press'd the car with polish'd brass inlay'd:
But left *Eurymedon* the reins to guide;
The fiery coursers snorted at his side.
On foot thro' all the martial ranks he moves,
265 And these encourages, and those reproves.
Brave Men! he cries (to such who boldly dare
Urge their swift steeds to face the coming war)

Your ancient valour on the foes approve;
Jove is with *Greece*, and let us trust in *Jove*.
'Tis not for us, but guilty *Troy* to dread,   270
Whose crimes sit heavy on her perjur'd head;
Her sons and matrons *Greece* shall lead in chains,
And her dead warriors strow the mournful plains.

    Thus with new ardour he the brave inspires;
Or thus the fearful with reproaches fires.   275
Shame to your country, scandal of your kind!
Born to the fate ye well deserve to find!
Why stand ye gazing round the dreadful plain,
Prepar'd for flight, but doom'd to fly in vain?
Confus'd and panting, thus, the hunted deer   280
Falls as he flies, a victim to his fear.
Still must ye wait the foes, and still retire,
'Till yon' tall vessels blaze with *Trojan* Fire?
Or trust ye, *Jove* a valiant foe shall chace,
To save a trembling, heartless, dastard race?   285

    This said, he stalk'd with ample strides along,
To *Crete*'s brave monarch and his martial throng;
High at their head he saw the chief appear,
And bold *Meriones* excite the rear.
At this the King his gen'rous joy exprest,   290
And clasp'd the warriour to his armed breast.
Divine *Idomeneus*! what thanks we owe
To worth like thine? what praise shall we bestow?
To thee the foremost honours are decreed,
First in the fight, and ev'ry graceful deed.   295
For this, in banquets, when the gen'rous bowls
Restore our blood, and raise the warriors souls,
Tho' all the rest with stated rules we bound,
Unmix'd, unmeasur'd are thy goblets crown'd.
Be still thyself; in arms a mighty name;   300
Maintain thy honours, and enlarge thy fame.

    To whom the *Cretan* thus his speech addrest;
Secure of me, O King! exhort the rest:
Fix'd to thy side, in ev'ry toil I share,
Thy firm associate in the day of war.   305
But let the signal be this moment giv'n;
To mix in fight is all I ask of heav'n.

The field shall prove how perjuries succeed,
And chains or death avenge their impious deed.

310   Charm'd with this heat, the King his course pursues,
And next the troops of either *Ajax* views:
In one firm orb the bands were rang'd around,
A cloud of heroes blacken'd all the ground.
Thus from the lofty promontory's brow

315 A swain surveys the gath'ring storm below;
Slow from the main the heavy vapours rise,
Spread in dim streams, and sail along the skies,
'Till black as night the swelling tempest shows,
The cloud condensing as the West-wind blows:

320 He dreads th' impending storm, and drives his flock
To the close covert of an arching rock.

    Such, and so thick, th' embattel'd squadrons stood,
With spears erect, a moving iron wood;
A shady light was shot from glimm'ring shields,

325 And their brown arms obscur'd the dusky fields.

    O heroes! worthy such a dauntless train,
Whose godlike virtue we but urge in vain,
(Exclaim'd the King) who raise your eager bands
With great examples more than loud commands.

330 Ah would the Gods but breathe in all the rest
Such souls as burn in your exalted breast!
Soon should our arms with just success be crown'd,
And *Troy*'s proud walls lie smoking on the ground.

    Then to the next the Gen'ral bends his course;

335 (His heart exults, and glories in his force)
There rev'rend *Nestor* ranks his *Pylian* bands,
And with inspiring eloquence commands,
With strictest order sets his train in arms,
The chiefs advises, and the soldiers warms.

340 *Alastor*, *Chromius*, *Hæmon* round him wait,
Bias the good, and *Pelagon* the great.
The horse and chariots to the front assign'd,
The foot (the strength of war) he rang'd behind;
The middle space suspected troops supply,

345 Inclos'd by both, nor left the pow'r to fly:
He gives command to curb the fiery steed,
Nor cause confusion, nor the ranks exceed;

Before the rest let none too rashly ride;
No strength nor skill, but just in time, be try'd:
The charge once made, no warriour turn the rein,   350
But fight, or fall; a firm, embody'd train.
He whom the fortune of the field shall cast
From forth his chariot, mount the next in haste;
Nor seek unpractis'd to direct the car,
Content with jav'lins to provoke the war.   355
Our great forefathers held this prudent course,
Thus rul'd their ardour, thus preserv'd their force,
By laws like these immortal conquests made,
And earth's proud tyrants low in ashes laid.

So spoke the master of the martial art,   360
And touch'd with transport great *Atrides*' heart.
Oh! had'st thou strength to match thy brave desires,
And nerves to second what thy soul inspires!
But wasting years that wither human race,
Exhaust thy spirits, and thy arms unbrace.   365
What once thou wert, oh ever might'st thou be!
And age the lot of any chief but thee.

Thus to th' experienc'd Prince *Atrides* cry'd;
He shook his hoary locks, and thus reply'd.
Well might I wish, could mortal wish renew   370
That strength which once in boiling youth I knew;
Such as I was, when *Ereuthalion* slain
Beneath this arm fell prostrate on the plain.
But heav'n its gifts not all at once bestows,
These years with wisdom crowns, with action those: 375
The field of combate fits the young and bold,
The solemn council best becomes the old:
To you the glorious conflict I resign,
Let sage advice, the palm of age, be mine.

He said. With joy the monarch march'd before,   380
And found *Menestheus* on the dusty shore,
With whom the firm *Athenian* Phalanx stands;
And next *Ulysses*, with his subject bands.
Remote their forces lay, nor knew so far
The peace infring'd, nor heard the sounds of war;   385
The tumult late begun, they stood intent
To watch the motion, dubious of th' event.

The King, who saw their squadrons yet unmov'd,
With hasty ardour thus the chiefs reprov'd.

390   Can *Peteus'* son forget a warriour's part,
And fears *Ulysses*, skill'd in ev'ry art?
Why stand you distant, and the rest expect
To mix in combate which your selves neglect?
From you 'twas hop'd among the first to dare

395   The shock of armies, and commence the war.
For this your names are call'd, before the rest,
To share the pleasures of the genial feast:
And can you, chiefs! without a blush survey
Whole troops before you lab'ring in the fray?

400   Say, is it thus those honours you requite?
The first in banquets, but the last in fight.

        Ulysses heard; The hero's warmth o'erspread
His cheek with blushes; and severe, he said.
Take back th' unjust reproach! Behold we stand

405   Sheath'd in bright arms, and but expect command.
If glorious deeds afford thy soul delight,
Behold me plunging in the thicket fight.
Then give thy warriour-chief a warriour's due,
Who dares to act whate'er thou dar'st to view.

410   Struck with his gen'rous wrath, the King replies;
Oh great in action, and in council wise!
With ours, thy care and ardour are the same,
Nor need I to command, nor ought to blame.
Sage as thou art, and learn'd in humankind,

415   Forgive the transport of a martial mind.
Haste to the fight, secure of just amends;
The Gods that make, shall keep the worthy, friends.

        He said, and pass'd where great *Tydides* lay,
His steeds and chariots wedg'd in firm array:

420   (The warlike *Sthenelus* attends his side)
To whom with stern reproach the monarch cry'd.
Oh Son of *Tydeus*! (he, whose strength could tame
The bounding steed, in arms a mighty Name)
Can'st thou, remote, the mingling hosts descry

425   With hands unactive, and a careless eye?
Not thus thy Sire the fierce encounter fear'd;
Still first in front the matchless Prince appear'd:

What glorious toils, what wonders they recite,
Who view'd him lab'ring thro' the ranks of fight!
I saw him once, when gath'ring martial pow'rs   430
A peaceful guest, he sought *Mycenæ*'s tow'rs;
Armies he ask'd, and armies had been giv'n,
Not we deny'd, but *Jove* forbad from heav'n;
While dreadful comets glaring from afar
Forewarn'd the horrours of the *Theban* war.   435
Next, sent by *Greece* from where *Asopus* flows,
A fearless envoy, he approach'd the foes;
Thebes' hostile walls, unguarded and alone,
Dauntless he enters, and demands the throne.
The tyrant feasting with his chiefs he found,   440
And dar'd to combate all those chiefs around;
Dar'd and subdu'd, before their haughty lord;
For *Pallas* strung his arm, and edg'd his sword.
Stung with the shame, within the winding way,
To bar his passage fifty warriours lay;   445
Two heroes led the secret squadron on,
Mæon the fierce, and hardy *Lycophon*;
Those fifty slaughter'd in the gloomy vale,
He spar'd but one to bear the dreadful tale.
Such *Tydeus* was, and such his martial fire;   450
Gods! how the son degen'rates from the sire?

      No words the godlike *Diomed* return'd,
But heard respectful, and in secret burn'd:
Not so fierce *Capaneus*' undaunted son,
Stern as his sire, the boaster thus begun.   455

      What needs, O monarch, this invidious praise,
Our selves to lessen, while our sires you raise?
Dare to be just, *Atrides*! and confess
Our valour equal, tho' our fury less.
With fewer troops we storm'd the *Theban* wall,   460
And happier, saw the sev'nfold city fall.
In impious acts the guilty fathers dy'd;
The sons subdu'd, for heav'n was on their side.
Far more than heirs of all our parents fame,
Our glories darken their diminish'd name.   465

      To him *Tydides* thus. My friend forbear,
Suppress thy passion, and the King revere:

His high concern may well excuse this rage,
Whose cause we follow, and whose war we wage;
470 His the first praise, were *Ilion*'s tow'rs o'erthrown,
And, if we fail, the chief disgrace his own.
Let him the *Greeks* to hardy toils excite,
'Tis ours, to labour in the glorious fight.

He spoke, and ardent, on the trembling ground
475 Sprung from his car; his ringing arms resound.
Dire was the clang, and dreadful from afar,
Of arm'd *Tydides* rushing to the war.
As when the winds, ascending by degrees,
First move the whitening surface of the seas,
480 The billows float in order to the shore,
The wave behind rolls on the wave before;
Till, with the growing storm, the deeps arise,
Foam o'er the rocks, and thunder to the skies.
So to the fight the thick *Battalions* throng,
485 Shields urg'd on shields, and men drove men along.
Sedate and silent move the num'rous bands;
No sound, no whisper, but the Chief's commands,
Those only heard; with awe the rest obey,
As if some God had snatch'd their voice away.

490 Not so the *Trojans*, from their host ascends
A gen'ral shout that all the region rends.
As when the fleecy flocks unnumber'd stand
In wealthy folds, and wait the milker's hand,
The hollow vales incessant bleating fills,
495 The lambs reply from all the neighb'ring hills:
Such clamours rose from various nations round,
Mix'd was the murmur, and confus'd the sound.
Each Host now joins, and each a God inspires,
These *Mars* incites, and those *Minerva* fires.

500 Pale *Flight* around, and dreadful *Terror* reign;
And *Discord* raging bathes the purple plain:
Discord! dire sister of the slaught'ring pow'r,
Small at her birth, but rising ev'ry hour,
While scarce the skies her horrid head can bound,
505 She stalks on earth, and shakes the world around;
The nations bleed, where–e'er her steps she turns,
The groan still deepens, and the combate burns.

Now shield with shield, with helmet helmet clos'd,
To armour armour, lance to lance oppos'd,
Host against host with shadowy squadrons drew,   510
The sounding darts in iron tempests flew,
Victors and vanquish'd join promiscuous cries,
And shrilling shouts and dying groans arise;
With streaming blood the slipp'ry fields are dy'd,
And slaughter'd heroes swell the dreadful tide.   515
　　As torrents roll, increas'd by num'rous rills,
With rage impetuous down their ecchoing hills;
Rush to the vales, and pour'd along the plain,
Roar thro' a thousand chanels to the main;
The distant shepherd trembling hears the sound: 520
So mix both hosts, and so their cries rebound.
　　The bold *Antilochus* the slaughter led,
The first who strook a valiant *Trojan* dead:
At great *Echepolus* the lance arrives,
Raz'd his high crest, and thro' his helmet drives;   525
Warm'd in the brain the brazen weapon lies,
And shades eternal settle o'er his eyes.
So sinks a tow'r, that long assaults had stood
Of force and fire; its walls besmear'd with blood.
Him, the bold *Leader of th' *Abantian* throng   530
Seiz'd to despoil, and dragg'd the corps along:
But while he strove to tug th' inserted dart,
Agenor's jav'lin reach'd the hero's heart.
His flank, unguarded by his ample shield,
Admits the lance: He falls, and spurns the field;   535
The nerves unbrac'd support his limbs no more;
The soul comes floating in a tide of gore.
Trojans and *Greeks* now gather round the slain;
The war renews, the warriours bleed again;
As o'er their prey rapacious wolves engage,   540
Man dies on man, and all is blood and rage.
　　In blooming youth fair *Simoïsius* fell,
Sent by great *Ajax* to the shades of hell:
Fair *Simoïsius*, whom his mother bore
Amid the flocks on silver *Simois*' shore: 545

* *Elphenor.*

The Nymph descending from the hills of *Ide*,
To seek her parents on his flow'ry side,
Brought forth the babe, their common care and joy,
And thence from *Simois* nam'd the lovely boy.
550   Short was his date! by dreadful *Ajax* slain
He falls, and renders all their cares in vain!
So falls a poplar, that in watry ground
Rais'd high the head, with stately branches crown'd,
(Fell'd by some artist with his shining steel,
555   To shape the circle of the bending wheel)
Cut down it lies, tall, smooth, and largely spread,
With all its beauteous honours on its head;
There left a subject to the wind and rain,
And scorch'd by suns, it withers on the plain.
560   Thus pierc'd by *Ajax*, *Simoïsius* lies
Stretch'd on the shore, and thus neglected dies.

    At *Ajax*, *Antiphus* his jav'lin threw;
The pointed lance with erring fury flew,
And *Leucus*, lov'd by wise *Ulysses*, slew.
565   He drops the corps of *Simoïsius* slain,
And sinks a breathless carcass on the plain.
This saw *Ulysses*, and with grief enrag'd
Strode where the foremost of the foes engag'd;
Arm'd with his spear, he meditates the wound,
570   In act to throw; but cautious, look'd around.
Struck at his sight the *Trojans* backward drew,
And trembling heard the jav'lin as it flew.
A Chief stood nigh who from *Abydos* came,
Old *Priam*'s son, *Democoön* was his name;
575   The weapon enter'd close above his ear,
Cold thro' his temples glides the whizzing spear;
With piercing shrieks the youth resigns his breath,
His eye-balls darken with the shades of death;
Pond'rous he falls; his clanging arms resound,
580   And his broad buckler rings against the ground.
    Seiz'd with affright the boldest foes appear;
Ev'n godlike *Hector* seems himself to fear;
Slow he gave way, the rest tumultuous fled;
The *Greeks* with shouts press on, and spoil the dead;

But *Phœbus* now from *Ilion*'s tow'ring height
Shines forth reveal'd, and animates the fight.
Trojans be bold, and force with force oppose;
Your foaming steeds urge headlong on the foes!
Nor are their bodies rocks, nor ribb'd with steel;
Your weapons enter, and your strokes they feel.
Have ye forgot what seem'd your dread before?
The great, the fierce *Achilles* fights no more.

   Apollo thus from *Ilion*'s lofty tow'rs
Array'd in terrours, rowz'd the *Trojan* pow'rs:
While War's fierce Goddess fires the *Grecian* foe,
And shouts and thunders in the fields below.

   Then great *Diores* fell, by doom divine,
In vain his valour, and illustrious line.
A broken rock the force of *Pirus* threw,
(Who from cold *Ænus* led the *Thracian* crew)
Full on his ankle dropt the pond'rous stone,
Burst the strong nerves, and crash'd the solid bone:
Supine he tumbles on the crimson'd sands, ⎤
Before his helpless friends, and native bands, ⎬
And spreads for aid his unavailing hands. ⎦
The foe rush'd furious as he pants for breath,
And thro' his navel drove the pointed death:
His gushing entrails smoak'd upon the ground,
And the warm life came issuing from the wound.

   His lance bold *Thoas* at the conqu'ror sent,
Deep in his breast above the pap it went,
Amid the lungs was fix'd the winged wood,
And quiv'ring in his heaving bosom stood:
'Till from the dying chief, approaching near,
Th' *Ætolian* warriour tugg'd his weighty spear:
Then sudden wav'd his flaming faulchion round,
And gash'd his belly with a ghastly wound.
The corps now breathless on the bloody plain,
To spoil his arms the victor strove in vain;
The *Thracian* bands against the victor prest;
A grove of lances glitter'd at his breast.
Stern *Thoas*, glaring with revengeful eyes,
In sullen fury slowly quits the prize.

585

590

595

600

605

610

615

620

Thus fell two Heroes; one the pride of *Thrace*,
625 And one the leader of th' *Epeian* race;
Death's sable shade at once o'ercast their eyes,
In dust the vanquish'd, and the victor lies.
With copious slaughter all the fields are red,
And heap'd with growing mountains of the dead.

630 Had some brave Chief this martial scene beheld,
By *Pallas* guarded thro' the dreadful field,
Might darts be bid to turn their points away,
And swords around him innocently play,
The war's whole art with wonder had he seen,
635 And counted Heroes where he counted Men.

So fought each host, with thirst of glory fir'd,
And crowds on crowds triumphantly expir'd.

OBSERVATIONS

ON THE

FOURTH BOOK

It was from the beginning of this book that *Virgil* has taken that of his tenth *Æneid*, as the whole tenour of the story in this and the last book is followed in his twelfth. The truce and the solemn oath, the breach of it by a dart thrown by *Tolumnius*, *Juturna*'s inciting the *Latines* to renew the war, the wound of *Æneas*, his speedy cure, and the battel ensuing, all these are manifestly copied from hence. The solemnity, surprize, and variety of these circumstances seem'd to him of importance enough, to build the whole catastrophe of his work upon them; tho' in *Homer* they are but openings to the general action, and such as in their warmth are still exceeded by all that follow them. They are chosen, we grant, by *Virgil* with great judgment, and conclude his poem with a becoming majesty: Yet the finishing his scheme with that which is but the coolest part of *Homer*'s action, tends in some degree to shew the disparity of the poetical fire in these two authors.

3. *Immortal* Hebè.] The Goddess of Youth is introduc'd as an attendant upon the banquets of the Gods, to shew that the divine beings enjoy an eternal youth, and that their life is a felicity without end.

Dacier.

9. *Two pow'rs divine.*] *Jupiter*'s reproaching these two Goddesses with neglecting to assist *Menelaus*, proceeds (as M. *Dacier* remarks) from the affection he bore to *Troy*: Since if *Menelaus* by their help had gain'd a complete victory, the siege had been rais'd, and the city deliver'd. On the contrary, *Juno* and *Minerva* might suffer *Paris* to escape, as the method to continue the war to the total destruction of *Troy*. And accordingly a few lines after we find them complotting together, and contriving a new scene of miseries to the *Trojans*.

18. *Tho' great* Atrides *gain'd the glorious strife.*] *Jupiter* here makes it a question, whether the foregoing combate should determine the controversy, or the peace be broken? His putting it thus, *that* Paris *is not killed, but* Menelaus *has the victory*, gives a hint for a dispute whether the conditions of the treaty were valid or annulled; that is to say, whether the controversy was to be determined by the *victory* or by the *death* of one of the combatants. Accordingly it has been disputed whether the articles were really binding to the *Trojans* or not? *Plutarch* has treated the question in his *Symposiacks l. 9. qu.* 13. The substance is this. In the first proposal of the challenge *Paris* mentions only the victory, *And who his rival shall in arms subdue*: Nor does *Hector* who carries it say any more. However *Menelaus* understands it of the death by what he replies: *Fall he that must beneath his rival's arms, And live the rest* – Iris to *Helen* speaks only of the former; and *Idæus* to *Priam* repeats the same words. But in the solemn oath *Agamemnon* specifies the latter, *If by* Paris *slain* – and *If by my brother's arms the* Trojan *bleed*. *Priam* also understands it of both, saying at his leaving the field, *What Prince shall fall heav'n only knows* – (I do not cite the *Greek* because the *English* has preserv'd the same nicety.) *Paris* himself confesses he has lost the victory, in his speech to *Helen*, which he would hardly have done, had the whole depended on that alone: And lastly *Menelaus* (after the conquest is clearly his by the flight of *Paris*) is still searching round the field to kill him, as if all were of no effect without the death of his adversary. It appears from hence that the *Trojans* had no ill pretence to break the treaty, so that *Homer* ought not to have been directly accus'd of making *Jupiter* the author of perjury in what follows, which is one of the chief of *Plato*'s objections against him.

31. *Tho' secret anger swell'd* Minerva's *breast.*] *Spondanus* takes notice that *Minerva*, who in the first book had restrain'd the anger of *Achilles*, had now an opportunity of exerting the same conduct in respect to herself. We may bring the parallel close, by observing that she had before her in like manner a superiour, who had provok'd her by sharp expressions, and whose counsels ran against her sentiments. In all which the poet takes care to preserve her still in the practice of that *Wisdom* of which she was Goddess.

55. *Let* Priam *bleed*, &c.] We find in *Persius*'s satyrs the name of *Labeo*, as an ill poet who made a miserable translation of the *Iliad*; one of whose verses is still preserv'd, and happens to be that of this place.

Crudum manduces Priamum, Priamique pisinnos.

[Might you devour Priam raw, as well as the children of Priam.]

It may seem from this, that his translation was servilely literal (as the old *Scholiast* on *Persius* observes.) And one cannot but take notice that *Ogilby*'s and *Hobbes*'s in this place are not unlike *Labeo*'s.

> *Both King and people thou would'st eat alive.*
> *And eat up* Priam *and his children all.*

61.   *But should this arm prepare to wreak our hate*
       On thy lov'd realms –]

Homer in this place has made *Jupiter* to prophecy the destruction of *Mycenæ* the favour'd city of *Juno*, which happen'd a little before the time of our author. *Strab. l. 8. The* Trojan *war being over, and the kingdom of* Agamemnon *destroy'd,* Mycenæ *daily decreas'd after the return of the* Heraclidæ: *For these becoming masters of* Peloponnesus, *cast out the old inhabitants; so that they who possess'd* Argos *overcame* Mycenæ *also, and contracted both into one body. A short time after,* Mycenæ *was destroy'd by the* Argives, *and not the least remains of it are now to be found.*

96. *Th' advice approv'd.*] This is one of the places for which *Homer* is blamed by *Plato*, who introduces *Socrates* reprehending it in his dialogue of the Republick. And indeed if it were granted that the *Trojans* had no right to break this treaty, the present machine where *Juno* is made to propose perjury, *Jupiter* to allow it, and *Minerva* to be commission'd to hasten the execution of it, would be one of the hardest to be reconciled to reason in the whole poem. Unless even then one might imagine, that *Homer*'s heaven is sometimes no more than an ideal world of abstracted beings; and so every motion which rises in the mind of man is attributed to the quality to which it belongs, with the name of the Deity who is suppos'd to preside over that quality superadded to it. In this sense the present allegory is easy enough. *Pandarus* thinks it *prudence* to gain honour and wealth at the hands of the *Trojans* by destroying *Menelaus*. This sentiment is also incited by a notion of *glory*, of which *Juno* is represented as Goddess. *Jupiter* who is suppos'd to know the thoughts of men, permits the action which he is not author of, but sends a prodigy at the same time to give warning of a coming mischief, and accordingly we find both armies descanting upon the sight of it in the following lines.

120. Pandarus *for strength renown'd.*] *Homer*, says *Plutarch* in his treatise of the *Pythian Oracle*, makes not the Gods to use all persons indifferently as their second agents, but each according to the powers he is endu'd with by art or nature. For a proof of this, he puts us in mind how *Minerva*, when she would persuade the *Greeks*, seeks for *Ulysses*; when she would break the truce, for *Pandarus*; and when she would conquer, for *Diomed*. If we consult the *Scholia* upon this instance, they give several reasons why *Pandarus* was particularly proper for the occasion. The Goddess went not to the *Trojans*, because they hated *Paris*, and (as we are told in the end of the foregoing book) would rather have given him up, than have done an ill action for him: She therefore looks among the allies, and finds *Pandarus* who was of a nation noted for perfidiousness, and had a soul avaricious enough to be capable of engaging in this treachery for the hopes of a reward from *Paris*: as appears by his being so covetous as not to bring horses to the siege for fear of the expence or loss of them; as he tells *Æneas* in the fifth book.

141. *Sixteen palms.*] Both the horns together made this length; and not each, as Madam *Dacier* renders it. I do not object it as an improbability that the horns were of sixteen Palms each; but that this would be an extravagant and unmanageable size for a bow is evident.

144. *This, by the* Greeks *unseen, the warriour bends.*] The poet having held us thro' the foregoing book in Expectation of a Peace, makes the conditions be here broken after such a manner, as should oblige the *Greeks* to act thro' the war with that irreconcileable fury, which affords him the opportunity of exerting the full fire of his own genius. The shot of *Pandarus* being therefore of such consequence (and as he calls it, the ἕρμα ὀδυνάων, the *foundation of future woes*) it was thought fit not to pass it over in a few words, like the flight of every common arrow, but to give it a description some way corresponding to its importance. For this, he surrounds it with a train of circumstances; the history of the bow, the bending it, the covering *Pandarus* with shields, the choice of the arrow, the prayer, and posture of the shooter, the sound of the string, and flight of the shaft; all most beautifully, and livelily painted. It may be observed too, how proper a time it was to expatiate in these particulars; when the armies being unemploy'd, and only one man acting, the poet and his readers had leisure to be the spectators of a single and deliberate action. I think it will be allow'd that the little circumstances which are sometimes thought too redundant in *Homer*, have a wonderful beauty in this place. *Virgil* has not fail'd to copy it, and with the greatest happiness imaginable.

> *Dixit, & aurata volucrem Threissa sagittam*
> *Deprompsit pharetra, cornuque infensa tetendit,*
> *Et duxit longe, donec curvata coirent*
> *Inter se capita, & manibus jam tangeret æquis,*
> *Læva aciem ferri, dextra nervoque papillam.*
> *Extemplo teli stridorem aurasque sonantes*
> *Audiit una Aruns, hæsitque in corpore ferrum.* [XI. 858–64]

> She said, and from her quiver chose with speed
> [The winged shaft, predestin'd for the deed:
> Then, to the stubborn Eugh her strength apply'd;
> Till the far-distant horns approach'd on either side,
> The bow-string touch'd her breast, so strong she drew;
> Whizzing in air the fatal arrow flew:
> At once the twanging bow, and sounding dart
> The traytor heard, and felt the point within his heart.]

160. Pallas *assists, and* (weaken'd in its force) *Diverts the weapon* –] For she only designed, by all this action, to encrease the glory of the *Greeks* in the taking of *Troy*: Yet some commentators have been so stupid as to wonder that *Pallas* should be employ'd first in the wounding of *Menelaus*, and after in the protecting him.

163. *Wafts th' envenom'd fly.*] This is one of those humble comparisons which *Homer* sometimes uses to diversify his subject, but a very exact one in its kind, and corresponding in all its parts. The care of the Goddess, the unsuspecting security of *Menelaus*, the ease with which she diverts the danger, and the danger itself, are all included in this short compass. To which it may be added, that if the providence of heavenly powers to their creatures is exprest by the love of a mother to her child, if men in regard to them are but as heedless sleeping infants, and if those dangers which may seem great to us, are by them as easily warded off as the simile implies; there will appear something sublime in this conception, however little or low the image may be thought at first sight in respect to a hero. A higher comparison would but have tended to lessen the disparity between the Gods and man, and the justness of the simile had been lost, as well as the grandeur of the sentiment.

170. *As when some stately trappings*, &c.] Some have judg'd the circumstances in this simile to be superfluous, and think it foreign to the purpose to take notice that this ivory was intended for the bosses of a bridle, was laid up for a Prince, or that a woman of *Caria* or *Mæonia* dy'd it. *Eustathius* was of a different opinion, who extols this passage for the variety it presents, and the learning it includes: We learn from hence that the *Lydians* and *Carians* were famous in the first times for their staining in purple, and that the women excell'd in works of ivory: As also that there were certain ornaments which only Kings and Princes were privileged to wear. But without having recourse to antiquities to justify this particular, it may be alledg'd, that the simile does not consist barely in the colours; it was but little to tell us, that the blood of *Menelaus* appearing on the whiteness of his skin, vyed with the purpled ivory; but this implies that the honourable wounds of a hero are the beautiful dress of war, and become him as much as the most gallant ornaments in which he takes the field. *Virgil*, 'tis true, has omitted the circumstance in his imitation of this comparison, *Æn.* 12. [67–8]

> *Indum sanguineo veluti violaverit ostro*
> *Si quis ebur –*

> [Thus *Indian* iv'ry shows,
> Which with the bord'ring paint of purple glows.]

But in this he judges only for himself, and does not condemn *Homer*. It was by no means proper that his ivory should have been a piece of martial accoutrement, when he apply'd it so differently, transferring it from the wounds of a hero to the blushes of the fair *Lavinia*.

177. *As down thy snowy thigh.*] *Homer* is very particular here, in giving the picture of the blood running in a long trace, lower and lower, as will appear from the words themselves.

> Τοῖοί τοι, Μενέλαε, μιάνθην αἵματι μηροὶ
> Εὐφυέες, κνῆμαί τε ἰδὲ σφυρὰ κάλ᾽ ὑπένερθε.

The translator has not thought fit to mention every one of these parts, first the thigh, then the leg, then the foot, which might be tedious in *English*: But the Author's design being only to image the streaming of the blood, it seem'd equivalent to make it trickle thro' the length of an *Alexandrian* line.

186. *Oh dear as life*, &c.] This incident of the wound of *Menelaus* gives occasion to *Homer* to draw a fine description of fraternal love in *Agamemnon*. On the first sight of it, he is struck with amaze and confusion, and now breaks out in tenderness and grief. He first accuses himself as the cause of this misfortune, by having consented to expose his brother to the single combate, which had drawn on this fatal consequence. Next he inveighs against the *Trojans* in general for their perfidiousness, as not yet knowing that it was the act of *Pandarus* only. He then comforts himself with the confidence that the Gods will revenge him upon *Troy*; but doubts by what hands this punishment may be inflicted, as fearing the death of *Menelaus* will force the *Greeks* to return with shame to their country. There is no contradiction in all this, but on the other side a great deal of nature, in the confused sentiments of *Agamemnon* on the occasion, as they are very well explained by *Spondanus*.

212. *While some proud* Trojan, &c.] *Agamemnon* here calls to mind how, upon the death of his brother, the ineffectual preparations and actions against *Troy* must become a derision to the world. This is in its own nature a very irritating sentiment, tho' it were never so carelessly exprest; but the Poet has found out a peculiar air of aggravation, in making him bring all the consequences before his eyes, in a picture of their *Trojan* enemies gathering round the tomb of the unhappy *Menelaus*, elated with pride, insulting the dead, and throwing out disdainful expressions and curses against him and his family. There is nothing which could more effectually represent a state of anguish, than the drawing such an image as this, which shews a man increasing his present unhappiness by the prospect of a future train of misfortunes.

222. *Let not thy words the warmth of* Greece *abate*.] In *Agamemnon*, *Homer* has shewn an example of a tender nature and fraternal affection, and now in *Menelaus* he gives us one of a generous warlike patience and presence of mind. He speaks of his own case with no other regard, but as this accident of his wound may tend to the discouragement of

the soldiers; and exhorts the General to beware of dejecting their spirits from the prosecution of the war.   *Spondanus.*

253. *The* Trojans *rush tumultuous to the war.*] They advanced to the enemy in the belief that the shot of *Pandarus* was made by order of the Generals.   *Dacier.*

256. *Nor had you seen.*] The Poet here changes his narration, and turns himself to the reader in an *Apostrophe. Longinus* in his 22*d* chapter commends this figure, as causing a reader to become a spectator, and keeping his mind fixed upon the action before him. *The* Apostrophe (says he) *renders us more awaken'd, more attentive, and more full of the thing describ'd.* Madam *Dacier* will have it, that it is the muse who addresses herself to the Poet in the second person: 'Tis no great matter which, since it has equally its effect either way.

264. *Thro' all the martial ranks he moves,* &c.] In the following review of the army, which takes up a great part of this book, we see all the spirit, art, and industry of a compleat General; together with the proper *characters* of those leaders whom he incites. *Agamemnon* considers at this sudden exigence, that he should first address himself to all in general; he divides his discourse to the brave and the fearful, using arguments which arise from confidence or despair, passions which act upon us most forcibly: To the brave, he urges their secure hopes of conquest, since the Gods must punish perjury; to the timorous, their inevitable destruction if the enemy should burn their ships. After this he flies from rank to rank, applying himself to each ally with particular artifice: He caresses *Idomeneus* as an old friend who had promised not to forsake him; and meets with an answer in that hero's true character, short, honest, hearty, and soldier-like. He praises the *Ajaxes* as warriours whose examples fired the army; and is received by them without any reply, as they were men who did not profess speaking. He passes next to *Nestor*, whom he finds talking to his soldiers as he marshal'd them; here he was not to part without a compliment on both sides; he wishes him the strength he had once in his youth, and is answer'd with an account of something which the old hero had done in his former days. From hence he goes to the troops which lay farthest from the place of action; where he finds *Menestheus* and *Ulysses*, not intirely unprepar'd nor yet in motion, as being ignorant of what had happen'd. He reproves *Ulysses* for this, with words agreeable to the hurry he is

in, and receives an answer which suits not ill with the twofold character of a wise and a valiant man: Hereupon *Agamemnon* appears present to himself, and excuses his hasty expressions. The next he meets is *Diomed*, whom he also rebukes for backwardness, but after another manner, by setting before him the example of his father. Thus is *Agamemnon* introduced, praising, terrifying, exhorting, blaming, excusing himself, and again relapsing into reproofs; a lively picture of a great mind in the highest emotion. And at the same time the variety is so kept up, with a regard to the different characters of the leaders, that our thoughts are not tired with running along with him over all his army.

296. *For this, in banquets.*] The ancients usually in their feasts divided to the guests by equal portions, except when they took some particular occasion to shew distinction and give the preference to any one person. It was then look'd upon as the highest mark of honour to be allotted the best portion of meat and wine, and to be allowed an exemption from the laws of the feast, in drinking wine unmingled and without stint. This custom was much more ancient than the time of the *Trojan* war, and we find it practised in the banquet given by *Joseph* to his brethren in *Ægypt*, Gen. 43. v. *ult. And he sent messes to them from before him, but* Benjamin's *mess was five times so much as any of theirs.*

Dacier.

336. *There rev'rend* Nestor *ranks his* Pylian *bands.*] This is the Prince whom *Homer* chiefly celebrates for martial discipline; of the rest he is content to say they were valiant, and ready to fight: The years, long observation and experience of *Nestor* render'd him the fittest person to be distinguished on this account. The disposition of his troops in this place (together with what he is made to say, that their forefathers used the same method) may be a proof that the art of war was well known in *Greece* before the time of *Homer*. Nor indeed can it be imagined otherwise, in an age when all the world made their acquisitions by force of arms only. What is most to be wonder'd at, is, that they had not the use of *cavalry*, all men engaging either on *foot*, or from *chariots* (a particular necessary to be known by every reader of *Homer*'s battels.) In these chariots there were always two persons, one of whom only fought, the other was wholly employ'd in managing the Horses. Madam *Dacier*, in her excellent preface to *Homer*, is of opinion, that there were no horsemen 'till near the time of *Saul*, threescore years after

the siege of *Troy*; so that altho' cavalry were in use in *Homer*'s days, yet he thought himself obliged to regard the customs of the age of which he writ, rather than those of his own.

344. *The middle space suspected troops supply.*] This artifice of placing those men whose behaviour was most to be doubted, in the middle (so as to put them under a necessity of engaging even against their inclinations) was followed by *Hannibal* in the battel of *Zama*; as is observed and praised by *Polybius*, who quotes this verse on that occasion in acknowledgment of *Homer*'s skill in military discipline. That our author was the first master of that art in *Greece* is the opinion of *Ælian, Tactic. c. 1. Frontinus* gives us another example of *Pyrrhus* King of *Epirus*'s following this instruction of *Homer. Vide Stratag. lib. 2. c.* 3. So *Ammianus Marcellinus l.* 14. *Imperator catervis peditum infirmis, medium inter acies spacium, secundum Homericam dispositionem, præstituit.* [The commander kept the weak troops of foot-soldiers in the middle of the battlefield, in the Homeric manner.]

352. *He whom the fortune of the field shall cast*
      From forth his chariot, mount the next – &c.]

The words in the original are capable of four different significations, as *Eustathius* observes. The first is, that whoever in fighting upon his chariot shall win a chariot from his enemy, he shall continue to fight, and not retire from the engagement to secure his prize. The second, that if any one be thrown out of his chariot, he who happens to be nearest shall hold forth his javelin to help him up into his own. The third is directly the contrary to the last, that if any one be cast from his chariot and would mount up into another man's, that other shall push him back with his javelin, and not admit him for fear of interrupting the combate. The fourth is the sense which is followed in the translation, as seeming much the most natural, that every one should be left to govern his own chariot, and the other who is admitted fight only with the javelin. The reason of this advice appears by the speech of *Pandarus* to *Æneas* in the next book: *Æneas* having taken him up into his chariot to go against *Diomed*, compliments him with the choice either to fight, or to manage the reins, which was esteem'd an office of honour. To this *Pandarus* answers, that it is more proper for *Æneas* to guide his own horses; lest they not feeling their accustomed master, should be ungovernable and bring them into danger.

Upon occasion of the various and contrary significations of which these words are said to be capable, and which *Eustathius* and *Dacier* profess to admire as an excellence; Mons. *de la Motte*, in his late discourse upon *Homer*, very justly animadverts, that if this be true, it is a grievous fault in *Homer*. For what can be more absurd than to imagine, that the orders given in a battel should be delivered in such ambiguous terms, as to be capable of many meanings? These double interpretations must proceed not from any design in the Author, but purely from the ignorance of the moderns in the *Greek* tongue: It being impossible for any one to possess the dead languages to such a degree, as to be certain of all the graces and negligences; or to know precisely how far the licences and boldnesses of expression were happy, or forced. But Criticks, to be thought learned, attribute to the Poet all the random senses that amuse them, and imagine they see in a single word a whole heap of things, which no modern language can express; so are oftentimes charmed with nothing but the confusion of their own ideas.

384. *Remote their forces lay.*] This is a reason why the troops of *Ulysses* and *Menestheus* were not yet in motion. Tho' another may be added in respect to the former, that it did not consist with the wisdom of *Ulysses* to fall on with his forces 'till he was well assured. Tho' courage be no inconsiderable part of his character, yet it is always join'd with great caution. Thus we see him soon after in the very heat of battel, when his friend was just slain before his eyes, first looking carefully about him, before he would throw his spear to revenge him.

430. *I saw him once, when,* &c.] This long narration concerning the history of *Tydeus*, is not of the nature of those for which *Homer* has been blam'd with some colour of justice: It is not a cold story, but a warm reproof, while the particularising the actions of the father is made the highest incentive to the son. Accordingly the air of this speech ought to be inspirited above the common narrative style. As for the story itself, it is finely told by *Statius* in the second book of the *Thebais*.

452. *No words the Godlike* Diomed *return'd.*] 'When *Diomed* is reproved by *Agamemnon*, he holds his peace in respect to his General; but *Sthenelus* retorts upon him with boasting and insolence. It is here worth observing in what manner *Agamemnon* behaves himself; he passes by *Sthenelus* without affording any reply; whereas just before,

when *Ulysses* testify'd his resentment, he immediately return'd him an answer. For as it is a mean and servile thing, and unbecoming the majesty of a Prince, to make apologies to every man in justification of what he has said or done; so to treat all men with equal neglect is mere pride and excess of folly. We also see of *Diomed*, that tho' he refrains from speaking in this place when the time demanded Action; he afterwards expresses himself in such a manner, as shews him not to have been insensible of this unjust rebuke: (*in the ninth book*) when he tells the King, he was the first who had dar'd to reproach him with want of courage.'   Plutarch *of reading the Poets.*

460. *We storm'd the* Theban *wall.*] The first *Theban* war, of which *Agamemnon* spoke in the preceding lines, was seven and twenty years before the war of *Troy*. *Sthenelus* here speaks of the second *Theban* war, which happen'd ten years after the first: when the sons of the seven captains conquer'd the city, before which their fathers were destroyed. *Tydeus* expired gnawing the head of his enemy, and *Capaneus* was thunder-struck while he blasphemed *Jupiter*.

                                            Vid. Stat. Thebaid.

478. *As when the winds.*] Madam *Dacier* thinks it may seem something odd, that an army going to conquer should be compared to the waves going to break themselves against the shore; and would solve the appearing absurdity by imagining the Poet laid not the stress so much upon this circumstance, as upon the same waves assaulting a rock, lifting themselves over its head, and covering it with foam as the *trophy of their victory* (as she expresses it.) But to this it may be answer'd, that neither did the *Greeks* get the better in this battel, nor will a comparison be allowed intirely beautiful, which instead of illustrating its subject, stands itself in need of so much illustration and refinement, to be brought to agree with it. The passage naturally bears this sense. *As when, upon the rising of the wind, the waves roll after one another to the shore; at first there is a distant motion in the sea, then they approach to break with noise on the strand, and lastly rise swelling over the rocks, and toss their foam above their heads: So the* Greeks, *at first, marched in order one after another silently to the fight* – Where the Poet breaks off from prosecuting the comparison, and by a *prolepsis*, leaves the reader to carry it on, and image to himself the future tumult, rage and force of the battel, in opposition to that silence in which he describes the troops at present, in the lines immediately ensuing. What confirms this exposition is, that *Virgil* has made use of the simile in the same sense in the seventh *Æneid* [528–30].

> *Fluctus uti primo cœpit cum albescere vento,*
> *Paulatim sese tollit mare, & altius undas*
> *Erigit; inde imo consurgit ad æthera fundo.*

> [Thus when a black-brow'd gust begins to rise,
> White foam at first on the curl'd ocean flies;
> Then roars the main, the billows mount the skies:
> 'Till by the fury of the storm full blown,
> The muddy bottom o'er the clouds is thrown.]

478. *As when the winds*, &c.] This is the first battel in *Homer*, and it is worthy observation with what grandeur it is described, and raised by one circumstance above another, 'till all is involved in horrour and tumult: The foregoing simile of the winds, rising by degrees into a general tempest, is an image of the progress of his own spirit in this description. We see first an innumerable army moving in order, and are amus'd with the pomp and silence, then waken'd with the noise and clamour; next they join, the adverse Gods are let down among them; the imaginary persons of *Terror, Flight, Discord* succeed to re-inforce them; then all is undistinguish'd fury and a confusion of horrours, only that at different openings we behold the distinct deaths of several heroes, and then are involv'd again in the same confusion.

502. *Discord, dire sister*, &c.] This is the passage so highly extoll'd by *Longinus*, as one of the most signal instances of the noble sublimity of this author: where it is said, that the image here drawn of discord, *whose head touch'd the heavens*, and *whose feet were on earth*, may as justly be apply'd to the vast reach and elevation of the genius of *Homer*. But Mons. *Boileau* informs us that neither the quotation nor these words were in the original of *Longinus*, but partly inserted by *Gabriel de Petra*. However, the best encomium is, that *Virgil* [*Aen.* IV. 176–7] has taken it word for word, and apply'd it to the person of *Fame*.

> *Parva metu primo, mox sese attollit in auras,*
> *Ingrediturque solo, & caput inter nubila condit.*

> [Soon grows the pygmee to gygantic size;
> Her feet on earth, her forehead in the skies.]

Aristides had formerly blamed *Homer* for admitting *Discord* into heaven, and *Scaliger* takes up the criticism to throw him below *Virgil*. *Fame* (he says) is properly feign'd to hide her head in the clouds, because the grounds and authors of rumours are commonly unknown. As if the same might not be alledg'd for *Homer*, since the grounds and authors of *Discord* are often no less secret. *Macrobius* has put this among the passages where he thinks *Virgil* has fallen short in his imitation of *Homer*, and brings these reasons for his opinion. *Homer* represents *Discord* to rise from small beginnings, and afterwards in her encrease to reach the heavens: *Virgil* has said this of *Fame*, but not with equal propriety; for the subjects are very different. *Discord*, tho' it reaches to war and devastation, is still *Discord*; nor ceases to be what it was at first. But *Fame*, when it grows to be universal, is *Fame* no longer, but becomes knowledge and certainty. For who calls any thing *Fame*, which is known from earth to heaven? Nor has *Virgil* equal'd the strength of *Homer*'s hyperbole, for one speaks of *heaven*, the other only of the *clouds. Macrob. Sat. l. 5. c. 13. Scaliger* is very angry at this last period, and by mistake blames *Gellius* for it, in whom there is no such thing. His words are so insolently dogmatical, that barely to quote them is to answer them, and the only answer which such a spirit of criticism deserves. *Clamant quod Maro de Fama dixit eam inter nubila caput condere, cum tamen Homerus unde ipse accepit, in cœlo caput Eridis constituit. Jam tibi pro me respondeo. Non sum imitatus, nolo imitari: non placet, non est verum, Contentionem ponere caput in cœlo. Ridiculum est, fatuum est, Homericum est, Græculum est.* [They complain that Virgil said of Fame that she hid her head in the clouds, while Homer – from whom Virgil himself borrowed it – placed the head of Discord in the heavens. Now to you I respond, as if I were Virgil. 'I am not an imitator, I do not wish to imitate: it does not please me, it is not true that Discord places her head in the heavens. That is ridiculous, it is foolish, it is Homeric, it is Greekish.'] *Poetic. l. 5. c. 3.*

This fine verse was also criticiz'd by Mons. *Perault*, who accuses it as a forc'd and extravagant hyperbole. M. *Boileau* answers, that hyperboles as strong are daily used even in common discourse, and that nothing is in effect more strictly true than that *Discord* reigns over all the earth, and in heaven itself; that is to say, among the Gods of *Homer*. It is not (continues this excellent critick) the description of a giant, as this censor would pretend, but a just allegory; and as he makes *Discord* an allegorical person, she may be of what size he pleases without shocking us; since it is what we regard only as an idea and creature of the fancy, and not as a material substance that has any being in nature. The expression in the *Psalms*, that the *impious man is lifted up as a cedar of* Libanus, does by no means imply that the impious man was a giant as tall as the cedar. Thus far *Boileau*; and upon the whole we may observe, that it seems not only the fate of great genius's to have met with the most malignant cricks, but of the finest and noblest passages in them to have been particulary pitch'd upon for impertinent criticisms. These are the divine boldnesses which in their very nature provoke ignorance and short-sightedness to shew themselves; and which whoever is capable of attaining, must also certainly know, that they will be attack'd by such as cannot reach them.

508. *Now shield with shield*, &c.] The verses which follow in the original are perhaps excell'd by none in *Homer*; and that he had himself a particular fondness for them, may be imagin'd from his inserting them again in the same words in the eighth book. They are very happily imitated by *Statius lib.* 7 [*Theb.* VIII. 398–9].

> *Jam clypeus clypeis, umbone repellitur umbo,*
> *Ense minax ensis, pede pes, & cuspide cuspis*, &c.

[Now shield is driven back by shield, boss by boss, fierce sword by sword, and spear by spear.]

516. *As torrents roll.*] This comparison of rivers meeting and roaring, with two armies mingling in battel, is an image of that nobleness, which (to say no more) was worthy the invention of *Homer* and the imitation of *Virgil* [*Aen.* XII. 523–5; II. 307–8].

> *Aut ubi decursu rapido de montibus altis,*
> *Dant sonitum spumosi amnes, & in æquora currunt,*
> *Quisque suum populatus iter; – Stupet inscius alto*
> *Accipiens sonitum saxi de vertice pastor.*

[Or as two neighb'ring torrents fall from high,
Rapid they run; the foamy waters fly:
They rowl to sea with unresisted force,
And down the rocks precipitate their course.
The shepherd climbs the cliff, and sees from far,
The wasteful ravage of the wat'ry war.]

The word *populatus* here has a beauty which one must be insensible not to observe. *Scaliger* prefers *Virgil*'s, and *Macrobius Homer*'s, without any reasons on either side, but only one critick's positive word against another's. The reader may judge between them.

522. *The bold* Antilochus.] *Antilochus* the son of *Nestor* is the first who begins the engagement. It seems as if the old hero having done the greatest service he was capable of at his years, in disposing the troops in the best order (as we have seen before) had taken care to set his son at the head of them, to give him the glory of beginning the battel.

540. *As o'er their prey rapacious wolves engage.*] This short comparison in the *Greek* consists only of two words, Λύκοι ὥς which *Scaliger* observes upon as too abrupt. But may it not be answer'd that such a place as this, where all things are in confusion, seems not to admit of any simile, except of one which scarce exceeds a metaphor in length? When two heroes are engag'd, there is a plain view to be given us of their actions, and there a long simile may be of use, to raise and enliven them by parallel circumstances; but when the troops fall in promiscuously upon one another, the confusion excludes distinct or particular images, and consequently comparisons of any length would be less natural.

542. *In bloom of youth fair* Simoïsius *fell.*] This Prince receiv'd his name from the River *Simoïs*, on whose banks he was born. It was the custom of the eastern people to give names to their children deriv'd from the most remarkable accidents of their birth. The holy scripture is full of examples of this kind. It is also usual in the Old Testament to compare Princes to trees, cedars, &c. as *Simoïsius* is here resembled to a poplar.   *Dacier.*

552. *So falls a poplar.*] *Eustathius* in *Macrobius* prefers to this simile that of *Virgil* in the second *Æneid* [626–31].

> *Ac veluti in summis antiquam montibus ornum,*
> *Cum ferro accisam crebrisque bipennibus instant*
> *Eruere agricolæ certatim; illa usque minatur,*
> *Et tremefacta comam concusso vertice nutat;*
> *Vulneribus donec paulatim evicta supremum*
> *Congemuit, traxitque jugis avulsa ruinam.*

[Rent like a mountain ash, which dared the winds;
 And stood the sturdy strokes of lab'ring binds:
About the roots the cruel ax resounds,
The stumps are pierc'd, with oft repeated wounds.
The war is felt on high, the nodding crown
Now threats a fall, and throws the leafy honours down.
To their united force it yields, though late;
And mourns with mortal groans th' approaching fate:
The roots no more their upper load sustain;
But down she falls, and spreads a ruin thro' the plain.]

Mr. *Hobbes*, in the preface to his translation of *Homer*, has discours'd upon this occasion very judiciously. *Homer* (says he) intended no more in this place than to shew how comely the body of *Simoïsius* appear'd as he lay dead upon the bank of *Scamander*, strait and tall, with a fair head of hair, like a strait and high poplar with the boughs still on; and not at all to describe the manner of his falling, which (when a man is wounded thro' the breast as he was with a spear) is always sudden. *Virgil*'s is the description of a great tree falling when many men together hew it down. He meant to compare the manner how *Troy* after many battels, and after the loss of many cities, conquer'd by the many nations under *Agamemnon* in a long war, was thereby weaken'd and at last overthrown, with a great tree hewn round about, and then falling by little and little leisurely. So that neither these two descriptions, nor the two comparisons, can be compared together. The image of a man lying on the ground is one thing; the image of falling (especially of a kingdom) is another. This therefore gives no advantage to *Virgil* over *Homer*. Thus Mr. *Hobbes*.

585. *But* Phœbus *now.*] *Homer* here introduces *Apollo* on the side of the *Trojans*: He had given them the assistance of *Mars* at the beginning of this battel; but *Mars* (which signifies courage without conduct) proving too weak to resist *Minerva* (or courage with conduct) which the Poet represents as constantly aiding his *Greeks*; they want some prudent management to rally them again: He therefore brings in a *wisdom* to assist *Mars*, under the appearance of *Apollo*.

592. Achilles *fights no more.*] *Homer* from time to time puts his readers in mind of *Achilles*, during his absence from the war; and finds occasions of celebrating his valour with the highest praises. There

cannot be a greater encomium than this, where *Apollo* himself tells the *Trojans* they have nothing to fear, since *Achilles* fights no longer against them.   *Dacier.*

630. *Had some brave Chief.*] The turning off in this place from the actions of the field, to represent to us a man with security and calmness walking thro' it, without being able to reprehend any thing in the whole action; this is not only a fine praise of the battel, but as it were a breathing place to the poetical spirit of the author, after having rapidly run along with the heat of the engagement: He seems like one who having got over a part of his journey, stops upon an eminence to look back upon the space he has pass'd, and concludes the book with an agreeable pause or respite.

The reader will excuse our taking notice of such a trifle, as that it was an old superstition, that this fourth book of the *Iliads* being laid under the head, was a cure for the *Quartern Ague. Serenus Sammonicus,* a celebrated physician in the time of the younger *Gordian,* and preceptor to that Emperor, has gravely prescrib'd it among other receipts in his medicinal precepts, *Præc.* 50.

Mæoniæ Iliados quartum suppone timenti.

[Place the fourth book of the Maeonian *Iliad* under the head of the person who is apprehensive about contending with this disease.]

I believe it will be found a true observation, that there never was anything so absurd or ridiculous, but has at one time or other been written even by some author of reputation: A reflection it may not be improper for writers to make, as being at once some mortification to their vanity, and some comfort to their infirmity.

THE

ILIAD

OF

HOMER

VOLUME II

AN ESSAY

ON

HOMER'S BATTELS

Perhaps it may be necessary in this place at the opening of *Homer*'s battels, to premise some observations upon them in general. I shall first endeavour to shew the *Conduct* of the Poet herein, and next collect some *Antiquities*, that tend to a more distinct understanding of those descriptions which make so large a part of the Poem.

One may very well apply to *Homer* himself what he says of his Heroes at the end of the fourth book, that whosoever should be guided thro' his battels by *Minerva*, and pointed to every scene of them, would see nothing through the whole but subjects of surprize and applause. When the reader reflects that no less than the compass of twelve books is taken up in these, he will have reason to wonder by what methods our author could prevent descriptions of such a length from being tedious. It is not enough to say, that tho' the subject itself be the same, the actions are always different; that we have now distinct combats, now promiscuous fights, now single duels, now general engagements; or that the scenes are perpetually vary'd; we are now in the fields, now at the fortification of the *Greeks*, now at the ships, now at the gates of *Troy*, now at the river *Scamander*: But we must look farther into the art of the poet to find the reasons of this astonishing variety.

We may first observe that *diversity* in the *deaths* of his *warriors*, which he has supply'd by the vastest fertility of invention. These he distinguishes several ways: Sometimes by the *characters* of the Men, their *age*, *office*, *profession*, *Nation*, *Family*, &c. One is a blooming *youth*, whose father dissuaded him from the war; one is a *priest* whose piety could not save him; one is a *sportsman* whom *Diana* taught in vain; one is the *Native* of a far-distant *country*, who is never to return; one is descended from a *noble line* which ends in his death; one is made remarkable by his *boasting*; another by his *beseeching*; and another who is distinguish'd no way else is mark'd by his *habit* and the singularity of his armour.

Sometimes he varies these deaths by the several *postures* in which his Heroes are represented either fighting or falling. Some of these are so exceedingly *exact*, that one may guess from the very position of the combatant, whereabouts the wound will light: Others so very *peculiar* and *uncommon*, that they could only be the effect of an imagination which had search'd thro' all the ideas of nature. Such is that picture of *Mydon* in the fifth book, whose arm being numb'd by a blow on the elbow, drops the reins that trail on the ground; and then being suddenly struck on the temples, falls headlong from the chariot in a soft and deep place; where he sinks up to the shoulders in the sands, and continues a while fix'd by the weight of his armour, with his legs quivering in the air, 'till he is trampled down by his horses.

Another cause of this variety is the difference of the *wounds* that are given in the *Iliad*: They are by no means like the wounds described by most other poets, which are commonly made in the self-same obvious places: The heart and head serve for all those in general who understand no anatomy, and sometimes for variety they kill men by wounds that are no where mortal but in their poems. As the whole human body is the subject of these, so nothing is more necessary to him who would describe them well, than a thorough knowledge of its structure, even tho' the poet is not professedly to write of them as an anatomist; in the same manner as an exact Skill in Anatomy is necessary to those painters that would excel in drawing the naked, tho' they are not to make every muscle as visible as in a book of chirurgery. It appears from so many passages in *Homer* that he was perfectly master of this science, that it would be needless to cite any in particular. One may only observe, that if we thoroughly examine all the wounds he has described, tho' so infinite in number, and so many ways diversify'd, we shall hardly find one which will contradict this observation.

I must just add a remark, That the various periphrases and circumlocutions by which *Homer* expresses the single act of *dying*, have supply'd *Virgil* and the succeeding Poets with all their manners of phrasing it. Indeed he repeats the same verse on that occasion more often than they – τὸν δὲ σκότος ὄσσ᾽ ἐκάλυψε – Ἀράβησε δὲ τεύχε᾽ ἐπ᾽ αὐτῷ, &c. But tho' it must be owned he had more frequent occasions for a line of this kind than any Poet, as no other has describ'd half so many deaths, yet one cannot ascribe this to any sterility of expression, but to the genius of his times, that delighted in those reiterated verses. We find repetitions of the same sort affected by the sacred writers, such as *He was gathered to his people*; *He slept with his fathers*, and the like. And upon the whole they have a certain antiquated harmony not unlike the burthen of a song, which the ear is willing to suffer, and as it were rests upon.

As the perpetual horrour of combats, and a succession of images of death, could not but keep the imagination very much on the stretch; *Homer* has been careful to contrive such reliefs and pauses as might divert the mind to some other scene, without losing sight of his principal object. His *comparisons* are the more frequent on this account; for a *comparison* serves this end the most effectually of any thing, as it is at once correspondent to, and differing from the subject. Those criticks who fancy that the use of comparisons distracts the attention, and draws it from the first image which should most employ it, (as that we lose the idea of the *battle* itself, while we are led by a simile to that of a *deluge* or a *storm*:) Those, I say, may as well imagine we lose the thought of the sun, when we see his reflection in the water, where he appears more distinctly, and is contemplated more at ease, than if we gaz'd directly at his beams. For it is with the eye of the imagination as it is with our corporeal eye, it must sometimes be taken off from the object in order to see it the better. The same criticks that are displeased to have their fancy distracted (as they call it) are yet so inconsistent with themselves as to object to *Homer* that his similes are too much alike, and are too often derived from the same animal. But is it not more reasonable (according to their own notion) to compare the same Man always to the same animal, than to see him sometimes a sun, sometimes a tree, and sometimes a river? Tho' *Homer* speaks of the same creature, he so diversifies the circumstances and accidents of the comparisons, that they always appear quite different. And to say truth, it is not so much the animal or the thing, as the action or posture of them that employs our imagination: Two different animals in the same action are more like to each other, than one and the same animal is to himself, in two different actions. And those who in reading *Homer* are shock'd that 'tis always a *lion*, may as well be angry that 'tis always a *man*.

What may seem more exceptionable is his inserting the same comparisons in the same words at length upon different occasions, by which management he makes one single image. afford many ornaments to several parts of the Poem. But may not one say *Homer* is in this like a skilful improver, who places a beautiful statue in a well-disposed garden so as to answer several vistas, and by that artifice one single figure seems multiply'd into as many objects as there are openings from whence it may be viewed?

What farther relieves and softens these descriptions of battels, is the Poet's wonderful art of introducing many pathetic circumstances about the deaths of the Heroes, which raise a different movement in the mind from what those images naturally inspire, I mean compassion and pity; when he causes us to look back upon the lost riches, possessions, and hopes of those who die: When he transports us to their native countries and paternal seats, to see the griefs of their aged fathers, the despair and tears of their widows, or the abandon'd condition of their orphans. Thus when *Protesilaus* falls, we are made to reflect on the lofty Palaces he left half finish'd; when the sons of *Phenops* are killed, we behold the mortifying distress of their wealthy father, who saw his estate divided before his eyes, and taken in trust for strangers. When *Axylus* dies, we are taught to compassionate the hard fate of that generous and hospitable man, whose house was the house of all men, and who deserv'd that glorious elogy of, *The friend of human kind*.

It is worth taking notice too, what use *Homer* every where makes of each little accident or circumstance that can naturally happen in a battel, thereby to cast a variety over his action; as well as of every turn of mind or emotion a Hero can possibly feel, such as resentment, revenge, concern, confusion, *&c*. The former of these makes his work resemble a large history-piece, where even the less important figures and actions have yet some convenient place or corner to be shewn in; and the latter gives it all the advantages of tragedy in those various turns of passion that animate the speeches of his Heroes, and render his whole Poem the most *Dramatick* of any Epick whatsoever.

It must also be observ'd that the constant *machines* of the *Gods* conduce very greatly to vary these long battels, by a continual change of the scene from earth to heaven. *Homer* perceiv'd them too necessary for this purpose to abstain from the use of them, even after *Jupiter* had enjoin'd the Deities not to act on either side. It is remarkable how many methods he has found to draw them into every book; where if they dare not assist the warriors, at least they are very helpful to the poet.

But there is nothing that more contributes to the variety, surprize, and *Eclat* of *Homer*'s battels, or is more perfectly admirable in itself, than that artful manner of taking measure, or (as one may say) *gaging* his Heroes by each other, and thereby elevating the character of one person by the opposition of it to that of some other whom he is made to excel. So that he many times describes one only to image another, and raises one only to raise another. I cannot better exemplify this remark, than by giving an instance in the character of *Diomed* that lies before me. Let us observe by what a scale of oppositions he elevates this Hero, in the fifth book, first to excel all human valour, and after to rival the Gods themselves. He distinguishes him first from the *Grecian* Captains in general, each of whom he represents conquering a single *Trojan*, while *Diomed* constantly encounters two at once; and while they are engag'd each in his distinct post, he only is drawn fighting in every quarter, and slaughtering on every side. Next he opposes him to *Pandarus*, next to *Æneas*, and then to *Hector*. So of the Gods he shews him first against *Venus*, then *Apollo*, then *Mars*, and lastly in the eighth book against *Jupiter* himself in the midst of his thunders. The same conduct is observable more or less in regard to every personage of his work.

This subordination of the Heroes is one of the causes that make each of his battels rise above the other in greatness, terrour, and importance, to the end of the Poem. If *Diomed* has perform'd all these wonders in the first combates, it is but to raise *Hector*, at whose appearance he begins to fear. If in the next battels *Hector* triumphs not only over *Diomed*, but over *Ajax* and *Patroclus*, sets fire to the fleet, wins the armour of *Achilles*, and singly eclipses all the Heroes; in the midst of all his glory, *Achilles* appears, *Hector* flies, and is slain.

The manner in which his Gods are made to act, no less advances the gradation we are speaking of. In the first battels they are seen only in short and separate excursions: *Venus* assists *Paris*, *Minerva Diomed*, or *Mars Hector*. In the next, a clear stage is left for *Jupiter*, to display his omnipotence and turn the fate of Armies alone. In the last, all the powers of heaven are engag'd and banded into regular parties, Gods encountring Gods, *Jove* encouraging them with his thunders, *Neptune* raising his tempests, heaven flaming, earth trembling, and *Pluto* himself starting from the throne of hell.

II. I am now to take notice of some customs of *antiquity*, relating to the *arms* and *art military* of those times, which are proper to be known in order to form a right notion of our author's descriptions of war.

That *Homer* copied the manners and customs of the age he writ of, rather than of that he lived in, has been observed in some instances. As that he no where represents *cavalry* or *trumpets* to have been used in the *Trojan* wars, tho' they apparently were in his own time. It is not therefore impossible but there may be found in his works some deficiencies in the art of war, which are not to be imputed to his ignorance, but to his judgment.

Horses had not been brought into *Greece* long before the siege of *Troy.* They were originally eastern animals, and if we find at that very period so great a number of them reckon'd up in the wars of the *Israelites*, it is the less a wonder, considering they came from *Asia.* The practice of riding them was so little known in *Greece* a few years before, that they look'd upon the *Centaurs* who first used it, as monsters compounded of men and horses. *Nestor* in the first *Iliad* says he had seen these *Centaurs* in his youth, and *Polypætes* in the second is said to have been born on the day that his father expelled them from *Pelion* to the desarts of *Æthica.* They had no other use of horses than to draw their chariots in battel, so that whenever *Homer* speaks of *fighting from an horse, taming an horse,* or the like, it is constantly to be understood of fighting from a chariot, or taming horses to that service. This (as we have said) was a piece of decorum in the Poet; for in his own time they were arrived to such a perfection in horsemanship, that in the fifteenth *Iliad,* v. 822, we have a *simile* taken from an extraordinary feat of activity, where one man manages four horses at once, and leaps from the back of one to another at full speed.

If we consider in what high esteem among warriours these noble animals must have been at their first coming into *Greece*, we shall the less wonder at the frequent occasions *Homer* has taken to describe and celebrate them. It is not so strange to find them set almost upon a level with men, at the time when a *horse* in the prizes was of equal value with a *captive.*

The *chariots* were in all probability very low. For we frequently find in the *Iliad,* that a person who stands erect on a chariot is killed (and sometimes by a stroke on the head) by a foot-soldier with a sword. This may farther appear from the ease and readiness with which they alight or mount on every occasion; to facilitate which, the chariots were made open behind. That the wheels were but small, may be guest from a custom they had of taking them off and setting them on, as they were laid by, or made use of. *Hebe* in the fifth book puts on the wheels of *Juno*'s chariot, when she calls for it in haste. And it seems to be with allusion to the same practice that it is said in *Exodus*, ch. 14. *The Lord*

took off their chariot-wheels, so that they drove them heavily. The sides
were also low; for whoever is killed in his Chariot throughout the
poem, constantly falls to the ground as having nothing to support him.
That the whole machine was very small and light, is evident from a
passage in the tenth *Iliad*, where *Diomed* debates whether he shall
draw the chariot of *Rhesus* out of the way, or carry it on his shoulders
to a place of safety. All the particulars agree with the representations of
the chariots on the most ancient *Greek* coins; where the tops of them
reach not so high as the backs of the horses, the wheels are yet lower,
and the Heroes who stand in them are seen from the knee upwards.
*This may serve to shew those Criticks are under a mistake, who
blame *Homer* for making his warriours sometimes retire behind their
chariots, as if it were a piece of cowardice: which was as little disgraceful
then, as it is now to alight from one's horse in a battel on any necessary
emergency.

There were generally two persons in each chariot, one of whom was
wholly employ'd in guiding the horses. They used indifferently two,
three, or four horses: From hence it happens, that sometimes when a
horse is killed, the hero continues the fight with the two or more that
remain; and at other times a warriour retreats upon the loss of one; not
that he has less courage than the other, but that he has fewer horses.

Their *swords* were all broad cutting swords, for we find they never
stab but with their spears. The *spears* were used two ways, either to
push with, or to cast from them, like the missive javelins. It seems
surprizing that a man should throw a dart or spear with such force as
to pierce thro' both sides of the armour and the body (as is often
described in *Homer*.) For if the strength of the men was gigantick, the
armour must have been strong in proportion. Some solution might be
given for this, if we imagin'd the armour was generally brass, and the
weapons pointed with iron; and if we could fancy that *Homer* call'd the
spears and swords *brazen* in the same manner that he calls the reins of
a bridle *ivory*, only from the ornaments about them. But there are
passages where the point of the spear is expressly said to be of brass, as
in the description of that of *Hector* in *Iliad 6. Pausanias, Laconicis*,
takes it for granted, that the arms, as well offensive as defensive, were
brass. He says the spear of *Achilles* was kept in his time in the temple
of *Minerva*, the top and point of which were of brass; and the sword of
Meriones, in that of *Æsculapius* among the *Nicomedians*, was entirely of

* *See the Collection of* Goltzius, &c.

the same metal. But be it as it will, there are examples even at this day of such a prodigious force in casting darts, as almost exceeds credibility. The *Turks* and *Arabs* will pierce thro' thick planks with darts of harden'd wood; which can only be attributed to their being bred (as the ancients were) to that exercise, and to the strength and agility acquir'd by a constant practice of it.

We may ascribe to the same cause their power of casting *stones* of a vast weight, which appears a common practice in these battels. Those are in a great error, who imagine this to be only a fictitious embellishment of the Poet, which was one of the exercises of war among the ancient *Greeks* and *Orientals.* *St *Jerome* tells us, it was an old custom in *Palestine*, and in use in his own time, to have round stones of a great weight kept in the castles and villages for the youth to try their strength with. And the custom is yet extant in some parts of *Scotland*, where stones for the same purpose are laid at the gates of great houses, which they call *putting-stones.*

Another consideration which will account for many things that may seem uncouth in *Homer*, is the reflection that before the use of *fire-arms* there was infinitely more scope for personal valour than in the modern battels. Now whensoever the personal strength of the combatants happen'd to be unequal, the declining a single combate could not be so dishonourable as it is in this age, when the arms we make use of put all men on a level. For a soldier of far inferior strength may manage a rapier or fire-arms so expertly as to be an overmatch to his adversary. This may appear a sufficient excuse for what in the modern construction might seem cowardice in *Homer*'s heroes, when they avoid engaging with others, whose bodily strength exceeds their own. The maxims of valour in all times were founded upon reason, and the cowardice ought rather in this case to be imputed to him who braves his inferiour. There was also more *leisure* in their battels before the

---

* Mos est in Urbibus Palestinæ, & usque hodie per omnem Judæam vetus consuetudo servatur, ut in viculis, oppidis, & castellis rotundi ponantur lapides gravissimi ponderis, ad quos juvenes exercere se solent, & eos pro varietate virium sublevare, alii ad genua, alii ad umbilicum, alii ad humeros, ad caput, non nulli super verticem, rectis junctique manibus, magnitudinem virium demonstrantes, pondus attollunt.

[There is a custom in the cities of Palestine, a custom that is observed even today throughout all Judaea, of placing round, very heavy stones in villages, towns, and forts; the young men exercise with these, and lift them with different degrees of strength – some to their knees, some to their navels, some to their heads; some lift the stones above their heads, and with their hands joined together in an upright manner, displaying a great deal of strength, they lift the weight.]

knowledge of fire-arms; and this in a good degree accounts for those harangues his heroes make to each other in the time of combate.

There was another practice frequently used by these ancient warriours, which was to spoil an enemy of his arms after they had slain him; and this custom we see them frequently pursuing with such eagerness as if they look'd on their victory not complete 'till this point was gain'd. Some modern Criticks have accused them of avarice on account of this practice, which might probably arise from the great value and scarceness of armour in that early time and infancy of war. It afterwards became a point of honour, like gaining a standard from the enemy. *Moses* and *David* speak of the pleasure of obtaining many spoils. They preserved them as monuments of victory, and even religion at last became interested herein, when those spoils were consecrated in the temples of the tutelar Deities of the conqueror.

The reader may easily see, I set down these heads just as they occur to my memory, and only as hints to farther observations; which any one who is conversant in *Homer* can not fail to make, if he will but think a little in the same track.

It is no part of my design to enquire what progress had been made in the *art of war* at this early period: The bare perusal of the Iliad will best inform us of it. But what I think tends more immediately to the better comprehension of these descriptions, is to give a short view of the *scene* of War, the *situation* of *Troy*, and those places which *Homer* mentions, with the proper *field* of each battel: Putting together, for this purpose, those passages in my Author that give any light to this matter.

The ancient City of *Troy* stood at a greater distance from the sea than those Ruins which have since been shewn for it. This may be gather'd from Iliad 5. v. (of the original) 791. where it is said that the *Trojans* never durst sally out of the *walls* of their town 'till the retirement of *Achilles*; but afterwards combated the *Grecians* at their very ships, *far from the city.* For had *Troy* stood (as *Strabo* observes) so nigh the *sea-shore*, it had been madness in the *Greeks* not to have built any fortification before their fleet till the tenth year of the siege, when the enemy was so near them: And on the other hand, it had been cowardice in the *Trojans* not to have attempted any thing all that time, against an army that lay unfortify'd and unintrench'd. Besides, the intermediate space had been too small to afford a field for so many various adventures and actions of war. The places about *Troy* particularly mentioned by *Homer* lie in this order.

1. The *Scæan gate*: This open'd to the field of battel, and was that thro' which the *Trojans* made their excursions. Close to this stood the *beech-tree*, sacred to *Jupiter*, which *Homer* generally mentions with it.

2. The *hill* of *wild fig-trees*. It join'd to the walls of *Troy* on one side, and extended to the high-way on the other. The first appears from what *Andromache* says in *Iliad* 6. v. 432, that *the walls were in danger of being scaled from this hill*; and the last from *Il.* 22. v. 145. *&c.*

3. The *two springs* of *Scamander*. These were a little higher on the same high-way. (*Ibid.*)

4. *Callicolone*, the name of a pleasant hill, that lay near the river *Simoïs*, on the other side of the town. *Il.* 20. v. 53.

5. *Bateia*, or the sepulchre of *Myrinne*, stood a little before the city in the plain. *Il.* 2. v. 318. *of the Catal.*

6. The *Monument of Ilus*: Near the middle of the plain. *Il.* 11. v. 166.

7. The tomb of *Æsyetes*, commanded the prospect of the fleet, and that part of the sea-coast. *Il.* 2. v. 301. *of the catalogue.*

It seems, by the 465*th* verse of the second Iliad, that the *Grecian* army was drawn up under the several leaders by the banks of *Scamander*, on that side toward the ships: In the mean time that of *Troy* and the auxiliaries was rang'd in order at *Myrinne*'s sepulchre. *Ibid.* v. 320 *of the Catal.* The place of the *first Battel* where *Diomed* performs his exploits, was near the joining of *Simoïs* and *Scamander*; for *Juno* and *Pallas* coming to him, alight at the confluence of those rivers. *Il.* 5. v. 776. and that the *Greeks* had not yet past the stream, but fought on that side next the fleet, appears from v. 791 of the same book, where *Juno* says *the* Trojans *now brave them at their very ships.* But in the beginning of the sixth book, the place of battel is specify'd to be between the rivers of *Simoïs* and *Scamander*; so that the *Greeks* (tho' *Homer* does not particularize when, or in what manner) had then cross'd the stream toward *Troy*.

The engagement in the eighth book is evidently close to the *Grecian* fortification on the shore. That night *Hector* lay at *Ilus*'s tomb in the field, as *Dolon* tells us *Lib.* 10. v. 415. And in the eleventh book the battel is chiefly about *Ilus*'s tomb.

In the twelfth, thirteenth, and fourteenth, about the fortification of the *Greeks*, and in the fifteenth at the *Ships*.

In the sixteenth, the *Trojans* being repulsed by *Patroclus*, they engage between the fleet, the river, and the *Grecian* wall: See v. 396. *Patroclus* still advancing, they fight at the gates of *Troy* v. 700. In the seventeenth, the fight about the body of *Patroclus* is under the *Trojan* wall, v. 403. His body being carried off, *Hector* and *Æneas* pursue the *Greeks* to the fortification, v. 760. And in the eighteenth, upon *Achilles*'s appearing, they retire and encamp without the fortification.

In the twentieth, the fight is still on that side next the sea; for the *Trojans* being pursued by *Achilles*, pass over the *Scamander* as they run toward *Troy*: See the beginning of book 21. The following battels are either in the river itself, or between that and the city, under whose walls *Hector* is kill'd in the twenty-second book, which puts an end to the battels of the *Iliad*.

N.B. *The verses above are cited according to the number of lines in the Greek.*

THE
FIFTH BOOK
OF THE
ILIAD

The ARGUMENT

The Acts of *Diomed*

Diomed, *assisted by* Pallas, *performs wonders in this day's battel.* Pandarus *wounds him with an Arrow, but the Goddess cures him, enables him to discern Gods from mortals, and prohibits him from contending with any of the former, excepting* Venus. Æneas *joins* Pandarus *to oppose him,* Pandarus *is killed, and* Æneas *in great danger but for the Assistance of* Venus; *who, as she is removing her son from the fight, is wounded on the hand by* Diomed. Apollo *seconds her in his rescue, and at length carries off* Æneas *to* Troy, *where he is heal'd in the temple of* Pergamus. Mars *rallies the* Trojans, *and assists* Hector *to make a stand. In the mean time* Æneas *is restor'd to the field, and they overthrow several of the* Greeks; *among the rest* Tlepolemus *is slain by* Sarpedon. Juno *and* Minerva *descend to resist* Mars; *the latter incites* Diomed *to go against that God; he wounds him, and sends him groaning to Heaven.*

The first battel continues thro' this book. The scene *is the same as in the former.*

But *Pallas* now *Tydidès'* soul inspires,
Fills with her force, and warms with all her fires,
Above the *Greeks* his deathless fame to raise,
And crown her Hero with distinguish'd praise.
5 High on his helm celestial lightnings play,
His beamy shield emits a living ray;
Th' unweary'd blaze incessant streams supplies,
Like the red star that fires th' autumnal skies,
When fresh he rears his radiant orb to sight,
10 And bath'd in Ocean, shoots a keener light.
Such Glories *Pallas* on the chief bestow'd,
Such, from his Arms, the fierce effulgence flow'd:
Onward she drives him, furious to engage,
Where the fight burns, and where the thickest rage.
15   The Sons of *Dares* first the Combate sought,
A wealthy priest, but rich without a fault;
In *Vulcan*'s fane the father's days were led,
The sons to toils of glorious battel bred;
These singled from their troops the fight maintain,
20 These from their steeds, *Tydides* on the plain.
Fierce for renown the brother chiefs draw near,
And first bold *Phegeus* cast his founding spear,
Which o'er the warriour's shoulder took its course,
And spent in empty air its erring force.
25 Not so, *Tydides*, flew thy lance in vain,
But pierc'd his breast, and stretch'd him on the plain.
Seiz'd with unusual fear, *Idæus* fled,
Left the rich chariot, and his brother dead;

And had not *Vulcan* lent celestial aid,
He too had sunk to death's eternal shade;
But in a smoaky cloud the God of fire
Preserv'd the son, in pity to the sire.
The steeds and chariot, to the navy led,
Encreas'd the spoils of gallant *Diomed*.

    Struck with amaze, and shame, the *Trojan* crew
Or slain, or fled, the sons of *Dares* view;
When by the blood-stain'd hand *Minerva* prest
The God of battels; and this speech addrest.

    Stern pow'r of war! by whom the mighty fall,
Who bathe in blood, and shake the lofty wall!
Let the brave chiefs their glorious toils divide;
And whose the conquest, mighty *Jove* decide:
While we from interdicted fields retire,
Nor tempt the wrath of heaven's avenging Sire.

    Her words allay th' impetuous warriour's heat,
The God of arms and martial Maid retreat;
Remov'd from fight, on *Xanthus* flow'ry bounds
They sate, and listen'd to the dying sounds.

    Meantime, the *Greeks* the *Trojan* race pursue,
And some bold chieftain ev'ry leader slew:
First *Odius* falls, and bites the bloody sand,
His death ennobled by *Atrides'* hand;
As he to flight his wheeling car addrest,
The speedy javelin drove from back to breast.
In dust the mighty *Halizonian* lay,
His arms resound, the spirit wings its way.

    Thy fate was next, O *Phæstus!* doom'd to feel
The great *Idomeneus'* protended steel;
Whom *Borus* sent (his son and only joy)
From fruitful *Tarne* to the fields of *Troy*.
The *Cretan* javelin reach'd him from afar,
And pierc'd his shoulder as he mounts his car;
Back from the car he tumbles to the ground,
And everlasting shades his eyes surround.

    Then dy'd *Scamandrius*, expert in the chace,
In woods and wilds to wound the savage race;
Diana taught him all her sylvan arts,
To bend the bow and aim unerring darts:

But vainly here *Diana*'s arts he tries,
70   The fatal lance arrests him as he flies;
From *Menelaüs*' arm the Weapon sent,
Thro' his broad back and heaving bosom went:
Down sinks the warriour with a thundring sound,
His brazen armour rings against the ground.

75   Next artful *Phereclus* untimely fell;
Bold *Merion* sent him to the realms of hell.
Thy father's skill, O *Phereclus*, was thine,
The graceful fabrick and the fair design;
For lov'd by *Pallas*, *Pallas* did impart
80   To him the shipwright's and the builder's art.
Beneath his hand the fleet of *Paris* rose,
The fatal cause of all his country's woes;
But he, the mystic will of heav'n unknown,
Nor saw his country's peril, nor his own.
85   The hapless artist, while confus'd he fled,
The spear of *Merion* mingled with the dead.
Thro' his right hip with forceful fury cast,
Between the bladder and the bone it past:
Prone on his knees he falls with fruitless cries,
90   And death in lasting slumber seals his eyes.

From *Meges*' force the swift *Pedæus* fled,
Antenor's offspring from a foreign bed,
Whose gen'rous spouse, *Theano*, heav'nly fair,
Nurs'd the young stranger with a mother's care.
95   How vain those cares! when *Meges* in the rear
Full in his nape infix'd the fatal spear;
Swift thro' his crackling jaws the weapon glides,
And the cold tongue and grinning teeth divides.

Then dy'd *Hypsenor*, gen'rous and divine,
100   Sprung from the brave *Dolopion*'s mighty line,
Who near ador'd *Scamander* made abode,
Priest of the stream, and honour'd as a God.
On him, amidst the flying numbers found,
Eurypilus inflicts a deadly wound;
105   On his broad shoulder fell the forceful brand,
Thence glancing downward lopp'd his holy hand,
Which stain'd with sacred blood the blushing sand.

Down sunk the Priest: the purple hand of death
Clos'd his dim eye, and fate suppress'd his breath.

    Thus toil'd the chiefs, in diff'ring parts engag'd,   110
In ev'ry quarter fierce *Tydides* rag'd,
Amid the *Greek*, amid the *Trojan* train,
Rapt thro' the ranks he thunders o'er the plain,
Now here, now there, he darts from place to place,
Pours on the rear, or lightens in their face.   115
Thus from high hills the torrents swift and strong
Deluge whole fields, and sweep the trees along,
Thro' ruin'd moles the rushing wave resounds,
O'erwhelms the bridge, and bursts the lofty bounds;
The yellow harvests of the ripen'd year,   120
And flatted vineyards, one sad waste appear!
While *Jove* descends in sluicy sheets of rain,
And all the labours of mankind are vain.

    So rag'd *Tydides*, boundless in his ire,
Drove armies back, and made all *Troy* retire.   125
With grief the *leader of the *Lycian* band
Saw the wide waste of his destructive hand:
His bended bow against the chief he drew;
Swift to the mark the thirsty arrow flew,
Whose forky point the hollow breast-plate tore,   130
Deep in his shoulder pierc'd, and drank the gore:
The rushing stream his brazen armour dy'd,
While the proud archer thus exulting cry'd.

    Hither ye *Trojans*, hither drive your steeds!
Lo! by our hand the bravest *Grecian* bleeds.   135
Not long the deathful dart he can sustain;
Or *Phœbus* urg'd me to these fields in vain.

    So spoke he, boastful; but the winged dart
Stopt short of life, and mock'd the shooter's art.
The wounded chief behind his car retir'd,   140
The helping Hand of *Sthenelus* requir'd;
Swift from his seat he leap'd upon the ground,
And tugg'd the weapon from the gushing wound;
When thus the King his guardian pow'r addrest,
The purple current wand'ring o'er his vest.   145

* Pandarus.

O Progeny of Jove! unconquer'd maid!
If e'er my Godlike sire deserv'd thy aid,
If e'er I felt thee in the fighting field;
Now, Goddess, now, thy sacred succour yield.
150 Oh give my lance to reach the *Trojan* Knight,
Whose arrow wounds the chief thou guard'st in fight;
And lay the boaster grov'ling on the shore,
That vaunts these eyes shall view the light no more.
    Thus pray'd *Tydides*, and *Minerva* heard,
155 His nerves confirm'd, his languid spirits chear'd;
He feels each limb with wonted vigour light;
His beating bosom claims the promis'd fight.
Be bold (she cry'd) in ev'ry combate shine,
War be thy province, thy protection mine;
160 Rush to the fight, and ev'ry foe controul;
Wake each paternal virtue in thy soul:
Strength swells thy boiling breast, infus'd by me,
And all thy Godlike father breathes in thee!
Yet more, from mortal mists I purge thy eyes,
165 And set to view the warring Deities.
These see thou shun, thro' all th' embattled plain,
Nor rashly strive where human force is vain.
If *Venus* mingle in the martial band,
Her shalt thou wound: So *Pallas* gives command.
170   With that, the blue-ey'd virgin wing'd her flight;
The Hero rush'd impetuous to the fight;
With tenfold ardour now invades the plain,
Wild with delay, and more enrag'd by pain.
As on the fleecy flocks, when hunger calls,
175 Amidst the field a brindled lyon falls;
If chance some shepherd with a distant dart
The savage wound, he rouses at the smart,
He foams, he roars; the shepherd dares not stay,
But trembling leaves the scatt'ring flocks a prey.
180 Heaps fall on heaps; he bathes with blood the ground,
Then leaps victorious o'er the lofty mound.
Not with less fury stern *Tydides* slew,
And two brave leaders at an instant slew:
Astynous breathless fell, and by his side
185 His people's pastor, good *Hypenor*, dy'd;

Astynous' breast the deadly lance receives,
Hypenor's shoulder his broad faulchion cleaves.
Those slain he left; and sprung with noble rage
Abas, and *Polyidus* to engage;
Sons of *Eurydamas*, who wise and old,   190
Could fates foresee, and mystic dreams unfold;
The youths return'd not from the doubtful plain,
And the sad father try'd his arts in vain;
No mystick dream could make their fates appear,
Tho' now determin'd by *Tydides*' spear.   195

   Young *Xanthus* next, and *Thoön* felt his rage,
The joy and hope of *Phœnops*' feeble age;
Vast was his wealth, and these the only heirs
Of all his labours, and a life of cares;
Cold death o'ertakes them in their blooming years,   200
And leaves the father unavailing tears:
To strangers now descends his heapy store,
The race forgotten, and the name no more.

   Two sons of *Priam* in one chariot ride,
Glitt'ring in arms, and combate side by side.   205
As when the lordly lyon seeks his food
Where grazing heifers range the lonely wood,
He leaps amidst them with a furious bound,
Bends their strong necks, and tears them to the ground:
So from their seats the brother-chiefs are torn,   210
Their steeds and chariot to the navy born.

   With deep concern divine *Æneas* view'd
The foe prevailing, and his friends pursu'd,
Thro' the thick storm of singing spears he flies,
Exploring *Pandarus* with careful eyes.   215
At length he found *Lycaon*'s mighty son;
To whom the chief of *Venus*' race begun.

   Where, *Pandarus*, are all thy honours now,
Thy winged arrows and unerring bow,
Thy matchless skill, thy yet-unrival'd fame,   220
And boasted glory of the *Lycian* name?
Oh pierce that mortal, if we mortal call
That wondrous force by which whole armies fall;
Or God incens'd, who quits the distant skies
To punish *Troy* for slighted sacrifice;   225

(Which oh avert from our unhappy state!
For what so dreadful as celestial hate?)
Whoe'er he be, propitiate *Jove* with pray'r;
If man, destroy; if God, entreat to spare.
230   To him the *Lycian.* Whom your eyes behold,
If right I judge, is *Diomed* the bold.
Such coursers whirl him o'er the dusty field,
So tow'rs his helmet, and so flames his shield.
If 'tis a God, he wears that Chief's disguise;
235   Or if that Chief, some guardian of the skies
Involv'd in clouds, protects him in the fray,
And turns unseen the frustrate dart away.
I wing'd an arrow, which not idly fell,
The stroke had fix'd him to the gates of hell,
240   And, but some God, some angry God withstands,
His fate was due to these unerring hands.

Skill'd in the bow, on foot I sought the war,
Nor join'd swift horses to the rapid car.
Ten polish'd chariots I possess'd at home,
245   And still they grace *Lycaon's* princely dome:
There veil'd in spacious coverlets they stand;
And twice ten coursers wait their Lord's command.
The good old warriour bade me trust to these,
When first for *Troy* I sail'd the sacred seas;
250   In fields, aloft, the whirling car to guide,
And thro' the ranks of death triumphant ride.
But vain with youth, and yet to thrift inclin'd,
I heard his counsels with unheedful mind,
And thought the steeds (your large supplies unknown)
255   Might fail of forage in the straiten'd town:
So took my bow and pointed darts in hand,
And left the chariots in my native land.

Too late, O friend! my rashness I deplore;
These shafts, once fatal, carry death no more.
260   *Tydeus'* and *Atreus'* sons their points have found,
And undissembled gore pursu'd the wound.
In vain they bled: This unavailing bow
Serves not to slaughter, but provoke the foe.
In evil hour these bended horns I strung,
265   And seiz'd the quiver where it idly hung.

Curs'd be the fate that sent me to the field,
Without a warriour's arms, the spear and shield!
If e'er with life I quit the *Trojan* plain,
If e'er I see my Spouse and Sire again,
This bow, unfaithful to my glorious aims,   270
Broke by my hand, shall feed the blazing flames.

    To whom the Leader of the *Dardan* race:
Be calm, nor *Phœbus*' honour'd gift disgrace.
The distant dart be prais'd, tho' here we need
The rushing chariot, and the bounding steed.   275
Against yon' Hero let us bend our course,
And, hand to hand, encounter force with force.
Now mount my seat, and from the chariot's height
Observe my father's steeds, renown'd in fight,
Practis'd alike to turn, to stop, to chace,   280
To dare the shock, or urge the rapid race:
Secure with these, thro' fighting fields we go,
Or safe to *Troy*, if *Jove* assist the foe.
Haste, seize the whip, and snatch the guiding rein:
The warriour's fury let this arm sustain;   285
Or if to combate thy bold heart incline,
Take thou the spear, the chariot's care be mine.

    O Prince! (*Lycaon*'s valiant son reply'd)
As thine the steeds, be thine the task to guide.
The horses practis'd to their Lord's command,   290
Shall hear the rein, and answer to thy hand.
But if unhappy, we desert the fight,
Thy voice alone can animate their flight:
Else shall our fates be number'd with the Dead,
And these, the victor's prize, in triumph led.   295
Thine be the guidance then: With spear and shield
My self will charge this terror of the field.

    And now both Heroes mount the glitt'ring car:
The bounding coursers rush amidst the war.
Their fierce approach bold *Sthenelus* espy'd,   300
Who thus, alarm'd, to great *Tydides* cry'd.

    O Friend! two chiefs of force immense I see,
Dreadful they come, and bend their rage on thee:
Lo the brave heir of old *Lycaon*'s line,
And great *Æneas*, sprung from race divine!   305

Enough is giv'n to fame. Ascend thy car;
And save a life, the bulwark of our war.
    At this the Hero cast a gloomy look,
Fix'd on the chief with scorn, and thus he spoke.
310 Me dost thou bid to shun the coming fight?
Me would'st thou move to base, inglorious flight?
Know, 'tis not honest in my soul to fear,
Nor was *Tydides* born to tremble here.
I hate the cumbrous chariot's slow advance,
315 And the long distance of the flying lance;
But while my nerves are strong, my force entire,
Thus front the foe, and emulate my Sire.
Nor shall yon' steeds that fierce to fight convey
Those threatning heroes, bear them both away;
320 One chief at least beneath this arm shall die;
So *Pallas* tells me, and forbids to fly.
But if she dooms, and if no God withstand,
That both shall fall by one victorious hand;
Then heed my words: My horses here detain,
325 Fix'd to the chariot by the straiten'd rein;
Swift to *Æneas*' empty seat proceed,
And seize the coursers of ætherial breed.
The race of those which once the thund'ring God
For ravish'd *Ganymede* on *Tros* bestow'd,
330 The best that e'er on earth's broad surface run,
Beneath the rising or the setting sun.
Hence great *Anchises* stole a breed, unknown,
By mortal *Mares*, from fierce *Laomedon*:
Four of this race his ample stalls contain,
335 And two transport *Æneas* o'er the plain.
These, were the rich immortal prize our own,
Thro' the wide world should make our glory known.
    Thus while they spoke, the foe came furious on,
And stern *Lycaon*'s warlike race begun.
340   Prince, thou art met. Tho' late in vain assail'd,
The spear may enter where the arrow fail'd.
    He said, then shook the pondrous lance, and flung,
On his broad shield the sounding weapon rung,
Pierc'd the tough orb, and in his cuirass hung.

He bleeds! The pride of *Greece*! (the boaster cries)   345
Our triumph now, the mighty warriour lies!
Mistaken vaunter! *Diomed* reply'd;
Thy dart has err'd, and now my spear be try'd:
Ye scape not both; one, headlong from his car,
With hostile blood shall glut the God of War.   350

   He spoke, and rising hurl'd his forceful dart,
Which driv'n by *Pallas*, pierc'd a vital part;
Full in his face it enter'd, and betwixt
The nose and eye-ball the proud *Lycian* fixt;
Crash'd all his jaws, and cleft the tongue within,   355
'Till the bright point look'd out beneath the chin.
Headlong he falls, his helmet knocks the ground;
Earth groans beneath him, and his arms resound;
The starting coursers tremble with affright;
The soul indignant seeks the realms of night.   360

   To guard his slaughter'd friend, *Æneas* flies,
His spear extending where the carcass lies;
Watchful he wheels, protects it ev'ry way,
As the grim lyon stalks around his prey.
O'er the fall'n trunk his ample shield display'd,   365
He hides the Hero with his mighty shade,
And threats aloud: The *Greeks* with longing eyes
Behold at distance, but forbear the prize.
Then fierce *Tydides* stoops; and from the fields
Heav'd with vast force, a rocky fragment wields.   370
Not two strong men th' enormous weight could raise,
Such men as live in these degen'rate days.
He swung it round; and gath'ring strength to throw,
Discharg'd the pond'rous ruin at the foe.
Where to the hip th' inserted thigh unites,   375
Full on the bone the pointed marble lights;
Thro' both the tendons broke the rugged stone,
And stripp'd the skin, and crack'd the solid bone.
Sunk on his knees, and stagg'ring with his pains,
His falling bulk his bended arm sustains;   380
Lost in a dizzy mist the Warriour lies;
A sudden cloud comes swimming o'er his eyes.
There the brave chief who mighty numbers sway'd
Oppress'd had sunk to death's eternal shade;

385   But Heav'nly *Venus*, mindful of the love
        She bore *Anchises* in th' *Idæan* grove,
        His danger views with anguish and despair,
        And guards her offspring with a mother's care.
        About her much-lov'd son her arms she throws,
390   Her arms whose whiteness match the falling snows.
        Screen'd from the foe behind her shining veil,
        The swords wave harmless, and the javelins fail:
        Safe thro' the rushing horse and feather'd flight
        Of sounding shafts, she bears him from the fight.

395   Nor *Sthenelus*, with unassisting hands,
        Remain'd unheedful of his Lord's commands:
        His panting steeds, remov'd from out the war,
        He fix'd with straiten'd traces to the car.
        Next rushing to the *Dardan* spoil, detains
400   The heav'nly coursers with the flowing manes.
        These in proud triumph to the fleet convey'd,
        No longer now a *Trojan* Lord obey'd.
        That charge to bold *Deïpylus* he gave,
        (Whom most he lov'd, as brave men love the brave)
405   Then mounting on his car, resum'd the rein,
        And follow'd where *Tydides* swept the plain.

        Meanwhile (his conquest ravish'd from his eyes)
        The raging chief in chace of *Venus* flies:
        No Goddess she, commission'd to the field,
410   Like *Pallas* dreadful with her sable shield,
        Or fierce *Bellona* thund'ring at the wall,
        While flames ascend, and mighty ruins fall;
        He knew soft combats suit the tender dame,
        New to the field, and still a foe to fame.
415   Thro' breaking ranks his furious course he bends,
        And at the Goddess his broad lance extends;
        Thro' her bright veil the daring weapon drove,
        Th' ambrosial veil, which all the Graces wove;
        Her snowy hand the razing steel profan'd,
420   And the transparent skin with crimson stain'd.
        From the clear vein a stream immortal flow'd,
        Such stream as issues from a wounded God:
        Pure Emanation! uncorrupted flood;
        Unlike our gross, diseas'd, terrestrial blood:

(For not the bread of man their life sustains,
Nor wine's inflaming juice supplies their veins.) 425
With tender shrieks the Goddess fill'd the place,
And dropt her offspring from her weak embrace.
Him *Phœbus* took: He casts a cloud around
The fainting chief, and wards the mortal wound. 430

    Then with a voice that shook the vaulted skies,
The King insults the Goddess as she flies.
Ill with *Jove*'s daughter bloody fights agree,
The field of combat is no scene for thee:
Go, let thy own soft sex employ thy care, 435
Go lull the coward, or delude the fair.
Taught by this stroke, renounce the war's alarms,
And learn to tremble at the name of arms.

    Tydides thus. The Goddess, seiz'd with dread,
Confus'd, distracted, from the conflict fled. 440
To aid her, swift the winged *Iris* flew,
Wrapt in a mist above the warring crew.
The Queen of Love with faded charms she found,
Pale was her cheek, and livid look'd the wound.
To *Mars*, who sate remote, they bent their way. 445
Far on the left, with clouds involv'd, he lay;
Beside him stood his lance, distain'd with gore,
And, rein'd with gold, his foaming steeds before.
Low at his knee, she begg'd, with streaming eyes,
Her brother's car, to mount the distant skies, 450
And shew'd the wound by fierce *Tydides* giv'n,
A mortal man, who dares encounter heav'n.

    Stern *Mars* attentive hears the Queen complain,
And to her hand commits the golden rein;
She mounts the seat oppress'd with silent woe, 455
Driv'n by the Goddess of the painted bow.
The lash resounds, the rapid chariot flies,
And in a moment scales the lofty skies.
There stopp'd the car, and there the coursers stood,
Fed by fair *Iris* with ambrosial food. 460
Before her mother Love's bright Queen appears,
O'erwhelm'd with anguish and dissolv'd in tears;
She rais'd her in her arms, beheld her bleed,
And ask'd, what God had wrought this guilty deed?

465   Then she: This insult from no God I found,
        An impious mortal gave the daring wound!
        Behold the deed of haughty *Diomed!*
        'Twas in the son's defence the mother bled.
        The war with *Troy* no more the *Grecians* wage;
470   But with the Gods (th' immortal Gods) engage.
            Dione then. Thy wrongs with patience bear,
        And share those griefs inferior pow'rs must share:
        Unnumber'd woes mankind from us sustain,
        And men with woes afflict the Gods again.
475   The mighty *Mars* in mortal fetters bound,
        And lodg'd in brazen dungeons under ground,
        Full thirteen moons imprison'd roar'd in vain;
        Otus and *Ephialtes* held the chain:
        Perhaps had perish'd; had not *Hermes*' care
480   Restor'd the groaning God to upper air.
        Great *Juno*'s self has born her weight of pain,
        Th' imperial partner of the heav'nly reign;
        Amphitryon's son infix'd the deadly dart,
        And fill'd with anguish her immortal heart.
485   Ev'n hell's grim King *Alcides*' pow'r confest,
        The shaft found entrance in his iron breast;
        To *Jove*'s high palace for a cure he fled,
        Pierc'd in his own dominions of the dead;
        Where *Pæon* sprinkling heav'nly balm around,
490   Assuag'd the glowing pangs, and clos'd the wound.
        Rash, impious man! to stain the blest abodes,
        And drench his arrows in the blood of Gods!
            But thou (tho' *Pallas* urg'd thy frantic deed)
        Whose spear ill-fated makes a Goddess bleed,
495   Know thou, whoe'er with heav'nly pow'r contends,
        Short is his date, and soon his glory ends;
        From fields of death when late he shall retire,
        No infant on his knees shall call him Sire.
        Strong as thou art, some God may yet be found,
500   To stretch thee pale and gasping on the ground;
        Thy distant wife, *Ægiale* the fair,
        Starting from sleep with a distracted air,
        Shall rouse thy slaves, and her lost Lord deplore,
        The brave, the great, the glorious, now no more!

This said, she wip'd from *Venus*' wounded palm   505
The sacred *Ichor*, and infus'd the balm.
Juno and *Pallas* with a smile survey'd,
And thus to *Jove* began the blue-ey'd maid.

Permit thy daughter, gracious *Jove!* to tell
How this mischance the *Cyprian* Queen befell.   510
As late she try'd with passion to inflame
The tender bosom of a *Grecian* dame,
Allur'd the fair with moving thoughts of joy,
To quit her country for some youth of *Troy*;
The clasping Zone, with golden buckles bound,   515
Raz'd her soft hand with this lamented wound.

The Sire of Gods and men superior smil'd,
And, calling *Venus*, thus addrest his child.
Not these, O daughter, are thy proper cares,
Thee milder arts befit, and softer wars;   520
Sweet smiles are thine, and kind endearing charms,
To *Mars* and *Pallas* leave the deeds of arms.

Thus they in heav'n: While on the plain below
The fierce *Tydides* charg'd his *Dardan* foe:
Flush'd with celestial blood pursu'd his way,   525
And fearless dar'd the threatning God of day;
Already in his hopes he saw him kill'd,
Tho' screen'd behind *Apollo*'s mighty shield.
Thrice rushing furious, at the chief he strook;
His blazing buckler thrice *Apollo* shook: 530
He try'd the fourth: When breaking from the cloud,
A more than mortal voice was heard aloud.

O Son of *Tydeus*, cease! be wise and see
How vast the diff'rence of the Gods and thee;
Distance immense! between the pow'rs that shine   535
Above, eternal, deathless, and divine,
And mortal man! a wretch of humble birth,
A short-liv'd reptile in the dust of earth.

So spoke the God who darts celestial fires;
He dreads his fury, and some steps retires.   540
Then *Phœbus* bore the chief of *Venus*' race
To *Troy*'s high fane, and to his holy place;
Latona there and *Phœbe* heal'd the wound,
With vigour arm'd him, and with glory crown'd.

545 This done, the patron of the silver bow
A phantom rais'd, the same in shape and show
With great *Æneas*; such the form he bore,
And such in fight the radiant arms he wore.
Around the spectre bloody wars are wag'd,
550 And *Greece* and *Troy* with clashing shields engag'd.
Meantime on *Ilion*'s tow'r *Apollo* stood,
And calling *Mars*, thus urg'd the raging God.

    Stern pow'r of arms! by whom the mighty fall,
Who bathe in blood, and shake th' embattel'd wall!
555 Rise in thy wrath! To hell's abhorr'd abodes
Dispatch yon' *Greek*, and vindicate the Gods.
First rosy *Venus* felt his brutal rage;
Me next he charg'd, and dares all heav'n engage:
The wretch would brave high heav'ns immortal Sire,
560 His triple thunder, and his bolts of fire.

    The God of battel issues on the plain,
Stirs all the ranks, and fires the *Trojan* train;
In form like *Acamas*, the *Thracian* guide,
Enrag'd, to *Troy*'s retiring chiefs he cry'd:

565   How long, ye Sons of *Priam!* will ye fly,
And unreveng'd see *Priam*'s people die?
Still unresisted shall the foe destroy,
And stretch the slaughter to the gates of *Troy?*
Lo brave *Æneas* sinks beneath his wound,
570 Not Godlike *Hector* more in arms renown'd:
Haste all, and take the gen'rous warriour's part.
He said; new courage swell'd each hero's heart.
Sarpedon first his ardent soul express'd,
And, turn'd to *Hector*, these bold words address'd.

575   Say, Chief, is all thy ancient valour lost,
Where are thy threats, and where thy glorious boast,
That propt alone by *Priam*'s race should stand
Troy's sacred walls, nor need a foreign hand?
Now, now thy country calls her wanted friends,
580 And the proud vaunt in just derision ends.
Remote they stand, while alien troops engage,
Like trembling hounds before the lion's rage.
Far distant hence I held my wide command,
Where foaming *Xanthus* laves the *Lycian* land,

With ample wealth (the wish of mortals) blest,   585
A beauteous wife, and infant at her breast;
With those I left whatever dear could be;
Greece, if she conquers, nothing wins from me.
Yet first in fight my *Lycian* bands I chear,
And long to meet this mighty man ye fear.   590
While *Hector* idle stands, nor bids the brave
Their wives, their infants, and their altars save.
Haste, warriour, haste! preserve thy threaten'd state;
Or one vast burst of all-involving fate
Full o'er your tow'rs shall fall, and sweep away   595
Sons, sires, and wives, an undistinguish'd prey.
Rouze all thy *Trojans*, urge thy aids to fight;
These claim thy thoughts by day, thy watch by night:
With force incessant the brave *Greeks* oppose;
Such cares thy friends deserve, and such thy foes.   600
    Stung to the heart the gen'rous *Hector* hears,
But just reproof with decent silence bears.
From his proud car the Prince impetuous springs;
On earth he leaps; his brazen armor rings.
Two shining spears are brandish'd in his hands;   605
Thus arm'd, he animates his drooping bands,
Revives their ardour, turns their steps from flight,
And wakes anew the dying flames of fight.
They turn, they stand: The *Greeks* their fury dare,
Condense their pow'rs, and wait the growing war.   610
    As when, on *Ceres'* sacred floor, the Swain
Spreads the wide fan to clear the golden grain,
And the light chaff, before the breezes born,
Ascends in clouds from off the heapy corn;
The grey dust, rising with collected winds,   615
Drives o'er the barn, and whitens all the hinds.
So white with dust the *Grecian* host appears,
From trampling steeds, and thundring charioteers,
The dusky clouds from labour'd earth arise,
And roll in smoking volumes to the skies.   620
Mars hovers o'er them with his sable shield,
And adds new horrors to the darken'd field;
Pleas'd with his charge, and ardent to fulfill
In *Troy*'s defence *Apollo*'s heav'nly will:

625   Soon as from fight the blue-ey'd maid retires,
       Each *Trojan* bosom with new warmth he fires.
       And now the God, from forth his sacred fane,
       Produc'd *Æneas* to the shouting train;
       Alive, unharm'd, with all his Peers around,
630   Erect he stood, and vig'rous from his wound:
       Enquiries none they made; the dreadful day
       No pause of words admits, no dull delay;
       Fierce *Discord* storms, *Apollo* loud exclaims,
       Fame calls, *Mars* thunders, and the field's in flames.

635   Stern *Diomed* with either *Ajax* stood,
       And great *Ulysses*, bath'd in hostile blood.
       Embodied close, the lab'ring *Grecian* train
       The fiercest shock of charging hosts sustain;
       Unmov'd and silent, the whole war they wait,
640   Serenely dreadful, and as fix'd as fate.
       So when th' embattel'd clouds in dark array
       Along the skies their gloomy lines display,
       When now the *North* his boist'rous rage has spent,
       And peaceful sleeps the liquid element,
645   The low-hung vapours, motionless and still,
       Rest on the summits of the shaded hill;
       'Till the mass scatters as the winds arise,
       Dispers'd and broken thro' the ruffled skies.
           Nor was the Gen'ral wanting to his train,
650   From troop to troop he toils thro' all the plain.
       Ye *Greeks*, be men! the charge of battle bear;
       Your brave associates, and Your selves revere!
       Let glorious acts more glorious acts inspire,
       And catch from breast to breast the noble fire!
655   On valour's side the odds of combate lie,
       The brave live glorious, or lamented die;
       The wretch who trembles in the field of fame,
       Meets death, and worse than death, eternal shame.
           These words he seconds with his flying lance,
660   To meet whose point was strong *Deicoon*'s chance;
       Æneas' friend, and in his native place
       Honour'd and lov'd like *Priam*'s royal race:
       Long had he fought the foremost in the field;
       But now the monarch's lance transpierc'd his shield:

His shield too weak the furious dart to stay,   665
Thro' his broad belt the weapon forc'd its way;
The grizly wound dismiss'd his soul to hell,
His arms around him rattled as he fell.
　　Then fierce *Æneas* brandishing his blade,
In dust *Orsilochus* and *Crethon* laid,   670
Whose sire *Diöcleus*, wealthy, brave and great,
In well built *Pheræ* held his lofty seat:
Sprung from *Alpheüs*, plenteous stream! that yields
Encrease of harvests to the *Pylian* fields.
He got *Orsilochus*, *Diöcleus* he,   675
And these descended in the third degree.
Too early expert in the martial toil,
In sable ships they left their native soil,
T' avenge *Atrides*: Now, untimely slain,
They fell with glory on the *Phrygian* plain.   680
So two young mountain lions, nurs'd with blood
In deep recesses of the gloomy wood,
Rush fearless to the plains, and uncontroul'd
Depopulate the stalls and waste the fold;
'Till pierc'd at distance from their native den,   685
O'erpow'r'd they fall beneath the force of men.
Prostrate on earth their beauteous bodies lay,
Like mountain firs, as tall and strait as they.
Great *Menelaus* views with pitying eyes,
Lifts his bright lance, and at the victor flies;   690
Mars urg'd him on; yet, ruthless in his hate,
The God but urg'd him to provoke his fate.
He thus advancing, *Nestor*'s valiant son
Shakes for his danger, and neglects his own;
Struck with the thought, should *Helen*'s lord be slain,   695
And all his country's glorious labours vain.
Already met the threat'ning heroes stand;
The spears already tremble in their hand:
In rush'd *Antilochus*, his aid to bring,
And fall or conquer by the *Spartan* King.   700
These seen, the *Dardan* backward turn'd his course,
Brave as he was, and shunn'd unequal force.
The breathless bodies to the *Greeks* they drew;
Then mix in combate and their toils renew.

705 First *Pylæmenes*, great in battel, bled,
Who sheath'd in brass the *Paphlagonians* led.
Atrides mark'd him where sublime he stood;
Fix'd in his throat, the javelin drank his blood.
The faithful *Mydon* as he turn'd from fight

710 His flying coursers, sunk to endless night:
A broken rock by *Nestor*'s son was thrown;
His bended arm receiv'd the falling stone,
From his numb'd hand the iv'ry-studded reins
Dropt in the dust are trail'd along the plains.

715 Meanwhile his temples feel a deadly wound;
He groans in death, and pondrous sinks to ground:
Deep drove his helmet in the sands, and there
The head stood fix'd, the quiv'ring legs in air:
'Till trampled flat beneath the courser's feet,

720 The youthful victor mounts his empty seat,
And bears the prize in triumph to the fleet.

 Great *Hector* saw, and raging at the view
Pours on the *Greeks*: The *Trojan* troops pursue;
He fires his host with animating cries,

725 And brings along the furies of the skies.
Mars, stern destroyer! and *Bellona* dread,
Flame in the front, and thunder at their head;
This swells the tumult and the rage of fight;
That shakes a spear that casts a dreadful light;

730 Where *Hector* march'd, the God of battels shin'd,
Now storm'd before him, and now rag'd behind.

 Tydides paus'd amidst his full carrier;
Then first the Hero's manly breast knew fear.
As when some simple swain his cot forsakes,

735 And wide thro' fens an unknown journey takes;
If chance a swelling brook his passage stay,
And foam impervious cross the wand'rer's way,
Confus'd he stops, a length of country past,
Eyes the rough waves, and tir'd, returns at last.

740 Amaz'd no less the great *Tydides* stands;
He stay'd, and turning, thus address'd his bands.

 No wonder, *Greeks!* that all to *Hector* yield,
Secure of fav'ring Gods, he takes the field;

His strokes they second, and avert our spears:
Behold where *Mars* in mortal arms appears!   745
Retire then warriours, but sedate and slow;
Retire, but with your faces to the foe.
Trust not too much your unavailing might;
'Tis not with *Troy*, but with the Gods ye fight.

   Now near the *Greeks* the black battalions drew;   750
And first two leaders valiant *Hector* slew,
His force *Anchialus* and *Mnesthes* found,
In ev'ry art of glorious war renown'd;
In the same car the chiefs to combate ride,
And fought united, and united dy'd.   755
Struck at the sight, the mighty *Ajax* glows
With thirst of vengeance, and assaults the foes.
His massy spear with matchless fury sent,
Thro' *Amphius*' Belt and heaving Belly went:
Amphius Apæsus' happy soil possess'd,   760
With herds abounding, and with treasure bless'd;
But Fate resistless from his country led
The Chief, to perish at his people's head.
Shook with his fall his brazen armour rung,
And fierce, to seize it, conqu'ring *Ajax* sprung: 765
Around his head an iron tempest rain'd;
A wood of spears his ample shield sustain'd;
Beneath one foot the yet-warm corps he prest,
And drew his javelin from the bleeding breast:
He could no more; the show'ring darts deny'd   770
To spoil his glitt'ring arms, and plumy pride.
Now foes on foes came pouring on the fields,
With bristling lances, and compacted shields;
'Till in the steely circle straiten'd round,
Forc'd he gives way, and sternly quits the ground.   775

   While thus they strive, *Tlepolemus* the great,
Urg'd by the force of unresisted fate,
Burns with desire *Sarpedon*'s strength to prove;
Alcides' offspring meets the son of *Jove*.
Sheath'd in bright arms each adverse Chief came on,   780
Jove's great descendant, and his greater son.
Prepar'd for combate, e're the lance he tost,
The daring *Rhodian* vents his haughty boast.

What brings this *Lycian* Counsellor so far,
785   To tremble at our arms, not mix in war?
Know thy vain self, nor let their flatt'ry move,
Who style thee son of cloud-compelling *Jove*.
How far unlike those Chiefs of race divine,
How vast the diff'rence of their deeds and thine?
790   *Jove* got such Heroes as my Sire, whose Soul
No fear could daunt, nor earth, nor hell controul.
Troy felt his arm, and yon' proud ramparts stand
Rais'd on the ruins of his vengeful hand:
With six small ships, and but a slender train,
795   He left the town a wide, deserted plain.
But what art thou? who deedless look'st around,
While unreveng'd thy *Lycians* bite the ground:
Small Aid to *Troy* thy feeble force can be,
But wert thou greater, thou must yield to me.
800   Pierc'd by my spear to endless darkness go!
I make this present to the shades below.
      The son of *Hercules*, the *Rhodian* guide,
Thus haughty spoke. The *Lycian* King reply'd.
      Thy Sire, O Prince! o'erturn'd the *Trojan* state,
805   Whose perjur'd monarch well deserv'd his fate;
Those heav'nly steeds the Hero sought so far,
False he detain'd, the just reward of war.
Nor so content, the gen'rous chief defy'd,
With base reproaches and unmanly pride.
810   But you, unworthy the high race you boast,
Shall raise my glory when thy own is lost:
Now meet thy fate, and by *Sarpedon* slain
Add one more ghost to *Pluto*'s gloomy reign.
      He said: Both Javelins at an instant flew;
815   Both struck, both wounded, but *Sarpedon*'s slew:
Full in the boaster's neck the weapon stood,
Transfix'd his throat, and drank the vital blood;
The soul disdainful seeks the caves of night,
And his seal'd eyes for ever lose the light.
820   Yet not in vain, *Tlepolemus*, was thrown
Thy angry lance; which piercing to the bone
Sarpedon's thigh, had robb'd the chief of breath;
But *Jove* was present, and forbad the death.

Born from the conflict by his *Lycian* throng,
The wounded Hero dragg'd the lance along.   825
(His friends, each busy'd in his sev'ral part,
Thro' haste, or danger, had not drawn the dart.)
The *Greeks* with slain *Tlepolemus* retir'd;
Whose fall *Ulysses* view'd, with fury fir'd;
Doubtful if *Jove*'s great son he should pursue,   830
Or pour his vengeance on the *Lycian* crew.
But heav'n and fate the first design withstand,
Nor this great death must grace *Ulysses*' hand.
Minerva drives him on the *Lycian* train;
Alastor, *Chromius*, *Halius* strow'd the plain,   835
Alcander, *Prytanis*, *Noëmon* fell,
And numbers more his sword had sent to hell:
But *Hector* saw; and furious at the sight,
Rush'd terrible amidst the ranks of fight.
With joy *Sarpedon* view'd the wish'd relief,   840
And faint, lamenting, thus implor'd the Chief.

   Oh suffer not the foe to bear away
My helpless corps, an unassisted prey.
If I, unblest, must see my son no more,
My much-lov'd consort, and my native shore,   845
Yet let me die in *Ilion*'s sacred wall;
Troy, in whose cause I fell, shall mourn my fall.

   He said, nor *Hector* to the Chief replies,
But shakes his plume, and fierce to combate flies,
Swift as a whirlwind drives the scatt'ring foes,   850
And dyes the ground with purple as he goes.

   Beneath a beech, *Jove*'s consecrated shade,
His mournful friends divine *Sarpedon* laid:
Brave *Pelagon*, his fav'rite Chief, was nigh,
Who wrench'd the javelin from his sinewy thigh.   855
The fainting soul stood ready wing'd for flight,
And o'er his eye-balls swum the shades of night;
But *Boreas* rising fresh, with gentle breath,
Recall'd his spirit from the gates of death.

   The gen'rous *Greeks* recede with tardy pace,   860
Tho' *Mars* and *Hector* thunder in their face;
None turn their backs to mean ignoble flight,
Slow they retreat, and ev'n retreating fight.

Who first, who last, by *Mars* and *Hector*'s hand

865   Stretch'd in their blood, lay gasping on the sand?

Teuthras the great, *Orestes* the renown'd

For manag'd steeds, and *Trechus* press'd the ground;

Next *Oenomaus*, and *Oenops'* offspring dy'd;

Oresbius last fell groaning at their side:

870   *Oresbius*, in his painted mitre gay,

In fat *Bœotia* held his wealthy sway,

Where lakes surround low *Hylè*'s watry plain;

A Prince and People studious of their gain.

    The carnage *Juno* from the skies survey'd,

875   And touch'd with grief bespoke the blue-ey'd maid.

Oh sight accurst! Shall faithless *Troy* prevail,

And shall our promise to our people fail?

How vain the word to *Menelaüs* giv'n

By *Jove*'s great daughter and the Queen of Heav'n,

880   Beneath his arms that *Priam*'s tow'rs should fall;

If warring Gods for ever guard the wall?

Mars, red with slaughter, aids our hated foes:

Haste, let us arm, and force with force oppose!

    She spoke; *Minerva* burns to meet the war:

885   And now Heav'ns Empress calls her blazing car.

At her command rush forth the steeds divine;

Rich with immortal gold their trappings shine.

Bright *Hebè* waits; by *Hebè*, ever young,

The whirling wheels are to the chariot hung.

890   On the bright axle turns the bidden wheel

Of sounding brass; the polish'd axle steel.

Eight brazen spokes in radiant order flame;

The circles gold, of uncorrupted frame,

Such as the Heav'ns produce: and round the gold

895   Two brazen rings of work divine were roll'd.

The bossie naves of solid silver shone;

Braces of gold suspend the moving throne:

The car behind an arching figure bore;

The bending concave form'd an arch before.

900   Silver the beam, th' extended yoke was gold,

And golden reins th' immortal coursers hold.

Herself, impatient, to the ready car

The coursers joins, and breathes revenge and war.

Pallas disrobes; her radiant veil unty'd,
With flow'rs adorn'd, with art diversify'd,   905
(The labour'd veil her heav'nly fingers wove)
Flows on the pavement of the court of *Jove.*
Now heav'ns dread arms her mighty limbs invest,
Jove's cuirass blazes on her ample breast;   910
Deck'd in sad triumph for the mournful field,
O'er her broad shoulders hangs his horrid shield,
Dire, black, tremendous! Round the margin roll'd,
A fringe of serpents hissing guards the gold:
Here all the terrors of grim war appear,
Here rages Force, here tremble Flight and Fear,   915
Here storm'd Contention, and here Fury frown'd,
And the dire orb portentous *Gorgon* crown'd.
The massy golden helm she next assumes,
That dreadful nods with four o'ershading plumes;
So vast, the broad circumference contains   920
A hundred armies on a hundred plains.
The Goddess thus th' imperial car ascends;
Shook by her arm the mighty javelin bends,
Pond'rous and huge; that when her fury burns,
Proud tyrants humbles, and whole hosts o'erturns.   925
     Swift at the scourge th' ethereal coursers fly,
While the smooth chariot cuts the liquid sky.
Heav'n gates spontaneous open to the pow'rs,
Heav'ns golden gates, kept by the winged hours;
Commission'd in alternate watch they stand,   930
The sun's bright portals and the skies command,
Involve in clouds th' eternal gates of day,
Or the dark barrier roll with ease away.
The sounding hinges ring: On either side
The gloomy volumes, pierc'd with light, divide.   935
The chariot mounts, where deep in ambient skies,
Confus'd, *Olympus*' hundred heads arise;
Where far apart the Thund'rer fills his throne,
O'er all the Gods, superior and alone.
There with her snowy hand the Queen restrains   940
The fiery steeds, and thus to *Jove* complains.
     O Sire! can no resentment touch thy soul?
Can *Mars* rebel, and does no thunder roll?

What lawless rage on yon' forbidden plain,
945 What rash destruction! and what heroes slain?
Venus, and *Phœbus* with the dreadful bow,
Smile on the slaughter, and enjoy my woe.
Mad, furious pow'r! whose unrelenting mind
No God can govern, and no justice bind.
950 Say, mighty father! Shall we scourge his pride,
And drive from fight th' impetuous homicide?
      To whom assenting, thus the Thund'rer said:
Go! and the great *Minerva* be thy aid.
To tame the Monster-god *Minerva* knows,
955 And oft afflicts his brutal breast with woes.
      He said; *Saturnia*, ardent to obey,
Lash'd her white steeds along th' aërial way.
Swift down the steep of heav'n the chariot rolls,
Between th' expanded earth and starry poles.
960 Far as a shepherd, from some point on high,
O'er the wide main extends his boundless eye;
Thro' such a space of air, with thund'ring sound,
At ev'ry leap th' immortal coursers bound,
Troy now they reach'd, and touch'd those banks divine
965 Where silver *Simoïs* and *Scamander* join.
There *Juno* stopp'd and (her fair steeds unloos'd)
Of air condens'd a vapour circumfus'd:
For these, impregnate with celestial dew
On *Simoïs*' brink ambrosial herbage grew.
970 Thence, to relieve the fainting *Argive* throng,
Smooth as the failing doves they glide along.
The best and bravest of the *Grecian* band
(A warlike circle) round *Tydides* stand:
Such was their look as lions bath'd in blood,
975 Or foaming boars, the terror of the wood.
Heaven's Empress mingles with the mortal crowd,
And shouts, in *Stentor*'s sounding voice, aloud:
Stentor the strong, endu'd with brazen lungs,
Whose throat surpass'd the force of fifty tongues.
980   Inglorious *Argives*! to your race a shame,
And only men in figure and in name!
Once from the walls your tim'rous foes engag'd,
While fierce in war divine *Achilles* rag'd;

Now issuing fearless they possess the plain,
Now win the shores, and scarce the seas remain. 985

    Her speech new fury to their hearts convey'd;
While near *Tydides* stood th' *Athenian* maid:
The King beside his panting steeds she found,
O'erspent with toil, reposing on the ground:
To cool his glowing wound he sate apart, 990
(The wound inflicted by the *Lycian* dart)
Large drops of sweat from all his limbs descend,
Beneath his pond'rous shield his sinews bend,
Whose ample belt that o'er his shoulder lay,
He eas'd; and wash'd the clotted gore away. 995
The Goddess leaning o'er the bending yoke,
Beside his coursers, thus her silence broke.

    Degen'rate Prince! and not of *Tydeus*' kind,
Whose little body lodg'd a mighty mind.
Foremost he press'd, in glorious toils to share, 1000
And scarce refrain'd when I forbad the war.
Alone, unguarded, once he dar'd to go,
And feast encircled by the *Theban* foe;
There brav'd, and vanquish'd, many a hardy Knight;
Such nerves I gave him, and such force in fight. 1005
Thou too no less hast been my constant care;
Thy hands I arm'd, and sent thee forth to war:
But thee or fear deters, or sloth detains;
No drop of all thy father warms thy veins.

    The Chief thus answer'd mild. Immortal maid! 1010
I own thy presence, and confess thy aid.
Not fear, thou know'st, withholds me from the plains,
Nor sloth hath seiz'd me, but thy word restrains:
From warring Gods thou bad'st me turn my spear,
And *Venus* only found resistance here. 1015
Hence, Goddess! heedful of thy high commands,
Loth I gave way, and warn'd our *Argive* bands:
For *Mars*, the homicide, these eyes beheld,
With slaughter red, and raging round the field.

    Then thus *Minerva.* Brave *Tydides*, hear! 1020
Not *Mars* himself, nor ought immortal fear.
Full on the God impel thy foaming horse:
Pallas commands, and *Pallas* lends thee force.

Rash, furious, blind, from these to those he flies,
1025   And ev'ry side of wav'ring combate tries;
Large promise makes, and breaks the promise made;
Now gives the *Grecians*, now the *Trojans* aid.
    She said, and to the steeds approaching near,
Drew from his seat the martial charioteer.
1030   The vig'rous pow'r the trembling car ascends,
Fierce for revenge; and *Diomed* attends.
The groaning axle bent beneath the load;
So great a Hero, and so great a God.
She snatch'd the reins, she lash'd with all her force,
1035   And full on *Mars* impell'd the foaming horse:
But first, to hide her heav'nly visage, spread
Black *Orcus*' helmet o'er her radiant head.
Just then gigantic *Periphas* lay slain,
The strongest warriour of th' *Ætolian* train;
1040   The God who slew him, leaves his prostrate prize
Stretch'd where he fell, and at *Tydides* flies.
Now rushing fierce, in equal arms appear,
The daring *Greek*; the dreadful God of war!
Full at the chief, above his courser's head,
1045   From *Mars* his arm th' enormous weapon fled:
Pallas oppos'd her hand, and caus'd to glance
Far from the car, the strong immortal lance.
Then threw the force of *Tydeus*' warlike son;
The javelin hiss'd; the Goddess urg'd it on:
1050   Where the broad cincture girt his armour round,
It pierc'd the God: His groin receiv'd the wound.
From the rent skin the warriour tugs again
The smoaking steel. *Mars* bellows with the pain:
Loud, as the roar encountring armies yield,
1055   When shouting millions shake the thund'ring field.
Both armies start, and trembling gaze around;
And earth and heav'n rebellow to the sound.
As vapours blown by *Auster*'s sultry breath,
Pregnant with plagues, and shedding seeds of death,
1060   Beneath the rage of burning *Sirius* rise,
Choak the parch'd earth, and blacken all the skies;
In such a cloud the God from combate driv'n,
High o'er the dusty whirlwind scales the heav'n.

Wild with his pain, he sought the bright abodes,
There sullen sate beneath the Sire of Gods, 1065
Show'd the celestial blood, and with a groan
Thus pour'd his plaints before th' immortal throne.
 Can *Jove*, supine, flagitious facts survey,
And brook the furies of this daring day?
For mortal men celestial pow'rs engage, 1070
And Gods on Gods exert eternal rage.
From thee, O father! all these ills we bear,
And thy fell daughter with the shield and spear:
Thou gav'st that fury to the realms of light,
Pernicious, wild, regardless of the right. 1075
All heav'n beside reveres thy sov'reign sway,
Thy voice we hear, and thy behests obey:
'Tis hers t'offend; and ev'n offending share
Thy breast, thy counsels, thy distinguish'd care:
So boundless she, and thou so partial grown, 1080
Well may we deem the wond'rous birth thy own.
Now frantic *Diomed*, at her command,
Against th' Immortals lifts his raging hand:
The heav'nly *Venus* first his fury found,
Me next encount'ring, me he dar'd to wound; 1085
Vanquish'd I fled: Ev'n I, the God of fight,
From mortal madness scarce was sav'd by flight.
Else had'st thou seen me sink on yonder plain,
Heap'd round, and heaving under loads of slain!
Or pierc'd with *Grecian* darts, for ages lie, 1090
Condemn'd to pain, tho' fated not to die.
 Him thus upbraiding, with a wrathful look
The Lord of thunders view'd, and stern bespoke.
To me, perfidious! this lamenting strain?
Of lawless force shall lawless *Mars* complain? 1095
Of all the Gods who tread the spangled skies,
Thou most unjust, most odious in our eyes!
Inhuman discord is thy dire delight,
The waste of slaughter, and the rage of fight.
No bound, no law thy fiery temper quells, 1100
And all thy mother in thy soul rebels.
In vain our threats, in vain our pow'r we use;
She gives th' example, and her son pursues.

Yet long th' inflicted pangs thou shalt not mourn,
1105 Sprung since thou art from *Jove*, and heav'nly born.
Else, sing'd with light'ning, had'st thou hence been
          thrown,
Where chain'd on burning rocks the *Titans* groan.
    Thus he who shakes *Olympus* with his nod;
Then gave to *Pœon*'s care the bleeding God.
1110 With gentle hand the balm he pour'd around,
And heal'd th' immortal flesh, and clos'd the wound.
As when the fig's prest juice, infus'd in cream,
To curds coagulates the liquid stream,
Sudden the fluids fix, the parts combin'd;
1115 Such, and so soon, th' ætherial texture join'd.
Cleans'd from the dust and gore, fair *Hebè* drest
His mighty limbs in an immortal vest.
Glorious he sate, in majesty restor'd,
Fast by the throne of heav'ns superior Lord.
1120 *Juno* and *Pallas* mount the blest abodes,
Their task perform'd, and mix among the Gods.

OBSERVATIONS
ON THE
FIFTH BOOK

The epigraph on the frontispiece of Volume II (Books 5–8) consists of the following lines:

> *Quis* Martem *tunica tectum adamantina*
> *Digne scripserit? aut pulvere* Troïco
> *Nigrum* Merionen? *aut ope* Palladis
> Tydiden *Superis parem?*

[Who is capable of writing, with the appropriate epic gravity, of Mars dressed in his adamantine tunic? or of Meriones blackened with Trojan dust? or of Tydides, who is the equal – with Pallas's help – of the gods? (Horace, *Carmina*, 1.6.13–16)]

1. *But* Pallas *now*, &c.] As in every just history-picture there is one principal figure, to which all the rest refer and are subservient; so in each battel of the *Iliad* there is one principal person, that may properly be call'd the Hero of that day or action. This conduct preserves the unity of the piece, and keeps the imagination from being distracted and confused with a wild number of independent figures, which have no subordination to each other. To make this probable; *Homer* supposes these extraordinary measures of courage to be the immediate gift of the Gods; who bestow them sometimes upon one, sometimes upon another, as they think fit to make them the instruments of their designs; an opinion conformable to true theology. Whoever reflects upon this, will not blame our Author for representing the same heroes brave at one time, and dispirited at another; just as the Gods assist, or abandon them, on different occasions.

1. Tydides.] That we may enter into the spirit and beauty of this book, it will be proper to settle the true character of *Diomed*, who is the hero of it. *Achilles* is no sooner retired, but *Homer* raises his other *Greeks* to supply his absence; like stars that shine each in his due revolution, till the principal hero rises again, and eclipses all others. As *Diomed* is the first in this office, he seems to have more of the character of *Achilles* than any besides. He has naturally an excess of boldness and too much fury in his temper, forward and intrepid like the other, and running after Gods or men promiscuously as they offer themselves. But what differences his character is, that he is soon reclaim'd by advice, hears those that are more experienced, and in a word, obeys *Minerva* in all things. He is assisted by the patroness of wisdom and arms, as he is eminent both for prudence and valor. That which characterizes his prudence is a quick sagacity and presence of mind in all emergencies, and an undisturb'd readiness in the very article of danger. And what is particular in his valor is agreeable to these qualities, his actions being always performed with remarkable dexterity, activity, and dispatch. As the gentle and manageable turn of his mind seems drawn with an opposition to the boisterous temper of *Achilles*, so his bodily excellencies seem design'd as in contraste to those of *Ajax*, who appears with great strength, but heavy and unwieldy. As he is forward to act in the field, so is he ready to speak in the council: But 'tis observable that his counsels still incline to war, and are byass'd rather on the side of bravery than caution. Thus he advises to reject the proposals of the *Trojans* in the seventh book, and not to accept of *Helen* her self, tho' *Paris* should offer her. In the ninth, he opposes *Agamemnon*'s proposition to return to *Greece*, in so strong a manner, as to declare he will stay and continue the siege himself, if the General should depart. And thus he hears without concern *Achilles*'s refusal of a reconciliation, and doubts not to be able to carry on the war without him. As for his private character, he appears a gallant lover of hospitality in his behaviour to *Glaucus* in the sixth book; a lover of wisdom in his assistance of *Nestor* in the eighth, and his choice of *Ulysses* to accompany him in the tenth; upon the whole, an open sincere friend, and a generous enemy.

The wonderful actions he performs in this battel, seem to be the effect of a noble resentment at the reproach he had receiv'd from *Agamemnon* in the foregoing book, to which these deeds are the answer. He becomes immediately the second hero of *Greece*, and dreaded equally with *Achilles* by the *Trojans*. At the first sight of him his enemies make a question, whether he is a man or a God. *Æneas* and *Pandarus* go against him, whose approach terrifies *Sthenelus*, and the apprehension of so great a warriour marvellously exalts the intrepidity of *Diomed*. *Æneas* himself is not sav'd but by the interposing of a Deity: He pursues and wounds that Deity, and *Æneas* again escapes only by the help of a stronger power, *Apollo*. He attempts *Apollo* too, retreats not till the God threatens him in his own voice, and even then retreats but a few steps. When he sees *Hector* and *Mars* himself in open arms against him, he had not retir'd tho' he was wounded, but in obedience to *Minerva*, and then retires with his face toward them. But as soon as she permits him to engage with that God, he conquers, and sends him groaning to heaven. What invention and what conduct appears in this whole episode? What boldness in raising a character to such a pitch, and what judgment in raising it by such degrees? While the most daring flights of poetry are employ'd to move our admiration, and at the same time the justest and closest allegory, to reconcile those flights to moral truth and probability? It may be farther remark'd, that the high degree to which *Homer* elevates this character, enters into the principal design of his whole poem; which is to shew, that the greatest personal qualities and forces are of no effect when union is wanting among the chief rulers, and that nothing can avail 'till they are reconciled so as to act in concert.

5. *High on his helm celestial light'nings play.*] This beautiful passage gave occasion to *Zoilus* for an insipid piece of raillery, who ask'd how it happen'd that the hero escap'd burning by these fires that continually broke from his armour? *Eustathius* answers, that there are several examples in history, of fires being seen to break forth from human bodies as presages of greatness and glory. Among the rest, *Plutarch* in the life of *Alexander* describes his helmet much in this manner. This is enough to warrant the fiction, and were there no such example, the same Author says very well, that the imagination of a Poet is not to be confined to strict physical truths. But all objections may easily be removed, if we consider it as done by *Minerva*, who had determined this day to raise *Diomed* above all the heroes, and caused this apparition to render him formidable. The power of a God makes it not only allowable, but highly noble, and greatly imagined by *Homer*; as well as correspondent to a miracle in holy scripture, where *Moses* is described with a glory shining on his face at his descent from mount *Sinai*, a parallel which *Spondanus* has taken notice of.

Virgil was too sensible of the beauty of this passage not to imitate it, and it must be owned he has surpassed his original.

> *Ardet apex capiti, cristisque ac vertice flamma*
> *Funditur, & vastos umbo vomit aureus ignes.*
> *Non secus ac liquida si quando nocte cometæ*
> *Sanguinei lugubre rubent: aut Sirius ardor,*
> *Ille sitim morbosque ferens mortalibus ægris,*
> *Nascitur, & lævo contristat lumine cœlum.*   Aen. x. v. 270

[The *Latians* saw from far, with dazl'd eyes,
The radiant crest that seem'd in flames to rise,
And dart diffusive fires around the field;
And the keen glitt'ring of the golden shield.
  Thus threatning comets, when by night they rise,
Shoot sanguine streams, and sadden all the skies:
So *Sirius*, flashing forth sinister lights,
Pale human kind with plagues, and with dry famine
      frights.]

In *Homer*'s comparison there is no other circumstance alluded to but that of a remarkable brightness: Whereas *Virgil*'s comparison, beside this, seems to foretel the immense slaughter his hero was to make, by comparing him first to a comet, which is vulgarly imagin'd a prognostick, if not the real cause, of much misery to mankind; and again to the dog-star, which appearing with the greatest brightness in the latter end of summer, is suppos'd the occasion of all the distempers of that sickly season. And methinks the objection of *Macrobius* to this place is not just, who thinks the simile unseasonably apply'd by *Virgil* to *Æneas*, because he was yet on his ship, and had not begun the battel. One may answer, that this miraculous appearance could never be more proper than at the first sight of the hero, to strike terror into the enemy, and to prognosticate his approaching victory.

27. Idæus *fled, Left the rich chariot.*] It is finely said by M. *Dacier*, that *Homer* appears perhaps greater by the criticisms that have been past upon him, than by the praises which have been given him. *Zoilus* had a cavil at this place; he thought it ridiculous in *Idæus* to descend from his chariot to fly, which he might have done faster by the help of his horses. Three things are said in answer to this: first, that *Idæus* knowing the passion which *Diomed* had for horses, might hope the pleasure of seizing these would retard him from pursuing him. Next, that *Homer* might design to represent in this action of *Idæus* the common effect of fear, which disturbs the understanding to such a degree, as to make men abandon the surest means to save themselves. And then, that *Idæus* might have some advantage of *Diomed* in swiftness, which he had reason to confide in. But I fancy one may add another solution which will better account for this passage. *Homer*'s word is ἔτλη, which I believe would be better translated *non perseveravit* [he did not continue steadfastly], than *non sustinuit defendere fratrem interfectum* [he did not venture to protect his slain brother]: and then the sense will be clear, that *Idæus* made an effort to save his brother's body, which proving impracticable, he was obliged to fly with the utmost precipitation. One may add, that his alighting from his chariot was not that he could run faster on foot, but that he could sooner escape by mixing with the crowd of common soldiers. There is a particular exactly of the same nature in the book of *Judges*, Ch. 4. v. 15. where *Sisera* alights to fly in the same manner.

40. *Who bathe in blood.*] It may seem something unnatural, that *Pallas*, at a time when she is endeavouring to work upon *Mars* under the appearance of benevolence and kindness, should make use of terms which seem so full of bitter reproaches; but these will appear very properly applied to this warlike Deity. For Persons of this martial character, who scorning equity and reason, carry all things by force, are better pleas'd to be celebrated for their power than their virtue. Statues are rais'd to the conquerors, that is, the destroyers of nations, who are complemented for excelling in the arts of ruine. *Demetrius* the son of *Antigonus* was celebrated by his flatterers with the title of *Poliorcetes*, a term equivalent to one here made use of.

46. *The God of arms and martial Maid retreat.*] The retreat of *Mars* from the *Trojans* intimates that courage forsook them: It may be said then, that *Minerva*'s absence from the *Greeks* will signify that wisdom deserted them also. It is true she does desert them, but it is at a time when there was more occasion for gallant actions than for wise counsels.

Eustathius.

48. *The* Greeks *the* Trojan *race pursue.*] *Homer* always appears very zealous for the honour of *Greece*, which alone might be a proof of his being of that country, against the opinion of those who would have him of other nations.

It is observable thro' the whole Iliad, that he endeavours every where to represent the *Greeks* as superior to the *Trojans* in valour and the art of war. In the beginning of the third book he describes the *Trojans* rushing on to the battel in a barbarous and confus'd manner, with loud shouts and cries, while the *Greeks* advance in the most profound silence and exact order. And in the latter part of the fourth book, where the two armies march to the engagement, the *Greeks* are animated by *Pallas*, while *Mars* instigates the *Trojans*, the Poet attributing by this plain allegory to the former a well-conducted valour, to the latter rash strength and brutal force: So that the abilities of each nation are distinguish'd by the characters of the Deities who assist them. But in this place, as *Eustathius* observes, the Poet being willing to shew how much the *Greeks* excell'd their enemies when they engag'd only with their proper force, and when each side was alike destitute of divine assistance, takes occasion to remove the Gods out of the battel, and then each *Grecian* Chief gives signal instances of valour superior to the *Trojans*.

A modern Critick observes that this constant superiority of the *Greeks* in the art of war, valour, and number, is contradictory to the main design of the poem, which is to make the return of *Achilles* appear necessary for the preservation of the *Greeks*; but this contradiction vanishes when we reflect that the affront given *Achilles* was the occasion of *Jupiter*'s interposing in favour of the *Trojans*. Wherefore the anger of *Achilles* was not pernicious to the *Greeks* purely because it kept him inactive, but because it occasion'd *Jupiter* to afflict them in such a manner, as made it necessary to appease *Achilles* in order to render *Jupiter* propitious.

63. *Back from the car he tumbles.*] It is in poetry as in painting, the postures and attitudes of each figure ought to be different: *Homer* takes care not to draw two persons in the same posture; one is tumbled from his chariot, another is slain as he ascends it, a third as he endeavours to escape on foot, a conduct which is every where observed by the Poet.   *Eustathius.*

75. *Next artful* Phereclus.] This character of *Phereclus* is finely imagined, and presents a noble moral in an uncommon manner. There ran a report, that the *Trojans* had formerly receiv'd an oracle, commanding

them to follow husbandry, and not apply themselves to navigation. *Homer* from hence takes occasion to feign, that the shipwright who presumed to build the fleet of *Paris* when he took his fatal voyage to *Greece*, was overtaken by the divine vengeance so long after as in this battel. One may take notice too in this, as in many other places, of the remarkable disposition *Homer* shews to *Mechanicks*; he never omits an opportunity either of describing a piece of workmanship, or of celebrating an artist.

93. *Whose gen'rous Spouse* Theano.] *Homer* in this remarkable passage commends the fair *Theano* for breeding up a bastard of her husband's with the same tenderness as her own children. This lady was a woman of the first quality, and (as it appears in the sixth *Iliad*) the high Priestess of *Minerva*: So that one cannot imagine the education of this child was imposed upon her by the authority or power of *Antenor*; *Homer* himself takes care to remove any such derogatory notion, by particularizing the motive of this unusual piece of humanity to have been to please her husband, χαριζομένη πόσεϊ ᾧ. Nor ought we to lessen this commendation by thinking the wives of those times in general were more complaisant than those of our own. The stories of *Phoenix*, *Clytemnestra*, *Medea*, and many others, are plain instances how highly the keeping of mistresses was resented by the married ladies. But there was a difference between the *Greeks* and *Asiaticks* as to their notions of marriage: For it is certain the latter allowed plurality of wives; *Priam* had many lawful ones, and some of them Princesses who brought great dowries. *Theano* was an *Asiatick*, and that is the most we can grant; for the son she nurs'd so carefully was apparently not by a wife, but by a mistress; and her passions were naturally the same with those of the *Grecian* women. As to the degree of regard then shewn to the bastards, they were carefully enough educated, tho' not (like this of *Antenor*) as the lawful issue, nor admitted to an equal share of inheritance. *Megapenthes* and *Nicostratus* were excluded from the inheritance of *Sparta*, becuase they were born of bond-women, as *Pausanias* says. But *Neoptolemus*, a natural son of *Achilles* by *Deïdamia*, succeeded in his father's kingdom, perhaps with respect to his mother's quality, who was a princess. Upon the whole, however that matter stood, *Homer* was very favourable to bastards, and has paid them more complements than one in his works. If I am not mistaken, *Ulysses* reckons himself one in the *Odysseis*. *Agamemnon* in the eighth *Iliad* plainly accounts it no disgrace, when charm'd with the

noble exploits of young *Teucer*, and praising him in the rapture of his heart, he just then takes occasion to mention his illegitimacy as a kind of panegyrick upon him. The reader may consult the passage, v. 284 of the original, and v. 343 of the translation. From all this I should not be averse to believe that *Homer* himself was a bastard, as *Virgil* was, of which I think this observation a better Proof, than what is said for it in the common lives of him.

100.   – Hypsenor, *gen'rous and divine,*
        Sprung from the brave Dolopion's *mighty line;*
        Who near ador'd Scamander *made abode;*
        Priest of the stream, and honour'd as a God.

From the number of circumstances put together here, and in many other passages, of the parentage, place of abode, profession, and quality of the persons our Author mentions; I think it is plain he composed his poem from some records or traditions of the actions of the times preceding, and complied with the truth of history. Otherwise these particular descriptions of genealogies and other minute circumstances would have been an affectation extremely needless and unreasonable. This consideration will account for several things that seem odd or tedious, not to add that one may naturally believe he took these occasions of paying a complement to many great men and families of his patrons, both in *Greece* and *Asia.*

108. *Down sinks the Priest.*] *Homer* makes him die upon the cutting off his arm, which is an instance of his skill; for the great flux of blood that must follow such a wound, would be the immediate cause of death.

116. *Thus from high hills Torrents swift and strong.*] This whole passage (says *Eustathius*) is extremely beautiful. It describes the hero carry'd by an enthusiastick valour into the midst of his enemies, and so mingled with their ranks as if himself were a *Trojan.* And the simile wonderfully illustrates this fury proceeding from an uncommon infusion of courage from heaven, in resembling it not to a constant river, but a torrent rising from an extraordinary burst of rain. This simile is one of those that draws along with it some foreign circumstances: We must not often expect from *Homer* those minute resemblances in every branch of a comparison, which are the pride of modern similes. If that

which one may call the main action of it, or the principal point of likeness, be preserved; he affects, as to the rest, rather to present the mind with a great image, than to fix it down to an exact one. He is sure to make a fine picture in the whole, without drudging on the under parts; like those free Painters who (one would think) had only made here and there a few very significant strokes, that give form and spirit to all the piece. For the present comparison, *Virgil* in the second *Æneid* [496–9] has inserted an imitation of it, which I cannot think equal to this, tho' *Scaliger* prefers *Virgil*'s to all our Author's similitudes from rivers put together.

> *Non sic aggeribus ruptis cum spumeus amnis*
> *Exiit, oppositasque evicit gurgite moles,*
> *Fertur in arva furens cumulo, camposque per omnes*
> *Cum stabulis armenta trahit –*

> Not with so fierce a rage, the foaming flood
> Roars, when he finds his rapid course withstood;
> Bears down the dams with unresisted sway,
> And sweeps the cattel and the cotts away.   *Dryden.*

133. *The* [. . .] *dart stopt short of life.*] *Homer* says it did not kill him, and I am at a loss why M. *Dacier* translates it, *The wound was slight*; when just after the arrow is said to have pierc'd *quite thro'*, and she herself there turns it, *Perçoit l'espaule d'outre en outre* [It pierced completely through his shoulder]. Had it been so slight, he would not have needed the immediate assistance of *Minerva* to restore his usual vigour, and enable him to continue the fight.

164. *From mortal mists I purge thy eyes.*] This fiction of *Homer* (says M. *Dacier*) is founded upon an important truth of religion, not unknown to the Pagans, that God only can open the eyes of men, and enable them to see what they cannot discover by their own capacity. There are frequent examples of this in the Old Testament. God opens the eyes of *Hagar* that she might see the fountain, in *Genes.* 21. v. 14. So *Numbers* 22. v. 31. *The Lord open'd the eyes of* Balaam, *and he saw the Angel of the Lord standing in his way, and his sword drawn in his hand.* A passage much resembling this of our Author. *Venus* in *Virgil*'s second *Æneid* performs the same office to *Æneas*, and shews him the Gods who were engag'd in the destruction of *Troy*.

> *Aspice; namque omnem quæ nunc obducta tuenti*
> *Mortales hebetat visus tibi, & humida circum*
> *Caligat, nubem eripiam —*   [604–6]
>
> *Apparent diræ facies, inimicaque Trojæ*
> *Numina magna Deum. —*   [622–3]

[Now cast your eyes around; while I dissolve
The mists and films that mortal eyes involve:
Purge from your sight the dross, and make you see
The shape of each avenging deity.

I look'd, I listen'd; dreadful sounds I hear;
And the dire forms of hostile Gods appear.]

Milton seems likewise to have imitated this where he makes *Michael* open *Adam*'s eyes to see the future revolutions of the world, and fortunes of his posterity, *book* 11.

> — *He purg'd with euphrasie and rue*
> *The visual nerve, for he had much to see,*
> *And from the well of life three drops distill'd.*

This distinguishing sight of *Diomed* was given him only for the present occasion and service in which he was employ'd by *Pallas*. For we find in the sixth book that upon meeting *Glaucus*, he is ignorant whether that Hero be a Man or a God.

194. *No mystic dream.*] This line in the original, Τοῖς οὐκ ἐρχομένοις ὁ γέρων ἐκρίνατ᾽ ὀνείρους, contains as puzzling a passage for the construction as I have met with in *Homer*. Most interpreters join the negative particle οὐκ with the verb ἐκρίνατο, which may receive three different meanings: That *Eurydamas* had not interpreted the dreams of his children when they went to the wars, or that he had foretold them by their dreams they should never return from the wars, or that he should now no more have the satisfaction to interpret their dreams at their return. After all, this construction seems forced, and no way agreeable to the general idiom of the *Greek* language, or to *Homer*'s simple diction in particular. If we join οὐκ with ἐρχομένοις, I think the most obvious sense will be this; *Diomed* attacks the two sons of *Eurydamas* an old interpreter of dreams; his children not returning, the Prophet sought by his dreams to know their fate; however they fall by the hands of *Diomed*. This interpretation seems natural and poetical, and tends to move compassion, which is almost constantly the design of the Poet, in his frequent short digressions concerning the circumstances and relations of dying persons.

202. *To strangers now descends his wealthy* [sic] *store.*] This is a circumstance than which nothing could be imagined more tragical, considering the character of the father. *Homer* says the trustees of the remote collateral relations seiz'd the estate before his eyes (according to a custom of those times) which to a covetous old man must be the greatest of miseries.

212. *Divine Æneas.*] It is here *Æneas* begins to act, and if we take a view of the whole episode of this Hero in *Homer*, where he makes but an under-part, it will appear that *Virgil* has kept him perfectly in the same character in his Poem, where he shines as the first Hero. His piety and his valour, tho' not drawn at so full a length, are mark'd no less in the original than in the copy. It is the manner of *Homer* to express very strongly the character of each of his persons in the first speech he is made to utter in the Poem. In this of *Æneas*, there is a great air of piety in those strokes, *Is he some God who punishes* Troy *for having neglected his sacrifices?* And then that sentence, *The anger of heaven is terrible.* When he is in danger afterwards, he is saved by the heavenly assistance of two Deities at once, and his wounds cured in the holy temple of *Pergamus* by *Latona* and *Diana.* As to his valour, he is second only to *Hector*, and in personal bravery as great in the *Greek* author as in the *Roman.* He is made to exert himself on emergencies of the first importance and hazard, rather than on common occasions: he checks *Diomed* here in the midst of his fury; in the thirteenth book defends his friend *Deiphobus* before it was his turn to fight, being placed in one of the hindmost ranks (which *Homer*, to take off all objections to his Valour, tells us happen'd because *Priam* had an animosity to him, tho' he was one of the bravest of the army.) He is one of those who rescue *Hector* when he is overthrown by *Ajax* in the fourteenth book. And what alone were sufficient to establish him a first-rate Hero, he is the first that dares resist *Achilles* himself at his return to the fight in all his rage for the loss of *Patroclus.* He indeed avoids encountering two at once, in the present book; and shews upon the whole a sedate and deliberate courage, which if not so glaring as that of some others, is yet more just. It is worth considering how thoroughly *Virgil* penetrated into all this, and saw into the very idea of

Homer; so as to extend and call forth the whole figure in its full dimensions and colours from the slightest hints and sketches which were but casually touch'd by *Homer*, and even in some points too where they were rather left to be understood, than express'd. And this, by the way, ought to be consider'd by those criticks who object to *Virgil*'s Hero the want of that sort of courage which strikes us so much in *Homer*'s *Achilles*. *Æneas* was not the creature of *Virgil*'s imagination, but one whom the world was already acquainted with, and expected to see continued in the same character; and one who perhaps was chosen for the Hero of the *Latin* Poem, not only as he was the founder of the *Roman* empire, but as this more calm and regular character better agreed with the temper and genius of the Poet himself.

242. *Skill'd in the bow*, &c.] We see thro' this whole discourse of *Pandarus* the character of a vain-glorious passionate Prince, who being skill'd in the use of the bow, was highly valued by himself and others for his excellence; but having been successless in two different trials of his skill, he is rais'd into an outragious passion, which vents itself in vain threats on his guiltless bow. *Eustathius* on this passage relates a story of a *Paphlagonian* famous like him for his archery, who having miss'd his aim at repeated trials, was so transported by rage, that breaking his bow and arrows, he executed a more fatal vengeance by hanging himself.

244. *Ten polish'd chariots.*] Among the many pictures *Homer* gives us of the simplicity of the heroic ages, he mingles from time to time some hints of an extraordinary magnificence. We have here a Prince who has all these chariots for pleasure at one time, with their particular sets of horses to each, and the most sumptuous coverings in their stables. But we must remember that he speaks of an *Asiatic* Prince, those *Barbarians* living in great luxury.   *Dacier.*

252. *Yet to thrift inclin'd.*] 'Tis *Eustathius* his remark, that *Pandarus* did this out of avarice, to save the expence of his horses. I like this conjecture, because nothing seems more judicious, than to give a man of a perfidious character a strong tincture of avarice.

261. *And undissembled gore pursu'd the wound.*] The *Greek* is ἀτρεκὲς αἷμα. He says he is sure it was real blood that follow'd his arrow; because it was anciently a custom, particularly among the *Spartans*, to

have ornaments and figures of a purple colour on their breast-plates, that the blood they lost might not be seen by the soldiers, and tend to their discouragement. *Plutarch* in his *Instit. Lacon.* takes notice of this point of antiquity, and I wonder it escap'd Madam *Dacier* in her translation.

273. *Nor* Phœbus' *honour'd gift disgrace.*] For *Homer* tells us in the second book, v. 334 of the catalogue, that the bow and shafts of *Pandarus* were given him by *Apollo.*

284. *Haste, seize the whip,* &c.] *Homer* means not here, that one of the Heroes should alight or descend from the chariot, but only that he should quit the reins to the management of the other, and stand on foot upon the chariot to fight from thence. As one might use the expression, *to descend from the ship,* to signify to quit the helm or oar, in order to take up arms. This is the note of *Eustathius,* by which it appears that most of the translators are mistaken in the sense of this passage, and among the rest Mr *Hobbes.*

320. *One chief at least beneath this arm shall die.*] It is the manner of our author to make his persons have some intimation from within, either of prosperous or adverse fortune, before it happens to them. In the present instance, we have seen *Æneas,* astonished at the great exploits of *Diomed,* proposing to himself the means of his escape by the swiftness of his horses, before he advances to encounter him. On the other hand, *Diomed* is so filled with assurance, that he gives orders here to *Sthenelus* to seize those horses, before they come up to him. The opposition of these two (as Mad. *Dacier* has remark'd) is very observable.

327. *The coursers of æthereal breed.*] We have already observed the great delight *Homer* takes in horses. He makes some horses, as well as heroes, of celestial race: and if he has been thought too fond of the genealogies of some of his warriours, in relating them even in a battel; we find him here as willing to trace that of his horses in the same circumstance. These were of that breed which *Jupiter* bestow'd upon *Tros,* and far superior to the common strain of *Trojan* horses. So that (according to *Eustathius*'s opinion) the translators are mistaken who turn Τρώϊοι ἵπποι, *the Trojan horses,* in v. 222 of the original, where *Æneas* extolls their qualities to *Pandarus.* The same Author takes notice, that frauds in the case of horses have been thought excusable in

all times, and commends *Anchises* for this piece of theft. *Virgil* was so well pleas'd with it as to imitate this passage in the seventh *Æneid* [280–83].

> *Absenti Æneæ currum, geminosque jugales*
> *Semine ab æthereo, spirantes naribus ignem,*
> *Illorum de gente, patri quos dædala Circe*
> *Supposita de matre nothos furata creavit.*

> [Then to his absent guest the King decreed
> A pair of coursers born of heav'nly breed:
> Who from their nostrils breath'd etherial fire;
> Whom *Circe* stole from her cœlestial sire:
> By substituting mares, produc'd on earth,
> Whose wombs conceiv'd a more than mortal birth.]

353. *Full in his face it enter'd.*] It has been ask'd, how *Diomed* being on foot, could naturally be suppos'd to give such a wound as is describ'd here. Were it never so improbable, the express mention that *Minerva* conducted the javelin to that part, would render this passage unexceptionable. But without having recourse to a miracle, such a wound might be receiv'd by *Pandarus* either if he stoop'd; or if his enemy took the advantage of a rising ground, by which means he might not impossibly stand higher, tho' the other were in a chariot. This is the solution given by the ancient *Scholia*, which is confirm'd by the lowness of the chariots, observed in the *Essay on* Homer's *battels*.

361. *To guard his slaughter'd friend Æneas flies.*] This protecting of the dead body was not only an office of piety agreeable to the character of *Æneas* in particular, but look'd upon as a matter of great importance in those times. It was believ'd that the very soul of the deceas'd suffer'd by the body's remaining destitute of the rites of sepulture, as not being else admitted to pass the waters of *Styx*. See what *Patroclus* his ghost says to *Achilles* in the 23d *Iliad*.

> *Hæc omnis, quam cernis, inops inhumataque turba est;*
> *Portitor ille, Charon; hi, quos vehit unda, sepulti.*
> *Nec ripas datur horrendas & rauca fluenta*
> *Transportare prius, quam sedibus ossa quierunt.*
> *Centum errant annos, volitantque hæc litora circum.*

Virg. Æn. 6 [325–9].

> [The ghosts rejected, are th' unhappy crew
> Depriv'd of sepulchers, and fun'ral due;
> The boatman *Charon*; those, the bury'd host,
> He ferries over to the farther coast.
> Nor dares his transport vessel cross the waves,
> With such whose bones are not compos'd in graves.
> A hundred years they wander on the shore.]

Whoever considers this, will not be surprized at those long and obstinate combates for the bodies of the Heroes, so frequent in the *Iliad*. *Homer* thought it of such weight, that he has put this circumstance of want of burial into the *Proposition* at the beginning of his Poem, as one of the chief misfortunes that befel the *Greeks*.

371. *Not two strong men.*] This opinion of a degeneracy of human size and strength in the process of ages, has been very general. *Lucretius, Lib. 2* [1150–52].

> *Jamque adeo fracta est ætas, effœtaque tellus*
> *Vix animalia parva creat, quæ cuncta creavit*
> *Sæcla, deditque ferarum ingentia corpora partu.*

[Even now indeed the power of life is broken, and the earth exhausted scarcely produces tiny creatures, she who once produced all kinds and gave birth to the huge bodies of wild beasts.]

The active life and temperance of the first men, before their native powers were prejudiced by luxury, may be supposed to have given them this advantage. *Celsus* in his first Book observes, that *Homer* mentions no sort of diseases in the old heroic times but what were immediately inflicted by heaven, as if their temperance and exercise preserved them from all besides. *Virgil* imitates this passage, with a farther allowance of the decay in proportion to the distance of his time from that of *Homer*. For he says it was an Attempt that exceeded the Strength of *twelve* Men, instead of *two*.

> *– Saxum circumspicit ingens –*
> *Vix illud lecti bis sex cervice subirent.*
> *Qualia nunc hominum producit corpora tellus.*

> [An antique stone he saw . . .
> So vast, that twelve strong men of modern days,
> Th' enormous weight from earth cou'd hardly raise.]

Juvenal has made an agreeable use of this thought in his fourteenth Satyr [xv. 69–70].

> *Nam genus hoc vivo jam decrescebat Homero,*
> *Terra malos homines nunc educat, atque pusillos.*

[For even in Homer's day the race of man was on the wane; earth now produces none but weak and wicked men.]

391. *Hid from the foe behind her shining veil.*] *Homer* says, she spread her veil that it might be a defence against the darts. How comes it then afterwards to be pierc'd thro', when *Venus* is wounded? It is manifest the veil was not impenetrable, and is said here to be a defence only as it render'd *Æneas* invisible, by being interposed. This is the observation of *Eustathius*, and was thought too material to be neglected in the translation.

403. *To bold* Deïpylus – *Whom most he lov'd.*] *Sthenelus* (says M. *Dacier*) loved *Deïpylus, parce qu'il avoit la mesme humeur que luy, la mesme sagesse* [Because he had the same temperament, the prudent and wise demeanour]. The words in the original are ὅτι οἱ φρεσὶν ἄρτια ᾔδη. *Because his mind was equal and consentaneous to his own.* Which I should rather translate, with regard to the character of *Sthenelus*, that he had the same *bravery*, than the same *wisdom.* For that *Sthenelus* was not remarkable for wisdom appears from many passages, and particularly from his speech to *Agamemnon* in the fourth book, upon which see *Plutarch*'s remark, v. 456.

408. *The chief in chace of* Venus *flies.*] We have seen with what ease *Venus* takes *Paris* out of the battel in the third book, when his life was in danger from *Menelaus*; but here when she has a charge of more importance and nearer concern, she is not able to preserve her self or her son from the fury of *Diomed.* The difference of success in two attempts so like each other, is occasion'd by that penetration of sight with which *Pallas* had endu'd her favourite. For the Gods in their intercourse with men are not ordinarily seen, but when they please to render themselves visible; wherefore *Venus* might think her self and her son secure from the insolence of this daring mortal; but was in this deceiv'd, being ignorant of that faculty, wherewith the hero was enabled to distinguish Gods as well as men.

419. *Her snowy hand the razing steel profan'd.*] *Plutarch* in his *Symposiacks l.* 9. tells us, that *Maximus* the Rhetorician propos'd this farfetch'd question at a banquet, *On which of her Hands* Venus *was wounded?* and that *Zopyrion* answer'd it by asking, *On which of his legs* Philip *was lame?* But *Maximus* reply'd, It was a different case: For *Demosthenes* left no foundation to guess at the one, whereas *Homer* gives a solution of the other, in saying that *Diomed* throwing his spear across, wounded her wrist: so that it was her right hand he hurt, her left being opposite to his right. He adds another humorous reason from *Pallas*'s reproaching her afterwards, as having got this wound while she was stroking and solliciting some *Grecian* Lady, and unbuckling her zone; *An action* (says this Philosopher) *in which no one would make use of the left hand.*

422. *Such stream as issues from a wounded God.*] This is one of those passages in *Homer* which have given occasion to that famous censure of *Tully* and *Longinus*, *That he makes Gods of his heroes, and mortals of his Gods.* This, taken in a general sense, appear'd the highest impiety to *Plato* and *Pythagoras*; one of whom has banish'd *Homer* from his commonwealth, and the other said he was tortured in hell, for fictions of this nature. But if a due distinction be made of a difference among beings superior to mankind, which both the Pagans and Christians have allowed, the fables may be easily accounted for. *Wounds inflicted on the dragon, bruising the serpent's head*, and other such metaphorical Images, are consecrated in holy writ, and apply'd to angelical and incorporeal natures. But in our Author's days they had a notion of Gods that were corporeal, to whom they ascribed bodies, tho' of a more subtil kind than those of mortals. So in this very place he supposes them to have blood, but blood of a finer or superior nature. Notwithstanding the foregoing censures, *Milton* has not scrupled to imitate and apply this to angels in the christian system, when *Satan* is wounded by *Michael* in his sixth book, v. 327.

> – Then Satan *first knew Pain,*
> *And writh'd him to and fro convolv'd; so sore*
> *The griding sword with discontinuous wound*
> *Pass'd thro' him; but th' Ætherial substance clos'd,*
> *Not long divisible, and from the gash*
> *A stream of nectarous humour issuing flow'd,*
> *Sanguin, such as celestial spirits may bleed –*

> *Yet soon he heal'd, for Spirits that live throughout,*
> *Vital in ev'ry part, not as frail man*
> *In entrails, head or heart, liver or reins,*
> *Cannot but by annihilating die.*

Aristotle, cap. 26. Art. Poet. excuses *Homer* for following fame and common opinion in his account of the Gods, tho' no way agreeable to truth. The religion of those times taught no other notions of the Deity, than that the Gods were beings of human forms and passions, so that any but a real *Anthropomorphite* would probably have past among the ancient *Greeks* for an impious heretick: They thought their religion, which worshipped the Gods in images of human shape, was much more refin'd and rational than that of *Ægypt* and other nations, who ador'd them in animal or monstrous forms. And certainly Gods of human shape cannot justly be esteemed or described otherwise, than as a celestial race, superior only to mortal men by greater abilities, and a more extensive degree of wisdom and strength, subject however to the necessary inconveniences consequent to corporeal beings. *Cicero*, in his book *de Nat. Deor.* urges this consequence strongly against the *Epicureans*, who tho' they depos'd the Gods from any power in creating or governing the world, yet maintain'd their existence in human forms. *Non enim sentitis quam multa vobis suscipienda sunt si impetraveritis ut concedamus eandem esse hominum & deorum figuram; omnis cultus & curatio corporis erit eadem adhibenda Deo quæ adhibetur homini, ingressus, cursus, accubatio, inclinatio, sessio, comprehensio, ad extremum etiam sermo & oratio. Nam quod & mares Deos & fœminas esse dicitis, quid sequatur videtis.* [You don't perceive what a number of things you are let in for, if we consent to admit that men and gods have the same form. You will have to assign to god exactly the same physical exercises and care of the person as are proper to men: he will walk, run, recline, bend, sit, hold things in the hand, and lastly even converse and make speeches. As for your saying that the gods are male and female, well, you must see what the consequence of that will be.]

This particular of the wounding of *Venus* seems to be a fiction of *Homer*'s own brain, naturally deducible from the doctrine of corporeal Gods abovementioned; and considered as poetry, no way shocking. Yet our Author, as if he had foreseen some objection, has very artfully inserted a justification of this bold stroke, in the speech *Dione* soon after makes to *Venus*. For as it was natural to comfort her daughter, by putting her in mind that many other deities had receiv'd as ill treatment from mortals by the permission of *Jupiter*; so it was of great use to the Poet, to enumerate those ancient fables to the same purpose, which being then generally assented to, might obtain credit for his own. This fine remark belongs to *Eustathius.*

424. *Unlike our gross, diseas'd, terrestrial blood,* &c.] The opinion of the incorruptibility of celestial matter seems to have been receiv'd in the time of *Homer.* For he makes the immortality of the Gods to depend upon the incorruptible nature of the nutriment by which they are sustained; As the mortality of men to proceed from the corruptible materials of which they are made, and by which they are nourished. We have several instances in him from whence this may be inferred, as when *Diomed* questions *Glaucus,* if he be a God or mortal, he adds, *One who is sustained by the fruits of the earth.*   Lib. 6. v. 175.

449. *Low at his knee she begg'd.*] All the former *English* translators make it, *she fell on her knees,* an oversight occasion'd by the want of a competent knowledge in antiquities (without which no man can tolerably understand this Author.) For the custom of praying on the knees was unknown to the *Greeks,* and in use only among the *Hebrews.*

472. *And share those griefs inferior pow'rs must share.*] The word *inferior* is added by the translator, to open the distinction *Homer* makes between the Divinity itself, which he represents impassible, and the subordinate celestial beings or spirits.

475. *The mighty* Mars, &c.] *Homer* in these fables, as upon many other occasions, makes a great show of his theological learning, which was the manner of all the *Greeks* who had travell'd into *Ægypt.* Those who would see these allegories explained at large, may consult *Eustathius* on this place. *Virgil* [*Aen.* I. 294–6] speaks much in the same figure, when he describes the happy peace with which *Augustus* had blest the world:

> – *Furor impius intus*
> *Sæva sedens super arma, & centum vinctus aënis*
> *Post tergum nodis, fremit horridus ore cruento.*

> [within remains
> Imprison'd fury, bound in brazen chains:
> High on a trophie rais'd, of useless arms,
> He sits, and threats the world with vain alarms.]

479. *Perhaps had perish'd.*] Some of *Homer's* censurers have inferred from this passage, that the Poet represents his Gods subject to death, when nothing but great misery is here described. It is a common way of speech to use *perdition* and destruction for *misfortune.* The language of scripture calls eternal punishment *perishing everlastingly.* There is a remarkable passage to this purpose in *Tacitus, An. 6.* which very livelily represents the miserable state of a distracted tyrant: It is the beginning of a Letter from *Tiberius* to the Senate, *Quid scribam vobis, P. C. aut quomodo scribam, aut quid omnino non scribam hoc tempore, Dii me deæque pejus* perdant *quam* perire *quotidie sentio, si scio* [What I shall write to you, conscript fathers, or how I shall write, or what I shall omit entirely at this time – may the gods and goddesses destroy me more savagely than I feel myself perishing today, if I can understand this question].

498. *No infant on his knees shall call him Sire.*] This is *Homer's* manner of foretelling that he shall perish unfortunately in battel, which is infinitely a more artful way of conveying that thought than by a direct expression. He does not simply say, he shall never return from the war, but intimates as much by describing the loss of the most sensible and affecting pleasure that a warriour can receive at his return. Of the like nature is the prophecy at the end of this speech of the hero's death, by representing it in a dream of his wife's. There are many fine strokes of this kind in the prophetical parts of the Old Testament. Nothing is more natural than *Dione's* forming these images of revenge upon *Diomed*, the hope of which vengeance was so proper a topick of consolation to *Venus.*

500. *To stretch thee pale,* &c.] *Virgil* has taken notice of this threatning denunciation of vengeance, tho' fulfill'd in a different manner, where *Diomed* in his answer to the Embassador of K. *Latinus* enumerates his misfortunes, and imputes the cause of them to this impious attempt upon *Venus.*   *Æneid, Lib.* XI [269–77].

> *Invidisse Deos patriis ut redditus oris*
> *Conjugium optatum & pulchram Calydona viderem?*
> *Nunc etiam horribili visu portenta sequuntur:*
> *Et socii amissi petierunt Æquora pennis:*
> *Fluminibusque vagantur aves (heu dira meorum*

Supplicia!) & scopulos, lachrymosis vocibus implent.
Hæc adeo ex illo mihi jam speranda fuerunt
Tempore, cum ferro cælestia corpora demens
Appetii, & Veneris violavi vulnere dextram.

[The Gods have envied me the sweets of life,
My much lov'd country, and my more lov'd wife:
Banish'd from both, I mourn; while in the sky
Transform'd to birds, my lost companions fly:
Hov'ring about the coasts they make their moan;
And cuff the cliffs with pinions not their own.
What squalid spectres, in the dead of night,
Break my short sleep, and skim before my sight!
I might have promis'd to my self those harms,
Mad as I was, when I with mortal arms
Presum'd against immortal pow'rs to move;
And violate with wounds the Queen of Love.]

501. *Thy distant wife.*] The Poet seems here to complement the fair
sex at the expence of truth, by concealing the character of *Ægiale*,
whom he has describ'd with the disposition of a faithful wife; tho' the
history of those times represents her as an abandon'd prostitute, who
gave up her own person and her husband's crown to her lover. So that
Diomed at his return from *Troy*, when he expected to be receiv'd with
all the tenderness of a loving spouse, found his bed and throne
possess'd by an adulterer, was forc'd to fly his country, and seek refuge
and subsistence in foreign lands. Thus the offended Goddess executed
her vengeance by the proper effects of her own power, by involving
the hero in a series of misfortunes proceeding from the incontinence of
his wife.

517. *The Sire of Gods and men superior smil'd.*] One may observe the
decorum and decency our Author constantly preserves on this Occa-
sion: *Jupiter* only *smiles*, the other Gods *laugh out*. That *Homer* was no
enemy to mirth may appear from several places of his poem; which so
serious as it is, is interspers'd with many gayeties, indeed more than he
has been follow'd in by the succeeding Epic Poets. *Milton*, who was
perhaps fonder of him than the rest, has given most into the ludicrous;
of which his *paradise of fools* in the third book, and his *jesting angels* in
the sixth, are extraordinary instances. Upon the confusion of *Babel*, he

says there was *great laughter in heaven*: as *Homer* calls the laughter of the Gods in the first book ἄσβεστος γέλως, an *inextinguishable laugh*: But the scripture might perhaps embolden the *English* Poet, which says, *The Lord shall laugh them to scorn*, and the like. *Plato* is very angry at *Homer* for making the Deities laugh, as a high indecency and offence to gravity. He says the Gods in our Author represent magistrates and persons in authority, and are designed as examples to such: On this supposition, he blames him for proposing immoderate laughter as a thing decent in great men. I forgot to take notice in its proper Place, that the epithet *inextinguishable* is not to be taken literally for dissolute or ceasless mirth, but was only a phrase of that time to signify chearfulness and seasonable gayety; in the same manner as we may now say, *to die with Laughter*, without being understood to be in danger of dying with it. The place, time, and occasion were all agreeable to mirth: It was at a banquet; and *Plato* himself relates several things that past at the banquet of *Agathon*, which had not been either decent or rational at any other season. The same may be said of the present passage: raillery could never be more natural than when two of the female sex had an opportunity of triumphing over another whom they hated. *Homer* makes wisdom her self not able, even in the presence of *Jupiter*, to resist the temptation. She breaks into a ludicrous speech, and the supreme being himself vouchsafes a smile at it. But this (as *Eustathius* remarks) is not introduced without judgment and precaution. For we see he makes *Minerva* first beg *Jupiter*'s permission for this piece of freedom, *Permit thy daughter, gracious* Jove; in which he asks the reader's leave to enliven his narration with this piece of gayety.

540. *He dreads his fury, and some steps retires.*] *Diomed* still maintains his intrepid character; he retires but a *step or two* even from *Apollo*. The conduct of *Homer* is remarkably just and rational here. He gives *Diomed* no sort of advantage over *Apollo*, because he would not feign what was entirely incredible, and what no allegory could justify. He wounds *Venus* and *Mars*, as it is morally possible to overcome the irregular passions which are represented by those Deities. But it is impossible to vanquish *Apollo*, in whatsoever capacity he is considered, either as the *sun*, or as *Destiny*: One may shoot at the sun, but not hurt him; and one may strive against destiny, but not surmount it.

Eustathius.

546. *A phantom rais'd.*] The fiction of a God's placing a phantom instead of the hero, to delude the enemy and continue the engagement, means no more than that the enemy thought he was in the battel. This is the language of poetry, which prefers a marvellous fiction to a plain and simple truth, the recital whereof would be cold and unaffecting. Thus *Minerva*'s guiding a javelin, signifies only that it was thrown with art and dexterity; *Mars* taking upon him the shape of *Acamas*, that the courage of *Acamas* incited him to do so, and in like manner of the rest. The present passage is copied by *Virgil* in the tenth *Æneid*, where the spectre of *Æneas* is raised by *Juno* or the *Air*, as it is here by *Apollo* or the *Sun*; both equally proper to be employ'd in forming an apparition. Whoever will compare the two authors on this subject, will observe with what admirable art, and what exquisite ornaments, the latter has improved and beautify'd his original. *Scaliger* in comparing these places, has absurdly censured the phantom of *Homer* for its inactivity; whereas it was only form'd to represent the hero lying on the ground, without any appearance of life or motion. *Spencer* in the eighth canto of the third book seems to have improved this imagination, in the creation of his false *Florimel*, who performs all the functions of life, and gives occasion for many adventures.

575. *The speech of* Sarpedon *to* Hector.] It will be hard to find a speech more warm and spirited than this of *Sarpedon*, or which comprehends so much in so few words. Nothing could be more artfully thought upon to pique *Hector*, who was so jealous of his country's glory, than to tell him he had formerly conceiv'd too great a notion of the *Trojan* valour; and to exalt the auxiliaries above his countrymen. The description *Sarpedon* gives of the little concern or interest himself had in the war, in opposition to the necessity and imminent danger of the *Trojans*, greatly strengthens this preference, and lays the charge very home upon their honour. In the latter part, which prescribes *Hector* his duty, there is a particular reprimand in telling him how much it behoves him to animate and encourage the auxiliaries; for this is to say in other words, you should exhort them, and they are forc'd on the contrary to exhort you.

611. *Ceres' sacred floor.*] *Homer* calls the threshing floor *sacred* (says *Eustathius*) not only as it was consecrated to *Ceres*, but in regard of its great use and advantage to human kind; in which sense also he frequently gives the same epithet to *cities*, &c. This simile is of an exquisite beauty.

641. *So when th' embattel'd Clouds.*] This simile contains as proper a comparison, and as fine a picture of nature as any in *Homer*: However it is to be fear'd the beauty and propriety of it will not be very obvious to many readers, because it is the description of a natural appearance which they have not had an opportunity to remark, and which can be observed only in a mountainous country. It happens frequently in very calm weather, that the atmosphere is charg'd with thick vapours, whose gravity is such, that they neither rise nor fall, but remain poiz'd in the air at a certain height, where they continue frequently for several days together. In a plain country this occasions no other visible appearance, but of an uniform clouded sky; but in a hilly region these vapours are to be seen covering the tops and stretch'd along the sides of the mountains; the clouded parts above being terminated and distinguish'd from the clear parts below by a strait line running parallel to the horizon, as far as the mountains extend. The whole compass of nature cannot afford a nobler and more exact representation of a numerous army, drawn up in line of battel, and expecting the charge. The long-extended even front, the closeness of the ranks; the firmness, order, and silence of the whole, are all drawn with great resemblance in this one comparison. The Poet adds, that this appearance is while *Boreas* and the other boisterous winds which disperse and break the clouds, are laid asleep. This is as exact as it is poetical; for when the winds arise, this regular order is soon dissolv'd. This circumstance is added to the description, as an ominous anticipation of the flight and dissipation of the *Greeks*, which soon ensued when *Mars* and *Hector* broke in upon them.

651. *Ye* Greeks, *be men,* &c.] If *Homer* in the longer Speeches of the *Iliad*, says all that could be said by eloquence, in the shorter he says all that can be said with judgment. Whatever some few modern Criticks have thought, it will be found upon due reflection, that the length or brevity of his speeches is determined as the occasions either allow leisure or demand haste. This concise oration of *Agamemnon* is a master-piece in the laconic way. The exigence required he should say something very powerful, and no time was to be lost. He therefore warms the brave and the timorous by one and the same exhortation, which at once moves by the love of glory, and the fear of death. It is short and full, like that of the brave *Scotch* General under *Gustavus*, who upon sight of the enemy, said only this; *See ye those Lads? Either fell them or they'll fell you.*

652. *Your brave associates and your selves revere.*] This noble exhortation of *Agamemnon* is correspondent to the wise scheme of *Nestor* in the second book: where he advised to rank the soldiers of the same nation together, that being known to each other, all might be incited either by a generous emulation or a decent shame. *Spondanus.*

691. Mars *urg'd him on.*] This is another instance of what has been in general observ'd in the discourse on the battels of *Homer*, his artful manner of making us measure one hero by another. We have here an exact scale of the valour of *Æneas* and of *Menelaus*; how much the former outweighs the latter, appears by what is said of *Mars* in these lines, and by the necessity of *Antilochus*'s assisting *Menelaus*: as afterwards what overbalance that assistance gave him, by *Æneas*'s retreating from them both. How very nicely are these degrees mark'd on either hand? This knowledge of the difference which nature itself sets between one man and another, makes our Author neither blame these two heroes for going against one, who was superior to each of them in strength; nor that one for retiring from both, when their conjunction made them an overmatch to him. There is great judgment in all this.

696. *And all his country's glorious labours vain.*] For (as *Agamemnon* said in the fourth book upon *Menelaus*'s being wounded) if he were slain, the war would be at an end, and the *Greeks* think only of returning to their country. *Spondanus.*

726. Mars, *stern destroyer*, &c.] There is a great nobleness in this passage. With what pomp is *Hector* introduced into the battel, where *Mars* and *Bellona* are his attendants: The retreat of *Diomed* is no less beautiful; *Minerva* had remov'd the mist from his eyes, and he immediately discovers *Mars* assisting *Hector*. His surprize on this occasion is finely imag'd by that of the traveller on the sudden sight of the river.

784. *What brings this* Lycian *Counsellor so far?*] There is a particular sarcasm in *Tlepolemus*'s calling *Sarpedon* in this place Λυκίων Βουληφόρε,

Lycian Counsellor, one better skill'd in oratory than war; as he was the Governor of a people who had long been in Peace, and probably (if we may guess from his character in *Homer*) remarkable for his speeches. This is rightly observed by *Spondanus*, tho' not taken notice of by M. *Dacier*.

792. Troy *felt his arm*.] He alludes to the history of the first destruction of *Troy* by *Hercules*, occasion'd by *Laomedon*'s refusing that hero the horses, which were the reward promis'd him for the delivery of his daughter *Hesione*.

809. *With base reproaches and unmanly pride*.] Methinks these Words κακῷ ἠνίπαπε μύθῳ include the chief sting of *Sarpedon*'s answer to *Tlepolemus*, which no Commentator that I remember has remark'd. He tells him *Laomedon* deserv'd his misfortune, not only for his perfidy, but for injuring a brave man with unmanly and scandalous reproaches; alluding to those which *Tlepolemus* had just before cast upon him.

848. *Nor* Hector *to the Chief replies*.] *Homer* is in nothing more admirable than in the excellent use he makes of the *silence* of the Persons he introduces. It would be endless to collect all the instances of this truth throughout his Poem; yet I cannot but put together those that have already occurr'd in the course of this work, and leave to the reader the pleasure of observing it in what remains. The silence of the two Heralds, when they were to take *Briseïs* from *Achilles* in *Lib.* 1. of which see *note* 39. In the third book, when *Iris* tells *Helen* the two rivals were to fight in her quarrel, and that all *Troy* were standing spectators; that guilty Princess makes no answer, but casts a veil over her face and drops a tear; and when she comes just after into the presence of *Priam*, she speaks not, till after he has in a particular manner encourag'd and commanded her. *Paris* and *Menelaus* being just upon the point to encounter, the latter declares his wishes and hopes of conquest to heaven; the former being engag'd in an unjust cause, says not a word. In the fourth book, when *Jupiter* has express'd his desire to favour *Troy*, *Juno* declaims against him, but the *Goddess of Wisdom*, tho' much concern'd, holds her peace. When *Agamemnon* too rashly reproves *Diomed*, that Hero remains silent, and in the true character of a rough warriour, leaves it to his actions to speak for him. In the present book, when *Sarpedon* has reproach'd *Hector* in an open and generous manner, *Hector* preserving the same warlike character, returns no answer, but

immediately hastens to the business of the field; as he also does in this place, where he instantly brings off *Sarpedon*, without so much as telling him he will endeavour his rescue. *Chapman* was not sensible of the beauty of this, when he imagined *Hector*'s silence here proceeded from the pique he had conceiv'd at *Sarpedon* for his late reproof of him. That Translator has not scrupled to insert this opinion of his in a groundless interpolation altogether foreign to the Author. But indeed it is a liberty he frequently takes, to draw any passage to some new, far--fetch'd conceit of his invention; insomuch, that very often before he translates any speech, to the sense or design of which he gives some fanciful turn of his own, he prepares it by several additional lines purposely to prepossess the reader of that meaning. Those who will take the trouble may see examples of this in what he sets before the speeches of *Hector*, *Paris*, and *Helena* in the sixth book, and innumerable other places.

858. *But* Boreas *rising fresh.*] *Sarpedon*'s fainting at the extraction of the dart, and reviving by the free air, shews the great judgment of our author in these matters. But how poetically has he told this truth in raising the God *Boreas* to his Hero's Assistance, and making a little machine of but one line? This manner of representing common things in figure and person, was perhaps the effect of *Homer*'s *Ægyptian* education.

860. *The gen'rous* Greeks, &c.] This flow and orderly retreat of the *Greeks*, with their front constantly turn'd to the enemy, is a fine encomium both of their courage and discipline. This manner of retreat was in use among the ancient *Lacedæmonians*, as were many other martial customs describ'd by *Homer*. This practice took its rise among that brave people from the apprehensions of being slain with a wound receiv'd in their backs. Such a misfortune was not only attended with the highest infamy, but they had found a way to punish them who suffer'd thus even after their death, by denying them (as *Eustathius* informs us) the rites of burial.

864.   *Who first, who last, by* Mars *and* Hector's *hand*
        Stretch'd in their blood, lay gasping on the sand?]

This manner of breaking into an interrogation, amidst the description of a battel, is what serves very much to awaken the reader. It is here an invocation to the muse that prepares us for something uncommon; and the Muse is suppos'd immediately to answer, Teuthras *the great*, &c. *Virgil*, I think, has improved the strength of this figure by addressing the apostrophe to the person whose exploits he is celebrating, as to *Camilla* in the eleventh book [664–5].

> *Quem telo primum, quem postremum, aspera virgo,*
> *Dejicis? aut quot humi morientia corpora fundis?*

> [Who formost, and who last, heroick maid,
> On the cold earth were by thy courage laid?]

885. *And now Heav'ns Empress calls her blazing car*, &c.] *Homer* seems never more delighted than when he has some occasion of displaying his skill in mechanicks. The detail he gives us of this chariot is a beautiful example of it, where he takes occasion to describe every different part with a happiness rarely to be found in descriptions of this nature.

904. Pallas *disrobes.*] This fiction of *Pallas* arraying herself with the arms of *Jupiter*, finely intimates (says *Eustathius*) that she is nothing else but the wisdom of the Almighty. The same author tells us, that the ancients mark'd this place with a star, to distinguish it as one of those that were perfectly admirable. Indeed there is a greatness and sublimity in the whole passage, which is astonishing, and superior to any imagination but that of *Homer*, nor is there any that might better give occasion for that celebrated saying, That *he was the only man who had seen the forms of the Gods, or the only man who had shewn them.* With what nobleness he describes the chariot of *Juno*, the armour of *Minerva*, the *Ægis* of *Jupiter*, fill'd with the Figures of *Horror*, *Affright*, *Discord*, and all the terrors of war, the effects of his wrath against men; and that spear with which his power and wisdom overturns whole armies, and humbles the pride of the Kings who offend him? But we shall not wonder at the unusual majesty of all these ideas, if we consider that they have a near resemblance to some descriptions of the same kind in the sacred writings, where the Almighty is represented arm'd with terror, and descending in majesty to be aveng'd on his enemies: The *chariot*, the *bow*, and the *shield of God* are expressions frequent in the *Psalms.*

913. *A fringe of serpents.*] Our author does not particularly describe this fringe of the *Ægis*, as consisting of serpents; but that it did so, may be learn'd from *Herodotus* in his fourth book. 'The *Greeks* (says he) borrowed the vest and shield of *Minerva* from the *Lybians*, only with this difference, that the *Lybian* shield was fringed with thongs of leather, the *Grecian* with serpents.' And *Virgil*'s description of the same *Ægis* agrees with this, *Æn.* 8. v. 435.

> *Ægidaque horriferam, turbatæ Palladis arma,*
> *Certatim squamis serpentum, auroque polibant,*
> *Connexosque angues –*

> [The rest refresh the scaly snakes, that fold
>   The shield of *Pallas*; and renew their gold.]

This note is taken from *Spondanus*, as is also *Ogilby*'s on this place, but he has translated the passage of *Herodotus* wrong, and made the *Lybian* shield have the serpents which were peculiar to the *Grecian*. By the way I must observe, that *Ogilby*'s notes are for the most part a transcription of *Spondanus*'s.

920. *So vast, the wide circumference contains A hundred armies.*] The words in the original are ἑκατὸν πόλεων πρυλέεσσ᾽ ἀραρυῖαν, which are capable of two meanings; either that this helmet of *Jupiter* was sufficient to have covered the armies of an hundred cities, or that the armies of an hundred cities were engraved upon it. It is here translated in such a manner that it may be taken either way, tho' the learned are most inclined to the former sense, as that idea is greater and more extraordinary, indeed more agreeable to *Homer*'s bold manner, and not extravagant if we call in the allegory to our assistance, and imagine it (with M. *Dacier*) an allusion to the providence of God that extends over all the universe.

928. *Heav'n gates spontaneous open'd.*] This marvellous circumstance of the gates of heav'n opening themselves of their own accord to the divinities that past thro' them, is copied by *Milton, Lib.* 5.

> – *At the gate*
> *Of Heav'n arriv'd, the gate self-open'd wide*
> *On golden hinges turning, as by work*
> *Divine the sov'reign Architect had fram'd.*

And again in the seventh book,

> – *Heav'n open'd wide*
> *Her everduring gates, harmonious sound,*
> *On golden hinges moving –*

As the fiction that the hours are the guards of those gates, gave him the hint of that beautiful passage in the beginning of his sixth,

> *– The morn*
> *Wak'd by the circling hours, with rosy hand*
> *Unbarr'd the gates of light, &c.*

This Expression of *the gates of heaven* is in the *Eastern* manner, where they said the *gates* of Heaven, or of Earth, for the *entrance* or *extremities* of Heaven or Earth; a phrase usual in the scriptures, as is observ'd by *Dacier.*

929. *Heav'ns golden gates, kept by the winged hours.*] By the *hours* here are meant the *seasons*; and so *Hobbes* translates it, but spoils the sense by what he adds,

> *Tho' to the seasons* Jove *the power gave*
> *Alone to judge of early and of late,*

Which is utterly unintelligible, and nothing like *Homer*'s thought. *Natalis Comes* explains it thus, *Lib.* 4. *c.* 5. *Homerus libro quinto Iliadis non solum has, Portas cœli servare, sed etiam nubes inducere & serenum facere, cum libuerit; quippe cum apertum cœlum, serenum nominent Poetæ, at clausum, tectum nubibus.* [Although *Homer*, in the fifth book of the *Iliad*, was pleased to have them not only guarding the gates of heaven but even spreading about clouds and bringing fair weather, clearly when the poets say 'open sky' they mean fair weather, and when they say 'closed sky' they mean covered with clouds.]

954. *To tame the Monster-god* Minerva *knows.*] For it is only *wisdom* that can master *strength.* It is worth while here to observe the conduct of *Homer.* He makes *Minerva*, and not *Juno*, to fight with *Mars*; because a combate between *Mars* and *Juno* could not be supported by any allegory to have authorized the fable: whereas the allegory of a battel between *Mars* and *Minerva* is very open and intelligible.

Eustathius.

960. *Far as a shepherd*, &c.] *Longinus* citing these verses as a noble instance of the sublime, speaks to this effect. 'In what a wonderful manner does *Homer* exalt his Deities; measuring the leaps of their very horses by the whole breadth of the horizon? Who is there that considering the magnificence of this hyperbole, would not cry out with reason, that if these heavenly steeds were to make a second leap, the world would want room for a third?' This puts me in mind of that Passage in *Hesiod*'s *Theogony*, where he describes the height of the Heavens, by saying a smith's anvil would be nine days in falling from thence to earth.

971. *Smooth as the gliding doves.*] This simile is intended to express the lightness and smoothness of the motion of these Goddesses. The doves to which *Homer* compares them, are said by the ancient scholiast to leave no impression of their steps. The word βάτην in the original may be render'd *ascenderunt* as well as *incesserunt*; so may imply (as M. *Dacier* translates it) moving without touching the earth, which *Milton* finely calls *smooth-gliding without step. Virgil* [*Aen.* V. 216–17] describes the gliding of one of these birds by an image parallel to that in this verse.

> — *Mox aëre lapsa quieto,*
> *Radit iter liquidum, celeres neque commovet alas.*

> [at length she springs,
> To smoother flight, and shoots upon her wings.]

This kind of movement was appropriated to the Gods by the *Egyptians*, as we see in *Heliodorus, Lib.* 3. *Homer* might possibly have taken this notion from them. And *Virgil* in that passage where *Æneas* discovers *Venus* by her gate, *Et vera incessu patuit Dea*, seems to allude to some manner of moving that distinguish'd divinities from mortals. This opinion is likewise hinted at by him in the fifth *Æneid* [647–9], where he so beautifully and briefly enumerates the distinguishing marks of a Deity,

> — *Divini signa decoris,*
> *Ardentesque notate oculos: qui spiritus illi,*
> *Qui vultus, vocisque sonus, vel gressus eunti!*

> [What terrours from her frowning front arise;
> Behold a Goddess in her ardent eyes!
> What rays around her heav'nly face are seen,
> Mark her majestic voice, and more than mortal meen!]

This passage likewise strengthens what is said in the notes on the first book, v. 268.

978. Stentor *the strong, endu'd with brazen lungs.*] There was a necessity for cryers whose voices were stronger than ordinary, in those ancient times, before the use of trumpets was known in their armies. And that they were in esteem afterwards may be seen from *Herodotus*, where he takes notice that *Darius* had in his train an *Egyptian*, whose voice was louder and stronger than any man's of his age. There is a farther propriety in *Homer*'s attributing this voice to *Juno*; because *Juno* is no other than the *Air*, and because the *Air* is the cause of *Sound*.   *Eustathius, Spondanus.*

998. *Degen'rate Prince,* &c.] This speech of *Minerva* to *Diomed* derives its whole force and efficacy from the offensive comparison she makes between *Tydeus* and his son. *Tydeus* when he was single in the city of his enemy, fought and overcame the *Thebans* even tho' *Minerva* forbade him; *Diomed* in the midst of his army, and with enemies inferior in number, declines the fight, tho' *Minerva* commands him. *Tydeus* disobeys her, to engage in the battel; *Diomed* disobeys her to avoid engaging; and that too after he had upon many occasions experienced the assistance of the Goddess. Madam *Dacier* should have acknowledged this remark to belong to *Eustathius.*

1024. *Rash, furious, blind, from these to those he flies.*] *Minerva* in this place very well paints the manners of *Mars*, whose business was always to fortify the weaker side, in order to keep up the broil. I think the passage includes a fine allegory of the nature of *War. Mars* is called *inconstant*, and a *breaker of his promises*, because the chance of war is wavering, and uncertain victory is perpetually changing sides. This latent meaning of the epithet ἀλλοπρόσαλλος is taken notice of by Eustathius.

1033. *So great a God.*] The translation has ventured to call a Goddess so; in imitation of the *Greek*, which uses the word Θεός promiscuously for either gender. Some of the *Latin* Poets have not scrupled to do the same. *Statius, Thebaid* 4 [425]. (speaking of *Diana*)

> *Nec caret umbra* Deo.

> [Nor is the shady spot without its goddess.]

And *Virgil, Æneid* 2 [632–3]. where *Æneas* is conducted by *Venus* thro' the dangers of the fire and the enemy.

Descendo, ac ducente Deo, *flammam inter & hostes*
Expedior –

[Descending thence, I scape through foes, and fire:
Before the Goddess, foes and flames retire.]

1037. *Black* Orcus' *helmet.*] As every thing that goes into the dark empire of *Pluto*, or *Orcus*, disappears and is seen no more; the *Greeks* from thence borrow'd this figurative expression, *to put on* Pluto's *helmet*, that is to say, *to become invisible. Plato* uses this proverb in the tenth book of his *Republick*, and *Aristophanes* in *Acharnens.*

Eusthathius.

1054. *Loud as the roar encountring armies yield.*] This *hyperbole* to express the roaring of *Mars*, so strong as it is, yet is not extravagant. It wants not a qualifying circumstance or two; the voice is not human, but that of a Deity, and the comparison being taken from an army, renders it more natural with respect to the God of War. It is less daring to say that a God could send forth a voice as loud as the shout of two armies, than that *Camilla*, a *Latian* nymph, could run so swiftly over the corn as not to bend an ear of it. Or, to alledge a nearer instance, that *Polyphemus* a meer mortal, shook all the island of *Sicily*, and made the deepest caverns of *Ætna* roar with his cries. Yet *Virgil* generally escapes the censure of those moderns who are shock'd with the bold flights of *Homer*. It is usual with those who are slaves to common opinion to overlook or praise the same things in one, that they blame in another. They think to depreciate *Homer* in extolling the judgment of *Virgil*, who never shew'd it more than when he followed him in these boldnesses. And indeed they who would take boldness from poetry, must leave dulness in the room of it.

1058. *As Vapors blown*, &c.] *Mars* after a sharp engagement amidst the rout of the *Trojans*, wrapt in a whirlwind of dust which was rais'd by so many thousand combatants, flies toward *Olympus. Homer* compares him in this estate, to those black clouds, which during a scorching southern wind in the dog-days, are sometimes born towards Heaven; for the wind at that time gathering the dust together, forms a dark cloud of it. The heat of the fight, the precipitation of the *Trojans*, together with the clouds of dust that flew above the army and took

Mars from the sight of his enemy, supply'd *Homer* with this noble image.   *Dacier.*

1074. *Thou gav'st that fury to the realms of light, Pernicious, wild,* &c.] It is very artful in *Homer*, to make Mars accuse *Minerva* of all those faults and enormities he was himself so eminently guilty of. Those people who are the most unjust and violent accuse others, even the best, of the same crimes: Every irrational man is a distorted rule, tries every thing by that wrong measure, and forms his judgment accordingly.   *Eustathius.*

1091. *Condemn'd to pain, tho' fated not to die.*] Those are mistaken who imagine our author represents his Gods as mortal. He only represents the inferior or corporeal Deities as capable of pains and punishments, during the will of *Jupiter*, which is not inconsistent with true theology. If *Mars* is said in *Dione*'s speech to *Venus* to have been near *perishing* by *Otus* and *Ephialtes*, it means no more than lasting misery, such as *Jupiter* threatens him with when he speaks of precipitating him into *Tartarus. Homer* takes care to tell us both of this God and of *Pluto* when *Pæon* cured them, that they were not mortal.

> Οὐ μὲν γάρ τι καταθνητός γ᾽ ἐτέτυκτο.

[He was not made in any way mortal.]

1096. *Of all the Gods – Thou most unjust, most odious,* &c.] *Jupiter*'s reprimand of *Mars* is worthy the justice and goodness of the great Governor of the world, and seems to be no more than was necessary in this place. *Homer* hereby admirably distinguishes between *Minerva* and *Mars*, that is to say, between *Wisdom* and ungovern'd *Fury*; the former is produced from *Jupiter* without a mother, to show that it proceeds from God alone; (and *Homer*'s alluding to that fable in the preceding speech shows that he was not unacquainted with this opinion.) The latter is born of *Jupiter* and *Juno*, because, as *Plato* explains it, whatever is created by the ministry of second causes, and the concurrence of matter, partakes of that original spirit of division which reigned in the *Chaos*, and is of a corrupt and rebellious nature. The reader will find this allegory pursued with great beauty in these two speeches; especially where *Jupiter* concludes with saying he will not destroy *Mars*, because he comes from himself; God will not annihilate *Passion*, which he created to be of use to *Reason*: 'Wisdom (says *Eustathius* upon this place) has occasion for passion, in the same manner as Princes have need of guards. Therefore reason and wisdom correct and keep passion in subjection, but do not entirely destroy and ruin it.'

1101. *And all thy mother in thy soul rebels*, &c.] *Jupiter* says of *Juno*, that *she has a temper which is insupportable, and knows not how to submit, tho' he is perpetually chastising her with his reproofs.* Homer says no more than this, but M. *Dacier* adds, *Si je ne la retenois par la severité des mes loix, il n'est rien qu'elle ne bouleversast dans l'Olympe & sous l'Olympe.* [If I do not restrain her by the severity of my laws, it is only in order that she not wreak havoc both on and below Olympus.] Upon which she makes a remark to this effect, 'that if it were not for the laws of providence, the whole world would be nothing but confusion.' This practice of refining and adding to *Homer*'s thought in the text, and then applauding the author for it in the notes, is pretty usual with the more florid modern translators. In the third *Iliad*, in *Helen*'s speech to *Priam*, v. 175. she wishes she had rather dy'd than follow'd *Paris* to *Troy*. To this is added in the *French*, *Mais je n'eus ni assez de courage ni assez de vertu* [But I did not have enough courage or virtue], for which there is not the least Hint in *Homer*. I mention this particular instance in pure justice, because in the treatise *de la Corruption du Gout Exam. de Liv.* 3. she triumphs over M. *de la Motte*, as if he had omitted the sense and moral of *Homer* in that place, when in truth he only left out her own interpolation.

1112. *As when the fig's prest Juice*, &c.] The sudden operation of the remedy administer'd by *Pæon*, is well express'd by this similitude. It is necessary just to take notice, that they anciently made use of the juice or sap of a fig for runnet, to cause their milk to coagulate. It may not be amiss to observe, that *Homer* is not very delicate in the choice of his allusions. He often borrowed his similes from low life, and provided they illustrated his thoughts in a just and lively manner, it was all he had regard to.

The allegory of this whole book lies so open, is carry'd on with such closeness, and wound up with so much fulness and strength, that it is a wonder how it could enter into the imagination of any critick, that these actions of *Diomed* were only a daring and extravagant fiction in

Homer, as if he affected the *marvellous* at any rate. The great moral of it is, that a brave man should not contend against Heaven, but resist only *Venus* and *Mars*, Incontinence and ungovern'd Fury. *Diomed* is propos'd as an example of a great and enterprizing nature, which would perpetually be venturing too far, and committing extravagancies or impieties, did it not suffer itself to be check'd and guided by *Minerva* or Prudence: For it is this *Wisdom* (as we are told in the very first lines of the book) that raises a Hero above all others. Nothing is more observable than the particular care *Homer* has taken to shew he designed this moral. He never omits any occasion throughout the book, to put it in express terms into the mouths of the Gods or persons of the greatest Weight. *Minerva*, at the beginning of the battel, is made to give this precept to *Diomed*; *fight not against the Gods, but give way to them, and resist only* Venus. The same Goddess opens his eyes, and enlightens him so far as to perceive when it is heaven that acts immediately against him, or when it is man only that opposes him. The hero himself, as soon as he has perform'd her dictates in driving away *Venus*, cries out, not as to the *Goddess*, but as to the *Passion*, *Thou hast no business with warriours, is it not enough that thou deceiv'st weak women?* Even the mother of *Venus* while she comforts her daughter, bears testimony to the moral: *That man* (says she) *is not long-liv'd who contends with the Gods.* And when *Diomed*, transported by his nature, proceeds but a step too far, *Apollo* discovers himself in the most solemn manner, and declares this truth in his own voice, as it were by direct revelation: *Mortal, forbear! consider, and know the vast difference there is between the Gods and thee. They are immortal and divine, but man a miserable reptile of the dust.*

THE
SIXTH BOOK
OF THE
ILIAD

The ARGUMENT

The Episodes of *Glaucus* and *Diomed*, and of *Hector* and *Andromache*

The Gods having left the field, the Grecians *prevail.* Helenus, *the chief augur of* Troy, *commands* Hector *to return to the city in order to appoint a solemn procession of the Queen and the* Trojan *matrons to the temple of* Minerva, *to entreat her to remove* Diomed *from the fight. The battel relaxing during the absence of* Hector, Glaucus *and* Diomed *have an interview between the two armies; where coming to the knowledge of the friendship and hospitality past between their ancestors, they make exchange of their arms.* Hector *having performed the orders of* Helenus, *prevail'd upon* Paris *to return to the battel, and taken a tender leave of his wife* Andromache, *hastens again to the field.*

The Scene *is first in the field of battel, between the rivers* Simois *and* Scamander, *and then changes to* Troy.

Now heav'n forsakes the fight: Th' immortals yield
To human force and human skill, the field:
Dark show'rs of javelins fly from foes to foes;
Now here, now there, the tyde of combate flows;
While *Troy*'s fam'd *streams that bound the deathful
5   plain
On either side run purple to the main.

   Great *Ajax* first to conquest led the way,
Broke the thick ranks, and turn'd the doubtful day.
The *Thracian Acamas* his faulchion found,
10 And hew'd th' enormous giant to the ground;
His thundring arm a deadly stroke imprest
Where the black horse-hair nodded o'er his crest:
Fix'd in his front the brazen weapon lies,
And seals in endless shades his swimming eyes.

15   Next *Teuthras*' son distain'd the sands with blood,
Axylus, hospitable, rich and good:
In fair *Arisba*'s walls (his native place)
He held his seat; a friend to human race.
Fast by the road, his ever-open door
20 Oblig'd the wealthy, and reliev'd the poor.
To stern *Tydides* now he falls a prey,
No friend to guard him in the dreadful day!
Breathless the good man fell, and by his side
His faithful servant, old *Calesius* dy'd.

Scamander and *Simoïs*.

By great *Euryalus* was *Dresus* slain, 25
And next he lay'd *Opheltius* on the plain.
Two twins were near, bold, beautiful and young,
From a fair *Naiad* and *Bucolion* sprung:
(*Laomedon*'s white flocks *Bucolion* fed,
That monarch's first-born by a foreign bed; 30
In secret woods he won the *Naiad*'s grace,
And two fair infants crown'd his strong embrace.)
Here dead they lay in all their youthful charms;
The ruthless victor stripp'd their shining arms.

   Astyalus by *Polypætes* fell; 35
Ulysses' spear *Pidytes* sent to hell;
By *Teucer*'s shaft brave *Aretäon* bled,
And *Nestor*'s son laid stern *Ablerus* dead.
Great *Agamemnon*, leader of the brave,
The mortal wound of rich *Elatus* gave, 40
Who held in *Pedasus* his proud abode,
And till'd the banks where silver *Satnio* flow'd.
Melanthius by *Eurypylus* was slain;
And *Phylacus* from *Leitus* flies in vain.

   Unblest *Adrastus* next at mercy lies 45
Beneath the *Spartan* spear, a living prize.
Scar'd with the din and tumult of the fight,
His headlong steeds, precipitate in flight,
Rush'd on a *Tamarisk*'s strong trunk, and broke
The shatter'd chariot from the crooked yoke. 50
Wide o'er the field, resistless as the wind,
For *Troy* they fly, and leave their lord behind.
Prone on his face he sinks beside the wheel;
Atrides o'er him shakes his vengeful steel;
The fallen chief in suppliant posture press'd 55
The victor's knees, and thus his pray'r address'd.

   Oh spare my youth, and for the life I owe
Large gifts of price my father shall bestow;
When fame shall tell, that not in battel slain
Thy hollow ships his captive son detain, 60
Rich heaps of brass shall in thy tent be told;
And steel well-temper'd, and persuasive gold.

   He said: compassion touch'd the hero's heart,
He stood suspended with the lifted dart:

65 As pity pleaded for his vanquish'd prize,
    Stern *Agamemnon* swift to vengeance flies,
    And furious, thus. Oh impotent of mind!
    Shall these, shall these *Atrides'* mercy find?
    Well hast thou known proud *Troy*'s perfidious land,
70 And well her natives merit at thy hand!
    Not one of all the race, nor sex, nor age,
    Shall save a *Trojan* from our boundless rage:
    Ilion shall perish whole, and bury all;
    Her babes, her infants at the breast, shall fall.
75 A dreadful lesson of exampled fate,
    To warn the nations, and to curb the great!
        The monarch spoke: the words with warmth addrest
    To rigid justice steel'd his brother's breast.
    Fierce from his knees the hapless chief he thrust;
80 The monarch's javelin stretch'd him in the dust.
    Then pressing with his foot his panting heart,
    Forth from the slain he tugg'd the reeking dart.
    Old *Nestor* saw, and rouz'd the warriour's rage;
    Thus, heroes! thus the vig'rous combate wage!
85 No son of *Mars* descend, for servile gains,
    To touch the booty, while a foe remains.
    Behold yon' glitt'ring host, your future spoil!
    First gain the conquest, then reward the toil.
        And now had *Greece* eternal fame acquir'd,
90 And frighted *Troy* within her walls retir'd;
    Had not sage *Helenus* her state redrest,
    Taught by the Gods that mov'd his sacred breast;
    Where *Hector* stood, with great *Æneas* join'd,
    The seer reveal'd the counsels of his mind.
95   Ye gen'rous chiefs! on whom th' immortals lay
    The cares and glories of this doubtful day,
    On whom your aid's, your country's hopes depend,
    Wise to consult, and active to defend!
    Here, at our gates, your brave efforts unite,
100 Turn back the routed, and forbid the flight;
    E're yet their wives soft arms the cowards gain,
    The sport and insult of the hostile train.
    When your commands have hearten'd ev'ry band,
    Our selves, here fix'd, will make the dang'rous stand;

Press'd as we are, and sore of former fight,   105
These straits demand our last remains of might.
Meanwhile, thou *Hector* to the town retire,
And teach our mother what the Gods require:
Direct the Queen to lead th' assembled train
Of *Troy*'s chief matrons to *Minerva*'s fane;   110
Unbar the sacred gates, and seek the pow'r
With offer'd vows, in *Ilion*'s topmost tow'r.
The largest mantle her rich wardrobes hold,
Most priz'd for art, and labour'd o'er with gold,
Before the Goddess' honour'd knees be spread;   115
And twelve young heifers to her altars led.
If so the pow'r, atton'd by fervent pray'r,
Our wives, our infants, and our city spare,
And far avert *Tydides'* wastful ire,
That mows whole troops, and makes all *Troy* retire.   120
Not thus *Achilles* taught our hosts to dread,
Sprung tho' he was from more than mortal bed;
Not thus resistless rul'd the stream of fight,
In rage unbounded, and unmatch'd in might.

 Hector obedient heard; and, with a bound,   125
Leap'd from his trembling chariot to the ground;
Thro' all his host, inspiring force, he flies,
And bids the thunder of the battel rise.
With rage recruited the bold *Trojans* glow,
And turn the tyde of conflict on the foe: 130
Fierce in the front he shakes two dazling spears;
All *Greece* recedes, and 'midst her triumph fears.
Some God, they thought, who rul'd the fate of wars,
Shot down avenging, from the vault of stars.

 Then thus, aloud. Ye dauntless *Dardans* hear!   135
And you whom distant nations send to war!
Be mindful of the strength your fathers bore;
Be still your selves, and *Hector* asks no more.
One hour demands me in the *Trojan* wall,
To bid our altars flame, and victims fall: 140
Nor shall, I trust, the matron's holy train
And rev'rend elders, seek the Gods in vain.

 This said, with ample strides the hero past;
The shield's large orb behind his shoulder cast,

145   His neck o'ershading, to his ancle hung;
      And as he march'd, the brazen buckler rung.
         Now paus'd the battel, (Godlike *Hector* gone)
      When daring *Glaucus* and great *Tydeus'* son
      Between both armies met: The chiefs from far
150   Observ'd each other, and had mark'd for war.
      Near as they drew, *Tydides* thus began.
         What art thou, boldest of the race of man?
      Our eyes, till now, that aspect ne'er beheld,
      Where fame is reap'd amid th' embattel'd field;
155   Yet far before the troops thou dar'st appear,
      And meet a lance the fiercest heroes fear.
      Unhappy they, and born of luckless sires,
      Who tempt our fury when *Minerva* fires!
      But if from heav'n, celestial thou descend;
160   Know, with immortals we no more contend.
      Not long *Lycurgus* view'd the golden light,
      That daring man who mix'd with Gods in fight;
      Bacchus, and *Bacchus'* votaries he drove
      With brandish'd steel from *Nyssa's* sacred grove,
165   Their consecrated spears lay scatter'd round,
      With curling vines and twisted ivy bound;
      While *Bacchus* headlong sought the briny flood,
      And *Thetis'* arms receiv'd the trembling God.
      Nor fail'd the crime th' immortals wrath to move,
170   (Th' immortals blest with endless ease above)
      Depriv'd of sight by their avenging doom,
      Chearless he breath'd, and wander'd in the gloom,
      Then sunk unpity'd to the dire abodes,
      A wretch accurst, and hated by the Gods!
175   I brave not heav'n: But if the fruits of earth
      Sustain thy life, and human be thy birth;
      Bold as thou art, too prodigal of breath,
      Approach, and enter the dark gates of death.
         What, or from whence I am, or who my sire,
180   (Reply'd the chief) can *Tydeus'* son enquire?
      Like leaves on trees the race of man is found,
      Now green in youth, now with'ring on the ground,
      Another race the following spring supplies,
      They fall successive, and successive rise;

So generations in their course decay,   185
So flourish these, when those are past away.
But if thou still persist to search my birth,
Then hear a tale that fills the spacious earth.
    A city stands on *Argos'* utmost bound,
(*Argos* the fair for warlike steeds renown'd)   190
Æolian Sysiphus, with wisdom blest,
In ancient time the happy walls possest,
Then call'd *Ephyre*: *Glaucus* was his son;
Great *Glaucus*, father of *Bellerophon*,
Who o'er the sons of men in beauty shin'd,   195
Lov'd for that valour which preserves mankind.
Then mighty *Prætus Argos'* sceptres sway'd,
Whose hard commands *Bellerophon* obey'd.
With direful jealousy the monarch rag'd,
And the brave Prince in num'rous toils engag'd.   200
For him, *Antæa* burn'd with lawless flame,
And strove to tempt him from the paths of fame:
In vain she tempted the relentless youth,
Endu'd with wisdom, sacred fear, and truth.
Fir'd at his scorn the Queen to *Prætus* fled,   205
And begg'd revenge for her insulted bed:
Incens'd he heard, resolving on his fate;
But hospitable laws restrain'd his hate:
To *Lycia* the devoted youth he sent,
With tablets seal'd, that told his dire intent.   210
Now blest by ev'ry pow'r who guards the good,
The chief arriv'd at *Xanthus'* silver flood:
There *Lycia's* monarch paid him honours due;
Nine days he feasted, and nine bulls he slew.
But when the tenth bright morning orient glow'd,   215
The faithful youth his monarch's mandate show'd:
The fatal tablets, till that instant seal'd,
The deathful secret to the King reveal'd.
First, dire *Chymæra's* conquest was enjoin'd;
A mingled monster, of no mortal kind;   220
Behind, a dragon's fiery tail was spread;
A goat's rough body bore a lion's head;
Her pitchy nostrils flaky flames expire;
Her gaping throat emits infernal fire.

225   This pest he slaughter'd (for he read the skies,
       And trusted heav'ns informing prodigies)
       Then met in arms the *Solymæan* crew,
       (Fiercest of men) and those the warriour slew.
       Next the bold *Amazon*'s whole force defy'd;
230   And conquer'd still, for heav'n was on his side.
          Nor ended here his toils: His *Lycian* Foes
       At his return, a treach'rous ambush rose,
       With levell'd spears along the winding shore;
       There fell they breathless, and return'd no more.
235   At length the monarch with repentant grief
       Confess'd the Gods, and God-descended chief;
       His daughter gave, the stranger to detain,
       With half the honours of his ample reign.
       The *Lycians* grant a chosen space of ground,
240   With woods, with vineyards, and with harvests crown'd.
       There long the chief his happy lot possess'd,
       With two brave sons and one fair daughter bless'd;
       (Fair ev'n in heav'nly eyes; her fruitful love
       Crown'd with *Sarpedon*'s birth th' embrace of *Jove*)
245   But when at last, distracted in his mind,
       Forsook by heav'n, forsaking human kind,
       Wide o'er th' *Aleian* field he chose to stray,
       A long, forlorn, uncomfortable way!
       Woes heap'd on woes comsum'd his wasted heart;
250   His beauteous daughter fell by *Phœbè*'s dart;
       His eldest-born by raging *Mars* was slain,
       In combate on the *Solymæan* plain.
       Hippolochus surviv'd; from him I came,
       The honour'd author of my birth and name;
255   By his decree I sought the *Trojan* town,
       By his instructions learn to win renown,
       To stand the first in worth as in command,
       To add new honours to my native land,
       Before my eyes my mighty sires to place,
260   And emulate the glories of our race.
          He spoke, and transport fill'd *Tydides*' heart;
       In earth the gen'rous warriour fix'd his dart,
       Then friendly, thus, the *Lycian* Prince addrest.
       Welcome, my brave hereditary guest!

Thus ever let us meet, with kind embrace,   265
Nor stain the sacred friendship of our race.

Know, chief, our grandsires have been guests of old;
Oeneus the strong, *Bellerophon* the bold:
Our ancient seat his honour'd presence grac'd,
Where twenty days in genial rites he pass'd.   270
The parting heroes mutual presents left;
A golden goblet was thy grandsire's gift;
Oeneus a belt of matchless work bestow'd,
That rich with *Tyrian* dye refulgent glow'd.
(This from his pledge I learn'd, which safely stor'd   275
Among my treasures, still adorns my board:
For *Tydeus* left me young, when *Thebè*'s wall
Beheld the sons of *Greece* untimely fall.)
Mindful of this, in friendship let us join;
If heav'n our steps to foreign lands incline,   280
My guest in *Argos* thou, and I in *Lycia* thine.
Enough of *Trojans* to this lance shall yield,
In the full harvest of yon' ample field;
Enough of *Greeks* shall die thy spear with gore;
But thou and *Diomed* be foes no more.   285
Now change we arms, and prove to either host
We guard the friendship of the line we boast.

    Thus having said, the gallant chiefs alight,
Their hands they join, their mutual faith they plight;
Brave *Glaucus* then each narrow thought resign'd,   290
(*Jove* warm'd his bosom and enlarg'd his mind)
For *Diomed*'s brass arms, of mean device,
For which nine oxen paid (a vulgar price)
He gave his own, of gold divinely wrought,
A hundred beeves the shining purchase bought.   295

    Meantime the guardian of the *Trojan* State,
Great *Hector*, enter'd at the *Scæan* gate.
Beneath the beech-tree's consecrated shades,
The *Trojan* matrons and the *Trojan* maids
Around him flock'd, all press'd with pious care   300
For husbands, brothers, sons, engag'd in war.
He bids the train in long procession go,
And seek the Gods, t' avert th' impending woe.

And now to *Priam*'s stately courts he came,
305   Rais'd on arch'd columns of stupendous frame;
O'er these a range of marble structure runs,
The rich pavillions of his fifty sons,
In fifty chambers lodg'd; and rooms of state
Oppos'd to those, where *Priam*'s daughters sate:
310   Twelve domes for them and their lov'd spouses shone,
Of equal beauty, and of polish'd stone.
Hither great *Hector* pass'd, nor pass'd unseen
Of royal *Hecuba*, his mother Queen.
(With her *Laodicè*, whose beauteous face
315   Surpass'd the nymphs of *Troy*'s illustrious race)
Long in a strict embrace she held her son,
And press'd his hand, and tender thus begun.

O *Hector!* say, what great occasion calls
My son from fight, when *Greece* surrounds our walls?
320   Com'st thou to supplicate th' almighty pow'r,
With lifted hands from *Ilion*'s lofty tow'r?
Stay, till I bring the cup with *Bacchus* crown'd, ⎫
In *Jove*'s high name, to sprinkle on the ground, ⎬
And pay due vows to all the Gods around. ⎭
325   Then with a plenteous draught refresh thy soul,
And draw new spirits from the gen'rous bowl;
Spent as thou art with long laborious fight,
The brave defender of thy country's right.

Far hence be *Bacchus*' gifts (the chief rejoin'd) ⎫
330   Inflaming wine, pernicious to mankind, ⎬
Unnerves the limbs, and dulls the noble mind. ⎭
Let chiefs abstain, and spare the sacred juice
To sprinkle to the Gods, its better use.
By me that holy office were prophan'd;
335   Ill fits it me, with human gore distain'd,
To the pure skies these horrid hands to raise,
Or offer heav'n's great Sire polluted praise.
You, with your matrons, go! a spotless train,
And burn rich odors in *Minerva*'s fane.
340   The largest mantle your full wardrobes hold,
Most priz'd for art, and labour'd o'er with gold,
Before the Goddess' honour'd knees be spread,
And twelve young heifers to her altar led.

So may the pow'r, atton'd by fervent pray'r,
Our wives, our infants, and our city spare,
And far avert *Tydides'* wastful ire,
Who mows whole troops, and makes all *Troy* retire.
Be this, O mother, your religious care;
I go to rouze soft *Paris* to the war;
If yet, not lost to all the sense of shame,
The recreant warriour hear the voice of fame.
Oh would kind earth the hateful wretch embrace,
That pest of *Troy*, that ruin of our race!
Deep to the dark abyss might he descend,
Troy yet should flourish, and my sorrows end.

This heard, she gave command; and summon'd came
Each noble matron, and illustrious dame.
The *Phrygian* Queen to her rich wardrobe went,
Where treasured odours breath'd a costly scent.
There lay the vestures, of no vulgar art,
Sidonian maids embroider'd ev'ry part,
Whom from soft *Sidon* youthful *Paris* bore,
With *Helen* touching on the *Tyrian* shore.
Here as the Queen revolv'd with careful eyes
The various textures and the various dies,
She chose a veil that shone superior far,
And glow'd refulgent as the morning star.
Herself with this the long procession leads;
The train majestically slow proceeds.
Soon as to *Ilion*'s topmost tow'r they come,
And awful reach the high *Palladian* dome,
Antenor's consort, fair *Theano*, waits
As *Pallas*' priestess, and unbars the gates.
With hands uplifted and imploring eyes,
They fill the dome with supplicating cries.
The Priestess then the shining veil displays,
Plac'd on *Minerva*'s knees, and thus she prays.

Oh awful goddess! ever-dreadful maid,
Troy's strong defence, unconquer'd *Pallas*, aid!
Break thou *Tydides*' spear, and let him fall
Prone on the dust before the *Trojan* wall.
So twelve young heifers, guiltless of the yoke,
Shall fill thy temple with a grateful smoke.

345

350

355

360

365

370

375

380

But thou, atton'd by penitence and pray'r,
385   Our selves, our infants, and our city spare!
So pray'd the priestess in her holy fane;
So vow'd the matrons, but they vow'd in vain.

  While these appear before the pow'r with pray'rs,
Hector to *Paris*' lofty dome repairs.
390   Himself the mansion rais'd, from ev'ry part
Assembling architects of matchless art.
Near *Priam*'s court and *Hector*'s Palace stands
The pompous structure, and the town commands.
A spear the hero bore of wondrous strength,
395   Of full ten cubits was the lance's length,
The steely point with golden ringlets join'd,
Before him brandish'd, at each motion shin'd.
Thus entring in the glitt'ring rooms, he found
His brother-chief, whose useless arms lay round,
400   His eyes delighting with their splendid show,
Bright'ning the shield, and polishing the bow.
Beside him, *Helen* with her virgins stands,
Guides their rich labours, and instructs their hands.

  Him thus unactive, with an ardent look
405   The Prince beheld, and high-resenting spoke.
Thy Hate to *Troy*, is this the time to show?
(Oh wretch ill-fated, and thy country's foe!)
Paris and *Greece* against us both conspire,
Thy close resentment, and their vengeful ire.
410   For thee great *Ilion*'s guardian heroes fall,
Till heaps of dead alone defend her wall;
For thee the soldier bleeds, the matron mourns,
And wastful war in all its fury burns.
Ungrateful man! deserves not this thy care,
415   Our troops to hearten, and our toils to share?
Rise, or behold the conqu'ring flames ascend,
And all the *Phrygian* glories at an end.

  Brother, 'tis just (reply'd the beauteous youth)
Thy free remonstrance proves thy worth and truth:
420   Yet charge my absence less, oh gen'rous chief!
On hate to *Troy*, than conscious shame and grief:
Here, hid from human eyes, thy brother sate,
And mourn'd in secret, his, and *Ilion*'s fate.

'Tis now enough: now glory spreads her charms,
And beauteous *Helen* calls her chief to arms. 425
Conquest to day my happier sword may bless,
'Tis man's to fight, but heav'ns to give success.
But while I arm, contain thy ardent mind;
Or go, and *Paris* shall not lag behind.

He said, nor answer'd *Priam*'s warlike son; 430
When *Helen* thus with lowly grace begun.

Oh gen'rous brother! if the guilty dame
That caus'd these woes, deserves a sister's name!
Would heav'n, e're all these dreadful deeds were done,
The day, that show'd me to the golden sun, 435
Had seen my death! Why did not whirlwinds bear
The fatal infant to the fowls of air?
Why sunk I not beneath the whelming tyde,
And 'midst the roarings of the waters dy'd?
Heav'n fill'd up all my ills, and I accurst 440
Bore all, and *Paris* of those ills the worst.
Helen at least a braver spouse might claim,
Warm'd with some virtue, some regard of fame!
Now tir'd with toils, thy fainting limbs recline,
With toils, sustain'd for *Paris*' sake and mine: 445
The Gods have link'd our miserable doom,
Our present woe, and infamy to come:
Wide shall it spread, and last thro' ages long,
Example sad! and theme of future song.

The chief reply'd: This time forbids to rest: 450
The *Trojan* bands by hostile Fury prest,
Demand their *Hector*, and his arm require;
The combate urges, and my soul's on fire.
Urge thou thy Knight to march where glory calls,
And timely join me, e're I leave the walls. 455
E're yet I mingle in the direful fray,
My wife, my infant, claim a moment's stay;
This day (perhaps the last that sees me here)
Demands a parting word, a tender tear:
This day, some God who hates our *Trojan* land 460
May vanquish *Hector* by a *Grecian* hand.

He said, and past with sad presaging heart
To seek his spouse, his soul's far dearer part;

At home he sought her, but he sought in vain;
465   She, with one maid of all her menial train,
Had thence retir'd; and with her second joy,
The young *Astyanax*, the hope of *Troy*.
Pensive she stood on *Ilion*'s tow'ry height,
Beheld the war, and sicken'd at the sight;
470   There her sad eyes in vain her Lord explore,
Or weep the wounds her bleeding country bore.
But he who found not whom his soul desir'd,
Whose virtue charm'd him as her beauty fir'd,
Stood in the gates, and ask'd what way she bent
475   Her parting step? If to the fane she went,
Where late the mourning matrons made resort;
Or sought her sisters in the *Trojan* court?
Not to the court, (reply'd th' attendant train)
Nor mix'd with matrons to *Minerva*'s fane:
480   To *Ilion*'s steepy tow'r she bent her way,
To mark the fortunes of the doubtful day.
Troy fled, she heard, before the *Grecian* sword;
She heard, and trembled for her absent Lord:
Distracted with surprize, she seem'd to fly,
485   Fear on her cheek, and sorrow in her eye.
The nurse attended with her infant boy,
The young *Astyanax*, the hope of *Troy*.
Hector, this heard, return'd without delay;
Swift thro' the town he trod his former way,
490   Thro' streets of palaces and walks of state;
And met the mourner at the *Scæan* gate.
With haste to meet him sprung the joyful fair,
His blameless wife, *Aëtion*'s wealthy heir:
(*Cilician Thebè* great *Aëtion* sway'd,
495   And *Hippoplacus*' wide-extended shade)
The nurse stood near, in whose embraces prest
His only hope hung smiling at her breast,
Whom each soft charm and early grace adorn,
Fair as the new-born star that gilds the morn.
500   To this lov'd infant *Hector* gave the name
Scamandrius, from *Scamander*'s honour'd stream;
Astyanax the *Trojans* call'd the boy,
From his great father, the defence of *Troy*.

Silent the warriour smil'd, and pleas'd resign'd
To tender passions all his mighty mind: 505
His beauteous Princess cast a mournful look,
Hung on his hand, and then dejected spoke;
Her bosom labour'd with a boding sigh,
And the big tear stood trembling in her eye.

    Too daring Prince! ah whither dost thou run? 510
Ah too forgetful of thy wife and son!
And think'st thou not how wretched we shall be,
A widow I, an helpless orphan he!
For sure such courage length of life denies,
And thou must fall, thy virtue's sacrifice. 515
Greece in her single heroes strove in vain;
Now hosts oppose thee, and thou must be slain!
Oh grant me Gods! e're *Hector* meets his doom,
All I can ask of heav'n, an early tomb!

    So shall my days in one sad tenour run, 520
And end with sorrows as they first begun.
No parent now remains, my griefs to share,
No father's aid, no mother's tender care.
The fierce *Achilles* wrapt our walls in fire,
Lay'd *Thebè* waste, and slew my warlike Sire! 525
His fate compassion in the victor bred;
Stern as he was, he yet rever'd the dead,
His radiant arms preserv'd from hostile spoil,
And lay'd him decent on the fun'ral pile;
Then rais'd a mountain where his bones were burn'd, 530
The mountain nymphs the rural tomb adorn'd,
Jove's sylvan daughters bade their elms bestow
A barren shade, and in his honour grow.

    By the same arm my sev'n brave brothers fell,
In one sad day beheld the gates of hell; 535
While the fat herds and snowy flocks they fed,
Amid their fields the hapless Heroes bled!
My mother liv'd to bear the victor's bands,
The Queen of *Hippoplacia*'s sylvan lands:
Redeem'd too late, she scarce beheld again 540
Her pleasing empire and her native plain,
When ah! opprest by life-consuming woe,
She fell a victim to *Diana*'s bow.

Yet while my *Hector* still survives, I see
545   My father, mother, brethren, all, in thee.
Alas! my parents, brothers, kindred, all,
Once more will perish if my *Hector* fall.
Thy wife, thy infant, in thy danger share:
Oh prove a husband's and a father's care!
550   That quarter most the skillful *Greeks* annoy,
Where yon' wild fig-trees join the wall of *Troy*:
Thou, from this tow'r defend th' important post;
There *Agamemnon* points his dreadful host,
That pass *Tydides*, *Ajax* strive to gain,
555   And there the vengeful *Spartan* fires his train.
Thrice our bold foes the fierce attack have giv'n,
Or led by hopes, or dictated from heav'n.
Let others in the field their arms employ,
But stay my *Hector* here, and guard his *Troy*.

560   The chief reply'd: That post shall be my care,
Nor that alone, but all the works of war.
How would the sons of *Troy*, in arms renown'd,
And *Troy*'s proud dames whose garments sweep the
        ground,
Attaint the lustre of my former name,
565   Should *Hector* basely quit the field of fame?
My early youth was bred to martial pains,
My soul impels me to th' embattel'd plains:
Let me be foremost to defend the throne,
And guard my father's glories, and my own.

570   Yet come it will, the day decreed by fates;
(How my heart trembles while my tongue relates!)
The day when thou, Imperial *Troy!* must bend,
And see thy warriors fall, thy glories end.
And yet no dire presage so wounds my mind,
575   My mother's death, the ruin of my kind,
Not *Priam*'s hoary hairs defil'd with gore,
Not all my brothers gasping on the shore;
As thine, *Andromache!* thy griefs I dread;
I see thee trembling, weeping, captive led!
580   In *Argive* looms our battels to design,
And woes, of which so large a part was thine!

To bear the victor's hard commands, or bring
The weight of waters from *Hyperia*'s spring.
There, while you groan beneath the load of life,
They cry, Behold the mighty *Hector*'s wife!   585
Some haughty *Greek*, who lives thy tears to see,
Embitters all thy woes, by naming me.
The thoughts of glory past, and present shame,
A thousand griefs shall waken at the name!
May I lie cold before that dreadful day,   590
Press'd with a load of monumental clay!
Thy *Hector*, wrapt in everlasting sleep,
Shall neither hear thee sigh, nor see thee weep.

    Thus having spoke, th' illustrious chief of *Troy*
Stretch'd his fond arms to clasp the lovely boy.   595
The babe clung crying to his nurse's breast,
Scar'd at the dazling helm, and nodding crest.
With secret pleasure each fond parent smil'd,
And *Hector* hasted to relieve his child,
The glitt'ring terrours from his brows unbound,   600
And plac'd the beaming helmet on the ground.
Then kist the child, and lifting high in air,
Thus to the Gods preferr'd a father's pray'r.

    O thou! whose glory fills th' ætherial throne,
And all ye deathless pow'rs! protect my son!   605
Grant him, like me, to purchase just renown,
To guard the *Trojans*, to defend the crown,
Against his country's foes the war to wage,
And rise the *Hector* of the future age!
So when triumphant from successful toils,   610
Of heroes slain he bears the reeking spoils,
Whole hosts may hail him with deserv'd acclaim,
And say, This chief transcends his father's fame:
While pleas'd amidst the gen'ral shouts of *Troy*,
His mother's conscious heart o'erflows with joy.   615

    He spoke, and fondly gazing on her charms,
Restor'd the pleasing burthen to her arms;
Soft on her fragrant breast the babe she laid,
Hush'd to repose, and with a smile survey'd.
The troubled pleasure soon chastiz'd by Fear,   620
She mingled with the smile a tender tear.

The soften'd chief with kind compassion view'd,
And dry'd the falling drops, and thus pursu'd.
   Andromache! my soul's far better part,
625 Why with untimely sorrows heaves thy heart?
No hostile hand can antedate my doom,
Till fate condemns me to the silent tomb.
Fix'd is the term to all the race of earth,
And such the hard condition of our birth.
630 No force can then resist, no flight can save,
All sink alike, the fearful and the brave.
No more – but hasten to thy tasks at home,
There guide the spindle, and direct the loom:
Me glory summons to the martial scene,
635 The field of combate is the sphere for men.
Where heroes war, the foremost place I claim,
The first in danger as the first in fame.
   Thus having said, the glorious chief resumes
His tow'ry helmet, black with shading plumes.
640 His princess parts with a prophetick sigh,
Unwilling parts, and oft' reverts her eye
That stream'd at ev'ry look: then, moving slow,
Sought her own palace, and indulg'd her woe.
There, while her tears deplor'd the godlike man,
645 Thro' all her train the soft infection ran,
The pious maids their mingled sorrows shed,
And mourn the living *Hector*, as the dead.
   But now, no longer deaf to honour's call,
Forth issues *Paris* from the palace wall.
650 In brazen arms that cast a gleamy ray,
Swift thro' the town the warriour bends his way.
The wanton courser thus, with reins unbound,
Breaks from his stall, and beats the trembling ground;
Pamper'd and proud, he seeks the wonted tides,
655 And laves, in height of blood, his shining sides;
His head now freed, he tosses to the skies;
His mane dishevel'd o'er his shoulders flies;
He snuffs the females in the distant plain,
And springs, exulting, to his fields again.
660 With equal triumph, sprightly, bold and gay,
In arms refulgent as the God of day,

The son of *Priam*, glorying in his might,
Rush'd forth with *Hector* to the fields of fight.
    And now the warriours passing on the way,
The graceful *Paris* first excus'd his stay.   665
To whom the noble *Hector* thus reply'd:
O Chief! in blood, and now in arms, ally'd!
Thy pow'r in war with justice none contest;
Known is thy courage, and thy strength confest.
What pity, sloth should seize a soul so brave,   670
Or godlike *Paris* live a woman's slave!
My heart weeps blood at what the *Trojans* say,
And hopes, thy deeds shall wipe the stain away.
Haste then, in all their glorious labours share;
For much they suffer, for thy sake, in war.   675
These ills shall cease, whene'er by *Jove*'s decree
We crown the bowl to *Heav'n* and *Liberty*:
While the proud foe his frustrate triumphs mourns,
And *Greece* indignant thro' her seas returns.

OBSERVATIONS

ON THE

SIXTH BOOK

7. *Great* Ajax.] *Ajax* performs his exploits immediately upon the departure of the Gods from the battel. It is observ'd that this hero is never assisted by the Deities, as most of the rest are; See his character in the notes on the seventh book. The expression of the *Greek* is, that he *brought light to his troops*, which M. *Dacier* takes to be metaphorical: I do not see but it may be literal; he broke the thick Squadrons of the enemy, and open'd a passage for the light.

9. *The* Thracian *Acamas.*] This *Thracian* Prince is the same in whose likeness *Mars* appears in the preceding book, rallying the *Trojans* and forcing the *Greeks* to retire. In the present description of his strength and size, we see with what propriety this personage was selected by the Poet as fit to be assumed by the God of war.

16. Axylus, *hospitable.*] This beautiful character of *Axylus* has not been able to escape the misunderstanding of some of the commentators, who thought *Homer* design'd it as a reproof of an undistinguish'd generosity. It is evidently a panegyrick on that virtue, and not improbably on the memory of some excellent, but unfortunate man in that country, whom the Poet honours with the noble title of *A friend to mankind.* It is indeed a severe reproof of the ingratitude of men, and a kind of satire on human race, while he represents this lover of his species miserably perishing without assistance from any of those numbers he had obliged. This death is very moving, and the circumstance of a faithful servant's dying by his side, well imagined, and natural to such a character. His manner of keeping house near a frequented highway, and relieving all travellers, is agreeable to that ancient hospitality which we now only read of. There is abundance of this spirit every where in the *Odyssey*. The Patriarchs in the Old Testament sit at their gates to see those who pass by, and entreat them to enter into their houses: This cordial manner of invitation is particularly described in the 18*th* and 19*th* chapters of *Genesis.* The *Eastern* nations seem to have had a peculiar disposition to these exercises of humanity, which continues in a great measure to this day. It is yet a piece of charity frequent with the *Turks,* to erect *Caravanserahs,* or inns for the reception of travellers. Since I am upon this head, I must mention one or two extraordinary examples of ancient hospitality. *Diodorus Siculus* writes of *Gallias* of *Agrigentum,* that having built several inns for the relief of strangers, he appointed persons at the gates to invite all who travelled to make use of them; and that this example was followed by many others who were inclined after the ancient manner to live in a human and beneficent correspondence with mankind. That this *Gallias* entertained and cloathed at one time no less than five hundred horsemen; and that there were in his cellars three hundred vessels, each of which contained an hundred hogsheads of wine. The same author tells us of another *Agrigentine,* that at the marriage of his daughter feasted all the people of his city, who at that time were above twenty thousand.

Herodotus in his seventh book has a story of this kind, which is prodigious, being of a private man so immensely rich as to entertain *Xerxes* and his whole army. I shall transcribe the passage as I find it translated to my hands.

'*Pythius* the Son of *Atys,* a *Lydian,* then residing in *Celæne,* entertain'd the King and all his army with great magnificence, and offered him his treasures towards the expence of the war; which liberality *Xerxes* communicating to the *Persians* about him, and asking who this *Pythius* was, and what riches he might have to enable him to make such an offer? received this answer: *Pythius,* said they, is the person who presented your father *Darius* with a plane-tree and vine of gold; and after you, is the richest man we know in the world. *Xerxes* surprized with these last words, asked him to what sum his treasures might amount. I shall conceal nothing from you, said *Pythius,* nor pretend to be ignorant of my own wealth; but being perfectly inform'd of the state of my accompts, shall tell you the truth with sincerity. When I heard you was ready to begin the march towards the *Grecian* sea, I resolved to present you with a sum of money towards the charge of the war; and to that end having taken an account of my riches, I found by computation that I had two thousand talents of silver, and three millions nine hundred ninety three thousand pieces of gold, bearing the stamp of *Darius.* These treasures I freely give you, because I shall be sufficiently furnish'd with whatever is necessary to life by the labour of my servants and husbandmen.

'*Xerxes* heard these words with pleasure, and in answer to *Pythius*, said; My *Lydian* host, since I parted from *Susa* I have not found a man besides your self, who has offered to entertain my army, or voluntarily to contribute his treasures to promote the present expedition. You alone have treated my army magnificently, and readily offered me immense riches: Therefore, in return of your kindness, I make you my host; and that you may be master of the intire sum of four millions of gold, I will give you seven thousand *Darian* pieces out of my own treasure. Keep then all the riches you now possess; and if you know how to continue always in the same good disposition, you shall never have reason to repent of your affection to me, either now or in future time.'

The sum here offer'd by *Pythius* amounts, by *Brerewood*'s computation, to three millions three hundred seventy five thousand pounds sterling, according to the lesser valuation of talents. I make no apology for inserting so remarkable a passage at length, but shall only add, that it was at last the fate of this *Pythius* (like our *Axylus*) to experience the ingratitude of man; his eldest son being afterwards cut in pieces by the same *Xerxes.*

57. *Oh spare my youth*, &c.] This passage, where *Agamemnon* takes away that *Trojan*'s life whom *Menelaus* had pardoned, and is not blamed by *Homer* for so doing, must be ascribed to the uncivilized manners of those times, when mankind was not united by the bonds of a rational Society, and is not therefore to be imputed to the Poet, who followed nature as it was in his days. The historical books of the old Testament abound in instances of the like cruelty to conquered enemies.

Virgil had this part of *Homer* in his view, when he described the death of *Magus* in the tenth *Æneid.* Those lines of his prayer, where he offers a ransome, are translated from this of *Adrastus*, but both the prayer and the answer *Æneas* makes when he refuses him mercy, are very much heighten'd and improved. They also receive a great addition of beauty and propriety from the occasion on which he inserts them: Young *Pallas* is just kill'd, and *Æneas* seeking to be revenged upon *Turnus*, meets this *Magus.* Nothing can be a more artful piece of address than the first lines of that supplication, if we consider the character of *Æneas*, to whom it is made.

> *Per patrios manes, per spes surgentis Iüli,*
> *Te precor, hanc animam serves natoque, patrique.*   [524–5]

[By young *Iulus*, by thy father's shade,
O spare my life, and send me back to see
My longing sire, and tender progeny.]

And what can exceed the closeness and fullness of that reply to it?

> *– Belli commercia Turnus*
> *Sustulit ista prior, jam tum Pallante perempto.*
> *Hoc patris Anchisæ manes, hoc sentit Iülus.*   [532–4]

[Thy *Turnus* broke
All rules of war, by one relentless stroke
When *Pallas* fell: So deems, nor deems alone,
My father's shadow, but my living son.]

This removes the imputation of cruelty from *Æneas*, which had less agreed with his character than it does with *Agamemnon*'s; whose reproof to *Menelaus* in this place is not unlike that of *Samuel* to *Saul* for not killing *Agag*.

74. *Her infants at the breast shall fall.*] Or, her infants *yet in the womb*, for it will bear either sense. But I think Madam *Dacier* in the right, in her affirmation that the *Greeks* were not arrived to that pitch of cruelty to rip up the wombs of women with child. *Homer* (says she) to remove all equivocal meaning from this phrase, adds the Words κοῦρον ἐόντα, *juvenem puerulum existentem* [being a little boy], which would be ridiculous were it said of a child yet unborn. Besides, he would never have represented one of his first heroes capable of so barbarous a crime, or at least would not have commended him (as he does just after) for such a wicked exhortation.

88. *First gain the conquest, then divide the spoil.*] This important maxim of war is very naturally introduced, upon *Nestor*'s having seen *Menelaus* ready to spare an enemy for the sake of a ransome. It was for such lessons as these (says M. *Dacier*) that *Alexander* so much esteem'd *Homer* and study'd his poem. He made his use of this precept in the battel of *Arbela*, when *Parmenio* being in danger of weakening the

main body to defend the baggage, he sent this message to him: Leave
the Baggage there; for if we gain the victory, we shall not only recover
what is our own, but be masters of all that is the enemy's. Histories
ancient and modern are fill'd with examples of enterprizes that have
miscarry'd, and battels that have been lost, by the greediness of
soldiers for pillage.

98. *Wise to consult, and active to defend.*] This is a two-fold branch of
praise, expressing the excellence of these princes both in council and in
battel. I think Madam *Dacier*'s translation does not come up to the
sense of the original. *Les plus hardis & les plus experimentez des nos
capitains.* [The boldest and most experienced of our captains.]

107. *Thou* Hector *to the town.*] It has been a modern objection to
Homer's conduct, that *Hector* upon whom the whole fate of the day
depended, is made to retire from the battel, only to carry a message to
Troy concerning a sacrifice, which might have been done as well by
any other. They think it absurd in *Helenus* to advise this, and in *Hector*
to comply with it. What occasioned this false criticism was that they
imagin'd it to be a Piece of *advice*, and not a *command*. *Helenus* was a
priest and augur of the highest rank, he enjoins it as a point of religion,
and *Hector* obeys him as one inspired from heaven. The *Trojan* army
was in the utmost distress, occasioned by the prodigious slaughter
made by *Diomed*: There was therefore more reason and necessity to
propitiate *Minerva* who assisted that hero; which *Helenus* might know,
tho' *Hector* would have chosen to have stay'd and trusted to the arm of
flesh. Here is nothing but what may agree with each of their characters.
Hector goes as he was obliged in religion, but not before he has
animated the troops, re-established the combate, repulsed the *Greeks* to
some distance, received a promise from *Helenus* that they would make
a stand at the gates, and given one himself to the army that he would
soon return to the fight: All which *Homer* has been careful to specify,
to save the honour, and preserve the character, of this hero. As to
Helenus his part, he saw the straits his countrymen were reduced to, he
knew his authority as a priest, and design'd to revive the courage of the
troops by a promise of divine assistance. Nothing adds more courage
to the minds of men than superstition, and perhaps it was the only
expedient then left; much like a modern practice in the army, to enjoin
a *fast* when they wanted provision. *Helenus* could no way have made
his promise more credible, than by sending away *Hector*; which look'd

like an assurance that nothing could prejudice them during his absence on such a religious account. No leader of less authority than *Hector* could so properly have enjoined this solemn act of religion; and lastly, no other whose valour was less known than his, could have left the army in this juncture without a taint upon his honour. *Homer* makes this piety succeed; *Paris* is brought back to the fight, the *Trojans* afterwards prevail, and *Jupiter* appears openly in their favour, *l*. 8. Tho' after all, I cannot dissemble my opinion, that the Poet's chief intention in this, was to introduce that fine episode of the parting of *Hector* and *Andromache*. This change of the scene to *Troy* furnishes him with a great number of beauties. *By this means* (says *Eustathius*) *his poem is for a time divested of the fierceness and violence of battels, and being as it were wash'd from slaughter and blood, becomes calm and smiling by the beauty of these various episodes.*

117. *If so the pow'r, atton'd.*] The Poet here plainly supposes *Helenus*, by his skill in augury or some other divine inspiration, well inform'd that the might of *Diomed* which wrought such great destruction among the *Trojans*, was the gift of *Pallas* incensed against them. The prophet therefore directs prayers, offerings, and sacrifices to be made to appease the anger of this offended Goddess; not to invoke the mercy of any propitious deity. This is conformable to the whole system of *Pagan* superstition, the worship whereof being grounded not on love but fear, seems directed rather to avert the malice and anger of a wrathful and mischievous Dæmon, than to implore the assistance and protection of a benevolent being. In this strain of religion this same prophet is introduced by *Virgil* in the third *Æneid* [435–9], giving particular direction to *Æneas* to appease the indignation of *Juno*, as the only means which could bring his labours to a prosperous end.

> *Unum illud tibi, nate Dea, præque omnibus unum*
> *Prædicam, & repetens iterumque iterumque monebo.*
> *Junonis magnæ primum prece numen adora:*
> *Junoni cane vota libens, dominamque potentem*
> *Supplicibus supera donis: –*

> [Do not this precept of your friend forget;
> Which therefore more than once I must repeat.
> Above the rest, great *Juno's* name adore:
> Pay vows to *Juno*; *Juno's* aid implore.
> Let gifts be to the mighty Queen design'd;
> And mollify with pray'rs her haughty mind.]

147. *The interview of* Glaucus *and* Diomed.] No passage in our Author has been the subject of more severe and groundless criticisms than this, where these two heroes enter into a long conversation (as they will have it) in the heat of a battel. Monsieur *Dacier*'s answer in defence of *Homer* is so full, that I cannot do better than to translate it from his remarks on the 26*th* chapter of *Aristotle*'s *Poetic*. There can be nothing more unjust than the criticisms past upon things that are the effect of custom. It was usual in ancient times for soldiers to talk together before they encounter'd. *Homer* is full of examples of this sort, and he very well deserves we should be so just as to believe, he had never done it so often, but that it was agreeable to the manners of his age. But this is not only a thing of custom, but founded on reason itself. The ties of hospitality in those times were held more sacred than those of blood; and it is on that account *Diomed* gives so long an audience to *Glaucus*, whom he acknowledges to be his guest, with whom it was not lawful to engage in combate. *Homer* makes an admirable use of this conjecture, to introduce an entertaining history after so many battels as he has been describing, and to unbend the mind of his reader by a recital of so much variety as the story of the family of *Sisyphus.* It may be farther observ'd, with what address and management he places this long conversation; it is not during the heat of an obstinate battel, which had been too unseasonable to be excused by any custom whatever; but he brings it in after he has made *Hector* retire into *Troy*, when the absence of so powerful an enemy had given *Diomed* that leisure which he could not have had otherwise. One need only read the judicious remark of *Eustathius* upon this place. *The Poet* (says he) *after having caus'd* Hector *to go out of the fight, interrupts the violence of wars, and gives some relaxation to the reader, in causing him to pass from the confusion and disorder of the action to the tranquillity and security of an historical narration. For by means of the happy episode of* Glaucus, *he casts a thousand pleasing wonders into his poem; as fables, that include beautiful allegories, histories, genealogies, sentences, ancient customs, and several other graces that tend to be diversifying of his work, and which by breaking (as one may say) the monotony of it, agreeably instruct the reader.* Let us observe, in how fine a manner *Homer* has hereby praised both *Diomed* and *Hector.* For he makes us know, that as long as *Hector* is in the field, the *Greeks* have not the least leisure to take breath; and that as soon as he quits it, all the *Trojans*, however they had regained all their advantages, were not able to employ *Diomed* so far as to prevent his entertaining himself with *Glaucus* without any

danger to his party. Some may think after all, that tho' we may justify *Homer*, yet we cannot excuse the manners of his time; it not being natural for men with swords in their hands to dialogue together in cold blood just before they engage. But not to alledge, that these very manners yet remain in those countries, which have not been corrupted by the commerce of other nations, (which is a great sign of their being natural) what reason can be offered that it is more natural to fall on at first sight with rage and fierceness, than to speak to an enemy before the encounter? Thus far Monsieur *Dacier*, and St *Evremont* asks humourously, if it might not be as proper in that country for men to harangue before they fought, as it is in *England* to make speeches before they are hanged.

That *Homer* is not in general apt to make unseasonable harangues (as these censurers would represent) may appear from that remarkable care he has shewn in many places to avoid them: as when in the fifth book *Æneas* being cured on a sudden in the middle of the fight, is seen with surprize by his soldiers; he specifies with particular caution, that they *asked him no questions how he became cured*, in a time of so much business and action. Again, when there is a necessity in the same book that *Minerva* should have a conference with *Diomed*, in order to engage him against *Mars* (after her prohibition to him to fight with the Gods) *Homer* chuses a time for that speech, just when the hero is retired behind his chariot to take breath, which was the only moment that could be spared during the hurry of that whole engagement. One might produce many instances of the same kind.

The discourse of *Glaucus* to *Diomed* is severely censured, not only on account of the circumstance of time and place, but likewise on the score of the subject, which is taxed as improper, and foreign to the end and design of the poem. But the Criticks who have made this objection, seem neither to comprehend the design of the Poet in general, nor the particular aim of this discourse. Many passages in the best ancient Poets appear unaffecting at present, which probably gave the greatest delight to their first readers, because they were very nearly interested in what was there related. It is very plain that *Homer* designed this Poem as a monument to the honour of the *Greeks*, who, tho' consisting of several independent societies, were yet very national in point of glory, being strongly affected with every thing that seemed to advance the honour of their common country, and resentful of any indignity offer'd to it. This disposition was the ground of that grand alliance which is the subject of this poem. To men so fond of their country's glory, what could be more agreeable than to read a history fill'd with wonders of a noble family transplanted from *Greece* into *Asia*? They might here learn with pleasure that the *Grecian* virtues did not degenerate by removing into distant climes: but especially they must be affected with uncommon delight to find that *Sarpedon* and *Glaucus*, the bravest of the *Trojan* auxiliaries, were originally *Greeks*.

Tasso in this manner has introduced an agreeable episode, which shews *Clorinda* the offspring of *Christian* parents, tho' engaged in the Service of the *Infidels*, Cant. 12.

149. *Between both armies met*, &c.] It is usual with *Homer*, before he introduces a hero, to make as it were a halt, to render him the more remarkable. Nothing could more prepare the attention and expectation of the reader, than this circumstance at the first meeting of *Diomed* and *Glaucus*. Just at the time when the mind begins to be weary with the battel, it is diverted with the prospect of a single combate, which of a sudden turns to an interview of friendship and an unexpected scene of sociable virtue. The whole air of the conversation between these two heroes has something heroically solemn in it.

159. *But if from heav'n,* &c.] A quick change of mind from the greatest impiety to as great superstition, is frequently observable in men who having been guilty of the most heinous crimes without any remorse, on the sudden are fill'd with doubts and scruples about the most lawful or indifferent actions. This seems the present case of *Diomed*, who having knowingly wounded and insulted the Deities, is now afraid to engage the first man he meets, lest perhaps a God might be conceal'd in that shape. This disposition of *Diomed* produces the question he puts to *Glaucus*, which without this consideration will appear impertinent, and so naturally occasions that agreeable episode of *Bellerophon* which *Glaucus* relates in answer to *Diomed*.

161. *Not long* Lycurgus, &c.] What *Diomed* here says is the effect of remorse, as if he had exceeded the commission of *Pallas* in encountring with the Gods, and dreaded the consequences of proceeding too far. At least he had no such commission now, and besides, was no longer capable of distinguishing them from men (a faculty she had given him in the foregoing book:) He therefore mentions this story of *Lycurgus* as an example that sufficed to terrify him from so rash an undertaking. The ground of the fable they say is this, *Lycurgus* caused most of the vines of his country to be rooted up, so that his subjects were obliged

to mix it with water when it was less plentiful: Hence it was feign'd that *Thetis* receiv'd *Bacchus* into her bosom.

170. *Immortals blest with endless ease.*] Tho' *Dacier's* and most of the versions take no notice of the epithet used in this place, Θεοὶ ῥεῖα ζώοντες, *Dii facile seu beate viventes*; the translator thought it a beauty which he could not but endeavour to preserve. *Milton* seems to have had this in his eye in his second book;

> *– Thou wilt bring me soon*
> *To that new world of light and bliss, among*
> *The* Gods *who live at ease –*

178. *Approach, and enter the dark gates of death.*] This haughty air which *Homer* gives his heroes was doubtless a copy of the manners and hyperbolical speeches of those times. Thus *Goliah* to *David, Sam.* 1. ch. 17. *Approach, and I will give thy flesh to the fowls of the air and the Beasts of the field.* The Orientals speak the same language to this day.

181. *Like leaves on trees.*] There is a noble gravity in the beginning of this speech of *Glaucus*, according to the true style of antiquity, *Few and evil are our days.* This beautiful thought of our Author, whereby the race of men are compared to the leaves of trees, is celebrated by *Simonides* in a fine fragment extant in *Stobæus.* The same thought may be found in *Ecclesiasticus*, ch. 14. v. 18. almost in the same words; *As of the green leaves on a thick tree, some fall, and some grow; so is the generation of flesh and blood, one cometh to an end, and another is born.*

The reader who has seen so many passages imitated from *Homer* by succeeding Poets, will no doubt be pleased to see one of an ancient Poet which *Homer* has here imitated: this is a fragment of *Musæus* preserv'd by *Clemens Alexandrinus* in his *Stromata, lib. 6.*

> Ὡς δ' αὔτως καὶ φύλλα φύει ζείδωρος ἄρουρα,
> Ἄλλα μὲν ἐν μελίῃσιν ἀποφθίνει, ἄλλα δὲ φύει,
> Ὡς δὲ καὶ ἀνθρώπου γενεὴ καὶ φύλλον ἑλίσσει.

[Just as the fruitful corn-field brings forth foliage, but some leaves perish upon the ash while others thrive; just so do the race of men and the leaves whirl round and round.]

Tho' this comparison be justly admired for its beauty in this obvious application to the mortality and succession of human life, it seems however design'd by the Poet in this place as a proper emblem of the transitory state not of men, but of Families, which being by their misfortunes or follies fallen and decayed, do again in a happier season revive and flourish in the fame and virtues of their posterity: In this sense it is a direct answer to what *Diomed* had asked, as well as a proper preface to what *Glaucus* relates of his own family, which having been extinct in *Corinth*, had recovered new life in *Lycia*.

193. *Then call'd* Ephyre.] It was the same which was afterwards called *Corinth*, and had that name in *Homer*'s time, as appears from his catalogue, v. 77.

196. *Lov'd for that valour which preserves mankind.*] This distinction of true valour, which has the good of mankind for its end, in opposition to the valour of tyrants or oppressors, is beautifully hinted by *Homer* in the epithet ἐρατεινή, *amiable valour*. Such as was that of *Bellerophon* who freed the land from monsters, and creatures destructive to his species. It is apply'd to this young hero with particular judgment and propriety, if we consider the innocence and gentleness of his manners appearing from the following story, which every one will observe has a great resemblance with that of *Joseph* in the scriptures.

216. *The faithful youth his monarch's mandate show'd.*] *Plutarch* much commends the virtue of *Bellerophon*, who faithfully carry'd those letters he might so justly suspect of ill consequence to him: The passage is in his discourse of *curiosity*, and worth transcribing. 'A man of curiosity is void of all faith, and it is better to trust letters or any important secrets to servants, than to friends and familiars of an inquisitive temper. *Bellerophon*, when he carry'd letters that order'd his own destruction, did not unseal them, but forbore touching the King's dispatches with the same continence, as he had refrained from injuring his bed: For curiosity is an incontinence as well as adultery.'

219. *First dire* Chimæra.] *Chimæra* was feign'd to have the head of a lion breathing flames, the body of a goat, and the tail of a dragon; because the mountain of that name in *Lycia* had a *Vulcano* on its top, and nourished lions, the middle part afforded pasture for goats, and the bottom was infested with serpents. *Bellerophon* destroying these, and rendring the mountain habitable, was said to have conquer'd *Chimæra*. He calls this monster Θεῖον γένος [divine offspring], in the

manner of the *Hebrews*, who gave to any thing vast or extraordinary the appellative of *Divine*. So the psalmist says, *The mountains of God*, &c.

227. *The* Solymæan *crew.*] These *Solymi* were an ancient nation inhabiting the mountainous parts of *Asia Minor* between *Lycia* and *Pisidia*. *Pliny* mentions them as an instance of a people so entirely destroyed, that no footsteps of them remained in his time. Some authors both ancient and modern, from a resemblance in sound to the *Latin* name of *Jerusalem*, have confounded them with the *Jews*. *Tacitus*, speaking of the various opinions concerning the origin of the *Jewish* nation, has these words, *Clara alii tradunt Judæorum initia, Solymos carminibus Homeri celebratam gentem, conditæ urbi Hierosolymam nomen e suo fecisse.* [Some describe illustrious origins for the *Jews*, namely that the Solymi are the race celebrated in the poems of Homer, and that they formed, from their own name, the name Jerusalem for the city that they founded.] Hist. Lib. 6.

239. *The* Lycians *grant a chosen space of ground.*] It was usual in the ancient times, upon any signal piece of service performed by the Kings or great men, to have a portion of land decreed by the publick as a reward to them. Thus when *Sarpedon* in the twelfth book incites *Glaucus* to behave himself valiantly, he puts him in mind of these possessions granted by his countrymen.

> Γλαῦκε, τίη δὴ νῶϊ τετιμήμεσθα μάλιστα – &c.
> Καὶ τέμενος νεμόμεσθα μέγα Ξάνθοιο παρ' ὄχθας
> Καλὸν, φυταλιῆς καὶ ἀρούρης πυροφόροιο;

> [Why boast we, *Glaucus*! our extended reign,
> Where *Xanthus*' streams enrich the *Lycian* plain,
> Our num'rous herds that range the fruitful field,
> And hills where vines their purple harvest yield.
> – Pope's translation, XII. 371–4.]

In the same manner in the ninth book [274] of *Virgil*, *Nisus* is promised by *Ascanius* the *fields* which were possessed by Latinus, as a reward for the service he undertook.

> – *Campi quod rex habet ipse Latinus.*

> [Whatever domain King Latinus himself possesses.]

Chapman has an interpolation in this place, to tell us that this *field* was afterwards called by the *Lycians*, *The field of wandrings*, from the wandrings and distraction of *Bellerophon* in the latter part of his life. But they were not these fields that were call'd Ἀλήϊοι, but those upon which he fell from the horse *Pegasus*, when he endeavoured (as the fable has it) to mount to heaven.

245. *But when at last*, &c.] The same Criticks who have taxed *Homer* for being too tedious in this story of *Bellerophon*, have censured him for omitting to relate the particular offence which had raised the anger of the Gods against a man formerly so highly favoured by them: But this relation coming from the mouth of his grandson, it is with great decorum and propriety he passes over in silence those crimes of his ancestor, which had provoked the divine vengeance against him. *Milton* has interwoven this story with what *Homer* here relates of *Bellerophon.*

> *Left from this flying steed unrein'd (as once*
> Bellerophon, *though from a lower clime)*
> *Dismounted on the* Aleian *field I fall,*
> *Erroneous there to wander and forlorn.*   Parad. Lost. B. 7.

Tully in his third book of *Tusculane* questions, having observ'd that persons oppress'd with woe naturally seek solitude, instances this Example of *Bellerophon*, and gives us his translation of two of these lines.

> *Qui miser in campos mœrens errabat Aleis,*
> *Ipse suum cor edens, hominum vestigia vitans.*

[Who, wretched, wandered grieving in Aleïsis, himself consuming his own heart, shunning every trace of humankind.]

267. *Our grandsires have been guests of old.*] The laws of hospitality were anciently held in great veneration. The friendship contracted hereby was so sacred, that they preferred it to all the bands of consanguinity and alliance, and accounted it obligatory even to the third and fourth generation. We have seen in the foregoing story of *Bellerophon*, that *Prœtus*, a Prince under the supposition of being injured in the highest degree, is yet afraid to revenge himself upon the criminal on this account: He is forced to send him into *Lycia* rather than be guilty of a breach of this law in his own country. And the King of *Lycia* having entertained the stranger before he unseal'd the letters, puts him upon expeditions abroad, in which he might be destroyed, rather than at his court. We here see *Diomed* and *Glaucus* agreeing not to be enemies during the whole course of a war, only because their grandfathers had been mutual guests. And we afterwards find *Teucer* engaged with the *Greeks* on this account against the *Trojans*, tho' he was himself of *Trojan* extraction, the nephew of *Priam* by the mother's side, and cousin german of *Hector*, whose life he pursues with the utmost violence. They preserved in their families the presents which had been made on these occasions, as obliged to transmit to their children the memorials of this right of hospitality.

Eustathius.

291. Jove *warm'd his bosom and enlarg'd his mind.*] The words in the original are ἐξέλετο φρένας, which may equally be interpreted, *he took away his sense*, or *he elevated his mind.* The former being a reflection upon *Glaucus*'s prudence, for making so unequal an exchange, the latter a praise of the magnanimity and generosity which induced him to it. *Porphyry* contends for its being understood in this last way, and *Eustathius*, Monsieur and Madam *Dacier* are of the same opinion. Notwithstanding it is certain that *Homer* uses the same words in the contrary sense in the seventeenth Iliad, v. 470. and in the nineteenth, v. 137. And it is an obvious remark, that the interpretation of *Porphyry* as much dishonours *Diomed* who proposed this exchange, as it does honour to *Glaucus* for consenting to it. However, I have followed it, if not as the juster, as the most heroic sense, and as it has the nobler air in poetry.

295. *A hundred beeves.*] I wonder the curious have not remarked from this place, that the proportion of the value of *gold* to *brass* in the time of the *Trojan* war, was but as an *hundred* to *nine*; allowing these armours of equal weight: which as they belonged to men of equal strength, is a reasonable supposition. As to this manner of computing the value of the armour by *beeves* or *oxen*, it might be either because the money was anciently stamped with those figures, or (which is most probable in this place) because in those times they generally purchased by exchange of commodities, as we see by a passage near the end of the seventh book.

329. *Far hence be* Bacchus' *gifts* – *Enflaming wine.*] This maxim of *Hector*'s concerning wine, has a great deal of truth in it. It is a vulgar mistake to imagine the use of wine either raises the spirits, or encreases strength. The best physicians agree with *Homer* in this point; whatever our modern soldiers may object to this old heroic *regimen*. One may take notice that *Sampson* as well as *Hector* was a water-drinker; for he was a *Nazarite* by vow, and as such was forbid the use of wine. To which *Milton* alludes in his *Sampson Agonistes*.

> *Where-ever Fountain or fresh current flow'd*
> *Against the eastern ray, translucent, pure,*
> *With touch æthereal of heav'ns fiery rod,*
> *I drank, from the clear milky juice allaying*
> *Thirst, and refresh'd; nor envy'd them the grape,*
> *Whose heads that turbulent liquor fills with fumes.*

335. *Ill fits it me, with human gore distain'd,* &c.] The custom which prohibits persons polluted with blood to perform any offices of divine worship before they were purified, is so ancient and universal, that it may in some sort be esteemed a precept of natural religion, tending to inspire an uncommon dread and religious horror of bloodshed. There is a fine passage in *Euripides* where *Iphigenia* argues how impossible it is that human sacrifices should be acceptable to the Gods, since they do not permit any defiled with blood, or even polluted with the touch of a dead body, to come near their altars. *Iphig. in Tauris.* v. 380. *Virgil* [II. 718–20] makes his *Æneas* say the same thing *Hector* does here.

> *Me bello e tanto digressum & cæde recenti*
> *Attrectare nefas, donec me flumine vivo*
> *Abluero.* –

> [In me 'tis impious holy things to bear,
> Red as I am with slaughter, new from war:
> 'Till in some living stream I cleanse the guilt
> Of dire debate, and blood in battel spilt.]

361. Sidonian *Maids.*] *Dictys Cretensis, lib.* 1. acquaints us that *Paris* returned not directly to *Troy* after the rape of *Helen*, but fetched a compass, probably to avoid pursuit. He touched at *Sidon*, where he surprized the King of *Phœnicia* by night, and carried off many of his treasures and captives, among which probably were these *Sidonian* women. The author of the ancient poem of the *Cypriacks* says, he sailed from *Sparta* to *Troy* in the space of three days: from which passage *Herodotus* concludes that poem was not *Homer's*. We find in the scriptures, that *Tyre* and *Sidon* were famous for works in gold, embroidery, &c. and for whatever regarded magnificence and luxury.

374. *With hands uplifted.*] The only gesture described by *Homer* as used by the ancients in the invocation of the Gods, is the lifting up their hands to heaven. *Virgil* frequently alludes to this practice; particularly in the second book [403–6] there is a passage, the beauty of which is much rais'd by this consideration.

> *Ecce trahebatur passis Priameia virgo*
> *Crinibus, a templo, Cassandra, adytisque Minervæ,*
> *Ad cælum tendens ardentia lumina frustra,*
> *Lumina! nam teneras arcebant vincula palmas.*

> [Behold the royal Prophetess, the fair
> *Cassandra*, drag'd by her dishevel'd hair;
> Whom not *Minerva*'s shrine, nor sacred bands,
> In safety cou'd protect from sacrilegious hands:
> On Heav'n she cast her eyes, she sigh'd, she cry'd,
> ('Twas all she cou'd) her tender arms were ty'd.]

378. *Oh awful Goddess*, &c.] This procession of the *Trojan* matrons to the temple of *Minerva*, with their offering, and the ceremonies; tho' it be a passage some moderns have criticis'd upon, seems to have particularly pleas'd *Virgil*. For he has not only introduced it among the figures in the picture at *Carthage* [I. 479–82],

> *Interea ad templum non æquæ Palladis ibant*
> *Crinibus Iliades passis, peplumque ferebant*
> *Suppliciter tristes; & tunsis pectora palmis.*
> *Diva solo fixos oculos aversa tenebat.*

> [Mean time the *Trojan* dames oppress'd with woe,
> To *Pallas* fane in long procession goe,
> In hopes to reconcile their heav'nly foe:
> They weep, they beat their breasts, they rend their hair,
> And rich embroider'd vests for presents bear:
> But the stern Goddess stands unmov'd with pray'r.]

But he has again copied it in the eleventh book, where the *Latian* dames make the same procession upon the approach of *Æneas* to their city. The prayer to the Goddess is translated almost word for word: v. 483.

> *Armipotens præses belli, Tritonia virgo,*
> *Frange manu telum Phrygii prædonis, & ipsum*
> *Pronum sterne solo portisque effunde sub altis.*

> [O patroness of arms, unspotted maid,
> Propitious hear, and lend thy *Latins* aid:
> Break short the pirat's lance; pronounce his fate,
> And lay the *Phrygian* low before the gate.]

This prayer in the *Latin* Poet seems introduced with less propriety, since *Pallas* appears no where interested in the conduct of affairs thro' the whole *Æneid*. The first line of the *Greek* here is translated more literally than the former versions; ἐρυσίπτολι, δῖα θεάων. I take the first epithet to allude to *Minerva*'s being the particular protectress of *Troy* by means of the *Palladium*, and not (as Mr *Hobbes* understands it) the protectress of all cities in general.

387. *But they vow'd in vain.*] For *Helenus* only ordered that prayers should be made to *Minerva* to drive *Diomed* from before the walls. But *Theano* prays that *Diomed* may perish, and perish flying, which is included in his falling *forward*. Madam *Dacier* is so free as to observe here, that women are seldom moderate in the prayers they make against their enemies, and therefore are seldom heard.

390. *Himself the mansion rais'd.*] I must own my self not so great an enemy to *Paris* as some of the commentators. His blind passion is the unfortunate occasion of the ruine of his country, and he has the ill fate to have all his fine qualities swallowed up in that. And indeed I cannot say he endeavours much to be a better man than his nature made him. But as to his parts and turn of mind, I see nothing that is either weak, or wicked, the general manners of those times considered. On the contrary, a gentle soul, patient of good advice, tho' indolent enough to forget it; and liable only to that frailty of love, which methinks might in his case as well as *Helen*'s be charged upon the *Stars*, and the *Gods*. So very amorous a constitution, and so incomparable a beauty to provoke it, might be temptation enough even to a wise man, and in some degree make him deserve compassion, if not pardon. It is remarkable, that *Homer* does not paint him and *Helen* (as some other Poets would have done) like monsters, odious to Gods and men, but allows their characters such esteemable qualifications as could consist, and in truth generally do, with tender frailties. He gives *Paris* several polite accomplishments, and in particular a turn to those sciences that are the result of a fine imagination. He makes him have a taste and addiction to *curious works* of all sorts, which caus'd him to transport *Sidonian* artists to *Troy*, and employ himself at home in adorning and finishing his armour: And now we are told that he assembled the most skilful builders from all parts of the country, to render his palace a compleat piece of *Architecture*. This, together with what *Homer* has said elsewhere of his skill in the *Harp*, which in those days included both *Musick* and *Poetry*, may I think establish him a *Bel Esprit* and a *fine genius*.

406. *Thy Hate to* Troy, &c.] All the commentators observe this Speech of *Hector* to be a piece of artifice; he seems to imagine that the retirement of *Paris* proceeds only from his resentment against the *Trojans*, and not from his indolence, luxury, or any other cause. *Plutarch* thus discourses upon it. 'As a discreet physician rather chuses to cure his patient by diet or rest, than by castoreum or scammony, so a good friend, a good master, or a good father, are always better pleased to make use of commendation than reproof, for the reformation of manners: For nothing so much assists a man who reprehends with frankness and liberty, nothing renders him less offensive, or better promotes his good design, than to reprove with calmness, affection, and temper. He ought not therefore to urge them too severely if they deny the fact, nor forestall their justification of themselves, but rather try to help them out, and furnish them artificially with honest and colourable pretences to excuse them; and tho' he sees that their fault proceeded from a more shameful cause, he should yet impute it to something less criminal. Thus *Hector* deals with *Paris*, when he tells him, *This is not the time to manifest your anger against the* Trojans: As if his retreat from the battel had not been absolutely a flight, but merely the effect of resentment and indignation.' Plut. *Of knowing a flatterer from a friend.*

418. *Brother, 'tis just*, &c.] *Paris* readily lays hold of the pretext *Hector* had furnished him with, and confesses he has partly touch'd

upon the true reason of his retreat, but that it was also partly occasioned by the concern he felt at the victory of his rival. Next he professes his readiness for the fight; but nothing can be a finer trait (if we consider his character) than what *Homer* puts into his mouth just in this place, that *he is now exhorted to it by* Helen: Which shews that not the danger of his country and parents, neither private shame, nor publick hatred, could so much prevail upon him, as the commands of his mistress, to go and recover his honour.

432. Helen's *speech.*] The repentance of *Helena* (which we have before observed *Homer* never loses an opportunity of manifesting) is finely touch'd again here. Upon the whole, we see the Gods are always concerned in what befalls an unfortunate beauty: Her Stars foredoom'd all the mischief, and Heaven was to blame in suffering her to live: Then she fairly gets quit of the infamy of her lover, and shews she has higher sentiments of honour than he. How very natural is all this in the like characters to this day?

462. *The Episode of* Hector *and* Andromache.] *Homer* undoubtedly shines most upon the great subjects, in raising our admiration or terrour: Pity, and the softer passions, are not so much of the nature of his Poem, which is formed upon anger and the violence of ambition. But we have cause to think his genius was no less capable of touching the heart with tenderness, than of firing it with glory, from the few sketches he has left us of his excellency in that way too. In the present Episode of the parting of *Hector* and *Andromache*, he has assembled all that love, grief, and compassion could inspire. The greatest censurers of *Homer* have acknowledged themselves charmed with this part; even Monsieur *Perault* translated it into *French* verse as a kind of penitential sacrifice for the sacrileges he had committed against this author.

This Episode tends very much to raise the character of *Hector* and endear him to every reader. This hero, tho' doubtful if he should ever see *Troy* again, yet goes not to his wife and child, till after he has taken care for the sacrifice, exhorted *Paris* to the fight, and discharged every duty to the Gods, and to his country; his Love of which, as we formerly remark'd, makes his chief character. What a beautiful con- traste has *Homer* made between the manners of *Paris* and those of *Hector*, as he here shews them one after the other in this domestic light, and in their regards to the fair sex? What a difference between the characters and behaviour of *Helen* and of *Andromache*? And what an amiable picture of conjugal love, opposed to that of unlawful passion?

I must not forget, that Mr *Dryden* has formerly translated this admirable Episode, and with so much success, as to leave me at least no hopes of improving or equalling it. The utmost I can pretend is to have avoided a few modern phrases and deviations from the original, which have escaped that great man. I am unwilling to remark upon an author to whom every *English* Poet owes so much; and shall therefore only take notice of a criticism of his which I must be obliged to answer in its place, as it is an accusation of *Homer* himself.

468. *Pensive she stood on* Ilion's *tow'ry height.*] It is a fine imagination to represent the tenderness of *Andromache* for *Hector*, by her standing upon the tower of *Troy*, and watching all his motions in the field; even the religious procession to *Minerva*'s temple could not draw her from this place, at a time when she thought her husband in danger.

473. *Whose Virtue charm'd him,* &c.] *Homer* in this verse particularizes the Virtue of *Andromache* in the epithet ἀμύμονα, *blameless*, or *without a fault*. I have used it literally in another part of this Episode.

487. Hector, *this heard, return'd.*] *Hector* does not stay to seek his wife on the tower of *Ilion*, but hastens where the business of the field calls him. *Homer* is never wanting in point of honour and decency, and while he constantly obeys the strictest rules, finds a way to make them contribute to the beauty of his poem. Here for instance he has managed it so, that this observance of *Hector*'s is the cause of a very pleasing surprize to the reader; for at first he is not a little disappointed to find that *Hector* does not meet *Andromache*, and is no less pleased afterwards to see them encounter by chance, which gives him a satisfaction he thought he had lost.   *Dacier.*

501. Scamandrius, *from* Scamander's *honour'd stream*, &c.] This manner of giving proper names to children derived from any place, accident, or quality belonging to them or their parents, is very ancient, and was customary among the *Hebrews.* The *Trojans* called the son of *Hector, Astyanax,* because (as it is said here and at the end of the twenty second book) *his father defended the city.* There are many instances of the same kind in the thirtieth chapter of *Genesis*, where the names given to *Jacob*'s children, and the reasons of those names, are enumerated.

524. *The fierce* Achilles, &c.] Mr *Dryden*, in the preface to the third volume of *Miscellany Poems*, has past a judgment upon part of this speech which is altogether unworthy of him. '*Andromache* (says he) in the midst of her concernment and fright for *Hector*, runs off her biass, to tell him a story of her pedigree, and of the lamentable death of her father, her mother, and her seven brothers. The Devil was in *Hector*, if he knew not all this matter, as well as she who told it him; for she had been his bedfellow for many years together: And if he knew it, then it must be confessed, that *Homer* in this long digression, has rather given us his own character, than that of the fair Lady whom he paints. His dear friends, the commentators, who never fail him at a pinch, will needs excuse him, by making the present sorrow of *Andromache*, to occasion the remembrance of all the past: But others think that she had enough to do with that grief which now oppressed her, without running for assistance to her family.' But may not it be answered, that nothing was more natural in *Andromache*, than to recollect her past calamities in order to represent her present distress to *Hector* in a stronger light, and shew her utter desertion if he should perish. What could more effectually work upon a generous and tender mind like that of *Hector*? What could therefore be more proper to each of their characters? If *Hector* be induced to refrain from the field, it proceeds from compassion to *Andromache*: If *Andromache* endeavour to persuade him, it proceeds from her fear for the life of *Hector*. *Homer* had yet a farther view in this recapitulation; it tends to raise his chief hero *Achilles*, and acquaints us with those great atchievements of his which preceded the opening of the Poem. Since there was a necessity that this hero should be absent from the action during a great part of the *Iliad*, the Poet has shewn his art in nothing more, than in the methods he takes from time to time to keep up our great idea of him, and to awaken our expectation of what he is to perform in the progress of the work. His greatest enemies cannot upbraid or complain of him, but at the same time they confess his glory, and describe his victories. When *Apollo* encourages the *Trojans* to fight, it is by telling them *Achilles* fights no more. When *Juno* animates the *Greeks*, it is by putting them in mind that they have to do with enemies who durst not appear out of their walls while *Achilles* engaged. When *Andromache* trembles for *Hector*, it is with remembrance of the resistless force of *Achilles*. And when *Agamemnon* would bribe him to a reconciliation, it is partly with those very treasures and spoils which had been won by *Achilles* himself.

528. *His arms preserv'd from hostile spoil.*] This circumstance of *Aetion*'s being burned with his arms will not appear trivial in this relation, when we reflect with what eager passion these ancient heroes fought to spoil and carry off the armour of a vanquished enemy; and therefore this action of *Achilles* is mentioned as an instance of uncommon favour and generosity. Thus *Æneas* in *Virgil* [*Aen.* X. 827–8] having slain *Lausus*, and being moved with compassion for this unhappy youth, gives him a promise of the like favour.

> *Arma, quibus lætatus, habe tua: teque parentum*
> *Manibus, & cineri, si qua est ea cura, remitto.*

> [Accept whate'er *Aeneas* can afford,
> Untouch'd thy arms, untaken be thy sword:
> And all that pleas'd the living still remain
> Inviolate, and sacred to the slain.
> Thy body on thy parents I bestow,
> To rest thy soul, at least if shadows know,
> Or have a sense of human things below.]

532. Jove's *sylvan daughters bade their elms bestow A barren shade*, &c.] It was the custom to plant about tombs only such trees as elms, alders, &c. that bear no fruit, as being most suitable to the dead. This passage alludes to that piece of antiquity.

543. *A victim to* Diana's *bow.*] The *Greeks* ascribed all sudden deaths of women to *Diana.* So *Ulysses* in *Odyss.* 11. asks *Antyclia* among the shades if she died by the darts of *Diana?* And in the present book, *Laodame* the daughter of *Bellerophon*, is said to have perished young by the arrows of this Goddess. Or perhaps it may allude to some disease fatal to women, such as *Macrobius* speaks of *Sat.* 1. 17. *Fœminas certis afflictas morbis* Σεληνοβλήτους καὶ Ἀρτεμιδοβλήτους *vocant.* [They call women stricken by certain diseases 'moonstruck' and 'stricken by Artemis'.]

550. *That quarter most – where yon' wild fig-trees.*] The artifice *Andromache* here uses to detain *Hector* in *Troy* is very beautifully imagined. She takes occasion from the three attacks that had been made by the enemy upon this place, to give him an honourable pretence for staying at that rampart to defend it. If we consider that those attempts must have been known to all in the city, we shall not think she talks like a soldier, but like a woman, who naturally enough makes use of any incident that offers, to persuade her lover to what she desires. The ignorance too which she expresses, of the reasons that moved the *Greeks* to attack this particular place, was what I doubt not *Homer* intended, to reconcile it the more to a female character.

583. Hyperia's *spring.*] Drawing water was the office of the meanest slaves. This appears by the holy scripture, where the *Gibeonites* who had deceiv'd *Josuah* are made slaves and subjected to draw water. *Josuah* pronounces the curse against them in these words: *Now therefore ye are cursed, and there shall none of you be freed from being bondmen, and hewers of wood, and drawers of water.* Josh. ch. 9. v. 23.

Dacier.

595. *Stretch'd his fond arms.*] There never was a finer piece of painting than this. *Hector* extends his arms to embrace his child; the child affrighted at the glittering of his helmet and the shaking of the plume, shrinks backward to the breast of his nurse; *Hector* unbraces his helmet, lays it on the ground, takes the infant in his arms, lifts him towards heaven, and offers a prayer for him to the Gods: then returns him to the mother *Andromache*, who receives him with a smile of pleasure, but at the same instant the fears for her husband make her burst into tears. All these are but small circumstances, but so artfully chosen, that every reader immediately feels the force of them, and represents the whole in the utmost liveliness to his imagination. This alone might be a confutation of that false criticism some have fallen into, who affirm that a poet ought only to collect the great and noble particulars in his paintings. But it is in the images of things as in the characters of persons; where a small action, or even a small circumstance of an action, lets us more into the knowledge and comprehension of them, than the material and principal parts themselves. As we find this in a history, so we do in a picture, where sometimes a small motion or turn of a finger will express the character and action of the figure more than all the other parts of the design. *Longinus* indeed blames an author's insisting too much on trivial circumstances; but in the same place extols *Homer* as 'the poet who best knew how to make

use of important and beautiful circumstances, and to avoid the mean and superfluous ones.' There is a vast difference betwixt a *small* circumstance and a *trivial* one, and the smallest become important if they are well chosen, and not confused.

604. Hector's *prayer for his son*.] It may be asked how *Hector*'s prayer, that his son might protect the *Trojans*, could be consistent with what he had said just before, that he certainly knew *Troy* and his parents would perish. We ought to reflect that this is only a prayer: *Hector* in the excess of a tender emotion for his son, entreats the Gods to preserve *Troy*, and permit *Astyanax* to rule there. It is at all times allowable to beseech heaven to appease its anger, and change its decrees; and we are taught that prayers can alter destiny. *Dacier*. Besides, it cannot be infer'd from hence, that *Hector* had any divine foreknowledge of his own fate, and the approaching ruine of his country; since in many following passages we find him possess'd with strong hopes and firm assurances to raise the siege, by the flight or destruction of the *Greeks*. So that these forebodings of his fate were only the apprehensions and misgivings of a soul dejected with sorrow and compassion, by considering the great dangers to which he saw all that was dear to him expos'd.

613. *Transcends his father's fame*.] The commendation *Hector* here gives himself, is not only agreeable to the openness of a brave man, but very becoming on such a solemn occasion; and a natural effect from the testimony of his own heart to his honour; at this time especially, when he knew not but he was speaking his last words. *Virgil* has not scrupled it, in what he makes *Æneas* say to *Ascanius* at his parting for the battel.

> *Et pater Æneas & avunculus excitet Hector.*
> *Disce puer virtutem ex me, verumque laborem,*
> *Fortunam ex aliis –*   Æn. 12. [440; 435–6]

> [Assert thy birthright; and in arms be known,
> For *Hector*'s nephew, and *Æneas*' son.

> My son, from my example learn the war,
> In camps to suffer, and in fields to dare:
> But happier chance than mine attend thy care.]

I believe he had this of *Homer* in his eye, tho' the pathetical mention of *fortune* in the last line seems an imitation of that prayer of *Sophocles*, copied also from hence, where *Ajax* wishes his son may be *like him in all things but in his misfortunes.*

615. *His mother's conscious heart.*] Tho' the chief beauty of this prayer consists in the paternal piety shewn by *Hector*, yet it wants not a fine stroke at the end, to continue him in the character of a tender lover of his wife, when he makes one of the motives of his wish, to be the joy she shall receive on hearing her son applauded.

628. *Fix'd is the term.*] The reason which *Hector* here urges to allay the affliction of his wife, is grounded on a very ancient and common opinion, that the fatal period of life is appointed to all men at the time of their birth; which as no precaution can avoid, so no danger can hasten. This sentiment is as proper to give comfort to the distress'd, as to inspire courage to the desponding; since nothing is so fit to quiet and strengthen our minds in times of difficulty, as a firm assurance that our lives are exposed to no real hazards, in the greatest appearances of danger.

649. *Forth issues Paris.*] *Paris* stung by the reproaches of *Hector*, goes to the battel. 'Tis a just remark of *Eustathius*, that all the reproofs and remonstrances in *Homer* have constantly their effect. The poet by this shews the great use of reprehensions when properly apply'd, and finely intimates that every worthy mind will be the better for them.

652. *The wanton courser thus*, &c.] This beautiful comparison being translated by *Virgil* in the eleventh *Æneid* [492–7]; I shall transcribe the originals, that the reader may have the pleasure of comparing them.

'Ὡς δ' ὅτε τις στατὸς ἵππος ἀκοστήσας ἐπὶ φάτνῃ,
Δεσμὸν ἀπορρήξας θείει πεδίοιο κροαίνων,
Εἰωθὼς λούεσθαι ἐϋρρεῖος ποταμοῖο,
Κυδιόων, ὑψοῦ δὲ κάρη ἔχει, ἀμφὶ δὲ χαῖται
Ὤμοις ἀΐσσονται· ὁ δ' ἀγλαΐηφι πεποιθὼς,
'Ρίμφα ἑ γοῦνα φέρει μετά τ' ἤθεα καὶ νομὸν ἵππων.

Qualis ubi abruptis fugit præsepia vinclis
Tandem liber equus, campoque potitus aperto,

Aut ille in pastus armentaque tendit equarum:
Aut assuetus aquæ perfundi flumine noto
Emicat, arrectisque fremit cervicibus alte
Luxurians; luduntque jubæ per colla, per armos.

[Freed from his keepers, thus with broken reins,
The wanton courser prances o're the plains:
Or in the pride of youth o're leaps the mounds;
And snuffs the females in forbidden grounds:
Or seeks his wat'ring in the well known flood,
To quench his thirst, and cool his fiery blood:
He swims luxuriant, in the liquid plain,
And o're his shoulder flows his waving mane:
He neighs, he snorts, he bears his head on high;
Before his ample chest the frothy waters fly.]

Tho' nothing can be translated better than this is by *Virgil*, yet in
Homer the simile seems more perfect, and the place more proper. *Paris*
had been indulging his ease within the walls of his palace, as the horse
in his stable, which was not the case of *Turnus.* The beauty and
wantonness of the steed agrees more exactly with the character of *Paris*
than with the other: And the insinuation of his love of the mares has
yet a nearer resemblance. The languishing Flow of that Verse,

Εἰωθώς λούεσθαι ἐΰρρεῖος ποταμοῖο,

finely corresponds with the ease and luxuriancy of the pamper'd
courser bathing in the flood; a beauty which *Scaliger* did not consider,
when he criticis'd particularly upon that line. *Tasso* has also imitated
this simile, *cant.* 9.

Come destrier, che da la regie stalle
Ove à l'uso de l'arme si reserba,
Fugge, e libero alfin per largo calle
Va tra gl' armenti, o al fiume usato, o a l'erba;
Scherzan su 'l collo i crini, e sù le spalle,
Si scote la cervice alta, e superba;
Suonano i pie nel corso, e par, ch'auvampi,
Di sonori nitriti empiendo i campi.

[As a fierce steed 'scap'd from his stall at large,
Where he had long been kept for warlike need,
Runs through the fields unto the flow'ry marge

Of some green forest where he used to feed,
His curled mane his shoulders broad doth charge,
And from his lofty crest doth spring and spread,
Thunder his feet, his nostrils fire breathe out,
And with his neigh the world resounds about.

– trans. Fairfax]

665. Paris *excus'd his stay.*] Here, in the original, is a short speech of *Paris* containing only these words; *Brother, I have detained you too long, and should have come sooner as you desired me.* This and some few others of the same nature in the Iliad, the translator has ventured to omit, expressing only the sense of them. A living author (whom future times will quote, and therefore I shall not scruple to do it) says that these short speeches, tho' they may be natural in other languages, can't appear so well in ours, which is much more stubborn and unpliant, and therefore are but as so many rubs in the story that are still turning the narration out of its proper course.

669. Known *is thy courage,* &c.] *Hector* here confesses the natural valour of *Paris*, but observes it to be overcome by the indolence of his temper and the love of pleasure. An ingenious *French* writer very well remarks, that the true character of this hero has a great resemblance with that of *Marc Anthony.* See the notes on the third book, v. 37, and 86.

677. *We crown the bowl to heav'n and liberty.*] The *Greek* is, κρητῆρα ἐλεύθερον, *the free bowl,* in which they made libations to *Jupiter* after the recovery of their liberty. The expression is observed by M. *Dacier* to resemble those of the *Hebrews; The cup of salvation, the cup of sorrow, the cup of benediction,* &c. *Athenæus* mentions those cups which the *Greeks* call'd γραμματικὰ ἐκπώματα, and were consecrated to the Gods in memory of some success. He gives us the inscription of one of this sort, which was, *ΔΙΟΣ ΣΩΤΗΡΟΣ.*

THE
SEVENTH BOOK
OF THE
ILIAD

The ARGUMENT

The single Combate of *Hector* and *Ajax*

The battel renewing with double ardour upon the return of Hector,
Minerva *is under apprehensions for the* Greeks. Apollo *seeing her descend
from* Olympus, *joins her near the Scæan gate. They agree to put off the
general engagement for that day, and incite* Hector *to challenge the*
Greeks *to a single combate. Nine of the Princes accepting the challenge,
the lot is cast, and falls upon* Ajax. *These heroes, after several attacks, are
parted by the night. The* Trojans *calling a council,* Antenor *proposes the
delivery of* Helen *to the* Greeks, *to which* Paris *will not consent, but offers
to restore them her riches.* Priam *sends a herald to make this offer, and to
demand a truce for burning the dead, the last of which only is agreed to by*
Agamemnon. *When the funerals are performed, the* Greeks, *pursuant to
the advice of* Nestor, *erect a fortification to protect their fleet and camp,
flank'd with towers, and defended by a ditch and palisades.* Neptune
testifies his jealousy at this work, but is pacified by a promise from
Jupiter. *Both armies pass the night in feasting, but* Jupiter *disheartens the*
Trojans *with thunder and other signs of his wrath.*

The three and twentieth day ends with the duel of Hector *and* Ajax:
*The next day the truce is agreed: Another is taken up in the funeral rites
of the slain; and one more in building the fortification before the ships: So
that somewhat above three days is employed in this book. The scene lies
wholly in the Field.*

So spoke the guardian of the *Trojan* state,
Then rush'd impetuous thro' the *Scæan* gate.
Him *Paris* follow'd to the dire alarms;
Both breathing slaughter, both resolv'd in arms.
5 As when to sailors lab'ring thro' the main,
That long had heav'd the weary oar in vain,
Jove bids at length th' expected gales arise;
The gales blow grateful, and the vessel flies:
So welcome these to *Troy*'s desiring train;
10 The bands are chear'd, the war awakes again.

　　Bold *Paris* first the work of death begun,
On great *Menesthius*, *Areïthous*' son;
Spring from the fair *Philomeda*'s embrace,
The pleasing *Arnè* was his native place.
15 Then sunk *Eioneus* to the shades below,
Beneath his steely casque he felt the blow
Full on his neck, from *Hector*'s weighty hand;
And roll'd, with limbs relax'd, along the land.
By *Glaucus*' spear the bold *Iphinous* bleeds,
20 Fix'd in the shoulder as he mounts his steeds;
Headlong he tumbles: His slack nerves unbound
Drop the cold useless members on the ground.

　　When now *Minerva* saw her *Argives* slain,
From vast *Olympus* to the gleaming plain
25 Fierce she descends: *Apollo* mark'd her flight,
Nor shot less swift from *Ilion*'s tow'ry height:
Radiant they met, beneath the beechen shade;
When thus *Apollo* to the blue-ey'd maid.

What cause, O daughter of almighty *Jove!*
Thus wings thy progress from the realms above?
Once more impetuous dost thou bend thy way,   30
To give to *Greece* the long divided day?
Too much has *Troy* already felt thy hate,
Now breathe thy rage, and hush the stern debate:
This day, the business of the field suspend;   35
War soon shall kindle, and great *Ilion* bend;
Since vengeful Goddesses confed'rate join
To raze her walls, tho' built by hands divine.

　　To whom the progeny of *Jove* replies:
I left, for this, the council of the skies: 40
But who shall bid conflicting hosts forbear,
What art shall calm the furious sons of war?
To her the God: Great *Hector*'s soul incite
To dare the boldest *Greek* to single fight,
Till *Greece*, provok'd, from all her numbers show   45
A warriour worthy to be *Hector*'s foe.

　　At this agreed, the heav'nly powers withdrew;
Sage *Helenus* their secret counsels knew:
Hector inspir'd he sought: To him addrest,
Thus told the dictates of his sacred breast.   50
O son of *Priam!* let thy faithful ear
Receive my words; thy friend and brother hear!
Go forth persuasive, and a while engage
The warring nations to suspend their rage;
Then dare the boldest of the hostile train   55
To mortal combate on the listed plain.
For not this day shall end thy glorious date;
The Gods have spoke it, and their voice is fate.
He said: The warriour heard the word with joy.
Then with his spear restrain'd the youth of *Troy*,   60
Held by the midst athwart. On either hand
The squadrons part; th' expecting *Trojans* stand.
Great *Agamemnon* bids the *Greeks* forbear;
They breathe, and hush the tumult of the war.
Th' *Athenian* Maid, and glorious God of day,   65
With silent joy the settling hosts survey:
In form like vultures, on the beech's height
They sit conceal'd, and wait the future fight.

The thronging troops obscure the dusky fields,
70   Horrid with bristling spears, and gleaming shields.
As when a gen'ral darkness veils the main,
(Soft *Zephyr* curling the wide wat'ry plain)
The waves scarce heave, the face of Ocean sleeps,
And a still horrour saddens all the deeps:
75   Thus in thick orders settling wide around,
At length compos'd they sit, and shade the ground.
Great *Hector* first amidst both armies broke
The solemn silence, and their pow'rs bespoke.

   Hear all ye *Trojan*, all ye *Grecian* bands,
80   What my soul prompts, and what some God commands.
Great *Jove*, averse our warfare to compose,
O'erwhelms the nations with new toils and woes;
War with a fiercer tide once more returns,
Till *Ilion* falls, or till yon' navy burns.
85   You then, O princes of the *Greeks*! appear;
'Tis *Hector* speaks, and calls the Gods to hear:
From all your troops select the boldest knight,
And him, the boldest, *Hector* dares to Fight.
Here if I fall, by chance of battel slain,
90   Be his my spoil, and his these arms remain;
But let my body, to my Friends return'd,
By *Trojan* hands and *Trojan* flames be burn'd.
And if *Apollo*, in whose aid I trust,
Shall stretch your daring champion in the dust;
95   If mine the glory to despoil the foe;
On *Phœbus'* temple I'll his arms bestow;
The breathless carcase to your navy sent,
Greece on the shore shall raise a monument;
Which when some future mariner surveys,
100   Wash'd by broad *Hellespont*'s resounding seas,
Thus shall he say, 'A valiant *Greek* lies there,
By *Hector* slain, the mighty man of war.'
The stone shall tell your vanquish'd hero's name,
And distant ages learn the victor's fame.

105   This fierce defiance *Greece* astonish'd heard,
Blush'd to refuse, and to accept it fear'd.
Stern *Menelaüs* first the silence broke,
And inly groaning, thus opprobrious spoke.

Women of *Greece!* Oh scandal of your race,
Whose coward souls your manly form disgrace.   110
How great the shame, when ev'ry age shall know
That not a *Grecian* met this noble foe!
Go then! resolve to earth, from whence ye grew,
A heartless, spiritless, inglorious crew!
Be what ye seem, unanimated clay!   115
Myself will dare the danger of the day.
'Tis Man's bold task the gen'rous strife to try,
But in the hands of God is victory.

    These words scarce spoke, with gen'rous ardour prest,
His manly limbs in azure arms he drest: 120
That day, *Atrides!* a superiour hand
Had stretch'd thee breathless on the hostile strand;
But all at once, thy fury to compose,
The Kings of *Greece*, an awful band, arose:
Ev'n he their Chief, great *Agamemnon*, press'd   125
Thy daring hand, and this advice address'd.
Whither, O *Menelaüs!* would'st thou run,
And tempt a fate which prudence bids thee shun?
Griev'd tho' thou art, forbear the rash design;
Great *Hector*'s arm is mightier far than thine.   130
Ev'n fierce *Achilles* learn'd its force to fear,
And trembling met this dreadful son of war.
Sit thou secure amidst thy social band;
Greece in our cause shall arm some pow'rful hand.
The mightiest warriour of th' *Achaian* name,   135
Tho' bold, and burning with desire of fame,
Content, the doubtful honour might forego,
So great the danger, and so brave the foe.

    He said, and turn'd his brother's vengeful mind;
He stoop'd to reason, and his rage resign'd,   140
No longer bent to rush on certain harms;
His joyful friends unbrace his azure arms.

    He, from whose lips divine persuasion flows,
Grave *Nestor*, then, in graceful act arose.
Thus to the Kings he spoke. What grief, what shame   145
Attend on *Greece*, and all the *Grecian* name?
How shall, alas! her hoary heroes mourn,
Their sons degen'rate, and their race a scorn?

What tears shall down thy silver beard be roll'd,
150   Oh *Peleus*, old in arms, in wisdom old!
Once with what joy the gen'rous Prince would hear
Of ev'ry chief who fought this glorious War,
Participate their fame, and pleas'd enquire
Each name, each action, and each hero's sire?
155   Gods! should he see our warriours trembling stand,
And trembling all before one hostile hand;
How would he lift his aged arms on high,
Lament inglorious *Greece*, and beg to die!
Oh! would to all th' immortal pow'rs above,
160   *Minerva*, *Phœbus*, and almighty *Jove!*
Years might again roll back, my youth renew,
And give this arm the spring which once it knew:
When fierce in war, where *Jardan's* waters fall,
I led my troops to *Phea's* trembling wall,
165   And with th' *Arcadian* spears my prowess try'd,
Where *Celadon* rolls down his rapid tide.
There *Ereuthalion* brav'd us in the field,
Proud, *Areïthous'* dreadful arms to wield;
Great *Areïthous*, known from shore to shore
170   By the huge, knotted iron-mace he bore;
No lance he shook, nor bent the twanging bow,
But broke, with this, the battel of the foe.
Him not by manly force *Lycurgus* slew,
Whose guileful javelin from the thicket flew,
175   Deep in a winding way his breast assail'd,
Nor aught the warriour's thund'ring mace avail'd.
Supine he fell: those Arms which *Mars* before
Had giv'n the vanquish'd, now the victor bore.
But when old age had dimm'd *Lycurgus'* eyes,
180   To *Ereuthalion* he consign'd the prize.
Furious with this, he crush'd our levell'd bands,
And dar'd the trial of the strongest hands;
Nor cou'd the strongest hands his fury stay;
All saw, and fear'd, his huge, tempestuous sway.
185   Till I, the youngest of the host, appear'd,
And youngest, met whom all our army fear'd.
I fought the chief: my arms *Minerva* crown'd:
Prone fell the Giant o'er a length of ground.

What then he was, Oh were your *Nestor* now!
Not *Hector*'s self should want an equal foe.   190
But Warriours, you, that youthful vigour boast,
The flow'r of *Greece*, th' examples of our host,
Sprung from such fathers, who such numbers sway,
Can you stand trembling, and desert the day?

 His warm reproofs the list'ning Kings inflame.   195
And nine, the noblest of the *Grecian* name,
Up-started fierce: But far before the rest
The King of Men advanc'd his dauntless breast:
Then bold *Tydides*, great in arms, appear'd;
And next his bulk gigantic *Ajax* rear'd: 200
Oïleus follow'd; *Idomen* was there,
And *Merion*, dreadful as the God of war:
With these *Eurypylus* and *Thoas* stand,
And wise *Ulysses* clos'd the daring band.
All these, alike inspir'd with noble rage,   205
Demand the fight. To whom the *Pylian* sage:

 Lest thirst of glory your brave souls divide,
What chief shall combate, let the lots decide.
Whom heav'n shall chuse, be his the chance to raise
His country's fame, his own immortal praise.   210

 The lots produc'd, each Hero signs his own;
Then in the Gen'rals helm the fates are thrown.
The people pray, with lifted eyes and hands,
And vows like these ascend from all the bands.
Grant, thou Almighty! in whose hand is fate,   215
A worthy champion for the *Grecian* state.
This task let *Ajax* or *Tydides* prove,
Or He, the King of Kings, belov'd by *Jove*.

 Old *Nestor* shook the casque. By heav'n inspir'd,
Leap'd forth the lot, of ev'ry *Greek* desir'd.   220
This from the right to left the herald bears,
Held out in order to the *Grecian* peers.
Each to his rival yields the mark unknown,
Till Godlike *Ajax* finds the lot his own;
Surveys th' inscription with rejoicing eyes,   225
Then casts before him, and with transport cries:

 Warriours! I claim the lot, and arm with joy;
Be mine the conquest of this chief of *Troy*.

Now, while my brightest arms my limbs invest,
230   To *Saturn*'s son be all your vows addrest:
But pray in secret, lest the foes should hear,
And deem your pray'rs the mean effect of fear.
Said I in secret? No, your vows declare,
In such a voice as fills the earth and air.

235   Lives there a chief whom *Ajax* ought to dread,
Ajax, in all the toils of battel bred?
From warlike *Salamis* I drew my birth,
And born to combates, fear no force of earth.

He said. The troops with elevated eyes,
240   Implore the God whose thunder rends the skies.
O Father of mankind, superior Lord!
On lofty *Ida*'s holy hill ador'd;
Who in the highest heav'n hast fix'd thy throne,
Supreme of Gods! unbounded, and alone:

245   Grant thou, that *Telamon* may bear away
The praise and conquest of this doubtful day;
Or if illustrious *Hector* be thy care,
That both may claim it, and that both may share.

Now *Ajax* brac'd his dazling armour on;
250   Sheath'd in bright steel the giant-warriour shone:
He moves to combate with majestic pace;
So stalks in arms the grizly God of *Thrace*,
When *Jove* to punish faithless men prepares,
And gives whole nations to the waste of wars.

255   Thus march'd the Chief, tremendous as a God;
Grimly he smil'd; earth trembled as he strode:
His massy jav'lin quiv'ring in his hand,
He stood, the bulwark of the *Grecian* band.
Thro' ev'ry *Argive* heart new transport ran;
260   All *Troy* stood trembling at the mighty man.
Ev'n *Hector* paus'd; and with new doubt opprest,
Felt his great heart suspended in his breast:
'Twas vain to seek retreat, and vain to fear;
Himself had challeng'd, and the foe drew near.

265   Stern *Telamon* behind his ample shield,
As from a brazen tow'r, o'erlook'd the field.
Huge was its orb, with sev'n thick folds o'ercast,
Of tough bull-hides; of solid brass the last.

(The work of *Tychius*, who in *Hylè* dwell'd,
And all in arts of armoury excell'd.)   270
This *Ajax* bore before his manly breast,
And threat'ning, thus his adverse chief addrest.

   Hector! approach my arm, and singly know
What strength thou hast, and what the *Grecian* foe.
Achilles shuns the fight; yet some there are   275
Not void of soul, and not unskill'd in war:
Let him, unactive on the sea-beat shore,
Indulge his wrath, and aid our arms no more;
Whole troops of heroes *Greece* has yet to boast,
And sends thee one, a sample of her host.   280
Such as I am, I come to prove thy might;
No more – be sudden, and begin the fight.

   O Son of *Telamon*, thy country's pride!
(To *Ajax* thus the *Trojan* Prince reply'd)
Me, as a boy or woman would'st thou fright,   285
New to the field, and trembling at the fight?
Thou meet'st a chief deserving of thy arms,
To combate born, and bred amidst alarms:
I know to shift my ground, remount the car,
Turn, charge, and answer ev'ry call of war;   290
To right, to left, the dext'rous lance I wield,
And bear thick battel on my sounding shield.
But open be our fight, and bold each blow;
I steal no conquest from a noble foe.

   He said, and rising, high above the field   295
Whirl'd the long lance against the sev'nfold shield.
Full on the brass descending from above
Thro' six bull-hides the furious weapon drove,
Till in the sev'nth it fix'd. Then *Ajax* threw,
Thro' *Hector*'s shield the forceful jav'lin flew,   300
His corslet enters, and his garment rends,
And glancing downwards near his flank descends.
The wary *Trojan* shrinks, and bending low
Beneath his buckler, disappoints the blow.
From their bor'd shields the chiefs their jav'lins drew,   305
Then close impetuous, and the charge renew:
Fierce as the mountain lions bath'd in blood,
Or foaming boars, the terrour of the wood.

At *Ajax Hector* his long lance extends;
310   The blunted point against the buckler bends.
But *Ajax* watchful as his foe drew near,
Drove thro' the *Trojan* targe the knotty spear;
It reach'd his neck, with matchless strength impell'd;
Spouts the black gore, and dimms his shining shield.

315   Yet ceas'd not *Hector* thus; but, stooping down,
In his strong hand up-heav'd a flinty stone,
Black, craggy, vast: To this his force he bends;
Full on the brazen boss the stone descends;
The hollow brass resounded with the shock.

320   Then *Ajax* seiz'd the fragment of a rock,
Apply'd each nerve, and swinging round on high,
With force tempestuous let the ruin fly:
The huge stone thund'ring thro' his buckler broke;
His slacken'd knees receiv'd the numbing stroke;

325   Great *Hector* falls extended on the field,
His Bulk supporting on the shatter'd shield.
Nor wanted heav'nly aid: *Apollo*'s might
Confirm'd his sinews, and restor'd to fight.
And now both heroes their broad faulchions drew:

330   In flaming circles round their heads they flew;
But then by heralds voice the word was giv'n,
The sacred ministers of earth and heav'n:
Divine *Talthybius* whom the *Greeks* employ,
And sage *Idæus* on the part of *Troy*,

335   Between the swords their peaceful sceptres rear'd;
And first *Idæus*' awful voice was heard.

Forbear, my sons! your farther force to prove,
Both dear to men, and both belov'd of *Jove*.
To either host your matchless worth is known,
340   Each sounds your praise, and war is all your own.
But now the night extends her awful shade;
The Goddess parts you: Be the night obey'd.

To whom great *Ajax* his high soul express'd.
O sage! to *Hector* be these words address'd.
345   Let him, who first provok'd our chiefs to fight,
Let him demand the sanction of the night:
If first he ask it, I content obey,
And cease the strife when *Hector* shows the way.

Oh first of *Greeks!* (his noble foe rejoin'd)
Whom heav'n adorns, superior to thy kind,
With strength of body, and with worth of mind!
Now martial law commands us to forbear;
Hereafter we shall meet in glorious war,
Some future day shall lengthen out the strife,
And let the Gods decide of death or life!
Since then the night extends her gloomy shade,
And heav'n enjoins it, be the night obey'd.
Return, brave *Ajax*, to thy *Grecian* friends,
And joy the nations whom thy arm defends;
As I shall glad each chief, and *Trojan* wife,
Who wearies heav'n with vows for *Hector*'s life.
But let us, on this memorable day,
Exchange some gift; that *Greece* and *Troy* may say,
'Not hate, but glory, made these chiefs contend;
And each brave foe was in his soul a friend.'

   With that, a sword with stars of silver grac'd,
The baldrick studded, and the sheath enchas'd,
He gave the *Greek*. The gen'rous *Greek* bestow'd
A radiant belt that rich with purple glow'd.
Then with majestic grace they quit the plain;
This seeks the *Grecian*, that the *Phrygian* train.

   The *Trojan* bands returning *Hector* wait,
And hail with joy the champion of their state:
Escap'd great *Ajax*, they survey'd him round,
Alive, unharm'd, and vig'rous from his wound.
To *Troy*'s high gates the god-like man they bear,
Their present triumph, as their late despair.

   But *Ajax*, glorying in his hardy deed,
The well-arm'd *Greeks* to *Agamemnon* lead.
A steer for sacrifice the King design'd,
Of full five years, and of the nobler kind.
The victim falls; they strip the smoking hide,
The beast they quarter, and the joints divide,
Then spread the tables, the repast prepare,
Each takes his seat, and each receives his share.
The King himself (an honorary sign)
Before great *Ajax* plac'd the mighty chine.

350

355

360

365

370

375

380

385

When now the rage of hunger was remov'd;
Nestor, in each persuasive art approv'd,
390   The sage whose counsels long had sway'd the rest,
In words like these his prudent thought exprest.

    How dear, O Kings! this fatal day has cost,
What *Greeks* are perish'd! what a people lost!
What tides of blood have drench'd *Scamander*'s shore?
395   What crowds of Heroes sunk, to rise no more?
Then hear me, Chief! nor let the morrow's light
Awake thy squadrons to new toils of fight.
Some space at least permit the war to breathe,
While we to flames our slaughter'd friends bequeathe,
400   From the red field their scatter'd bodies bear,
And nigh the fleet a fun'ral structure rear:
So decent urns their snowy bones may keep,
And pious children o'er their ashes weep.
Here, where on one promiscuous pile they blaz'd,
405   High o'er them all a gen'ral tomb be rais'd;
Next, to secure our camp, and naval pow'rs,
Raise an embattel'd wall, with lofty tow'rs;
From space to space be ample gates around,
For passing chariots, and a trench profound.
410   So *Greece* to combate shall in safety go,
Nor fear the fierce incursions of the foe.
   'Twas thus the Sage his wholsome counsel mov'd;
The sceptred Kings of *Greece* his words approv'd.

    Meanwhile, conven'd at *Priam*'s palace-gate,
415   The *Trojan* peers in nightly council sate:
A senate void of order, as of choice,
Their hearts were fearful, and confus'd their voice.
Antenor rising, thus demands their ear:
Ye *Trojans*, *Dardans*, and auxiliars hear!
420   'Tis heav'n the counsel of my breast inspires,
And I but move what ev'ry God requires:
Let *Sparta*'s treasures be this hour restor'd,
And *Argive Helen* own her ancient Lord.
The ties of faith, the sworn alliance broke,
425   Our impious battels the just Gods provoke.
As this advice ye practise, or reject,
So hope success, or dread the dire effect.

The senior spoke, and sate. To whom reply'd
The graceful husband of the *Spartan* bride.
Cold counsels, *Trojan*, may become thy years,   430
But sound ungrateful in a warriour's ears:
Old man, if void of fallacy or art
Thy words express the purpose of thy heart,
Thou, in thy time, more sound advice hast giv'n;
But wisdom has its date, assign'd by heav'n.   435
Then hear me, Princes of the *Trojan* name!
Their treasures I'll restore, but not the dame;
My treasures too, for peace, I will resign;
But be this bright possession ever mine.

    'Twas then, the growing discord to compose,   440
Slow from his seat the rev'rend *Priam* rose.
His god-like aspect deep attention drew:
He paus'd, and these pacific words ensue.

    Ye *Trojans*, *Dardans*, and auxiliar bands!
Now take refreshment as the hour demands:
Guard well the walls, relieve the watch of night,   445
Till the new sun restores the chearful light:
Then shall our herald to th' *Atrides* sent,
Before their ships proclaim my son's intent.
Next let a truce be ask'd, that *Troy* may burn   450
Her slaughter'd heroes, and their bones in-urn.
That done, once more the fate of war be try'd,
And whose the conquest, mighty *Jove* decide!

    The monarch spoke: the warriours snatch'd with haste
(Each at his post in arms) a short repaste.   455
Soon as the rosy morn had wak'd the day,
To the black ships *Idæus* bent his way;
There, to the sons of *Mars*, in council found,
He rais'd his voice: The hosts stood list'ning round.

    Ye Sons of *Atreus*, and ye *Greeks*, give ear!   460
The words of *Troy*, and *Troy*'s great Monarch hear.
Pleas'd may ye hear (so heav'n succeed my pray'rs)
What *Paris*, author of the war, declares.
The spoils and treasures he to *Ilion* bore,
(Oh had he perish'd e'er they touch'd our shore)   465
He proffers injur'd *Greece*; with large encrease
Of added *Trojan* wealth to buy the peace.

But to restore the beauteous bride again,
This *Greece* demands, and *Troy* requests in vain.
470 Next, O ye chiefs! we ask a truce to burn
Our slaughter'd heroes, and their bones in-urn.
That done, once more the fate of war be try'd,
And whose the conquest, mighty *Jove* decide!

The *Greeks* gave ear, but none the silence broke;
475 At length *Tydides* rose, and rising spoke.
Oh take not, friends! defrauded of your fame,
Their proffer'd wealth, nor ev'n the *Spartan* dame.
Let conquest make them ours: Fate shakes their wall,
And *Troy* already totters to her fall.
480 Th' admiring chiefs, and all the *Grecian* name,
With gen'ral shouts return'd him loud acclaim.
Then thus the King of Kings rejects the peace:
Herald! in him thou hear'st the voice of *Greece*.
For what remains; let fun'ral flames be fed
485 With heroes corps: I war not with the dead:
Go search your slaughter'd chiefs on yonder plain,
And gratify the *Manes* of the slain.
Be witness, *Jove!* whose thunder rolls on high!
He said, and rear'd his sceptre to the sky.

490 To sacred *Troy*, where all her Princes lay
To wait th' event, the herald bent his way.
He came, and standing in the midst, explain'd
The peace rejected, but the truce obtain'd.
Strait to their sev'ral cares the *Trojans* move,
495 Some search the plain, some fell the sounding grove:
Nor less the *Greeks*, descending on the shore,
Hew'd the green forests, and the bodies bore.
And now from forth the chambers of the main,
500 To shed his sacred light on earth again,
Arose the golden chariot of the day,
And tipt the mountains with a purple ray.
In mingled throngs, the *Greek* and *Trojan* train
Thro' heaps of carnage search'd the mournful plain.
Scarce could the friend his slaughter'd friend explore,
505 With dust dishonour'd, and deform'd with gore.
The wounds they wash'd, their pious tears they shed,
And, lay'd along their cars, deplor'd the dead.

Sage *Priam* check'd their grief: With silent haste
The bodies decent on the piles were plac'd:
With melting hearts the cold remains they burn'd;
And sadly slow, to sacred *Troy* return'd.   510

Nor less the *Greeks* their pious sorrows shed,
And decent on the pile dispose the dead;
The cold remains consume with equal care;
And slowly, sadly, to their fleet repair.   515

Now, e're the morn had streak'd with red'ning light
The doubtful confines of the day and night;
About the dying flames the *Greeks* appear'd,
And round the pile a gen'ral tomb they rear'd.

Then, to secure the camp and naval pow'rs,   520
They rais'd embattel'd walls with lofty tow'rs:
From space to space were ample gates around,
For passing chariots; and a trench profound,
Of large extent, and deep in earth below
Strong piles infix'd stood adverse to the foe.   525

So toil'd the *Greeks*: Meanwhile the Gods above
In shining circle round their father *Jove*,
Amaz'd beheld the wondrous works of man:
Then *he, whose trident shakes the earth, began.

What mortals henceforth shall our pow'r adore,   530
Our fanes frequent, our oracles implore,
If the proud *Grecians* thus successful boast
Their rising bulwarks on the sea-beat coast?
See the long walls extending to the main,
No God consulted, and no victim slain!   535
Their fame shall fill the world's remotest ends,
Wide, as the morn her goldern beam extends.
While old *Laömedon*'s divine abodes,
Those radiant structures rais'd by lab'ring Gods,
Shall, raz'd and lost, in long oblivion sleep.   540
Thus spoke the hoary monarch of the deep.

Th' Almighty Thund'rer with a frown replies,
That clouds the world, and blackens half the skies.
Strong God of Ocean! Thou, whose rage can make
The solid earth's eternal basis shake!   545

*Neptune.

What cause of fear from mortal works cou'd move
The meanest subject of our realms above?
Where-e'er the sun's refulgent rays are cast,
Thy pow'r is honour'd, and thy fame shall last.
550   But yon' proud work no future age shall view,
No trace remain where once the glory grew.
The sapp'd foundations by thy force shall fall,
And whelm'd beneath thy waves, drop the huge wall:
Vast drifts of sand shall change the former shore;
555   The ruin vanish'd, and the name no more.
     Thus they in heav'n: while, o'er the *Grecian* train,
The rolling sun descending to the main
Beheld the finish'd work. Their bulls they slew;
Black from the tents the sav'ry vapours flew.
560   And now the fleet, arriv'd from *Lemnos'* strands,
With *Bacchus'* blessings chear'd the gen'rous bands.
Of fragrant wines the rich *Eunæus* sent
A thousand measures to the royal tent.
(*Eunæus*, whom *Hypsipyle* of yore
565   To *Jason*, shepherd of his people, bore)
The rest they purchas'd at their proper cost,
And well the plenteous freight supply'd the host:
Each, in exchange, proportion'd treasures gave;
Some brass or iron, some an oxe, or slave.
570   All night they feast, the *Greek* and *Trojan* pow'rs;
Those on the fields, and these within their tow'rs.
But *Jove* averse the signs of wrath display'd,
And shot red light'nings thro' the gloomy shade:
Humbled they stood; pale horrour seiz'd on all,
575   While the deep thunder shook th' aërial hall.
Each pour'd to *Jove* before the bowl was crown'd,
And large libations drench'd the thirsty ground:
Then late refresh'd with sleep from toils of fight,
Enjoy'd the balmy blessings of the night.

OBSERVATIONS

ON THE

SEVENTH BOOK

2. *Thro' the* Scæan *gate.*] This gate is not here particularized by *Homer*, but it appears by the 491st verse of the sixth book that it could be no other. *Eustathius* takes notice of the difference of the words ἐξέσσυτο and χίε, the one apply'd to *Hector*, the other to *Paris*: by which the motion of the former is described as an impetuous sallying forth, agreeable to the violence of a warriour; and that of the latter as a calmer movement, correspondent to the gentler character of a lover. But perhaps this remark is too refined, since *Homer* plainly gives *Paris* a character of bravery in what immediately precedes and follows this verse.

5. *As when to sailors*, &c.] This simile makes it plain that the battel had relax'd during the absence of *Hector* in *Troy*; and consequently that the conversation of *Diomed* and *Glaucus* in the former book, was not (as *Homer*'s censurers would have it) in the heat of the engagement.

23. *When now* Minerva, &c.] This machine of the two Deities meeting to part the two armies is very noble. *Eustathius* tells us it is an allegorical *Minerva* and *Apollo*: *Minerva* represents the prudent valour of the *Greeks*, and *Apollo* who stood for the *Trojans*, the power of destiny: So that the meaning of the allegory may be, that the valour and wisdom of the *Greeks* had now conquer'd *Troy*, had not destiny withstood. *Minerva* therefore complies with *Apollo*, an intimation that wisdom can never oppose fate. But if you take them in the literal sense as a real God and Goddess, it may be ask'd what necessity there was for the introduction of two such Deities? To this *Eustathius* answers, that the last book was the only one in which both armies were destitute

of the aid of Gods: In consequence of which there is no gallant action atchiev'd, nothing extraordinary done, especially after the retreat of *Hector*; but here the Gods are again introduced to usher in a new scene of great actions. The same author offers this other solution: *Hector* finding the *Trojan* army overpower'd, considers how to stop the fury of the present battel; this he thinks may best be done by the proposal of a single combate: Thus *Minerva* by a very easy and natural fiction may signify that wisdom or courage (she being the Goddess of both) which suggests the necessity of diverting the war; and *Apollo*, that seasonable stratagem by which he effected it.

37. *Vengeful Goddesses.*] ῾Υμῖν ἀθανάτῃσι in this place must signify *Minerva* and *Juno*, the word being of the feminine gender.

Eustathius.

48. *Sage* Helenus *their sacred counsels knew.*] *Helenus* was the priest of *Apollo*, and might therefore be supposed to be informed of this by his God, or taught by an oracle that such was his will. Or else being an *Augur*, he might learn it from the flight of those birds, into which the Deities are here feigned to transform themselves, (perhaps for that reason, as it would be a very poetical manner of expressing it.) The fiction of these divinities sitting on the beech-tree in the shape of *Vulturs*, is imitated by *Milton* in the fourth book of *Paradise lost*, where *Satan* leaping over the boundaries of *Eden*, sits in the form of a cormorant upon the tree of life.

57. *For not this day shall end thy glorious date.*] *Eustathius* justly observes that *Homer* here takes from the greatness of *Hector*'s intrepidity, by making him foreknow that he should not fall in this combate; whereas *Ajax* encounters him without any such encouragement. It may perhaps be difficult to give a reason for this management of the Poet, unless we ascribe it to that commendable prejudice, and honourable partiality he bears his countrymen, which makes him give a superiority of courage to the heroes of his own nation.

60. *Then with his spear restrain'd the youth of* Troy, *Held by the midst athwart.* –] The remark of *Eustathius* here is observable: He tells us that the warriors of those times (having no trumpets, and because the voice of the loudest herald would be drown'd in the noise of a battel) address'd themselves to the eyes, and that grasping the middle of the

spear denoted a request that the fight might a while be suspended; the holding the spear in that position not being the posture of a warriour; and thus *Agamemnon* understands it without any farther explication. But however it be, we have a lively picture of a general who stretches his spear across, and presses back the most advanced soldiers of his army.

71. *As when a gen'ral darkness*, &c.] The thick ranks of the troops composing themselves, in order to sit and hear what *Hector* was about to propose, are compar'd to the waves of the sea just stirr'd by the *West* wind; the simile partly consisting in the *darkness* and *stillness*. This is plainly different from those images of the sea, given us on other occasions, where the armies in their engagement and confusion are compared to the waves in their *agitation* and *tumult*: And that the contrary is the drift of this simile appears particularly from *Homer's* using the word εἶατο, *sedebant*, twice in the application of it. All the other versions seem to be mistaken here: What caused the difficulty was the expression ὀρνυμένοιο νέον, which may signify the *west* wind *blowing on a sudden*, as well as *first rising*. But the design of *Homer* was to convey an image both of the gentle motion that arose over the field from the helmets and spears before their armies were quite settled; and of the repose and awe which ensued, when *Hector* began to speak.

79. *Hear all ye* Trojan, *all ye* Grecian *bands*.] The appearance of *Hector*, his formal challenge, and the affright of the *Greeks* upon it, have a near resemblance to the description of the challenge of *Goliah* in the first book of *Samuel*, ch. 17. *And he stood and cried to the Armies of* Israel — *Chuse you a man for you, and let him come down to me. If he be able to fight with me, and to kill me, then will we be your servants: but if I prevail against him, and kill him, then shall ye be our servants.* — *When* Saul *and all* Israel *heard the words of the* Philistine, *they were dismayed, and greatly afraid*, &c.

There is a fine air of gallantry and bravery in this challenge of *Hector*. If he seems to speak too vainly, we should consider him under the character of a challenger, whose business it is to defy the enemy. Yet at the same time we find a decent modesty in his manner of expressing the conditions of the combate: He says simply, *If my enemy kills me*; but of himself, *If* Apollo *grant me victory*. It was an imagination equally agreeable to a man of generosity and a lover of glory, to mention the monument to be erected over his vanquish'd enemy; tho' we see he considers it not so much an honour paid to the conquer'd as a trophy to the conqueror. It was natural too to dwell most upon the thought that pleas'd him best; for he takes no notice of any monument that should be raised over himself, if he should fall unfortunately. He no sooner allows himself to expatiate, but the prospect of glory carries him away thus far beyond his first intention, which was only to allow the enemy to inter their champion with decency.

96. *On* Phœbus' *temple I'll his arms bestow.*] It was the manner of the ancients to dedicate trophies of this kind to the temples of the Gods. The particular reason for consecrating the arms in this place to *Apollo*, is not only as he was the constant protector of *Troy*, but as this thought of the challenge was inspired by him.

98. Greece *on the shore shall raise a monument.*] *Homer* took the hint of this from several tombs of the ancient heroes who had fought at *Troy*, remaining in his time upon the shore of the *Hellespont.* He gives that sea the epithet *broad,* to distinguish the particular place of those tombs, which was on the *Rhœtean* or *Sigœan* coast, where the *Hellespont* (which in other parts is narrow) opens itself to the *Ægean* sea. *Strabo* gives an account of the monument of *Ajax* near *Rhœteum,* and of *Achilles* at the promontory of *Sigœum.* This is one among a thousand proofs of our author's exact knowledge in geography and antiquities. Time (says *Eustathius*) has destroy'd those tombs which were to have preserv'd *Hector*'s glory; but *Homer*'s poetry more lasting than monuments and proof against ages, will for ever support and convey it to the latest posterity.

105. *All* Greece *astonish'd heard.*] It seems natural to enquire, why the *Greeks*, before they accepted *Hector*'s challenge, did not demand reparation for the former treachery of *Pandarus,* and insist upon delivering up the author of it; which had been the shortest way for the *Trojans* to have wip'd off that stain: It was very reasonable for the *Greeks* to reply to this challenge, that they could not venture a second single combate for fear of such another insidious Attempt upon their champion. And indeed I wonder that *Nestor* did not think of this excuse for his countrymen, when they were so backward to engage. One may make some sort of answer to this, if we consider the clearness of *Hector*'s character, and his words at the beginning of the foregoing speech, where he first complains of the revival of the war as a

misfortune common to them both (which is at once very artful and decent) and lays the blame of it upon *Jupiter*. Tho', by the way, his charging the *Trojan* breach of faith upon the Deity looks a little like the reasoning of some modern saints in the doctrine of absolute reprobation, making God the author of sin, and may serve for some instance of the antiquity of that false tenet.

109. *Women of* Greece! &c.] There is a great deal of fire in this speech of *Menelaus*, which very well agrees with his character and circumstances. Methinks while he speaks one sees him in a posture of emotion, pointing with contempt at the commanders about him. He upbraids their cowardice, and wishes they may become (according to the literal words) *earth and water*: that is, be resolved into those principles they sprung from, or die. Thus *Eustathius* explains it very exactly from a verse he cites of *Zenophanes*.

Πάντες γὰρ γαίης τε καὶ ὕδατος ἐκγενόμεσθα.

[We are all sprung from earth and water.]

131. *Ev'n fierce* Achilles *learn'd his force to fear.*] The Poet every where takes occasion to set the brotherly love of *Agamemnon* toward *Menelaus* in the most agreeable light: When *Menelaus* is wounded, *Agamemnon* is more concern'd than he; and here dissuades him from a danger, which he offers immediately after to undertake himself. He makes use of *Hector*'s superior courage to bring him to a compliance; and tells him that even *Achilles* dares not engage with *Hector*. This (says *Eustathius*) is not true, but only the affection for his brother thus breaks out into a kind extravagance. *Agamemnon* likewise consults the honour of *Menelaus*, for it will be no disgrace to him to decline encountering a man whom *Achilles* himself is afraid of. Thus he artfully provides for his safety and honour at the same time.

135. *The mightiest warrior*, &c.] It cannot with certainty be concluded from the words of *Homer*, who is the person to whom *Agamemnon* applies the last lines of this speech; the interpreters leave it as undetermin'd in their translations as it is in the original. Some would have it understood of *Hector*, that the *Greeks* would send such an antagonist against him, from whose hands *Hector* might be glad to escape. But this interpretation seems contrary to the plain design of *Agamemnon*'s discourse, which only aims to deter his brother from so

rash an undertaking as engaging with *Hector*. So that instead of dropping any expression which might depreciate the power or courage of this hero, he endeavours rather to represent him as the most formidable of men, and dreadful even to *Achilles*. This passage therefore will be most consistent with *Agamemnon*'s design, if it be consider'd as an argument offer'd to *Menelaus*, at once to dissuade him from the engagement, and to comfort him under the appearance of so great a disgrace as refusing the challenge; by telling him that any warriour, how bold and intrepid soever, might be content to sit still and rejoice that he is not expos'd to so hazardous an engagement. The Words αἴ κε φύγῃσι Δηΐου ἐκ πολέμοιο, signify not to escape out of the combate (as the translators take it) but to avoid entring into it.

The Phrase of γόνυ κάμψειν, which is literally *to bend the knee*, means (according to *Eustathius*) to *rest*, to sit down, καθεσθῆναι, and is used so by *Æschylus* in *Prometheo*. Those interpreters were greatly mistaken who imagin'd it signify'd *to kneel down*, to thank the Gods for escaping from such a combate; whereas the custom of kneeling in prayer (as we before observ'd) was not in use among these nations.

145. *The speech of* Nestor.] This speech, if we consider the occasion of it, could be made by no person but *Nestor*. No young warriour could with decency exhort others to undertake a combate which he himself declin'd. Nothing could be more in his character than to represent to the *Greeks* how much they would suffer in the opinion of another old man like himself. In naming *Peleus* he sets before their eyes the expectations of all their fathers, and the shame that must afflict them in their old age if their Sons behaved themselves unworthily. The account he gives of the conversations he had formerly held with that King, and his jealousy for the glory of *Greece*, is a very natural picture of the warm dialogues of two old warriours upon the commencement of a new war. Upon the whole, *Nestor* never more displays his oratory than in this place: You see him rising with a sigh, expressing a pathetick sorrow, and wishing again for his youth that he might wipe away this disgrace from his country. The humour of story-telling, so natural to old men, is almost always mark'd by *Homer* in the speeches of *Nestor*: The apprehension that their age makes them contemptible, puts them upon repeating the brave deeds of their youth. *Plutarch* justifies the praises *Nestor* here gives himself, and the vaunts of his valour, which on this occasion were only exhortations to those he address'd them to: By these he restores courage to the *Greeks*

who were astonish'd at the bold challenge of *Hector*, and causes nine of the princes to rise and accept it. If any man had a right to commend himself, it was this venerable prince, who in relating his own actions did no more than propose examples of virtue to the young. *Virgil*, without any such softening qualification, makes his hero say of himself,

> *Sum pius Æneas, fama super æthera notus.*   [I. 378–9]

> [The good *Aeneas* am I call'd, a name,
> While fortune favour'd, not unknown to fame.]

And comfort a dying warriour with these words,

> *Ænea magni dextra cadis.* –   [X. 830]

> [There to thy fellow ghosts with glory tell,
> 'Twas by the great *Aeneas* hand I fell.]

The same Author also imitates the wish of *Nestor* for a return of his youth, where *Evander* cries out,

> *O mihi præteritos referat si Jupiter annos!*
> *Qualis eram, cum primam aciem Præneste sub ipsa*
> *Stravi, scutorumque incendi victor acervos,*
> *Et regem hac Herilum dextra sub Tartara misi!*
>
> > [VIII. 560–63]

> [Wou'd Heav'n, said he, my strength and youth recall,
> Such as I was beneath *Præneste*'s wall;
> Then when I made the foremost foes retire,
> And set whole heaps of conquer'd shields on fire.
> When *Herilus* in single fight I slew;
> Whom with three lives *Feronia* did endue:
> And thrice I sent him to the *Stygian* shore;
> Till the last ebbing soul return'd no more.]

As for the narration of the *Arcadian* war introduced here, it is a part of the true history of those times, as we are inform'd by *Pausanias*.

177. *Those arms which* Mars *before Had giv'n.*] *Homer* has the peculiar happiness of being able to raise the obscurest circumstance into the strongest point of light. *Areithous* had taken these arms in battel, and this gives occasion to our Author to say they were the present of *Mars*.
                                                                    Eustathius.

188. *Prone fell the Giant o'er a length of ground.*] *Nestor*'s insisting upon this circumstance of the fall of *Ereuthalion*, which paints his vast body lying extended on the earth, has a particular beauty in it, and recalls into the old man's mind the joy he felt on the sight of his enemy after he was slain. These are the fine and natural strokes that give life to the descriptions of poetry.

196. *And nine, the noblest*, &c.] In this catalogue of the nine warriors, who offer themselves as champions for *Greece*, one may take notice of the first and the last who rises up. *Agamemnon* advanced foremost, as it best became the General, and *Ulysses* with his usual caution took time to deliberate till seven more had offer'd themselves. *Homer* gives a great encomium of the eloquence of *Nestor* in making it produce so sudden an effect; especially when *Agamemnon*, who did not proffer himself before, even to save his brother, is now the first that steps forth: One would fancy this particular circumstance was contrived to shew, that eloquence has a greater power than even nature itself.

208. *Let the Lots decide.*] This was a very prudent Piece of Conduct in *Nestor*: he does not chuse any of these nine himself, but leaves the Determination entirely to Chance. Had he named the Hero, the rest might have been griev'd to have seen another prefer'd before them; and he well knew that the Lot could not fall upon a wrong Person, where all were valiant.   *Eustathius.*

209.   *Whom heav'n shall chuse, be his the chance to raise*
         His country's fame, his own immortal praise.]

The original of this passage is somewhat confused; the interpreters render it thus: 'Cast the lots, and he who shall be chosen, if he escapes from this dangerous combat, will do an eminent service to the *Greeks*, and also have cause to be greatly satisfied himself.' But the sense will appear more distinct and rational if the words οὗτος and αὐτός be not understood of the same person: and the meaning of *Nestor* will then be, 'He who is chosen for the engagement by the lot, will do his country great service, and he likewise who is not, will have reason to rejoice for escaping so dangerous a combate.' The expression αἴ κε φύγῃσι Δηΐου ἐκ πολέμοιο, is the same *Homer* uses in v. 118, 119. of this book, which we explained in the same sense in the note on v. 135.

213. *The people pray.*] *Homer*, who supposes every thing on earth to proceed from the immediate disposition of heaven, allows not even the lots to come up by chance, but places them in the hands of God. The people pray to him for the disposal of them, and beg that *Ajax*, *Diomed*, or *Agamemnon* may be the person. In which the Poet seems to make the army give his own sentiments, concerning the preference of valour in his heroes, to avoid an odious comparison in downright terms, which might have been inconsistent with his design of complementing the *Grecian* families. They afterwards offer up their prayers again, just as the combate is beginning, that if *Ajax* does not conquer, at least he may divide the glory with *Hector*; in which the Commentators observe *Homer* prepares the readers for what is to happen in the sequel.

225. *Surveys th' inscription.*] There is no necessity to suppose that they put any letters upon these lots, at least not their names, because the herald could not tell to whom the lot of *Ajax* belong'd, till he claimed it himself. It is more probable that they made some private mark or signet each upon his own lot. The lot was only a piece of wood, a shell, or any thing that lay at hand.   *Eustathius.*

227. *Warriours! I claim the lot.*] This is the first speech of *Ajax* in the Iliad. He is no Orator, but always expresses himself in short, generally bragging, or threatning, and very positive. The appellation of ἕρκος Ἀχαιῶν, the *bulwark of the* Greeks, which *Homer* almost constantly gives him, is extremely proper to the bulk, strength, and immobility of this heavy hero, who on all occasions is made to stand to the business, and support the brunt. These qualifications are given him, that he may last out, when the rest of the chief heroes are wounded: this makes him of excellent use in Iliad 13, &c. He there puts a stop to the whole force of the enemy, and a long time prevents the firing of the ships. It is particularly observable, that he is never assisted by any Deity, as the others are. Yet one would think *Mars* had been no improper patron for him, there being some resemblance in the boisterous character of that God and this hero. However it be, this consideration may partly account for a particular which else might very well raise a question: Why *Ajax*, who is in this book superior in strength to *Hector*, should afterward in the Iliad shun to meet him, and appear his inferior? We see the Gods make this difference: *Hector* is not only assisted by them in his own person, but his men second him, whereas those of *Ajax* are dispirited by heaven: To which one may add another which is a natural reason, *Hector* in this book expresly tells *Ajax*, 'he will now make use of no skill or art in fighting with him'. The *Greek* in bare brutal Strength proved too hard for *Hector*, and therefore he might be supposed afterwards to have exerted his dexterity against him.

251. *He moves to combate*, &c.] This description is full of the sublime imagery so peculiar to our author. The *Grecian* champion is drawn in all that terrible glory with which he equals his Heroes to the Gods: He is no less dreadful than *Mars* moving to battel, to execute the decrees of *Jove* upon mankind, and determine the fate of nations. His march, his posture, his countenance, his bulk, his tow'r-like shield; in a word, his whole figure, strikes our eyes in all the strongest colours of Poetry. We look upon him as a Deity, and are not astonished at those emotions which *Hector* feels at the sight of him.

269. *The Work of* Tychius.] I shall ask leave to transcribe here the story of this *Tychius*, as we have it in the ancient *Life of Homer*, attributed to *Herodotus*. '*Homer* falling into poverty, determined to go to *Cuma*, and as he past thro' the Plain of *Hermus*, came to a place called *the new wall*, which was a colony of the *Cumæans*. Here (*after he had recited five verses in celebration of* Cuma) he was received by a leather-dresser, whose name was *Tychius*, into his house, where he shewed to his host and his company, a poem on the expedition of *Amphiaraus*, and his *hymns*. The admiration he there obtained procured him a present subsistence. They shew to this day with great veneration the place where he sate when he recited his verses, and a poplar which they affirm to have grown there in his time.' If there be any thing in this story, we have reason to be pleased with the grateful temper of our Poet, who took this occasion of immortalizing the name of an ordinary tradesman, who had obliged him. The same account of his life takes notice of several other instances of his gratitude in the same kind.

270. *In arts of armoury.*] I have called *Tychius* an armourer rather than a leather-dresser or currier; his making the shield of *Ajax* authorizes one expression as well as the other; and tho' that which *Homer* uses had no lowness or vulgarity in the *Greek*, it is not to be admitted into *English* heroic verse.

273. Hector, *approach my arm*, &c.] I think it needless to observe how exactly this speech of *Ajax* corresponds with his blunt and soldier-like character. The same propriety, in regard to this hero, is maintained throughout the *Iliad*. The business he is about is all that employs his head, and he speaks of nothing but fighting. The last line is an image of his mind at all times.

> *No more – be sudden, and begin the fight.*

285. *Me, as a boy or woman, would'st thou fright?*] This reply of *Hector* seems rather to allude to some gesture *Ajax* had used in his approach to him, as *shaking his spear*, or the like, than to any thing he had said in his speech. For what he had told him amounts to no more than that there were several in the *Grecian* army who had courted the honour of this combate as well as himself. I think one must observe many things of this kind in *Homer*, that allude to the particular attitude or action in which the author supposes the person to be at that time.

290. *Turn, charge, and answer ev'ry call of war.*] The *Greek* is, *To move my feet to the sound of* Mars, which seems to shew that those military dances were in use even in *Homer*'s time, which were afterwards practised in *Greece*.

305. *From their bor'd shields the chiefs their jav'lins drew.*] *Homer* in this combate makes his heroes perform all their exercises with all sorts of weapons; first darting lances at distance, then advancing closer, and pushing with spears, then casting stones, and lastly attacking with swords; in every one of which the Poet gives the superiority to his countryman. It is farther observable (as *Eustathius* remarks) that *Ajax* allows *Hector* an advantage in throwing the first spear.

327. Apollo's *Might.*] In the beginning of this book we left *Apollo* perch'd upon a tree, in the shape of a vultur, to behold the combate: He comes now very opportunely to save his favourite *Hector*. *Eustathius* says that *Apollo* is the same with *Destiny*, so that when *Homer* says *Apollo* saved him, he means no more than that it was not his fate yet to die, as *Helenus* had foretold him.

331. *Heralds, the sacred ministers*, &c.] The heralds of old were sacred persons, accounted the delegates of *Mercury*, and inviolable by the law of nations. The ancient histories have many examples of the severity exercised against those who committed any outrage upon them. Their office was to assist in the sacrifices and councils, to proclaim war or peace, to command silence at ceremonies or single combates, to part the combatants, and to declare the conqueror, &c.

333. *Divine* Talthybius, &c.] This interposition of the two heralds to part the combatants, on the approach of the night, is applied by *Tasso* to the single combate of *Tancred* and *Argantes* in the sixth book of his *Jerusalem.* The herald's speech, and particularly that remarkable injunction to *obey the night*, are translated literally by that author. The combatants there also part not without a promise of meeting again in battel, on some more favourable opportunity.

336. *And first* Idæus.] *Homer* observes a just decorum in making *Idæus* the *Trojan* herald speak first, to end the combate wherein *Hector* had the disadvantage. *Ajax* is very sensible of this difference, when in his reply he requires that *Hector* should first ask for a cessation, as he was the challenger.   *Eustathius.*

349. *O first of* Greeks, &c.] *Hector*, how hardly soever he is prest by his present circumstance, says nothing to obtain a truce that is not strictly consistent with his honour. When he praises *Ajax*, it lessens his own disadvantage, and he is careful to extol him only above the *Greeks*, without acknowledging him more valiant than himself or the *Trojans*: *Hector* is always jealous of the honour of his country. In what follows we see he keeps himself on a level with his adversary; *Hereafter we shall meet.* – *Go thou, and give the same joy to thy* Grecians *for thy escape, as I shall to my* Trojans. The *point of honour* in all this is very nicely preserved.

361. *Who wearies heav'n with vows for* Hector's *life.*] *Eustathius* gives many solutions of the difficulty in these words, Θεῖον ἀγῶνα: They mean either that the *Trojan* Ladies will pray to the Gods for him (ἀγωνίως, or *certatim*) with the utmost zeal and transport; or that they will go in procession to the temples for him (εἰς θεῖον ἀγῶνα, *cœtum Deorum*;) or that they will pray to him as to a God, ὅσα θεῷ τινι εὔξονταί μοι.

363. *Exchange some gift.*] There is nothing that gives us a greater pleasure in reading an heroic Poem, than the generosity, which one brave enemy shews to another. The proposal made here by *Hector*, and so readily embraced by *Ajax*, makes the parting of these two heroes more glorious to them than the continuance of the combate could have been. A *French* critick is shocked at *Hector*'s making proposals to *Ajax* with an air of equality; he says a man that is vanquished, instead of talking of presents, ought to retire with shame from his conqueror. But that *Hector* was vanquished is by no means to be allowed; *Homer* had told us that his strength was restored by *Apollo*, and that the two combatants were engaging again upon equal terms with their swords. So that this criticism falls to nothing. For the rest, 'tis said that this exchange of presents between *Hector* and *Ajax* gave birth to a proverb, that the presents of enemies are generally fatal. For *Ajax* with this sword afterwards killed himself, and *Hector* was dragged by this belt at the chariot of *Achilles.*

387. *Before great* Ajax *plac'd the mighty chine.*] This is one of those passages that will naturally fall under the ridicule of a true modern critick. But what *Agamemnon* here bestows on *Ajax* was in former times a great mark of respect and honour: Not only as it was customary to distinguish the quality of their guests by the largeness of the portions assigned them at their tables, but as this part of the victim peculiarly belonged to the King himself. It is worth remarking on this occasion, that the simplicity of those times allowed the eating of no other flesh but beef, mutton, or kid. This is the food of the Heroes of *Homer*, and the Patriarchs and Warriours of the Old Testament. Fishing and fowling were the arts of more luxurious nations, and came much later into *Greece* and *Israel.*

One cannot read this passage without being pleased with the wonderful simplicity of the old heroic ages. We have here a gallant warriour returning victorious (for that he thought himself so, appears from those words κεχαρηότα νίκῃ [rejoicing in his victory] from a single combate with the bravest of his enemies; and he is no otherwise rewarded than with a larger portion of the sacrifice at supper. Thus an upper seat or a more capacious bowl was a recompence for the greatest actions; and thus the only reward in the olympic games was a pine branch, or a chaplet of parsley or wild olive. The latter part of this note belongs to *Eustathius.*

399. *While we to flames,* &c.] There is a great deal of artifice in this counsel of *Nestor* or burning the dead and raising a fortification; for

tho' piety was the specious pretext, their security was the real aim of the truce, which they made use of to finish their works. Their doing this at the same time they erected the funeral piles, made the imposition easy upon the enemy, who might naturally mistake one work for the other. And this also obviates a plain objection, *viz.* Why the *Trojans* did not interrupt them in this work? The truce determined no exact time, but as much as was needful for discharging the rites of the dead.

I fancy it may not be unwelcome to the reader to enlarge a little upon the way of disposing the dead among the ancients. It may be proved from innumerable instances that the *Hebrews* interred their dead; thus *Abraham*'s burying-place is frequently mentioned in scripture: And that the *Ægyptians* did the same is plain from their embalming them. Some have been of opinion that the usage of burning the dead was originally to prevent any outrage to the bodies from their enemies; which imagination is rendered not improbable by that passage in the first book of *Samuel*, where the *Israelites* burn the bodies of *Saul* and his sons after they had been misused by the *Philistines*, even tho' their common custom was to bury their dead. And so *Sylla* among the *Romans* was the first of his family who ordered his body to be burnt, for fear the barbarities he had exercised on that of *Marius* might be retaliated upon his own. Tully *de legibus, lib.* 2. *Procul dubio cremandi ritus a Græcis venit, nam sepultum legimus Numam ad Anienis fontem; totique genti Corneliæ solenne fuisse sepulcrum, usque ad Syllam, qui primus ex ea gente crematus est.* [Without a doubt, the custom of burning bodies came from the Greeks, for we read that Numa was buried near the source of the river Anio; and that, for the family of Cornelia, this was the customary burial place up to the time of Sulla, who was the first member of his family to be cremated.] The *Greeks* used both ways of interring and burning; *Patroclus* was burned, and *Ajax* laid in the ground, as appears from *Sophocles*'s *Ajax*, lin. 1165.

Σπεῦσον κοίλην κάπετόν τιν' ἰδεῖν
Τῷδε . . . τάφον. –

Hasten (says the Chorus) *to prepare a hollow hole, a grave for this Man.*

Thucidydes, in his second book, mentions λάρνακας κυπαρισσίνας: coffins or chests made of cypress wood, in which the *Athenians* kept the bones of their friends that died in the Wars.

The *Romans* derived from the *Greeks* both these customs of burning and burying: *In urbe neve* SEPELITO *neve* URITO [neither buried nor burned in the city], says the law of the twelve tables. The place where they burn'd the dead was set apart for this religious use, and called *Glebe*; from which practice the name is yet apply'd to all the grounds belonging to the church.

Plutarch observes that *Homer* is the first who mentions one general tomb for a number of dead persons. Here is a *Tumulus* built round the *Pyre*, not to bury their bodies, for they were to be burn'd; nor to receive the bones, for those were to be carry'd to *Greece*; but perhaps to inter their ashes, (which custom may be gathered from a passage in *Iliad* 23. v. 255.) or it might be only a *Cenotaph* in remembrance of the dead.

415. *The* Trojan *peers in nightly council sate.*] There is a great Beauty in the two Epithets *Homer* gives to this council, δεινή, τετρηχυῖα, *timida, turbulenta.* The unjust side is always fearful and discordant. I think M. *Dacier* has not entirely done justice to this thought in her translation. *Horace* seems to have accounted this an useful and necessary part, that contained the great moral of the *Iliad*, as may be seen from his selecting it in particular from the rest, in his epistle to *Lollius.*

> *Fabula, qua Paridis propter narratur amorem,*
> *Græcia Barbariæ lento collisa duello,*
> *Stultorum regum & populorum continet æstus.*
> *Antenor censet belli præcidere causam.*
> *Quid Paris? Ut salvus regnet, vivatque beatus,*
> *Cogi posse negat. –*

[The story in which it is told how, because of Paris' love, Greece clashed in tedious war with a foreign land, embraces the passions of foolish kings and peoples. Antenor moves to cut away the cause of the war. What of Paris? To reign in safety and to live in happiness – nothing, he says, can force him.]

441. *The rev'rend* Priam *rose.*] *Priam* rejects the wholsome advice of *Antenor*, and complies with his son. This is indeed extremely natural to the indulgent character and easy nature of the old King, of which the whole *Trojan* war is a proof; but I could wish *Homer* had not just in this place celebrated his wisdom in calling him Θεόφιν μήστωρ ἀτάλαντος [a counsellor equal in wisdom to the gods]. *Spondanus* refers this blindness of *Priam* to the power of fate, the time now approaching when *Troy* was to be punish'd for its injustice. Something like this weak fondness of a father is described in the scripture, in the story of *David* and *Absalom.*

450. *Next let a truce be ask'd.*] The conduct of *Homer* in this place is remarkable: He makes *Priam* propose in council to send to the *Greeks* to ask a truce to bury the dead. This the *Greeks* themselves had before determined to propose: But it being more honourable to his country, the Poet makes the *Trojan* herald prevent any proposition that could be made by the *Greeks.* Thus they are requested to do what they themselves were about to request, and have the honour to comply with a proposal which they themselves would otherwise have taken as a favour.

Eustathius.

455. *Each at his post in arms.*] We have here the manner of the *Trojans* taking their repast: Not promiscuously, but each at his post. *Homer* was sensible that military men ought not to remit their guard, even while they refresh themselves, but in every action display the soldier.

Eustathius.

460. *The speech of* Idæus.] The proposition of restoring the treasures, and not *Helen*, is sent as from *Paris* only; in which his father seems to permit him to treat by himself as a sovereign Prince, and the sole author of the war. But the herald seems to exceed his commission in what he tells the *Greeks. Paris* only offered to restore the treasures he took from *Greece*, not including those he brought from *Sidon* and other coasts, where he touched in his voyage: But *Idæus* here proffers all that he had brought to *Troy.* He adds, as from himself, a wish that *Paris* had perish'd in that voyage. Some ancient expositors suppose those words to be spoken aside, or in a low voice, as it is usual in Dramatic Poetry. But without that *Salvo*, a generous love for the welfare of his country might transport *Idæus* into some warm expressions against the author of its woes. He lays aside the Herald to act the Patriot, and speaks with indignation against *Paris*, that he may influence the *Grecian* captains to give a favourable answer. *Eustathius.*

474. *The* Greeks *gave ear, but none the silence broke.*] This silence of the *Greeks* might naturally proceed from an opinion that however desirous they were to put an end to this long war, *Menelaus* would never consent to relinquish *Helen*, which was the thing insisted upon by *Paris. Eustathius* accounts for it in another manner, and it is from him M. *Dacier* has taken her remark. The Princes (says he) were silent, because it was the part of *Agamemnon* to determine in matters of this nature; and *Agamemnon* is silent, being willing to hear the inclinations of the Princes. By this means he avoided the imputation of exposing the *Greeks* to dangers for his advantage and glory; since he only gave the answer which is put into his mouth by the Princes, with a general applause of the army.

476. *Oh take not,* Greeks! &c.] There is a peculiar decorum in making *Diomed* the author of this advice, to reject even *Helen* herself if she were offer'd; this had not agreed with an amorous husband like *Menelaus*, nor with a cunning politician like *Ulysses*, nor with a wise old man like *Nestor*. But it is proper to *Diomed*, not only as a young fearless warriour, but as he is in particular an enemy to the interests of *Venus*.

507. *And lay'd along the*[ir] *Cars.*] These probably were not Chariots, but Carriages; for *Homer* makes *Nestor* say in v. 332. that this was to be done with Mules and Oxen, which were not commonly join'd to Chariots, and the word κυκλήσομεν there, may be apply'd to any Vehicle that runs on Wheels. Ἅμαξα signifies indifferently *Plaustrum* and *Currus*; and our *English* word *Car* implies either. But if they did use Chariots in bearing their Dead, it is at least evident, that those Chariots were drawn by Mules and Oxen at Funeral Solemnities. *Homer's* using the word ἅμαξα and not δίφρος, confirms this Opinion.

520. *Then, to secure the camp,* &c.] *Homer* has been accus'd of an offence against probability, in causing this fortification to be made so late as in the last year of the war. Mad. *Dacier* answers to this objection, that the *Greeks* had no occasion for it till the departure of *Achilles*: He alone was a greater defence to them; and *Homer* had told the reader in a preceding book, that the *Trojans* never durst venture out of the walls of *Troy* while *Achilles* fought: these Intrenchments therefore serve to raise the glory of his principal hero, since they become necessary as soon as he withdraws his aid. She might have added, that *Achilles* himself says all this, and makes *Homer's* apology in the ninth Book, v. 460. The same author, speaking of this fortification, seems to doubt whether the use of intrenching camps was known in the *Trojan* war, and is rather inclined to think *Homer* borrowed it from what was practised in his own time. But I believe (if we consider the caution with which he has been observed, in some instances already given, to preserve the manners of the age he writes of, in contradistinction to what was practised in his own;) we may reasonably conclude the art of fortification was in use even so long before him, and in the degree of perfection that he here describes it. If it was not, and if *Homer* was fond of describing an improvement in this art made in his own days; nothing could be better contrived than his feigning *Nestor* to be the author of it, whose Wisdom and Experience in War render'd it probable that he might carry his projects farther than the rest of his contemporaries. We have here a fortification as perfect as any in the modern times: A strong wall is thrown up, towers are built upon it from space to space, gates are made to issue out at, and a ditch sunk, deep, wide and long: to all which palisades are added to compleat it.

526. *Meanwhile the Gods.*] The fiction of this wall raised by the *Greeks*, has given no little advantage to *Homer*'s Poem, in furnishing him with an opportunity of changing the scene, and in a great degree the subject and accidents of his battels; so that the following descriptions of war are totally different from all the foregoing. He takes care at the first mention of it to fix in us a great idea of this work, by making the Gods immediately concerned about it. We see *Neptune* jealous lest the glory of his own work, the walls of *Troy*, should be effaced by it; and *Jupiter* comforting him with a prophecy that it shall be totally destroyed in a short time. *Homer* was sensible that as this was a building of his imagination only, and not founded (like many other of his descriptions) upon some antiquities or traditions of the country, so posterity might convict him of a falsity when no remains of any such wall should be seen on the coast. Therefore (as *Aristotle* observes) he has found this way to elude the censure of an improbable fiction: The word of *Jove* was fulfilled, the hands of the Gods, the force of the rivers, and the waves of the sea, demolish'd it. In the twelfth book he digresses from the subject of his poem to describe the execution of this prophecy. The verses there are very noble, and have given the hint to *Milton* for those in which he accounts, after the same poetical manner, for the vanishing of the terrestrial paradise.

>   – *All fountains of the deep*
> *Broke up, shall heave the ocean to usurp*
> *Beyond all bounds, till inundation rise*
> *Above the highest hills: Then shall this mount*
> *Of* Paradise *by might of waves be mov'd*
> *Out of its place, push'd by the horned flood,*
> *With all its verdure spoil'd, and trees adrift,*

> *Down the great river to the opening gulf,*
> *And there take root an island salt and bare,*
> *The Haunt of seals and orcs, and sea-mews clang.*

560. *And now the fleet,* &c.] The verses from hence to the end of the book afford us the knowledge of some points of history and antiquity. As that *Jason* had a Son by *Hypsipyle*, who succeeded his mother in the kingdom of *Lemnos*: That the isle of *Lemnos* was anciently famous for its wines, and drove a traffick in them; and that coined money was not in use in the time of the *Trojan* war, but the trade of countries carried on by exchange in gross, brass, oxen, slaves, &c. I must not forget the particular term used here for Slave, ἀνδράποδον, which is literally the same with our modern word *footman*.

572. *But* Jove *averse,* &c.] The signs by which *Jupiter* here shews his wrath against the *Grecians*, are a prelude to those more open declarations of his anger which follow in the next book, and prepare the mind of the reader for that machine, which might otherwise seem too bold and violent.

THE
EIGHTH BOOK
OF THE
ILIAD

The ARGUMENT

The second Battel, and the Distress of the *Greeks*

Jupiter *assembles a council of the Deities, and threatens them with the pains of* Tartarus *if they assist either side:* Minerva *only obtains of him that she may direct the* Greeks *by her counsels. The armies join battel;* Jupiter *on Mount* Ida *weighs in his balances the fates of both, and affrights the* Greeks *with his thunders and lightnings.* Nestor *alone continues in the field in great danger;* Diomed *relieves him; whose exploits, and those of* Hector, *are excellently described.* Juno *endeavours to animate* Neptune *to the assistance of the* Greeks, *but in vain. The acts of* Teucer, *who is at length wounded by* Hector *and carry'd off.* Juno *and* Minerva *prepare to aid the* Grecians, *but are restrained by* Iris, *sent from* Jupiter. *The night puts an end to the battel.* Hector *keeps the field (the* Greeks *being driven to their fortification before the ships) and gives orders to keep the watch all night in the camp, to prevent the enemy from reimbarking and escaping by flight. They kindle fires through all the field, and pass the night under arms.*

The time *of seven and twenty days is employed from the opening of the Poem to the end of this book. The* scene *here (except of the celestial machines) lies in the field toward the sea-shore.*

Aurora now, fair daughter of the dawn,
Sprinkled with rosy light the dewy lawn,
When *Jove* conven'd the senate of the skies,
Where high *Olympus'* cloudy tops arise.
5   The Sire of Gods his awful silence broke;
The heav'ns attentive trembled as he spoke.
    Celestial states, immortal Gods! give ear,
Hear our decree, and rev'rence what ye hear;
The fix'd decree which not all heav'n can move;
10 Thou Fate! fulfill it; and ye pow'rs! approve!
What God but enters yon' forbidden field,
Who yields assistance, or but wills to yield;
Back to the skies with shame he shall be driv'n,
Gash'd with dishonest wounds, the scorn of heav'n:
15 Or far, oh far from steep *Olympus* thrown,
Low in the dark *Tartarean* gulf shall groan,
With burning chains fix'd to the brazen floors,
And lock'd by hell's inexorable doors;
As deep beneath th' infernal centre hurl'd,
20 As from that centre to th' æthereal world.
Let him who tempts me, dread those dire abodes;
And know, th' almighty is the God of Gods.
League all your forces then, ye pow'rs above,
Join all, and try th' omnipotence of *Jove*:
25 Let down our golden everlasting chain,
Whose strong embrace holds heav'n, and earth, and main:
Strive all, of mortal and immortal birth,
To drag, by this, the Thund'rer down to earth:

Ye strive in vain! If I but stretch this hand,
I heave the Gods, the Ocean, and the Land,
I fix the chain to great *Olympus'* height,   30
And the vast world hangs trembling in my sight!
For such I reign, unbounded and above;
And such are Men, and Gods, compar'd to *Jove*.

    Th' Almighty spoke, nor durst the pow'rs reply,   35
A rev'rend horrour silenc'd all the sky;
Trembling they stood before their sov'reign's look;
At length his best-loved, the pow'r of *Wisdom*, spoke.

    Oh first and greatest! God by Gods ador'd!
We own thy might, our father and our Lord!   40
But ah! permit to pity human state:
If not to help, at least lament their fate.
From fields forbidden we submiss refrain,
With arms unaiding mourn our *Argives* slain;
Yet grant my counsels still their breasts may move,   45
Or all must perish in the wrath of *Jove*.

    The cloud-compelling God her suit approv'd,
And smil'd superior on his best-belov'd.
Then call'd his coursers, and his chariot took;
The stedfast firmament beneath them shook: 50
Rapt by th' æthereal steeds the chariot roll'd;
Brass were their hoofs, their curling manes of gold.
Of heav'ns undrossy gold the God's array
Refulgent, flash'd intolerable day.
High on the throne he shines: His Coursers fly,   55
Between th' extended earth and starry sky.
But when to *Ida*'s topmost height he came,
(Fair nurse of fountains, and of savage game)
Where o'er her pointed summits proudly rais'd,
His fane breath'd odours, and his altar blaz'd: 60
There, from his radiant car, the sacred Sire
Of Gods and men releas'd the steeds of fire:
Blue ambient mists th' immortal steeds embrac'd;
High on the cloudy point his seat he plac'd;
Thence his broad eye the subject world surveys,   65
The town, the tents, and navigable seas.

    Now had the *Grecians* snatch'd a short repaste,
And buckled on their shining arms with haste.

Troy rowz'd as soon; for on this dreadful day
70   The fate of fathers, wives, and infants lay.
The gates unfolding pour forth all their train;
Squadrons on squadrons cloud the dusky plain:
Men, steeds, and chariots shake the trembling ground;
The tumult thickens, and the skies resound.
75   And now with shouts the shocking armies clos'd,
To lances, lances, shields to shields oppos'd,
Host against host with shadowy legions drew,
The sounding darts in iron tempests flew,
Victors and vanquish'd join promiscuous cries,
80   Triumphant shouts and dying groans arise;
With streaming blood the slipp'ry fields are dy'd,
And slaughter'd heroes swell the dreadful tide.
Long as the morning beams encreasing bright,
O'er heav'ns clear azure spread the sacred light;
85   Commutual death the fate of war confounds,
Each adverse battel goar'd with equal wounds.
But when the Sun the height of heav'n ascends;
The Sire of Gods his golden scales suspends,
With equal hand: In these explor'd the fate
90   Of *Greece* and *Troy*, and pois'd the mighty weight.
Press'd with its load, the *Grecian* balance lies
Low sunk on earth, the *Trojan* strikes the skies.
Then *Jove* from *Ida*'s top his horrours spreads;
The clouds burst dreadful o'er the *Grecian* heads;
95   Thick lightnings flash; the mutt'ring thunder rolls;
Their strength he withers, and unmans their souls.
Before his wrath the trembling hosts retire;
The God in terrours, and the skies on fire.
Nor great *Idomeneus* that sight could bear,
100   Nor each stern *Ajax*, thunderbolts of war:
Nor he, the King of Men, th' alarm sustain'd;
Nestor alone amidst the storm remain'd.
Unwilling he remain'd, for *Paris*' dart
Had pierc'd his courser in a mortal part;
105   Fix'd in the forehead where the springing mane
Curl'd o'er the brow, it stung him to the brain:
Mad with his anguish, he begins to rear,
Paw with his hoofs aloft, and lash the air.

Scarce had his faulchion cut the reins, and freed
Th' incumber'd chariot from the dying steed,
When dreadful *Hector*, thund'ring thro' the war, 110
Pour'd to the tumult on his whirling car.
That day had stretch'd beneath his matchless hand
The hoary monarch of the *Pylian* band,
But *Diomed* beheld; from forth the crowd 115
He rush'd, and on *Ulysses* call'd aloud.
 Whither, oh whither does *Ulysses* run?
Oh flight unworthy great *Laërtes'* Son!
Mix'd with the vulgar shall thy fate be found,
Pierc'd in the back, a vile, dishonest wound? 120
Oh turn and save from *Hector*'s direful rage
The glory of the *Greeks*, the *Pylian* sage.
His fruitless words are lost unheard in air;
Ulysses seeks the ships, and shelters there.
But bold *Tydides* to the rescue goes, 125
A single Warriour 'midst a host of foes;
Before the coursers with a sudden spring
He leap'd, and anxious thus bespoke the King.
 Great perils, father! wait th' unequal fight;
These younger champions will oppress thy might. 130
Thy veins no more with ancient vigour glow,
Weak is thy servant, and thy coursers slow.
Then haste, ascend my seat, and from the car
Observe the steeds of *Tros*, renown'd in war,
Practis'd alike to turn, to stop, to chace, 135
To dare the fight, or urge the rapid race;
These late obey'd *Æneas'* guiding rein;
Leave thou thy chariot to our faithful train:
With these against yon' *Trojans* will we go,
Nor shall great *Hector* want an equal foe, 140
Fierce as he is, ev'n he may learn to fear
The thirsty fury of my flying spear.
 Thus said the chief; and *Nestor*, skill'd in war,
Approves his counsel, and ascends the car:
The steeds he left, their trusty servants hold, 145
Eurymedon and *Sthenelus* the bold.
The rev'rend charioteer directs the course,
And strains his aged arm to lash the horse.

Hector they face; unknowing how to fear,
150 Fierce he drove on; *Tydides* whirl'd his spear.
The spear with erring haste mistook its way,
But plung'd in *Eniopeus'* bosom lay.
His opening hand in death forsakes the rein;
The steeds fly back: He falls, and spurns the plain.
155 Great *Hector* sorrows for his servant kill'd,
Yet unreveng'd permits to press the field;
Till to supply his place and rule the car,
Rose *Archeptolemus*, the fierce in war.
And now had death and horrour cover'd all;
160 Like tim'rous flocks the *Trojans* in their wall
Inclos'd had bled: but *Jove* with awful sound
Roll'd the big thunder o'er the vast profound:
Full in *Tydides'* face the light'ning flew;
The ground before him flam'd with sulphur blue;
165 The quiv'ring steeds fell prostrate at the sight;
And *Nestor's* trembling hand confess'd his fright;
He drop'd the reins; and shook with sacred dread,
Thus, turning, warn'd th' intrepid *Diomed*.
      O chief! too daring in thy friend's defence,
170 Retire advis'd, and urge the chariot hence.
This day, averse, the sov'reign of the skies
Assists great *Hector*, and our palm denies.
Some other sun may see the happier hour,
When *Greece* shall conquer by his heav'nly pow'r.
175 'Tis not in man his fix'd decree to move:
The great will glory to submit to *Jove*.
      O rev'rend Prince! (*Tydides* thus replies)
Thy years are awful, and thy words are wise.
But ah! what grief? should haughty *Hector* boast,
180 I fled inglorious to the guarded coast.
Before that dire disgrace shall blast my fame,
O'erwhelm me, earth! and hide a warriour's shame.
To whom *Gerenian Nestor* thus reply'd:
Gods! can thy courage fear the *Phrygian's* pride?
185 *Hector* may vaunt, but who shall heed the boast? ⎫
Not those who felt thy arm, the *Dardan* host, ⎬
Nor *Troy*, yet bleeding in her heroes lost;   ⎭

Not ev'n a *Phrygian* dame, who dreads the sword
Thay lay'd in dust her lov'd, lamented lord.
He said, and hasty, o'er the gasping throng   190
Drives the swift steeds; the chariot smoaks along.
The shouts of *Trojans* thicken in the wind;
The storm of hissing javelins pours behind.
Then with a voice that shakes the solid skies,
Pleas'd *Hector* braves the warriour as he flies.   195
Go, mighty hero! grac'd above the rest
In seats of council and the sumptuous feast:
Now hope no more those honours from thy train;
Go, less than woman, in the form of man!
To scale our walls, to wrap our tow'rs in flames,   200
To lead in exile the fair *Phrygian* dames,
Thy once proud hopes, presumptuous Prince! are fled;
This arm shall reach thy heart, and stretch thee dead.

　　Now fears dissuade him, and now hopes invite,
To stop his coursers, and to stand the fight;   205
Thrice turn'd the chief, and thrice imperial *Jove*
On *Ida*'s summits thunder'd from above.
Great *Hector* heard; he saw the flashing light,
(The sign of conquest) and thus urg'd the fight.

　　Hear ev'ry *Trojan*, *Lycian*, *Dardan* band,   210
All fam'd in war, and dreadful hand to hand.
Be mindful of the wreaths your arms have won,
Your great forefathers glories, and your own.
Heard ye the voice of *Jove*? Success and fame
Await on *Troy*, on *Greece* eternal shame.   215
In vain they skulk behind their boasted wall,
Weak bulwarks! destin'd by this arm to fall.
High o'er their slighted trench our steeds shall bound,
And pass victorious o'er the levell'd mound.
Soon as before yon' hollow ships we stand,   220
Fight each with flames, and toss the blazing brand;
Till their proud navy wrapt in smoke and fires,
All *Greece*, encompass'd, in one blaze expires.

　　Furious he said; then bending o'er the yoke,
Encourag'd his proud steeds, while thus he spoke.   225
Now *Xanthus*, *Æthon*, *Lampus*! urge the chace,
And thou, *Podargus*! prove thy gen'rous race:

Be fleet, be fearless, this important day,
And all your master's well-spent care repay.
230 For this, high fed in plenteous stalls ye stand,
Serv'd with pure wheat, and by a Princess' hand;
For this my spouse of great *Aëtion*'s line
So oft' has steep'd the strength'ning grain in wine.
Now swift pursue, now thunder uncontroll'd;
235 Give me to seize rich *Nestor*'s shield of gold;
From *Tydeus*' shoulders strip the costly load,
Vulcanian arms, the labour of a God:
These if we gain, then Victory, ye pow'rs!
This night, this glorious night, the fleet is ours.
240   That heard, deep anguish stung *Saturnia*'s soul;
She shook her throne that shook the starry pole:
And thus to *Neptune*: Thou! whose force can make
The stedfast earth from her foundations shake,
See'st thou the *Greeks* by fates unjust opprest,
245 Nor swells thy heart in that immortal breast?
Yet *Ægæ*, *Helicè*, thy pow'r obey,
And gifts unceasing on thine altars lay.
Would all the Deities of *Greece* combine,
In vain the gloomy Thund'rer might repine:
250 Sole should he sit, with scarce a God to friend,
And see his *Trojans* to the shades descend:
Such be the scene from his *Idæan* bow'r;
Ungrateful prospect to the sullen pow'r!
    Neptune with wrath rejects the rash design:
255 What rage, what madness, furious Queen! is thine?
I war not with the Highest. All above
Submit and tremble at the hand of *Jove*.
    Now Godlike *Hector*, to whose matchless might
Jove gave the glory of the destin'd fight,
260 Squadrons on squadrons drives, and fills the fields
With close-rang'd chariots, and with thicken'd shields.
Where the deep trench in length extended lay,
Compacted troops stand wedg'd in firm array,
A dreadful front! they shake the brands, and threat
265 With long-destroying flames the hostile fleet.
The King of Men, by *Juno*'s self inspir'd,
Toil'd thro' the tents, and all his army fir'd,

Swift as he mov'd, he lifted in his hand
His purple robe, bright ensign of command.
High on the midmost bark the King appear'd;   270
There, from *Ulysses'* deck, his voice was heard.
To *Ajax* and *Achilles* reach'd the sound,
Whose distant ships the guarded navy bound.
Oh *Argives!* shame of human race; he cry'd,
(The hollow vessels to his voice reply'd)   275
Where now are all your glorious Boasts of yore,
Your hasty triumphs on the *Lemnian* shore?
Each fearless hero dares an hundred foes,
While the feast lasts, and while the goblet flows;
But who to meet one martial man is found,   280
When the fight rages, and the flames surround?
Oh mighty *Jove!* oh sire of the distress'd!
Was ever King like me, like me oppress'd?
With pow'r immense, with justice arm'd in vain;
My glory ravish'd, and my people slain!   285
To thee my vows were breath'd from ev'ry shore;
What altar smoak'd not with our victims gore?
With fat of bulls I fed the constant flame,
And ask'd destruction to the *Trojan* name.
Now, gracious God! far humbler our demand;   290
Give these at least to 'scape from *Hector*'s hand,
And save the reliques of the *Grecian* land!
      Thus pray'd the King, and heav'ns great Father heard
His Vows, in bitterness of soul preferr'd;
The wrath appeas'd, by happy signs declares,   295
And gives the people to their monarch's pray'rs.
His eagle, sacred bird of heav'n! he sent,
A fawn his talons truss'd (divine portent)
High o'er the wond'ring hosts he soar'd above,
Who paid their vows to *Panomphæan Jove*;   300
Then let the prey before his altar fall;
The *Greeks* beheld, and transport seiz'd on all:
Encourag'd by the sign, the troops revive,
And fierce on *Troy* with doubled fury drive.
Tydides first, of all the *Grecian* force,   305
O'er the broad ditch impell'd his foaming horse,

Pierc'd the deep ranks, their strongest battel tore,
And dy'd his jav'lin red with *Trojan* gore.
Young *Ageläus* (*Phradmon* was his sire)
310 With flying coursers shun'd his dreadful ire:
Strook thro' the back, the *Phrygian* fell opprest;
The dart drove on, and issu'd at his breast:
Headlong he quits the car; his arms resound;
His pond'rous buckler thunders on the ground.
315 Forth rush a tide of *Greeks*, the passage freed;
Th' *Atridæ* first, th' *Ajaces* next succeed:
Meriones, like *Mars* in arms renown'd,
And Godlike *Idomen*, now pass'd the mound;
Euæmon's son next issues to the foe,
320 And last, young *Teucer* with his bended bow.
Secure behind the *Telamonian* shield
The skilful archer wide survey'd the field,
With ev'ry shaft some hostile victim slew,
Then close beneath the seven-fold orb withdrew.
325 The conscious Infant so, when Fear alarms,
Retires for safety to the mother's arms.
Thus *Ajax* guards his brother in the field,
Moves as he moves, and turns the shining shield.
Who first by *Teucer*'s mortal arrows bled?
330 *Orsilochus*; then fell *Ormenus* dead:
The god-like *Lycophon* next press'd the plain,
With *Chromius*, *Dætor*, *Ophelestes* slain:
Bold *Hamopäon* breathless sunk to ground;
The bloody pile great *Melanippus* crown'd.
335 Heaps fell on heaps, sad trophies of his art,
A *Trojan* ghost attending ev'ry dart.
Great *Agamemnon* views with joyful eye
The ranks grow thinner as his arrows fly:
Oh youth for ever dear! (the monarch cry'd)
340 Thus, always thus, thy early worth be try'd;
Thy brave example shall retrieve our host,
Thy country's saviour, and thy father's boast!
Sprung from an alien's bed thy sire to grace,
The vig'rous offspring of a stol'n embrace,
345 Proud of his boy, he own'd the gen'rous flame,
And the brave son repays his cares with fame.

Now hear a monarch's vow: If heav'ns high pow'rs
Give me to raze *Troy*'s long defended tow'rs;
Whatever treasures *Greece* for me design,
The next rich honorary gift be thine: 350
Some golden tripod, or distinguish'd car,
With coursers dreadful in the ranks of war,
Or some fair captive whom thy eyes approve,
Shall recompence the warriour's toils with love.

　　To this the chief: With praise the rest inspire,   355
Nor urge a soul already fill'd with fire.
What strength I have, be now in battel try'd,
Till ev'ry shaft in *Phrygian* blood be dy'd.
Since rallying from our wall we forc'd the foe,
Still aim'd at *Hector* have I bent my bow;   360
Eight forky arrows from this hand have fled,
And eight bold heroes by their points lie dead:
But sure some God denies me to destroy
This fury of the field, this dog of *Troy*.

　　He said, and twang'd the string. The weapon flies   365
At *Hector*'s breast, and sings along the skies:
He miss'd the mark; but pierc'd *Gorgythio*'s heart,
And drench'd in royal blood the thirsty dart.
(Fair *Castianira*, nymph of form divine,
This offspring added to King *Priam*'s line)   370
As full-blown poppies overcharg'd with rain
Decline the head, and drooping kiss the plain;
So sinks the youth: his beauteous head, depress'd
Beneath his helmet, drops upon his breast.
Another shaft the raging archer drew: 375
That other shaft with erring fury flew,
(From *Hector Phœbus* turn'd the flying wound)
Yet fell not dry or guiltless to the ground:
Thy breast, brave *Archeptolemus!* it tore,
And dipp'd its feathers in no vulgar gore.   380
Headlong he falls: his sudden fall alarms
The steeds that startle at his sounding arms.
Hector with grief his charioteer beheld,
All pale and breathless on the sanguin field.
Then bids *Cebriones* direct the rein,   385
Quits his bright car, and issues on the plain.

Dreadful he shouts: from earth a stone he took,
And rush'd on *Teucer* with the lifted rock.
The youth already strain'd the forceful yew;
390   The shaft already to his shoulder drew;
The feather in his hand, just wing'd for flight,
Touch'd where the neck and hollow chest unite:
There, where the juncture knits the channel bone,
The furious chief discharg'd the craggy stone:
395   The bowstring burst beneath the pondrous blow,
And his numb'd hand dismiss'd his useless bow.
He fell: But *Ajax* his broad shield display'd,
And screen'd his brother with a mighty shade;
Till great *Alastor*, and *Mecistheus*, bore
400   The batter'd archer groaning to the shore.

Troy yet found grace before th' *Olympian* Sire,
He arm'd their hands, and fill'd their breasts with fire.
The *Greeks*, repuls'd, retreat behind their wall,
Or in the trench on heaps confus'dly fall.
405   First of the foe great *Hector* march'd along,
With terrour cloath'd, and more than mortal strong.
As the bold hound that gives the lion chace,
With beating bosom, and with eager pace,
Hangs on his haunch, or fastens on his heels,
410   Guards as he turns, and circles as he wheels:
Thus oft' the *Grecians* turn'd, but still they flew;
Thus following *Hector* still the hindmost slew.
When flying they had pass'd the trench profound,
And many a chief lay gasping on the ground;
415   Before the ships a desp'rate stand they made,
And fir'd the troops, and call'd the Gods to aid.
Fierce on his ratt'ling chariot *Hector* came;
His eyes like *Gorgon* shot a sanguin flame
That wither'd all their host; Like *Mars* he stood,
420   Dire as the monster, dreadful as the God!
Their strong distress the wife of *Jove* survey'd;
Then pensive thus, to War's triumphant maid.

Oh daughter of that God, whose Arm can wield
Th' avenging bolt, and shake the sable shield!
425   Now, in this moment of her last despair,
Shall wretched *Greece* no more confess our care,

Condemn'd to suffer the full force of fate,
And drain the dregs of heav'ns relentless hate?
Gods! shall one raging hand thus level all?
What numbers fell! what numbers yet shall fall!   430
What pow'r divine shall *Hector*'s wrath assuage?
Still swells the slaughter, and still grows the rage!

  So spoke th' imperial regent of the skies;
To whom the Goddess with the azure eyes:
Long since had *Hector* stain'd these fields with gore,   435
Stretch'd by some *Argive* on his native shore;
But He above, the Sire of heav'n withstands,
Mocks our attempts, and slights our just demands.
The stubborn God, inflexible and hard,
Forgets my service and deserv'd reward: 440
Sav'd I, for this, his fav'rite *son distress'd,
By stern *Eurystheus* with long labours press'd?
He begg'd, with tears he begg'd, in deep dismay;
I shot from heav'n, and gave his arm the day.
Oh had my wisdom known this dire event,   445
When to grim *Pluto*'s gloomy gates he went;
The triple dog had never felt his chain,
Nor *Styx* been cross'd, nor hell explor'd in vain.
Averse to me of all his heav'n of Gods,
At *Thetis*' suit the partial thund'rer nods.   450
To grace her gloomy, fierce, resenting son,
My hopes are frustrate, and my *Greeks* undone.
Some future day, perhaps he may be mov'd
To call his blue-ey'd maid his best-belov'd.
Haste, launch thy chariot, thro' yon' ranks to ride;   455
My self will arm, and thunder at thy side.
Then Goddess! say, shall *Hector* glory then,
(That terrour of the *Greeks*, that Man of men)
When *Juno*'s self, and *Pallas* shall appear,
All dreadful in the crimson walks of war?   460
What mighty *Trojan* then, on yonder shore, }
Expiring, pale, and terrible no more,
Shall feast the fowls, and glut the dogs with gore?

*Hercules.

She ceas'd, and *Juno* rein'd the Steeds with Care;
465 (Heav'ns awful empress, *Saturn*'s other heir)
Pallas, meanwhile, her various veil unbound,
With flow'rs adorn'd, with art immortal crown'd;
The radiant robe her sacred fingers wove
Floats in rich waves, and spreads the court of *Jove*.
470 Her father's arms her mighty limbs invest,
His cuirass blazes on her ample breast.
The vig'rous pow'r the trembling car ascends;
Shook by her arm, the massy jav'lin bends;
Huge, pond'rous, strong! that when her fury burns,
475 Proud tyrants humbles, and whole hosts o'erturns.
Saturnia lends the lash; the coursers fly;
Smooth glides the chariot thro' the liquid sky.
Heav'n gates spontaneous open to the pow'rs,
Heav'ns golden gates, kept by the winged *Hours*,
480 Commission'd in alternate watch they stand,
The Sun's bright portals and the skies command;
Close, or unfold, th' eternal gates of day,
Bar heav'n with clouds, or roll those clouds away.
The sounding hinges ring, the clouds divide;
485 Prone down the steep of heav'n their course they guide.
But *Jove* incens'd from *Ida*'s top survey'd,
And thus enjoin'd the many-colour'd Maid.
Thaumantia! mount the winds, and stop their car;
Against the Highest who shall wage the war?
490 If furious yet they dare the vain debate,
Thus have I spoke, and what I spake is Fate.
Their coursers crush'd beneath the wheels shall lie,
Their car in fragments scatter'd o'er the sky;
My light'ning these rebellious shall confound,
495 And hurl them flaming, headlong to the ground,
Condemn'd for ten revolving years to weep
The wounds impress'd by burning thunder deep.
So shall *Minerva* learn to fear our ire,
Nor dare to combate her's and natures Sire.
500 For *Juno*, headstrong and imperious still,
She claims some title to transgress our will.
Swift as the wind, the various-colour'd Maid
From *Ida*'s top her golden wings display'd;

To great *Olympus'* shining gates she flies,
There meets the chariot rushing down the skies,
Restrains their progress from the bright abodes,
And speaks the mandate of the Sire of Gods.

    What frenzy, Goddesses! what rage can move
Celestial minds to tempt the wrath of *Jove?*
Desist, obedient to his high command;
This is his word; and know his word shall stand.
His light'ning your rebellion shall confound,
And hurl ye headlong, flaming to the ground:
Your horses crush'd beneath the wheels shall lie,
Your car in fragments scatter'd o'er the sky;
Your selves condemn'd ten rolling years to weep
The wounds impress'd by burning thunder deep.
So shall *Minerva* learn to fear his ire,
Nor dare to combate her's and nature's Sire.
For *Juno*, headstrong and imperious still,
She claims some title to transgress his will:
But thee what desp'rate insolence has driv'n,
To lift thy lance against the King of heav'n?

    Then mounting on the pinions of the wind,
She flew; and *Juno* thus her rage resign'd.

    O daughter of that God, whose arm can wield
Th' avenging bolt, and shake the dreadful shield!
No more let beings of superiour birth
Contend with *Jove* for this low race of earth:
Triumphant now, now miserably slain,
They breathe or perish, as the fates ordain.
But *Jove's* high counsels full effect shall find,
And ever constant, ever rule mankind.

    She spoke, and backward turn'd her steeds of light,
Adorn'd with manes of gold, and heav'nly bright.
The *Hours* unloos'd them, panting as they stood,
And heap'd their mangers with ambrosial food.
There ty'd, they rest in high celestial stalls;
The chariot propt against the crystal walls.
The pensive Goddesses, abash'd, controul'd,
Mix with the Gods, and fill their seats of gold.

    And now the Thund'rer meditates his flight
From *Ida's* summits to th' *Olympian* height.

505

510

515

520

525

530

535

540

Swifter than thought the wheels instinctive fly,
545 Flame thro' the vast of air, and reach the sky.
'Twas *Neptune*'s charge his coursers to unbrace,
And fix the car on its immortal base;
There stood the chariot beaming forth its rays,
Till with a snowy veil he screen'd the blaze.

550 He, whose all–conscious eyes the world behold,
Th' eternal Thunderer, sate thron'd in gold.
High heav'n the footstool of his feet he makes,
And wide beneath him, all *Olympus* shakes.
Trembling afar th' offending pow'rs appear'd,
555 Confus'd and silent, for his frown they fear'd.
He saw their soul, and thus his word imparts;
Pallas and *Juno!* say, why heave your hearts?
Soon was your battel o'er: Proud *Troy* retir'd
Before your face, and in your wrath expir'd.

560 But know, whoe'er almighty pow'r withstand!
Unmatch'd our force, unconquer'd is our hand:
Who shall the sov'reign of the skies controul?
Not all the Gods that crown the starry pole.
Your hearts shall tremble, if our arms we take,
565 And each immortal nerve with horrour shake.
For thus I speak, and what I speak shall stand;
What pow'r soe'er provokes our lifted hand,
On this our hill no more shall hold his place,
Cut off, and exil'd from th' æthereal race.

570 *Juno* and *Pallas* grieving hear the doom,
But feast their souls on *Ilion*'s woes to come.
Tho' secret anger swell'd *Minerva*'s breast,
The prudent Goddess yet her wrath represt:
But *Juno*, impotent of rage, replies.

575 What hast thou said, Oh tyrant of the skies!
Strength and Omnipotence invest thy throne;
'Tis thine to punish; ours to grieve alone.
For *Greece* we grieve, abandon'd by her fate
To drink the dregs of thy unmeasur'd hate:
580 From fields forbidden we submiss refrain,
With arms unaiding see our *Argives* slain;
Yet grant our counsels still their breasts may move,
Lest all should perish in the rage of *Jove*.

The Goddess thus: and thus the God replies
Who swells the clouds, and blackens all the skies.   585
The morning sun, awak'd by loud alarms,
Shall see th' Almighty Thunderer in arms.
What heaps of *Argives* then shall load the plain,
Those radiant eyes shall view, and view in vain.
Nor shall great *Hector* cease the rage of fight,   590
The navy flaming, and thy *Greeks* in flight,
Ev'n till the day, when certain fates ordain
That stern *Achilles* (his *Patroclus* slain)
Shall rise in vengeance, and lay waste the plain.
For such is Fate, nor can'st thou turn its course   595
With all thy rage, with all thy rebel force.
Fly, if thou wilt, to earth's remotest bound,
Where on her utmost verge the seas resound;
Where curs'd *Iäpetus* and *Saturn* dwell,
Fast by the brink, within the steams of hell;   600
No Sun e'er gilds the gloomy horrours there,
No chearful gales refresh the lazy air;
There arm once more the bold *Titanian* band;
And arm in vain: For what I will, shall stand.

Now deep in Ocean sunk the lamp of light,   605
And drew behind the cloudy veil of night:
The conqu'ring *Trojans* mourn his beams decay'd;
The *Greeks* rejoicing bless the friendly shade.

The victors keep the field; and *Hector* calls
A martial council near the navy-walls: 610
These to *Scamander*'s bank apart he led,
Where thinly scatter'd lay the heaps of dead.
Th' assembled chiefs, descending on the ground,
Attend his order, and their Prince surround.
A massy spear he bore of mighty strength,   615
Of full ten cubits was the lance's length;
The point was brass, refulgent to behold,
Fix'd to the wood with circling rings of gold:
The noble *Hector* on this lance reclin'd,
And bending forward, thus reveal'd his mind.   620
Ye valiant *Trojans*, with attention hear!
Ye *Dardan* bands, and gen'rous Aids give ear!

This Day, we hop'd, would wrap in conq'ring flame
Greece with her ships, and crown our toils with fame:
625 But darkness now, to save the cowards, falls,
And guards them trembling in their wooden walls.
Obey the Night, and use her peaceful hours
Our steeds to forage, and refresh our pow'rs.
Strait from the town be sheep and oxen sought,
630 And strength'ning bread, and gen'rous wine be brought.
Wide o'er the field, high-blazing to the sky,
Let num'rous fires the absent sun supply,
The flaming piles with plenteous fuel raise,
Till the bright morn her purple beam displays:
635 Left in the silence and the shades of night,
Greece on her sable ships attempt her flight.
Not unmolested let the wretches gain
Their lofty decks, or safely cleave the main;
Some hostile wound let ev'ry dart bestow,
640 Some lasting token of the *Phrygian* foe,
Wounds, that long hence may ask their spouses' care,
And warn their children from a *Trojan* war.
Now thro' the circuit of our *Ilian* wall,
Let sacred heralds sound the solemn call;
645 To bid the Sires with hoary honours crown'd,
And beardless youths, our battlements surround.
Firm be the guard, while distant lie our pow'rs,
And let the matrons hang with lights the tow'rs:
Lest under covert of the midnight shade,
650 Th' insidious foe the naked town invade.
Suffice, to-night, these orders to obey;
A nobler charge shall rouze the dawning day.
The Gods, I trust, shall give to *Hector*'s hand,
From these detested foes to free the land,
655 Who plow'd, with fates averse, the wat'ry way;
For *Trojan* vultures a predestin'd prey.
Our common safety must be now the care;
But soon as morning paints the fields of air,
Sheath'd in bright arms let ev'ry troop engage,
660 And the fir'd fleet behold the battel rage.
Then, then shall *Hector* and *Tydides* prove,
Whose fates are heaviest in the scale of *Jove*.

Tomorrow's light (oh haste the glorious morn!)
Shall see his bloody spoils in triumph born,
With this keen jav'lin shall his breast be gor'd,   665
And prostrate heroes bleed around their lord.
Certain as this, oh! might my days endure,
From age inglorious and black death secure;
So might my life and glory know no bound,
Like *Pallas* worship'd, like the sun renown'd!   670
As the next dawn, the last they shall enjoy,
Shall crush the *Greeks*, and end the woes of *Troy*.

    The leader spoke. From all his hosts around
Shouts of applause along the shores resound.
Each from the yoke the smoking steeds unty'd,   675
And fix'd their headstalls to his chariot-side.
Fat sheep and oxen from the town are led,
With gen'rous wine, and all-sustaining bread.
Full hecatombs lay burning on the shore;
The winds to heav'n the curling vapours bore.   680
Ungrateful off'ring to th' immortal pow'rs,
Whose wrath hung heavy o'er the *Trojan* tow'rs;
Nor *Priam* nor his sons obtain'd their grace;
Proud *Troy* they hated, and her guilty race.

    The Troops exulting sate in order round,   685
And beaming fires illumin'd all the ground.
As when the Moon, refulgent lamp of night!
O'er heav'ns clear azure spreads her sacred light,
When not a breath disturbs the deep serene,
And not a cloud o'ercasts the solemn scene;   690
Around her throne the vivid planets roll,
And stars unnumber'd gild the glowing pole,
O'er the dark trees a yellower verdure shed,
And tip with silver ev'ry mountain's head;
Then shine the vales, the rocks in prospect rise,   695
A flood of glory bursts from all the skies:
The conscious swains, rejoicing in the sight,
Eye the blue vault, and bless the useful light.
So many flames before proud *Ilion* blaze,
And lighten glimm'ring *Xanthus* with their rays.   700
The long reflections of the distant fires
Gleam on the walls, and tremble on the spires.

A thousand piles the dusky horrours gild,
And shoot a shady lustre o'er the field.
705 Full fifty guards each flaming pile attend,
Whose umber'd arms, by fits, thick flashes send.
Loud neigh the coursers o'er their heaps of corn,
And ardent warriours wait the rising morn.

OBSERVATIONS

ON THE

EIGHTH BOOK

Homer, like most of the *Greeks*, is thought to have travelled into *Ægypt*, and brought from the priests there, not only their learning, but their manner of conveying it in fables and hieroglyphicks. This is necessary to be considered by those who would thoroughly penetrate into the beauty and design of many parts of this author: For whoever reflects that this was the mode of learning in those times, will make no doubt but there are several mysteries both of natural and moral philosophy involv'd in his fictions, which otherwise in the literal meaning appear too trivial or irrational; and it is but just, when these are not plain or immediately intelligible, to imagine that something of this kind may be hid under them. Nevertheless, as *Homer* travelled not with a direct view of writing philosophy or theology, so he might often use these hieroglyphical fables and traditions as embellishments of his poetry only, without taking the pains to open their mystical meaning to his readers, and perhaps without diving very deeply into it himself.

16. *Low in the dark Tartarean Gulf*, &c.] This opinion of *Tartarus*, the place of torture for the impious after death, might be taken from the *Ægyptians*: for it seems not improbable, as some writers have observed, that some tradition might then be spread in the Eastern parts of the world, of the fall of the angels, the punishment of the damned, and other sacred truths which were afterwards more fully explained and taught by the Prophets and Apostles. These *Homer* seems to allude to in this and other passages; as where *Vulcan* is said to be precipitated from heaven in the first book, where *Jupiter* threatens *Mars* with *Tartarus* in the fifth, and where the Dæmon of Discord is cast out of heaven in the nineteenth. *Virgil* has translated a part of these lines in the sixth *Æneid*.

> *– Tum Tartarus ipse*
> *Bis patet in præceps tantum, tenditque sub umbras,*
> *Quantus ad æthereum cœli suspectus Olympum.*

> [The gaping gulph, low to the centre lies;
> And twice as deep as earth is distant from the skies.]

And *Milton* in his first book,

> *As far remov'd from God and light of heav'n,*
> *As from the centre thrice to th' utmost pole.*

It may not be unpleasing just to observe the gradation in these three great Poets, as if they had vied with each other, in extending this idea of the depth of hell. *Homer* says as far, *Virgil* twice as far, *Milton* thrice.

25. *Let down our golden everlasting chain.*] The various opinions of the ancients concerning this passage are collected by *Eustathius. Jupiter* says, *If he holds this chain of gold, the force of all the Gods is unable to draw him down, but he can draw up them, the seas, and the earth, and cause the whole universe to hang unactive.* Some think that *Jupiter* signifies the *Æther*, the golden chain the *Sun*: If the *Æther* did not temper the rays of the sun as they pass thro' it, his beams would not only drink up and exhale the Ocean in vapours, but also exhale the moisture from the veins of the earth, which is the cement that holds it together: by which means the whole creation would become unactive, and all its powers suspended.

Others affirm, that by this golden chain may be meant the days of the world's duration, ἡμέρας αἰῶνας, which are as it were painted by the lustre of the sun, and follow one another in a successive chain till they arrive at their final period: While *Jupiter* or the *Æther* (which the ancients called the soul of all things) still remains unchanged.

Plato in his *Theætetus* says that by this golden chain is meant the sun, whose rays enliven all nature and cement the parts of the universe.

The *Stoicks* will have it, that by *Jupiter* is implied destiny, which over-rules every thing both upon and above the earth.

Others (delighted with their own conceits) imagine that *Homer* intended to represent the excellence of monarchy; that the sceptre ought to be sway'd by one hand, and that all the wheels of government should be put in motion by one person.

But I fancy a much better interpretation may be found for this, if we allow (as there is great reason to believe) that the *Ægyptians* understood the true system of the world, and that *Pythagoras* first learn'd it from them. They held that the planets were kept in their orbits by gravitation upon the sun, which was therefore called *Jovis carcer* [the prison of *Jove*]; and sometimes by the sun (as *Macrobius* informs us) is meant *Jupiter* himself: We see too that the most prevailing opinion of antiquity fixes it to the *sun*; so that I think it will be no strained interpretation to say, that by the inability of the Gods to pull *Jupiter* out of his place with this *Catena* [chain], may be understood the superior attractive force of the sun, whereby he continues unmoved, and draws all the rest of the planets toward him.

35. *Th' Almighty spoke.*] *Homer* in this whole passage plainly shews his belief of one supreme, omnipotent God, whom he introduces with a majesty and superiority worthy the great ruler of the universe. Accordingly *Justin Martyr* cites it as a proof of our Author's attributing the power and government of all things to one first God, whose divinity is so far superiour to all other Deities, that if compared to him they may be rank'd among mortals. *Admon. ad gentes.* Upon this account, and with the authority of that learned father, I have ventur'd to apply to *Jupiter* in this place such appellatives as are suitable to the supreme Deity: a practice I would be cautious of using in many other passages where the notions and descriptions of our Author must be own'd to be unworthy of the divinity.

39. *O first and greatest!* &c.] *Homer* is not only to be admir'd for keeping up the characters of his Heroes, but for adapting his speeches to the characters of his Gods. Had *Juno* here given the reply, she would have begun with some mark of resentment, but *Pallas* is all submission; *Juno* would probably have contradicted him, but *Pallas* only begs leave to be sorry for those whom she must not assist; *Juno* would have spoken with the prerogative of a wife, but *Pallas* makes her address with the obsequiousness of a prudent daughter.

Eustathius.

69. *For on this dreadful day The fate of fathers, wives, and infants lay.*] It may be necessary to explain why the *Trojans* thought themselves obliged to fight in order to defend their wives and children. One would think they might have kept within their walls; the *Grecians* made no attempt to batter them, neither were they invested; and the country was open on all sides except towards the sea, to give them provisions. The most natural thought is, that they and their auxiliaries being very numerous, could not subsist but from a large country about them; and perhaps not without the sea, and the rivers, where the *Greeks* encamp'd: That in time the *Greeks* would have surrounded them, and blocked up every avenue to their town: That they thought themselves obliged to defend the country with all the inhabitants of it, and that indeed at first this was rather a war between two nations, and became not properly a siege till afterwards.

71. *The gates unfolding*, &c.] There is a wonderful sublimity in these lines; one sees in the description the gates of a warlike city thrown open, and an army pouring forth; and hears the trampling of men and horses rushing to the battel.

These verses are, as *Eustathius* observes, only a repetition of a former passage, which shews that the Poet was particularly pleased with them, and that he was not ashamed of a repetition when he could not express the same image more happily than he had already done.

84. *The sacred light.*] *Homer* describing the advance of the day from morning till noon, calls it ἱερὸν, or sacred, says *Eustathius*, who gives this reason for it, because that part of the day was allotted to sacrifice and religious worship.

88. *The Sire of Gods his golden scales suspends.*] This figure representing God as weighing the destinies of men in his balances, was first made use of in holy writ. In the book of *Job*, which is acknowledged to be one of the most ancient of the scriptures, he prays to be *weighed in an even balance, that God may know his integrity. Daniel* declares from God to *Belshazzar, thou art weighed in the balances, and found light.* And *Proverbs*, ch. 16. v. 11. *A just weight and balance are the Lord's.* Our Author has it again in the twenty second *Iliad*, and it appear'd so beautiful to succeeding Poets, that *Æschylus* (as we are told by *Plutarch de aud. Poetis*) writ a whole tragedy upon this foundation, which he called *Psychostasia*, or the *weighing of souls*. In this he introduced *Thetis* and *Aurora* standing on either side of *Jupiter*'s scales, and praying each for her son while the heroes fought.

> Καὶ τότε δὴ χρύσεια πατὴρ ἐτίταινε τάλαντα,
> Ἐν δ' ἐτίθει δύο κῆρε τανηλεγέος θανάτοιο,
> Ἕλκε δὲ μέσσα λαβών· ῥέπε δ' Ἕκτορος αἴσιμον ἦμαρ.

[*Jove* lifts the golden balances, that show
  The fates of mortal men, and things below:
  Here each contending hero's lot he tries,
  And weighs, with equal hand, their destinies.
  Low sinks the scale surcharg'd with *Hector*'s fate;
  Heavy with death it sinks, and hell receives the weight.]

It has been copied by *Virgil* in the last *Æneid* [725–7].

> *Jupiter ipse duas æquato examine lances*
> *Sustinet, & fata imponit diversa duorum:*
> *Quem damnet labor, & quo vergat pondere lethum.*

[*Jove* sets the beam; in either scale he lays
  The champions fate, and each exactly weighs.
  On this side life, and lucky chance ascends:
  Loaded with death, that other scale descends.]

I cannot agree with Madam *Dacier* that these verses are inferior to *Homer*'s; but *Macrobius* observes with some colour, that the application of them is not so just as in our author; for *Virgil* had made *Juno* say before, that *Turnus* would certainly perish. [XII. 149–51].

> *Nunc juvenem imparibus video concurrere fatis,*
> *Parcarumque dies & vis inimica propinquat.*

[But now he struggles with unequal fate;
  And goes with Gods averse, o'ermatch'd in might,
  To meet th' inevitable death in fight.]

So that there was less reason for weighing his fate with that of *Æneas* after that declaration. *Scaliger* trifles miserably, when he says *Juno* might have learned this from the fates, tho' *Jupiter* did not know it, before he consulted them by weighing the scales. But *Macrobius*'s excuse in behalf of *Virgil* is much better worth regard: I shall transcribe it entire, as it is perhaps the finest period in all that author. *Hæc & alia ignoscenda Virgilio, qui studii circa Homerum nimietate excedit modum. Et revera non poterat non in aliquibus minor videri, qui per omnem poësim suam hoc uno est præcipue usus Archetypo. Acriter enim in Homerum oculos intendit, ut æmularetur ejus non modo magnitudinem sed & simplicitatem, & præsentiam orationis, & tacitam majestatem. Hinc diversarum inter Heroas suos personarum varia magnificatio, hinc Deorum interpositio, hinc autoritas fabulosa, hinc affectuum naturalium expressio,*

hinc monumentorum persecutio, hinc parabolarum exaggeratio, hinc torren-
tis orationis sonitus, hinc rerum singularum cum splendore fastigium.
[These things and others should be pardoned in Virgil, who trans-
gresses the mean through an excess of zeal in his admiration of Homer.
And, in fact, he could not but have seemed the lesser in some matters,
since throughout his own poem he made use, principally, of this one
original. For he kept his eyes ardently fixed upon Homer so that he
might emulate not only his greatness, but also his simplicity, the effect
of his style, and his quiet grandeur. From Homer he derives that
many-sided ennobling of diverse persons among his heroes, from him,
the intervention of the gods; from him, the ancient and fabled
example and the expression of emotions drawn from nature; the
fondness for antiquities, the heaping of similes; from him, the sound
of vehement eloquence; from him, the ability to depict particulars with
both brilliance and dignity.] Sat. *l.* 5. c. 13.

As to the ascent or descent of the scales, *Eustathius* explains it in
this manner. The descent of the scale toward earth signifies unhappi-
ness and death, the earth being the place of misfortune and mortality;
the Mounting of it signifies prosperity and life, the superior regions
being the seats of felicity and immortality.

Milton has admirably improved upon this fine fiction, and with an
alteration agreeable to a Christian Poet. He feigns that the Almighty
weighed *Satan* in such scales, but judiciously makes this difference,
that the mounting of his scale denoted ill success; whereas the same
circumstance in *Homer* points the victory. His reason was, because
Satan was immortal, and therefore the sinking of his scale could not
signify death, but the mounting of it did his *lightness*, conformable to
the expression we just now cited from *Daniel.*

> *Th' Eternal, to prevent such horrid fray,*
> *Hung forth in heav'n his golden scales, yet seen*
> *Between* Astræa *and the* Scorpion *sign:*
> *Wherein all things created first he weigh'd,*
> *The pendulous round earth, with balanc'd air,*
> *In counterpoise; now ponders all events,*
> *Battels and realms: In these he put two weights,*
> *The sequel each of parting and of fight:*
> *The latter quick up-flew, and kick'd the beam.*

I believe upon the whole this may with justice be preferr'd both to
Homer's and *Virgil*'s, on account of the beautiful allusion to the sign of

Libra in the heavens, and that noble imagination of the Maker's weighing the whole world at the creation, and all the events of it since; so correspondent at once to philosophy, and to the style of the scriptures.

93. *Then* Jove *from* Ida's *top, &c.*] This distress of the *Greeks* being suppos'd, *Jupiter's* presence was absolutely necessary to bring them into it: for the inferiour Gods that were friendly to *Greece* were rather more in number and superiour in force to those that favoured *Troy*; and the Poet had shew'd before, when both Armies were left to themselves, that the *Greeks* could overcome the *Trojans*; besides it would have been an indelible reflection upon his countrymen to have been vanquish'd by a smaller number. Therefore nothing less than the immediate interposition of *Jupiter* was requisite, which shews the wonderful address of the Poet in his machinery. *Virgil* makes *Turnus* say in the last *Æneid* [895],

– Dii me terrent & Jupiter hostis.

['Tis hostile heaven I dread; and partial *Jove*.]

And indeed this defeat of the *Greeks* seems more to their glory than all their victories, since even *Jupiter's* omnipotence could with difficulty effect it.

95. *Thick lightnings flash.*] This notion of *Jupiter's* declaring against the *Greeks* by thunder and lightning, is drawn (says *Dacier*) from truth itself. *Sam.* 1. *ch.* 7. *And as* Samuel *was offering up the burnt-offering, the* Philistines *drew near to battel against* Israel: *But the Lord thunder'd with a great thunder on that day upon the* Philistines, *and discomfited them, and they were smitten before* Israel. To which may be added that in the 18*th* Psalm. *The Lord thundered in the heavens, and the Highest gave his voice; hailstones and coals of fire. Yea, he sent out his arrows and scattered them; he shot out lightnings and discomfited them.*

Upon occasion of the various successes given by *Jupiter*, now to *Grecians*, now to *Trojans*, whom he suffers to perish interchangeably; some have fancied this supposition injurious to the nature of the Sovereign Being, as representing him variable or inconstant in his rewards and punishments. It may be answered, that as God makes use of some people to chastise others, and none are totally void of crimes, he often decrees to punish those very persons for lesser sins, whom he makes his instruments to punish others for greater: so purging them from their own iniquities before they become worthy to be chastisers of other men's. This is the case of the *Greeks* here, whom *Jupiter* permits to suffer many ways, tho' he had destin'd them to revenge the rape of *Helen* upon *Troy.* There is a history in the Bible just of this nature. In the 20*th* chapter of *Judges,* the *Israelites* are commanded to make war against the tribe of *Benjamin,* to punish a rape on the wife of a *Levite* committed in the city of *Gibeah:* When they have laid siege to the place, the *Benjamites* sally upon them with so much vigour, that a great number of the besiegers are destroy'd: they are astonish'd at these defeats, as having undertaken the siege in obedience to the command of God: But they are still order'd to persist, till at length they burn the city, and almost extinguish the race of *Benjamin.* There are many instances in scripture, where heaven is represented to change its decrees according to the repentance or relapses of men: *Hezechias* is order'd to prepare for death, and afterwards fifteen years are added to his life. It is foretold to *Achab,* that he shall perish miserably, and then upon his humiliation God defers the punishment till the reign of his successor, &c.

I must confess, that in comparing passages of the sacred books with our Author one ought to use a great deal of caution and respect. If there are some places in scripture that in compliance to human understanding represent the Deity as acting by motives like those of men; there are infinitely more that shew him as he is, all perfection, justice, and beneficence; whereas in *Homer* the general tenour of the Poem represents *Jupiter* as a being subject to passion, inequality, and imperfection. I think M. *Dacier* has carried these comparisons too far, and is too zealous to defend him upon every occasion in the points of theology and doctrine.

115. *But* Diomed *beheld.*] The whole following Story of *Nestor* and *Diomed* is admirably contriv'd to raise the character of the latter. He maintains his intrepidity, and ventures singly to bring off the old hero, notwithstanding the general consternation. The art of *Homer* will appear wonderful to any one who considers all the circumstances of this part, and by what degrees he reconciles this flight of *Diomed* to that undaunted character. The thunderbolt falls just before him; that is not enough; *Nestor* advises him to submit to heaven; this does not prevail, he cannot bear the thoughts of flight: *Nestor* drives back the

chariot without his consent; he is again inclined to go on till *Jupiter* again declares against him. These two heroes are very artfully placed together, because none but a person of *Nestor*'s authority and wisdom could have prevailed upon *Diomed* to retreat: A younger warriour could not so well in honour have given him such counsel, and from no other would he have taken it. To cause *Diomed* to fly, required both the counsel of *Nestor*, and the thunder of *Jupiter*.

121. *Oh turn and save*, &c.] There is a decorum in making *Diomed* call *Ulysses* to the assistance of his brother sage; for who better knew the importance of *Nestor*, than *Ulysses*? But the question is, whether *Ulysses* did not drop *Nestor* as one great minister would do another, and fancied he should be the wise man when the other was gone? *Eustathius* indeed is of opinion that *Homer* meant not to cast any aspersion on *Ulysses*, nor would have given him so many noble appellations, when in the same breath he reflected upon his courage. But perhaps the contrary opinion may not be ill grounded, if we observe the manner of *Homer*'s expression. *Diomed* call'd *Ulysses*, but *Ulysses* was deaf, he *did not hear*; and whereas the Poet says of the rest, that they had not the *hardiness* to stay, *Ulysses* is not only said to *fly*, but παρήιξεν, to make *violent haste* towards the navy. *Ovid* at least understood it thus, for he puts an objection in *Ajax*'s mouth, *Metam.* 13. drawn from this passage, which would have been improper had not *Ulysses* made more speed than he ought; since *Ajax* on the same occasion retreated as well as he.

142. *The thirsty fury of my flying spear.*] *Homer* has figures of that boldness which it is impossible to preserve in another language. The words in the original are Δόρυ μαίνεται, Hector *shall see if my spear is mad in my hands.* The translation pretends only to have taken some shadow of this, in animating the spear, giving it *fury*, and strengthning the figure with the epithet *thirsty*.

159. *And now had death*, &c.] *Eustathius* observes how wonderfully *Homer* still advances the character of *Diomed*: when all the leaders of *Greece* were retreated, the Poet says that had not *Jupiter* interposed, *Diomed* alone had driven the whole army of *Troy* to their walls, and with his single hand have vanquish'd an Army.

164. *The Ground before him flam'd.*] Here is a battel describ'd with so

much fire, that the warmest imagination of an able painter cannot add
a circumstance to heighten the surprize or horrour of the picture. Here
is what they call the *Fracas*, or hurry and tumult of the action in the
utmost strength of colouring, upon the foreground; and the *repose* or
solemnity at a distance, with great propriety and judgment. First, in the
Eloignement, we behold *Jupiter* in golden armour, surrounded with
glory, upon the summit of Mount *Ida*; his chariot and horses by him,
wrapt in dark clouds. In the next place below the horizon, appear the
clouds rolling and opening, thro' which the lightning flashes in the
face of the *Greeks*, who are flying on all sides; *Agamemnon* and the rest
of the commanders in the rear, in postures of astonishment. Towards
the middle of the piece, we see *Nestor* in the utmost distress, one of his
horses having a deadly wound in the forehead with a dart, which
makes him rear and writhe, and disorder the rest. *Nestor* is cutting the
harness with his sword, while *Hector* advances driving full speed.
Diomed interposes, in an action of the utmost fierceness and intrepidity:
These two heroes make the principal figures and subject of the picture.
A burning thunderbolt falls just before the feet of *Diomed*'s horses,
from whence a horrid flame of sulphur rises.

This is only a specimen of a single picture designed by *Homer*, out
of the many with which he has beautified the *Iliad*. And indeed every
thing is so natural and so lively, that the History painter would
generally have no more to do but to delineate the forms, and copy the
circumstances just as he finds them described by this great master. We
cannot therefore wonder at what has been so often said of *Homer*'s
furnishing Ideas to the most famous Painters of antiquity.

194. *The solid skies.*] *Homer* sometimes calls the Heavens *Brazen*,
Ὀυρανὸν πολύχαλκον, and *Jupiter*'s palace, χαλκοβατὲς δῶ. One might
think from hence that the notion of the *solidity of the heavens*, which is
indeed very ancient, had been generally receiv'd. The scripture uses
expressions agreeable to it, *A Heaven of brass*, and the *firmament*.

214. *Heard ye the voice of* Jove?] It was a noble and effectual manner
of encouraging the troops, by telling them that God was surely on
their side: This, it seems, has been an ancient practice, as it has been
used in modern times by those who never read *Homer*.

226. *Now* Xanthus, Æthon, &c.] There have been Criticks who blame
this manner, introduced by *Homer* and copied by *Virgil*, of making a

hero address his discourse to his horses. *Virgil* has given human
sentiments to the horse of *Pallas*, and made him weep for the death of
his master. In the tenth *Æneid*, *Mezentius* speaks to his horse in the
same manner as *Hector* does here. Nay, he makes *Turnus* utter a
speech to his spear, and invoke it as a divinity. All this is agreeable to
the art of oratory, which makes it a precept to speak to every thing,
and make every thing speak; of which there are innumerable applauded
instances in the most celebrated orators. Nothing can be more spirited
and affecting than this enthusiasm of *Hector*, who, in the transport of
his joy at the sight of *Diomed* flying before him, breaks out into this
apostrophe to his horses, as he is pursuing. And indeed the air of this
whole speech is agreeable to a man drunk with the hopes of success,
and promising himself a series of conquests. He has in imagination
already forced the *Grecian* retrenchments, set the fleet in flames, and
destroyed the whole army.

231. *For this my spouse.*] There is (says M. *Dacier*) a secret beauty in
this passage, which perhaps will only be perceiv'd by those who are
particularly vers'd in *Homer*. He describes a Princess so tender in her
love to her husband, that she takes care constantly to go and meet him
at his return from every battel, and in the joy of seeing him again, runs
to his horses, and gives them bread and wine as a testimony of her
acknowledgment to them for bringing him back. Notwithstanding the
raillery that may be past upon this remark, I take a Lady to be the best
judge to what actions a woman may be carried by fondness to her
husband. *Homer* does not expressly mention bread, but wheat; and the
commentators are not agreed whether she gave them wine to drink, or
steep'd the grain in it. *Hobbes* translates it as I do.

237. Vulcanian *arms, the labour of a God.*] These were the arms
that *Diomed* had received from *Glaucus*, and a prize worthy *Hector*,
being (as we are told in the sixth book) entirely of gold. I do not
remember any other place where the shield of *Nestor* is celebrated
by *Homer*.

246. *Yet Ægæ, Helicè.*] These were two cities of *Greece* in which
Neptune was particularly honoured, and in each of which there was a
temple and statue of him.

262. *Where the deep trench.*] That is to say, the space betwixt the ditch and the wall was filled with the men and chariots of the *Greeks: Hector* not having yet past the ditch.   *Eustathius.*

269. *His purple robe.*] *Agamemnon* here addresses himself to the eyes of the army; his voice might have been lost in the confusion of a retreat, but the motion of this purple robe could not fail of attracting the regards of the soldiers. His speech also is very remarkable; he first endeavours to shame them into courage, and then begs of *Jupiter* to give that courage success; at least so far as not to suffer the whole army to be destroyed.   *Eustathius.*

270. *High on the midmost bark,* &c.] We learn from hence the situation of the ships of *Ulysses, Achilles,* and *Ajax.* The two latter being the strongest heroes of the army, were placed to defend either end of the fleet as most obnoxious to the incursions or surprizes of the enemy; and *Ulysses* being the ablest head, was allotted the middle place, as more safe and convenient for the council, and that he might be the nearer if any emergency required his advice.   *Eustathius, Spondanus.*

293. *Thus pray'd the King, and heav'ns great Father heard.*] It is to be observ'd in general, that *Homer* hardly ever makes his heroes succeed, unless they have first offer'd a prayer to heaven. Whether they engage in war, go upon an embassy, undertake a voyage; in a word, whatever they enterprize, they almost always supplicate some God; and whenever we find this omitted, we may expect some adversity to befall them in the course of the story.

297. *The eagle, sacred bird!*] *Jupiter* upon the prayers of *Agamemnon* sends an omen to encourage the *Greeks.* The application of it is obvious: The eagle signified *Hector,* the fawn denoted the fear and flight of the *Greeks,* and being dropt at the altar of *Jupiter,* shew'd that they would be saved by the protection of that God. The word Πανομφαῖος (says *Eustathius*) has a great significancy in this place. The *Greeks* having just received this happy omen from *Jupiter,* were offering oblations to him under the title of the *Father of Oracles.* There may also be a natural reason for this appellation, as *Jupiter* signified the *Æther,* which is the vehicle of all sounds.

Virgil has a fine imitation of this passage, but diversify'd with many more circumstances, where he make *Juturna* shew a prodigy of the like nature to encourage the *Latins, Æn.* 12 [247–56].

Namque volans rubra fulvus Jovis ales in æthra,
Litoreas agitabat aves, turbamque sonantem
Agminis aligeri: subito cum lapsus ad undas
Cycnum excellentem pedibus rapit improbus uncis.
Arrexere animos Itali: cunctæque volucres
Convertunt clamore fugam (mirabile visu)
Ætheraque obscurant pennis, hostemque per auras
Facta nube premunt: donec vi victus & ipso
Pondere defecit, prædamque ex unguibus ales
Projecit fluvio, penitusque in nubila fugit.

[For, sudden, in the fiery tracts above,
Appears in pomp th' imperial bird of *Jove*:
A plump of fowl he spies, that swim the lakes;
And o'er their heads his sounding pinions shakes:
Then stooping on the fairest of the train,
In his strong tallons truss'd a silver swan.
Th' *Italians* wonder at th' unusual sight;
But while he lags, and labours in his flight,
Behold the dastard fowl return anew;
And with united force the foe pursue:
Clam'rous around the royal hawk they fly;
And thick'ning in a cloud, o'reshade the sky.
They cuff, they scratch, they cross his airy course;
Nor can th' encumber'd bird sustain their force:
But vex'd, not vanquish'd, drops the pond'rous prey,
And, lighten'd of his burthen, wings his way.]

305. Tydides *first.*] *Diomed*, as we have before seen, was the last that retreated from the thunder of *Jupiter*; he is now the first that returns to the battel. It is worth while to observe the behaviour of the hero upon this occasion: He retreats with the utmost reluctancy, and advances with the utmost ardour, he flies with greater impatience to meet danger, than he could before to put himself in safety.

Eustathius.

321. *Secure behind the* Telamonian *shield.*] *Eustathius* observes that *Teucer* being an excellent Archer, and using only the bow, could not wear any arms which would incumber him, and render him less expedite in his archery. *Homer* to secure him from the enemy,

represents him as standing behind *Ajax*'s shield, and shooting from thence. Thus the Poet gives us a new circumstance of a battel, and tho' *Ajax* atchieves nothing himself, he maintains a superiority over *Teucer*: *Ajax* may be said to kill these *Trojans* with the arrows of *Teucer*.

There is also a wonderful tenderness in the simile with which he illustrates the Retreat of *Teucer* behind the shield of *Ajax*: Such tender circumstances soften the horrours of a battel, and diffuse a sort of serenity over the soul of the reader.

337. *Great* Agamemnon *views.*] *Eustathius* observes that *Homer* would here teach the duty of a general in a battel. He must observe the behaviour of his soldiers: He must honour the hero, reproach the coward, reduce the disorderly; and for the encouragement of the deserving, he must promise rewards, that desert in arms may not be paid with glory only.

343. *Sprung from an alien's bed.*] *Agamemnon* here in the height of his commendations of *Teucer*, tells him of his spurious birth: This (says *Eustathius*) was reckon'd no disgrace among the ancients; nothing being more common than for heroes of old to take their female captives to their beds; and as such captives were then given for a reward of valour, and as a matter of glory, it could be no reproach to be descended from them. Thus *Teucer* (says *Eustathius*) was descended from *Telamon*, and *Hesione* the sister of *Priam*, a female captive.

364. *This dog of* Troy.] This is literal from the *Greek*, and I have ventured it as no improper expression of the rage of *Teucer* for having been so often disappointed in his aim, and of his passion against that enemy who had so long prevented all the hopes of the *Grecians. Milton* was not scrupulous of imitating even these, which the modern refiners call unmannerly strokes of our author, (who knew to what extremes human passions might proceed, and was not ashamed to copy them.) He has put this very expression into the mouth of God himself, who upon beholding the havock which *Sin* and *Death* made in the world, is moved in his indignation to cry out,

> *See with what heat these dogs of hell advance!*

367. *He miss'd the mark.*] These words, says *Eustathius*, are very artfully inserted; the reader might wonder why so skilful an archer

should so often miss his mark, and it was necessary that *Teucer* should miss *Hector* because *Homer* could not falsify the History: This difficulty he removes by the intervention of *Apollo*, who wafts the arrow aside from him: The poet does not tell us that this was done by the hand of a God, 'till the arrow of *Teucer* came so near *Hector* as to kill his charioteer, which made some such contrivance necessary.

371. *As full-blown poppies.*] This simile is very beautiful, and exactly represents the manner of *Gorgythion*'s death: There is such a sweetness in the comparison, that it makes us pity the youth's fall, and almost feel his wound. *Virgil* has applied it to the death of *Euryalus* [IX. 434–7].

> – *Inque humeros cervix collapsa recumbit:*
> *Purpureus veluti cum flos succisus aratro*
> *Languescit moriens; lassove papavera collo*
> *Demisere caput, pluvia cum forte gravantur.*

> [His snowy neck reclines upon his breast,
> Like a fair flow'r by the keen share oppress'd:
> Like a white poppy sinking on the plain,
> Whose heavy head is overcharg'd with rain.]

This is finely improved by the *Roman* author, with the particulars of *succisus aratro*, and *lasso collo*. But it may on the other hand be observ'd in the favour of *Homer*, that the circumstance of the head being oppress'd and weigh'd down by the helmet is so remarkably just, that it is a wonder *Virgil* omitted it; and the rather because he had particularly taken notice before that it was the helmet of *Euryalus* which occasioned the discovery and unfortunate death of this young hero and his friend.

One may make a general observation, that *Homer* in those comparisons that breath an air of tenderness, is very exact, and adapts them in every point to the subject which he is to illustrate: But in other comparisons, where he is to inspire the soul with sublime sentiments, he gives a loose to his fancy, and does not regard whether the images exactly correspond. I take the Reason of it to be this: In the first, the copy must be like the original to cause it to affect us; the glass needs only to return the real image to make it beautiful: whereas in the other, a succession of noble ideas will cause the like sentiments in the soul; and tho' the glass should enlarge the image, it only strikes us with such thoughts as the Poet intended to raise, sublime and great.

393. *There, where the juncture knits the channel bone.*] *Hector* struck *Teucer* (it seems) just about the articulation of the arm, with the shoulder; which cut the tendon or wounded it so, that the arm lost its force: This is a true description of the effect of such a blow.

407. *As the bold hound that gives the lion chace.*] This simile is the justest imaginable; and gives the most lively picture of the manner in which the *Grecians* fled, and *Hector* pursued them, still slaughtering the hindmost. *Gratius* and *Oppian* have given us particular descriptions of those sort of dogs, of prodigious strength and size, which were employed to hunt and tear down wild beasts. To one of these fierce animals he compares *Hector*, and one cannot but observe his care not to disgrace his *Grecian* countrymen by an unworthy comparison: Tho' he is obliged to represent them flying, he makes them fly like lions, and as they fly, turn frequently back upon their pursuer: so that it is hard to say, if they, or he, be in the greater danger. On the contrary, when any of the *Grecian* heroes pursue the *Trojans*, it is he that is the lion, and the flyers are but sheep or trembling deer.

439. *The stubborn God, inflexible and hard.*] It must be owned that this speech of *Minerva* against *Jupiter*, shocks the Allegory more than perhaps any in the poem. Unless the Deities may sometimes be thought to mean no more than Beings that presided over those parts of nature, or those passions and faculties of the mind. Thus as *Venus* suggests unlawful as well as lawful desires, so *Minerva* may be described as the Goddess not only of Wisdom but of Craft; that is, both of true and false Wisdom. So the moral of *Minerva*'s speaking rashly of *Jupiter* may be, that the wisest of finite Beings is liable to passion and indiscretion, as the commentators have already observed.

461. *What mighty* Trojan *then, on yonder shore.*] She means *Hector*, whose death the Poet makes her foresee in such a lively manner, as if the image of the hero lay bleeding before her. This Picture is noble, and agreeable to the observation we formerly made of *Homer*'s method of prophecying in the spirit of poetry.

469. *Floats in rich Waves.*] The *Greek* word is κατέχευεν, *pours* the veil on the pavement. I must just take notice that here is a repetition of the same beautiful verses which the author had used in the fifth book.

477. *Smooth glides the chariot,* &c.] One would almost think *Homer* made his Gods and Goddesses descend from *Olympus*, only to mount again, and mount only to descend again, he is so remarkably delighted with the descriptions of their horses, and their manner of flight. We have no less than three of these in the present book.

500. *For* Juno *headstrong and imperious still, She claims,* &c.] *Eustathius* observes here, if a good man does us a wrong, we are justly angry at it, but if it proceeds from a bad one, it is no more than we expected, we are not at all surprized, and we bear it with patience.

There are many such passages as these in *Homer*, which glance obliquely at the fair sex; and *Jupiter* is here forced to take upon himself the severe husband, to teach *Juno* the duty of a wife.

522. *But thee what desp'rate insolence.*] It is observable that *Homer* generally makes his messengers, divine as well as human, very punctual in delivering their messages in the very words of the persons who commissioned them. *Iris* however in the close of her speech has ventured to go beyond her instructions and all rules of decorum, by adding these expressions of bitter reproach to a Goddess of superior rank. The words of the original, Κύον ἀδδεές [shameless bitch], are too gross to be literally translated.

525. Juno *her rage resign'd.*] *Homer* never intended to give us the picture of a good wife in the description of *Juno*: She obeys *Jupiter*, but it is a forced obedience: She submits rather to the governour than to the husband, and is more afraid of his lightning than his commands.

Her behaviour in this place is very natural to a person under a disappointment: She had set her heart upon preferring the *Greeks*, but failing in that point, she assumes an air of indifference, and says, whether they live or die, she is unconcerned.

531. *They breathe or perish as the fates ordain.*] The translator has turn'd this line in compliance to an old observation upon *Homer*, which *Macrobius* has written, and several others have since fallen into: They say he was so great a fatalist, as not so much as to name the word *Fortune* in all his works, but constantly *Fate* instead of it. This remark seems curious enough, and indeed does agree with the general tenour and doctrine of this Poet; but unluckily it is not true, the word which

they have proscribed being implied in the original of this v. 430. Ὅς κε
τύχῃ.

547. *And fix the car on its immortal base.*] It is remarked by *Eustathius*
that the word βωμοὶ signifies not only *altars*, but *pedestals* or *bases*, of
statues, &c. I think our language will bear this literally, tho' M. *Dacier*
durst not venture it in the *French.* The solemnity with which this
chariot of *Jupiter* is set up, by the hands of a God, and covered with a
fine veil, makes it easy enough to imagine that this distinction also
might be shewn it.

570. Juno *and* Pallas.] In the beginning of this Book *Juno* was silent,
and *Minerva* replied: Here, says *Eustathius*, *Homer* makes *Juno* reply
with great propriety to both their characters. *Minerva* resents the
usage of *Jupiter*, but the reverence she bears to her father, and her
King, keeps her silent; she has not less anger than *Juno*, but more
reason. *Minerva* there spoke with all the submission and deference that
was owing from a child to a father, or from a subject to a King; but
Juno is more free with her husband, she is angry, and lets him know it
by the first word she utters.

Juno here repeats the same words which had been used by *Minerva*
to *Jupiter* near the beginning of this book. What is there uttered by
wisdom herself, and approved by him, is here spoken by a Goddess
who (as *Homer* tells us at this very time) imprudently manifested her
passion, and whom *Jupiter* answers with anger. To deal fairly, I cannot
defend this in my Author, any more than some other of his repetitions;
as when *Ajax* in the fifteenth Iliad, v. 668 uses the same speech word
for word to encourage the *Greeks*, which *Agamemnon* had made in the
fifth, v. 529. I think it equally an extreme, to vindicate all the
repetitions of *Homer*, and to excuse none. However *Eustathius* very
ingeniously excuses this, by saying that the same speeches become
entirely different by the different manner of introducing them. *Minerva*
addressed herself to *Jupiter* with words full of respect, but *Juno*
with terms of resentment. This, says he, shews the effect of opening
our speeches with art: It prejudices the audience in our favour, and
makes us speak to friends: whereas the auditor naturally denies that
favour, which the Orator does not seem to ask; so that what he
delivers, tho' it has equal merit, labours under this disadvantage, that
his judges are his enemies.

590. *Nor shall great* Hector *cease,* &c.] Here, says *Eustathius,* the Poet prepares the reader for what is to succeed: he gives us the outlines of his piece, which he is to fill up in the progress of the poem. This is so far from cloying the reader's appetite, that it raises it, and makes him desirous to see the picture drawn in its full length.

621. *Ye valiant* Trojans, &c.] *Eustathius* observes that *Hector* here speaks like a soldier: He bears a spear, not a sceptre in his hand; he harangues like a soldier, but like a victor; he seems to be too much pleased with himself, and in this vein of self-flattery, he promises a compleat conquest over the *Greeks.*

648. *And let the matrons.*] I have been more observant of the decorum in this line than my Author himself. He calls the women Θηλύτεραι [weaker (of the two sexes)], an epithet of scandalous import, upon which *Porphyry* and the *Greek* scholiast have said but too much. I know no man that has yet had the impudence to translate that remark, in regard of which it is politeness to imitate the Barbarians, and say, *Græcum est, non legitur* [It is Greek, it is not spoken]. For my part, I leave it as a motive to some very curious persons of both sexes to study the *Greek* language.

679. *Full hecatombs,* &c.] The six lines that follow being a translation of four in the original, are added from the authority of *Plato* in Mr *Barnes* his edition: That author cites them in his second *Alcibiades.* There is no doubt of their being genuine, but the question is only whether they are rightly placed here? I shall not pretend to decide upon a point which will doubtless be the speculation of future criticks.

687. *As when the moon,* &c.] This comparison is inferior to none in *Homer.* It is the most beautiful night-piece that can be found in poetry. He presents you with a prospect of the heavens, the seas, and the earth: The stars shine, the air is serene, the world enlighten'd, and the moon mounted in glory. *Eustathius* remarks that φαεινὴν does not signify the moon at full, for then the light of the stars is diminish'd or lost in the greater brightness of the moon. And others correct the word φαιεινὴν, to φάει νῆν, for φάει νέην, but this criticism is forced, and I see no necessity why the moon may not be said to be bright, tho' it is not in the full. A Poet is not obliged to speak with the exactness of philosophy, but with the liberty of Poetry.

703. *A thousand piles.*] *Homer* in his catalogue of the *Grecian* ships, tho' he does not recount expertly the number of the *Greeks*, has given some hints from whence the sum of their army may be collected. But in the same book where he gives an account of the *Trojan* army, and relates the names of the leaders and nations of the auxiliaries, he says nothing by which we may infer the number of the army of the besieged. To supply therefore that omission, he has taken occasion by this piece of poetical arithmetick, to inform his reader, that the *Trojan* army amounted to fifty thousand. That the assistant nations are to be included herein, appears from what *Dolon* says in *l.* 10. that the auxiliaries were encamped that night with the *Trojans.*

This passage gives me occasion to animadvert upon a mistake of a modern writer, and another of my own. The *Abbé Terasson* in a late treatise against *Homer*, is under a grievous error, in saying that all the forces of *Troy* and the auxiliaries cannot be reasonably suppos'd from *Homer* to be above ten thousand men. He had entirely overlook'd this place, which says there were a thousand fires, and fifty men at each of them. See my observation on the second book, where these fires by a slip of my memory are called funeral piles: I should be glad it were the greatest error I have committed in these notes.

707. *The coursers o'er their heaps of corn.*] I durst not take the same liberty with M. *Dacier*, who has omitted this circumstance, and does not mention the horses at all. In the following line, the last of the book, *Homer* has given to the *Morning* the epithet *fair-sphear'd*, or *bright-throned*, ἐΰθρονον ἠῶ. I have already taken notice in the preface of the method of translating the epithets of *Homer*, and must add here, that it is often only the uncertainty the moderns lie under, of the true genuine signification of an ancient word, which causes the many various constructions of it. So that it is probable the author's own words, at the time he used them, never meant half so many things as we translate them into. Madam *Dacier* generally observes one practice as to these throughout her version: She renders almost every such epithet in *Greek* by two or three in *French*, from a fear of losing the least part of its significance. This perhaps may be excusable in prose; tho' at best it makes the whole much more verbose and tedious, and is rather like writing a dictionary than rendring an author: But in verse, every reader knows such a redoubling of epithets would not be tolerable. A Poet has therefore only to chuse that, which most agrees with the tenour and main intent of the particular passage, or with the genius of poetry itself.

It is plain that too scrupulous an adherence to many of these, gives the translation an exotic, pedantic, and whimsical air, which it is not to be imagined the original ever had. To call a hero the *great artificer of flight*, the *swift of foot*, or the *horse-tamer*, these give us ideas of little peculiarities, when in the author's time they were epithets used only in general to signify alacrity, agility, and vigour. A common reader would imagine from these servile versions, that *Diomed* and *Achilles* were foot-racers, and *Hector* a horse-courser, rather than that any of them were heroes. A man shall be called a faithful translator for rendring πόδας ὠκύς in *English*, *swift-footed*; but laugh'd at if he should translate our *English* word *dext'rous* into any other language, *right-handed*.

THE
ILIAD
OF
HOMER

VOLUME III

THE
NINTH BOOK
OF THE
ILIAD

The ARGUMENT

The Embassy to *Achilles*

Agamemnon, *after the last day's defeat, proposes to the* Greeks *to quit the siege, and return to their country.* Diomed *opposes this, and* Nestor *seconds him, praising his wisdom and resolution. He orders the guard to be strengthened, and a council summon'd to deliberate what measures were to be follow'd in this emergency.* Agamemnon *pursues this advice, and* Nestor *farther prevails upon him to send ambassadors to* Achilles, *in order to move him to a reconciliation.* Ulysses *and* Ajax *are made choice of, who are accompanied by old* Phœnix. *They make, each of them, very moving and pressing speeches, but are rejected with roughness by* Achilles, *who notwithstanding retains* Phœnix *in his tent. The ambassadors return unsuccessfully to the camp, and the troops betake themselves to sleep.*

This book, and the next following, take up the space of one night, *which is the twenty-seventh from the beginning of the poem. The* scene *lies on the sea-shore, the station of the* Grecian *ships.*

Thus joyful *Troy* maintain'd the watch of night;
While Fear, pale comrade of inglorious flight,
And heav'n-bred horrour, on the *Grecian* part,
Sate on each face, and sadden'd ev'ry heart.
5 As from its cloudy dungeon issuing forth,
A double tempest of the west and north
Swells o'er the sea, from *Thracia*'s frozen shore,
Heaps waves on waves, and bids th' *Ægean* roar;
This way and that, the boiling deeps are tost;
10 Such various passions urg'd the troubled host.
Great *Agamemnon* griev'd above the rest;
Superiour sorrows swell'd his royal breast;
Himself his orders to the heralds bears,
To bid to council all the *Grecian* Peers,
15 But bid in whispers: these surround their Chief,
In solemn sadness, and majestic grief.
The King amidst the mournful circle rose;
Down his wan cheek a briny torrent flows:
So silent fountains, from a rock's tall head,
20 In sable streams soft-trickling waters shed.
With more than vulgar grief he stood opprest;
Words, mixt with sighs, thus bursting from his breast.
    Ye Sons of *Greece!* partake your Leader's care,
Fellows in arms, and Princes of the war!
25 Of partial *Jove* too justly we complain,
And heav'nly oracles believ'd in vain;
A safe return was promis'd to our toils,
With conquest honour'd, and enrich'd with spoils:

Now shameful flight alone can save the host;
Our wealth, our people, and our glory lost.   30
So *Jove* decrees, Almighty Lord of all!
Jove, at whose nod whole empires rise or fall,
Who shakes the feeble props of human trust,
And tow'rs and armies humbles to the dust.
Haste then, for ever quit these fatal fields,   35
Haste to the joys our native country yields;
Spread all your canvas, all your oars employ,
Nor hope the fall of heav'n–defended *Troy*.

He said; deep silence held the *Grecian* band,
Silent, unmov'd, in dire dismay they stand,
A pensive scene! 'till *Tydeus*' warlike son   40
Roll'd on the King his eyes, and thus begun.

When Kings advise us to renounce our fame,
First let him speak, who first has suffer'd shame.
If I oppose thee, Prince! thy wrath with-hold,
The laws of council bid my tongue be bold.   45
Thou first, and thou alone, in fields of fight,
Durst brand my courage, and defame my might;
Nor from a friend th' unkind reproach appear'd,
The *Greeks* stood witness, all our army heard.   50
The Gods, O Chief! from whom our honours spring,
The Gods have made thee but by halves a King;
They gave thee scepters, and a wide command,
They gave dominion o'er the seas and land,
The noblest pow'r that might the world controul   55
They gave thee not – a brave and virtuous soul.
Is this a Gen'ral's voice, that would suggest
Fears like his own to ev'ry *Grecian* breast?
Confiding in our want of worth, he stands,
And if we fly, 'tis what our King commands.   60
Go thou inglorious! from th' embattel'd plain;
Ships thou hast store, and nearest to the main,
A nobler care the *Grecians* shall employ,
To combate, conquer, and extirpate *Troy*.
Here *Greece* shall stay; or if all *Greece* retire,   65
My self will stay, till *Troy* or I expire;
My self, and *Sthenelus*, will fight for fame;
God bad us fight, and 'twas with God we came.

He ceas'd: the *Greeks* loud acclamations raise,
70   And voice to voice resounds *Tydides'* praise.
Wise *Nestor* then his rev'rend figure rear'd;
He spoke: the host in still attention heard.
    O truly great! in whom the Gods have join'd
Such strength of body, with such force of mind;
75   In conduct, as in courage, you excel,
Still first to act what you advise so well.
Those wholsome counsels which thy wisdom moves,
Applauding *Greece* with common voice approves.
Kings thou canst blame; a bold, but prudent youth;
80   And blame ev'n Kings with praise, because with truth.
And yet those years that since thy birth have run,
Would hardly stile thee *Nestor*'s youngest son.
Then let me add what yet remains behind,
A thought unfinish'd in that gen'rous mind;
85   Age bids me speak; nor shall th' advice I bring
Distaste the people, or offend the King:
    Curs'd is the man, and void of law and right,
Unworthy property, unworthy light,
Unfit for publick rule, or private care;
90   That wretch, that monster, who delights in war:
Whose lust is murder, and whose horrid joy,
To tear his country, and his kind destroy!
This night, refresh and fortify thy train;
Between the trench and wall, let guards remain:
95   Be that the duty of the young and bold;
But thou, O King, to council call the old:
Great is thy sway, and weighty are thy cares;
Thy high commands must spirit all our wars.
With *Thracian* wines recruit thy honour'd guests,
100   For happy counsels flow from sober feasts.
Wise, weighty counsels aid a state distrest,
And such a Monarch as can chuse the best.
See! what a blaze from hostile tents aspires,
How near our fleet approach the *Trojan* fires!
105   Who can, unmov'd, behold the dreadful light,
What eye beholds 'em, and can close to night?
This dreadful interval determines all;
To-morrow, *Troy* must flame, or *Greece* must fall.

Thus spoke the hoary sage: the rest obey;
Swift thro' the gates the guards direct their way.   110
His son was first to pass the lofty mound,
The gen'rous *Thrasymed*, in arms renown'd:
Next him *Ascalaphus*, *Iälmen*, stood,
The double offspring of the Warriour-God.
Deïpyrus, *Aphareus*, *Merion* join,   115
And *Lycomed*, of *Creon*'s noble line.
Sev'n were the leaders of the nightly bands,
And each bold Chief a hundred spears commands.
The fires they light, to short repasts they fall,
Some line the trench, and others man the wall.   120

The King of men, on publick counsels bent,
Conven'd the Princes in his ample tent;
Each seiz'd a portion of the kingly feast,
But stay'd his hand when thirst and hunger ceast.
Then *Nestor* spoke, for wisdom long approv'd,   125
And slowly rising, thus the council mov'd.

Monarch of nations! whose superior sway
Assembled states, and Lords of earth obey,
The laws and scepters to thy hand are giv'n,
And millions own the care of thee and heav'n.   130
O King! the counsels of my age attend;
With thee my cares begin, in thee must end;
Thee, Prince! it fits alike to speak and hear,
Pronounce with judgment, with regard give ear,
To see no wholesome motion be withstood,   135
And ratify the best for publick good.
Nor, tho' a meaner give advice, repine,
But follow it, and make the wisdom thine.
Hear then a thought, not now conceiv'd in haste,
At once my present judgment, and my past;   140
When from *Pelides'* tent you forc'd the maid,
I first oppos'd, and faithful, durst dissuade;
But bold of soul, when headlong fury fir'd,
You wrong'd the man, by men and Gods admir'd:
Now seek some means his fatal wrath to end,   145
With pray'rs to move him, or with gifts to bend.

To whom the King. With justice hast thou shown
A Prince's faults, and I with reason own.

That happy man whom *Jove* still honours most,
150 Is more than armies, and himself an host.
Blest in his love, this wond'rous hero stands;
Heav'n fights his war, and humbles all our bands.
Fain wou'd my heart, which err'd thro' frantic rage,
The wrathful Chief and angry Gods assuage.
155 If gifts immense his mighty soul can bow,
Hear, all ye *Greeks*, and witness what I vow.
Ten weighty talents of the purest gold,
And twice ten vases of refulgent mold;
Sev'n sacred tripods, whose unsully'd frame
160 Yet knows no office, nor has felt the flame:
Twelve steeds unmatch'd in fleetness and in force,
And still victorious in the dusty course:
(Rich were the man whose ample stores exceed
The prizes purchas'd by their winged speed)
165 Sev'n lovely captives of the *Lesbian* line,
Skill'd in each art, unmatch'd in form divine,
The same I chose for more than vulgar charms,
When *Lesbos* sunk beneath the hero's arms.
All these, to buy his friendship, shall be paid,
170 And join'd with these, the long-contested Maid;
With all her charms, *Briseïs* I resign,
And solemn swear those charms were never mine;
Untouch'd she stay'd, uninjur'd she removes,
Pure from my arms, and guiltless of my loves,
175 These instant shall be his; and if the pow'rs
Give to our arms proud *Ilion*'s hostile tow'rs,
Then shall he store (when *Greece* the spoil divides)
With gold and brass his loaded navy's sides.
Besides full twenty nymphs of *Trojan* race,
180 With copious love shall crown his warm embrace;
Such as himself will chuse; who yield to none,
Or yield to *Helen*'s heav'nly charms alone.
Yet hear me farther: when our wars are o'er,
If safe we land on *Argos*' fruitful shore,
185 There shall he live my son, our honours share,
And with *Orestes*' self divide my care.
Yet more – three daughters in my court are bred,
And each well worthy of a royal bed;

Laodice and *Iphigenia* fair,
And bright *Chrysothemis* with golden hair;   190
Her let him choose, whom most his eyes approve,
I ask no presents, no reward for love.
My self will give the dow'r; so vast a store,
As never father gave a child before.
Sev'n ample cities shall confess his sway,   195
Him *Enope*, and *Phæræ* him obey,
Cardamyle with ample turrets crown'd,
And sacred *Pedasus*, for vines renown'd;
Æpea fair, the Pastures *Hyra* yields,
And rich *Antheia* with her flow'ry fields: 200
The whole extent to *Pylos*' sandy plain
Along the verdant margin of the main.
There heifers graze, and lab'ring oxen toil;
Bold are the men, and gen'rous is the soil;
There shall he reign with pow'r and justice crown'd,   205
And rule the tributary realms around.
All this I give, his vengeance to controul,
And sure all this may move his mighty soul.
Pluto, the grizly God who never spares,
Who feels no mercy, and who hears no pray'rs,   210
Lives dark and dreadful in deep Hell's abodes,
And mortals hate him, as the worst of Gods.
Great tho' he be, it fits him to obey;
Since more than his my years, and more my sway.

   The monarch thus: the rev'rend *Nestor* then: 215
Great *Agamemnon!* glorious King of Men!
Such are thy offers as a Prince may take,
And such as fits a gen'rous King to make.
Let chosen delegates this hour be sent,
(Myself will name them) to *Pelides*' tent: 220
Let *Phœnix* lead, rever'd for hoary age,
Great *Ajax* next, and *Ithacus* the sage.
Yet more to sanctify the word you send,
Let *Hodius* and *Eurybates* attend.
Now pray to *Jove* to grant what *Greece* demands;   225
Pray, in deep silence, and with purest hands.
   He said, and all approv'd. The heralds bring
The cleansing water from the living spring.

The youth with wine the sacred goblets crown'd,
230   And large libations drench'd the sands around.
The rite perform'd, the chiefs their thirst allay,
Then from the royal tent they take their way;
Wise *Nestor* turns on each his careful eye,
Forbids t' offend, instructs them to apply:
235   Much he advis'd them all, *Ulysses* most,
To deprecate the Chief, and save the host.
Thro' the still night they march, and hear the roar
Of murm'ring billows on the sounding shore.
To *Neptune*, ruler of the seas profound,
240   Whose liquid arms the mighty globe surround,
They pour forth vows their embassy to bless,
And calm the rage of stern *Æacides*.
And now arriv'd, where, on the sandy bay
The *Myrmidonian* tents and vessels lay;
245   Amus'd at ease, the god-like man they found,
Pleas'd with the solemn harp's harmonious Sound.
(The well-wrought harp from conquer'd *Thebæ* came,
Of polish'd silver was its costly frame;)
With this he sooths his angry soul, and sings
250   Th' immortal deeds of Heroes and of Kings.
Patroclus only of the royal train,
Plac'd in his tent, attends the lofty strain:
Full opposite he sate, and listen'd long,
In silence waiting till he ceas'd the song.
255   Unseen the *Grecian* embassy proceeds
To his high tent; the great *Ulysses* leads.
Achilles starting, as the Chiefs he spy'd,
Leap'd from his seat, and laid the harp aside.
With like surprize arose *Menætius'* son:
260   *Pelides* grasp'd their hands, and thus begun.
    Princes all hail! whatever brought you here,
Or strong necessity, or urgent fear;
Welcome, tho' *Greeks!* for not as foes ye came;
To me more dear than all that bear the name.
265   With that, the Chiefs beneath his roof he led,
And plac'd in seats with purple carpets spread.
Then thus – *Patroclus*, crown a larger bowl,
Mix purer wine, and open ev'ry soul.

Of all the warriours yonder host can send,
Thy friend most honours these, and these thy friend.   270
    He said; *Patroclus* o'er the blazing fire
Heaps in a brazen vase three chines entire:
The brazen vase *Automedon* sustains,
Which flesh of porket, sheep, and goat contains:
Achilles at the genial feast presides,   275
The parts transfixes, and with skill divides.
Mean while *Patroclus* sweats the fire to raise;
The tent is brightned with the rising blaze:
Then, when the languid flames at length subside,
He strows a bed of glowing embers wide,   280
Above the coals the smoaking fragments turns,
And sprinkles sacred salt from lifted urns;
With bread the glitt'ring canisters they load,
Which round the board *Menætius'* son bestow'd;
Himself, oppos'd t' *Ulysses* full in sight,   285
Each portion parts, and orders ev'ry rite.
The first fat off'rings, to th' Immortals due,
Amidst the greedy flames *Patroclus* threw;
Then each, indulging in the social feast,
His thirst and hunger soberly represt.   290
That done, to *Phœnix Ajax* gave the sign;
Not unperceiv'd; *Ulysses* crown'd with wine
The foaming bowl, and instant thus began,
His speech addressing to the god-like man.
    Health to *Achilles!* happy are thy guests!   295
Not those more honour'd whom *Atrides* feasts:
Tho' gen'rous plenty crown thy loaded boards,
That, *Agamemnon's* regal tent affords;
But greater cares sit heavy on our souls,
Not eas'd by banquets or by flowing bowls.   300
What scenes of slaughter in yon fields appear!
The dead we mourn, and for the living fear;
Greece on the brink of fate all doubtful stands,
And owns no help but from thy saving hands:
Troy and her aids for ready vengeance call;   305
Their threat'ning tents already shade our wall:
Hear how with shouts their conquest they proclaim,
And point at ev'ry ship their vengeful flame!

For them the Father of the Gods declares,
310 Theirs are his omens, and his thunder theirs.
See, full of *Jove*, avenging *Hector* rise!
See! Heav'n and earth the raging Chief defies;
What fury in his breast, what light'ning in his eyes!
He waits but for the morn, to sink in flame
315 The ships, the *Greeks*, and all the *Grecian* name.
Heav'ns! how my country's woes distract my mind,
Lest fate accomplish all his rage design'd.
And must we, Gods! our heads inglorious lay
In *Trojan* dust, and this the fatal day?
320 Return, *Achilles!* oh return, tho' late,
To save thy *Greeks*, and stop the course of fate;
If in that heart, or grief, or courage lies,
Rise to redeem; ah yet, to conquer, rise!
The day may come, when all our warriours slain,
325 That heart shall melt, that courage rise in vain.
Regard in time, O prince divinely brave!
Those wholsome counsels which thy father gave.
When *Peleus* in his aged arms embrac'd
His parting son, these accents were his last.
330 My child! with strength, with glory and success,
Thy arms may *Juno* and *Minerva* bless!
Trust that to heav'n: – but thou, thy cares engage
To calm thy passions, and subdue thy rage:
From gentler manners let thy glory grow,
335 And shun contention, the sure source of woe;
That young and old may in thy praise combine,
The virtues of humanity be thine –
This, now despis'd advice, thy father gave;
Ah! check thy anger, and be truly brave.
340 If thou wilt yield to great *Atrides'* pray'rs,
Gifts worthy thee his royal hand prepares;
If not – but hear me, while I number o'er
The proffer'd presents, an exhaustless store.
Ten weighty talents of the purest gold,
345 And twice ten vases of refulgent mold;
Sev'n sacred tripods, whose unsully'd frame
Yet knows no office, nor has felt the flame:

Twelve steeds unmatch'd in fleetness and in force,
And still victorious in the dusty course:
(Rich were the man, whose ample stores exceed   350
The prizes purchas'd by their winged speed)
Sev'n lovely captives of the *Lesbian* line,
Skill'd in each art, unmatch'd in form divine,
The same he chose for more than vulgar charms,
When *Lesbos* sunk beneath thy conqu'ring arms.   355
All these, to buy thy friendship, shall be paid,
And join'd with these the long contested maid;
With all her charms, *Briseïs* he'll resign,
And solemn swear those charms were only thine;
Untouch'd she stay'd, uninjur'd she removes,   360
Pure from his arms, and guiltless of his loves.
These instant shall be thine; and if the pow'rs
Give to our arms proud *Ilion*'s hostile tow'rs,
Then shalt thou store (when *Greece* the spoil divides)
With gold and brass thy loaded navy's sides.   365
Besides full twenty nymphs of *Trojan* race,
With copious love shall crown thy warm embrace;
Such as thy self shall chuse; who yield to none,
Or yield to *Helen*'s heav'nly charms alone.
Yet hear me farther: when our wars are o'er,   370
If safe we land on *Argos*' fruitful shore,
There shalt thou live his son, his honours share,
And with *Orestes*' self divide his care.
Yet more – three daughters in his court are bred,
And each well worthy of a royal bed;   375
Laodice and *Iphigenia* fair,
And bright *Chrysothemis* with golden hair;
Her shalt thou wed whom most thy eyes approve;
He asks no presents, no reward for love:
Himself will give the dow'r; so vast a store,   380
As never father gave a child before.
Sev'n ample cities shall confess thy sway,
Thee *Enope*, and *Phæræ* thee obey,
Cardamyle with ample turrets crown'd,
And sacred *Pedasus*, for vines renown'd;   385
Æpea fair, the pastures *Hyra* yields,
And rich *Antheia* with her flow'ry fields:

The whole extent to *Pylos'* sandy plain
Along the verdant margin of the main.
390 There heifers graze, and lab'ring oxen toil;
Bold are the men, and gen'rous is the soil.
There shalt thou reign with pow'r and justice crown'd,
And rule the tributary realms around.
Such are the proffers which this day we bring,
395 Such the repentance of a suppliant King.
But if all this relentless thou disdain,
If honour, and if int'rest plead in vain;
Yet some redress to suppliant *Greece* afford,
And be, amongst her guardian Gods, ador'd.
400 If no regard thy suff'ring country claim,
Hear thy own glory, and the voice of fame:
For now that chief, whose unresisted ire
Made nations tremble, and whole hosts retire,
Proud *Hector*, now, th' unequal fight demands,
405 And only triumphs to deserve thy hands.

Then thus the Goddess-born. *Ulysses*, hear
A faithful speech, that knows nor art, nor fear;
What in my secret soul is understood,
My tongue shall utter, and my deeds make good.
410 Let *Greece* then know, my purpose I retain,
Nor with new treaties vex my peace in vain.
Who dares think one thing, and another tell,
My heart detests him as the gates of hell.

Then thus in short my fixt resolves attend,
415 Which nor *Atrides*, nor his *Greeks* can bend;
Long toils, long perils in their cause I bore,
But now th' unfruitful glories charm no more.
Fight or not fight, a like reward we claim,
The wretch and hero find their prize the same;
420 Alike regretted in the dust he lies,
Who yields ignobly, or who bravely dies.
Of all my dangers, all my glorious pains,
A life of labours, lo! what fruit remains?
As the bold bird her helpless young attends,
425 From danger guards them, and from want defends;
In search of prey she wings the spacious air,
And with th' untasted food supplies her care:

For thankless *Greece* such hardships have I brav'd,
Her wives, her infants by my labours sav'd;
Long sleepless nights in heavy arms I stood,   430
And sweat laborious days in dust and blood.
I sack'd twelve ample cities on the main,
And twelve lay smoking on the *Trojan* plain:
Then at *Atrides'* haughty feet were laid
The wealth I gather'd, and the spoils I made.   435
Your mighty Monarch these in peace possest;
Some few my soldiers had, himself the rest.
Some present too to ev'ry Prince was paid;
And ev'ry Prince enjoys the gift he made;
I only must refund, of all his train;   440
See what preheminence our merits gain!
My spoil alone his greedy soul delights;
My spouse alone must bless his lustful nights:
The woman, let him (as he may) enjoy;
But what's the quarrel then of *Greece* to *Troy*?   445
What to these shores th' assembled nations draws,
What calls for vengeance but a woman's cause?
Are fair endowments and a beauteous face
Belov'd by none but those of *Atreus'* race?
The wife whom choice and passion both approve,   450
Sure ev'ry wife and worthy man will love.
Nor did my fair one less distinction claim;
Slave as she was, my soul ador'd the dame.
Wrong'd in my love, all proffers I disdain;
Deceiv'd for once, I trust not Kings again.   455
Ye have my answer – what remains to do,
Your King, *Ulysses*, may consult with you.
What needs he the defence this arm can make?
Has he not walls no human force can shake?
Has he not fenc'd his guarded navy round,   460
With piles, with ramparts, and a trench profound?
And will not these (the wonders he has done)
Repel the rage of *Priam*'s single son?
There was a time ('twas when for *Greece* I fought)
When *Hector*'s prowess no such wonders wrought;   465
He kept the verge of *Troy*, nor dar'd to wait ⎤
Achilles' fury at the *Scæan* gate;   ⎬
He try'd it once, and scarce was sav'd by fate. ⎦

But now those ancient enmities are o'er;
470   To-morrow we the fav'ring Gods implore,
Then shall you see our parting vessels crown'd,
And hear with oars the *Hellespont* resound.
The third day hence, shall *Pthia* greet our sails,
If mighty *Neptune* send propitious gales;
475   *Pthia* to her *Achilles* shall restore
The wealth he left for this detested shore:
Thither the spoils of this long war shall pass,
The ruddy gold, the steel, and shining brass;
My beauteous captives thither I'll convey,
480   And all that rests of my unravish'd prey.
One only valu'd gift your tyrant gave,
And that resum'd; the fair *Lyrnessian* slave.
Then tell him; loud, that all the *Greeks* may hear,
And learn to scorn the wretch they basely fear;
485   (For arm'd in impudence, mankind he braves,
And meditates new cheats on all his slaves;
Tho' shameless as he is, to face these eyes
Is what he dares not; if he dares, he dies)
Tell him, all terms, all commerce I decline,
490   Nor share his council, nor his battel join;
For once deceiv'd, was his; but twice, were mine.
No – let the stupid Prince, whom *Jove* deprives
Of sense and justice, run where frenzy drives;
His gifts are hateful: Kings of such a kind
495   Stand but as slaves before a noble mind.
Not tho' he proffer'd all himself possest,
And all his rapine cou'd from others wrest;
Not all the golden tides of wealth that crown
The many-peopled *Orchomenian* town;
500   Not all proud *Thebes'* unrival'd walls contain,
The world's great empress on th' *Ægyptian* plain,
(That spreads her conquests o'er a thousand states,
And pours her heroes thro' a hundred gates,
Two hundred horsemen, and two hundred cars
505   From each wide portal issuing to the wars)
Tho' bribes were heap'd on bribes, in number more
Than dust in fields, or sands along the shore;

Should all these offers for my friendship call;
'Tis he that offers, and I scorn them all.
Atrides' daughter never shall be led 510
(An ill-match'd consort) to *Achilles'* bed;
Like golden *Venus* tho' she charm'd the heart,
And vy'd with *Pallas* in the works of art.
Some greater *Greek* let those high nuptials grace,
I hate alliance with a tyrant's race. 515
If heav'n restore me to my realms with life,
The rev'rend *Peleus* shall elect my wife;
Thessalian nymphs there are, of form divine,
And Kings that sue to mix their blood with mine.
Blest in kind love, my years shall glide away, 520
Content with just hereditary sway;
There deaf for ever to the martial strife,
Enjoy the dear prerogative of life.
Life is not to be bought with heaps of gold;
Not all *Apollo*'s *Pythian* treasures hold, 525
Or *Troy* once held, in peace and pride of sway,
Can bribe the poor possession of a day!
Lost herds and treasures, we by arms regain,
And steeds unrival'd on the dusty plain:
But from our lips the vital spirit fled, 530
Returns no more to wake the silent dead.
My fates long since by *Thetis* were disclos'd,
And each alternate, life or fame propos'd;
Here, if I stay, before the *Trojan* town,
Short is my date, but deathless my renown: 535
If I return, I quit immortal praise
For years on years, and long-extended days.
Convinc'd, tho' late, I find my fond mistake,
And warn the *Greeks* the wiser choice to make:
To quit these shores, their native seats enjoy, 540
Nor hope the fall of heav'n-defended *Troy*.
Jove's arm display'd asserts her from the skies;
Her hearts are strengthen'd, and her glories rise.
Go then, to *Greece* report our fixt design;
Bid all your counsels, all your armies join, 545
Let all your forces, all your arts conspire,
To save the ships, the troops, the chiefs from fire.

One stratagem has fail'd, and others will:
Ye find, *Achilles* is unconquer'd still.
550   Go then – digest my message as ye may –
But here this night let rev'rend *Phœnix* stay:
His tedious toils, and hoary hairs demand
A peaceful death in *Pthia*'s friendly land.
But whether he remain, or sail with me,
555   His age be sacred, and his will be free.

    The son of *Peleus* ceas'd: the chiefs around
In silence wrapt, in consternation drown'd,
Attend the stern reply. Then *Phœnix* rose;
(Down his white beard a stream of sorrow flows)
560   And while the fate of suff'ring *Greece* he mourn'd,
With accent weak these tender words return'd.

    Divine *Achilles!* wilt thou then retire,
And leave our hosts in blood, our fleets on fire?
If wrath so dreadful fill thy ruthless mind,
565   How shall thy friend, thy *Phœnix*, stay behind?
The royal *Peleus*, when from *Pthia*'s coast
He sent thee early to th' *Achaian* host;
Thy youth as then in sage debates unskill'd,
And new to perils of the direful field:
570   He bade me teach thee all the ways of war.
To shine in councils, and in camps to dare.
Never, ah never let me leave thy side!
No time shall part us, and no fate divide.
Not tho' the God, that breath'd my life, restore
575   The bloom I boasted, and the port I bore,
When *Greece* of old beheld my youthful flames,
(Delightful *Greece*, the land of lovely dames.)
My father, faithless to my mother's arms,
Old as he was, ador'd a stranger's charms.
580   I try'd what youth could do (at her desire)
To win the damsel, and prevent my sire.
My sire with curses loads my hated head,
And cries, 'Ye furies! barren be his bed.
Infernal *Jove*, the vengeful fiends below,
585   And ruthless *Proserpine*, confirm'd his vow.
Despair and grief distract my lab'ring mind;
Gods! what a crime my impious heart design'd?

I thought (but some kind God that thought supprest)
To plunge the ponyard in my father's breast:
Then meditate my flight; my friends in vain   590
With pray'rs entreat me, and with force detain;
On fat of rams, black bulls, and brawny swine,
They daily feast, with draughts of fragrant wine:
Strong guards they plac'd, and watch'd nine nights
        entire;
The roofs and porches flam'd with constant fire.   595
The tenth, I forc'd the gates, unseen of all;
And favour'd by the night, o'erleap'd the wall.
My travels thence thro' spacious *Greece* extend;
In *Pthia*'s court at last my labours end.
Your sire receiv'd me, as his son caress'd,   600
With gifts enrich'd, and with possessions bless'd.
The strong *Dolopians* thenceforth own'd my reign,
And all the coast that runs along the main.
By love to thee his bounties I repaid,
And early wisdom to thy soul convey'd: 605
Great as thou art, my lessons made thee brave,
A child I took thee, but a hero gave.
Thy infant breast a like affection show'd;
Still in my arms (an ever-pleasing load)
Or at my knee, by *Phœnix* wouldst thou stand;   610
No food was grateful but from *Phœnix*' hand.
I pass my watchings o'er thy helpless years,
The tender labours, the compliant cares;
The Gods (I thought) revers'd their hard decree,
And *Phœnix* felt a father's joys in thee: 615
Thy growing virtues justify'd my cares,
And promis'd comfort to my silver hairs.
Now by thy rage, thy fatal rage, resign'd;
A cruel heart ill suits a manly mind:
The Gods (the only great, and only wise)   620
Are mov'd by off'rings, vows, and sacrifice;
Offending man their high compassion wins,
And daily pray'rs attone for daily sins.
Pray'rs are *Jove*'s daughters, of celestial race,
Lame are their feet, and wrinkled is their face;   625

With humble mien, and with dejected eyes,
Constant they follow, where *Injustice* flies:
Injustice swift, erect, and unconfin'd,
Sweeps the wide earth, and tramples o'er mankind, }
630   While *Pray'rs*, to heal her wrongs, move slow behind.
Who hears these daughters of almighty *Jove*,
For him they mediate to the throne above:
When man rejects the humble suit they make,
The sire revenges for the daughter's sake;
635   From *Jove* commission'd, fierce *Injustice* then
Descends, to punish unrelenting men.
Oh let not headlong passion bear the sway;
These reconciling Goddesses obey:
Due honours to the seed of *Jove* belong;
640   Due honours calm the fierce, and bend the strong.
Were these not paid thee by the terms we bring,
Were rage still harbour'd in the haughty King,
Nor *Greece*, nor all her fortunes, should engage
Thy friend to plead against so just a rage.
645   But since what honour asks, the Gen'ral sends,
And sends by those whom most thy heart commends,
The best and noblest of the *Grecian* train;
Permit not these to sue, and sue in vain!
Let me (my son) an ancient fact unfold,
650   A great example drawn from times of old;
Hear what our fathers were, and what their praise,
Who conquer'd their revenge in former days.

    Where *Calydon* on rocky mountains stands,
Once fought th' *Ætolian* and *Curetian* bands;
655   To guard it those, to conquer, these advance;
And mutual deaths were dealt with mutual chance.
The silver *Cynthia* bade *Contention* rise,
In Vengeance of neglected Sacrifice;
On *Oeneus*' fields she sent a monstrous boar,
660   That level'd harvests, and whole forests tore:
This beast, (when many a chief his tusks had slain)
Great *Meleager* stretch'd along the plain.
Then, for his spoils, a new debate arose,
The neighbour nations thence commencing foes.

Strong as they were, the bold *Curetes* fail'd, 665
While *Meleager*'s thund'ring arm prevail'd:
Till rage at length inflam'd his lofty breast,
(For rage invades the wisest and the best.)
     Curs'd by *Althæa*, to his wrath he yields,
And in his wife's embrace forgets the fields. 670
(She from *Marpessa* sprung, divinely fair,
And matchless *Idas*, more than man in war;
The God of day ador'd the mother's charms;
Against the God the father bent his arms;
Th' afflicted pair, their sorrows to proclaim, 675
From *Cleopatra* chang'd this daughter's name,
And call'd *Alcyone*; a name to show
The father's grief, the mourning mother's woe.)
To her the chief retir'd from stern debate,
But found no peace from fierce *Althæa*'s hate: 680
Althæa's hate th' unhappy warriour drew,
Whose luckless hand his royal uncle slew;
She beat the ground, and call'd the pow'rs beneath
On her own son to wreak her brother's death:
Hell heard her curses from the realms profound, 685
And the red fiends that walk the nightly round.
In vain *Ætolia* her deliv'rer waits,
War shakes her walls, and thunders at her gates.
She sent embassadors, a chosen band,
Priests of the Gods, and elders of the land; 690
Besought the chief to save the sinking state:
Their pray'rs were urgent, and their proffers great:
(Full fifty acres of the richest ground,
Half pasture green, and half with vin'yards crown'd.)
His suppliant father, aged *Oeneus*, came; 695
His sisters follow'd; ev'n the vengeful dame,
Althæa sues; His friends before him fall:
He stands relentless, and rejects 'em all.
Mean while the victor's shouts ascend the skies;
The walls are scal'd; the rolling flames arise; 700
At length his wife (a form divine) appears,
With piercing cries, and supplicating tears;
She paints the horrors of a conquer'd town,
The heroes slain, the palaces o'erthrown,

705 The matrons ravish'd, the whole race enslav'd:
The warriour heard, he vanquish'd, and he sav'd.
Th'*Ætolians*, long disdain'd, now took their turn,
And left the chief their broken faith to mourn.
Learn hence, betimes to curb pernicious ire,
710 Nor stay, till yonder fleets ascend in fire:
Accept the presents; draw thy conqu'ring sword;
And be amongst our guardian Gods ador'd.
    Thus he: The stern *Achilles* thus reply'd.
My second father, and my rev'rend guide!
715 Thy friend, believe me, no such gifts demands,
And asks no honours from a mortal's hands:
Jove honours me, and favours my designs;
His pleasure guides me, and his will confines:
And here I stay, (if such his high behest)
720 While life's warm spirit beats within my breast.
Yet hear one word, and lodge it in thy heart;
No more molest me on *Atrides*' part:
Is it for him these tears are taught to flow,
For him these sorrows? for my mortal foe?
725 A gen'rous friendship no cold medium knows,
Burns with one love, with one resentment glows;
One should our int'rests, and our passions be;
My friend must hate the man that injures me.
Do this, my *Phœnix*, 'tis a gen'rous part,
730 And share my realms, my honours, and my heart.
Let these return: Our voyage, or our stay,
Rest undetermin'd till the dawning day.
    He ceas'd; then order'd for the sage's bed
A warmer couch with num'rous carpets spread.
735 With that, stern *Ajax* his long silence broke,
And thus, impatient, to *Ulysses* spoke.
    Hence, let us go – why waste we time in vain?
See what effect our low submissions gain!
Lik'd or not lik'd, his words we must relate,
740 The *Greeks* expect them, and our heroes wait.
Proud as he is, that iron-heart retains
Its stubborn purpose, and his friends disdains.
Stern, and unpitying! if a brother bleed,
On just attonement, we remit the deed;

A sire the slaughter of his son forgives;   745
The price of blood discharg'd, the murd'rer lives:
The haughtiest hearts at length their rage resign,
And gifts can conquer ev'ry soul but thine.
The Gods that unrelenting breast have steel'd,
And curs'd thee with a mind that cannot yield.   750
One woman-slave was ravish'd from thy arms:
Lo, sev'n are offer'd, and of equal charms.
Then hear, *Achilles!* be of better mind;
Revere thy roof, and to thy guests be kind;
And know the men, of all the *Grecian* host,   755
Who honour worth, and prize thy valour most.

   Oh soul of battels, and thy people's guide!
(To *Ajax* thus the first of *Greeks* reply'd)
Well hast thou spoke; but at the tyrant's name
My rage rekindles, and my soul's on flame: 760
'Tis just resentment, and becomes the brave;
Disgrac'd, dishonour'd, like the vilest slave!
Return then heroes! and our answer bear,
The glorious combat is no more my care;
Not till amidst yon' sinking navy slain,   765
The blood of *Greeks* shall dye the sable main;
Not till the flames, by *Hector*'s fury thrown,
Consume your vessels, and approach my own;
Just there, th' impetuous homicide shall stand,
There cease his battel, and there feel our hand.   770

   This said, each prince a double goblet crown'd,
And cast a large libation on the ground;
Then to their vessels, thro' the gloomy shades,
The chiefs return; divine *Ulysses* leads.
Meantime *Achilles'* slaves prepar'd a bed,   775
With fleeces, carpets, and soft linen spread:
There, till the sacred morn restor'd the day,
In slumbers sweet the rev'rend *Phœnix* lay.
But in his inner tent, an ampler space,
Achilles slept; and in his warm embrace   780
Fair *Diomedè* of the *Lesbian* race.
Last, for *Patroclus* was the couch prepar'd,
Whose nightly joys the beauteous *Iphis* shar'd:

Achilles to his friend consign'd her charms,
785　When *Scyros* fell before his conqu'ring arms.
　　　And now th' elected chiefs whom *Greece* had sent,
　　　Pass'd thro' the hosts, and reach'd the royal tent.
　　　Then rising all, with goblets in their hands,
　　　The peers and leaders of th' *Achaian* bands
790　Hail'd their return: *Atrides* first begun.
　　　Say what success? divine *Laertes'* son!
　　　Achilles' high resolves declare to all;
　　　Returns the chief, or must our navy fall?
　　　Great King of nations! (*Ithacus* reply'd)
795　Fixt is his wrath, unconquer'd is his pride;
　　　He slights thy friendship, thy proposals scorns,
　　　And thus implor'd, with fiercer fury burns.
　　　To save our army, and our fleets to free,
　　　Is not his care; but left to *Greece* and thee.
800　Your eyes shall view, when morning paints the sky,
　　　Beneath his oars the whitening billows fly.
　　　Us too he bids our oars and sails employ,
　　　Nor hope the fall of heav'n-protected *Troy*;
　　　For *Jove* o'ershades her with his arm divine,
805　Inspires her war, and bids her glory shine.
　　　Such was his word: What farther he declar'd,
　　　These sacred heralds and great *Ajax* heard.
　　　But *Phœnix* in his tent the chief retains,
　　　Safe to transport him to his native plains,
810　When morning dawns: if other he decree,
　　　His age is sacred, and his choice is free.
　　　　Ulysses ceas'd: The great *Achaian* host,
　　　With sorrow seiz'd, in consternation lost,
　　　Attend the stern reply. *Tydides* broke
815　The gen'ral silence, and undaunted spoke.
　　　Why shou'd we gifts to proud *Achilles* send,
　　　Or strive with pray'rs his haughty soul to bend?
　　　His country's woes he glories to deride,
　　　And pray'rs will burst that swelling heart with pride.
820　Be the fierce impulse of his rage obey'd;
　　　Our battels let him, or desert, or aid;
　　　Then let him arm when *Jove* or he think fit;
　　　That, to his madness, or to heav'n commit.

What for our selves we can, is always ours;
This night, let due repast refresh our pow'rs;   825
(For strength consists in spirits and in blood,
And those are ow'd to gen'rous wine and food)
But when the rosy messenger of day
Strikes the blue mountains with her golden ray,
Rang'd at the ships, let all our squadrons shine,   830
In flaming arms, a long-extended line:
In the dread front let great *Atrides* stand,
The first in danger, as in high command.

    Shouts of acclaim the list'ning heroes raise,
Then each to heav'n the due libations pays;   835
Till sleep descending o'er the tents, bestows
The grateful blessings of desir'd repose.

OBSERVATIONS

ON THE

NINTH BOOK

The epigraph on the frontispiece of Volume III (Books 9–12) consists of the following lines:

> – *Det primos versibus annos*
> *Mæoniumque bibat fœlici pectore fontem.*   PETR.

[May he give his youth to poetry and
may he drink, with a fortunate soul,
of the Maeonian (i.e. Homeric) fount.
                    (Petronius, *Satyricon*, 5 v. 11)]

We have here a new scene of action opened; the Poet has hitherto given us an account of what happened by day only: the two following books relate the adventures of the night.

It may be thought that *Homer* has crowded a great many actions into a very short time. In the ninth book a council is conven'd, an embassy sent, a considerable time passes in the speeches and replies of the embassadors and *Achilles*: In the tenth book a second council is call'd; after this a debate is held, *Dolon* is intercepted, *Diomed* and *Ulysses* enter into the enemy's camp, kill *Rhesus*, and bring away his horses: and all this done in the narrow compass of one night.

It must therefore be remember'd that the ninth book takes up the first part of the night only; that after the first council was dissolv'd, there pass'd some time before the second was summon'd, as appears by the leaders being awakened by *Menelaus*. So that it was almost morning before *Diomed* and *Ulysses* set out upon their design, which is very evident from the words of *Ulysses*, Book 10. v. 251.

Ἀλλ' ἴομεν, μάλα γὰρ νὺξ ἄνεται, ἐγγύθι δ' ἠώς.

So that altho' a great many incidents are introduc'd, yet every thing might easily have been perform'd in the allotted time.

7. *From* Thracia*'s shore.*] *Homer* has been suppos'd by *Eratosthenes* and others, to have been guilty of an error, in saying that *Zephyrus*, or the west wind, blows from *Thrace*, whereas in truth it blows toward it. But the poet speaks so either because it is fabled to be the rendezvous of all the winds; or with respect to the particular situation of *Troy* and the *Ægean* Sea. Either of these replies are sufficient to solve that objection.

The particular parts of this comparison agree admirably with the design of *Homer*, to express the distraction of the *Greeks*: the two winds representing the different opinions of the armies, one part of which were inclin'd to return, the other to stay.   *Eustathius.*

15. *But bid in whispers.*] The reason why *Agamemnon* commands his heralds to summon the leaders in silence, is for fear the enemy should discover their consternation, by reason of their nearness, or perceive what their designs were in this extremity.   *Eustathius.*

23. Agamemnon*'s speech.*] The criticks are divided in their opinion whether this speech, which is word for word the same with that he makes in *Lib.* 2. be only a feint to try the army, as it is there, or the real sentiments of the General. *Dionysius* of *Halicarnassus* explains it as the former, with whom Madam *Dacier* concurs; she thinks they must be both counterfeit, because they are both the same, and believes *Homer* would have varied them, had the design been different. She takes no notice that *Eustathius* is of the contrary opinion; as is also Monsieur *de la Motte*, who argues as if he had read them. '*Agamemnon* (says he) in the second Iliad, thought himself assured of victory from the dream which *Jupiter* had sent to him, and in that confidence was desirous to bring the *Greeks* to a battel; but in the ninth book his circumstances are changed, he is in the utmost distress and despair upon his defeat, and therefore his proposal to raise the siege is in all probability sincere. If *Homer* had intended we should think otherwise, he would have told us so, as he did on the former occasion; and some of the officers would have suspected a feint the rather, because they had been impos'd upon by the same speech before. But none of them

suspect him at all. *Diomed* thinks him so much in earnest as to reproach his cowardice, *Nestor* applauds *Diomed*'s liberty, and *Agamemnon* makes not the least defence for himself.'

Dacier answers, that *Homer* had no occasion to tell us this was counterfeit, because the officers could not but remember it to have been so before; and as for the answers of *Diomed* and *Nestor*, they only carry on the same feint, as *Dionysius* has prov'd, whose reasons may be seen in the following note.

I do not pretend to decide upon this point; but which way soever it be, I think *Agamemnon*'s design was equally answer'd by repeating the same speech: so that the repetition at least is not to be blamed in *Homer*. What obliged *Agamemnon* to that feint in the second book was the hatred he had incurred in the army by being the cause of *Achilles*'s departure; this made it but a necessary precaution in him to try, before he came to a battel, whether the *Greeks* were dispos'd to it: And it was equally necessary, in case the event should prove unsuccessful, to free himself from the odium of being the occasion of it. Therefore when they were now actually defeated, to repeat the same words, was the readiest way to put them in mind that he had propos'd the same advice to them before the battel; and to make it appear unjust that their ill fortune should be charged upon him. See the 5*th* and 8*th* notes on the second Iliad.

43. *The Speech of* Diomed.] I shall here translate the Criticism of *Dionysius* on this passage. He asks, 'What can be the drift of *Diomed*, when he insults *Agamemnon* in his griefs and distresses? For what *Diomed* here says seems not only very ill tim'd, but inconsistent with his own opinion, and with the respect he had shewn in the beginning of this very speech.

> *If I upbraid thee, Prince, thy wrath with-hold,*
> *The laws of council bid my tongue be bold.*

This is the introduction of a man in temper, who is willing to soften and excuse the liberty of what is to follow, and what necessity only obliges him to utter. But he subjoins a resentment of the reproach the King had formerly thrown upon him, and tells him that *Jupiter* had given him power and dominion without courage and virtue. These are things which agree but ill together, that *Diomed* should upbraid *Agamemnon* in his adversity with past injuries, after he had endur'd his reproaches with so much moderation, and had reproved *Sthenelus* so warmly for the contrary practice in the fourth book. If any one answer, that *Diomed* was warranted in this freedom by the bravery of his warlike behaviour since that reproach, he supposes this Hero very ignorant how to demean himself in prosperity. The truth is, this whole accusation of *Diomed*'s is only a feint to serve the designs of *Agamemnon*. For being desirous to persuade the *Greeks* against their departure, he effects that design by this counterfeited anger, and license of speech: and seeming to resent, that *Agamemnon* should be capable of imagining the army would return to *Greece*, he artificially makes use of these reproaches to cover his argument. This is farther confirm'd by what follows, when he bids *Agamemnon* return, if he pleases, and affirms that the *Grecians* will stay without him. Nay, he carries the matter so far, as to boast, that if all the rest should depart, himself and *Sthenelus* alone would continue the war, which would be extremely childish and absurd in any other view than this.'

53. *They gave thee sceptres,* &c.] This is the language of a brave man, to affirm and say boldly, that courage is above scepters and crowns. Scepters and crowns were indeed in former times not hereditary, but the recompence of valour. With what art and haughtiness *Diomed* sets himself indirectly above *Agamemnon!*   *Eustathius.*

62. *And nearest to the main.*] There is a secret stroke of satyr in these words: *Diomed* tells the King that his squadron lies next the sea, insinuating that they were the most distant from the battel, and readiest for flight.   *Eustathius.*

68. *God bade us fight, and 'twas with God we came.*] This is literal from the *Greek*, and therein may be seen the style of holy scripture, where 'tis said that they *come with God*, or that they are not come *without God*, meaning that they did not come without his order: *Numquid sine Domino ascendi in terram istam?* [Have I come up against his country without God's help?] says *Rabshekah* to *Hezekiah* in *Isaiah* 36. v. 8. This passage seems to me very beautiful. *Homer* adds it to shew that the valour of *Diomed*, which puts him upon remaining alone with *Sthenelus*, when all the *Greeks* were gone, is not a rash and mad boldness, but a reasonable one, and founded on the promises of God himself, who cannot lye.   *Dacier.*

73. *The speech of* Nestor.] Dionysius gives us the design of this speech in the place above cited. '*Nestor* (says he) seconds the oration of

Diomed: We shall perceive the artifice of his discourse, if we reflect to how little purpose it would be without this design. He praises *Diomed* for what he has said, but does it not without declaring, that he had not spoken fully to the purpose, but fallen short in some points, which he ascribes to his youth, and promises to supply them. Then after a long preamble, when he has turn'd himself several ways, as if he was sporting in a new and uncommon vein of oratory, he concludes by ordering the watch to their stations, and advising *Agamemnon* to invite the elders of the army to a supper, there, out of many counsels, to chuse the best. All this at first sight appears absurd: But we must know that *Nestor* too speaks in figure. *Diomed* seems to quarrel with *Agamemnon* purely to gratify him; but *Nestor* praises his liberty of speech, as it were to vindicate a real quarrel with the King. The end of all this is only to move *Agamemnon* to supplicate *Achilles*; and to that end he so much commends the young man's freedom. In proposing to call a council only of the eldest, he consults the dignity of *Agamemnon*, that he might not be expos'd to make this condescension before the younger officers. And he concludes by an artful inference of the absolute necessity of applying to *Achilles* from the present posture of their affairs.

> *See what a blaze from hostile tents aspires,*
> *How near our fleets* [sic] *approach the* Trojan *fires!*

This is all *Nestor* says at this time before the general assembly of the *Greeks*; but in his next speech, when the elders only are present, he explains the whole matter at large, and openly declares that they must have recourse to *Achilles*.' *Dion. Hal.* περὶ ἐσχηματισμένων, ρ. 2.

Plutarch de aud. Poetis, takes notice of this piece of decorum in *Nestor*, who when he intended to move for a mediation with *Achilles*, chose not to do it in publick, but propos'd a private meeting of the chiefs to that end. If what these two great authors have said be consider'd, there will be no room for the trivial objection some moderns have made to this proposal of *Nestor*'s, as if in the present distress he did no more than impertinently advise them to go to supper.

73. *Oh truly great.*] *Nestor* could do no less than commend *Diomed*'s valour, he had lately been a witness of it when he was preserv'd from falling into the enemy's hands till he was rescu'd by *Diomed*.

Eustathius.

87. *Curs'd is the man.*] *Nestor*, says the same author, very artfully brings in these words as a general maxim, in order to dispose *Agamemnon* to a reconciliation with *Achilles*: he delivers it in general terms, and leaves the King to make the application. This passage is translated with liberty, for the original comprizes a great deal in a very few words, ἀφρήτωρ, ἀθέμιστος, ἀνέστιος; it will be proper to give a particular explication of each of these; αφρήτωρ, says *Eustathius*, signifies one who is a vagabond or foreigner. The *Athenians* kept a register, in which all that were born were enroll'd, whence it easily appear'd who were citizens, or not; ἀφρήτωρ therefore signifies one who is depriv'd of the privilege of a citizen. Ἀθέμιστος is one who had forfeited all title to be protected by the laws of his country. Ἀνέστιος, one that has no habitation, or rather one that was not permitted to partake of any family sacrifice. For Ἑστία is a family Goddess; and *Jupiter* sometimes is called Ζεὺς ἑστιοῦχος.

There is a sort of gradation in these words. Ἀθέμιστος signifies a man that has lost the privileges of his country; ἀφρήτωρ those of his own tribe, and ἀνέστιος those of his own family.

94. *Between the trench and wall.*] It is almost impossible to make such particularities as these appear with any tolerable elegance in poetry: And as they cannot be rais'd, so neither must they be omitted. This particular space here mention'd between the trench and wall, is what we must carry in our mind thro' this and the following book: Otherwise we shall be at a loss to know the exact scene of the actions and councils that follow.

119. *The fires they light.*] They lighted up these fires that they might not seem to be under any consternation, but to be called upon their guard against any alarm.   *Eustathius.*

124. *When thirst and hunger ceast.*] The conduct of *Homer* in this place is very remarkable; he does not fall into a long description of the entertainment, but complies with the exigence of affairs, and passes on to the consultation.   *Eustathius.*

138. *And make the wisdom thine.*] *Eustathius* thought that *Homer* said this, because in council, as in the army, all is attributed to the Princes, and the whole honour ascrib'd to them: but this is by no means *Homer*'s thought. What he here says, is a maxim drawn from the profoundest philosophy. That which often does men the most harm, is

envy, and the shame of yielding to advice, which proceeds from others. There is more greatness and capacity in following good advice, than in proposing it; by executing it, we render it our own, and we ravish even the property of it from its author; and *Eustathius* seems to incline to this thought, when he afterwards says, *Homer* makes him that follows good advice, equal to him that gives it; but he has not fully express'd himself.   *Dacier.*

140. *At once my present judgment and my past.*] *Nestor* here by the word πάλαι, means the advice he gave at the time of the quarrel in the first book: He says, as it was his opinion then that *Agamemnon* ought not to disgrace *Achilles*, so after the maturest deliberation, he finds no reason to alter it. *Nestor* here launches out into the praises of *Achilles*, which is a secret argument to induce *Agamemnon* to regain his friendship, by shewing the importance of it.   *Eustathius.*

151. *This wondrous hero.*] It is remarkable that *Agamemnon* here never uses the name of *Achilles*: tho' he is resolv'd to court his friendship, yet he cannot bear the mention of his name. The impression which the dissention made, is not yet worn off, tho' he expatiates in commendation of his valour.   *Eustathius.*

155. *If gifts immense his mighty soul can bow.*] The Poet, says *Eustathius*, makes a wise choice of the gifts that are to be proffer'd to *Achilles*. Had he been ambitious of wealth, there are golden tripods, and ten talents of gold to bribe his resentment. If he had been addicted to the fair sex, there was a King's daughter and seven fair captives to win his favour. Or if he had been ambitious of greatness, there were seven wealthy cities and a kingly power to court him to a reconciliation: But he takes this way to shew us that his anger was stronger than all his other passions. It is farther observable, that *Agamemnon* promises these presents at three different times; first, at this instant; secondly, on the taking of *Troy*; and lastly, after their return to *Greece.* This division in some degree multiplies them.   *Dacier.*

157. *Ten weighty Talents.*] The ancient criticks have blamed one of the verses in the enumeration of these presents, as not sufficiently flowing and harmonious, the pause is ill placed, and one word does not fall easily into the other. This will appear very plain if we compare it with a more numerous verse.

Ἄκρον ἐπὶ ῥηγμῖνος ἁλὸς πολιοῖο θέεσκον.

[They would run along the top of the surf of the grey salt
water.]

Ἀίθωνας δὲ λέβητας ἐείκοσι, δώδεκα δ' ἵππους.

[Twenty shining cauldrons, and twelve horses.]

The ear immediately perceives the musick of the former line, every
syllable glides smoothly away, without offending the ear with any such
roughness, as is found in the second. The first runs as swiftly as the
coursers describes; but the latter is a broken, interrupted, uneven
verse. But it is certainly pardonable in this place, where the musick of
poetry is not necessary; the mind is entirely taken up in learning what
presents *Agamemnon* intended to make *Achilles*: and is not at leisure to
regard the ornaments of versification; and even those pauses are not
without their beauties, as they would of necessity cause a stop in the
delivery, and so give time for each particular to sink into the mind of
Achilles.

Eustathius.

159. *Sev'n sacred tripods.*] There were two kinds of tripods: in the one
they used to boil water, the other was entirely for shew, to mix wine
and water in, says *Athenæus*: the first were called λέβητας, or cauldrons,
for common use, and made to bear the fire; the other were ἄπυροι, and
made chiefly for ornament. It may be ask'd why this could be a proper
present for *Achilles*, who was a martial man, and regarded nothing but
arms? It may be answer'd, that these presents were very well suited to
the person to whom they were sent, as tripods in ancient days were the
usual prizes in games, and they were given by *Achilles* himself in those
which he exhibited in honour of *Patroclus*: the same may be said of the
female captives, which were also among the prizes in the games of
Patroclus.

Eustathius.

161. *Twelve steeds unmatch'd.*] From hence it is evident that games used
to be celebrated in the *Grecian* army during the time of war; perhaps in
honour of the deceased Heroes. For had *Agamemnon* given *Achilles* horses
that had been victorious before the beginning of the *Trojan* war, they
would by this time have been too old to be of any value. *Eustathius*.

189. Laodice *and* Iphigenia, &c.] These are the names of *Agamemnon*'s
daughters, among which we do not find *Electra*. But some affirm, says

Eustathius, that *Laodice* and *Electra* are the same, (as *Iphianassa* is the same with *Iphigenia*) and she was called so either by way of surname, or by reason of her complexion, which was ἠλεκτρῶδες, *flava*; or by way of derision ἠλέκτρα *quasi* ἄλεκτρον [unbedded], because she was an old maid, as appears from *Euripides*, who says that she remained long a virgin.

Παρθένε, μακρὸν δὴ μῆκος Ἠλέκτρα, χρόνου.

[Elektra, for a long time chaste.]

And in *Sophocles* she says of herself, Ἀνύμφευτος αἰὲν οἰχνῶ, *I wander a disconsolate unmarry'd virgin*, which shews that it was ever looked upon as a disgrace to continue long so.

192. *I ask no presents – My self will give the dow'r.*] For in *Greece* the bridegroom, before he married, was obliged to make two presents, one to his betroth'd wife, and the other to his father-in-law. This custom is very ancient; it was practised by the *Hebrews* in the time of the patriarchs. *Abraham*'s servant gave necklaces and ear-rings to *Rebecca* whom he demanded for *Isaac. Genesis* 24. 22. *Shechem* son of *Hamor* says to *Jacob* and his sons, whose sister he was desirous to espouse, 'Ask me never so much dowry and gifts,' *Genesis* 34. 12. For the dowry was for the daughter. This present serv'd for her dowry, and the other presents were for the father. In the first Book of *Samuel* 18. 25. *Saul* makes them say to *David*, who by reason of his poverty said he could not be son-in-law to the King: 'The King desireth not any dowry.' And in the two last passages, we see the presents were commonly regulated by the father of the bride. There is no mention in *Homer* of any present made to the father, but only of that which was given to the married daughter, which was called ἕδνα. The dowry which the father gave to his daughter was called μείλια: Wherefore *Agamemnon* says here ἐπὶ μείλια δώσω.   *Dacier.*

209. Pluto, *the grizly God, who never spares.*] The meaning of this may be gather'd from *Æschylus*, cited here by *Eustathius.*

Μόνος θεῶν θάνατος οὐ δώρων ἐρᾷ,
Οὐδ' ἄν τι θύων οὐδ' ἐπισπένδων λάβοις,
Οὐδ' ἔστι βωμός, οὐδὲ παιωνίζεται.

'Death is the only God who is not moved by offerings, whom you cannot conquer by sacrifices and oblations, and therefore he is the only God to whom no altar is erected, and no hymns are sung.'

221. *Let* Phœnix *lead.*] How comes it to pass that *Phœnix* is in the *Grecian* camp: when undoubtedly he retired with his pupil *Achilles*? *Eustathius* says the ancients conjectured that he came to the camp to see the last battel: and indeed nothing is more natural to imagine, than that *Achilles* would be impatient to know the event of the day, when he was himself absent from the fight: and as his revenge and glory were to be satisfied by the ill success of the *Grecians*, it is highly probable that he sent *Phœnix* to enquire after it. *Eustathius* farther observes, *Phœnix* was not an embassador, but only the conductor of the embassy. This is evident from the words themselves, which are all along delivered in the dual number; and farther, from *Achilles*'s requiring *Phœnix* to stay with him when the other two departed.

222. *Great* Ajax *next, and* Ithacus *the sage.*] The choice of these persons is made with a great deal of judgment. *Achilles* could not but reverence the venerable *Phœnix* his guardian and tutor. *Ajax* and *Ulysses* had been disgrac'd in the first book, line 145, as well as he, and were therefore proper persons to persuade him to forgive as they had forgiven: besides it was the greatest honour that could be done to *Achilles* to send the most worthy personages in the army to him. *Ulysses* was inferior to none in eloquence but to *Nestor*. *Ajax* was second to none in valour but to *Achilles*.

Ajax might have an influence over him as a relation, by descent from *Æacus, Ulysses* as an orator: to these are join'd *Hodius* and *Eurybates*, two heralds, which tho it were not customary, yet was necessary in this place, both to certify *Achilles* that this embassage was the act of *Agamemnon* himself, and also to make these persons who had been witnesses before God and man of the wrong done to *Achilles* in respect to *Briseïs*, witnesses also of the satisfaction given him.

Eustathius.

235. *Much he advis'd them all,* Ulysses *most.*] There is a great propriety in representing *Nestor* as so particularly applying himself on this occasion to *Ulysses.* Tho' he of all Men had the least need of his instructions; yet it is highly natural for one wise man to talk most to another.

246. *Pleas'd with the solemn harp's harmonious sound.*] 'Homer (says *Plutarch*) to prove what an excellent use may be made of musick, feign'd *Achilles* to compose by this means the wrath he had conceived against *Agamemnon.* He sung to his harp the noble actions of the valiant, and the atchievements of Heroes and Demigods, a subject worthy of *Achilles. Homer* moreover teaches us in this fiction the proper season for musick, when a man is at leisure and unemploy'd in greater affairs. For *Achilles,* so valorous as he was, had retir'd from Action thro' his displeasure to *Agamemnon.* And nothing was better suited to the martial disposition of this hero, than these heroick songs, that prepared him for the deeds and toils he afterwards undertook, by the celebration of the like in those who had gone before him. Such was the ancient musick, and to such purposes it was applied.' *Plut. of Musick.* The same author relates in the life of *Alexander,* that when the Lyre of *Paris* was offered to that Prince, he made answer, 'He had little value for it, but much desired that of *Achilles,* on which he sung the actions of heroes in former times.'

261. *Princes all hail!*] This short speech is wonderfully proper to the occasion, and to the temper of the speaker. One is under a great expectation of what *Achilles* will say at the sight of these Heroes, and I know nothing in nature that could satisfy it, but the very thing he here accosts them with.

268. *Mix purer wine.*] The meaning of this word ζωρότερον is very dubious; some say it signifies warm wine, from ζέω, *ferveo*: According to *Aristotle,* it is an adverb, and implies to mix wine *quickly.* And others think it signifies pure wine. In this last sense *Herodotus* uses it. Ἐπὰν ζωρότερον βούλωνται Σπαρτιῆται πιεῖν, ἐπισκύθισον λέγουσιν, ὡς ἀπὸ τῶν Σκυθῶν, οἵ, φησιν, εἰς Σπάρτην ἀφικόμενοι πρέσβεις ἐδίδαξαν τὸν Κλεομένην ἀκρατοποτεῖν. Which in *English* is thus: 'When the *Spartans* have an inclination to drink their wine pure and not diluted, they propose to drink after the manner of the *Scythians*; some of whom coming embassadors to *Sparta,* taught *Cleomenes* to drink his wine unmix'd.' I think this sense of the word is most natural, and *Achilles* might give this particular order not to dilute the wine so much as usually, because the embassadors who were brave men, might be supposed to be much fatigued in the late battel, and to want a more than usual refreshment. *Eustathius.* See *Plutarch Symp. l.* 4. *c.* 5.

271. Patroclus *o'er the blazing fire,* &c.] The reader must not expect to find much beauty in such descriptions as these: they give us an exact account of the simplicity of that age, which for all we know might be a part of *Homer*'s design; there being, no doubt, a considerable change of customs in *Greece* from the time of the *Trojan* war to those wherein our author lived; and it seemed demanded of him to omit nothing that might give the *Greeks* an idea of the manners of their predecessors. But however that matter stood, it should methinks be a pleasure to a modern reader to see how such mighty men, whose actions have surviv'd their persons three thousand years, lived in the earliest ages of the world. The embassadors found this hero, says *Eustathius*, without any attendants; he had no ushers or waiters to introduce them, no servile parasites about him: the latter ages degenerated into these pieces of state and pageantry.

The supper also is described with an equal simplicity: three Princes are busied in preparing it, and they who made the greatest figure in the field of battel, thought it no disparagement to prepare their own repast. The objections some have made, that *Homer*'s Gods and Heroes do every thing for themselves, as if several of those offices were unworthy of them, proceeds from the corrupt idea of modern luxury and grandeur: Whereas in truth it is rather a weakness and imperfection to stand in need of the assistance and ministry of others. But however it be, methinks those of the nicest taste might relish this entertainment of *Homer*'s, when they consider these great men as soldiers in a camp, in whom the least appearance of luxury would have been a crime.

271. Patroclus *o'er the blazing fire.*] Madam *Dacier*'s general note on this passage deserves to be transcribed. '*Homer*, says she, is in the right not to avoid these descriptions, because nothing can properly be called vulgar which is drawn from the manner and usages of persons of the first dignity; and also because in his tongue even the terms of cookery are so noble, and of so agreeable a sound, and he likewise knows how to place them so well, as to extract a perfect harmony from them: so that he may be said to be as excellent a Poet when he describes these small matters, as when he treats of the greatest subjects. 'Tis not so either with our manners, or our language. Cookery is left to servants, and all its terms so low and disagreeable, even in the sound, that nothing can be made of them, that has not some taint of their meanness. This great disadvantage made me at first think of abridging this preparation of the repast; but when I had well considered it, I was resolv'd to preserve and give *Homer* as he is, without retrenching any thing from the simplicity of the heroick manners. I do not write to enter the lists against *Homer*, I will dispute nothing with him; my design is only to give an idea of him, and to make him understood: the reader will therefore forgive me if this description has none of its original graces.'

272. *In a brazen vase.*] The word κρεῖον signifies the vessel, and not the meat itself, as *Euphorion* conjectured, giving it as a reason that *Homer* makes no mention of boiled meat: but this does not hinder but that the meat might be parboil'd in the vessel to make it roast the sooner. This, with some other notes on the particulars of this passage, belong to *Eustathius*, and Madam *Dacier* ought not to have taken to herself the merit of his explanations.

282. *And sprinkles sacred salt.*] Many reasons are given why salt is called sacred or divine, but the best is because it preserves things incorrupt, and keeps them from dissolution. 'So thunder (says *Plutarch Sympos. l. 5. qu. 10.*) is called divine, because bodies struck with thunder will not putrify; besides generation is divine, because God is the principle of all things, and salt is most operative in generation. *Lycophron* calls it ἁγνίτην τὸν ἅλα [most hallowed salt]: For this reason *Venus* was feign'd by the poets to spring from the sea.'

291. *To* Phœnix Ajax *gave the sign.*] *Ajax*, who was a rough soldier and no orator, is impatient to have the business over: he makes a sign to *Phœnix* to begin, but *Ulysses* prevents him. Perhaps *Ulysses* might flatter himself that his oratory would prevail upon *Achilles*, and so obtain the honour of making the reconciliation himself: or if he were repuls'd, there yet remain'd a second and third resource in *Ajax* and *Phœnix*, who might renew the attempt, and endeavour to shake his resolution: there would still be some hopes of success, as one of these was his guardian, the other his relation. One may farther add to these reasons of *Eustathius*, that it would have been improper for *Phœnix* to have spoken first, since he was not an embassador; and therefore *Ulysses* was the fitter person, as being empower'd by that function to make an offer of the presents in the name of the King.

295. *Health to* Achilles.] There are no discourses in the Iliad better placed, better tim'd, or that give a greater idea of *Homer*'s genius, than these of the embassadors to *Achilles*. These Speeches are not only necessarily demanded by the occasion, but disposed with art, and in such an order, as raises more and more the pleasure of the reader.

Ulysses speaks the first, the character of whose discourse is a well-address'd eloquence; so the mind is agreeably engag'd by the choice of his reasons and applications: *Achilles* replies with a magnanimous freedom, whereby the mind is elevated with the sentiments of the hero: *Phœnix* discourses in a manner touching and pathetick, whereby the heart is moved; and *Ajax* concludes with a generous disdain, that leaves the soul of the reader inflamed. This order undoubtedly denotes a great poet, who knows how to command attention as he pleases by the arrangement of his matter; and I believe it is not possible to propose a better model for the happy disposition of a subject. These words are Monsieur *de la Motte*'s, and no testimony can be more glorious to *Homer* than this, which comes from the mouth of an enemy.

296. *Not those more honour'd whom* Atrides *feasts.*] I must just mention *Dacier*'s observation: With what cunning *Ulysses* here slides in the odious name of *Agamemnon*, as he praises *Achilles*, that the ear of this impetuous man might be familiarized to that name.

314. *He waits but for the morn, to sink in flame The ships, the* Greeks, &c.] There is a circumstance in the original which I have omitted, for fear of being too particular in an oration of this warmth and importance; but as it preserves a piece of antiquity, I must not forget it here. He says that *Hector* will not only fire the fleet, but bear off the *statues of the Gods*, which were carv'd on the prows of the vessels. These were hung up in the temples, as a monument of victory, according to the custom of those times.

342. *But hear me, while I number o'er The proffer'd presents.*] Monsieur *de la Motte* finds fault with *Homer* for making *Ulysses* in this place repeat all the offers of *Agamemnon* to *Achilles*. Not to answer that it was but necessary to make known to *Achilles* all the proposals, or that this distinct enumeration served the more to move him, I think one may appeal to any person of common taste, whether the solemn recital of these circumstances does not please him more than the simple narration could have done, which Monsieur *de la Motte* would have put in its stead. *Ulysses made all the offers* Agamemnon *had commissioned him.*

406. *Achilles's Speech.*] Nothing is more remarkable than the conduct of *Homer* in this speech of *Achilles.* He begins with some degree of coolness, as in respect to the embassadors, whose persons he esteem'd, yet even there his temper just shews itself in the insinuation that *Ulysses* had dealt artfully with him, which in two periods rises into an open detestation of all artifice. He then falls into a sullen declaration of his resolves, and a more sedate representation of his past services; but warms as he goes on, and every minute he but names his wrongs, flies out into extravagance. His rage, awaken'd by that injury, is like a fire blown by a wind that sinks and rises by fits, but keeps continually burning, and blazes but the more for those intermissions.

424. *As the bold Bird*, &c.] This simile (says *La Motte*) must be allowed to be just, but was not fit to be spoken in a passion. One may answer, that the tenderness of the comparison renders it no way the less proper to a man in a passion: it being natural enough, the more one is disgusted at present, the more to recollect the kindness we have formerly shewn to those who are ungrateful. *Eustathius* observes, that so soft as the simile seems, it has nevertheless its *fierté*; for *Achilles* herein expresses his contempt for the *Greeks*, as a weak defenceless people, who must have perished if he had not preserved them. And indeed, if we consider what is said in the preceding note, it will appear that the passion of *Achilles* ought not as yet to be at the height.

432. *I sack'd twelve ample cities.*] *Eustathius* says, that the anger of *Achilles* not only throws him into tautology, but also into ambiguity: For, says he, these words may either signify that he destroy'd twelve cities with his ships, or barely cities with twelve ships. But *Eustathius* in this place is like many other commentators, who can see a meaning in a sentence that never entered into the thoughts of an author. It is not easy to conceive how *Achilles* could have express'd himself more clearly. There is no doubt but δώδεκα agrees with the same word that ἔνδεκα does, in the following line, which is certainly πόλεις; and there is a manifest enumeration of the places he had conquer'd by sea, and by land.

450. *The wife whom choice and passion both approve, Sure ev'ry wise and worthy man will love.*] The argument of *Achilles* in this place is very a-propos with reference to the case of *Agamemnon*. If I translated it verbatim, I must say in plain *English*, *Every honest man loves his wife*. Thus *Homer* has made this rash, this fiery soldier govern'd by his passions, and in the rage of youth, bear testimony to his own respect for the ladies. But it seems *Poltis* King of *Thrace* was of another opinion, who would have parted with two wives, out of pure good-nature to two mere strangers; as I have met with the story somewhere in *Plutarch.* When the *Greeks* were raising forces against *Troy*, they sent ambassadors to this *Poltis* to desire his assistance. He enquir'd the cause of the war, and was told it was the injury *Paris* had done *Menelaus* in taking his wife from him. 'If that be all, said the good King, let me accommodate the difference: Indeed it is not just the *Greek* Prince should lose a wife, and on the other side it is pity the *Trojan* should want one. Now I have two wives, and to prevent all this mischief, I'll send one of them to *Menelaus*, and the other to *Paris*.' It is a shame this story is so little known, and that poor *Poltis* yet remains uncelebrated: I cannot but recommend him to the modern Poets.

457. *Your King,* Ulysses, *may consult with you.*] *Achilles* still remembers what *Agamemnon* said to him when they quarrel'd, *Other brave warriours will be left behind to follow me in battel*, as we have seen in the first book. He answers here without either sparing *Ajax* or *Ulysses*; as much his friends as they are, they have their share in this stroke of raillery.   *Eustathius.*

459. *Has he not walls?*] This is a bitter satire (says *Eustathius*) against *Agamemnon*, as if his only deeds were the making of this wall, this ditch, these pallisades, to defend himself against those whom he came to besiege: There was no need of these retrenchments, whilst *Achilles* fought. But (as *Dacier* observes) this satire does not affect *Agamemnon* only, but *Nestor* too, who had advis'd the making of these retrenchments, and who had said in the second book, *If there are a few who separate themselves from the rest of the army, let them stay and perish,* v. 346. Probably this had been reported to *Achilles*, and that Hero revenges himself here by mocking these retrenchments.

473. *The third day hence shall* Pthia, &c.] Monsieur *de la Motte* thinks the mention of these minute circumstances not to agree with the passionate character of the speaker; that *he shall arrive at* Pthia *in three days*, that *he shall find there all the riches he left when he came to the siege*, and that *he shall carry other treasures home. Dacier* answers, that we need only consider the present situation of *Achilles*, and his cause of complaint against *Agamemnon*, and we shall be satisfied here is nothing but what is exactly agreeable to the occasion. To convince the

ambassadors that he will return home, he instances the easiness of doing it in the space of three days. *Agamemnon* had injured him in the point of booty, he therefore declares he had sufficient treasures at home, and that he will carry off spoils enough, and women enough, to make amends for those that Prince had ravish'd from him. Every one of these particulars marks his passion and resentment.

481. *One only valu'd gift your tyrant gave.*] The injury which *Agamemnon* offer'd to *Achilles* is still uppermost in his thoughts; he has but just dismiss'd it, and now returns to it again. These repetitions are far from being faults in *Achilles*'s wrath, whose Anger is perpetually breaking out upon the same injury.

494. *Kings of such a kind stand but as slaves before a noble mind.*] The words in the *Greek* are, *I despise him as a Carian.* The *Carians* were People of *Bœotia*, the first that sold their valour, and were ready to fight for any that gave them their pay. This was look'd upon as the vilest of actions in those heroical ages. I think there is at present but one nation in the world distinguish'd for this practice, who are ready to prostitute their hands to kill for the highest bidder.

Eustathius endeavours to give many other solutions of this place, as that ἐν καρός may be mistaken for ἔγκαρος from ἔγκαρ, *pediculus* [louse]; but this is too mean and trivial to be *Homer*'s sentiment. There is more probability that it comes from κῆρ, κηρός, and so καρός by the change of the *Eta* into *Alpha*; and then the meaning will be, that *Achilles* hates him as much as hell or death, agreeable to what he had said a little before.

’Εχθρὸς μέν μοι κεῖνος ὁμῶς ’Αἴδαο πύλῃσι.

500. *Not all proud* Thebes, &c.] These several circumstances concerning *Thebes* are thought by some not to suit with that emotion with which *Achilles* here is suppos'd to speak: but the contrary will appear true, if we reflect that nothing is more usual for persons transported with anger, than to insist, and return to such particulars as most touch them; and that exaggeration is a figure extremely natural in passion. *Achilles* therefore, by shewing the greatness of *Thebes*, its wealth, and extent, does in effect but shew the greatness of his own soul, and of that insuperable resentment which renders all these riches (tho' the greatest in the world) contemptible in his sight, when he compares them with the indignity his honour has receiv'd.

500. *Proud* Thebes' *unrival'd walls*, &c.] 'The city which the *Greeks* call *Thebes*, the *Ægyptians Dios* (says *Diodorus lib. 1. part. 2.*), was in Circuit a hundred and forty stadia, adorned with stately buildings, magnificent temples, and rich donations. It was not only the most beautiful and noble city of *Ægypt*, but of the whole world. The fame of its wealth and grandeur was so celebrated in all parts, that the poet took notice of it in these words.

$$- \text{οὐδ' ὅσα Θήβας}$$
Αἰγυπτας, ὅθι πλεῖστα δόμοις ἐν κτήματα κεῖται,
Αἴ θ' ἑκατόμπυλοί εἰσι, διηκόσιοι δ' ἂν ἑκάστας
Ἀνέρες ἐξοιχνεῦσι σὺν ἵπποισι καὶ ὄχεσφιν. v. 381

Tho' others affirm it had not a hundred gates, but several vast porches to the temples; from whence the city was call'd the *Hundred-gated*, only as having many gates. Yet it is certain it furnished twenty thousand chariots of war; for there were a hundred stables along the river, from *Memphis* to *Thebes* towards *Lybia*, each of which contain'd two hundred horses, the ruins whereof are shewn at this day. The Princes from time to time made it their care to beautify and enlarge this city, to which none under the sun was equal in the many and magnificent treasures of gold, silver, and ivory; with innumerable *colossus*'s, and obelisques of one entire stone. There were four temples admirable in beauty and greatness, the most ancient of which was in circuit thirteen *stadia*, and five and forty cubits in height, with a wall of four and twenty foot broad. The ornaments and offerings within were agreeable to this magnificence, both in value and workmanship. The fabrick is yet remaining, but the gold, silver, ivory, and precious stones were ransack'd by the *Persians* when *Cambyses* burn'd the temples of *Ægypt*. There were found in the rubbish above three hundred talents of gold, and no less than two thousand three hundred of silver.' The same author proceeds to give many instances of the magnificence of this great city. The description of the sepulchres of their Kings, and particularly that of *Osymanduas*, is perfectly astonishing, to which I refer the reader.

Strabo farther informs us, that the Kings of *Thebes* extended their conquests as far as *Scythia*, *Bactria*, and *India*.

525. *Not all* Apollo's *Pythian treasures.*] The temple of *Apollo* at *Delphos* was the richest temple in the world, by the offerings which were brought to it from all parts; there were statues of massy gold of a

human size, figures of animals in gold, and several other treasures. A great sign of its wealth is, that the *Phocians* pillag'd it in the time of *Philip* the Son of *Amyntas*, which gave occasion to the holy war. 'Tis said to have been pillag'd before, and that the great riches of which *Homer* speaks, had been carried away.   *Eustathius.*

530. *The vital Spirit fled, Returns no more.*] Nothing sure could be better imagin'd, or more strongly paint *Achilles*'s resentment, than this commendation which *Homer* puts into his mouth of a long and peaceable life. That hero, whose very soul was possess'd with love of glory, and who prefer'd it to life itself, lets his anger prevail over this his darling passion: He despises even glory, when he cannot obtain that, and enjoy his revenge at the same time; and rather than lay this aside, becomes the very reverse of himself.

532. *My fates long since by* Thetis *were disclos'd.*] It was very necessary for *Homer* to put the reader more than once in mind of this piece of *Achilles*'s story: There is a remark of Monsieur *de la Motte* which deserves to be transcribed entire on this occasion.

'The generality of people who do not know *Achilles* by the Iliad, and who upon a most noted fable conceive him invulnerable all but in the heel, find it ridiculous that he should be placed at the head of heroes; so true it is, that the idea of valour implies it always in danger.

'Should a giant, well arm'd, fight against a legion of children, whatever slaughter he should make, the pity any one would have for them would not turn at all to any admiration of him, and the more he should applaud his own courage, the more one would be offended at his pride.

'*Achilles* had been in this case, if *Homer*, besides all the superiority of strength he has given him, had not found the art of putting likewise his greatness of soul out of all suspicion.

'He has perfectly well succeeded in feigning that *Achilles* before his setting out to the *Trojan* war, was sure of meeting his death. The destinies had proposed to him by the mouth of *Thetis*, the alternative of a long and happy, but obscure life, if he staid in his own state; or of a short, but glorious one, if he embrac'd the vengeance of the *Greeks.* He wishes for glory in contempt of death; and thus all his actions, all his motions are so many proofs of his courage; he runs, in hastening his exploits, to a death which he knows infallibly attends him; what does it avail him, that he routs every thing almost without resistance? It is still true, that he every moment encounters and faces the sentence of his destiny, and that he devotes himself generously for glory. *Homer* was so sensible that this idea must force a concern for his hero, that he scatters it throughout his poem, to the end that the reader having it always in view, may esteem *Achilles* even for what he performs without the least danger.'

565. *How shall thy friend, thy* Phœnix *stay behind.*] This is a strong argument to persuade *Achilles* to stay, but dress'd up in the utmost tenderness: the venerable old man rises with tears in his eyes, and speaks the language of affection. He tells him that he would not be left behind him, tho' the Gods would free him from the burthen of old age, and restore him to his youth: but in the midst of so much fondness, he couches a powerful argument to persuade him not to return home, by adding that his father sent him to be his guide and guardian; *Phœnix* ought not therefore to follow the inclinations of *Achilles*, but *Achilles* the directions of *Phœnix*.   *Eustathius.*

'The art of this speech of *Phœnix* (says *Dionysius* περὶ ἐσχηματισμέ-νων, *lib.* 1.) consists in his seeming to agree with all that *Achilles* had said: *Achilles*, he sees, will depart, and he must go along with him; but in assigning the reasons why he must go with him, he proves that *Achilles* ought not to depart. And thus while he seems only to shew his love to his pupil in his inability to stay behind him, he indeed challenges the other's gratitude for the benefits he had confer'd upon him in his infancy and education. At the same time that he moves *Achilles*, he gratifies *Agamemnon*; and that this was the real design which he disguised in that manner, we are inform'd by *Achilles* himself in the reply he makes: for *Homer*, and all the authors that treat of this figure, generally contrive it so, that the answers made to these kind of speeches, discover all the art and structure of them. *Achilles* therefore asks him,

> *Is it for him these tears are taught to flow,*
> *For him these sorrows, for my mortal foe?*

You see the scholar reveals the art and dissimulation of his master; and as *Phœnix* had recounted the benefits done him, he takes off that expostulation by promising to divide his empire with him, as may be seen in the same answer.'

567. *He sent thee early to th' Achaian host.*] *Achilles* (says *Eustathius*) according to some of the ancients, was but twelve years old when he went to the wars of *Troy*; (πέμπε νήπιον [he sent a child]) and it may be gather'd from what the Poet here relates of the education of *Achilles* under *Phœnix*, that the fable of his being tutor'd by *Chiron* was the invention of latter ages, and unknown to *Homer*.

Mr *Bayle*, in his article of *Achilles*, has very well proved this. He might indeed, as he grew up, have learn'd musick and physick of *Chiron*, without having him formally as his tutor; for it is plain from this speech that he was put under the direction of *Phœnix* as his governor in morality, when his father sent him along with him to the siege of *Troy*.

578. *My father, faithless to my mother's arms*, &c.] *Homer* has been blamed for introducing two long stories into this speech of *Phœnix*; this concerning himself is said not to be in the proper place, and what *Achilles* must needs have heard over and over: it also gives (say they) a very ill impression of *Phœnix* himself, and makes him appear a very unfit person to be a teacher of morality to the young hero. It is answer'd, that tho' *Achilles* might have known the story before in general, 'tis probable *Phœnix* had not till now so pressing an occasion to make him discover the excess his fury had transported him to, in attempting the life of his own father: the whole story tends to represent the dreadful effects of passion: and I cannot but think the example is the more forcible, as it is drawn from his own experience.

581. *To win the Damsel.*] The counsel that this mother gives to her son *Phœnix* is the same that *Achitophel* gave to *Absolom*, to hinder him from ever being reconciled to *David*. *Et ait Achitophel ad Absolom: ingredere ad concubinos patris tui, quas dimisit ad custodiendam domum, ut cum audierit omnis Israel quod fœdaveris patrem tuum, roborentur tecum manus eorum.* [And Achitophel said to Absalom: 'Go to your father's concubines, whom he left to look after the house; so that, when all Israel hears that you have disgraced your father, the hands of those who are with you will be strengthened.'] 2 Sam. 14. 20.

Dacier.

581. *Prevent my sire.*] This Decency of *Homer* is worthy observation, who to remove all the disagreeable ideas which might proceed from this intrigue of *Phœnix* with his father's mistress, took care to give us to understand in one single word, that *Amyntor* had no share in her affections, which makes the action of *Phœnix* the more excusable. He

does it only in obedience to his mother, in order to reclaim his father, and oblige him to live like her husband: besides, his father had yet no commerce with this mistress to whose love he pretended. Had it been otherwise, and had *Phœnix* committed this sort of incest, *Homer* would neither have presented this image to his reader, nor *Peleus* chosen *Phœnix* to be governor to *Achilles.*   *Dacier.*

584. *Infernal* Jove.] The *Greek* is Ζεύς τε καταχθόνιος. The ancients gave the name of *Jupiter* not only to the God of heaven, but likewise to the God of hell, as is seen here; and to the God of the sea, as appears from *Æschylus.* They thereby meant to shew that one sole deity governed the world; and it was to teach the same truth, that the ancient statuaries made statues of *Jupiter*, which had three eyes. *Priam* had one of them in that manner in the court of his palace, which was there in *Laomedon*'s time: after the taking of *Troy*, when the *Greeks* shared the booty, it fell to *Sthenelus*'s lot, who carried it into *Greece.*
                                                                        Dacier.

586. *Despair and grief distract*, &c.] I have taken the liberty to replace here four verses which *Aristarchus* had cut out, because of the horror which the idea gave him of a son who is going to kill his father; but perhaps *Aristarchus*'s niceness was too great. These verses seem to me necessary, and have a very good effect; for *Phœnix*'s aim is to shew *Achilles*, that unless we overcome our wrath, we are exposed to commit the greatest crimes: he was going to kill his own father. *Achilles* in the same manner is going to let his father *Phœnix* and all the *Greeks* perish, if he does not appease his wrath. *Plutarch* relates these four verses in his treatise of reading the poets; and adds, '*Aristarchus* frightened at this horrible crime, cut out these verses; but they do very well in this place, and on this occasion, *Phœnix* intending to shew *Achilles* what wrath is, and to what abominable excesses it hurries men who do not obey reason, and who refuse to follow the counsels of those that advise them.' These sort of curtailings from *Homer*, often contrary to all reason, gave room to *Lucian* to feign that being in the fortunate islands, he asked *Homer* a great many questions. 'Among other things (says he in his second book of his true history) I ask'd him whether he had made all the verses which had been rejected in his poem? he assur'd me they were all his own, which made me laugh at the impertinent and bold criticisms of *Zenodorus* and *Aristarchus*, who had retrenched them.'   *Dacier.*

612. *I pass my watchings o'er thy helpless years.*] In the original of this place *Phœnix* tells *Achilles*, that as he placed him in his infancy on his lap, *he has often cast up the wine he had drank upon his cloaths.* I wish I had any authority to say these verses were foisted into the text: for tho' the idea be indeed natural, it must be granted to be so very gross as to be utterly unworthy of *Homer*; nor do I see any colour to soften the meanness of it: such images in any age or country, must have been too nauseous to be described.

624. Pray'rs *are* Jove's *daughters.*] Nothing can be more beautiful, noble, or religious, than this divine allegory. We have here Goddesses of *Homer*'s creation; he sets before us their pictures in lively colours, and gives these fancied beings all the features that resemble mankind who offer injuries, or have recourse to prayers.

Prayers are said to be the daughters of *Jove*, because it is he who teaches man to pray. They are lame, because the posture of a suppliant is with his knee on the ground. They are wrinkled, because those that pray have a countenance of dejection and sorrow. Their eyes are turn'd aside, because thro' an awful regard to heaven they dare not lift them thither. They follow *Ate* or *Injury*, because nothing but prayers can attone for the wrongs that are offered by the injurious. *Ate* is said to be strong and swift of foot, *&c.* because injurious men are swift to do mischief. This is the explanation of *Eustathius*, with whom *Dacier* agrees, but when she allows the circumstance of lameness to intimate the custom of kneeling in prayer, she forgets that this contradicts her own assertion in one of the remarks on Iliad 7. where she affirms that no such custom was used by the *Greeks.* And indeed the contrary seems inferred in several places in *Homer*, particularly where *Achilles* says in the 608*th* verse of the eleventh book, *The* Greeks *shall stand round his knees supplicating to him.* The phrases in that language that signify praying, are derived from the knee, only as it was usual to lay hold on the knee of the person to whom they supplicated.

A modern author imagines *Ate* to signify *divine Justice*; a notion in which he is single, and repugnant to all the mythologists. Besides, the whole context in this place, and the very application of the allegory to the present case of *Achilles*, whom he exhorts to be moved by prayers, notwithstanding the injustice done him by *Agamemnon*, makes the contrary evident.

643. *Nor Greece, nor all her fortunes.*] *Plato* in the third book of his Republick condemns this passage, and thinks it very wrong, that *Phœnix* should say to *Achilles* that if they did not offer him great presents, he would not advise him to be appeased; but I think there is some injustice in this censure, and that *Plato* has not rightly entered into the sense of *Phœnix*, who does not look upon these presents on the side of interest, but honour, as a mark of *Agamemnon*'s repentance, and of the satisfaction he is ready to make: wherefore he says, that honour has a mighty power over great spirits.   *Dacier.*

648. *Permit not these to sue, and sue in vain!*] In the original it is – τῶν μὴ σύ γε μῦθον ἐλέγξῃς Μηδὲ πόδας [Do not bring disgrace upon their words or their feet]. – I am pretty confident there is not any manner of speaking like this used throughout all *Homer*; nor two substantives so oddly coupled to a verb, as μῦθον and πόδας in this Place. We may indeed meet with such little Affectations in *Ovid*, – *Aurigam pariter animaque, rotisque, Expulit* [He cleanly thrust out the driver along with his soul and his wheels] – and the like; but the taste of the ancients in general was too good for these fooleries. I must have leave to think the verse Μηδὲ πόδας, &c. an interpolation; the sense is compleat without it, and the latter part of the line, πρὶν δ᾽ οὔ τι νεμεσσητὸν κεχολῶσθαι [although, before this, it was not reprehensible to be angry], seems but a tautology, after what is said in the six verses preceding.

649. *Let me, my son, an ancient fact unfold.*] *Phœnix*, says *Eustathius*, lays down, as the foundation of his story, that great men in former ages were always appeas'd by presents and entreaties; and to confirm this position, he brings *Meleager* as an instance; but it may be objected that *Meleager* was an ill-chosen instance, being a person whom no entreaties could move. The superstructure of this story seems not to agree with the foundation. *Eustathius* solves the difficulty thus. *Homer* did not intend to give an instance of a hero's compliance with the entreaties of his friends, but to shew that they who did not comply were sufferers themselves in the end. So that the connection of the story is thus: The heroes of former times were used always to be won by presents and entreaties; *Meleager* only was obstinate, and suffer'd because he was so.

The length of this narration cannot be taxed as unseasonable; it was at full leisure in the tent, and in the night, a time of no action. Yet I cannot answer but the tale may be tedious to a modern reader. I have translated it therefore with all possible shortness, as will appear upon a comparison. The piece itself is very valuable, as it preserves to us a part of ancient history that had otherwise been entirely lost, as *Quintilian* has remark'd. The same great Critick commends *Homer*'s manner of relating it: *Narrare quis significantius potest, quam qui Curetum Ætolorumque prælia exponit?* [Who can narrate more vividly than he who describes the battle between the Curetes and Aetolians?] *lib.* 10. *c.* 1.

677. Alcyone, *a name to show*, &c.] It appears (says Madam *Dacier*) by this passage, and by others already observed, that the *Greeks* often gave names, as did the *Hebrews*, not only with respect to the circumstances, but likewise to the accidents which happened to the fathers and mothers of those they named: Thus *Cleopatra* is called *Alcyone*, from the lamentations of her mother. I cannot but think this digression concerning *Idas* and *Marpessa* too long, and not very much to the purpose.

703.   *She paints the horrors of a conquer'd town,*
         The heroes slain, the palaces o'erthrown,
         The matrons ravish'd, the whole race enslav'd.]

It is remarkable with what art *Homer* here in a few words sums up the miseries of a city taken by assault.

It had been unpardonable for *Cleopatra* to have made a long representation to *Meleager* of these miseries, when every moment that kept him from the battel could not be spared. It is also to be observed how perfectly the features of *Meleager* resemble *Achilles*; they are both brave men, ambitious of glory, both of them describ'd as giving victory to their several armies while they fought, and both of them implacable in their resentment.   *Eustathius.*

713. Achilles's *answer to* Phœnix.] The character of *Achilles* is excellently sustained in all his speeches: To *Ulysses* he returns a flat denial, and threatens to leave the *Trojan* shores in the morning: To *Phœnix* he gives a much gentler answer, and begins to mention *Agamemnon* with less disrespect 'Ατρείδη ἥρωϊ [the hero Atrides]: After *Ajax* had spoken, he seems determined not to depart, but yet refuses to bear arms, till it is to defend his own squadron. Thus *Achilles*'s character is every where of a piece: He begins to yield, and not to have done so, would not have spoke him a man; to have made him perfectly inexorable had shewn him a monster. Thus the Poet draws the heat of his passion cooling by slow degrees, which is very natural: To have done otherwise, had not been agreeable to *Achilles*'s temper, nor the reader's expectation, to whom it would have been shocking to have seen him passing from the greatest storm of anger to a quiet calmness. *Eustathius.*

720. *While life's warm spirit beats within my breast.*] *Eustathius* observes here with a great deal of penetration, that these words of *Achilles* include a sort of oracle, which he does not understand: For it sometimes happens that men full of their objects say things, which besides the sense natural and plain to every body, include another supernatural, which they themselves do not understand, and which is understood by those only who have penetration enough to see through the obscurity of it. Thus *Oedipus* often speaks in *Sophocles*; and holy scripture furnishes us with great examples of enthusiastick speeches, which have a double sense. Here we manifestly see that *Achilles* in speaking a very simple and common thing, foretells without thinking of it, that his abode on that fatal shore will equal the course of his life, and consequently that he shall die there: and this double meaning gives a sensible pleasure to the reader. *Dacier.*

737. *The Speech of* Ajax.] I have before spoken of this short soldier-like speech of *Ajax*; *Dionysius* of *Halicarnassus* says of it, 'That the person who entreats most, and with most liberty, who supplicates most, and presses most, is *Ajax*.' It is probable that *Ajax* rises up when he speaks the word, *Let us go.* He does not vouchsafe to address himself to *Achilles*, but turns himself to *Ulysses*, and speaks with a martial eloquence.

746. *The price of blood discharg'd.*] It was the custom for the murderer to go into banishment one year, but if the relations of the person murdered were willing, the criminal by paying them a certain fine, might buy off the exile, and remain at home. (It may not be amiss to observe, that ποινή, quasi φοίνη, properly signifies a mulct paid for murder.) *Ajax* sums up this argument with a great deal of strength: We see, says he, a brother forgive the murder of his brother, a father that of his son: But *Achilles* will not forgive the injury offered him by taking away one captive woman. *Eustathius.*

754. *Revere the roof, and to thy guests be kind.*] *Eustathius* says there is some difficulty in the original of this place. Why should *Ajax* draw an argument to influence *Achilles*, by putting him in mind to reverence his own habitation? The latter part of the verse explains the former: We, says *Ajax*, are under your roof, and let that protect us from any ill usage; send us not away from your house with contempt, who came hither as friends, as supplicants, as embassadors.

759. *Well hast thou spoke, but at the tyrant's name My rage rekindles.*] We have here the true picture of an angry man, and nothing can be better imagin'd to heighten *Achilles*'s wrath; he owns that reason would induce him to a reconciliation, but his anger is too great to listen to reason. He speaks with respect to them, but upon mentioning *Agamemnon*, he flies into rage: Anger is in nothing more like madness, than that madmen will talk sensibly enough upon any indifferent matter; but upon the mention of the subject that caused their disorder, they fly out into their usual extravagance.

806. *Such was his word.*] It may be ask'd here why *Ulysses* speaks only of the answer which *Achilles* made him at first, and says nothing of the disposition to which the discourses of *Phœnix* and *Ajax* had brought him. The question is easily answer'd; it is because *Achilles* is obstinate in his resentment; and that, if at length a little mov'd by *Phœnix*, and shaken by *Ajax*, he seem'd dispos'd to take arms, it is not out of regard to the *Greeks*, but only to save his own squadron, when *Hector*, after having put the *Greeks* to the sword, shall come to insult it. Thus this inflexible man abates nothing of his rage. It is therefore prudent in *Ulysses* to make this report to *Agamemnon*, to the end that being put out of hopes of the aid with which he flatter'd himself, he may concert with the leaders of the army the measures necessary to save his fleet and troops.   *Eustathius.*

816. *Why should we Gifts,* &c.] This speech is admirably adapted to the character of *Diomed*, every word is animated with a martial courage, and worthy to be delivered by a gallant soldier. He advis'd fighting in the beginning of the book, and continues still in that opinion; and he is no more concern'd at the speech of *Achilles* now, than he was at that of *Agamemnon* before.

THE
TENTH BOOK
OF THE
ILIAD

The ARGUMENT

The Night-Adventure of *Diomed* and *Ulysses*

Upon the refusal of Achilles *to return to the army, the Distress of* Agamemnon *is described in the most lively manner. He takes no rest that night, but passes thro' the camp, awaking the leaders, and contriving all possible methods for the publick safety.* Menelaus, Nestor, Ulysses *and* Diomed *are employ'd in raising the rest of the captions. They call a council of war, and determine to send scouts into the enemy's camp to learn their posture and discover their intentions.* Diomed *undertakes this hazardous enterprize, and makes choice of* Ulysses *for his companion. In their passage they surprize* Dolon, *whom* Hector *had sent on a like design to the camp of the* Grecians. *From him they are inform'd of the situation of the* Trojan *and auxiliary forces, and particularly of* Rhesus *and the* Thracians *who were lately arrived. They pass on with success, kill* Rhesus, *with several of his officers, and seize the famous horses of that Prince with which they return in triumph to the camp.*

The same night continues; the scene *lies in the two camps.*

All night the Chiefs before their vessels lay,
And lost in sleep the labours of the day:
All but the King; with various thoughts opprest,
His country's cares lay rowling in his breast.
5   As when by light'nings *Jove*'s ætherial pow'r
Foretells the ratling hail, or weighty show'r,
Or sends soft snows to whiten all the shore,
Or bids the brazen throat of war to roar;
By fits one flash succeeds, as one expires,
10   And heav'n flames thick with momentary fires.
So bursting frequent from *Atrides'* breast,
Sighs following sighs his inward fears confest.
Now o'er the fields, dejected, he surveys
From thousand *Trojan* fires the mounting blaze;
15   Hears in the passing wind their music blow,
And marks distinct the voices of the foe.
Now looking backwards to the fleet and coast,
Anxious he sorrows for th' endanger'd host.
He rends his hairs, in sacrifice to *Jove*,
20   And sues to him that ever lives above:
Inly he groans; while glory and despair
Divide his heart, and wage a doubtful war.
     A thousand cares his lab'ring breast revolves;
To seek sage *Nestor* now the Chief resolves,
25   With him, in wholsome counsels, to debate
What yet remains to save th' afflicted state.
He rose, and first he cast his mantle round,
Next on his feet the shining sandals bound;

A lion's yellow spoils his back conceal'd;
His warlike hand a pointed jav'lin held.
Mean while his brother, prest with equal woes,   30
Alike deny'd the gifts of soft repose,
Laments for *Greece*; that in his cause before
So much had suffer'd, and must suffer more.
A leopard's spotted hide his shoulders spread;   35
A brazen helmet glitter'd on his head:
Thus (with a jav'lin in his hand) he went
To wake *Atrides* in the royal tent.
Already wak'd, *Atrides* he descry'd,
His armour buckling at his vessel's side.   40
Joyful they met; the *Spartan* thus begun:
Why puts my brother his bright armour on?
Sends he some spy, amidst these silent hours,
To try yon' camp, and watch the *Trojan* pow'rs?
But say, what hero shall sustain that task?   45
Such bold exploits uncommon courage ask,
Guideless, alone, through night's dark shade to go,
And 'midst a hostile camp explore the foe?

   To whom the King. In such distress we stand,
No vulgar counsels our affairs demand;   50
Greece to preserve, is now no easy part,
But asks high wisdom, deep design, and art.
For *Jove*, averse, our humble pray'r denies,
And bows his head to *Hector*'s sacrifice.
What eye has witness'd, or what ear believ'd,   55
In one great day, by one great arm atchiev'd,
Such wond'rous deeds as *Hector*'s hand has done,
And we beheld, the last revolving sun?
What honours the belov'd of *Jove* adorn!
Sprung from no God, and of no Goddess born,   60
Yet such his acts, as *Greeks* unborn shall tell,
And curse the battel where their fathers fell.

   Now speed thy hasty course along the fleet,
There call great *Ajax*, and the Prince of *Crete*;
Our self to hoary *Nestor* will repair;   65
To keep the guards on duty, be his care;
(For *Nestor*'s influence best that quarter guides,
Whose son, with *Merion*, o'er the watch presides.)

To whom the *Spartan*: These thy orders born,
70 Say shall I stay, or with dispatch return?
There shalt thou stay (the King of men reply'd)
Else may we miss to meet, without a guide,
The paths so many, and the camp so wide.
Still, with your voice, the sloathful soldiers raise,
75 Urge by their father's fame, their future praise.
Forget we now our state and lofty birth;
Not titles here, but works, must prove our worth.
To labour is the lot of man below;
And when *Jove* gave us life, he gave us woe.

80   This said, each parted to his sev'ral cares;
The King to *Nestor*'s sable ship repairs;
The sage protector of the *Greeks* he found
Stretch'd in his bed with all his arms around;
The various-colour'd scarf, the shield he rears,
85 The shining helmet, and the pointed spears:
The dreadful weapons of the warriour's rage,
That, old in arms, disdain'd the peace of age.
Then leaning on his hand his watchful head,
The hoary Monarch rais'd his eyes, and said.

90   What art thou, speak, that on designs unknown
While others sleep, thus range the camp alone?
Seek'st thou some friend, or nightly centinel?
Stand off, approach not, but thy purpose tell.

    O Son of *Neleus* (thus the King rejoin'd)
95 Pride of the *Greeks*, and glory of thy kind!
Lo here the wretched *Agamemnon* stands,
Th' unhappy Gen'ral of the *Grecian* bands;
Whom *Jove* decrees with daily cares to bend,
And woes, that only with his life shall end!
100 Scarce can my knees these trembling limbs sustain,
And scarce my heart support its load of pain.
No taste of sleep these heavy eyes have known;
Confus'd, and sad, I wander thus alone,
With fears distracted, with no fix'd design;
105 And all my people's miseries are mine.
If ought of use thy waking thoughts suggest,
(Since cares, like mine, deprive thy soul of rest)

Impart thy counsel, and assist thy friend;
Now let us jointly to the trench descend,
At ev'ry gate the fainting guard excite,   110
Tir'd with the toils of day, and watch of night:
Else may the sudden foe our works invade,
So near, and favour'd by the gloomy shade.

    To him thus *Nestor.* Trust the Pow'rs above,
Nor think proud *Hector*'s hopes confirm'd by *Jove*:   115
How ill agree the views of vain mankind,
And the wise counsels of th' eternal mind?
Audacious *Hector*, if the Gods ordain
That great *Achilles* rise and rage again,
What toils attend thee, and what woes remain?   120
Lo faithful *Nestor* thy command obeys;
The care is next our other Chiefs to raise:
Ulysses, Diomed we chiefly need;
Mages for strength, *Oileus* fam'd for speed.
Some other be dispatch'd, of nimbler feet,   125
To those tall ships, remotest of the fleet,
Where lie great *Ajax* and the King of *Crete*.
To rouse the *Spartan* I my self decree;
Dear as he is to us, and dear to thee,
Yet must I tax his sloth, that claims no share   130
With his great brother in this martial care:
Him it behov'd to ev'ry chief to sue,
Preventing ev'ry part perform'd by you;
For strong necessity our toils demands,
Claims all our hearts, and urges all our hands.   135

    To whom the King: With rev'rence we allow
Thy just rebukes, yet learn to spare them now.
My gen'rous brother is of gentle kind,
He seems remiss, but bears a valiant mind;
Thro' too much def'rence to our sov'reign sway,   140
Content to follow when we lead the way.
But now, our ills industrious to prevent,
Long e'er the rest, he rose, and sought my tent.
The chiefs you nam'd, already, at his call,
Prepare to meet us near the navy-wall;   145
Assembling there, between the trench and gates,
Near the night-guards, our chosen council waits.

Then none (said *Nestor*) shall his rule withstand,
For great examples justify command.
150 With that, the venerable warriour rose;
The shining greaves his manly legs inclose;
His purple mantle golden buckles join'd,
Warm with the softest wool, and doubly lin'd.
Then rushing from his tent, he snatch'd in haste
155 His steely lance, that lighten'd as he past.
The camp he travers'd thro' the sleeping crowd,
Stopped at *Ulysses'* tent, and call'd aloud.
Ulysses, sudden as the voice was sent,
Awakes, starts up, and issues from his tent.
160 What new distress, what sudden cause of fright
Thus leads you wand'ring in the silent night?
O prudent chief! (the *Pylian* sage reply'd)
Wise as thou art, be now thy wisdom try'd:
Whatever means of safety can be sought,
165 Whatever counsels can inspire our thought,
Whatever methods, or to fly, or fight;
All, all depend on this important night!
  He heard, return'd, and took his painted shield:
Then join'd the chiefs, and follow'd thro' the field.
170 Without his tent, bold *Diomed* they found,
All sheath'd in arms; his brave companions round:
Each sunk in sleep, extended on the field,
His head reclining on his bossy shield.
A wood of spears stood by, that fixt upright,
175 Shot from their flashing points a quiv'ring light.
A bull's black hide compos'd the hero's Bed;
A splendid carpet roll'd beneath his head.
Then, with his foot, old *Nestor* gently shakes
The slumb'ring chief, and in these words awakes.
180 Rise, Son of *Tydeus!* to the brave and strong
Rest seems inglorious, and the night too long.
But sleep'st thou now? when from yon' hill the foe
Hangs o'er the fleet, and shades our walls below?
  At this, soft slumber from his eyelids fled;
185 The warriour saw the hoary chief, and said.
Wond'rous old man! whose soul no respite knows,
Tho' years and honours bid thee seek repose.

Let younger *Greeks* our sleeping warriours wake;
Ill fits thy age these toils to undertake.
My friend, (he answer'd) gen'rous is thy care,   190
These toils, my subjects and my sons might bear,
Their loyal thoughts and pious loves conspire
To ease a sov'reign, and relieve a sire.
But now the last despair surrounds our host;
No hour must pass, no moment must be lost;   195
Each single *Greek*, in this conclusive strife,
Stands on the sharpest edge of death or life:
Yet if my years thy kind regard engage,
Employ thy youth as I employ my age;
Succeed to these my cares, and rouze the rest;   200
He serves me most, who serves his country best.

This said, the hero o'er his shoulders flung
A lion's spoils, that to his ankles hung;
Then seiz'd his pond'rous lance, and strode along.
Meges the bold, with *Ajax* fam'd for speed,   205
The warriour rouz'd, and to th' entrenchments led.

And now the chiefs approach the nightly guard;
A wakeful squadron, each in arms prepar'd:
Th' unweary'd watch their list'ning leaders keep,
And couching close, repel invading sleep.   210
So faithful dogs their fleecy charge maintain,
With toil protected from the prowling train;
When the gaunt lioness, with hunger bold,
Springs from the mountains tow'rd the guarded fold:
Thro' breaking woods her rust'ling course they hear;   215
Loud, and more loud, the clamours strike their ear
Of hounds and men; they start, they gaze around,
Watch ev'ry side, and turn to ev'ry sound.
Thus watch'd the *Grecians*, cautious of surprize,
Each voice, each motion, drew their ears and eyes;   220
Each step of passing feet increas'd th' affright;
And hostile *Troy* was ever full in sight.
Nestor with joy the wakeful band survey'd,
And thus accosted thro' the gloomy shade.
'Tis well, my sons, your nightly cares employ,   225
Else must our host become the scorn of *Troy*.

Watch thus, and *Greece* shall live – The hero said;
Then o'er the trench the following chieftains led.
His Son, and godlike *Merion* march'd behind,
230   (For these the Princes to their council join'd)
The trenches past, th' assembl'd Kings around
In silent state the consistory crown'd.
A place there was, yet undefil'd with gore,
The spot where *Hector* stop'd his rage before,
235   When night descending, from his vengeful hand
Repriev'd the relicks of the *Grecian* band:
(The plain beside with mangled corps was spread,
And all his progress mark'd by heaps of dead.)
There sate the mournful Kings: when *Neleus'* son
240   The council opening, in these words begun.

Is there (said he) a chief so greatly brave,
His life to hazard, and his country save?
Lives there a man, who singly dares to go
To yonder camp, or seize some stragling foe?
245   Or favour'd by the night, approach so near,
Their speech, their counsels, and designs to hear?
If to besiege our navies they prepare,
Or *Troy* once more must be the seat of war?
This could he learn, and to our peers recite,
250   And pass unharm'd the dangers of the night;
What fame were his thro' all succeeding days,
While *Phœbus* shines, or men have tongues to praise?
What gifts his grateful country would bestow?
What must not *Greece* to her deliv'rer owe?
255   A sable ewe each leader should provide,
With each a sable lambkin by her side;
At ev'ry rite his share should be increas'd,
And his the foremost honours of the feast.

Fear held them mute: Alone, untaught to fear,
260   *Tydides* spoke – The man you seek, is here.
Thro' yon' black camps to bend my dang'rous way,
Some God within commands, and I obey.
But let some other chosen warriour join,
To raise my hopes, and second my design.
265   By mutual confidence, and mutual aid,
Great deeds are done, and great discov'ries made;

The wise new prudence from the wise acquire,
And one brave hero fans another's fire.
　　Contending leaders at the word arose;
Each gen'rous breast with emulation glows: 270
So brave a task each *Ajax* strove to share,
Bold *Merion* strove, and *Nestor*'s valiant heir;
The *Spartan* wish'd the second place to gain,
And great *Ulysses* wish'd, nor wish'd in vain.
Then thus the King of men the contest ends: 275
Thou first of warriours, and thou best of friends,
Undaunted *Diomed!* what chief to join
In this great enterprize, is only thine.
Just be thy choice, without affection made,
To birth, or office, no respect be paid;   280
Let worth determine here. The Monarch spake,
And inly trembled for his brother's sake.
　　Then thus (the God-like *Diomed* rejoin'd)
My choice declares the impulse of my mind.
How can I doubt, while great *Ulysses* stands   285
To lend his counsels, and assist our hands?
A chief, whose safety is *Minerva*'s care;
So fam'd, so dreadful, in the works of war:
Blest in his conduct, I no aid require,
Wisdom like his might pass thro' flames of fire.   290
　　It fits thee not, before these chiefs of fame,
(Reply'd the Sage) to praise me, or to blame:
Praise from a friend, or censure from a foe,
Are lost on hearers that our merits know.
But let us haste – night rolls the hours away,   295
The red'ning Orient shows the coming day,
The stars shine fainter on th' ætherial plains,
And of night's empire but a third remains.
　　Thus having spoke, with gen'rous ardour prest,
In arms terrific their huge limbs they drest.   300
A two–edg'd faulchion *Thrasymed* the brave,
And ample buckler, to *Tydides* gave:
Then in a leathern helm he cas'd his head,
Short of its crest, and with no plume o'erspread;
(Such as by youths unus'd to arms, are worn;   305
No spoils enrich it, and no studs adorn.)

Next him *Ulysses* took a shining sword,
A bow and quiver, with bright arrows stor'd:
A well-prov'd casque with leather braces bound
310 (Thy gift, *Meriones*) his temples crown'd;
Soft wool within; without, in order spread,
A boar's white teeth grinn'd horrid o'er his head.
This from *Amyntor*, rich *Ormenus'* son,
Autolychus by fraudful rapine won,
315 And gave *Amphydamas*; from him the prize
Molus receiv'd, the Pledge of social ties;
The helmet next by *Merion* was possess'd,
And now *Ulysses'* thoughtful temples press'd.
Thus sheath'd in arms, the counsel they forsake,
320 And dark thro' paths oblique their progress take.
Just then, in sign she favour'd their intent,
A long-wing'd heron great *Minerva* sent;
This, tho' surrounding shades obscur'd their view,
By the shrill clang and whistling wings, they knew.
325 As from the right she soar'd, *Ulysses* pray'd,
Hail'd the glad omen, and address'd the maid.

　　O daughter of that God, whose arm can wield
Th' avenging bolt, and shake the dreadful shield!
O thou! for ever present in my way,
330 Who, all my motions, all my toils survey!
Safe may we pass beneath the gloomy shade,
Safe by thy succour to our ships convey'd;
And let some deed this signal night adorn,
To claim the tears of *Trojans* yet unborn.

335 　　Then god-like *Diomed* preferr'd his pray'r:
Daughter of *Jove*, unconquer'd *Pallas!* hear.
Great Queen of arms, whose favour *Tydeus* won,
As thou defend'st the sire, defend the son.
When on *Æsopus'* banks the banded pow'rs
340 Of *Greece* he left, and sought the *Theban* tow'rs,
Peace was his charge; receiv'd with peaceful show,
He went a legate, but return'd a foe:
Then help'd by thee, and cover'd by thy shield,
He fought with numbers, and made numbers yield.
345 So now be present, Oh celestial maid!
So still continue to the race thine aid!

A youthful steer shall fall beneath the stroke,
Untam'd, unconscious of the galling yoke,
With ample forehead, and with spreading horns,
Whose taper tops refulgent gold adorns.   350

    The Heroes pray'd, and *Pallas* from the skies,
Accords their vow, succeeds their enterprize.
Now, like two lions panting for the prey,
With deathful thoughts they trace the dreary way,
Thro' the black horrors of th' ensanguin'd plain,   355
Thro' dust, thro' blood, o'er arms, and hills of slain.

    Nor less bold *Hector*, and the sons of *Troy*,
On high designs the wakeful hours employ;
Th' assembled peers their lofty chief inclos'd;
Who thus the counsels of his breast propos'd.   360

    What glorious man, for high attempts prepar'd,
Dares greatly venture for a rich reward?
Of yonder fleet a bold discov'ry make,
What watch they keep, and what resolves they take?
If now subdu'd they meditate their flight,   365
And spent with toil neglect the watch of night?
His be the chariot that shall please him most,
Of all the plunder of the vanquish'd host;
His the fair steeds that all the rest excel,
And his the glory to have serv'd so well.   370

    A youth there was among the tribes of *Troy*,
Dolon his name, *Eumedes'* only boy,
(Five girls beside the rev'rend herald told)
Rich was the son in brass, and rich in gold;
Not blest by nature with the charms of face,   375
But swift of foot, and matchless in the race.
Hector! (he said) my courage bids me meet
This high atchievement, and explore the fleet:
But first exalt thy sceptre to the skies,
And swear to grant me the demanded prize;   380
Th' immortal coursers, and the glitt'ring car,
That bear *Pelides* thro' the ranks of war.
Encourag'd thus, no idle scout I go,
Fulfill thy wish, their whole intention know,
Ev'n to the royal tent pursue my way,   385
And all their counsels, all their aims betray.

The chief then heav'd the golden sceptre high,
Attesting thus the monarch of the sky.
Be witness thou! immortal Lord of all!
390   Whose thunder shakes the dark aerial hall:
By none but *Dolon* shall this prize be born,
And him alone th' immortal steeds adorn.

Thus *Hector* swore: the Gods were call'd in vain;
But the rash youth prepares to scour the plain:
395   A-cross his back the bended bow he flung,
A wolf's grey hide around his shoulders hung.
A ferret's downy fur his helmet lin'd,
And in his hand a pointed jav'lin shin'd.
Then (never to return) he sought the shore,
400   And trod the path his feet must tread no more.
Scarce had he pass'd the steeds and *Trojan* throng,
(Still bending forward as he cours'd along)
When, on the hollow way, th' approaching tread
Ulysses mark'd, and thus to *Diomed.*

405   O Friend! I hear some step of hostile feet,
Moving this way, or hast'ning to the fleet;
Some spy perhaps, to lurk beside the main;
Or nightly pillager that strips the slain.
Yet let him pass, and win a little space;
410   Then rush behind him, and prevent his pace.
But if too swift of foot he flies before,
Confine his course along the fleet and shore,
Betwixt the camp and him our spears employ,
And intercept his hop'd return to *Troy.*

415   With that they step'd aside, and stoop'd their head,
(As *Dolon* pass'd) behind a heap of dead:
Along the path the spy unwary flew;
Soft, at just distance, both the chiefs pursue.
So distant they, and such the space between,
420   As when two teams of mules divide the green,
(To whom the hind like shares of land allows)
When now few furrows part th' approaching ploughs.
Now *Dolon* list'ning, heard them as they past;
Hector (he thought) had sent, and check'd his hast,
425   Till scarce at distance of a jav'lin's throw,
No voice succeeding, he perceiv'd the Foe.

As when two skilful hounds the lev'ret winde,
Or chase thro' woods obscure the trembling hinde;
Now lost, now seen, they intercept his way,
And from the herd still turn the flying prey:
So fast, and with such fears, the *Trojan* flew;   430
So close, so constant, the bold *Greeks* pursue.
Now almost on the fleet the dastard falls,
And mingles with the guards that watch the walls;
When brave *Tydides* stopp'd; a gen'rous thought   435
(Inspir'd by *Pallas*) in his bosom wrought,
Lest on the foe some forward *Greek* advance,
And snatch the glory from his lifted lance.
Then thus aloud: whoe'er thou art, remain;
This jav'lin else shall fix thee to the plain.   440
He said, and high in air the weapon cast,
Which wilful err'd, and o'er his shoulder past;
Then fix'd in earth. Against the trembling wood
The wretch stood propp'd, and quiver'd as he stood;
A sudden palsy seiz'd his turning head;   445
His loose teeth chatter'd, and his colour fled:
The panting warriours seize him as he stands,
And with unmanly tears his life demands.

O spare my youth, and for the breath I owe,
Large gifts of price my father shall bestow: 450
Vast heaps of brass shall in your ships be told,
And steel well-temper'd, and refulgent gold.

To whom *Ulysses* made this wise reply;
Whoe'er thou art, be bold, nor fear to die.
What moves thee, say, when sleep has clos'd the sight,   455
To roam the silent fields in dead of night?
Cam'st thou the secrets of our camp to find,
By *Hector* prompted, or thy daring mind?
Or art some wretch by hopes of plunder led
Thro' heaps of carnage to despoil the dead?   460

Then thus pale *Dolon* with a fearful look,
(Still, as he spoke, his limbs with horror shook)
Hither I came, by *Hector*'s words deceiv'd;
Much did he promise, rashly I believ'd:
No less a bribe than great *Achilles*' car,   465
And those swift steeds that sweep the ranks of war,

Urg'd me, unwilling, this attempt to make;
To learn what counsels, what resolves you take,
If now subdu'd, you fix your hopes on flight,
470   And tir'd with toils, neglect the watch of night?
    Bold was thy aim, and glorious was the prize,
(*Ulysses*, with a scornful smile, replies)
Far other rulers those proud steeds demand,
And scorn the guidance of a vulgar hand;
475   Ev'n great *Achilles* scarce their rage can tame,
Achilles sprung from an immortal dame.
But say, be faithful, and the truth recite!
Where lies encamp'd the *Trojan* chief to-night?
Where stand his coursers? In what quarter sleep
480   Their other Princes? tell what watch they keep?
Say, since this conquest, what their counsels are? ⎫
Or here to combat, from their city far, ⎬
Or back to *Ilion*'s walls transfer the war? ⎭
    Ulysses thus, and thus *Eumedes'* son:
485   What *Dolon* knows, his faithful tongue shall own.
Hector, the peers assembling in his tent,
A council holds at *Ilus'* monument.
No certain guards the nightly watch partake;
Where-e'er yon' fires ascend, the *Trojans* wake:
490   Anxious for *Troy*, the guard the natives keep;
Safe in their cares, th' auxiliar forces sleep,
Whose wives and infants, from the danger far,
Discharge their souls of half the fears of war.
    Then sleep those aids among the *Trojan* train,
495   (Enquir'd the chief) or scatter'd o'er the plain?
    To whom the spy: Their pow'rs they thus dispose:
The *Pæons*, dreadful with their bended bows,
The *Carians*, *Caucons*, the *Pelasgian* host,
And *Leleges*, encamp along the coast.
500   Not distant far, lie higher on the land
The *Lycian*, *Mysian*, and *Mæonian* Band,
And *Phrygia*'s horse, by *Thymbras'* ancient wall;
The *Thracians* utmost, and a-part from all.
These *Troy* but lately to her succour won,
505   Led on by *Rhesus*, great *Eioneus'* son:

I saw his coursers in proud triumph go,
Swift as the wind, and white as winter-snow:
Rich silver plates his shining car infold;
His solid arms, refulgent, flame with gold;
No mortal shoulders suit the glorious load,   510
Celestial *Panoply*, to grace a God!
Let me, unhappy, to your fleet be born,
Or leave me here, a captive's fate to mourn,
In cruel chains; till your return reveal
The truth or falshood of the news I tell.   515

   To this *Tydides*, with a gloomy frown:
Think not to live, tho' all the truth be shown:
Shall we dismiss thee, in some future strife
To risk more bravely thy now forfeit life?
Or that again our camps thou may'st explore?   520
No – once a traytor, thou betray'st no more.

   Sternly he spoke, and as the wretch prepar'd
With humble blandishment to stroke his beard,
Like light'ning swift the wrathful faulchion flew,
Divides the neck, and cuts the nerves in two;
One instant snatch'd his trembling soul to hell,   525
The head, yet speaking, mutter'd as it fell.
The furry helmet from his brow they tear,
The wolf's grey hide, th' unbended bow and spear;
These great *Ulysses* lifting to the skies,
To fav'ring *Pallas* dedicates the prize.   530

   Great Queen of arms! receive this hostile spoil,
And let the *Thracian* steeds reward our toil:
Thee first of all the heav'nly host we praise;
Oh speed our labours, and direct our ways!
This said, the spoils with dropping gore defac'd,   535
High on a spreading tamarisk he plac'd;
Then heap'd with reeds and gather'd boughs the plain,
To guide their footsteps to the place again.

   Thro' the still night they cross the devious fields,   540
Slipp'ry with blood, o'er arms and heaps of shields.
Arriving where the *Thracian* Squadrons lay,
And eas'd in sleep the labours of the day,
Rang'd in three lines they view the prostrate band:
The horses yok'd beside each warriour stand;   545

Their arms in order on the ground reclin'd,
Thro' the brown shade the fulgid weapons shin'd.
Amidst, lay *Rhesus*, stretch'd in sleep profound,
And the white steeds behind his chariot bound.
550 The welcome sight *Ulysses* first descries,
And points to *Diomed* the tempting prize.
The man, the coursers, and the car behold!
Describ'd by *Dolon*, with the arms of gold.
Now, brave *Tydides!* now thy courage try,
555 Approach the chariot, and the steeds untye;
Or if thy soul aspire to fiercer deeds,
Urge thou the slaughter, while I seize the steeds.
  Pallas (this said) her hero's bosom warms,
Breath'd in his heart, and strung his nervous arms;
560 Where e'er he pass'd, a purple stream pursu'd;
His thirsty faulchion, fat with hostile blood,
Bath'd all his footsteps, dy'd the fields with gore,
And a low groan remurmur'd thro' the shore.
So the grim lion, from his nightly den,
565 O'erleaps the fences, and invades the pen;
On sheep or goats, resistless in his way,
He falls, and foaming rends the guardless prey.
Nor stopp'd the fury of his vengeful hand,
Till twelve lay breathless of the *Thracian* band.
570 *Ulysses* following, as his part'ner slew,
Back by the foot each slaughter'd warriour drew;
The milk-white coursers studious to convey
Safe to the ships, he wisely clear'd the way,
Lest the fierce steeds, not yet to battels bred,
575 Should start, and tremble at the heaps of dead.
Now twelve dispatch'd, the monarch last they found;
Tydides' faulchion fix'd him to the ground.
Just then a deathful dream *Minerva* sent;
A warlike form appear'd before his tent,
580 Whose visionary steel his bosom tore:
So dream'd the monarch, and awak'd no more.
  Ulysses now the snowy steeds detains,
And leads them, fasten'd by the silver reins;
These, with his bow unbent, he lash'd along;
585 (The scourge forgot, on *Rhesus* chariot hung.)

Then gave his friend the signal to retire;
But him, new dangers, new atchievements fire:
Doubtful he stood, or with his reeking blade
To send more heroes to th' infernal shade,
Drag off the car where *Rhesus'* armour lay,   590
Or heave with manly force, and lift away.
While unresolv'd the son of *Tydeus* stands,
Pallas appears, and thus her chief commands.

    Enough, my son, from farther slaughter cease,
Regard thy safety, and depart in peace;   595
Haste to the ships, the gotten spoils enjoy,
Nor tempt too far the hostile Gods of *Troy.*

    The voice divine confess'd the martial maid;
In haste he mounted, and her word obey'd;
The coursers fly before *Ulysses'* bow,   600
Swift as the wind, and white as winter-snow.

    Not unobserv'd they pass'd: the God of light
Had watch'd his *Troy,* and mark'd *Minerva's* flight,
Saw *Tydeus'* son with heav'nly succour blest,
And vengeful anger fill'd his sacred breast.   605
Swift to the *Trojan* camp descends the pow'r,
And wakes *Hippocoön* in the morning-hour,
(On *Rhesus'* side accustom'd to attend,
A faithful kinsman, and instructive friend.)
He rose, and saw the field deform'd with blood,   610
An empty space where late the coursers stood,
The yet-warm *Thracians* panting on the coast;
For each he wept, but for his *Rhesus* most:
Now while on *Rhesus'* name he calls in vain,
The gath'ring tumult spreads o'er all the plain;   615
On heaps the *Trojans* rush, with wild affright,
And wond'ring view the slaughters of the night.

    Mean while the chiefs, arriving at the shade
Where late the spoils of *Hector's* spy were laid,
Ulysses stopp'd; to him *Tydides* bore   620
The trophy, dropping yet with *Dolon's* gore:
Then mounts again; again their nimble feet
The coursers ply, and thunder tow'rds the fleet.

    Old *Nestor* first perceiv'd th' approaching sound,
Bespeaking thus the *Grecian* peers around.   625

Methinks the noise of tramp'ling steeds I hear
Thick'ning this way, and gath'ring on my ear;
Perhaps some horses of the *Trojan* breed
(So may, ye Gods! my pious hopes succeed)
630   The great *Tydides* and *Ulysses* bear,
Return'd triumphant with this prize of war.
Yet much I fear (ah may that fear be vain)
The chiefs out-number'd by the *Trojan* train:
Perhaps, ev'n now pursu'd, they seek the shore;
635   Or oh! perhaps those heroes are no more.

Scarce had he spoke, when lo! the chiefs appear,
And spring to earth; the *Greeks* dismiss their fear:
With words of friendship and extended hands
They greet the Kings; and *Nestor* first demands:
640   Say thou, whose praises all our host proclaim,
Thou living glory of the *Grecian* name!
Say whence these coursers? by what chance bestow'd,
The spoil of foes, or present of a God?
Not those fair steeds so radiant and so gay,
645   That draw the burning chariot of the day.
Old as I am, to age I scorn to yield,
And daily mingle in the martial field;
But sure till now no coursers struck my sight
Like these, conspicuous thro' the ranks of fight.
650   Some God, I deem, conferr'd the glorious prize,
Blest as ye are, and fav'rites of the skies;
The care of him who bids the thunder roar,
And *her, whose fury bathes the world with gore.

Father! not so, (sage *Ithacus* rejoin'd)
655   The gifts of heav'n are of a nobler kind.
Of *Thracian* lineage are the steeds ye view,
Whose hostile King the brave *Tydides* slew;
Sleeping he dy'd, with all his guards around,
And twelve beside lay gasping on the ground.
660   These other spoils from conquer'd *Dolon* came,
A wretch, whose swiftness was his only fame,
By *Hector* sent our forces to explore,
He now lies headless on the sandy shore.

*Minerva.

Then o'er the trench the bounding coursers flew;
The joyful *Greeks* with loud acclaim pursue.   665
Strait to *Tydides'* high pavilion born,
The matchless steeds his ample stalls adorn:
The neighing coursers their new fellows greet,
And the full racks are heap'd with gen'rous wheat.
But *Dolon*'s armour, to his ships convey'd,   670
High on the painted stern *Ulysses* laid,
A trophy destin'd to the blue-ey'd maid.

   Now from nocturnal sweat, and sanguine stain,
They cleanse their bodies in the neighb'ring main:
Then in the polish'd bath, refresh'd from toil,   675
Their joints they supple with dissolving oil,
In due repast indulge the genial hour,
And first to *Pallas* the libations pour:
They sit, rejoicing in her aid divine,
And the crown'd goblet foams with floods of wine.   680

OBSERVATIONS

ON THE

TENTH BOOK

It is observable, says *Eustathius*, that the Poet very artfully repairs the loss of the last day by this nocturnal stratagem; and it is plain that such a contrivance was necessary: the army was dispirited and *Achilles* inflexible; but by the success of this adventure the scale is turn'd in favour of the *Grecians*.

3. *All but the King,* &c.] *Homer* here with a very small alteration repeats the verses which begin the second book: he introduces *Agamemnon* with the same pomp as he did *Jupiter*; he ascribes to the one the same watchfulness over men, as the other exercis'd over the Gods, and *Jove* and *Agamemnon* are the only persons awake, while heaven and earth are asleep.   *Eustathius.*

7. *Or sends soft snows.*] *Scaliger*'s criticism against this passage, that it never lightens and snows at the same time, is sufficiently refuted by experience. See *Bossu* of the Epic poem *lib.* 3. *c.* 7. and *Barnes*'s note on this place.

8. *Or bids the brazen throat of war to roar.*] There is something very noble and sublime in this image: the *vast jaws of war* is an expression that very poetically represents the voraciousness of war, and gives us a lively idea of an insatiate monster.   *Eustathius.*

9. *By fits one flash succeeds,* &c.] It requires some skill in *Homer* to take the chief point of his similitudes; he has often been misunderstood in that respect, and his comparisons have frequently been strain'd to comply with the fancies of commentators. This comparison which is brought to illustrate the frequency of *Agamemnon*'s sighs, has been

usually thought to represent in general the groans of the King; whereas what *Homer* had in his view was only the quick succession of them.

13. *Now o'er the fields*, &c.] *Aristotle* answers a criticism of some censurers of *Homer* on this place. They asked how it was that *Agamemnon*, shut up in his tent in the night, could see the *Trojan* camp at one view, and the fleet at another, as the poet represents it? It is (says *Aristotle*) only a metaphorical manner of speech; *to cast one's eye*, means but *to reflect upon*, or *to revolve in one's mind*: and that employ'd *Agamemnon*'s thoughts in his tent, which had been the chief object of his eyes the day before.

19. *He rends his hairs in sacrifice to* Jove.] I know this action of *Agamemnon* has been taken only as a common expression of grief, and so indeed it was render'd by *Accius*, as cited by *Tully*, *Tusc. quæst. l.* 3. *Scindens dolore identidem intonsam comam* [tearing incessantly, in grief, his uncut hair]. But whoever reads the context will, I believe, be of opinion, that *Jupiter* is mention'd here on no other account than as he was apply'd to in the offering of these hairs, in an humble supplication to the offended deity who had so lately manifested his anger.

27. *He rose, and first he cast his mantle round.*] I fancy it will be entertaining to the reader to observe how well the poet at all times suits his descriptions to the circumstances of the persons; we must remember that this book continues the actions of one night; the whole army is now asleep, and *Homer* takes this opportunity to give us a description of several of his heroes suitable to their proper characters. *Agamemnon*, who is every where describ'd as anxious for the good of his people, is kept awake by a fatherly care for their preservation. *Menelaus*, for whose sake the *Greeks* had suffer'd so greatly, shares all their misfortunes, and is restless while they are in danger. *Nestor*, a provident, wise old man, sacrifices his rest even in the extremity of age, to his love for his country. *Ulysses*, a Person next to *Nestor* in wisdom, is ready at the first summons; he finds it hard, while the *Greeks* suffer, to compose himself to sleep, but is easily awak'd to march to its defence; but *Diomed*, who is every where describ'd as a daring warriour, sleeps unconcern'd at the nearness of the enemy, and is not awaked without some violence: he is said to be asleep, but he sleeps like a soldier in compleat arms.

I could not pass over one circumstance in this place in relation to

Nestor. It is a pleasure to see what care the poet takes of his favourite counsellor: he describes him lying in a soft bed, wraps him up in a warm cloak, to preserve his age from the coldness of the night; but *Diomed*, a gallant young hero, sleeps upon the ground in open air; and indeed every warriour is dress'd in Arms peculiar to that season: the Hide of a lion or leopard is what they all put on, being not to engage an enemy, but to meet their friends in council.   *Eustathius.*

43. *Sends he some spy?* &c.] *Menelaus* in this place starts a design which is afterwards proposed by *Nestor* in council; the poet knew that the project would come with greater weight from the age of the one, than from the youth of the other: and that the valiant would be ready to execute a design, which so venerable a counsellor had form'd.

                                                                  Eustathius.

57. *Such wondrous deeds as* Hector's *hand,* &c.] We hear *Agamemnon* in this place launching into the praises of a gallant enemy; but if any one think that he raises the actions of *Hector* too high, and sets him above *Achilles* himself, this objection will vanish if he considers that he commends him as the bravest of mere men, but still he is not equal to *Achilles*, who was descended from a goddess. *Agamemnon* undoubtedly had *Achilles* in his thoughts when he says,

> *Sprung from no God,* &c.

But his anger will not let him even name the man whom he thus obliquely praises.

Eastathius proceeds to observe, that the poet ascribes the gallant exploits of *Hector* to his piety; and had he not been favour'd by *Jove*, he had not been this victorious.

He also remarks that there is a double tautology in this speech of *Agamemnon*, as δηθά τε καὶ δολιχόν, μέρμερα μητίσασθαι [for a long time he has long devised things that will be remembered], and ἔργα ἔρρεξε [he performed actions]. This proceeds from the wonder which the King endeavours to express at the greatness of *Hector*'s actions: he labours to make his words answer the great idea he had conceived of them; and while his mind dwells upon the same object, he falls into the same manner of expressing it. This is very natural to a person in his circumstances, whose thoughts are as it were pent up, and struggle for an utterance.

73. *The paths so many,* &c.] 'Tis plain from this verse, as well as from many others, that the art of fortification was in some degree of perfection in *Homer*'s days: here are lines drawn that traverse the camp ev'ry way; the ships are drawn up in the manner of a rampart, and sally ports made at proper distances, that they might without difficulty either retire or issue out, as the occasion should require.

Eustathius.

92. *Seek'st thou some friend or nightly centinel?*] It has been thought that *Nestor* asks this question upon the account of his son *Thrasymedes*, who commanded the guard that night. He seems to be under some apprehension lest he should have remitted the watch. And it may also be gathered from this passage, that in those times the use of the watchword was unknown; because *Nestor* is obliged to crowd several questions together, before he can learn whether *Agamemnon* be a friend or an enemy. The shortness of the questions agrees admirably with the occasion upon which they were made; it being necessary that *Nestor* should be immediately informed who he was that passed along the camp: if a spy, that he might stand upon his guard; if a friend, that he might not cause an alarm to be given to the army, by multiplying questions.

Eustathius.

96. *Lo here the wretched* Agamemnon *stands.*] *Eustathius* observes, that *Agamemnon* here paints his distress in a very pathetical manner: while the meanest soldier is at rest, the General wanders about disconsolate, and is superiour now in nothing so much as in sorrow: but this sorrow proceeds not from a base abject spirit, but from a generous disposition; he is not anxious for the loss of his own glory, but for the sufferings of his people: it is a noble sorrow, and springs from a commendable tenderness and humanity.

138. *My gen'rous brother is of gentle kind.*] *Agamemnon* is every where represented as the greatest example of brotherly affection; and he at all times defends *Menelaus*, but never with more address than now: *Nestor* had accused *Menelaus* of sloth; the King is his advocate, but pleads his excuse only in part: he does not entirely acquit him, because he would not contradict so wise a man as *Nestor*; nor does he condemn him, because his brother at this time was not guilty; but he very artfully turns the imputation of *Nestor* to the praise of *Menelaus*; and affirms, that what might seem to be remissness in his character was only a

deference to his authority, and that his seeming inactivity was but an unwillingness to act without command.   *Eustathius.*

174. *A wood of spears stood by,* &c.] The picture here given us of *Diomed* sleeping in his arms, with his soldiers about him, and the spears sticking upright in the earth, has a near resemblance to that in the first book of *Samuel*, Ch. 26. v. 7. Saul *lay sleeping within the trench, and his spear stuck in the ground at his bolster; but* Abner *and the people lay round about him.*

182. *From yon' hill the foe,* &c.] It is necessary, if we would form an exact idea of the battels of *Homer*, to carry in our minds the place where each Action was fought. It will therefore be proper to enquire where that eminence stood, upon which the *Trojans* encamp'd this night. *Eustathius* is inclinable to believe it was *Callicolone*, (the situation of which you will find in the map of *Homer*'s battels [not included in this edition]) but it will appear from what *Dolon* says, v. 415. (of *Hector*'s being encamp'd at the monument of *Ilus*) that this eminence must be the *Tumulus* on which that monument was situate, and so the old scholiast rightly explains it.

194. *But now the last despair surrounds our host.*] The different behaviour of *Nestor* upon the same occasion, to different persons, is worthy observation: *Agamemnon* was under a concern and dejection of spirit from the danger of his army: To raise his courage, *Nestor* gave him hopes of success, and represented the state of affairs in the most favourable view. But he applies himself to *Diomed*, who is at all times enterprizing and incapable of despair, in a far different manner: He turns the darkest side to him, and gives the worst prospect of their condition. This conduct (says *Eustathius*) shews a great deal of prudence: 'tis the province of wisdom to encourage the dishearten'd with hopes, and to qualify the forward courage of the daring with fears; that the valour of the one may not sink thro' despair, nor that of the other fly out into rashness.

207. *And now the chiefs approach the nightly guard.*] It is usual in poetry to pass over little circumstances, and carry on the greater. *Menelaus* in this book was sent to call some of the leaders; the poet has too much judgment to dwell upon the trivial particulars of his performing his message, but lets us know by the sequel that he had performed

it. It would have clogged the poetical narration to have told us how *Menelaus* waked the heroes to whom he was dispatched, and had been but a repetition of what the poet had fully described before: He therefore (says the same author) drops these particularities, and leaves them to be supplied by the imagination of the reader. 'Tis so in painting, the painter does not always draw at the full length, but leaves what is wanting to be added by the fancy of the beholder.

211. *So faithful dogs,* &c.] This simile is in all its parts just to the description it is meant to illustrate. The dogs represent the watch, the flock the *Greeks*, the fold their camp, and the wild beast that invades them, *Hector.* The place, posture, and circumstance, are painted with the utmost life and nature.

Eustathius takes notice of one particular in this description, which shews the manner in which their centinels kept the guard. The poet tells us, that they *sate down with their arms in their hands*. I think that this was not so prudent a method as is now used; it being almost impossible for a man that stands, to drop asleep, whereas one that is seated may easily be overpowered by the fatigue of a long watch.

228. *Then o'er the trench the following chieftains led.*] The reason why *Nestor* did not open the council within the trenches, was with a design to encourage the guards, and those whom he intended to send to enter the *Trojan* Camp. It would have appeared unreasonable to send others over the entrenchments upon a hazardous enterprize, and not to have dared himself to set a foot beyond them. This also could not fail of inflaming the courage of the *Grecian* spies, who would know themselves not to be far from assistance, while so many of the princes were passed over the ditch as well as they.   *Eustathius.*

241. *Is there (said he) a chief so greatly brave?*] *Nestor* proposes his design of sending spies into the *Trojan* army with a great deal of address: He begins with a general sentence, and will not choose any one hero, for fear of disgusting the rest: Had *Nestor* named the person, he would have paid him a complement that was sure to be attended with the hazard of his life; and that person might have believed that *Nestor* exposed him to a danger, which his honour would not let him decline; while the rest might have resented such a partiality, which would have seemed to give the preference to another before them. It therefore was wisdom in *Nestor* to propose the design in general terms, whereby all the gallant men that offered themselves satisfied their honour, by being willing to share the danger with *Diomed*; and it was no disgrace to be left behind, after they had offered to hazard their lives for their country.   *Eustathius.*

244. *Or seize some straggling foe?*] It is worthy observation with how much caution *Nestor* opens this design, and with how much courage *Diomed* accepts it. *Nestor* forms it with coolness, but *Diomed* embraces it with warmth and resolution. *Nestor* only proposes that some man would approach the enemy and intercept some straggling *Trojan*, but *Diomed* offers to penetrate the very camp. *Nestor* was afraid lest no one should undertake it: *Diomed* overlooks the danger, and presents himself, as willing to march against the whole army of *Troy*.   *Eustathius.*

280. *To birth or office no respect be paid.*] *Eustathius* remarks that *Agamemnon* artfully steals away his brother from danger; the fondness he bears to him makes him think him unequal to so bold an enterprize, and prefer his safety to his glory. He farther adds, that the Poet intended to condemn that faulty modesty which makes one sometimes prefer a nobleman before a person of more real worth. To be greatly born is an happiness, but no merit; whereas personal virtues shew a man worthy of that greatness to which he is not born.

It appears from hence, how honourable it was of old to go upon these parties by night, or undertake those offices which are now only the task of common soldiers. *Gideon* in the book of *Judges* (as *Dacier* observes) goes as a spy into the camp of *Midian*, tho' he was at that time General of the *Israelites*.

289. *Blest in his conduct.*] There required some address in *Diomed* to make his choice without offending the *Grecian* Princes; each of them might think it an indignity to be refus'd such a place of honour. *Diomed* therefore chuses *Ulysses* not because he is braver than the rest, but because he is wiser. This part of his character was allow'd by all the leaders of the army; and none of them thought it a disparagement to themselves as they were men of valour, to see the first place given to *Ulysses* in point of wisdom. No doubt but the poet, by causing *Diomed* to make this choice, intended to insinuate that valour ought always to be temper'd with wisdom; to the end that what is design'd with prudence may be executed with resolution.   *Eustathius.*

291. *It fits thee not to praise me or to blame.*] The Modesty of *Ulysses* in this passage is very remarkable; tho' undoubtedly he deserved to be praised, yet he interrupts *Diomed* rather than he would be a hearer of his own commendation. What *Diomed* spoke in praise of *Ulysses*, was utter'd to justify his choice of him to the leaders of the army; otherwise the praise he had given him, would have been no better than flattery.

Eustathius.

295. *– Night rolls the hours away,*
The stars shine fainter on th' ætherial plains,
And of night's empire but a third remains.]

It has been objected that *Ulysses* is guilty of a threefold tautology, when every word he utter'd shews the necessity of being concise: If the night was nigh spent, there was the less time to lose in tautologies. But this is so far from being a fault, that it is a beauty: *Ulysses* dwells upon the shortness of the time before the day appears, in order to urge *Diomed* to the greater speed in prosecuting the design.   *Eustathius.*

298. *But a third remains.*] One ought to take notice with how much exactness *Homer* proportions his incidents to the time of action: These two books take up no more than the compass of one night; and this design could not have been executed in any other part of it. The Poet had before told us, that all the plain was enlightened by the fires of *Troy*, and consequently no spy could pass over to their camp, till they were almost sunk and extinguish'd, which could not be till near the morning.

'Tis observable that the Poet divides the night into three parts, from whence we may gather, that the *Grecians* had three watches during the night: The first and second of which were over, when *Diomed* and *Ulysses* set out to enter the enemy's camp.   *Eustathius.*

301. *A two-edg'd faulchion* Thrasymed *the brave*, &c.] It is a very impertinent remark of *Scaliger*, that *Diomed* should not have gone from his tent without a sword. The expedition he now goes upon could not be foreseen by him at the time he rose: He was awak'd of a sudden, and sent in haste to call some of the Princes: Besides, he went but to council, and even then carry'd his spear with him, as *Homer* had already inform'd us. I think if one were to study the art of cavilling, there would be more occasion to blame *Virgil* for what *Scaliger* praises him, giving a sword to *Euryalus* when he had one before, *Æn.* 9. v. 303.

303. *Then in a leathern helm.*] It may not be improper to observe how conformably to the design the Poet arms these two heroes: *Ulysses* has a bow and arrows, that he might be able to wound the enemy at a distance, and so retard his flight till he could overtake him; and for fear of a discovery, *Diomed* is arm'd with an helmet of leather, that the glittering of it might not betray him.   *Eustathius.*

There is some resemblance in this whole story to that of *Nisus* and *Euryalus* in *Virgil*: and as the heroes are here successful, and in *Virgil* unfortunate, it was perhaps as great an instance of *Virgil*'s judgment to describe the unhappy youth in a glittering Helmet, which occasion'd his discovery, as it was in *Homer* to arm his successful one in the contrary manner.

309. *A well-prov'd casque.*] Mr *Barnes* has a pretty remark on this place, that it was probably from this description, πῖλος ἀρήρει [fitted with felt], that the ancient Painters and tragic Poets constantly represented *Ulysses* with the *Pileus* [a felt cap] on his head; but this particularity could not be preserved with any grace in the translation.

313. *This from* Amyntor, &c.] The succession of this helmet descending from one hero to another, is imitated by *Virgil* in the story of *Nisus* and *Euryalus.*

> *Euryalus phaleras Rhamnetis, & aurea bullis*
> *Cingula, Tiburti Remulo ditissimus olim*
> *Quæ mittit dona, hospitio cum jungeret absens*
> *Cædicus, ille suo moriens dat habere nepoti.*
> *Post mortem bello Rutuli pugnaque potiti.*

[Nor did his eyes less longingly behold
The girdle-belt, with nails of burnish'd gold.
This present *Cedicus* the rich, bestow'd
On *Remulus*, when friendship first they vow'd:
And absent, join'd in hospitable tyes;
He dying, to his heir bequeath'd the prize:
Till by the conqu'ring *Ardean* troops oppress'd
He fell; and they the glorious gift possess'd.]

It was anciently a custom to make these military presents to brave adventurers. So *Jonathan* in the first book of *Samuel*, *stript himself of the robe that was upon him, and gave it to* David; *and his garments, even to his sword, and his bow, and his girdle.* Ch. 18. v. 4.

326. Ulysses *hail'd the glad omen.*] This passage sufficiently justifies *Diomed* for his choice of *Ulysses*: *Diomed*, who was most renown'd for valour, might have given a wrong interpretation to this omen, and so have been discourag'd from proceeding in the attempt. For tho' it really signify'd, that as the bird was not seen, but only heard by the sound of its wings, so they should not be discover'd by the *Trojans*, but perform actions which all *Troy* should hear with sorrow; yet on the other hand it might imply, that as they discover'd the bird by the noise of its wings, so they should be betray'd by the noise they should make in the *Trojan* army. The reason why *Pallas* does not send the bird that is sacred to her self, but the heron, is because it is a bird of prey, and denoted that they should spoil the *Trojans*.

Eustathius.

356. *Thro' dust, thro' blood*, &c.] *Xenophon* (says *Eustathius*) has imitated this passage; but what the poet gives us in one line, the historian protracts into several sentences. Ἐπεὶ δὲ ἔληξεν ἡ μάχη, παρῆν ἰδεῖν, τὴν μὲν γῆν αἵματι πεφυρμένην, &c. 'When the battel was over, one might behold *through the whole extent of the field*, the ground dy'd red with blood, *the bodies of friends and enemies stretch'd over each other, the shields pierc'd, the spears broken, and the drawn swords, some scatter'd on the earth, some plung'd in the bodies of the slain, and some yet grasp'd in the hands of the soldiers.*'

357. *Nor less bold* Hector, &c.] It is the remark of *Eustathius*, that *Homer* sends out the *Trojan* spy in this place in a very different manner from the *Grecian* ones before. Having been very particular in describing the counsel of the *Greeks*, he avoids tiring the reader here with parallel circumstances, and passes it in general terms. In the first, a wise old man proposes the adventure with an air of deference; in the second, a brave young man with an air of authority. The one promises a small gift, but very honourable and certain; the other a great one, but uncertain and less honourable, because 'tis given as a reward. So that *Diomed* and *Ulysses* are inspired with the love of glory, *Dolon* is possest with a thirst of gain: they proceed with a sage and circumspect

valour, he with rashness and vanity; they go in conjunction, he alone; they cross the fields out of the road, he follows the common track. In all this there is a contraste that is admirable, and a moral that strikes every reader at first sight.

372. Dolon *his name.*] 'Tis scarce to be conceiv'd with what conciseness the poet has here given us the name, the fortunes, the pedigree, the office, the shape, the swiftness of *Dolon*. He seems to have been eminent for nothing so much as for his wealth, tho' undoubtedly he was by place one of the first rank in *Troy*: *Hector* summons him to this assembly amongst the chiefs of *Troy*; nor was he unknown to the *Greeks*, for *Diomed* immediately after he had seiz'd him, calls him by his name. Perhaps being an herald, he had frequently pass'd between the armies in the execution of his office.

The ancients observ'd upon this place, that it was the office of *Dolon* which made him offer himself to *Hector*. The sacred character gave him hopes that they would not violate his person, should he happen to be taken; and his riches he knew were sufficient to purchase his liberty; besides all which advantages, he had hopes from his swiftness to escape any pursuers.   *Eustathius.*

375. *Not blest by nature with the charms of face.*] The original is,

Ὃς δή τοι εἶδος μὲν ἔην κακός, ἀλλὰ ποδώκης.

[He was unattractive but swift-footed.]

Which some ancient criticks thought to include a contradiction, because the man who is ill-shap'd can hardly be swift in running; taking the word εἶδος as apply'd in general to the air of the whole person. But *Aristotle* acquaints us that word was as proper in regard to the face only, and that it was usual with the *Cretans* to call a man with a handsome face, εὐειδής. So that *Dolon* might want a good face, and yet be well-shap'd enough to make an excellent racer. *Poet. c.* 26.

380. *Swear to grant me,* &c.] It is evident from this whole narration, that *Dolon* was a man of no worth or courage; his covetousness seems to be the sole motive of his undertaking this exploit: and whereas *Diomed* neither desired any reward, nor when promis'd requir'd any assurance of it; *Dolon* demands an oath, and will not trust the promise of *Hector*; he every where discovers a base spirit, and by the sequel it

will appear, that this vain boaster instead of discovering the army of
the enemy, becomes a traytor to his own.   *Eustathius.*

381. *Th' immortal coursers, and the glitt'ring car.*] *Hector* in the forego-
ing speech promises the best horses in the *Grecian* army, as a reward to
any one who would undertake what he propos'd. *Dolon* immediately
demands those of *Achilles*, and confines the general promise of *Hector*
to the particular horses of that brave hero.

There is something very extraordinary in *Hector*'s taking a solemn
oath, that he will give the chariots and steeds of *Achilles* to *Dolon.* The
Ancients, says *Eustathius*, knew not whose vanity most to wonder at,
that of *Dolon*, or *Hector*; the one for demanding this, or the other for
promising it. Though we may take notice, that *Virgil* lik'd this
extravagance so well as to imitate it, where *Ascanius* (without being
asked) promises the horses and armour of *Turnus* to *Nisus*, on his
undertaking a like enterprize.

> *Vidisti, quo Turnus equo, quibus ibat in armis,*
> *Aureus; ipsum illum, clypeum cristasque rubentes*
> *Excipiam sorti, jam nunc tua præmia, Nise.*

> [Thou saw'st the courser by proud *Turnus* press'd,
> That, *Nisus*, and his arms and nodding crest,
> And shield, from chance exempt, shall be thy share.]

Unless one should think the rashness of such a promise better agreed
with the ardour of this youthful prince, than with the character of an
experienc'd warriour like *Hector*.

419. *– Such the space between, As when two teams of mules,* &c.] I
wonder *Eustathius* takes no notice of the manner of ploughing used by
the ancients, which is describ'd in these verses, and of which we have
the best account from *Dacier*. She is not satisfied with the explanation
given by *Didymus*, that *Homer* meant the space which mules by their
swiftness gain upon oxen that plow in the same field. 'The *Grecians*
(says she) did not plow in the manner now in use. They first broke up
the ground with oxen, and then plow'd it more lightly with mules.
When they employed two plows in a Field, they measured the space
they could plow in a day, and set their plows at the two ends of that
space, and those plows proceeded toward each other. This intermediate
space was constantly fix'd, but less in proportion for two plows of oxen

than for two of mules; because oxen are slower and toil more in a field that has not been yet turn'd up, whereas mules are naturally swifter, and make greater speed in a ground that has already had the first plowing. I therefore believe that what *Homer* calls ἐπίουροι, is the space left by the husbandmen between two plows of mules which till the same field: and as this space was so much the greater in a field already plow'd by oxen, he adds what he says of mules, that they are swifter and fitter to give the second plowing than oxen, and therefore distinguishes the field so plowed by the epithet of *deep*, νειοῖο βαθείης: for that space was certain, of so many acres or perches, and always larger than in a field as yet untill'd, which being heavier and more difficult, requir'd the interval to be so much the less between two plows of oxen, because they could not dispatch so much work. *Homer* could not have serv'd himself of a juster comparison for a thing that pass'd in the fields; at the same time he shews his experience in the art of agriculture, and gives his verses a most agreeable ornament, as indeed all the images drawn from this art are peculiarly entertaining.'

This manner of measuring a space of ground by a comparison from plowing, seems to have been customary in those times, from that passage in the first book of *Samuel*, Ch. 14. v. 14. *And the first slaughter which* Jonathan *and his armour-bearer made, was about twenty men, within as it were half a furrow of an acre of land, which a yoke of oxen might plow.*

444. *Quiver'd as he stood,* &c.] The Poet here gives us a very lively picture of a person in the utmost agonies of fear: *Dolon*'s swiftness forsakes him, and he stands shackled by his cowardice. The very words express the thing he describes by the broken turn of the *Greek* verses. And something like it is aimed at in the *English*.

$$- ὁ δ᾽ ἄρ᾽ ἔστη τάρβησέν τε$$
$$Βαμβαίνων, ἄραβος δὲ διὰ στόμα γίγνετ᾽ ὀδόντων,$$
$$Χλωρὸς ὑπαὶ δείους. -$$

454. *Be bold, nor fear to die.*] 'Tis observable what caution the poet here uses in reference to *Dolon*: *Ulysses* does not make him any promises of life, but only bids him very artfully not to think of dying: so that when *Diomed* kills him, he was not guilty of a breach of promise, and the spy was deceiv'd rather by the art and subtlety of *Ulysses*, than by his falshood. *Dolon*'s understanding seems entirely to

be disturb'd by his fears; he was so cautious as not to believe a friend just before without an oath, but here he trusts an enemy without so much as a promise.   *Eustathius.*

467. *Urg'd me unwilling.*] 'Tis observable that the cowardice of *Dolon* here betrays him into a falshood: tho' *Eustathius* is of opinion that the word in the original means no more than *contrary to my judgment.*

478. *Where lies encamp'd.*] The Night was now very far advanc'd, the morning approach'd, and the two heroes had their whole design still to execute: *Ulysses* therefore complies with the necessity of the time, and makes his questions very short, tho' at the same time very full. In the like manner when *Ulysses* comes to shew *Diomed* the chariot of *Rhesus*, he uses a sudden transition without the usual form of speaking.

488. *No certain guards.*] *Homer* to give an air of probability to this narration, lets us understand that the *Trojan* camp might easily be enter'd without a discovery, because there were no centinels to guard it. This might happen partly thro' the security which their late success had thrown them into, and partly thro' the fatigues of the former day. Besides which, *Homer* gives us another very natural reason, the negligence of the auxiliar forces, who being foreigners, had nothing to lose by the fall of *Troy.*

489. *Where e'er yon fires ascend.*] This is not to be understood of those fires which *Hector* commanded to be kindled at the beginning of this night, but only of the houshold fires of the *Trojans*, distinct from the auxiliars. The expression in the original is somewhat remarkable; but implies those people that were natives of *Troy*; ἱστία and ἐσχάρα πυρός signifying the same thing. So that ἱστίας ἔχειν and ἐσχάρας ἔχειν mean to have houses or hearths in *Troy.*   *Eustathius.*

525. *Divides the neck.*] It may seem a piece of barbarity in *Diomed* to kill *Dolon* thus, in the very act of supplicating for mercy. *Eustathius* answers, that it was very necessary that it should be so, for fear, if he had defer'd his death, he might have cry'd out to the *Trojans*, who hearing his voice, would have been upon their guard.

578. *Just then a deathful dream* Minerva *sent.*] All the circumstances of this action, the night, *Rhesus* buried in a profound sleep, and

Diomed with the sword in his hand hanging over the head of that prince, furnish'd *Homer* with the idea of this fiction, which represents *Rhesus* dying fast asleep, and as it were beholding his enemy in a dream plunging a sword into his bosom. This image is very natural, for a man in this condition awakes no farther than to see confusedly what environs him, and to think it not a reality, but a vision.

Eustathius, Dacier.

607. *And wakes* Hippocoön.] *Apollo*'s waking the *Trojans* is only an allegory to imply that the light of the morning awaken'd them.

Eustathius.

624. *Old* Nestor *first perceiv'd*, &c.] It may with an appearance of reason be ask'd, whence it could be that *Nestor*, whose sense of hearing might be suppos'd to be impair'd by his great age, should be the first person among so many youthful warriours who hears the tread of the horse's feet at a distance? *Eustathius* answers, that *Nestor* had a particular concern for the safety of *Diomed* and *Ulysses* on this occasion, as he was the person who, by proposing the undertaking, had exposed them to a very signal danger; and consequently his extraordinary care for their preservation, did more than supply the disadvantage of his age. This agrees very well with what immediately follows; for the old man breaks out into a transport at the sight of them, and in a wild sort of joy asks some questions, which could not have proceeded from him, but while he was under that happy surprize.   *Eustathius.*

656. *Of* Thracian *Lineage*, &c.] It is observable, says *Eustathius*, that *Homer* in this place unravels the series of this night's exploits, and inverts the order of the former narration. This is partly occasion'd by a necessity of *Nestor*'s enquiries, and partly to relate the same thing in a different way, that he might not tire the reader with an exact repetition of what he knew before.

659. *And twelve beside*, &c.] How comes it to pass that the Poet should here call *Dolon* the thirteenth that was slain, whereas he had already number'd up thirteen besides him? *Eustathius* answers, that he mentions *Rhesus* by himself, by way of eminence. Then coming to recount the *Thracians*, he reckons twelve of them; so that taking *Rhesus* separately, *Dolon* will make the thirteenth.

674. *They cleanse their bodies in the main,* &c.] We have here a regimen very agreeable to the simplicity and austerity of the old heroic times. These warriours plunge into the sea to wash themselves; for the salt water is not only more purifying than any other, but more corroborates the nerves. They afterwards enter into a bath, and rub their bodies with oil, which by softening and moistening the flesh prevents too great a dissipation, and restores the natural strength.

Eustathius.

677. *In due repast,* &c.] It appears from hence with what preciseness *Homer* distinguishes the time of these actions. 'Tis evident from this passage, that immediately after their return, it was day-light; that being the time of taking such a repast as is here describ'd.

I cannot conclude the notes to this book without observing, that what seems the principal beauty of it, and what distinguishes it among all the others, is the liveliness of its paintings: The reader sees the most natural night scene in the world; he is led step by step with the adventurers, and made the companion of all their expectations, and uncertainties. We see the very colour of the sky, know the time to a minute, are impatient while the heroes are arming, our imagination steals out after them, becomes privy to all their doubts, and even to the secret wishes of their hearts sent up to *Minerva.* We are alarmed at the approach of *Dolon,* hear his very footsteps, assist the two chiefs in pursuing him, and stop just with the spear that arrests him. We are perfectly acquainted with the situation of all the forces, with the figure in which they lie, with the disposition of *Rhesus* and the *Thracians,* with the posture of his chariot and horses. The marshy spot of ground where *Dolon* is killed, the tamarisk, or aquatic plants upon which they hang his spoils, and the reeds that are heap'd together to mark the place, are circumstances the most picturesque imaginable. And tho' it must be owned, that the human figures in this piece are excellent, and disposed in the properest actions; I cannot but confess my opinion, that the chief beauty of it is in the prospect, a finer than which was never drawn by any pencil.

THE
ELEVENTH BOOK
OF THE
ILIAD

The ARGUMENT

The third Battel, and the acts of *Agamemnon*

Agamemnon *having arm'd himself, leads the* Grecians *to battel:* Hector *prepares the* Trojans *to receive them; while* Jupiter, Juno, *and* Minerva *give the signals of war.* Agamemnon *bears all before him; and* Hector *is commanded by* Jupiter (*who sends* Iris *for that purpose*) *to decline the engagement, till the King shall be wounded and retire from the field. He then makes a grèat slaughter of the enemy;* Ulysses *and* Diomed *put a stop to him for a while; but the latter being wounded by* Paris *is obliged to desert his companion, who is encompassed by the* Trojans, *wounded, and in the utmost danger, till* Menelaus *and* Ajax *rescue him.* Hector *comes against* Ajax, *but that hero alone opposes multitudes, and rallies the* Greeks. *In the mean time* Machaon, *in the other wing of the army, is pierced with an arrow by* Paris, *and carried from the fight in* Nestor's *chariot.* Achilles (*who overlooked the action from his ship*) *sends* Patroclus *to enquire which of the* Greeks *was wounded in that manner?* Nestor *entertains him in his tent with an account of the accidents of the day, and a long recital of some former wars which he remembered, tending to put* Patroclus *upon persuading* Achilles *to fight for his countrymen, or at least to permit him to do it, clad in* Achilles's *armour.* Patroclus *in his return meets* Eurypilus *also wounded, and assists him in that distress.*

This book opens with the eight and twentieth day of the poem; and the same day, with its various actions and adventures, is extended thro' the twelfth, thirteenth, fourteenth, fifteenth, sixteenth, seventeenth, and part of the eighteenth books. The scene lies in the field near the monument of Ilus.

The saffron morn, with early blushes spread,
Now rose refulgent from *Tithonus*' bed;
With new-born day to gladden mortal sight,
And gild the courts of heav'n with sacred light.
5   When baleful *Eris*, sent by *Jove*'s command,
The torch of discord blazing in her hand,
Thro' the red skies her bloody sign extends,
And wrapt in tempests, o'er the fleet descends.
High on *Ulysses*' bark her horrid stand
10 She took, and thunder'd thro' the seas and land.
Ev'n *Ajax* and *Achilles* heard the sound,
Whose ships, remote, the guarded navy bound.
Thence the black Fury thro' the *Grecian* throng
With horrour sounds the loud *Orthian* song:
15 The navy shakes, and at the dire alarms
Each bosom boils, each warriour starts to arms.
No more they sigh, inglorious to return,
But breathe revenge, and for the combat burn.
      The King of men his hardy host inspires
20 With loud command, with great example fires;
Himself first rose, himself before the rest
His mighty limbs in radiant armour drest.
And first he cas'd his manly legs around
In shining greaves, with silver buckles bound:
25 The beaming cuirass next adorn'd his breast,
The same which once King *Cinyras* possest:
(The fame of *Greece* and her assembled host
Had reach'd that monarch on the *Cyprian* coast;

'Twas then, the friendship of the chief to gain,
This glorious gift he sent, nor sent in vain.)
Ten rows of azure steel the work infold,   30
Twice ten of tin, and twelve of ductile gold;
Three glitt'ring dragons to the gorget rise,
Whose imitated scales against the skies
Reflected various light, and arching bow'd,   35
Like colour'd rainbows o'er a show'ry cloud.
(*Jove*'s wond'rous bow, of three celestial dyes,
Plac'd as a sign to man amid the skies.)
A radiant baldrick, o'er his shoulder ty'd,
Sustain'd the sword that glitter'd at his side: 40
Gold was the hilt, a silver sheath encas'd
The shining blade, and golden hangers grac'd.
His buckler's mighty orb was next display'd,
That round the warriour cast a dreadful shade;
Ten zones of brass its ample Brims surround,   45
And twice ten bosses the bright convex crown'd;
Tremendous *Gorgon* frown'd upon its field,
And circling terrours fill'd th' expressive shield:
Within its concave hung a silver thong,
On which a mimic serpent creeps along,   50
His azure length in easy waves extends,
Till in three heads th' embroider'd monster ends.
Last o'er his brows his fourfold helm he plac'd,
With nodding horse-hair formidably grac'd;
And in his hands two steely jav'lins wields,   55
That blaze to heav'n, and lighten all the fields.

That instant, *Juno* and the martial Maid
In happy thunders promis'd *Greece* their aid;
High o'er the chief they clash'd their arms in air,
And leaning from the clouds, expect the war.   60

Close to the limits of the trench and mound,
The fiery coursers to their chariots bound
The squires restrain'd: The Foot, with those who wield
The lighter arms, rush forward to the field.
To second these, in close array combin'd,   65
The squadrons spread their sable wings behind.
Now shouts and tumults wake the tardy sun,
As with the light the warriours toils begun.

Ev'n *Jove*, whose thunder spoke his wrath, distill'd
70 Red drops of blood o'er all the fatal field;
The woes of men unwilling to survey,
And all the slaughters that must stain the day.
    Near *Ilus'* tomb, in order rang'd around,
The *Trojan* lines possess'd the rising ground.
75 There wise *Polydamas* and *Hector* stood;
Æneas, honour'd as a guardian God;
Bold *Polybus*, *Agenor* the divine;
The brother warriours of *Antenor*'s line;
With youthful *Acamas*, whose beauteous face
80 And fair proportion match'd th' etherial race.
Great *Hector*, cover'd with his spacious shield,
Plies all the troops, and orders all the field.
As the red star now shows his sanguine fires
Thro' the dark clouds, and now in night retires;
85 Thus thro' the ranks appear'd the God-like man,
Plung'd in the rear, or blazing in the van;
While streamy sparkles, restless as he flies,
Flash from his arms as light'ning from the skies.
As sweating reapers in some wealthy field,
90 Rang'd in two bands, their crooked weapons wield,
Bear down the furrows, till their labours meet;
Thick fall the heapy harvests at their feet.
So *Greece* and *Troy* the field of war divide,
And falling ranks are strow'd on ev'ry side.
95 None stoop'd a thought to base inglorious flight;
But horse to horse, and man to man they fight.
Not rabid wolves more fierce contest their prey;
Each wounds, each bleeds, but none resign the day.
Discord with joy the scene of death descries,
100 And drinks large slaughter at her sanguine eyes:
Discord alone, of all th' immortal train,
Swells the red horrors of this direful plain:
The Gods in peace their golden mansions fill,
Rang'd in bright order on th' *Olympian* hill;
105 But gen'ral murmurs told their griefs above,
And each accus'd the partial will of *Jove*.
Mean while apart, superiour, and alone,
Th' eternal Monarch, on his awful throne,

Wrapt in the blaze of boundless glory sate;
And fix'd, fulfill'd the just decrees of fate.   110
On earth he turn'd his all-consid'ring eyes,
And mark'd the spot where *Ilion*'s tow'rs arise;
The sea with ships, the fields with armies spread,
The victor's rage, the dying, and the dead.

Thus while the morning-beams increasing bright   115
O'er heav'ns pure azure spread the growing light,
Commutual death the fate of war confounds,
Each adverse battel goar'd with equal wounds.
But now (what time in some sequester'd vale
The weary woodman spreads his sparing meal,   120
When his tir'd arms refuse the axe to rear,
And claim a respite from the sylvan war;
But not till half the prostrate forests lay
Stretch'd in long ruin, and expos'd to day)
Then, nor till then, the *Greeks* impulsive might   125
Pierc'd the black *Phalanx*, and let in the light.
Great *Agamemnon* then the slaughter led,
And slew *Bienor* at his people's head:
Whose Squire *Oïleus*, with a sudden spring,
Leap'd from the chariot to revenge his King,   130
But in his front he felt the fatal wound,
Which pierc'd his brain, & stretch'd him on the ground:
Atrides spoil'd, and left them on the plain;
Vain was their youth, their glitt'ring armour vain:
Now soil'd with dust, and naked to the sky,   135
Their snowy limbs and beauteous bodies lie.

Two sons of *Priam* next to battel move,
The product one of marriage, one of love;
In the same car the brother warriours ride,
This took the charge to combat, that to guide: 140
Far other task! than when they wont to keep,
On *Ida*'s tops, their father's fleecy sheep.
These on the mountains once *Achilles* found,
And captive led, with pliant osiers bound;
Then to their sire for ample sums restor'd;   145
But now to perish by *Atrides*' sword:
Pierc'd in the breast the base-born *Isus* bleeds;
Cleft thro' the head, his brother's fate succeeds.

Swift to the spoil the hasty victor falls,
150   And stript, their features to his mind recalls.
The *Trojans* see the youths untimely die,
But helpless tremble for themselves, and fly.
So when a lion, ranging o'er the lawns,
Finds, on some grassy lare, the couching fawns,
155   Their bones he cracks, their reeking vitals draws,
And grinds the quiv'ring flesh with bloody jaws;
The frighted hind beholds, and dares not stay,
But swift thro' rustling thickets bursts her way;
All drown'd in sweat the panting mother flies,
160   And the big tears roll trickling from her eyes.

Amidst the tumult of the routed train,
The sons of false *Antimachus* were slain;
He, who for bribes his faithless counsels sold,
And voted *Helen*'s stay for *Paris*' gold.
165   *Atrides* mark'd as these their safety sought,
And slew the children for the father's fault;
Their headstrong horse unable to restrain,
They shook with fear, and dropp'd the silken rein;
Then in their chariot, on their knees they fall,
170   And thus with lifted hands for mercy call.

Oh spare our youth, and for the life we owe,
Antimachus shall copious gifts bestow;
Soon as he hears, that not in battel slain,
The *Grecian* ships his captive sons detain,
175   Large heaps of brass in ransom shall be told,
And steel well-temper'd, and persuasive gold.

These words, attended with a flood of tears,
The youths address'd to unrelenting ears:
The vengeful monarch gave this stern reply;
180   If from *Antimachus* ye spring, ye die:
The daring wretch who once in council stood
To shed *Ulysses*' and my brother's blood,
For proffer'd peace! And sues his seed for grace?
No, die, and pay the forfeit of your race.

185   This said, *Pisander* from the car he cast,
And pierc'd his breast: supine he breath'd his last.
His brother leap'd to earth; but as he lay,
The trenchant faulchion lopp'd his hands away;

His sever'd head was toss'd among the throng,
And rolling, drew a bloody trail along.   190
Then, where the thickest fought, the victor flew;
The King's example all his *Greeks* pursue.
Now by the foot the flying foot were slain,
Horse trod by horse, lay foaming on the Plain.
From the dry fields thick clouds of dust arise,   195
Shade the black host, and intercept the skies.
The brass-hoof'd steeds tumultuous plunge and bound,
And the thick thunder beats the lab'ring ground.
Still slaught'ring on, the King of men proceeds;
The distanc'd army wonders at his deeds.   200
As when the winds with raging flames conspire,
And o'er the forests roll the flood of fire,
In blazing heaps the grove's old honours fall,
And one refulgent ruin levels all.
Before *Atrides'* rage so sinks the foe,   205
Whole squadrons vanish, and proud heads lie low.
The steeds fly trembling from his waving sword;
And many a car, now lighted of its Lord,
Wide o'er the field with guideless fury rolls,
Breaking their ranks, and crushing out their souls;   210
While his keen faulchion drinks the warriors lives;
More grateful, now, to vultures than their wives!

   Perhaps great *Hector* then had found his fate,
But *Jove* and destiny prolong'd his date.
Safe from the darts, the care of heav'n he stood,   215
Amidst alarms, and death, and dust, and blood.

   Now past the tomb where ancient *Ilus* lay,
Thro' the mid field the routed urge their way.
Where the wild figs th' adjoining summit crown,
That path they take, and speed to reach the town.   220
As swift *Atrides* with loud shouts pursu'd,
Hot with his toil, and bath'd in hostile blood.
Now near the beech-tree, and the *Scæan* gates,
The hero haults, and his associates waits.
Mean while on ev'ry side, around the plain,   225
Dispers'd, disorder'd, fly the *Trojan* train.
So flies a herd of beeves, that hear dismay'd
The lion's roaring thro' the midnight shade;

On heaps they tumble with successless haste;
230   The savage seizes, draws, and rends the last:
Not with less fury stern *Atrides* flew,
Still press'd the rout, and still the hindmost slew;
Hurl'd from their cars the bravest chiefs are kill'd,
And rage, and death, and carnage, load the field.

235   Now storms the victor at the *Trojan* wall;
Surveys the tow'rs, and meditates their fall.
But *Jove* descending shook th' *Idæan* hills,
And down their summits pour'd a hundred rills:
Th' unkindled light'ning in his hand he took,
240   And thus the many-colour'd maid bespoke.

Iris, with haste thy golden wings display,
To god-like *Hector* this our word convey.
While *Agamemnon* wastes the ranks around,
Fights in the front, and bathes with blood the ground,
245   Bid him give way; but issue forth commands,
And trust the war to less important hands:
But when, or wounded by the spear, or dart,
That chief shall mount his chariot, and depart:
Then *Jove* shall string his arm, and fire his breast,
250   Then to her ships shall flying *Greece* be press'd,
Till to the main the burning sun descend,
And sacred night her awful shade extend.

He spoke, and *Iris* at his word obey'd;
On wings of winds descends the various maid.
255   The chief she found amidst the ranks of war,
Close to the bulwarks, on his glitt'ring car.
The Goddess then: O son of *Priam* hear!
From *Jove* I come, and his high mandate bear.
While *Agamemnon* wastes the ranks around,
260   Fights in the front, and bathes with blood the ground,
Abstain from fight; yet issue forth commands,
And trust the war to less important hands.
But when, or wounded by the spear, or dart,
The chief shall mount his chariot, and depart;
265   Then *Jove* shall string thy arm, and fire thy breast,
Then to her ships shall flying *Greece* be prest,
'Till to the main the burning sun descend,
And sacred night her awful shade extend.

She said, and vanish'd: *Hector*, with a bound,
Springs from his chariot on the trembling ground,   270
In clanging arms: he grasps in either hand
A pointed lance, and speeds from band to band;
Revives their ardour, turns their steps from flight,
And wakes anew the dying flames of fight.
They stand to arms: the *Greeks* their onset dare,   275
Condense their pow'rs, and wait the coming war.
New force, new spirit to each breast returns;
The fight renew'd with fiercer fury burns:
The King leads on; all fix on him their eye,
And learn from him, to conquer, or to die.   280
   Ye sacred nine, celestial Muses! tell,
Who fac'd him first, and by his prowess fell?
The great *Iphidamas*, the bold and young;
From sage *Antenor* and *Theano* sprung;
Whom from his youth his grandsire *Cisseus* bred,   285
And nurs'd in *Thrace* where snowy flocks are fed.
Scarce did the down his rosy cheeks invest,
And early honour warm his gen'rous breast,
When the kind sire consign'd his daughter's charms
(*Theano*'s sister) to his youthful arms.   290
But call'd by glory to the wars of *Troy*,
He leaves untasted the first fruits of joy;
From his lov'd bride departs with melting eyes,
And swift to aid his dearer country flies.
With twelve black ships he reach'd *Percope*'s strand,   295
Thence took the long, laborious march by land.
Now fierce for fame, before the ranks he springs,
Tow'ring in arms, and braves the King of Kings.
Atrides first discharg'd the missive spear;
The *Trojan* stoop'd, the jav'lin pass'd in air.   300
Then near the corselet, at the monarch's heart,
With all his strength the youth directs his dart;
But the broad belt, with plates of silver bound,
The point rebated, and repell'd the wound.
Encumber'd with the dart, *Atrides* stands,   305
Till grasp'd with force, he wrench'd it from his hands.
At once, his weighty sword discharg'd a wound
Full on his neck, that fell'd him to the ground.

Stretch'd in the dust th' unhappy warriour lies,
310   And sleep eternal seals his swimming eyes.
Oh worthy better fate! oh early slain!
Thy country's friend; and virtuous, tho' in vain!
No more the youth shall join his consort's side,
At once a virgin, and at once a bride!
315   No more with presents her embraces meet,
Or lay the spoils of conquest at her feet,
On whom his passion, lavish of his store,
Bestow'd so much, and vainly promis'd more!
Unwept, uncover'd, on the plain he lay,
320   While the proud victor bore his arms away.
     Coön, *Antenor*'s eldest hope, was nigh:
Tears, at the sight, came starting from his eye,
While pierc'd with grief the much-lov'd youth he view'd,
And the pale features now deform'd with blood.
325   Then with his spear, unseen, his time he took,
Aim'd at the King, and near his elbow strook.
The thrilling steel transpierc'd the brawny part,
And thro' his arm stood forth the barbed dart.
Surpriz'd the monarch feels, yet void of fear
330   On *Coön* rushes with his lifted spear:
His brother's corps the pious *Trojan* draws,
And calls his country to assert his cause,
Defends him breathless on the sanguine field,
And o'er the body spreads his ample shield.
335   *Atrides*, marking an unguarded part,
Transfix'd the warriour with his brazen dart;
Prone on his brother's bleeding breast he lay,
The Monarch's faulchion lopp'd his head away:
The social shades the same dark journey go,
340   And join each other in the realms below.
     The vengeful victor rages round the fields,
With ev'ry weapon, art or fury yields:
By the long lance, the sword, or pond'rous stone,
Whole ranks are broken, and whole troops o'erthrown.
345   This, while yet warm, distill'd the purple flood;
But when the wound grew stiff with clotted blood,
Then grinding tortures his strong bosom rend,
Less keen those darts the fierce *Ilythiæ* send,

(The pow'rs that cause the teeming matron's throes,
Sad mothers of unutterable woes!)   350
Stung with the smart, all panting with the pain,
He mounts the car, and gives his squire the rein:
Then with a voice which fury made more strong,
And pain augmented, thus exhorts the throng.

    O friends! O *Greeks!* assert your honours won;   355
Proceed, and finish what this arm begun:
Lo! angry *Jove* forbids your chief to stay,
And envies half the glories of the day.

    He said; the driver whirls his lengthful thong;
The horses fly; the chariot smoaks along.   360
Clouds from their nostrils the fierce coursers blow,
And from their sides the foam descends in snow;
Shot thro' the battel in a moment's space,
The wounded Monarch at his tent they place.

    No sooner *Hector* saw the King retir'd,   365
But thus his *Trojans* and his aids he fir'd.
Hear all ye *Dardan,* all ye *Lycian* race!
Fam'd in close fight, and dreadful face to face.
Now call to mind your ancient trophies won,
Your great forefathers virtues, and your own.   370
Behold, the Gen'ral flies! deserts his pow'rs!
Lo *Jove* himself declares the conquest ours!
Now on yon' ranks impel your foaming steeds;
And, sure of glory, dare immortal deeds.

    With words like these the fiery chief alarms   375
His fainting host, and ev'ry bosom warms.
As the bold hunter chears his hounds to tear
The brindled lion, or the tusky bear,
With voice and hand provokes their doubting heart,
And springs the foremost with his lifted dart: 380
So God-like *Hector* prompts his troops to dare;
Nor prompts alone, but leads himself the war.
On the black body of the foes he pours:
As from the cloud's deep bosom swell'd with show'rs,
A sudden storm the purple ocean sweeps,   385
Drives the wild waves, and tosses all the deeps.
Say Muse! when *Jove* the *Trojan*'s glory crown'd,
Beneath his arm what heroes bit the ground?

Assæus, *Dolops*, and *Autonous* dy'd,

390   *Opites* next was added to their side,

Then brave *Hipponous* fam'd in many a fight,

Opheltius, *Orus*, sunk to endless night,

Æsymnus, *Agelaus*; all chiefs of name;

The rest were vulgar deaths, unknown to fame.

395   As when a western whirlwind, charg'd with storms,

Dispels the gather'd clouds that *Notus* forms;

The gust continu'd, violent, and strong,

Rolls sable clouds in heaps on heaps along;

Now to the skies the foaming billows rears,

400   Now breaks the surge, and wide the bottom bares.

Thus raging *Hector*, with resistless hands,

O'erturns, confounds, and scatters all their bands.

Now the last ruin the whole host appalls;

Now *Greece* had trembled in her wooden walls;

405   But wise *Ulysses* call'd *Tydides* forth,

His soul rekindled, and awak'd his worth.

And stand we deedless, O eternal shame!

Till *Hector*'s arm involve the ships in flame?

Haste, let us join, and combat side by side.

410   The warriour thus, and thus the friend reply'd.

    No martial toil I shun, no danger fear;

Let *Hector* come; I wait his fury here.

But *Jove* with conquest crowns the *Trojan* train;

415   And, *Jove* our foe, all human force is vain.

    He sigh'd; but sighing, rais'd his vengeful steel,

And from his car the proud *Thymbræus* fell:

Molion, the charioteer, pursu'd his Lord,

His death ennobled by *Ulysses*' sword.

There slain, they left them in eternal night;

420   Then plung'd amidst the thickest ranks of fight.

So two wild boars outstrip the foll'owing hounds,

Then swift revert, and wounds return for wounds.

Stern *Hector*'s conquests in the middle plain

Stood check'd a while, and *Greece* respir'd again.

425   The sons of *Merops* shone amidst the war;

Tow'ring they rode in one refulgent car:

In deep prophetic arts their father skill'd,

Had warn'd his children from the *Trojan* field;

Fate urg'd them on; the father warn'd in vain,
They rush'd to fight, and perish'd on the plain!
Their breasts no more the vital spirit warms;
The stern *Tydides* strips their shining arms.
Hypirochus by great *Ulysses* dies,
And rich *Hippodamus* becomes his prize.
Great *Jove* from *Ide* with slaughter fills his sight,
And level hangs the doubtful scale of fight.
By *Tydeus'* lance *Agastrophus* was slain,
The far-fam'd hero of *Pæonian* strain;
Wing'd with his fears, on foot he strove to fly,
His steeds too distant, and the foe too nigh;
Thro' broken orders, swifter than the wind,
He fled, but flying, left his life behind.
This *Hector* sees, as his experienc'd eyes
Traverse the files, and to the rescue flies;
Shouts, as he past, the crystal regions rend,
And moving armies on his march attend.
Great *Diomed* himself was seiz'd with fear,
And thus bespoke his brother of the war.

   Mark how this way yon' bending squadrons yield!
The storm rolls on, and *Hector* rules the field:
Here stand his utmost force – The warriour said;
Swift at the word, his pondrous jav'lin fled;
Nor miss'd its aim, but where the plumage danc'd,
Raz'd the smooth cone, and thence obliquely glanc'd.
Safe in his helm (the gift of *Phœbus'* hands)
Without a wound the *Trojan* hero stands;
But yet so stunn'd, that stagg'ring on the plain,
His arm and knee his sinking bulk sustain;
O'er his dim sight the misty vapours rise,
And a short darkness shades his swimming eyes.
Tydides follow'd to regain his lance;
While *Hector* rose, recover'd from the trance,
Remounts his car, and herds amidst the crowd;
The *Greek* pursues him, and exults aloud.

   Once more thank *Phœbus* for thy forfeit breath,
Or thank that swiftness which outstrips the death.
Well by *Apollo* are thy pray'rs repaid,
And oft' that partial pow'r has lent his aid.

430

435

440

445

450

455

460

465

Thou shalt not long the death deserv'd withstand,
If any God assist *Tydides'* hand.
Fly then, inglorious! but thy flight, this day,
Whole hecatombs of *Trojan* ghosts shall pay.

    Him, while he triumph'd, *Paris* ey'd from far,
(The spouse of *Helen*, the fair cause of war)
475 Around the field his feather'd shafts he sent,
From ancient *Ilus'* ruin'd monument;
Behind the column plac'd, he bent his bow,
And wing'd an arrow at th' unwary foe;
Just as he stoop'd, *Agastrophus's* crest
480 To seize, and drew the corselet from his breast.
The bow-string twang'd; nor flew the shaft in vain,
But pierc'd his foot, and nail'd it to the plain.
The laughing *Trojan*, with a joyful spring
Leaps from his ambush, and insults the King.

485   He bleeds! (he cries) some God has sped my dart;
Would the same God had fixt it in his heart!
So *Troy* reliev'd from that wide-wasting hand
Shall breathe from slaughter, and in combat stand,
Whose sons now tremble at his darted spear,
490 As scatter'd lambs the rushing lion fear.

    He, dauntless, thus: Thou conqu'ror of the fair,
Thou woman-warriour with the curling hair;
Vain archer! trusting to the distant dart,
Unskill'd in arms to act a manly part!
495 Thou hast but done what boys or women can;
Such hands may wound, but not incense a man.
Nor boast the scratch thy feeble arrow gave,
A coward's weapon never hurts the brave.
Not so this dart, which thou may'st one day feel;
500 Fate wings its flight, and death is on the steel,
Where this but lights, some noble life expires,
Its touch makes orphans, bathes the cheeks of sires,
Steeps earth in purple, gluts the birds of air,
And leaves such objects as distract the fair.

505   *Ulysses* hastens with a trembling heart,
Before him steps, and bending draws the dart:
Forth flows the blood; an eager pang succeeds;
Tydides mounts, and to the navy speeds.

Now on the field *Ulysses* stands alone,
The *Greeks* all fled, the *Trojans* pouring on: 510
But stands collected in himself and whole,
And questions thus his own unconquer'd soul.

What farther subterfuge, what hopes remain?
What shame, inglorious if I quit the plain?
What danger, singly if I stand the ground,   515
My friends all scatter'd, all the foes around?
Yet wherefore doubtful? Let this truth suffice;
The brave meets danger, and the coward flies:
To die, or conquer, proves a hero's heart;
And knowing this, I know a soldier's part.   520

Such thoughts revolving in his careful breast,
Near, and more near, the shady cohorts prest;
These, in the warriour, their own fate inclose;
And round him deep the steely circle grows.
So fares a boar, whom all the troop surrounds   525
Of shouting Huntsmen and of clam'rous hounds;
He grinds his iv'ry tusks; he foams with ire;
His sanguine eyeballs glare with living fire;
By these, by those, on ev'ry part is ply'd;
And the red slaughter spreads on ev'ry side.   530
Pierc'd thro' the shoulder, first *Deiopis* fell;
Next *Ennomus* and *Thoön* sunk to hell;
Chersidamas, beneath the navel thrust,
Falls prone to earth, and grasps the bloody dust.
Charops, the son of *Hippasus*, was near;   535
Ulysses reach'd him with the fatal spear;
But to his aid his brother *Socus* flies,
Socus, the brave, the gen'rous, and the wise:
Near as he drew, the warriour thus began.

O great *Ulysses*, much-enduring man!   540
Not deeper skill'd in ev'ry martial slight,
Than worn to toils, and active in the fight!
This day, two brothers shall thy conquest grace,
And end at once the great *Hippasian* race,
Or thou beneath this lance must press the field —   545
He said, and forceful pierc'd his spacious shield:
Thro' the strong brass the ringing javelin thrown,
Plow'd half his side, and bar'd it to the bone.

By *Pallas'* care, the spear, tho' deep infix'd,
550 Stop'd short of life, nor with his entrails mix'd.
      The wound not mortal wise *Ulysses* knew,
Then furious thus, (but first some steps withdrew.)
Unhappy man! whose death our hands shall grace!
Fate calls thee hence, and finish'd is thy race.
555 No longer check my conquests on the foe;
But pierc'd by this, to endless darkness go,
And add one spectre to the realms below!
      He spoke, while *Socus* seiz'd with sudden fright,
Trembling gave way, and turn'd his back to flight,
560 Between his shoulders pierc'd the following dart,
And held its passage thro' the panting heart.
Wide in his breast appear'd the grizly wound;
He falls; his armour rings against the ground.
Then thus *Ulysses*, gazing on the slain.
565 Fam'd son of *Hippasus!* there press the plain;
There ends thy narrow span assign'd by fate,
Heav'n owes *Ulysses* yet a longer date.
Ah wretch! no father shall thy corps compose,
Thy dying eyes no tender mother close,
570 But hungry birds shall tear those balls away,
And hov'ring vultures scream around their prey.
Me *Greece* shall honour, when I meet my doom,
With solemn fun'rals and a lasting tomb.
      Then raging with intolerable smart,
575 He writhes his body, and extracts the dart.
The dart a tide of spouting gore pursu'd,
And gladden'd *Troy* with sight of hostile blood.
Now troops on troops the fainting chief invade,
Forc'd he recedes, and loudly calls for aid.
580 Thrice to its pitch his lofty voice he rears;
The well-known voice thrice *Menelaüs* hears:
Alarm'd, to *Ajax Telamon* he cry'd,
Who shares his labours, and defends his side.
O friend! *Ulysses'* shouts invade my ear;
585 Distress'd he seems, and no assistance near:
Strong as he is; yet, one oppos'd to all,
Oppress'd by multitudes, the best may fall.

Greece, robb'd of him, must bid her host despair,
And feel a loss not ages can repair.

Then, where the cry directs, his course he bends;　590
Great *Ajax*, like the God of war, attends.
The prudent chief in sore distress they found,
With bands of furious *Trojans* compass'd round.
As when some huntsman, with a flying spear,
From the blind thicket wounds a stately deer;　595
Down his cleft side while fresh the blood distills,
He bounds aloft, and scuds from hills to hills:
Till Life's warm vapour issuing thro' the wound,
Wild mountain-wolves the fainting beast surround;
Just as their jaws his prostrate limbs invade,　600
The Lion rushes thro' the woodland shade,
The wolves, tho' hungry, scour dispers'd away;
The lordly savage vindicates his prey.
Ulysses thus, unconquer'd by his pains,
A single warriour, half an host sustains:　605
But soon as *Ajax* heaves his tow'r-like shield,
The scatter'd crowds fly frighted o'er the field;
Atrides' arm the sinking hero stays,
And sav'd from numbers, to his car conveys.

Victorious *Ajax* plies the routed crew;　610
And first *Doryclus*, *Priam*'s son, he slew,
On strong *Pandocus* next inflicts a wound,
And lays *Lysander* bleeding on the ground.
As when a torrent, swell'd with wintry rains,
Pours from the mountains o'er the delug'd plains,　615
And pines and oaks, from their foundations torn,
A country's ruins! to the seas are born:
Fierce *Ajax* thus o'erwhelms the yielding throng,
Men, steeds, and chariots, roll in heaps along.

But *Hector*, from this scene of slaughter far,　620
Rag'd on the left, and rul'd the tide of war:
Loud groans proclaim his progress thro' the plain,
And deep *Scamander* swells with heaps of slain.
There *Nestor* and *Idomeneus* oppose
The warriour's fury, there the battel glows;　625
There fierce on foot, or from the chariot's height,
His sword deforms the beauteous ranks of fight.

The spouse of *Helen* dealing darts around,
Had pierc'd *Machaon* with a distant wound:
630 In his right shoulder the broad shaft appear'd,
And trembling *Greece* for her physician fear'd.
To *Nestor* then *Idomeneus* begun;
Glory of *Greece*, old *Neleus*' valiant son!
Ascend thy chariot, haste with speed away,
635 And great *Machaon* to the ships convey.
A wise physician, skill'd our wounds to heal,
Is more than armies to the publick weal.
    Old *Nestor* mounts the seat: Beside him rode
The wounded offspring of the healing God.
640 He lends the lash; the steeds with sounding feet
Shake the dry field, and thunder tow'rd the fleet.
    But now *Cebriones*, from *Hector*'s car,
Survey'd the various fortune of the war.
While here (he cry'd) the flying *Greeks* are slain;
645 *Trojans* on *Trojans* yonder load the plain.
Before great *Ajax* see the mingled throng
Of men and chariots driv'n in heaps along!
I know him well, distinguish'd o'er the field
By the broad glitt'ring of the sev'nfold shield.
650 Thither, O *Hector*, thither urge thy steeds;
There danger calls, and there the combat bleeds,
There horse and foot in mingled deaths unite,
And groans of slaughter mix with shouts of fight.
    Thus having spoke, the driver's lash resounds;
655 Swift thro' the ranks the rapid chariot bounds;
Stung by the stroke, the coursers scour the fields
O'er heaps of carcasses, and hills of shields.
The horses hoofs are bath'd in heroes gore,
And dashing, purple all the car before,
660 The groaning axle sable drops distills,
And mangled carnage clogs the rapid wheels.
Here *Hector* plunging thro' the thickest fight
Broke the dark *Phalanx*, and let in the light.
(By the long lance, the sword, or pondrous stone,
665 The ranks lie scatter'd, and the troops o'erthrown)
Ajax he shuns, thro' all the dire debate,
And fears that arm whose force he felt so late.

But partial *Jove*, espousing *Hector*'s part,
Shot heav'n-bred horrour thro' the *Grecian*'s heart;
Confus'd, unnerv'd in *Hector*'s presence grown,   670
Amaz'd he stood, with terrours not his own.
O'er his broad back his moony shield he threw,
And glaring round, by tardy steps withdrew.
Thus the grim lion his retreat maintains,
Beset with watchful dogs, and shouting swains,   675
Repuls'd by numbers from the nightly stalls,
Tho' rage impells him, and tho' hunger calls,
Long stands the show'ring darts, and missile fires;
Then sow'rly slow th' indignant beast retires.
So turn'd stern *Ajax*, by whole hosts repell'd,   680
While his swoln heart at ev'ry step rebell'd.

  As the slow beast with heavy strength indu'd,
In some wide field by troops of boys pursu'd,
Tho' round his sides a wooden tempest rain,
Crops the tall harvest, and lays waste the plain;   685
Thick on his hide the hollow blows resound,
The patient animal maintains his ground,
Scarce from the field with all their efforts chas'd,
And stirs but slowly when he stirs at last.
On *Ajax* thus a weight of *Trojans* hung,   690
The strokes redoubled on his buckler rung;
Confiding now in bulky strength he stands,
Now turns, and backward bears the yielding bands;
Now stiff recedes, yet hardly seems to fly,
And threats his followers with retorted eye.   695
Fix'd as the bar between two warring pow'rs,
While hissing darts descend in iron show'rs:
In his broad buckler many a weapon stood,
Its surface bristled with a quiv'ring wood;
And many a javelin, guiltless on the plain,   700
Marks the dry dust, and thirsts for blood in vain.
But bold *Eurypylus* his aid imparts,
And dauntless springs beneath a cloud of darts;
Whose eager javelin launch'd against the foe,
Great *Apisaon* felt the fatal blow;   705
From his torn liver the red current flow'd,
And his slack knees desert their dying load.

The victor rushing to despoil the dead,
From *Paris'* bow a vengeful arrow fled.
710   Fix'd in his nervous thigh the weapon stood,
Fix'd was the point, but broken was the wood.
Back to the lines the wounded *Greek* retir'd,
Yet thus, retreating, his associates fir'd.
    What God, O *Grecians!* has your hearts dismay'd?
715   Oh, turn to arms; 'tis *Ajax* claims your aid.
This hour he stands the mark of hostile rage,
And this the last brave battel he shall wage;
Haste, join your forces; from the gloomy grave
The warriour rescue, and your country save.
720   Thus urg'd the chief; a gen'rous troop appears,
Who spread their bucklers, and advance their spears,
To guard their wounded friend: While thus they stand
With pious care, great *Ajax* joins the band:
Each takes new courage at the hero's sight;
725   The hero rallies and renews the fight.
    Thus rag'd both armies like conflicting fires,
While *Nestor*'s chariot far from fight retires:
His coursers steep'd in sweat, and stain'd with gore,
The *Greeks* preserver, great *Machaon* bore.
730   That hour, *Achilles* from the topmost height
Of his proud fleet, o'erlook'd the fields of fight;
His feasted eyes beheld around the plain
The *Grecian* rout, the slaying, and the slain.
His friend *Machaon* singled from the rest,
735   A transient pity touch'd his vengeful breast.
Strait to *Mænetius'* much-lov'd son he sent;
Graceful as *Mars*, *Patroclus* quits his tent,
(In evil hour! Then fate decreed his doom;
And fix'd the date of all his woes to come!)
740   Why calls my friend? thy lov'd injunctions lay,
Whate'er thy will, *Patroclus* shall obey.
    O first of friends! (*Pelides* thus reply'd)
Still at my heart, and ever at my side!
The time is come, when yon' despairing host
745   Shall learn the value of the man they lost:
Now at my knees the *Greeks* shall pour their moan,
And proud *Atrides* tremble on his throne.

Go now to *Nestor*, and from him be taught
What wounded warriour late his chariot brought?
For seen at distance, and but seen behind,   750
His form recall'd *Machaon* to my mind;
Nor could I, thro' yon' cloud, discern his face,
The coursers past me with so swift a pace.

    The hero said. His friend obey'd with haste,
Thro' intermingled ships and tents he past;   755
The chiefs descending from their car he found;
The panting steeds *Eurymedon* unbound.
The warriours standing on the breezy shore,
To dry their sweat, and wash away the gore,
Here paus'd a moment, while the gentle gale   760
Convey'd that freshness the cool seas exhale;
Then to consult on farther methods went,
And took their seats beneath the shady tent.
The draught prescrib'd, fair *Hecamede* prepares,
Arsinous' daughter, grac'd with golden hairs: 765
(Whom to his aged arms, a royal slave,
Greece, as the prize of *Nestor's* wisdom, gave)
A table first with azure feet she plac'd;
Whose ample orb a brazen charger grac'd:
Honey new-press'd, the sacred flow'r of wheat,   770
And wholsome garlick crown'd the sav'ry treat.
Next her white hand an antique goblet brings,
A goblet sacred to the *Pylian* Kings,
From eldest times: emboss'd with studs of gold,
Two feet support it, and four handles hold;   775
On each bright handle, bending o'er the brink,
In sculptur'd gold two turtles seem to drink:
A massy weight, yet heav'd with ease by him,
When the brisk nectar overlook'd the brim.
Temper'd in this, the nymph of form divine   780
Pours a large potion of the *Pramnian* wine;
With goat's-milk cheese a flav'rous taste bestows,
And last with flour the smiling surface strows.
This for the wounded Prince the dame prepares;
The cordial bev'rage rev'rend *Nestor* shares: 785
Salubrious draughts the warriour's thirst allay,
And pleasing conference beguiles the day.

Mean time *Patroclus*, by *Achilles* sent,
Unheard approach'd, and stood before the tent.
790   Old *Nestor* rising then, the hero led
To his high seat; the chief refus'd, and said.
'Tis now no season for these kind delays;
The great *Achilles* with impatience stays.
To great *Achilles* this respect I owe;
795   Who asks what hero, wounded by the foe,
Was born from combat by thy foaming steeds?
With grief I see the great *Machaon* bleeds.
This to report, my hasty course I bend;
Thou know'st the fiery temper of my friend.
800   Can then the sons of *Greece* (the sage rejoin'd)
Excite compassion in *Achilles*' mind?
Seeks he the sorrows of our host to know?
This is not half the story of our woe.
Tell him, not great *Machaon* bleeds alone,
805   Our bravest heroes in the navy groan,
Ulysses, Agamemnon, Diomed,
And stern *Eurypylus*, already bleed.
But ah! what flatt'ring hopes I entertain?
Achilles heeds not, but derides our pain:
810   Ev'n till the flames consume our fleet, he stays,
And waits the rising of the fatal blaze.
Chief after Chief the raging foe destroys;
Calm he looks on, and ev'ry death enjoys.
Now the slow course of all-impairing time
815   Unstrings my nerves, and ends my manly prime;
Oh! had I still that strength my youth possess'd,
When this bold arm th' *Epeian* pow'rs oppress'd,
The bulls of *Elis* in glad triumph led,
And stretch'd the great *Itymonæus* dead!
820   Then, from my fury fled the trembling swains,
And ours was all the plunder of the plains:
Fifty white flocks, full fifty herds of swine,
As many goats, as many lowing kine;
And thrice the number of unrival'd steeds,
825   All teeming females, and of gen'rous breeds.
These, as my first essay of arms, I won;
Old *Neleus* glory'd in his conqu'ring son.

Thus *Elis* forc'd, her long arrears restor'd,
And shares were parted to each *Pylian* Lord.
The state of *Pyle* was sunk to last despair,
When the proud *Elians* first commenc'd the war. 830
For *Neleus'* sons *Alcides'* rage had slain;
Of twelve bold brothers, I alone remain!
Oppress'd, we arm'd; and now, this conquest gain'd,
My sire three hundred chosen sheep obtain'd. 835
(That large reprizal he might justly claim,
For prize defrauded, and insulted fame,
When *Elis'* Monarch at the publick course
Detain'd his chariot and victorious horse.)
The rest the people shar'd; my self survey'd 840
The just partition, and due victims pay'd.
Three days were past, when *Elis* rose to war,
With many a courser, and with many a car;
The sons of *Actor* at their army's head
(Young as they were) the vengeful squadrons led. 845
High on a rock fair *Thryoëssa* stands,
Our utmost frontier on the *Pylian* lands;
Not far the streams of fam'd *Alphæus* flow;
The stream they pass'd, and pitch'd their tents below.
Pallas, descending in the shades of night, 850
Alarms the *Pylians*, and commands the fight.
Each burns for fame, and swells with martial pride;
My self the foremost; but my sire deny'd;
Fear'd for my youth expos'd to stern alarms;
And stopp'd my chariot, and detain'd my arms. 855
My sire deny'd in vain: On foot I fled
Amidst our chariots: for the goddess led.
    Along fair *Arene's* delightful plain,
Soft *Minyas* rolls his waters to the main.
There, horse and foot, the *Pylian* troops unite, 860
And sheath'd in arms, expect the dawning light.
Thence, e'er the sun advanc'd his noonday flame,
To great *Alphæus'* sacred source we came.
There first to *Jove* our solemn rites were paid;
An untam'd heifer pleas'd the blue-ey'd maid, 865
A bull *Alphæus*; and a bull was slain
To the blue Monarch of the wat'ry main.

In Arms we slept, beside the winding flood,
While round the town the fierce *Epeians* stood.
870   Soon as the sun, with all-revealing ray,
Flam'd in the front of heav'n, and gave the day;
Bright scenes of arms, and works of war appear;
The nations meet; there *Pylos*, *Elis* here.
The first who fell, beneath my javelin bled;
875   King *Augias'* son, and spouse of *Agamede*:
(She that all simples' healing virtues knew,
And ev'ry herb that drinks the morning dew.)
I seiz'd his car, the van of battel led;
Th' *Epeians* saw, they trembled, and they fled.
880   The foe dispers'd, their bravest warriour kill'd,
Fierce as a whirlwind now I swept the field:
Full fifty captive chariots grac'd my train;
Two chiefs from each, fell breathless to the plain.
Then *Actor's* sons had dy'd, but *Neptune* shrouds
885   The youthful heroes in a veil of clouds.
O'er heapy shields, and o'er the prostrate throng,
Collecting spoils, and slaught'ring all along,
Thro' wide *Buprasian* fields we forc'd the foes,
Where o'er the vales th' *Olenian* rocks arose;
890   Till *Pallas* stopp'd us where *Alisium* flows.
Ev'n there, the hindmost of their rear I slay,
And the same arm that led, concludes the day;
Then back to *Pyle* triumphant take my way.
There to high *Jove* were publick thanks assign'd
895   As first of Gods, to *Nestor*, of mankind.
Such then I was, impell'd by youthful blood;
So prov'd my valour for my country's good.
     Achilles with unactive fury glows,
And gives to passion what to *Greece* he owes.
900   How shall he grieve, when to th' eternal shade
Her hosts shall sink, nor his the pow'r to aid?
O friend! my memory recalls the day,
When gath'ring aids along the *Grecian* sea,
I, and *Ulysses*, touch'd at *Pthia's* port,
905   And enter'd *Peleus'* hospitable court.
A bull to *Jove* he slew in sacrifice,
And pour'd libations on the flaming thighs.

Thy self, *Achilles*, and thy rev'rend sire
Menætius, turn'd the fragments on the fire.
Achilles sees us, to the feast invites;   910
Social we sit, and share the genial rites.
We then explain'd the cause on which we came,
Urg'd you to arms, and found you fierce for fame.
Your ancient fathers gen'rous precepts gave;
Peleus said only this, – 'My son! be brave.'   915
Menætius thus; 'Tho' great *Achilles* shine
In strength superior, and of race divine,
Yet cooler thoughts thy elder years attend;
Let thy just counsels aid, and rule thy friend.'
Thus spoke your father at *Thessalia*'s court: 920
Words now forgot, tho' now of vast import.
Ah! try the utmost that a friend can say,
Such gentle force the fiercest minds obey;
Some fav'ring God *Achilles*' heart may move;
Tho' deaf to glory, he may yield to love.   925
If some dire oracle his breast alarm,
If ought from heav'n with-hold his saving arm;
Some beam of comfort yet on *Greece* may shine,
If thou but lead the *Myrmidonian* line;
Clad in *Achilles*' arms, if thou appear,   930
Proud *Troy* may tremble, and desist from war;
Press'd by fresh forces her o'er-labour'd train
Shall seek their walls, and *Greece* respire again.
    This touch'd his gen'rous heart, and from the tent
Along the shore with hasty strides he went;   935
Soon as he came, where, on the crouded strand,
The publick mart and courts of justice stand,
Where the tall fleet of great *Ulysses* lies,
And altars to the guardian Gods arise;
There sad he met the brave *Evæmon*'s son,   940
Large painful drops from all his members run,
An arrow's head yet rooted in his wound,
The sable blood in circles mark'd the ground,
As faintly reeling he confess'd the smart;
Weak was his pace, but dauntless was his heart.   945
Divine compassion touch'd *Patroclus*' breast,
Who sighing, thus his bleeding friend addrest.

Ah hapless leaders of the *Grecian* host!
Thus must ye perish on a barb'rous coast?
950 Is this your fate, to glut the dogs with gore,
Far from your friends, and from your native shore?
Say, great *Eurypylus!* shall *Greece* yet stand?
Resists she yet the raging *Hector*'s hand?
Or are her heroes doom'd to die with shame,
955 And this the period of our wars and fame?
    Eurypylus replies: No more (my friend)
Greece is no more! this day her glories end.
Ev'n to the ships victorious *Troy* pursues,
Her force encreasing, as her toil renews.
960 Those chiefs, that us'd her utmost rage to meet,
Lie pierc'd with wounds and bleeding in the fleet.
But thou, *Patroclus!* act a friendly part,
Lead to my ships, and draw this deadly dart;
With lukewarm water wash the gore away,
965 With healing balms the raging smart allay,
Such as sage *Chiron*, Sire of *Pharmacy*,
Once taught *Achilles*, and *Achilles* thee.
Of two fam'd surgeons, *Podalirius* stands
This hour surrounded by the *Trojan* bands;
970 And great *Machaon*, wounded in his tent,
Now wants that succour which so oft' he lent.
    To him the chief. What then remains to do?
Th' event of things the Gods alone can view.
Charg'd by *Achilles*' great command I fly,
975 And bear with haste the *Pylian* King's reply:
But thy distress this instant claims relief.
He said, and in his arms upheld the chief.
The slaves their master's slow approach survey'd,
And hides of oxen on the floor display'd:
980 There stretch'd at length the wounded hero lay,
Patroclus cut the forky steel away.
Then in his hands a bitter root he bruis'd;
The wound he wash'd, the styptick juice infus'd.
The closing flesh that instant ceas'd to glow,
985 The wound to torture, and the blood to flow.

OBSERVATIONS

ON THE

ELEVENTH BOOK

As *Homer*'s invention is in nothing more wonderful than in the great variety of characters with which his poems are diversify'd, so his judgment appears in nothing more exact, than in that propriety with which each character is maintained. But this exactness must be collected by a diligent attention to his conduct thro' the whole: and when the particulars of each character are laid together, we shall find them all proceeding from the same temper and disposition of the person. If this observation be neglected, the Poet's conduct will lose much of its true beauty and harmony.

I fancy it will not be unpleasant to the reader, to consider the picture of *Agamemnon*, drawn by so masterly an hand as that of *Homer*, in its full length, after having seen him in several views and lights since the beginning of the poem.

He is a master of policy and stratagem, and maintains a good understanding with his council; which was but necessary, considering how many different, independent nations and interests he had to manage: He seems fully conscious of his own superior authority, and always knows the time when to exert it: He is personally very valiant, but not without some mixture of fierceness: Highly resentful of the injuries done his family, even more than *Menelaus* himself: Warm both in his passions and affections, particularly in the love he bears his brother. In short, he is (as *Homer* himself in another place describes him) both a good King, and a great warriour.

᾽Αμφότερον, βασιλεύς τ᾽ ἀγαθός, κρατερός τ᾽ αἰχμητής.

It is very observable how this hero rises in the esteem of the reader as the poem advances: It opens with many circumstances very much to the disadvantage of his character; he insults the priest of *Apollo*, and outrages *Achilles*: but in the second book he grows sensible of the effects of his rashness, and takes the fault entirely upon himself: In the fourth he shews himself a skilful commander, by exhorting, reproving and performing all the offices of a good general: In the eighth he is deeply touched by the sufferings of his army, and makes all the peoples calamities his own: In the ninth he endeavours to reconcile himself to *Achilles*, and condescends to be the petitioner, because it is for the publick good: In the tenth, finding those endeavours ineffectual, his concern keeps him the whole night awake, in contriving all possible methods to assist them: And now in the eleventh as it were resolving himself to supply the want of *Achilles*, he grows prodigiously in his valour, and performs wonders in his single person.

Thus we see *Agamemnon* continually winning upon our esteem, as we grow acquainted with him; so that he seems to be like that Goddess the Poet describes, who was low at the first, but rising by degrees, at last reaches the very heavens.

5. *When baleful* Eris, &c.] With what a wonderful sublimity does the Poet begin this book? He awakens the reader's curiosity, and sounds an alarm to the approaching battel. With what magnificence does he usher in the deeds of *Agamemnon*? He seems for a while to have lost all view of the main battel, and lets the whole action of the poem stand still, to attend the motions of this single hero. Instead of a Herald, he brings down a Goddess to inflame the army; instead of a trumpet or such warlike musick, *Juno* and *Minerva* thunder over the field of battel: *Jove* rains down drops of blood, and averts his eyes from such a scene of horrours.

By the Goddess *Eris* is meant that ardour and impatience for the battel which now inspired the *Grecian* army: They who just before were almost in despair, now burn for the fight, and breath nothing but war.   *Eustathius.*

14. Orthian *Song.*] This is a kind of an *Odaic* song, invented and sung on purpose to fire the soul to noble deeds in war. Such was that of *Timotheus* before *Alexander the Great*, which had such an influence upon him, that he leaped from his seat and laid hold on his arms.
                                                                          Eustathius.

26. *King* Cinyras.] 'Tis probable this passage of *Cinyras*, King of

Cyprus, alludes to a true history; and what makes it the more so, is that this island was famous for its mines of several metals.   *Eustathius.*

35. *Arching bow'd, &c.*] *Eustathius* observes, that the poet intended to represent the bending figure of these serpents as well as their colour, by comparing them to rainbows. *Dacier* observes here how close a parallel this passage of *Homer* bears to that in *Genesis*, where God tells *Noah, I have set my bow in the clouds, that it may be for a sign of the covenant between me and the earth.*

63. *The foot, and those who wield The lighter arms, rush forward.*] Here we see the order of battel is inverted, and opposite to that which *Nestor* proposed in the fourth book: For it is the cavalry which is there sustained by the infantry; here the infantry by the cavalry. But to deliver my opinion, I believe it was the nearness of the enemy that obliged *Agamemnon* to change the disposition of the battel: He would break their battalions with his infantry, and complete their defeat by his cavalry, which should fall upon the flyers.   *Dacier.*

70. *Red drops of blood.*] These prodigies, with which *Homer* embellishes his poetry, are the same with those which history relates not as ornaments, but as truths. Nothing is more common in history than showers of blood, and philosophy gives us the reason of them: The two battels which had been fought on the plains of *Troy*, had so drenched them with blood, that a great quantity of it might be exhaled in vapours and carried into the air, and being there condens'd, fall down again in dews and drops of the same colour.

Eustathius. [See Notes on *lib.* 16. v. 560.]

83. *As the red star.*] We have just seen at full length the picture of the General of the *Greeks*: Here we see *Hector* beautifully drawn in miniature. This proceeded from the great judgment of the Poet: 'twas necessary to speak fully of *Agamemnon*, who was to be the chief hero of this battel, and briefly of *Hector*, who had so often been spoken of at large before. This is an instance that the Poet well knew when to be concise, and when to be copious. It is impossible that any thing should be more happily imagin'd than this similitude: It is so lively, that we see *Hector* sometimes shining in arms at the head of his troops; and then immediately lose sight of him, while he retires in the ranks of the army.   *Eustathius.*

89. *As sweating reapers.*] 'Twill be necessary for the understanding of this similitude, to explain the method of mowing in *Homer*'s days: They mowed in the same manner as they plowed, beginning at the extremes of the field, which was equally divided, and proceeded till they met in the middle of it. By this means they raised an emulation between both parties, which should finish their share first. If we consider this custom, we shall find it a very happy comparison to the two armies advancing against each other, together with an exact resemblance in every circumstance the Poet intended to illustrate.

119. *What time in some sequester'd vale The weary woodman,* &c.] One may gather from hence, that in *Homer*'s time they did not measure the day by hours, but by the progression of the sun; and distinguished the parts of it by the most noted employments; as in the 12 of the *Odysseis*, v. 439. from the rising of the judges, and here from the dining of the labourer.

It may perhaps be entertaining to the reader to see a general account of the mensuration of time among the ancients, which I shall take from *Spondanus.* At the beginning of the world it is certain there was no distinction of time but by the light and darkness, and the whole day was included in the general terms of the evening and the morning. *Munster* makes a pretty observation upon this custom: Our long-liv'd forefathers (says he) had not so much occasion to be exact observers how the day pass'd, as their frailer sons, whose shortness of life makes it necessary to distinguish every part of time, and suffer none of it to slip away without their observation.

It is not improbable but that the *Chaldæans*, many ages after the flood, were the first who divided the day into hours; they being the first who applied themselves with any success to astrology. The most ancient sun-dial we read of is that of *Achaz*, mention'd in the second book of Kings, ch. 20. about the time of the building of *Rome*: But as these were of no use in clouded days and in the night, there was another invention of measuring the parts of time by water; but that not being sufficiently exact, they laid it aside for another by sand.

'Tis certain the use of dials was earlier among the *Greeks* than the *Romans*; 'twas above three hundred years after the building of *Rome* before they knew any thing of them: But yet they had divided the day and night into twenty-four hours, as appears from *Varro* and *Macrobius*, though they did not count the hours as we do, numerically, but from midnight to midnight, and distinguish'd them by particular names, as by the cock-crowing, the dawn, the mid-day, &c. The first sun-dial we read of among the *Romans* which divided the day into hours, is mention'd by *Pliny, lib.* 1. *cap.* 20. fixt upon the temple of *Quirinus* by *L. Papyrius* the censor, about the 12th year of the wars with *Pyrrhus.* But the first that was of any use to the publick was set up near the *rostra* in the *forum* by *Valerius Messala* the consul, after the taking of *Catana* in *Sicily*; from whence it was brought, thirty years after the first had been set up by *Papyrius*: but this was still an imperfect one, the lines of it not exactly corresponding with the several hours. Yet they made use of it many years, till *Q. Marcius Philippus* placed another by it greatly improved: but these had still one common defect of being useless in the night, and when the skies were overcast. All these inventions being thus ineffectual, *Scipio Nasica* some years after measur'd the day and night into hours from the dropping of water.

Yet near this time, it may be gather'd that sun-dials were very frequent in *Rome*, from a fragment preserv'd by *Aulus Gellius* and ascrib'd to *Plautus*: The lines are so beautiful, that I cannot deny the reader the satisfaction of seeing them. They are supposed to be spoken by an hungry parasite, upon a sight of one of these dials.

> *Ut illum Dii perdant, primus qui horas repperit;*
> *Quique adeo primus statuit heic solarium:*
> *Qui mihi comminuit misero, articulatim, diem!*
> *Nam me puero uterus hic erat solarium,*
> *Multo omnium istorum optimum & verissumum,*
> *Ubi iste monebat esse, nisi cum nihil erat.*
> *Nunc etiam quod est, non est, nisi Soli lubet:*
> *Itaque adeo jam oppletum est oppidum solariis,*
> *Major pars populi aridi reptant fame.*

[Might the gods destroy the man who first discovered the hours, and who first set up a sun-dial in this place – he who broke up the day into pieces, and made me miserable! For, when I was a child, my belly – by far the best and most accurate of such indicators – was what instructed me where to be, unless there was nothing to be gained there. But now, even when there is something to be gained, it's hopeless. And so, the town is now so full of sun-dials, that most of its inhabitants, shriveled up in hunger, crawl along the streets.]

We find frequent mention of the *Hours* in the course of this poem; but to prevent any mistake, it may not be improper to take notice, that they must always be understood to mean the seasons, and not the division of the day by hours.

125. *The* Greeks *impulsive might.*] We had just before seen that all the Gods were withdrawn from the battel; that *Jupiter* was resolv'd, even against the inclinations of them all, to honour the *Trojans.* Yet we here see the *Greeks* breaking thro' them: the love the poet bears to his countrymen makes him aggrandize their valour, and over-rule even the decrees of fate. To vary his battels, he supposes the Gods to be absent this day; and they are no sooner gone, but the courage of the *Greeks* prevails, even against the determination of *Jupiter.*   *Eustathius.*

135. *Naked to the sky.*] *Eustathius* refines upon this place, and believes that *Homer* intended, by particularizing the whiteness of the limbs, to ridicule the effeminate education of these unhappy youths. But as such an interpretation may be thought below the majesty of an Epic poem, and a kind of barbarity to insult the unfortunate, I thought it better to give the passage an air of compassion. As the words are equally capable of either meaning, I imagin'd the reader would be more pleas'd with the humanity of the one, than with the satyr of the other.

143. *These on the mountains once* Achilles *found.*] *Homer,* says *Eustathius,* never lets any opportunity pass of mentioning the hero of his poem, *Achilles:* he gives here an instance of his former resentment, and at once varies his poetry, and exalts his character. Nor does he mention him cursorily; he seems unwilling to leave him; and when he pursues the thread of the story in a few lines, takes occasion to speak again of him. This is a very artful conduct; by mentioning him so frequently, he takes care that the reader should not forget him, and shews the importance of that hero, whose anger is the subject of his poem.

181. Antimachus [sic], *who once.*] 'Tis observable that *Homer* with a great deal of art interweaves the true history of the *Trojan* war in his poem; he here gives a circumstance that carries us back from the tenth year of the war to the very beginning of it. So that although the action of the poem takes up but a small part of the last year of the war, yet by such incidents as these we are taught a great many particulars that happen thro' the whole series of it.   *Eustathius.*

188. *Lopp'd his hands away.*] I think one cannot but compassionate the fate of these brothers, who suffer for the sins of their father, notwithstanding the justice which the commentators find in this action of *Agamemnon.* And I can much less imagine that his cutting off their hands was meant for an express example against bribery, in revenge for the gold which *Antimachus* had received from *Paris. Eustathius* is very refining upon this point; but the grave *Spondanus* outdoes them all, who has found there was an excellent conceit in cutting off the hands and head of the son; the first, because the father had been for *laying hands* on the *Grecian embassadors*; and the second, because it was from his *head* that the advice proceeded of detaining *Helena.*

193. *Now by the foot the flying Foot,* &c.] After *Homer* with a poetical justice has punished the sons of *Antimachus* for the crimes of the father; he carries on the narration, and presents all the terrours of the battel to our view: we see in the lively description the men and chariots overthrown, and hear the trampling of the horses feet. Thus the Poet very artfully, by such sudden alarms, awakens the attention of the reader, that is apt to be tired and grow remiss by a plain and more cool narration.

197. *The brass-hoof'd steeds.*] *Eustathius* observes that the custom of shoeing horses was in use in *Homer*'s time, and calls the shoes σεληναῖα [moonlit], from the figure of an half-moon.

212. *More grateful, now, to vultures than their wives.*] This is a reflection of the Poet, and such an one as arises from a sentiment of compassion; and indeed there is nothing more moving than to see those heroes, who were the love and delight of their spouses, reduced suddenly to such a condition of horrour, that those very wives durst not look upon them. I was very much surprized to find a remark of *Eustathius* upon this, which seems very wrong and unjust: he would have it that there is in this place an *Ellipsis*, which comprehends a severe raillery: 'For, says he, *Homer* would imply that those dead warriours were now more agreeable to vultures, than they had ever been in all their days to their wives.' This is very ridiculous; to suppose that these unhappy women did not love their husbands, is to insult them barbarously in their affliction; and every body can see that such a thought in this place would have appear'd mean, frigid, and out of season. *Homer*, on the contrary, always endeavours to excite

compassion by the grief of the wives, whose husbands are kill'd in the battel.   *Dacier.*

217. *Now past the tomb where ancient* Ilus *lay.*] By the exactness of *Homer*'s description we see as in a landscape the very place where this battel was fought. *Agamemnon* drives the *Trojans* from the tomb of *Ilus*, where they encamp'd all the night; that tomb stood in the middle of the plain: from thence he pursues them by the wild fig-tree to the beech-tree, and from thence to the very *Scæan* gate. Thus the scene of action is fix'd, and we see the very rout through which the one retreats and the other advances.   *Eustathius.*

241. Iris *with haste thy golden wings display.*] 'Tis evident that some such contrivance as this was necessary; the *Trojans*, we learn from the beginning of this book, were to be victorious this day; but if *Jupiter* had not now interpos'd, they had been driven even within the walls of *Troy.* By this means also the Poet consults both for the honour of *Hector* and that of *Agamemnon. Agamemnon* has time enough to shew the greatness of his valour, and it is no disgrace to *Hector* not to encounter him when *Jupiter* interposes.

Eustathius observes, that the Poet gives us here a sketch of what is drawn out at large in the story of this whole book: This he does to raise the curiosity of the reader, and make him impatient to hear those great actions which must be perform'd before *Agamemnon* can retire, and *Hector* be victorious.

281. *Ye sacred nine!*] The Poet, to win the attention of the reader, and seeming himself to be struck with the exploits of *Agamemnon* while he recites them (who when the battel was rekindled, rushes out to engage his enemies) invokes not one muse as he did in the beginning of the poem, but as if he intended to warn us that he was about to relate something surprizing, he invokes the whole nine; and then, as if he had received their inspiration, goes on to deliver what they suggested to him. By means of this apostrophe, the imagination of the reader is so fill'd, that he seems not only present, but active in the scene to which the skill of the Poet has transported him.   *Eustathius.*

283. Iphidamas *the bold and young.*] *Homer* here gives us the history of this *Iphidamas*, his parentage, the place of his birth, and many circumstances of his private life. This he does to diversify his poetry, and to soften with some amiable embellishments the continual horrours that must of necessity strike the imagination in an uninterrupted narration of blood and slaughter.   *Eustathius.*

290. *Theano's sister.*] That the reader may not be shock'd at the marriage of *Iphidamas* with his mother's sister, it may not be amiss to observe from *Eustathius*, that consanguinity was no impediment in *Greece* in the days of *Homer*: nor is *Iphidamas* singular in this kind of marriage, for *Diomed* was married to his own aunt as well as he.

348. *The fierce* Ilythiæ.] These *Ilythiæ* are the Goddesses that *Homer* supposes to preside over child-birth: he arms their hands with a kind of an instrument, from which a pointed dart is shot into the distressed mother, as an arrow is from a bow: so that as *Eris* has her torch and *Jupiter* his thunder, these Goddesses have their darts which they shoot into women in travail. He calls them the daughters of *Juno*, because she presides over the marriage-bed.   *Eustathius.*   Here (says *Dacier*) we find the style of the holy scripture, which to express a severe pain, usually compares it to that of women in labour. Thus *David, Pain came upon them as upon a woman in travail*; and *Isaiah, They shall grieve as a woman in travail.* And all the Prophets are full of the like expressions.

357. *Lo angry* Jove *forbids your chief to stay.*] *Eustathius* remarks upon the behaviour of *Agamemnon* in his present distress: *Homer* describes him as rack'd with almost intolerable pains, yet he does not complain of the anguish he suffers, but that he is obliged to retire from the fight.

This indeed, as it prov'd his undaunted spirit, so did it likewise his wisdom: had he shew'd any unmanly dejection, it would have dispirited the army; but his intrepidity makes them believe his wound less dangerous, and renders them not so highly concern'd for the absence of their General.

387. *Say, Muse, when* Jove *the* Trojan's *glory crown'd.*] The Poet just before has given us an invocation of the muses, to make us attentive to the great exploits of *Agamemnon.* Here we have one with regard to *Hector*, but this last may perhaps be more easily accounted for than the other. For in that, after so solemn an invocation, we might reasonably have expected wonders from the hero: whereas in reality he kills but one man before he himself is wounded; and what he does afterwards seems to proceed from a frantic valour, arising from the smart of the wound: we do not find by the text that he kills one man, but overthrows several in his fury, and then retreats: So that one would imagine he invoked the muses only to describe his retreat.

But upon a nearer view, we shall find that *Homer* shews a commendable partiality to his own countryman and hero *Agamemnon*: he seems to detract from the greatness of *Hector*'s actions, by ascribing them to *Jupiter*; whereas *Agamemnon* conquers by the dint of bravery: and that this is a just observation, will appear by what follows. Those *Greeks* that fall by the sword of *Hector*, he passes over as if they were all vulgar men: he says nothing of them but that they died; and only briefly mentions their names, as if he endeavour'd to conceal the overthrow of the *Greeks*. But when he speaks of his favourite *Agamemnon*, he expatiates and dwells upon his actions; and shews us, that those that fell by his hand were all men of distinction, such as were the sons of *Priam*, of *Antenor*, and *Antimachus*. 'Tis true, *Hector* kill'd as many leaders of the *Greeks* as *Agamemnon* of the *Trojans*, and more of the common soldiers; but by particularizing the deaths of the chiefs of *Troy*, he sets the deeds of *Agamemnon* in the strongest point of light, and by his silence in respect to the leaders whom *Hector* slew, he casts a shade over the greatness of the action, and consequently it appears less conspicuous.

405. *But wise* Ulysses *call'd* Tydides *forth.*] There is something instructive in those which seem the most common passages of *Homer*, who by making the wise *Ulysses* direct the brave *Diomed* in all the enterprizes of the last book, and by maintaining the same conduct in this, intended to shew this moral, that valour should always be under the guidance of wisdom. Thus in the eighth book, when *Diomed* could scarce be restrain'd by the thunder of *Jupiter*, *Nestor* is at hand to moderate his courage; and this hero seems to have made a very good use of those instructions; his valour no longer runs out into rashness: tho' he is too brave to decline the fight, yet he is too wise to fight against *Jupiter*.

447. *Great* Diomed *himself was seiz'd with fear.*] There seems to be some difficulty in these words: this brave warriour, who has frequently met *Hector* in the battel, and offer'd himself for the single combat, is here said to be seiz'd with fear at the very sight of him: this may be thought not to agree with his usual behaviour, and to derogate from the general character of his intrepidity: but we must remember that *Diomed* himself has but just told us, that *Jupiter* fought against the *Grecians*; and that all the endeavours of himself and *Ulysses* would be in vain: this fear therefore of *Diomed* is far from being dishonourable: it is not *Hector*, but *Jupiter* of whom he is afraid.   *Eustathius.*

476. Ilus' *Monument.*] I thought it necessary just to put the reader in mind that the battel still continues near the tomb of *Ilus*: by a just observation of that, we may with pleasure see the various turns of the fight, and how every step of ground is won or lost as the armies are repuls'd or victorious.

479.   *Just as he stoop'd,* Agastrophus's *crest*
        To seize, and draw the corselet from his breast.]

One would think that the poet at all times endeavoured to condemn the practice of stripping the dead, during the heat of action; he frequently describes the victor wounded, while he is so employ'd about the bodies of the slain; thus in the present book we see *Agamemnon, Diomed, Ulysses, Elephenor,* and *Eurypylus,* all suffer as they strip the men they slew; and in the sixth book he brings in the wise *Nestor* directly forbidding it.   *Eustathius.*

482. *But pierc'd his foot.*] It cannot but be a satisfaction to the reader to see the Poet smitten with the love of his country, and at all times consulting its glory; This day was to be glorious to *Troy,* but *Homer* takes care to remove with honour most of the bravest *Greeks* from the field of battel, before the *Trojans* can conquer. Thus *Agamemnon, Diomed,* and *Ulysses* must bleed, before the Poet can allow his countrymen to retreat.   *Eustathius.*

483. *The laughing* Trojan.] *Eustathius* is of opinion that *Homer* intended to satirize in this place the unwarlike behaviour of *Paris*: such an effeminate laugh and gesture is unbecoming a brave warriour, but agrees very well with the character of *Paris*: he is before said to be more delighted with the soft amorous lyre, than with the warlike sound of the battel: nor do I remember that in the whole Iliad any one Person is describ'd in such an indecent transport, tho' upon a much more glorious or successful action. He concludes his ludicrous insult with a circumstance very much to the honour of *Diomed,* and very

much to the disadvantage of his own character; for he reveals to an enemy the fears of *Troy*, and compares the *Greeks* to lions, and the *Trojans* to sheep. *Diomed* is the very reverse of him; he despises and lessens the wound he receiv'd, and in the midst of his pain, would not gratify his enemy with the little joy he might give him by letting him know it.

512. *And questions thus his own unconquer'd soul.*] This is a passage which very much strikes me: we have here a brave hero making a noble soliloquy, or rather calling a council within himself, when he was singly to encounter an army: 'tis impossible for the reader not to be in pain for so gallant a man in such an imminent danger; he must be impatient for the event, and his whole curiosity must be awaken'd till he knows the fate of *Ulysses*, who scorn'd to fly, tho' encompass'd by an army.

549. *By* Pallas' *care.*] It is a just observation, that there is no moral so evident, or so constantly carried on through the Iliad, as the necessity mankind at all times has of divine assistance. Nothing is perform'd with success, without particular mention of this; *Hector* is not saved from a dart without *Apollo*, or *Ulysses* without *Minerva*. *Homer* is perpetually acknowledging the hand of God in all events, and ascribing to that only all the victories, triumphs, rewards, or punishments of men. Thus the grand moral he laid down at the entrance of his poem, Διὸς δ' ἐτελείετο βουλή, *The will of God was fulfill'd*, runs thro' his whole work, and is with a most remarkable care and conduct put into the mouths of his greatest and wisest persons on every occasion.

Homer generally makes some peculiar God attend on each hero: For the ancients believed that every man had his particular tutelary deity; these in succeeding times were called *Dæmons* or *Genii*, who (as they thought) were given to men at the hour of their birth, and directed the whole course of their lives. See *Cebes*'s *Tablet*. *Menander*, as he is cited by *Ammianus Marcellinus*, styles them μυσταγωγὸι βίου, *the invisible guides of life.*

565. *Fam'd Son of* Hippasus.] *Homer* has been blamed by some late censurers for making his heroes address discourses to the dead. *Dacier* replies that passion dictates these speeches, and it is generally to the dying, not to the dead, that they are addressed. However, one may say, that they are often rather reflections than insults. Were it otherwise,

Homer deserves not to be censured for feigning what histories have reported as truth. We find in *Plutarch* that *Mark Antony* upon sight of the dead body of *Brutus*, stopp'd and reproach'd him with the death of his Brother *Caius*, whom *Brutus* had killed in *Macedonia* in revenge for the murder of *Cicero*. I must confess I am not altogether pleased with the railleries he sometimes uses to a vanquished warriour, which inhumanities, if spoken to the dying, would I think be yet worse than after they were dead.

571. *And hov'ring vultures scream around their prey.*] This is not literally translated, what the Poet says gives us the most lively picture imaginable of the vultures in the act of tearing their prey with their bills: They beat the body with their wings as they rend it, which is a very natural circumstance, but scarce possible to be copied by a translator without losing the beauty of it.

572. *Me* Greece *shall honour when I meet my doom, With solemn fun'rals.* –] We may see from such passages as these that honours paid to the ashes of the dead have been greatly valued in all ages: This posthumous honour was paid as a publick acknowledgment that the person deceased had deserved well of his country, and consequently was an incitement to the living to imitate his actions: In this view there is no man but would be ambitious of them, not as they are testimonies of titles or riches, but of distinguished merit.

591. *Great* Ajax *like the God of War attends.*] The silence of other heroes on many occasions is very beautiful in *Homer*, but peculiarly so in *Ajax*, who is a gallant rough soldier, and readier to act than to speak: The present necessity of *Ulysses* required such a behaviour, for the least delay might have been fatal to him: *Ajax* therefore complying both with his own inclinations, and the urgent condition of *Ulysses*, makes no reply to *Menelaus*, but immediately hastens to his relief. The reader will observe how justly the Poet maintains this character of *Ajax* throughout the whole Iliad, who is often silent when he has an opportunity to speak, and when he speaks, 'tis like a soldier, with a martial air, and always with brevity.   *Eustathius.*

636. *A wise Physician.*] The Poet passes a very signal commendation upon Physicians: The army had seen several of their bravest heroes wounded, yet were not so much dispirited for them all, as they were at the single danger of *Machaon*: But the person whom he calls a Physician, seems rather to be a Surgeon. The cutting out of arrows, and the applying of anodynes being the province of the latter: However (as *Eustathius* says) we must conclude that *Machaon* was both a Physician and Surgeon, and that those two Professions were practised by one person.

It is reasonable to think, from the frequency of their wars, that the profession in those days was chiefly chirurgical: *Celsus* says expressly that the *Diætetic* was long after invented; but that *Botany* was in great esteem and practice, appears from the stories of *Medea*, *Circe*, &c. We often find mention among the most ancient writers, of women eminent in that art; as of *Agamede* in this very book, v. 876. who is said (like *Solomon*) to have known the virtues of every plant that grew on the earth, and of *Polydamne* in the fourth book of the *Odysseis*, v. 227, &c.

Homer, I believe, knew all that was known in his time of the practice of these arts. His methods of extracting of arrows, stanching of blood by the bitter root, fomenting of wounds with warm water, applying proper bandages and remedies, are all according to the true precepts of art. There are likewise several passages in his works that shew his knowledge of the virtues of plants, even of those qualities which are commonly (tho' perhaps erroneously) ascribed to them, as of the *Moly* against enchantments, the willow which causes barrenness, the *nepenthe*, &c.

668. But partial Jove, &c.] The address of *Homer* in bringing off *Ajax* with decency is admirable: He makes *Hector* afraid to approach him: He brings down *Jupiter* himself to terrify him; so that he retreats not from a mortal, but from a God.

This whole passage is inimitably just and beautiful: we see *Ajax* drawn in the most bold and strong colours, and in a manner alive in the description. We see him slowly and sullenly retreat between two armies, and even with a look repulse the one, and protect the other: There is not one line but what resembles *Ajax*; the character of a stubborn but undaunted warriour is perfectly maintain'd, and must strike the reader at the first view. He compares him first to the lion for his undauntedness in fighting, and then to the ass for his stubborn slowness in retreating; tho' in the latter comparison there are many other points of likeness that enliven the image: The havock he makes in the field is represented by the tearing and trampling down the harvests; and we see the bulk, strength, and obstinacy of the hero, when the *Trojans* in respect to him are compared but to troops of boys that impotently endeavour to drive him away.

Eustathius is silent as to those objections which have been raised against this last simile, for a pretended want of delicacy: This alone is conviction to me that they are all of a later date: For else he would not have failed to have vindicated his favourite Poet in a passage that had been applauded many hundreds of years, and stood the test of ages.

But Monsieur *Dacier* has done it very well in his remarks upon *Aristotle*. 'In the time of *Homer* (says that author) an ass was not in such circumstances of contempt as in ours: The name of that animal was not then converted into a term of reproach, but it was a beast upon which Kings and Princes might be seen with dignity. And it will not be very discreet to ridicule this comparison, which the holy scripture has put into the mouth of *Jacob*, who says in the benediction of his children, Issachar *shall be as a strong Ass*.' Monsieur *de la Motte* allows this point, and excuses *Homer* for his choice of this animal, but is unhappily disgusted at the circumstance of the boys, and the obstinate gluttony of the Ass, which he says are images too mean to represent the determined valour of *Ajax*, and the fury of his enemies. It is answered by Madam *Dacier*, that what Homer here images is not the gluttony, but the patience, the obstinacy, and strength of the Ass, (as *Eustathius* had before observ'd.) To judge rightly of comparisons, we are not to examine if the subject from whence they are deriv'd be great or little, noble or familiar; but we are principally to consider if the image produc'd be clear and lively, if the Poet has the skill to dignify it by poetical words, and if it perfectly paints the thing it is intended to represent. A company of boys whipping a top is very far from a great and noble subject, yet *Virgil* has not scrupled to draw from it a similitude which admirably expresses a princess in the violence of her Passion.

> *Ceu quondam torto volitans sub verbere turbo,*
> *Quem pueri magno in gyro vacua atria circum*
> *Intenti ludo exercent; ille actus habena*
> *Curvatis fertur spatiis: stupet inscia supra*
> *Impubesque manus, mirata volubile buxum:*
> *Dant animos plagæ* – &c.   Æn. lib. 7.

[And, as young striplings whip the top for sport,
  On the smooth pavement of an empty court;

    The wooden engine flies and whirls about,
    Admir'd, with clamours, of the beardless rout;
    They lash aloud, each other they provoke,
    And lend their little souls at ev'ry stroke.]

However, upon the whole, a translator owes so much to the taste of the age in which he lives, as not to make too great a complement to a former; and this induced me to omit the mention of the word *Ass* in the translation. I believe the reader will pardon me, if on this occasion I transcribe a passage from Mr *Boileau*'s notes on *Longinus*.

'There is nothing (says he) that more disgraces a composition than the use of mean and vulgar words; insomuch that (generally speaking) a mean thought expressed in noble terms, is more tolerable than a noble thought expressed in mean ones. The reason whereof is, that all the world are not capable to judge of the justness and force of a thought; but there's scarce any man who cannot, especially in a living language, perceive the least meanness of words. Nevertheless very few writers are free from this vice: *Longinus* accuses *Herodotus*, the most polite of all the *Greek* historians, of this defect; and *Livy*, *Salust*, and *Virgil* have not escaped the same censure. Is it not then very surprizing, that no reproach on this account has been ever cast upon *Homer*? tho' he has composed two poems each more voluminous than the *Æneid*; and tho' no author whatever has descended more frequently than he into a detail of little particularities. Yet he never uses terms which are not noble, or if he uses humble words or phrases, it is with so much art that, as *Dionysius* observes, they become noble and harmonious. Undoubtedly, if there had been any cause to charge him with this fault, *Longinus* had spared him no more than *Herodotus*. We may learn from hence the ignorance of those modern criticks, who resolving to judge of the *Greek* without the knowledge of it, and never reading *Homer* but in low and inelegant translations, impute the meannesses of his translators to the Poet himself; and ridiculously blame a man who spoke in one language, for speaking what is not elegant in another. They ought to know that the words of different languages are not always exactly correspondent; and it may often happen that a word which is very noble in *Greek*, cannot be render'd in another tongue but by one which is very mean. Thus the word *asinus* in *Latin*, and *ass* in *English*, are the vilest imaginable, but that which signifies the same animal in *Greek* and *Hebrew*, is of dignity enough to be employed on the most magnificent occasions. In like manner the terms of *hog-herd* and *cow-keeper* in our language are insufferable, but those which answer to them in *Greek*, συβώτης and βουκόλος, are graceful and harmonious: and *Virgil*, who in his own tongue entitled his Eclogs *Bucolica*, would have been ashamed to have called them in ours, the *Dialogues of Cowkeepers.*'

712. *Back to the lines the wounded* Greek *retires.*] We see here almost all the chiefs of the *Grecian* army withdrawn: *Nestor* and *Ulysses*, the two great counsellors; *Agamemnon*, *Diomed*, and *Eurypylus*, the bravest warriours; all retreated: So that now in this necessity of the *Greeks*, there was occasion for the Poet to open a new scene of action, or else the *Trojans* had been victorious, and the *Grecians* driven from the shores of *Troy*. To shew the distress of the *Greeks* at this period, from which the poem takes a new turn, 'twill be convenient to cast a view on the posture of their affairs: All human aid is cut off by the wounds of their heroes, and all assistance from the Gods forbid by *Jupiter*: Whereas the *Trojans* see their General at their head, and *Jupiter* himself fights on their side. Upon this hinge turns the whole poem; the distress of the *Greeks* occasions first the assistance of *Patroclus*, and then the death of that hero draws on the return of *Achilles*. It is with great art that the Poet conducts all these incidents: He lets *Achilles* have the pleasure of seeing that the *Greeks* were no longer able to carry on the war without his assistance: and upon this depends the great catastrophe of the poem.   *Eustathius.*

730. *That hour*, Achilles, &c.] Tho' the resentment of *Achilles* would not permit him to be an actor in the battel, yet his love of war inclines him to be a spectator: And as the Poet did not intend to draw the character of a perfect man in *Achilles*, he makes him delighted with the destruction of the *Greeks*, because it conspired with his revenge: That resentment which is the subject of the poem, still prevails over all his other passions, even the love of his country; for tho' he begins now to pity his countrymen, yet his anger stifles those tender emotions, and he seems pleas'd with their distress, because he judges it will contribute to his glory.   *Eustathius.*

734. *His Friend* Machaon, &c.] It may be ask'd why *Machaon* is the only person whom *Achilles* pities? *Eustathius* answers, that it was either because he was his countryman, a *Thessalian*; or because *Æsculapius*, the father of *Machaon*, presided over physick, the profession of his preceptor *Chiron*. But perhaps it may be a better reason to say that a physician is a publick good, and was valued by the whole army; and it is not improbable but he might have cured *Achilles* of a wound during the course of the *Trojan* wars.

746. *Now at my knees the* Greeks *shall pour their moan.*] The Poet by putting these Words into the mouth of *Achilles*, leaves room for a second embassy, and (since *Achilles* himself mentions it) one may think it would not have been unsuccessful: But the Poet, by a more happy management, makes his friend *Patroclus* the advocate of the *Greeks*, and by that means his return becomes his own choice. This conduct admirably maintains the character of *Achilles*, who does not assist the *Greeks* thro' his kindness to them, but from a desire of revenge upon the *Trojans*: His present anger for the death of his friend, blots out the former one for the injury of *Agamemnon*; and as he separated from the army in a rage, so he joins it again in the like disposition.

Eustathius.

763. *And took their seats beneath the shady tent.*] The Poet here steals away the reader from the battel, and relieves him by the description of *Nestor*'s entertainment. I hope to be pardon'd for having more than once repeated this observation, which extends to several passages of *Homer*. Without this piece of conduct, the frequency and length of his battels might fatigue the reader, who could not be so long delighted with continued scenes of blood.

773. *A goblet sacred to the* Pylian *Kings.*] There are some who can find out a mystery in the plainest things; they can see what the author never meant, and explain him into the greatest obscurities. *Eustathius* here gives us a very extraordinary instance of this nature: The bowl by an allegory figures the world; the spherical form of it represents its roundness; the *Greek* word which signifies the *doves* being spell'd almost like the *Pleiades*, is said to mean that constellation; and because the Poet tells us the bowl was studded with gold, those studs must needs imply the stars.

778. *Yet heav'd with ease by him.*] There has ever been a great dispute about this passage; nor is it apparent for what reason the Poet should tell us that *Nestor* even in his old age could more easily lift this bowl than any other man. This has drawn a great deal of raillery upon the

old man, as if he had learn'd to lift it by frequent use, an insinuation that *Nestor* was no enemy to wine. Others with more justice to his character have put another construction upon the words, which solves the improbability very naturally. According to this opinion, the word which is usually supposed to signify *another man*, is render'd *another old man*, meaning *Machaon*, whose wound made him incapable to lift it. This would have taken away the difficulty without any violence to the construction. But *Eustathius* tells us, the propriety of speech would require the word to be, not ἄλλος but ἕτερος, when spoken but of two. But why then may it not signify any other *old man*?

781. *Pours a large potion.*] The potion which *Hecamede* here prepares for *Machaon*, has been thought a very extraordinary one in the case of a wounded person, and by some criticks held in the same degree of repute with the balsam of *Fierabras* in *Don Quixot.* But it is rightly observed by the commentators, that *Machaon* was not so dangerously hurt, as to be obliged to a different regimen from what he might use at another time. *Homer* had just told us that he stay'd on the sea-side to refresh himself, and he now enters into a long conversation with *Nestor*; neither of which would have been done by a man in any great pain or danger: his loss of blood and spirits might make him not so much in fear of a feaver, as in want of a cordial; and accordingly this potion is rather alimentary than medicinal. If it had been directly improper in this case, I cannot help fancying that *Homer* would not have fail'd to tell us of *Machaon*'s rejecting it. Yet after all, some answer may be made even to the grand objection, that wine was too inflammatory for a wounded man. *Hippocrates* allows wine in acute cases, and even without water in cases of indigestion. He says indeed in his book of ancient medicine, that the ancients were ignorant both of the good and bad qualities of wine: and yet the potion here prescrib'd will not be allow'd by physicians to be an instance that they were so; for wine might be proper for *Machaon* not only as a cordial, but as an *opiate. Asclepiades*, a physician who flourish'd at *Rome* in the time of *Pompey*, prescrib'd wine in feavers, and even in phrensies to cause sleep. *Cælius Aurelianus, lib.* 4. *c.* 14.

800. *Can then the Sons of* Greece, &c.] It is customary with those who translate or comment on an author, to use him as they do their mistress; they can see no faults, or convert his very faults into beauties; but I cannot be so partial to *Homer*, as to imagine that this speech of

Nestor's is not greatly blameable for being too long: he crouds incident upon incident, and when he speaks of himself, he expatiates upon his own great actions, very naturally indeed to old age, but unseasonably in the present juncture. When he comes to speak of his killing the son of *Augeas*, he is so pleas'd with himself, that he forgets the distress of the army, and cannot leave his favourite subject till he has given us the pedigree of his relations, his wife's name, her excellence, the command he bore, and the fury with which he assaulted him. These and many other circumstances, as they have no visible allusion to the design of the speech, seem to be unfortunately introduc'd. In short, I think they are not so valuable upon any other account, as because they preserve a piece of ancient history, which had otherwise been lost.

What tends yet farther to make this story seem absurd, is what *Patroclus* said at the beginning of the speech, that he *had not leisure even to sit down*; so that *Nestor* detains him in the tent standing, during the whole narration.

They that are of the contrary opinion observe, that there is a great deal of art in some branches of the discourse; that when *Nestor* tells *Patroclus* how he had himself disobey'd his father's commands for the sake of his country, he says it to make *Achilles* reflect that he disobeys his father by the contrary behaviour: that what he did himself was to retaliate a small injury, but *Achilles* by fighting may save the *Grecian* army. He mentions the wound of *Agamemnon* at the very beginning, with an intent to give *Achilles* a little revenge, and that he may know how much his greatest enemy has suffer'd by his absence. There are many other arguments brought in the defence of particular parts; and it may not be from the purpose to observe, that *Nestor* might designedly protract the speech, that *Patroclus* might himself behold the distress of the army: thus every moment he detain'd him, enforced his arguments, by the growing misfortunes of the *Greeks*. Whether this was the intention or not, it must be allow'd that the stay of *Patroclus* was very happy for the *Greeks*; for by this means he met *Eurypylus* wounded, who confirm'd him into a certainty that their affairs were desperate, without *Achilles*'s aid.

As for *Nestor*'s second story, it is much easier to be defended; it tends directly to the matter in hand, and is told in such a manner as to affect both *Patroclus* and *Achilles*; the circumstances are well adapted to the person to whom they are spoken, and by repeating their father's instructions, he as it were brings them in, seconding his admonitions.

818. *The bulls of* Elis *in glad triumph led.*] *Elis* is the whole southern part of *Peloponnesus*, between *Achaia* and *Messenia*; it was originally divided into several districts or principalities, afterwards it was reduc'd to two; the one of the *Elians*, who were the same with the *Epeians*, the other of *Nestor*. This remark is necessary for the understanding what follows. In *Homer's* time the city *Elis* was not built.   *Dacier.*

838. *At the publick course Detain'd his chariot.*] 'Tis said that these were particular games, which *Augeas* had establish'd in his own state; and that the *Olympic* games cannot be here understood, because *Hercules* did not institute them till he had kill'd this King, and deliver'd his kingdom to *Phyleus*, whom his father *Augeas* had banish'd. The prizes of these games of *Augeas* were prizes of wealth, as golden tripods, &c. whereas the prizes of the *Olympic* games were only plain chaplets of leaves or branches: besides, 'tis probable *Homer* knew nothing of these chaplets given at the games, nor of the triumphal crowns, nor of the garlands wore at feasts; if he had, he would somewhere or other have mention'd them.   *Eustathius.*

844. *The sons of* Actor.] These are the same whom *Homer* calls the two *Molions*, namely, *Eurytus* and *Cteatus. Thryoëssa,* in the lines following, is the same town which he calls *Thryon* in the catalogue. The river *Minyas* is the same with *Anygrus,* about half way between *Pylos* and *Thryoëssa,* call'd *Minyas* from the *Minyans* who liv'd on the banks of it. It appears from what the Poet says of the time of their march, that it is half a day's march between *Pylos* and *Thryoëssa.*
                              Eustathius. Strabo, lib. 8.

894.   *There to high* Jove *were publick thanks assign'd*
             As first of Gods, to Nestor, of mankind.]

There is a resemblance between this passage and one in the sacred scripture, where all the congregation *blessed the Lord God of their fathers, and bowed down their heads, and worshipped the Lord, and the King.*
                              1 Chron. 29. 20.

915. Peleus *said only this, – 'My son, be brave.*] The conciseness of this advice is very beautiful; *Achilles* being hasty, active, and young, might not have burthen'd his memory with a long discourse: therefore *Peleus* comprehends all his instructions in one sentence. But *Menœtius* speaks more largely to *Patroclus*, he being more advanced in years, and mature in judgment; and we see by the manner of the expression, that he was sent with *Achilles*, not only as a companion but as a monitor, of which *Nestor* puts him in mind, to shew that it is rather his duty to give good advice to *Achilles*, than to follow his caprice, and espouse his resentment.   *Eustathius.*

922. *Ah try the utmost,* &c.] It may not be ungrateful to the reader to see at one view the aim and design of *Nestor*'s speech. By putting *Patroclus* in mind of his father's injunctions, he provokes him to obey him by a like zeal for his country: by the mention of the sacrifice, he reprimands him for a breach of those engagements to which the Gods were witnesses: by saying that the very arms of *Achilles* would restore the fortunes of *Greece*, he makes a high complement to that hero, and offers a powerful insinuation to *Patroclus* at the same time, by giving him to understand, that he may personate *Achilles.*   *Eustathius.*

927. *If ought from heav'n with-hold his saving arm.*] *Nestor* says this upon account of what *Achilles* himself spoke in the ninth book; and it is very much to the purpose, for nothing could sooner move *Achilles* than to make him think it was the general report in the army, that he shut himself up in his tent for no other reason, but to escape death, with which his mother had threaten'd him in discovering to him the decrees of the destinies.   *Dacier.*

968. *Of two fam'd surgeons.*] Tho' *Podalirius* is mention'd first for the sake of the verse, both here and in the catalogue, *Machaon* seems to be the person of the greatest character upon many accounts; besides, it is to him that *Homer* attributes the cure of *Philoctetes*, who was lame by having let an arrow dipt in the gall of the *Hydra* of *Lerna* fall upon his foot; a plain mark that *Machaon* was an abler physician than *Chiron* the centaure, who could not cure himself of such a wound. *Podalirius* had a son named *Hypolochus*, from whom the famous *Hippocrates* was descended.

976. *But this distress this instant claims relief.*] *Eustathius* remarks, that *Homer* draws a great advantage for the conduct of his poem from this incident of the stay of *Patroclus*; for while he is employ'd in the friendly task of taking care of *Eurypylus*, he becomes an eye-witness of the attack upon the entrenchments, and finds the necessity of using his utmost efforts to move *Achilles*.

THE
TWELFTH BOOK
OF THE
ILIAD

The ARGUMENT

The Battel at the *Grecian* Wall

The Greeks *being retired into their entrenchments,* Hector *attempts to force them; but it proving impossible to pass the ditch,* Polydamas *advises to quit their chariots, and manage the attack on foot. The* Trojans *follow his counsel, and having divided their army into five bodies of foot, begin the assault. But upon the signal of an eagle with a serpent in his talons, which appear'd on the left hand of the* Trojans, Polydamas *endeavours to withdraw them again. This* Hector *opposes, and continues the attack; in which, after many actions,* Sarpedon *makes the first breach in the wall:* Hector *also casting a stone of a vast size, forces open one of the gates, and enters at the head of his troops, who victoriously pursue the* Grecians *even to their ships.*

While thus the hero's pious cares attend
The cure and safety of his wounded friend,
Trojans and *Greeks* with clashing shields engage,
And mutual deaths are dealt with mutual rage.
5 Nor long the trench or lofty walls oppose;
With Gods averse th' ill-fated works arose;
Their pow'rs neglected, and no victim slain,
The walls were rais'd, the trenches sunk in vain.
    Without the Gods, how short a period stands
10 The proudest monument of mortal hands!
This stood, while *Hector* and *Achilles* rag'd,
While sacred *Troy* the warring hosts engag'd;
But when her sons were slain, her city burn'd,
And what surviv'd of *Greece* to *Greece* return'd;
15 Then *Neptune* and *Apollo* shook the shore,
Then *Ida*'s summits pour'd their wat'ry store;
Rhesus and *Rhodius* then unite their rills,
Caresus roaring down the stony hills,
Æsepus, *Granicus*, with mingled force,
20 And *Xanthus* foaming from his fruitful source;
And gulphy *Simois*, rolling to the main
Helmets, and shields, and god-like heroes slain:
These, turn'd by *Phœbus* from their wonted ways,
Delug'd the rampire nine continual days;
25 The weight of waters saps the yielding wall,
And to the sea the floating bulwarks fall.
Incessant cataracts the Thund'rer pours,
And half the skies descend in sluicy show'rs.

The God of Ocean, marching stern before,
With his huge trident wounds the trembling shore,   30
Vast stones and piles from their foundation heaves,
And whelms the smoaky ruin in the waves.
Now smooth'd with sand, and levell'd by the flood,
No fragment tells where once the wonder stood;
In their old bounds the rivers roll again,   35
Shine 'twixt the hills, or wander o'er the plain.
  But this the Gods in later times perform;
As yet the bulwark stood, and brav'd the storm;
The strokes yet echo'd of contending pow'rs;
War thunder'd at the gates, and blood distain'd the
    tow'rs.   40
Smote by the arm of *Jove*, and dire dismay,
Close by their hollow ships the *Grecians* lay:
Hector's approach in ev'ry wind they hear,
And *Hector*'s fury ev'ry moment fear.
He, like a whirlwind, toss'd the scatt'ring throng,   45
Mingled the troops, and drove the field along.
So 'midst the dogs and hunter's daring bands,
Fierce of his might, a boar or lion stands;
Arm'd foes around a dreadful circle form,
And hissing jav'lins rain an iron storm: 50
His pow'rs untam'd their bold assault defy,
And where he turns, the rout disperse, or die:
He foams, he glares, he bounds against them all,
And if he falls, his courage makes him fall.
With equal rage encompass'd *Hector* glows;   55
Exhorts his armies, and the trenches shows.
The panting steeds impatient fury breathe,
But snort and tremble at the gulph beneath;
Just on the brink, they neigh, and paw the ground,
And the turf trembles, and the skies resound.   60
Eager they view'd the prospect dark and deep,
Vast was the leap, and headlong hung the steep;
The bottom bare, (a formidable show!)
And bristled thick with sharpen'd stakes below.
The foot alone this strong defence could force,   65
And try the pass impervious to the horse.

This saw *Polydamas*; who, wisely brave,
Restrain'd great *Hector*, and this counsel gave.
   Oh thou! bold leader of our *Trojan* bands,
70 And you, confed'rate chiefs from foreign lands!
What entrance here can cumb'rous chariots find,
The stakes beneath, the *Grecian* walls behind?
No pass thro' those, without a thousand wounds,
No space for combat in yon' narrow bounds.
75 Proud of the favours mighty *Jove* has shown,
On certain dangers we too rashly run:
If 'tis his will our haughty foes to tame,
Oh may this instant end the *Grecian* name!
Here, far from *Argos*, let their heroes fall,
80 And one great day destroy, and bury all!
But should they turn, and here oppress our train,
What hopes, what methods of retreat remain?
Wedg'd in the trench, by our own troops confus'd,
In one promiscuous carnage crush'd and bruis'd,
85 All *Troy* must perish, if their arms prevail,
Nor shall a *Trojan* live to tell the tale.
Hear then ye warriours! and obey with speed;
Back from the trenches let your steeds be led;
Then all alighting, wedg'd in firm array,
90 Proceed on foot, and *Hector* lead the way.
So *Greece* shall stoop before our conqu'ring pow'r,
And this (if *Jove* consent) her fatal hour.
   This counsel pleas'd: the god-like *Hector* sprung
Swift from his seat; his clanging armour rung.
95 The chief's example follow'd by his train,
Each quits his car, and issues on the plain.
By orders strict the charioteers enjoin'd,
Compel the coursers to their ranks behind.
The forces part in five distinguish'd bands,
100 And all obey their sev'ral chief's commands.
The best and bravest in the first conspire,
Pant for the fight, and threat the fleet with fire:
Great *Hector* glorious in the van of these,
Polydamas, and brave *Cebriones*.
105 Before the next the graceful *Paris* shines,
And bold *Alcathous*, and *Agenor* joins.

The sons of *Priam* with the third appear,
Deïphobus, and *Helenus* the seer:
In arms with these the mighty *Asius* stood,
Who drew from *Hyrtacus* his noble blood,   110
And whom *Arisba*'s yellow coursers bore,
The coursers fed on *Selle*'s winding shore.
Antenor's sons the fourth battalion guide,
And great *Æneas*, born on fount-full *Ide*.
Divine *Sarpedon* the last band obey'd,   115
Whom *Glaucus* and *Asteropæus* aid,
Next him, the bravest at their army's head,
But he more brave than all the hosts he led.

   Now with compacted shields, in close array,
The moving legions speed their headlong way: 120
Already in their hopes they fire the fleet,
And see the *Grecians* gasping at their feet.

   While ev'ry *Trojan* thus, and ev'ry Aid,
Th' advice of wise *Polydamas* obey'd;
Asius alone, confiding in his car,   125
His vaunted coursers urg'd to meet the war.
Unhappy hero! and advis'd in vain!
Those wheels returning ne'er shall mark the plain;
No more those coursers with triumphant joy
Restore their master to the gates of *Troy!*   130
Black death attends behind the *Grecian* wall,
And great *Idomeneus* shall boast thy fall!
Fierce to the left he drives, where from the plain
The flying *Grecians* strove their ships to gain;
Swift thro' the wall their horse and chariots past,   135
The gates half-open'd to receive the last.
Thither, exulting in his force, he flies;
His following host with clamours rend the skies;
To plunge the *Grecians* headlong in the main,
Such their proud hopes, but all their hopes were vain!   140

   To guard the gates, two mighty chiefs attend,
Who from the *Lapiths* warlike race descend;
This *Polypætes*, great *Perithous*' heir,
And that *Leonteus*, like the God of war.
As two tall oaks, before the wall they rise;   145
Their roots in earth, their heads amidst the skies,

Whose spreading arms with leafy honours crown'd,
Forbid the tempest, and protect the ground;
High on the hills appears their stately form,
150   And their deep roots for ever brave the storm.
So graceful these, and so the shock they stand
Of raging *Asius*, and his furious band.
Orestes, *Acamas* in front appear,
And *Oenomaus* and *Thoön* close the rear;
155   In vain their clamours shake the ambient fields,
In vain around them beat their hollow shields;
The fearless brothers on the *Grecians* call,
To guard their navies, and defend the wall.
Ev'n when they saw *Troy*'s sable Troops impend,
160   And *Greece* tumultuous from her tow'rs descend,
Forth from the portals rush'd th' intrepid pair,
Oppos'd their breasts, and stood themselves the war.
So two wild boars spring furious from their den,
Rouz'd with the cries of dogs, and voice of men;
165   On ev'ry side the crackling trees they tear,
And root the shrubs, and lay the forest bare;
They gnash their tusks, with fire their eye-balls roll,
Till some wide wound lets out their mighty soul.
Around their heads the whistling jav'lins sung;
170   With sounding strokes their brazen targets rung:
Fierce was the fight, while yet the *Grecian* pow'rs
Maintain'd the walls and mann'd the lofty tow'rs:
To save their fleet, the last efforts they try,
And stones and darts in mingled tempests fly.

175   As when sharp *Boreas* blows abroad, and brings
The dreary winter on his frozen wings;
Beneath the low-hung clouds the sheets of snow
Descend, and whiten all the fields below.
So fast the darts on either army pour,
180   So down the rampires rolls the rocky show'r;
Heavy, and thick, resound the batter'd shields,
And the deaf echo rattles round the fields.

With shame repuls'd, with grief and fury driv'n,
The frantic *Asius* thus accuses heav'n.
185   In pow'rs immortal who shall now believe?
Can those too flatter, and can *Jove* deceive?

What man could doubt but *Troy*'s victorious pow'r
Should humble *Greece*, and this her fatal hour?
But look how wasps from hollow crannies drive,
To guard the entrance of their common hive,   190
Dark'ning the rock, while with unweary'd wings
They strike th' assailants, and infix their stings;
A race determin'd, that to death contend:
So fierce, these *Greeks* their last retreats defend.
Gods! shall two warriours only guard their gates,   195
Repel an army, and defraud the fates?

These empty accents mingled with the wind,
Nor mov'd great *Jove*'s unalterable mind;
To God-like *Hector* and his matchless might
Was ow'd the glory of the destin'd fight.   200
Like deeds of arms thro' all the forts were try'd,
And all the gates sustain'd an equal tide;
Thro' the long walls the stony show'rs were heard,
The blaze of flames, the flash of arms appear'd.
The spirit of a God my breast inspire,   205
To raise each act to life, and sing with fire!
While *Greece* unconquer'd kept alive the war,
Secure of death, confiding in despair;
And all her guardian Gods, in deep dismay,
With unassisting arms deplor'd the day.   210

Ev'n yet the dauntless *Lapithæ* maintain
The dreadful pass, and round them heap the slain.
First *Damasus*, by *Polypætes*' steel,
Pierc'd thro' his helmet's brazen vizor, fell;
The weapon drank the mingled brains and gore;   215
The warriour sinks, tremendous now no more!
Next *Ormenus* and *Pylon* yield their breath:
Nor less *Leonteus* strows the field with death;
First thro' the belt *Hippomachus* he goar'd,
Then sudden wav'd his unresisted sword;   220
Antiphates, as thro' the ranks he broke,
The faulchion strook, and fate pursu'd the stroke;
Iämenus, *Orestes*, *Menon*, bled;
And round him rose a monument of dead.

Mean-time the bravest of the *Trojan* crew   225
Bold *Hector* and *Polydamas* pursue;

Fierce with impatience on the works to fall,
And wrap in rowling flames the fleet and wall.
These on the farther bank now stood and gaz'd,
230 By heav'n alarm'd, by prodigies amaz'd:
A signal omen stopp'd the passing host,
Their martial fury in their wonder lost.
Jove's bird on sounding pinions beat the skies;
A bleeding serpent of enormous Size,
235 His talons truss'd; alive, and curling round,
He stung the bird, whose throat receiv'd the wound:
Mad with the smart, he drops the fatal prey,
In airy circles wings his painful way,
Floats on the winds, and rends the heav'ns with cries:
240 Amidst the host the fallen serpent lies.
They, pale with terrour, mark its spires unroll'd,
And *Jove*'s portent with beating hearts behold.
Then first *Polydamas* the silence broke,
Long weigh'd the signal, and to *Hector* spoke.

245   How oft, my brother, thy reproach I bear,
For words well meant, and sentiments sincere?
True to those counsels which I judge the best,
I tell the faithful dictates of my breast.
To speak his thought, is ev'ry freeman's right,
250 In peace and war, in council and in fight;
And all I move, deferring to thy sway,
But tends to raise that pow'r which I obey.
Then hear my words, nor may my words be vain:
Seek not, this day, the *Grecian* ships to gain;
255 For sure to warn us *Jove* his omen sent,
And thus my mind explains its clear event.
The victor eagle, whose sinister flight
Retards our host, and fills our hearts with fright,
Dismiss'd his conquest in the middle skies,
260 Allow'd to seize, but not possess the prize;
Thus tho' we gird with fires the *Grecian* fleet,
Tho' these proud bulwarks tumble at our feet,
Toils unforeseen, and fiercer, are decreed;
More woes shall follow, and more heroes bleed.
265 So bodes my soul, and bids me thus advise;
For thus a skilful seer would read the skies.

To him then *Hector* with disdain return'd;
(Fierce as he spoke, his eyes with fury burn'd)
Are these the faithful counsels of thy tongue?
Thy will is partial, not thy reason wrong: 270
Or if the purpose of thy heart thou vent,
Sure heav'n resumes the little sense it lent.
What coward counsels would thy madness move,
Against the word, the will reveal'd of *Jove*?
The leading sign, th' irrevocable nod,   275
And happy thunders of the fav'ring God,
These shall I slight? and guide my wav'ring mind
By wand'ring birds, that flit with ev'ry wind?
Ye vagrants of the sky! your wings extend,
Or where the suns arise, or where descend;   280
To right, to left, unheeded take your way,
While I the dictates of high heav'n obey.
Without a sign his sword the brave man draws,
And asks no omen but his country's cause.
But why should'st thou suspect the war's success?   285
None fears it more, as none promotes it less:
Tho' all our chiefs amid yon' ships expire,
Trust thy own cowardice t' escape their fire.
Troy and her sons may find a gen'ral grave,
But thou can'st live, for thou can'st be a slave.   290
Yet should the fears that wary mind suggests
Spread their cold poison thro' our soldier's breasts,
My jav'lin can revenge so base a part,
And free the soul that quivers in thy heart.

Furious he spoke, and rushing to the wall,   295
Calls on his host; his host obey the call;
With ardour follow where their leader flies:
Redoubling clamours thunder in the skies.
Jove breaths a whirlwind from the hills of *Ide*,
And drifts of dust the clouded navy hide: 300
He fills the *Greeks* with terrour and dismay,
And gives great *Hector* the predestin'd day.
Strong in themselves, but stronger in his aid,
Close to the works their rigid siege they laid.
In vain the mounds and massy beams defend,   305
While these they undermine, and those they rend;

Upheave the piles that prop the solid wall;
And heaps on heaps the smoaky ruins fall.
Greece on her rampart stands the fierce alarms;
310   The crowded bulwarks blaze with waving arms,
Shield touching shield, a long-refulgent row;
Whence hissing darts, incessant, rain below.
The bold *Ajaces* fly from tow'r to tow'r,
And rouze, with flame divine, the *Grecian* pow'r.
315   The gen'rous impulse ev'ry *Greek* obeys;
Threats urge the fearful, and the valiant, Praise.

    Fellows in arms! whose deeds are known to Fame,
And you whose ardour hopes an equal name!
Since not alike endu'd with force or art,
320   Behold a day when each may act his part!
A day to fire the brave, and warm the cold,
To gain new glories, or augment the old.
Urge those who stand, and those who faint excite;
Drown *Hector's* vaunts in loud exhorts of fight;
325   Conquest, not safety, fill the thoughts of all;
Seek not your fleet, but sally from the wall;
So *Jove* once more may drive their routed train,
And *Troy* lie trembling in her walls again.

    Their ardour kindles all the *Grecian* pow'rs;
330   And now the stones descend in heavier show'rs.
As when high *Jove* his sharp artill'ry forms,
And opes his cloudy magazine of storms;
In winter's bleak, uncomfortable reign,
A snowy inundation hides the plain;
335   He stills the winds, and bids the skies to sleep;
Then pours the silent tempest, thick, and deep:
And first the mountain tops are cover'd o'er,
Then the green fields, and then the sandy shore;
Bent with the weight the nodding woods are seen,
340   And one bright waste hides all the works of men:
The circling seas alone absorbing all,
Drink the dissolving fleeces as they fall.
So from each side increas'd the stony rain,
And the white ruin rises o'er the plain.

345   Thus God-like *Hector* and his Troops contend
To force the ramparts, and the gates to rend;

Nor *Troy* could conquer, nor the *Greeks* would yield,
Till great *Sarpedon* tow'r'd amid the field;
For mighty *Jove* inspir'd with martial flame
His matchless son, and urg'd him on to fame.   350
In arms he shines, conspicuous from afar,
And bears aloft his ample shield in air;
Within whose orb the thick bull-hides were roll'd,
Pond'rous with brass, and bound with ductile gold:
And while two pointed jav'lins arm his hands,   355
Majestick moves along, and leads his *Lycian* bands.
  So press'd with hunger, from the mountain's brow
Descends a lion on the flocks below;
So stalks the lordly savage o'er the plain,
In sullen majesty, and stern disdain: 360
In vain loud mastives bay him from afar,
And shepherds gaul him with an iron war;
Regardless, furious, he pursues his way;
He foams, he roars, he rends the panting prey.
  Resolv'd alike, divine *Sarpedon* glows   365
With gen'rous rage that drives him on the foes.
He views the tow'rs, and meditates their fall,
To sure destruction dooms th' aspiring wall;
Then casting on his friend an ardent look,
Fir'd with the thirst of glory, thus he spoke.   370
  Why boast we, *Glaucus!* our extended reign,
Where *Xanthus'* streams enrich the *Lycian* plain,
Our num'rous herds that range the fruitful field,
And hills where vines their purple harvest yield,
Our foaming bowls with purer nectar crown'd,   375
Our feasts enhanc'd with music's sprightly sound?
Why on those shores are we with joy survey'd,
Admir'd as heroes, and as Gods obey'd?
Unless great acts superior merit prove,
And vindicate the bount'ous pow'rs above.   380
'Tis ours, the dignity they give, to grace;
The first in valour, as the first in place.
That when with wond'ring eyes our martial bands
Behold our deeds transcending our commands,
Such, they may cry, deserve the sov'reign state,   385
Whom those that envy, dare not imitate!

Could all our care elude the gloomy grave,
Which claims no less the fearful than the brave,
For lust of fame I should not vainly dare
390   In fighting fields, nor urge thy soul to war.
But since, alas! ignoble age must come,
Disease, and death's inexorable doom;
The life which others pay, let us bestow,
And give to fame what we to nature owe;
395   Brave tho' we fall, and honour'd if we live,
Or let us glory gain, or glory give!
        He said; his words the list'ning chief inspire
With equal warmth, and rouze the warriour's fire;
The troops pursue their leaders with delight,
400   Rush to the foe, and claim the promis'd fight.
Menestheus from on high the storm beheld,
Threat'ning the fort, and black'ning in the field;
Around the walls he gaz'd, to view from far
What aid appear'd t' avert th' approaching war,
405   And saw where *Teucer* with th' *Ajaces* stood,
Of fight insatiate, prodigal of blood.
In vain he calls; the din of helms and shields
Rings to the skies, and echoes thro' the fields,
The brazen hinges fly, the walls resound,
Heav'n trembles, roar the mountains, thunders all the
410   ground.
        Then thus to Thoös; – hence with speed, (he said)
And urge the bold *Ajaces* to our aid;
Their strength, united, best may help to bear
The bloody labours of the doubtful war:
415   Hither the *Lycian* Princes bend their course,
The best and bravest of the hostile force.
But if too fiercely there the foes contend,
Let *Telamon*, at least, our tow'rs defend,
And *Teucer* haste with his unerring bow,
420   To share the danger, and repel the foe.
        Swift as the word, the herald speeds along
The lofty ramparts, through the martial throng;
And finds the heroes bath'd in sweat and gore,
Oppos'd in combat on the dusty shore.
425   Ye valiant leaders of our warlike bands!

Your aid (said *Thoös*) *Peteus'* son demands,
Your strength, united, best may help to bear
The bloody labours of the doubtful war:
Thither the *Lycian* Princes bend their course,
The best and bravest of the hostile force.   430
But if too fiercely, here, the foes contend,
At least, let *Telamon* those tow'rs defend,
And *Teucer* haste, with his unerring bow,
To share the danger, and repel the foe.

   Strait to the fort great *Ajax* turn'd his care,   435
And thus bespoke his brothers of the war.
Now valiant *Lycomede!* exert your might,
And brave *Oïleus*, prove your force in fight:
To you I trust the fortune of the field,
Till by this arm the foe shall be repell'd;   440
That done, expect me to compleat the day –
Then, with his sev'nfold shield, he strode away.
With equal steps bold *Teucer* press'd the shore,
Whose fatal bow the strong *Pandion* bore.

   High on the walls appear'd the *Lycian* pow'rs,   445
Like some black tempest gath'ring round the tow'rs;
The *Greeks*, oppress'd, their utmost force unite,
Prepar'd to labour in th' unequal fight;
The war renews, mix'd shouts and groans arise;
Tumultuous clamour mounts, and thickens in the skies.   450
Fierce *Ajax* first th' advancing host invades,
And sends the brave *Epicles* to the shades,
Sarpedon's friend; across the warriour's way,
Rent from the walls a rocky fragment lay;
In modern ages not the strongest swain   455
Could heave th' unwieldy burthen from the plain.
He pois'd, and swung it round; then toss'd on high,
It flew with force, and labour'd up the sky;
Full on the *Lycian*'s helmet thund'ring down,
The pond'rous ruin crush'd his batter'd crown.   460
As skilful divers, from some airy steep,
Headlong descend, and shoot into the deep,
So falls *Epicles*; then in groans expires,
And murm'ring to the shades the soul retires.

465   While to the ramparts daring *Glaucus* drew,
From *Teucer*'s hand a winged arrow flew;
The bearded shaft the destin'd passage found,
And on his naked arm inflicts a wound.
The chief, who fear'd some foe's insulting boast
470   Might stop the progress of his warlike host,
Conceal'd the wound, and leaping from his height,
Retir'd reluctant from th' unfinish'd fight.
Divine *Sarpedon* with regret beheld
Disabl'd *Glaucus* slowly quit the field;
475   His beating breast with gen'rous ardour glows,
He springs to fight, and flies upon the foes.
Alcmäon first was doom'd his force to feel;
Deep in his breast he plung'd the pointed steel;
Then, from the yawning wound with fury tore
480   The spear, pursu'd by gushing streams of gore;
Down sinks the warriour with a thund'ring sound,
His brazen armour rings against the ground.
    Swift to the battlement the victor flies,
Tugs with full force, and ev'ry nerve applies;
485   It shakes; the pond'rous stones disjointed yield;
The rowling ruins smoak along the field.
A mighty breach appears; the walls lie bare;
And, like a deluge, rushes in the war.
At once bold *Teucer* draws the twanging bow,
490   And *Ajax* sends his jav'lin at the foe;
Fix'd in his belt the feather'd weapon stood,
And thro' his buckler drove the trembling wood;
But *Jove* was present in the dire debate,
To shield his offspring, and avert his fate.
495   The Prince gave back, not meditating flight,
But urging vengeance, and severer fight;
Then rais'd with hope, and fir'd with glory's charms,
His fainting squadrons to new fury warms.
O where, ye *Lycians!* is the strength you boast?
500   Your former fame, and ancient virtue lost!
The breach lies open, but your chief in vain
Attempts alone the guarded pass to gain:
Unite, and soon that hostile fleet shall fall;
The force of pow'rful union conquers all.

This just rebuke inflam'd the *Lycian* crew,   505
They join, they thicken, and th' assault renew;
Unmov'd th' embody'd *Greeks* their fury dare,
And fix'd support the weight of all the war;
Nor could the *Greeks* repel the *Lycian* pow'rs,
Nor the bold *Lycians* force the *Grecian* tow'rs.   510
As on the confines of adjoining grounds,
Two stubborn swains with blows dispute their bounds;
They tugg, they sweat; but neither gain, nor yield,
One foot, one inch, of the contended field:
Thus obstinate to death, they fight, they fall;   515
Nor these can keep, nor those can win the wall.
Their manly breasts are pierc'd with many a wound,
Loud strokes are heard, and rattling arms resound,
The copious slaughter covers all the shore,
And the high ramparts drop with human gore.   520
    As when two scales are charg'd with doubtful loads,
From side to side the trembling balance nods,
(While some laborious matron, just and poor,
With nice exactness weighs her woolly store)
Till pois'd aloft, the resting beam suspends   525
Each equal weight; nor this, nor that, descends.
So stood the war, till *Hector*'s matchless might
With fates prevailing, turn'd the scale of fight.
Fierce as a whirlwind up the walls he flies,
And fires his host with loud repeated cries.   530
Advance, ye *Trojans!* lend your valiant hands,
Hast to the fleet, and toss the blazing brands!
They hear, they run, and gath'ring at his call,
Raise scaling engines, and ascend the wall:
Around the works a wood of glitt'ring spears   535
Shoots up, and all the rising host appears.
A pond'rous stone bold *Hector* heav'd to throw,
Pointed above, and rough and gross below:
Not two strong men th' enormous weight could raise,
Such men as live in these degen'rate days.   540
Yet this, as easy as a swain could bear
The snowy fleece, he toss'd, and shook in air:
For *Jove* upheld, and lighten'd of its load
Th' unweildy rock, the labour of a God.

545   Thus arm'd, before the folded gates he came,
     Of massy substance and stupendous frame;
     With iron bars and brazen hinges strong,
     On lofty beams of solid timber hung.
     Then thund'ring thro' the planks, with forceful sway,
550   Drives the sharp rock; the solid beams give way,
     The folds are shatter'd; from the crackling door
     Leap the resounding bars, the flying hinges roar.
     Now rushing in, the furious chief appears,
     Gloomy as night! and shakes two shining spears:
555   A dreadful gleam from his bright armour came,
     And from his eye-balls flash'd the living flame.
     He moves a God, resistless in his course,
     And seems a match for more than mortal force.
     Then pouring after, thro' the gaping space,
560   A tyde of *Trojans* flows, and fills the place;
     The *Greeks* behold, they tremble, and they fly;
     The shore is heap'd with death, and tumult rends the
          sky.

OBSERVATIONS

ON THE

TWELFTH BOOK

It may be proper here to take a general View of the conduct of the Iliad: the whole design turns upon the wrath of *Achilles*: that wrath is not to be appeas'd but by the calamities of the *Greeks*, who are taught by their frequent defeats the importance of this hero: for in Epic, as in Tragic poetry, there ought to be some evident and necessary incident at the winding up of the catastrophe, and that should be founded upon some visible distress. This conduct has an admirable effect, not only as it gives an air of probability to the relation, by allowing leisure to the wrath of *Achilles* to cool and die away by degrees, (who is every where described as a person of a stubborn resentment, and consequently ought not to be easily reconcil'd) but also as it highly contributes to the honour of *Achilles*, which was to be fully satisfy'd before he could relent.

9. *Without the Gods how short a period*, &c.] *Homer* here teaches a truth conformable to sacred scripture, and almost in the very words of the *Psalmist*; *Unless the Lord build the house, they labour in vain that build it.*

15. *Then* Neptune *and* Apollo, &c.] This whole episode of the destruction of the wall is spoken as a kind of prophecy, where *Homer* in a poetical enthusiasm relates what was to happen in future ages. It has been conjectur'd from hence that our author flourish'd not long after the *Trojan* war; for had he lived at a greater distance, there had been no occasion to have recourse to such extraordinary means to destroy a wall, which would have been lost and worn away by time alone. *Homer* (says *Aristotle*) foresaw the question might be ask'd, how it came to pass that no ruins remain'd of so great a work? and therefore contrived

to give his fiction the nearest resemblance to truth. Inundations and earthquakes are sufficient to abolish the strongest works of man, so as not to leave the least remains where they stood. But we are told this in a manner wonderfully noble and poetical: we see *Apollo* turning the course of the rivers against the wall, *Jupiter* opening the cataracts of heaven, and *Neptune* rending the foundations with his trident: that is, the sun exhales the vapours, which descend in rain from the air or *Æther*; this rain causes an inundation, and that inundation overturns the wall. Thus the poetry of *Homer*, like magick, first raises a stupendous object, and then immediately causes it to vanish.

What farther strengthens the opinion that *Homer* was particularly careful to avoid the objection which those of his own age might raise against the probability of this fiction, is, that the verses which contain this account of the destruction of the wall seem to be added after the first writing of the Iliad, by *Homer* himself. I believe the Reader will incline to my opinion, if he considers the manner in which they are introduced, both here and in the seventh book, where first this wall is mentioned. There, describing how it was made, he ends with this line,

> Ὣς οἱ μὲν πονέοντο καρηκομόωντες Ἀχαιοί.

[Thus the Achaians, with their flowing locks, laboured.]

After which is inserted the debate of the Gods concerning the method of its destruction, at the conclusion whereof immediately follows a verse that seems exactly to connect with the former.

> Δύσετο δ᾽ ἠέλιος, τετέλεστο δὲ ἔργον Ἀχαιῶν.

[The sun set, and the work of the Achaians was completed.]

In like manner, in the present book, after the fourth verse,

> Τάφρος ἔτι σχήσειν Δαναῶν καὶ τεῖχος ὕπερθεν.

[The ditch of the Greeks and the wall above.]

That which is now the thirty sixth, seems originally to have follow'd.

> Τεῖχος ἐΰδμητον, κανάχιζε δὲ δούρατα πύργων, &c.

[The well-built wall, and the timbers of the tower rattled, etc.]

And all the lines between (which break the course of the narration, and are introduced in a manner not usual in *Homer*) seem to have been added for the reason above-said. I do not insist much upon this observation, but I doubt not several will agree to it upon a review of the passages.

24. *Nine continual days.*] Some of the ancients thought it incredible that a wall which was built in one day by the *Greeks*, should resist the joint efforts of three deities nine days: to solve this difficulty, *Crates* the *Mallesian* was of opinion, that it should be writ, ἐν ἦμαρ, *one day*. But there is no occasion to have recourse to so forc'd a solution; it being sufficient to observe, that nothing but such an extraordinary power could have so entirely ruin'd the wall, that not the least remains of it should appear; but such a one, as we have before said, *Homer* stood in need of.   *Eustathius.*

99. *The forces part in five distinguish'd bands.*] The *Trojan* army is divided into five parts, perhaps because there were five gates in the wall, so that an attack might be made upon every gate at the same instant: By this means the *Greeks* would be obliged to disunite, and form themselves into as many bodies, to guard five places at the same time.

The Poet here breaks the thread of his narration, and stops to give us the names of the leaders of every battalion: By this conduct he prepares us for an action entirely new, and different from any other in the poem.   *Eustathius.*

125. Asius *alone confiding in his car.*] It appears from hence that the three captains who commanded each battalion, were not subordinate one to the other, but commanded separately, each being impowered to order his own troop as he thought fit: For otherwise *Asius* had not been permitted to keep his chariot when the rest were on foot. One may observe from hence, that *Homer* does not attribute the same regular discipline in war to the barbarous nations, which he had given to his *Grecians*; and he makes some use too of this defect, to cast the more variety over this part of the description.   *Dacier.*

127. *Unhappy hero!* &c.] *Homer* observes a poetical justice in relation to *Asius*; he punishes his folly and impiety with death, and shews the danger of despising wise counsel, and blaspheming the Gods. In pursuance of this prophecy, *Asius* is killed in the thirteenth book by *Idomeneus.*

143. *This* Polypœtes – *And that* Leonteus, &c.] These heroes are the originals of *Pandarus* and *Bitias* in *Virgil.* We see two gallant officers exhorting their soldiers to act bravely; but being deserted by them, they execute their own commands, and maintain the pass against the united force of the battalions of *Asius:* Nor does the Poet transgress the bounds of probability in the story: The *Greeks* from above beat off some of the *Trojans* with stones, and the gate-way being narrow, it was easy to be defended.   *Eustathius.*

185. *The Speech of* Asius.] This speech of *Asius* is very extravagant: He exclaims against *Jupiter* for a breach of promise, not because he had broken his word, but because he had not fulfill'd his own vain imaginations. This conduct, tho' very blameable in *Asius*, is very natural to Persons under a disappointment, who are ever ready to blame heaven, and turn their misfortunes into a crime.
                                                    Eustathius.

233. Jove's *bird on sounding pinions*, &c.] *Virgil* has imitated this passage in the eleventh *Æneid*, v. 751.

> *Utque volans alte raptum cum fulva draconem*
> *Fert aquila, implicuitque pedes, atque unguibus hæsit;*
> *Saucius at serpens sinuosa volumina versat,*
> *Arrectisque horret squamis, & sibilat ore*
> *Arduus insurgens; illa haud minus urget obunco*
> *Luctantem rostro; simul æthera verberat alis.*

[So stoops a yellow eagle from on high,
 And bears a speckled serpent thro' the sky;
 Fast'ning his crooked tallons on the prey:
 The pris'ner hisses thro' the liquid way,
 Resists the royal hawk, and tho' opprest,
 She fights in volumes, and erects her crest:
 Turn'd to her foe, she stiffens ev'ry scale;
 And shoots her forky tongue, and whisks her threat'ning
         tail.
 Against the victour all defence is weak;
 Th' imperial bird still plies her with his beak:

He tears her bowels, and her breast he gores;
Then claps his pinions, and securely soars.]

Which *Macrobius* compares with this of *Homer*, and gives the preference to the original, on account of *Virgil*'s having neglected to specify the *Omen. His prætermissis, (quod sinistra veniens vincentium prohibebat accessum, & accepto a serpente morsu prædam dolore dejecit; factoque Tripudio solistimo, cum clamore dolorem testante, prætervolat) quæ animam Parabolæ dabant, velut exanime in latinis versibus corpus remansit.* [These details having been omitted by Virgil (that by approaching from the left [the eagle] forbade the advance of the victors, and that, bitten by the serpent, it dropped its prey; and that, once this omen most favorable [to the Greeks] had been made manifest, it flew by with a cry that bore witness to its pain) – details that were the very life of the simile, there remained in the Latin verses, as it were, only a lifeless corpse.] *Sat. l. 5. c.* 14. But methinks this criticism might have been spared, had he considered that *Virgil* had no design, or occasion, to make an *Omen* of it; but took it only as a natural image, to paint the posture of two warriours struggling with each other.

245. *The Speech of* Polydamas.] The address of *Polydamas* to *Hector* in this speech is admirable: He knew that the daring spirit of that hero would not suffer him to listen to any mention of a retreat: He had already storm'd the walls in imagination, and consequently the advice of *Polydamas* was sure to meet with a bad reception. He therefore softens every expression, and endeavours to flatter *Hector* into an assent; and tho' he is assured he gives a true interpretation of the prodigy, he seems to be diffident: but that his personated distrust may not prejudice the interpretation, he concludes with a plain declaration of his opinion, and tells him that what he delivers is not conjecture, but science, and appeals for the truth of it to the augurs of the army.

Eustathius.

267. *The Speech of* Hector.] This speech of *Hector*'s is full of spirit: His Valour is greater than the skill of *Polydamas*, and he is not to be argu'd into a retreat. There is something very heroic in that line,

– *His sword the brave man draws,*
And asks no omen but his country's cause.

And if any thing can add to the beauty of it, it is in being so well adapted to the character of him who speaks it, who is every where described as a great lover of his country.

It may seem at the first view that *Hector* uses *Polydamas* with too much severity in the conclusion of his speech: But he will be sufficiently justified, if we consider that the interpretation of the omen given by *Polydamas* might have discouraged the army; and this makes it necessary for him to decry the prediction, and insinuate that the advice proceeded not from his skill but his cowardice.   *Eustathius.*

281. *To right, to left, unheeded take your way.*] *Eustathius* has found out four meanings in these two lines, and tells us that the words may signify East, West, North, and South. This is writ in the true spirit of a Critick, who can find out a mystery in the plainest words, and is ever learnedly obscure: For my part, I cannot imagine how any thing can be more clearly express'd; I care not, says *Hector*, whether the eagle flew on the right, towards the sun-rising, which was propitious, or on the left towards his setting, which was unlucky.

299. *Jove* rais'd *a whirlwind.*] It is worth our notice to observe how the least circumstance grows in the hand of a great Poet. In this battel it is to be supposed that the *Trojans* had got the advantage of the wind of the *Grecians*, so that a cloud of dust was blown upon their army: This gave room for this fiction of *Homer*, which supposes that *Jove*, or the air, rais'd the dust, and drove it in the face of the *Grecians.*
    Eustathius.

348. *Till great* Sarpedon, &c.] The Poet here ushers in *Sarpedon* with abundance of pomp: He forces him upon the observation of the reader by the greatness of the description, and raises our expectations of him, intending to make him perform many remarkable actions in the sequel of the poem, and become worthy to fall by the hand of *Patroclus.*
    Eustathius.

357. *So press'd with hunger, from the mountain's brow, Descends a Lion.*] This comparison very much resembles that of the Prophet *Isaiah*, Ch. 31. v. 4. where God himself is compared to a lion: *Like as the lion, and the young lion roaring on his prey, when a multitude of shepherds is call'd forth against him, he will not be afraid of their voice, nor abase himself for the noise of them: So shall the Lord of Hosts come down that he may fight upon mount* Sion.   *Dacier.*

371. *The speech of* Sarpedon *to* Glaucus.] In former times Kings were look'd upon as the generals of armies, who to return the honours that were done them, were obliged to expose themselves first in the battel, and be an example to their soldiers. Upon this *Sarpedon* grounds his discourse, which is full of generosity and nobleness. We are, says he, honour'd like Gods; and what can be more unjust, than not to behave our selves like men? he ought to be superior in virtue, who is superior in dignity; What strength is there, and what greatness in that thought? it includes justice, gratitude, and magnanimity; justice, in that he scorns to enjoy what he does not merit; gratitude, because he would endeavour to recompense his obligations to his subjects; and magnanimity, in that he despises death, and thinks of nothing but glory.

Eustathius. Dacier.

387. *Could all our care,* &c.] There is not a more forcible argument than this, to make men contemn dangers, and seek glory by brave actions. Immortality with eternal youth, is certainly preferable to glory purchas'd with the loss of life; but glory is certainly better than an ignominious life; which at last, tho' perhaps late, must end. It is ordain'd that all men shall die, nor can our escaping danger secure us immortality; it can only give us a longer continuance in disgrace, and even that continuance will be but short, tho' the infamy everlasting. This is incontestable, and whoever weighs his actions in these scales, can never hesitate in his choice: but what is most worthy of remark is, that *Homer* does not put this in the mouth of an ordinary person, but ascribes it to the son of *Jupiter.*   *Eustathius. Dacier.*

I ought not to neglect putting the reader in mind that this speech of *Sarpedon* is excellently translated by Sir *John Denham*, and if I have done it with any spirit, it is partly owing to him.

444. *Whose fatal bow the strong* Pandion *bore.*] It is remarkable that *Teucer*, who is excellent for his skill in archery, does not carry his own bow, but has it born after him by *Pandion*: I thought it not improper to take notice of this, by reason of its unusualness. It may be suppos'd that *Teucer* had chang'd his arms in this fight, and comply'd with the exigence of the battel which was about the wall; he might judge that some other weapon might be more necessary upon this occasion, and therefore committed his bow to the care of *Pandion.*   *Eustathius.*

454. *A rocky fragment,* &c.] In this book both *Ajax* and *Hector* are

describ'd throwing stones of a prodigious size. But the Poet, who loves
to give the preference to his countrymen, relates the action much to
the advantage of *Ajax*: *Ajax*, by his natural strength, performs what
Hector could not do without the assistance of *Jupiter*.　　*Eustathius.*

455. *In modern ages.*] The difference which our author makes between
the heroes of his poem, and the men of his age, is so great, that some
have made use of it as an argument that *Homer* liv'd many ages after
the war of *Troy*: but this argument does not seem to be of any weight;
for supposing *Homer* to have writ two hundred and fifty or two
hundred and sixty years after the destruction of *Troy*, this space is
long enough to make such a change as he speaks of; peace, luxury, or
effeminacy would do it in a much less time.　　　　　　　*Dacier.*

483. *Swift to the battlement the victor flies.*] From what *Sarpedon* here
performs, we may gather that this wall of the *Greeks* was not higher
than a tall man: from the great depth and breadth of it, as it is
described just before, one might have concluded that it had been much
higher: but it appears to be otherwise from this passage; and conse-
quently the thickness of the wall was answerable to the wideness of the
ditch.　　　　　　　　　　　　　　　　　　　　　*Eustathius.*

511. *As on the confines of adjoining ground.*] This simile, says *Eustath-
ius*, is wonderfully proper; it has one circumstance that is seldom to be
found in *Homer*'s allusions; it corresponds in every point with the
subject it was intended to illustrate: the measures of the two neighbours
represent the spears of the combatants: the confines of the field shew
that they engag'd hand to hand; and the wall which divides the armies
gives us a lively idea of the large stones that were fix'd to determine
the bounds of adjoining fields.

521. *As when two scales,* &c.] This comparison is excellent on account
of its justness; for there is nothing better represents an exact equality
than a balance: but *Homer* was particularly exact, in having neither
describ'd a woman of wealth and condition, for such a one is never
very exact, not valuing a small inequality; nor a slave, for such a one is
ever regardless of his master's interest: but he speaks of a poor woman
that gains her livelihood by her labour, who is at the same time just
and honest; for she will neither defraud others, nor be defrauded her

self. She therefore takes care that the scales be exactly of the same weight.

It was an ancient tradition, (and is countenanced by the author of *Homer*'s life ascribed to *Herodotus*) that the Poet drew this comparison from his own family; being himself the son of a woman who maintained her self by her own industry; he therefore to extol her honesty, (a qualification very rare in poverty) gives her a place in his poem.

Eustathius.

THE
ILIAD
OF
HOMER

VOLUME IV

THE
THIRTEENTH BOOK
OF THE
ILIAD

The ARGUMENT

The fourth battel continued, in which *Neptune* assists the *Greeks*: The acts of *Idomeneus*

Neptune, *concern'd for the loss of the* Grecians, *upon seeing the fortification forc'd by* Hector, *(who had enter'd the gate near the station of the* Ajaxes*) assumes the shape of* Calchas, *and inspires those heroes to oppose him: Then in the form of one of the generals, encourages the other* Greeks *who had retir'd to their vessels. The* Ajaxes *form their troops in a close phalanx, and put a stop to* Hector *and the* Trojans. *Several deeds of valour are perform'd;* Meriones *losing his spear in the encounter, repairs to seek another at the tent of* Idomeneus. *This occasions a conversation between those two warriours, who return together to the battel.* Idomeneus *signalizes his courage above the rest; he kills* Othryoneus, Asius, *and* Alcathous. Deïphobus *and* Æneas *march against him, and at length* Idomeneus *retires.* Menelaus *wounds* Helenus, *and kills* Pisander. *The* Trojans *are repuls'd in the left wing;* Hector *still keeps his ground against the* Ajaxes, *till being gaul'd by the* Locrian *slingers and archers,* Polydamas *advises to call a council of war:* Hector *approves his advice, but goes first to rally the* Trojans; *upbraids* Paris, *rejoins* Polydamas, *meets* Ajax *again, and renews the attack.*

The eight and twentieth day still continues. The scene is between the Grecian *wall and the sea-shore.*

When now the Thund'rer, on the sea-beat coast,
Had fix'd great *Hector* and his conqu'ring host;
He left them to the fates, in bloody fray
To toil and struggle thro' the well-fought day.
5   Then turn'd to *Thracia* from the field of fight
Those eyes, that shed insufferable light,
To where the *Mysians* prove their martial force,
And hardy *Thracians* tame the savage horse;
And where the far-fam'd *Hippemolgian* strays,
10 Renown'd for justice and for length of days,
Thrice happy race! that, innocent of blood,
From milk, innoxious, seek their simple food:
Jove sees delighted, and avoids the scene
Of guilty *Troy*, of arms, and dying men:
15 No aid, he deems, to either host is giv'n,
While his high law suspends the pow'rs of heav'n.
    Mean time the *Monarch of the watry main
Observ'd the Thund'rer, not observ'd in vain.
In *Samothracia*, on a mountain's brow,
20 Whose waving woods o'erhung the deeps below,
He sate; and round him cast his azure eyes,
Where *Ida*'s misty tops confus'dly rise;
Below, fair *Ilion*'s glitt'ring spires were seen,
The crowded ships, and sable seas between.
25 There, from the crystal chambers of the main,
Emerg'd, he sate; and mourn'd his *Argives* slain.

*Neptune.

At *Jove* incens'd, with grief and fury stung,
Prone down the rocky steep, he rush'd along;
Fierce as he past, the lofty mountains nod,
The forests shake! earth trembled as he trod,   30
And felt the footsteps of th' immortal God.
From realm to realm three ample strides he took,
And, at the fourth, the distant *Ægæ* shook.

   Far in the bay his shining palace stands,
Eternal frame! not rais'd by mortal hands: 35
This having reach'd, his brass-hoof'd steeds he reins,
Fleet as the winds, and deck'd with golden manes.
Refulgent arms his mighty limbs infold,
Immortal arms, of adamant and gold.
He mounts the car, the golden scourge applies;   40
He sits superior, and the chariot flies.
His whirling wheels the glassy surface sweep;
Th' enormous monsters, rolling o'er the deep,
Gambol around him, on the watry way;
And heavy whales in aukward measures play: 45
The sea subsiding spreads a level plain,
Exults, and owns the monarch of the main;
The parting waves before his coursers fly;
The wond'ring waters leave his axle dry.

   Deep in the liquid regions lies a cave,   50
Between where *Tenedos* the surges lave,
And rocky *Imbrus* breaks the rolling wave:
There the great ruler of the azure round
Stop'd his swift chariot, and his steeds unbound,
Fed with ambrosial herbage from his hand,   55
And link'd their fetlocks with a golden band,
Infrangible, immortal: There they stay.
The father of the floods pursues his way;
Where, like a tempest, dark'ning heav'n around,
Or fiery deluge that devours the ground,   60
Th' impatient *Trojans*, in a gloomy throng,
Embattel'd roll'd, as *Hector* rush'd along.
To the loud tumult and the barb'rous cry,
The heav'ns re-echo, and the shores reply;
They vow destruction to the *Grecian* name,   65
And, in their hopes, the Fleets already flame.

But *Neptune*, rising from the seas profound,
The God whose earthquakes rock the solid ground,
Now wears a mortal form; like *Calchas* seen,
70 Such his loud voice, and such his manly mien;
His shouts incessant ev'ry *Greek* inspire,
But most th' *Ajaces*, adding fire to fire.

    'Tis yours, O warriors, all our hopes to raise;
Oh recollect your ancient worth and praise!
75 'Tis yours to save us, if you cease to fear;
Flight, more than shameful, is destructive here.
On other works tho' *Troy* with fury fall,
And pour her armies o'er our batter'd wall;
There, *Greece* has strength: but this, this part o'erthrown,
80 Her strength were vain; I dread for you alone.
Here *Hector* rages like the force of fire,
Vaunts of his Gods, and calls high *Jove* his sire.
If yet some heav'nly pow'r your breast excite,
Breathe in your hearts, and string your arms to fight,
85 *Greece* yet may live, her threat'ned fleet maintain,
And *Hector*'s force, and *Jove*'s own aid, be vain.

    Then with his sceptre that the deep controuls,
He touch'd the chiefs, and steel'd their manly souls;
Strength, not their own, the touch divine imparts,
90 Prompts their light limbs, and swells their daring hearts.
Then, as a falcon from the rocky height,
Her quarry seen, impetuous at the sight,
Forth-springing instant, darts her self from high,
Shoots on the wing, and skims along the sky:
95 Such, and so swift, the pow'r of Ocean flew;
The wide horizon shut him from their view.

    Th' inspiring God, *Oïleus'* active son
Perceiv'd the first, and thus to *Telamon*.

    Some God, my friend, some God in human form
100 Fav'ring descends, and wills to stand the storm.
Not *Calchas* this, the venerable seer;
Short as he turn'd, I saw the pow'r appear:
I mark'd his parting, and the steps he trod;
His own bright evidence reveals a God.
105 Ev'n now some energy divine I share,
And seem to walk on wings, and tread in air!

With equal ardour (*Telamon* returns)
My soul is kindled, and my bosom burns;
New rising spirits all my force alarm,
Lift each impatient limb, and brace my arm.   110
This ready arm, unthinking, shakes the dart;
The blood pours back, and fortifies my heart;
Singly methinks, yon' tow'ring chief I meet,
And stretch the dreadful *Hector* at my feet.

    Full of the God that urg'd their burning breast,   115
The heroes thus their mutual warmth express'd.
Neptune meanwhile the routed *Greeks* inspir'd;
Who breathless, pale, with length of labours tir'd,
Pant in the ships; while *Troy* to conquest calls,
And swarms victorious o'er their yielding walls:
Trembling before th' impending storm they lie,   120
While tears of rage stand burning in their eye.
Greece sunk they thought, and this their fatal hour;
But breathe new courage as they feel the pow'r.
Teucer and *Leitus* first his words excite;   125
Then stern *Peneleus* rises to the fight;
Thoas, *Deïpyrus*, in arms renown'd,
And *Merion* next, th' impulsive fury found;
Last *Nestor*'s son the same bold ardour takes,
While thus the God the martial fire awakes.   130

    Oh lasting infamy, oh dire disgrace
To chiefs of vig'rous youth, and manly race!
I trusted in the Gods, and you, to see
Brave *Greece* victorious, and her navy free:
Ah no – the glorious combate you disclaim,   135
And one black day clouds all her former fame.
Heav'ns! what a prodigy these eyes survey,
Unseen, unthought, till this amazing day!
Fly we at length from *Troy*'s oft-conquer'd bands,
And falls our fleet by such inglorious hands?   140
A rout undisciplin'd, a straggling train,
Not born to glories of the dusty plain;
Like frighted fawns from hill to hill pursu'd,
A prey to every savage of the wood:
Shall these, so late who trembled at your name,   145
Invade your camps, involve your ships in flame?

A change so shameful, say what cause has wrought?
The soldiers baseness, or the gen'ral's fault?
Fools! will ye perish for your leader's vice?
150   The purchase infamy, and life the price!
'Tis not your cause, *Achilles'* injur'd fame:
Another's is the crime, but yours the shame.
Grant that our chief offend thro' rage or lust,
Must you be cowards, if your king's unjust?
155   Prevent this evil, and your country save:
Small thought retrieves the spirits of the brave.
Think, and subdue! on dastards dead to fame
I waste no anger, for they feel no shame:
But you, the pride, the flow'r of all our host,
160   My heart weeps blood to see your glory lost!
Nor deem this day, this battel, all you lose;
A day more black, a fate more vile, ensues.
Let each reflect, who prizes fame or breath,
On endless infamy, on instant death.
165   For lo! the fated time, th' appointed shore;
Hark! the gates burst, the brazen barriers roar!
Impetuous *Hector* thunders at the wall;
The hour, the spot, to conquer, or to fall.

These words the *Grecians* fainting hearts inspire,
170   And list'ning armies catch the godlike fire.
Fix'd at his post was each bold *Ajax* found,
With well-rang'd squadrons strongly circled round:
So close their order, so dispos'd their Fight,
As *Pallas'* self might view with fixt delight;
175   Or had the God of war inclin'd his eyes,
The God of war had own'd a just surprize.
A chosen Phalanx, firm, resolv'd as Fate,
Descending *Hector* and his battel wait.
An iron scene gleams dreadful o'er the fields,
180   Armour in armour lock'd, and shields in shields,
Spears lean on spears, on targets targets throng,
Helms stuck to helms, and man drove man along.
The floating plumes unnumber'd wave above,
As when an earthquake stirs the nodding grove;
185   And levell'd at the skies with pointing rays,
Their brandish'd lances at each motion blaze.

Thus breathing death, in terrible array,
The close-compacted legions urg'd their way:
Fierce they drove on, impatient to destroy;
Troy charg'd the first, and *Hector* first of *Troy.*   190
As from some mountain's craggy forehead torn,
A rock's round fragment flies, with fury born,
(Which from the stubborn stone a torrent rends)
Precipitate the pond'rous mass descends:
From steep to steep the rolling ruin bounds;   195
At ev'ry shock the crackling wood resounds;
Still gath'ring force, it smoaks; and, urg'd amain,
Whirls, leaps, and thunders down, impetuous to the
          plain:
There stops – So *Hector.* Their whole force he prov'd,
Resistless when he rag'd, and when he stop'd, unmov'd.   200

On him the war is bent, the darts are shed,
And all their faulchions wave around his head.
Repuls'd he stands, nor from his stand retires;
But with repeated shouts his army fires.
Trojans! be firm; this arm shall make your way   205
Thro' yon' square body, and that black array:
Stand, and my spear shall rout their scatt'ring pow'r,
Strong as they seem, embattel'd like a tow'r.
For he that *Juno*'s heav'nly bosom warms,
The first of Gods, this day inspires our arms.   210

He said, and rouz'd the soul in ev'ry breast;
Urg'd with desire of fame, beyond the rest,
Forth march'd *Deïphobus*; but marching, held
Before his wary steps, his ample shield.
Bold *Merion* aim'd a stroke (nor aim'd it wide)   215
The glitt'ring jav'lin pierc'd the tough bull-hide;
But pierc'd not thro': Unfaithful to his hand,
The point broke short, and sparkled in the sand.
The *Trojan* Warriour, touch'd with timely fear,
On the rais'd orb to distance bore the spear: 220
The *Greek* retreating mourn'd his frustrate blow,
And curs'd the treach'rous lance that spar'd a foe;
Then to the ships with surly speed he went,
To seek a surer jav'lin in his tent.

225   Meanwhile with rising rage the battel glows,
       The tumult thickens, and the clamour grows.
       By *Teucer*'s arm the warlike *Imbrius* bleeds,
       The son of *Mentor*, rich in gen'rous steeds.
       E're yet to *Troy* the sons of *Greece* were led,
230   In fair *Pedæus*' verdant pastures bred,
       The youth had dwelt; remote from war's alarms,
       And bless'd in bright *Medesicaste*'s arms:
       (This nymph, the fruit of *Priam*'s ravish'd joy,
       Ally'd the warriour to the house of *Troy*.)
235   To *Troy*, when glory call'd his arms, he came,
       And match'd the bravest of her chiefs in fame:
       With *Priam*'s sons, a guardian of the throne,
       He liv'd, belov'd and honour'd as his own.
       Him *Teucer* pierc'd between the throat and ear;
240   He groans beneath the *Telamonian* spear.
       As from some far-seen mountain's airy crown,
       Subdu'd by steel, a tall ash tumbles down,
       And foils its verdant tresses on the ground:
       So falls the youth; his arms the fall resound.
245   Then *Teucer* rushing to despoil the dead,
       From *Hector*'s hand a shining jav'lin fled:
       He saw, and shun'd the death; the forceful dart
       Sung on, and pierc'd *Amphimachus* his heart,
       Cteatus' son, of *Neptune*'s forceful line;
250   Vain was his courage, and his race divine!
       Prostrate he falls; his clanging arms resound,
       And his broad buckler thunders on the ground.
       To seize his beamy helm the victor flies,
       And just had fastned on the dazling prize,
255   When *Ajax*' manly arm a jav'lin flung;
       Full on the shield's round boss the weapon rung;
       He felt the shock, nor more was doom'd to feel,
       Secure in mail, and sheath'd in shining steel.
       Repuls'd he yields; the victor *Greeks* obtain
260   The spoils contested, and bear off the slain.
       Between the leaders of th' *Athenian* line,
       (*Stichius* the brave, *Menestheus* the divine,)
       Deplor'd *Amphimachus*, sad object! lies;
       Imbrius remains the fierce *Ajaces*' prize.

As two grim lions bear across the lawn,   265
Snatch'd from devouring hounds, a slaughter'd fawn,
In their fell jaws high-lifting thro' the wood,
And sprinkling all the shrubs with drops of blood;
So these the chief: Great *Ajax* from the dead
Strips his bright arms, *Oïleus* lops his head: 270
Toss'd like a ball, and whirl'd in air away,
At *Hector*'s feet the goary visage lay.

    The God of Ocean, fir'd with stern disdain,
And pierc'd with sorrow for his *grandson slain,
Inspires the *Grecian* hearts, confirms their hands.   275
And breathes destruction to the *Trojan* bands.
Swift as a whirlwind rushing to the fleet,
He finds the lance-fam'd *Idomen* of *Crete*;
His pensive brow the gen'rous care exprest
With which a wounded soldier touch'd his breast,   280
Whom in the chance of war a jav'lin tore,
And his sad comrades from the battel bore;
Him to the Surgeons of the camp he sent;
That office paid, he issu'd from his tent,
Fierce for the fight: To him the God begun,   285
In *Thoas*' voice, *Andræmon*'s valiant son,
Who rul'd where *Calydon*'s white rocks arise,
And *Pleuron*'s chalky cliffs emblaze the skies.
    Where's now th' imperious vaunt, the daring boast
Of *Greece* victorious, and proud *Ilion* lost?   290

    To whom the King. On *Greece* no blame be thrown,
Arms are her trade, and war is all her own.
Her hardy heroes from the well-fought plains
Nor fear with-holds, nor shameful sloth detains.
'Tis Heav'n, alas! and *Jove*'s all-pow'rful doom,   295
That far, far distant from our native home
Wills us to fall, inglorious! Oh my friend!
Once foremost in the fight, still prone to lend
Or arms, or counsels; now perform thy best,
And what thou canst not singly, urge the rest.   300

    Thus he; and thus the God, whose force can make
The solid globe's eternal basis shake.

Amphimachus.

Ah! never may he see his native land,
But feed the vulturs on this hateful strand,
305 Who seeks ignobly in his ships to stay,
Nor dares to combate on this signal day!
For this, behold! in horrid arms I shine,
And urge thy soul to rival acts with mine:
Together let us battel on the plain;
310 Two, not the worst; nor ev'n this succour vain.
Not vain the weakest, if their force unite;
But ours, the bravest have confess'd in fight.

This said, he rushes where the combate burns;
Swift to his tent the *Cretan* King returns.
315 From thence, two jav'lins glitt'ring in his hand,
And clad in arms that lighten'd all the strand,
Fierce on the foe th' impetuous hero drove;
Like light'ning bursting from the arm of *Jove*,
Which to pale man the wrath of heav'n declares,
320 Or terrifies th' offending world with wars;
In streamy sparkles, kindling all the skies,
From pole to pole the trail of glory flies.
Thus his bright armour o'er the dazled throng
Gleam'd dreadful, as the Monarch flash'd along.
325 Him, near his tent, *Meriones* attends;
Whom thus he questions: Ever best of friends!
O say, in ev'ry art of battel skill'd,
What holds thy courage from so brave a field?
On some important message art thou bound,
330 Or bleeds my friend by some unhappy wound?
Inglorious here, my soul abhors to stay,
And glows with prospects of th' approaching day.

O Prince! (*Meriones* replies) whose care
Leads forth th' embattel'd sons of *Crete* to war;
335 *This* speaks my grief; this headless lance I wield;
The rest lies rooted in a *Trojan* shield.

To whom the *Cretan*: Enter, and receive
The wanted weapons; those my tent can give.
Spears I have store, (and *Trojan* lances all)
340 That shed a lustre round th' illumin'd wall.
Tho' I, disdainful of the distant war,
Nor trust the dart, or aim th' uncertain spear,

Yet hand to hand I fight, and spoil the slain;
And thence these trophies and these arms I gain.
Enter, and see on heaps the helmets roll'd,   345
And high-hung spears, and shields that flame with gold.

    Nor vain (said *Merion*) are our martial toils;
We too can boast of no ignoble spoils.
But those my ship contains, whence distant far,
I fight conspicuous in the van of war.   350
What need I more? If any *Greek* there be
Who knows not *Merion*, I appeal to thee.

    To this, *Idomeneus*. The fields of fight
Have prov'd thy valour and unconquer'd might;
And were some ambush for the foes design'd,   355
Ev'n there, thy courage would not lag behind.
In that sharp service, singled from the rest,
The fear of each, or valour, stands confest.
No force, no firmness, the pale coward shows;
He shifts his place, his colour comes and goes;   360
A dropping sweat creeps cold on ev'ry part;
Against his bosom beats his quiv'ring heart;
Terrour and death in his wild eye-balls stare;
With chatt'ring teeth he stands, and stiff'ning hair,
And looks a bloodless image of despair!   365
Not so the brave – still dauntless, still the same,
Unchang'd his colour, and unmov'd his frame;
Compos'd his thought, determin'd is his eye,
And fix'd his soul, to conquer or to die:
If ought disturb the tenour of his breast,   370
'Tis but the wish to strike before the rest.

    In such assays thy blameless worth is known,
And ev'ry art of dang'rous war thy own.
By chance of fight whatever wounds you bore,
Those wounds were glorious all, and all before;   375
Such as may teach, 'twas still thy brave delight
T' oppose thy bosom where the foremost fight.
But why, like infants, cold to honour's charms,
Stand we to talk, when glory calls to arms?
Go – from my conquer'd spears, the choicest take,   380
And to their owners send them nobly back.

Swift as the word bold *Merion* snatch'd a spear,
And breathing slaughter, follow'd to the war.
So *Mars* armipotent invades the plain,
385   (The wide destroyer of the race of man)
Terrour, his best lov'd son, attends his course,
Arm'd with stern boldness, and enormous force;
The pride of haughty Warriours to confound,
And lay the strength of tyrants on the ground:
390   From *Thrace* they fly, call'd to the dire alarms
Of warring *Phlegyans*, and *Ephyrian* arms;
Invok'd by both, relentless they dispose
To these, glad conquest, murd'rous rout to those.
So march'd the leaders of the *Cretan* train,
395   And their bright arms shot horrour o'er the plain.
    Then first spake *Merion*: Shall we join the right,
Or combate in the centre of the fight?
Or to the left our wanted succour lend?
Hazard and fame all parts alike attend.
400   Not in the centre, (*Idomen* reply'd)
Our ablest chieftains the main battel guide;
Each godlike *Ajax* makes that post his care,
And gallant *Teucer* deals destruction there:
Skill'd, or with shafts to gall the distant field,
405   Or bear close battel on the sounding shield.
These can the rage of haughty *Hector* tame:
Safe in their arms, the navy fears no flame;
Till *Jove* himself descends, his bolts to shed,
And hurl the blazing Ruin at our Head.
410   Great must he be, of more than human birth,
Nor feed like mortals on the fruits of earth,
Him neither rocks can crush, nor steel can wound,
Whom *Ajax* fells not on th' ensanguin'd ground.
In standing fight he mates *Achilles'* force,
415   Excell'd alone in swiftness in the course.
Then to the left our ready arms apply,
And live with glory, or with glory die.
    He said; and *Merion* to th' appointed place,
Fierce as the God of battels, urg'd his pace.
420   Soon as the foe the shining chiefs beheld
Rush like a fiery torrent o'er the field,

Their force embody'd in a tide they pour;
The rising combate sounds along the shore.
As warring winds, in *Sirius'* sultry reign,
From diff'rent quarters sweep the sandy plain;   425
On ev'ry side the dusty whirlwinds rise,
And the dry fields are lifted to the skies:
Thus by despair, hope, rage, together driv'n,
Met the black hosts, and meeting, darken'd heav'n.
All dreadful glar'd the iron face of war,   430
Bristled with upright spears, that flash'd afar;
Dire was the gleam, of breast-plates, helms and shields,
And polish'd arms emblaz'd the flaming fields:
Tremendous scene! that gen'ral horror gave,
But touch'd with joy the bosoms of the brave.   435

    Saturn's great sons in fierce contention vy'd,
And crowds of heroes in their anger dy'd.
The sire of earth and heav'n, by *Thetis* won
To crown with glory *Peleus'* godlike son,
Will'd not destruction to the *Grecian* pow'rs,   440
But spar'd a while the destin'd *Trojan* tow'rs:
While *Neptune* rising from his azure main, ⎫
Warr'd on the King of heav'n with stern disdain, ⎬
And breath'd revenge, and fir'd the *Grecian* train, ⎭
Gods of one source, of one ethereal race,   445
Alike divine, and heav'n their native place;
But *Jove* the greater, first-born of the skies,
And more than men, or Gods, supremely wise.
For this, of *Jove*'s superiour might afraid,
Neptune in human form conceal'd his aid.   450
These pow'rs infold the *Greek* and *Trojan* train
In War and Discord's adamantine chain;
Indissolubly strong, the fatal tye
Is stretch'd on both, and close-compell'd they die.

    Dreadful in arms, and grown in combats grey,   455
The bold *Idomeneus* controuls the day.
First by his hand *Othryoneus* was slain,
Swell'd with false hopes, with mad ambition vain!
Call'd by the voice of war to martial fame,
From high *Cabesus'* distant walls he came;   460

Cassandra's love he sought with boasts of pow'r,
And promis'd conquest was the proffer'd dow'r.
The King consented, by his Vaunts abus'd;
The King consented, but the fates refus'd.
465 Proud of himself, and of th' imagin'd bride,
The field he measur'd with a larger stride.
Him, as he stalk'd, the *Cretan* jav'lin found;
Vain was his breast-plate to repel the wound:
His dream of glory lost, he plung'd to hell;
470 The plains resounded as the boaster fell.

The great *Idomeneus* bestrides the dead:
And thus (he cries) behold thy promise sped!
Such is the help thy arms to *Ilion* bring,
And such the contract of the *Phrygian* King!
475 Our offers now, illustrious Prince! receive;
For such an aid what will not *Argos* give?
To conquer *Troy*, with ours thy forces join,
And count *Atrides'* fairest daughter thine.
Meantime, on farther methods to advise,
480 Come, follow to the fleet thy new allies;
There hear what *Greece* has on her part to say.
He spoke, and dragg'd the goary corse away.

This *Asius* view'd, unable to contain,
Before his chariot warring on the plain;
485 (His valu'd Coursers, to his squire consign'd,
Impatient panted on his neck behind)
To vengeance rising with a sudden spring,
He hop'd the conquest of the *Cretan* King.
The wary *Cretan*, as his foe drew near,
490 Full on his throat discharg'd the forceful spear:
Beneath the chin the point was seen to glide,
And glitter'd, extant at the farther side.
As when the mountain-oak, or poplar tall,
Or Pine, fit mast for some great Admiral,
495 Groans to the oft-heav'd axe, with many a wound,
Then spreads a length of ruin o'er the ground.
So sunk proud *Asius* in that dreadful day,
And stretch'd before his much-lov'd coursers lay.
He grinds the dust distain'd with streaming gore,
500 And, fierce in death, lies foaming on the shore.

Depriv'd of motion, stiff with stupid fear,
Stands all aghast his trembling charioteer,
Nor shuns the foe, nor turns the steeds away,
But falls transfix'd, an unresisting prey:
Pierc'd by *Antilochus*, he pants beneath   505
The stately car, and labours out his breath.
Thus *Asius'* steeds (their mighty master gone)
Remain the prize of *Nestor's* youthful son.

  Stabb'd at the sight, *Deïphobus* drew nigh,
And made, with force, the vengeful weapon fly.   510
The *Cretan* saw; and stooping, caus'd to glance
From his slope shield, the disappointed lance.
Beneath the spacious targe (a blazing round,
Thick with bull-hides, and brazen orbits bound,
On his rais'd arm by two strong braces stay'd)   515
He lay collected, in defensive Shade.
O'er his safe head the jav'lin idly sung,
And on the tinkling verge more faintly rung.
Ev'n then, the spear the vig'rous arm confest,
And pierc'd, obliquely, King *Hypsenor's* breast: 520
Warm'd in his liver, to the ground it bore
The chief, his people's guardian now no more!

  Not unattended (the proud *Trojan* cries)
Nor unreveng'd, lamented *Asius* lies:
For thee, tho' hell's black portals stand display'd,   525
This mate shall joy thy melancholy shade.

  Heart-piercing anguish, at this haughty boast,
Touch'd ev'ry *Greek*, but *Nestor's* son the most.
Griev'd as he was, his pious arms attend,
And his broad buckler shields his slaughter'd friend;   530
Till sad *Mecistheus* and *Alastor* bore
His honour'd body to the tented shore.

  Nor yet from fight *Idomeneus* withdraws;
Resolv'd to perish in his country's cause,
Or find some foe, whom heav'n and he shall doom   535
To wail his fate in death's eternal gloom.
He sees *Alcathous* in the front aspire:
Great *Æsyetes* was the hero's sire;
His spouse *Hippodamè*, divinely fair,
Anchises' eldest hope, and darling care;   540

Who charm'd her parent's and her husband's heart,
With beauty, sense, and ev'ry work or art:
He once, of *Ilion*'s youth, the loveliest boy,
The fairest she, of all the fair of *Troy.*
545 By *Neptune* now the hapless hero dies,
Who covers with a cloud those beauteous eyes,
And fetters ev'ry limb: yet bent to meet
His fate he stands; nor shuns the lance of *Crete.*
Fixt as some column, or deep-rooted oak,
550 (While the winds sleep) his breast receiv'd the stroke.
Before the pond'rous stroke his corselet yields,
Long us'd to ward the death in fighting fields.
The riven armour sends a jarring sound:
His lab'ring heart, heaves, with so strong a bound,
555 The long lance shakes, and vibrates in the wound:
Fast-flowing from its source, as prone he lay,
Life's purple tide, impetuous, gush'd away.

   Then *Idomen*, insulting o'er the slain;
Behold, *Deïphobus!* nor vaunt in vain.
560 See! on one *Greek* three *Trojan* ghosts attend,
This, my third victim, to the shades I send.
Approaching now, thy boasted might approve,
And try the prowess of the seed of *Jove.*
From *Jove*, enamour'd on a mortal dame,
565 Great *Minos*, guardian of his country, came:
Deucalion, blameless Prince! was *Minos'* heir;
His first-born I, the third from *Jupiter*:
O'er spacious *Crete*, and her bold sons I reign,
And thence my ships transport me thro' the main;
570 Lord of a host, o'er all my host I shine,
A scourge to thee, thy father, and thy line.

   The *Trojan* heard; uncertain, or to meet
Alone, with vent'rous arms, the King of *Crete*;
Or seek auxiliar force; at length decreed
575 To call some hero to partake the deed.
Forthwith *Æneas* rises to his thought;
For him, in *Troy*'s remotest lines, he sought,
Where he, incens'd at partial *Priam*, stands,
And sees superior posts in meaner hands.

To him, ambitious of so great an aid, 580
The bold *Deïphobus* approach'd, and said.
    Now, *Trojan* Prince, employ thy pious arms,
If e'er thy bosom felt fair honour's charms.
Alcathous dies, thy brother and thy friend!
Come, and the warriour's lov'd remains defend. 585
Beneath his cares thy early youth was train'd,
One table fed you, and one roof contain'd.
This deed to fierce *Idomeneus* we owe;
Haste, and revenge it on th' insulting foe.
    Æneas heard, and for a space resign'd 590
To tender pity all his manly mind;
Then rising in his rage, he burns to fight:
The *Greek* awaits him, with collected might.
As the fell boar on some rough mountain's head,
Arm'd with wild terrours, and to slaughter bred, 595
When the loud rusticks rise, and shout from far,
Attends the tumult, and expects the war;
O'er his bent back the bristly horrours rise,
Fires stream in light'ning from his sanguin eyes,
His foaming tusks both dogs and men engage, 600
But most his hunters rouze his mighty rage.
So stood *Idomeneus*, his jav'lin shook,
And met the *Trojan* with a low'ring look.
Antilochus, *Deïpyrus* were near,
The youthful offspring of the God of war, 605
Merion, and *Aphareus*, in field renown'd:
To these the warriour sent his Voice around.
Fellows in arms! your timely aid unite;
Lo, great *Æneas* rushes to the fight:
Sprung from a God, and more than mortal bold; 610
He fresh in youth, and I in arms grown old.
Else should this hand, this hour, decide the strife,
The great dispute, of glory, or of life.
    He spoke, and all as with one soul obey'd;
Their lifted bucklers cast a dreadful shade 615
Around the chief. *Æneas* too demands
Th' assisting forces of his native bands:
Paris, *Deïphobus*, *Agenor* join;
(Co-aids and captains of the *Trojan* line.)

620   In order follow all th' embody'd train;
      Like *Ida*'s flocks proceeding o'er the plain;
      Before his fleecy care, erect and bold,
      Stalks the proud ram, the father of the fold:
      With joy the swain surveys them, as he leads
625   To the cool fountains, thro' the well-known meads.
      So joys *Æneas*, as his native band
      Moves on in rank, and stretches o'er the land.
          Round dead *Alcathous* now the battel rose;
      On ev'ry side the steely circle grows;
630   Now batter'd breast-plates and hack'd helmets ring,
      And o'er their heads unheeded jav'lins sing.
      Above the rest, two tow'ring chiefs appear,
      There great *Idomeneus*, *Æneas* here.
      Like Gods of war, dispensing fate, they stood,
635   And burn'd to drench the ground with mutual blood.
      The *Trojan* weapon whizz'd along in air;
      The *Cretan* saw, and shun'd the brazen spear:
      Sent from an arm so strong, the missive wood
      Stuck deep in earth, and quiver'd where it stood.
      But *Oenomas* receiv'd the *Cretan*'s stroke,
      The forceful spear his hollow corselet broke,
      It ripp'd his belly with a ghastly wound,
      And roll'd the smoaking entrails to the ground.
      Stretch'd on the plain, he sobs away his breath,
645   And furious, grasps the bloody dust in death.
      The victor from his breast the weapon tears;
      (His spoils he could not, for the show'r of spears.)
      Tho' now unfit an active war to wage,
      Heavy with cumb'rous arms, stiff with cold age,
650   His listless limbs unable for the course;
      In standing fight he yet maintains his force:
      Till faint with labour, and by foes repell'd,
      His tir'd, slow steps, he drags from off the field.
          Deiphobus beheld him as he past,
655   And, fir'd with hate, a parting jav'lin cast:
      The jav'lin err'd, but held its course along,
      And pierc'd *Ascalaphus*, the brave and young:
      The son of *Mars* fell gasping on the ground,
      And gnash'd the dust all bloody with his wound.

Nor knew the furious father of his fall;   660
High-thron'd amidst the great *Olympian* hall,
On golden clouds th' immortal synod sate;
Detain'd from bloody war by *Jove* and *Fate*.

Now, where in dust the breathless hero lay,
For slain *Ascalaphus* commenc'd the fray.   665
Deiphobus to seize his helmet flies,
And from his temples rends the glitt'ring prize;
Valiant as *Mars*, *Meriones* drew near,
And on his loaded arm discharg'd his spear:
He drops the weight, disabled with the pain;   670
The hollow helmet rings against the plain.
Swift as a vultur leaping on his prey,
From his torn arm the *Grecian* rent away
The reeking jav'lin, and rejoin'd his friends.
His wounded brother good *Polites* tends;   675
Around his waste his pious arms he threw,
And from the rage of combate gently drew:
Him his swift coursers, on his splendid car
Rapt from the less'ning thunder of the war;
To *Troy* they drove him, groaning from the shore,   680
And sprinkling, as he past, the sands with gore.

Meanwhile fresh slaughter bathes the sanguin ground,
Heaps fall on heaps, and heav'n and earth resound.
Bold *Aphareus* by great *Æneas* bled;
As tow'rd the chief he turn'd his daring head,   685
He pierc'd his throat; the bending head deprest
Beneath his helmet, nods upon his breast;
His shield revers'd o'er the fall'n warriour lies;
And everlasting slumber seals his eyes.
Antilochus, as *Thoön* turn'd him round,   690
Transpierc'd his back with a dishonest wound:
The hollow vein that to the neck extends
Along the chine, his eager jav'lin rends:
Supine he falls, and to his social Train
Spreads his imploring arms, but spreads in vain.   695
Th' exulting victor leaping where he lay,
From his broad shoulders tore the spoils away;
His time observ'd; for clos'd by foes around,
On all sides thick, the peals of arms resound.

700   His shield emboss'd the ringing storm sustains,
       But he impervious and untouch'd remains.
       (Great *Neptune*'s care preserv'd from hostile rage
       This youth, the joy of *Nestor*'s glorious age)
       In arms intrepid, with the first he fought,
705   Fac'd ev'ry foe, and ev'ry danger sought;
       His winged lance, resistless as the wind,
       Obeys each motion of the master's mind,
       Restless it flies, impatient to be free,
       And meditates the distant enemy.
710   The Son of *Asius, Adamas*, drew near,
       And struck his target with the brazen spear,
       Fierce in his front: but *Neptune* wards the blow,
       And blunts the jav'lin of th' eluded foe.
       In the broad buckler half the weapon stood;
715   Splinter'd on earth flew half the broken wood.
       Disarm'd, he mingled in the *Trojan* crew;
       But *Merion*'s spear o'ertook him as he flew,
       Deep in the belly's rim an entrance found,
       Where sharp the pang, and mortal is the wound.
720   Bending he fell, and doubled to the ground,
       Lay panting. Thus an oxe, in fetters ty'd,
       While death's strong pangs distend his lab'ring side,
       His bulk enormous on the field displays;
       His heaving heart beats thick, as ebbing life decays.
725   The spear, the conqu'ror from his body drew,
       And death's dim shadows swam before his view.
       Next brave *Deipyrus* in dust was lay'd:
       King *Helenus* wav'd high the *Thracian* blade,
       And smote his temples, with an arm so strong,
730   The helm fell off, and roll'd amid the throng:
       There, for some luckier *Greek* it rests a prize,
       For dark in death the godlike owner lies!
       With raging grief great *Menelaus* burns,
       And fraught with vengeance, to the victor turns;
735   That shook the pond'rous lance, in act to throw,
       And this stood adverse with the bended bow:
       Full on his breast the *Trojan* arrow fell,
       But harmless bounded from the plated steel.

As on some ample barn's well-harden'd floor,
(The winds collected at each open door)   740
While the broad fan with force is whirl'd around,
Light leaps the golden grain, resulting from the ground:
So from the steel that guards *Atrides'* heart,
Repell'd to distance flies the bounding dart.

Atrides, watchful of th' unwary foe,   745
Pierc'd with his lance the hand that grasp'd the bow,
And nail'd it to the eugh: The wounded hand
Trail'd the long lance that mark'd with blood the sand.

But good *Agenor* gently from the wound   750
The spear sollicites, and the bandage bound;
A sling's soft wool, snatch'd from a soldier's side,
At once the tent and ligature supply'd.

  Behold! *Pisander*, urg'd by fate's decree,
Springs thro' the ranks to fall, and fall by thee,   755
Great *Menelaüs!* to enhance thy fame;
High-tow'ring in the front, the warriour came.
First the sharp lance was by *Atrides* thrown;
The lance far distant by the winds was blown.
Nor pierc'd *Pisander* thro' *Atrides'* shield;
Pisander's spear fell shiver'd on the field.   760
Not so discourag'd, to the future blind,
Vain dreams of conquest swell his haughty mind;
Dauntless he rushes where the *Spartan* lord
Like light'ning brandish'd his far-beaming sword.
His left arm high oppos'd the shining shield;   765
His right, beneath, the cover'd pole-axe held;
(An olive's cloudy grain the handle made,
Distinct with studs; and brazen was the blade)
This on the helm discharg'd a noble blow;
The plume dropp'd nodding to the plain below,   770
Shorn from the crest. *Atrides* wav'd his steel:
Deep thro' his front the weighty faulchion fell.
The crashing bones before its force gave way;
In dust and blood the groaning hero lay;
Forc'd from their ghastly orbs, and spouting gore,   775
The clotted eye-balls tumble on the shore.
The fierce *Atrides* spurn'd him as he bled,
Tore off his arms, and loud-exulting, said.

Thus, *Trojans*, thus, at length be taught to fear;
780 O race perfidious, who delight in war!
Already noble deeds ye have perform'd,
A Princess rap'd transcends a navy storm'd:
In such bold feats your impious might approve,
Without th' assistance, or the fear of *Jove.*
785 The violated rites, the ravish'd dame,
Our heroes slaughter'd, and our ships on flame;
Crimes heap'd on crimes, shall bend your glory down,
And whelm in ruins yon' flagitious town.
O thou, great Father! Lord of earth and skies,
790 Above the thought of man, supremely wise!
If from thy hand the fates of mortals flow,
From whence this favour to an impious foe?
A godless crew, abandon'd and unjust,
Still breathing rapine, violence, and lust!
795 The best of things beyond their measure, cloy;
Sleeps balmy blessing, love's endearing joy;
The feast, the dance; whate'er mankind desire,
Ev'n the sweet charms of sacred numbers tire.
But *Troy* for ever reaps a dire delight
800 In thirst of slaughter, and in lust of fight.
    This said, he seiz'd (while yet the carcass heav'd)
The bloody armour, which his train receiv'd:
Then sudden mix'd among the warring crew,
And the bold son of *Pylæmenes* slew.
805 *Harpalion* had thro' *Asia* travell'd far,
Following his martial father to the war;
Thro' filial love he left his native shore,
Never, ah never, to behold it more!
His unsuccessful spear he chanc'd to fling
810 Against the target of the *Spartan* King;
Thus of his lance disarm'd, from death he flies,
And turns around his apprehensive eyes.
Him, thro' the hip transpiercing as he fled,
The shaft of *Merion* mingled with the dead.
815 Beneath the bone the glancing point descends,
And driving down, the swelling bladder rends:
Sunk in his sad companion's arms he lay,
And in short pantings sobb'd his soul away;

(Like some vile worm extended on the ground)
While life's red torrent gush'd from out the wound.   820
    Him on his car the *Paphlagonian* train
In slow procession bore from off the plain.
The pensive father, father now no more!
Attends the mournful pomp along the shore,
And unavailing tears profusely shed,   825
And unreveng'd, deplor'd his offspring dead.
    Paris from far the moving sight beheld,
With pity soften'd, and with fury swell'd:
His honour'd host, a youth of matchless grace,
And lov'd of all the *Paphlagonian* race!   830
With his full strength he bent his angry bow,
And wing'd the feather'd vengeance at the foe.
A chief there was, the brave *Euchenor* nam'd,
For riches much, and more for virtue fam'd,
Who held his seat in *Corinth*'s stately town;   835
Polydus' son, a seer of old renown.
Oft' had the father told his early doom,
By arms abroad, or slow disease at home:
He climb'd his vessel, prodigal of breath,
And chose the certain, glorious path to death.   840
Beneath his ear the pointed arrow went;
The soul came issuing at the narrow vent:
His limbs, unnerv'd, drop useless on the ground,
And everlasting darkness shades him round.
    Nor knew great *Hector* how his legions yield,   845
(Wrapt in the cloud and tumult of the field)
Wide on the left the force of *Greece* commands,
And conquest hovers o'er th' *Achaian* bands:
With such a tide superiour virtue sway'd,
And *he that shakes the solid earth, gave aid.   850
But in the centre *Hector* fix'd remain'd,
Where first the gates were forc'd, and bulwarks gain'd;
There, on the margin of the hoary deep,
(Their naval station where th' *Ajaces* keep,
And where low walls confine the beating tides   855
Whose humble barrier scarce the foes divides;

*Neptune.

Where late in fight, both foot and horse engag'd,
And all the thunder of the battel rag'd)
There join'd, the whole *Bœotian* strength remains,
860 The proud *Ionians* with their sweeping trains,
Locrians and *Pthians*, and th' *Epœan* force;
But join'd, repel not *Hector*'s fiery course.
The Flow'r of *Athens*, *Stichius*, *Phidas* led,
Bias, and great *Menestheus* at their head.
865 *Meges* the strong th' *Epeian* bands controul'd,
And *Dracius* prudent, and *Amphion* bold;
The *Pthians Medon*, fam'd for martial might,
And brave *Podarces*, active in the fight.
This drew from *Phylacus* his noble line;
870 *Iphyclus*' son: and that (*Oileus*) thine:
(Young *Ajax* brother, by a stol'n embrace;
He dwelt far distant from his native place,
By his fierce stepdame from his father's reign
Expell'd and exil'd, for her brother slain.)
875 These rule the *Pthians*, and their arms employ
Mixt with *Bœotians*, on the shores of *Troy*.
    Now side by side, with like unweary'd care,
Each *Ajax* labour'd thro' the field of war.
So when two lordly bulls, with equal toil,
880 Force the bright plowshare thro' the fallow soil,
Join'd to one yoke, the stubborn earth they tear,
And trace large furrows with the shining share;
O'er their huge limbs the foam descends in snow,
And streams of sweat down their sow'r foreheads flow.
885 A train of heroes follow'd thro' the field,
Who bore by turns great *Ajax*' sev'nfold shield;
Whene'er he breath'd, remissive of his might,
Tir'd with th' incessant slaughters of the fight.
No following troops his brave associate grace,
890 In close engagement an unpractised race:
The *Locrian* squadrons nor the jav'lin wield,
Nor bear the helm, nor lift the moony shield;
But skill'd from far the flying shaft to wing,
Or whirl the sounding pebble from the sling,
895 Dext'rous with these they aim a certain wound,
Or fell the distant warriour to the ground.

Thus in the van, the *Telamonian* train
Throng'd in bright arms, a pressing fight maintain;
Far in the rear the *Locrian* archers lie,
Whose stones and arrows intercept the sky,   900
The mingled tempest on the foes they pour;
Troy's scatt'ring orders open to the show'r.

 Now had the *Greeks* eternal fame acquir'd,
And the gall'd *Ilians* to their walls retir'd;
But sage *Polydamas*, discreetly brave,   905
Address'd great *Hector*, and this counsel gave.

 Tho' great in all, thou seem'st averse to lend
Impartial audience to a faithful friend:
To Gods and men thy matchless worth is known,
And ev'ry art of glorious war thy own;   910
But in cool thought and counsel to excel,
How widely differs this from warring well?
Content with what the bounteous Gods have giv'n,
Seek not alone t' engross the gifts of heav'n.
To some the pow'rs of bloody war belong,   915
To some, sweet music, and the charm of song;
To few, and wond'rous few, has *Jove* assign'd
A wise, extensive, all-consid'ring mind;
Their guardians these, the nations round confess,
And towns and empires for their safety bless.   920
If heav'n have lodg'd this virtue in my breast,
Attend, O *Hector*, what I judge the best.
See, as thou mov'st, on dangers dangers spread,
And war's whole fury burns around thy head.
Behold! distress'd within yon' hostile wall,   925
How many *Trojans* yield, disperse, or fall?
What troops, out-number'd, scarce the war maintain?
And what brave heroes at the ships lie slain?
Here cease thy fury; and the Chiefs and Kings
Convok'd to council, weigh the sum of things.   930
Whether (the Gods succeeding our desires)
To yon' tall ships to bear the *Trojan* fires;
Or quit the fleet, and pass unhurt away,
Contented with the conquest of the day.
I fear, I fear, lest *Greece* (not yet undone)   935
Pay the large debt of last revolving sun;

Achilles, great *Achilles*, yet remains
On yonder decks, and yet o'erlooks the plains!
    The counsel pleas'd; and *Hector*, with a bound,
940 Leap'd from his chariot on the trembling ground;
Swift as he leap'd, his clanging arms resound.
To guard this post (he cry'd) thy art employ,
And here detain the scatter'd youth of *Troy*:
Where yonder heroes faint, I bend my way,
945 And hasten back to end the doubtful Day.
    This said; the tow'ring Chief prepares to go,
Shakes his white plumes that to the breezes flow,
And seems a moving mountain topt with snow.
Thro' all his host, inspiring force, he flies,
950 And bids anew the martial thunder rise.
To *Panthus'* son, at *Hector's* high command,
Haste the bold leaders of the *Trojan* band:
But round the battlements, and round the plain,
For many a chief he look'd, but look'd in vain;
955 *Deïphobus*, nor *Helenus* the seer,
Nor *Asius'* son, nor *Asius'* self appear.
For these were pierc'd with many a ghastly wound,
Some cold in death, some groaning on the ground;
Some low in dust (a mournful object) lay,
960 High on the wall some breath'd their souls away.
    Far on the left, amid the throng he found
(Cheering the troops, and dealing deaths around)
The graceful *Paris*; whom, with fury mov'd,
Opprobrious, thus, th' impatient chief reprov'd.
965   Ill-fated *Paris!* Slave to womankind,
As smooth of face as fraudulent of mind!
Where is *Deïphobus*, where *Asius* gone?
The godlike father, and th' intrepid son?
The force of *Helenus*, dispensing fate,
970 And great *Othryoneus*, so fear'd of late?
Black fate hangs o'er thee from th' avenging Gods,
Imperial *Troy* from her foundations nods;
Whelm'd in thy country's ruins shalt thou fall,
And one devouring vengeance swallow all.
975   When *Paris* thus: My brother and my friend,
Thy warm impatience makes thy tongue offend.

In other battels I deserv'd thy blame,
Tho' then not deedless, nor unknown to fame:
But since yon' rampart by thy arms lay low,
I scatter'd slaughter from my fatal bow.   980
The chiefs you seek on yonder shore lie slain;
Of all those heroes, two alone remain;
Deïphobus, and *Helenus* the seer:
Each now disabled by a hostile spear.
Go then, successful, where thy soul inspires;   985
This heart and hand shall second all thy fires:
What with this arm I can, prepare to know,
Till death for death be paid, and blow for blow.
But 'tis not ours, with forces not our own
To combate; strength is of the Gods alone.   990
    These words the hero's angry mind asswage:
Then fierce they mingle where the thickest rage.
Around *Polydamas*, distain'd with blood,
Cebrion, *Phalces*, stern *Orthæus* stood,
Palmus, with *Polypætes* the divine,   995
And two bold brothers of *Hippotion*'s line:
(Who reach'd fair *Ilion*, from *Ascania* far,
The former day; the next, engag'd in war.)
As when from gloomy clouds a whirlwind springs,
That bears *Jove*'s thunder on its dreadful wings,   1000
Wide o'er the blasted fields the tempest sweeps,
Then gather'd, settles on the hoary deeps;
Th' afflicted deeps, tumultuous, mix and roar;
The waves behind impel the waves before,
Wide-rolling, foaming high, and tumbling to the
        shore.   1005
Thus rank on rank the thick battalions throng,
Chief urg'd on chief, and man drove man along:
Far o'er the plains, in dreadful order bright,
The brazen arms reflect a beamy light.
Full in the blazing van great *Hector* shin'd,   1010
Like *Mars* commission'd to confound mankind.
Before him flaming, his enormous shield
Like the broad sun, illumin'd all the field:
His nodding helm emits a streamy ray;
His piercing eyes thro' all the battel stray,   1005

And, while beneath his targe he flash'd along,
Shot terrours round, that wither'd ev'n the strong.
   Thus stalk'd he, dreadful; death was in his Look;
Whole nations fear'd: but not an *Argive* shook.
1020   The tow'ring *Ajax*, with an ample stride,
Advanc'd the first, and thus the chief defy'd.
   Hector! come on, thy empty threats forbear:
'Tis not thy arm, 'tis thund'ring *Jove* we fear:
The skill of war to us not idly giv'n,
1025   Lo! *Greece* is humbled not by *Troy*, but heav'n.
Vain are the hopes that haughty mind imparts,
To force our fleet: The *Greeks* have hands, and hearts.
Long e'er in flames our lofty navy fall,
Your boasted city and your god-built wall
1030   Shall sink beneath us, smoking on the ground;
And spread a long, unmeasur'd ruin round.
The time shall come, when chas'd along the plain
Ev'n thou shalt call on *Jove*, and call in vain;
Ev'n thou shalt wish, to aid thy desp'rate course,
1035   The wings of falcons for thy flying horse;
Shalt run, forgetful of a warriour's fame,
While clouds of friendly dust conceal thy shame.
   As thus he spoke, behold, in open view,
On sounding wings a dexter eagle flew.
1040   To *Jove*'s glad omen all the *Grecians* rise,
And hail, with shouts, his progress thro' the skies:
Far-echoing clamours bound from side to side;
They ceas'd; and thus the Chief of *Troy* reply'd.
   From whence this menace, this insulting strain?
1045   Enormous boaster! doom'd to vaunt in vain.
So may the Gods on *Hector* life bestow,
(Not that short life which mortals lead below,
But such as those of *Jove*'s high lineage born,
The blue-ey'd Maid, or he that gilds the morn.)
1050   As this decisive day shall end the fame
Of *Greece*, and *Argos* be no more a name.
And thou, imperious! if thy madness wait
The lance of *Hector*, thou shalt meet thy fate:
That giant-corse, extended on the shore,
1055   Shall largely feast the fowls with fat and gore.

He said, and like a lion stalk'd along:
With shouts incessant earth and ocean rung,
Sent from his foll'wing host: The *Grecian* train
With answ'ring thunders fill'd the echoing plain;
A shout that tore heav'ns concave, and above   1060
Shook the fix'd splendors of the throne of *Jove*.

OBSERVATIONS
ON THE
THIRTEENTH BOOK

The epigraph on the frontispiece of Volume IV (Books 13–16) consists of the following lines:

> *Men' moveat cimex Pantilius? aut cruciet quod*
> *Vellicat absentem Demetrius? aut quod ineptus*
> *Fannius Hermogenis lædat conviva Tigelli?*
> *Plotius, & Varius, Mæcenas, Vergiliusque,*
> *Valgius, & probet hæc Octavius optimus. –*   HOR.

[Shall that bug Pantilius disturb my composure? or shall I be tormented because Demetrius criticizes me behind my back? or because that absurd Fannius, who feasts upon the hospitality of Tigellius, tries to harm me? Let but Plotius and Varius, Mæcenas and Virgil, and Vulgius, and the unexampled Octavius approve of my writing
(Horace, *Sermones*, I.10. 78–83)]

5. *Then turn'd to* Thracia *from the field of fight.*] One might fancy at the first reading of this passage, that *Homer* here turn'd aside from the main view of his Poem, in a vain ostentation of learning, to amuse himself with a foreign and unnecessary description of the manners and customs of these nations. But we shall find, upon better consideration, that *Jupiter's* turning aside his eyes was necessary to the conduct of the work, as it gives Opportunity to *Neptune* to assist the *Greeks*, and thereby causes all the adventures of this book. Madam *Dacier* is too refining on this occasion; when she would have it, that *Jupiter's averting his eyes* signifies his abandoning the *Trojans*; in the same manner, as the scripture represents the Almighty *turning his face* from those whom he deserts. But at this rate *Jupiter* turning his eyes from the battel, must desert both the *Trojans* and the *Greeks*; and it is evident from the context, that *Jupiter* intended nothing less than to let the *Trojans* suffer.

9. *And where the far-fam'd* Hippemolgian *strays.*] There is much dispute among the Criticks, which are the proper names, and which the epithets, in these verses: some making ἀγαυοί the Epithet to ἱππημολγοί, others ἱππημολγοί the epithet to ἀγαυοί; and ἄβιοι, which by the common interpreters is thought only an epithet, is by *Strabo* and *Ammianus Marcellinus* made the proper name of a people. In this diversity of opinions, I have chosen that which I thought would make the best figure in poetry. It is a beautiful and moral imagination, to suppose that the long life of the *Hippemolgians* was an effect of their simple diet, and a reward of their justice: And that the Supreme Being, displeased at the continued scenes of human violence and dissension, as it were recreated his eyes in contemplating the simplicity of these people.

It is observable that the same custom of living on milk is preserv'd to this day by the *Tartars*, who inhabit the same country.

27.　　*At* Jove *incens'd, with grief and fury flung,*
　　　Prone down the rocky steep he rush'd. –

Mons. *de la Motte* has play'd the critick upon this passage a little unadvisedly. '*Neptune*, says he, is impatient to assist the *Greeks. Homer* tells us that this God goes first to seek his chariot in a certain place; next he arrives at another place nearer the camp; there he takes off his horses, and then he locks them fast to secure them at his return. The detail of so many particularities no way suits the majesty of a God, or the impatience in which he is described.' Another *French* writer makes answer, that however impatient *Neptune* is represented to be, none of the Gods ever go to the war without their arms; and the arms, chariot and horses of *Neptune* were at *Ægæ*. He makes but four steps to get thither; so that what M. *de la Motte* calls being slow, is swiftness itself. The God puts on his arms, mounts his chariot, and departs: nothing is more rapid than his course; he flies over the waters: The verses of *Homer* in that place run swifter than the God himself. It is sufficient to have ears, to perceive the rapidity of *Neptune*'s chariot in the very sound of those three lines, each of which is entirely compos'd of dactyles, excepting that one spondee which must necessarily terminate the verse.

Βῆ δ' ἐλάαν ἐπὶ κύματ', ἄταλλε δὲ κήτε' ὑπ' αὐτοῦ
Γηθοσύνη δὲ θάλασσα διίστατο, τοὶ δὲ πέτοντο
Ῥίμφα μάλ', οὐδ' ὑπένερθε διαίνετο χάλκεος ἄξων.

29.   – *The lofty mountains nod,*
        The forests shake! earth trembled as he trod,
        And felt the footsteps of th' immortal God.]

Longinus confesses himself wonderfully struck with the sublimity of this passage. That Critick, after having blamed the defects with which *Homer* draws the manners of his Gods, adds, that he has much better succeeded in describing their figure and persons. He owns that he often paints a God such as he is, in all his majesty and grandeur, and without any mixture of mean and terrestrial images; of which he produces this passage as a remarkable instance, and one that had challenged the admiration of all antiquity.

The book of *Psalms* affords us a description of the like sublime manner of imagery, which is parallel to this. *O God, when thou wentest forth before thy people, when thou didst march through the wilderness, the earth shook, the heavens dropped at the presence of God, even* Sinai *itself was moved at the presence of God, the God of* Israel. Ps. 68.

32.   – *Three ample strides he took.*] This is a very grand imagination, and equals, if not transcends, what he has feign'd before of the passage of this God. We are told, that at four steps he reach'd *Ægæ*, which (supposing it meant of the town of that name in *Eubœa*, which lay the nighest to *Thrace*) is hardly less than a degree at each step. One may, from a view of the map, imagine him striding from promontory to promontory, his first step on mount *Athos*, his second on *Pallene*, his third upon *Pelion*, and his fourth in *Eubœa*. *Dacier* is not to be forgiven for omitting this miraculous circumstance, which so perfectly agrees with the marvellous air of the whole passage, and without which the sublime image of *Homer* is not compleat.

33.   – *The distant Ægæ shook.*] There were three places of this name, which were all sacred to *Neptune*; an island in the *Ægean* sea mentioned by *Nicostratus*, a town in *Peloponnesus*, and another in *Eubœa*. *Homer* is supposed in this passage to speak of the last; but the question is put, why *Neptune* who stood upon a hill in *Samothrace*, instead of going on the left to *Troy*, turns to the right, and takes a way contrary to that

which leads to the army? This difficulty is ingeniously solv'd by the old Scholiast; who says, that *Jupiter* being now on mount *Ida*, with his eyes turn'd towards *Thrace*, *Neptune* could not take the direct way from *Samo-thrace* to *Troy* without being discover'd by him, and therefore fetches this compass to conceal himself. *Eustathius* is contented to say, that the Poet made *Neptune* go so far about, for the opportunity of those fine descriptions of the palace, the chariot, and the passage of this God.

43. *Th' enormous monsters rolling o'er the deep.*] This description of *Neptune* rises upon us; his passage by water is yet more pompous than that by land. The God driving thro' the seas, the whales acknowledging him, and the waves rejoicing and making way for their monarch, are full of that *marvellous* so natural to the imagination of our author. And I cannot but think the verses of *Virgil* in the fifth *Æneid* are short of his original:

> *Cæruleo per summa levis volat æquora curru:*
> *Subsidunt undæ, tumidumque; sub axe tonanti*
> *Sternitur æquor aquis: fugiunt vasto æthere nimbi.*
> *Tum variæ comitum facies, immania cete,* &c.

> [High on the waves his azure car he guides,
> Its axles thunder, and the sea subsides;
> And the smooth ocean rowls her silent tides.
> The tempests fly before their father's face,
> Trains of inferiour Gods his triumph grace;
> And monster whales before their master play.]

I fancy *Scaliger* himself was sensible of this, by his passing in silence a passage which lay so obvious to comparison.

79.   – *This part o'erthrown,*
         Our strength were vain; I dread for you alone.]

What address, and at the same time, what strength is there in these words? *Neptune* tells the two *Ajaces*, that he is only afraid for their post, and that the *Greeks* will perish by that gate, since it is *Hector* who assaults it: at every other quarter, the *Trojans* will be repuls'd. It may therefore be properly said, that the *Ajaces* only are vanquished, and that their defeat draws destruction upon all the *Greeks.* I don't think that any thing better could be invented to animate couragious men, and make them attempt even impossibilities.   *Dacier.*

83. *If yet some heav'nly pow'r, &c.*] Here *Neptune*, considering how the *Greeks* were discouraged by the knowledge that *Jupiter* assisted *Hector*, insinuates, that notwithstanding *Hector*'s confidence in that assistance, yet the power of some other God might countervail it on their part; wherein he alludes to his own aiding them, and seems not to doubt his ability of contesting the point with *Jove* himself. 'Tis with the same confidence he afterwards speaks to *Iris*, of himself and his power, when he refuses to submit to the order of *Jupiter* in the fifteenth book. *Eustathius* remarks, what an incentive it must be to the *Ajaces*, to hear those who could stand against *Hector* equall'd, in this oblique manner, to the Gods themselves.

97. *Th' inspiring God,* Oïleus' *active son – Perceiv'd the first.*] The reason has been ask'd, why the lesser *Ajax* is the first to perceive the assistance of the God? And the ancient solution of this question was very ingenious. They said that the greater *Ajax*, being slow of apprehension, and naturally valiant, could not be sensible so soon of this accession of strength as the other, who immediately perceiv'd it as not owing so much to his natural courage.

102. *Short as he turn'd, I saw the pow'r.*] This opinion, that the majesty of the Gods was such that they could not be seen face to face by men, seems to have been generally receiv'd in most nations. *Spondanus* observes, that it might be derived from sacred truth, and founded upon what God says to *Moses* in *Exodus*, ch. 33. v. 20, 23. *Man shall not see me and live: Thou shalt see my back parts, but my face thou shalt not behold.* For the farther particulars of this notion among the Heathens, see the notes on *lib.* I. v. 268 and on the 5th, v. 971.

131. *The speech of* Neptune *to the* Greeks.] After *Neptune* in his former discourse to the *Ajaces*, who yet maintain'd a retreating fight, had encouraged them to withstand the attack of the *Trojans*; he now addresses himself to those, who having fled out of the battel, and retired to the ships, had given up all for lost. These he endeavours to bring again to the engagement, by one of the most noble and spirited speeches in the whole Iliad. He represents that their present miserable condition was not to be imputed to their want of power, but to their want of resolution to withstand the enemy, whom by experience they had often found unable to resist them. But what is particularly artful, while he is endeavouring to prevail upon them, is that he does not attribute their present dejection of mind to a cowardly spirit, but to a resentment and indignation of their general's usage of their favourite hero *Achilles.* With the same softning art, he tells them, he scorns to speak thus to cowards, but is only concern'd for their misbehaviour as they are the bravest of the army. He then exhorts them for their own sake to avoid destruction, which would certainly be inevitable, if for a moment longer they delay'd to oppose so imminent a danger.

141. *A rout undisciplin'd,* &c.] I translate this line,

Αὔτως ἠλάσκουσαι, ἀνάλκιδες, οὐδ' ἔπι χάρμη,

[Thus they wander about, in a cowardly fashion, devoid of fighting spirit,]

with allusion to the want of military discipline among the *Barbarians,* so often hinted at in *Homer.* He is always opposing to this the exact and regular disposition of his *Greeks,* and accordingly a few lines after, we are told that the *Grecian* phalanxes were such, that *Mars* or *Minerva* could not have found a defect in them.

155. *Prevent this evil,* &c.] The verse in the original,

᾽Αλλ᾽ ἀκεώμεθα θᾶσσον, ἀκεσταί τοι φρένες ἐσθλῶν.

may be capable of receiving another sense to this effect. If it be your resentment of *Agamemnon*'s usage of *Achilles,* that withholds you from the battel, *that evil (viz.* the dissension of those two chiefs) *may soon be remedy'd, for the minds of good men are easily calm'd and compos'd.* I had once translated it,

> *Their future strife with speed we shall redress,*
> *For noble minds are soon compos'd to peace.*

But upon considering the whole context more attentively, the other explanation (which is that of *Didymus*) appeared to me the more natural and unforc'd, and I have accordingly follow'd it.

171. *Fix'd at his post was each bold* Ajax *found,* &c.] We must here take notice of an old story, which however groundless and idle it seems, is related by *Plutarch, Philostratus* and others. *Ganictor* the son of *Amphidamas* King of *Eubœa,* celebrating with all solemnity the funeral of his father, proclaimed according to custom several publick games, among which was the prize for Poetry. *Homer* and *Hesiod* came to dispute for it. After they had produced several pieces on either side, in all which the audience declar'd for *Homer*, *Panides*, the brother of the deceased, who fate as one of the judges, order'd each of the contending Poets to recite that part of his works which he esteem'd the best. *Hesiod* repeated those lines which make the beginning of his second book,

> Πληϊάδων Άτλαγενέων ἐπιτελλομενάων,
> Άρχεσθ' ἀμήτου ἀρότοιό τε δυσομενάων, &c.

[Begin your harvest when the Pleiades, sprung from Atlas, are rising; and when they set, begin your ploughing.]

Homer answer'd with the verses which follow here: But the Prince preferring the peaceful subject of *Hesiod* to the martial one of *Homer*, contrary to the expectation of all, adjudg'd the Prize to *Hesiod.* The commentators upon this occasion are very rhetorical, and universally exclaim against so crying a piece of injustice. All the hardest names which learning can furnish, are very liberally bestow'd upon poor *Panides. Spondanus* is mighty smart, calls him *Midas*, takes him by the ear, and asks the dead Prince as many insulting questions, as any of his author's own heroes could have done. *Dacier* with all gravity tells us, that posterity prov'd a more equitable judge than *Panides.* And if I had not told this tale in my turn, I must have incurred the censure of all the schoolmasters in the nation.

173. *So close their order,* &c.] When *Homer* retouches the same subject, he has always the art to rise in his ideas above what he said before. We shall find an instance of it in this place; if we compare this manner of commending the exact discipline of an army, with what he had made use of on the same occasion at the end of the fourth Iliad. There it is said, that the most experienc'd warriour could not have reprehended any thing, had he been led by *Pallas* thro' the battel; but here he carries it farther, in affirming that *Pallas* and the God of war themselves must have admir'd this disposition of the *Grecian* forces.   *Eustathius.*

177. *A chosen Phalanx, firm,* &c.] *Homer* in these lines has given us a description of the ancient *Phalanx*, which consisted of several ranks of men closely ranged in this order. The first line stood with their spears levell'd directly forward; the second rank being armed with spears two cubits longer, levell'd them likewise forward thro' the interstices of the first; and the third in the same manner held forth their spears yet

longer, thro' the two former ranks; so that the points of the spears of the three ranks terminated in one line. All the other ranks stood with their spears erected, in readiness to advance, and fill the vacant places of such as fell. This is the account *Eustathius* gives of the Phalanx, which he observes was only fit for a body of men acting on the defensive, but improper for the attack: And accordingly *Homer* here only describes the *Greeks* ordering their battel in this manner, when they had no other view but to stand their ground against the furious assault of the *Trojans*. The same Commentator observes from *Hermolytus*, an ancient writer of *Tacticks*, that this manner of ordering the Phalanx was afterwards introduc'd among the *Spartans* by *Lycurgus*, among the *Argives* by *Lysander*, among the *Thebans* by *Epaminondas*, and among the *Macedonians* by *Charidemus*.

191. *As from some mountain's craggy forehead torn*, &c.] This is one of the noblest similes in all *Homer*, and the most justly corresponding in its circumstances to the thing described. The furious descent of *Hector* from the wall represented by a stone that flies from the top of a rock, the hero push'd on by the superior force of *Jupiter*, as the stone driven by a torrent, the ruins of the wall falling after him, all things yielding before him, the clamour and tumult around him, all imag'd in the violent bounding and leaping of the stone, the crackling of the woods, the shock, the noise, the rapidity, the irresistibility, and the augmentation of force in its progress. All these points of likeness make but the first part of this admirable simile. Then the sudden stop of the stone when it comes to the plain, as of *Hector* at the Phalanx of the *Ajaces* (alluding also to the natural situation of the ground, *Hector* rushing down the declivity of the shore, and being stopped on the level of the sea.) And lastly, the immobility of both when so stopp'd, the enemy being as unable to move him back, as he to get forward: This last branch of the comparison is the happiest in the world, and tho' not hitherto observ'd, is what methinks makes the principal beauty and force of it. The simile is copied by *Virgil*, *Æn.* 12.

> *Ac veluti montis saxum de vertice præceps,*
> *Cum ruit avulsum vento, seu turbidus imber*
> *Proluit, aut annis solvit sublapsa vetustas:*
> *Fertur in abruptum magno mons improbus actu*
> *Exultatque solo; sylvas, armenta, virosque*
> *Involvens secum. Disjecta per agmina Turnus*
> *Sic urbis ruit ad muros —*

[As when a fragment, from a mountain torn
By nagging tempests, or by torrents born,
Or sapp'd by time, or loosen'd from the roots,
Prone through the void the rocky ruine shoots,
Rowling from crag to crag, from steep to steep;
Down sink, at once the shepherds and their sheep,
Involv'd alike, they rush to neather ground,
Stunn'd with the shock they fall, and stunn'd from earth
        rebound:
So *Turnus*, hasting headlong to the town,
Should'ring and shoving, bore the squadrons down.
Still pressing onward, to the walls he drew.]

And *Tasso* has again copied it from *Virgil* in his 18*th* book.

Qual gran sasso tal hor, ch' ò la vecchiezza
Solve d'un monte, o svelle ira de' venti
Ruinoso dirupa, e porta, e spezza
Le selve, e con le case anco gli armenti
Tal giù trahea de la sublime altezza
L'horribil trave e merli, e arme, e gente,
Diè la torre a quel moto uno, o duo crolli;
Tremar le mura, e rimbombaro i colli.

[As an old rock, which age or stormy wind
Tears from some craggy hill or mountain steep,
Doth break, doth bruise, and into dust doth grind
Woods, houses, hamlets, herds, and folds of sheep;
So fell the beam and down with it all kind
Of arms, of weapons, and of men did sweep,
Wherewith the towers once or twice did shake,
Trembled the walls, the hills and mountains quake.]

It is but justice to *Homer* to take notice how infinitely inferior both these similes are to their original. They have taken the image without the likeness, and lost those corresponding circumstances which raise the justness and sublimity of *Homer*'s. In *Virgil* it is only the violence of *Turnus* in which the whole application consists: And in *Tasso* it has no farther allusion than to the fall of a tower in general.

There is yet another beauty in the numbers of this part. As the verses themselves make us see, the sound of them makes us hear what they represent, in the noble roughness, rapidity, and sonorous cadence that distinguishes them.

Ῥήξας, ἀσπέτῳ ὄμβρῳ ἀναιδέος ἔχματα πέτρης, &c.

[In the aftermath of a torrential downpour, tearing away the moorings of a huge boulder.]

The translation, however short it falls of these beauties, may serve to shew the reader, that there was at least an Endeavour to imitate them.

278. Idomen of Crete.] *Idomeneus* appears at large in this book, whose character (if I take it right) is such as we see pretty often in common life: A person of the first rank, sufficient enough of his high birth, growing into years, conscious of his decline in strength and active qualities; and therefore endeavouring to make it up to himself in dignity, and to preserve the veneration of others. The true picture of a stiff old soldier, not willing to lose any of the reputation he has acquir'd; yet not inconsiderate in danger; but by the sense of his age, and by his experience in battel, become too cautious to engage with any great odds against him: Very careful and tender of his soldiers, whom he had commanded so long that they were become old acquaintance; (so that it was with great judgment *Homer* chose to introduce him here, in performing a kind office to one of them who was wounded.) Talkative upon subjects of war, as afraid that others might lose the memory of what he had done in better days, of which the long conversation with *Meriones*, and *Ajax*'s Reproach of him in Iliad 23. v. 478 of the original, are sufficient proofs. One may observe some strokes of lordliness and state in his character: That Respect *Agamemnon* seems careful to treat him with, and the particular distinctions shewn him at table, are mention'd in a manner that insinuates they were points upon which this Prince not a little insisted. *Il.* 4. v. 257, &c. The vaunting of his family in this book, together with his sarcasms and contemptuous railleries on his dead enemies, favour of the same turn of mind. And it seems there was among the ancients a tradition of *Idomeneus* which strengthens this conjecture of his pride: For we find in the *Heroicks* of *Philostratus*, that before he would come to the *Trojan* war, he demanded a share in the sovereign command with *Agamemnon* himself.

I must, upon this occasion, make an observation once for all, which will be applicable to many passages in *Homer*, and afford a solution of many difficulties. It is that our Author drew several of his characters with an eye to the histories then known of famous persons, or the traditions that past in those times. One cannot believe otherwise of a

Poet, who appears so nicely exact in observing all the customs of the age he described; nor can we imagine the infinite number of minute circumstances relating to particular persons, which we meet with every where in his poem, could possibly have been invented purely as ornaments to it. This reflection will account for a hundred seeming oddnesses not only in the *characters*, but in the *speeches* of the Iliad: For as no author is more true than *Homer* to the character of the person he introduces speaking, so no one more often suits his oratory to the character of the person spoken to. Many of these beauties must needs be lost to us, yet this supposition will give a new light to several particulars. For instance, the speech I have been mentioning of *Agamemnon* to *Idomeneus* in the 4th book, wherein he puts this hero in mind of the magnificent entertainments he had given him, becomes in this view much less odd and surprizing. Or who can tell but it had some allusion to the manners of the *Cretans* whom he commanded, whose character was so well known, as to become a proverb: *The* Cretans, *evil beasts, and slow bellies.*

283. *The surgeons of the camp.*] *Podalirius* and *Machaon* were not the only physicians in the army; it appears from some passages in this poem, that each body of troops had one peculiar to themselves. It may not be improper to advertise, that the ancient physicians were all surgeons.   *Eustathius.*

325. – Meriones *attends, Whom thus he questions* –] This conversation between *Idomeneus* and *Meriones* is generally censured as highly improper and out of place, and as such is given up even by M. *Dacier*, the most zealous of our Poet's defenders. However, if we look closely into the occasion and drift of this discourse, the accusation will, I believe, appear not so well grounded. Two persons of distinction, just when the enemy is put to a stop by the *Ajaces*, meet behind the army: Having each on important occasions retired out of the fight, the one to help a wounded soldier, the other to seek a new weapon. *Idomeneus*, who is superiour in years as well as authority, returning to the battel, is surprized to meet *Meriones* out of it, who was one of his own officers (θεράπων, as *Homer* here calls him) and being jealous of his soldier's honour, demands the cause of his quitting the fight. *Meriones* having told him it was the want of a spear, he yet seems unsatisfy'd with the excuse; adding, that he himself did not approve of that distant manner of fighting with a spear. *Meriones* being touch'd to the quick with this reproach, replies, that he of all the *Greeks* had the least reason to suspect his courage: Whereupon *Idomeneus* perceiving him highly piqued, assures him he entertains no such hard thoughts of him, since he had often known his courage prov'd on such occasions, where the danger being greater, and the number smaller, it was impossible for a coward to conceal his natural infirmity: But now recollecting that a malicious mind might give a sinister interpretation to their inactivity during this discourse, he immediately breaks it off upon that reflection. As therefore this conversation has its rise from a jealousy in the most tender point of honour, I think the Poet cannot justly be blamed for suffering a discourse so full of warm sentiments to run on for about forty verses; which after all cannot be suppos'd to take up more than two or three minutes from action.

335. *This headless Lance*, &c.] We have often seen several of *Homer*'s combatants lose and break their spears, yet they do not therefore retire from the battel to seek other weapons; why therefore does *Homer* here send *Meriones* on this errand? It may be said, that in the kind of fight which the *Greeks* now maintain'd drawn up into the phalanx, *Meriones* was useless without this weapon.

339. *Spears I have store*, &c.] *Idomeneus* describes his tent as a magazine, stored with variety of arms won from the enemy, which were not only laid up as useless trophies of his victories, but kept there in order to supply his own, and his friend's occasions. And this consideration shews us one reason why these warriours contended with such eagerness to carry off the arms of a vanquish'd enemy.

This gives me an occasion to animadvert upon a false remark of *Eustathius*, which is inserted in the notes on the 11*th* book, 'that *Homer*, to shew us nothing is so unseasonable in a battel as to stay to despoil the slain, feigns that most of the warriours who do it, are kill'd, wounded, or unsuccessful.' I am astonish'd how so great a mistake should fall from any man who had read *Homer*, much more from one who had read him so thoroughly, and even superstitiously, as the old Archbishop of *Thessalonica*. There is scarce a book in *Homer* that does not abound with instances to the contrary, where the conquerors strip their enemies, and bear off their spoils in triumph. It was (as I have already said in the essay on *Homer*'s battels) as honourable an exploit in those days to carry off the arms, as it is now to gain a standard. But it is a strange consequence, that because our author sometimes represents a man unsuccessful in a glorious attempt, he therefore discommends the attempt itself; and is as good an argument against encountring an enemy living, as against despoiling him dead. One ought not to confound this with plundering, between which *Homer* has so well mark'd the distinction; when he constantly speaks of the spoils as glorious, but makes *Nestor* in the 6*th* book, and *Hector* in the 15*th*, directly forbid the pillage, as a practice that has often prov'd fatal in the midst of a victory, and sometimes even after it.

353. *To this*, Idomeneus.] There is a great deal more dialogue in *Homer* than in *Virgil*. The *Roman* Poet's are generally set speeches, those of the *Greek* more in conversation. What *Virgil* does by two words of a narration, *Homer* brings about by a speech; he hardly raises one of his heroes out of bed without some talk concerning it. There are not only replies, but rejoinders in *Homer*, a thing scarce ever to be found in *Virgil*; the consequence whereof is, that there must be in the Iliad many continued conversations (such as this of our two heroes) a little resembling common chit-chat. This renders the poem more natural and animated, but less grave and majestic. However, that such was the way of writing generally practised in those ancient times, appears from the like manner used in most of the books of the old Testament; and it particularly agreed with our Author's warm imagination, which delighted in perpetual imagery, and in painting every circumstance of what he described.

355. *In that sharp service*, &c.] In a general battel cowardise may be the more easily conceal'd, by reason of the number of the combatants; but in an ambuscade, where the soldiers are few, each must be discovered to be what he is; this is the reason why the ancients entertain'd so great an idea of this sort of war; the bravest men were always chosen to serve upon such occasions.   *Eustathius.*

384. *So* Mars *armipotent*, &c.] *Homer* varies his similitudes with all imaginable art, sometimes deriving them from the properties of animals, sometimes from natural passions, sometimes from the occurrences of life, and sometimes (as in the simile before us) from history. The invention of *Mars*'s passage from *Thrace*, (which was feign'd to be the country of that God) to the *Phlegyans* and *Ephyrians*, is a very beautiful and poetical manner of celebrating the martial genius of that people, who lived in perpetual wars.

Methinks there is something of a fine enthusiasm, in *Homer*'s manner of fetching a compass, as it were, to draw in new images besides those in which the direct point of likeness consists. *Milton* perfectly well understood the beauty of these digressive images, as we may see from the following simile, which is in a manner made up of them.

> *Thick as autumnal leaves that strow the brooks*
> *In* Vallombrosa *(where th' Etrurian shades*
> *High-overarch'd embow'r.) Or scatter'd sedge*
> *Afloat, when with fierce winds* Orion *arm'd*
> *Hath vex'd the* Red sea-*coast, (whose wave o'erthrew*
> Busiris *and his* Memphian *chivalry,*
> *While with perfidious hatred they pursu'd*
> *The sojourners of* Goshen, *who beheld*
> *From the safe shore their floating carcasses,*
> *And broken chariot-wheels) — So thick bestrown*
> *Abject and lost lay these. —*

As for the general purport of this comparison of *Homer*, it gives us a noble and majestic idea, at once of *Idomeneus* and *Meriones*, represented by *Mars* and his son *Terrour*; in which each of these heroes is greatly elevated, yet the just distinction between them preserved. The beautiful simile of *Virgil* in his 12*th Æneid* is drawn with an eye to this of our Author.

> *Qualis apud gelidi cum flumina concitus Hebri*
> *Sanguineus Mavors clypeo increpat, atque furentes*
> *Bella movens immittit equos; illi æquore aperto*
> *Ante Notos Zephyrumque volant: gemit ultima pulsu*
> *Thraca pedum: circumque atræ Formidinis ora,*
> *Iræque, Insidiæque, Dei comitatus, aguntur.*

> [Thus on the bank of *Hebrus* freezing flood
> The God of battles in his angry mood,
> Clashing his sword against his brazen shield,
> Let loose the reins, and scours along the field:
> Before the wind his fiery coursers fly,
> Groans the sad earth, resounds the rattling sky.
> Wrath, terror, treason, tumult, and despair,
> Dire faces, and deform'd, surround the car;
> Friends of the God, and followers of the war.]

396. – *Shall we join the right,*
Or combat in the centre of the fight,
Or to the left our wanted succour lend?]

The common interpreters have to this question of *Meriones* given a
meaning which is highly impertinent, if not downright nonsense;
explaining it thus. *Shall we fight on the right, or in the middle, or on the
left, for no where else doe the* Greeks *so much want assistance?* which
amounts to this: 'Shall we engage where our assistance is most wanted,
or where it is not wanted?' The context, as well as the words of the
original, oblige us to understand it in this obvious meaning; *Shall we
bring our assistance to the right, to the left, or to the centre? Since the*
Greeks *being equally press'd and engag'd on all sides, equally need our aid
in all parts.*

400. *Not in the centre*, &c.] There is in this answer of *Idomeneus* a
small circumstance which is overlooked by the commentators, but in
which the whole spirit and reason of what is said by him consists.
He says he is in no fear for the centre, since it is defended by
Teucer and *Ajax*; *Teucer* being not only most famous for the use of
the bow, but likewise excellent ἐν σταδίῃ ὑσμίνῃ, in a *close standing
fight*: And as for *Ajax*, tho' not so swift of foot as *Achilles*, yet he
was equal to him ἐν αὐτοσταδίῃ, in the same *stedfast* manner of
fighting; hereby intimating that he was secure for the centre, because
that post was defended by two persons both accomplished in that
part of war, which was most necessary for the service they were then
engaged in; the two expressions before mentioned peculiarly signify-
ing a firm and steady way of fighting, most useful in maintaining a
post.

452. *In war and discord's adamantine chain.*] It will be necessary, for
the better understanding the conduct of *Homer* in every battel he
describes, to reflect on the particular kind of fight, and the circum-
stances that distinguish each. In this view therefore we ought to
remember thro' this whole book, that the battel describ'd in it, is a
fix'd close fight, wherein the armies engage in a gross compact body,
without any skirmishes or feats of activity so often mentioned in the
foregoing engagements. We see at the beginning of it the *Grecians*
form a *Phalanx*, v. 177. which continues unbroken at the very end, v.

1106. The chief weapon made use of is a *spear*, being most proper for this manner of combat; nor do we see any other use of a chariot, but to carry off the dead or wounded (as in the instance of *Harpalion* and *Deïphobus.*)

From hence we may observe with what judgment and propriety *Homer* introduces *Idomeneus* as the chief in action on this occasion: For this hero being declined from his prime, and somewhat stiff with years, was only fit for this kind of engagement, as *Homer* expressly says in the 512*th* verse of the present book.

> Οὐ γὰρ ἔτ' ἔμπεδα γυῖα ποδῶν ἦν ὁρμηθέντι,
> Οὔτ' ἄρ' ἐπαῖξαι μεθ' ἑὸν βέλος, οὔτ' ἀλέασθαι,
> Τῶ ῥα καὶ ἐν σταδίῃ μὲν ἀμύνετο νηλεὲς ἦμαρ.

(See the translation, v. 648, &c.)

452. This short but comprehensive allegory is very proper to give us an idea of the present condition of the two contending armies, who being both powerfully sustain'd by the assistance of superiour Deities, join and mix together in a close and bloody engagement, without any remarkable advantage on either side. To image to us this state of things, the Poet represents *Jupiter* and *Neptune* holding the two armies close bound by a mighty chain, which he calls the knot of contention and war, and of which the two Gods draw the extremities, whereby the enclos'd armies are compelled together, without any possibility on either side to separate or conquer. There is not perhaps in *Homer* any image at once so exact and so bold. Madam *Dacier* acknowledges, that despairing to make this passage shine in her language, she purposely omitted it in her translation: But from what she says in her annotations, it seems that she did not rightly apprehend the propriety and beauty of it. *Hobbes* too was not very sensible of it, when he translated it so oddly.

> *And thus the Saw from brother unto brother*
> *Of cruel war was drawn alternately,*
> *And many slain on one side and the other.*

471. *The great* Idomeneus *bestrides the dead:*
      And thus (he cries) –]

It seems (says *Eustathius* on this place) that the Iliad being an heroick Poem, is of too serious a nature to admit of raillery: Yet *Homer* has found the secret of joining two things that are in a manner incompatible. For this piece of raillery is so far from raising laughter, that it becomes a hero, and is capable to enflame the courage of all who hear it. It also elevates the character of *Idomeneus*, who notwithstanding he is in the midst of imminent dangers, preserves his usual gaiety of temper, which is the greatest evidence of an uncommon courage.

I confess I am of an opinion very different from this of *Eustathius*, which is also adopted by M. *Dacier*. So severe and bloody an irony to a dying person is a fault in morals, if not in poetry itself. It should not have place at all, or if it should, is ill placed here. *Idomeneus* is represented a brave man, nay a man of a compassionate nature, in the circumstance he was introduc'd in, of assisting a wounded soldier. What provocation could such an one have, to insult so barbarously an unfortunate Prince, being neither his rival nor particular enemy? True courage is inseparable from humanity, and all generous warriours regret the very victories they gain, when they reflect what a price of blood they cost. I know it may be answer'd, that these were not the manners of *Homer*'s time, a spirit of violence and devastation then reigned, even among the chosen people of God, as may be seen from the actions of *Joshua*, &c. However, if one would forgive the *cruelty*, one cannot forgive the *gaiety* on such an occasion. These inhuman jests the Poet was so far from being oblig'd to make, that he was on the contrary forced to break through the general serious air of his poem to introduce them. Would it not raise a suspicion, that (whatever we see of his superiour genius in other respects) his own views of morality were not elevated above the barbarity of his age? I think indeed the thing by far the most shocking in this Author, is that spirit of cruelty which appears too manifestly in the Iliad.

Virgil was too judicious to imitate *Homer* in these licences, and is much more reserv'd in his sarcasms and insults. There are not above four or five in the whole *Æneid*. That of *Pyrrhus* to *Priam* in the second book, tho' barbarous in itself, may be accounted for as intended to raise a character of horrour, and render the action of *Pyrrhus* odious; whereas *Homer* stains his most favourite characters with these barbarities. That of *Ascanius* over *Numanus* in the ninth, was a fair opportunity where *Virgil* might have indulg'd the humour of a cruel raillery, and have been excus'd by the youth and gaiety of the speaker; yet it is no more than a very moderate answer to the insolences with which he had just been provok'd by his enemy, only retorting two of his own words upon him.

> – I, verbis virtutem illude superbis!
> Bis capti Phryges hæc Rutulis responsa remittunt.

> [Go now, vain boaster, and true valor scorn;
>   The *Phrygians* twice subdu'd, yet make this third
>   return.]

He never suffers his *Æneas* to fall into this practice, but while he is on fire with indignation after the death of his friend *Pallas*: That short one to *Mezentius* is the least that could be said to such a tyrant.

> – Ubi nunc Mezentius acer, & illa
> Effera vis animi? –

> [Now, where are now thy vaunts, the fierce disdain
>   Of proud *Mezentius*, and the lofty strain?]

The worst-natur'd one I remember (which yet is more excusable than *Homer*'s) is that of *Turnus* to *Eumedes* in the 12th book.

> En, agros, & quam bello, Trojane, petisti,
> Hesperiam metire jacens: hæc præmia, qui me
> Ferro ausi tentare, ferunt: sic mœnia condunt.

> [Possess, said he, the fruit of all thy pains,
>   And measure, at thy length, our *Latian* plains.
>   Thus are my foes rewarded by my hand,
>   Thus may they build their town, and thus enjoy the
>   land.]

474. *And such the contract of the* Phrygian *King*, &c.] It was but natural to raise a question, on occasion of these and other passages in *Homer*, how it comes to pass that the heroes of different nations are so well acquainted with the stories and circumstances of each other? *Eustathius*'s solution is no ill one, that the warriours on both sides might learn the story of their enemies from the captives they took, during the course of so long a war.

511. *The* Cretan *saw, and stooping*, &c.] Nothing could paint in a more lively manner this whole action, and every circumstance of it, than the following lines. There is the posture of *Idomeneus* upon seeing the lance flying toward him; the lifting the shield obliquely to turn it aside; the arm discover'd in that position; the form, composition, materials, and ornaments of the shield distinctly specify'd; the flight of the dart over it; the sound of it first as it flew, then as it fell; and the decay of that sound on the edge of the buckler, which being thinner than the other parts, rather tinkled than rung, especially when the first force of the stroke was spent on the orb of it. All this in the compass of so few lines, in which every word is an image, is something more beautifully particular, than I remember to have met with in any Poet.

543. *He, once of* Ilion's *youth the loveliest boy.*] Some manuscripts, after these words, ὥριστος ἐνὶ Τροίῃ εὐρείῃ, insert the three following verses,

> Πρὶν 'Αντηνορίδας τραφέμεν καὶ Πάνθοου υἷας
> Πριαμίδας θ' οἳ Τρωσὶ μετέπρεπον ἱπποδάμοισιν
> Ἕως ἔθ' ἤβην εἶχεν, ὄφελλε δὲ κούριον ἄνθος;

which I have not translated, as not thinking them genuine. Mr *Barnes* is of the same opinion.

554. *His lab'ring Heart, heaves, with so strong a bound,*
The long lance shakes, and vibrates in the wound.]

We cannot read *Homer* without observing a wonderful variety in the wounds and manner of dying. Some of these wounds are painted with very singular circumstances, and those of uncommon art and beauty. This passage is a masterpiece in that way; *Alcathous* is pierc'd into the heart, which throbs with so strong a pulse, that the motion is communicated even to the distant end of the spear, which is vibrated thereby. This circumstance might appear too bold, and the effect beyond nature, were we not inform'd by the most skilful anatomists of the wonderful force of this muscle, which some of them have computed to be equal to the weight of several thousand pounds.

Lower, de Corde. Borellus & alii.

578. *Incens'd at partial* Priam, &c.] *Homer* here gives the reason why *Æneas* did not fight in the foremost ranks. It was against his inclination that he serv'd *Priam*, and he was rather engag'd by honour and reputation to assist his country, than by any disposition to aid that Prince. This passage is purely historical, and the ancients have preserv'd to us a tradition which serves to explain it. They say that *Æneas* became suspected by *Priam*, on account of an oracle which prophesied he should in process of time rule over the *Trojans.* The King therefore shew'd him no great degree of esteem or consideration, with design to discredit, and render him despicable to the people. *Eustathius.* This envy of *Priam*, and this report of the oracle, are mention'd by *Achilles* to *Æneas* in the 20th Book.

> — ἢ σέ γε θυμὸς ἐμοὶ μαχέσασθαι ἀνώγει,
> Ἐλπόμενον Τρώεσσιν ἀνάξειν ἱπποδάμοισι,
> Τιμῆς τῆς Πριάμου; ἀτὰρ εἴ κεν ἔμ᾽ ἐξεναρίξῃς
> Οὔ τοι τοὔνεκά γε Πρίαμος γέρας ἐν χερὶ θήσει.
> Εἰσὶν γὰρ οἱ παῖδες. —

(See v. 216, &c. of the translation.)

And *Neptune* in the same book,

> Ἤδη γὰρ Πριάμου γενεὴν ἤχθηρε Κρονίων.
> Νῦν δὲ δὴ Αἰνείαο βίη Τρώεσσιν ἀνάξει,
> Καὶ παίδων παῖδες, τοί κεν μετόπισθε γένωνται.

(In the translation, v. 355, &c.)

I shall conclude this note with the character of *Æneas*, as it is drawn by *Philostratus*, wherein he makes mention of the same tradition. '*Æneas* (says this Author) was inferior to *Hector* in battel only, in all else equal, and in prudence superior. He was likewise skilful in whatever related to the Gods, and conscious of what destiny had reserv'd for him after the taking of *Troy.* Incapable of fear, never discompos'd, and particularly possessing himself in the article of danger. *Hector* is reported to have been call'd the hand, and *Æneas* the head of the *Trojans*; and the latter more advantag'd their affairs by his caution, than the former by his fury. These two heroes were much of the same age, and the same stature: The air of *Æneas* had something in it less bold and forward, but at the same time more fix'd and constant.'

Philostrat. Heroic.

621. *Like* Ida's *flocks*, &c.] *Homer*, whether he treats of the customs of men or beasts, is always a faithful interpreter of nature. When sheep leave the pasture and drink freely, it is a certain sign, that they have found good pasturage, and that they are all found; 'tis therefore upon this account, that *Homer* says the shepherd rejoices. *Homer*, we find, well understood what *Aristotle* many ages after him remark'd, *viz.* that sheep grow fat by drinking. This therefore is the reason, why shepherds are accustom'd to give their flocks a certain quantity of salt every five days in the summer, that they may by this means drink the more freely.   *Eustathius.*

655. *And, fir'd with hate.*] *Homer* does not tell us the occasion of this hatred; but since his days, *Simonides* and *Ibycus* write, that *Idomeneus* and *Deïphobus* were rivals, and both in love with *Helen.* This very well agrees with the ancient tradition which *Euripides* and *Virgil* have follow'd: for after the death of *Paris,* they tell us she was espous'd to *Deïphobus.*   *Eustathius.*

720. *Bending he fell, and doubled to the ground, Lay panting.* –] The original is,

> — ὁ δ᾽ ἑσπόμενος περὶ δουρὶ,
> Ἤσπαιρ᾽. —

The versification represents the short broken pantings of the dying warriour, in the short sudden break at the second syllable of the second line. And this beauty is, as it happens, precisely copied in the *English.* It is not often that a Translator can do this justice to *Homer,* but he must be content to imitate these graces and proprieties at more distance, by endeavouring at something parallel, tho' not the same.

728. *King* Helenus.] The appellation of King was not anciently confin'd to those only who bore the sovereign dignity, but applied also to others. There was in the island of *Cyprus* a whole order of officers call'd Kings, whose business it was to receive the relations of informers, concerning all that happen'd in the island, and to regulate affairs accordingly.   *Eustathius.*

739. *As on some ample barn's well-harden'd floor.*] We ought not to be shock'd at the frequency of these similes taken from the ideas of a rural life. In early times, before politeness had rais'd the esteem of arts subservient to luxury, above those necessary to the subsistence of mankind, agriculture was the employment of persons of the greatest esteem and distinction: We see in sacred history Princes busy at sheep-shearing; and in Time of the *Roman* common-wealth, a Dictator taken from the plough. Wherefore it ought not to be wonder'd at that allusions and comparisons of this kind are frequently used by ancient heroic writers, as well to raise, as illustrate their descriptions. But since these arts are fallen from their ancient dignity, and become the drudgery of the lowest people, the images of them are likewise sunk into meanness, and without this consideration, must appear to common readers unworthy to have place in Epic poems. It was perhaps thro' too much deference to such tastes, that *Chapman* omitted this simile in his translation.

751.   *A sling's soft wool, snatch'd from a soldier's side,*
  At once the tent and ligature supply'd.]

The words of the original are these,

’Αυτὴν δὲ ξυνέδησεν ἐΰστρεφεῖ οἰὸς ἀώτῳ
Σφενδόνῃ, ἣν ἄρα οἱ θεράπων ἔχε ποιμένι λαῶν.

This passage, by the Commentators ancient and modern, seems rightly understood in the sense express'd in this translation: The word σφενδόνη properly signifying a *Sling*; which (as *Eustathius* observes from an old Scholiast) was anciently made of woollen strings. *Chapman* alone dissents from the common interpretation, boldly pronouncing that slings are no where mention'd in the Iliad, without giving any reason for his opinion. He therefore translates the word σφενδόνη, a *scarf*, by no other authority but that he says, *it was a fitter thing to hang a wounded arm in, than a Sling*; and very prettily wheedles his reader into this opinion by a most gallant imagination, that *his squire might carry this scarf about him as a favour of his own or of his master's mistress.* But for the use he has found for this scarf, there is not any pretence from the original; where it is only said the wound was bound up, without any mention of hanging the arm. After all, he is hard put to it in his translation; for being resolv'd to have a *Scarf*, and oblig'd to mention *Wool*, we are left entirely at a loss to know from whence he got the latter.

A like passage recurs near the end of this book, where the Poet says the *Locrians* went to war without shield or spear, only armed,

Τόξοισι καὶ ἐΰστρόφεῖ οἰὸς ἀώτῳ.   v. 716.

Which last expression, as all the Commentators agree, signifies a *sling*, tho' the word σφενδόνη is not used. *Chapman* here likewise, without any colour of authority, dissents from the common opinion; but very inconstant in his errours, varies his mistake, and assures us, *this expression is the true Periphrasis of a light kind of armour, call'd a* Jack, *by which all our archers used to serve in of old, and which were ever quilted with wool.*

766. *The cover'd pole-axe.*] *Homer* never ascribes this weapon to any but the *Barbarians*, for the battel-axe was not used in war by the politer nations. It was the favourite weapon of the *Amazons.*

Eustathius.

779. *The speech of* Menelaus.] This speech of *Menelaus* over his dying enemy, is very different from those with which *Homer* frequently makes his heroes insult the vanquish'd, and answers very well the character of this good-natur'd Prince. Here are no insulting taunts, no cruel sarcasms, nor any sporting with the particular misfortunes of the dead: The invectives he makes are general, arising naturally from a remembrance of his wrongs, and being almost nothing else but a recapitulation of them. These reproaches come most justly from this Prince, as being the only person among the *Greeks* who had receiv'd any personal injury from the *Trojans.* The apostrophe he makes to *Jupiter*, wherein he complains of his protecting a wicked people, has given occasion to censure *Homer* as guilty of impiety, in making his heroes tax the Gods with Injustice: But since, in the former part of this speech, it is expressly said, that *Jupiter* will certainly punish the *Trojans* by the destruction of their city for violating the laws of hospitality, the latter part ought only to be consider'd as a complaint to *Jupiter* for delaying that vengeance: This reflection being no more than what a pious suffering mind, griev'd at the flourishing condition of prosperous wickedness, might naturally fall into. Not unlike this is the complaint of the prophet *Jeremiah*, ch. 12. v. 1. *Righteous art thou, O Lord, when I plead with thee: yet let me talk with thee of thy judgments. Wherefore doth the way of the wicked prosper? Wherefore are all they happy that deal very treacherously?*

Nothing can more fully represent the cruelty and injustice of the *Trojans*, than the observation with which *Menelaus* finishes their character, by saying, that they have a more strong, constant, and insatiable appetite after bloodshed and rapine, than others have to satisfy the most agreeable pleasures and natural desires.

795. *The best of things beyond their measure cloy.*] These words comprehend a very natural sentiment, which perfectly shews the wonderful folly of men: They are soon weary'd with the most agreeable things, when they are innocent, but never with the most toilsome things in the world, when injust and criminal.   *Eustathius. Dacier.*

797. *The dance.*] In the Original it is call'd ἀμύμων, *the blameless dance*; to distinguish (says *Eustathius*) what sort of dancing it is that *Homer* commends. For there were two kinds of dancing practis'd among the ancients, the one reputable, invented by *Minerva*, or by *Castor* and *Pollux*; the other dishonest, of which *Pan*, or *Bacchus*, was the author. They were distinguish'd by the name of the tragic, and the comic or satyric dance. But those which probably our Author commends were certain military dances used by the greatest heroes. One of this sort was known to the *Macedonians* and *Persians*, practis'd by *Antiochus* the Great, and the famous *Polyperchon*. There was another which was danc'd in compleat armour, call'd the *Pyrrhick*, from *Pyrrhicus* the *Spartan* its inventor, which continu'd in fashion among the *Lacedæmonians*. *Scaliger* the father remarks, that this dance was too laborious to remain long in use even among the ancients; however it seems that labour could not discourage this bold Critick from reviving that laudable kind of dance in the presence of the Emperor *Maximilian* and his whole court. It is not to be doubted but the performance rais'd their admiration; nor much to be wonder'd at, if they desir'd to see more than once so extraordinary a spectacle, as we have it in his own Words. *Poëtices, lib.* 1. *cap.* 18. *Hanc saltationem* [Pyrrhicam] *nos & sæpe, & diu, coram Divo Maximiliano, jussu Bonifacii patrui,* non sine stupore totius Germaniæ, *repræsentavimus.* [Long and often have we performed this Pyrrhic dance before divine Maximilian by the command of his uncle Boniface, to the amazement of all Germany.]

819. *Like some vile worm extended on the ground.*] I cannot be of *Eustathius*'s opinion, that this simile was design'd to debase the character of *Harpalion*, and to represent him in a mean and disgraceful view, as one who had nothing noble in him. I rather think from the character he gives of this young man, whose piety carry'd him to the wars to attend his father, and from the air of this whole passage, which is tender and pathetick, that he intended this humble comparison only as a mortifying picture of human misery and mortality. As to the verses which *Eustathius* alledges for a proof of the cowardice of *Harpalion*,

Ἂψ δ' ἑτάρων εἰς ἔθνος ἐχάζετο κῆρ' ἀλεείνων
Πάντοσε παπταίνων. –

[Shunning death, he fell back into the band of his companions, looking cautiously about, in every direction.]

The retreat described in the first verse is common to the greatest
heroes in *Homer*; the same words are applied to *Deïphobus* and *Meriones*
in this book, and to *Patroclus* in the 16*th*, v. 817 of the *Greek*. The
same thing in other words is said even of the great *Ajax*, *Il.* 15. v. 728.
And we have *Ulysses* describ'd in the 4*th*, v. 497. with the same circum-
spection and fear of the darts: tho' none of those warriours have the
same reason as *Harpalion* for their retreat or caution, he alone being
unarm'd, which circumstance takes away all imputation of cowardice.

823. *The pensive father.*] We have seen in the 5*th* Iliad the death of
Pylæmenes general of the *Paphlagonians*: How comes he then in this
place to be introduced as following the funeral of his son? *Eustathius*
informs us of a most ridiculous solution of some criticks, who thought
it might be the ghost of this unhappy father, who not being yet
interr'd, according to the opinion of the ancients, wander'd upon the
earth. *Zenodotus* not satisfy'd with this (as indeed he had little reason
to be) chang'd the name of *Pylæmenes* into *Kylæmenes*. *Didymus* thinks
there were two of the same name; as there are in *Homer* two *Schedius*'s,
two *Eurymedon*'s, and three *Adrastus*'s. And others correct the verse by
adding a negative, μετὰ δ᾽ οὔ σφι πατὴρ κίε; *his father did* not *follow his
chariot with his face bath'd in tears.* Which last, if not of more weight
than the rest, is yet more ingenious.   *Eustathius. Dacier.*

> Nor did his valiant father (now no more)
> Pursue the mournful pomp along the shore,
> No sire surviv'd, to grace th' untimely bier,
> Or sprinkle the cold ashes with a tear.

840. *And chose the certain, glorious path to death.*] Thus we see
Euchenor is like *Achilles*, who fail'd to *Troy*, tho' he knew he should
fall before it: This might somewhat have prejudic'd the character of
Achilles, every branch of which ought to be single, and superior to all
others, as he ought to be without a rival in every thing that speaks a
hero: Therefore we find two essential differences between *Euchenor*
and *Achilles*, which preserve the superiority of the hero of the poem.
Achilles, if he had not fail'd to *Troy*, had enjoy'd a long life; but
Euchenor had been soon cut off by some cruel disease. *Achilles* being
independent, and as a King, could have liv'd at ease at home, without
being obnoxious to any disgrace; but *Euchenor* being but a private
man, must either have gone to the war, or been expos'd to an
ignominious penalty.   *Eustathius. Dacier.*

845. *Nor knew great Hector,* &c.] Most part of this book being employ'd to describe the brave resistance the *Greeks* made on their left under *Idomeneus* and *Meriones*; the Poet now shifts the scene, and returns to *Hector*, whom he left in the center of the army, after he had pass'd the wall, endeavouring in vain to break the phalanx where *Ajax* commanded. And that the reader might take notice of this change of place, and carry distinctly in his mind each scene of action, *Homer* is very careful in the following lines to let us know that *Hector* still continues in the place where he had first pass'd the wall, at that part of it which was lowest, (as appears from *Sarpedon*'s having pull'd down one of its battlements on foot, *lib.* 12.) and which was nearest the station where the ships of *Ajax* were laid, because that hero was probably thought a sufficient guard for that part. As the poet is so very exact in describing each scene as in a chart or plan, the reader ought to be careful to trace each action in it; otherwise he will see nothing but confusion in things which are in themselves very regular and distinct. This observation is the more necessary, because even in this place, where the Poet intended to prevent any such mistake, *Dacier* and other interpreters have apply'd to the present action what is only a recapitulation of the time and place describ'd in the former book.

861. Pthians.] These *Pthians* are not the troops of *Achilles*, for those were call'd *Pthiotes*; but they were the troops of *Protesilaus* and *Philoctetes.*   *Eustathius.*

879. *So when two lordly bulls,* &c.] The image here given of the *Ajaces* is very lively and exact; there being no circumstance of their present condition that is not to be found in the comparison, and no particular in the comparison that does not resemble the action of the heroes. Their strength and labour, their unanimity and nearness to each other, the difficulties they struggle against, and the sweat occasion'd by the struggling, perfectly corresponding with the simile.

937.   Achilles, *great* Achilles, *yet remains*
         On yonder decks, and yet o'erlooks the plains.]

There never was a nobler encomium than this of *Achilles.* It seems enough to so wise a counsellor as *Polydamas*, to convince so intrepid a warriour as *Hector*, in how great danger the *Trojans* stood, to say, Achilles *sees us.* 'Tho' he abstains from the fight, he still casts his eye on the battel; it is true, we are a brave army, and yet keep our ground, but still *Achilles* sees us, and we are not safe.' This reflection makes him a God, a single regard of whom can turn the fate of armies, and determine the destiny of a whole people. And how nobly is this thought extended in the progress of the poem, where we shall see in the 16*th* book the *Trojans* fly at the first sight of his armour, worn by *Patroclus*; and in the 18*th* their defeat compleated by his sole appearance, unarm'd, on his ship.

939. Hector, *with a bound, Leap'd from his chariot.*] *Hector* having in the last book alighted, and caused the *Trojans* to leave their chariots behind them, when they pass'd the trench, and no mention of any chariot but that of *Asius* since occurring in the battel; we must necessarily infer, either that *Homer* has neglected to mention the advance of the chariots, (a circumstance which should not have been omitted) or else, that he is guilty here of a great mistake in making *Hector* leap from his chariot. I think it evident, that this is really a slip of the Poet's memory: For in this very book, v. 533 (of the original) we see *Polites* leads off his wounded brother to the place where his chariot remain'd behind the army. And again in the next book, *Hector* being wounded, is carried out of the battel in his soldier's arms to the place where his horses and chariot waited at a distance from the battel,

> — τὸν δ' ἄρ' ἑταῖροι
> Χερσὶν ἀείραντες φέρον ἐκ πόνου, ὄφρ' ἵκεθ' ἵππους
> Ὠκέας οἵ οἱ ὄπισθε μάχης ἠδὲ πτολέμοιο
> Ἕστασαν.   *Lib.* 14. v. 428.

[His companions carried him out of the battle, raising him up with their hands until they reached their swift horses, where they had placed them, to the rear of the fighting and the battle.]

But what puts it beyond dispute, that the chariots continued all this time in the place where they first quitted them, is a passage in the beginning of the fifteenth book, where the *Trojans* being overpower'd by the *Greeks*, fly back over the wall and trench till they came to the place where their chariots stood,

> Οἱ μὲν δὴ παρ' ὄχεσφιν ἐρητύοντο μένοντες.   *Lib.* 15. v. 3.

[They restrained themselves, remaining by their chariots.]

Neither *Eustathius* nor *Dacier* have taken any notice of this incongruity, which would tempt one to believe they were willing to overlook what they could not excuse. I must honestly own my opinion, that there are several other negligences of this kind in *Homer*. I cannot think otherwise of the passage in the present book concerning *Pylæmenes*, notwithstanding the excuses of the Commentators which are there given. The very using the same name in different places for different persons, confounds the reader in the story, and is what certainly would be better avoided: So that 'tis to no purpose to say, there might as well be two *Pylæmenes*'s as two *Schedius*'s, two *Eurymedons*, two *Ophelestes*'s, &c. since it is more blameable to be negligent in many instances than in one. *Virgil* is not free from this, as *Macrobius* has observ'd. *Sat. l. 5. c. 15.* But the above-mention'd names are proofs of that Critick's being greatly mistaken in affirming that *Homer* is not guilty of the same. It is one of those many errors he was led into, by his partiality to *Homer* above *Virgil*.

948. *And seems a moving mountain topt with snow.*] This simile is very short in the original, and requires to be open'd a little to discover its full beauty. I am not of Mad. *Dacier*'s opinion, that the lustre of *Hector*'s armour was that which furnish'd *Homer* with this image; it seems rather to allude to the plume upon his helmet, in the action of shaking which, this hero is so frequently painted by our Author, and from thence distinguish'd by the remarkable epithet κορυθαίολος. This is a very pleasing image, and very much what Painters call *picturesque*. I fancy it gave the hint for a very fine one in *Spenser*, where he represents the person of *Contemplation* in the figure of a venerable old man almost consum'd with study.

> *His snowy locks adown his shoulders spread,*
> *As hoary frost with spangles doth attire*
> *The mossy branches of an oak half dead.*

965. *Ill-fated* Paris.] The reproaches which *Hector* here casts on *Paris*, give us the character of this hero, who in many things resembles *Achilles*; being (like him) injust, violent, and impetuous, and making no distinction between the innocent and criminal. 'Tis he who is obstinate in attacking the entrenchments, yet asks an account of those who were slain in the attack from *Paris*; and tho' he ought to blame himself for their deaths, yet he speaks to *Paris*, as if thro' his cowardice he had suffer'd these to be slain, whom he might have preserv'd if he had fought courageously.

Eustathius.

1005. *Wide-rowling, foaming high, and tumbling to the shore.*] I have endeavour'd in this verse to imitate the confusion, and broken sound of the original, which images the tumult and roaring of many waters.

> Κύματα παφλάζοντα πολυφλοίσβοιο θαλάσσης
> Κυρτὰ, φαληριόωντα. –

1037. *Clouds of rolling dust.*] A Critick might take occasion from hence, to speak of the exact time of the year in which the actions of the Iliad are suppos'd to have happen'd. And (according to the grave manner of a learned Dissertator) begin by informing us, that he has found it must be the *summer* season, from the frequent mention made of clouds of *dust*: Tho' what he discovers might be full as well inferr'd from common sense, the summer being the natural season for a campaign. However he should quote all these passages at large; and adding to the article of *dust* as much as he can find of the *sweat* of the heroes, it might fill three pages very much to his own satisfaction. It would look well to observe farther, that the fields are describ'd flowery, *Il.* 2. v. 546. that the branches of a tamarisk tree are flourishing, *Il.* 10. v. 767. that the warriours sometimes wash themselves in the sea, *Il.* 10. v. 674. and sometimes refresh themselves by cool breezes from the sea, *Il.* 11. v. 762. that *Diomed* sleeps out of his tent on the ground, *Il.* 10. v. 170. that the flies are very busy about the dead body of *Patroclus*, *Il.* 19. v. 30. that *Apollo* covers the body of *Hector* with a cloud to prevent its being scorch'd, *Il.* 23. All this would prove the very thing which was said at first, that it was *summer*. He might next proceed to enquire, what precise critical time of summer? And here the mention of new-made Honey in *Il.* 11. v. 771. might be of great service in the investigation of this important matter: He would conjecture from hence, that it must be near the end of summer, honey being seldom taken till that time; to which having added the plague which rages in book 1. and remark'd, that infections of that kind generally proceed from the extremest heats, which heats are not till near the *autumn*; the learned enquirer might hug himself in this discovery, and conclude with triumph.

If any one think this too ridiculous to have been ever put in practice, he may see what *Bossu* has done to determine the precise season of the *Æneid*, *lib.* 3. *ch.* 12. The memory of that learned Critick fail'd him, when he produc'd as one of the proofs that it was autumn, a passage in the 6*th* book, where the fall of the leaf is only mention'd in a *simile.* He has also found out a beauty in *Homer*, which few even of his greatest admirers can believe he intended; which is, that to the *violence* and *fury* of the *Iliad* he artfully adapted the *heat* of *summer*, but to the *Odyssey* the *cooler and maturer* Season of *autumn*, to correspond with the *sedateness* and *prudence* of *Ulysses*.

THE
FOURTEENTH BOOK
OF THE
ILIAD

The ARGUMENT

Juno deceives *Jupiter* by the Girdle of *Venus*

Nestor *sitting at the table with* Machaon, *is alarm'd with the encreasing clamour of the war, and hastens to* Agamemnon: *On his way he meets that Prince with* Diomed *and* Ulysses, *whom he informs of the extremity of the danger.* Agamemnon *proposes to make their escape by night, which* Ulysses *withstands; to which* Diomed *adds his advice, that, wounded as they were, they should go forth and encourage the army with their presence; which advice is pursued.* Juno *seeing the partiality of* Jupiter *to the* Trojans, *forms a design to over-reach him; she sets off her charms with the utmost care, and (the more surely to enchant him) obtains the magick girdle of* Venus. *She then applies herself to the God of* Sleep, *and with some difficulty, persuades him to seal the eyes of* Jupiter; *this done, she goes to Mount* Ida, *where the God, at first sight, is ravish'd with her beauty, sinks in her embraces, and is laid asleep.* Neptune *takes advantage of his slumber, and succours the* Greeks: Hector *is struck to the ground with a prodigious stone by* Ajax, *and carry'd off from the battel: Several actions succeed; till the* Trojans *much distress'd, are obliged to give way: The lesser* Ajax *signalizes himself in a particular manner.*

But nor the genial feast, nor flowing bowl,
Could charm the cares of *Nestor*'s watchful soul;
His startled ears th' encreasing cries attend;
Then thus, impatient, to his wounded friend.
5   What new alarm, divine *Machaon*, say,
What mixt events attend this mighty day?
Hark! how the shouts divide, and how they meet,
And now come full, and thicken to the fleet!
Here, with the cordial draught dispel thy care,
10   Let *Hecamede* the strength'ning bath prepare,
Refresh thy wound, and cleanse the clotted gore;
While I th' adventures of the day explore.
      He said: and seizing *Thrasimedes'* shield,
(His valiant offspring) hasten'd to the field;
15   (That day, the son his father's buckler bore)
Then snatch'd a lance, and issu'd from the door.
Soon as the prospect open'd to his view,
His wounded eyes the scene of sorrow knew;
Dire disarray! the tumult of the fight,
20   The wall in ruins, and the *Greeks* in flight.
As when old Ocean's silent surface sleeps,
The waves just heaving on the purple deeps;
While yet th' expected tempest hangs on high,
Weighs down the cloud, and blackens in the sky,
25   The mass of waters will no wind obey;
Jove sends one gust, and bids them roll away.
While wav'ring counsels thus his mind engage,
Fluctuates, in doubtful thought, the *Pylian* sage;

To join the host, or to the Gen'ral haste,
Debating long, he fixes on the last: 30
Yet, as he moves, the fight his bosom warms;
The field rings dreadful with the clang of arms;
The gleaming faulchions flash, the jav'lins fly;
Blows echo blows, and all or kill, or die.

    Him, in his march, the wounded Princes meet,   35
By tardy steps ascending from the fleet.
The King of men, *Ulysses* the divine,
And who to *Tydeus* owes his noble line.
(Their ships at distance from the battel stand,
In lines advanc'd along the shelving strand;   40
Whose bay, the fleet unable to contain
At length, beside the margin of the main,
Rank above rank, the crowded ships they moor;
Who landed first lay highest on the shore.)
Supported on their spears, they took their way,   45
Unfit to fight, but anxious for the day.
Nestor's approach alarm'd each *Grecian* breast,
Whom thus the Gen'ral of the host addrest.

    O grace and glory of th' *Achaian* name!
What drives thee, *Nestor*, from the field of fame?   50
Shall then proud *Hector* see his boast fulfill'd,
Our fleets in ashes, and our heroes kill'd?
Such was his threat, ah now too soon made good,
On many a *Grecian* bosom writ in blood.
Is ev'ry heart inflam'd with equal rage   55
Against your King, nor will one chief engage?
And have I liv'd to see with mournful eyes
In ev'ry *Greek* a new *Achilles* rise?

    Gerenian Nestor then. So Fate has will'd;
And all-confirming Time has Fate fulfill'd.   60
Not he that thunders from th' aërial bow'r,
Not *Jove* himself, upon the past has pow'r.
The wall, our late inviolable bound,
And best defence, lies smoking on the ground:
Ev'n to the ships their conqu'ring arms extend,   65
And groans of slaughter'd *Greeks* to heav'n ascend.
On speedy measures then employ your thought;
In such distress if counsel profit ought;

Arms cannot much: Tho' *Mars* our souls incite,
70 These gaping wounds withhold us from the fight.
        To him the Monarch. That our army bends,
    That *Troy* triumphant our high fleet ascends,
    And that the rampart, late our surest trust,
    And best defence, lies smoaking in the dust:
75 All this from *Jove*'s afflictive hand we bear,
    Who, far from *Argos*, wills our ruin here.
    Past are the days when happier *Greece* was blest,
    And all his favour, all his aid confest;
    Now heav'n averse, our hands from battel ties,
80 And lifts the *Trojan* glory to the skies.
    Cease we at length to waste our blood in vain,
    And launch what ships lie nearest to the main;
    Leave these at anchor till the coming night: ⎫
    Then if impetuous *Troy* forbear the fight,   ⎬
85 Bring all to sea, and hoist each sail for flight. ⎭
    Better from evils, well foreseen, to run,
    Than perish in the danger we may shun.
        Thus he. The sage *Ulysses* thus replies,
    While anger flash'd from his disdainful eyes.
90 What shameful words (unkingly as thou art)
    Fall from that trembling tongue, and tim'rous heart?
    Oh were thy sway the curse of meaner pow'rs,
    And thou the shame of any host but ours!
    A Host, by *Jove* endu'd with martial might,
95 And taught to conquer, or to fall in fight:
    Advent'rous combats and bold wars to wage,
    Employ'd our youth, and yet employs our age.
    And wilt thou thus desert the *Trojan* plain?
    And have whole streams of blood been spilt in vain?
100 In such base sentence if thou couch thy fear,
    Speak it in whispers, lest a *Greek* should hear.
    Lives there a man so dead to fame, who dares
    To think such meanness, or the thought declares?
    And comes it ev'n from him whose sov'reign sway
105 The banded legions of all *Greece* obey?
    Is this a Gen'ral's voice, that calls to flight,
    While war hangs doubtful, while his soldiers fight?

What more could *Troy*? What yet their fate denies
Thou giv'st the foe: all *Greece* becomes their prize.
No more the troops, (our hoisted sails in view,   110
Themselves abandon'd) shall the fight pursue,
Thy ships first flying with despair shall see,
And owe destruction to a Prince like thee.

 Thy just reproofs (*Atrides* calm replies)
Like arrows pierce me, for thy words are wise.   115
Unwilling as I am to lose the host,
I force not *Greece* to quit this hateful coast.
Glad I submit, whoe'er, or young or old,
Ought, more conducive to our weal, unfold.

 Tydides cut him short, and thus began.   120
Such counsel if you seek, behold the man
Who boldly gives it, and what he shall say,
Young tho' he be, disdain not to obey:
A youth, who from the mighty *Tydeus* springs,
May speak to councils and assembled Kings.   125
Hear then in me the great *Oenides*' son,
Whose honour'd dust (his race of glory run)
Lies whelm'd in ruins of the *Theban* wall,
Brave in his life, and glorious in his fall.
With three bold sons was gen'rous *Prothous* blest,   130
Who *Pleuron*'s walls and *Calydon* possest;
Melas and *Agrius*, but (who surpast
The rest in courage) *Oeneus* was the last.
From him, my sire. From *Calydon* expell'd,
He past to *Argos*, and in exile dwell'd;   135
The monarch's daughter there (so *Jove* ordain'd)
He won, and flourish'd where *Adrastus* reign'd;
There rich in fortune's gifts, his acres till'd, ⎫
Beheld his vines their liquid harvest yield, ⎬
And num'rous flocks that whiten'd all the field. ⎭   140
Such *Tydeus* was, the foremost once in fame!
Nor lives in *Greece* a stranger to his name.
Then, what for common good my thoughts inspire,
Attend, and in the son, respect the sire.
Tho' fore of battel, tho' with wounds opprest,   145
Let each go forth, and animate the rest,

Advance the glory which he cannot share,
Tho' not partaker, witness of the war.
But lest new wounds on wounds o'erpower us quite,
150 Beyond the missile jav'lin's sounding flight,
Safe let us stand; and from the tumult far,
Inspire the ranks, and rule the distant war.

He added not: The list'ning Kings obey,
Slow moving on; *Atrides* leads the way.
155 The God of ocean (to inflame their rage)
Appears a warriour furrow'd o'er with age;
Prest in his own, the Gen'ral's hand he took,
And thus the venerable hero spoke.

Atrides, lo! with what disdainful eye
160 *Achilles* sees his country's forces fly;
Blind impious man! whose anger is his guide,
Who glories in unutterable pride!
So may he perish, so may *Jove* disclaim
The wretch relentless, and o'erwhelm with shame!
165 But heav'n forsakes not thee: O'er yonder sands
Soon shalt thou view the scatter'd *Trojan* bands
Fly diverse; while proud Kings, and Chiefs renown'd,
Driv'n heaps on heaps, with clouds involv'd around
Of rolling dust, their winged wheels employ
170 To hide their ignominious heads in *Troy*.

He spoke, then rush'd amid the warriour crew;
And sent his voice before him as he flew,
Loud, as the shout encountring armies yield,
When twice ten thousand shake the lab'ring field;
175 Such was the voice, and such the thund'ring sound
Of him, whose trident rends the solid ground.
Each *Argive* bosom beats to meet the fight,
And grizly war appears a pleasing sight.

Meantime *Saturnia* from *Olympus'* brow,
180 High-thron'd in gold, beheld the fields below;
With joy the glorious conflict she survey'd,
Where her great brother gave the *Grecians* aid.
But plac'd aloft, on *Ida*'s shady height
She sees her *Jove*, and trembles at the sight.
185 *Jove* to deceive, what methods shall she try,
What arts, to blind his all-beholding eye?

At length she trusts her pow'r; resolv'd to prove
'The old, yet still successful, cheat of love':
Against his wisdom to oppose her charms,
And lull the Lord of Thunders in her arms.   190
   Swift to her bright apartment she repairs,
Sacred to dress, and beauty's pleasing cares:
With skill divine had *Vulcan* form'd the bow'r,
Safe from access of each intruding pow'r.
Touch'd with her secret key, the doors unfold: 195
Self-clos'd behind her shut the valves of gold.
Here first she bathes; and round her body pours
Soft oils of fragrance, and ambrosial show'rs:
The winds perfum'd, the balmy gale convey
Thro' heav'n, thro' earth, and all th' aërial way: 200
Spirit divine! whose exhalation greets
The sense of Gods with more than mortal sweets.
Thus while she breath'd of heav'n, with decent pride
Her artful hands the radiant tresses ty'd;
Part on her head in shining ringlets roll'd,   205
Part o'er her shoulders wav'd like melted gold.
Around her next a heav'nly mantle flow'd,
That rich with *Pallas'* labour'd colours glow'd;
Large clasps of gold the foldings gather'd round,
A golden zone her swelling bosom bound.   210
Far-beaming pendants tremble in her ear,
Each gemm illumin'd with a triple star.
Then o'er her head she casts a veil more white
Then new fal'n snow, and dazling as the light.
Last her fair feet celestial sandals grace.   215
Thus issuing radiant, with majestic pace,
Forth from the dome th' imperial Goddess moves,
And calls the Mother of the *Smiles* and *Loves.*
   How long (to *Venus* thus apart she cry'd)
Shall human strifes celestial minds divide?   220
Ah yet, will *Venus* aid *Saturnia's* joy,
And set aside the cause of *Greece* and *Troy*?
   Let heav'n's dread empress (*Cytherǽa* said)
Speak her request, and deem her will obey'd.
Then grant me (said the Queen) those conqu'ring
      charms,   225
That pow'r, which mortals and immortals warms,

That love, which melts mankind in fierce desires,
And burns the sons of heav'n with sacred fires!
    For lo! I haste to those remote abodes,
230 Where the great parents (sacred source of Gods!)
Ocean and *Tethys* their old empire keep,
On the last limits of the land and deep.
In their kind arms my tender years were past;
What-time old *Saturn*, from *Olympus* cast,
235 Of upper heav'n to *Jove* resign'd the reign,
Whelm'd under the huge mass of earth and main.
For strife, I hear, has made the union cease,
Which held so long that ancient pair in peace.
What honour, and what love shall I obtain,
240 If I compose those fatal feuds again?
Once more their minds in mutual ties engage,
And what my youth has ow'd, repay their age.
    She said. With awe divine the Queen of Love
Obey'd the sister and the wife of *Jove*:
245 And from her fragrant breast the zone unbrac'd,
With various skill and high embroid'ry grac'd.
In this was ev'ry art, and ev'ry charm,
To win the wisest, and the coldest warm:
Fond love, the gentle vow, the gay desire,
250 The kind deceit, the still-reviving fire,
Persuasive speech, and more persuasive sighs,
Silence that spoke, and eloquence of eyes.
This on her hand the *Cyprian* Goddess laid;
Take this, and with it all thy wish, she said:
255 With smiles she took the charm; and smiling prest
The pow'rful *Cestus* to her snowy breast.
    Then *Venus* to the courts of *Jove* withdrew;
Whilst from *Olympus* pleas'd *Saturnia* flew.
O'er high *Pieria* thence her course she bore,
260 O'er fair *Emathia*'s ever pleasing shore,
O'er *Hæmus*' hills with snows eternal crown'd;
Nor once her flying foot approach'd the ground.
Then taking wing from *Athos*' lofty steep,
She speeds to *Lemnos* o'er the rowling deep,
265 And seeks the cave of Death's half-brother, *Sleep.*

Sweet pleasing Sleep! (*Saturnia* thus began)
Who spread'st thy empire o'er each God and man;
If e'er obsequious to thy *Juno*'s will,
O Pow'r of Slumbers! hear, and favour still.
Shed thy soft dews on *Jove*'s immortal eyes,   270
While sunk in love's entrancing joys he lies.
A splendid footstool, and a throne, that shine
With gold unfading, *Somnus*, shall be thine;
The work of *Vulcan*; to indulge thy ease,
When wine and feasts thy golden humours please.   275
    Imperial Dame (the balmy pow'r replies)
Great *Saturn*'s heir, and empress of the skies!
O'er other Gods I spread my easy chain;
The Sire of all, old *Ocean*, owns my reign,
And his hush'd waves lie silent on the main.   280
But how, unbidden, shall I dare to steep
Jove's awful temples in the dew of sleep?
Long since too vent'rous, at thy bold command,
On those eternal lids I laid my hand;
What-time, deserting *Ilion*'s wasted plain,   285
His conqu'ring son, *Alcides*, plow'd the main:
When lo! the deeps arise, the tempests roar,
And drive the hero to the *Coan* shore:
Great *Jove* awaking, shook the blest abodes
With rising wrath, and tumbled Gods on Gods;   290
Me chief he sought, and from the realms on high
Had hurl'd indignant to the nether sky,
But gentle *Night*, to whom I fled for aid,
(The friend of earth and heav'n) her wings display'd;
Impow'r'd the wrath of Gods and men to tame,   295
Ev'n *Jove* rever'd the venerable dame.
    Vain are thy fears (the Queen of heav'n replies,
And speaking, rolls her large, majestic eyes)
Think'st thou that *Troy* has *Jove*'s high favour won,
Like great *Alcides*, his all-conqu'ring son?   300
Hear, and obey the mistress of the skies,
Nor for the deed expect a vulgar prize;
For know, thy lov'd-one shall be ever thine,
The youngest *Grace*, *Pasithaë* the divine.

305   Swear then (he said) by those tremendous floods
       That roar thro' hell, and bind th' invoking Gods:
       Let the great parent Earth one hand sustain,
       And stretch the other o'er the sacred main.
       Call the black *Titans* that with *Chronos* dwell,
310   To hear, and witness from the depths of hell;
       That she, my lov'd one, shall be ever mine,
       The youngest *Grace*, *Pasithaë* the divine.
       The Queen assents, and from th' infernal bow'rs
       Invokes the sable subtartarean pow'rs,
315   And those who rule th' inviolable floods,
       Whom mortals name the dread *Titanian* Gods.
       Then swift as wind, o'er *Lemnos* smoaky isle,
       They wing their way, and *Imbrus*' sea-beat soil,
       Thro' air unseen involv'd in darkness glide,
320   And light on *Lectos*, on the point of *Ide*.
       (Mother of savages, whose echoing hills
       Are heard resounding with a hundred rills)
       Fair *Ida* trembles underneath the God;
       Hush'd are her mountains, and her forests nod.
325   There on a fir, whose spiry branches rise
       To join its summit to the neighb'ring skies,
       Dark in embow'ring shade, conceal'd from sight,
       Sate *Sleep*, in likeness of the bird of night.
       (*Chalcis* his name with those of heav'nly birth,
330   But call'd *Cymindis* by the race of earth.)
       To *Ida*'s top successful *Juno* flies;
       Great *Jove* surveys her with desiring eyes:
       The God, whose light'ning sets the heav'ns on fire,
       Thro' all his bosom feels the fierce desire;
335   Fierce as when first by stealth he seiz'd her charms,
       Mix'd with her soul, and melted in her arms.
       Fix'd on her eyes he fed his eager look,
       Then press'd her hand, and thus with transport spoke.
       Why comes my Goddess from th' æthereal sky,
340   And not her steeds and flaming chariot nigh?
       Then she – I haste to those remote abodes,
       Where the great parents of the deathless Gods,
       The rev'rend *Ocean* and grey *Tethys* reign,
       On the last limits of the land and main.

I visit these, to whose indulgent cares   345
I owe the nursing of my tender years.
For strife, I hear, has made that union cease,
Which held so long this ancient pair in peace.
The steeds, prepar'd my chariot to convey
O'er earth and seas, and thro' th' aërial way,   350
Wait under *Ide*: Of thy superiour pow'r
To ask consent, I leave th' *Olympian* bow'r;
Nor seek, unknown to thee, the sacred cells
Deep under seas, where hoary *Ocean* dwells.

   For that (said *Jove*) suffice another day;   355
But eager love denies the least delay.
Let softer cares the present hour employ,
And be these moments sacred all to joy.
Ne'er did my soul so strong a passion prove,
Or for an earthly, or a heav'nly love: 360
Not when I press'd *Ixion*'s matchless dame,
Whence rose *Perithous* like the Gods in fame.
Not when fair *Danaë* felt the show'r of gold
Stream into life, whence *Perseus* brave and bold.
Not thus I burn'd for either *Theban* dame,   365
(*Bacchus* from this, from that *Alcides* came).
Not *Phœnix*' daughter, beautiful and young,
Whence godlike *Rhadamanth* and *Minos* sprung.
Not thus I burn'd for fair *Latona*'s face,
Nor comelier *Ceres*' more majestick grace.   370
Not thus ev'n for thyself I felt desire,
As now my veins receive the pleasing fire.

   He spoke; the Goddess with the charming eyes
Glows with celestial red, and thus replies.
Is this a scene for love? On *Ida*'s height,   375
Expos'd to mortal, and immortal sight;
Our joys prophan'd by each familiar eye;
The sport of heav'n, and fable of the sky!
How shall I e'er review the blest abodes,
Or mix among the senate of the Gods?   380
Shall I not think, that, with disorder'd charms,
All heav'n beholds me recent from thy arms?
With skill divine has *Vulcan* form'd thy bow'r,
Sacred to love and to the genial hour;

385 If such thy will, to that recess retire,
And secret there indulge thy soft desire.
    She ceas'd, and smiling with superiour love,
Thus answer'd mild the cloud-compelling *Jove.*
Nor God, nor mortal shall our joys behold,
390 Shaded with clouds, and circumfus'd in gold,
Not ev'n the sun, who darts thro' heav'n his rays,
And whose broad eye th' extended earth surveys.
    Gazing he spoke, and kindling at the view,
His eager arms around the Goddess threw.
395 Glad earth perceives, and from her bosom pours
Unbidden herbs, and voluntary flow'rs;
Thick new-born vi'lets a soft carpet spread,
And clust'ring *Lotos* swell'd the rising bed,
And sudden hyacinths the turf bestrow,
400 And flamy *Crocus* made the mountain glow.
There golden clouds conceal the heav'nly pair,
Steep'd in soft joys, and circumfus'd with air;
Celestial dews, descending o'er the ground,
Perfume the mount, and breathe *Ambrosia* round.
405 At length with love and sleep's soft pow'r opprest,
The panting Thund'rer nods, and sinks to rest.
    Now to the navy born on silent wings,
To *Neptune*'s ear soft *Sleep* his message brings;
Beside him sudden, unperceiv'd he stood,
410 And thus with gentle words address'd the God.
    Now, *Neptune!* now, th' important hour employ,
To check a while the haughty hopes of *Troy*:
While *Jove* yet rests, while yet my vapours shed
The golden vision round his sacred head;
415 For *Juno*'s love, and *Somnus*' pleasing ties,
Have clos'd those awful and eternal eyes.
    Thus having said, the pow'r of slumber flew,
On human lids to drop the balmy dew.
Neptune, with zeal encreas'd, renews his care,
420 And tow'ring in the foremost ranks of war,
Indignant thus – Oh once of martial fame!
O *Greeks!* if yet ye can deserve the name!
This half-recover'd day shall *Troy* obtain?
Shall *Hector* thunder at your ships again?

Lo still he vaunts, and threats the fleet with fires,   425
While stern *Achilles* in his wrath retires.
One hero's loss too tamely you deplore,
Be still your selves, and we shall need no more.
Oh yet, if glory any bosom warms,
Brace on your firmest helms, and stand to arms: 430
His strongest spear each valiant *Grecian* wield,
Each valiant *Grecian* seize his broadest shield;
Let, to the weak, the lighter arms belong,
The pond'rous targe be wielded by the strong.
(Thus arm'd) not *Hector* shall our presence stay;   435
My self, ye *Greeks!* my self will lead the way.

   The troops assent; their martial arms they change,
The busy chiefs their banded legions range.
The Kings, tho' wounded, and oppress'd with pain,
With helpful hands themselves assist the train.   440
The strong and cumb'rous arms the valiant wield,
The weaker warriour takes a lighter shield.
Thus sheath'd in shining brass, in bright array,
The legions march, and *Neptune* leads the way:
His brandish'd faulchion flames before their eyes,   445
Like light'ning flashing thro' the frighted skies.
Clad in his might th' earth-shaking pow'r appears;
Pale mortals tremble, and confess their fears.

   Troy's great defender stands alone unaw'd,
Arms his proud host, and dares oppose a God: 450
And lo! the God, and wond'rous man appear;
The sea's great ruler there, and *Hector* here.
The roaring main, at her great master's call,
Rose in huge ranks, and form'd a watry wall
Around the ships: Seas hanging o'er the shores,   455
Both armies join: Earth thunders, Ocean roars.
Not half so loud the bellowing deeps resound,
When stormy winds disclose the dark profound;
Less loud the winds, that from th' *Æolian* hall
Roar thro' the woods, and make whole forests fall;   460
Less loud the woods, when flames in torrents pour,
Catch the dry mountain, and its shades devour.

   With such a rage the meeting hosts are driv'n,
And such a clamour shakes the sounding heav'n.

465   The first bold jav'lin urg'd by *Hector*'s force,
       Direct at *Ajax*' bosom wing'd its course;
       But there no pass the crossing belts afford,
       (One brac'd his shield, and one sustain'd his sword.)
       Then back the disappointed *Trojan* drew,
470   And curs'd the lance that unavailing flew:
       But scap'd not *Ajax*; his tempestuous hand
       A pond'rous stone up-heaving from the sand,
       (Where heaps lay'd loose beneath the warriour's feet,
       Or serv'd to ballast, or to prop the fleet)
475   Toss'd round and round, the missive marble flings;
       On the raz'd shield the falling ruin rings:
       Full on his breast and throat with force descends;
       Nor deaden'd there its giddy fury spends,
       But whirling on, with many a fiery round,
480   Smokes in the dust, and ploughs into the ground.
       As when the bolt, red-hissing from above,
       Darts on the consecrated plant of *Jove*,
       The mountain-oak in flaming ruin lies,
       Black from the blow, and smoaks of sulphur rise;
485   Stiff with amaze the pale beholders stand,
       And own the terrours of th' almighty hand!
       So lies great *Hector* prostrate on the shore;
       His slacken'd hand deserts the lance it bore;
       His following shield the fallen chief o'erspread;
490   Beneath his helmet drop'd his fainting head;
       His load of armour, sinking to the ground,
       Clanks on the field; a dead, and hollow sound.
       Loud Shouts of triumph fill the crowded plain;
       Greece sees, in hope, *Troy*'s great defender slain:
495   All spring to seize him; storms of arrows fly;
       And thicker jav'lins intercept the sky.
       In vain an iron tempest hisses round;
       He lies protected, and without a wound.
       Polydamas, *Agenor* the divine,
       The pious warriour of *Anchises*' line,
       And each bold leader of the *Lycian* band;
       With cov'ring shields (a friendly circle) stand.
       His mournful followers, with assistant care,
       The groaning hero to his chariot bear;

His foaming coursers, swifter than the wind,   505
Speed to the town, and leave the war behind.
  When now they touch'd the mead's enamel'd side,
Where gentle *Xanthus* rolls his easy tyde,
With watry drops the chief they sprinkle round,
Plac'd on the margin of the flow'ry ground.   510
Rais'd on his knees, he now ejects the gore;
Now faints anew, low-sinking on the shore;
By fits he breathes, half views the fleeting skies,
And seals again, by fits, his swimming eyes.
  Soon as the *Greeks* the chief's retreat beheld,   515
With double fury each invades the field.
Oïlean Ajax first his jav'lin sped,
Pierc'd by whose point, the son of *Enops* bled;
(*Satnius* the brave, whom beauteous *Neis* bore
Amidst her flocks on *Satnio*'s silver shore)   520
Struck thro' the belly's rim, the warriour lies
Supine, and shades eternal veil his eyes.
An arduous battel rose around the dead;
By turns the *Greeks*, by turns the *Trojans* bled.
Fir'd with revenge, *Polydamas* drew near,   525
And at *Prothœnor* shook the trembling spear;
The driving jav'lin thro' his shoulder thrust,
He sinks to earth, and grasps the bloody dust.
Lo thus (the victor cries) we rule the field,
And thus their arms the race of *Panthus* wield: 530
From this unerring hand there flies no dart
But bathes its point within a *Grecian* heart.
Propt on that spear to which thou ow'st thy fall,
Go, guide thy darksome steps, to *Pluto*'s dreary hall!
  He said, and sorrow touch'd each *Argive* breast: 535
The soul of *Ajax* burn'd above the rest.
As by his side the groaning warriour fell,
At the fierce foe he launch'd his piercing steel;
The foe reclining, shunn'd the flying death;
But fate, *Archelochus*, demands thy breath: 540
Thy lofty birth no succour could impart,
The wings of death o'ertook thee on the dart,
Swift to perform heav'n's fatal will it fled,
Full on the juncture of the neck and head,

545 And took the joint, and cut the nerves in twain:
The dropping head first tumbled to the plain.
So just the stroke, that yet the body stood
Erect, then roll'd along the sands in blood.

Here, proud *Polydamas*, here turn thy eyes!
550 (The tow'ring *Ajax* loud-insulting cries)
Say, is this chief extended on the plain,
A worthy vengeance for *Prothœnor* slain?
Mark well his port! his figure and his face
Nor speak him vulgar, nor of vulgar race;
555 Some lines, methinks, may make his lineage known,
Antenor's brother, or perhaps his son.

He spake, and smil'd severe, for well he knew
The bleeding youth: *Troy* sadden'd at the view.
But furious *Acamas* aveng'd his cause;
560 As *Promachus* his slaughter'd brother draws,
He pierc'd his heart – Such fate attends you all,
Proud *Argives!* destin'd by our arms to fall.
Not *Troy* alone, but haughty *Greece* shall share
The toils, the sorrows, and the wounds of war.
565 Behold your *Promachus* depriv'd of breath,
A victim ow'd to my brave brother's death.
Not unappeas'd, he enters *Pluto*'s gate,
Who leaves a brother to revenge his fate.

Heart-piercing anguish struck the *Grecian* host,
570 But touch'd the breast of bold *Peneleus* most:
At the proud boaster he directs his course;
The boaster flies, and shuns superior force.
But young *Ilioneus* receiv'd the spear,
Ilioneus, his father's only care:
(*Phorbas* the rich, of all the *Trojan* train
Whom *Hermes* lov'd, and taught the arts of gain)
Full in his eye the weapon chanc'd to fall,
And from the fibres scoop'd the rooted ball,
Drove thro' the neck, and hurl'd him to the plain;
580 He lifts his miserable arms in vain!
Swift his broad faulchion fierce *Peneleus* spread,
And from the spouting shoulders struck his head;
To earth at once the head and helmet fly;
The lance, yet sticking thro' the bleeding eye,

The victor seiz'd; and as aloft he shook   585
The goary visage, thus insulting spoke.
 Trojans! your great *Ilioneus* behold!
Haste, to his father let the tale be told:
Let his high roofs resound with frantic woe,
Such, as the house of *Promachus* must know;   590
Let doleful tidings greet his mother's ear,
Such, as to *Promachus'* sad spouse we bear;
When we, victorious, shall to *Greece* return,
And the pale matron in our triumphs mourn.

 Dreadful he spoke, then toss'd the head on high;   595
The *Trojans* hear, they tremble, and they fly:
Aghast they gaze around the fleet and wall,
And dread the ruin that impends on all.

 Daughters of *Jove!* that on *Olympus* shine,
Ye all–beholding, all–recording nine!   600
O say, when *Neptune* made proud *Ilion* yield,
What chief, what hero first embru'd the field?
Of all the *Grecians*, what immortal name,
And whose blest trophies, will ye raise to fame?

 Thou first, great *Ajax!* on th' ensanguin'd plain   605
Laid *Hyrtius*, leader of the *Mysian* train.
Phalces and *Mermer*, *Nestor*'s son o'erthrew.
Bold *Merion*, *Morys* and *Hippotion* slew.
Strong *Periphætes* and *Prothoön* bled,
By *Teucer*'s arrows mingled with the dead.   610
Pierc'd in the flank by *Menelaüs'* steel,
His people's pastor, *Hyperenor* fell;
Eternal darkness wrapt the warriour round,
And the fierce soul came rushing thro' the wound.
But stretch'd in heaps before *Oileus'* son,   615
Fall mighty numbers; mighty numbers run;
Ajax the less, of all the *Grecian* race
Skill'd in pursuit, and swiftest in the chace.

OBSERVATIONS

ON THE

FOURTEENTH BOOK

The Poet, to advance the character of *Nestor*, and give us a due esteem for his conduct and circumspection, represents him as deeply sollicitous for the common good: In the very article of mirth or relaxation from the toils of war, he is all attention to learn the fate and issue of the battel: And through his long use and skill in martial events, he judges from the nature of the uproar still encreasing, that the fortune of the day is held no longer in suspense, but inclines to one side.

Eustathius.

1. *But nor the genial feast.*] At the end of the 11*th* book we left *Nestor* at the table with *Machaon*. The attack of the entrenchments, describ'd thro' the 12*th* and 13*th* books, happen'd while *Nestor* and *Machaon* sate at the table; nor is there any improbability herein, since there is nothing performed in those two books, but what might naturally happen in the space of two hours. *Homer* constantly follows the thread of his narration, and never suffers his reader to forget the train of action, or the time it employs.   *Dacier.*

10. *Let* Hecamede *the bath prepare.*] The custom of women officiating to men in the bath was usual in ancient times. Examples are frequent in the *Odyssey*. And it is not at all more odd, or to be sneered at, than the custom now used in *France*, of *Valets de Chambres* dressing and undressing the ladies.

21. *As when old Ocean's silent surface sleeps.*] There are no where more finish'd pictures of nature, than those which *Homer* draws in several of his comparisons. The beauty however of some of these will be lost to many, who cannot perceive the resemblance, having never had opportu-

nity to observe the things themselves. The life of this description will be most sensible to those who have been at sea in a calm: In this Condition the water is not entirely motionless, but swells gently in smooth waves, which fluctuate backwards and forwards in a kind of balancing motion: This state continues till a rising wind gives a determination to the waves, and rolls 'em one certain way. There is scarce any thing in the whole compass of nature that can more exactly represent the state of an irresolute mind, wavering between two different designs, sometimes inclining to the one, sometimes to the other, and then moving to that point to which its resolution is at last determined. Every circumstance of this comparison is both beautiful and just; and it is the more to be admired, because it is very difficult to find sensible images proper to represent the motions of the mind; wherefore we but rarely meet with such comparisons even in the best Poets. There is one of great beauty in *Virgil*, upon a subject very like this, where he compares his hero's mind, agitated with a great variety and quick succession of thoughts, to a dancing light reflected from a vessel of water in motion.

> *Cuncta videns, magno curarum fluctuat æstu,*
> *Atque animum, nunc huc, celerem, nunc dividit illuc,*
> *In partesque; rapit varias, perque omnia versat.*
> *Sicut aquæ tremulum labris ubi lumen ahenis*
> *Sole repercussum, aut radiantis imagine lunæ,*
> *Omnia pervolitat late loca; jamque sub auras*
> *Erigitur, summique ferit laquearia tecti.*   Æn. l. 8. v. 19.

> [This way and that he turns his anxious mind;
> Thinks, and rejects the counsels he design'd:
> Explores himself in vain, in ev'ry part,
> And gives no rest to his distracted heart.
>   So when the sun by day, or moon by night,
> Strike, on the polish'd brass, their trembling light,
> The glitt'ring species here and there divide;
> And cast their dubious beams from side to side:
> Now on the walls, now on the pavement play,
> And to the ceiling flash the glaring day.]

30. *He fixes on the last.*] *Nestor* appears in this place a great friend to his Prince; for upon deliberating whether he should go through the body of the *Grecian* host, or else repair to *Agamemnon*'s tent; he

determines at last, and judges it the best way to go to the latter. Now because it had been ill concerted to have made a man of his age walk a great way round about in quest of his commander, *Homer* has ordered it so that he should meet *Agamemnon* in his way thither. And nothing could be better imagined than the reason, why the wounded Princes left their tents; they were impatient to behold the battel, anxious for its success, and desirous to inspirit the soldiers by their presence. The Poet was obliged to give a reason; for in *Epic* Poetry, as well as in *Dramatic*, no person ought to be introduced without some necessity, or at least some probability, for his appearance.   *Eustathius.*

39. *Their Ships at distance,* &c.] *Homer* being always careful to distinguish each scene of action, gives a very particular description of the station of the ships, shewing in what manner they lay drawn up on the land. This he had only hinted at before; but here taking occasion on the wounded heroes coming from their ships, which were at a distance from the fight (while others were engaged in the defence of those ships where the wall was broke down) he tells us, that the shore of the bay (comprehended between the *Rhætean* and *Sigæan* promontories) was not sufficient to contain the ships in one line; which they were therefore obliged to draw up in ranks, ranged in parallel lines along the shore. How many of these lines there were, the Poet does not determine. M. *Dacier*, without giving any reason for her opinion, says they were but two; one advanced near the wall, the other on the verge of the sea. But it is more than probable, that there were several intermediate lines; since the order in which the vessels lay is here described by a metaphor taken from the steps of a *scaling-ladder*; which had been no way proper to give an image only of two ranks, but very fit to represent a greater, tho' undetermined number. That there were more than two lines, may likewise be inferred from what we find in the beginning of the 11*th* book; where it is said, that the voice of *Discord*, standing on the ship of *Ulysses, in the middle of the fleet*, was heard as far as the stations of *Achilles* and *Ajax, whose ships were drawn up in the two extremities*: Those of *Ajax* were nearest the wall (as is expresly said in the 682d verse of the 13*th* book, *in the orig.*) and those of *Achilles* nearest the sea, as appears from many passages scatter'd thro' the Iliad.

It must be supposed that those ships were drawn highest upon land, which first approached the shore; the first line therefore consisted of those who first disembarked, which were the ships of *Ajax* and

Protesilaus; the latter of whom seems mentioned in the verse above cited of the 13*th* book, only to give occasion to observe this, for he was slain as he landed first of the *Greeks*. And accordingly we shall see in the 15*th* book, it is his ship that is first attacked by the *Trojans*, as it lay the nearest to them.

We may likewise guess how it happens, that the ships of *Achilles* were placed nearest to the sea; for in the answer of *Achilles* to *Ulysses* in the 9*th* book, v. 432. he mentions a naval expedition he had made while *Agamemnon* lay safe in the camp: So that his ships at their return did naturally lie next the sea; which, without this consideration, might appear a station not so becoming this hero's courage.

47. Nestor*'s approach alarm'd.*] That so laborious a person as *Nestor* has been described, so indefatigable, so little indulgent of his extreme age, and one that never receded from the battel, should approach to meet them; this it was that struck the Princes with amazement, when they saw he had left the field.   *Eustathius.*

81. *Cease we at length,* &c.] *Agamemnon* either does not know what course to take in this distress, or only sounds the sentiments of his nobles (as he did in the second book of the whole army.) He delivers himself first after *Nestor*'s speech, as it became a counseller to do. But knowing this advice to be dishonourable, and unsuitable to the character he assumes elsewhere, ἰδρώσει μέν τευ τελαμών [his sword-belt will sweat, *Il.* II. 388], *&c.* and considering that he should do no better than abandon his post, when before he had threaten'd the deserters with death; he reduces his counsel into the form of a proverb, disguising it as handsomly as he can under a sentence. *It is better to shun an evil,* &c. It is observable too how he has qualified the expression: He does not say, to *shun the battel*, for that had been unsoldierly; but he softens the phrase, and calls it, to shun *evil*: and this word *Evil* he applies twice together, in advising them to leave the engagement.

It is farther remarked, that this was the noblest opportunity for a General to try the temper of his officers; for he knew that in a calm of affairs, it was common with most people either out of flattery or respect to submit to their leaders: But in imminent danger, fear does not bribe them, but every one discovers his very soul, valuing all other considerations, in regard to his safety, but in the second place. He knew the men he spoke to were prudent persons, and not easy to cast themselves into a precipitate flight. He might likewise have a mind to recommend himself to his army by the means of his officers; which he was not very able to do of himself, angry as they were at him, for the affront he had offered *Achilles*, and by consequence thinking him the author of all their present calamities. *Eustathius.*

92.　*Oh were thy sway the curse of meaner pow'rs,*
　　And thou the shame of any host but ours.]

This is a noble complement to his country and to the *Grecian* army, to shew that it was an impossibility for them to follow even their General in any thing that was cowardly, or shameful; tho' the lives and safeties of 'em all were concerned in it.

104.　*And comes it ev'n from him whose sov'reign sway*
　　The banded legions of all Greece *obey?*]

As who should say, that another man might indeed have utter'd the same advice, but it could not be a person of prudence; or if he had prudence, he could not be a governour, but a private man; or if a governour, yet one who had not a well-disciplin'd and obedient army; or lastly, if he had an army so condition'd, yet it could not be so large and numerous an one as that of *Agamemnon.* This is a fine climax, and of wonderful strength. *Eustathius.*

118.　*Whoe'er, or young, or old,* &c.] This nearly resembles an ancient custom at *Athens*, where in times of trouble and distress, every one, of what age or quality soever, was invited to give in his opinion with freedom by the publick cryer. *Eustathius.*

120.] This speech of *Diomed* is naturally introduced, beginning with an answer, as if he had been call'd upon to give his advice. The counsel he proposes was that alone which could be of any real service in their present exigency: However, since he ventures to advise where *Ulysses* is at a loss, and *Nestor* himself silent, he thinks it proper to apologize for this liberty by reminding them of his birth and descent, hoping thence to add to his counsel a weight and authority which he could not from his years and experience. It can't indeed be deny'd that this historical digression seems more out of season than any of the same kind which we so frequently meet with in *Homer*, since his birth and parentage must have been sufficiently known to all at the siege, as he here tells them. This must be own'd a defect not altogether to be excus'd in the Poet, but which may receive some alleviation, if consider'd as a fault of temperament. For he had certainly a strong inclination to genealogical stories, and too frequently takes occasion to gratify this humour.

135. *He fled to* Argos.] This is a very artful colour: He calls the flight of his father for killing one of his brothers, *travelling and dwelling at* Argos, without mentioning the cause and occasion of his retreat. What immediately follows (*so* Jove *ordain'd*) does not only contain in it a disguise of his crime, but is a just motive likewise for our compassion.

Eustathius.

146. *Let each go forth and animate the rest.*] It is worth a remark, with what management and discretion the Poet has brought these four Kings, and no more, towards the engagement, since these are sufficient alone to perform all that he requires. For *Nestor* proposes to them to enquire, if there be any way or means which prudence can direct for their security. *Agamemnon* attempts to discover that method. *Ulysses* refutes him as one whose method was dishonourable, but proposes no other project. *Diomed* supplies that deficiency, and shews what must be done: that wounded as they are, they should go forth to the battel; for though they were not able to engage, yet their presence would reestablish their affairs by detaining in arms those who might otherwise quit the field. This counsel is embrac'd, and readily obey'd by the rest.

Eustathius.

179. *The Story of* Jupiter *and* Juno.] I don't know a bolder fiction in all antiquity, than this of *Jupiter*'s being deceiv'd and laid asleep, or that has a greater air of impiety and absurdity. 'Tis an observation of Mons. *de St Evremond* upon the ancient poets, which every one will agree to: 'that it is surprizing enough to find them so scrupulous to preserve probability, in actions purely human; and so ready to violate it, in representing the actions of the Gods. Even those who have spoken more sagely than the rest, of their nature, could not forbear to speak extravagantly of their conduct. When they establish their being and their attributes, they make them immortal, infinite, almighty, perfectly wise, and perfectly good: But the moment they represent them acting, there's no weakness to which they do not make 'em stoop, and no folly or wickedness they do not make 'em commit.' The same

author answers this in another place by remarking, 'that truth was not the inclination of the first ages: a foolish lye or a lucky falshood gave reputation to impostors, and pleasure to the credulous. 'Twas the whole secret of the great and the wise to govern the simple and ignorant herd. The vulgar, who pay a profound reverence to mysterious errors, would have despised plain truth, and it was thought a piece of prudence to deceive them. All the discourses of the ancients were fitted to so advantagious a design. There was nothing to be seen but fictions, allegories, and similitudes, and nothing was to appear as it was in itself.'

I must needs, upon the whole, as far as I can judge, give up the morality of this fable; but what colour of excuse for it *Homer* might have from ancient tradition, or what mystical or allegorical sense might attone for the appearing impiety, is hard to be ascertain'd at this distant period of time. That there had been before his age a tradition of *Jupiter*'s being laid asleep, appears from the story of *Hercules* at *Coos*, referr'd to by our author, v. 285. There is also a passage in *Diodorus*, *lib.* 1. *c.* 7. which gives some small light to this fiction. Among other reasons which that historian lays down to prove that *Homer* travell'd into *Egypt*, he alledges this passage of the interview of *Jupiter* and *Juno*, which he says was grounded upon an *Egyptian* festival, *whereon the nuptial ceremonies of these two deities were celebrated, at which time both their tabernacles, adorned with all sorts of flowers, are carry'd by the priests to the top of a high mountain.* Indeed as the greatest part of the ceremonies of the ancient religions consisted in some symbolical representations of certain actions of their Gods, or rather deify'd mortals, so a great part of ancient poetry consisted in the description of the actions exhibited in those ceremonies. The loves of *Venus* and *Adonis* are a remarkable instance of this kind, which, tho' under different names, were celebrated by annual representations, as well in *Egypt* as in several nations of *Greece* and *Asia*: and to the images which were carry'd in these festivals, several ancient poets were indebted for their most happy descriptions. If the truth of this observation of *Diodorus* be admitted, the present passage will appear with more dignity, being grounded on religion; and the conduct of the poet will be more justifiable, if that, which has been generally counted an indecent, wanton fiction, should prove to be the representation of a religious solemnity. Considering the great ignorance we are in of many ancient ceremonies, there may be probably in *Homer* many incidents entirely of this nature; wherefore we ought to be reserv'd in our censures, lest what we decry as wrong in the Poet, should prove only a fault in his religion. And indeed it would be a very unfair way to tax any people, or any age whatever, with grossness in general, purely from the gross or absurd ideas or practices that are to be found in their religions.

In the next place, if we have recourse to allegory, (which softens and reconciles every thing) it may be imagin'd that by the congress of *Jupiter* and *Juno*, is meant the mingling of the *æther* and the *air* (which are generally said to be signify'd by these two deities.) The ancients believ'd the *æther* to be igneous, and that by its kind influence upon the air it was the cause of all vegetation: To which nothing more exactly corresponds, than the fiction of the earth putting forth her flowers immediately upon this congress. *Virgil* has some lines in the second *Georgic*, that seem a perfect explanation of the fable into this sense. In describing the spring, he hints as if something of a vivifying influence was at that time spread from the upper heavens into the air. He calls *Jupiter* expressly *Æther*, and represents him operating upon his spouse for the production of all things.

> *Tum pater omnipotens fœcundis imbribus æther*
> *Conjugis in gremio lætæ descendit, & omnes*
> *Magnus alit, magno commixtus corpore, fœtus.*
> *Parturit omnis ager,* &c.

> [For then almighty *Jove* descends and pours
> Into his buxom bride his fruitful show'rs.
> And mixing his large limbs with hers, he feeds
> Her births with kindly juice, and fosters teeming seeds.
> Then fields the blades of bury'd corn disclose, . . .]

But, be all this as it will, it is certain, that whatever may be thought of this fable in a theological or philosophical view, it is one of the most beautiful pieces that ever was produc'd by Poetry. Neither does it want its moral: an ingenious modern writer [*Tatler* 147] (whom I am pleas'd to take any occasion of quoting) has given it us in these words.

'This passage of *Homer* may suggest abundance of instruction to a woman who has a mind to preserve or recall the affection of her husband. The care of her person and dress, with the particular blandishments woven in the *Cestus*, are so plainly recommended by this fable, and so indispensably necessary in every female who desires to please, that they need no farther explanation. The discretion likewise in covering all matrimonial quarrels from the knowledge of others, is taught in the pretended visit to *Tethys*, in the speech where *Juno* addresses herself to *Venus*; as the chaste and prudent management of a wife's charms is intimated by the same pretence for her appearing before *Jupiter*, and by the Concealment of the *Cestus* in her bosom. I shall leave this tale to the consideration of such good houswives who are never well dress'd but when they are abroad, and think it necessary to appear more agreeable to all men living than their husbands: As also to those prudent ladies, who, to avoid the appearance of being over-fond, entertain their husbands with indifference, aversion, sullen silence, or exasperating language.'

191. *Swift to her bright apartment she repairs,* &c.] This passage may be of consideration to the ladies, and, for their sakes, I take a little pains to observe upon it. *Homer* tells us that the very Goddesses, who are all over charms, never dress in sight of any one: The Queen of Heaven adorns herself in private, and the doors lock after her. In *Homer* there are no *Dieux des Ruelles*, no Gods are admitted to the toilette.

I am afraid there are some earthly Goddesses of less prudence, who have lost much of the adoration of mankind by the contrary practice. *Lucretius* (a very good judge in gallantry) prescribes as a cure to a desperate lover, the frequent sight of his mistress undress'd. *Juno* herself has suffer'd a little by the very *Muse*'s peeping into her chamber, since some nice criticks are shock'd in this place of *Homer* to find that the Goddess washes herself, which presents some idea as if she was dirty. Those who have delicacy will profit by this remark.

198. *Soft oils of fragrance.*] The practice of *Juno* in anointing her body with perfumed oils was a remarkable part of ancient *Cosmeticks*, tho' entirely disused in the modern arts of dress. It may possibly offend the niceness of modern ladies; but such of 'em as paint, ought to consider that this practice might, without much greater difficulty, be reconciled to cleanliness. This passage is a clear instance of the antiquity of this custom, and clearly determines against *Pliny*, who is of opinion that it was not so ancient as those times, where, speaking of perfum'd un-guents, he says, *Quis primus invenerit non traditur; Iliacis temporibus non erant* [Who first discovered them has not been recorded; at the time of the *Trojan* war, they did not exist], lib. 13. c. 1. Besides the

custom of anointing Kings among the *Jews*, which the Christians have borrow'd, there are several allusions in the Old Testament which shew that this practice was thought ornamental among them. The *Psalmist*, speaking of the gifts of God, mentions wine and oil, the former to make glad the heart of man, and the latter to give him a chearful countenance. It seems most probable that this was an eastern invention, agreeable to the luxury of the *Asiaticks*, among whom the most proper ingredients for these unguents were produc'd; from them this custom was propagated among the *Romans*, by whom it was esteem'd a pleasure of a very refin'd nature. Whoever is curious to see instances of their expence and delicacy therein, may be satisfied in the three first chapters of the thirteenth book of *Pliny*'s natural history.

203. *Thus while she breath'd of Heav'n,* &c.] We have here a compleat picture from head to foot of the dress of the fair sex, and of the mode between two and three thousand years ago. May I have leave to observe the great simplicity of *Juno*'s dress, in comparison with the innumerable equipage of a modern toilette? The Goddess, even when she is setting herself out on the greatest occasion, has only her own locks to tie, a white veil to cast over them, a mantle to dress her whole body, her pendants, and her sandals. This the Poet expresly says was *all her dress* [πάντα κόσμον;] and one may reasonably conclude it was all that was used by the greatest princesses and finest beauties of those times. The good *Eustathius* is ravish'd to find, that here are no washes for the face, no dyes for the hair, and none of those artificial embellishments since in practice; he also rejoices not a little, that *Juno* has no looking-glass, tire-woman, or waiting maid. One may preach till dooms-day on this subject, but all the commentators in the world will never prevail upon a lady to stick one pin the less in her gown, except she can be convinced, that the ancient dress will better set off her person.

As the *Asiaticks* always surpass'd the *Grecians* in whatever regarded magnificence and luxury, so we find their women far gone in the contrary extreme of dress. There is a passage in *Isaiah*, Ch. 3. that gives us a particular of their wardrobe, with the number and uselessness of their ornaments; and which I think appears very well in contrast to this of *Homer*. *The bravery of their tinkling ornaments about their feet, and their cauls, and their round tires like the moon: The chains, and the bracelets, and the mufflers, the bonnets, and the ornaments of the legs, and the headbands, and the tablets, and the ear-rings, the rings and nose-jewels, the changeable suits of apparel, and the mantles, and the wimples, and the crisping-pins, the glasses, and the fine linen, and the hoods, and the veils.*

I could be glad to ask the ladies which they should like best to imitate, the *Greeks*, or the *Asiaticks*? I would desire those that are handsome and well-made, to consider, that the dress of *Juno* (which is the same they see in *statues*) has manifestly the advantage of the present, in displaying whatever is beautiful: That the charms of the *neck* and *breast* are not less laid open, than by the modern stays; and that those of the *leg* are more gracefully discover'd, than even by the hoop-petticoat: That the fine turn of the *arms* is better observ'd; and that several natural graces of the *shape* and *body* appear much more conspicuous. It is not to be deny'd but the *Asiatic* and our present modes were better contriv'd to conceal some people's defects, but I don't speak to such people: I speak only to ladies of that beauty, who can make any fashion prevail by their being seen in it; and who put others of their sex under the wretched necessity of being like them in their habits, or not being like them at all. As for the rest, let 'em follow the mode of *Judæa*, and be content with the name of *Asiaticks*.

216. *Thus issuing radiant,* &c.] Thus the Goddess comes from her apartment against her spouse in compleat armour. The pleasures of women mostly prevail by pure cunning, and the artful management of their persons; for there is but one way for the weak to subdue the mighty, and that is by pleasure. The Poet shews at the same time, that men of understanding are not master'd without a great deal of artifice and address. There are but three ways, whereby to overcome another, by violence, by persuasion, or by craft: *Jupiter* was invincible by main force; to think of persuading was as fruitless, after he had pass'd his nod to *Achilles*; therefore *Juno* was obliged of necessity to turn her thoughts entirely upon craft; and by the force of pleasure it is, that she insnares and manages the God.   *Eustathius.*

218. *And calls the Mother of the* Smiles *and* Loves.] Notwithstanding all the Pains *Juno* has been at, to adorn herself, she is still conscious that neither the natural beauty of her person, nor the artificial one of her dress, will be sufficient to work upon a husband. She therefore has recourse to the *Cestus* of *Venus*, as a kind of love-charm, not doubting to enflame his mind by *magical enchantment*; a folly which in all ages has possest her sex. To procure this, she applies to the Goddess of Love; from whom hiding her real design under a feign'd story, (another propriety in the character of the fair) she obtains the valuable present of this wonder-working girdle. The allegory of the *Cestus* lies very open, though the impertinences of *Eustathius* on this head are unspeakable. In it are comprized the most powerful *incentives* to love, as well as the strongest *effects* of the passion. The just admiration of this passage has been always so great and universal, that the *Cestus* of *Venus* is become proverbial. The beauty of the lines which in a few words comprehend this agreeable fiction, can scarce be equall'd. So beautiful an original has produc'd very fine imitations, wherein we may observe a few additional figures, expressing some of the improvements which the affectation, or artifice, of the fair sex have introduc'd into the art of love since *Homer*'s days. *Tasso* has finely imitated this description in the magical girdle of *Armida. Gierusalemme liberata*, Cant. 16.

> *Teneri Sdegni, e placide e tranquille*
> *Repulse, e cari vezzi, e liete paci,*
> *Sorrisi, parrolette, e dolci stille*
> *Di pianto, e sospir tronchi, e molli baci.*

[Of mild denays, of tender scorns, of sweet
Repulses, war, peace, hope, despair, joy, fear,
Of smiles, jests, mirth, wo, grief, and sad regret,
Sighs, sorrows, tears, embracements, kisses dear.]

Mons. *de la Motte*'s imitation of this fiction is likewise wonderfully beautiful.

> *Ce tissu, le simbole, & la cause à la fois,*
> *Du pouvoir d'l'amour, du charme de ses loix.*
> *Elle enflamme les yeux, de cet ardeur qui touche;*
> *D'un sourire enchanteur, elle anime la bouche;*
> *Passionne la voix, en adoucit les sons,*
> *Prête ces tours heureux, plus forts que les raisons;*
> *Inspire, pour toucher, ces tendres stratagêmes,*
> *Ces resus attirans, l'ecueil des sages mêmes.*
> *Et la nature enfin, y voulut renfermer,*
> *Tout ce qui persuade, & ce qui fait aimer.*
> *   En prenant ce tissu, que Venus lui presente,*
> *Junon n'etoit que belle, elle devient charmante.*
> *Les graces, & les ris, les plaisirs, & les jeux,*
> *Surpris cherchent Venus, doutent qui l'est des deux.*

L'amour même trompé, trouve Junon plus belle;
Et son arc à la main, déjà vole après elle.

[This garment, the symbol and, at the same time, the
      cause
of the power of love, of the spell cast by its laws.
It sets the eyes on fire with that ardour that so moves the
      soul;
with a captivating smile it animates the mouth;
it impassions the voice, it softens its sounds,
it lends to it that tone of sweet suggestiveness that is
      stronger than reason;
it inspires those tender stratagems that are so affecting,
those enticing refusals that have shipwrecked even the
      wise.
And nature has, in a word, wished to contain within it
all that is persuasive, all that inspires love.
      Upon taking up this garment that Venus had given to
      her,
Juno was not only beautiful, but she became captivating.
Gracefulness, laughter, pleasure, and playfulness –
all astonished – expect to find Venus, and wonder which
      of the two goddesses she is.
Cupid, himself deceived, finds Juno the more beautiful;
and, bow in hand, he immediately flies after her.]

Spencer, in his 4*th* book, Canto 5. describes a girdle of *Venus* of a very
different nature; for as this had the power to raise up loose desires in
others, that had a more wonderful faculty to suppress them in the
person that wore it: But it had a most dreadful quality, to burst
asunder whenever tied about any but a chaste bosom. Such a girdle,
'tis to be fear'd, would produce effects very different from the other:
Homer's *Cestus* would be a peace-maker to reconcile man and wife; but
Spencer's *Cestus* would probably destroy the good agreement of many a
happy couple.

255. – *And prest The pow'rful* Cestus *to her snowy breast.*] *Eustathius*
takes notice, that the word *Cestus* is not the name, but epithet only, of
Venus's girdle; tho' the epithet has prevail'd so far as to become the
proper name in common use. This has happen'd to others of our
Author's epithets; the word *Pygmy* is of the same nature. *Venus* wore

this girdle below her neck, and in open sight, but *Juno* hides it in her bosom, to shew the difference of the two characters: It suits well with *Venus* to make a shew of whatever is engaging in her; but *Juno*, who is a matron of prudence and gravity, ought to be more modest.

264.　*She speeds to* Lemnos *o'er the rolling deep,*
　　　And seeks the cave of Death's half-brother, Sleep.]

In this fiction *Homer* introduces a new divine personage: It does not appear whether this God of *Sleep* was a God of *Homer*'s creation, or whether his pretensions to divinity were of more ancient date. The Poet indeed speaks of him as of one formerly active in some heavenly transactions. Be this as it will, succeeding Poets have always acknowledg'd his title. *Virgil* would not let his *Æneid* be without a person so proper for poetical machinery; tho' he has employ'd him with much less art than his master, since he appears in the fifth book without provocation or commission, only to destroy the *Trojan* pilot. The criticks, who cannot see all the allegories which the commentators pretend to find in *Homer*'s divinities, must be obliged to acknowledge the reality and propriety of this; since every thing that is here said of this imaginary Deity is justly applicable to Sleep. He is called the *Brother of Death*; said to be protected by *Night*; and is employed very naturally to lull a husband to rest in the embraces of his wife; which effect of this *conjugal opiate* even the modest *Virgil* has remark'd in the persons of *Vulcan* and *Venus*, probably with an eye to this passage of *Homer*.

　　　– Placidumque petivit
　　Conjugis infusus gremio per membra soporem.

　　[He snatch'd the willing Goddess to his arms;
　　'Till in her lap infus'd, he lay possess'd
　　Of full desire, and sunk to pleasing rest.]

264. *To* Lemnos.] The commentators are hard put to it, to give a reason why *Juno* seeks for *Sleep* in *Lemnos.* Some finding out that *Lemnos* anciently abounded with wine, inform us that it was a proper place of residence for him, wine being naturally a great provoker of sleep. Others will have it, that this God being in love with *Pasithaë*, who resided with her sister the wife of *Vulcan*, in *Lemnos*, it was very probable he might be found haunting near his mistress. Other

commentators perceiving the weakness of these conjectures, will have it that *Juno* met *Sleep* here by mere accident; but this is contradictory to the whole thread of the narration. But who knows whether *Homer* might not design this fiction as a piece of raillery upon the sluggishness of the *Lemnians*; tho' this character of them does not appear? A kind of satire like that of *Ariosto*, who makes the Angel find *Discord* in a monastery? Or like that of *Boileau* in his *Lutrin*, where he places *Mollesse* in a dormitory of the Monks of St *Bernard*?

266. *Sweet-pleasing Sleep*, &c.] *Virgil* has copied some part of this conversation between *Juno* and *Sleep*, where he introduces the same Goddess making a request to *Æolus*. *Scaliger*, who is always eager to depreciate *Homer*, and zealous to praise his favourite Author, has highly censured this passage: But notwithstanding this critick's judgment, an impartial reader will find, I don't doubt, much more art and beauty in the original than the copy. In the former, *Juno* endeavours to engage *Sleep* in her design by the promise of a proper and valuable present; but having formerly run a great hazard in a like attempt, he is not prevail'd upon. Hereupon the Goddess, knowing his passion for one of the *Graces*, engages to give her to his desires: This hope brings the lover to consent, but not before he obliges *Juno* to confirm her promise by an oath in a most solemn manner, the very words and ceremony whereof he prescribes to her. These are all beautiful and poetical circumstances, most whereof are untouch'd by *Virgil*, and which *Scaliger* therefore calls low and vulgar. He only makes *Juno* demand a favour from *Æolus*, which he had no reason to refuse; and promise him a reward, which it does not appear he was fond of. The *Latin* Poet has indeed with great judgment added one circumstance concerning the promise of children,

> – & *pulchra faciat te prole parentem.*

[And make thee father of a happy line.]

And this is very conformable to the religion of the *Romans*, among whom *Juno* was suppos'd to preside over human births; but it does not appear she had any such office in the *Greek* theology.

272. *A splendid footstool.*] Notwithstanding the cavils of *Scaliger*, it may be allow'd, that an easy chair was no improper present for *Sleep*. As to the footstool, Mad. *Dacier*'s observation is a very just one; that

besides its being a conveniency, it was a mark of honour, and was far from presenting any low or trivial idea. 'Tis upon that account we find it so frequently mention'd in scripture, where the earth is call'd *the footstool of the throne of God.* In *Jeremiah, Judæa* is call'd (as a mark of distinction) the footstool of the feet of God. *Lament.* 2. v. 1. *And he remember'd not the footstool of his feet, in the day of his wrath.* We see here the same image, founded no doubt upon the same customs.

Dacier.

279. *The Sire of all, old* Ocean.] '*Homer* (says *Plutarch*) calls the Sea *Father of All,* with a view to this doctrine, that all things were generated from water. *Thales* the *Milesian,* the head of the *Ionick* sect who seems to have been the first author of Philosophy, affirmed water to be the principle from whence all things spring, and into which all things are resolved; because the prolific seed of all animals is a moisture; all Plants are nourished by moisture; the very sun and stars, which are fire, are nourished by moist vapours and exhalations; and consequently he thought the world was produced from this element.' Plut. *Opin. of Philos.* lib. 1. c. 3.

281. *But how, unbidden,* &c.] This particularity is worth remarking; *Sleep* tells *Juno* that he dares not approach *Jupiter* without his own order; whereby he seems to intimate, that a spirit of a superiour kind may give itself up to a voluntary cessation of thought and action, tho' it does not want this relaxation from any weakness or necessity of its nature.

285. *What-time deserting* Ilion'*s wasted plain,* &c.] One may observe from hence, that to make falsity in fables useful and subservient to our designs, it is not enough to cause the story to resemble truth, but we are to corroborate it by parallel places; which method the Poet uses elsewhere. Thus many have attempted great difficulties, and sur-mounted 'em. So did *Hercules,* so did *Juno,* so did *Pluto.* Here therefore the Poet feigning that *Sleep* is going to practise insidiously upon *Jove,* prevents the strangeness and incredibility of the tale, by squaring it to an ancient story; which ancient story was, that *Sleep* had once before got the mastery of *Jove* in the case of *Hercules.*

Eustathius.

296. *Ev'n* Jove *rever'd the venerable dame.*] *Jupiter* is represented as unwilling to do any thing that might be offensive or ungrateful to *Night*; the Poet (says *Eustathius*) instructs us by this, that a wise and honest man will curb his wrath before any awful and venerable persons: Such was *Night* in regard of *Jupiter*, feign'd as an ancestor, and honourable on account of her antiquity and power. For the *Greek* theology teaches that *Night* and *Chaos* were before all things. Wherefore it was held sacred to obey the *Night* in the conflicts of war, as we find by the admonitions of the heralds to *Hector* and *Ajax* in the 7th Iliad.

Milton has made a fine use of this ancient opinion in relation to *Chaos* and *Night*, in the latter part of his second book, where he describes the passage of *Satan* thro' their empire. He calls them,

> — *Eldest* Night
> *And* Chaos, *ancestors of nature;* —

And alludes to the same, in those noble verses,

> — *Behold the throne*
> *Of* Chaos, *and his dark pavillion spread*
> *Wide on the wasteful deep: with him enthron'd*
> *Sate sable-vested* Night, *eldest of things*
> *The consort of his reign.* —

That fine apostrophe of *Spenser* has also the same allusion, book 1.

> *O thou, most ancient grandmother of all,*
> *More old than* Jove, *whom thou at first didst breed,*
> *Or that great house of Gods cœlestial;*
> *Which was begot in* Dæmogorgon's *hall,*
> *And saw'st the secrets of the world unmade.*

307. *Let the great parent Earth one hand sustain,*
      And stretch the other o'er the sacred main, &c.]

There is something wonderfully solemn in this manner of swearing proposed by *Sleep* to *Juno*. How answerable is this idea to the dignity of the Queen of the Goddesses, where Earth, Ocean, and Hell itself, where the whole creation, all things visible and invisible, are called to be witnesses of the oath of the Deity.

311. *That she, my lov'd one,* &c.] *Sleep* is here made to repeat the words of *Juno*'s promise, than which repetition nothing, I think, can be more beautiful or better placed. The lover fired with these hopes,

insists on the promise, dwelling with pleasure on each circumstance that relates to his fair one. The throne and footstool, it seems, are quite out of his head.

323. *Fair* Ida *trembles.*] It is usually supposed at the approach or presence of any heavenly being, that upon their motion all should shake that lies beneath them. Here the Poet giving a description of the descent of these Deities upon the ground at *Lectos*, says that the loftiest of the wood trembled under their feet: Which expression is to intimate the lightness and swiftness of the motions of heavenly beings; the wood does not shake under their feet from any corporeal weight, but from a certain awful dread and horrour.　　　　　　*Eustathius.*

328. *In likeness of a bird of night.*] This is a bird about the size of a hawk, entirely black; and that is the reason why *Homer* describes *Sleep* under its form. Here (says *Eustathius*) *Homer* lets us know, as well as in many other places, that he is no stranger to the language of the Gods. *Hobbes* has taken very much from the dignity of this supposition, in translating the present lines in this manner.

> *And there sate* Sleep *in likeness of a fowl,*
> *Which Gods do* Chalcis *call, but men an owl.*

We find in *Plato*'s *Cratylus* a discourse of great subtilty, grounded chiefly on this observation of *Homer*, that the Gods and men call the same thing by different names. The Philosopher supposes that in the original language every thing was express'd by a word, whose sound was naturally apt to mark the nature of the thing signified. This great work he ascribes to the Gods, since it required more knowledge both in the nature of sounds and things, than man had attained to. This resemblance, he says, was almost lost in modern languages by the unskilful alterations men had made, and the great licence they had taken in compounding of words. However, he observes there were yet among the *Greeks* some remains of this original language, of which he gives a few instances, adding, that many more were to be found in some of the barbarous languages, that had deviated less from the original, which was still preserved entire among the Gods. This appears a notion so uncommon, that I could not forbear to mention it.

345. – *To whose indulgent cares I owe the nursing,* &c.] The allegory of this is very obvious. *Juno* is constantly understood to be the *air*; and

we are here told she was nourished by the vapours which rise from
the *Ocean* and the *Earth*. For *Tethys* is the same with *Rhea*.

Eustathius.

359.] This Courtship of *Jupiter* to *Juno* may possibly be thought
pretty singular. He endeavours to prove the ardour of his passion to
her, by the instances of its warmth to other women. A great many
people will look upon this as no very likely method to recommend
himself to *Juno*'s favour. Yet, after all, something may be said in
defence of *Jupiter*'s way of thinking, with respect to the Ladies. Perhaps
a man's love to the sex in general may be no ill recommendation of
him to a particular. And to be known, or thought to have been
successful with a good many, is what some moderns have found no
unfortunate qualification in gaining a lady, even a most virtuous one
like *Juno*, especially one who (like her) has had the experience of a
married state.

395. *Glad earth perceives,* &c.] It is an observation of *Aristotle* in the
25*th* chapter of his Poeticks, that when *Homer* is obliged to describe
any thing of itself absurd or too improbable, he constantly contrives to
blind and dazle the judgment of his readers with some shining descrip-
tion. This passage is a remarkable instance of that artifice, for having
imagined a fiction of very great absurdity, that the Supreme Being
should be laid aside in a female embrace, he immediately, as it were to
divert his reader from reflecting on his boldness, pours forth a great
variety of poetical ornaments; by describing the various flowers the
earth shoots up to compose their couch, the golden clouds that
encompassed them, and the bright heav'nly dews that were shower'd
round them. *Eustathius* observes it as an instance of *Homer*'s modest
conduct in so delicate an affair, that he has purposely adorn'd the bed
of *Jupiter* with such a variety of beautiful flowers, that the reader's
thoughts being entirely taken up with these ornaments, might have no
room for loose imaginations. In the same manner an ancient scholiast
has observ'd, that the golden cloud was contriv'd to lock up this action
from any farther enquiry of the reader.

395.] I cannot conclude the notes on this story of *Jupiter* and *Juno*,
without observing with what particular care *Milton* has imitated the
several beautiful parts of this episode, introducing them upon different
occasions as the subjects of his poem would admit. The circumstance

of *Sleep*'s sitting in likeness of a bird on the fir-tree upon mount *Ida*, is alluded to in his *4th* book, where *Satan* sits in likeness of a cormorant on the tree of life. The creation is made to give the same tokens of joy at the performance of the nuptial rites of our first parents, as she does here at the congress of *Jupiter* and *Juno*.   *Lib.* 8.

> — *To the nuptial bow'r*
> *I led her blushing like the morn, all heav'n*
> *And happy constellations on that hour*
> *Shed their selectest influence; the earth*
> *Gave sign of gratulation, and each hill;*
> *Joyous the birds; fresh gales and gentle airs*
> *Whisper'd it to the woods, and from their wings*
> *Flung rose, flung odours from the spicy shrub.*

Those lines also in the *4th* book are manifestly from the same original.

> — *Roses and jessamine*
> *Rear'd high their flourish'd heads between, and wrought*
> *Mosaic, underfoot the violet,*
> *Crocus and hyacinth with rich inlay*
> *Broider'd the ground.* —

Where the very turn of *Homer*'s verses is observed, and the cadence, and almost the words, finely translated.

But it is with wonderful judgment and decency he has used that exceptionable passage of the dalliance, ardour, and enjoyment: That which seems in *Homer* an impious fiction, becomes a moral lesson in *Milton*; since he makes that lascivious rage of the passion the immediate effect of the sin of our first parents after the fall. *Adam* expresses it in the words of *Jupiter*.

> *For never did thy beauty since the day*
> *I saw thee first, and wedded thee, adorn'd*
> *With all perfections, so enflame my sense,*
> *With ardour to enjoy thee, fairer now*
> *Than ever; bounty of this virtuous tree!*
> *So said he, and forbore not glance or toy*
> *Of amorous intent, well understood*
> *Of* Eve, *whose eye darted contagious fire.*
> *Her hand he seiz'd, and to a shady bank*
> *Thick over-head with verdant roof embow'r'd,*

> *He led her, nothing loath: flow'rs were the couch,*
> *Pansies, and violets, and asphodel,*
> *And hyacinth; earth's freshest, softest lap.*
> *There they their fill of love and love's disport*
> *Took largely, of their mutual guilt the seal;*
> *The solace of their sin, till dewy* Sleep
> *Oppress'd them, weary of their amorous play.*   Milton, *l.* 9.

417. *The pow'r of slumbers flew.*] M. *Dacier* in her translation of this passage has thought fit to dissent from the common interpretation, as well as obvious sense of the words. She restrains the general expression ἐπὶ κλυτὰ φῦλ' ἀνθρώπων, *the famous nations of men*, to signify only the country of the *Lemnians*, who, she says, were much *celebrated* on account of *Vulcan*. But this strain'd interpretation cannot be admitted, especially when the obvious meaning of the words express what is very proper and natural. The God of *Sleep* having hastily delivered his message to *Neptune*, immediately leaves the hurry of the battel, (which was no proper scene for him) and retires among the tribes of mankind. The word κλυτά [famous], on which M. *Dacier* grounds her criticism, is an expletive epithet very common in *Homer*, and no way fit to point out one certain nation, especially in an author one of whose most distinguishing characters is particularity in description.

442. *The weaker warriour takes a lighter shield.*] *Plutarch* seems to allude to this passage in the beginning of the life of *Pelopidas*. '*Homer*, says he, makes the bravest and stoutest of his warriours march to battel in the best arms. The *Grecian* legislators punish'd those who cast away their shields, but not those who lost their spears or their swords, as an intimation that the care of preserving and defending our selves is preferable to the wounding our enemy, especially in those who are Generals of armies, or Governors of states.' *Eustathius* has observ'd, that the Poet here makes the best warriours take the largest shields and longest spears, that they might be ready prepar'd, with proper arms, both offensive and defensive, for a new kind of fight, in which they are soon to be engaged when the fleet is attack'd. Which indeed seems the most rational account that can be given for *Neptune*'s advice in this exigence.

Mr. *Hobbes* has committed a great oversight in this place; he makes the wounded princes (who it is plain were unfit for the battel, and do not engage in the ensuing fight) put on arms as well as the others; whereas they do no more in *Homer* than see their orders obey'd by the rest as to this change of arms.

444. *The legions march, and* Neptune *leads the way.*] The chief Advantage the *Greeks* gain by the Sleep of *Jupiter* seems to be this: *Neptune* unwilling to offend *Jupiter*, has hitherto concealed himself in disguised shapes; so that it does not appear that *Jupiter* knew of his being among the *Greeks*, since he takes no notice of it. This precaution hinders him from assisting the *Greeks* otherwise than by his advice. But upon the intelligence receiv'd of what *Juno* had done, he assumes a form that manifests his divinity, inspiring courage into the *Grecian* chiefs, appearing at the head of their army, brandishing a sword in his hand, the sight of which struck such a terrour into the *Trojans* that, as *Homer* says, none durst approach it. And therefore it is not to be wonder'd, that the *Trojans* who are no longer sustain'd by *Jupiter*, immediately give way to the enemy.

452. *And lo the God, and wondrous man appear.*] What magnificence and nobleness is there in this idea? where *Homer* opposes *Hector* to *Neptune*, and equalizes him in some degree to a God. *Eustathius.*

453. *The roaring main,* &c.] This swelling and inundation of the sea towards the *Grecian* camp, as if it had been agitated by a storm, is meant for a prodigy, intimating that the waters had the same resentments with their commander *Neptune*, and seconded him in his quarrel.   *Eustathius.*

457. *Not half so loud,* &c.] The Poet having ended the episode of *Jupiter* and *Juno*, returns to the battel, where the *Greeks* being animated and led on by *Neptune*, renew the fight with vigour. The noise and outcry of this fresh onset, he endeavours to express by these three sounding comparisons; as if he thought it necessary to awake the reader's attention, which by the preceding descriptions might be lull'd into a forgetfulness of the fight. He might likewise design to shew how soundly *Jupiter* slept, since he is not awak'd by so terrible an uproar.

This passage cannot be thought justly liable to the objections which have been made against heaping comparisons one upon another, whereby the principal object is lost amidst too great a variety of different images. In this case the principal image is more strongly impressed on the mind by a multiplication of similes, which are the natural product of an imagination labouring to express something very vast: But finding no single idea sufficient to answer its conceptions, it endeavours by redoubling the comparisons to supply this defect: The different sounds of waters, winds, and flames, being as it were united in one. We have several instances of this sort even in so castigated and reserv'd a Writer as *Virgil*, who has joined together the images of this passage in the 4*th Georgic*, v. 261. and apply'd them, beautifully softened by a kind of parody, to the buzzing of a bee-hive.

> *Frigidus ut quondam sylvis immurmurat Auster,*
> *Ut mare sollicitum stridet refluentibus undis,*
> *Æstuat ut clausis rapidus fornacibus ignis.*

[As when the woods by gentle winds are stirred;
Such stifled noise as the close furnace hides,
Or dying murmurs of departing tides.]

Tasso has not only imitated this particular passage of *Homer*, but likewise added to it.   *Cant.* 9. *st.* 22.

> *Rapido sì che torbida procella*
> *De cavernosi monti esce piu tarda:*
> *Fiume, ch' alberi insieme, e case svella:*
> *Folgore, che le torri abbatta, & arda:*
> *Terremoto, che'l mondo empia d' horrore,*
> *Son picciole sembianze al suo furore.*

[As swift as hideous *Boreas'* hasty blast,
From hollow rocks when first his storms out burst,
The raging floods that trees and rocks down cast,
Thunders that towns and towers drive to dust:
   Earthquakes, to tear the world in twain that threat,
   Are nought, compared to his fury great.]

480. *Smokes in the dust, and ploughs into the ground.*]

> Στρόμβον δ' ὡς ἔσσευε βαλών, &c.

[Having thrown the rock, he (Ajax) sent it (or him, i.e. Hector) spinning, like a top.]

These words are translated by several as if they signify'd that *Hector* was turn'd round with the blow, like a whirlwind; which would enhance the wonderful greatness of *Ajax*'s strength. *Eustathius* rather inclines to refer the words to the stone itself, and the violence of its motion. *Chapman*, I think, is in the right to prefer the latter, but he should not have taken the interpretation to himself. He says, it is above the wit of man to give a more fiery illustration both of *Ajax*'s strength and *Hector*'s; of *Ajax*, for giving such a force to the stone, that it could not spend itself on *Hector*; but afterwards turn'd upon the earth with that violence; and of *Hector*, for standing the blow so solidly; for without that consideration, the stone could never have recoil'd so fiercely. This image, together with the noble simile following it, seem to have given *Spencer* the hint of those sublime verses.

> *As when almighty* Jove, *in wrathful mood,*
> *To wreak the guilt of mortal sins is bent,*
> *Hurls forth his thund'ring dart, with deadly food*
> *Enroll'd, of flames, and smouldring dreariment:*
> *Thro' riven clouds, and molten firmament,*
> *The fierce three-forked engine making way,*
> *Both lofty tow'rs and highest trees hath rent,*
> *And all that might his dreadful passage stay,*
> *And shooting in the earth, casts up a mound of clay.*
> *His boist'rous club so bury'd in the ground,*
> *He could not rear again,* &c. –

533. *Propt on that spear*, &c.] The occasion of this sarcasm of *Poly-damas* seems taken from the attitude of his falling enemy, who is transfixed with a spear thro' his right shoulder. This posture bearing some resemblance to that of a man leaning on a staff, might probably suggest the conceit.

The speech of *Polydamas* begins a long string of sarcastick raillery, in which *Eustathius* pretends to observe very different characters. This of *Polydamas*, he says, is *pleasant*, that of *Ajax*, *heroic*; that of *Acamas*, *plain*; and that of *Peneleus*, *pathetick*.

599. *Daughters of* Jove! &c.] Whenever we meet with these fresh invocations in the midst of action, the Poets would seem to give their readers to understand, that they are come to a point where the description being above their own strength, they have occasion for supernatural assistance; by this artifice at once exciting the reader's attention, and gracefully varying the narration. In the present case, *Homer* seems to triumph in the advantage the *Greeks* had gain'd in the flight of the *Trojans*, by invoking the *Muses* to snatch the brave actions of his heroes from oblivion, and set them in the light of eternity. This power is vindicated to them by the Poets on every occasion, and it is to this task they are so solemnly and frequently summoned by our Author. *Tasso* has, I think, introduced one of these invocations in a very noble and peculiar manner; where, on occasion of a battel by night, he calls upon the *Night* to allow him to draw forth those mighty deeds which were performed under the concealment of her shades, and to display their glories, notwithstanding that disadvantage, to all posterity.

> *Notte, che nel profondo oscuro seno*
> *Chiudesti, e ne l' oblio fatto si grande;*
> *Piacciati, ch' io nel tragga, e'n bel sereno*
> *A la future età lo spieghi, e mande.*
> *Viva la fame loro, e trà lor gloria*
> *Splenda del fosco tuo l' alta memoria.*

> [Worthy of royal lists and brightest day,
> Worthy a golden trump and laurel crown,
> The actions were and wonders of that fray,
> Which sable night did in black bosom drown:
> Yet, night, consent that I their acts display,
> And make their deeds to future ages known,
>   And in records of long enduring story,
>   Enroll their praise, their fame, their worth and glory.]

THE
FIFTEENTH BOOK
OF THE
ILIAD

The ARGUMENT

The fifth Battel, at the Ships; and the Acts of *Ajax*

Jupiter *awaking, sees the* Trojans *repuls'd from the trenches,* Hector *in a swoon, and* Neptune *at the head of the Greeks: He is highly incens'd at the artifice of* Juno, *who appeases him by her submissions; she is then sent to* Iris *and* Apollo. Juno *repairing to the assembly of the Gods, attempts with extraordinary address to incense them against* Jupiter; *in particular she touches* Mars *with a violent resentment: He is ready to take arms, but is prevented by* Minerva. Iris *and* Apollo *obey the orders of* Jupiter; Iris *commands* Neptune *to leave the battel, to which, after much reluctance and passion, he consents.* Apollo *re-inspires* Hector *with vigour, brings him back to the battel, marches before him with his Ægis, and turns the fortune of the fight. He breaks down great part of the* Grecian *wall; the* Trojans *rush in and attempt to fire the first line of the fleet, but are, as yet, repell'd by the greater* Ajax *with a prodigious slaughter.*

Now in swift flight they past the trench profound,
And many a chief lay gasping on the ground:
Then stopp'd, and panted, where the chariots lie;
Fear on their cheek, and horrour in their eye.
5   Meanwhile awaken'd from his dream of Love,
On *Ida*'s summit sate imperial *Jove*:
Round the wide fields he cast a careful view,
There saw the *Trojans* fly, the *Greeks* pursue,
These proud in arms, those scatter'd o'er the plain;
10 And, 'midst the war, the Monarch of the main.
Not far, great *Hector* on the dust he spies,
(His sad associates round with weeping eyes)
Ejecting blood, and panting yet for breath,
His senses wandring to the verge of death.
15 The God beheld him with a pitying look,
And thus, incens'd, to fraudful *Juno* spoke.
    O thou, still adverse to th' eternal will,
For ever studious in promoting ill!
Thy arts have made the god-like *Hector* yield,
20 And driv'n his conqu'ring squadrons from the field.
Can'st thou, unhappy in thy wiles! withstand
Our pow'r immense, and brave th' almighty hand?
Hast thou forgot, when bound and fix'd on high,
From the vast concave of the spangled sky,
25 I hung thee trembling, in a golden chain;
And all the raging Gods oppos'd in vain?
Headlong I hurl'd them from th' *Olympian* hall,
Stunn'd in the whirl, and breathless with the fall.

For godlike *Hercules* these deeds were done,
Nor seem'd the vengeance worthy such a son;
When by thy wiles induc'd, fierce *Boreas* tost   30
The shipwrack'd hero on the *Coan* coast:
Him thro' a thousand forms of death I bore,
And sent to *Argos*, and his native shore.
Hear this, remember, and our fury dread,
Nor pull th' unwilling vengeance on thy head,   35
Lest arts and blandishments successless prove,
Thy soft deceits, and well-dissembled love.

    The Thund'rer spoke: Imperial *Juno* mourn'd,
And trembling, these submissive words return'd.   40

    By ev'ry oath that pow'rs immortal ties,
The foodful earth, and all-infolding skies,
By thy black waves, tremendous *Styx!* that flow
Thro' the drear realms of gliding ghosts below:
By the dread honours of thy sacred head,   45
And that unbroken vow, our virgin bed!
Not by my arts the ruler of the main
Steeps *Troy* in blood, and rages round the plain;
By his own ardour, his own pity sway'd
To help his *Greeks*; he fought, and disobey'd: 50
Else had thy *Juno* better counsels giv'n,
And taught submission to the Sire of heav'n.

    Think'st thou with me? fair Empress of the skies!
(Th' immortal Father with a smile replies!)
Then soon the haughty Sea-God shall obey,   55
Nor dare to act, but when we point the way.
If truth inspires thy tongue, proclaim our will
To yon' bright synod on th' *Olympian* hill;
Our high decree let various *Iris* know,
And call the God that bears the silver bow.   60
Let her descend, and from th' embattel'd plain
Command the Sea-god to his wat'ry reign:
While *Phœbus* hastes, great *Hector* to prepare
To rise afresh, and once more wake the war,
His lab'ring bosom re-inspires with breath,   65
And calls his senses from the verge of death.
Greece chas'd by *Troy* ev'n to *Achilles'* fleet,
Shall fall by thousands at the hero's feet.

He, not untouch'd with pity, to the plain
70 Shall send *Patroclus*, but shall send in vain.
What youth he slaughters under *Ilion*'s walls?
Ev'n my lov'd son, divine *Sarpedon* falls!
Vanquish'd at last by *Hector*'s lance he lies.
Then, nor till then, shall great *Achilles* rise:
75 And lo! that instant, godlike *Hector* dies.
From that great hour the war's whole fortune turns,
Pallas assists, and lofty *Ilion* burns.
Not till that day shall *Jove* relax his rage,
Nor one of all the heav'nly host engage
80 In aid of *Greece.* The promise of a God
I gave, and seal'd it with th' almighty nod,
Achilles' glory to the stars to raise;
Such was our word, and fate the word obeys.
    The trembling Queen (th' almighty order giv'n)
85 Swift from th' *Idæan* summit shot to heav'n.
As some way-faring man, who wanders o'er
In thought, a length of lands he trod before,
Sends forth his active mind from place to place,
Joins hill to dale, and measures space with space:
90 So swift flew *Juno* to the blest abodes,
If thought of man can match the speed of Gods.
There sate the pow'rs in awful synod plac'd;
They bow'd, and made obeysance as she pass'd,
Thro' all the brazen dome: With goblets crown'd
95 They hail her Queen; the *Nectar* streams around.
Fair *Themis* first presents the golden bowl,
And anxious asks, what cares disturb her soul?
    To whom the white-arm'd Goddess thus replies:
Enough thou know'st the tyrant of the skies,
100 Severely bent his purpose to fulfill,
Unmov'd his mind, and unrestrain'd his will.
Go thou, the feasts of heav'n attend thy call;
Bid the crown'd Nectar circle round the hall;
But *Jove* shall thunder thro' th' ethereal dome,
105 Such stern decrees, such threatned woes to come,
As soon shall freeze mankind with dire surprize,
And damp th' eternal banquets of the skies.

The Goddess said, and sullen took her place;
Blank horrour sadden'd each celestial face.
To see the gath'ring grudge in ev'ry breast,   110
Smiles on her lips a spleenful joy exprest,
While on her wrinkled front, and eyebrow bent,
Sate stedfast care, and low'ring discontent.
Thus she proceeds – Attend ye pow'rs above!
But know, 'tis madness to contest with *Jove*:   115
Supreme he sits; and sees, in pride of sway,
Your vassal Godheads grudgingly obey;
Fierce in the majesty of pow'r controuls,
Shakes all the thrones of Heav'n, and bends the poles.
Submiss, immortals! all he wills, obey;   120
And thou, great *Mars*, begin and shew the way.
Behold *Ascalaphus!* behold him die,
But dare not murmur, dare not vent a sigh;
Thy own lov'd boasted offspring lies o'erthrown,
If that lov'd boasted offspring be thy own.   125

  Stern *Mars*, with anguish for his slaughter'd son,
Smote his rebelling breast, and fierce begun.
Thus then, Immortals! thus shall *Mars* obey;
Forgive me, Gods, and yield my vengeance way:
Descending first to yon' forbidden plain,   130
The God of battels dares avenge the slain;
Dares, tho' the thunder bursting o'er my head
Should hurl me blazing on those heaps of dead.

  With that, he gives command to *Fear* and *Flight*
To join his rapid coursers for the fight: 135
Then grim in arms, with hasty vengeance flies;
Arms, that reflect a radiance thro' the skies.
And now had *Jove*, by bold rebellion driv'n,
Discharg'd his wrath on half the host of heav'n;
But *Pallas* springing thro' the bright abode,   140
Starts from her azure throne to calm the God.
Struck for th' immortal race with timely fear,
From frantic *Mars* she snatch'd the shield and spear;
Then the huge helmet lifting from his head,
Thus, to th' impetuous homicide she said.   145

  By what wild passion, furious! art thou tost?
Striv'st thou with *Jove*? Thou art already lost.

Shall not the Thund'rer's dread command restrain,
And was imperial *Juno* heard in vain?
150　Back to the skies would'st thou with shame be driv'n,
And in thy guilt involve the host of heav'n?
Ilion and *Greece* no more should *Jove* engage;
The skies would yield an ampler scene of rage,
Guilty and guiltless find an equal fate,
155　And one vast ruin whelm th' *Olympian* state.
Cease then thy offspring's death unjust to call;
Heroes as great have dy'd, and yet shall fall.
Why should heav'n's law with foolish man comply,
Exempted from the race ordain'd to die?
160　　This menace fix'd the warriour to his throne;
Sullen he sate, and curb'd the rising groan.
Then *Juno* call'd (*Jove*'s orders to obey)
The winged *Iris*, and the God of Day.
Go wait the Thund'rer's will (*Saturnia* cry'd)
165　On yon' tall summit of the fount-ful *Ide*:
There in the father's awful presence stand,
Receive, and execute his dread command.
　　She said, and sate: the God that gilds the day,
And various *Iris* wing their airy way.
170　Swift as the wind, to *Ida*'s hills they came,
(Fair nurse of fountains and of savage game.)
There sate th' Eternal; he, whose nod controuls
The trembling world, and shakes the steady poles.
Veil'd in a mist of fragrance him they found,
175　With clouds of gold and purple circled round.
Well-pleas'd the Thund'rer saw their earnest care,
And prompt obedience to the Queen of Air;
Then (while a smile serenes his awful brow)
Commands the Goddess of the show'ry bow.
180　　*Iris!* descend, and what we here ordain
Report to yon' mad tyrant of the main.
Bid him from fight to his own deeps repair,
Or breathe from slaughter in the fields of air.
If he refuse, then let him timely weigh
185　Our elder birthright, and superiour sway.
How shall his rashness stand the dire alarms,
If heav'ns omnipotence descend in arms?

Strives he with me, by whom his pow'r was giv'n,
And is there equal to the Lord of Heav'n?
      Th' Almighty spoke; the Goddess wing'd her flight   190
To sacred *Ilion* from th' *Idæan* height.
Swift as the rat'ling hail, or fleecy snows
Drive thro' the skies, when *Boreas* fiercely blows;
So from the clouds descending *Iris* falls;
And to blue *Neptune* thus the Goddess calls.   195
      Attend the mandate of the Sire above,
In me behold the messenger of *Jove*:
He bids thee from forbidden wars repair
To thy own deeps, or to the fields of air.
This if refus'd, he bids thee timely weigh   200
His elder birthright, and superiour sway.
How shall thy rashness stand the dire alarms,
If heav'ns omnipotence descend in arms?
Striv'st thou with him, by whom all pow'r is giv'n?
And art thou equal to the Lord of Heav'n?   205
      What means the haughty Sov'reign of the skies,
(The King of Ocean thus, incens'd, replies)
Rule as he will his portion'd realms on high;
No vassal God, nor of his train am I.
Three Brother Deities from *Saturn* came,   210
And ancient *Rhea*, earth's immortal dame:
Assign'd by lot, our triple rule we know;
Infernal *Pluto* sways the shades below;
O'er the wide clouds, and o'er the starry plain,
Ethereal *Jove* extends his high domain;   215
My court beneath the hoary waves I keep,
And hush the roarings of the sacred deep:
Olympus, and this earth, in common lie;
What claim has here the tyrant of the sky?
Far in the distant clouds let him controul,   220
And awe the younger brothers of the pole;
There to his children his commands be giv'n,
The trembling, servile, second race of heav'n.
      And must I then (said she) O Sire of Floods!
Bear this fierce answer to the King of Gods?   225
Correct it yet, and change thy rash intent;
A noble mind disdains not to repent.

To elder brothers guardian fiends are giv'n,
To scourge the wretch insulting them and heav'n.
230   Great is the profit (thus the God rejoin'd)
When ministers are blest with prudent mind:
Warn'd by thy words, to pow'rful *Jove* I yield,
And quit, tho' angry, the contended field.
Not but his threats with justice I disclaim,
235 The same our honours, and our birth the same.
If yet, forgetful of his promise giv'n
To *Hermes*, *Pallas*, and the Queen of heav'n;
To favour *Ilion*, that perfidious place,
He breaks his faith with half th' ethereal race;
240 Give him to know, unless the *Grecian* train
Lay yon' proud structures level with the plain,
Howe'er th' offence by other Gods be past,
The wrath of *Neptune* shall for ever last.
        Thus speaking, furious from the field he strode,
245 And plung'd into the bosom of the flood.
The Lord of Thunders from his lofty height
Beheld, and thus bespoke the Source of light.
        Behold! the God whose liquid arms are hurl'd
Around the globe, whose earthquakes rock the world;
250 Desists at length his rebel-war to wage,
Seeks his own seas, and trembles at our rage!
Else had my wrath, heav'ns thrones all shaking round,
Burn'd to the bottom of the seas profound;
And all the gods that round old *Saturn* dwell,
255 Had heard the thunders to the deeps of hell.
Well was the crime, and well the vengeance spar'd;
Ev'n pow'r immense had found such battel hard.
Go thou, my son! the trembling *Greeks* alarm,
Shake my broad *Ægis* on thy active arm,
260 Be godlike *Hector* thy peculiar care,
Swell his bold heart, and urge his strength to war:
Let *Ilion* conquer, till th' *Achaian* train
Fly to their ships and *Hellespont* again:
Then *Greece* shall breathe from toils – the Godhead said;
265 His will divine the son of *Jove* obey'd.
Not half so swift the sailing falcon flies,
That drives a turtle thro' the liquid skies;

As *Phœbus* shooting from th' *Idæan* brow,
Glides down the mountain to the plain below.
There *Hector* seated by the stream he sees,   270
His sense returning with the coming breeze;
Again his pulses beat, his spirits rise;
Again his lov'd companions meet his eyes;
Jove thinking of his pains, they past away.
To whom the God who gives the golden day.   275
   Why sits great *Hector* from the field so far,
What grief, what wound, withholds him from the war?
   The fainting hero, as the vision bright
Stood shining o'er him, half unseal'd his sight:
What blest immortal, with commanding breath,   280
Thus wakens *Hector* from the sleep of death?
Has fame not told, how, while my trusty sword
Bath'd *Greece* in slaughter, and her battel gor'd,
The mighty *Ajax* with a deadly blow
Had almost sunk me to the shades below?   285
Ev'n yet, methinks, the gliding ghosts I spy,
And hell's black horrours swim before my eye.
   To him *Apollo*. Be no more dismay'd;
See, and be strong! the Thund'rer sends thee aid,
Behold! thy *Phœbus* shall his arms employ,   290
Phœbus, propitious still to thee, and *Troy*.
Inspire thy warriours then with manly force,
And to the ships impel thy rapid horse:
Ev'n I will make thy fiery coursers way,
And drive the *Grecians* headlong to the sea.   295
   Thus to bold *Hector* spoke the son of *Jove*,
And breath'd immortal ardour from above.
As when the pamper'd steed, with reins unbound,
Breaks from his stall, and pours along the ground;
With ample strokes he rushes to the flood,   300
To bathe his sides and cool his fiery blood.
His head now freed, he tosses to the skies;
His mane dishevel'd o'er his shoulders flies;
He snuffs the females in the well known plain,
And springs, exulting, to his fields again: 305
Urg'd by the voice divine, thus *Hector* flew,
Full of the God; and all his hosts pursue.

As when the force of men and dogs combin'd
Invade the mountain goat, or branching hind;
310 Far from the hunter's rage secure they lie,
Close in the rock, (not fated yet to die)
When lo! a Lion shoots across the way:
They fly; at once the chasers and the prey.
So *Greece*, that late in conq'ring troops pursu'd,
315 And mark'd their progress thro' the ranks in blood,
Soon as they see the furious chief appear,
Forget to vanquish, and consent to fear.

   Thoas with grief observ'd his dreadful course,
Thoas, the bravest of th' *Ætolian* force:
320 Skill'd to direct the jav'lin's distant flight,
And bold to combate in the standing fight;
Nor more in councils fam'd for solid sense,
Than winning words and heav'nly eloquence.
Gods! what portent (he cry'd) these eyes invades?
325 Lo! *Hector* rises from the *Stygian* shades!
We saw him, late, by thund'ring *Ajax* kill'd:
What God restores him to the frighted field;
And not content that half of *Greece* lie slain,
Pours new destruction on her sons again?
330 He comes not, *Jove!* without thy pow'rful will;
Lo! still he lives, pursues, and conquers still!
Yet hear my counsel, and his worst withstand;
The *Greek*'s main body to the fleet command;
But let the few whom brisker spirits warm,
335 Stand the first onset, and provoke the storm:
Thus point your arms; and when such foes appear,
Fierce as he is, let *Hector* learn to fear.

   The warriour spoke, the list'ning *Greeks* obey,
Thick'ning their ranks, and form a deep array.
340 Each *Ajax*, *Teucer*, *Merion*, gave command,
The valiant leader of the *Cretan* band,
And *Mars*-like *Meges*: These the chiefs excite,
Approach the foe, and meet the coming fight.
Behind, unnumber'd multitudes attend,
345 To flank the navy, and the shores defend.
Full on the front the pressing *Trojans* bear,
And *Hector* first came tow'ring to the war.

Phœbus himself the rushing battel led;
A veil of clouds involv'd his radiant head:
High-held before him, *Jove*'s enormous shield   350
Portentous shone, and shaded all the field,
Vulcan to *Jove* th' immortal gift consign'd,
To scatter hosts, and terrify mankind.
The *Greeks* expect the shock; the clamours rise
From diff'rent parts, and mingle in the skies.   355
Dire was the hiss of darts, by heroes flung,
And arrows leaping from the bowstring sung;
These drink the life of gen'rous warriours slain;
Those guiltless fall, and thirst for blood in vain.
As long as *Phœbus* bore unmov'd the shield,   360
Sate doubtful Conquest hov'ring o'er the field;
But when aloft he shakes it in the skies,
Shouts in their ears, and lightens in their eyes,
Deep horrour seizes ev'ry *Grecian* breast,
Their force is humbled, and their fear confest.   365
So flies a herd of oxen, scatter'd wide,
No swain to guard 'em, and no day to guide,
When two fell Lions from the mountain come,
And spread the carnage thro' the shady gloom.
Impending *Phœbus* pours around 'em fear,   370
And *Troy* and *Hector* thunder in the rear.
Heaps fall on heaps: the slaughter *Hector* leads;
First great *Arcesilas*, then *Stichius* bleeds;
One to the bold *Bœotians* ever dear,
And one *Menestheus*' friend, and fam'd compeer.   375
Medon and *Iäsus*, *Æneas* sped;
This sprung from *Phelus*, and th' *Athenians* led;
But hapless *Medon* from *Oïleus* came;
Him *Ajax* honour'd with a brother's name,
Tho' born of lawless love: From home expell'd,   380
A banish'd man, in *Phylace* he dwell'd,
Press'd by the vengeance of an angry wife;
Troy ends, at last, his labours and his life.
Mecystes next, *Polydamas* o'erthrew;
And thee, brave *Clonius!* great *Agenor* slew.   385
By *Paris*, *Deiochus* inglorious dies,
Pierc'd thro' the shoulder as he basely flies.

Polites' arm laid *Echius* on the plain;
Stretch'd on one heap, the victors spoil the slain.
390   The *Greeks* dismay'd, confus'd, disperse or fall,
Some seek the trench, some skulk behind the wall,
While these fly trembling, others pant for breath,
And o'er the slaughter stalks gigantic Death.
On rush'd bold *Hector*, gloomy as the night,
395   Forbids to plunder, animates the fight,
Points to the fleet: For by the Gods, who flies,
Who dares but linger, by this hand he dies:
No weeping sister his cold eye shall close,
No friendly hand his fun'ral pyre compose.
400   Who stops to plunder, in this signal hour,
The birds shall tear him, and the dogs devour.
     Furious he said; the smarting scourge resounds;
The coursers fly; the smoking chariot bounds:
The hosts rush on; loud clamours shake the shore;
405   The horses thunder, earth and ocean roar!
Apollo, planted at the trench's bound,
Push'd at the bank: down sunk th' enormous mound:
Roll'd in the ditch the heapy ruin lay;
A sudden road! A long and ample way.
410   O'er the dread fosse (a late-impervious space)
Now steeds, and men, and cars, tumultuous pass.
The wond'ring crowds the downward level trod;
Before them flam'd the shield, and march'd the God.
Then with his hand he shook the mighty wall;
415   And lo! the turrets nod, the bulwarks fall.
Easy, as when ashore an infant stands,
And draws imagin'd houses in the sands;
The sportive wanton, pleas'd with some new play,
Sweeps the slight works and fashion'd domes away.
420   Thus vanish'd, at thy touch, the tow'rs and walls;
The toil of thousands in a moment falls.
     The *Grecians* gaze around with wild despair,
Confus'd, and weary all the pow'rs with pray'r;
Exhort their men, with praises, threats, commands;
425   And urge the Gods, with voices, eyes, and hands.
Experienc'd *Nestor* chief obtests the skies,
And weeps his country with a father's eyes.

O *Jove!* if ever, on his native shore,
One *Greek* enrich'd thy shrine with offer'd gore;
If e'er, in hope our country to behold,
We paid the fattest firstlings of the fold;   430
If e'er thou sign'st our wishes with thy nod;
Perform the promise of a gracious God!
This day, preserve our navies from the flame,
And save the reliques of the *Grecian* name.
   Thus pray'd the sage: Th' Eternal gave consent,   435
And peals of thunder shook the firmament.
Presumptuous *Troy* mistook th' accepting sign,
And catch'd new fury at the voice divine.
As, when black tempests mix the seas and skies,
The roaring deeps in watry mountains rise,   440
Above the sides of some tall ship ascend,
Its womb they deluge, and its ribs they rend:
Thus loudly roaring, and o'erpow'ring all,
Mount the thick *Trojans* up the *Grecian* wall;
Legions on legions from each side arise;   445
Thick sound the keels; the storm of arrows flies.
Fierce on the ships above, the cars below,
These wield the mace, and those the jav'lin throw.
   While thus the thunder of the battel rag'd,   450
And lab'ring armies round the works engag'd;
Still in the tent *Patroclus* sate, to tend
The good *Eurypylus*, his wounded friend.
He sprinkles healing balmes, to anguish kind,
And adds discourse, the med'cine of the mind.   455
But when he saw, ascending up the fleet,
Victorious *Troy*: then, starting from his seat,
With bitter groans his sorrows he exprest,
He wrings his hands, he beats his manly breast.
Tho' yet thy state require redress (he cries)   460
Depart I must: What horrours strike my eyes?
Charg'd with *Achilles'* high commands I go,
A mournful witness of this scene of woe:
I haste to urge him, by his country's care,
To rise in arms, and shine again in war.   465
Perhaps some fav'ring God his soul may bend;
The voice is pow'rful of a faithful friend.

He spoke; and speaking, swifter than the wind
Sprung from the tent, and left the war behind.
470 Th' embody'd *Greeks* the fierce attack sustain,
But strive, tho' num'rous, to repulse in vain.
Nor could the *Trojans*, thro' that firm array,
Force, to the fleet and tents, th' impervious way.
As when a shipwright, with *Palladian* art,
475 Smooths the rough wood, and levels ev'ry part;
With equal hand he guides his whole design,
By the just rule, and the directing line.
The martial leaders, with like skill and care,
Preserv'd their line, and equal kept the war.
480 Brave deeds of arms thro' all the ranks were try'd,
And ev'ry ship sustain'd an equal tide.
At one proud bark, high-tow'ring o'er the fleet
Ajax the great, and God-like *Hector* meet:
For one bright prize the matchless chiefs contend;
485 Nor this the ships can fire, nor that defend;
One kept the shore, and one the vessel trod;
That fix'd as Fate, this acted by a God.
The Son of *Clytius*, in his daring hand,
The deck approaching, shakes a flaming brand;
490 But pierc'd by *Telamon*'s huge lance expires;
Thund'ring he falls, and drops th' extinguish'd fires.
Great *Hector* view'd him with a sad survey,
As stretch'd in dust before the stern he lay.
Oh! all of *Trojan*, all of *Lycian* race!
495 Stand to your arms, maintain this arduous space!
Lo! where the son of royal *Clytius* lies,
Ah save his arms, secure his obsequies!
This said, his eager jav'lin sought the foe:
But *Ajax* shunn'd the meditated blow.
500 Not vainly yet the forceful lance was thrown;
It stretch'd in dust unhappy *Lycophron*:
An exile long, sustain'd at *Ajax*' board,
A faithful servant to a foreign lord;
In peace, in war, for ever at his side,
505 Near his lov'd master, as he liv'd, he dy'd.
From the high poop he tumbles on the sand,
And lies, a lifeless load, along the land.

With anguish *Ajax* views the piercing sight,
And thus inflames his brother to the fight.

   Teucer, behold! extended on the shore   510
Our friend, our lov'd companion! now no more!
Dear as a parent, with a parent's care,
To fight our wars, he left his native air.
This death deplor'd to *Hector*'s rage we owe;
Revenge, revenge it on the cruel foe.   515
Where are those darts on which the Fates attend?
And where the bow, which *Phœbus* taught to bend?

   Impatient *Teucer*, hastening to his aid,
Before the chief his ample bow display'd;
The well-stor'd quiver on his shoulders hung: 520
Then hiss'd his arrow, and the bowstring sung.
Clytus, *Pisenor*'s son, renown'd in fame,
(To thee, *Polydamas!* an honour'd name)
Drove thro' the thickest of th' embattel'd plains
The startling steeds, and shook his eager reins.   525
As all on glory ran his ardent mind,
The pointed death arrests him from behind:
Thro' his fair neck the thrilling arrow flies;
In youth's first bloom reluctantly he dies.
Hurl'd from the lofty seat, at distance far,   530
The headlong coursers spurn his empty car;
Till sad *Polydamas* the steeds restrain'd,
And gave, *Astynous*, to thy careful hand;
Then, fir'd to vengeance, rush'd amidst the foe;
Rage edg'd his sword, and strengthen'd ev'ry blow.   535

   Once more bold *Teucer*, in his country's cause,
At *Hector*'s breast a chosen arrow draws;
And had the weapon found the destin'd way,
Thy fall, great *Trojan!* had renown'd that day.
But *Hector* was not doom'd to perish then: 540
Th' all-wise Disposer of the fates of men,
(Imperial *Jove*) his present death withstands;
Nor was such glory due to *Teucer*'s hands.
At his full stretch, as the tough string he drew,
Struck by an arm unseen, it burst in two;   545
Down drop'd the bow: the shaft with brazen head
Fell innocent, and on the dust lay dead.

Th' astonish'd archer to great *Ajax* cries;
Some God prevents our destin'd enterprize:
550 Some God, propitious to the *Trojan* foe,
Has, from my arm unfailing, struck the bow,
And broke the nerve my hands had twin'd with art,
Strong to impel the flight of many a dart.

Since Heav'n commands it (*Ajax* made reply)
555 Dismiss the bow, and lay thy arrows by;
Thy arms no less suffice the lance to wield,
And quit the quiver for the pond'rous shield.
In the first ranks indulge thy thirst of fame,
Thy brave example shall the rest inflame.
560 Fierce as they are, by long successes vain;
To force our fleet, or ev'n a ship to gain,
Asks toil, and sweat, and blood: Their utmost might
Shall find its match – No more: 'Tis ours to fight.

Then *Teucer* laid his faithless bow aside;
565 The four-fold buckler o'er his shoulder ty'd;
On his brave head a crested helm he plac'd,
With nodding horse-hair formidably grac'd;
A dart, whose point with brass refulgent shines,
The warriour wields; and his great brother joins.

570   This *Hector* saw, and thus express'd his joy.
Ye troops of *Lycia*, *Dardanus*, and *Troy!*
Be mindful of yourselves, your ancient fame,
And spread your glory with the navy's flame.
Jove is with us; I saw his hand, but now,
575 From the proud archer strike his vaunted bow.
Indulgent *Jove!* how plain thy favours shine,
When happy nations bear the marks divine!
How easy then, to see the sinking state
Of realms accurs'd, deserted, reprobate!
580 Such is the fate of *Greece*, and such is ours:
Behold, ye warriours, and exert your pow'rs.
Death is the worst; a fate which all must try;
And, for our country, 'tis a bliss to die.
The gallant man, tho' slain in fight he be,
585 Yet leaves his nation safe, his children free;
Entails a debt on all the grateful state;
His own brave friends shall glory in his fate;

His wife live honour'd, all his race succeed;
And late posterity enjoy the deed!

This rouz'd the soul in ev'ry *Trojan* breast: 590
The god-like *Ajax* next his *Greeks* addrest.
How long, ye warriours of the *Argive* race,
(To gen'rous *Argos* what a dire disgrace!)
How long, on these curs'd confines will ye lie,
Yet undetermin'd, or to live, or die!   595
What hopes remain, what methods to retire,
If once your vessels catch the *Trojan* fire?
Mark how the flames approach, how near they fall,
How *Hector* calls, and *Troy* obeys his call!
Not to the dance that dreadful voice invites,   600
It calls to death, and all the rage of fights.
'Tis now no time for wisdom or debates;
To your own hands are trusted all your fates:
And better far, in one decisive strife,
One day should end our labour, or our life;   605
Than keep this hard-got inch of barren sands,
Still press'd, and press'd by such inglorious hands.

The list'ning *Grecians* feel their Leader's Flame,
And ev'ry kindling bosom pants for fame.
Then mutual slaughters spread on either side;   610
By *Hector* here the *Phocian Schedius* dy'd;
There pierc'd by *Ajax*, sunk *Laodamas*,
Chief of the foot, of old *Antenor*'s race.
Polydamas laid *Otus* on the sand,
The fierce commander of th' *Epeian* band.   615
His lance bold *Meges* at the victor threw;
The victor stooping, from the death withdrew:
(That valu'd life, O *Phœbus!* was thy care)
But *Cræsmus'* bosom took the flying spear:
His corps fell bleeding on the slipp'ry shore;   620
His radiant arms triumphant *Meges* bore.
Dolops, the son of *Lampus* rushes on,
Sprung from the race of old *Laomedon*,
And fam'd for prowess in a well-fought field;
He pierc'd the centre of his sounding shield: 625
But *Meges*, *Phyleus'* ample breastplate wore,
(Well known in fight on *Selles'* winding shore,

For King *Euphetes* gave the golden mail,
Compact, and firm with many a jointed scale)
630 Which oft, in cities storm'd, and battels won,
Had sav'd the father, and now saves the son.
Full at the *Trojan*'s head he urg'd his lance,
Where the high plumes above the helmet dance,
New ting'd with *Tyrian* dye: In dust below,
635 Shorn from the crest, the purple honours glow.
Meantime their fight the *Spartan* King survey'd,
And stood by *Meges*' side, a sudden aid,
Thro' *Dolops*' shoulder urg'd his forceful dart,
Which held its passage thro' the panting heart,
640 And issu'd at his breast. With thund'ring sound
The warriour falls, extended on the ground.
In rush the conqu'ring *Greeks* to spoil the slain;
But *Hector*'s voice excites his kindred train;
The hero most, from *Hicetaon* sprung,
645 Fierce *Melanippus*, gallant, brave, and young.
He (e'er to *Troy* the *Grecians* cross'd the main)
Fed his large oxen on *Percote*'s plain;
But when oppress'd, his country claim'd his care,
Return'd to *Ilion*, and excell'd in war:
650 For this, in *Priam*'s court he held his place,
Belov'd no less than *Priam*'s royal race.
Him *Hector* singled, as his troops he led,
And thus inflam'd him, pointing to the dead.

    Lo *Melanippus!* lo where *Dolops* lies;
655 And is it thus our royal kinsman dies?
O'ermatch'd he falls; to two at once a prey,
And lo! they bear the bloody arms away!
Come on – a distant war no longer wage,
But hand to hand thy country's foes engage:
660 Till *Greece* at once, and all her glory end;
Or *Ilion* from her tow'ry height descend,
Heav'd from the lowest stone; and bury all,
In one sad sepulchre, one common fall.

    Hector (this said) rush'd forward on the foes:
665 With equal ardour *Melanippus* glows:
Then *Ajax* thus – Oh *Greeks!* respect your fame,
Respect your selves, and learn an honest shame:

Let mutual reverence mutual warmth inspire,
And catch from breast to breast the noble fire.
On valour's side the odds of combate lie,   670
The brave live glorious, or lamented die;
The wretch that trembles in the field of fame,
Meets death, and worse than death, eternal shame.

    His gen'rous sense he not in vain imparts;
It sunk, and rooted in the *Grecian* hearts.   675
They join, they throng, they thicken at his call,
And flank the navy with a brazen wall;
Shields touching shields in order blaze above,
And stop the *Trojans*, tho' impell'd by *Jove.*
The fiery *Spartan* first, with loud applause,   680
Warms the bold son of *Nestor* in his cause.
Is there (he said) in arms a youth like you,
So strong to fight, so active to pursue?
Why stand you distant, nor attempt a deed?
Lift the bold lance, and make some *Trojan* bleed.   685

    He said, and backward to the lines retir'd;
Forth rush'd the youth, with martial fury fir'd,
Beyond the foremost ranks; his lance he threw,
And round the black battalions cast his view.
The troops of *Troy* recede with sudden fear,   690
While the swift jav'lin hiss'd along in air.
Advancing *Melanippus* met the dart
With his bold breast, and felt it in his heart:
Thund'ring he falls; his falling arms resound,
And his broad buckler rings against the ground.   695
The victor leaps upon his prostrate prize;
Thus on a roe the well-breath'd beagle flies,
And rends his side, fresh-bleeding with the dart
The distant hunter sent into his heart.

Observing *Hector* to the rescue flew;   700
Bold as he was, *Antilochus* withdrew:
So when a savage, ranging o'er the plain,
Has torn the shepherd's dog, or shepherd swain;
While conscious of the deed, he glares around,
And hears the gath'ring multitude resound,   705
Timely he flies the yet-untasted food,
And gains the friendly shelter of the wood.

So fears the youth; all *Troy* with shouts pursue,
While stones and darts in mingled tempest flew;
710 But enter'd in the *Grecian* ranks, he turns
His manly breast, and with new fury burns.
        Now on the fleet the Tydes of *Trojans* drove,
Fierce to fulfill the stern decrees of *Jove*:
The Sire of Gods, confirming *Thetis*' pray'r,
715 The *Grecian* ardour quench'd in deep despair;
But lifts to glory *Troy*'s prevailing bands,
Swells all their hearts, and strengthens all their hands.
On *Ida*'s top he waits with longing eyes,
To view the navy blazing to the skies;
720 Then, nor till then, the scale of war shall turn,
The *Trojans* fly, and conquer'd *Ilion* burn.
These fates revolv'd in his almighty mind,
He raises *Hector* to the work design'd,
Bids him with more than mortal fury glow,
725 And drives him, like a light'ning, on the foe.
So *Mars*, when human crimes for vengeance call,
Shakes his huge jav'lin, and whole armies fall.
Not with more rage a conflagration rolls,
Wraps the vast mountains, and involves the poles.
730 He foams with wrath; beneath his gloomy brow
Like fiery meteors his red eye-balls glow:
The radiant helmet on his temples burns,
Waves when he nods, and lightens as he turns:
For *Jove* his splendour round the chief had thrown,
735 And cast the blaze of both the hosts on one.
Unhappy glories! for his fate was near,
Due to stern *Pallas*, and *Pelides*' spear:
Yet *Jove* deferr'd the death he was to pay,
And gave what fate allow'd, the honours of a day!
740   Now all on fire for fame, his breast, his eyes
Burn at each foe, and single ev'ry prize;
Still at the closest ranks, the thickest fight,
He points his ardour, and exerts his might.
The *Grecian* phalanx moveless as a tow'r,
745 On all sides batter'd, yet resists his pow'r:
So some tall rock o'erhangs the hoary main,
By winds assail'd, by billows beat in vain,

Unmov'd it hears, above, the tempest blow,
And sees the watry mountains break below.
Girt in surrounding flames, he seems to fall   750
Like fire from *Jove*, and bursts upon them all:
Bursts as a wave, that from the clouds impends,
And swell'd with tempests on the ship descends;
White are the decks with foam; the winds aloud
Howl o'er the masts, and sing thro' ev'ry shroud: 755
Pale, trembling, tir'd, the sailors freeze with fears;
And instant death on ev'ry wave appears.
So pale the *Greeks* the eyes of *Hector* meet,
The chief so thunders, and so shakes the fleet.

    As when a lion, rushing from his den,   760
Amidst the plain of some wide-water'd fen,
(Where num'rous oxen, as at ease they feed,
At large expatiate o'er the ranker mead;)
Leaps on the herds before the herdsman's eyes;
The trembling herdsman far to distance flies: 765
Some lordly bull (the rest dispers'd and fled)
He singles out; arrests, and lays him dead.
Thus from the rage of *Jove*-like *Hector* flew
All *Greece* in heaps; but one he seiz'd, and slew.
Mycenian Periphes, a mighty name,   770
In wisdom great, in arms well known to fame:
The minister of stern *Euristheus'* ire
Against *Alcides*, *Copreus*, was his sire:
The son redeem'd the honours of the race,
A son as gen'rous as the sire was base;   775
O'er all his country's youth conspicuous far,
In ev'ry virtue, or of peace or war:
But doom'd to *Hector*'s stronger force to yield!
Against the margin of his ample shield
He struck his hasty foot: his heels up-sprung;   780
Supine he fell; his brazen helmet rung.
On the fall'n chief th' invading *Trojan* prest,
And plung'd the pointed jav'lin in his breast.
His circling friends, who strove to guard too late
Th' unhappy hero; fled, or shar'd his fate.   785
    Chas'd from the foremost line, the *Grecian* train
Now man the next, receding tow'rd the main:

Wedg'd in one body at the tents they stand,
Wall'd round with sterns, a gloomy, desp'rate band.
790   Now manly shame forbids th' inglorious flight;
Now fear itself confines them to the fight:
Man courage breathes in man; but *Nestor* most
(The sage preserver of the *Grecian* host)
Exhorts, adjures, to guard these utmost shores;
795   And by their parents, by themselves, implores.
      O Friends! be men: your gen'rous breasts inflame
With mutual honour, and with mutual shame!
Think of your hopes, your fortunes; all the care
Your wives, your infants, and your parents share:
800   Think of each living father's rev'rend head;
Think of each ancestor with glory dead;
Absent, by me they speak, by me they sue;
They ask their safety and their fame from you:
The Gods their fates on this one action lay,
805   And all are lost, if you desert the day.
      He spoke, and round him breath'd heroic fires;
Minerva seconds what the sage inspires.
The mist of darkness *Jove* around them threw,
She clear'd, restoring all the war to view;
810   A sudden ray shot beaming o'er the plain,
And shew'd the shores, the navy, and the main:
Hector they saw, and all who fly, or fight,
The scene wide-opening to the blaze of light.
First of the field, great *Ajax* strikes their eyes,
815   His port majestick, and his ample size:
A pond'rous mace, with studs of iron crown'd,
Full twenty cubits long, he swings around.
Nor fights like others, fix'd to certain stands,
But looks a moving tow'r above the bands;
820   High on the decks, with vast gigantic stride,
The godlike hero stalks from side to side.
So when a horseman from the watry mead
(Skill'd in the manage of the bounding steed)
Drives four fair coursers, practis'd to obey,
825   To some great city thro' the publick way;
Safe in his art, as side by side they run,
He shifts his seat, and vaults from one to one;
And now to this, and now to that he flies; ·

Admiring numbers follow with their eyes.
From ship to ship thus *Ajax* swiftly flew,   830
No less the wonder of the warring crew.
As furious, *Hector* thunder'd threats aloud,
And rush'd enrag'd before the *Trojan* croud:
Then swift invades the ships, whose beaky prores
Lay rank'd contiguous on the bending shores.   835
So the strong eagle from his airy height,
Who marks the swan's or crane's embody'd flight,
Stoops down impetuous, while they light for food,
And stooping, darkens with his wings the flood.
Jove leads him on with his almighty hand,   840
And breathes fierce spirits in his following band.
The warring nations meet, the battel roars,
Thick beats the combat on the sounding prores.
Thou wouldst have thought, so furious was their fire,
No force could tame them, and no toil could tire;   845
As if new vigour from new fights they won,
And the long battel was but then begun.
Greece yet unconquer'd, kept alive the war,
Secure of death, confiding in despair;
Troy in proud hopes already view'd the main   850
Bright with the blaze, and red with heroes slain!
Like strength is felt, from hope, and from despair,
And each contends, as his were all the war.
    'Twas thou, bold *Hector!* whose resistless hand
First seiz'd a ship on that contested strand;   855
The same which dead *Protesilaüs* bore,
The first that touch'd th' unhappy *Trojan* shore:
For this in arms the warring nations stood,
And bath'd their gen'rous breasts with mutual blood.
No room to poize the lance, or bend the bow;   860
But hand to hand, and man to man they grow.
Wounded, they wound; and seek each other's hearts
With faulchions, axes, swords, and shorten'd darts.
The faulchions ring, shields rattle, axes sound,
Swords flash in air, or glitter on the ground;   865
With streaming blood the slipp'ry shores are dy'd,
And slaughter'd heroes swell the dreadful tyde.
    Still raging *Hector* with his ample hand
Grasps the high stern, and gives this loud command.

870   Haste, bring the flames! the toil of ten long years
       Is finish'd; and the day desir'd appears!
       This happy day with acclamations greet,
       Bright with destruction of yon' hostile fleet.
       The coward-counsels of a tim'rous throng
875   Of rev'rend dotards, check'd our glory long:
       Too long *Jove* lull'd us with lethargic charms,
       But now in peals of thunder calls to arms;
       In this great day he crowns our full desires,
       Wakes all our force, and seconds all our fires.

880   He spoke – The warriours, at his fierce command,
       Pour a new deluge on the *Grecian* band.
       Ev'n *Ajax* paus'd (so thick the jav'lins fly)
       Step'd back, and doubted or to live, or die.
       Yet where the oars are plac'd, he stands to wait
885   What chief approaching dares attempt his fate;
       Ev'n to the last, his naval charge defends,
       Now shakes his spear, now lifts, and now protends,
       Ev'n yet, the *Greeks* with piercing shouts inspires,
       Amidst attacks, and deaths, and darts, and fires.

890   O friends! O heroes! names for ever dear,
       Once Sons of *Mars*, and thunderbolts of war!
       Ah! yet be mindful of your old renown,
       Your great forefathers virtues, and your own.
       What aids expect you in this utmost strait?
895   What bulwarks rising between you and fate?
       No aids, no bulwarks your retreat attend,
       No friends to help, no city to defend.
       This spot is all you have, to lose or keep;
       There stand the *Trojans*, and here rolls the deep.
900   'Tis hostile ground you tread; your native lands
       Far, far from hence: your fates are in your hands.

       Raging he spoke; nor farther wastes his breath,
       But turns his jav'lin to the work of death.
       Whate'er bold *Trojan* arm'd his daring hands,
905   Against the sable ships with flaming brands,
       So well the chief his naval weapon sped,
       The luckless warriour at his stern lay dead:
       Full twelve, the boldest, in a moment fell,
       Sent by great *Ajax* to the shades of hell.

OBSERVATIONS

ON THE

FIFTEENTH BOOK

Adam, in *Paradise lost*, awakes from the Embrace of *Eve*, in much the same humour with *Jupiter* in this place. Their Circumstance is very parallel; and each of them, as soon as his passion is over, full of that resentment natural to a superiour, who is imposed upon by one of less worth and Sense than himself, and imposed upon in the worst manner, by shews of tenderness and love.

23. *Hast thou forgot*, &c.] It is in the original to this effect. *Have you forgot how you swung in the air when I hung a load of two anvils at your feet, and a chain of gold on your hands?* 'Tho' it is not my design,' says M. *Dacier*, 'to give a reason for every story in the pagan theology, yet I can't prevail upon my self to pass over this in silence. The physical allegory seems very apparent to me: *Homer* mysteriously in this place explains the nature of the *Air*, which is *Juno*; the two anvils which she had at her feet are the two elements, earth and water; and the chains of gold about her Hands are the *æther*, or fire, which fills the superiour region: The two grosser elements are called anvils, to shew us, that in these two elements only, arts are exercis'd. I don't know but that a moral allegory may here be found, as well as a physical one; the Poet by these masses tied to the feet of *Juno*, and by the chain of gold with which her hands were bound, might signify, that not only domestick affairs should like Fetters detain the wife at home; but that proper and beautiful works like chains of gold ought to employ her hands.'

The physical part of this note belongs to *Heraclides Ponticus*, *Eustathius*, and the Scholiast: M. *Dacier* might have been contented with the credit of the moral one, as it seems an observation no less singular in a Lady.

23.] *Eustathius* tells us, that there were in some manuscripts of *Homer* two verses which are not to be found in any of the printed editions, (which *Hen. Stephens* places here.)

Πρίν γ' ὅτε δὴ σ' ἀπέλυσα ποδῶν, μύδρους δ' ἐνὶ Τροίη
Κάββαλον ὄφρα πέλοιτο καὶ ἐσσομένοισι πυθέσθαι.

[Before I loosed your feet from the fetters, I cast down into Troy masses of burning metal as a lesson to future generations.]

By these two verses *Homer* shews us, that what he says of the punishment of *Juno* was not an invention of his own, but founded upon an ancient tradition. There had probably been some statue of *Juno* with anvils at her feet, and chains on her hands; and nothing but chains and anvils being left by time, superstitious people rais'd this story; so that *Homer* only follow'd common report. What farther confirms it, is what *Eustathius* adds, that there were shewn near *Troy* certain ruins, which were said to be the remains of these masses.   *Dacier.*

43. *And thy black waves, tremendous* Styx!] The epithet *Homer* here gives to *Styx* is κατειβόμενον, *subterlabens* [flowing in the depths], which I take to refer to its passage thro' the infernal regions. But there is a refinement upon it, as if it signify'd *ex alto stillans*, falling drop by drop from on high. *Herodotus* in his sixth book, writes thus. 'The *Arcadians* say, that near the city *Nonacris* flows the water of *Styx*, and that it is a small rill, which distilling from an exceeding high rock, falls into a little cavity or bason, environ'd with a hedge.' *Pausanias*, who had seen the place, gives light to this passage of *Herodotus*. 'Going from *Phereus*, says he, in the country of the *Arcadians*, and drawing towards the West, we find on the left the city of *Clytorus*, and on the right that of *Nonacris*, and the fountain of *Styx*, which from the height of a shaggy precipiece falls drop by drop upon an exceeding high rock, and before it has travers'd this rock, flows into the river *Crathis*; this water is mortal both to man and beast, and therefore it is said to be an infernal fountain. *Homer* gives it a place in his Poems, and by the description which he delivers, one would think he had seen it.' This shews the wonderful exactness of *Homer* in the description of places which he mentions. The Gods swore by *Styx*, and this was the strongest oath they could take; but we likewise find that men too swore by this fatal water: for *Herodotus* tells us, that *Cleomenes* going to

Arcadia to engage the *Arcadians* to follow him in a war against *Sparta*, had a design to assemble at the city *Nonacris*, and make them swear by the water of this fountain.   *Dacier. Eustath.* in *Odyss.*

47. *Not by my arts,* &c.] This apology is well contriv'd; *Juno* could not swear that she had not deceiv'd *Jupiter*, for this had been entirely false, and *Homer* would be far from authorizing perjury by so great an example. *Juno*, we see, throws part of the fault on *Neptune*, by shewing she had not acted in concert with him.   *Eustathius.*

67. Greece *chas'd by* Troy, &c.] In this discourse of *Jupiter*, the Poet opens his design, by giving his reader a sketch of the principal events he is to expect. As this conduct of *Homer* may to many appear no way artful, and since it is a principal article of the charge brought against him by some late *French* criticks, it will not be improper here to look a little into this dispute. The case will be best stated by translating the following passage from Mr *de la Motte*'s *Reflections sur la Critique.*

'I could not forbear wishing that *Homer* had an art, which he seems to have neglected, that of preparing events without making them known beforehand, so that when they happen one might be surprized agreeably. I could not be quite satisfied to hear *Jupiter*, in the middle of the Iliad, give an exact abridgment of the remainder of the action. Mad. *Dacier* alledges as an excuse, that this past only between *Jupiter* and *Juno*; as if the reader was not let into the secret, and had not as much share in the confidence.'

She adds, 'that as we are capable of a great deal of pleasure at the representation of a tragedy which we have seen before, so the surprizes which I require are no way necessary to our entertainment. This I think a pure piece of Sophistry: One may have two sorts of pleasure at the representation of a tragedy; in the first place, that of taking part in an action of importance the first time it passes before our eyes, of being agitated by fear and hope for the persons one is most concern'd about, and in fine, of partaking their felicity or misfortune, as they happen to succeed, or be disappointed.

'This therefore is the first pleasure which the poet should design to give his auditors, to transport them by pathetick surprizes which excite terrour or pity. The second pleasure must proceed from a view of that art which the author has shewn in raising the former.

''Tis true, when we have seen a piece already, we have no longer that first pleasure of the surprize, at least not in all its vivacity; but there still remains the second, which could never have its turn, had not the poet labour'd successfully to excite the first, it being upon that indispensable obligation that we judge of his art.

'The art therefore consists in telling the hearer only what is necessary to be told him, and in telling him only as much as is requisite to the design of pleasing him. And although we know this already when we read it a second time, we yet taste the pleasure of that order and conduct which the art required.

'From hence it follows, that every poem ought to be contrived for the first impression it is to make. If it be otherwise, it gives us (instead of two pleasures which we expected) two sorts of disgusts; the one, that of being cool and untouch'd when we should be mov'd and transported; the other, that of perceiving the defect which caus'd that disgust.

'This, in one word, is what I have found in the Iliad. I was not interested or touch'd by the adventures, and I saw it was this cooling preparation that prevented my being so.'

It appears clearly that M. *Dacier*'s Defence no way excuses the poet's conduct; wherefore I shall add two or three considerations which may chance to set it in a better light. It must be own'd that a surprize artfully managed, which arises from unexpected revolutions of great actions, is extremely pleasing. In this consists the principal pleasure of a Romance or well writ Tragedy. But besides this, there is in the relation of great events a different kind of pleasure which arises from the artful unravelling a knot of actions, which we knew before in the gross. This is a delight peculiar to History and Epic Poetry, which is founded on History. In these kinds of writing, a preceding summary knowledge of the events described does no way damp our curiosity, but rather makes it more eager for the detail. This is evident in a good history, where generally the reader is affected with a greater delight in proportion to his preceding knowledge of the facts described: The pleasure in this case is like that of an Architect's first view of some magnificent building, who was before well acquainted with the proportions of it. In an Epic Poem the case is of a like nature; where, as if the historical Fore-knowledge were not sufficient, the most judicious poets never fail to excite their reader's curiosity by some small sketches of their design; which like the outlines of a fine picture, will necessarily raise in us a greater desire to see it in its finish'd colouring.

Had our author been inclined to follow the method of managing our passions by surprizes, he could not well have succeeded by this manner in the subject he chose to write upon, which being a story of great importance, the principal events of which were well known to the *Greeks*, it was not possible for him to alter the ground-work of his piece; and probably he was willing to mark, sometimes by anticipation, sometimes by recapitulations, how much of his story was founded on historical truths, and that what is superadded were the poetical ornaments.

There is another consideration worth remembering on this head, to justify our author's conduct. It seems to have been an opinion in those early times, deeply rooted in most countries and religions, that the actions of men were not only foreknown, but predestinated by a superior being. This sentiment is very frequent in the most ancient writers both sacred and prophane, and seems a distinguishing character of the writings of the greatest antiquity. *The word of the Lord was fulfill'd* is the principal observation in the history of the Old Testament, and Διὸς δ' ἐτελείετο βουλή [the will of Zeus was being fulfilled] is the declared and most obvious moral of the Iliad. If this great moral be fit to be represented in poetry, what means so proper to make it evident, as this introducing *Jupiter* foretelling the events which he had decreed?

86. *As some way-faring man,* &c.] The discourse of *Jupiter* to *Juno* being ended, she ascends to heaven with wonderful celerity, which the poet explains by this comparison. On other occasions he has illustrated the action of the mind by sensible images from the motion of the bodies; here he inverts the case, and shews the great velocity of *Juno*'s flight by comparing it to the quickness of thought. No other comparison could have equall'd the speed of an heavenly being. To render this more beautiful and exact, the poet describes a traveller who revolves in his mind the several places which he has seen, and in an instant passes in imagination from one distant part of the earth to another. *Milton* seems to have had it in his eye in that elevated passage,

> – *The speed of Gods*
> *Time counts not, tho' with swiftest minutes wing'd.*

As the sense in which we have explain'd this passage is exactly literal, as well as truly sublime, one cannot but wonder what should induce both *Hobbes* and *Chapman* to ramble so wide from it in their translations.

> *This said, went* Juno *to* Olympus *high.*
> *As when a man looks o'er an ample plain,*
> *To any distance quickly goes his eye:*
> *So swiftly* Juno *went with little pain.*

Chapman's is yet more foreign to the subject,

> *But as the mind of such a man, that hath a great way gone,*
> *And either knowing not his way, or then would let alone*
> *His purpos'd journey; is distract, and in his vexed mind*
> *Resolves now not to go, now goes, still many ways inclin'd —*

102. *Go thou, the feasts of heav'n attend thy call.*] This is a passage worthy our observation. *Homer* feigns, that *Themis*, that is Justice, presides over the feasts of the Gods; to let us know, that she ought much more to preside over the feasts of men.   *Eustathius.*

114. Juno's *speech to the Gods.*] It was no sort of exaggeration what the ancients have affirm'd of *Homer*, that the examples of all kinds of oratory are to be found in his works. The present speech of *Juno* is a masterpiece in that sort, which seems to say one thing, and persuades another: For while she is only declaring to the Gods the orders of *Jupiter*, at the time that she tells them they must obey, she fills them with a reluctance to do it. By representing so strongly the superiority of his power, she makes them uneasy at it, and by particularly advising that God to submit, whose temper could least brook it, she incites him to downright rebellion. Nothing can be more sly and artfully provoking, than that stroke on the death of his darling son. *Do thou, O* Mars, *teach obedience to us all, for 'tis upon thee that* Jupiter *has put the severest trial:* Ascalaphus *thy son lies slain by his means: Bear it with so much temper and moderation, that the world may not think he was thy son.*

134. *To* Fear *and* Flight. —] *Homer* does not say, that *Mars* commanded they should join his horses to his chariot, which horses were call'd *Fear* and *Flight*. *Fear* and *Flight* are not the names of the horses of *Mars*, but the names of two furies in the service of this God: It appears likewise by other passages, that they were his children, book 13. v. 299. This is a very ancient mistake; *Eustathius* mentions it as an error of *Antimachus*, yet *Hobbes* and most others have fallen into it.

164. *Go wait the Thund'rer's Will.*] 'Tis remarkable, that whereas it is familiar with the Poet to repeat his errands and messages, here he introduces *Juno* with very few words, where she carries a dispatch from *Jupiter* to *Iris* and *Apollo.* She only says, '*Jove* commands you to attend him on Mount *Ida*,' and adds nothing of what had pass'd between herself and her consort before. The reason of this brevity is not only that she is highly disgusted with *Jupiter*, and so unwilling to tell her tale from the anguish of her heart; but also because *Jupiter* had given her no commission to relate fully the subject of their discourse: wherefore she is cautious of declaring what possibly he would have concealed. Neither does *Jupiter* himself in what follows reveal his decrees: For he lets *Apollo* only so far into his will, that he would have him discover and rout the *Greeks*: Their good fortune, and the success which was to ensue, he hides from him, as one who favour'd the cause of *Troy.* One may remark in this passage *Homer*'s various conduct and discretion concerning what ought to be put in practice, or left un-done; whereby his reader may be inform'd how to regulate his own affairs.   *Eustathius.*

210.   *Three brother deities, from* Saturn *came,*
          And ancient Rhea, *earth's immortal dame:*
          Assign'd by lot, our triple rule we know, &c.

Some have thought the *Platonic* Philosophers drew from hence the notion of their *Triad* (which the Christian *Platonists* since imagined to be an obscure hint of the *Sacred Trinity*.) The *Trias* of *Plato* is well known, τὸ αὐτὸ ὄν, ὁ νοῦς ὁ δημιουργός, ἡ τοῦ κόσμου ψυχή [the one itself, the intelligence and master-craftsman, the soul of the Universe]. In his *Gorgias* he tells us, τὸν Ὅμηρον (*auctorem sc. fuisse*) τῆς τῶν δημιουργικῶν Τριαδικῆς ὑποστάσεως [that *Homer* was the originator of the tripartite essence of the master-craftsman]. See *Proclus in Plat. Theol. lib.* 1. *c.* 5. *Lucian Philopatr. Aristotle de cœlo, l.* 1. *c.* 1. speaking of the *Ternarian* Number from *Pythagoras*, has these words; Τὰ τρία πάντα, καὶ τὸ τρὶς πάντη. Καὶ πρὸς τὰς ἁγιστείας τῶν θεῶν χρώμεθα τῷ ἀριθμῷ τούτῳ. Καθάπερ γάρ φασι καὶ οἱ Πυθαγόρειοι, τὸ πᾶν καὶ τὰ πάντα τοῖς τρισὶν ὥρισται. Τελευτὴ γὰρ καὶ μέσον καὶ ἀρχὴ τὸν ἀριθμὸν ἔχει τὸν τοῦ παντός· ταῦτα τὸν τῆς τριάδος [All things are three, and three is in all things. And we make use of this number in the worship of the Gods. For, as the Pythagoreans say, the 'all' and everything that makes up the all are determined by these three (dimensions). For the end, the middle, and the beginning have the number of the 'all'. And these same things have the number of the triad]. From which passage *Trapezuntius* endeavour'd very seriously to prove, that *Aristotle* had a perfect knowledge of the *Trinity*. *Duport* (who furnish'd me with this note, and who seems to be sensible of the folly of *Trapezuntius*) nevertheless in his *Gnomologia Homerica*, or comparison of our author's sentences with those of the Scripture, has placed opposite to this verse that of St *John*. *There are three who give testimony in heaven, the Father, the Son, and the Holy Ghost.* I think this the strongest instance I ever met with of the manner of thinking of such men, whose too much learning has made them mad.

Lactantius, de Fals. Relig. lib. 1. *cap.* 11. takes this fable to be a remain of ancient history, importing, that the empire of the then known world was divided among the three brothers; to *Jupiter* the oriental part, which was call'd Heaven, as the Region of light, or the sun: to *Pluto* the occidental, or darker regions: and to *Neptune* the sovereignty of the seas.

228. *To elder brothers.*] *Iris*, that she may not seem to upbraid *Neptune* with weakness of judgment, out of regard to the greatness and dignity of his person, does not say that *Jupiter* is stronger or braver; but attacking him from a motive not in the least invidious, superiority of age, she says sententiously, that the *Furies* wait upon our elders. The *Furies* are said to wait upon men in a double sense: either for evil, as they did upon *Orestes* after he had slain his mother; or else for their good, as upon elders when they are injur'd, to protect them and avenge their wrongs. This is an instance that the Pagans look'd upon birthright as a right divine. *Eustathius.*

252. *Else had our wrath,* &c.] This representation of the terrours which must have attended the conflict of two such mighty powers as *Jupiter* and *Neptune*, whereby the elements had been mix'd in confusion, and the whole frame of nature endangered, is imaged in these few lines with a nobleness suitable to the occasion. *Milton* has a thought very like it in his fourth book, where he represents what must have happen'd if *Satan* and *Gabriel* had encounter'd.

> — *Not only* Paradise
> *In this commotion, but the starry cope*
> *Of heav'n, perhaps, and all the elements*
> *At least had gone to wrack, disturb'd and torn*

With violence of this conflict, had not soon
Th' Almighty, to prevent such horrid fray, &c.

274. Jove *thinking of his pains, they past away.*] *Eustathius* observes, that this is a very sublime representation of the power of *Jupiter*, to make *Hector*'s pains cease from the moment wherein *Jupiter* first turn'd his thoughts towards him. *Apollo* finds him so far recovered, as to be able to sit up, and know his friends. Thus much was the work of *Jupiter*; the God of health perfects the cure.

298. *As when the pamper'd steed.*] This comparison is repeated from the sixth book, and we are told that the ancient criticks retain'd no more than the two first verses and the four last in this place, and that they gave the verses two marks; by the one (which was the *asterism*) they intimated, that the four lines were very beautiful; but by the other (which was the *obelus*) that they were ill placed. I believe an impartial reader who considers the two places will be of the same opinion.

Tasso has improv'd the justness of this simile in his sixteenth book [xxviii], where *Rinaldo* returning from the arms of *Armida* to battel, is compared to the steed that is taken from his pastures and mares to the service of the war: The reverse of the circumstance better agreeing with the occasion.

> *Qual feroce destrier, ch'al faticoso*
> *Honor de l'arme vincitor sia tolto,*
> *E lascivo marito in vil riposo*
> *Frà gli armenti, e ne' paschi erri disciolto;*
> *Se'l desta o suon di tromba, o luminoso*
> *Acciar, colà tosto annittendo è volto;*
> *Già già brama l'arringo, e l'huom sùl dorso*
> *Portando, urtato riurtar nel corso.*

[As the fierce steed for age withdrawn from war,
  Wherein the glorious beast had always won,
  That in vile rest, from fight sequester'd far,
  Feeds with the males at rest, his service done;
  If arms he see, or hear the trumpet's jar,
  He neigheth loud, and thither fast doth run,
    And wisheth on his back the armed knight,
      Longing for jousts, for tournaments, and fight.]

311. *Far from the hunters rage.*] *Dacier* has a pretty remark on this passage, that *Homer* extended destiny (that is, the care of providence) even over the beasts of the field; an opinion that agrees perfectly with true theology. In the book of *Jonas*, the regard of the creator extending to the meanest rank of his creatures, is strongly express'd in those words of the Almighty, where he makes his compassion to the brute beasts one of the reasons against destroying *Nineveh. Shall I not spare the great city, in which there are more than sixscore thousand persons, and also much cattel?* And what is still more parallel to this passage, in St *Matth.* ch. 10. *Are not two sparrows sold for a farthing? And yet one of them shall not fall to the ground, without your father.*

362. *But when aloft he shakes.*] *Apollo* in this passage, by the mere shaking his *Ægis*, without acting offensively, annoys and puts the *Greeks* into disorder. *Eustathius* thinks that such a motion might possibly create the same confusion, as hath been reported by historians to proceed from *panic fears*: or that it might intimate some dreadful confusion in the air, and a noise issuing from thence; a notion which seems to be warranted by *Apollo*'s outcry, which presently follows in the same verse. But perhaps we need not go so far to account for this fiction of *Homer*: The sight of a hero's armour often has the like effect in an Epic Poem: The Shield of Prince *Arthur* in *Spencer* works the same wonders with this *Ægis* of *Apollo*.

386.   *By* Paris, Deiochus *inglorious dies,*
        Pierc'd thro' the shoulder as he basely flies.]

Here is one that falls under the spear of *Paris*, smitten in the extremity of his shoulder, as he was flying. This gives occasion to a pretty observation in *Eustathius*, that this is the only *Greek* who falls by a wound in the back, so careful is *Homer* of the honour of his countrymen. And this remark will appear not ill grounded, if we except the death of *Eioneus* in the beginning of *lib.* 6.

396. *For by the Gods, who flies,* &c.] It sometimes happens (says *Longinus*) that a writer in speaking of some person, all on a sudden puts himself in that other's place, and acts his part; a figure which marks the impetuosity and hurry of passion. It is this which *Homer* practises in these verses; the Poet stops his narration, forgets his own person, and instantly, without any notice, puts this precipitate menace into the mouth of his furious and transported hero. How must his discourse have languish'd, had he stay'd to tell us, Hector *then said these, or the like words?* Instead of which, by this unexpected transition he prevents the reader, and the transition is made before the Poet himself seems sensible he had made it. The true and proper place for this figure is when the time presses, and when the occasion will not allow of any delay: It is elegant then to pass from one person to another, as in that of *Hecatæus. The herald, extremely discontented at the orders he had received, gave command to the* Heraclidæ *to withdraw. – It is no way in my power to help you; if therefore you would not perish entirely, and if you would not involve me too in your ruin, depart, and seek a retreat among some other people.* Longinus, *ch.* 23.

416. *As when ashore an infant stands.*] This simile of the sand is inimitable; it is not easy to imagine any thing more exact and emphatical to describe the tumbling and confus'd heap of a wall, in a moment. Moreover the comparison here taken from sand is the juster, as it rises from the very place and scene before us. For the wall here demolished, as it was founded on the coast, must needs border on the sand; wherefore the similitude is borrowed immediately from the subject matter under view. *Eustathius.*

428. *Oh Jove! if ever,* &c.] The form of *Nestor*'s prayer in this place resembles that of *Chryses* in the first book. And it is worth remarking, that the Poet well knew what shame and confusion the reminding one of past benefits is apt to produce. From the same topick *Achilles* talks with his mother, and *Thetis* herself accosts *Jove*; and likewise *Phœnix* where he holds a parley with *Achilles.* This righteous prayer hath its wished accomplishment. *Eustathius.*

438. *Presumptuous* Troy *mistook the sign.*] The thunder of *Jupiter* is design'd as a mark of his acceptance of *Nestor*'s prayers, and a sign of his favour to the *Greeks.* However, there being nothing in the prodigy particular to the *Greeks*, the *Trojans* expound it in their own favour, as they seem warranted by their present success. This self-partiality of men in appropriating to themselves the protection of heaven, has always been natural to them. In the same manner *Virgil* makes *Turnus* explain the transformation of the *Trojan* ships into nymphs, as an ill omen to the *Trojans.*

Trojanos hæc monstra petunt, his Jupiter ipse
Auxilium solitum eripuit. —

[These monsters for the *Trojans* fate are meant,
And are by *Jove* for black presages sent.]

History furnishes many instances of oracles, which by reason of this partial interpretation, have proved an occasion to lead men into great misfortunes: It was the case of *Cræsus* in his wars with *Cyrus*; and a like mistake engaged *Pyrrhus* to make war upon the *Romans*.

448. *On the ships above, the cars below.*] This is a new sort of battel, which *Homer* has never before mentioned; the *Greeks* on their ships, and the *Trojans* in their chariots, fight as on a plain.   *Eustathius.*

472. *Nor could the* Trojans — *Force to the fleet and tents th' impervious way.*] *Homer* always marks distinctly the place of battel; he here shews us clearly, that the *Trojans* attacked the first line of the fleet that stood next the wall, or the vessels which were drawn foremost on the land: These vessels were a strong rampart to the tents, which were pitch'd behind, and to the other line of the navy which stood nearer to the sea; to penetrate therefore to the tents, they must necessarily force the first line, and defeat the troops which defended it.   *Eustathius.*

582. *Death is the worst,* &c.] 'Tis with very great address, that to the bitterness of death, he adds the advantages that were to accrue after it. And the ancients are of opinion, that 'twou'd be as advantageous for young soldiers to read this lesson, concise as it is, as all the volumes of *Tyrtæus,* wherein he endeavours to raise the spirits of his countrymen. *Homer* makes a noble enumeration of the parts wherein the happiness of a city consists. For having told us in another place, the three great evils to which a town, when taken, is subject; the slaughter of the men, the destruction of the place by fire; the leading of their wives and children into captivity: now he reckons up the blessings that are contrary to those calamities. To the slaughter of the men indeed he makes no opposition; because it is not necessary to the well-being of a city, that every individual should be saved, and not a man slain.

Eustathius.

590. *The god-like* Ajax *next.*] The oration of *Hector* is more splendid and shining that that of *Ajax*, and also more solemn, from his sentiments concerning the favour and assistance of *Jupiter*. But that of *Ajax* is the more politick, fuller of management, and apter to persuade: For it abounds with no less than seven generous arguments to inspire resolution. He exhorts his people even to death, from the danger to which their navy was exposed, which if once consumed, they were never like to get home. And as the *Trojans* were bid to die, so he bids his men dare to die likewise: and indeed with great necessity, for the *Trojans* may recruit after the engagement, but for the *Greeks*, they had no better way than to hazard their lives; and if they should gain nothing else by it, yet at least they would have a speedy dispatch, not a lingring and dilatory destruction.   *Eustathius.*

677. *And flank the Navy with a brazen wall.*] The Poet has built the *Grecians* a new sort of Wall out of their Arms; and perhaps one might say, 'twas from this Passage *Apollo* borrow'd that Oracle which he gave to the *Athenians* about their Wall of Wood; in like manner, the *Spartans* were said to have a Wall of Bones: If so, we must allow the God not a little obliged to the Poet.   *Eustathius.*

723. *He raises* Hector, &c.] This picture of *Hector*, impuls'd by *Jupiter*, is a very finish'd piece, and excels all the drawings of this hero which *Homer* has given us in so various attitudes. He is here represented as an instrument in the hand of *Jupiter*, to bring about those designs the God had long projected: And as his fatal hour now approaches, *Jove* is willing to recompence his hasty death with this short-liv'd glory. Accordingly, this being the last scene of victory he is to appear in, the Poet introduces him with all imaginable pomp, and adorns him with all the terrour of a conqueror: His Eyes sparkle with fire, his mouth foams with fury, his figure is compared to the God of War, his rage is equall'd to a conflagration and a storm, and the destruction he causes is resembled to that which a lion makes among the herds. The Poet, by this heap of comparisons, raises the idea of the hero higher than any single description could reach.

736. – *His fate was near* – *Due to stern* Pallas.] It may be ask'd, what *Pallas* has to do with the *Fates*, or what power has she over them? *Homer* speaks thus, because *Minerva* has already resolv'd to succour *Achilles*, and deceive *Hector* in the combate between these two heroes, as we find in book 22. Properly speaking, *Pallas* is nothing but the knowledge and wisdom of *Jove*, and it is wisdom which presides

over the councels of his providence; therefore she may be look'd upon as drawing all things to the fatal term to which they are decreed.   *Dacier.*

752. *Bursts as a Wave*, &c.] *Longinus*, observing that oftentimes the principal beauty of writing consists in the judicious assembling together of the great circumstances, and the strength with which they are marked in the proper place, chuses this passage of *Homer* as a plain instance of it. 'Where (says that noble critick) in describing the terrour of a tempest, he takes care to express whatever are the accidents of most dread and horrour in such a situation: He is not content to tell us that the mariners were in danger, but he brings them before our eyes, as in a picture, upon the Point of being every Moment overwhelmed by every wave; nay the very words and syllables of the description give us an image of their peril.' He shews, that a Poet of less judgment would amuse himself in less important circumstances, and spoil the whole effect of the image by minute, ill-chosen, or superfluous particulars. Thus *Aratus* endeavouring to refine upon that line,

> *And instant death on ev'ry wave appears!*

He turn'd it thus,

> *A slender plank preserves them from their fate.*

Which, by flourishing upon the thought, has lost the loftiness and terrour of it, and is so far from improving the image, that it lessens and vanishes in his management. By confining the danger to a single line, he has scarce left the shadow of it; and indeed the word *preserves* takes away even that. The same critick produces a fragment of an old poem on the *Arimaspians*, written in this false taste, whose Author, he doubts not, imagined he had said something wonderful in the following affected verses. I have done my best to give 'em the same turn, and I believe there are those, who will not think 'em bad ones.

> *Ye pow'rs! what madness! How, on ships so frail,*
> *(Tremendous thought!) can thoughtless mortals sail?*
> *For stormy seas they quit the pleasing plain,*
> *Plant woods in waves, and dwell amidst the main.*
> *Far o'er the deep (a trackless path) they go,*
> *And wander oceans, in pursuit of woe.*
> *No ease their hearts, no rest their eyes can find,*

On heav'n their looks, and on the waves their mind;
Sunk are their spirits, while their arms they rear;
And Gods are weary'd with their fruitless pray'r.

796. Nestor's *speech.*] This popular harangue of *Nestor* is justly extoll'd as the strongest and most persuasive piece of oratory imaginable. It contains in it every motive by which men can be affected; the preservation of their wives and children, the secure possession of their fortunes, the respect of their living parents, and the due regard for the memory of those that were departed: By these he diverts the *Grecians* from any thoughts of flight in the article of extreme peril.   *Eustathius.*

This noble exhortation is finely imitated by *Tasso, Jerusalem. l.* 20 [xx. xxv–xxvi].

> *– O valoroso, hor via con questa*
> *Faccia, a ritor la preda a noi rapita.*
> *L'imagine ad alcuno in mente desta,*
> *Glie la figura quasi, e glie l'addita*
> *De la pregante patria e de la mesta*
> *Supplice famiglivola sbigottita.*
> *Credi (dicea) che la tua patria spieghi*
> *Per la mia lingua in tui parole i preghi.*
>
> *Guarda tù le mie leggi, e i sacri Tempi*
> *Fà, ch'io del sangue mio non bagni, e lavi,*
> *Assicura le virgini da gli empi,*
> *E i sepolchri, e le cinere de gli avi.*
> *A te piangendo i lor passati tempi*
> *Mostran la bianca chioma i vecchi gravi:*
> *A tè la moglie, e le mammelle, e'l petto,*
> *Le cune, e i figli, e'l marital suo letto.*

[But to the bold, 'Go, hardy knight (he says),
His prey out of this lion's paws go tear.'
To some before his thoughts the shape he lays,
And makes therein the image true appear,
How his sad country him entreats and prays,
His house, his loving wife, his children dear:
    'Suppose (quoth he) thy country doth beseech
    And pray thee thus: suppose this is her speech:
"Defend my laws, uphold my temples brave,
My blood from washing of my streets withhold;

From ravishing my virgins keep, and save
Thine ancestors' dead bones and ashes cold;
To thee thy fathers' dear and parents' grave
Show their uncover'd heads, white, hoary, old;
    To thee thy wife, her breasts with tears o'erspread,
    Thy sons their cradles show, their marriage bed." ']

814. *First of the field, great* Ajax.] In this book, *Homer*, to raise the valour of *Hector*, gives him *Neptune* for an antagonist; and to raise that of *Ajax*, he first opposed to him *Hector*, supported by *Apollo*, and now the same *Hector* impelled and seconded by *Jupiter* himself. These are strokes of a master-hand.   *Eustathius.*

824. *Drives four fair coursers,* &c.] The comparison which *Homer* here introduces, is a demonstration that the art of mounting and managing horses was brought to so great a perfection in these early times, that one man could manage four at once, and leap from one to the other even when they run full speed. But some object, that the custom of riding was not known in *Greece* at the time of the *Trojan* war: Besides, they say the comparison is not just, for the horses are said to run full speed, whereas the ships stand firm and unmoved. Had *Homer* put the comparison in the mouth of one of his heroes, the objection had been just, and he guilty of an inconsistency: but it is he himself who speaks: Saddle-horses were in use in his age, and any poet may be allowed to illustrate pieces of antiquity by images familiar to his own times. This is sufficient for the first objection; nor is the second more reasonable; for it is not absolutely necessary that comparisons should correspond in every particular; it suffices if there be a general resemblance. This is only introduced to shew the Agility of *Ajax*, who passes swiftly from one vessel to another, and is therefore entirely just.   *Eustathius.*

856. *The same that dead* Protesilaus *bore.*] *Homer* feigns that *Hector* laid hold on the ship of the dead *Protesilaus*, rather than on that of any other, that he might not disgrace any of his *Grecian* Generals.
    Eustathius.

874.   *The coward-counsels of a tim'rous throng*
      Of rev'rend dotards. –]

Homer adds this with a great deal of art and prudence, to answer beforehand all the objections which he well foresaw might be made, because *Hector* never till now attacks the *Grecians* in their camp, or endeavours to burn their navy. He was retained by the elders of *Troy*, who frozen with fear at the sight of *Achilles*, never suffered him to march from the ramparts. Our Author forgets nothing that has the resemblance of truth; but he had yet a farther reason for inserting this, as it exalts the glory of his principal hero: These elders of *Troy* thought it less difficult to defeat the *Greeks*, tho' defended with strong entrenchments, while *Achilles* was not with them; than to overcome them without entrenchments when he assisted them. And this is the reason that they prohibited *Hector* before, and permit him now, to sally upon the enemy.   *Dacier.*

877. *But now* Jove *calls to arms,* &c.] *Hector* seems to be sensible of an extraordinary impulse from heaven, signified by these words, *the most mighty hand of* Jove *pushing him on.* 'Tis no more than any other person would be ready to imagine, who should rise from a state of distress or indolence, into one of good fortune, vigour, and activity.
                                                      Eustathius.

890. *The speech of* Ajax.] There is great strength, closeness, and spirit in this speech, and one might (like many criticks) employ a whole page in extolling and admiring it in general terms. But sure the perpetual rapture of such commentators, who are always giving us exclamations instead of criticisms, may be a mark of great admiration, but of little judgment. Of what use is this either to a reader who has a taste, or to one who has not? To admire a fine passage is what the former will do without us, and what the latter cannot be taught to do by us. However we ought gratefully to acknowledge the good nature of most people, who are not only pleased with this superficial applause given to fine passages, but are likewise inclined to transfer to the critick, who only points at these beauties, part of the admiration justly due to the Poet. This is a cheap and easy way to fame, which many writers ancient and modern have pursued with great success. Formerly indeed this sort of authors had modesty, and were humbly content to call their performances only *Florilegia* or *Posies*: But some of late have passed such collections on the world for criticisms of great depth and learning, and seem to expect the same flowers should please us better, in these paltry nosegays of their own making up, than in the native gardens where they grew. As this practice of extolling without giving reasons is very

convenient for most writers, so it excellently suits the ignorance or laziness of most readers, who will come into any sentiment rather than take the trouble of refuting it. Thus the complement is mutual: For as such criticks do not tax their readers with any thought to understand them, so their readers in return advance nothing in opposition to such criticks. They may go roundly on, admiring and exclaiming in this manner; *What an exquisite spirit of poetry – How beautiful a circumstance – What delicacy of sentiments – With what art has the Poet – In how sublime and just a manner – How finely imagined – How wonderfully beautiful and poetical* – And so proceed, without one reason to interrupt the course of their eloquence, most comfortably and ignorantly apostrophising to the end of the chapter.

THE
SIXTEENTH BOOK
OF THE
ILIAD

The ARGUMENT

The sixth battel: The acts and death of *Patroclus*

Patroclus *(in pursuance of the request of* Nestor *in the eleventh book)* *entreats* Achilles *to suffer him to go to the assistance of the* Greeks *with* Achilles's *troops and armour. He agrees to it, but at the same time charges him to content himself with rescuing the fleet, without farther pursuit of the enemy. The armour, horses, soldiers, and officers of* Achilles *are described.* Achilles *offers a libation for the success of his friend, after which* Patroclus *leads the* Myrmidons *to battel. The* Trojans *at the sight of* Patroclus *in* Achilles's *armour, taking him for that hero, are cast into the utmost consternation: He beats them off from the vessels,* Hector *himself flies,* Sarpedon *is kill'd, tho'* Jupiter *was averse to his fate. Several other particulars of the battel are described; in the heat of which,* Patroclus, *neglecting the orders of* Achilles, *pursues the foe to the walls of* Troy; *where* Apollo *repulses and disarms him,* Euphorbus *wounds him, and* Hector *kills him, which concludes the book.*

So warr'd both armies on th' ensanguin'd shore,
While the black vessels smoak'd with human gore.
Meantime *Patroclus* to *Achilles* flies;
The streaming tears fall copious from his eyes;
5   Not faster, trickling to the plains below,
From the tall rock the sable waters flow.
Divine *Pelides*, with compassion mov'd,
Thus spoke, indulgent to his best belov'd.

Patroclus, say, what grief thy bosom bears,
10   That flows so fast in these unmanly tears?
No girl, no infant whom the mother keeps
From her lov'd breast, with fonder passion weeps;
Not more the mother's soul that infant warms,
Clung to her knees, and reaching at her arms,
15   Than thou hast mine! Oh tell me, to what end
Thy melting sorrows thus pursue thy friend?

Griev'st thou for me, or for my martial band?
Or come sad tidings from our native land?
Our fathers live, (our first, most tender care)
20   Thy good *Menœtius* breathes the vital air,
And hoary *Peleus* yet extends his days;
Pleas'd in their age to hear their children's praise.

Or may some meaner cause thy pity claim?
Perhaps yon' reliques of the *Grecian* name,
25   Doom'd in their ships to sink by fire and sword,
And pay the forfeit of their haughty lord?
Whate'er the cause, reveal thy secret care,
And speak those sorrows which a friend would share.

A sigh, that instant, from his bosom broke,
Another follow'd, and *Patroclus* spoke.   30
   Let *Greece* at length with pity touch thy breast,
Thy self a *Greek*; and, once, of *Greeks* the best!
Lo! ev'ry chief that might her fate prevent,
Lies pierc'd with wounds, and bleeding in his tent.
Eurypylus, *Tydides*, *Atreus'* son,   35
And wise *Ulysses*, at the navy groan
More for their country's wounds, than for their own.
Their pain, soft arts of pharmacy can ease,
Thy breast alone no lenitives appease.
   May never rage like thine my soul enslave,   40
O great in vain! unprofitably brave!
Thy country slighted in her last distress,
What friend, what man, from thee shall hope redress?
No – men unborn, and ages yet behind,
Shall curse that fierce, that unforgiving mind.   45
   O man unpitying! if of man thy race;
But sure thou spring'st not from a soft embrace,
Nor ever am'rous hero caus'd thy birth,
Nor ever tender Goddess brought thee forth.
Some rugged rock's hard entrails gave thee form,   50
And raging seas produc'd thee in a storm,
A soul well-suiting that tempestuous kind,
So rough thy manners, so untam'd thy mind.
   If some dire Oracle thy breast alarm,
If ought from *Jove*, or *Thetis*, stop thy arm,   55
Some beam of comfort yet on *Greece* may shine,
If I but lead the *Myrmidonian* line:
Clad in thy dreadful arms if I appear,
Proud *Troy* shall tremble, and desert the war:
Without thy person *Greece* shall win the day,   60
And thy mere image chase her foes away.
Press'd by fresh forces, her o'erlabour'd train
Shall quit the ships, and *Greece* respire again.
   Thus, blind to fate! with supplicating breath,
Thou beg'st his arms, and in his arms, thy death.   65
Unfortunately good! a boding sigh
Thy friend return'd; and with it, this reply.

Patroclus! thy *Achilles* knows no fears;
Nor words from *Jove*, nor *oracles* he hears;
70   Nor ought a mother's caution can suggest;
The tyrant's pride lies rooted in my breast.
My wrongs, my wrongs, my constant thought engage,
Those, my sole oracles, inspire my rage:
I made him tyrant; gave him pow'r to wrong
75   Ev'n me: I felt it; and shall feel it long.
The maid, my black-ey'd maid, he forc'd away,
Due to the toils of many a well-fought day;
Due to my conquest of her father's reign;
Due to the votes of all the *Grecian* train.
80   From me he forc'd her; me, the bold and brave;
Disgrac'd, dishonour'd, like the meanest slave.
But bear we this – the wrongs I grieve, are past;
'Tis time our fury should relent at last:
I fix'd its date; the day I wish'd appears:
85   Now *Hector* to my ships his battel bears,
The flames my eyes, the shouts invade my ears.
Go then *Patroclus!* court fair honour's charms
In *Troy's* fam'd fields, and in *Achilles'* arms:
Lead forth my martial *Myrmidons* to fight,
90   Go save the fleets, and conquer in my right.
See the thin reliques of their baffled band,
At the last edge of yon' deserted land!
Behold all *Ilion* on their ships descends;
How the cloud blackens, how the storm impends!
95   It was not thus, when, at my sight amaz'd,
Troy saw and trembled, as this helmet blaz'd:
Had not th' injurious King our friendship lost,
Yon' ample trench had bury'd half her host.
No camps, no bulwarks now the *Trojans* fear,
100   Those are not dreadful, no *Achilles* there:
No longer flames the lance of *Tydeus'* son;
No more your Gen'ral calls his heroes on;
Hector, alone, I hear; his dreadful breath
Commands your slaughter, or proclaims your death.
105   Yet now, *Patroclus*, issue to the plain;
Now save the ships, the rising fires restrain,
And give the *Greeks* to visit *Greece* again.

But heed my words, and mark a friend's command
Who trusts his fame and honours in thy hand,
And from thy deeds expects, th' *Achaian* host   110
Shall render back the beauteous maid he lost:
Rage uncontroul'd thro' all the hostile crew,
But touch not *Hector*, *Hector* is my due.
Tho' *Jove* in thunder should command the war,
Be just, consult my glory, and forbear.   115
The fleet once sav'd, desist from farther chace,
Nor lead to *Ilion*'s walls the *Grecian* race;
Some adverse God thy rashness may destroy;
Some God, like *Phœbus*, ever kind to *Troy*.
Let *Greece*, redeem'd from this destructive strait,   120
Do her own work, and leave the rest to fate.
Oh! would to all th' immortal pow'rs above,
Apollo, *Pallas*, and almighty *Jove!*
That not one *Trojan* might be left alive,
And not a *Greek* of all the race survive;   125
Might only we the vast destruction shun,
And only we destroy th' accursed town!

 Such conf'rence held the chiefs: while on the strand,
Great *Jove* with conquest crown'd the *Trojan* band.
Ajax no more the sounding storm sustain'd,   130
So thick, the darts an iron tempest rain'd:
On his tir'd arm the weighty buckler hung;
His hollow helm with falling jav'lins rung;
His breath, in quick, short pantings, comes, and goes,
And painful sweat from all his members flows.   135
Spent and o'erpow'r'd, he barely breathes at most;
Yet scarce an army stirs him from his post:
Dangers on dangers all around him grow,
And toil to toil, and woe succeeds to woe.

 Say, Muses, thron'd above the starry frame,   140
How first the navy blaz'd with *Trojan* flame?

 Stern *Hector* wav'd his sword; and standing near
Where furious *Ajax* ply'd his ashen spear,
Full on the lance a stroke so justly sped,
That the broad faulchion lopp'd its brazen head: 145
His pointless spear the warriour shakes in vain;
The brazen head falls sounding on the plain.

Great *Ajax* saw, and own'd the hand divine,
Confessing *Jove*, and trembling at the sign;
150   Warn'd, he retreats. Then swift from all sides pour
The hissing brands; thick streams the fiery show'r;
O'er the high stern the curling volumes rise,
And sheets of rolling smoke involve the skies.
    Divine *Achilles* view'd the rising flames,
155   And smote his thigh, and thus aloud exclaims.
Arm, arm, *Patroclus!* Lo, the blaze aspires!
The glowing ocean reddens with the fires.
Arm, e'er our vessels catch the spreading flame;
Arm, e'er the *Grecians* be no more a name;
160   I haste to bring the troops. – The hero said;
The friend with ardour and with joy obey'd.
    He cas'd his limbs in brass, and first around
His manly legs, with silver buckles bound
The clasping greaves; then to his breast applies
165   The flamy cuirass, of a thousand dyes;
Emblaz'd with studs of gold his faulchion shone,
In the rich belt, as in a starry zone.
Achilles' shield his ample shoulders spread,
Achilles' helmet nodded o'er his head.
170   Adorn'd in all his terrible array,
He flash'd around intolerable day.
Alone, untouch'd, *Pelides'* jav'lin stands,
Not to be pois'd but by *Pelides'* hands:
From *Pelion*'s shady brow the plant entire
175   Old *Chiron* rent, and shap'd it for his sire;
Whose son's great arm alone the weapon wields,
The death of heroes, and the dread of fields.
    Then brave *Automedon* (an honour'd name,
The second to his Lord in love and fame,
180   In peace his friend, and part'ner of the war)
The winged coursers harness'd to the car.
Xanthus and *Balius*, of immortal breed,
Sprung from the wind, and like the wind in speed;
Whom the wing'd *Harpye*, swift *Podarge*, bore,
185   By *Zephyr* pregnant on the breezy shore.
Swift *Pedasus* was added to their side,
(Once great *Aëtion*'s, now *Achilles'* pride)

Who, like in strength, in swiftness, and in grace,
A mortal courser match'd th' immortal race.

    Achilles speeds from tent to tent, and warms   190
His hardy *Myrmidons* to blood and arms.
All breathing death, around their chief they stand,
A grim, terrific, formidable band:
Grim as voracious wolves that seek the springs
When scalding thirst their burning bowels wrings   195
(When some tall stag, fresh-slaughter'd in the wood,
Has drench'd their wide, insatiate throats with blood)
To the black fount they rush, a hideous throng,
With paunch distended, and with lolling tongue,
Fire fills their eye, their black jaws belch the gore,   200
And gorg'd with slaughter, still they thirst for more.
Like furious rush'd the *Myrmidonian* crew,
Such their dread strength, and such their deathful view.

    High in the midst the great *Achilles* stands,
Directs their order, and the war commands.   205
He, lov'd of *Jove*, had launch'd for *Ilion*'s shores
Full fifty vessels, mann'd with fifty oars:
Five chosen leaders the fierce bands obey,
Himself supreme in valour, as in sway.

    First march'd *Menestheus*, of celestial birth,   210
Deriv'd from thee, whose waters wash the earth,
Divine *Sperchius! Jove*-descended flood!
A mortal mother mixing with a God.
Such was *Menestheus*, but miscall'd by fame
The son of *Borus*, that espous'd the dame.   215

    Eudorus next; whom *Polymele* the gay,
Fam'd in the graceful dance, produc'd to day.
Her, sly *Cyllenius* lov'd; on her would gaze,
As with swift step she form'd the running maze:
To her high chamber, from *Diana*'s quire,   220
The God pursu'd her, urg'd, and crown'd his fire.
The son confess'd his father's heav'nly race,
And heir'd his mother's swiftness in the chace.
Strong *Echeclëus*, blest in all those charms
That pleas'd a God, succeeded to her arms;   225
Not conscious of those loves, long hid from fame,
With gifts of price he sought and won the dame;

Her secret offspring to her sire she bare;
Her sire caress'd him with a parent's care.
230   *Pisander* follow'd; matchless in his art
To wing the spear, or aim the distant dart;
No hand so sure of all th' *Emathian* line,
Or if a surer, great *Patroclus!* thine.
The fourth by *Phœnix*' grave command was grac'd;
235   *Laërces*' valiant offspring led the last.
Soon as *Achilles*, with superiour care,
Had call'd the chiefs, and order'd all the war,
This stern remembrance to his troops he gave:
Ye far-fam'd *Myrmidons*, ye fierce and brave!
140   Think with what threats you dar'd the *Trojan* throng,
Think what reproach these ears endur'd so long,
'Stern Son of *Peleus* (thus ye us'd to say,
While restless, raging, in your ships you lay)
Oh nurs'd with gall, unknowing how to yield!
245   Whose rage defrauds us of so fam'd a field.
If that dire fury must for ever burn,
What make we here? Return, ye Chiefs, return!'
Such were your words – Now Warriours grieve no more.
Lo there the *Trojans!* bath your swords in gore!
250   This day shall give you all your soul demands;
Glut all your hearts! and weary all your hands!
Thus while he rowz'd the fire in ev'ry breast,
Close, and more close, the list'ning cohorts prest;
Ranks wedg'd in ranks; of arms a steely ring
255   Still grows, and spreads, and thickens round the King.
As when a circling wall the builder forms,
Of strength defensive against winds and storms,
Compacted stones the thick'ning work compose,
And round him wide the rising structure grows.
260   So helm to helm, and crest to crest they throng,
Shield urg'd on shield, and man drove man along:
Thick, undistinguish'd plumes, together join'd,
Float in one sea, and wave before the wind.
Far o'er the rest, in glitt'ring pomp appear,
265   There, bold *Automedon*; *Patroclus* here;
Brothers in arms, with equal fury fir'd;
Two friends, two bodies with one soul inspir'd.

But mindful of the Gods, *Achilles* went
To the rich coffer, in his shady tent:
There lay on heaps his various garments roll'd,   270
And costly furs, and carpets stiff with gold.
(The presents of the silver-footed dame)
From thence he took a bowl, of antique frame,
Which never man had stain'd with ruddy wine,
Nor rais'd in off'rings to the pow'rs divine,   275
But *Peleus'* son; and *Peleus'* son to none
Had rais'd in off'rings, but to *Jove* alone.
This ting'd with sulphur, sacred first to flame,
He purg'd; and wash'd it in the running stream.
Then cleans'd his hands; and fixing for a space   280
His eyes on heaven, his feet upon the place
Of sacrifice, the purple draught he pour'd
Forth in the midst; and thus the God implor'd.

Oh thou Supreme! high-thron'd, all height above!
Oh Great! *Pelasgic, Dodonæan Jove!*   285
Who 'midst surrounding frosts, and vapours chill,
Preside on bleak *Dodona's* vocal hill:
(Whose groves, the *Selli*, race austere! surround,
Their feet unwash'd, their slumbers on the ground;
Who hear, from rustling oaks, thy dark decrees;   290
And catch the fates, low-whisper'd in the breeze.)
Hear, as of old! Thou gav'st, at *Thetis* pray'r,
Glory to me, and to the *Greeks* despair:
Lo to the dangers of the fighting field
The best, the dearest of my friends, I yield: 295
Tho' still determin'd, to my ships confin'd,
Patroclus gone, I stay but half behind.
Oh! be his guard thy providential care,
Confirm his heart, and string his arm to war:
Press'd by his single force, let *Hector* see   300
His Fame in Arms not owing all to me.
But when the fleets are sav'd from foes and fire,
Let him with conquest and renown retire;
Preserve his arms, preserve his social train,
And safe return him to these eyes again!   305

Great *Jove* consents to half the chief's request,
But heav'ns eternal doom denies the rest;

To free the fleet was granted to his pray'r;
His safe return, the winds dispers'd in air.
310 Back to his tent the stern *Achilles* flies,
And waits the combate with impatient eyes.
     Meanwhile the troops beneath *Patroclus'* care,
Invade the *Trojans*, and commence the war.
As wasps, provok'd by children in their play,
315 Pour from their mansions by the broad high-way,
In swarms the guiltless traveller engage,
Whet all their stings, and call forth all their rage;
All rise in arms, and with a gen'ral cry
Assert their waxen domes, and buzzing progeny.
320 Thus from the tents the fervent legion swarms,
So loud their clamours, and so keen their arms.
Their rising rage *Patroclus'* breath inspires,
Who thus inflames them with heroick fires.
     Oh warriors, part'ners of *Achilles'* praise!
325 Be mindful of your deeds in ancient days:
Your godlike master let your acts proclaim,
And add new glories to his mighty name.
Think, your *Achilles* sees you fight: Be brave,
And humble the proud monarch whom you save.
330   Joyful they heard, and kindling as he spoke,
Flew to the fleet, involv'd in fire and smoke.
From shore to shore the doubling shouts resound,
The hollow ships return a deeper sound.
The war stood still, and all around them gaz'd,
335 When great *Achilles'* shining armour blaz'd:
Troy saw, and thought the dread *Achilles* nigh,
At once they see, they tremble, and they fly.
     Then first thy spear, divine *Patroclus!* flew,
Where the war rag'd, and where the tumult grew.
340 Close to the stern of that fam'd ship, which bore
Unblest *Protesilaus* to *Ilion's* shore,
The great *Pæonian*, bold *Pyrechmes*, stood;
(Who led his bands from *Axius'* winding flood)
His shoulder-blade receives the fatal wound;
345 The groaning warrior pants upon the ground.
His troops, that see their country's glory slain,
Fly diverse, scatter'd o'er the distant plain.

Patroclus' arm forbids the spreading fires,
And from the half-burn'd ship proud *Troy* retires:
Clear'd from the smoke the joyful navy lies;   350
In heaps on heaps the foe tumultuous flies;
Triumphant *Greece* her rescu'd decks ascends,
And loud acclaim the starry region rends.
So when thick clouds inwrap the mountain's head,
O'er heav'ns expanse like one black cieling spread;   355
Sudden, the Thund'rer, with a flashing ray,
Bursts thro' the darkness, and lets down the day:
The hills shine out, the rocks in prospect rise,
And streams, and vales, and forests strike the eyes;
The smiling scene wide opens to the sight,   360
And all th' unmeasur'd *Æther* flames with light.

But *Troy* repuls'd, and scatter'd o'er the plains,
Forc'd from the navy, yet the fight maintains.
Now ev'ry *Greek* some hostile hero slew,
But still the foremost, bold *Patroclus* flew: 365
As *Areilycus* had turn'd him round,
Sharp in his thigh he felt the piercing wound;
The brazen-pointed spear, with vigour thrown,
The thigh transfix'd, and broke the brittle bone:
Headlong he fell. Next *Thoas* was thy chance,   370
Thy breast, unarm'd, receiv'd the *Spartan* lance.
Phylides' dart (as *Amphiclus* drew nigh)
His blow prevented, and transpierc'd his thigh,
Tore all the brawn, and rent the nerves away:
In darkness, and in death, the warriour lay.   375

In equal arms two sons of *Nestor* stand,
And two bold brothers of the *Lycian* band:
By great *Antilochus*, *Atymnius* dies,
Pierc'd in the flank, lamented youth! he lies.
Kind *Maris*, bleeding in his brother's wound,   380
Defends the breathless carcase on the ground;
Furious he flies, his murd'rer to engage,
But godlike *Thrasimed* prevents his rage,
Between his arm and shoulder aims a blow;
His arm falls spouting on the dust below: 385
He sinks, with endless darkness cover'd o'er,
And vents his soul effus'd with gushing gore.

Slain by two brothers, thus two brothers bleed,
Sarpedon's friends, *Amisodarus*' seed;
390 *Amisodarus*, who by furies led,
The bane of men, abhorr'd *Chimæra* bred;
Skill'd in the dart in vain, his sons expire,
And pay the forfeit of their guilty Sire.
Stopp'd in the tumult *Cleobulus* lies,
395 Beneath *Oileus*' arm, a living prize;
A living prize not long the *Trojan* stood;
The thirsty faulchion drank his reeking blood:
Plung'd in his throat the smoking weapon lies;
Black death, and fate unpitying, seal his eyes.
400 Amid the ranks, with mutual thirst of fame,
Lycon the brave, and fierce *Peneleus* came;
In vain their jav'lins at each other flew,
Now, met in Arms, their eager Swords they drew.
On the plum'd crest of his *Bæotian* foe,
405 The daring *Lycon* aim'd a noble blow;
The sword broke short; but his, *Peneleus* sped
Full on the juncture of the neck and head:
The head, divided by a stroke so just,
Hung by the skin: the body sunk to dust.
410 O'ertaken *Neamas* by *Merion* bleeds,
Pierc'd thro' the shoulder as he mounts his steeds;
Back from the car he tumbles to the ground:
His swimming eyes eternal shades surround.
Next *Erymas* was doom'd his fate to feel,
415 His open'd mouth receiv'd the *Cretan* steel:
Beneath the brain the point a passage tore,
Crash'd the thin bones, and drown'd the teeth in gore:
His mouth, his eyes, his nostrils pour a flood;
He sobs his soul out in the gush of blood.
420 As when the flocks neglected by the swain
(Or kids, or lambs) lie scatter'd o'er the plain,
A troop of wolves th' unguarded charge survey,
And rend the trembling, unresisting prey.
Thus on the foe the *Greeks* impetuous came;
425 *Troy* fled, unmindful of her former fame.
But still at *Hector* godlike *Ajax* aim'd,
Still, pointed at his breast, his jav'lin flam'd:

The *Trojan* chief, experienc'd in the field,
O'er his broad shoulders spread the massy shield,
Observ'd the storm of darts the *Grecians* pour,　　　430
And on his buckler caught the ringing show'r.
He sees for *Greece* the scale of conquest rise,
Yet stops, and turns, and saves his lov'd allies.

　　As when the hand of *Jove* a tempest forms,
And rolls the cloud to blacken heav'n with storms,　　　435
Dark o'er the fields th' ascending vapour flies,
And shades the sun, and blots the golden skies:
So from the ships, along the dusky plain,
Dire *Flight* and *Terrour* drove the *Trojan* train.
Ev'n *Hector* fled; thro' heaps of disarray　　　440
The fiery coursers forc'd their Lord away:
While far behind, his *Trojans* fall confus'd,
Wedg'd in the trench, in one vast carnage bruis'd.
Chariots on chariots roll; the clashing spokes
Shock; while the madding steeds break short their yokes:　　　445
In vain they labour up the steepy mound;
Their Charioteers lie foaming on the ground.
Fierce on the rear, with Shouts, *Patroclus* flies;
Tumultuous clamour fills the fields and skies;
Thick drifts of dust involve their rapid flight,　　　450
Clouds rise on clouds, and heav'n is snatch'd from sight.
Th' affrighted steeds, their dying Lords cast down,
Scour o'er the fields, and stretch to reach the town.
Loud o'er the rout was heard the victor's cry,
Where the war bleeds, and where the thickest die.　　　455
Where horse and arms, and chariots lie o'erthrown,
And bleeding heroes under axles groan.
No stop, no check, the steeds of *Peleus* knew;
From bank to bank th' immortal coursers flew,
High-bounding o'er the fosse: the whirling car　　　460
Smoaks thro' the ranks, o'ertakes the flying war,
And thunders after *Hector*; *Hector* flies,
Patroclus shakes his lance; but fate denies.
Not with less noise, with less impetuous force,
The tyde of *Trojans* urge their desp'rate course,　　　465
Than when in Autumn *Jove* his fury pours,
And earth is loaden with incessant show'rs,

(When guilty mortals break th' eternal laws,
And judges brib'd, betray the righteous cause)
470   From their deep beds he bids the rivers rise,
And opens all the floodgates of the skies:
Th' impetuous torrents from their hills obey,
Whole fields are drown'd, and mountains swept away;
Loud roars the deluge till it meets the main;
475   And trembling man sees all his labours vain!
  And now the chief (the foremost troops repell'd)
Back to the ships his destin'd progress held,
Bore down half *Troy* in his resistless way,
And forc'd the routed ranks to stand the day.
480   Between the space where silver *Simois* flows,
Where lay the fleets, and where the rampires rose,
All grim in dust and blood, *Patroclus* stands,
And turns the slaughter on the conqu'ring bands.
First *Pronous* dy'd beneath his fiery dart,
485   Which pierc'd below the shield his valiant heart.
Thestor was next; who saw the chief appear,
And fell the victim of his coward fear;
Shrunk up he sate, with wild and haggard eye,
Nor stood to combate, nor had force to fly:
490   *Patroclus* mark'd him as he shunn'd the war,
And with unmanly tremblings shook the car,
And dropp'd the flowing reins. Him 'twixt the jaws
The jav'lin sticks, and from the chariot draws:
As on a rock that overhangs the main,
495   An angler, studious of the line and cane,
Some mighty fish draws panting to the shore;
Not with less ease the barbed jav'lin bore
The gaping dastard: As the spear was shook,
He fell, and life his heartless breast forsook.
500   Next on *Eryalus* he flies; a stone
Large as a rock, was by his fury thrown.
Full on his crown the pond'rous fragment flew,
And burst the helm, and cleft the head in two:
Prone to the ground the breathless warriour fell,
505   And death involv'd him with the shades of hell.
Then low in dust *Epaltes*, *Echius*, lie;
Ipheas, *Evippus*, *Polymelus*, die;

Amphoterus, and *Erymas* succeed,
And last, *Tlepolemus* and *Pyres* bleed.
Where'er he moves, the growing slaughters spread   510
In heaps on heaps; a monument of dead.

When now *Sarpedon* his brave friends beheld
Grov'ling in dust, and gasping on the field,
With this reproach his flying host he warms,
Oh stain to honour! oh disgrace to arms!   515
Forsake, inglorious, the contended plain;
This hand, unaided, shall the war sustain:
The task be mine this hero's strength to try,
Who mows whole troops, and makes an army fly.

He spake; and speaking, leaps from off the car;   520
Patroclus lights, and sternly waits the war.
As when two vulturs on the mountain's height
Stoop with resounding pinions to the fight;
They cuff, they tear, they raise a screaming cry:
The desert echoes, and the rocks reply: 525
The warriors thus oppos'd in arms, engage
With equal clamours, and with equal rage.

Jove view'd the combate, whose event foreseen,
He thus bespoke his Sister and his Queen.
The hour draws on; the destinies ordain,   530
My godlike son shall press the *Phrygian* plain:
Already on the verge of death he stands,
His life is ow'd to fierce *Patroclus'* hands.
What passions in a parent's breast debate!
Say, shall I snatch him from impending Fate,   535
And send him safe to *Lycia*, distant far
From all the dangers and the toils of war;
Or to his doom my bravest offspring yield,
And fatten, with celestial blood, the field?

Then thus the goddess with the radiant eyes: 540
What words are these, O sov'reign of the skies?
Short is the date prescrib'd to mortal man;
Shall *Jove*, for one, extend the narrow span,
Whose bounds were fix'd before his race began?
How many sons of Gods, foredoom'd to death,   545
Before proud *Ilion*, must resign their breath!

Were thine exempt, debate would rise above,
And murm'ring pow'rs condemn their partial *Jove*.
Give the bold chief a glorious fate in fight;
550   And when th' ascending soul has wing'd her flight,
Let *Sleep* and *Death* convey, by thy command,
The breathless body to his native land.
His friends and people, to his future praise,
A marble tomb and pyramid shall raise,
555   And lasting honours to his ashes give;
His fame ('tis all the dead can have!) shall live.
      She said; the cloud-compeller overcome,
Assents to Fate, and ratifies the Doom.
Then, touch'd with grief, the weeping heav'ns distill'd
560   A show'r of blood o'er all the fatal field.
The God, his eyes averting from the plain,
Laments his son, predestin'd to be slain,
Far from the *Lycian* shores, his happy native reign.
      Now met in arms, the combatants appear,
565   Each heav'd the shield, and pois'd the lifted spear:
From strong *Patroclus'* hand the jav'lin fled,
And pass'd the groin of valiant *Thrasymed*,
The nerves unbrac'd no more his bulk sustain,
He falls, and falling bites the bloody plain.
570   Two sounding darts the *Lycian* leader threw;
The first aloof with erring fury flew,
The next transpierc'd *Achilles'* mortal steed,
The gen'rous *Pedasus*, of *Theban* breed;
Fix'd in the shoulders joint, he reel'd around;
Rowl'd in the bloody dust, and paw'd the slipp'ry
575   ground.
His sudden fall th' entangled harness broke;
Each axle crackled, and the chariot shook:
When bold *Automedon*, to disengage
The starting coursers, and restrain their rage,
580   Divides the traces with his Sword, and freed
Th' incumber'd chariot from the dying steed:
The rest move on, obedient to the rein;
The car rowls slowly o'er the dusty plain.
      The tow'ring chiefs to fiercer fight advance,
585   And first *Sarpedon* whirl'd his weighty lance,

Which o'er the warriour's shoulder took its course,
And spent in empty air its dying force.
Not so *Patroclus'* never-erring dart;
Aim'd at his breast, it pierc'd the mortal part
Where the strong fibres bind the solid heart. 590
Then, as the mountain oak, or poplar tall,
Or pine (fit mast for some great admiral)
Nods to the axe, till with a groaning sound
It sinks, and spreads its honours on the ground:
Thus fell the King; and laid on earth supine, 595
Before his chariot stretch'd his form divine:
He grasp'd the dust distain'd with streaming gore,
And pale in death, lay groaning on the shore.
So lies a bull beneath the lion's paws,
While the grim savage grinds with foamy jaws 600
The trembling limbs, and sucks the smoaking blood;
Deep groans, and hollow roars, rebellow thro' the wood.

    Then to the leader of the *Lycian* band
The dying chief address'd his last command.
Glaucus, be bold; thy task be first to dare 605
The glorious dangers of destructive war,
To lead my troops, to combate at their head,
Incite the living, and supply the dead.
Tell 'em, I charg'd them with my latest breath
Not unreveng'd to bear *Sarpedon*'s death. 610
What grief, what shame must *Glaucus* undergo,
If these spoil'd arms adorn a *Grecian* foe?
Then as a friend, and as a warriour, fight;
Defend my body, conquer in my right;
That taught by great examples, all may try 615
Like thee to vanquish, or like me to die.

    He ceas'd; the fates suppress'd his lab'ring breath,
And his eyes darken'd with the shades of death.
Th' insulting victor with disdain bestrode
The prostrate prince, and on his bosom trod; 620
Then drew the weapon from his panting heart,
The reeking fibres clinging to the dart;
From the wide wound gush'd out a stream of blood,
And the soul issu'd in the purple flood.

625   His flying Steeds the *Myrmidons* detain,
       Unguided now, their mighty master slain.
       All-impotent of aid, transfix'd with grief,
       Unhappy *Glaucus* heard the dying chief.
       His painful arm, yet useless with the smart
630   Inflicted late by *Teucer's* deadly dart,
       Supported on his better hand he stay'd;
       To *Phœbus* then ('twas all he could) he pray'd.
           All-seeing Monarch! whether *Lycia's* coast
       Or sacred *Ilion*, thy bright presence boast,
635   Pow'rful alike to ease the wretche's smart;
       Oh hear me! God of ev'ry healing art!
       Lo! stiff with clotted blood, and pierc'd with pain,
       That thrills my arm and shoots thro' ev'ry vein,
       I stand unable to sustain the spear,
640   And sigh, at distance from the glorious war.
       Low in the dust is great *Sarpedon* laid,
       Nor *Jove* vouchsaf'd his hapless off'ring aid.
       But thou, O God of Health! thy succour lend,
       To guard the reliques of my slaughter'd friend.
645   For thou, tho' distant, can'st restore my might,
       To head my *Lycians*, and support the fight.
           Apollo heard; and suppliant as he stood,
       His heav'nly hand restrain'd the flux of blood;
       He drew the dolours from the wounded part,
650   And breath'd a spirit in his rising heart.
       Renew'd by art divine, the hero stands,
       And owns th' assistance of immortal hands.
       First to the fight his native troops he warms,
       Then loudly calls on *Troy's* vindictive arms;
655   With ample strides he stalks from place to place,
       Now fires *Agenor*, now *Polydamas*;
       Æneas next, and *Hector* he accosts;
       Inflaming thus the rage of all their hosts.
           What thoughts, regardless chief! thy breast employ?
660   Oh too forgetful of the friends of *Troy*!
       Those gen'rous friends, who, from their country far,
       Breathe their brave souls out in another's war.
       See! where in dust the great *Sarpedon* lies,
       In action valiant, and in council wise,

Who guarded right, and kept his people free;   665
To all his *Lycians* lost, and lost to thee!
Stretch'd by *Patroclus'* arm on yonder plains,
Oh save from hostile rage his lov'd remains:
Ah let not *Greece* his conquer'd trophies boast,
Nor on his corpse revenge her heroes lost.   670

He spoke; each leader in his grief partook,
Troy, at the loss, thro' all her legions shook.
Tranfix'd with deep regret, they view o'erthrown
At once his country's pillar, and their own;
A chief, who led to *Troy*'s beleaguer'd wall   675
A host of heroes, and outshin'd them all.
Fir'd, they rush on; First *Hector* seeks the foes,
And with superiour vengeance greatly glows.

But o'er the dead the fierce *Patroclus* stands,
And rouzing *Ajax*, rouz'd the list'ning bands.   680

Heroes, be men! be what you were before;
Or weigh the great occasion, and be more.
The chief who taught our lofty walls to yield,
Lies pale in death, extended on the field.
To guard his body *Troy* in numbers flies;   685
'Tis half the glory to maintain our prize.
Haste, strip his arms, the slaughter round him spread,
And send the living *Lycians* to the dead.

The heroes kindle at his fierce command;
The martial squadrons close on either hand: 690
Here *Troy* and *Lycia* charge with loud alarms,
Thessalia there, and *Greece*, oppose their arms.
With horrid shouts they circle round the slain;
The clash of armour rings o'er all the plain.
Great *Jove*, to swell the horrors of the fight,   695
O'er the fierce armies pours pernicious night,
And round his son confounds the warring hosts,
His fate ennobling with a croud of ghosts.

Now *Greece* gives way, and great *Epigeus* falls;
Agacleus' son, from *Budium*'s lofty walls: 700
Who chas'd for murder thence, a suppliant came
To *Peleus*, and the silver-footed dame;
Now sent to *Troy*, *Achilles'* arms to aid,
He pays due vengeance to his kinsman's shade.

705 Soon as his luckless hand had touch'd the dead,
 A rock's large fragment thunder'd on his head;
 Hurl'd by *Hectorean* force, it cleft in twain
 His shatter'd helm, and stretch'd him o'er the slain.
  Fierce to the van of fight *Patroclus* came;
710 And, like an eagle darting at his game,
 Sprung on the *Trojan* and the *Lycian* band;
 What grief thy heart, what fury urg'd thy hand,
 Oh gen'rous *Greek!* when with full vigour thrown
 At *Stenelaüs* flew the weighty stone,
715 Which sunk him to the dead: when *Troy*, too near
 That arm, drew back; and *Hector* learn'd to fear.
 Far as an able hand a lance can throw,
 Or at the lists, or at the fighting foe;
 So far the *Trojans* from their lines retir'd;
720 Till *Glaucus*' turning, all the rest inspir'd.
 Then *Bathyclæus* fell beneath his rage,
 The only hope of *Chalcon*'s trembling age:
 Wide o'er the land was stretch'd his large domain,
 With stately seats, and riches, blest in vain:
725 Him, bold with youth, and eager to pursue
 The flying *Lycians*, *Glaucus* met, and slew;
 Pierc'd thro' the bosom with a sudden wound,
 He fell, and falling, made the fields resound.
 Th' *Achaians* sorrow for their hero slain;
730 With conqu'ring shouts the *Trojans* shake the plain,
 And crowd to spoil the dead: The *Greeks* oppose;
 An iron circle round the carcase grows.
  Then brave *Laogonus* resign'd his breath,
 Dispatch'd by *Merion* to the shades of death:
735 On *Ida*'s holy hill he made abode,
 The Priest of *Jove*, and honour'd like his God.
 Between the jaw and ear the jav'lin went;
 The soul, exhaling, issu'd at the vent.
 His Spear *Æneas* at the victor threw,
740 Who stooping forward from the death withdrew;
 The lance hiss'd harmless o'er his cov'ring shield,
 And trembling strook, and rooted in the field;
 There yet scarce spent, it quivers on the plain,
 Sent by the great *Æneas*' arm in vain.

Swift as thou art (the raging hero cries)   745
And skill'd in dancing to dispute the prize,
My spear, the destin'd passage had it found,
Had fix'd thy active vigour to the ground.

 Oh valiant leader of the *Dardan* host!
(Insulted *Merion* thus retorts the boast)   750
Strong as you are, 'tis mortal force you trust,
An arm as strong may stretch thee in the dust.
And if to this my lance thy Fate be giv'n,
Vain are thy vaunts; Success is still from heav'n;
This instant sends thee down to *Pluto*'s coast,   755
Mine is the glory, his thy parting ghost.

 O friend (*Menœtius*' son this answer gave)
With words to combate, ill befits the brave:
Not empty boasts the sons of *Troy* repell,
Your swords must plunge them to the shades of hell.   760
To speak, beseems the council; but to dare
In glorious action, is the task of war.

 This said, *Patroclus* to the battel flies;
Great *Merion* follows, and new shouts arise:
Shields, helmets rattle, as the warriours close;   765
And thick and heavy sounds the storm of blows.
As thro' the shrilling vale, or mountain ground,
The labours of the woodman's axe resound;
Blows following blows are heard re-echoing wide,
While crackling forests fall on ev'ry side.   770
Thus echo'd all the fields with loud alarms,
So fell the warriours, and so rung their arms.

 Now great *Sarpedon*, on the sandy shore,
His heav'nly form defac'd with dust and gore,
And stuck with darts by warring heroes shed,   775
Lies undistinguish'd from the vulgar dead.
His long-disputed corpse the chiefs inclose,
On ev'ry side the busy combate grows;
Thick, as beneath some shepherd's thatch'd abode,
(The pails high-foaming with a milky flood,)   780
The buzzing flies, a persevering train,
Incessant swarm, and chas'd, return again.

 Jove view'd the combate with a stern survey,
And eyes that flash'd intolerable day;

785   Fix'd on the field his sight, his breast debates
       The vengeance due, and meditates the fates;
       Whether to urge their prompt effect, and call
       The force of *Hector* to *Patroclus'* fall,
       This instant see his short-liv'd trophies won,
790   And stretch him breathless on his slaughter'd son;
       Or yet, with many a soul's untimely flight,
       Augment the fame and horrour of the fight?
       To crown *Achilles'* valiant friend with praise
       At length he dooms; and that his last of days
795   Shall set in glory; bids him drive the foe;
       Nor unattended, see the shades below.
       Then *Hector*'s mind he fills with dire dismay;
       He mounts his car, and calls his hosts away;
       Sunk with *Troy*'s heavy fates, he sees decline
800   The scales of *Jove*, and pants with awe divine.
         Then, nor before, the hardy *Lycians* fled,
       And left their monarch with the common dead:
       Around, in heaps on heaps, a dreadful wall
       Of carnage rises, as the heroes fall.
805   (So *Jove* decreed!) At length the *Greeks* obtain
       The prize contested, and despoil the slain.
       The radiant arms are by *Patroclus* born,
       Patroclus' ships the glorious spoils adorn.
         Then thus to *Phœbus*, in the realms above,
810   Spoke from his throne the cloud-compelling *Jove*.
       Descend, my *Phœbus!* on the *Phrygian* plain,
       And from the fight convey *Sarpedon* slain;
       Then bathe his body in the crystal flood,
       With dust dishonour'd, and deform'd with blood:
815   O'er all his limbs ambrosial odours shed,
       And with celestial robes adorn the dead.
       Those rites discharg'd, his sacred corpse bequeath
       To the soft arms of silent *Sleep* and *Death*;
       They to his friends the mournful charge shall bear,
820   His friends a tomb and pyramid shall rear;
       What honours mortals after death receive,
       Those unavailing honours we may give!
         Apollo bows, and from mount *Ida*'s height,
       Swift to the field precipitates his flight;

Thence from the war the breathless hero bore,   825
Veil'd in a cloud, to silver *Simoïs'* shore:
There bath'd his honourable wounds, and drest
His manly members in th' immortal vest;
And with perfumes of sweet ambrosial dews,
Restores his freshness, and his form renews.   830
Then *Sleep* and *Death*, two twins of winged race,
Of matchless swiftness, but of silent pace,
Receiv'd *Sarpedon*, at the God's command,
And in a moment reach'd the *Lycian* land;
The corpse amidst his weeping Friends they laid,   835
Where endless honours wait the sacred shade.

    Meanwhile *Patroclus* pours along the plains,
With foaming coursers, and with loosen'd reins.
Fierce on the *Trojan* and the *Lycian* crew,
Ah blind to fate! thy headlong fury flew: 840
Against what fate and pow'rful *Jove* ordain,
Vain was thy friend's command, thy courage vain.
For he, the God, whose counsels uncontroll'd,
Dismay the mighty, and confound the bold:
The God who gives, resumes, and orders all,   845
He urg'd thee on, and urg'd thee on to fall.

    Who first, brave hero! by that arm was slain,
Who last, beneath thy vengeance, press'd the plain;
When heav'n itself thy fatal fury led,
And call'd to fill the number of the dead?   850
Adrestus first; *Autonous* then succeeds;
Echeclus follows; next young *Megas* bleeds;
Epistor, *Menalippus*, bite the ground;
The slaughter, *Elasus* and *Mulius* crown'd:
Then sunk *Pylartes* to eternal night;   855
The rest dispersing, trust their fates to flight.

    Now *Troy* had stoop'd beneath his matchless pow'r,
But flaming *Phœbus* kept the sacred tow'r.
Thrice at the battlements *Patroclus* strook,
His blazing *Ægis* thrice *Apollo* shook: 860
He try'd the fourth; when, bursting from the cloud,
A more than mortal voice was heard aloud.

    Patroclus! cease: This Heav'n-defended wall
Defies thy lance; not fated yet to fall;

865   Thy friend, thy greater far, it shall withstand,
     Troy shall not stoop ev'n to *Achilles'* hand.
      So spoke the God who darts celestial fires:
     The *Greek* obeys him, and with awe retires.
     While *Hector* checking at the *Scæan* gates
870   His panting coursers, in his breast debates,
     Or in the field his forces to employ,
     Or draw the troops within the walls of *Troy*.
     Thus while he thought, beside him *Phœbus* stood,
     In *Asius'* shape, who reign'd by *Sangar*'s flood;
875   (Thy brother, *Hecuba!* from *Dymas* sprung;
     A valiant warriour, haughty, bold, and young.)
     Thus he accosts him. What a shameful sight!
     Gods! is it *Hector* that forbears the fight?
     Were thine my vigour, this successful spear
880   Should soon convince thee of so false a fear.
     Turn then, ah turn thee to the field of fame,
     And in *Patroclus'* blood efface thy shame.
     Perhaps *Apollo* shall thy arms succeed,
     And heav'n ordains him by thy lance to bleed.
885   So spoke th' inspiring God; then took his flight,
     And plung'd amidst the tumult of the fight.
     He bids *Cebrion* drive the rapid car;
     The lash resounds; the coursers rush to war.
     The God the *Grecians* sinking souls deprest,
890   And pour'd swift spirits thro' each *Trojan* breast.
     Patroclus lights, impatient for the fight;
     A spear his left, a stone employs his right:
     With all his nerves he drives it at the foe;
     Pointed above, and rough and gross below:
895   The falling ruin crush'd *Cebrion*'s head,
     (The lawless offspring of King *Priam*'s bed,)
     His front, brows, eyes, one undistinguish'd wound,
     The bursting balls drop sightless to the ground.
     The charioteer, while yet he held the rein,
900   Struck from the car, falls headlong on the plain.
     To the dark shades the soul unwilling glides,
     While the proud victor thus his fall derides,
      Good heav'ns! what active feats yon' artist shows,
     What skilful divers are our *Phrygian* foes!

Mark with what ease they sink into the sand!   905
Pity! that all their practice is by land.
   Then rushing sudden on his prostrate prize,
To spoil the carcase fierce *Patroclus* flies:
Swift as a lion, terrible and bold,
That sweeps the fields, depopulates the fold;   910
Pierc'd thro' the dauntless heart, then tumbles slain;
And from his fatal courage finds his bane.
At once bold *Hector* leaping from his car,
Defends the body, and provokes the war.
Thus for some slaughter'd hind, with equal rage,   915
Two lordly rulers of the wood engage;
Stung with fierce hunger, each the prey invades,
And echoing roars rebellow thro' the shades.
Stern *Hector* fastens on the warriour's head,
And by the foot *Patroclus* drags the dead.   920
While all around, confusion, rage, and fright
Mix the contending hosts in mortal fight.
So pent by hills, the wild winds roar aloud
In the deep bosom of some gloomy wood;
Leaves, arms, and trees aloft in air are blown,   925
The broad oaks crackle, and the *Sylvans* groan;
This way and that, the ratt'ling thicket bends,
And the whole forest in one crash descends.
Not with less noise, with less tumultuous rage,
In dreadful shock the mingled hosts engage.   930
Darts show'r'd on darts, now round the carcase ring;
Now flights of arrows bounding from the string:
Stones follow stones; some clatter on the fields,
Some, hard and heavy, shake the sounding shields.
But where the rising whirlwind clouds the plains,   ⎫   835
Sunk in soft dust the mighty chief remains,   ⎬
And stretch'd in death, forgets the guiding reins!   ⎭
   Now flaming from the *Zenith*, *Sol* had driv'n
His fervid orb thro' half the vault of heav'n;
While on each host with equal tempest fell   940
The show'ring darts, and numbers sunk to hell.
But when his ev'ning wheels o'erhung the main,
Glad conquest rested on the *Grecian* train.

Then from amidst the tumult and alarms,
945 They draw the conquer'd corpse, and radiant arms.
Then rash *Patroclus* with new fury glows,
And breathing slaughter, pours amid the foes.
Thrice on the press like *Mars* himself he flew,
And thrice three heroes at each onset slew.
950 There ends thy glory! there the fates untwine
The last, black remnant of so bright a line.
Apollo dreadful stops thy middle way;
Death calls, and heav'n allows no longer day!

For lo! the God, in dusky clouds enshrin'd,
Approaching dealt a stagg'ring blow behind.
995 The weighty shock his neck and shoulders feel;
His eyes flash sparkles, his stunn'd senses reel
In giddy darkness: Far to distance flung,
His bounding helmet on the champain rung.
960 *Achilles'* plume is stain'd with dust and gore;
That plume, which never stoop'd to earth before,
Long us'd, untouch'd, in fighting fields to shine,
And shade the temples of the man divine.
Jove dooms it now on *Hector*'s helm to nod;
965 Not long – for fate pursues him, and the God.

His spear in shivers falls: His ample shield
Drops from his arm: His baldrick strows the field:
The corselet his astonish'd breast forsakes:
Loose is each joint; each nerve with Horrour shakes.
970 Stupid he stares, and all-assistless stands:
Such is the force of more than mortal hands!

A *Dardan* youth there was, well-known to fame,
From *Panthus* sprung, *Euphorbus* was his name;
Fam'd for the manage of the foaming horse,
975 Skill'd in the dart, and matchless in the course:
Full twenty Knights he tumbled from the car,
While yet he learn'd his rudiments of war.
His vent'rous spear first drew the hero's gore;
He strook, he wounded, but he durst no more;
980 Nor tho' disarm'd, *Patroclus*' fury stood:
But swift withdrew the long-protended wood,
And turn'd him short, and herded in the croud.

Thus, by an arm divine, and mortal spear,
Wounded at once, *Patroclus* yields to fear,
Retires for succour to his social train,   985
And flies the fate, which heav'n decreed, in vain.
Stern *Hector*, as the bleeding chief he views,
Breaks thro' the ranks, and his retreat pursues:
The lance arrests him with a mortal wound;
He falls, earth thunders, and his arms resound.   990
With him all *Greece* was sunk; that moment all
Her yet-surviving heroes seem'd to fall.
So scorch'd with heat along the desart shore,
The roaming lion meets a bristly boar,
Fast by the spring; they both dispute the flood,   995
With flaming eyes, and jaws besmear'd with blood;
At length the sov'reign savage wins the strife,
And the torn boar resigns his thirst and life.
Patroclus thus, so many chiefs o'erthrown,
So many lives effus'd, expires his own.   1000
As dying now at *Hector*'s feet he lies,
He sternly views him, and triumphing cries.

    Lie there *Patroclus!* and with thee, the joy
Thy pride once promis'd, of subverting *Troy*;
The fancy'd scenes of *Ilion* wrapt in flames,   1005
And thy soft pleasures serv'd with captive dames!
Unthinking man! I fought, those tow'rs to free,
And guard that beauteous race from lords like thee:
But thou a prey to vulturs shalt be made!
Thy own *Achilles* cannot lend thee aid;   1010
Tho much at parting that great chief might say,
And much enjoin thee, this important day.
'Return not, my brave friend (perhaps he said)
Without the bloody arms of *Hector* dead':
He spoke, *Patroclus* march'd, and thus he sped.   1015
    Supine, and wildly gazing on the skies,
With faint, expiring breath, the chief replies.

    Vain boaster! cease, and know the pow'rs divine;
Jove's and *Apollo*'s is this deed, not thine;
To heav'n is ow'd whate'er your own you call,   1020
And heav'n itself disarm'd me e'er my fall.

Had twenty mortals, each thy match in might,
Oppos'd me fairly, they had sunk in fight:
By fate and *Phœbus* was I first o'erthrown,
1025 *Euphorbus* next; the third mean part thy own.
But thou, imperious! hear my latest breath;
The Gods inspire it, and it sounds thy death.
Insulting man! thou shalt be soon, as I;
Black fate hangs o'er thee, and thy hour draws nigh;
1030 Ev'n now on life's last verge I see thee stand,
I see thee fall, and by *Achilles'* hand.

He faints; the soul unwilling wings her way,
(The beauteous body left a load of clay)
Flits to the lone, uncomfortable coast;
1035 A naked, wand'ring, melancholy ghost!

Then *Hector* pausing, as his eyes he fed
On the pale carcase, thus address'd the dead.

From whence this boding speech, the stern decree
Of death denounc'd, or why denounc'd to me?
1040 Why not as well *Achilles'* fate be giv'n
To *Hector*'s lance? Who knows the will of heav'n?

Pensive he said; then pressing as he lay
His breathless bosom, tore the lance away;
And upwards cast the corps: The reeking spear
1045 He shakes, and charges the bold charioteer.
But swift *Automedon* with loosned reins
Rapt in the chariot o'er the distant plains,
Far from his rage th' immortal coursers drove;
Th' immortal coursers were the gift of *Jove*.

OBSERVATIONS

ON THE

SIXTEENTH BOOK

We have at the entrance of this book one of the most beautiful parts of the Iliad. The two different characters are admirably sustain'd in the dialogue of the two heroes, wherein there is not a period but strongly marks not only their natural temper, but that particular disposition of mind in either, which arises from the present state of affairs. We see *Patroclus* touch'd with the deepest compassion for the misfortune of the *Greeks*, (whom the *Trojans* had forc'd to retreat to their ships, and which ships were on the point of burning) prostrating himself before the vessel of *Achilles*, and pouring out his tears at his feet. *Achilles*, struck with the grief of his friend, demands the cause of it. *Patroclus*, pointing to the ships, where the flames already began to rise, tells him he is harder than the rocks or sea which lay in prospect before them, if he is not touch'd with so moving a spectacle, and can see in cold blood his friends perishing before his eyes. As nothing can be more natural and affecting than the speech of *Patroclus*, so nothing is more lively and picturesque than the attitude he is here describ'd in.

The *Pathetic* of *Patroclus*'s speech is finely contrasted by the *Fierté* of that of *Achilles*. While the former is melting with sorrow for his countrymen, the utmost he can hope from the latter, is but to borrow his armour and troops; to obtain his personal assistance he knows is impossible. At the very instant that *Achilles* is mov'd to ask the cause of his friend's concern, he seems to say that nothing could deserve it but the death of their fathers: and in the same breath speaks of the total destruction of the *Greeks* as of too slight a cause for tears. *Patroclus*, at the opening of this speech, dares not name *Agamemnon* even for being wounded; and after he has tried to bend him by all the arguments that could affect an human breast, concludes by supposing that some oracle or supernatural inspiration is the cause that with-holds his arms. What can match the fierceness of his answer? Which implies, that not the oracles of heaven itself should be regarded, if they stood in competition with his resentment: That if he yields, it must be thro' his own mere motive: The only reason he has ever to yield, is that nature itself cannot support anger eternally: And if he yields now, it is only because he had before determin'd to do so at a certain time, (*Il.* 9. v. 773). That time was not till the flames should approach to his own ships, till the last article of danger, and that not of danger to *Greece*, but to himself. Thus his very pity has the sternest qualifications in the world. After all, what is it he yields to? Only to suffer his friend to go in his stead, just to save them from present ruin, but he expressly forbids him to proceed any farther in their assistance, than barely to put out the fires, and secure his own and his friend's return into their country: And all this concludes with a wish, that (if it were possible) every *Greek* and every *Trojan* might perish except themselves. Such is that *Wrath* of *Achilles*, that more than wrath, as the *Greek* μῆνις implies, which *Homer* has painted in so strong a colouring.

8. *Indulgent to his best belov'd.*] The friendship of *Achilles* and *Patroclus* is celebrated by all antiquity: And *Homer*, notwithstanding the anger of *Achilles* was his profess'd subject, has found the secret to discover, thro' that very anger, the softer parts of his character. In this view we shall find him generous in his temper, despising gain and booty, and as far as his honour is not concern'd, fond of his mistress, and easy to his friend: Not proud, but when injur'd; and not more revengeful when ill us'd, than grateful and gentle when respectfully treated. '*Patroclus* (says *Philostratus*, who probably grounds his assertion on some ancient tradition) was not so much elder than *Achilles* as to pretend to direct him, but of a tender, modest, and unassuming nature; constant and diligent in his attendance, and seeming to have no affections but those of his friend.' The same author has a very pretty passage, where *Ajax* is introduced enquiring of *Achilles*, 'Which of all his warlike actions were the most difficult and dangerous to him? He answers, Those which he undertook for the sake of his friends. And which (continues *Ajax*) were the most pleasing and easy? The very same, replies *Achilles*. He then asks him, Which of all the wounds he ever bore in battel was the most painful to him? *Achilles* answers, That which he receiv'd from *Hector*. But *Hector*, says *Ajax*, never gave you a wound. Yes, replies *Achilles*, a mortal one, when he slew my friend *Patroclus*.'

It is said in the life of *Alexander the Great*, that when that Prince visited the monuments of the heroes at *Troy*, and plac'd a crown upon the tomb of *Achilles*; his Friend *Hephæstion* plac'd another on that of *Patroclus*, as an intimation of his being to *Alexander* what the other was to *Achilles*. On which occasion the saying of *Alexander* is recorded; *That* Achilles *was happy indeed, for having had such a* Friend *to love him living, and such a* Poet *to celebrate him dead.*

11. *No girl, no infant,* &c.] I know the obvious translation of this passage makes the comparison consist only in the tears of the infant, applied to those of *Patroclus*. But certainly the idea of the simile will be much finer, if we comprehend also in it the mother's fondness and concern, awaken'd by this uneasiness of the child, which no less aptly corresponds with the tenderness of *Achilles* on the sight of his friend's affliction. And there is yet a third branch of the comparison, in that pursuit, and constant application the infant makes to the mother, in the same manner as *Patroclus* follows *Achilles* with his grief, till he forces him to take notice of it. I think (all these circumstances laid together) nothing can be more affecting or exact in all its views, than this similitude; which without that regard, has perhaps seem'd but low and trivial to an unreflecting reader.

31. *Let* Greece *at length with pity touch thy breast.*] The commentators labour to prove, that the words in the Original, which begin this speech, Μὴ νεμέσα, *Be not angry*, are not meant to desire *Achilles* to bear no farther resentment against the *Greeks*, but only not to be displeas'd at the tears which *Patroclus* sheds for their misfortune. *Patroclus* (they say) was not so imprudent to begin his intercession in that manner, when there was need of something more insinuating. I take this to be an excess of refinement: The purpose of every period in his speech is to persuade *Achilles* to lay aside his anger; why then may he not begin by desiring it? The whole question is, whether he may speak openly in favour of the *Greeks* in the first half of the verse, or in the latter? For in the same line he represents their distress.

– τοῖον γὰρ ἄχος βεβίηκεν Ἀχαιούς.

[such distress has befallen the Achaians]

'Tis plain he treats him without much reserve, calls him implacable, inexorable, and even mischievous (for αἰναρέτη implies no less.) I don't see wherein the caution of this speech consists; it is a generous, unartful petition, whereof *Achilles*'s nature would much more approve, than of all the artifice of *Ulysses* (to which he express'd his hatred in the ninth book, v. 310.)

35.   Eurypylus, Tydides, Atreus' *son,*
      And wise Ulysses. –]

Patroclus in mentioning the wounded Princes to *Achilles*, takes care not to put *Agamemnon* first, lest that odious name striking his ear on a sudden, should shut it against the rest of his discourse: Neither does he name him last, for fear *Achilles* dwelling upon it should fall into passion: But he slides it into the middle, mixing and confounding it with the rest, that it might not be taken too much notice of, and that the names which precede and follow it may diminish the hatred it might excite. Wherefore he does not so much as accompany it with an epithet.

I think the foregoing remark of *Eustathius* is very ingenious, and I have given into it so far, as to chuse rather to make *Patroclus* call him *Atreus'* son than *Agamemnon*, which yet farther softens it, since thus it might as well be imagin'd he spoke of *Menelaus*, as of *Agamemnon*.

61. *And thy mere image chase her foes away.*] It is hard to conceive a greater complement, or one that could more touch the warlike ambition of *Achilles*, than this which *Homer* puts into the mouth of *Patroclus.* It was also an encomium which he could not suspect of flattery; since the person who made it desires to hazard his life upon the security that the enemy could not support the sight of the very armour of *Achilles*: And indeed *Achilles* himself seems to entertain no less a thought, in the answer to this speech, where he ascribes the flight of *Troy* to the blazing of his helmet: a circumstance wonderfully fine, and nobly exalting the idea of this hero's terrible character. Besides all this, *Homer* had it in his view to prepare hereby the wonderful incident that is to ensue in the eighteenth book, where the very sight of *Achilles* from his ship turns the fortune of the war.

101. *No longer flames the lance of* Tydeus' *son.*] By what *Achilles* here says, joining *Diomede* to *Agamemnon* in this taunting reflection, one may justly suspect there was some particular disagreement and emula-tion between these two Heroes. This we may suppose to be the more natural, because *Diomede* was of all the *Greeks* confessedly the nearest in fame and courage to *Achilles*, and therefore the most likely to move

his envy, as being the most likely to supply his place. The same sentiments are to be observ'd in *Diomede* with regard to *Achilles*; he is always confident in his own valour, and therefore· in their greatest extremities he no where acknowledges the necessity of appeasing *Achilles*, but always in council appears most forward and resolute to carry on the war without him. For this reason he was not thought a fit embassador to *Achilles*; and upon return from the embassy, he breaks into a severe reflection, not only upon *Achilles*, but even upon *Agamemnon* who had sent this embassy to him. *I wish thou hadst not sent these supplications and gifts to* Achilles; *his insolence was extreme before, but now his arrogance will be intolerable; let us not mind whether he goes or stays, but do our duty and prepare for the battel.* *Eustathius* observes, that *Achilles* uses this particular expression concerning *Diomede*,

Οὐ γὰρ Τυδεΐδεω Διομήδεος ἐν παλάμῃσι
Μαίνεται ἐγχείη –

[No longer flames the lance of *Tydeus'* son]

because it was the same boasting expression *Diomed* had apply'd to himself, *Il.* 8. v. 111 of the original. But this having been said only to *Nestor* in the heat of fight, how can we suppose *Achilles* had notice of it? This observation shews the great diligence, if not the judgment, of the good archbishop.

111. *Shall render back the beauteous maid.*] But this is what the *Greeks* had already offer'd to do, and which he has refus'd; this then is an inequality in *Achilles*'s manners. Not at all: *Achilles* is still ambitious; when he refused these presents, the *Greeks* were not low enough, he would not receive them till they were reduced to the last extremity, and till he was sufficiently reveng'd by their losses.   *Dacier.*

113. *But touch not* Hector.] This injunction of *Achilles* is highly correspondent to his ambitious character: He is by no means willing that the conquest of *Hector* should be atchiev'd by any hand but his own: In that point of glory he is jealous even of his dearest friend. This also wonderfully strengthens the idea we have of his implacability and resentment; since at the same time that nothing can move him to assist the *Greeks* in the battel, we see it is the utmost force upon his nature to abstain from it, by the fear he manifests lest any other should subdue this hero.

The verse I am speaking of,

> Τοὺς ἄλλους ἐνάριζ᾽ · ἀπὸ δ᾽ Ἕκτορος ἴσχεο χεῖρας,

[Go ahead and slay the others; but don't touch *Hector*]

is cited by *Diogenes Laertius* as *Homer*'s, but not to be found in the editions before that of *Barnes*. It is certainly one of the instructions of *Achilles* to *Patroclus*, and therefore properly placed in this speech; but I believe better after

> – ποτὶ δ᾽, ἀγλαὰ δῶρα πόρωσιν,

[and they will bring me shining gifts]

than where he has inserted it four lines above: For *Achilles*'s instructions not beginning till v. 83.

> Πείθεο δ᾽, ὥς τοι ἐγὼ μύθου τέλος ἐν φρεσὶ θείω,

[Obey this decisive word I shall put before your mind]

it is not so proper to divide this material one from the rest. Whereas (according to the method I propose) the whole context will lie in this order. *Obey my injunctions, as you consult my interest and honour. Make as great a slaughter of the* Trojans *as you will, but abstain from* Hector. *And as soon as you have repuls'd them from the ships, be satisfy'd and return: For it may be fatal to pursue the victory to the walls of* Troy.

115. *Consult my glory, and forbear.*] *Achilles* tells *Patroclus*, that if he pursues the foe too far, whether he shall be victor or vanquish'd, it must prove either way prejudicial to his glory. For by the former, the *Greeks* having no more need of *Achilles*'s aid, will not restore him his captive, nor try any more to appease him by presents: By the latter, his arms would be left in the enemy's hands, and he himself upbraided with the death of *Patroclus*.   *Dacier.*

122. *Oh would to all*, &c.] *Achilles* from his overflowing gall vents this execration: The *Trojans* he hates as professed enemies, and he detests the *Grecians* as people who had with calmness overlooked his wrongs. Some of the ancient cricks not entring into the manners of *Achilles*, would have expunged this imprecation, as uttering an universal malevolence to mankind. This violence agrees perfectly with his implacable character. But one may observe at the same time the mighty force of friendship, if for the sake of his dear *Patroclus* he will protect and secure those *Greeks*, whose destruction he wishes. What a little qualifies this bloody wish, is that we may suppose it spoken with great unreservedness, as in secret, and between friends.

Mons. *de la Motte* has a lively remark upon the absurdity of this wish. Upon the supposition that *Jupiter* had granted it, if all the *Trojans* and *Greeks* were destroy'd, and only *Achilles* and *Patroclus* left to conquer *Troy*, he asks, what would be the victory without any enemies, and the triumph without any spectators? But the answer is very obvious; *Homer* intends to paint a man in passion; the wishes and schemes of such an one are seldom conformable to reason; and the manners are preserved the better, the less they are represented to be so.

This brings into my mind that curse in *Shakespear*, where that admirable master of nature makes *Northumberland*, in the rage of his passion, wish for an universal destruction.

> *– Now let not nature's hand*
> *Keep the wild flood confin'd! Let order die,*
> *And let the world no longer be a stage*
> *To feed contention in a lingring act:*
> *But let one spirit of the first–born* Cain
> *Reign in all bosoms, that each heart being set*
> *On bloody courses, the rude scene may end,*
> *And darkness be the burier of the dead!*

130. Ajax *no more,* &c.] This description of *Ajax* wearied out with battel, is a passage of exquisite life and beauty: Yet what I think nobler than the description itself, is what he says at the end of it, that his hero even in this excess of fatigue and languor, could scarce be moved from his post by the efforts of a whole army. *Virgil* has copied the description very exactly, *Æn.* 9.

> *Ergo nec clypeo juvenis subsistere tantum*
> *Nec dextra valet: injectis sic undique telis*
> *Obruitur. Strepit assiduo cava tempora circum*
> *Tinnitu galea, & saxis solida æra fatiscunt:*
> *Discussæque jubæ capiti, nec sufficit umbo*
> *Ictibus: ingeminant hastis & Troes, & ipse*
> *Fulmineus Mnestheus; tum toto corpore sudor*

Liquitur, & piceum, nec respirare potestas,
Flumen agit; fessos quatit æger anhelitus artus.

[With labour spent, no longer can he wield
The heavy faulchion, or sustain the shield:
O'erwhelm'd with darts, which from afar they fling,
The weapons round his hollow temples ring:
His golden helm gives way: with strong blows
Batter'd, and flat, and beaten to his brows.
His crest is rash'd away; his ample shield
Is falsify'd, and round with jav'lins fill'd.
    The foe now faint, the *Trojans* overwhelm:
And *Mnesteus* lays hard load upon his helm.
Sick sweat succeeds, he drops at ev'ry pore,
With driving dust his cheeks are pasted o're.
Shorter and shorter ev'ry gasp he takes,
And vain efforts, and hurtless blows he makes.]

The circumstances which I have mark'd in a different character are
improvements upon *Homer*, and the last verse excellently expresses, in
the short catching up of the numbers, the quick, short panting,
represented in the image. The reader may add to the comparison an
imitation of the same place in *Tasso*, Canto 9. *St.* 97.

Fatto intanto hà il Soldan cio, ch'e concesso
Fare a terrena forza, hor piu non puote:
Tutto e sangue e sudore; un grave, e spesso
Anhelar gli ange il petto, e i fianche scote.
Langue sotto lo scudo il brachio oppresso,
Gira la destra il ferro in pigre rote;
Spessa, e non taglia, e divenendo ottuso
Perduto il brando omai di brando hà l'uso.

[Meanwhile the Soldan in this latest charge
Had done as much as human force was able,
All sweat and blood appear'd his members large,
His breath was short, his courage wax'd unstable,
His arm grew weak to bear his mighty targe,
His hand to rule his heavy sword unable,
    Which bruis'd, not cut, so blunted was the blade
    It lost the use for which a sword was made.]

148.   *Great* Ajax *saw, and own'd the hand divine,*
        Confessing Jove, *and trembling at the sign.*]

In the *Greek* there is added an explication of this sign, which has no other allusion to the action but a very odd one in a single phrase, or metaphor.

> – ὅ ῥα πάγχυ μάχης ἐπὶ μήδεα κείρει
> Ζεὺς ὑψιβρεμέτης, Τρώεσσι δὲ βούλετο νίκην.

Which may be translated,

> *So seem'd their hopes cut off by heav'ns high Lord,*
> *So doom'd to fall before the* Trojan *sword.*

Chapman endeavours to account for the meanness of this conceit, by the gross wit of *Ajax*; who seeing the head of his lance cut off, took it into his fancy that *Jupiter* would in the same manner cut off the counsels and schemes of the *Greeks.* For to understand this far-fetch'd apprehension gravely, as the commentators have done, is indeed (to use the words of *Chapman*) most *dull and Ajantical.* I believe no man will blame me for leaving these lines out of the text.

154. Achilles *view'd the rising flames.*] This event is prepared with a great deal of art and probability. That effect which a multitude of speeches was not able to accomplish, one lamentable spectacle, the sight of the flames, at length brings to pass, and moves *Achilles* to compassion. This it was (say the ancients) that moved the tragedians to make visible representations of misery; for the spectators beholding people in unhappy circumstances, find their souls more deeply touch'd, than by all the strains of rhetorick.   *Eustathius.*

162. *He cas'd his limbs in brass,* &c.] *Homer* does not amuse himself here to describe these arms of *Achilles* at length, for besides that the time permits it not, he reserves this description for the new armour which *Thetis* shall bring that hero; a description which will be plac'd in a more quiet moment, and which will give him all the leisure of making it, without requiring any force to introduce it.   *Eustathius.*

172. *Alone untouch'd* Pelides' *jav'lin stands.*] This passage affords another instance of the stupidity of the commentators, who are here most absurdly inquisitive after the reasons why *Patroclus* does not take the

spear, as well as the other arms of *Achilles?* He thought himself a very happy man, who first found out, that *Homer* had certainly given this spear to *Patroclus*, if he had not foreseen that when it should be lost in his future unfortunate engagement, *Vulcan* could not furnish *Achilles* with another; being no joiner, but only a smith. *Virgil*, it seems, was not so precisely acquainted with *Vulcan*'s disability to profess the two trades: since he has, without any scruple, employed him in making a spear, as well as the other arms for *Æneas.* Nothing is more obvious than this thought of *Homer*, who intended to raise the idea of his hero, by giving him such a spear as no other could wield: The description of it in this place is wonderfully pompous.

183. *Sprung from the wind.*] It is a beautiful invention of the poet to represent the wonderful swiftness of the horses of *Achilles*, by saying they were begotten by the western wind. This fiction is truly poetical, and very proper in the way of natural allegory. However, it is not altogether improbable our author might have designed it even in the literal sense: Nor ought the notion to be thought very extravagant in a Poet, since grave naturalists have seriously vouched the truth of this kind of generation. Some of these relate as an undoubted piece of natural history, that there was anciently a breed of this kind of horses in *Portugal*, whose damms were impregnated by a western Wind: *Varro*, *Collumella*, and *Pliny*, are all of this opinion. I shall only mention the words of *Pliny*, Nat. Hist. lib. 8. cap. 42. *Constat in Lusitania circa Olyssiponem oppidum, & Tagum amnem, equas Favonio flante obversas animalem concipere spiritum, idque partum fieri & gigni pernicissimum* [It is well known in Lusitania, in the area around the town of Olisipo (Lisbon) and the river Tagus, when the West Wind is blowing, that the mares who are facing it conceive a living spirit, and that in this way is born an extremely swift colt]. See also the same author, *l.* 4. *c.* 22. *l.* 16. *c.* 25. Possibly *Homer* had this opinion in view, which we see has authority more than sufficient to give it place in poetry. *Virgil* has given us a description of this manner of conception, *Georgic* 3.

> *Continuoque avidis ubi subdita flamma medullis,*
> *Vere magis (quia vere calor redit ossibus) illæ*
> *Ore omnes versæ in Zephyrum, stant rupibus altis,*
> *Exceptantque leves auras: & sæpe sine ullis*
> *Conjugiis, vento gravidæ (mirabile dictu)*

Saxa per & scopulos & depressas convalles
Diffugiunt. –

[When, at the spring's approach, their marrow burns,
 (For with the spring their genial warmth returns),
 The mares to cliffs of rugged rocks repair,
 And with wide nostrils snuff the western air:
 When (wondrous to relate!) the parent wind,
 Without the stallion, propagates the kind,
 Then, fir'd with am'rous rage, they take their flight
 Through plains, and mount the hills' unequal height.]

186. *Swift* Pedasus *was added to their side.*] Here was a necessity for a spare horse (as in another place *Nestor* had occasion for the same) that if by any misfortune one of the other horses should fall, there might be a fresh one ready at hand to supply his place. This is good management in the Poet, to deprive *Achilles* not only of his charioteer and his arms, but of one of his inestimable horses.   *Eustathius.*

194. *Grim as voracious wolves,* &c.] There is scarce any picture in *Homer* so much in the savage and terrible way, as this comparison of the *Myrmidons* to wolves: It puts one in mind of the pieces of *Spagnolett*, or *Salvator Rosa*: Each circumstance is made up of images very strongly coloured, and horridly lively. The principal design is to represent the stern looks and fierce appearance of the *Myrmidons*, a gaunt and ghastly train of raw-bon'd bloody-minded Fellows. But besides this, the Poet seems to have some farther views in so many different particulars of the comparison: Their eager desire of fight is hinted at by the wolves thirsting after water: Their strength and vigour for the battel is intimated by their being filled with food: And as these beasts are said to have their thirst sharper after they are gorged with Prey; so the *Myrmidons* are strong and vigorous with ease and refreshment, and therefore more ardently desirous of the combate. This image of their *strength* is inculcated by several expressions, both in the simile and the application, and seems design'd in contraste to the other *Greeks*, who are all wasted and spent with toil.

We have a picture much of this kind given us by *Milton, lib.* 10. where *Death* is let loose into the new creation, to glut his appetite, and discharge his rage upon all nature.

> — *As when a flock*
> *Of rav'nous fowls, tho' many a league remote,*
> *Against the day of battel, to a field*
> *Where armies lie encamp'd, come flying, lur'd*
> *With scent of living carcasses, design'd*
> *For Death the following day, in bloody fight.*
> *So scented the grim feature, and upturn'd*
> *His nostril wide into the murky air,*
> *Sagacious of his quarry from afar.*

And by *Tasso*, Canto 10. *St.* 2. of the furious *Soldan* covered with blood, and thirsting for fresh slaughter.

> *Come dal chiuso ovil cacciato viene*
> *Lupo tal' hor, che fugge, e si nasconde;*
> *Che se ben del gran ventre omai ripiene*
> *Ha l' ingorde voragini profonde.*
> *Avido pur di sangue anco fuor tiene*
> *La lingua, e'l sugge da le labbra immonde;*
> *Tal' ei sen gia dopo il sanguigno stratio*
> *De la sua cupa fame anco non satio.*

> [As when a savage wolf, chas'd from the fold,
> To hide his head runs to some holt or wood,
> Who though he filled hath while it might hold
> His greedy paunch, yet hung'reth after food,
> With sanguine tongue out of his lips forth roll'd,
> About his jaws that licks up foam and blood;
>   So from his bloody fray the Soldan hied,
>   His rage unquench'd, his wrath unsatisfied.]

211. *Deriv'd from thee, whose waters, &c.*] *Homer* seems resolved that every thing about *Achilles* shall be miraculous. We have seen his very horses are of celestial origine; and now his commanders, tho' vulgarly reputed the sons of men, are represented as the real offspring of some Deity. The Poet thus enhances the admiration of his chief hero by every circumstance with which his imagination could furnish him.

220. *To her high chamber.*] It was the custom of those times to assign the uppermost rooms to the women, that they might be the farther removed from commerce: Wherefore *Penelope* in the *Odysseis* mounts up into a garret, and there sits to her business. So *Priam*, in the 16*th* book, v. 248. had chambers for the ladies of his court, under the roof of his palace.

The *Lacedæmonians* call'd these high apartments ῷα, and as the word also signifies *eggs*, 'tis probable it was this that gave occasion to the fable of *Helen*'s birth, who is said to be born from an *egg*.

Eustathius.

283. *And thus the God implor'd.*] Tho' the character of *Achilles* every where shews a mind sway'd with unbounded passions, and entirely regardless of all human authority and law; yet he preserves a constant respect to the Gods, and appears as zealous in the sentiments and actions of piety as any hero of the Iliad; who indeed are all remarkable this way. The present passage is an exact description and perfect ritual of the ceremonies on these occasions. *Achilles*, tho' an urgent affair call'd for his friend's assistance, would not yet suffer him to enter the fight, till in a most solemn manner he had recommended him to the protection of *Jupiter*: And this I think a stronger proof of his tenderness and affection for *Patroclus*, than either the grief he express'd at his death, or the fury he shew'd to revenge it.

285. Dodonæan Jove.] The frequent mention of *Oracles* in *Homer* and the ancient Authors, may make it not improper to give the reader a general account of so considerable a part of the *Grecian* superstition; which I cannot do better than in the words of my friend Mr *Stanyan*, in his excellent and judicious abstract of the *Grecian* History.

'The *Oracles* were rank'd among the noblest and most religious kinds of divination; the design of them being to settle such an immediate way of converse with their Gods, as to be able by them not only to explain things intricate and obscure, but also to anticipate the knowledge of future events; and that with far greater certainty than they could hope for from men, who out of ignorance and prejudice must sometimes either conceal or betray the truth. So that this became the only safe way of deliberating upon affairs of any consequence, either publick or private. Whether to proclaim war, or conclude a peace, to institute a new form of government, or enact new laws, all was to be done with the advice and approbation of the oracle, whose determinations were always held sacred and inviolable. As to the causes of Oracles, *Jupiter* was look'd upon as the first cause of this, and all other sorts of divination; he had the book of fate before him, and out of that reveal'd either more or less, as he pleas'd, to inferior dæmons. But to argue more rationally, this way of access to the Gods has been branded as one of the earliest and grossest pieces of priestcraft, that obtain'd in the world. For the priests, whose dependance was on the Oracles, when they found the cheat had got sufficient footing, allow'd no man to consult the gods without costly sacrifices and rich presents to themselves: And as few could bear this expence, it serv'd to raise their credit among the common people, by keeping them at an awful distance. And to heighten their esteem with the better and wealthier sort, even they were only admitted upon a few stated days: By which the thing appear'd still more mysterious, and for want of this good management, must quickly have been seen through, and fall to the ground. But whatever juggling there was as to the religious part, Oracles had certainly a good effect as to the publick; being admirably suited to the genius of a people, who would join in the most desperate expedition, and admit of any change of government, when they understood by the Oracle it was the irresistible will of the Gods. This was the method *Minos*, *Lycurgus*, and all the famous law-givers took; and indeed they found the people so entirely devoted to this part of religion, that it was generally the easiest, and sometimes the only way of winning them into a compliance. And then they took care to have them deliver'd in such ambiguous terms, as to admit of different constructions according to the exigency of the times; so that they were generally interpreted to the advantage of the state, unless sometimes there happen'd to be bribery, or flattery in the case; as when *Demosthenes* complain'd that the *Pythia* spoke as *Philip* would have her. The most numerous, and of greatest repute were the Oracles of *Apollo*, who in subordination to *Jupiter*, was appointed to preside over, and inspire all sorts of prophets and diviners. And amongst these, the *Delphian* challeng'd the first place, not so much in respect of its antiquity, as its perspicuity and certainty; insomuch that the answers of the *Tripos* came to be used proverbially for clear and infallible truths. Here we must not omit the first *Pythia* or priestess of this famous Oracle in heroic verse. They found a secret charm in numbers, which made every thing look pompous and weighty. And hence it became the general practice of legislators, and philosophers, to deliver their laws and maxims in that dress: And scarce any thing in those ages was writ of excellence or moment but in verse. This was the dawn of poetry, which soon grew into repute; and so long as it serv'd to such noble purposes as religion and government, poets were highly honour'd, and admitted into a share of the administration. But by that time it arriv'd to any perfection, they pursu'd more mean and servile ends; and as they prostituted their muse, and debased the subject, they sunk proportionably in their esteem and dignity. As to the history of Oracles, we find them mention'd in the very infancy of *Greece*; and it is as uncertain when they were finally extinct, as when they began. For they often lost their prophetick faculty for some time, and recover'd it again. I know 'tis a common opinion, that they were universally silenc'd upon our Saviour's appearance in the world: And if the Devil had been permitted for so many ages to delude mankind, it might probably have been so. But we are assur'd from history, that several of them continu'd till the reign of *Julian* the apostate, and were consulted by him: And therefore I look upon the whole business as of human contrivance; an egregious imposture founded upon superstition, and carry'd on by policy and interest, till the brighter Oracles of the holy scriptures dispell'd these mists of error and enthusiasm.'

285. Pelasgic, Dodonæan Jove.] *Achilles* invokes *Jupiter* with these particular appellations, and represents to him the services perform'd by these priests and prophets, making these honours paid in his own country, his claim for the protection of this Deity. *Jupiter* was look'd upon as the first cause of all divination and Oracles, from whence he had the appellation of πανομφαῖος [author of all omens], *Il.* 8. v. 250. The first Oracle of *Dodona* was founded by the *Pelasgi*, the most ancient of all the inhabitants of *Greece*, which is confirm'd by this verse of *Hesiod*, preserv'd by the Scholiast on *Sophocles Trachin.*

Δωδώνην, φηγόν τε Πελασγῶν ἕδρανον ἧκεν.

[He came to Dodona, the oak and abode of the Pelasgi.]

The oaks of this place were said to be endow'd with voice, and prophetic spirit; the priests who gave answers concealing themselves in these trees; a practice which the pious frauds of succeeding ages have render'd not improbable.

288. *Whose groves the* Selli, *race austere!* &c.] *Homer* seems to me to say clearly enough, that these priests lay on the ground and forbore the bath, to honour by these austerities the God they serv'd; for he says, σοὶ ναίουσ᾽ ἀνιπτόποδες [who, to please you, keep their feet unwashed] and this σοὶ can in my opinion only signify *for you*, that is to say, *to* *please you*, and *for your honour.* This example is remarkable, but I do not think it singular; and the earliest antiquity may furnish us with the like of pagans, who by an austere life try'd to please their Gods. Nevertheless I am obliged to say, that *Strabo*, who speaks very much at large of these *Selli* in his 7*th* book, has not taken this austerity of life for an effect of their devotion, but for a remain of the grossness of their ancestors; who being barbarians, and straying from country to country, had no bed but the earth, and never used a bath. But it is no way unlikely that what was in the first *Pelasgians* (who founded this Oracle) only custom and use, might be continu'd by these priests thro' devotion. How many things do we at this day see, which were in their original only ancient manner, and which are continu'd thro' zeal and a spirit of religion? It is very probable that these priests by this hard living had a mind to attract the admiration and confidence of a people who lov'd luxury and delicacy so much. I was willing to search into antiquity for the original of these *Selli*, priests of *Jupiter*, but found nothing so ancient as *Homer*: *Herodotus* writes in his second book, that the Oracle of *Dodona* was the ancientest in *Greece*, and that it was a long time the only one; but what he adds, that it was founded by an *Egyptian* woman, who was the priestess of it, is contradicted by this passage of *Homer*, who shews, that in the time of the *Trojan* war this temple was serv'd by men call'd *Selli*, and not by women. *Strabo* informs us of a curious ancient tradition, importing, that this temple was at first built in *Thessaly*, that from thence it was carry'd into *Dodona*, that several women who had plac'd their devotion there follow'd it, and that in process of time the priestesses used to be chosen from among the descendents of those women. To return to these *Selli*, *Sophocles*, who of all the *Greek* poets is he who has most imitated *Homer*, speaks in like manner of these priests in one of his plays, where *Hercules* says to his son *Hillus*; 'I will declare to thee a new Oracle, which perfectly agrees with this ancient one; I my self having enter'd into the sacred wood inhabited by the austere *Selli*, who lie on the ground, writ this answer of the oak, which is consecrated to my father *Jupiter*, and which renders his oracles in all languages.'   *Dacier.*

288.] *Homer* in this verse uses a word which I think singular and remarkable, ὑποφῆται [under-prophets]. I cannot believe that it was put simply for προφῆται, but am persuaded that this term includes some particular sense, and shews some custom but little known, which I would willingly discover. In the scholia of *Didymus* there is this remark: 'They call'd those who serv'd in the temple, and who explain'd the Oracles render'd by the priests, *hypothets*, or *under-prophets.*' It is certain that there were in the temples servitors, or subaltern ministers, who for the sake of gain, undertook to explain the Oracles which were obscure. This custom seems very well establish'd in the *Ion* of *Euripides*; where that young child (after having said that the priestess is seated on the tripod, and renders the Oracles which *Apollo* dictates to her) addresses himself to those who serve in the temple, and bids them go and wash in the *Castalian* fountain, to come again into the temple and explain the Oracles to those who should demand the explication of them. *Homer* therefore means to shew, that these *Selli* were, in the temple of *Dodona*, those subaltern ministers that interpreted the Oracles. But this, after all, does not appear to agree with the present passage: For, besides that the custom was not establish'd in *Homer*'s time, and that there is no footstep of it founded in that early age; these *Selli* (of whom *Homer* speaks) are not here ministers subordinate to others, they are plainly the chief priests. The explication of this word therefore must be elsewhere sought, and I shall offer my conjecture, which I ground upon the nature of this Oracle of *Dodona*, which was very different from all the other Oracles: In all other temples the priests deliver'd the Oracles which they had receiv'd from their Gods, immediately: But in the temple of *Dodona*, *Jupiter* did not utter his oracles to his priests, but to his *Selli*; he render'd them to the oaks, and the wonderful oaks render'd them to the priests, who declared them to those who consulted them: So these priests were not properly προφῆται, prophets, since they did not receive those answers from the mouth of their God immediately; but they were ὑποφῆται, under-prophets, because they receiv'd them from the mouth of the oaks, if I may say so. The oaks, properly speaking, were the prophets, the first interpreters of *Jupiter*'s Oracles; and the *Selli* were ὑποφῆται, under-prophets, because they pronounc'd what the Oaks had said. Thus *Homer* in one single word includes a very curious piece of antiquity.   *Dacier.*

306. *Great* Jove *consents to half.*] *Virgil* has finely imitated this in his 11*th Æneid.*

> *Audiit, & voti Phœbus succedere partem*
> *Mente dedit; partem volucres dispersit in auras.*
> *Sterneret ut subita turbatam morte Camillam*
> *Annuit oranti; reducem ut patria alta videret*
> *Non dedit, inque notos vocem vertere procellæ.*

> [*Apollo* heard, and granting half his pray'r,
> Shuffled in winds the rest, and toss'd in empty air.
> He gives the death desir'd; his safe return
> By southern tempests to the seas is borne.]

314. *As wasps, provok'd,* &c.] One may observe, that tho' *Homer* sometimes takes his similitudes from the meanest and smallest things in nature, yet he orders it so as by their appearance to signalize and give lustre to his greatest heroes. Here he likens a body of *Myrmidons* to a nest of wasps, not on account of their strength and bravery, but of their heat and resentment. *Virgil* has imitated these humble comparisons, as when he compares the builders of *Carthage* to bees. *Homer* has carry'd it a little farther in another place, where he compares the soldiers to flies, for their busy industry and perseverance about a dead body; not diminishing his heroes by the size of these small animals, but raising his comparisons from certain properties inherent in them, which deserve our observation.   *Eustathius.*

This brings into my mind a pretty rural simile in *Spencer*, which is very much in the simplicity of the old father of poetry.

> *As gentle shepherd in sweet even-tide,*
> *When ruddy* Phœbus *'gins to welke in west,*
> *High on a hill, his flock to viewen wide,*
> *Marks which do bite their hasty supper best;*
> *A cloud of cumb'rous gnats do him molest,*
> *All striving to infix their feeble stings,*
> *That from their noyance he no whit can rest,*
> *But with his clownish hand their tender wings*
> *He brusheth oft, and oft doth mar their murmurings.*

354. *So when thick clouds,* &c.] All the commentators take this comparison in a sense different from that in which it is here translated. They suppose *Jupiter* is here described cleaving the air with a flash of lightning, and spreading a gleam of light over a high mountain, which a black cloud held bury'd in Darkness. The application is made to *Patroclus* falling on the *Trojans*, and giving respite to the *Greeks*, who were plung'd in obscurity. *Eustathius* gives this interpretation, but at the same time acknowledges it improper in this comparison to represent the extinction of the flames by the darting of lightning. This explanation is solely founded on the expression στεροπηγερέτα Ζεύς [Zeus the lightning-compellor], *fulgurator Jupiter*, which epithet is often applied when no such action is supposed. The most obvious signification of the words in this passage, gives a more natural and agreeable image, and admits of a juster application. The simile seems to be of *Jupiter* dispersing a black cloud which had cover'd a high mountain, whereby a beautiful prospect, which was before hid in darkness, suddenly appears. This is applicable to the present state of the *Greeks*, after *Patroclus* had extinguish'd the flames, which began to spread clouds of smoak over the fleet. It is *Homer*'s design in his comparisons to apply them to the most obvious and sensible image of the thing to be illustrated; which his commentators too frequently endeavour to hide by moral and allegorical refinements; and thus injure the Poet more, by attributing to him what does not belong to him, than by refusing him what is really his own.

It is much the same image with that of *Milton* in his second book, tho' apply'd in a very different way.

> *As when from mountain tops the dusky clouds*
> *Ascending, while the north wind sleeps, o'erspread*
> *Heav'ns chearful face; the low'ring element*
> *Scowls o'er the darkned landskip snow or show'r;*
> *If chance the radiant sun with farewell sweet*
> *Extend his evening beam, the fields revive,*
> *The birds their notes renew, the bleating herds*
> *Attest their joy, that hill and vally rings.*

390. Amisodarus, *who*, &c.] *Amisodarus* was King of *Caria*; *Bellerophon* married his daughter. The ancients guess'd from this passage that the *Chimæra* was not a fiction, since *Homer* marks the time wherein she liv'd, and the Prince with whom she liv'd; they thought it was some beast of that Prince's herds, who being grown furious and mad, had done a great deal of mischief, like the *Calydonian* boar.   *Eustathius.*

433. *Yet stops, and turns, and saves his lov'd allies.]* *Homer* represents *Hector*, as he retires, making a stand from time to time, to save his troops: And he expresses it by this single word ἀνέμιμνε; for ἀναμί μνειν does not only signify to *stay*, but likewise in retiring to stop from time to time; for this is the power of the preposition ἀνά, as in the word ἀναμάχεσθαι, which signifies to *fight by fits and starts;* ἀναπαλαί- ειν, to *wrestle several times*, and in many others.   *Eustathius.*

459. *From bank to bank th' immortal coursers flew*, &c.] *Homer* has made of *Hector*'s horses all that poetry could make of common and mortal horses; they stand on the bank of the ditch foaming and neighing for madness that they cannot leap it. But the immortal horses of *Achilles* find no obstacle; they leap the ditch, and fly into the plain.

Eustathius.

466.   *As when in autumn* Jove *his fury pours* –
       – *When guilty mortals* &c.]

The Poet in this image of an inundation, takes occasion to mention a sentiment of great piety, that such calamities were the effects of divine justice punishing the sins of mankind. This might probably refer to the tradition of an universal deluge, which was very common among the ancient heathen writers; most of them ascribing the cause of this deluge to the wrath of heaven provoked by the wickedness of men. *Diodorus Siculus, l.* 15. *c.* 5. speaking of an earthquake and inundation, which destroyed a great part of *Greece* in the 101*st Olympiad*, has these Words. *There was a great dispute concerning the cause of this calamity: The natural philosophers generally ascribed such events to necessary causes, not to any divine hand: But they who had more devout sentiments gave a more probable account hereof; asserting, that it was the divine vengeance alone that brought this destruction upon men who had offended the Gods with their impiety.* And then proceeds to give an account of those crimes which drew down this punishment upon them.

This is one, among a thousand instances, of *Homer*'s indirect and oblique manner of introducing moral sentences and instructions. These agreeably break in upon his reader even in descriptions and poetical parts, where one naturally expects only painting and amusement. We have virtue put upon us by surprize, and are pleas'd to find a thing where we should never have look'd to meet with it. I must do a noble *English* poet the justice to observe, that it is this particular art that is the very distinguishing excellence of *Cooper's-Hill*; throughout which, the descriptions of places, and images rais'd by the Poet, are still tending to some hint, or leading into some reflection, upon moral life or political institution: Much in the same manner as the real sight of such scenes and prospects is apt to give the mind a compos'd turn, and incline it to thoughts and contemplations that have a relation to the object.

480. *Between the space where silver* Simoïs *flows,*
Where lay the ships, and where the rampires rose.]

It looks at first sight as if *Patroclus* was very punctual in obeying the orders of *Achilles*, when he hinders the *Trojans* from ascending to their town, and holds an engagement with 'em between the ships, the river, and the wall. But he seems afterwards thro' very haste to have slipt his commands, for his orders were that he should drive 'em from the ships, and then presently return; but he proceeds farther, and his death is the consequence. *Eustathius.*

512. *When now* Sarpedon, &c.] The Poet preparing to recount the death of *Sarpedon*, it will not be improper to give a sketch of some particulars which constitute a character the most faultless and amiable in the whole Iliad. This hero is by birth superiour to all the chiefs of either side, being the only son of *Jupiter* engaged in this war. His qualities are no way unworthy his descent, since he every where appears equal in valour, prudence, and eloquence, to the most admired heroes: Nor are these excellences blemish'd with any of those defects with which the most distinguishing characters of the Poem are stain'd. So that the nicest criticks cannot find any thing to offend their delicacy, but must be obliged to own the manners of this hero perfect. His valour is neither rash nor boisterous; his prudence neither timorous nor tricking; and his eloquence neither talkative nor boasting. He never reproaches the living, or insults the dead: but appears uniform thro' his conduct in the war, acted with the same generous sentiments that engaged him in it, having no interest in the quarrel but to succour his allies in distress. This noble life is ended with a death as glorious; for in his last moments he has no other concern, but for the honour of his friends, and the event of the day.

Homer justly represents such a character to be attended with universal esteem: As he was greatly honour'd when living, he is as much lamented when dead, as the chief prop of *Troy.* The Poet by his death, even before that of *Hector*, prepares us to expect the destruction of that town, when its two great defenders are no more: and in order to make it the more signal and remarkable, it is the only death in the Iliad attended with prodigies: Even his funeral is perform'd by divine assistance, he being the only hero whose body is carried back to be interr'd in his native country, and honour'd with monuments erected to his fame. These peculiar and distinguishing honours seem appropriated by our author to him alone, as the reward of a merit superior to all his other less perfect heroes.

522. *As when two vulturs.*] *Homer* compares *Patroclus* and *Sarpedon* to two vulturs, because they appeared to be of equal strength and abilities, when they had dismounted from their chariots. For this reason he has chosen to compare them to birds of the same kind; as on another occasion, to image the like equality of strength, he resembles both *Hector* and *Patroclus* to lions; But a little after this place, diminishing the force of *Sarpedon*, he compares him to a bull, and *Patroclus* to a lion. He has placed these vulturs upon a high rock, because it is their nature to perch there, rather than in the boughs of trees. Their crooked talons make them unfit to walk on the ground, they could not fight steadily in the air, and therefore their fittest place is the rock.   *Eustathius.*

535. *Say, shall I snatch him from impending Fate.*] It appears by this passage, that *Homer* was of opinion, that the power of God could over-rule fate or destiny. It has puzzled many to distinguish exactly the notion of the heathens as to this point. Mr *Dryden* contends that *Jupiter* was limited by the destinies, or (to use his expression) was no better than book-keeper to them. He grounds it upon a passage in the tenth book of *Virgil*, where *Jupiter* mentions this instance of *Sarpedon* as a proof of his yielding to the fates. But both that and his citation from *Ovid*, amounts to no more than that *Jupiter* gave way to destiny, not that he could not prevent it; the contrary to which is plain from his doubt and deliberation in this place. And indeed whatever may be inferr'd of other poets, *Homer*'s opinion at least, as to the dispensations of God to man, has ever seem'd to me very clear, and distinctly agreeable to truth. We shall find, if we examine his whole works with an eye to this doctrine, that he assigns three causes of all the good and evil that happens in this world, which he takes a particular care to distinguish. First the *will of God*, superiour to all.

   – Διὸς δ' ἐτελείετο βουλή.   *Il.* 1.

[And the will of God was working out.]

   – Θεὸς διὰ πάντα τελευτᾷ.   *Il.* 19. v. 90.

[God brings all things to pass.]

– Ζεὺς ἀγαθόν τε κακόν τε διδοῖ, – &c.

[Zeus sometimes brings good and sometimes evil.

Od. 4. 237.]

Secondly, *destiny* or *fate*, meaning the laws and order of nature affecting the constitutions of men, and disposing them to good or evil, prosperity or misfortune; which the supreme being, if it be his pleasure, may over-rule (as he is inclin'd to do in this place) but which he generally suffers to take effect. Thirdly, our own *free will*, which either by prudence overcomes those natural influences and passions, or by folly suffers us to fall under them.   *Odyss.* 1. v. 32.

'Ω πόποι, οἶον δή νυ Θεοὺς βροτοὶ αἰτιόωνται.
Ἐξ ἡμέων γάρ φασι κάκ᾽ ἔμμεναι· οἱ δὲ καὶ αὐτοὶ
Σφῆσιν ἀτασθαλίῃσιν ὑπὲρ μόρον ἄλγε᾽ ἔχουσιν.

Why charge mankind on heav'n their own offence,
And call their woes the crime of providence?
Blind! who themselves their miseries create,
And perish by their folly, not their fate.

551.   *Let Sleep and Death convey, by thy command,*
       The breathless body to his native land.]

The history or fable receiv'd in *Homer*'s time imported, that *Sarpedon* was interr'd in *Lycia*, but it said nothing of his death. This gave the Poet the liberty of making him die at *Troy*, provided that after his death he was carried into *Lycia*, to preserve the fable. The Expedient proposed by *Juno* solves all; *Sarpedon* dies at *Troy*, and is interr'd at *Lycia*; and what renders this probable, is, that in those times, as at this day, Princes and persons of quality who died in foreign parts, were carried into their own country to be laid in the tombs of their fathers. The antiquity of this custom cannot be doubted, since it was practis'd in the Patriarchs times: *Jacob* dying in *Egypt*, orders his children to carry him into the land of *Canaan*, where he desired to be buried. *Gen.* 49. 29.   *Dacier.*

560.   *A show'r of blood.*] As to showers of a bloody colour, many both ancient and modern naturalists agree in asserting the reality of such appearances, tho' they account for 'em differently. You may see a very odd solution of 'em in *Eustathius*, Note on v. 7 of the eleventh Iliad.

What seems the most probable, is that of *Fromondus* in his *Meteorology*, who observ'd, that a shower of this kind, which gave great cause of wonder, was nothing but a quantity of very small red insects, beat down to the earth by a heavy shower, whereby the ground was spotted in several places, as with drops of blood.

572. – Achilles' *mortal steed,*
       The gen'rous Pedasus –.]

For the other two horses of *Achilles*, *Xanthus* and *Balius*, were immortal, as we have already seen in this book. 'Tis a merry conceit of *Eustathius*, that *Pedasus* is only said to be mortal, because of the three horses he only was a gelding. 'Tis pity poor *Pedasus* had not a better fate, to have recompensed the loss of his immortality.

605. Glaucus, *be bold*, &c.] This dying speech of *Sarpedon* deserves particular notice, being made up of noble sentiments, and fully answering the character of this brave and generous Prince, which he preserves in his last moments. Being sensible of approaching death, without any transports of rage, or desire of revenge, he calls to his friend to take care to preserve his body and arms from becoming a prey to the enemy: And this he says without any regard to himself, but out of the most tender concern for his friend's reputation, who must for ever become infamous if he fails in this point of honour and duty. If we conceive this said by the expiring hero, his dying looks fix'd on his wounded disconsolate friend, the spear remaining in his body, and the victor standing by in a kind of extasy surveying his conquest; these circumstances will form a very moving picture. *Patroclus* all this time, either out of humanity or surprize, omits to pull out the spear, which however he does not long forbear, but with it drawing forth his vitals, puts a period to this gallant life.

637. – *pierc'd with pain*
       That thrils my arm, and shoots thro' ev'ry vein.]

There seems to be an oversight in this place. *Glaucus* in the twelfth book had been wounded with an arrow by *Teucer* at the attack of the wall; and here so long after, we find him still on the field, *in the sharpest anguish of his wound, the blood not being yet stanch'd,* &c. In the speech that next follows to *Hector*, there is also something liable to censure, when he imputes to the negligence of the *Trojans* the death of

Sarpedon, of which they knew nothing till that very speech inform'd 'em. I beg leave to pass over these things without exposing or defending them, tho' such as these may be sufficient grounds for a most inveterate war among the criticks.

696. *Great* Jove – *O'er the fierce armies pours pernicious night.*] *Homer* calls here by the name of night, the whirlwinds of thick dust which rise from beneath the feet of the combatants, and which hinders them from knowing one another. Thus poetry knows how to convert the most natural things into miracles; these two armies are buried in dust round *Sarpedon*'s body; 'tis *Jupiter* who pours upon them an obscure night, to make the battel bloodier, and to honour the funeral of his son by a greater number of victims.   *Eustathius.*

746. *And skill'd in dancing.*] This stroke of raillery upon *Meriones* is founded on the custom of his country. For the *Cretans* were peculiarly addicted to this exercise, and in particular are said to have invented the *Pyrrhic* dance, which was perform'd in complete armour. See Note on v. 797. the thirteenth book.

831. *Then Sleep and Death*, &c.] It is the Notion of *Eustathius*, that by this interment of *Sarpedon*, where *Sleep* and *Death* are concerned, *Homer* seems to intimate, that there was nothing else but an empty monument of that hero in *Lycia*, for he delivers him not to any real or solid persons, but to certain unsubstantial phantoms to conduct his body thither. He was forced (continues my author) to make use of these machines, since there were no other deities he could with any likelihood employ about this work; for the ancients (as appears from *Euripides*, *Hippolyto*) had a superstition that all dead bodies were offensive to the Gods, they being of a nature celestial and uncorruptible. But this last remark is impertinent, since we see in this very place *Apollo* is employ'd in adorning and embalming the body of *Sarpedon.*

What I think better accounts for the passage, is what *Philostratus in Heroicis* affirms, that this alludes to a piece of antiquity. 'The *Lycians* shew'd the body of *Sarpedon*, strew'd over with aromatical spices, in such a graceful composure, that he seem'd to be only asleep: And it was this that gave rise to the fiction of *Homer*, that his rites were perform'd by *Sleep* and *Death*.'

But after all these refin'd observations, it is probable the Poet intended only to represent the death of this favourite Son of *Jupiter*, and one of his most amiable characters, in a gentle and agreeable view, without any circumstances of dread or horrour; intimating by this fiction, that he was delivered out of all the tumults and miseries of life by two imaginary deities, *Sleep* and *Death*, who alone can give mankind ease and exemption from their misfortunes.

847. *Who, first, brave hero!* &c.] The Poet in a very moving and solemn way turns his discourse to *Patroclus.* He does not accost his muse, as it is usual with him to do, but enquires of the hero himself who was the first, and who the last, who fell by his hand? This address distinguishes and signalizes *Patroclus*, (to whom *Homer* uses it more frequently, than I remember on any other occasion) as if he was some genius or divine being, and at the same time it is very pathetical and apt to move our compassion. The same kind of apostrophe is used by *Virgil* to *Camilla.*

> *Quem telo primum, quem postremum, aspera virgo!*
> *Dejicis? Aut quot humi morientia corpora fundis?*

> [Who foremost, and who last, heroick maid,
> On the cold earth were by thy courage laid?
> Thy spear, of mountain ash, *Eumenius* first,
> With fury driv'n, from side to side transpierc'd.]

904. *What skilful divers,* &c.] The original is literally thus: *'Tis pity he is not nearer the sea, he would furnish good quantities of excellent oisters, and the storms would not frighten him; see how he exercises and plunges from the top of his chariot into the plain! Who would think that there were such good divers at* Troy? This seems to be a little too long; and if this passage be really *Homer*'s, I could almost swear that he intended to let us know, that a good soldier may be an indifferent jester. But I very much doubt whether this passage be his: It is very likely these five last verses were added by some of the ancient criticks, whose caprices *Homer* has frequently undergone; or perhaps some of the rhapsodists, who in reciting his verses, made additions of their own to please their auditors. And what persuades me of its being so, is, that 'tis by no means probable that *Patroclus*, who had lately blamed *Meriones* for his little raillery against *Æneas*, and told him, 'that 'twas not by raillery or invective that they were to repel the *Trojans*, but by dint of blows; that council required words, but war deeds:' It is by no means probable, I say, that the same *Patroclus* should forget that

excellent precept, and amuse himself with raillery, especially in the sight of *Hector.* I am therefore of opinion that *Patroclus* said no more than this verse, Ω πόποι, &c. *Good Gods! what an active* Trojan *it is, and how cleverly he dives,* and that the five following are strangers, tho' very ancient.

Dacier.

I must just take notice, that however mean or ill placed these railleries may appear, there have not been wanting such fond lovers of *Homer* as have admired and imitated them. *Milton* himself is of this number, as may be seen from those very low jests, which he has put into the mouth of *Satan* and his angels in the sixth book. What *Æneas* says to *Meriones* upon his dancing is nothing so trivial as those lines, where after the displosion of their diabolical enginry, angel rowling on archangel, they are thus derided.

> – *When we propounded terms*
> *Of composition, strait they chang'd their minds,*
> *Flew off, and into strange vagaries fell,*
> *As they would dance; yet for a dance they seem'd*
> *Somewhat extravagant and wild, perhaps*
> *For joy of offer'd peace –* &c.
>   – *Terms that amus'd 'em all,*
> *And stumbled many; who receives them right*
> *Had need from head to foot well understand:*
> *Not understood, this gift they have besides,*
> *They show us when our foes walk not upright.*

952. Apollo *dreadful,* &c.] If *Homer* is resolv'd to do any thing extraordinary, or arbitrary, which his readers may not very well relish, he takes care however to prepare them by degrees for receiving such innovations. He had before given us a sketch of this trick of the Gods in the 13*th* book, where *Neptune* serves *Alcathous* much in the same manner. *Apollo* here carries it a little farther; and both these are specimens of what we are to expect from *Minerva* at the death of *Hector* in *Il.* 22.

1003. *Lie there,* Patroclus! &c.] There is much spirit in this sarcasm of *Hector* upon *Patroclus:* Nor is *Achilles* exempt from the severity of the reflection, who (as he imagines) had persuaded his dearest friend to attempt exploits that were impracticable. He touches him also, for staying at home in security himself, and encouraging *Patroclus* to

undertake this perilous adventure, and to seek after spoils which he
was never like to enjoy.   *Eustathius.*

1026. *– Hear my latest breath,*
        The Gods inspire it. –]

It is an opinion of great antiquity, that when the soul is on the point of
being delivered from the body, and makes a nearer approach to the
divine nature, at such a time its views are stronger and clearer, and the
mind endow'd with a spirit of true prediction. So *Artemon* of *Miletum*
says in his book of dreams, that when the soul hath collected all its
powers from every limb and part of the body, and is just ready to
be severed from it, at that time it becomes prophetical. *Socrates* also
in his defence to the *Athenians*, 'I am now arrived at the verge of
life, wherein it is familiar with people to foretell what will come to
pass.'   *Eustathius.*

This opinion seems alluded to in those admirable lines of *Waller*:

> *Leaving the old, both worlds at once they view,*
> *Who stand upon the threshold of the new.*

1032. *The death of* Patroclus.] I sometimes think I am in respect to
Homer much like *Sancho Panca* with regard to *Don Quixote.* I believe
upon the whole that no mortal ever came near him for wisdom,
learning, and all good qualities. But sometimes there are certain starts
which I cannot tell what to make of, and am forced to own that my
master is a little out of the way, if not quite beside himself. The
present passage of the death of *Patroclus*, attended with so many odd
circumstances to overthrow this hero (who might, for all I can see, as
decently have fallen by the force of *Hector*) are what I am at a loss to
excuse, and must indeed (in my own opinion) give them up to the
criticks. I really think almost all those parts in *Homer* which have been
objected against with most clamour and fury, are honestly defensible,
and none of them (to confess my private sentiment) seem to me to be
faults of any consideration, except this conduct in the death of *Patro-
clus*; the length of *Nestor*'s discourse in *Lib.* 11. the speech of *Achilles*'s
horse in the 19*th.* the conversation of that hero with *Æneas* in *Lib.* 20.
and the manner of *Hector*'s flight round the walls of *Troy* in *Lib.* 22. I
hope, after so free a confession, no reasonable modern will think me
touch'd with the Ὁμηρομανία of Madam *Dacier* and others. I am
sensible of the extremes which mankind run into, in extolling and

depreciating authors: We are not more violent and unreasonable in attacking those who are not yet establish'd in fame, than in defending those who are, even in every minute trifle. Fame is a debt, which when we have kept from people as long as we can, we pay with a prodigious interest, which amounts to twice the value of the principal. Thus 'tis with ancient works as with ancient coins, they pass for a vast deal more than they were worth at first; and the very obscurities and deformities which time has thrown upon them, are the sacred rust, which enhances their value with all true lovers of antiquity.

But as I have own'd what seem my author's faults, and subscribed to the opinion of *Horace*, that *Homer* sometimes nods; I think I ought to add that of *Longinus* as to such negligences. I can no way so well conclude the notes to this book as with the translation of it.

'It may not be improper to discuss the question in general, which of the two is the more estimable, a faulty sublime, or a faultless mediocrity? And consequently, if of two works, one has the greater number of beauties, and the other attains directly to the sublime, which of these shall in equity carry the prize? I am really persuaded that the true sublime is incapable of that purity which we find in compositions of a lower strain, and in effect that too much accuracy sinks the spirit of an author; whereas the case is generally the same with the favourites of nature, and those of fortune, who with the best oeconomy cannot, in the great abundance they are blest with, attend to the minuter articles of their expence. Writers of a cool imagination are cautious in their management, and venture nothing, merely to gain the character of being correct; but the sublime is bold and enterprizing, notwithstanding that on every advance the danger encreaseth. Here probably some will say that men take a malicious satisfaction in exposing the blemishes of an author; that his errors are never forgot, while the most exquisite beauties leave but very imperfect traces on the memory. To obviate this objection, I will solemnly declare, that in my criticisms on *Homer* and other authors, who are universally allowed to be authentic standards of the sublime, tho' I have censur'd their failings with as much freedom as any one, yet I have not presum'd to accuse them of voluntary faults, but have gently remark'd some little defects and negligences, which the mind being intent on nobler ideas did not condescend to regard. And on these principles I will venture to lay it down for a maxim, that the sublime (purely on account of its grandeur) is preferable to all other kinds of style, however it may fall into some inequalities. The Argonauticks of *Apollonius* are faultless in their kind;

and *Theocritus* hath shewn the happiest vein imaginable for pastorals, excepting those in which he has deviated from the country: And yet if it were put to your choice, would you have your name descend to posterity with the reputation of either of those poets, rather than with that of *Homer?* Nothing can be more correct than the *Erigone* of *Eratosthenes*: but is he therefore a greater poet than *Archilochus*, in whose composures perspicuity and order are often wanting; the divine fury of his genius being too impatient for restraint, and superior to law? Again, do you prefer the odes of *Bacchilides* to *Pindar*'s, or the scenes of *Ion* of *Chios* to those of *Sophocles?* Their writings are allow'd to be correct, polite, and delicate; whereas, on the other hand, *Pindar* and *Sophocles* sometimes hurry on with the greatest impetuosity, and like a devouring flame seize and set on fire whatever comes in their way; but on a sudden the conflagration is extinguish'd, and they miserably flag when no body expects it. Yet none have so little discernment as not to prefer the single *Oedipus* of *Sophocles* to all the tragedies that *Ion* ever brought on the stage.

'In our decisions therefore on the Characters of these great men, who have illustrated what is useful and necessary with all the graces and elevation of style; we must impartially confess that, with all their errors, they have more perfections than the nature of man can almost be conceiv'd capable of attaining: For 'tis merely human to excel in other kinds of writing, but the sublime ennobleth our nature, and makes near approaches to divinity: He who commits no faults, is barely read without censure; but a genius truly great excites admiration. In short, the magnificence of a single period in one of these admirable authors is sufficient to attone for all their defects: Nay farther, if any one should collect from *Homer*, *Demosthenes*, *Plato*, and other celebrated heroes of antiquity, the little errors that have escap'd them; they would not bear the least proportion to the infinite beauties to be met with in every page of their writings. 'Tis on this account that envy, thro' so many ages, hath never been able to wrest from them the prize of eloquence which their merits have so justly acquir'd: An Acquisition which they still are, and will, in all probability continue possess'd of,

> '*As long as streams in silver mazes rove,*
> *Or spring with annual green renews the grove.*'
>
> Mr FENTON.

THE
ILIAD
OF
HOMER

VOLUME V

THE
SEVENTEENTH BOOK
OF THE
ILIAD

The ARGUMENT

The seventh Battel, for the Body of *Patroclus*: The Acts of *Menelaus*

Menelaus, *upon the death of* Patroclus, *defends his body from the enemy:* Euphorbus *who attempts it, is slain.* Hector *advancing,* Menelaus *retires, but soon returns with* Ajax, *and drives him off. This* Glaucus *objects to* Hector *as a flight, who thereupon puts on the armour he had won from* Patroclus, *and renews the battel. The* Greeks *give way, till* Ajax *rallies them:* Æneas *sustains the* Trojans. Æneas *and* Hector *attempt the chariot of* Achilles, *which is borne off by* Automedon. *The horses of* Achilles *deplore the loss of* Patroclus: *Jupiter covers his body with a thick darkness: The noble prayer of* Ajax *on that occasion.* Menelaus *sends* Antilochus *to* Achilles, *with the news of* Patroclus's *death: Then returns to the fight, where, tho' attack'd with the utmost fury, he, and* Meriones *assisted by the* Ajaxes, *bear off the body to the ships.*

The time is the evening of the eight and twentieth day. The scene lies in the fields before Troy.

On the cold earth divine *Patroclus* spread,
Lies pierc'd with wounds among the vulgar dead.
Great *Menelaüs*, touch'd with gen'rous woe,
Springs to the front, and guards him from the foe:
5   Thus round her new fal'n young, the heifer moves,
Fruit of her throes, and first-born of her loves,
And anxious, (helpless as he lies, and bare)
Turns, and re-turns her, with a mother's care.
Oppos'd to each, that near the carcase came,
10   His broad shield glimmers, and his lances flame.

    The son of *Panthus*, skill'd the dart to send,
Eyes the dead hero and insults the friend.
This hand, *Atrides*, laid *Patroclus* low;
Warriour! desist, nor tempt an equal blow:
15   To me the spoils my prowess won, resign;
Depart with life, and leave the glory mine.

    The *Trojan* thus: The *Spartan* monarch burn'd
With generous anguish, and in scorn return'd.
Laugh'st thou not, *Jove!* from thy superiour throne,
20   When mortals boast of prowess not their own?
Not thus the lion glories in his might,
Nor panther braves his spotted foe in fight,
Nor thus the boar (those terrours of the plain)
Man only vaunts his force, and vaunts in vain.
25   But far the vainest of the boastful kind
These sons of *Panthus* vent their haughty mind.
Yet 'twas but late, beneath my conqu'ring steel
This boaster's brother, *Hyperenor*, fell,

Against our arm which rashly he defy'd,
Vain was his vigour, and as vain his pride.   30
These eyes beheld him on the dust expire,
No more to chear his spouse, or glad his sire.
Presumptuous youth! like his shall be thy doom,
Go, wait thy brother to the *Stygian* gloom;
Or while thou may'st, avoid the threaten'd fate;   35
Fools stay to feel it, and are wise too late.
　　Unmov'd, *Euphorbus* thus: That action known,
Come, for my brother's blood repay thy own.
His weeping father claims thy destin'd head,
And spouse, a widow in her bridal bed.   40
On these thy conquer'd spoils I shall bestow,
To sooth a consort's and a parent's woe.
No longer then defer the glorious strife,
Let heav'n decide our fortune, fame, and life.
　　Swift as the word, the missile lance he flings,   45
The well-aim'd weapon on the buckler rings,
But blunted by the brass innoxious falls.
On *Jove* the father, great *Atrides* calls,
Nor flies the jav'lin from his arm in vain,
It pierc'd his throat, and bent him to the plain;   50
Wide thro' the neck appears the grizly wound,
Prone sinks the warriour, and his arms resound.
The shining circlets of his golden hair,
Which ev'n the Graces might be proud to wear,
Instarr'd with gems and gold, bestrow the shore,   55
With dust dishonour'd, and deform'd with gore.
　　As the young olive, in some sylvan scene,
Crown'd by fresh fountains with eternal green,
Lifts the gay head, in snowy flow'rets fair,
And plays and dances to the gentle air;   60
When lo! a whirlwind from high heav'n invades
The tender plant, and withers all its shades;
It lies uprooted from its genial bed,
A lovely ruin, now defac'd and dead.
Thus young, thus beautiful, *Euphorbus* lay,   65
While the fierce *Spartan* tore his arms away.
Proud of his deed, and glorious in the prize,
Affrighted *Troy* the tow'ring victor flies,

Flies, as before some mountain lion's ire
70 The village curs, and trembling swains retire;
When o'er the slaughter'd bull they hear him roar,
And see his jaws distil with smoking gore;
All pale with fear, at distance scatter'd round,
They shout incessant, and the vales resound.

75   Meanwhile *Apollo* view'd with envious eyes,
And urg'd great *Hector* to dispute the prize,
(In *Mentes'* shape, beneath whose martial care
The rough *Ciconians* learn'd the trade of war)
Forbear, he cry'd, with fruitless speed to chace
80 *Achilles'* coursers of æthereal race;
They stoop not, these, to mortal man's command,
Or stoop to none but great *Achilles'* hand.
Too long amus'd with a pursuit so vain,
Turn, and behold the brave *Euphorbus* slain!
85 By *Sparta* slain! for ever now supprest
The fire which burn'd in that undaunted breast!

    Thus having spoke, *Apollo* wing'd his flight
And mix'd with mortals in the toils of fight:
His words infix'd unutterable care
90 Deep in great *Hector*'s soul: Thro' all the war
He darts his anxious eye; and instant, view'd
The breathless hero in his blood imbru'd,
(Forth welling from the wound, as prone he lay)
And in the victor's hands the shining prey.

95 Sheath'd in bright arms, thro' cleaving ranks he flies,
And sends his voice in thunder to the skies:
Fierce as a flood of flame by *Vulcan* sent,
It flew, and fir'd the nations as it went.
Atrides from the voice the storm divin'd,
100 And thus explor'd his own unconquer'd mind.

    Then shall I quit *Patroclus* on the plain,
Slain in my cause, and for my honour slain,
Desert the arms, the relicks of my friend?
Or singly, *Hector* and his troops attend?
105 Sure where such partial favour heav'n bestow'd,
To brave the hero were to brave the God:
Forgive me, *Greece*, if once I quit the field;
'Tis not to *Hector*, but to heav'n I yield.

Yet, nor the God, nor heav'n, shou'd give me fear,
Did but the voice of *Ajax* reach my ear: 110
Still would we turn, still battle on the plains,
And give *Achilles* all that yet remains
Of his and our *Patroclus* – This, no more,
The Time allow'd: *Troy* thicken'd on the shore,
A sable scene! The terrors *Hector* led.   115
Slow he recedes, and sighing, quits the dead.
    So from the fold th'unwilling lion parts,
Forc'd by loud clamours, and a storm of darts;
He flies indeed, but threatens as he flies,
With heart indignant and retorted eyes.   120
Now enter'd in the *Spartan* ranks, he turn'd
His manly breast, and with new fury burn'd,
O'er all the black battalions sent his view,
And thro' the cloud the god-like *Ajax* knew;
Where lab'ring on the left the warriour stood,   125
All grim in arms, and cover'd o'er with blood,
There breathing courage, where the God of day
Had sunk each heart with terrour and dismay.
To him the King. Oh *Ajax*, oh my friend!
Haste, and *Patroclus*' lov'd remains defend: 130
The body to *Achilles* to restore,
Demands our care; Alas! we can no more!
For naked now, despoil'd of arms he lies;
And *Hector* glories in the dazling prize.
He said, and touch'd his heart. The raging pair   135
Pierce the thick battel, and provoke the war.
Already had stern *Hector* seiz'd his head,
And doom'd to *Trojan* dogs th'unhappy dead;
But soon as *Ajax* rear'd his tow'rlike shield,
Sprung to his car, and measur'd back the field.   140
His train to *Troy* the radiant armour bear,
To stand a trophy of his fame in war.
    Meanwhile great *Ajax* (his broad shield display'd)
Guards the dead hero with the dreadful shade;
And now before, and now behind he stood: 145
Thus in the center of some gloomy wood,
With many a step the lioness surrounds
Her tawny young, beset by men and hounds;

Elate her heart, and rouzing all her pow'rs,
150 Dark o'er the fiery balls, each hanging eye-brow low'rs.
Fast by his side, the gen'rous *Spartan* glows
With great revenge, and feeds his inward woes.
     But *Glaucus*, leader of the *Lycian* aids,
On *Hector* frowning, thus his flight upbraids.
155 Where now in *Hector* shall we *Hector* find?
A manly form, without a manly mind.
Is this, O Chief! a hero's boasted fame?
How vain, without the merit is the name?
Since battel is renounc'd, thy thoughts employ
160 What other methods may preserve thy *Troy*?
'Tis time to try if *Ilion*'s state can stand
By thee alone, nor ask a foreign hand;
Mean, empty boast! but shall the *Lycians* stake
Their lives for you? those *Lycians* you forsake?
165 What from thy thankless arms can we expect?
Thy friend *Sarpedon* proves thy base neglect:
Say, shall our slaughter'd bodies guard your walls,
While unreveng'd the great *Sarpedon* falls?
Ev'n where he dy'd for *Troy*, you left him there,
170 A feast for dogs, and all the fowls of air.
On my command if any *Lycian* wait,
Hence let him march, and give up *Troy* to fate.
Did such a spirit as the Gods impart
Impel one *Trojan* hand, or *Trojan* heart;
175 (Such, as shou'd burn in ev'ry soul, that draws
The sword for glory, and his country's cause);
Ev'n yet our mutual arms we might employ,
And drag yon' carcass to the walls of *Troy*.
Oh! were *Patroclus* ours, we might obtain
180 *Sarpedon*'s arms and honour'd corse again!
Greece with *Achilles*' friend shou'd be repaid,
And thus due honours purchas'd to his shade.
But words are vain – Let *Ajax* once appear,
And *Hector* trembles and recedes with fear;
185 Thou dar'st not meet the Terrours of his eye;
And lo! already, thou prepar'st to fly.
     The *Trojan* chief with fixt resentment ey'd
The *Lycian* leader, and sedate reply'd.

Say, is it just (my friend) that *Hector*'s ear
From such a warriour such a speech shou'd hear?   190
I deem'd thee once the wisest of thy kind,
But ill this insult suits a prudent mind.
I shun great *Ajax*? I desert my train?
'Tis mine to prove the rash assertion vain;
I joy to mingle where the battel bleeds,   195
And hear the thunder of the sounding steeds.
But *Jove*'s high will is ever uncontroll'd,
The strong he withers, and confounds the bold,
Now crowns with fame the mighty man, and now
Strikes the fresh garland from the victor's brow!   200
Come, thro' yon' squadrons let us hew the way,
And thou be witness, if I fear to day;
If yet a *Greek* the sight of *Hector* dread,
Or yet their hero dare defend the dead.

    Then turning to the martial hosts, he cries,   205
Ye *Trojans*, *Dardans*, *Lycians*, and Allies!
Be men (my friends) in action as in name,
And yet be mindful of your ancient fame.
Hector in proud *Achilles*' arms shall shine,
Torn from his friend, by right of conquest mine.   210

    He strode along the field, as thus he said:
(The sable plumage nodded o'er his head)
Swift thro' the spacious plain he sent a look;
One instant saw, one instant overtook
The distant band, that on the sandy shore   215
The radiant spoils to sacred *Ilion* bore.
There his own mail unbrac'd, the field bestrow'd;
His train to *Troy* convey'd the massy load.
Now blazing in th'immortal arms he stands,
The work and present of celestial hands;   220
By aged *Peleus* to *Achilles* given,
As first to *Peleus* by the court of heav'n:
His father's arms not long *Achilles* wears,
Forbid by fate to reach his father's years.

    Him, proud in triumph, glitt'ring from afar,   225
The God whose thunder rends the troubled air,
Beheld with pity; as apart he sate,
And conscious, look'd thro' all the scene of fate.

He shook the sacred honours of his head;
230   *Olympus* trembled, and the Godhead said:
        Ah wretched man! unmindful of thy end!
A moment's glory! and what fates attend?
In heav'nly panoply divinely bright
Thou stand'st, and armies tremble at thy sight
235   As at *Achilles* self! Beneath thy dart
Lies slain the great *Achilles*' dearer part:
Thou from the mighty dead those arms hast torn
Which once the greatest of mankind had worn.
Yet live! I give thee one illustrious day,
240   A blaze of glory e'er thou fad'st away.
For ah! no more *Andromache* shall come,
With joyful tears to welcome *Hector* home;
No more officious, with endearing charms,
From thy tir'd limbs unbrace *Pelides*' arms!
245   Then with his sable brow he gave the nod,
That seals his word; the sanction of the God.
The stubborn arms (by *Jove*'s command dispos'd)
Conform'd spontaneous, and around him clos'd;
Fill'd with the God, enlarg'd his members grew,
250   Thro' all his veins a sudden vigour flew,
The blood in brisker tides began to roll,
And *Mars* himself came rushing on his soul.
Exhorting loud thro' all the field he strode,
And look'd, and mov'd, *Achilles*, or a God.
255   Now *Mesthles*, *Glaucus*, *Medon* he inspires,
Now *Phorcys*, *Chromius*, and *Hippothous* fires;
The great *Thersilochus* like fury found,
Asteropæus kindled at the sound,
And *Ennomus*, in augury renown'd.
260   Hear all ye hosts, and hear, unnumber'd bands
Of neighb'ring nations, or of distant lands!
'Twas not for state we summon'd you so far,
To boast our numbers, and the pomp of war;
Ye came to fight; a valiant foe to chase,
265   To save our present, and our future race.
For this, our wealth, our products you enjoy,
And glean the relicks of exhausted *Troy*.

Now then to conquer or to die prepare,
To die, or conquer, are the terms of war.
Whatever hand shall win *Patroclus* slain,   270
Whoe'er shall drag him to the *Trojan* train,
With *Hector*'s self shall equal honours claim;
With *Hector* part the spoil, and share the fame.

 Fir'd by his words, the troops dismiss their fears,
They join, they thicken, they protend their spears;   275
Full on the *Greeks* they drive in firm array,
And each from *Ajax* hopes the glorious prey:
Vain hope! what numbers shall the field o'erspread,
What victims perish round the mighty dead?

 Great *Ajax* mark'd the growing storm from far,   280
And thus bespoke his brother of the war.
Our fatal day, alas! is come (my friend)
And all our wars and glories at an end!
'Tis not this corpse alone we guard in vain,
Condemn'd to vulturs on the *Trojan* plain;   285
We too must yield: The same sad fate must fall
On thee, on me, perhaps (my friend) on all.
See what a tempest direful *Hector* spreads,
And lo! it bursts, it thunders on our heads!
Call on our *Greeks*, if any hear the call,   290
The bravest *Greeks*: This hour demands them all.

 The warriour rais'd his voice, and wide around
The field re-echo'd the distressful sound.
Oh chiefs! oh princes! to whose hand is giv'n
The rule of men; whose glory is from heav'n!   295
Whom with due honours both *Atrides* grace:
Ye guides and guardians of our *Argive* race!
All, whom this well-known voice shall reach from far,
All, whom I see not thro' this cloud of war,
Come all! let gen'rous rage your arms employ,   300
And save *Patroclus* from the dogs of *Troy*.

 Oïlean Ajax first the voice obey'd,
Swift was his pace, and ready was his aid;
Next him *Idomeneus*, more slow with age,
And *Merion*, burning with a hero's rage.   305
The long-succeeding numbers who can name?
But all were *Greeks* and eager all for fame.

Fierce to the charge great *Hector* led the throng;
Whole *Troy* embodied, rush'd with shouts along.
310 Thus, when a mountain billow foams and raves,
Where some swoln river disembogues his waves,
Full in the mouth is stopp'd the rushing tide,
The boiling ocean works from side to side,
The river trembles to his utmost shore,
315 And distant rocks rebellow to the roar.
   Nor less resolv'd, the firm *Achaian* band
With brazen shields in horrid circle stand:
Jove, pouring darkness o'er the mingled fight,
Conceals the warriours' shining helms in night:
320 To him, the chief for whom the hosts contend,
Had liv'd not hateful, for he liv'd a friend:
Dead, he protects him with superior care,
Nor dooms his carcase to the birds of air.
   The first attack the *Grecians* scarce sustain,
325 Repuls'd, they yield; the *Trojans* seize the slain:
Then fierce they rally, to revenge led on
By the swift rage of *Ajax Telamon.*
(*Ajax*, to *Peleus'* son the second name,
In graceful stature next, and next in fame.)
330 With headlong force the foremost ranks he tore;
So thro' the thicket bursts the mountain boar,
And rudely scatters, far to distance round,
The frighted hunter and the baying hound.
   The son of *Lethus*, brave *Pelasgus'* heir,
335 *Hippothous*, dragg'd the carcase thro' the war;
The sinewy ancles bor'd, the feet he bound
With thongs, inserted thro' the double wound:
Inevitable fate o'ertakes the deed;
Doom'd by great *Ajax'* vengeful lance to bleed;
340 It cleft the helmet's brazen cheeks in twain;
The shatter'd crest, and horse-hair, strow the plain:
With nerves relax'd he tumbles to the ground:
The brain comes gushing thro' the ghastly wound;
He drops *Patroclus'* foot, and o'er him spread
345 Now lies, a sad companion of the dead:
Far from *Larissa* lies, his native air,
And ill requites his parent's tender care.

Lamented youth! in life's first bloom he fell,
Sent by great *Ajax* to the shades of hell.

 Once more at *Ajax*, *Hector*'s jav'lin flies;   350
The *Grecian* marking as it cut the Skies,
Shunn'd the descending death; which hissing on,
Stretch'd in the dust the great *Iphytus*' son,
Schedius the brave, of all the *Phocian* Kind
The boldest warriour, and the noblest mind: 355
In little *Panope* for strength renown'd,
He held his seat, and rul'd the realms around.
Plung'd in his throat, the weapon drank his blood,
And deep transpiercing, thro' the shoulder stood;
In clanging arms the hero fell, and all   360
The fields resounded with his weighty fall.

 Phorcys, as slain *Hippothous* he defends,
The *Telamonian* lance his belly rends;
The hollow armour burst before the stroke,
And thro' the wound the rushing entrails broke.   365
In strong convulsions panting on the sands
He lies, and grasps the dust with dying hands.

 Struck at the sight, recede the *Trojan* train:
The shouting *Argives* strip the heroes slain.
And now had *Troy*, by *Greece* compell'd to yield,   370
Fled to her ramparts, and resign'd the field;
Greece, in her native fortitude elate,
With *Jove* averse, had turn'd the scale of fate:
But *Phœbus* urg'd *Æneas* to the fight;
He seem'd like aged *Periphas* to sight.   375
(A herald in *Anchises*' love grown old,
Rever'd for prudence, and with prudence, bold.)

 Thus he – what methods yet, oh chief! remain,
To save your *Troy*, tho' heav'n its fall ordain?
There have been heroes, who by virtuous care,   380
By valour, numbers, and by arts of war,
Have forc'd the pow'rs to spare a sinking state,
And gain'd at length the glorious odds of fate.
But you, when fortune smiles, when *Jove* declares
His partial favour, and assists your wars,   385
Your shameful efforts 'gainst your selves employ,
And force th'unwilling God to ruin *Troy*.

Æneas thro the form assum'd descries
The pow'r conceal'd, and thus to *Hector* cries.
390   Oh lasting shame! to our own fears a prey,
We seek our ramparts, and desert the day.
A God (nor is he less) my bosom warms,
And tells me, *Jove* asserts the *Trojan* arms.
        He spoke, and foremost to the combate flew:
395   The bold example all his hosts pursue.
Then first, *Leocritus* beneath him bled,
In vain belov'd by valiant *Lycomede*;
Who view'd his fall, and grieving at the chance,
Swift to revenge it, sent his angry lance;
400   The whirling lance with vig'rous force addrest,
Descends, and pants in *Apisaon*'s breast:
From rich *Pæonias*' vales the warriour came,
Next thee, *Asteropeus!* in place and fame.
Asteropeus with grief beheld the slain,
405   And rush'd to combate, but he rush'd in vain:
Indissolubly firm, around the dead,
Rank within rank, on buckler buckler spread,
And hemm'd with bristled spears, the *Grecians* stood;
A brazen bulwark, and an iron wood.
410   Great *Ajax* eyes them with incessant care,
And in an orb, contracts the crowded war,
Close in their ranks commands to fight or fall,
And stands the center and the soul of all:
Fixt on the spot they war; and wounded, wound;
415   A sanguine torrent steeps the reeking ground;
On heaps the *Greeks*, on heaps the *Trojans* bled,
And thick'ning round 'em, rise the hills of dead.
        Greece, in close order and collected might,
Yet suffers least, and sways the wav'ring fight;
420   Fierce as conflicting fires, the combate burns,
And now it rises, now it sinks by turns.
In one thick darkness all the fight was lost;
The sun, the moon, and all th'etherial host
Seem'd as extinct: day ravish'd from their eyes,
425   And all heav'n's splendors blotted from the skies.
Such o'er *Patroclus* body hung the night,
The rest in sunshine fought, and open light:

Unclouded there, th' aerial azure spread,
No vapour rested on the mountain's head,
The golden sun pour'd forth a stronger ray,   430
And all the broad expansion flam'd with day.
Dispers'd around the plain, by fits they fight,
And here, and there, their scatter'd arrows light:
But death and darkness o'er the carcase spread,
There burn'd the war, and there the mighty bled.   435

    Meanwhile the sons of *Nestor*, in the rear,
(Their fellows routed) toss the distant spear,
And skirmish wide: So *Nestor* gave command,
When from the ships he sent the *Pylian* band.
The youthful brothers thus for fame contend,   440
Nor knew the fortune of *Achilles'* friend;
In thought they view'd him still, with martial joy,
Glorious in arms, and dealing deaths to *Troy*.

    But round the corse, the heroes pant for breath,
And thick and heavy grows the work of death: 445
O'erlabour'd now, with dust, and sweat and gore,
Their knees, their legs, their feet are cover'd o'er;
Drops follow drops, the clouds on clouds arise,
And carnage clogs their hands, and darkness fills their
      eyes.
As when a slaughter'd bull's yet reeking Hide,   450
Strain'd with full force, and tugg'd from side to side,
The brawny curriers stretch; and labour o'er
Th'extended surface, drunk with fat and gore;
So tugging round the corps both armies stood;
The mangled body bath'd in sweat and blood: 455
While *Greeks* and *Ilians* equal strength employ,
Now to the ships to force it, now to *Troy*.
Not *Pallas'* self, her breast when fury warms,
Nor he, whose anger sets the world in arms,
Could blame this scene; such rage, such horror reign'd; 460
Such, *Jove* to honour the great dead ordain'd.

    Achilles in his ships at distance lay,
Nor knew the fatal fortune of the day;
He, yet unconscious of *Patroclus'* fall,
In dust extended under *Ilion's* wall,   465

Expects him glorious from the conquer'd plain,
And for his wish'd return prepares in vain;
Tho' well he knew, to make proud *Ilion* bend,
Was more than heav'n had destin'd to his friend,
470 Perhaps to him: This *Thetis* had reveal'd;
The rest, in pity to her son, conceal'd.

Still rag'd the conflict round the hero dead,
And heaps on heaps by mutual wounds they bled.
Curs'd be the man (ev'n private *Greeks* would say)
475 Who dares desert this well-disputed day!
First may the cleaving earth before our eyes
Gape wide, and drink our blood for sacrifice!
First perish all, e'er haughty *Troy* shall boast
We lost *Patroclus*, and our glory lost.

480 Thus they. While with one voice the *Trojans* said,
Grant this day, *Jove!* or heap us on the dead!
Then clash their sounding arms; the clangors rise,
And shake the brazen concave of the skies.

Meantime, at distance from the scene of blood,
485 The pensive steeds of great *Achilles* stood;
Their godlike master slain before their eyes,
They wept, and shar'd in human miseries.
In vain *Automedon* now shakes the rein,
Now plies the lash, and sooths and threats in vain;
490 Nor to the fight, nor *Hellespont* they go;
Restive they stood, and obstinate in woe:
Still as a tomb-stone, never to be mov'd,
On some good man, or woman unreprov'd
Lays its eternal weight; or fix'd as stands
495 A marble courser by the sculptor's hands,
Plac'd on the hero's grave. Along their face,
The big round drops cours'd down with silent pace,
Conglobing on the dust. Their manes, that late
Circled their arching necks, and wav'd in state,
500 Trail'd on the dust beneath the yoke were spread,
And prone to earth was hung their languid head:
Nor *Jove* disdain'd to cast a pitying look,
While thus relenting to the steeds he spoke.

Unhappy coursers of immortal strain!
505 Exempt from age, and deathless now in vain;

Did we your race on mortal man bestow,
Only alas! to share in mortal woe?
For ah! what is there, of inferiour birth,
That breathes or creeps upon the dust of earth;
What wretched creature of what wretched kind,   510
Than man more weak, calamitous, and blind?
A miserable race! But cease to mourn.
For not by you shall *Priam*'s son be born
High on the splendid car: one glorious prize
He rashly boasts; the rest our will denies.   515
Ourself will swiftness to your nerves impart,
Ourself with rising spirits swell your heart.
Automedon your rapid flight shall bear
Safe to the navy thro' the storm of war.
For yet 'tis giv'n to *Troy*, to ravage o'er   520
The field, and spread her slaughters to the shore;
The sun shall see her conquer, till his fall
With sacred darkness shades the face of all.

   He said; and breathing in th'immortal horse
Excessive spirit, urg'd 'em to the course;   525
From their high manes they shake the dust, and bear
The kindling chariot thro' the parted war:
So flies a vulture thro' the clam'rous train
Of geese, that scream, and scatter round the plain.
From danger now with swiftest speed they flew,   530
And now to conquest with like speed pursue;
Sole in the seat the charioteer remains,
Now plies the jav'lin, now directs the reins:
Him brave *Alcimedon* beheld distrest,
Approach'd the chariot, and the chief addrest.   535

   What God provokes thee, rashly thus to dare,
Alone, unaided, in the thickest war?
Alas! thy friend is slain, and *Hector* wields
Achilles' arms triumphant in the fields.

   In happy time (the charioteer replies)   540
The bold *Alcimedon* now greets my eyes;
No *Greek* like him, the heav'nly steeds restrains,
Or holds their fury in suspended reins:
Patroclus, while he liv'd, their rage cou'd tame,
But now *Patroclus* is an empty name!   545

To thee I yield the seat, to thee resign
The ruling charge: the task of fight be mine.
    He said. *Alcimedon*, with active heat,
Snatches the reins, and vaults into the seat.
550 His friend descends. The chief of *Troy* descry'd,
And call'd *Æneas* fighting near his side.
Lo, to my sight beyond our hope restor'd,
Achilles' car, deserted of its Lord!
The glorious steeds our ready arms invite,
555 Scarce their weak drivers guide them thro' the fight:
Can such opponents stand, when we assail?
Unite thy force, my friend, and we prevail.
    The son of *Venus* to the counsel yields;
Then o'er their backs they spread their solid shields;
560 With brass refulgent the broad surface shin'd,
And thick bull-hides the spacious concave lin'd.
Them *Chromius* follows, *Aretus* succeeds,
Each hopes the conquest of the lofty steeds:
In vain, brave youths, with glorious hopes ye burn,
565 In vain advance! not fated to return.
    Unmov'd, *Automedon* attends the fight,
Implores th'Eternal, and collects his might.
Then turning to his friend, with dauntless mind:
Oh keep the foaming coursers close behind!
570 Full on my shoulders let their nostrils blow,
For hard the fight, determin'd is the foe;
'Tis *Hector* comes; and when he seeks the prize,
War knows no mean: he wins it, or he dies.
    Then thro' the field he sends his voice aloud,
575 And calls th'*Ajaces* from the warring croud,
With great *Atrides*. Hither turn (he said)
Turn, where distress demands immediate aid;
The dead, encircled by his friends, forego,
And save the living from a fiercer foe.
580 Unhelp'd we stand, unequal to engage
The force of *Hector*, and *Æneas'* rage:
Yet mighty as they are, my force to prove,
Is only mine: th'event belongs to *Jove*.
    He spoke, and high the sounding jav'lin flung,
585 Which pass'd the shield of *Aretus* the young;

It pierc'd his belt, emboss'd with curious art;
Then in the lower belly stuck the dart.
As when the pond'rous axe descending full,
Cleaves the broad forehead of some brawny bull;
Struck 'twixt the horns, he springs with many a bound,   590
Then tumbling rolls enormous on the ground:
Thus fell the youth; the air his soul receiv'd,
And the spear trembled as his entrails heav'd.
    Now at *Automedon* the *Trojan* foe
Discharg'd his lance; the meditated blow,   595
Stooping, he shun'd; the jav'lin idly fled,
And hiss'd innoxious o'er the hero's head:
Deep rooted in the ground, the forceful spear
In long vibrations spent its fury there.
With clashing falchions now the chiefs had clos'd,   600
But each brave *Ajax* heard, and interpos'd;
Nor longer *Hector* with his *Trojans* stood,
But left their slain companion in his blood:
His arms *Automedon* divests, and cries,
Accept, *Patroclus!* this mean sacrifice.   605
Thus have I sooth'd my griefs, and thus have paid
Poor as it is, some off'ring to thy shade.
    So looks the lion o'er a mangled boar,
All grim with rage, and horrible with gore;
High on the chariot at one bound he sprung,   610
And o'er his seat the bloody trophies hung.
    And now *Minerva*, from the realms of air
Descends impetuous, and renews the war;
For, pleas'd at length the *Grecian* arms to aid,
The Lord of Thunders sent the blue-ey'd Maid.   615
As when high *Jove*, denouncing future woe,
O'er the dark clouds extends his purple bow,
(In sign of tempests from the troubled air,
Or from the rage of man, destructive war).
The drooping cattel dread th'impending skies,   620
And from his half-till'd field the lab'rer flies.
In such a form the Goddess round her drew
A livid cloud, and to the battle flew.
Assuming *Phœnix'* shape, on earth she falls
And in his well-known voice to *Sparta* calls.   625

And lies *Achilles'* friend, belov'd by all,
A prey to dogs beneath the *Trojan* wall?
What shame to *Greece* for future times to tell,
To thee the greatest, in whose cause he fell!
630   O chief, oh father! (*Atreus'* son replies)
O full of days! by long experience wise!
What more desires my soul, than here, unmov'd,
To guard the body of the man I lov'd?
Ah would *Minerva* send me strength to rear
635   This weary'd arm, and ward the storm of war!
But *Hector*, like the rage of fire, we dread,
And *Jove*'s own glories blaze around his head.
    Pleas'd to be first of all the pow'rs addrest,
She breathes new vigour in her hero's breast,
640   And fills with keen revenge, with fell despight,
Desire of blood, and rage, and lust of fight.
So burns the vengeful hornet (soul all o'er)
Repuls'd in vain, and thirsty still of gore;
(Bold son of Air and Heat) on angry wings
645   Untam'd, untir'd, he turns, attacks, and stings.
Fir'd with like ardour fierce *Atrides* flew,
And sent his soul with ev'ry lance he threw.
    There stood a *Trojan* not unknown to fame,
Eëtion's son, and *Podes* was his name;
650   With riches honour'd, and with courage blest,
By *Hector* lov'd, his comrade, and his guest;
Thro' his broad belt the spear a passage found,
And pond'rous as he falls, his arms resound.
Sudden at *Hector*'s side *Apollo* stood,
655   Like *Phænops*, *Asius'* son, appear'd the God;
(*Asius* the great, who held his wealthy reign
In fair *Abydos* by the rolling main.)
    Oh Prince (he cry'd) oh foremost once in fame!
What *Grecian* now shall tremble at thy name?
660   Dost thou at length to *Menelaus* yield?
A chief, once thought no terrour of the field;
Yet singly, now, the long disputed prize
He bears victorious, while our army flies.
By the same arm illustrious *Podes* bled,
665   The friend of *Hector*, unreveng'd, is dead!

This heard, o'er *Hector* spreads a cloud of woe,
Rage lifts his lance, and drives him on the foe.
    But now th'Eternal shook his sable shield,
That shaded *Ide*, and all the subject field
Beneath its ample verge. A rolling cloud   670
Involv'd the mount; the thunder roar'd aloud;
Th'affrighted hills from their foundations nod,
And blaze beneath the lightnings of the God:
At one regard of his all-seeing eye,
The vanquish'd triumph, and the victors fly.   675
    Then trembled *Greece*: The flight *Peneleus* led;
For as the brave *Bœotian* turn'd his head
To face the foe, *Polydamas* drew near,
And raz'd his shoulder with a shorten'd spear:
By *Hector* wounded, *Leitus* quits the plain,   680
Pierc'd thro' the wrist; and raging with the pain
Grasps his once formidable lance in vain.
    As *Hector* follow'd, *Idomen* addrest
The flaming jav'lin to his manly breast;
The brittle point before his corselet yields;   685
Exulting *Troy* with clamour fills the fields:
High on his chariot as the *Cretan* stood,
The Son of *Priam* whirl'd the missive wood;
But erring from its aim, th'impetuous spear
Strook to the dust the squire, and charioteer   690
Of martial *Merion*: *Cœranus* his name,
Who left fair *Lyctus* for the fields of fame.
On foot bold *Merion* fought; and now laid low,
Had grac'd the triumphs of his *Trojan* foe;
But the brave squire the ready coursers brought,   695
And with his life his master's safety bought.
Between his cheek and ear the weapon went,
The teeth it shatter'd, and the tongue it rent.
Prone from the seat he tumbles to the plain;
His dying hand forgets the falling rein: 700
This *Merion* reaches, bending from the car,
And urges to desert the hopeless war;
Idomeneus consents; the lash applies;
And the swift chariot to the navy flies.

705   Nor *Ajax* less the will of heav'n descry'd,
And Conquest shifting to the *Trojan* side,
Turn'd by the hand of *Jove*. Then thus begun,
To *Atreus'* seed, the godlike *Telamon*.
    Alas! who sees not *Jove*'s almighty hand
710 Transfers the glory to the *Trojan* band?
Whether the weak or strong discharge the dart,
He guides each arrow to a *Grecian* heart:
Not so our spears: incessant tho' they rain,
He suffers ev'ry lance to fall in vain.
715 Deserted of the God, yet let us try
What human strength and prudence can supply;
If yet this honour'd corps, in triumph born,
May glad the fleets that hope not our return,
Who tremble yet, scarce rescu'd from their fates,
720 And still hear *Hector* thund'ring at their gates.
Some hero too must be dispatch'd to bear
The mournful message to *Pelides'* ear;
For sure he knows not, distant on the shore,
His friend, his lov'd *Patroclus*, is no more.
725 But such a chief I spy not thro' the host:
The men, the steeds, the armies all are lost
In gen'ral darkness – Lord of Earth and Air!
Oh King! oh Father! hear my humble pray'r:
Dispel this cloud, the light of heav'n restore;
730 Give me to see, and *Ajax* asks no more:
If *Greece* must perish, we thy will obey,
But let us perish in the face of day!
    With tears the hero spoke, and at his pray'r
The God relenting, clear'd the clouded air;
735 Forth burst the sun with all-enlight'ning ray;
The blaze of armour flash'd against the day.
Now, now, *Atrides!* cast around thy sight,
If yet *Antilochus* survives the fight,
Let him to great *Achilles'* ear convey
740 The fatal news – *Atrides* hastes away.
    So turns the lion from the nightly fold,
Tho high in courage, and with hunger bold,
Long gall'd by herdsmen, and long vex'd by hounds,
Stiff with fatigue, and fretted sore with wounds;

The darts fly round him from an hundred hands, 745
And the red terrours of the blazing brands:
Till late, reluctant, at the dawn of day
Sow'r he departs, and quits th'untasted prey.
So mov'd *Atrides* from his dang'rous place
With weary limbs, but with unwilling pace; 750
The foe, he fear'd, might yet *Patroclus* gain,
And much admonish'd, much adjur'd his train.

   Oh guard these relicks to your charge consign'd,
And bear the merits of the dead in mind;
How skill'd he was in each obliging art; 755
The mildest manners, and the gentlest heart:
He was, alas! but fate decreed his end;
In death a hero, as in life a friend!

   So parts the chief; from rank to rank he flew,
And round on all sides sent his piercing view. 760
As the bold bird, endu'd with sharpest eye
Of all that wing the mid aërial sky,
The sacred eagle, from his walks above
Looks down, and sees the distant thicket move;
Then stoops, and sowsing on the quiv'ring hare, 765
Snatches his life amid the clouds of air.
Not with less quickness, his exerted sight
Pass'd this, and that way, thro' the ranks of fight:
Till on the left the chief he sought, he found;
Chearing his men, and spreading deaths around. 770

   To him the King. Belov'd of *Jove!* draw near,
For sadder tydings never touch'd thy ear;
Thy eyes have witness'd what a fatal turn!
How *Ilion* triumphs, and th'*Achaians* mourn.
This is not all: *Patroclus* on the shore, 775
Now pale and dead, shall succour *Greece* no more.
Fly to the fleet, this instant fly, and tell
The sad *Achilles* how his lov'd one fell:
He too may haste the naked corps to gain;
The arms are *Hector*'s, who despoil'd the slain. 780

   The youthful warriour heard with silent woe,
From his fair eyes the tears began to flow;
Big with the mighty grief, he strove to say
What sorrow dictates, but no word found way.

785 To brave *Laodocus* his arms he flung,
     Who near him wheeling, drove his steeds along;
     Then ran, the mournful message to impart,
     With tear-ful eyes, and with dejected heart.
         Swift fled the youth; nor *Menelaus* stands,
790 (Tho' sore distrest) to aid the *Pylian* bands;
     But bids bold *Thrasymede* those troops sustain;
     Himself returns to his *Patroclus* slain.
     Gone is *Antilochus* (the hero said)
     But hope not, warriors! for *Achilles'* aid:
795 Tho' fierce his rage, unbounded be his woe,
     Unarm'd, he fights not with the *Trojan* foe.
     'Tis in our hands alone our hopes remain,
     'Tis our own vigour must the dead regain;
     And save our selves, while with impetuous hate
800 *Troy* pours along, and this way rolls our fate.
         'Tis well (said *Ajax*) be it then thy care
     With *Merion*'s aid, the weighty corse to rear;
     Myself, and my bold brother will sustain
     The shock of *Hector* and his charging train:
805 Nor fear we armies, fighting side by side;
     What *Troy* can dare, we have already try'd,
     Have try'd it, and have stood. The hero said.
     High from the ground the warriours heave the dead;
     A gen'ral clamour rises at the sight:
810 Loud shout the *Trojans*, and renew the fight.
     Not fiercer rush along the gloomy wood,
     With rage insatiate and with thirst of blood,
     Voracious hounds, that many a length before
     Their furious hunters, drive the wounded boar;
815 But if the savage turns his glaring eye,
     They howl aloof, and round the forest fly.
     Thus on retreating *Greece* the *Trojans* pour,
     Wave their thick falchions, and their jav'lins show'r:
     But *Ajax* turning, to their fears they yield,
820 All pale they tremble, and forsake the field.
         While thus aloft the hero's corse they bear,
     Behind them rages all the storm of war;
     Confusion, tumult, Horrour, o'er the throng
     Of men, steeds, chariots, urg'd the rout along:

Less fierce the winds with rising flames conspire,   825
To whelm some city under waves of fire;
Now sink in gloomy clouds the proud abodes;
Now crack the blazing temples of the Gods;
The rumbling torrent thro' the ruin rolls,
And sheets of smoak mount heavy to the poles.   830
The heroes sweat beneath their honour'd load:
As when two mules, along the rugged road,
From the steep mountain with exerted strength
Drag some vast beam, or mast's unwieldy length;
Inly they groan, big drops of sweat distill,   835
Th'enormous timber lumbring down the hill:
So these – Behind, the bulk of *Ajax* stands,
And breaks the torrent of the rushing bands.
Thus when a river swell'd with sudden rains
Spreads his broad waters o'er the level plains,   840
Some interposing hill the stream divides,
And breaks its force, and turns the winding tides.
Still close they follow, close the rear engage;
Æneas storms, and *Hector* foams with rage:
While *Greece* a heavy, thick retreat maintains,   845
Wedg'd in one body like a flight of cranes,
That shriek incessant, while the faulcon hung
High on pois'd pinions, threats their callow young.
So from the *Trojan* chiefs the *Grecians* fly,
Such the wild Terrour, and the mingled cry.   850
Within, without the trench, and all the way,
Strow'd in bright heaps, their arms and armour lay;
Such horrour *Jove* imprest! Yet still proceeds
The work of death, and still the battel bleeds.   854

OBSERVATIONS

ON THE

SEVENTEENTH BOOK

The epigraph on the frontispiece of Volume V (Books 17–21) consists of the following lines:

> – *Sanctos ausus recludere fontes.*   VIRG.

[Having dared to set free the sacred founts.
                    (Virgil, *Georgics* II. 175)]

This is the only book of the Iliad which is a continued description of a battel, without any digression or episode, that serves for an interval to refresh the reader. The heav'nly machines too are fewer than in any other. *Homer* seems to have trusted wholly to the force of his own genius, as sufficient to support him, whatsoever lengths he was carried by it. But that spirit which animates the original, is what I am sensible evaporates so much in my hands; that, tho' I can't think my author tedious, I should have made him seem so, if I had not translated this book with all possible conciseness. I hope there is nothing material omitted, tho' the version consists but of sixty five lines more than the original.

However, one may observe there are more turns of fortune, more defeats, more rallyings, more accidents, in this battel, than in any other; because it was to be the last wherein the *Greeks* and *Trojans* were upon equal terms, before the Return of *Achilles*: And besides, all this serves to introduce the chief hero with the greater pomp and dignity.

3. *Great Menelaus* –] The poet here takes occasion to clear *Menelaus* from the imputations of idle and effeminate, cast on him in some parts

of the Poem; he sets him in the front of the army, exposing himself to dangers in defending the body of *Patroclus*, and gives him the conquest of *Euphorbus* who had the first hand in his Death. He is represented as the foremost who appears in his defence, not only as one of a like disposition of mind with *Patroclus*, a kind and generous friend; but as being more immediately concern'd in honour to protect from injuries the body of a hero that fell in his cause.   *Eustathius.* See Note on v. 271. of the third book.

5. *Thus round her new fal'n young*, &c.] In this comparison, as *Eustathius* has very well observed, the Poet accommodating himself to the occasion, means only to describe the affection *Menelaus* had for *Patroclus*, and the manner in which he presented himself to defend his body: And this comparison is so much the more just and agreeable, as *Menelaus* was a Prince full of goodness and mildness. He must have little sense or knowledge in Poetry, who thinks that it ought to be suppress'd. It is true, we shou'd not use it now-a-days, by reason of the low ideas we have of the animals from which it is derived; but those not being the ideas of *Homer*'s time, they could not hinder him from making a proper use of such a comparison.   *Dacier.*

id. Thus round her new fal'n young, &c.] It seems to me remarkable, that the several comparisons to illustrate the concern for *Patroclus*, are taken from the most tender sentiments of nature. *Achilles* in the beginning of the sixteenth book, considers him as a child, and himself as his mother. The sorrow of *Menelaus* is here described as that of a heifer for her young one. Perhaps these are design'd to intimate the excellent temper and goodness of *Patroclus*, which is expressed in that fine elogy of him in this book, v. 671. Πᾶσιν γὰρ ἐπίστατο μείλιχος εἶναι. *He knew how to be good-natur'd to all men.* This gave all mankind these sentiments for him, and no doubt the same is strongly pointed at by the uncommon concern of the whole army to rescue his body.

The dissimilitude of manners between these two friends, *Achilles* and *Patroclus*, is very observable: Such friendships are not uncommon, and I have often assign'd this reason for them, that it is natural for men to seek the assistance of those qualities in others, which they want themselves. That is still better if apply'd to providence, which associates men of different and contrary qualities, in order to make a more perfect system. But, whatever is customary in nature, *Homer* had a good poetical reason for it; for it affords many incidents to illustrate the manners of them both more strongly; and is what they call a contrast in painting.

11. *The Son of Panthus.*] The conduct of *Homer* is admirable in bringing *Euphorbus* and *Menelaus* together upon this occasion; for hardly any thing but such a signal revenge for the death of his brother, could have made *Euphorbus* stand the encounter. *Menelaus* putting him in mind of the death of his brother, gives occasion (I think) to one of the finest answers in all *Homer*; in which the insolence of *Menelaus* is retorted in a way to draw pity from every reader; and I believe there is hardly one, after such a speech, that would not wish *Euphorbus* had the better of *Menelaus*: A writer of Romances would not have fail'd to have giv'n *Euphorbus* the victory. But however, it was fitter to make *Menelaus*, who had received the greatest injury, do the most revengeful actions.

55. *Instarr'd with gems and gold.*] We have here a *Trojan* who used gold and silver to adorn his hair; which made *Pliny* say, that he doubted whether the women were the first that used those ornaments. *Est quidem apud eundem* [Homerum] *virorum crinibus aurum implexum, ideo nescio an prior usus a fœminis cœperit* [Indeed, according to Homer, men braided their hair with gold; and so I do not know whether this custom originated with the women] lib. 33. chap. 1. He might likewise have strengthened his doubt by the custom of the *Athenians*, who put into their hair little grashoppers of gold.   *Dacier.*

57. *As the young olive*, &c.] This exquisite Simile finely illustrates the beauty and sudden fall of *Euphorbus*, in which the allusion to that circumstance of his comely hair is peculiarly happy. *Porphyry* and *Jamblicus* acquaint us of the particular affection *Pythagoras* had for these verses, which he set to the harp, and used to repeat as his own *Epicedion.* Perhaps it was his fondness of them, which put it into his head to say, that his soul transmigrated to him from this hero. However it was, this conceit of *Pythagoras* is famous in antiquity, and has given occasion to a dialogue in *Lucian* entitled *The Cock*, which is, I think, the finest piece of that author.

65. *Thus young, thus beautiful* Euphorbus *lay.*] This is the only *Trojan* whose death the Poet laments, that he might do the more honour to *Patroclus*, his hero's friend. The comparison here used is very proper,

for the olive always preserves its beauty. But where the Poet speaks of the *Lapithæ*, a hardy and warlike people, he compares them to *Oaks*, that stand unmoved in storms and tempests; and where *Hector* falls by *Ajax*, he likens him to an *Oak* struck down by *Jove*'s thunder. Just after this soft comparison upon the beauty of *Euphorbus*, he passes to another full of strength and terrour, that of the lion.   *Eustathius.*

110. *Did but the voice of* Ajax *reach my ear.*] How observable is *Homer*'s art of illustrating the valour and glory of his heroes? *Menelaus*, who sees *Hector* and all the *Trojans* rushing upon him, would not retire if *Apollo* did not support them; and though *Apollo* does support them, he would oppose even *Apollo*, were *Ajax* but near him. This is glorious for *Menelaus*, and yet more glorious for *Ajax*, and very suitable to his character; for *Ajax* was the bravest of the *Greeks*, next to *Achilles*.   *Dacier. Eustathius.*

117. *So from the fold th'unwilling lion.*] The Beauty of the retreat of *Menelaus* is worthy notice. *Homer* is a great observer of natural imagery, that brings the thing represented before our view. It is indeed true, that lions, tygers, and beasts of prey are the only objects that can properly represent warriours; and therefore 'tis no wonder they are so often introduced: The inanimate things, as floods, fires, and storms, are the best, and only images of battels.

137. *Already had stern* Hector, &c.] *Homer* takes care, so long before hand, to lessen in his reader's mind the horror he may conceive from the cruelty that *Achilles* will exercise upon the body of *Hector*. That cruelty will be only the punishment of this which *Hector* here exercises upon the body of *Patroclus*; he drags him, he designs to cut off his head, and to leave his body upon the ramparts, expos'd to dogs and birds of prey.   *Eustathius.*

169. *You left him there a feast to dogs.*] It was highly dishonourable in *Hector* to forsake the body of a friend and guest, and against the laws of *Jupiter Xenius*, or *hospitalis*. For *Glaucus* knew nothing of *Sarpedon*'s being honoured with burial by the Gods, and sent embalmed into *Lycia*.   *Eustathius.*

193. *I shun great Ajax?*] *Hector* takes no notice of the affronts that *Glaucus* had thrown upon him, as knowing he had in some respects a

just cause to be angry, but he cannot put up what he had said of his fearing *Ajax*, to which part he only replies: This is very agreeable to his heroic character.   *Eustathius.*

209. Hector *in proud* Achilles' *arms shall shine.*] The ancients have observed that *Homer* causes the arms of *Achilles* to fall into *Hector*'s power, to equal in some sort those two heroes, in the battel wherein he is going to engage them. Otherwise it might be urged, that *Achilles* could not have kill'd *Hector* without the advantage of having his armour made by the hand of a God, whereas *Hector*'s was only of the hand of a mortal; but since both were clad in armour made by *Vulcan*, *Achilles*'s victory will be compleat, and in its full lustre. Besides this reason (which is for necessity and probability) there is also another, for ornament; for *Homer* here prepares to introduce that beautiful episode of the divine armour, which *Vulcan* makes for *Achilles.*   *Eustathius.*

216. *The radiant arms to sacred Ilion bore.*] A difficulty may arise here, and the question may be asked why *Hector* sent these arms to *Troy?* Why did not he take them at first? There are three answers, which I think are all plausible. The first, that *Hector* having killed *Patroclus*, and seeing the day very far advanced, had no need to take those arms for a fight almost at an end. The second, that he was impatient to shew to *Priam* and *Andromache* those glorious spoils. Thirdly, he perhaps at first intended to hang them up in some temple. *Glaucus*'s speech makes him change his resolution, he runs after those arms to fight against *Ajax*, and to win *Patroclus*'s body from him.   *Dacier.*

Homer (says *Eustathius*) does not suffer the arms to be carried into *Troy* for these reasons. That *Hector* by wearing them might the more encourage the *Trojans*, and be the more formidable to the *Greeks*: That *Achilles* may recover them again when he kills *Hector*: And that he may conquer him, even when he is strengthened with that divine armour.

231. Jupiter'*s Speech to* Hector.] The Poet prepares us for the death of *Hector*, perhaps to please the *Greek* readers, who might be troubled to see him shining in their hero's arms. Therefore *Jupiter* expresses his sorrow at the approaching fate of this unfortunate Prince, promises to repay his loss of life with glory, and nods to give a certain confirmation to his words. He says, *Achilles* is the bravest *Greek*, as *Glaucus* had just said before; the Poet thus giving him the greatest commendations, by putting his praise in the mouth of a God, and of an enemy, who were neither of them like to be prejudiced in his favour.   *Eustathius.*

How beautiful is that sentiment upon the miserable state of mankind, introduced here so artfully, and so strongly enforced, by being put into the mouth of the supreme being! And how pathetic the denunciation of *Hector*'s death, by that circumstance of *Andromache*'s disappointment, when she shall no more receive her hero glorious from the battel, in the armour of his conquered enemy!

247. *The stubborn arms* &c.] The words are,

> Ἦ, καὶ κυανέῃσιν ἐπ᾽ ὀφρύσι νεῦσε Κρονίων,
> Ἕκτορι δ᾽ ἥρμοσε τεύχε᾽ ἐπὶ χροΐ.

[The son of Kronos spoke, and with his dark brows he
   nodded,
And the armour was fitted on to Hector's body.]

If we give ἥρμοσε a passive signification, it will be, the arms fitted *Hector*; but if an active (as those take it who would put a greater difference between *Hector* and *Achilles*) then it belongs to *Jupiter*; and the sense will be, *Jupiter* made the arms fit for him, which were too large before: I have chosen the last as the more poetical sense.

260. *Unnumber'd bands of neighb'ring nations.*] *Eustathius* has very well explained the artifice of this speech of *Hector*, who indirectly answers all *Glaucus*'s invectives, and humbles his vanity. *Glaucus* had just spoken as if the *Lycians* were the only allies of *Troy*; and *Hector* here speaks of the numerous troops of different nations, which he expressly designs by calling them borderers upon his kingdom, thereby in some manner to exclude the *Lycians*, who were of a country more remote; as if he did not vouchsafe to reckon them. He afterwards confutes what *Glaucus* said, 'that if the *Lycians* would take his advice they would return home'; for he gives them to understand, that being hired troops, they are obliged to perform their bargain, and to fight till the war is at an end.   *Dacier.*

290. *Call on our Greeks.*] *Eustathius* gives three reasons why *Ajax* bids *Menelaus* call the *Greeks* to their assistance; instead of calling them himself. He might be ashamed to do it, lest it should look like fear and turn to his dishonour: Or the chiefs were more likely to obey *Menelaus*:

Or he had too much business of the war upon his hands, and wanted leisure more than the other.

302. *Oïlean Ajax first.*] *Ajax Oïleus* (says *Eustathius*) is the first that comes, being brought by his love to the other *Ajax*, as it is natural for one friend to fly to the assistance of another: To which we may add, he might very probably come first, because he was the swiftest of all the heroes.

318. Jove *pouring Darkness.*] *Homer*, who in all his former descriptions of battels is so fond of mentioning the lustre of the arms, here shades them in darkness, perhaps alluding to the clouds of dust that were raised; or to the throng of combatants; or else to denote the loss of *Greece* in *Patroclus*; or lastly, that as the heav'ns had mourned *Sarpedon* in showers of blood, so they might *Patroclus* in clouds of darkness.

Eustathius.

356. Panope *renown'd.*] *Panope* was a small town twenty *stadia* from *Chæronea*, on the side of mount *Parnassus*, and it is hard to know why *Homer* gives it the epithet of *renown'd*, and makes it the residence of *Schedius*, King of the *Phocians*; when it was but nine hundred paces in circuit, and had no palace, nor gymnasium, nor theatre, nor market, nor fountain; nothing in short that ought to have been in a town which is the residence of a King. *Pausanias* (in *Phocic.*) gives the reason of it; he says, that as *Phocis* was exposed on that side to the inroads of the *Bœotians*, *Schedius* made use of *Panope* as a sort of citadel, or place of arms.

Dacier.

375. *He seem'd like aged* Periphas.] The speech of *Periphas* to *Æneas* hints at the double fate, and the necessity of means. It is much like that of St *Paul*, after he was promised that no body should perish; he says, *except these abide, ye cannot be saved.*

422. *In one thick darkness,* &c.] The darkness spread over the body of *Patroclus* is artful upon several accounts. First, a fine Image of poetry. Next, a token of *Jupiter*'s love to a righteous man: But the chief design is to protract the action; which, if the *Trojans* had seen the spot, must have been decided one way or other, in a very short time. Besides, the *Trojans* having the better in the action, must have seized the body contrary to the intention of the author. There are innumerable instances of these little niceties and particularities of conduct in *Homer*.

436. *Meanwhile the sons of Nestor, in the rear,* &c.] It is not without reason *Homer* in this place makes particular mention of the sons of *Nestor*. It is to prepare us against he sends one of them to *Achilles*, to tell him the death of his friend.

450. *As when a slaughter'd bull's yet reeking hide.*] *Homer* gives us a most lively description of their drawing the body on all sides, and instructs us in the ancient manner of stretching hides, being first made soft and supple with oil. And tho' this comparison be one of those mean and humble ones which some have objected to, yet it has also its admirers for being so expressive, and for representing to the imagination the most strong and exact idea of the subject in hand.

Eustathius.

458. *Not* Pallas *self,* &c.] *Homer* says in the original, '*Minerva* could not have found fault, tho' she were angry.' Upon which *Eustathius* ingeniously observes, how common and natural it is for persons in anger to turn criticks, and find faults where there are none.

468.   *To make proud* Ilion *bend,*
            Was more than heav'n had promis'd to his friend,
            Perhaps to him:]

In these words the Poet artfully hints at *Achilles*'s death; he makes him not absolutely to flatter himself with the hopes of ever taking *Troy*, in his own person, however he does not say this expresly, but passes it over as an ungrateful subject.   *Eustathius.*

471. *The rest, in pity to her son conceal'd.*] Here, (says the same author) we have two rules laid down for common use. One, not to tell our friends all their mischances at once, it being often necessary to hide part of them, as *Thetis* does from *Achilles*: The other, not to push men of courage upon all that is possible for them to do. Thus *Achilles*, tho' he thought *Patroclus* able to drive the *Trojans* back to their gates, yet he does not order him to do so much, but only to save the ships, and beat them back into the field.

Homer's admonishing the reader that *Achilles*'s mother had concealed the circumstance of the death of his friend when she instructed him in his fate; and that all he knew, was only that *Troy* could not be taken at that time; this is a great instance of his care of the probability, and of his having the whole plan of the Poem at once in his head. For upon the supposition that *Achilles* was instructed in his fate, it was a natural objection, how came he to hazard his friend? If he was ignorant on the other hand of the impossibility of *Troy*'s being taken at that time, he might for all he knew, be robbed by his friend (of whose valour he had so good an opinion) of that glory, which he was unwilling to part with.

484. *At distance from the scene of blood.*] If the horses had not gone aside out of the war, *Homer* could not have introduced so well what he design'd to their honour. So he makes them weeping in secret (as their master *Achilles* used to do) and afterwards coming into the battel, where they are taken notice of and pursued by *Hector. Eustathius.*

485. *The pensive steeds of great* Achilles, &c.] It adds a great beauty to the poem when inanimate things act like animate. Thus the Heavens tremble at *Jupiter*'s nod, the sea parts it self to receive *Neptune*, the groves of *Ida* shake beneath *Juno*'s feet, &c. As also to find animate or brute creatures addrest to, as if rational: So *Hector* encourages his horses; and one of *Achilles*'s is endued not only with speech, but with fore-knowledge of future events. Here they weep for *Patroclus*, and stand fix'd and immoveable with grief: Thus is this hero universally mourn'd, and every thing concurs to lament his loss.   *Eustathius.*

As to the particular fiction of the horses weeping, it is countenanc'd both by naturalists and historians. *Aristotle* and *Pliny* write, that these animals often deplore their masters lost in battel, and even shed tears for them. So *Solinus* c. 47. *Ælian* relates the like of elephants, when they are carried from their native country, *De animal.* lib. 10. c. 17. *Suetonius* in the life of *Cæsar*, tells us, that several horses which at the passage of the *Rubicon* had been consecrated to *Mars*, and turn'd loose on the banks, were observed for some days after to abstain from feeding, and to weep abundantly. *Proximis diebus, equorum greges quos in trajiciendo* Rubicone *flumine Marti consecrarat, ac sine custode vagos dimiserat, comperit pabulo pertinacissime abstinere, ubertimque flere.* cap. 81.

Virgil could not forbear copying this beautiful circumstance, in those fine lines on the horse of *Pallas.*

> Post bellator equus, positis insignibus, Æthon,
> It lacrymans, guttisque humectat grandibus ora.

[To close the pomp, *Æthon*, the steed of state,
 Is led, the fun'rals of his lord to wait.
 Stripp'd of his trappings, with a sullen pace
 He walks, and the big tears run rolling down his face.]

494. *Or fix'd, as stands a marble courser,* &c.] *Homer* alludes to the custom in those days of placing columns upon tombs, on which columns there were frequently chariots with two or four horses. This furnish'd *Homer* with this beautiful image, as if these horses meant to remain there, to serve for an immortal monument to *Patroclus.*

Dacier.

I believe M. *Dacier* refines too much in this note. *Homer* says, – ἠὲ γυναικός [or of a lady], and seems to turn the thought only on the firmness of the column, and not on the imagery of it: Which would give it an air a little too modern, like that of *Shakespear, She sate like* Patience *on a monument, smiling at* Grief. – Be it as it will, this conjecture is ingenious; and the whole comparison is as beautiful as just. The horses standing still to mourn for their master, could not be more finely represented than by the dumb sorrow of images standing over a tomb. Perhaps the very posture in which these horses are described, their heads bowed down, and their manes falling in the dust, has an allusion to the attitude in which those statues on monuments were usually represented: There are *Bas-Reliefs* that favour this conjecture.

522. *The sun shall see* Troy *conquer.*] It is worth observing with what art and oeconomy *Homer* conducts his fable, to bring on the catastrophe. *Achilles* must hear of *Patroclus*'s death; *Hector* must fall by his hand: This cannot happen if the armies continue fighting about the body of *Patroclus* under the walls of *Troy.* Therefore, to change the face of affairs, *Jupiter* is going to raise the courage of the *Trojans*, and make them repulse and chase the *Greeks* again as far as their fleet; this obliges *Achilles* to go forth tho' without arms, and thereby every thing comes to an issue.

Dacier.

555. *Scarce their weak Drivers.*] There was but one driver, since *Alcimedon* was alone upon the chariot; and *Automedon* was got down to fight.

But in poetry, as well as in painting, there is often but one moment to be taken hold on. *Hector* sees *Alcimedon* mount the chariot, before *Automedon* was descended from it; and thereupon judging of their intention, and feeling them both as yet upon the chariot, he calls to *Æneas.* He terms them both drivers in mockery, because he saw them take the reins one after the other; as if he said, that chariot had two drivers, but never a fighter. 'Tis one single *moment* that makes this image. In reading the Poets one often falls into great perplexities, for want of rightly distinguishing the point of time in which they speak.   *Dacier.*

The art of *Homer*, in this whole passage concerning *Automedon*, is very remarkable; in finding out the only proper occasion, for so renowned a person as the charioteer of *Achilles* to signalize his valour.

564. *In vain, brave youths, with glorious hopes ye burn,*
            In vain advance! not fated to return.]

These beautiful anticipations are frequent in the Poets, who affect to speak in the character of prophets, and men inspired with the knowledge of futurity. Thus *Virgil* to *Turnus,*

> *Nescia mens hominum fati. – Turno tempus erit,* &c.

> [O mortals! blind is fate, who never know. –
>   The time shall come when *Turnus . . .*]

So *Tasso*, Cant. 12. when *Argante* had vowed the destruction of *Tancred.*

> *O vani giuramenti! Ecco contrari*
> *Seguir tosto gli effetti a l' alta speme:*
> *E cader questi in tenzon pari estinto*
> *Sotto colui, ch' ei fà già preso, e vinto.*

> [O promise vain! it otherwise fell out:
>   Men purpose, but high Gods dispose above;
>   For underneath his sword this boaster died,
>   Whom thus he scorn'd and threaten'd in his pride.]

And *Milton* makes the like apostrophe to *Eve* at her leaving *Adam* before she met the serpent.

> – *She to him engag'd*
> *To be return'd by noon amid the bower,*

> *And all things in best order to invite*
> *Noontide repast, or afternoon's repose.*
> *O much deceiv'd, much failing, hapless* Eve!
> *Thou never from that hour, in paradise,*
> *Found'st either sweet repast, or sound repose.*

642. *So burns the vengeful hornet, &c.*] It is literally in the *Greek, She inspir'd the hero with the boldness of a fly.* There is no impropriety in the comparison, this animal being of all others the most persevering in its attacks, and the most difficult to be beaten off: The occasion also of the comparison being the resolute persistance of *Menelaus* about the dead body, renders it still the more just. But our present idea of the fly is indeed very low, as taken from the littleness and insignificancy of this creature. However, since there is really no meanness in it, there ought to be none in expressing it; and I have done my best in the translation to keep up the dignity of my author.

651. *By* Hector *lov'd, his comrade and his guest.*] *Podes* the favourite and companion of *Hector*, being kill'd on this occasion, seems a parallel circumstance to the death of *Achilles*'s favourite and companion; and was probably put in here on purpose to engage *Hector* on a like occasion with *Achilles.*

721. *Some hero too must be dispatch'd, &c.*] It seems odd that they did not sooner send this message to *Achilles*; but there is some apology for it from the darkness, and the difficulty of finding a proper person. It was not every body that was proper to send but one who was a particular friend to *Achilles*, who might condole with him. Such was *Antilochus* who is sent afterwards, and who, besides, had that necessary qualification of being πόδας. ὠκύς [swift-footed].   *Eustathius.*

731. *If* Greece *must perish, we thy will obey;*
   But let us perish in the face of day!]

This thought has been look'd upon as one of the sublimest in *Homer*: *Longinus* represents it in this manner. 'The thickest darkness had on a sudden cover'd the *Grecian* army, and hindered them from fighting: When *Ajax*, not knowing what course to take, cries out, *Oh Jove! disperse this darkness which covers the Greeks, and if we must perish, let us perish in the light!* This is a sentiment truly worthy of *Ajax*, he does not pray for life; that had been unworthy a hero: But because in that darkness he could not employ his valour to any glorious purpose, and vex'd to stand idle in the field of battel, he only prays that the day may appear, as being assured of putting an end to it worthy his great heart, tho' *Jupiter* himself should happen to oppose his efforts.'

M. *l' Abbé Terasson* (in his dissertation on the Iliad) endeavours to prove that *Longinus* has misrepresented the whole context and sense of this passage of *Homer*. The fact (says he) is, that *Ajax* is in a very different situation in *Homer* from that wherein *Longinus* describes him. He has not the least intention of fighting, he thinks only of finding out some fit person to send to *Achilles*; and this darkness hindering him from seeing such an one, is the occasion of his prayer. Accordingly it appears by what follows, that as soon as *Jupiter* has dispersed the cloud, *Ajax* never falls upon the enemy, but in consequence of his former thought orders *Menelaus* to look for *Antilochus*, to dispatch him to *Achilles* with the news of the death of his friend. *Longinus* (continues this author) had certainly forgot the place from whence he took this thought; and it is not the first citation from *Homer* which the ancients have quoted wrong. Thus *Aristotle* attributes to *Calypso*, the words of *Ulysses* in the twelfth book of the *Odyssey*; and confounds together two passages, one of the second, the other of the fifteenth book of the Iliad. [*Ethic. ad Nicom.* l. 2. c. 9. and l. 3. c. 11.] And thus *Cicero* ascribed to *Agamemnon* a long discourse of *Ulysses* in the second Iliad; [*De divinatione* l. 2.] and cited as *Ajax*'s, the speech of *Hector* in the seventh. [See *Aul. Gellius* l. 15. c. 6.] One has no cause to wonder at this, since the ancients having *Homer* almost by heart, were for that very reason the more subject to mistake in citing him by memory.

To this I think one may answer, that granting it was partly the occasion of *Ajax*'s prayer to obtain light, in order to send to *Achilles* (which he afterwards does) yet the thought which *Longinus* attributes to him, is very consistent with it; and the last line expresses nothing else but an heroic desire rather to die in the light, than escape with safety in the darkness.

’Εν δέ φάει καὶ ὅλεσσον, ἐπεί νύ τοι εὔαδεν οὕτως.

[Destroy us in broad daylight, if it so pleases you to destroy us.]

But indeed the whole speech is only meant to paint the concern and distress of a brave general: the thought of sending a messenger is only a result from that concern and distress, and so but a small circumstance; which cannot be said to occasion the pray'r.

Mons. *Boileau* has translated this passage in two lines.

> *Grand Dieu! chasse la nuit qui nous couvre les yeux,*
> *Et combats contre nous à la clarté des cieux.*

[Great God! drive out the night that covers our eyes,
And fight against us under clear skies.]

And Mr *la Motte* yet better in one.

> *Grand Dieu! rends nous le jour, & combats contre nous!*

[Great God! Give us daylight, and fight against us!]

But both these (as *Dacier* very justly observes) are contrary to *Homer*'s sense. He is far from representing *Ajax* of such a daring impiety, as to bid *Jupiter* combate against him; but only makes him ask for light, that if it be his will the *Greeks* shall perish, they may perish in open day. Καὶ ὄλεσσον – (says he) that is, abandon us, withdraw from us your assistance; for those who are deserted by *Jove* must perish infallibly. This decorum of *Homer* ought to have been preserved.

756. *The mildest manners, and the gentlest heart.*] This is a fine elogium of *Patroclus*: *Homer* dwells upon it on purpose, lest *Achilles*'s character should be mistaken; and shews by the praises he bestows here upon goodness, that *Achilles*'s character is not commendable for morality. *Achilles*'s manners, entirely opposite to those of *Patroclus*, are not morally good; they are only poetically so, that is to say, they are well mark'd; and discover before-hand what resolutions that hero will take: As hath been at large explain'd upon *Aristotle*'s Poeticks.   *Dacier.*

781. *The youthful warriour heard with silent woe.*] *Homer* ever represents an excess of grief by a deep horrour, silence, weeping, and not enquiring into the manner of the friend's death: Nor could *Antilochus* have express'd his sorrow in any manner so moving as silence.
                                                        Eustathius.

785. *To brave* Laodocus *his arms he flung.*] *Antilochus* leaves his armour, not only that he might make the more haste, but (as the ancients conjecture) that he might not be thought to be absent by the enemies; and that seeing his armour on some other person, they might think him still in the fight.   *Eustathius.*

794.   *But hope not, Warriours! for Achilles' aid:*
       Unarm'd –]

This is an ingenious way of making the valour of *Achilles* appear the greater; who, tho' without arms, goes forth, in the next book, contrary to the expectation of *Ajax* and *Menelaus*.   *Dacier.*

825, *&c.* The heap of images which *Homer* throws together at the end of this book, makes the same action appear with a very beautiful variety. The *Description* of the burning of a city is short but very lively. That of *Ajax* alone bringing up the rear guard, and shielding those that bore the body of *Patroclus* from the whole *Trojan* host, gives a prodigious idea of *Ajax*; and as *Homer* has often hinted, makes him just second to *Achilles*. The image of the beam paints the great stature of *Patroclus*: That of the hill dividing the stream is noble and natural.

He compares the *Ajaxes* to a boar, for their fierceness and boldness; to a long bank that keeps off the course of the waters, for their standing firm and immoveable in the battel: Those that carry the dead body, to mules dragging a vast beam thro' rugged paths, for their laboriousness: The body carried, to a beam, for being heavy and inanimate: The *Trojans* to dogs, for their boldness; and to water for their agility and moving backwards and forwards: The *Greeks* to a flight of starlings and jays, for their timorousness, and swiftness.

                                        Eustathius.

THE
EIGHTEENTH BOOK
OF THE
ILIAD

The ARGUMENT

The grief of *Achilles*, and new armour
made him by *Vulcan*

The news of the death of Patroclus, *is brought to* Achilles *by* Antilochus. Thetis *hearing his lamentations, comes with all her sea-nymphs to comfort him. The speeches of the mother and son on this occasion.* Iris *appears to* Achilles *by the command of* Juno, *and orders him to shew himself at the head of the intrenchments. The sight of him turns the fortune of the day, and the body of* Patroclus *is carried off by the* Greeks. *The* Trojans *call a council, where* Hector *and* Polydamas *disagree in their opinions; but the advice of the former prevails, to remain encamped in the field: The grief of* Achilles *over the body of* Patroclus.

Thetis *goes to the palace of* Vulcan *to obtain new arms for her son. The description of the wonderful works of* Vulcan, *and lastly, that noble one of the shield of* Achilles.

The latter part of the nine and twentieth day, and the night ensuing, take up this book. The scene is at Achilles's *tent on the sea-shore, from whence it changes to the palace of* Vulcan.

Thus like the rage of fire the combat burns,
And now it rises, now it sinks by turns.
Meanwhile, where *Hellespont*'s broad waters flow,
Stood *Nestor*'s son, the messenger of woe:
5   There sate *Achilles*, shaded by his sails,
On hoisted yards extended to the gales;
Pensive he sate; for all that fate design'd
Rose in sad prospect to his boding mind.
Thus to his soul he said. Ah! what constrains
10 The *Greeks*, late victors, now to quit the plains?
Is this the day, which heav'n so long ago
Ordain'd, to sink me with the weight of woe?
(So *Thetis* warn'd) when by a *Trojan* hand,
The bravest of the *Myrmidonian* band
15 Should lose the light? Fulfill'd is that decree;
Fal'n is the warriour, and *Patroclus* he!
In vain I charg'd him soon to quit the plain,
And warn'd to shun *Hectorean* force in vain!

    Thus while he thinks, *Antilochus* appears,
20 And tells the melancholy tale with tears.
Sad tydings, son of *Peleus!* thou must hear;
And wretched I, th'unwilling messenger!
Dead is *Patroclus!* For his corps they fight;
His naked corps; His arms are *Hector*'s right.
25   A sudden horrour shot thro' all the chief,
And wrapt his senses in the cloud of grief;
Cast on the ground, with furious hands he spread
The scorching ashes o'er his graceful head;

His purple garments, and his golden hairs,
Those he deforms with dust, and these he tears: 30
On the hard soil his groaning breast he threw,
And roll'd and grovel'd, as to earth he grew.
The virgin captives, with disorder'd charms,
(Won by his own, or by *Patroclus'* arms)
Rush'd from the tents with cries; and gath'ring round,   35
Beat their white breasts, and fainted on the ground:
While *Nestor*'s son sustains a manlier part,
And mourns the warriour with a warriour's heart;
Hangs on his arms, amidst his frantic woe,
And oft prevents the meditated blow.   40
  Far in the deep abysses of the main,
With hoary *Nereus*, and the watry train,
The Mother Goddess from her crystal throne
Heard his loud cries, and answer'd groan for groan.
The circling *Nereids* with their mistress weep,   45
And all the sea-green sisters of the deep.
Thalia, *Glauce*, (ev'ry wat'ry name)
Nesæa mild, and silver *Spio* came.
Cymothoë and *Cymodoce* were nigh,
And the blue languish of soft *Alia*'s eye.   50
Their locks *Actæa* and *Limnoria* rear,
Then *Proto*, *Doris*, *Panope* appear,
Thoa, *Pherusa*, *Doto*, *Melita*;
Agave gentle, and *Amphithoë* gay:
Next *Callianira*, *Callianassa* show   55
Their sister looks; *Dexamene* the slow,
And swift *Dynamene*, now cut the tides:
Iæra now the verdant wave divides:
Nemertes with *Apseudes* lifts the head,
Bright *Galatea* quits her pearly bed;   60
These *Orythia*, *Clymene*, attend,
Mæra, *Amphinome*, the train extend,
And black *Janira*, and *Janassa* fair,
And *Amatheia* with her amber hair.
All these, and all that deep in ocean held   65
Their sacred seats, the glimm'ring grotto fill'd;
Each beat her iv'ry breast with silent woe,
Till *Thetis'* sorrows thus began to flow.

Hear me, and judge, ye sisters of the main!
How just a cause has *Thetis* to complain?
How wretched, were I mortal, were my fate!
How more than wretched in th'immortal state!
Sprung from my bed a god-like hero came,
The bravest far that ever bore the name;
Like some fair olive, by my careful hand
He grew, he flourish'd, and adorn'd the land:
To *Troy* I sent him; but the fates ordain
He never, never must return again.
So short a space the light of heav'n to view,
So short alas! and fill'd with anguish too?
Hear how his sorrows echo thro' the shore!
I cannot ease them, but I must deplore;
I go at least to bear a tender part,
And mourn my lov'd one with a mother's heart.

She said, and left the caverns of the main.
All bath'd in tears, the melancholy train
Attend her way. Wide-opening part the tides,
While the long pomp the silver wave divides.
Approaching now, they touch'd the *Trojan* land;
Then, two by two, ascended up the strand.
Th'immortal mother, standing close beside
Her mournful offspring, to his sighs reply'd;
Along the coast their mingled clamours ran,
And thus the silver-footed dame began.

Why mourns my son? thy late preferr'd request
The God has granted, and the *Greeks* distrest:
Why mourns my son? thy anguish let me share,
Reveal the cause, and trust a parent's care.

He, deeply groaning – To this cureless grief
Not ev'n the Thund'rer's favour brings relief.
Patroclus – Ah! – say, Goddess can I boast
A pleasure now? revenge itself is lost;
Patroclus, lov'd of all my martial train,
Beyond mankind, beyond my self, is slain!
Lost are those arms the Gods themselves bestow'd
On *Peleus*; *Hector* bears the glorious load.
Curs'd be that day, when all the pow'rs above
Thy charms submitted to a mortal love:

Oh had'st thou still, a sister of the main,
Pursu'd the pleasures of the wat'ry reign;   110
And happier *Peleus*, less ambitious, led
A mortal beauty to his equal bed!
E'er the sad fruit of thy unhappy womb
Had caus'd such sorrows past, and woes to come.
For soon alas! that wretched offspring slain,   115
New woes, new sorrows shall create again:
'Tis not in fate th'alternate now to give;
Patroclus dead, *Achilles* hates to live.
Let me revenge it on proud *Hector*'s heart,
Let his last spirit smoak upon my dart;   120
On these conditions will I breathe: Till then,
I blush to walk among the race of men.
    A flood of tears, at this, the Goddess shed;
Ah then, I see thee dying, see thee dead!
When *Hector* falls, thou dy'st. – Let *Hector* die,   125
And let me fall! (*Achilles* made reply)
Far lyes *Patroclus* from his native plain!
He fell, and falling, wish'd my aid in vain.
Ah then, since from this miserable day
I cast all hope of my return away,   130
Since unreveng'd, a hundred ghosts demand
The fate of *Hector* from *Achilles*' hand;
Since here, for brutal courage far renown'd,
I live an idle burden to the ground,
(Others in council fam'd for nobler skill,   135
More useful to preserve, than I to kill)
Let me – But oh! ye gracious pow'rs above!
Wrath and revenge from men and Gods remove:
Far, far too dear to ev'ry mortal breast,
Sweet to the soul, as honey to the taste;   140
Gath'ring like vapours of a noxious kind
From fiery blood, and dark'ning all the mind.
Me *Agamemnon* urg'd to deadly hate;
'Tis past – I quell it; I resign to fate.
Yes – I will meet the murd'rer of my friend,   145
Or (if the Gods ordain it) meet my end.
The stroke of fate the bravest cannot shun:
The great *Alcides*, *Jove*'s unequal'd son,

To *Juno*'s hate at length resign'd his breath,
150   And sunk the victim of all-conqu'ring Death.
So shall *Achilles* fall! stretch'd pale and dead,
No more the *Grecian* hope, or *Trojan* dread!
Let me, this instant, rush into the fields,
And reap what glory life's short harvest yields.
155   Shall I not force some widow'd dame to tear
With frantic hands her long dishevell'd hair?
Shall I not force her breast to heave with sighs,
And the soft tears to trickle from her eyes?
Yes, I shall give the Fair those mournful charms —
160   In vain you hold me — Hence! my arms, my arms!
Soon shall the sanguine torrent spread so wide,
That all shall know, *Achilles* swells the tide.

      My Son (*Cærulean Thetis* made reply,
To fate submitting with a secret sigh)
165   The host to succour, and thy friends to save,
Is worthy thee; the duty of the brave.
But can'st thou, naked, issue to the plains?
Thy radiant arms the *Trojan* foe detains.
Insulting *Hector* bears the Spoils on high,
170   But vainly glories, for his fate is nigh.
Yet, yet awhile, thy gen'rous ardour stay;
Assur'd, I meet thee at the dawn of day,
Charg'd with refulgent arms (a glorious load)
Vulcanian arms, the labour of a God.

175   Then turning to the daughters of the main,
The Goddess thus dismiss'd her azure train.

      Ye sister *Nereids!* to your deeps descend,
Haste, and our father's sacred seat attend,
I go to find the architect divine,
180   Where vast *Olympus*' starry summits shine:
So tell our hoary sire — This charge she gave:
The sea-green sisters plunge beneath the wave:
Thetis once more ascends the blest abodes,
And treads the brazen threshold of the Gods.

185   And now the *Greeks*, from furious *Hector*'s force,
Urge to broad *Hellespont* their headlong course:
Nor yet their chiefs *Patroclus*' body bore
Safe thro' the tempest to the tented shore.

The horse, the foot, with equal fury join'd,
Pour'd on the rear, and thunder'd close behind;   190
And like a flame thro' fields of ripen'd corn,
The rage of *Hector* o'er the ranks was born.
Thrice the slain hero by the foot he drew;
Thrice to the skies the *Trojan* clamours flew:
As oft' th' *Ajaces* his assault sustain;   195
But check'd, he turns; repuls'd, attacks again.
With fiercer shouts his ling'ring troops he fires,
Nor yields a step, nor from his post retires;
So watchful sheperds strive to force, in vain,
The hungry lion from a carcase slain.   200
Ev'n yet, *Patroclus* had he born away,
And all the glories of th'extended day;
Had not high *Juno*, from the realms of air,
Secret, dispatch'd her trusty messenger.
The various Goddess of the show'ry bow,   205
Shot in a whirlwind to the shore below;
To great *Achilles* at his ships she came,
And thus began the many-colour'd dame.
    Rise, Son of *Peleus!* rise divinely brave!
Assist the combate, and *Patroclus* save: 210
For him the slaughter to the fleet they spread,
And fall by mutual wounds around the dead.
To drag him back to *Troy* the foe contends;
Nor with his death the rage of *Hector* ends:
A prey to dogs he dooms the corse to lie,   215
And marks the place to fix his head on high.
Rise, and prevent (if yet thou think of fame)
Thy friend's disgrace, thy own eternal shame!
    Who sends thee, Goddess! from th'etherial skies?
Achilles thus. And *Iris* thus replies.   220
I come, *Pelides!* from the Queen of *Jove*,
Th'immortal Empress of the realms above;
Unknown to him who sits remote on high,
Unknown to all the synod of the sky.
Thou com'st in vain, he cries (with fury warm'd);   225
Arms I have none, and can I fight unarm'd?
Unwilling as I am, of force I stay,
Till *Thetis* bring me at the dawn of day

Vulcanian arms: What other can I wield?
230 Except the mighty *Telamonian* shield?
That, in my friend's defence, has *Ajax* spread,
While his strong lance around him heaps the dead:
The gallant chief defends *Menœtius'* son,
And does, what his *Achilles* should have done.

235   Thy want of arms (said *Iris*) well we know,
But tho unarm'd, yet clad in terrours, go!
Let but *Achilles* o'er yon' trench appear,
Proud *Troy* shall tremble, and consent to fear;
Greece from one glance of that tremendous eye
240 Shall take new courage, and disdain to fly.

She spoke, and past in air. The hero rose;
Her *Ægis*, *Pallas* o'er his shoulder throws;
Around his brows a golden cloud she spread;
A stream of glory flam'd above his head.

245 As when from some beleaguer'd town arise
The smokes high-curling to the shaded skies;
(See from some island, o'er the main afar,
When men distrest hang out the sign of war)
Soon as the sun in ocean hides his rays,
250 Thick on the hills the flaming beacons blaze;
With long-projected beams the seas are bright,
And Heav'ns high arch reflects the ruddy light;
So from *Achilles'* head the splendors rise,
Reflecting blaze on blaze against the skies.

255 Forth march'd the chief, and distant from the croud,
High on the rampart rais'd his voice aloud;
With her own shout *Minerva* swells the sound;
Troy starts astonish'd, and the shores rebound.
As the loud trumpet's brazen mouth from far
260 With shrilling clangor sounds th'alarm of war;
Struck from the walls, the echoes float on high,
And the round bulwarks and thick towr's reply;
So high his brazen voice the hero rear'd:
Hosts dropp'd their arms, and trembled as they heard;
265 And back the chariots roll, and coursers bound,
And steeds and men lie mingled on the ground.
Aghast they see the living light'nings play,
And turn their eye-balls from the flashing ray.

Thrice from the trench his dreadful voice he rais'd;
And thrice they fled, confounded and amaz'd. 270
Twelve in the tumult wedg'd, untimely rush'd
On their own spears, by their own chariots crush'd:
While shielded from the darts, the *Greeks* obtain
The long-contended carcase of the slain.

A lofty bier the breathless warriour bears; 275
Around, his sad companions melt in tears:
But chief *Achilles*, bending down his head,
Pours unavailing sorrows o'er the dead.
Whom late, triumphant with his steeds and car,
He sent refulgent to the field of war, 280
(Unhappy change!) now senseless, pale, he found,
Stretch'd forth, and gash'd with many a gaping wound.

Meantime, unweary'd with his heavenly way,
In ocean's waves th'unwilling light of day
Quench his red orb, at *Juno*'s high command, 285
And from their labours eas'd th'*Achaian* band.
The frighted *Trojans* (panting from the war,
Their steeds unharness'd from the weary car)
A sudden council call'd: Each chief appear'd
In haste, and standing; for to sit they fear'd. 290
'Twas now no season for prolong'd debate;
They saw *Achilles*, and in him their fate.
Silent they stood: *Polydamas* at last,
Skill'd to discern the future by the past,
The son of *Panthus*, thus exprest his fears; 295
(The friend of *Hector*, and of equal years:
The self-same night to both a being gave,
One wise in council, on in action brave.)

In free debate, my friends, your sentence speak;
For me, I move, before the morning break 300
To raise our camp: Too dang'rous here our post,
Far from *Troy* walls, and on a naked coast.
I deem'd not *Greece* so dreadful, while engag'd
In mutual feuds, her King and hero rag'd;
Then, while we hop'd our armies might prevail, 305
We boldly camp'd beside a thousand sail.
I dread *Pelides* now: his rage of mind
Not long continues to the shores confin'd,

Nor to the fields, where long in equal fray
310   Contending nations won and lost the day;
For *Troy*, for *Troy*, shall henceforth be the strife,
And the hard contest not for fame, but life.
Haste then to *Ilion*, while the fav'ring night
Detains those terrours, keeps that arm from fight;
315   If but the morrow's sun behold us here,
That arm, those terrours, we shall feel, not fear;
And hearts that now disdain, shall leap with joy,
If heav'n permits them then to enter *Troy*.
Let not my fatal prophecy be true,
320   Nor what I tremble but to think, ensue.
Whatever be our fate, yet let us try
What force of thought and reason can supply;
Let us on counsel for our guard depend;
The town, her gates and bulwarks shall defend.
325   When morning dawns, our well-appointed pow'rs
Array'd in arms, shall line the lofty tow'rs.
Let the fierce hero then, when fury calls,
Vent his mad vengeance on our rocky walls,
Or fetch a thousand circles round the plain,
330   Till his spent coursers seek the fleet again:
So may his rage be tir'd, and labour'd down;
And dogs shall tear him e'er he sack the town.

    Return? (said *Hector*, fir'd with stern disdain)
What, coop whole armies in our walls again?
335   Was't not enough, ye valiant warriours say,
Nine years imprison'd in those tow'rs ye lay?
Wide o'er the world was *Ilion* fam'd of old
For brass exhaustless, and for mines of gold:
But while inglorious in her walls we stay'd,
340   Sunk were her treasures, and her stores decay'd;
The *Phrygians* now her scatter'd spoils enjoy,
And proud *Mæonia* wasts the fruits of *Troy*.
Great *Jove* at length my arms to conquest calls,
And shuts the *Grecians* in their wooden walls:
345   Dar'st thou dispirit whom the Gods incite?
Flies any *Trojan*? I shall stop his flight.
To better counsel then attention lend;
Take due refreshment, and the watch attend.

If there be one whose riches cost him care,
Forth let him bring them, for the troops to share;   350
'Tis better gen'rously bestow'd on those,
Than left the plunder of our country's foes.
Soon as the morn the purple Orient warms
Fierce on yon' navy will we pour our arms.
If great *Achilles* rise in all his might,   355
His be the danger: I shall stand the fight.
Honor, ye Gods! or let me gain, or give;
And live he glorious, whosoe'er shall live!
Mars is our common Lord, alike to all;
And oft' the victor triumphs, but to fall.   360
    The shouting host in loud applauses join'd;
So *Pallas* robb'd the many of their mind,
To their own sense condemn'd! and left to chuse
The worst advice, the better to refuse.
    While the long night extends her sable reign,   365
Around *Patroclus* mourn'd the *Grecian* train.
Stern in superiour grief *Pelides* stood;
Those slaught'ring arms, so us'd to bathe in blood,
Now clasp his clay-cold limbs: then gushing start
The tears, and sighs burst from his swelling heart.   370
The lion thus, with dreadful anguish stung,
Roars thro' the desart, and demands his young;
When the grim savage to his rifled den
Too late returning, snuffs the track of men,
And o'er the vales, and o'er the forrest bounds;   375
His clam'rous grief the bellowing wood resounds.
So grieves *Achilles*; and impetuous, vents
To all his *Myrmidons*, his loud laments.
    In what vain promise, Gods! did I engage?
When to console *Menætius*' feeble age,   380
I vow'd his much-lov'd offspring to restore,
Charg'd with rich spoils, to fair *Opuntia*'s shore!
But mighty *Jove* cuts short, with just disdain,
The long, long views of poor, designing man!
One fate the warriour and the friend shall strike,   385
And *Troy*'s black sands must drink our blood alike:
Me too, a wretched mother shall deplore,
An aged father never see me more!

Yet, my *Patroclus!* yet a space I stay,
390   Then swift pursue thee on the darksome way.
E'er thy dear relicks in the grave are laid,
Shall *Hector*'s head be offer'd to thy shade;
That, with his arms, shall hang before thy shrine;
And twelve, the noblest of the *Trojan* line,
395   Sacred to vengeance, by this hand expire;
Their lives effus'd around thy flaming pyre.
Thus let me lie till then! thus, closely prest,
Bathe thy cold face, and sob upon thy breast!
While *Trojan* captives here thy mourners stay,
400   Weep all the night, and murmur all the day:
Spoils of my arms, and thine; when, wasting wide,
Our swords kept time, and conquer'd side by side.

He spoke, and bid the sad attendants round
Cleanse the pale corse, and wash each honour'd wound.
405   A massy caldron of stupendous frame
They brought, and plac'd it o'er the rising flame:
Then heap the lighted wood; the flame divides
Beneath the vase, and climbs around the sides:
In its wide womb they pour the rushing stream;
410   The boiling water bubbles to the brim.
The body then they bathe with pious toil,
Embalm the wounds, anoint the limbs with oil;
High on a bed of state extended laid,
And decent cover'd with a linen shade;
415   Last o'er the dead the milk-white veil they threw;
That done, their sorrows and their sighs renew.

Meanwhile to *Juno*, in the realms above,
(His wife and sister) spoke almighty *Jove.*
At last thy will prevails: Great *Peleus*' son
420   Rises in arms: Such grace thy *Greeks* have won.
Say (for I know not) is their race divine,
And thou the mother of that martial line?

What words are these (th'imperial dame replies,
While anger flash'd from her majestick eyes)
425   Succour like this a mortal arm might lend,
And such success mere human wit attend:
And shall not I, the second pow'r above,
Heav'ns Queen, and consort of the thund'ring *Jove,*

Say, shall not I one nation's fate command,
Not wreak my vengeance on one guilty land?   430
   So they. Meanwhile the silver-footed dame
Reach'd the *Vulcanian* dome, eternal frame!
High-eminent amid the works divine,
Where heav'ns far-beaming, brazen mansions shine.
There the lame architect the Goddess found,   435
Obscure in smoak, his forges flaming round,
While bath'd in sweat from fire to fire he flew,
And puffing loud, the roaring bellows blew.
That day no common task his labour claim'd:
Full twenty tripods for his hall he fram'd,   440
That plac'd on living wheels of massy gold,
(Wond'rous to tell) instinct with spirit roll'd
From place to place, around the blest abodes,
Self-mov'd, obedient to the beck of Gods:
For their fair handles now, o'erwrought with flow'rs,   445
In molds prepar'd, the glowing ore he pours.
Just as responsive to his thought, the frame
Stood prompt to move, the azure Goddess came:
Charis, his spouse, a grace divinely fair,
(With purple fillets round her braided hair)   450
Observ'd her ent'ring; her soft hand she press'd,
And smiling, thus the wat'ry Queen address'd.
   What, Goddess! this unusual favour draws?
All hail, and welcome! whatsoe'er the cause:
Till now a stranger, in a happy hour   455
Approach, and taste the dainties of the bow'r.
   High on a throne, with stars of silver grac'd
And various artifice, the Queen she plac'd;
A footstool at her feet: then calling, said,
Vulcan draw near, 'tis *Thetis* asks your aid.   460
   Thetis (reply'd the God) our pow'rs may claim,
An ever dear, and ever honour'd name!
When my proud mother hurl'd me from the sky,
(My awkward form, it seems, displeas'd her eye)
She, and *Eurynome*, my griefs redrest,   465
And soft receiv'd me on their silver breast.
Ev'n then, these arts employ'd my infant thought;
Chains, bracelets, pendants, all their toys I wrought.

Nine years kept secret in the dark abode,
470 Secure I lay, conceal'd from man and God:
Deep in a cavern'd rock my days were led;
The rushing ocean murmur'd o'er my head.
Now since her presence glads our mansion, say,
For such desert what service can I pay?
475 Vouchsafe, O *Thetis!* at our board to share
The genial rites, and hospitable fare;
While I the labours of the forge forego,
And bid the roaring bellows cease to blow.

Then from his anvil the lame artist rose;
480 Wide with distorted legs, oblique he goes,
And stills the bellows, and (in order laid)
Locks in their chests his instruments of trade.
Then with a sponge the sooty workman drest
His brawny arms imbrown'd, and hairy breast.
485 With his huge scepter grac'd, and red attire,
Came halting forth the Sov'reign of the fire:
The monarch's steps two female forms uphold,
That mov'd, and breath'd, in animated gold;
To whom was voice, and sense, and science giv'n
490 Of works divine (such wonders are in heav'n!)
On these supported, with unequal gait,
He reach'd the throne where pensive *Thetis* sate;
There plac'd beside her on the shining frame,
He thus address'd the silver-footed dame.

495 Thee, welcome Goddess! what occasion calls,
(So long a stranger) to these honour'd walls?
'Tis thine, fair *Thetis,* the command to lay,
And *Vulcan*'s joy and duty to obey.

To whom the mournful mother thus replies,
500 (The crystal drops stood trembling in her eyes)
Oh *Vulcan!* say, was ever breast divine
So pierc'd with sorrows, so o'erwhelm'd as mine?
Of all the Goddesses, did *Jove* prepare
For *Thetis* only such a weight of care?
505 I, only I, of all the wat'ry race,
By force subjected to a man's embrace,
Who, sinking now with age, and sorrow, pays
The mighty fine impos'd on length of days.

Sprung from my bed, a god-like hero came,
The bravest sure that ever bore the name;   510
Like some fair plant beneath my careful hand
He grew, he flourish'd, and he grac'd the land:
To *Troy* I sent him! but his native shore
Never, ah never, shall receive him more;
(Ev'n while he lives, he wastes with secret woe)   515
Nor I, a Goddess, can retard the blow!
Robb'd of the prize the *Grecian* Suffrage gave,
The King of nations forc'd his royal slave:
For this he griev'd; and till the *Greeks* opprest
Requir'd his arm, he sorrow'd unredrest.   520
Large gifts they promise, and their elders send;
In vain – He arms not, but permits his friend
His arms, his steeds, his forces to employ;
He marches, combates, almost conquers *Troy*:
Then slain by *Phœbus* (*Hector* had the name)   525
At once resigns his armour, life, and fame.
But thou, in pity, by my pray'r be won:
Grace with immortal arms this short-liv'd son,
And to the field in martial pomp restore,
To shine with glory, till he shines no more!   530
    To her the Artist-god. Thy griefs resign,
Secure, what *Vulcan* can, is ever thine.
O could I hide him from the fates as well,
Or with these hands the cruel stroke repel,
As I shall forge most envy'd arms, the gaze   535
Of wond'ring ages, and the world's amaze!
    Thus having said, the father of the fires
To the black labours of his forge retires.
Soon as he bade them blow, the bellows turn'd
Their iron mouths; and where the furnace burn'd,   540
Resounding breath'd: At once the blast expires,
And twenty forges catch at once the fires;
Just as the God directs, now loud, now low,
They raise a tempest, or they gently blow.
In hissing flames huge silver bars are roll'd,   545
And stubborn brass, and tin, and solid gold:
Before, deep fix'd, th'eternal anvils stand;
The pond'rous hammer loads his better hand,

His left with tongs turns the vex'd metal round,
550   And thick, strong strokes, the doubling vaults rebound.
      Then first he form'd th'immense and solid *shield*;
      Rich, various artifice emblaz'd the field;
      Its utmost verge a threefold circle bound;
      A silver chain suspends the massy round,
555   Five ample plates the broad expanse compose,
      And god-like labours on the surface rose.
      There shone the image of the master Mind:
      There earth, there heav'n, there ocean he design'd;
      Th'unweary'd sun, the moon compleatly round;
560   The starry lights that heav'ns high convex crown'd;
      The *Pleiads*, *Hyads*, with the northern team;
      And great *Orion*'s more refulgent beam;
      To which, around the axle of the sky,
      The *Bear* revolving, points his golden eye,
565   Still shines exalted on th'ætherial plain,
      Nor bathes his blazing forehead in the main.
      Two cities radiant on the shield appear,
      The image one of peace, and one of war.
      Here sacred pomp, and genial feast delight,
570   And solemn dance, and *Hymenæal* rite;
      Along the street the new-made brides are led,
      With torches flaming, to the nuptial bed;
      The youthful dancers in a circle bound
      To the soft flute, and cittern's silver sound:
575   Thro' the fair streets, the matrons in a row,
      Stand in their porches, and enjoy the show.
      There, in the *Forum* swarm a num'rous train;
      The subject of debate, a townsman slain:
      One pleads the fine discharg'd, which one deny'd,
580   And bade the publick and the laws decide:
      The witness is produc'd on either hand;
      For this, or that, the partial people stand:
      Th'appointed heralds still the noisy bands,
      And form a ring, with scepters in their hands;
585   On seats of stone, within the sacred place,
      The rev'rend elders nodded o'er the case;
      Alternate, each th'attesting scepter took,
      And rising solemn, each his sentence spoke.

Two golden talents lay amidst, in sight,
The prize of him who best adjudg'd the right.   590
   Another part (a prospect diff'ring far)
Glow'd with refulgent arms, and horrid war.
Two mighty hosts a leaguer'd town embrace,
And one would pillage, one wou'd burn the place.
Meantime the townsmen, arm'd with silent care,   595
A secret ambush on the foe prepare:
Their wives, their children, and the watchful band,
Of trembling parents on the turrets stand.
They march; by *Pallas* and by *Mars* made bold;
Gold were the Gods, their radiant garments Gold,   600
And gold their armour: These the Squadron led,
August, divine, superiour by the head!
A place for ambush fit, they found, and stood
Cover'd with shields, beside a silver flood.
Two spies at distance lurk, and watchful seem   605
If sheep or oxen seek the winding stream.
Soon the white flocks proceeded o'er the plains,
And steers slow-moving, and two shepherd swains;
Behind them, piping on their reeds, they go,
Nor fear an ambush, nor suspect a foe.   610
In arms the glitt'ring squadron rising round
Rush sudden; hills of slaughter heap the ground,
Whole flocks and herds lie bleeding on the plains,
And, all amidst them, dead, the shepherd swains!
The bellowing oxen the besiegers hear;   615
They rise, take horse, approach, and meet the war;
They fight, they fall, beside the silver flood;
The waving silver seem'd to blush with blood.
There tumult, there contention stood confest;
One rear'd a dagger at a captive's breast,   620
One held a living foe, that freshly bled
With new-made wounds; another dragg'd a dead;
Now here, now there, the carcasses they tore:
Fate stalk'd amidst them, grim with human gore.
And the whole war came out, and met the eye;   625
And each bold figure seem'd to live, or die.
   A field deep-furrow'd, next the God design'd,
The third time labour'd by the sweating hind;

The shining shares full many plowmen guide,
630   And turn their crooked yokes on ev'ry side.
Still as at either end they wheel around,
The master meets 'em with his goblet crown'd;
The hearty draught rewards, renews their toil,
Then back the turning plow-shares cleave the soil:
635   Behind, the rising earth in ridges roll'd,
And sable look'd, tho form'd of molten gold.
    Another field rose high with waving grain;
With bended sickles stand the reaper-train:
Here stretch'd in ranks the level'd swarths are found,
640   Sheaves heap'd on sheaves, here thicken up the ground.
With sweeping stroke the mowers strow the lands;
The gath'rers follow, and collect in bands;
And last the children, in whose arms are born
(Too short to gripe them) the brown sheaves of corn.
645   The rustic monarch of the field descries
With silent glee, the heaps around him rise.
A ready banquet on the turf is laid,
Beneath an ample oak's expanded shade.
The victim-ox the sturdy youth prepare;
650   The reaper's due repast, the women's care.
    Next, ripe in yellow gold, a vineyard shines,
Bent with the pond'rous harvest of its vines;
A deaper dye the dangling clusters show,
And curl'd on silver props, in order glow:
655   A darker metal mixt, intrench'd the place;
And pales of glitt'ring tin th'enclosure grace.
To this, one pathway gently winding leads,
Where march a train with baskets on their heads,
(Fair maids, and blooming youths) that smiling bear
660   The purple product of th'autumnal year.
To these a youth awakes the warbling strings,
Whose tender lay the fate of *Linus* sings;
In measur'd dance behind him move the train,
Tune soft the voice, and answer to the strain.
665   Here, herds of oxen march, erect and bold,
Rear high their horns, and seem to lowe in gold,
And speed to meadows on whose sounding shores
A rapid torrent thro' the rushes roars:

Four golden herdsmen as their guardians stand,
And nine sour dogs compleat the rustic band. 670
Two lions rushing from the wood appear'd;
And seiz'd a bull, the master of the herd:
He roar'd: in vain the dogs, the men withstood,
They tore his flesh, and drank the sable blood.
The dogs (oft' chear'd in vain) desert the prey, 675
Dread the grim terrours, and at distance bay.
   Next this, the eye the art of *Vulcan* leads
Deep thro' fair forests, and a length of meads;
And stalls, and folds, and scatter'd cotts between;
And fleecy flocks, that whiten all the scene. 680
   A figur'd dance succeeds: Such once was seen
In lofty *Gnossus*, for the *Cretan* Queen,
Form'd by *Dædalean* art. A comely band
Of youths and maidens, bounding hand in hand:
The maids in soft cymarrs of linen drest; 685
The youths all graceful in the glossy vest;
Of those the locks with flow'ry wreaths inroll'd,
Of these the sides adorn'd with swords of gold,
That glitt'ring gay, from silver belts depend.
Now all at once they rise, at once descend, 690
With well-taught feet: Now shape, in oblique ways,
Confus'dly regular, the moving maze:
Now forth at once, too swift for sight they spring,
And undistinguish'd blend the flying ring:
So whirls a wheel, in giddy circle tost, 695
And rapid as it runs, the single spokes are lost.
The gazing multitudes admire around;
Two active tumblers in the center bound;
Now high, now low, their pliant limbs they bend,
And gen'ral songs the sprightly revel end. 700
   Thus the broad shield complete the artist crown'd
With his last hand, and pour'd the ocean round:
In living silver seem'd the waves to roll,
And beat the buckler's verge, and bound the whole.
   This done, whate'er a warriour's use requires 705
He forg'd; the cuirass that outshone the fires;
The greaves of ductile tin, the helm imprest
With various sculpture, and the golden crest.

At *Thetis'* feet the finish'd labour lay;
710   She, as a falcon cuts th'Aerial way,
Swift from *Olympus'* snowy summit flies,
And bears the blazing present through the skies.

OBSERVATIONS

ON THE

EIGHTEENTH BOOK

1. *Thus like the rage of fire,* &c.] This phrase is usual in our Author, to signify a sharp battel fought with heat and fury on both parts; such an engagement like a flame, preying upon all sides, and dying the sooner, the fiercer it burns.   *Eustathius.*

6. *On hoisted yards.*] The epithet ὀρθοκραιράων in this place has a more than ordinary signification. It implies that the sail-yards were hoisted up, and *Achilles*'s ships on the point to set sail. This shews that it was purely in compliance to his friend that he permitted him to succour the *Greeks*; he meant to leave 'em as soon as *Patroclus* return'd; he still remembered what he told the embassadors in the ninth Book; v. 360. *To morrow you shall see my fleet set sail.* Accordingly this is the day appointed, and he is fixed to his resolution: This circumstance wonderfully strengthens his implacable character.

7. *Pensive he sate.*] *Homer* in this artful manner prepares *Achilles* for the fatal message, and gives him these forebodings of his misfortunes, that they might be no less than he expected.

His Expressions are suitable to his concern, and delivered confusedly. 'I bad him (says he) after he had saved the ships, and repulsed the *Trojans*, to return back, and not engage himself too far.' Here he breaks off, when he should have added; 'But he was so unfortunate as to forget my advice.' As he is reasoning with himself, *Antilochus* comes in, which makes him leave the sense imperfect.   *Eustathius.*

15.   *Fulfill'd is that decree;*
        Fal'n is the warriour, and Patroclus *he!*

It may be objected, that *Achilles* seems to contradict what had been said in the foregoing book, that *Thetis* concealed from her son the death of *Patroclus* in her prediction. Whereas here he says, that she had foretold he should lose the bravest of the *Thessalians*. There is nothing in this but what is natural and common among mankind: And it is still more agreeable to the hasty and inconsiderate temper of *Achilles*, not to have made that reflection till it was too late. Prophecies are only marks of divine prescience, not warnings to prevent human misfortunes; for if they were, they must hinder their own accomplishment.

21.   *Sad tydings, Son of* Peleus!]

This speech of *Antilochus* ought to serve as a model for the brevity with which so dreadful a piece of news ought to be delivered; for in two verses it comprehends the whole Affair of the death of *Patroclus*, the person that killed him, the contest for his body, and his arms in the possession of his enemy. Besides, it shou'd be observed that grief has so crowded his words, that in these two verses he leaves the verb ἀμφιμάχονται, *they fight*, without its nominative, *the Greeks* or *Trojans*. *Homer* observes this brevity upon all the like occasions. The *Greek* tragic Poets have not always imitated this discretion. In great distresses there is nothing more ridiculous than a messenger who begins a long story with pathetic descriptions; he speaks without being heard; for the person to whom he addresses himself has no time to attend him: The first word, which discovers to him his misfortune, has made him deaf to all the rest.   *Eustathius*.

25.   *A sudden horrour*, &c.] A modern *French* writer has drawn a parallel of the conduct of *Homer* and *Virgil*, in relation to the deaths of *Patroclus* and of *Pallas*. The latter is killed by *Turnus*, as the former by *Hector*; *Turnus* triumphs in the spoils of the one, as *Hector* is clad in the arms of the other; *Æneas* revenges the death of *Pallas* by that of *Turnus*, as *Achilles* the death of *Patroclus* by that of *Hector*. The grief of *Achilles* in *Homer* on the score of *Patroclus*, is much greater than that of *Æneas* in *Virgil*, for the sake of *Pallas*. *Achilles* gives himself up to despair with a weakness which *Plato* could not pardon in him, and which can only be excused on account of the long and close friendship between 'em: That of *Æneas* is more discreet, and seems more worthy of a hero. It was not possible that *Æneas* could be so deeply interested

for any man, as *Achilles* was interested for *Patroclus*: For *Virgil* had no colour to kill *Ascanius*, who was little more than a child; besides, that his hero's interest in the war of *Italy* was great enough of itself, not to need to be animated by so touching a concern as the fear of losing his son. On the other hand, *Achilles* having but very little personal concern in the war of *Troy* (as he had told *Agamemnon* in the beginning of the Poem) and knowing, besides, that he was to perish there, required some very pressing motive to engage him to persist in it, after such disgusts and Insults as he had received. It was this which made it necessary for these two great Poets to treat a subject so much in its own nature alike, in a manner so different. But as *Virgil* found it admirable in *Homer*, he was willing to approach it, as near as the oeconomy of his work would permit.

27. *Cast on the ground*, &c.] This is a fine picture of the grief of *Achilles*: We see on the one hand, the posture in which the hero receives the news of his friend's death; he falls upon the ground, he rends his hair, he snatches the ashes and casts them on his head, according to the manner of those times; (but what much enlivens it in this place, is his sprinkling embers instead of ashes in the violence of his passion.) On the other side, the captives are running from their tents, ranging themselves about him, and answering to his groans: Beside him stands *Antilochus*, fetching deep Sighs, and hanging on the arms of the hero, for fear his despair and rage should cause some desperate attempt upon his own life: There is no painter but will be touch'd with this image.

33. *The virgin captives.*] The captive maids lamented either in pity for their Lord, or in gratitude to the memory of *Patroclus*, who was remarkable for his goodness and affability; or under these pretences mourn'd for their own misfortunes and slavery.   *Eustathius.*

75. *Like some fair olive, by my careful hand.*] This passage, where the mother compares her son to a tender plant, raised and preserved with care; has a most remarkable resemblance to that in the *Psalms*, *Thy children like branches of olive trees round thy table.* Psal. 127.

100, 125. *The two speeches of* Achilles *to* Thetis.] It is not possible to imagine more lively and beautiful strokes of nature and passion, than those which our author ascribes to *Achilles* throughout these admirable speeches. They contain all, that the truest friend, the most tender son, and the most generous hero, could think or express in this delicate and affecting circumstance. He shews his excess of love to his mother, by wishing he had never been born or known to the world, rather than she should have endured so many sufferings on his account: He shews no less love for his friend, in resolving to revenge his death upon *Hector*, tho' his own would immediately follow. We see him here ready to meet his fate for the sake of his friend, and in the *Odyssey* we find him wishing to live again only to maintain his father's honour against his enemies. Thus he values neither life nor death, but as they conduce to the good of his friend and parents, or the encrease of his glory.

After having calmly considered the present state of his life, he deliberately embraces his approaching fate; and comforts himself under it, by a reflection on those great men, whom neither their illustrious actions, nor their affinity to heaven, could save from the general doom. A thought very natural to him, whose business it was in peace to sing their praises, and in war to imitate their actions. *Achilles*, like a man passionate of glory, takes none but the finest models; he thinks of *Hercules*, who was the son of *Jupiter*, and who had filled the universe with the noise of his immortal actions: These are the sentiments of a real hero.   *Eustathius.*

137. *Let me – But oh ye gracious powers*, &c.] *Achilles*'s words are these; 'Now since I am never to return home, and since I lie here an useless person, losing my best friend, and exposing the *Greeks* to so many dangers by my own folly; I who am superior to them all in battel – Here he breaks off, and says – May contention perish everlastingly, *&c. Achilles* leaves the sentence thus suspended, either because in his heat he had forgot what he was speaking of, or because he did not know how to end it; for he should have said, – 'Since I have done all this, I'll perish to revenge him:' Nothing can be finer than this sudden execration against discord and revenge, which breaks from the hero in the deep sense of the miseries those passions had occasioned.

Achilles could not be ignorant that he was superior to others in battel; and it was therefore no fault in him to say so. But he is so ingenuous as to give himself no farther commendation than what he undoubtedly merited; confessing at the same time, that many exceeded him in speaking: Unless one may take this as said in contempt of oratory, not unlike that of *Virgil*,

Orabunt caussas melius – &c.

[Plead better at the bar.]

153. *Let me, this instant.*] I shall have time enough for inglorious rest when I am in the grave, but now I must act like a living hero: I shall indeed lie down in death, but at the same time rise higher in glory.

Eustathius.

162. *That all shall know*, Achilles.] There is a great stress on δηρόν [long] and ἐγώ [I]. They shall soon find that their victories have been owing to the *long absence* of a hero, and that hero *Achilles*. Upon which the ancients have observed, that since *Achilles*'s anger there past in reality but a few days: To which it may be replied, that so short a time as this might well seem long to *Achilles*, who thought all unactive hours tedious and insupportable; and if the poet himself had said that *Achilles* was long absent, he had not said it because a great many days had past, but because so great a variety of incidents had happened in that time.

Eustathius.

171. – This promise of *Thetis* to present her son with a suit of armour, was the most artful method of hindering him from putting immediately in practice his resolution of fighting, which according to his violent manners, he must have done: Therefore the interposition of *Thetis* here was absolutely necessary; it was *dignus vindice nodus* [an impediment worthy of a protector].

219. *Who sends thee Goddess*, &c.] *Achilles* is amazed, that a moment after the Goddess his mother had forbid him fighting, he should receive a contrary order from the Gods: Therefore he asks what God sent her?

Dacier.

226. *Arms I have none.*] It is here objected against *Homer*, that since *Patroclus* took *Achilles*' armour, *Achilles* could not want arms while he had those of *Patroclus*; but (besides that *Patroclus* might have given his armour to his squire *Automedon*, the better to deceive the *Trojans* by making them take *Automedon* for *Patroclus*, as they took *Patroclus* for *Achilles*) this objection may be very solidly answered by saying that *Homer* has prevented it, since he made *Achilles*'s armour fit *Patroclus*'s body not without a miracle, which the Gods wrought in his favour.

Furthermore, it does not follow that because the armour of a large man fits one that is smaller, the armour of a little man should fit one that is larger.   *Eustathius.*

230. *Except the mighty* Telamonian *shield.*] *Achilles* seems not to have been of so large a stature as *Ajax*: Yet his shield 'tis likely might be fit enough for him, because his great strength was sufficient to wield it. This passage, I think, might have been made use of by the defenders of the shield of *Achilles* against the criticks, to shew that *Homer* intended the buckler of his hero for a very large one: And one would think he put it into this place, just a little before the description of that shield, on purpose to obviate that objection.

236. *But as thou art, unarm'd.*] A hero so violent and so outragious as *Achilles*, and who had but just lost the man he loved best in the world, is not likely to refuse shewing himself to the enemy, for the single reason of having no armour. Grief and despair in a great soul are not so prudent and reserv'd; but then on the other side, he is not to throw himself into the midst of so many enemies arm'd and flush'd with victory. *Homer* gets out of this nice circumstance with great dexterity, and gives to *Achilles*'s character every thing he ought to give to it, without offending either against reason or probability. He judiciously feigns, that *Juno* sent this order to *Achilles*, for *Juno* is the Goddess of royalty, who has the care of princes and kings; and who inspires them with the sense of what they owe to their dignity and character.   *Dacier.*

237. *Let but* Achilles *o'er yon' trench appear.*] There cannot be a greater instance, how constantly *Homer* carried his whole design in his head, as well as with what admirable art he raises one great idea upon another, to the highest sublime, than this passage of *Achilles*'s appearance to the army, and the preparations by which we are led to it. In the thirteenth book, when the *Trojans* have the victory, they check their pursuit of it, in the mere thought that *Achilles sees them*: In the sixteenth, they are put into the utmost consternation at the sight of his armour and chariot: In the seventeenth, *Menelaus* and *Ajax* are in despair, on the consideration that *Achilles* cannot succour them for want of armour: In the present book, beyond all expectation he does but shew himself unarm'd, and the very sight of him gives the victory to *Greece*: How extremely noble is this gradation!

246. *The smokes high-curling.*] For fires in the day appear nothing but smoak, and in the night flames are visible because of the darkness. And thus it is said in *Exodus*, That God led his people in the day with a pillar of smoak, and in the night with a pillar of fire. *Per diem in Columna nubis, & per noctem in columna ignis.*   Dacier.

247. *Seen from some Island.*] *Homer* makes choice of a town placed in an island, because such a place being besieged has no other means of making its distress known than by signals of fire; whereas a town upon the continent has other means to make known to its neighbours the necessity it is in.   *Dacier.*

259. *As the loud trumpet's,* &c.] I have already observ'd, that when the poet speaks as from himself, he may be allowed to take his comparisons from things which were not known before his time. Here he borrows a comparison from the *Trumpet*, as he has elsewhere done from *saddle-horses*, tho' neither one nor the other were used in *Greece* at the time of the *Trojan* war. *Virgil* was less exact in this respect, for he describes the trumpet as used in the sacking of *Troy*:

> *Exoritur clamorque virum clangorque tubarum.*

> [New clamours and new clangours now arise,
>   The sound of trumpets mixed with fighting-cries.]

And celebrates *Misenus* as the trumpeter of *Æneas.* But as *Virgil* wrote at a time more remote from those heroic ages, perhaps this liberty may be excused. But a Poet had better confine himself to customs and manners, like a painter; and it is equally a fault in either of them to ascribe to times and nations any thing with which they were unacquainted.

One may add an observation to this note of M. *Dacier*, that the trumpet's not being in use at that time, makes very much for *Homer*'s purpose in this place. The terrour raised by the voice of his hero, is much the more strongly imaged by a sound that was unusual, and capable of striking more from its very novelty.

315. *If but the morrow's sun,* &c.] *Polydamas* says in the original, 'If *Achilles* comes to morrow *in his armour.*' There seems to lie an objection against this passage, for *Polydamas* knew that *Achilles*'s armour was won by *Hector*, he must also know that no other man's

armour would fit him; how then could he know that new arms were
made for him that very night? Those who are resolved to defend
Homer, may answer, it was by his skill in prophecy; but to me this
seems to be a slip of our author's memory, and one of those little *nods*
which *Horace* speaks of.

333. *The Speech of* Hector.] *Hector* in this severe answer to *Polydamas*,
takes up several of his words and turns them another way.

Polydamas had said Πρῶϊ δ' ὑπηοῖοι σὺν τεύχεσι θωρηχθέντες
Στησόμεθ' ἄμ πύργους, 'To morrow by break of day let us put on our
arms, and defend the castles and city walls,' to which *Hector* replies,
Πρῶϊ δ' ὑπηοῖοι σὺν τεύχεσι θωρηχθέντες Νηυσὶν ἔπι γλαφυρῇσιν ἐγεί-
ρομεν ὀξὺν Ἄρηα, 'To morrow by break of day let us put on our arms,
not to defend our selves at home, but to fight the *Greeks* before their
own ships.'

Polydamas, speaking of *Achilles*, had said τῷ δ' ἄλγιον αἴ κ' ἐθέ-
λῃσιν, &c. 'if he comes after we are within the walls of our city, 'twill
be the worse for him, for he may drive round the city long enough
before he can hurt us.' To which, *Hector* answers; 'If *Achilles* should
come Ἄλγιον, αἴ κ' ἐθέλῃσι, τῷ ἔσσεται· οὔ μιν ἐγώ γε φεύξομαι ἐκ πολέ-
μοιο, &c. "Twill be the worse for him, as you say, because I'll fight
him: οὔ μιν ἐγώ γε φεύξομαι, says *Hector*, in reply to *Polydamas*'s
saying, ὅς κε φύγῃ. But *Hector* is not so far gone in passion or pride,
as to forget himself; and accordingly in the next lines he modestly puts
it in doubt, which of them shall conquer.   *Eustathius.*

340. *Sunk were her treasures, and her stores decay'd.*] As well by reason
of the convoys, which were necessarily to be sent for with ready
money; as by reason of the great allowances which were to be given to
the auxiliary troops, who came from *Phrygia* and *Mæonia.* *Hector's*
meaning is, that since all the riches of *Troy* are exhausted, it is no
longer necessary to spare themselves, or shut themselves up within
their walls.   *Dacier.*

349. *If there be one*, &c.] This noble and generous proposal is worthy
of *Hector*, and at the same time very artful to ingratiate himself with
the soldiers. *Eustathius* farther observes that it is said with an eye to
Polydamas, as accusing him of being rich, and of not opening the
advice he had given, for any other end than to preserve his great
wealth; for riches commonly make men cowards, and the desire of

saving them has often occasioned men to give advice very contrary to the publick welfare.

379. *In what vain promise.*] The lamentation of *Achilles* over the body of *Patroclus* is exquisitely touch'd: It is sorrow in the extreme, but the sorrow of *Achilles*. It is nobly usher'd in by that simile of the grief of the lion: An Idea which is fully answered in the savage and bloody conclusion of this speech. One would think by the beginning of it, that *Achilles* did not know his fate, till after his departure from *Opuntium*; and yet how does that agree with what is said of his choice of the short and active life, rather than the long and inglorious one? Or did not he flatter himself sometimes, that his fate might be changed? This may be conjectured from several other passages, and is indeed the most natural solution.

404. *Cleanse the pale corse,* &c.] This custom of washing the dead, is continued amongst the *Greeks* to this Day; and 'tis a pious duty performed by the dearest friend or relation, to see it washed and anointed with a perfume, after which they cover it with linen exactly in the manner here related.

417. Jupiter *and* Juno.] *Virgil* has copied the speech of *Juno* to *Jupiter. Ast ego quæ divum incedo regina* [But I, who walk in awful state above], &c. But it is exceeding remarkable, that *Homer* should upon every occasion make marriage and discord inseparable: 'Tis an unalterable rule with him, to introduce the husband and wife in a quarrel.

440. *Full twenty tripods.*] Tripods were vessels supported on three feet, with handles on the sides; they were of several kinds, and for several uses; some were consecrated to sacrifices, some used as tables, some as seats, others hung up as ornaments on walls of houses or temples; these of *Vulcan* have an addition of wheels, which was not usual, which intimates them to be made with clock-work. Mons. *Dacier* has commented very well on this passage. If *Vulcan* (says he) had made ordinary tripods, they had not answered the greatness, power, and skill of a God. It was therefore necessary that his work should be above that of men: To effect this, the tripods were animated, and in this *Homer* doth not deviate from the probability; for every one is fully persuaded, that a God can do things more difficult than these, and that all matter will obey him. What has not been said of the statues of *Dædalus*? *Plato* writes, that they walked alone, and if they had not taken care to tie them, they would have got loose, and run from their master. If a writer in prose can speak hyperbollically of a man, may not *Homer* do it much more of a God? Nay, this circumstance with which *Homer* has embellished his poem, would have had nothing too surprizing tho' these tripods had been made by a man; for what may not be done in clock-work by an exact management of springs? This criticism is then ill grounded, and *Homer* does not deserve the ridicule they would cast on him.

The same author applies to this passage of *Homer* that rule of *Aristotle*, *Poetic.* Chap. 26. which deserves to be alledged at large on this occasion.

'When a poet is accused of saying any thing that is impossible; we must examine that impossibility, either with respect to *poetry*, with respect to that which is *best*, or with respect to *common fame*. First, with regard to *poetry*, The *probable impossible* ought to be preferred to the *possible, which hath no verisimilitude*, and which would not be believed; and 'tis thus that *Zeuxis* painted his pieces. Secondly, with respect to that which is *best*, we see that a thing is more excellent and more wonderful this way, and that the originals ought always to surpass. Lastly, in respect to *fame*, It is prov'd that the poet need only follow common opinion. All that appears absurd may be also justified by one of these three ways; or else by the maxim we have already laid down, that it is probable, that a great many things may happen against probability.'

A late critick has taken notice of the conformity of this passage of *Homer* with that in the first chapter of *Ezekiel*, *The spirit of the living creatures was in the wheels; when those went, these went, and when those stood, these stood; and when those were lifted up, the wheels were lifted up over against them; for the spirit of the living creature was in the wheels.*

459. *A footstool at her feet.*] It is at this day the usual honour paid amongst the *Greeks*, to visiters of superior quality, to set them higher than the rest of the company, and put a footstool under their feet. See note on v. 179. Book 14. This, with innumerable other customs, are still preserved in the eastern nations.

460. Vulcan *draw near, 'tis* Thetis *asks your aid.*] The story the ancients tell of *Plato*'s application of this verse is worth observing. That great philosopher had in his youth a strong inclination to poetry, and not being satisfied to compose little pieces of gallantry and amour, he tried his forces in tragedy and epic poetry; but the success was not answerable to his hopes: He compared his performance with that of *Homer*, and was very sensible of the difference. He therefore abandoned a sort of writing wherein at best he could only be the second, and turn'd his views to an other, wherein he despaired not to become the first. His anger transported him so far, as to cast all his verses into the fire. But while he was burning them, he could not help citing a verse of the very poet who had caused his chagrin. It was the present line, which *Homer* has put into the mouth of *Charis*, when *Thetis* demands arms for *Achilles*.

Ἥφαιστε πρόμολ' ὧδε, Θέτις νύ τι σεῖο χατίζει.

Plato only inserted his own name instead of that of *Thetis*.

Vulcan *draw near*, '*tis* Plato *asks your aid*.

If we credit the ancients, it was the discontentment his own poetry gave him, that raised in him all the Indignation he afterwards expressed against the art itself. In which (say they) he behaved like those lovers, who speak ill of the beauties whom they cannot prevail upon.

Fraguier, Parall. de Hom. & de Platon.

461. Thetis *(reply'd the God) our pow'rs may claim*, &c.] *Vulcan* throws by his work to perform *Thetis*'s request, who had laid former obligations upon him; the Poet in this example giving us an excellent precept, that gratitude should take place of all other concerns.

The motives which should engage a God in a new work in the night-time upon a suit of armour for a mortal, ought to be strong; and therefore artfully enough put upon the foot of gratitude: Besides, they afford at the same time a noble occasion for *Homer* to retail his theology, which he is always very fond of.

The allegory of *Vulcan*, or fire (according to *Heraclides*) is this. His Father is *Jupiter*, or the *Æther*, his mother *Juno*, or the *Air*, from whence he fell to us, whether by lightning, or otherwise. He is said to be lame, that is, to want Support, because he cannot subsist without the continual subsistance of fuel. The ætherial fire, *Homer* calls *Sol* or *Jupiter*, the inferior *Vulcan*; the one wants nothing of perfection, the other is subject to decay, and is restored by accession of materials. *Vulcan* is said to fall from heaven, because at first, when the opportunity of obtaining fire was not so frequent, men prepared instruments of brass, by which they collected the beams of the sun; or else they gained it from accidental lightning, that set fire to some combustible matter. *Vulcan* had perished when he fell from heaven unless *Thetis* and *Eurynome* had received him; that is, unless he had been preserved by falling into some convenient receptacle, or subterranean place; and so was afterwards distributed for the common necessities of mankind. To understand these strange explications, it must be known, that *Thetis* is derived from τίθημι to *lay up*, and *Eurynome* from εὐρύς and νομή, a *wide distribution*. They are called daughters of the ocean, because the vapours and exhalations of the sea forming themselves into clouds, find nourishment for lightnings.

488. *Two female forms,*
    That mov'd and breath'd in animated gold.]

It is very probable, that *Homer* took the idea of these from the statues of *Dædalus*, which might be extant in his time. The ancients tell us, they were made to imitate life, in rolling their eyes, and in all other motions. From whence indeed it should seem, that the excellency of *Dædalus* consisted in what we call clock-work, or the management of moving figures by springs, rather than in sculpture or imagery: And accordingly, the fable of his fitting wings to himself and his son, is formed entirely upon the foundation of the former.

517. *Robb'd of the Prize*, &c.] *Thetis* to compass her design, recounts every thing to the advantage of her son; she therefore suppresses the episode of the embassy, the prayers that had been made use of to move him, and all that the *Greeks* had suffered after the return of the ambassadors; and artfully puts together two very distant things, as if they had followed each other in the same moment. He declined, says she, to succour the *Greeks*, but he sent *Patroclus*. Now between his refusing to help the *Greeks*, and his sending *Patroclus*, terrible things had fallen out; but she suppresses them, for fear of offending *Vulcan* with the recital of *Achilles*'s inflexible obduracy, and thereby create in that God an aversion to her son.   *Eustathius.*

525. *Then slain by* Phœbus (Hector *had the name*)] It is a passage worth taking notice of, that *Brutus* is said to have consulted the *Sortes Homericæ*, and to have drawn one of these lines, wherein the death of *Patroclus* is ascribed to *Apollo*: After which, unthinkingly, he gave the name of that God for the word of battel. This is remarked as an unfortunate omen by some of the ancients, tho' I forget where I met with it.

537. *The father of the fires,* &c.] The ancients (says *Eustathius*) have largely celebrated the philosophical mysteries which they imagined to be shadowed under these descriptions, especially *Damo* (supposed the Daughter of *Pythagoras*) whose explication is as follows. *Thetis,* who receives the arms, means the apt order and disposition of all things in the creation. By the fire and the wind raised by the bellows, are meant *air* and *fire* the most active of all the elements. The emanations of the fire are those *golden maids* that waited on *Vulcan.* The circular shield is the *World,* being of a sphærical figure. The Gold, the brass, the silver, and the tin are the *elements*: Gold is fire, the firm brass is earth, the silver is air, and the soft tin, water. And thus far (say they) *Homer* speaks a little obscurely, but afterwards he names them expressly, ἐν μὲν γαῖαν ἔτευξ', ἐν δ' οὐρανόν, ἐν δὲ θάλασσαν, to which, for the fourth element, you must add *Vulcan,* who makes the shield. The extreme circle that runs round the shield which he calls *splendid* and *threefold,* is the Zodiack; threefold in its breadth, within which all the planets move; splendid, because the sun passes always thro' the midst of it. The silver handle by which the shield is fastened at both extremities, is the *Axis* of the world, imagined to pass thro it, and upon which it turns. The five folds are those parallel circles that divide the world, the *Polar,* the *Tropicks,* and the *Æquator.*

Heraclides Ponticus thus pursues the allegory. *Homer* (says he) makes the working of his shield, that is the world, to be begun by *night*; as indeed all matter lay undistinguished in an original and universal *night*; which is called *Chaos* by the poets.

To bring the matter of the shield to separation and form, *Vulcan* presides over the work, or as we may say, an *essential warmth: All things,* says *Heraclitus, being made by the operation of fire.*

And because the *architect* is at this time to give a form and ornament to the world he is making, it is not rashly that he is said to be married to one of the graces.

> *On the broad shield the* maker's *hand engraves*
> *The earth and seas beneath, the pole above,*
> *The sun unwearied, and the circled moon.*

Thus in the beginning of the world, he first lays the earth as the foundation of a building, whose vacancies are fill'd up with the flowings of the sea. Then he spreads out the sky for a kind of divine roof over it, and lights the elements, now separated from their former confusion, with the *Sun*, the *Moon*,

> *And all those stars that crown the skies with fire:*

Where, by the word *crown*, which gives the idea of roundness, he again hints at the figure of the world; and tho' he cou'd not particularly name the Stars like *Aratus* (who professed to write upon them) yet he has not omitted to mention the principal. From hence he passes to represent two *allegorical* cities, one of *peace*, the other of *war*; *Empedocles* seems to have taken from *Homer* his assertion, that all things had their original from *strife* and *friendship*.

All these refinements (not to call 'em absolute whimsies) I leave just as I found 'em, to the Reader's Judgment or Mercy. They call it *Learning* to have read 'em, but I fear it is *Folly* to quote 'em.

566. *Nor bends his blazing forehead to the main.*] The criticks make use of this passage, to prove that *Homer* was ignorant of Astronomy; since he believed, that the *Bear* was the only constellation which never bathed itself in the ocean, that is to say that did not set, and was always visible; for say they, this is common to other constellations of the artick circle, as the lesser Bear, the Dragon, the greatest part of *Cepheus*, &c. To salve *Homer*, *Aristotle* answers, That he calls it the only one, to shew that 'tis the only one of those constellations he had spoken of, or that he has put the *only*, for the *principal* or the *most known*. *Strabo* justifies this after another manner, in the beginning of his first book, 'Under the Name of the *Bear* and the *Chariot*, *Homer* comprehends all the artick circle; for there being several other stars in that circle which never set, he could not say, that the Bear was the only one which did not bath itself in the ocean; wherefore those are deceived, who accuse the poet of ignorance, as if he knew one Bear only when there are two; for the lesser was not distinguished in his time. The *Phœnicians* were the first who observed it and made use of it in their navigation; and the figure of that sign passed from them to the *Greeks*: The same thing happened in regard to the constellation of *Berenice*'s hair, and that of *Canopus*, which received those names very lately; and as *Aratus* says well, there are several other stars which have no names. *Crates* was then in the wrong to endeavour to correct this passage, in putting οἶος for οἴη, for he tries to avoid that which there is no occasion to avoid. *Heraclitus* did better, who put the Bear for the artick circle as *Homer* has done. *The Bear* (says he) *is the limit of the rising and setting of the stars.* Now it is the *Artic Circle*, and not the *Bear* which is that limit. 'Tis therefore evident, that by the word *Bear*, which he calls the *Wagon*, and which he says observes *Orion*, he understands the artick circle; that by the ocean he means the horizon where the stars rise and set; and by those words, *which turns in the same place, and doth not bath itself in the ocean*, he shews that the artick circle is the most northern part of the horizon, &c.'

Dacier on *Arist.*

Mons. *Terasson* combates this passage with great warmth. But it will be a sufficient vindication of our author to say, that some other constellations, which are likewise perpetually above the horizon in the latitude where *Homer* writ, were not at that time discovered; and that whether *Homer* knew that the Bear's not setting was occasioned by the latitude, and that in a smaller latitude it would set, is of no consequence; for if he had known it, it was still more poetical not to take notice of it.

567. *Two cities*, &c.] In one of these cities are represented all the advantages of *peace*: And it was impossible to have chosen two better emblems of peace, than *Marriages* and *Justice.* 'Tis said this city was *Athens*, for marriages were first instituted there by *Cecrops*; and Judgment upon murder was first founded there. The ancient state of *Attica* seems represented in the neighbouring fields, where the ploughers and reapers are at work, and a king is overlooking them; for *Triptolemus* who reigned there, was the first who sowed corn: This was the imagination of *Agallias Cercyreus*, as we find him cited by *Eustathius.*

579. *The fine discharg'd.*] Murder was not always punished with death, or so much as banishment; but when some fine was paid, the criminal was suffered to remain in the city. So *Iliad* 9.

> – Καὶ μέν τίς τε κασιγνήτοιο φόνοιο
> Ποινὴν, ἢ οὗ παιδὸς ἐδέξατο τεθνηῶτος.
> Καὶ ῥ' ὁ μὲν ἐν δήμῳ μένει αὐτοῦ πόλλ' ἀποτίσας.

> – *If a brother bleed,*
> *On just atonement, we remit the deed;*
> *A sire the slaughter of his son forgives,*
> *The price of blood discharg'd, the murd'rer lives.*

590. *The prize of him who best adjudg'd the right.*] *Eustathius* informs us, that it was anciently the custom to have a reward given to that judge who pronounced the best sentence. M. *Dacier* opposes this authority, and will have it, that this reward was given to the person who upon the decision of the suit appeared to have the justest cause. The difference between these two customs, in the reason of the thing, is very great: For the one must have been an encouragement to justice, the other a provocation to dissension. It were to be wanting in a due reverence to the wisdom of the ancients, and of *Homer* in particular, not to chuse the former sense: And I have the honour to be confirmed in this opinion, by the ablest judge, as well as the best practiser, of equity, my Lord *Harcourt*, at whose seat I translated this Book.

591. *Another part (a prospect diff'rent far)* &c.] The same *Agallias*, cited above, would have this city in war to be meant of *Eleusina*, but upon very slight reasons. What is wonderful is, that all the accidents and events of *war* are set before our eyes in this short compass. The several scenes are excellently disposed to represent the whole affair. Here is in the space of thirty lines a siege, a sally, an ambush, the surprize of a convoy, and a battel; with scarce a single circumstance proper to any of these, omitted.

619. There *tumult*, &c.] This is the first place in the whole description of the buckler, where *Homer* rises in his style, and uses the allegorical ornaments of Poetry; so natural was it for his imagination, (now heated with the fighting scenes of the *Iliad*) to take fire, when the image of a battel was presented to it.

627. *A field deep-furrow'd,* &c.] Here begin the descriptions of rural life, in which *Homer* appears as great a master as in the great and terrible parts of poetry. One would think, he did this on purpose to rival his contemporary *Hesiod*, on those very subjects to which his genius was particularly bent. Upon this occasion, I must take notice of that *Greek* poem, which is commonly ascribed to *Hesiod* under the Title of Ἀσπὶς Ἡρακλέος [*The Shield of Hercules*]. Some of the ancients mention such a work as *Hesiod*'s, but that amounts to no proof that this is the same: Which indeed is not an express poem upon the shield of *Hercules*, but a fragment of the story of that hero. What regards the shield is a manifest copy from this of *Achilles*; and consequently it is not of *Hesiod*. For if he was not more ancient, he was at least contemporary with *Homer*: And neither of them could be supposed to borrow so shamelessly from the other, not only the plan of entire descriptions, (as those of the marriage, the harvest, the vineyard, the ocean round the margin, &c.) but also whole verses together: Those of the *Parca*, in the battel, are repeated word for word,

$$- \dot{\epsilon}\nu \; \delta' \; \dot{o}\lambda o \dot{\eta} \; K \dot{\eta} \rho,$$
$$\H{A}\lambda\lambda o\nu \; \zeta\omega\grave{o}\nu \; \H{\epsilon}\chi o\upsilon\sigma\alpha \; \nu\epsilon o\acute{\upsilon}\tau\alpha\tau o\nu, \; \H{a}\lambda\lambda o\nu \; \H{a}o\upsilon\tau o\nu$$
$$\H{A}\lambda\lambda o\nu \; \tau\epsilon\theta\nu\epsilon\eta\H{\omega}\tau\alpha \; \kappa\alpha\tau\grave{\alpha} \; \mu\acute{o}\theta o\nu \; \H{\epsilon}\lambda\kappa\epsilon \; \pi o\delta o\hat{\iota}\nu$$
$$E\hat{\iota}\mu\alpha \; \delta' \; \H{\epsilon}\chi' \; \H{a}\mu\phi' \; \H{\omega}\mu o\iota\sigma\iota \; \delta\alpha\phi o\iota\nu\epsilon\grave{o}\nu \; \alpha\H{\iota}\mu\alpha\tau\iota \; \phi\omega\tau\hat{\omega}\nu.$$

[And on the shield was deadly Fate holding one man just wounded, another unharmed, and another – who was dead – she dragged by his feet through the press of battle. On her shoulders she wore a garment red with men's blood.]

And indeed half the poem is but a sort of *Cento* composed out of *Homer*'s verses. The reader need only cast an eye on these two descriptions, to see the vast difference of the original and the copy; and I dare say he will readily agree with the sentiment of Monsieur *Dacier*, in applying to them that famous verse of *Sannazarius*,

Illum hominem dices, hunc posuisse Deum.

[You will say that a man composed that, but a god
composed this.]

id.] I ought not to forget the many apparent allusions to the descriptions on this shield, which are to be found in those pictures of peace and war, the city and country, in the eleventh book of *Milton*: Who was doubtless fond of any occasion to shew, how much he was charmed with the beauty of all these lively images. He makes his angel paint those objects which he shews to *Adam*, in the colours, and almost the very strokes of *Homer*. Such is that passage of the harvest field,

His eye he open'd, and beheld a field
Part arable and tilth, whereon were sheaves
New-reap'd; the other part sheep-walks and folds.
In midst an altar, as the landmark, stood,
Rustic, of grassy ford, &c.

That of the marriages,

They light the nuptial torch, and bid invoke

> Hymen *(then first to marriage rites invok'd)*
> *With feast and musick all the tents resound.*

But more particularly, the following lines are in a manner a translation of our author.

> *One way, a band select from forage drives*
> *A herd of beeves, fair oxen, and fair kine*
> *From a fat Meadow ground; or fleecy flock,*
> *Ewes and their bleating lambs, across the plain,*
> *Their booty: Scarce with life the shepherds fly,*
> *But call in aid, which makes a bloody fray,*
> *With cruel tournament the squadrons join*
> *Where cattel pastur'd late, now scatter'd lies*
> *With carcasses and arms th'ensanguin'd Field*
> *Deserted. – Others to a city strong*
> *Lay siege, encamp'd; by battery, scale, and mine*
> *Assaulting; others from the wall defend*
> *With dart and jav'lin, stones, and sulph'rous fire:*
> *On each hand slaughter and gigantic deeds.*
> *   In other part, the scepter'd heralds call*
> *To council in the city gates: anon*
> *Grey-headed men and grave, with warriours mixt,*
> *Assemble, and harangues are heard –*

645. *The rustic monarch of the field.*] *Dacier* takes this to be a piece of ground given to a hero in reward of his services. It was in no respect unworthy such a person, in those days, to see his harvest got in, and to overlook his reapers: It is very conformable to the manners of the ancient patriarchs, such as they are describ'd to us in the holy scriptures.

662. *The fate of* Linus.] There are two interpretations of this verse in the original: That which I have chosen is confirmed by the testimony of *Herodotus* lib. 2. and *Pausanias, Bœoticis. Linus* was the most ancient name in Poetry, the first upon record who invented verse and measure among the *Grecians*: He past for the son of *Apollo* or *Mercury*, and was præceptor to *Hercules, Thamyris,* and *Orpheus.* There was a solemn custom among the *Greeks* of bewailing annually the death of their first poet: *Pausanias* informs us, that before the yearly sacrifice to the muses on mount *Helicon*, the obsequies of *Linus* were performed, who had a statue and altar erected to him, in that place. *Homer* alludes to that custom in this passage, and was doubtless fond of paying this respect to the old father of poetry. *Virgil* has done the same in that fine celebration of him, *Eclog.* 6.

> *Tum canit errantem Permessi ad flumina Gallum,*
> *Utque viro Phœbi chorus assurrexerit omnis;*
> *Ut* Linus *hæc illi, divino carmine, pastor*
> *(Floribus atque apio crines ornatus amaro)*
> *Dixerit* – &c.

> [Then sang, how *Gallus* by a Muse's hand,
> Was led and welcom'd to the sacred strand:
> The senate rising to salute their guest;
> And *Linus* thus their gratitude express'd.]

And again in the fourth *Eclogue.*

> *Non me carminibus vincet nec* Thracius Orpheus,
> *Nec* Linus*; huic mater, quamvis atque huic pater adsit,*
> Orpheo Calliopea, Lino *formosus* Apollo.

> [Not *Thracian Orpheus* should transcend my layes,
> Nor *Linus* crown'd with never-fading bayes:
> Though each his heav'nly parent shou'd inspire;
> The muse instruct the voice, and *Phœbus* tune the lyre.]

681. *A figur'd dance.*] There were two sorts of dances, the Pyrrhick, and the common dance: *Homer* has joined both in this description. We see the Pyrrhick, or military, is performed by the youths who have swords on, the other by the virgins crowned with garlands.

Here the ancient scholiasts say, that whereas before it was the custom for men and women to dance separately, the contrary practice was afterwards brought in, by seven youths, and as many virgins, who were saved by *Theseus* from the labyrinth; and that this dance was taught them by *Dædalus*: To which *Homer* here alludes. See *Dion. Halic. Hist.* l. 7. c. 68.

It is worth observing that the *Grecian* dance is still performed in this manner in the *Oriental* nations: The youths and maids dance in a ring, beginning slowly; by degrees the musick plays a quicker time, till at last they dance with the utmost swiftness: And towards the conclusion, they sing (as it is said here) in a general chorus.

702. *And pour'd the ocean round.*] *Vulcan* was the God of fire, and passes over this part of the description negligently; for which reason *Virgil* (to take a different walk) makes half his description of *Æneas*'s buckler consist in a sea fight. For the same reason he has laboured the sea-piece among his *games*, more than any other, because *Homer* had described nothing of this kind at the funeral of *Patroclus*.

OBSERVATIONS

ON THE

SHIELD OF *ACHILLES*

The Poet intending to shew in its full lustre, his Genius for description, makes choice of this interval from action and the leisure of the night, to display that talent at large in the famous buckler of *Achilles.* His intention was no less, than to draw the picture of the whole world in the compass of this shield. We see first the universe in general; the heavens are spread, the stars are hung up, the earth is stretched forth, the seas are poured round: We next see the world in a nearer and more particular view; the cities, delightful in peace, or formidable in war; the labours of the country, and the fruit of those labours, in the harvests and the vintages; the pastoral life in its pleasures and its dangers: In a word, all the occupations, all the ambitions, and all the diversions of mankind. This noble and comprehensive design he has executed in a manner that challenged the admiration of all the ancients: And how right an idea they had of this grand design, may be judged from that verse of *Ovid, Met.* 13. where he calls it

> *Clypeus* vasti *cœlatus imagine* mundi.

> ['The shield, carved with an image of the vast universe.']

It is indeed astonishing how after this the arrogance of some moderns could unfortunately chuse the noblest part of the noblest poet for the object of their blind censures. Their criticisms, however just enough upon other parts, yet, when employed on this buckler, are to the utmost weak and impotent.

> – *postquam arma Dei ad Vulcania ventum est*
> *Mortalis mucro glacies seu futiles, icta*
> *Dissiluit –*

[But vain against the great Vulcanian shield,
The mortal-temper'd steel deceiv'd his hand:
The shiver'd fragments shone amid the sand.]

I design to give the reader the sum of what has been said on this subject. First, a reply to the loose and scattered objections of the criticks, by M. *Dacier*: Then the regular plan and distribution of the shield, by Mons. *Boivin*: And lastly, I shall attempt what has not yet been done, to consider it as a work of *Painting*, and prove it in all respects conformable to the most just ideas and established rules of that art.

I

It is the fate (says M. *Dacier*) of these arms of *Achilles*, to be still the occasion of quarrels and disputes. *Julius Scaliger* was the first who appeared against this part, and was followed by a whole herd. These object in the first place, that 'tis impossible to represent the movement of the figures; and in condemning the manner, they take the liberty to condemn also the subject, which they say is trivial, and not well understood. 'Tis certain that *Homer* speaks of the figures on this buckler, as if they were alive: And some of the ancients taking his expressions to the strictness of the letter, did really believe that they had all sorts of motion. *Eustathius* shewed the absurdity of that sentiment by a passage of *Homer* himself; 'That poet, says he, to shew that his figures are not animated, as some have pretended by an excessive affection for the prodigious, took care to say that they *moved and fought*, as if *they were living men.*' The ancients certainly founded this ridiculous opinion on a rule of *Aristotle*: For they thought the poet could not make his description more *admirable* and *marvellous*, than in making his figures animated, since (as *Aristotle* says) the *original should always excel the copy*. That shield is the work of a God: 'Tis the original, of which the engraving and painting of men is but an imperfect copy; and there is nothing impossible to the Gods. But they did not perceive, that by this *Homer* would have fallen into an extravagant admirable which would not have been probable. Therefore, 'tis without any necessity *Eustathius* adds, 'That 'tis possible all those figures did not stick close to the shield, but that they were detached from it, and moved by springs, in such a manner that they appeared to have motion; as *Æschylus* has feigned something like it, in his *seven*

Captains against Thebes.' But without having recourse to that conjecture, we can shew that there is nothing more simple and natural than the description of that shield, and there is not one word which *Homer* might not have said of it, if it had been the work of a man; for there is a great deal of difference between the work itself, and the description of it.

Let us examine the particulars for which they blame *Homer*. They say he describes two towns on his shield which *speak different languages.* 'Tis the *Latin* translation, and not *Homer*, that says so; the word μερό-πων [of mortals], is a common epithet of men, and which signifies only, that they have *an articulate voice.* These towns could not speak different languages, since, as the ancients have remarked, they were *Athens* and *Eleusina*, both which spake the same language. But tho' that epithet should signify, *which spake different languages*, there would be nothing very surprizing; for *Virgil* said what *Homer* it seems must not:

> *Victæ longo ordine gentes,*
> *Quam variæ linguis. –*

[Vast crowds of vanquish'd nations march along:
Various in arms, in habit, and in tongue.]   *Aen.* 8.

If a painter should put into a picture one town of *France* and another of *Flanders*, might not one say they were two towns which spake different languages?

Homer (they tell us) says in another place, that *we hear the harangues of two pleaders.* This is an unfair exaggeration: He only says, *two men pleaded*, that is, were represented pleading. Was not the same said by *Pliny* of *Nicomachus*, that he had painted two *Greeks*, which spake one after another? Can we express ourselves otherwise of these two arts, which tho' they are mute, yet have a language? Or in explaining a painting of *Raphael* or *Poussin*, can we prevent animating the figures, in making them speak conformably to the design of the painter? But how could the engraver represent those young shepherds and virgins that dance first in a ring, and then in setts? Or those troops which were in ambuscade? This would be difficult indeed if the workman had not the liberty to make his persons appear in different circumstances. All the objections against the young man who sings at the same time that he plays on the harp, the bull that roars whilst he is devoured by a lion, and against the musical consorts, are childish; for we can never speak of painting if we banish those expressions. *Pliny* says of *Apelles*, that he painted *Clytus* on horseback going to battel, and demanding his helmet of his squire: Of *Aristides*, that he drew a beggar whom he could almost understand, *pene cum voce* [almost with a voice]: Of *Ctesilochus*, that he had painted *Jupiter* bringing forth *Bacchus*, and crying out like a woman, *& muliebriter ingemiscentem* [groaning like a woman]: And of *Nicearchus*, that he had drawn a piece, in which *Hercules* was seen very melancholy on reflection of his madness, *Herculem tristem, insaniae pœnitentia* [a woeful Hercules, repenting his madness]. No one sure will condemn those ways of expression which are so common. The same author has said much more of *Apelles*; he tells us, he painted those things which could not be painted, as thunder; *pinxit quæ pingi non possunt*: And of *Timanthus*, that in all his Works there was something more understood than was seen; and tho' there was all the art imaginable, yet there was still more ingenuity than art: *Atque in omnibus ejus operibus, intelligitur plus semper quam pingitur; & cum ars summa sit, ingenium tamen ultra artem est.* If we take the pains to compare these expressions with those of *Homer*, we shall find him altogether excusable in his *manner* of describing the buckler.

We come now to the *matter*. If this shield (says a modern critick) had been made in a wiser age, it would have been more correct and less charged with objects. There are two things which cause the censurers to fall into this false criticism: The first is, that they think the shield was no broader than the brims of a hat, whereas it was large enough to cover a whole man. The other is, that they did not know the design of the poet, and imagined this description was only the whimsy of an irregular wit, who did it by chance, and not following nature; for they never so much as entered into the intention of the poet, nor knew the shield was designed as a representation of the universe.

'Tis happy that *Virgil* has made a buckler for *Æneas*, as well as *Homer* for *Achilles.* The *Latin* poet, who imitated the *Greek* one, always took care to accommodate those things which time had changed, so as to render them agreeable to the palate of his readers; yet he hath not only charged his shield with a great deal more work, since he paints all the actions of the *Romans* from *Ascanius* to *Augustus*; but has not avoided any of those manners of expression which offend the criticks. We see there the wolf of *Romulus* and *Remus*, who gives them her dugs *one after another, Mulcere alternos, & corpora fingere lingua* [She licked their tender limbs, and formed them as she fed. (Dryden)]: The rape of the *Sabines* and the war which followed it, *subitoque novum consurgere bellum* [And then suddenly a new war broke out.]: *Metius* torn by four Horses, and *Tullus* who draws his entrails thro' the Forest: *Porsenna* commanding the *Romans* to receive *Tarquin*, and besieging *Rome*: The geese flying to the porches of the capitol, and giving notice by their *cries* of the attack of the *Gauls*.

> *Atque, hic auratis volitans argenteus anser,*
> *Porticibus, Gallos in limine adesse* canebat.

> [The silver goose before the shining gate
> There flew; and by her cackle, sav'd the state.
> She told the *Gauls* approach.]

We see the *Salian* dance, hell, and the pains of the damn'd; and farther off, the place of the blessed, where *Cato* presides: We see the famous battel of *Actium*, where we may distinguish the captains: *Agrippa* with the Gods, and the winds favourable; and *Anthony* leading on all the forces of the *East*, *Egypt*, and the *Bactrians*: The fight begins, The sea is red with blood, *Cleopatra* gives the signal for a retreat, and calls her troops with a *systrum*. *Patrio vocat agmina systro.* The Gods, or rather the monsters of *Egypt*, fight against *Neptune*, *Venus*, *Minerva*, *Mars* and *Apollo*: We see *Anthony's* fleet beaten, and the *Nile* sorrowfully opening his bosom to receive the conquered: *Cleopatra* looks pale and almost dead at the thought of that death she had already determined; nay we see the very wind *Iapis*, which hastens her flight: We see the three triumphs of *Augustus*; that Prince consecrates three hundred temples, the Altars are filled with ladies offering up sacrifices, *Augustus* sitting at the entrance of *Apollo's* temple, receives presents, and hangs them on the pillars of the temple; while all the conquered Nations pass by, who *speak different languages*, and are differently equipped and armed.

> – *Incedunt victæ longo ordine gentes,*
> *Quam variæ linguis, habitu tum vestis & armis.*

> [Vast crowds of vanquish'd nations march along:
> Various in arms, in habit, and in tongue.]

Nothing can better justify *Homer*, or shew the wisdom and judgment of *Virgil*: He was charmed with *Achilles's* shield, and therefore would give the same ornament to his poem. But as *Homer* had painted the universe, he was sensible that nothing remained for him to do; he had no other way to take than that of prophecy, and shew what the descendant of his hero should perform; and he was not afraid to go

beyond *Homer*, because there is nothing improbable in the hands of a
God. If the criticks say, that this is justifying one fault by another; I
desire they would agree among themselves; for *Scaliger*, who was the
first that condemned *Homer*'s shield, admires *Virgil*'s; but suppose they
should agree, 'twould be foolish to endeavour to persuade us, that what
Homer and *Virgil* have done by the approbation of all ages, is not good;
and to make us think that their particular taste should prevail over that
of all other men. Nothing is more ridiculous than to trouble one's self
to answer men, who shew so little reason in their criticisms, that we
can do them no greater favour, than to ascribe it to their ignorance.

Thus far the objections are answered by Mons. *Dacier*. Since when,
some others have been started, as that the objects represented on the
buckler have no reference to the poem, no Agreement with *Thetis* who
procured it, *Vulcan* who made it, or *Achilles* for whom it was made.

To this it is replied, that the representation of the sea was agreeable
enough to *Thetis*; that the spheres and celestial fires were so to *Vulcan*;
(tho' the truth is, any piece of workmanship was equally fit to come
from the hands of this God) and that the images of a town besieged, a
battel, and an ambuscade, were objects sufficiently proper for *Achilles*.
But after all, where was the necessity that they should be so? They had
at least been as fit for one hero as for another; and *Æneas*, as *Virgil* tells
us, knew not what to make of the figures on his shield.

Rerumque Ignarus, imagine gaudet.

[Unknown the names, he yet admires the grace.]

I I

But still the main objection, and that in which the vanity of the
moderns has triumphed the most, is, that the shield is crowded with
such a multiplicity of figures, as could not possibly be represented in
the compass of it. The late dissertation of Mons. *Boivin* has put an end
to this cavil, and the reader will have the pleasure to be convinced of it
by ocular demonstration, in the print annexed.

This author supposes the buckler to have been perfectly round: He
divides the convex surface into four concentrick circles.

The circle next the center contains the globe of the earth and the
sea, in miniature; he gives this circle the dimension of three inches.

The second circle is allotted for the heavens and the stars: He allows
the space of ten inches between this, and the former circle.

The third shall be eight inches distant from the second. The space between these two circles shall be divided into twelve compartiments, each of which makes a picture of ten or eleven inches deep.

The fourth circle makes the margin of the buckler: And the interval between this and the former, being of three inches, is sufficient to represent the waves and currents of the ocean.

All these together make but four foot in the whole in diameter. The print of these circles and divisions will serve to prove, that the figures will neither be crowded nor confused, if disposed in the proper place and order.

As to the size and figure of the shield, it is evident from the poets, that in the time of the *Trojan* war there were shields of an extraordinary magnitude. The buckler of *Ajax* is often compared by *Homer* to a tower, and in the sixth Iliad that of *Hector* is described to cover him from the shoulders to the ankles.

> Ἀμφὶ δὲ οἱ σφυρὰ τύπτε καὶ αὐχένα δέρμα κελαινὸν
> Ἄντυξ ἣ πυμάτη θέεν ἀσπίδος ὀμφαλοέσσης.   v. 117.

[The shield's large orb behind his shoulder cast,
His neck o'ershading, to his ancle hung;
And as he march'd, the brazen buckler rung.
(Pope's trans., 143–5)]

In the second verse of the description of this buckler of *Achilles*, it is said that *Vulcan* cast round it a radiant circle.

> Περὶ δ' ἄντυγα βάλλε φαεινήν.   v. 479.

[He cast a shining rim around it.]

Which proves the figure to have been round. But if it be alledged that ἄντυξ [rim] as well signifies *oval* as *circular*, it may be answered, that the circular figure better agrees to the spheres represented in the center, and to the course of the ocean at the circumference.

We may very well allow four foot diameter to this buckler: As one may suppose a larger size would have been too unwieldy, so a less would not have been sufficient to cover the breast and arm of a man of a stature so large as *Achilles.*

In allowing four foot diameter to the whole, each of the twelve compartiments may be of ten or eleven inches in depth, which will be enough to contain, without any confusion, all the objects which *Homer* mentions. Indeed in this print, each compartiment being but of one inch, the principal figures only are represented; but the reader may easily imagine the advantage of nine or ten inches more. However, if the criticks are not yet satisfied there is room enough, it is but taking in the literal sense the words πάντοσε δαιδάλλων [decorating it on every side], with which *Homer* begins his description, and the buckler may be supposed engraven on both sides, which supposition will double the size of each piece: The one side may serve for the general description of heaven and earth, and the other for all the particulars.

III

It having been now shewn, that the shield of *Homer* is blameless as to its design and disposition, and that the subject (so extensive as it is) may be contracted within the due limits; not being one vast unproportioned heap of figures, but divided into twelve regular compartments: What remains, is to consider this piece as a complete *idea* of *painting*, and a sketch for what one may call an *universal picture.* This is certainly the light in which it is chiefly to be admired, and in which alone the criticks have neglected to place it.

There is reason to believe that *Homer* did in this, as he has done in other arts, (even in mechanicks) that is, comprehend whatever was known of it in his time; if not (as is highly probable) from thence extend his ideas yet farther, and give a more enlarged notion of it. Accordingly it is very observable, that there is scarce a species or branch of this art which is not here to be found, whether history, battel painting, landskip, architecture, fruits, flowers, animals, &c.

I think it possible that painting was arrived to a greater degree of perfection, even at that early period, than is generally supposed by those who have written upon it. *Pliny* expressly says, that it was not known in the time of the *Trojan* war. The same author, and others, represent it in a very imperfect state in *Greece*, in, or near the days of *Homer.* They tell us of one painter, that he was the first who begun to shadow; and of another, that he filled his outlines only with a single colour, and that laid on every where alike: But we may have a higher notion of the art, from those descriptions of statues, carvings, tapestries, sculptures upon armour, and ornaments of all kinds, which every where occur in our author; as well as from what he says of their beauty, the relievo, and their emulation of life itself. If we consider how much it is his constant practice to confine himself to the custom of the times whereof he writ, it will be hard to doubt but that painting and sculpture must have been then in great practice and repute.

The shield is not only described as a piece of sculpture but of painting; the outlines may be supposed engraved, and the rest enameled, or inlaid with various-coloured metals. The variety of colours is plainly distinguished by *Homer*, where he speaks of the *blackness* of the new-open'd earth, of the *several colours* of the grapes and vines; and in other places. The different metals that *Vulcan* is feigned to cast into the furnace, were sufficient to afford all the necessary colours: But if to those which are natural to the metals, we add also those which they are capable of receiving from the operation of fire, we shall find, that *Vulcan* had as great a variety of colours to make use of as any modern painter. That enamelling, or fixing colours by fire, was practised very anciently, may be conjectured from what *Diodorus* reports of one of the walls of *Babylon*, built by *Semiramis*, that *the bricks of it were painted before they were burned, so as to represent all sorts of animals.* lib. 2. chap. 4. Now it is but natural to infer, that men had made use of ordinary colours for the representation of objects, before they learnt to represent them by such as are given by the operation of Fire; one being much more easy and obvious than the other, and that sort of painting by means of fire being but an imitation of the painting with a pencil and colours. The same inference will be farther enforced from the works of tapestry, which the women of those times interweaved with many colours; as appears from the description of that veil which *Hecuba* offers to *Minerva* in the sixth Iliad, and from a passage in the twenty second where *Andromache* is represented working flowers in a piece of this kind. They must certainly have known the use of the colours themselves for painting, before they could think of dying threads with those colours, and weaving those threads close to one another, in order only to a more laborious imitation of a thing so much more easily performed by a pencil. This observation I owe to the *Abbé Fraguier*.

It may indeed be thought, that a Genius so vast and comprehensive as that of *Homer*, might carry his views beyond the rest of mankind, and that in this buckler of *Achilles* he rather designed to give a scheme of what might be performed, than a description of what really was so: And since he made a God the artist, he might excuse himself from a strict confinement to what was known and practised in the time of the *Trojan* war. Let this be as it will, it is certain that he had, whether by learning, or by strength of genius, (tho' the latter be more glorious for *Homer*) a full and exact idea of painting in all its parts; that is to say, in the *invention*, the *composition*, the *expression*, &c.

The *invention* is shewn in finding and introducing, in every subject, the *greatest*, the most *significant*, and most *suitable* objects. Accordingly in every single picture of the shield, *Homer* constantly finds out either those objects which are naturally the principal, those which most conduce to shew the subject, or those which set it in the liveliest and most agreeable light: These he never fails to dispose in the most advantagious manners, situations, and oppositions.

Next, we find all his figures differently *characterized*, in their expressions and attitudes, according to their several natures: The Gods (for instance) are distinguished in air, habit, and proportion, from men, in the fourth picture; masters from servants, in the eighth; and so of the rest.

Nothing is more wonderful than his exact observation of the *contrast*, not only between figure and figure, but between subject and subject. The city in peace is a contrast to the city in war: Between the siege in the fourth picture, and the battel in the sixth, a piece of paisage is introduced, and rural Scenes follow after. The country too is represented in war in the fifth, as well as in peace in the seventh, eighth, and ninth. The very animals are shewn in these two different states, in the tenth and eleventh. Where the subjects appear the same, he contrastes them some other way: Thus the first picture of the town in peace having a predominant air of gaiety, in the dances and pomps of the marriage; the second has a character of earnestness and sollicitude, in the dispute and pleadings. In the pieces of rural life, that of the plowing is of a different character from the harvest, and that of the harvest from the vintage. In each of these there is a contrast of the *labour* and *mirth* of the country people: In the first, some are plowing, others taking a cup of good liquor; in the next, we see the reapers working in one part, and the banquet prepared in another; in the last, the labour of the vineyard is relieved with musick and a dance. The persons are no less varied, old and young, men and women: There being women in two pictures together, namely the eighth and ninth, it is remarkable that those in the latter are of a different character from the former; they who dress the supper being ordinary women, the others who carry baskets in the vineyard, young and beautiful virgins: And these again are of an inferior character to those in the twelfth piece, who are distinguish'd as people of condition by a more elegant dress. There are three dances in the buckler; and these too are varied: That at the wedding is in a circular figure, that of the vineyard in a row, that in the last picture, a mingled one. Lastly, there is a manifest contrast in the colours; nay, ev'n in the back-grounds of the several pieces: For example, that of the plowing is of a dark tinct, that of the harvest yellow, that of the pasture green, and the rest in like manner.

That he was not a stranger to aerial *perspective*, appears in his expresly marking the distance of object from object: He tells us, for instance, that the two spies lay a little remote from the other figures; and that the oak under which was spread the banquet of the reapers, stood apart. What he says of the valley sprinkled all over with cottages and flocks, appears to be a description of a large country in perspective. And indeed a general argument for this may be drawn from the number of figures on the shield; which could not be all expressed in their full magnitude: And this is therefore a sort of proof that the art of lessening them according to perspective was known at that time.

What the criticks call the *three unities*, ought in reason as much to be observed in a picture as in a play; each should have only *one principal action*, one *instant of time*, and one *point of view*. In this method of examination also, the shield of *Homer* will bear the test: He has been more exact than the greatest painters, who have often deviated from one or other of these rules; whereas (when we examine the detail of each compartment) it will appear,

First, that there is but one principal action in each picture, and that no supernumerary figures or actions are introduced. This will answer all that has been said of the confusion and crowd of figures on the shield, by those who never comprehended the plan of it.

Secondly, that no action is represented in one piece, which could not happen in the same instant of time. This will overthrow the objection against so many different actions appearing in one shield; which, in this case, is much as absurd as to object against so many of *Raphael*'s cartoons appearing in one gallery.

Thirdly, It will be manifest that there are no objects in any one picture which could not be seen in one point of view. Hereby the *Abbé Terasson*'s whole criticism will fall to the ground, which amounts but to this, that the general objects of the heavens, stars and sea, with the particular prospects of towns, fields, &c. could never be seen all at once. *Homer* was incapable of so absurd a thought, nor could these heavenly bodies (had he intended them for a picture) have ever been seen together from one point; for the constellations and the full moon, for example, could never be seen at once with the sun. But the celestial bodies were placed on the boss, as the ocean at the margin of the shield: These were no parts of the painting, but the former was only an ornament to the projection in the middle, and the latter a frame round about it: In the same manner as the divisions, projections, or angles of a roof are left to be ornamented at the discretion of the painter, with foliage, architecture, grotesque, or what he pleases: However his judgment will be still more commendable, if he contrives to make even these extrinsical parts, to bear some allusion to the main design: It is this which *Homer* has done, in placing a sort of sphere in the middle, and the ocean at the border, of a work, which was so expressly intended to represent the universe.

I proceed now to the detail of the shield; in which the words of *Homer* being first translated, an attempt will be made to shew with what exact order all that he describes may enter into the composition, according to the rules of painting.

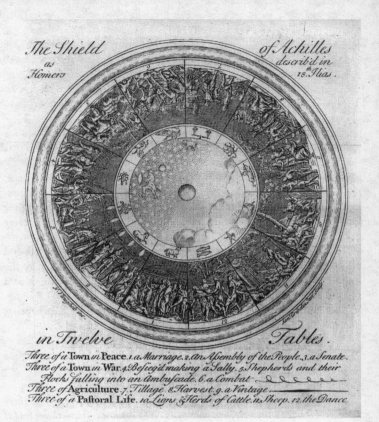

The Shield *as Homers* of Achilles *describ'd in 18.th Ilias.*

in Twelve Tables.

Three of a Town in Peace. 1. a Marriage. 2. An Assembly of the People. 3. a Senate.
Three of a Town in War. 4. Besieg'd making a Sally. 5. Shepherds and their Flocks falling into an Ambuscade. 6. a Combat
Three of Agriculture. 7. Tillage. 8. Harvest. 9. a Vintage.
Three of a Pastoral Life. 10. Lions & Herds of Cattle. 11. Sheep. 12. the Dance

The Shield of Achilles

Engraving from the 1743 edition.
Reproduction courtesy Jack Liu

THE
SHIELD OF *ACHILLES*
Divided into its several Parts

The BOSS *of the* SHIELD

483. *Ἐν μὲν γαῖαν, &c.*] *Here* Vulcan *represented the earth, the heaven, the sea, the indefatigable course of the sun, the moon in her full, all the celestial signs that crown* Olympus, *the* Pleiades, *the* Hyades, *the great* Orion, *and the* Bear, *commonly call'd the* Wain, *the only constellation which never bathing itself in the ocean, turns about the pole and osberves the course of* Orion.

The sculpture of these resembled somewhat of our terrestrial and celestial globes, and took up the center of the shield: 'Tis plain by the huddle in which *Homer* expresses this, that he did not describe it as a picture for a point of sight.

The circumference is divided into twelve compartments, each being a separate picture: as follow.

First Compartment. *A Town in Peace*

Ἐν δὲ δύω ποίησε πόλεις, &c.] *He engraved two cities; in one of them were represented nuptials and festivals. The spouses from their bridal chambers, were conducted thro' the town by the light of torches. Every mouth sung the* hymenæal *song: The youths turn'd rapidly about in a circular dance: The flute and the lyre resounded: The women, every one in the street, standing in the porches, beheld and admired.*

In this picture, the brides preceded by torch-bearers are on the fore-ground: The dance in circles, and musicians behind them: The street in perspective on either side, the women and spectators, in the porches, &c. dispersed thro' all the architecture.

Second Compartiment. *An Assembly of People*

Λαοὶ δ' εἰν ἀγορῇ, &c.] *There was seen a number of people in the market-place, and two men disputing warmly: The occasion was the payment of a fine for a murder, which one affirm'd before the people he had paid, the other denied to have received; both demanded, that the affair should be determined by the judgment of an arbiter: The acclamations of the multitude favoured sometimes the one party, sometimes the other.*

Here is a fine plan for a master-piece of *expression*; any judge of painting will see our author has chosen that *cause* which of all others, would give occasion to the greatest variety of expression: The father, the murderer, the witnesses, and the different passions of the assembly, would afford an ample field for this talent even to *Raphael* himself.

Third Compartiment. *The Senate*

Κήρυκες δ' ἄρα λαὸν.ἐρήτυον, &c.] *The heralds rang'd the people in order: The reverend elders were seated on seats of polish'd stone, in the sacred circle; they rose up and declared their judgment, each in his turn, with the scepter in his hand: Two talents of gold were laid in the middle of the circle, to be given to him who should pronounce the most equitable judgment.*

The judges are seated in the center of the picture; one (who is the principal figure) standing up as speaking, another in an action of rising, as in order to speak: The ground about 'em a prospect of the Forum, fill'd with auditors and spectators.

Fourth Compartiment. *A Town in War*

Τὴν δ' ἑτέρην πόλιν, &c.] *The other City was besieged by two glittering armies: They were not agreed, whether to sack the town, or divide all the booty of it into two equal parts, to be shared between them: Meantime the besieged secretly armed themselves for an ambuscade. Their wives, children, and old men were posted to defend the walls: The warriours marched from the town with* Pallas *and* Mars *at their head: The deities were of gold, and had golden armours, by the glory of which they were distinguished above the men, as well as by their superiour stature, and more elegant proportions.*

This subject may be thus disposed: The town pretty near the eye, a-cross the whole picture, with the old men on the walls: The chiefs of each army on the foreground: Their different opinions for putting the town to the sword, or sparing it on account of the booty, may be express'd by some having their hands on their swords, and looking up to the city, others stopping them, or in an action of persuading against it. Behind, in prospect, the townsmen may be seen going out from the back gates, with the two deities at their head.

Homer here gives a clear instance of what the ancients always practised; the distinguishing the Gods and Goddesses by characters of majesty or beauty somewhat superiour to nature; we constantly find this in their statues, and to this the modern masters owe the grand taste in the perfection of their figures.

Fifth Compartiment. *An Ambuscade*

Οἱ δ᾽ ὅτε δὴ ῥ᾽ ἵκανον, &c.] *Being arrived at the river where they designed their ambush (the place where the cattel were watered) they disposed themselves along the bank, covered with their arms: Two spies lay at a distance from them, observing when the oxen and sheep should come to drink. They came immediately, followed by two shepherds, who were playing on their pipes, without any apprehension of their danger.*

This quiet picture is a kind of *Repose* between the last, and the following, active pieces. Here is a scene of a river and trees, under which lie the soldiers, next the eye of the spectator; on the farther bank are placed the two spies on one hand, and the flocks and shepherds appear coming at a greater distance on the other.

Sixth Compartiment. *The Battle*

Οἱ μὲν τὰ προϊδόντες, &c.] *The people of the town rushed upon them, carried off the oxen and sheep, and killed the shepherds. The besiegers sitting before the town, heard the outcry, and mounting their horses, arrived at the bank of the river; where they stopped, and encountered each other with their spears. Discord, tumult, and fate raged in the midst of them. There might you see cruel* Destiny *dragging a dead soldier thro' the battel; two others she seized alive; one of which was mortally wounded; the other not yet hurt: The garment on her shoulders was stained with human blood: The figures appeared as if they lived, moved, and fought, you would think they really dragged off their dead.*

The sheep and two shepherds lying dead upon the fore-ground. A battle-piece fills the picture. The allegorical figure of the *Parca* or *Destiny* is the principal. This had been a noble occasion for such a painter as *Rubens*, who has with most happiness and learning, imitated the ancients in these fictitious and symbolical persons.

Seventh Compartiment. *Tillage*

'Εν δ' ἐτίθει νειὸν μαλακήν.] *The next piece represented a large field, a deep and fruitful soil, which seemed to have been three times plowed; the labourers appeared turning their plows on every side. As soon as they came to a land's end, a man presented them a bowl of wine; cheared with this, they turned, and worked down a new furrow, desirous to hasten to the next land's end. The field was of gold, but looked black behind the plows, as if it had really been turned up; the surprizing effect of the art of* Vulcan.

The plowmen must be represented on the fore-ground, in the action of turning at the end of the furrow. The invention of *Homer* is not content with barely putting down the figures, but enlivens them prodigiously with some remarkable circumstance: The giving a cup of wine to the plowmen must occasion a fine expression in the faces.

Eighth Compartiment. *The Harvest*

'Εν δ' ἐτίθει τέμενος, &c.] *Next he represented a field of corn, in which the reapers worked with sharp sickles in their hands; the corn fell thick along the furrows in equal rows: Three binders were employed in making up the sheaves: The boys attending them, gathered up the loose swarths, and carried them in their arms to be bound: The lord of the field standing in the midst of the heaps, with a scepter in his hand, rejoices in silence: His officers, at a distance, prepare a feast under the shade of an oak, and hold an ox ready to be sacrificed; while the women mix the flower of wheat for the reaper's supper.*

The reapers on the fore-ground, with their faces towards the spectators; the gatherers behind, and the children on the farther ground. The master of the field, who is the chief figure, may be set in the middle of the picture with a strong light upon him, in the action of directing and pointing with his scepter: The oak, with the Servants under it, the sacrifice, &c. on a distant ground, would altogether make a beautiful grouppe of great variety.

Ninth Compartment. *The Vintage*

'Εν δ' ἐτίθει σταφυλῇσι, &c.] *He then engraved a vineyard loaden with its grapes: The vineyard was gold, but the grapes black, and the props of them silver. A trench of a dark metal, and a palisade of tin encompassed the whole vineyard. There was one path in it, by which the labourers in the vineyard passed: Young men and maids carried the fruit in woven baskets: In the middle of them a youth played on the lyre, and charmed them with his tender voice, as he sung to the strings (or as he sung the song of Linus:) The rest striking the ground with their feet in exact time, followed him in a dance, and accompanied his voice with their own.*

The vintage scarce needs to be painted in any colours but *Homer*'s. The youths and maids toward the eye, as coming out of the vineyard: The enclosure, pales, gate, &c. on the fore-ground. There is something inexpressibly *riant* in this piece, above all the rest.

Tenth Compartment. *Animals*

'Εν δ' ἀγέλην ποίησε Βοῶν, &c.] *He graved a herd of oxen, marching with their heads erected; these oxen (inlaid with gold and tin) seemed to bellow as they quitted their stall, and run in haste to the meadows, through which a rapid river rolled with resounding streams amongst the rushes: Four herdsmen of gold attended them, followed by nine large dogs: Two terrible lions seized a bull by the throat, who roared as they dragged him along; the dogs and the herdsmen ran to his rescue, but the lions having torn the bull, devoured his entrails, and drank his blood, the herdsmen came up with their dogs and heartened them in vain; they durst not attack the lions, but standing at some distance, barked at them and shunned them.*

We have next a fine piece of animals, tame and savage: But what is remarkable, is, that these animals are not coldly brought in to be gazed upon: The herds, dogs, and lions are put into action, enough to exercise the warmth and spirit of *Rubens*, or the great taste of *Julio Romano*.

The lions may be next the eye, one holding the bull by the throat, the other tearing out his entrails: A herdsman or two heartening the dogs: All these on the fore-ground. On the second ground another grouppe of oxen, that seem to have been gone before, tossing their heads and running; other herdsmen and dogs after 'em: And beyond them, a prospect of the river.

Eleventh Compartiment. *Sheep*

'Ἐν δὲ νομόν, &c.] *The divine artist then engraved a large flock of white sheep, feeding along a beautiful valley. Innumerable folds, cottages, and enclosed shelters, were scattered thro' the prospect.*

This is an entire landscape without human figures, an image of nature solitary and undisturbed: The deepest repose and tranquillity is that which distinguishes it from the others.

Twelfth Compartiment. *The Dance*

'Ἐν δὲ χορόν, &c.] *The skilful* Vulcan *then designed the figure and various motions of a dance, like that which* Dædalus *of old contrived in* Gnossus *for the fair* Ariadne. *There the young men and maidens danced hand in hand; the maids were dressed in linen garments, the men in rich and shining stuffs: The maids had flowery crowns on their heads; the men had swords of gold hanging from their sides in belts of silver. Here they seemed to run in a ring with active feet, as swiftly as a wheel runs round when tried by the hand of the potter. There, they appeared to move in many figures, and sometimes to meet, sometimes to wind from each other. A multitude of spectators stood round, delighted with the dance. In the middle, two nimble tumblers exercised themselves in feats of activity, while the song was carried on by the whole circle.*

This picture includes the greatest number of persons: *Homer* himself has group'd them, and marked the manner of the composition. This piece would excell in the different *airs of beauty* which might be given to the young men and women, and the graceful attitudes in the various manners of dancing: On which account the subject might be fit for

Guido, or perhaps could be no where better executed than in our own country.

The BORDER *of the* SHIELD

'Εν δ' ἐτίθει ποταμοῖο, &c.] *Then lastly, he represented the rapid course of the great ocean, which he made to roll its waves round the extremity of the whole circumference.*

This (as has been said before) was only the frame to the whole shield; and is therefore but slightly touched upon, without any mention of particular objects.

I ought not to end this essay, without vindicating myself from the vanity of treating of an art, which I love so much better than I understand: But I have been very careful to consult both the best performers and judges in painting. I can't neglect this occasion of saying, how happy I think myself in the favour of the most distin-guish'd masters of that Art. Sir *Godfrey Kneller* in particular allows me to tell the world, that he entirely agrees with my sentiments on this subject: And I can't help wishing, that he who gives this testimony to *Homer*, would ennoble so great a design by his own execution of it. *Vulcan* never wrought for *Thetis* with more readiness and affection than Sir *Godfrey* has done for me: And so admirable a picture of the whole universe could not be a more agreeable present than he has obliged me with, in the portraits of some of those persons who are to me the dearest objects in it.

THE
NINETEENTH BOOK
OF THE
ILIAD

The ARGUMENT

The reconciliation of *Achilles* and *Agamemnon*

Thetis *brings to her son the armour made by* Vulcan. *She preserves the body of his friend from corruption, and commands him to assemble the army, to declare his resentment at an end.* Agamemnon *and* Achilles *are solemnly reconciled: The Speeches, presents, and ceremonies on that occasion.* Achilles *is with great difficulty persuaded to refrain from the battel till the troops have refreshed themselves, by the advice of* Ulysses. *The presents are conveyed to the tent of* Achilles; *where* Briseïs *laments over the body of* Patroclus. *The hero obstinately refuses all repast, and gives himself up to lamentations for his friend.* Minerva *descends to strengthen him, by the order of* Jupiter. *He arms for the fight; his appearance described. He addresses himself to his horses, and reproaches them with the death of* Patroclus. *One of them is miraculously endued with voice, and inspired to prophecy his fate; but the hero, not astonished by that prodigy, rushes with fury to the combate.*

The thirtieth day. The scene is on the sea-shore.

Soon as *Aurora* heav'd her orient head
Above the waves that blush'd with early red,
(With new-born day to gladden mortal sight,
And gild the courts of heav'n with sacred light,)
5 Th'immortal arms the Goddess-mother bears
Swift to her son: Her son she finds in tears,
Stretch'd o'er *Patroclus'* corse; while all the rest
Their Sov'reign's sorrows in their own exprest.
A ray divine her heav'nly presence shed,
10 And thus, his hand soft-touching, *Thetis* said.
     Suppress (my Son) this rage of grief, and know
It was not man, but heav'n that gave the blow;
Behold what arms by *Vulcan* are bestow'd,
Arms worthy thee, or fit to grace a god.
15   Then drops the radiant burden on the ground;
Clang the strong arms, and ring the shores around:
Back shrink the *Myrmidons* with dread surprize,
And from the broad effulgence turn their eyes.
Unmov'd, the hero kindles at the show,
20 And feels with rage divine his bosom glow:
From his fierce eye-balls living flames expire,
And flash incessant like a stream of fire:
He turns the radiant gift; and feeds his mind
On all th'immortal artist had design'd.
25   Goddess (he cry'd) these glorious arms that shine
With matchless art, confess the hand divine.
Now to the bloody battel let me bend:
But ah! the relicks of my slaughter'd friend!

In those wide wounds thro' which his spirit fled,
Shall flies, and worms obscene, pollute the dead?   30
    That unavailing care be laid aside,
(The azure Goddess to her son reply'd)
Whole years untouch'd, uninjur'd shall remain
Fresh as in life, the carcase of the slain.
But go, *Achilles*, (as affairs require)   35
Before the *Grecian* Peers renounce thine ire:
Then uncontroll'd in boundless war engage,
And heav'n with strength supply the mighty rage!
    Then in the nostrils of the slain she pour'd
Nectareous drops, and rich ambrosia showr'd   40
O'er all the corse. The flies forbid their prey,
Untouch'd it rests, and sacred from decay.
Achilles to the strand obedient went;
The Shores resounded with the voice he sent.
The heroes heard, and all the naval train   45
That tend the ships, or guide them o'er the main,
Alarm'd, transported, at the well-known sound,
Frequent and full, the great assembly crown'd;
Studious to see that terrour of the plain,
Long lost to battel, shine in arms again.   50
    Tydides and *Ulysses* first appear,
Lame with their wounds, and leaning on the spear;
These on the sacred seats of council plac'd,
The King of men, *Atrides*, came the last:
He too sore wounded by *Agenor*'s son.   55
Achilles (rising in the midst) begun.
    Oh Monarch! better far had been the fate
Of thee, of me, of all the *Grecian* state,
If, (e'er the day when by mad passion sway'd,
Rash we contended for the black-ey'd maid)   60
Preventing *Dian* had dispatch'd her dart,
And shot the shining mischief to the heart!
Then many a hero had not press'd the shore,
Nor *Troy*'s glad fields been fatten'd with our gore:
Long, long shall *Greece* the woes we caus'd, bewail,   65
And sad posterity repeat the tale.
But this, no more the subject of debate,
Is past, forgotten, and resign'd to fate:

Why should (alas) a mortal man, as I,
70 Burn with a fury that can never die?
Here then my anger ends: Let war succeed,
And ev'n as *Greece* has bled, let *Ilion* bleed.
Now call the hosts, and try, if in our sight,
Troy yet shall dare to camp a second night?
75 I deem, their mightiest, when this arm he knows,
Shall 'scape with transport, and with joy repose.

    He said: His finish'd wrath with loud acclaim
The *Greeks* accept, and shout *Pelides*' name.
When thus, not rising from his lofty throne,
80 In state unmov'd, the King of men begun.

    Hear me ye Sons of *Greece!* with silence hear!
And grant your monarch an impartial ear;
Awhile your loud, untimely joy suspend,
And let your rash, injurious clamours end:
85 Unruly murmurs, or ill-tim'd applause,
Wrong the best speaker, and the justest cause.
Nor charge on me, ye *Greeks*, the dire debate;
Know, angry *Jove*, and all-compelling *Fate*,
With fell *Erynnis*, urg'd my wrath that day
90 When from *Achilles*' arms I forc'd the prey.
What then cou'd I, against the will of heav'n?
Not by my self, but vengeful *Ate* driv'n;
She, *Jove*'s dread daughter, fated to infest
The race of mortals, enter'd in my breast.
95 Not on the ground that haughty fury treads,
But prints her lofty footsteps on the heads
Of mighty men; inflicting as she goes
Long-fest'ring wounds, inextricable woes!
Of old, she stalk'd amid the bright abodes;
100 And *Jove* himself, the Sire of Men and Gods,
The world's great ruler, felt her venom'd dart;
Deceiv'd by *Juno*'s wiles, and female art.
For when *Alcmena*'s nine long months were run,
And *Jove* expected his immortal son;
105 To Gods and Goddesses th'unruly joy
He show'd, and vaunted of his matchless boy:
From us (he said) this day an infant springs,
Fated to rule, and born a King of Kings.

Saturnia ask'd an oath, to vouch the truth,
And fix dominion on the favour'd youth.   110
The Thund'rer, unsuspicious of the fraud,
Pronounc'd those solemn words that bind a God.
The joyful Goddess, from *Olympus'* height,
Swift to *Achaian Argos* bent her flight;
Scarce sev'n moons gone, lay *Sthenelus* his wife;   115
She push'd her ling'ring infant into life:
Her charms *Alcmena's* coming labours stay,
And stop the babe, just issuing to the day.
Then bids *Saturnius* bear his oath in mind;
'A youth (said she) of *Jove's* immortal kind   120
Is this day born: From *Sthenelus* he springs,
And claims thy promise to be King of Kings.'
Grief seiz'd the Thund'rer, by his oath engag'd;
Stung to the soul, he sorrow'd, and he rag'd.
From his ambrosial head, where perch'd she sate,   125
He snatch'd the Fury-Goddess of Debate,
The dread, th'irrevocable oath he swore,
Th'immortal seats should ne'er behold her more;
And whirl'd her headlong down, for ever driv'n
From bright *Olympus* and the starry heav'n: 130
Thence on the nether world the fury fell;
Ordain'd with man's contentious race to dwell.
Full oft' the God his son's hard toils bemoan'd,
Curs'd the dire fury, and in secret groan'd.
Ev'n thus, like *Jove* himself, was I misled,   135
While raging *Hector* heap'd our camps with dead.
What can the errors of my rage attone?
My martial troops, my treasures, are thy own:
This instant from the navy shall be sent
Whate'er *Ulysses* promis'd at thy tent: 140
But thou! appeas'd, propitious to our pray'r,
Resume thy arms, and shine again in war.

O King of Nations! whose superiour sway
(Returns *Achilles*) all our hosts obey!
To keep, or send the presents, be thy care;   145
To us, 'tis equal: All we ask is war.
While yet we talk, or but an instant shun
The fight, our glorious work remains undone.

Let ev'ry *Greek* who sees my spear confound
150 The *Trojan* ranks, and deal destruction round,
With emulation, what I act, survey,
And learn from thence the business of the day.
    The Son of *Peleus* thus: And thus replies
The great in councils, *Ithacus* the wise.
155 Tho' godlike thou art by no toils opprest,
At least our armies claim repast and rest:
Long and laborious must the combate be,
When by the Gods inspir'd, and led by thee.
Strength is deriv'd from spirits and from blood,
160 And those augment by gen'rous wine and food;
What boastful son of war, without that stay,
Can last a hero thro' a single day?
Courage may prompt; but, ebbing out his strength,
Mere unsupported man must yield at length;
165 Shrunk with dry famine, and with toils declin'd,
The dropping body will desert the mind:
But built anew with strength-conferring fare,
With limbs and soul untam'd, he tires a war.
Dismiss the people then, and give command,
170 With strong repast to hearten ev'ry band;
But let the presents, to *Achilles* made,
In full assembly of all *Greece* be laid.
The King of men shall rise in publick sight,
And solemn swear (observant of the rite)
175 That spotless as she came, the maid removes,
Pure from his arms, and guiltless of his loves.
That done, a sumptuous banquet shall be made,
And the full price of injur'd honour paid.
Stretch not henceforth, O Prince! thy sov'reign might,
180 Beyond the bounds of reason and of right;
'Tis the chief praise that e'er to Kings belong'd,
To right with justice, whom with pow'r they wrong'd.
    To him the monarch. Just is thy decree,
Thy words give joy, and wisdom breathes in thee.
185 Each due atonement gladly I prepare;
And heav'n regard me as I justly swear!
Here then awhile let *Greece* assembled stay,
Nor great *Achilles* grudge this short delay;

Till from the fleet our presents be convey'd,
And, *Jove* attesting, the firm compact made.   190
A train of noble youth the charge shall bear;
These to select, *Ulysses*, be thy care:
In order rank'd let all our gifts appear,
And the fair train of captives close the rear:
Talthybius shall the victim boar convey,   195
Sacred to *Jove*, and yon' bright orb of day.
　For this (the stern *Æacides* replies)
Some less important season may suffice,
When the stern fury of the war is o'er,
And wrath extinguish'd burns my breast no more.   200
By *Hector* slain, their faces to the sky,
All grim with gaping wounds, our heroes lie:
Those call to war! and might my voice incite,
Now, now, this instant, shou'd commence the fight.
Then, when the day's complete, let gen'rous bowls   205
And copious banquets, glad your weary souls.
Let not my palate know the taste of food,
Till my insatiate rage be cloy'd with blood:
Pale lies my friend, with wounds disfigur'd o'er,
And his cold feet are pointed to the door.   210
Revenge is all my soul! no meaner care,
Int'rest, or thought, has room to harbour there;
Destruction be my feast, and mortal wounds,
And scenes of blood, and agonizing sounds.
　O first of *Greeks* (*Ulysses* thus rejoin'd)   215
The best and bravest of the warriour-kind!
Thy praise it is in dreadful camps to shine,
But old experience and calm wisdom, mine.
Then hear my counsel, and to reason yield,
The bravest soon are satiate of the field;   220
Tho' vast the heaps that strow the crimson plain,
The bloody harvest brings but little gain:
The scale of conquest ever wav'ring lies,
Great *Jove* but turns it, and the victor dies!
The great, the bold, by thousands daily fall,   225
And endless were the grief, to weep for all.
Eternal sorrows what avails to shed?
Greece honours not with solemn fasts the dead:

Enough, when death demands the brave, to pay
230   The tribute of a melancholy day.
One chief with patience to the grave resign'd,
Our care devolves on others left behind.
Let gen'rous food supplies of strength produce,
Let rising spirits flow from sprightly juice,
235   Let their warm heads with scenes of battle glow,
And pour new furies on the feebler foe.
Yet a short interval, and none shall dare
Expect a second summons to the war;
Who waits for that, the dire effect shall find,
240   If trembling in the ships he lags behind.
Embodied, to the battel let us bend,
And all at once on haughty *Troy* descend.

     And now the delegates *Ulysses* sent,
To bear the presents from the royal tent.
245   The sons of *Nestor*, *Phyleus'* valiant heir,
Thias and *Merion*, thunderbolts of war,
With *Lycomedes* of *Creiontian* strain,
And *Melanippus*, form'd the chosen train.
Swift as the word was giv'n, the youths obey'd;
250   Twice ten bright vases in the midst they laid;
A row of six fair tripods then succeeds;
And twice the number of high-bounding steeds;
Sev'n captives next a lovely line compose;
The eighth *Briseïs*, like the blooming rose,
255   Clos'd the bright band: Great *Ithacus*, before,
First of the train, the golden talents bore;
The rest in publick view the chiefs dispose,
A splendid scene! Then *Agamemnon* rose:
The boar *Talthybius* held: The *Grecian* Lord
260   Drew the broad cutlace sheath'd beside his sword;
The stubborn bristles from the victim's brow
He crops, and off'ring meditates his vow.
His hands uplifted to th'attesting skies,
On heav'ns broad marble roof were fix'd his eyes,
265   The solemn words a deep attention draw,
And *Greece* around sate thrill'd with sacred awe.
     Witness thou first! thou greatest pow'r above!
All-good, all-wise, and all-surveying *Jove!*

And mother-earth, and heav'ns revolving light,
And ye, fell furies of the realms of night,   270
Who rule the dead, and horrid woes prepare
For perjur'd Kings, and all who falsely swear!
The black-ey'd maid inviolate removes,
Pure and unconscious of my manly loves.
If this be false, heav'n all its vengeance shed,   275
And level'd thunder strike my guilty head!

    With that, his weapon deep inflicts the wound;
The bleeding savage tumbles to the ground:
The sacred herald rolls the victim slain
(A feast for fish) into the foaming main.   280

    Then thus *Achilles*. Hear, ye *Greeks!* and know
Whate'er we feel, 'tis *Jove* inflicts the woe:
Not else *Atrides* could our rage inflame,
Nor from my arms, unwilling, force the dame.
'Twas *Jove*'s high will alone, o'eruling all,   285
That doom'd our strife, and doom'd the *Greeks* to fall.
Go then ye chiefs! indulge the genial rite;
Achilles waits ye, and expects the fight.

    The speedy council at his word adjourn'd:
To their black vessels all the *Greeks* return'd.   290
Achilles sought his tent. His train before
March'd onward, bending with the gifts they bore.
Those in the tents the squires industrious spread:
The foaming coursers to the stalls they led.
To their new seats the female captives move;   295
Briseïs, radiant as the Queen of love,
Slow as she past, beheld with sad survey
Where gash'd with cruel wounds, *Patroclus* lay.
Prone on the body fell the heav'nly fair,
Beat her sad breast, and tore her golden hair;   300
All-beautiful in grief, her humid eyes
Shining with tears, she lifts, and thus she cries.

    Ah youth! for ever dear, for ever kind,
Once tender friend of my distracted mind!
I left thee fresh in life, in beauty gay;   305
Now find thee cold, inanimated clay!
What woes my wretched race of life attend?
Sorrows on sorrows, never doom'd to end!

The first lov'd consort of my virgin bed
310   Before these eyes in fatal battel bled:
My three brave brothers in one mournful day
All trod the dark, irremeable way:
Thy friendly hand uprear'd me from the plain,
And dry'd my sorrows for a husband slain;
355   *Achilles'* care you promis'd I shou'd prove,
The first, the dearest partner of his love,
That rites divine should ratify the band,
And make me empress in his native land.
Accept these grateful tears! For thee they flow,
320   For thee, that ever felt another's woe!

        Her sister captives echo'd groan for groan,
Nor mourn'd *Patroclus'* fortunes, but their own.
The leaders press'd the chief on ev'ry side;
Unmov'd, he heard them, and with sighs deny'd.
325   If yet *Achilles* have a friend, whose care
Is bent to please him; this request forbear:
Till yonder sun descend, ah let me pay
To grief and anguish one abstemious day.

        He spoke, and from the warriours turn'd his face:
330   Yet still the Brother-Kings of *Atreus'* race,
Nestor, Idomeneus, Ulysses sage,
And *Phœnix*, strive to calm his grief and rage:
His rage they calm not, nor his grief controul;
He groans, he raves, he sorrows from his soul.
335   Thou too, *Patroclus!* (thus his heart he vents)
Once spread th'inviting banquet in our tents:
Thy sweet society, thy winning care,
Once stay'd *Achilles*, rushing to the war.
But now alas! to death's cold arms resign'd,
340   What banquet but revenge can glad my mind?
What greater sorrow could afflict my breast,
What more, if hoary *Peleus* were deceast?
(Who now, perhaps, in *Phthia* dreads to hear
His son's sad fate, and drops a tender tear.)
345   What more, should *Neoptolemus* the brave
(My only offspring) sink into the grave?
If yet that offspring lives, (I distant far,
Of all neglectful, wage a hateful war.)

I cou'd not this, this cruel stroke attend;
Fate claim'd *Achilles*, but might spare his friend.   350
I hop'd *Patroclus* might survive, to rear
My tender orphan with a parent's care,
From *Scyros* isle conduct him o'er the main,
And glad his eyes with his paternal reign,
The lofty palace, and the large domain.   355
For *Peleus* breaths no more the vital air;
Or drags a wretched life of age and care,
But till the news of my sad fate invades
His hastening soul, and sinks him to the shades.

    Sighing he said: His grief the heroes join'd,   360
Each stole a tear for what he left behind.
Their mingled grief the Sire of heav'n survey'd,
And thus, with pity, to his blue-ey'd maid.

    Is then *Achilles* now no more thy care,
And dost thou thus desert the great in war?   365
Lo, where yon' sails their canvas wings extend,
All comfortless he sits, and wails his friend:
E'er thirst and want his forces have opprest,
Haste and infuse ambrosia in his breast.

    He spoke, and sudden as the word of *Jove*   370
Shot the descending Goddess from above.
So swift thro' æther the shrill *Harpye* springs,
The wide air floating to her ample wings.
To great *Achilles* she her flight addrest,
And pour'd divine Ambrosia in his breast,   375
With nectar sweet, (refection of the Gods!)
Then, swift ascending, sought the bright abodes.

    Now issued from the ships the warriour train,
And like a deluge pour'd upon the plain.
As when the piercing blasts of *Boreas* blow,   380
And scatter o'er the fields the driving snow;
From dusky clouds the fleecy winter flies,
Whose dazling lustre whitens all the skies:
So helms succeeding helms, so shields from shields
Catch the quick beams, and brighten all the fields;   385
Broad-glitt'ring breastplates, spears with pointed rays
Mix in one stream, reflecting blaze on blaze:

Thick beats the center as the coursers bound,
With splendour flame the skies, and laugh the fields
      around.
390   Full in the midst, high tow'ring o'er the rest,
His limbs in arms divine *Achilles* drest;
Arms which the father of the fire bestow'd,
Forg'd on th'eternal anvils of the God.
Grief and revenge his furious heart inspire,
395 His glowing eye-balls roll with living fire,
He grinds his teeth, and furious with delay
O'erlooks th'embattled host, and hopes the bloody day.
     The silver cuishes first his thighs infold:
Then o'er his breast was brac'd the hollow gold:
400 The brazen sword a various baldrick ty'd,
That, starr'd with gems, hung glitt'ring at his side;
And like the moon, the broad refulgent shield
Blaz'd with long rays, and gleam'd athwart the field.
     So to night-wand'ring sailors, pale with fears,
425 Wide o'er the wat'ry waste, a light appears,
Which on the far-seen mountain blazing high,
Streams from some lonely watch-tow'r to the sky:
With mournful eyes they gaze, and gaze again;
Loud howls the storm, and drives them o'er the main.
410   Next, his high head the helmet grac'd; behind
The sweepy crest hung floating in the wind:
Like the red star, that from his flaming hair
Shakes down diseases, pestilence and war;
So stream'd the golden honours from his head,
Trembled the sparkling plumes, and the loose glories
415   shed.
     The chief beholds himself with wond'ring eyes;
His arms he poises, and his motions tries;
Buoy'd by some inward force, he seems to swim,
And feels a pinion lifting ev'ry limb.
420   And now he shakes his great paternal spear,
Pond'rous and huge! which not a *Greek* could rear.
From *Pelion*'s cloudy top an ash entire
Old *Chiron* fell'd, and shap'd it for his sire;
A spear which stern *Achilles* only wields,
425 The death of heroes, and the dread of fields.

Automedon and *Alcimus* prepare
Th' immortal coursers, and the radiant car,
(The silver traces sweeping at their side)
Their fiery mouths resplendent bridles ty'd,
The iv'ry-studded reins, return'd behind,   430
Wav'd o'er their backs, and to the chariot join'd.
The charioteer then whirl'd the lash around,
And swift ascended at one active bound.
All bright in heav'nly arms, above his squire
Achilles mounts, and sets the field on fire;   435
Not brighter, *Phœbus* in th'ethereal way,
Flames from his chariot, and restores the day.
High o'er the host, all terrible he stands,
And thunders to his steeds these dread commands.

   Xanthus and *Balius!* of *Podarges'* strain,   440
(Unless ye boast that heav'nly race in vain)
Be swift, be mindful of the load ye bear,
And learn to make your master more your care:
Thro' falling squadrons bear my slaught'ring sword,
Nor, as ye left *Patroclus*, leave your Lord.   445

   The gen'rous *Xanthus*, as the words he said,
Seem'd sensible of woe, and droop'd his head:
Trembling he stood before the golden wain,
And bow'd to dust the honours of his mane,
When, strange to tell! (So *Juno* will'd) he broke   450
Eternal silence, and portentous spoke.

   Achilles! yes! this day at least we bear
Thy rage in safety thro' the files of war:
But come it will, the fatal time must come,
Nor ours the fault, but God decrees thy doom.   455
Not thro' our crime, or slowness in the course,
Fell thy *Patroclus*, but by heav'nly force;
The bright far-shooting God who gilds the day,
(Confest we saw him) tore his arms away.
No – could our swiftness o'er the winds prevail,   460
Or beat the pinions of the western gale,
All were in vain – The fates thy death demand,
Due to a mortal and immortal hand.

   Then ceas'd for ever, by the *Furies* ty'd,
His fate-ful voice. Th' intrepid chief reply'd   465

With unabated rage – So let it be!
Portents and prodigies are lost on me.
I know my fates: To die, to see no more
My much-lov'd parents, and my native shore –
470   Enough – When heav'n ordains, I sink in night;
Now perish *Troy!* he said, and rush'd to fight.

OBSERVATIONS

ON THE

NINETEENTH BOOK

13. *Behold what arms,* &c.] 'Tis not poetry only which has had this idea, of giving divine arms to a hero; we have a very remarkable example of it in our holy books. In the second of *Maccabees*, chap. 16. *Judas* sees in a dream the prophet *Jeremiah* bringing to him a sword as from God: Tho' this was only a dream, or a vision, yet still it is the same idea. This example is likewise so much the more worthy of observation, as it is much later than the age of *Homer*; and as thereby it is seen, that the same way of thinking continued a long time amongst the oriental nations.   *Dacier.*

30. *Shall flies, and worms obscene pollute the dead?*] The care which *Achilles* takes in this place to drive away the flies from the dead body of *Patroclus*, seems to us a mean employment, and a care unworthy of a hero. But that office was regarded by *Homer*, and by all the *Greeks* of his time, as a pious duty consecrated by custom and religion; which obliged the kindred and friends of the deceased to watch his corps, and prevent any corruption before the solemn day of his funerals. It is plain this devoir was thought an indispensable one, since *Achilles* could not discharge himself of it by imposing it upon his mother. It is also clear, that in those times the preservation of a dead body was accounted a very important matter, since the Goddesses themselves, nay the most delicate of the Goddesses, made it the subject of their utmost attention. As *Thetis* preserves the body of *Patroclus*, and chases from it those insects that breed in the wounds and cause putrefaction, so *Venus* is employed day and night about that of *Hector*, in driving away the dogs to which *Achilles* had exposed it. *Apollo*, on his part, covers it with a thick cloud, and preserves its freshness amidst the greatest heats of the sun: And this care of the deities over the dead was looked upon by men as a fruit of their piety.

There is an excellent remark upon this passage in *Bossu*'s admirable treatise of the epic poem, lib. 3. c. 10. 'To speak (says this Author) of the arts and sciences as a poet ought, we should veil them under names and actions of persons fictitious and allegorical. *Homer* will not plainly say that salt has the virtue to preserve dead bodies, and prevent the flies from engendering worms in them; he will not say, that the sea presented *Achilles* a remedy to preserve *Patroclus* from putrefaction; but he will make the Sea a Goddess, and tell us, that *Thetis* to comfort *Achilles*, engaged to perfume the body with an ambrosia which should keep it a whole year from corruption: It is thus *Homer* teaches the poets to speak of arts and sciences. This example shews the nature of the things, that flies cause putrefaction, that salt preserves bodies from it; but all this is told us poetically, the whole is reduced into action, the sea is made a person who speaks and acts, and this *prosopopœia* is accompanied with passion, tenderness and affection; in a word, there is nothing which is not (according to *Aristotle*'s precept) endued with manners.'

61.   *Preventing* Dian *had dispatch'd her dart,*
       And shot the shining mischief to the heart.]

Achilles wishes *Briseïs* had died before she had occasioned so great calamities to his countreymen: I will not say, to excuse him, that his virtue here overpowers his love, but that the wish is not so very barbarous as it may seem by the phrase to a modern reader. It is not, that *Diana* had actually killed her, as by a particular stroke or judgment from heaven; it means no more than a natural death, as appears from this passage in *Odyss.* 15.

> *When age or sickness have unnerv'd the strong,*
> Apollo *comes, and* Cynthia *comes along,*
> *They bend the silver bows for sudden ill,*
> *And every shining arrow flies to kill.*

And he does not wish her death now, after she had been his mistress, but only that she had died, before he knew, or loved her.

93.   *She,* Jove's *dread daughter.*] This speech of *Agamemnon*, consisting of little else than the long story of *Jupiter*'s casting *Discord* out of

heaven, seems odd enough at first sight; and does not indeed answer what I believe every reader expects, at the conference of these two Princes. Without excusing it from the justness, and proper application of the allegory in the present case, I think it a piece of artifice, very agreeable to the character of *Agamemnon*, which is a mixture of haughtiness and cunning: he cannot prevail with himself any way to lessen the dignity of the royal character, of which he every where appears jealous: Something he is obliged to say in publick, and not brooking directly to own himself in the wrong, he slurs it over with this tale. With what stateliness is it that he yields? 'I was misled (says he) but I was misled like *Jupiter*. We invest you with our powers, take our troops and our treasures: Our royal promise shall be fulfilled, but be you pacified.'

93.   *She,* Jove's *dread daughter, fated to infest*
       The race of mortals –]

It appears from hence, that the ancients owned a *Dæmon*, created by God himself, and totally taken up in doing mischief.

   This fiction is very remarkable, in as much as it proves that the *Pagans* knew that a dæmon of discord and malediction was in heaven, and afterwards precipitated to earth, which perfectly agrees with holy history. St. *Justin* will have it, that *Homer* attained to the knowledge thereof in *Egypt*, and that he had even read what *Isaiah* writes, chap. 14. *How art thou fal'n from heaven, O* Lucifer, *son of the morning, how art thou cut down to the ground which didst weaken the nations?* But our poet could not have seen the prophecy of *Isaiah*, because he lived 100, or 150 years before that prophet; and this anteriority of time makes this passage the more observable. *Homer* therein bears authentick witness to the truth of the story, of an angel thrown from heaven, and gives this testimony above 100 years before one of the greatest prophets spoke of it.   *Dacier.*

145.   *To keep or send the presents, be thy care.*] *Achilles* neither refuses nor demands *Agamemnon*'s presents: The first would be too contemptuous, and the other would look too selfish. It would seem as if *Achilles* fought only for pay like a mercenary, which would be utterly unbecoming a hero, and dishonourable to that character: *Homer* is wonderful as to the manners.   *Spond. Dac.*

159.   *Strength is deriv'd from Spirits,* &c.] This advice of *Ulysses* that

the troops should refresh themselves with eating and drinking, was extremely necessary, after a battle of so long continuance as that of the day before: And *Achilles*'s desire that they should charge the enemy immediately, without any reflection on the necessity of that refreshment, was also highly natural to his violent character. This forces *Ulysses* to repeat that advice, and insist upon it so much: Which those criticks did not see into, who thro' a false delicacy are shock'd at his insisting so warmly upon eating and drinking. Indeed to a common reader who is more fond of heroick and romantick, than of just and natural images, this at first sight may have an air of ridicule; but I'll venture to say there is nothing ridiculous in the thing itself, nor mean and low in *Homer*'s manner of expressing it: And I believe the same of this translation, tho' I have not soften'd or abated of the Idea they are so offended with.

197. *The stern Æacides replies.*] The *Greek* verse is

  Τὸν δ' ἀπαμειβόμενος προσέφη πόδας ὠκὺς 'Αχιλλεύς.

[And then, in turn, swift-footed Achilles answered.]

Which is repeated very frequently throughout the Iliad. It is a very just remark of a *French* critick, that what makes it so much taken notice of, is the rumbling sound and length of the word ἀπαμειβόμενος: This is so true, that if in a poem or romance of the same length as the Iliad, we should repeat *The hero answer'd*, full as often, we should never be sensible of that repetition. And if we are not shocked at the like frequency of those expressions in the Æneid, *sic ore refert, talia voce refert, talia dicta dabat, vix ea fatus erat,* &c. it is only because the sound of the *Latin* words does not fill the ear like that of the *Greek* ἀπαμειβόμενος.

The discourse of the same critick upon these sort of repetitions in general, deserves to be transcribed. That useless nicety (says he) of avoiding every repetition which the delicacy of later Times has introduced, was not known to the first ages of antiquity: The books of *Moses* abound with them. Far from condemning their frequent use in the most ancient of all the poets, we should look upon them as the certain character of the age in which he liv'd: They spoke so in his time, and to have spoken otherwise had been a fault. And indeed nothing is in itself so contrary to the true sublime, as that painful and frivolous exactness, with which we avoid to make use of a proper word because it was used before. It is certain that the *Romans* were less scrupulous as to this point: You have often in a single page of *Tully*, the same word five or six times over. If it were really a fault, it is not to be conceived how an author who so little wanted variety of expressions as *Homer*, could be so very negligent herein? On the contrary, he seems to have affected to repeat the same things in the same words, on many occasions.

It was from two principles equally true, that among several people, and in several ages, two practices entirely different took their rise. *Moses*, *Homer*, and the writers of the first times, had found that repetitions of the same Words recalled the ideas of things, imprinted them much more strongly, and rendered the discourse more intelligible. Upon this principle, the custom of repeating words, phrases, and even entire speeches, insensibly established itself both in prose and poetry, especially in narrations.

The writers who succeeded them observed, even from *Homer* himself, that the greatest beauty of style consisted in variety. This they made their principle: They therefore avoided repetitions of words, and still more of whole sentences; they endeavoured to vary their transitions; and found out new turns and manners of expressing the same things.

Either of these Practices is good, but the excess of either vicious: We should neither on the one hand, thro' a love of simplicity and clearness, continually repeat the same words, phrases, or discourses; nor on the other, for the pleasure of variety, fall into a childish affectation of expressing every thing twenty different ways, tho' it be never so natural and common.

Nothing so much cools the warmth of a piece or puts out the fire of poetry, as that perpetual care to vary incessantly even in the smallest circumstances. In this, as in many other points, *Homer* has despised the ungrateful labour of too scrupulous a nicety. He has done like a great painter, who does not think himself obliged to vary all his pieces to that degree, as not one of them shall have the least resemblance to another: If the principal figures are entirely different, we easily excuse a resemblance in the landscapes, the skies, or the draperies. Suppose a gallery full of pictures, each of which represents a particular subject: In one I see *Achilles* in fury, menacing *Agamemnon*; in another the same hero with regret delivers up *Briseïs* to the heralds; in a third 'tis still *Achilles*, but *Achilles* overcome with grief, and lamenting to his mother. If the air, the gesture, the countenance, the character of

Achilles, are the same in each of these three pieces; if the ground of one of these be the same with that of the others in the composition and general design, whether it be landscape, or architecture; then indeed one should have reason to blame the painter for the uniformity of his figures and grounds. But if there be no sameness but in the folds of a few draperies, in the structure of some part of a building, or in the figure of some tree, mountain, or cloud, it is what no one would regard as a fault. The application is obvious: *Homer* repeats, but they are not the great strokes which he repeats, not those which strike and fix our attention: They are only the little parts, the transitions, the general circumstances, or familiar images, which recur naturally, and upon which the reader but casts his eye carelessly: Such as the descriptions of sacrifices, repasts, or embarquements; such in short, as are in their own nature much the same, which it is sufficient just to shew, and which are in a manner incapable of different ornaments.

209. *Pale lies my friend,* &c.] It is in the *Greek, lies extended in my tent with his face turned towards the door,* ἀνὰ πρόθυρον τετραμμένος, that is to say, as the scholiast has explained it, *having his feet turned towards the door.* For it was thus the *Greeks* placed their dead in the porches of their houses, as likewise in *Italy,*

> *In portam rigidos calces extendit.*   Persius.

> [He stretches his stiff heels towards the door.]

> – *Recepitque ad limina gressum*
> *Corpus ubi exanimi positum Pallantis Acetes*
> *Servabat senior –*

> [he took his way,
> Where, new in death, lamented *Pallas* lay:
> *Acoetes* watch'd the corps.]

Thus we are told by *Suetonius,* of the body of *Augustus – Equester ordo suscepit, urbique intulit, atque in vestibulo domus collocavit* [The equestrian order took it up, carried it into the city, and laid it out in a vestibule in the house].

221. *Tho' vast the heaps,* &c.] *Ulysses*'s expression in the original is very remarkable; he calls καλάμη, *straw* or *chaff,* such as are killed in the battel; and he calls ἄμητος, the *crop,* such as make their escape.

This is very conformable to the language of holy scripture, wherein those who perish are called *chaff*, and those who are saved are called *corn*.   *Dacier.*

237.   *– None shall dare*
                    Expect a second summons to the war.]

This is very artful; *Ulysses*, to prevail upon *Achilles* to let the troops take repast, and yet in some sort to second his impatience, gives with the same breath orders for battel, by commanding the troops to march, and expect no farther orders. Thus tho' the troops go to take repast, it looks as if they do not lose a moment's time, but are going to put themselves in array of battel.   *Dacier.*

279–280. *Rolls the victim . . . into the main.*] For it was not lawful to eat the flesh of the victims, that were sacrificed in confirmation of oaths; such were victims of malediction.   *Eustathius.*

281. *Hear, ye* Greeks, &c.] *Achilles*, to let them see that he is entirely appeas'd, justifies *Agamemnon* himself, and enters into the reasons with which that Prince had coloured his fault. But in that justification he perfectly well preserves his character, and illustrates the advantage he has over that King who offended him.   *Dacier.*

303, *&c. The lamentation of* Briseïs *over* Patroclus.] This speech (says *Dionysius* of *Halicarnassus*) is not without its artifice: While *Briseïs* seems only to be deploring *Patroclus*, she represents to *Achilles* who stands by, the breach of the promises he had made her, and upbraids him with the neglect he had been guilty of in resigning her up to *Agamemnon.* He adds, that *Achilles* hereupon acknowledges the justice of her complaint, and makes answer that his promises should be performed: It was a slip in that great critick's memory, for the verse he cites is not in this part of the author, [Περὶ ἐσχηματισμένων, Part 2.]

315. Achilles' *care you promis'd,* &c.] In these days when our manners are so different from those of the ancients, and we see none of those dismal catastrophes which laid whole kingdoms waste and subjected princesses and queens to the power of the conqueror; it will perhaps seem astonishing, that a princess of *Briseïs*'s birth, the very day that her father, brothers, and husband were killed by *Achilles*, should suffer her self to be comforted and even flattered with the hopes of becoming the spouse of the murderer. But such were the manners of those times, as ancient history testifies: And a poet represents them as they were; but if there was a necessity for justifying them, it might be said that slavery was at that time so terrible, that in truth a princess like *Briseïs* was pardonable, to chuse rather to become *Achilles*'s wife than his slave.

Dacier.

322. *Nor mourn'd* Patroclus *fortunes but their own.*] *Homer* adds this touch, to heighten the character of *Briseïs*, and to shew the difference there was between her and the other captives. *Briseïs*, as a well-born princess, really bewail'd *Patroclus* out of *gratitude*; but the others, by pretending to bewail him, wept only out of *interest.*   *Dacier.*

335. *Thou too* Patroclus, &c.] This lamentation is finely introduced: While the Generals are persuading him to take some refreshment, it naturally awakens in his mind the remembrance of *Patroclus*, who had so often brought him food every morning before they went to battel: This is very natural, and admirably well conceals the art of drawing the subject of his discourse from the things that present themselves.

Spondanus.

351. *I hop'd* Patroclus *might survive*, &c.] *Patroclus* was young, and *Achilles* who had but a short time to live, hoped that after his death his dear friend would be as a father to his son, and put him into the possession of his kingdom: *Neoptolemus* would in *Patroclus* find *Peleus* and *Achilles*; whereas when *Patroclus* was dead, he must be an orphan indeed. *Homer* is particularly admirable for the sentiments, and always follows nature.   *Dacier.*

384.   *So helms succeeding helms, so shields from shields*
     Catch the quick beams, and brighten all the fields.]

It is probable the reader may think the words, *shining*, *splendid*, and others derived from the lustre of arms, too frequent in these books. My author is to answer for it, but it may be alledged in his excuse, that when it was the custom for every soldier to serve in armour, and when those arms were of brass before the use of iron became common, these images of lustre were less avoidable, and more necessarily frequent in descriptions of this nature.

390. *Achilles arming himself,* &c.] There is a wonderful pomp in this description of *Achilles*'s arming himself; every reader without being pointed to it, will see the extreme grandeur of all these images; but what is particular, is, in what a noble scale they rise one above another, and how the hero is set still in a stronger point of light than before; till he is at last in a manner covered over with glories: He is at first likened to the moonlight, then to the flames of a beacon, then to a comet, and lastly to the sun it self.

450.   *When, strange to tell! (so* Juno *will'd) he broke*
         Eternal silence, and portentous spoke.]

It is remark'd, in excuse of this extravagant fiction of a horse speaking, that *Homer* was authorized herein by fable, tradition, and history. *Livy* makes mention of two oxen that spoke on different occasions, and recites the speech of one, which was, *Roma cave tibi* [Rome, beware!]. *Pliny* tells us, these animals were particularly gifted this way, l. 8. c. 45. *Est frequens in prodigiis priscorum, bovem locutum* [It is common, in the prodigies of the ancients, for the ox to speak]. Besides *Homer* had prepared us for expecting something miraculous from these horses of *Achilles*, by representing them to be immortal. We have seen them already sensible, and weeping at the death of *Patroclus*: And we must add to all this, that a Goddess is concerned in working this wonder: It is *Juno* that does it. *Oppian* alludes to this in a beautiful passage of his first book: Not having the original by me, I shall quote (what I believe is no less beautiful) Mr. *Fenton*'s translation of it.

> *Of all the prone creation, none display*
> *A friendlier sense of man's superiour sway:*
> *Some in the silent pomp of grief complain,*
> *For the brave chief, by doom of battel slain:*
> *And when young* Peleus *in his rapid car*
> *Rush'd on, to rouze the thunder of the war,*
> *With human voice inspir'd, his steed deplor'd*
> *The fate impending dreadful o'er his Lord.*   Cyneg. lib. 1.

Spondanus and *Dacier* fail not to bring up *Balaam*'s ass on this occasion. But methinks the commentators are at too much pains to discharge the poet from the imputation of extravagant fiction, by accounting for wonders of this kind: I am afraid, that next to the extravagance of inventing them, is that of endeavouring to reconcile such fictions to probability. Would not one general answer do better, to say once for all, that the above cited authors lived in the *age of wonders*: The taste of the world has been generally turned to the miraculous; wonders were what the people would have, and what not only the poets, but the priests, gave 'em.

464. *Then ceas'd for ever, by the furies ty'd,*
His fate-ful voice –]

The poet had offended against probability if he had made *Juno* take away the voice, for *Juno* (which signifies the air) is the cause of the voice. Besides, the poet was willing to intimate that the privation of the voice is a thing so dismal and melancholy, that none but the *Furies* can take upon them so cruel an employment.   *Eustathius.*

THE
TWENTIETH BOOK
OF THE
ILIAD

The ARGUMENT

The battel of the Gods, and the acts of *Achilles*

Jupiter *upon* Achilles's *returning to the battel, calls a council of the Gods, and permits them to assist either party. The terrors of the combate described, when the Deities are engaged.* Apollo *encourages* Æneas *to meet* Achilles. *After a long conversation, these two heroes encounter; but* Æneas *is preserved by the assistance of* Neptune. Achilles *falls upon the rest of the* Trojans, *and is upon the point of killing* Hector, *but* Apollo *conveys him away in a cloud.* Achilles *pursues the* Trojans *with a great slaughter.*

The same day continues. The scene is in the field before Troy.

Thus round *Pelides* breathing war and blood,
Greece sheath'd in arms, beside her vessels stood;
While near impending from a neighb'ring height,
Troy's black battalions wait the shock of fight.
5   Then *Jove* to *Themis* gives command, to call
The Gods to council in the starry hall:
Swift o'er *Olympus'* hundred hills she flies,
And summons all the senate of the skies.
These shining on, in long procession come
10 To *Jove*'s eternal adamantine dome.
Not one was absent; not a rural pow'r
That haunts the verdant gloom, or rosy bow'r,
Each fair-hair'd Dryad of the shady wood,
Each azure sister of the silver flood;
15 All but old Ocean, hoary Sire! who keeps
His ancient seat beneath the sacred deeps.
On marble thrones with lucid columns crown'd,
(The work of *Vulcan*) sate the Pow'rs around.
Ev'n *he whose trident sways the watry reign,
20 Heard the loud summons, and forsook the main,
Assum'd his throne amid the bright abodes,
And question'd thus the Sire of Men and Gods.
    What moves the God who heav'n and earth commands,
And grasps the thunder in his awful hands,
25 Thus to convene the whole ætherial state?
Is *Greece* and *Troy* the subject in debate?

*Neptune

Already met, the low'ring hosts appear,
And death stands ardent on the edge of war.
     'Tis true (the cloud-compelling pow'r replies)
This day, we call the council of the skies   30
In care of human race; ev'n *Jove*'s own eye
Sees with regret unhappy mortals die.
Far on *Olympus*' top in secret state
Ourself will sit, and see the hand of Fate
Work out our will. Celestial pow'rs! descend,   35
And as your minds direct, your succour lend
To either host. *Troy* soon must lie o'erthrown,
If uncontroll'd *Achilles* fights alone:
Their troops but lately durst not meet his eyes;
What can they now, if in his rage he rise?   40
Assist them, Gods! or *Ilion*'s sacred wall
May fall this day, tho' Fate forbids the fall.
     He said, and fir'd their heav'nly breasts with rage:
On adverse parts the warring Gods engage.
Heav'ns awful Queen; and he whose azure round   45
Girds the vast globe; the maid in arms renown'd;
Hermes, of profitable arts the sire,
And *Vulcan*, the black sov'reign of the fire:
These to the fleet repair with instant flight;
The vessels tremble as the Gods alight.   50
In aid of *Troy*, *Latona*, *Phœbus* came,
Mars fiery-helm'd, the laughter-loving Dame,
Xanthus whose streams in golden currents flow,
And the chast huntress of the silver bow.
E'er yet the Gods their various aid employ,   55
Each *Argive* bosom swell'd with manly joy,
While great *Achilles*, (terrour of the plain)
Long lost to battel, shone in arms again.
Dreadful he stood in front of all his host;
Pale *Troy* beheld, and seem'd already lost;   60
Her bravest heroes pant with inward fear,
And trembling see another God of war.
     But when the pow'rs descending swell'd the fight,
Then Tumult rose; fierce rage and pale affright
Vary'd each face; then Discord sounds alarms,   65
Earth echoes, and the nations rush to arms.

Now thro' the trembling shores *Minerva* calls.
And now she thunders from the *Grecian* walls.
Mars hov'ring o'er his *Troy*, his terrour shrouds
70 In gloomy tempests, and a night of clouds:
Now thro' each *Trojan* heart he fury pours
With voice divine from *Ilion*'s topmost tow'rs,
Now shouts to *Simoïs*, from her beauteous *hill;
The mountain shook, the rapid stream stood still.
75 Above, the Sire of Gods his thunder rolls,
And peals on peals redoubled rend the poles.
Beneath, stern *Neptune* shakes the solid ground;
The forests wave, the mountains nod around;
Thro' all their summits tremble *Ida*'s woods,
80 And from their sources boil her hundred floods.
Troy's turrets totter on the rocking plain;
And the toss'd navies beat the heaving main.
Deep in the dismal regions of the dead,
Th'infernal Monarch rear'd his horrid head,
85 Leap'd from his throne, lest *Neptune*'s arm should lay
His dark dominions open to the day,
And pour in light on *Pluto*'s drear abodes,
Abhorr'd by men, and dreadful ev'n to Gods.
    Such war th'immortals wage: Such horrors rend
90 The world's vast concave, when the Gods contend.
First silver-shafted *Phœbus* took the plain
Against blue *Neptune*, Monarch of the main:
The God of arms his giant bulk display'd,
Oppos'd to *Pallas*, war's triumphant maid.
95 Against *Latona* march'd the son of *May*;
The quiver'd *Dian*, sister of the Day,
(Her golden arrows sounding at her side)
Saturnia, Majesty of heav'n, defy'd.
With fiery *Vulcan* last in battel stands
100 The sacred flood that rolls on golden sands;
Xanthus his name with those of heavenly birth,
But call'd *Scamander* by the sons of earth.
    While thus the Gods in various league engage,
Achilles glow'd with more than mortal rage:

*Callicolone.

Hector he sought; in search of *Hector* turn'd   105
His eyes around, for *Hector* only burn'd;
And burst like light'ning thro' the ranks, and vow'd
To glut the God of Battels with his blood.

　　Æneas was the first who dar'd to stay;
Apollo wedg'd him in the warrior's way,   110
But swell'd his bosom with undaunted might,
Half-forc'd, and half-persuaded to the fight.
Like young *Lycaon*, of the royal line,
In voice and aspect, seem'd the pow'r divine;
And bade the chief reflect, how late with scorn   115
In distant threats he brav'd the Goddess-born.

　　Then thus the hero of *Anchises'* strain.
To meet *Pelides* you persuade in vain:
Already have I met, nor void of fear
Observ'd the fury of his flying spear;   120
From *Ida*'s woods he chas'd us to the field,
Our force he scatter'd, and our herds he kill'd;
Lyrnessus, *Pedasus* in ashes lay;
But (*Jove* assisting) I surviv'd the day.
Else had I sunk opprest in fatal fight,   125
By fierce *Achilles* and *Minerva*'s might.
Where'ere he mov'd, the Goddess shone before,
And bath'd his brazen lance in hostile gore.
What mortal man *Achilles* can sustain?   ⎫
Th' immortals guard him thro' the dreadful plain, ⎬   130
And suffer not his dart to fall in vain.   ⎭
Were God my aid, this arm should check his pow'r,
Tho' strong in battel as a brazen tow'r.

　　To whom the Son of *Jove*, That God implore,
And be, what great *Achilles* was before.   135
From heav'nly *Venus* thou deriv'st thy strain,
And he, but from a sister of the main;
An aged Sea God, father of his line,
But *Jove* himself the sacred source of thine.
Then lift thy weapon for a noble blow,   140
Nor fear the vaunting of a mortal foe.

　　This said, and spirit breath'd into his breast,
Thro' the thick troops th'embolden'd hero prest:

His vent'rous act the white-arm'd Queen survey'd,
145 And thus, assembling all the pow'rs, she said.
    Behold an action, Gods! that claims your care,
Lo great *Æneas* rushing to the war;
Against *Pelides* he directs his course,
Phœbus impels, and *Phœbus* gives him force.
150 Restrain his bold career; at least, t'attend
Our favour'd hero, let some pow'r descend.
To guard his life, and add to his renown,
We, the great armament of heav'n, came down.
Hereafter let him fall, as Fates design,
155 That spun so short his life's illustrious line:
But lest some adverse God now cross his way,
Give him to know, what pow'rs assist this day:
For how shall mortal stand the dire alarms,
When heav'ns refulgent host appear in arms?
160   Thus she, and thus the God whose force can make
The solid globe's eternal basis shake.
Against the might of man, so feeble known,
Why shou'd cœlestial pow'rs exert their own?
Suffice, from yonder mount to view the scene;
165 And leave to war the fates of mortal men.
But if th'Armipotent, or God of Light,
Obstruct *Achilles*, or commence the fight,
Thence on the Gods of *Troy* we swift descend:
Full soon, I doubt not, shall the conflict end,
170 And these, in ruin and confusion hurl'd,
Yield to our conqu'ring arms the lower world.
    Thus having said, the tyrant of the sea,
Cœrulean Neptune, rose, and led the way.
Advanc'd upon the field there stood a mound
175 Of earth congested, wall'd, and trench'd around;
In elder times to guard *Alcides* made,
(The Work of *Trojans*, with *Minerva*'s aid)
What time, a vengeful monster of the main
Swept the wide shore, and drove him to the plain.
180   Here *Neptune*, and the Gods of *Greece* repair,
With clouds encompass'd, and a veil of air:
The adverse pow'rs, around *Apollo* laid,
Crown the fair hills that silver *Simoïs* shade.

In circle close each heav'nly party sate,
Intent to form the future scheme of Fate; 185
But mix not yet in fight, tho' *Jove* on high
Gives the loud signal, and the heav'ns reply.

    Meanwhile the rushing armies hide the ground;
The trampled center yields a hollow sound:
Steeds cas'd in mail, and chiefs in armour bright, 190
The gleamy champain glows with brazen light.
Amid both hosts (a dreadful space) appear
There, great *Achilles*, bold *Æneas* here.
With tow'ring strides *Æneas* first advanc'd;
The nodding plumage on his helmet danc'd, 195
Spread o'er his breast the fencing shield he bore,
And, as he mov'd, his jav'lin flam'd before.
Not so *Pelides*; furious to engage,
He rush'd impetuous. Such the lion's rage,
Who viewing first his foes with scornful eyes, 200
Tho' all in arms the peopled city rise,
Stalks careless on, with unregarding pride;
Till at the length, by some brave youth defy'd,
To his bold spear the savage turns alone,
He murmurs fury with an hollow groan; 205
He grins, he foams, he rolls his eyes around;
Lash'd by his tail his heaving sides resound;
He calls up all his rage; he grinds his teeth,
Resolv'd on vengeance, or resolv'd on death.
So fierce *Achilles* on *Æneas* flies; 210
So stands *Æneas*, and his force defies.
E'er yet the stern encounter join'd, begun
The seed of *Thetis* thus to *Venus*' son.

    Why comes *Æneas* thro' the ranks so far?
Seeks he to meet *Achilles*' arm in war, 215
In hope the realms of *Priam* to enjoy,
And prove his merits to the throne of *Troy*?
Grant that beneath thy lance *Achilles* dies,
The partial monarch may refuse the prize;
Sons he has many; those thy pride may quell; 220
And 'tis his fault to love those sons too well.
Or, in reward of thy victorious hand,
Has *Troy* propos'd some spacious tract of land?

An ample forest, or a fair domain,
225 Of hills for vines, and arable for grain?
Ev'n this, perhaps, will hardly prove thy lot.
But can *Achilles* be so soon forgot?
Once (as I think) you saw this brandish'd spear,
And then the great *Æneas* seem'd to fear.
230 With hearty haste from *Ida*'s mount he fled,
Nor, till he reach'd *Lyrnessus*, turn'd his head.
Her lofty walls not long our progress stay'd;
Those, *Pallas*, *Jove*, and we, in ruins laid:
In *Grecian* chains her captive race were cast;
235 'Tis true, the great *Æneas* fled too fast.
Defrauded of my conquest once before,
What then I lost, the Gods this day restore.
Go; while thou may'st, avoid the threaten'd fate;
Fools stay to feel it, and are wise too late.
240   To this *Anchises'* son. Such words employ
To one that fears thee, some unwarlike boy:
Such we disdain; the best may be defy'd
With mean reproaches, and unmanly pride:
Unworthy the high race from which we came,
245 Proclaim'd so loudly by the voice of fame,
Each from illustrious fathers draws his Line;
Each Goddess-born; half human, half divine.
Thetis' this day, or *Venus'* offspring dies,
And tears shall trickle from coelestial eyes:
250 For when two heroes, thus deriv'd, contend,
'Tis not in words the glorious strife can end.
If yet thou farther seek to learn my birth
(A tale resounded thro' the spacious earth)
Hear how the glorious origine we prove
255 From ancient *Dardanus*, the first from *Jove*:
Dardania's walls he rais'd; for *Ilion*, then,
(The city since of many-languag'd men)
Was not. The natives were content to till
The shady foot of *Ida*'s fount-ful hill.
260 From *Dardanus*, great *Erichthonius* springs,
The richest, once, of *Asia*'s wealthy kings;
Three thousand mares his spacious pastures bred,
Three thousand foals beside their mothers fed.

Boreas, enamour'd of the sprightly train,
Conceal'd his Godhead in a flowing mane, 265
With voice dissembled to his loves he neigh'd,
And cours'd the dappled beauties o'er the mead:
Hence sprung twelve others of unrival'd kind,
Swift as their mother mares, and father wind.
These lightly skimming, when they swept the plain, 270
Nor ply'd the grass, nor bent the tender grain;
And when along the level seas they flew,
Scarce on the surface curl'd the briny dew.
Such *Erichthonius* was: From him there came
The sacred *Tros*, of whom the *Trojan* name. 275
Three sons renown'd adorn'd his nuptial bed,
Ilus, *Assaracus*, and *Ganymed*:
The matchless *Ganymed*, divinely fair,
Whom heaven enamour'd snatch'd to upper air,
To bear the cup of *Jove* (ætherial guest) 280
The grace and glory of th'ambrosial feast.
The two remaining sons the line divide:
First rose *Laomedon* from *Ilus'* side;
From him *Tithonus*, now in cares grown old,
And *Priam*, (blest with *Hector*, brave and bold:) 285
Clytius and *Lampus*, ever-honour'd pair;
And *Hicetaon*, thunderbolt of war.
From great *Assaracus* sprung *Capys*, he
Begat *Anchises*, and *Anchises* me.
Such is our race: 'Tis fortune gives us birth, 290
But *Jove* alone endues the soul with worth:
He, source of pow'r and might! with boundless sway,
All human courage gives, or takes away.
Long in the field of words we may contend,
Reproach is infinite, and knows no end, 295
Arm'd or with truth or falshood, right or wrong,
So voluble a weapon is the tongue;
Wounded, we wound; and neither side can fail,
For ev'ry man has equal strength to rail:
Women alone, when in the streets they jar, 300
Perhaps excel us in this wordy war;
Like us they stand, encompass'd with the crowd,
And vent their anger, impotent and loud.

Cease then – Our business in the field of fight
305 Is not to question, but to prove our might.
To all those insults thou hast offer'd here,
Receive this answer: 'Tis my flying spear.
    He spoke. With all his force the jav'lin flung,
Fix'd deep, and loudly in the buckler rung.
310 Far on his out-stretch'd arm, *Pelides* held
(To meet the thund'ring lance) his dreadful shield,
That trembled as it stuck; nor void of fear
Saw, e'er it fell, th'immeasurable spear.
His fears were vain; impenetrable charms
315 Secur'd the temper of th'ætherial arms.
Thro' two strong plates the point its passage held,
But stopp'd, and rested, by the third repell'd;
Five plates of various metal, various mold,
Compos'd the shield; of brass each outward fold,
320 Of tin each inward, and the middle gold:
There stuck the lance. Then rising e'er he threw,
The forceful spear of great *Achilles* flew,
And pierc'd the *Dardan* shield's extremest bound,
Where the shrill brass return'd a sharper sound:
325 Thro' the thin verge the *Pelian* weapon glides.
And the slight cov'ring of expanded hides.
Æneas his contracted body bends,
And o'er him high the riven targe extends,
Sees, thro' its parting plates, the upper air,
330 And at his back perceives the quiv'ring spear:
A fate so near him, chills his soul with fright,
And swims before his eyes the many-colour'd light.
Achilles, rushing in with dreadful cries,
Draws his broad blade, and at *Æneas* flies:
335 *Æneas* rouzing as the foe came on,
(With force collected) heaves a mighty stone:
A mass enormous! which in modern days
No two of earth's degen'rate sons could raise.
But Ocean's God, whose earthquakes rock the ground,
340 Saw the distress, and mov'd the pow'rs around.
    Lo! on the brink of fate *Æneas* stands,
An instant victim to *Achilles'* hands:

By *Phœbus* urg'd; but *Phœbus* has bestow'd
His aid in vain: The man o'erpow'rs the God.
And can ye see this righteous chief attone   345
With guiltless blood, for vices not his own?
To all the Gods his constant vows were paid;
Sure, tho' he wars for *Troy*, he claims our aid.
Fate wills not this; nor thus can *Jove* resign
The future father of the *Dardan* line: 350
The first great ancestor obtain'd his grace,
And still his love descends on all the race.
For *Priam* now, and *Priam*'s faithless kind,
At length are odious to th'all-seeing mind;
On great *Æneas* shall devolve the reign,   355
And sons succeeding sons, the lasting line sustain.

   The great earth-shaker thus: To whom replies
Th'imperial Goddess with the radiant eyes.
Good as he is, to immolate or spare
The *Dardan* Prince, O *Neptune*, be thy care;   360
Pallas and I, by all that Gods can bind,
Have sworn destruction to the *Trojan* kind;
Not ev'n an instant to protract their fate,
Or save one member of the sinking state;
Till her last flame be quench'd with her last gore,   365
And ev'n her crumbling ruins are no more.

   The King of Ocean to the fight descends,
Thro' all the whistling darts his course he bends,
Swift interpos'd between the warriours flies,
And casts thick darkness o'er *Achilles*' eyes.   370
From great *Æneas*' shield the spear he drew,
And at its master's feet the weapon threw.
That done, with force divine, he snatch'd on high
The *Dardan* Prince, and bore him thro' the sky,
Smooth-gliding without step, above the heads   375
Of warring heroes, and of bounding steeds.
Till at the battel's utmost verge they light,
Where the slow *Caucons* close the rear of fight:
The Godhead there (his heav'nly form confess'd)
With words like these the panting chief address'd.   380

   What Pow'r, O Prince, with force inferior far,
Urg'd thee to meet *Achilles*' arm in war?

Henceforth beware, nor antedate thy doom,
Defrauding Fate of all thy fame to come.
385 But when the day decreed (for come it must)
Shall lay this dreadful hero in the dust,
Let then the furies of that arm be known,
Secure, no *Grecian* force transcends thy own.
        With that, he left him wond'ring as he lay,
390 Then from *Achilles* chas'd the mist away:
Sudden, returning with the stream of light,
The scene of war came rushing on his sight.
Then thus, amaz'd: What wonders strike my mind!
My spear, that parted on the wings of wind,
395 Laid here before me! and the *Dardan* Lord
That fell this instant, vanish'd from my sword!
I thought alone with mortals to contend,
But pow'rs cœlestial sure this foe defend.
Great as he is, our arm he scarce will try,
400 Content for once, with all his Gods, to fly.
Now then let others bleed – This said, aloud
He vents his fury, and inflames the crowd.
O *Greeks* (he cries, and every rank alarms)
Join battel, man to man, and arms to arms!
405 'Tis not in me, tho' favour'd by the sky,
To mow whole troops, and make whole armies fly:
No God can singly such a host engage,
Not *Mars* himself, nor great *Minerva*'s rage.
But whatsoe'er *Achilles* can inspire,
410 Whate'er of active force, or acting fire,
Whate'er this heart can prompt, or hand obey;
All, all *Achilles*, *Greeks*! is yours to–day.
Thro' yon wide host this arm shall scatter fear,
And thin the squadrons with my single spear.
415   He said: Nor less elate with martial joy,
The god-like *Hector* warm'd the troops of *Troy*.
Trojans to war! Think *Hector* leads you on;
Nor dread the vaunts of *Peleus*' haughty son.
Deeds must decide our fate. Ev'n those with words
420 Insult the brave, who tremble at their swords:
The weakest atheist-wretch all heav'n defies,
But shrinks and shudders, when the thunder flies.

Nor from yon' boaster shall your chief retire,
Not tho' his heart were steel, his hands were fire;
That fire, that steel, your *Hector* shou'd withstand,   425
And brave that vengeful heart, that dreadful hand.
     Thus (breathing rage thro' all) the hero said;
A wood of lances rises round his head,
Clamours on clamours tempest all the air,
They join, they throng, they thicken to the war.   430
But *Phœbus* warns him from high heav'n to shun
The single fight with *Thetis'* god-like son;
More safe to combate in the mingled band,
Nor tempt too near the terrours of his hand.
He hears, obedient to the God of Light,   435
And plung'd within the ranks, awaits the fight.
     Then fierce *Achilles*, shouting to the skies,
On *Troy*'s whole force with boundless fury flies.
First falls *Iphytion*, at his army's head;
Brave was the chief, and brave the host he led;   440
From great *Otrynteus* he deriv'd his blood,
His mother was a *Naïs* of the flood;
Beneath the shades of *Tmolus*, crown'd with snow,
From *Hyde*'s walls, he rul'd the lands below.
Fierce as he springs, the sword his head divides;   445
The parted visage falls on equal sides:
With loud-resounding arms he strikes the plain;
While thus *Achilles* glories o'er the slain.
     Lye there *Otryntides!* the *Trojan* earth
Receives thee dead, tho' *Gygæ* boast thy birth;   450
Those beauteous fields where *Hyllus'* waves are roll'd,
And plenteous *Hermus* swells with tides of gold,
Are thine no more – Th' insulting hero said,
And left him sleeping in eternal shade.
The rolling wheels of *Greece* the body tore,   455
And dash'd their axles with no vulgar gore.
     Demoleon next, *Antenor*'s offspring, laid
Breathless in dust, the price of rashness paid.
Th' impatient steel with full-descending sway
Forc'd thro' his brazen helm its furious way,   460
Resistless drove the batter'd skull before,
And dash'd and mingled all the brains with gore.

This sees *Hippodamas*, and seiz'd with fright,
Deserts his chariot for a swifter flight:
465 The lance arrests him: an ignoble wound
The panting *Trojan* rivets to the ground.
He groans away his soul: Not louder roars
At *Neptune*'s shrine on *Helice*'s high shores
The victim bull; the rocks rebellow round,
470 And Ocean listens to the grateful sound.

    Then fell on *Polydore* his vengeful rage,
The youngest hope of *Priam*'s stooping age:
(Whose feet for swiftness in the race surpast)
Of all his sons, the dearest, and the last.
475 To the forbidden field he takes his flight
In the first folly of a youthful knight,
To vaunt his swiftness, wheels around the plain,
But vaunts not long, with all his swiftness slain.
Struck where the crossing belts unite behind,
480 And golden rings the double back-plate join'd:
Forth thro' the navel burst the thrilling steel;
And on his knees with piercing shrieks he fell;
The rushing entrails pour'd upon the ground
His hands collect; and darkness wraps him round.

485 When *Hector* view'd, all ghastly in his gore
Thus sadly slain, th' unhappy *Polydore*;
A cloud of sorrow overcast his sight,
His soul no longer brook'd the distant fight,
Full in *Achilles'* dreadful front he came,
490 And shook his jav'lin like a waving flame.
The son of *Peleus* sees, with joy possest,
His heart high-bounding in his rising breast:
And, lo! the man, on whom black fates attend;
The man, that slew *Achilles*, in his friend!
495 No more shall *Hector*'s and *Pelides'* spear
Turn from each other in the walks of war –
Then with revengeful eyes he scan'd him o'er:
Come, and receive thy fate! He spake no more.

    Hector, undaunted, thus. Such words employ
500 To one that dreads thee, some unwarlike boy:
Such we could give, defying and defy'd,
Mean intercourse of obloquy and pride!

I know thy force to mine superiour far;
But heav'n alone confers success in war:
Mean as I am, the Gods may guide my dart,   505
And give it entrance in a braver heart.

    Then parts the lance: But *Pallas'* heav'nly breath,
Far from *Achilles* wafts the winged death:
The bidden dart again to *Hector* flies,
And at the feet of its great master lies.   510
Achilles closes with his hated foe,
His heart and eyes with flaming fury glow:
But present to his aid, *Apollo* shrouds
The favour'd hero in a veil of clouds.
Thrice struck *Pelides* with indignant heart,   515
Thrice in impassive air he plung'd the dart:
The spear a fourth time bury'd in the cloud,
He foams with fury, and exclaims aloud.

    Wretch! thou hast scap'd again. Once more thy flight
Has sav'd thee, and the partial God of Light.   520
But long thou shalt not thy just fate withstand,
If any pow'r assist *Achilles'* hand.
Fly then inglorious! But thy flight this day
Whole hecatombs of *Trojan* ghosts shall pay.

    With that, he gluts his rage on numbers slain: 525
Then *Dryops* tumbled to th'ensanguin'd plain,
Pierc'd thro' the neck: He left him panting there,
And stopp'd *Demuchus*, great *Philetor*'s heir,
Gigantick chief! Deep gash'd th'enormous blade,
And for the soul an ample passage made.   530
Laogonus and *Dardanus* expire,
The valiant sons of an unhappy sire;
Both in one instant from the chariot hurl'd,
Sunk in one instant to the nether world;
This diff'rence only their sad fates afford,   535
That one the spear destroy'd, and one the sword.

    Nor less unpity'd young *Alastor* bleeds;
In vain his youth, in vain his beauty pleads:
In vain he begs thee with a suppliant's moan,
To spare a form, an age so like thy own!   540
Unhappy boy! no pray'r, no moving art
E'er bent that fierce, inexorable heart!

While yet he trembled at his knees, and cry'd,
The ruthless falchion op'd his tender side;
545   The panting liver pours a flood of gore,
That drowns his bosom, till he pants no more.
    Thro' *Mulius'* head then drove th'impetuous spear,
The Warriour falls, transfix'd from ear to ear.
Thy life, *Echeclus!* next the sword bereaves,
550   Deep thro' the front the pond'rous falchion cleaves;
Warm'd in the brain the smoaking weapon lies,
The purple death comes floating o'er his eyes.
Then brave *Deucalion* dy'd: The dart was flung
Where the knit nerves the pliant elbow strung;
555   He dropp'd his arm, an unassisting weight,
And stood all impotent, expecting fate:
Full on his neck the falling falchion sped,
From his broad shoulders hew'd his crested head:
Forth from the bone the spinal marrow flies,
560   And sunk in dust, the corps extended lies.
Rhigmus, whose race from fruitful *Thracia* came,
(The son of *Pireus*, an illustrious name,)
Succeeds to fate: The spear his belly rends;
Prone from his car the thund'ring chief descends:
565   The squire who saw expiring on the ground
His prostrate master, rein'd the steeds around:
His back scarce turn'd, the *Pelian* jav'lin gor'd;
And stretch'd the servant o'er his dying Lord.
As when a flame the winding valley fills,
570   And runs on crackling shrubs between the hills;
Then o'er the stubble up the mountain flies,
Fires the high woods, and blazes to the skies,
This way and that, the spreading torrent roars;
So sweeps the hero thro' the wasted shores.
575   Around him wide, immense destruction pours,
And earth is delug'd with the sanguine show'rs.
As with autumnal harvests cover'd o'er,
And thick bestrown, lies *Ceres'* sacred floor,
When round and round, with never-weary'd pain,
580   The trampling steers beat out th'unnumber'd grain.
So the fierce coursers, as the chariot rolls,
Tread down whole ranks, and crush out Heroes souls.

Dash'd from their hoofs while o'er the dead they fly,
Black, bloody drops the smoking chariot dye:
The spiky wheels thro' heaps of carnage tore;   585
And thick the groaning axles dropp'd with gore.
High o'er the scene of death *Achilles* stood,
All grim with dust, all horrible in blood:
Yet still insatiate, still with rage on flame;
Such is the lust of never-dying Fame!   590

5. *Then* Jove *to* Themis *gives command,* &c.] The poet is now to bring his hero again into action, and he introduces him with the utmost pomp and grandeur: The Gods are assembled only upon this account, and *Jupiter* permits several Deities to join with the *Trojans,* and hinder *Achilles* from over-ruling destiny itself.

The circumstance of sending *Themis* to assemble the Gods is very beautiful; she is the Goddess of justice; the *Trojans* by the rape of *Helen,* and by repeated perjuries having broken her laws, she is the properest messenger to summon a synod to bring them to punishment.

Eustathius.

Proclus has given a farther Explanation of this. *Themis* or *Justice* (says he) is made to assemble the Gods round *Jupiter,* because it is from him that all the powers of Nature take their virtue, and receive their orders; and *Jupiter* sends them to the relief of both parties, to shew that nothing falls out but by his permission, and that neither angels, nor men, nor the elements, act but according to the power which is given them.

15. *All but old Ocean.*] *Eustathius* gives two reasons why *Oceanus* was absent from this assembly: The one is because he is fabled to be the original of all the Gods, and it would have been a piece of indecency for him to see the Deities, who were all his descendents, war upon one another by joining adverse parties: The other reason he draws from the allegory of *Oceanus,* which signifies the element of water, and consequently the whole element could not ascend into the Æther; But whereas *Neptune,* the rivers, and the fountains are said to have been present, this is no way impossible, if we consider it in an allegorical sense, which implies, that the rivers, seas, and fountains supply the air with vapours, and by that means ascend into the æther.

35.   *Cœlestial pow'rs! descend,*
           And as your minds direct, your succour lend
           To either host –]

Eustathius informs us, that the ancients were very much divided upon this passage of *Homer*. Some have criticised it, and others have answered their criticism; but he reports nothing more than the objection, without transmitting the answer to us. Those who condemned *Homer*, said *Jupiter* was for the *Trojans*; he saw the *Greeks* were the strongest, so permitted the Gods to declare themselves and go to the battel. But therein that God is deceived, and does not gain his point; for the Gods who favour the *Greeks* being stronger than those who favour the *Trojans*, the *Greeks* will still have the same advantage. I do not know what answer the partisans of *Homer* made, but for my part, I think this objection is more ingenious than solid. *Jupiter* does not pretend that the *Trojans* should be stronger than the *Greeks*, he has only a mind that the decree of destiny should be executed. Destiny had refused to *Achilles* the glory of taking *Troy*, but if *Achilles* fights singly against the *Trojans*, he is capable of forcing destiny; as *Homer* has already elsewhere said, that there had been brave men who had done so. Whereas if the Gods took part, tho' those who followed the *Grecians* were stronger than those who were for the *Trojans*, the latter would however be strong enough to support destiny, and to hinder *Achilles* from making himself master of *Troy*: This was *Jupiter*'s sole view. Thus is this passage far from being blameable, it is on the contrary very beautiful, and infinitely glorious for *Achilles*.   *Dacier*.

41.   *– Or* Ilion's *sacred wall*
           May fall this day, tho' Fate forbid the fall.]

Mons. *de la Motte* criticizes on this passage, as thinking it absurd and contradictory to *Homer*'s own system, to imagine, that what Fate had ordained should not come to pass. *Jupiter* here seems to fear that *Troy* will be taken this very day in spite of destiny, ὑπὲρ μόρον. M. *Boivin* answers, that the explication hereof depends wholly upon the principles of the ancient pagan theology and their doctrine concerning Fate. It is certain, according to *Homer* and *Virgil*, that what destiny had decreed did not constantly happen in the precise time marked by destiny, the fatal moment was not to be retarded, but might be hastened: For example, that of the death of *Dido* was advanced by the blow she gave herself; her hour was not then come.

> *– Nec fato, merita nec morte peribat,*
> *Sed misera ante diem –*

> [For since she dy'd, not doom'd by heav'ns decree,
> Or her own crime; but human casualty.]

Every violent death was accounted ὑπὲρ μόρον, that is, before the fated time, or (which is the same thing) against the natural order, *turbato mortalitatis ordine*, as the *Romans* expressed it. And the same might be said of any misfortunes which men drew upon themselves by their own ill conduct. (See the note on v. 560. *lib.* 16.) In a word, it must be allowed that it was not easy, in the pagan religion, to form the justest ideas upon a doctrine so difficult to be cleared; and upon which it is no great wonder if a poet should not always be perfectly consistent with himself, when it has puzzel'd such a number of divines and philosophers.

44.   *On adverse parts the warring Gods engage,*
      Heav'ns awful Queen, &c.]

Eustathius has a very curious remark upon this division of the Gods in *Homer*, which M. *Dacier* has entirely borrowed (as indeed no commentator ever borrowed more, or acknowledged less, than she has every where done from *Eustathius.*) This division, says he, is not made at random, but founded upon very solid reasons, drawn from the nature of those two nations. He places on the side of the *Greeks* all the Gods who preside over arts and sciences, to signify how much in that respect the *Greeks* excelled all other nations. *Juno, Pallas, Neptune, Mercury* and *Vulcan* are for the *Greeks*; *Juno*, not only as the Goddess who presides over marriage, and who is concerned to revenge an injury done to the nuptial bed, but likewise as the Goddess who represents monarchical government, which was better established in *Greece* than any where else; *Pallas*, because being the Goddess of war and wisdom, she ought to assist those who are wronged; besides the *Greeks* understood the art of war better than the *Barbarians*; *Neptune*, because he was an enemy to the *Trojans* upon account of *Laomedon*'s perfidiousness, and because most of the *Greeks* being come from islands or peninsula's they were in some sort his subjects; *Mercury*, because he is a God who presides over stratagems of war, and because *Troy* was taken by that of the wooden horse; and lastly *Vulcan*, as the declared enemy of *Mars* and of all adulterers, and as the father of arts.

52. *Mars fiery-helm'd, the laughter-loving Dame.*] The reasons why *Mars* and *Venus* engage for the *Trojans* are very obvious; the point in hand was to favour ravishers and debauchees. But the same reason, you will say, does not serve for *Apollo*, *Diana* and *Latona.* It is urged that *Apollo* is for the *Trojans*, because of the darts and arrows which were the principal strength of the *Barbarians*; and *Diana*, because she presided over dancing, and those *Barbarians* were great dancers; and *Latona*, as influenced by her children. *Xanthus* being a *Trojan* river is interested for his countrey.   `Eustathius.`

75. *Above the Sire of Gods,* &c.] 'The images (says *Longinus*) which *Homer* gives of the combate of the Gods, have in 'em something prodigiously great and magnificent. We see in these verses, the earth opened to its very center, hell ready to disclose itself, the whole machine of the world upon the point to be destroyed and overturned: To shew that in such a conflict, heaven and hell, all things mortal and immortal, the whole creation in short was engaged in this battel, and all the extent of nature in danger.'

> *Non secus ac si qua penitus vi terra dehiscens*
> *Infernas reseret sedes & regna recludat*
> *Pallida, Diis invisa, superque immane barathrum*
> *Cernatur, trepidentque immisso lumine manes.*   Virgil.

> [So the pent vapours with a rumbling sound
> Heave from below; and rend the hollow ground:
> A sounding flaw succeeds: And from on high,
> The Gods, with hate beheld the neather sky:
> The ghosts repine at violated night.]

Madam *Dacier* rightly observes that this copy is inferior to the original on this account, that *Virgil* has made a comparison of that which *Homer* made an action. This occasions an infinite difference, which is easy to be perceived.

One may compare with this noble passage of *Homer*, the battel of the Gods and Giants in *Hesiod*'s *Theogony*, which is one of the sublimest parts of that author; and *Milton*'s battel of the *Angels* in the sixth book: The elevation, and enthusiasm of our great countryman seems owing to this original.

91. *First silver-shafted* Phœbus *took the plain,* &c.] With what art does the poet engage the Gods in this conflict! *Neptune* opposes *Apollo,* which implies that things moist and dry are in continual discord: *Pallas* fights with *Mars,* which signifies that rashness and wisdom always disagree: *Juno* is against *Diana,* that is, nothing more differs from a marriage state, than celibacy: *Vulcan* engages *Xanthus,* that is, fire and water are in perpetual variance. Thus we have a fine allegory concealed under the veil of excellent poetry, and the reader receives a double satisfaction at the same time from beautiful verses, and an instructive moral.   *Eustathius.*

119. *Already have I met,* &c.] *Eustathius* remarks that the poet lets no opportunity pass of inserting into his poem the actions that preceded the tenth year of the war, especially the actions of *Achilles* the hero of it. In this place he brings in *Æneas* extolling the bravery of his enemy and confessing himself to have formerly been vanquish'd by him: At the same time he preserves a piece of ancient history by inserting into the poem the hero's conquest of *Pedasus* and *Lyrnessus.*

121.   From Ida's *woods he chas'd us –*
            But Jove *assisting I surviv'd.*]

It is remarkable that *Æneas* owed his safety to his flight from *Achilles,* but it may seem strange that *Achilles* who was so fam'd for his Swiftness, should not be able to overtake him, even with *Minerva* for his guide. *Eustathius* answers, that this might proceed from the better knowledge *Æneas* might have of the ways and defiles: *Achilles* being a stranger, and *Æneas* having long kept his father's flocks in those parts.

He farther observes, that the word φάος [light] discovers that it was in the night that *Achilles* pursued *Æneas.*

174. *Advanc'd upon the field there stood a mound,* &c.] It may not be unnecessary to explain this passage to make it understood by the reader: The poet is very short in the description, as supposing the fact already known, and hastens to the combat between *Achilles* and *Æneas.* This is very judicious in *Homer* not to dwell on a piece of history that had no relation to his action, when he has raised the reader's expectation by so pompous an introduction, and made the Gods themselves his spectators.

The story is as follows. *Laomedon* having defrauded *Neptune* of the reward he promised him for the building the walls of *Troy*, *Neptune* sent a monstrous whale, to which *Laomedon* exposed his daughter *Hesione*: But *Hercules* having undertaken to destroy the monster, the *Trojans* raised an intrenchment to defend *Hercules* from his pursuit: This being a remarkable piece of conduct in the *Trojans*, it gave occasion to the poet to adorn a plain narration with fiction by ascribing the work to *Pallas* the Goddess of wisdom.   *Eustathius.*

180. *Here* Neptune, *and the Gods,* &c.] I wonder why *Eustathius* and all other commentators should be silent upon this recess of the Gods: It seems strange at the first view, that so many deities, after having entered the scene of action, should perform so short a part, and immediately become themselves spectators? I conceive the reason of this conduct in the poet to be, that *Achilles* has been inactive during the greatest part of the poem; and as he is the hero of it, ought to be the chief character in it: The poet therefore withdraws the Gods from the field that *Achilles* may have the whole honour of the day, and not act in subordination to the deities: Besides, the poem now draws to a conclusion, and it is necessary for *Homer* to enlarge upon the exploits of *Achilles*, that he may leave a noble idea of his valour upon the mind of the reader.

214, &c. *The conversation of* Achilles *and* Æneas.] I shall lay before the reader the words of *Eustathius* in defence of this passage, which I confess seems to me to be faulty in the poet. The reader (says he) would naturally expect some great and terrible atchievements should ensue from *Achilles* upon his first entrance upon action. The poet seems to prepare us for it, by his magnificent introduction of him into the field: But instead of a storm, we have a calm; he follows the same method in this book as he did in the third, where when both armies were ready to engage in a general conflict, he ends the day in a single combat between two heroes: Thus he always agreeably surprizes his readers. Besides the admirers of *Homer* reap a farther advantage from this conversation of the Heroes: There is a chain of ancient history as well as a series of poetical beauties.

Madam *Dacier*'s excuse is very little better: And to shew that this is really a fault in the poet, I believe I may appeal to the taste of every reader who certainly finds himself disappointed: Our expectation is raised to see Gods and heroes engage, when suddenly it all sinks into such a combat in which neither party receives a wound; and (what is more extraordinary) the Gods are made the spectators of so small an action! What occasion was there for thunder, earthquakes, and descending deities, to introduce a matter of so little importance? Neither is it any excuse to say he has given us a piece of ancient history; we expected to read a poet, not an historian. In short, after the greatest preparation for action imaginable, he suspends the whole narration, and from the heat of a poet, cools at once into the simplicity of an historian.

258. *The natives were content to till*
The shady foot of Ida's *fount-ful hill.*]

Κτίσσε δὲ Δαρδανίην, ἐπεὶ οὔ πω Ἴλιος ἱρὴ
Ἐν πεδίῳ πεπόλιστο πόλις μερόπων ἀνθρώπων
Ἀλλ' ἔθ' ὑπωρείας ᾤκεον πολυπίδακος Ἴδης.

[cf. trans. Pope, 256–9]

Plato and *Strabo* understand this passage as favouring the opinion that the mountainous parts of the world were first inhabited, after the universal deluge; and that mankind by degrees descended to dwell in the lower parts of the hills (which they would have the word ὑπώρεια signify) and only in greater process of time ventured into the valleys: *Virgil* however seems to have taken this word in a sense something different where he alludes to this passage.   *Æn.* 3. 109.

– *Nondum Ilium et arces*
Pergameæ steterant, habitabant vallibus imis.

[E'er *Ilium* and the *Trojan* tow'rs arose,
In humble vales they built their soft abodes:]

262. *Three thousand mares,* &c.] The number of the horses and mares of *Ericthonius* may seem incredible, were we not assured by *Herodotus* that there were in the stud of *Cyrus* at one time (besides those for the service of war) eight hundred horses and six thousand six hundred mares.   *Eustathius.*

264. Boreas, *enamour'd,* &c.] *Homer* has the happiness of making the least circumstance considerable; the subject grows under his hands, and the plainest matter shines in his dress of poetry: Another poet would have said these horses were as swift as the wind, but *Homer* tells you that they sprung from *Boreas* the God of the wind; and thence drew their swiftness.

270. *These lightly skimming, as they swept the plain.*] The poet illustrates the swiftness of these horses by describing them as running over the standing corn, and surface of waters, without making any impression. *Virgil* has imitated these lines, and adapts what *Homer* says of these horses to the swiftness of *Camilla*.   *Æn.* 7. 809.

> *Illa vel intactæ segetis per summa volaret*
> *Gramina; nec teneras cursu læsisset aristas:*
> *Vel mare per medium, fluctu supensa tumenti*
> *Ferret iter, celeres nec tingeret æquore plantas.*

> [Flew o'er the fields, nor hurt the bearded grain:
> She swept the seas, and as she skim'd along,
> Her flying feet unbath'd on billows hung.]

The reader will easily perceive that *Virgil*'s is almost a literal translation: He has imitated the very run of the verses, which flow nimbly away in dactyls, and as swift as the wind they describe.

I cannot but observe one thing in favour of *Homer*, that there can no greater commendation be given to him, than by considering the conduct of *Virgil*: who, tho' undoubtedly the greatest poet after him, seldom ventures to vary much from his original in the passages he takes from him, as in a despair of improving, and contented if he can but equal them.

280. *To bear the cup of* Jove.] To be a cup-bearer has in all ages and nations been reckon'd an honourable employment: *Sappho* mentions it in honour of her brother *Larichus*, that he was cup-bearer to the nobles of *Mitylene*: The son of *Menelaus* executed the same office, *Hebe* and *Mercury* served the Gods in the same station.

It was the custom in the pagan worship to employ noble youths to pour the wine upon the sacrifice: In this office *Ganymede* might probably attend upon the altar of *Jupiter*, and from thence was fabled to be his cup-bearer.   *Eustath.*

339. *But Ocean's God*, &c.] The conduct of the poet in making *Æneas*

owe his safety to *Neptune* in this place is remarkable: *Neptune* is an enemy to the *Trojans*, yet he dares not suffer so pious a man to fall, lest *Jupiter* should be offended: This shews, says *Eustathius*, that piety is always under the protection of God; and that favours are sometimes conferred not out of kindness, but to prevent a greater detriment; thus *Neptune* preserves *Æneas*, lest *Jupiter* should revenge his death upon the *Grecians.*

345. *And can ye see this righteous chief,* &c.] Tho' *Æneas* is represented a man of great courage, yet his piety is his most shining character: This is the reason why he is always the care of the Gods, and they favour him constantly thro' the whole poem with their immediate protection.

'Tis in this light that *Virgil* has presented him to the view of the reader: His valour bears but the second place in the *Æneis.* In the *Ilias* indeed he is drawn in miniature, and in the *Æneis* at full length; but there are the same Features in the copy, which are in the original, and he is the same *Æneas* in *Rome* as he was in *Troy.*

355. *On great Æneas shall devolve the reign,*
    And sons succeeding sons the lasting line sustain.]

The story of *Æneas* his founding the *Roman* empire gave *Virgil* the finest occasion imaginable of paying a complement to *Augustus*, and his countrymen, who were fond of being thought the descendants of *Troy.* He has translated these two lines literally, and put them in the nature of a prophecy; as the favourers of the opinion of *Æneas*'s sailing into *Italy*, imagine *Homer*'s to be.

> – Αἰνείαο βίη Τρώεσσιν ἀνάξει
> Καὶ παῖδες παίδων τοί κεν μετόπισθε γένωνται.

[The might of Aeneas shall rule over the Trojans,
  And the sons of his sons, and those who are born
      thereafter shall continue to rule over them.]

Hic domus Æneæ cunctis dominabitur oris,
Et nati natorum & qui nascentur ab illis.

[Through the wide world th' *Æneian* house shall reign,
  And children's children shall the crown sustain.]

There has been a very ancient alteration made (as *Strabo* observes) in

these two lines by substituting πάντεσσι (over all) in the room of Τρώ-
εσσι (over the Trojans). It is not improbable but *Virgil* might give
occasion for it, by his *cunctis dominabitur oris* ([the house of Aeneas]
shall rule over all lands).

Eustathius does not entirely discountenance this story: If it be
understood, says he, as a prophecy, the poet might take it from the
Sibylline oracles. He farther remarks that the poet artfully interweaves
into his poem not only the things which happened before the commence-
ment, and in the prosecution of the *Trojan* war; but other matters of
importance which happened even after that war was brought to a
conclusion. Thus for instance, we have here a piece of history not
extant in any other author, by which we are informed that the house of
Æneas succeeded to the crown of *Troas*, and to the kingdom of *Priam.*

Eustathius.

This passage is very considerable, for it ruins the famous chimæra of
the *Roman* empire, and of the family of the *Cæsars*, who both pretended
to deduce their original from *Venus* by *Æneas*, alledging that after the
taking of *Troy*, *Æneas* came into *Italy*, and this pretension is hereby
actually destroyed. This testimony of *Homer* ought to be looked upon
as an authentick act, the fidelity and verity whereof cannot be ques-
tioned. *Neptune*, as much an enemy as he is to the *Trojans*, declares
that *Æneas*, and after him his posterity, shall reign over the *Trojans.*
Wou'd *Homer* have put this prophecy in *Neptune*'s mouth, if he had not
known that *Æneas* did not leave *Troy*, but that he reigned there, and if
he had not seen in his time the descendants of that Prince reign there
likewise? That poet wrote 260 Years, or thereabouts, after the taking of
Troy, and what is very remarkable he wrote in some of the towns of
Ionia, that is to say, in the neighbourhood of *Phrygia*, so that the time
and place give such a weight to his deposition that nothing can
invalidate it. All that the historians have written concerning *Æneas*'s
voyage into *Italy*, ought to be considered as a romance, made on
purpose to destroy all historical truth, for the most ancient is posterior
to *Homer* by some ages. Before *Dionysius* of *Halicarnassus*, some
writers being sensible of the strength of this passage of *Homer*,
undertook to explain it so as to reconcile it with this fable, and they
said that *Æneas*, after having been in *Italy*, returned to *Troy*, and left
his son *Ascanius* there. *Dionysius* of *Halicarnassus*, little satisfied with
this solution, which did not seem to him to be probable, has taken
another method: He would have it that by these words, 'He shall reign
over the *Trojans*,' *Homer* meant, he shall reign over the *Trojans* whom

he shall carry with him into *Italy*. 'For is it not possible,' says he, 'that *Æneas* should reign over the *Trojans*, whom he had taken with him, though settled elsewhere?'

That historian, who wrote in *Rome* itself, and in the very reign of *Augustus*, was willing to make his court to that Prince, by explaining this passage of *Homer* so as to favour the chimæra he was possessed with. And this is a reproach that may with some justice be cast on him; for poets may by their fictions flatter Princes and welcome: 'Tis their trade. But for historians to corrupt the gravity and severity of history, to substitute fable in the place of truth, is what ought not to be pardoned. *Strabo* was much more scrupulous, for tho' he wrote his books of geography towards the beginning of *Tiberius*'s reign, yet he had the courage to give a right explication to this passage of *Homer*, and to aver, that this poet said, and meant, that *Æneas* remained at *Troy*, that he reigned therein, *Priam*'s whole Race being extinguished, and that he left the kingdom to his children after him. *lib.* 13. You may see this whole matter discussed in a Letter from M. *Bochart* to M. *de Segrais*, who has prefixed it to his remarks upon the translation of *Virgil.*

378. *Where the slow* Caucons *close the rear.*] The *Caucones* (says *Eustathius*) were of *Paphlagonian* extract: And this perhaps was the reason why they are not distinctly mentioned in the catalogue, they being included under the general name of *Paphlagonians*: Tho' two lines are quoted which are said to have been left out by some transcriber, and immediately followed this,

$$K\rho\hat{\omega}\mu\nu\alpha\nu \ \tau' \ \alpha\dot{\imath}\gamma\iota\alpha\lambda\acute{o}\nu \ \tau\epsilon \ \kappa\alpha\dot{\imath} \ \dot{\upsilon}\psi\eta\lambda o\dot{\upsilon}s \ \ \rm{'}E\rho\upsilon\theta\acute{\imath}\nu o\upsilon s.$$

[The Cromnian shore and the Erythinian highlands.]

Which verses are these,

$$K\alpha\acute{\upsilon}\kappa\omega\nu\alpha s \ \alpha\mathring{\upsilon}\tau' \ \mathring{\eta}\gamma\epsilon \ \pi o\lambda\acute{\upsilon}\kappa\lambda\epsilon os \ \upsilon\mathring{\imath}\grave{o}s \ \mathring{\alpha}\mu\acute{\upsilon}\mu\iota o\nu.$$

[The famous, blameless son led the Caucones.]

Or as others read it, ᾿Aμειβos (new recruit).

$$O\mathring{\imath} \ \pi\epsilon\rho\grave{\imath} \ \pi\alpha\rho\theta\acute{\epsilon}\nu\iota o\nu \ \pi o\tau\alpha\mu\grave{o}\nu \ \kappa\lambda\upsilon\tau\grave{\alpha} \ \delta\acute{\omega}\mu\alpha\tau' \ \acute{\epsilon}\nu\alpha\iota o\nu.$$

[They dwelled in their shining homes, along the virgin river.]

Or according to others,

Κατὰ δώματ᾽ ἔναιον.

[They inhabited homes.]

Yet I believe these are not *Homer*'s lines, but rather the addition of some transcriber, and 'tis evident by consulting the passage from which they are said to have been curtail'd, that they would be absurd in that place; for the second line is actually there already, and as these *Caucons* are said to live upon the banks of the *Parthenius*, so are the *Paphlagonians* in the above-mentioned passage. It is therefore more probable that the *Caucons* are included in the *Paphlagonians.*

467. – *Not louder roars*
       At Neptune's *shrine on* Helice's *high shores,* &c.]

In *Helice*, a town of *Achaia*, three quarters of a league from the gulph of *Corinth*, *Neptune* had a magnificent temple where the *Ionians* offered every year to him a sacrifice of a bull; and it was with these people an auspicious sign, and a certain mark, that the sacrifice would be accepted, if the bull bellowed as he was led to the altar. After the *Ionic* migration, which happened about 140 years after the taking of *Troy*, the *Ionians* of *Asia* assembled in the fields of *Priene* to celebrate the same festival in honour of *Heliconian Neptune*; and as those of *Priene* valued themselves upon being originally of *Helice*, they chose for the King of the sacrifice a young *Prienian.* It is needless to dispute from whence the poet has taken his comparison; for as he lived 100, or 120 years after the *Ionic* migration, it cannot be doubted but he took it in the *Asian Ionia*, and at *Priene* itself; where he had probably often assisted at that sacrifice, and been witness of the ceremonies therein observed. This poet always appears strongly addicted to the customs of the *Ionians*, which makes some conjecture that he was an *Ionian* himself.   *Eustathius. Dacier.*

471. *Then fell on* Polydore *his vengeful rage.*] *Euripides* in his *Hecuba* has followed another tradition when he makes *Polydorus* the son of *Priam*, and of *Hecuba*, and slain by *Polymnestor* King of *Thrace*, after the taking of *Troy*; for according to *Homer*, he is not the son of *Hecuba*, but of *Laothoë*, as he says in the following book, and is slain by *Achilles*: *Virgil* too has rather chosen to follow *Euripides* than *Homer*.

489. *Full in* Achilles' *dreadful front he came.*] The great judgment of
the poet in keeping the character of his hero is in this place very
evident: When *Achilles* was to engage *Æneas* he holds a long conference
with him, and with patience bears the reply of *Æneas*: Had he pursued
the same Method with *Hector*, he had departed from his character.
Anger is the prevailing passion in *Achilles*: He left the field in a rage
against *Agamemnon*, and enter'd it again to be reveng'd of *Hector*: The
poet therefore judiciously makes him take fire at the sight of his
enemy: He describes him as impatient to kill him, he gives him a
haughty challenge, and that challenge is comprehended in a single line:
His impatience to be reveng'd, would not suffer him to delay it by a
length of words.

513. *But present to his aid,* Apollo.] It is a common observation that a
God should never be introduced into a poem but where his presence is
necessary. And it may be asked why the life of *Hector* is of such
importance that *Apollo* should rescue him from the hand of *Achilles*
here, and yet suffer him to fall so soon after? *Eustathius* answers, that
the poet had not yet sufficiently exalted the valour of *Achilles*, he takes
time to enlarge upon his atchievements, and rises by degrees in his
character, till he completes both his courage and resentment at one
blow in the death of *Hector*. And the poet, adds he, pays a great
complement to his favourite countryman, by shewing that nothing but
the intervention of a God could have sav'd *Æneas* and *Hector* from the
hand of *Achilles.*

541. *– No Pray'r, no moving art*
       E'er bent that fierce, inexorable heart!]

I confess it is a Satisfaction to me, to observe with what art the poet
pursues his subject: The opening of the poem professes to treat of the
Anger of *Achilles*; that anger draws on all the great events of the story:
And *Homer* at every opportunity awakens the reader to an attention to
it, by mentioning the effects of it: So that when we see in this place the
hero deaf to youth, and compassion, it is what we expect: Mercy in
him would offend, because it is contrary to his character. *Homer*
proposes him not as a pattern for imitation; but the moral of the poem
which he design'd the Reader should draw from it, is, that we should
avoid anger, since it is ever pernicious in the event.

580. *The trampling steers beat out the unnumber'd grain.*] In *Greece*, instead of threshing the corn as we do, they caused it to be trod out by oxen; this was likewise practised in *Judæa*, as is seen by the law of God, who forbad the *Jews* to muzzle the ox who trod out the corn, *Non ligabis os bovis terentis in area fruges tuas* ('Thou shalt not muzzle the ox when he treadeth out the corn' [King James version]). Deuteron. 25. *Dacier.*

The same practice is still preserved among the *Turks* and modern *Greeks.*

The similes at the end.] It is usual with our author to heap his similes very thick together at the conclusion of a book. He has done the same in the seventeenth: 'Tis the natural discharge of a vast imagination, heated in its progress, and giving itself vent in this crowd of images.

I cannot close the notes upon this book, without observing the dreadful idea of *Achilles*, which the poet leaves upon the mind of the reader. He drives his chariot over shields and mangled heaps of slain: The wheels, the axle-tree, and the horses are stain'd with blood, the hero's eyes burn with fury, and his hands are red with slaughter. A painter might form from this passage the picture of *Mars* in the fulness of his terrours, as well as *Phidias* is said to have drawn from another, that of *Jupiter* in all his majesty.

THE
TWENTY-FIRST BOOK
OF THE
ILIAD

The ARGUMENT

The battel in the river *Scamander*

The Trojans *fly before* Achilles, *some towards the town, others to the river* Scamander: *He falls upon the latter with great slaughter, takes twelve captives alive, to sacrifice to the shade of* Patroclus; *and kills* Lycaon *and* Asteropæus. Scamander *attacks him with all his waves;* Neptune *and* Pallas *assist the Hero;* Simois *joins* Scamander; *at length* Vulcan, *by the instigation of* Juno, *almost dries up the river. This combate ended, the other Gods engage each other. Meanwhile* Achilles *continues the slaughter, drives the rest into* Troy; Agenor *only makes a stand, and is conveyed away in a cloud by* Apollo; *who (to delude* Achilles*) takes upon him* Agenor's *shape, and while he pursues him in that disguise, gives the* Trojans *an opportunity of retiring into their city.*

The same day continues. The scene is on the banks, and in the stream, of Scamander.

And now to *Xanthus'* gliding stream they drove,
Xanthus, immortal progeny of *Jove.*
The river here divides the flying train.
Part to the town fly diverse o'er the plain,
5   Where late their troops triumphant bore the fight,
Now chas'd, and trembling in ignoble flight:
(These with a gather'd mist *Saturnia* shrouds,
And rolls behind the rout a heap of clouds)
Part plunge into the stream: Old *Xanthus* roars,
10 The flashing billows beat the whiten'd shores:
With cries promiscuous all the banks resound,
And here, and there, in eddies whirling round,
The flouncing steeds and shrieking warriours
      drown'd.
As the scorch'd locusts from their fields retire,
15 While fast behind them runs the blaze of fire;
Driv'n from the land before the smoky cloud,
The clust'ring legions rush into the flood:
So plung'd in *Xanthus* by *Achilles'* force,
Roars the resounding surge with men and horse.
20 His bloody lance the hero casts aside,
(Which spreading tam'risks on the margin hide)
Then, like a God, the rapid billows braves,
Arm'd with his sword, high-brandish'd o'er the waves:
Now down he plunges, now he whirls it round,
25 Deep groan'd the waters with the dying sound;
Repeated wounds the red'ning river dy'd,
And the warm purple circled on the tide.

Swift thro' the foamy flood the *Trojans* fly,
And close in rocks or winding caverns lie.
So the huge Dolphin tempesting the main,   30
In shoals before him fly the scaly train,
Confus'dly heap'd they seek their inmost caves,
Or pant and heave beneath the floating waves.
Now tir'd with slaughter, from the *Trojan* band
Twelve chosen youths he drags alive to land;   35
With their rich belts their captive arms constrains,
(Late their proud ornaments, but now their chains.)
These his attendants to the ships convey'd,
Sad Victims! destin'd to *Patroclus'* shade.

    Then, as once more he plung'd amid the flood,   40
The young *Lycaon* in his passage stood;
The son of *Priam*, whom the hero's hand
But late made captive in his father's land,
(As from a sycamore, his sounding steel
Lopp'd the green arms to spoke a chariot wheel)   45
To *Lemnos'* isle he sold the royal slave,
Where *Jason*'s son the price demanded gave;
But kind *Eëtion* touching on the shore,
The ransom'd Prince to fair *Arisbe* bore.
Ten Days were past, since in his father's reign   50
He felt the sweets of liberty again;
The next, that God whom men in vain withstand,
Gives the same youth to the same conqu'ring hand;
Now never to return! and doom'd to go
A sadder journey to the shades below.   55
His well-known face when great *Achilles* ey'd,
(The helm and visor he had cast aside
With wild affright, and dropt upon the field
His useless lance and unavailing shield.)
As trembling, panting, from the stream he fled,   60
And knock'd his fault'ring knees, the hero said.

    Ye mighty Gods! what Wonders strike my view!
Is it in vain our conqu'ring arms subdue?
Sure I shall see yon' heaps of *Trojans* kill'd
Rise from the shades, and brave me on the field: 65
As now the captive, whom so late I bound
And sold to *Lemnos*, stalks on *Trojan* ground!

Not him the sea's unmeasur'd deeps detain,
That barr such numbers from their native plain:
70 Lo! he returns! Try then, my flying spear!
Try, if the grave can hold the wanderer;
If earth at length this active Prince can seize,
Earth, whose strong grasp has held down *Hercules.*
    Thus while he spake, the *Trojan* pale with fears
75 Approach'd, and sought his knees with suppliant tears;
Loth as he was to yield his youthful breath,
And his soul shiv'ring at th' approach of death.
Achilles rais'd the spear, prepar'd to wound;
He kiss'd his feet, extended on the ground:
80 And while above the spear suspended stood,
Longing to dip its thirsty point in blood,
One hand embrac'd them close, one stopt the Dart;
While thus these melting words attempt his heart.
    Thy well-known captive, great *Achilles!* see,
85 Once more *Lycaon* trembles at thy knee.
Some pity to a suppliant's name afford,
Who shar'd the gifts of *Ceres* at thy board;
Whom late thy conqu'ring arm to *Lemnos* bore,
Far from his father, friends, and native shore;
90 A hundred oxen were his price that day,
Now sums immense thy mercy shall repay.
Scarce respited from woes I yet appear,
And scarce twelve morning suns have seen me here;
Lo! *Jove* again submits me to thy hands,
95 Again, her victim cruel fate demands!
I sprung from *Priam,* and *Laothöe* fair,
(Old *Alte*'s daughter, and *Lelegia*'s heir;
Who held in *Pedasus* his fam'd abode,
And rul'd the fields where silver *Satnio* flow'd)
100 Two sons (alas, unhappy sons) she bore;
For ah! one spear shall drink each brother's gore,
And I succeed to slaughter'd *Polydore.*
How from that arm of terrour shall I fly?
Some Dæmon urges! 'tis my doom to die!
105 If ever yet soft pity touch'd thy mind,
Ah! think not me too much of *Hector*'s kind!

Not the same mother gave thy suppliant breath,
With his, who wrought thy lov'd *Patroclus'* death.
      These words, attended with a show'r of tears,
The youth addrest to unrelenting ears: 110
Talk not of life, or ransom, (he replies)
Patroclus dead, whoever meets me, dies:
In vain a single *Trojan* sues for grace;
But least, the sons of *Priam*'s hateful race.
Die then, my friend! what boots it to deplore?   115
The great, the good *Patroclus* is no more!
He, far thy better, was foredoom'd to die,
And thou, dost thou, bewail mortality?
See'st thou not me, whom nature's gifts adorn,
Sprung from a hero, from a Goddess born;   120
The day shall come (which nothing can avert)
When by the spear, the arrow, or the dart,
By night, or day, by force or by design,
Impending death and certain fate are mine.
Die then – he said; and as the word he spoke   125
The fainting stripling sunk, before the stroke;
His hand forgot its grasp, and left the spear:
While all his trembling frame confest his fear.
Sudden, *Achilles* his broad sword display'd,
And buried in his neck the reeking blade.   130
Prone fell the youth; and panting on the land,
The gushing purple dy'd the thirsty sand:
The victor to the stream the carcass gave,
And thus insults him, floating on the wave.
      Lie there, *Lycaon!* let the fish surround   135
Thy bloated corse, and suck thy goary wound:
There no sad mother shall thy fun'rals weep,
But swift *Scamander* roll thee to the deep,
Whose ev'ry wave some wat'ry monster brings,
To feast unpunish'd on the fat of kings.   140
So perish *Troy*, and all the *Trojan* line!
Such ruin theirs, and such compassion mine.
What boots ye now *Scamander*'s worship'd stream,
His earthly honours, and immortal name;
In vain your immolated bulls are slain,   145
Your living coursers glut his gulphs in vain:

Thus he rewards you, with this bitter fate;
Thus, till the *Grecian* vengeance is compleat;
Thus is aton'd *Patroclus'* honour'd shade,
150   And the short absence of *Achilles* paid.
      These boastful words provoke the raging God;
With fury swells the violated flood.
What means divine may yet the pow'r employ,
To check *Achilles*, and to rescue *Troy*?
155   Meanwhile the hero springs in arms, to dare
The great *Asteropeus* to mortal war;
The Son of *Pelagon*, whose lofty line
Flows from the source of *Axius*, stream divine!
(Fair *Peribæa*'s love the God had crown'd,
160   With all his refluent waters circled round)
On him *Achilles* rush'd: He fearless stood,
And shook two spears, advancing from the flood;
The flood impell'd him, on *Pelides*' head
T'avenge his waters choak'd with heaps of dead.
165   Near as they drew, *Achilles* thus began.
      What art thou, boldest of the race of man?
Who, or from whence? Unhappy is the sire,
Whose son encounters our resistless ire.
      O Son of *Peleus!* what avails to trace
170   (Reply'd the warrior) our illustrious race?
From rich *Pæonia*'s valleys I command
Arm'd with protended spears, my native band;
Now shines the tenth bright morning since I came
In aid of *Ilion* to the fields of fame:
175   *Axius*, who swells with all the neighb'ring rills,
And wide around the floated region fills,
Begot my sire, whose spear such glory won:
Now lift thy arm, and try that hero's son!
      Threat'ning he said: The hostile chiefs advance;
180   At once *Asteropeus* discharg'd each lance,
(For both his dext'rous hands the lance cou'd wield)
One struck, but pierc'd not the *Vulcanian* shield;
One raz'd *Achilles* hand; the spouting blood
Spun forth, in earth the fasten'd weapon stood.
185   Like lightning next the *Pelian* jav'lin flies;
Its erring fury hiss'd along the skies;

Deep in the swelling bank was driv'n the spear,
Ev'n to the middle earth'd; and quiver'd there.
Then from his side the sword *Pelides* drew,
And on his foe with doubled fury flew.   190
The foe thrice tugg'd, and shook the rooted wood;
Repulsive of his might the weapon stood:
The fourth, he tries to break the spear in vain;
Bent as he stands, he tumbles to the plain;
His belly open'd with a ghastly wound,   195
The reeking entrails pour upon the ground.
Beneath the hero's feet he panting lies,
And his eye darkens, and his spirit flies:
While the proud victor thus triumphing said,
His radiant armour tearing from the dead: 200
    So ends thy glory! Such the fate they prove
Who strive presumptuous with the sons of *Jove*.
Sprung from a river didst thou boast thy line,
But great *Saturnius* is the source of mine.
How durst thou vaunt thy wat'ry progeny?   205
Of *Peleus*, *Æacus*, and *Jove*, am I;
The race of these superiour far to those,
As he that thunders to the stream that flows.
What rivers can, *Scamander* might have shown;
But *Jove* he dreads, nor wars against his son.   210
Ev'n *Achelöus* might contend in vain,
And all the roaring billows of the main.
Th'eternal Ocean, from whose fountains flow
The seas, the rivers, and the Springs below,
The thund'ring Voice of *Jove* abhors to hear,   215
And in his deep abysses shakes with fear.
    He said; then from the bank his jav'lin tore,
And left the breathless warriour in his gore.
The floating tides the bloody carcass lave,
And beat against it, wave succeeding wave;   220
Till roll'd between the banks, it lies the food
Of curling eels, and fishes of the flood.
All scatter'd round the stream (their mightiest slain)
Th'amaz'd *Pæonians* scour along the plain:
He vents his fury on the flying crew,   225
Thrasius, *Astypylus*, and *Mnesus* slew;

Mydon, Thersilochus, with *Ænius* fell;
And numbers more his lance had plung'd to hell;
But from the bottom of his gulphs profound,
230   *Scamander* spoke; the shores return'd the sound.
        O first of mortals! (for the Gods are thine)
In valour matchless, and in force divine!
If *Jove* have giv'n thee every *Trojan* head,
'Tis not on me thy rage should heap the dead.
235   See! my choak'd streams no more their course can keep,
Nor roll their wonted tribute to the deep.
Turn then, impetuous! from our injur'd flood;
Content, thy slaughters could amaze a God.
        In human form confess'd before his eyes
240   The river thus; and thus the Chief replies.
O sacred stream! thy word we shall obey;
But not till *Troy* the destin'd vengeance pay,
Not till within her tow'rs the perjur'd train
Shall pant, and tremble at our arms again;
245   Not till proud *Hector*, guardian of her wall,
Or stain this lance, or see *Achilles* fall.
        He said; and drove with fury on the foe.
Then to the Godhead of the silver bow
The yellow Flood began: O son of *Jove!*
250   Was not the mandate of the Sire above
Full and express? that *Phœbus* should employ
His sacred arrows in defence of *Troy*,
And make her conquer, till *Hyperion*'s fall
In awful darkness hide the face of all?
255   He spoke in vain – the chief without dismay
Ploughs thro' the boiling surge his desp'rate way.
Then rising in his rage above the shores,
From all his deep the bellowing river roars,
Huge heaps of slain disgorges on the coast,
260   And round the banks the ghastly dead are tost.
While all before, the billows rang'd on high
(A wat'ry bulwark) screen the bands who fly.
Now bursting on his head with thund'ring sound,
The falling deluge whelms the hero round:
265   His loaded shield bends to the rushing tide;
His feet, upborn, scarce the strong flood divide,

Slidd'ring, and stagg'ring. On the border stood
A spreading elm, that overhung the flood;
He seiz'd a bending bough, his steps to stay;
The plant uprooted to his weight gave way,   270
Heaving the bank, and undermining all;
Loud flash the waters to the rushing fall
Of the thick foliage. The large trunk display'd
Bridg'd the rough flood across: The hero stay'd
On this his weight, and rais'd upon his hand,   275
Leap'd from the chanel, and regain'd the land.

Then blacken'd the wild waves; the murmur rose;
The God pursues, a huger billow throws,
And bursts the bank, ambitious to destroy
The man whose fury is the fate of *Troy*.   280
He, like the warlike eagle speeds his pace,
(Swiftest and strongest of th'aërial race)
Far as a spear can fly, *Achilles* springs
At ev'ry bound; his clanging armour rings:
Now here, now there, he turns on ev'ry side,   285
And winds his course before the following tide;
The waves flow after, wheresoe'er he wheels,
And gather fast, and murmur at his heels.
So when a peasant to his garden brings
Soft rills of water from the bubbling springs,   290
And calls the floods from high, to bless his bow'rs
And feed with pregnant streams the plants and flow'rs;
Soon as he clears whate'er their passage staid,
And marks the future current with his spade,
Swift o'er the rolling pebbles, down the hills   295
Louder and louder purl the falling rills,
Before him scatt'ring, they prevent his pains,
And shine in mazy wand'rings o'er the plains.

    Still flies *Achilles*, but before his eyes
Still swift *Scamander* rolls where'er he flies: 300
Not all his speed escapes the rapid floods;
The first of men, but not a match for Gods.
Oft' as he turn'd the torrent to oppose,
And bravely try if all the pow'rs were foes;
So oft' the surge, in wat'ry mountains spread,   305
Beats on his back, or bursts upon his head.

Yet dauntless still the adverse flood he braves,
And still indignant bounds above the waves.
Tir'd by the tides, his knees relax with toil;
310   Wash'd from beneath him, slides the slimy Soil;
When thus (his eyes on heav'n's expansion thrown)
Forth bursts the hero with an angry groan.

Is there no God *Achilles* to befriend,
No pow'r t'avert his miserable end?
315   Prevent, oh *Jove!* this ignominious date,
And make my future life the sport of Fate.
Of all heav'ns oracles believ'd in vain,
But most of *Thetis*, must her son complain;
By *Phœbus'* darts she prophesy'd my fall,
320   In glorious arms before the *Trojan* wall.
Oh! had I dy'd in fields of battel warm,
Stretch'd like a hero, by a hero's arm!
Might *Hector's* spear this dauntless bosom rend,
And my swift soul o'ertake my slaughter'd friend!
325   Ah no! *Achilles* meets a shameful fate,
Oh how unworthy of the brave and great!
Like some vile swain, whom on a rainy day,
Crossing a ford, the torrent sweeps away,
An unregarded carcase to the sea.

330   *Neptune* and *Pallas* haste to his relief,
And thus in human form address the chief:
The pow'r of Ocean first. Forbear thy fear,
O son of *Peleus!* Lo thy Gods appear!
Behold! from *Jove* descending to thy aid,
335   Propitious *Neptune*, and the blue-ey'd maid.
Stay, and the furious flood shall cease to rave:
'Tis not thy fate to glut his angry wave.
But thou, the counsel heav'n suggests, attend!
Nor breathe from combate, nor thy sword suspend,
340   Till *Troy* receive her flying sons, till all
Her routed squadrons pant behind their wall:
Hector alone shall stand his fatal chance,
And *Hector's* blood shall smoke upon thy lance.
Thine is the glory doom'd. Thus spake the Gods;
345   Then swift ascended to the bright abodes.

Stung with new ardour, thus by heav'n impell'd,
He springs impetuous, and invades the field:
O'er all th'expanded plain the waters spread;
Heav'd on the bounding billows danc'd the dead,
Floating midst scatter'd arms; while casques of gold   350
And turn'd up bucklers glitter'd as they roll'd.
High o'er the surging tide, by leaps and bounds,
He wades, and mounts; the parted wave resounds.
Not a whole river stops the hero's course,
While *Pallas* fills him with immortal force.   355
With equal rage, indignant *Xanthus* roars,
And lifts his billows, and o'erwhelms his shores.

Then thus to *Simoïs*: Haste, my brother flood!
And check this mortal that controuls a God:
Our bravest heroes else shall quit the fight,   360
And *Ilion* tumble from her tow'ry height.
Call then thy subject streams, and bid them roar,
From all thy fountains swell thy wat'ry store,
With broken rocks, and with a load of dead,
Charge the black surge, and pour it on his head.   365
Mark how resistless thro' the floods he goes,
And boldly bids the warring Gods be foes!
But nor that force, nor form divine to sight
Shall ought avail him, if our rage unite:
Whelm'd under our dark gulphs those arms shall lie,   370
That blaze so dreadful in each *Trojan* eye;
And deep beneath a sandy mountain hurl'd,
Immers'd remain this terrour of the world.
Such pond'rous ruin shall confound the place,
No *Greek* shall e'er his perish'd relicks grace,   375
No hand his bones shall gather, or inhume;
These his cold rites, and this his wat'ry tomb.

He said; and on the chief descends amain,
Increas'd with gore, and swelling with the slain.
Then murm'ring from his beds, he boils, he raves,   380
And a foam whitens on the purple waves.
At ev'ry step, before *Achilles* stood
The crimson surge, and delug'd him with blood.
Fear touch'd the Queen of heav'n: She saw dismay'd,
She call'd aloud, and summon'd *Vulcan*'s aid.   385

Rise to the war! th'insulting flood requires
Thy wasteful arm: Assemble all thy fires!
While to their aid, by our command enjoin'd,
Rush the swift Eastern and the western wind:
390 These from old Ocean at my word shall blow,
Pour the red torrent on the wat'ry foe,
Corses and arms to one bright ruin turn,
And hissing rivers to their bottoms burn.
Go, mighty in thy rage! display thy pow'r,
395 Drink the whole flood, the crackling trees devour,
Scorch all the banks! and (till our voice reclaim)
Exert th'unweary'd furies of the flame!
     The Pow'r Ignipotent her word obeys:
Wide o'er the plain he pours the boundless blaze;
400 At once consumes the dead, and dries the soil;
And the shrunk waters in their chanel boil:
As when autumnal *Boreas* sweeps the sky,
And instant blows the water'd gardens dry:
So look'd the field, so whiten'd was the ground,
While *Vulcan* breath'd the fiery blast around.
Swift on the sedgy reeds the ruin preys;
Along the margin winds the running blaze:
The trees in flaming rows to ashes turn,
The flow'ry *Lotos*, and the tam'risk burn,
410 Broad elm, and cypress rising in a spire;
The wat'ry willows hiss before the fire.
Now glow the waves, the fishes pant for breath,
The eels lie twisting in the pangs of death:
Now flounce aloft, now dive the scaly fry,
415 Or gasping, turn their bellies to the sky.
At length the river rear'd his languid head,
And thus, short-panting, to the God he said.
     O *Vulcan*, oh! what pow'r resists thy might?
I faint, I sink, unequal to the fight –
420 I yield – Let *Ilion* fall; if Fate decree –
Ah – bend no more thy fiery arms on me!
     He ceas'd; wide conflagration blazing round;
The bubbling waters yield a hissing sound.
As when the flames beneath a caldron rise,
425 To melt the fat of some rich sacrifice,

Amid the fierce embrace of circling fires
The waters foam, the heavy smoak aspires:
So boils th' imprison'd flood, forbid to flow,
And choak'd with vapours, feels his bottom glow.
To *Juno* then, imperial Queen of Air,   430
The burning river sends his earnest pray'r.

    Ah why, *Saturnia*! must thy son engage
Me, only me, with all his wastfull rage?
On other Gods his dreadful arm employ,
For mightier Gods assert the cause of *Troy*.   435
Submissive I desist, if thou command,
But ah! withdraw this all-destroying hand.
Hear then my solemn oath, to yield to Fate
Unaided *Ilion*, and her destin'd state,
Till *Greece* shall gird her with destructive flame,   440
And in one ruin sink the *Trojan* name.

    His warm intreaty touch'd *Saturnia*'s ear:
She bade th' Ignipotent his rage forbear,
Recall the flame, nor in a mortal cause
Infest a God: Th'obedient flame withdraws: 445
Again, the branching streams begin to spread,
And soft re-murmur in their wonted bed.

    While these by *Juno*'s will the strife resign,
The warring Gods in fierce contention join:
Re-kindling rage each heavenly breast alarms;   450
With horrid clangor shock th' ætherial arms:
Heav'n in loud thunder bids the trumpet sound;
And wide beneath them groans the rending ground.
Jove, as his sport, the dreadful scene descries,
And views contending Gods with careless eyes.   455
The pow'r of battels lifts his brazen spear,
And first assaults the radiant Queen of War,

    What mov'd thy madness, thus to disunite
Æthereal minds, and mix all heav'n in fight?
What wonder this, when in thy frantick mood   460
Thou drov'st a mortal to insult a God;
Thy impious hand *Tydides*' jav'lin bore,
And madly bath'd it in celestial gore.

    He spoke, and smote the loud-resounding shield,
Which bears *Jove*'s thunder on its dreadful field;   465

The adamantine *Ægis* of her Sire,
That turns the glancing bolt, and forked fire.
Then heav'd the Goddess in her mighty hand
A stone, the limit of the neighb'ring land,
470   There fix'd from eldest times; black, craggy, vast:
This, at the heav'nly homicide she cast.
Thund'ring he falls; a mass of monstrous size,
And sev'n broad acres covers as he lies.
The stunning stroke his stubborn nerves unbound;
475   Loud o'er the fields his ringing arms resound:
The scornful dame her conquest views with smiles,
And glorying thus, the prostrate God reviles.
   Hast thou not yet, insatiate fury! known
How far *Minerva*'s force transcends thy own?
480   *Juno*, whom thou rebellious dar'st withstand,
Corrects thy folly thus by *Pallas*' hand;
Thus meets thy broken faith with just disgrace,
And partial aid to *Troy*'s perfidious race.
   The Goddess spoke, and turn'd her eyes away,
485   That beaming round, diffus'd celestial day.
Jove's *Cyprian* daughter, stooping on the land,
Lent to the wounded God her tender hand:
Slowly he rises, scarcely breathes with pain,
And propt on her fair arm, forsakes the plain.
490   This the bright Empress of the heav'ns survey'd,
And scoffing, thus, to War's victorious maid.
   Lo, what an aid on *Mars*'s side is seen!
The *Smiles* and *Love*'s unconquerable Queen!
Mark with what insolence, in open view,
495   She moves: Let *Pallas*, if she dares, pursue.
   Minerva smiling heard, the pair o'ertook,
And slightly on her breast the wanton strook:
She, unresisting, fell; (her spirits fled)
On earth together lay the lovers spread.
500   And like these heroes, be the fate of all
(*Minerva* cries) who guard the *Trojan* wall!
To *Grecian* Gods such let the *Phrygian* be,
So dread, so fierce, as *Venus* is to me;
Then from the lowest stone shall *Troy* be mov'd –
505   Thus she, and *Juno* with a smile approv'd.

Meantime, to mix in more than mortal fight,
The God of Ocean dares the God of Light.
What sloth has seiz'd us, when the fields around
Ring with conflicting pow'rs, and heav'n returns the
      sound?
Shall ignominious we with shame retire,   510
No deed perform'd, to our *Olympian* Sire?
Come, prove thy arm! for first the war to wage,
Suits not my greatness, or superiour age.
Rash as thou art to prop the *Trojan* throne,
(Forgetful of my wrongs, and of thy own)   515
And guard the race of proud *Laomedon!*
Hast thou forgot, how at the monarch's pray'r,
We shar'd the lengthen'd labours of a year?
Troy walls I rais'd (for such were *Jove*'s commands)
And yon' proud bulwarks grew beneath my hands: 520
Thy task it was, to feed the bellowing droves
Along fair *Ida*'s vales, and pendent groves.
But when the circling seasons in their train
Brought back the grateful day that crown'd our pain;
With menace stern the fraudful King defy'd   525
Our latent Godhead, and the prize deny'd:
Mad as he was, he threaten'd servile bands,
And doom'd us exiles far in barb'rous lands.
Incens'd, we heav'nward fled with swiftest wing,
And destin'd vengeance on the perjur'd King.   530
Dost thou, for this, afford proud *Ilion* grace,
And not like us, infest the faithless race?
Like us, their present, future sons destroy,
And from its deep foundations heave their *Troy*?
  Apollo thus: To combat for mankind   535
Ill suits the wisdom of celestial mind:
For what is man? Calamitous by birth,
They owe their life and nourishment to earth;
Like yearly leaves, that now, with beauty crown'd,
Smile on the sun; now, wither on the ground: 540
To their own hands commit the frantick scene,
Nor mix immortals in a cause so mean.
    Then turns his face, far-beaming heav'nly fires,
And from the Senior Pow'r, submiss retires;

545   Him, thus retreating, *Artemis* upbraids,
       The quiver'd huntress of the *sylvan* shades.
              And is it thus the youthful *Phœbus* flies,
       And yields to Ocean's hoary Sire, the prize?
       How vain that martial pomp, and dreadful show
550   Of pointed arrows, and the silver bow!
       Now boast no more in yon' celestial bow'r,
       Thy force can match the great Earth-shaking Pow'r.
              Silent, he heard the Queen of Woods upbraid:
       Not so *Saturnia* bore the vaunting maid;
555   But furious thus. What insolence has driv'n
       Thy pride to face the Majesty of Heav'n?
       What tho' by *Jove* the female plague design'd,
       Fierce to the feeble race of womankind,
       The wretched matron feels thy piercing dart;
560   Thy Sex's tyrant, with a tyger's heart?
       What tho' tremendous in the woodland chase,
       Thy certain arrows pierce the savage race?
       How dares thy rashness on the pow'rs divine
       Employ those arms, or match thy force with mine?
565   Learn hence, no more unequal war to wage –
       She said, and seiz'd her wrists with eager rage;
       These in her left hand lock'd, her right unty'd
       The bow, the quiver, and its plumy pride.
       About her temples flies the busy bow;
570   Now here, now there, she winds her from the blow;
       The scatt'ring arrows rattling from the case,
       Drop round, and idly mark the dusty place.
       Swift from the field the baffled huntress flies,
       And scarce restrains the torrent in her eyes:
575   So, when the falcon wings her way above,
       To the cleft cavern speeds the gentle dove,
       (Not fated yet to die) There safe retreats,
       Yet still her heart against the marble beats.
              To her, *Latona* hasts with tender care;
580   Whom *Hermes* viewing, thus declines the war.
       How shall I face the dame, who gives delight
       To him whose thunders blacken heav'n with night?
       Go matchless Goddess! triumph in the skies,
       And boast my conquest, while I yield the prize.

He spoke; and past: *Latona*, stooping low,   585
Collects the scatter'd shafts, and fallen bow,
That glitt'ring on the dust, lay here and there;
Dishonour'd relicks of *Diana*'s war.
Then swift pursu'd her to her blest abode,
Where, all confus'd, she sought the Sov'reign God;   590
Weeping she grasp'd his knees: Th' ambrosial vest
Shook with her sighs, and panted on her breast.
    The Sire, superiour smil'd; and bade her show,
What heav'nly hand had caus'd his daughter's woe?
Abash'd, she names his own imperial spouse;   595
And the pale crescent fades upon her brows.
    Thus they above: While swiftly gliding down,
Apollo enters *Ilion*'s sacred town:
The Guardian God now trembled for her wall,
And fear'd the *Greeks*, tho' Fate forbade her fall.   600
Back to *Olympus*, from the war's alarms,
Return the shining bands of Gods in arms;
Some proud in triumph, some with rage on fire;
And take their thrones around th' æthereal Sire.
    Thro' blood, thro' death, *Achilles* still proceeds,   605
O'er slaughter'd heroes, and o'er rolling steeds
As when avenging flames with fury driv'n,
On guilty towns exert the wrath of heav'n;
The pale inhabitants, some fall, some fly;
And the red vapours purple all the sky.   610
So rag'd *Achilles*: Death, and dire dismay,
And toils, and terrours, fill'd the dreadful day.
    High on a turret hoary *Priam* stands,
And marks the waste of his destructive hands;
Views, from his arm, the *Trojans* scatter'd flight,   615
And the near hero rising on his sight!
No stop, no check, no aid! With feeble pace,
And settled sorrow on his aged face,
Fast as he could, he sighing quits the walls;
And thus, descending, on the guards he calls.   620
    You to whose care our city gates belong,
Set wide your portals to the flying throng.
For lo! he comes, with unresisted sway;
He comes, and desolation marks his way!

625　But when within the walls our troops take breath,
　　Lock fast the brazen bars, and shut out death.
　　Thus charg'd the rev'rend monarch: Wide were flung
　　The opening folds; the sounding hinges rung.
　　Phœbus rush'd forth, the flying bands to meet,
630　Strook slaughter back, and cover'd the retreat.
　　On heaps the *Trojans* crowd to gain the gate,
　　And gladsome see their last escape from Fate:
　　Thither, all parch'd with thirst, a heartless train,
　　Hoary with dust, they beat the hollow plain;
635　And gasping, panting, fainting, labour on
　　With heavier strides, that lengthen tow'rd the town.
　　Enrag'd *Achilles* follows with his spear;
　　Wild with revenge, insatiable of war.
　　　　Then had the *Greeks* eternal praise acquir'd,
640　And *Troy* inglorious to her walls retir'd;
　　But *he, the God who darts æthereal flame,
　　Shot down to save her, and redeem her fame.
　　To young *Agenor* force divine he gave,
　　(*Antenor*'s offspring, haughty, bold and brave)
645　In aid of him, beside the beech he sate,
　　And wrapt in clouds, restrain'd the hand of Fate.
　　When now the gen'rous youth *Achilles* spies,
　　Thick beats his heart, the troubled motions rise,
　　(So, e're a storm, the waters heave and roll)
650　He stops, and questions thus his mighty soul.
　　　　What, shall I fly this terrour of the plain?
　　Like others fly, and be like others slain?
　　Vain hope! to shun him by the self-same road
　　Yon' line of slaughter'd *Trojans* lately trod.
655　No: with the common heap I scorn to fall —
　　What if they pass'd me to the *Trojan* wall,
　　While I decline to yonder path, that leads
　　To *Ida*'s forests and surrounding shades?
　　So may I reach, conceal'd, the cooling flood,
660　From my tir'd body wash the dirt and blood,
　　As soon as night her dusky veil extends,
　　Return in safety to my *Trojan* friends,

　　*Apollo.

What if? – But wherefore all this vain debate?
Stand I to doubt, within the reach of Fate?
Ev'n now perhaps, e'er yet I turn the wall,   665
The fierce *Achilles* sees me, and I fall:
Such is his swiftness, 'tis in vain to fly,
And such his valour, that who stands must die.
Howe'er, 'tis better, fighting for the state,
Here, and in publick view, to meet my fate.   670
Yet sure he too is mortal; He may feel
(Like all the sons of earth) the force of steel;
One only soul informs that dreadful frame;
And *Jove*'s sole favour gives him all his fame.

He said, and stood, collected in his might;   675
And all his beating bosom claim'd the fight.
So from some deep-grown wood a panther starts,
Rouz'd from his thicket by a storm of darts:
Untaught to fear or fly, he hears the sounds
Of shouting hunters, and of clam'rous hounds;   680
Tho' struk, tho' wounded, scarce perceives the pain,
And the barb'd jav'lin stings his breast in vain:
On their whole war, untam'd the savage flies;
And tears his hunter, or beneath him dies.
Not less resolv'd, *Antenor*'s valiant heir   685
Confronts *Achilles*, and awaits the war,
Disdainful of retreat: High-held before,
His shield (a broad circumference) he bore;
Then graceful as he stood, in act to throw
The lifted jav'lin, thus bespoke the foe.   690

How proud *Achilles* glories in his fame!
And hopes this day to sink the *Trojan* name
Beneath her ruins! Know, that hope is vain;
A thousand woes, a thousand toils remain.
Parents and children our just arms employ,   695
And strong, and many, are the sons of *Troy*.
Great as thou art, ev'n thou may'st stain with gore
These *Phrygian* fields, and press a foreign shore.

He said: With matchless force the jav'lin flung
Smote on his knee; the hollow cuishes rung   700
Beneath the pointed steel; but safe from harms
He stands impassive in th'æthereal arms.

Then fiercely rushing on the daring foe,
His lifted arm prepares the fatal blow.
705   But jealous of his fame, *Apollo* shrouds
The god-like *Trojan* in a veil of clouds;
Safe from pursuit, and shut from mortal view,
Dismiss'd with fame, the favour'd youth withdrew.
Meanwhile the God, to cover their escape,
710   Assumes *Agenor*'s habit, voice, and shape,
Flies from the furious chief in this disguise,
The furious chief still follows where he flies:
Now o'er the fields they stretch with lengthen'd strides,
Now urge the course where swift *Scamander* glides:
715   The God now distant scarce a stride before,
Tempts his pursuit, and wheels about the shore:
While all the flying troops their speed employ,
And pour on heaps into the walls of *Troy*.
No stop, no stay; no thought to ask, or tell,
720   Who scap'd by flight, or who by battel fell.
'Twas tumult all, and violence of flight;
And sudden joy confus'd, and mix'd affright:
Pale *Troy* against *Achilles* shuts her gate;
And nations breathe, deliver'd from their fate.

OBSERVATIONS

ON THE

TWENTY-FIRST BOOK

This book is entirely different from all the foregoing: Tho' it be a battel, it is entirely of a new and surprizing kind, diversify'd with a vast variety of imagery and description. The scene is totally chang'd, he paints the combate of his hero with the rivers, and describes a battel amidst an inundation. It is observable that tho' the whole war of the *Iliad* was upon the banks of these rivers, *Homer* has artfully left out the machinery of River-Gods in all the other battels, to aggrandize this of his hero. There is no book of the poem that has more force of imagination, or in which the great and inexhausted invention of our author is more powerfully exerted. After this description of an inundation, there follows a very beautiful contrast in that of the drought: The part of *Achilles* is admirably sustained, and the new strokes which *Homer* gives to his picture are such as are deriv'd from the very source of his character, and finish the entire draught of this Hero.

How far all that appears wonderful or extravagant in this episode, may be reconciled to probability, truth, and natural reason, will be considered in a distinct note on that head: The reader may find it on v. 447.

2. Xanthus, *immortal progeny of* Jove.] The river is here said to be the Son of *Jupiter*, on account of its being supply'd with waters that fall from *Jupiter*, that is, from heaven.   *Eustathius.*

14. *As the scorch'd locusts,* &c.] *Eustathius* observes that several countries have been much infested with armies of locusts; and that, to prevent their destroying the fruits of the earth, the countrymen by kindling large fires drove them from their fields; the locusts to avoid the intense heat were forc'd to cast themselves into the water. From

this observation the Poet draws his allusion, which is very much to the honour of *Achilles*, since it represents the *Trojans* with respect to him as no more than so many insects.

The same commentator takes notice, that because the Island of *Cyprus* in particular was used to practise this method with the locusts, some authors have conjectured that *Homer* was of that country; but if this were a sufficient reason for such a supposition, he might be said to be born in almost all the countries of the world, since he draws his observations from the customs of them all.

We may hence account for the innumerable armies of these locusts, mention'd among the Plagues of *Ægypt*, without having recourse to an immediate creation, as some good Men have imagin'd, whereas the miracle indeed consists in the wonderful manner of bringing them upon the *Ægyptians*: I have often observ'd with pleasure the similitude which many of *Homer*'s expressions bear with the holy scriptures, and that the most ancient heathen writer in the world often speaks in the idiom of *Moses*: Thus as the locusts in *Exodus* are said to be driven into *the sea*, so in *Homer* they are forc'd into a *river*.

30. *So the huge dolphin,* &c.] It is observable with what justness the author diversifies his comparisons according to the different scenes and elements he is engaged in: *Achilles* has been hitherto on the land, and compared to land animals, a lion, &c. Now he is in the water, the Poet derives his images from thence, and likens him to a dolphin.   *Eustathius.*

34. *Now tir'd with slaughter.*] This is admirably well suited to the character of *Achilles*, his rage bears him headlong on the enemy, he kills all that oppose him, and stops not till nature itself could not keep pace with his anger; he had determin'd to reserve twelve noble youths to sacrifice them to the *Manes* of *Patroclus*, but his resentment gives him no time to think of them, till the hurry of his passion abates, and he is tir'd with slaughter: Without this circumstance, I think an objection might naturally be raised, that in the time of a pursuit *Achilles* gave the enemy too much leisure to escape, while he busy'd himself with tying these prisoners: Tho' it is not absolutely necessary to suppose he tyed them with his own hands.

35. *Twelve chosen youths.*] This piece of cruelty in *Achilles* has appeared shocking to many, and indeed is what I think can only be

excused by considering the ferocious and vindictive spirit of this hero.
'Tis however certain that the cruelties exercised on enemies in war
were authorised by the military laws of those times; nay, religion itself
became a sanction to them. It is not only the fierce *Achilles*, but the
pious and religious *Æneas*, whose very character is virtue and compas-
sion, that reserves several young unfortunate captives taken in battel,
to sacrifice them to the *Manes* of his favourite hero. *Æn.* 10. v. 517.

> *– Sulmone creatos*
> *Quattuor hic juvenes, totidem quos educat Ufens*
> *Viventes rapit; inferias quos immolet umbris,*
> *Captivoque rogi perfundat sanguine flammas.*

> [Four sons of *Sulmo*, four whom *Ufens* bred,
> He took in fight, and living victims led,
> To please the ghost of *Pallas*; and expire
> In sacrifice, before his fun'ral fire.]

And *Æn.* 11. v. 81.

> *Vinxerat & post terga manus, quos mitteret umbris,*
> *Inferias, cæso sparsuros sanguine flammam.*

> [Then, pinioned with their hands behind, appear
> The unhappy captives, marching in the rear,
> Appointed offerings in the victor's name,
> To sprinkle with their blood the funeral flame.]

And (what is very particular) the *Latin* poet expresses no disapproba-
tion of the action, which the *Grecian* does in plain terms, speaking of
this in *Iliad* 23. v. 176.

> *– Κακὰ δὲ φρεσὶ μήδετο ἔργα.*

> [Evil were the deeds he pondered doing in his heart.]

41. *The young* Lycaon, &c.] *Homer* has a wonderful art and judgment
in contriving such incidents as set the characteristick qualities of his
heroes in the highest point of light. There is hardly any in the whole
Iliad more proper to move pity than this circumstance of *Lycaon*, or
to raise terror, than this view of *Achilles*. It is also the finest picture of
them both imaginable: We see the different attitude of their persons,
and the different passions which appeared in their countenances: At
first *Achilles* stands erect, with surprize in his looks, at the sight of one

whom he thought it impossible to find there; while *Lycaon* is in the posture of a suppliant, with looks that plead for compassion; with one hand holding the hero's lance, and his knee with the other: Afterwards, when at his death he lets go the spear and places himself on his knees, with his arms extended, to receive the mortal wound; how lively and how strongly is this painted? I believe every one perceives the beauty of this passage, and allows that poetry (at least in *Homer*) is truly a speaking picture.

84, &c. *The speeches of* Lycaon *and* Achilles.] It is impossible for any thing to be better imagin'd than these two speeches; that of *Lycaon* is moving and compassionate, that of *Achilles* haughty and dreadful; the one pleads with the utmost tenderness, the other denies with the utmost sternness: One would think it impossible to amass so many moving arguments in so few words as those of *Lycaon*: He forgets no circumstance to soften his enemy's anger, he flatters the memory of *Patroclus*, is afraid of being thought too nearly related to *Hector*, and would willingly put himself upon him as a suppliant, and consequently as an inviolable person: But *Achilles* is immoveable, his resentment makes him deaf to entreaties, and it must be remembered that anger, not mercy, is his character.

I must confess I could have wish'd *Achilles* had spared him: There are so many circumstances that speak in his favour, that he deserved his life, had he not asked it in terms a little too abject.

There is an air of greatness in the conclusion of the speech of *Achilles*, which strikes me very much: He speaks very unconcernedly of his own death, and upbraids his enemy for asking life so earnestly, a life that was of so much less importance than his own.

121.   *The day shall come –*
   When by the spear, the arrow, or the dart.

This is not spoken at random, but with an air of superiority; when *Achilles* says he shall fall by an arrow, a dart, or a spear, he insinuates that no man will have the courage to approach him in a close fight, or engage him hand to hand.   *Eustathius.*

146. *Your living coursers glut his gulphs in vain.*] It was an ancient custom to cast living horses into the sea, and into rivers, to honour, as it were, by these victims, the rapidity of their streams. This practice continued a long time, and history supplies us with examples of it: *Aurelius Victor* says of *Pompey* the younger, *Cum mari feliciter uteretur,* Neptuni *se filium confessus est, eumque bobus auratis & equo placavit* [When he wanted to use the sea with auspicious results, he confessed himself to be the son of Neptune and appeased him with golden cattle and a horse]. He offered oxen in Sacrifice, and threw a living horse into the sea, as appears from *Dion*; which is perfectly conformable to this of *Homer.*   *Eustath. Dacier.*

152. *With fury swells the violated flood.*] The poet has been preparing us for the episode of the river *Xanthus* ever since the beginning of the last book; and here he gives us an account why the river wars upon *Achilles*: It is not only because he is a river of *Troas*, but, as *Eustathius* remarks, because it is in defence of a man that was descended from a brother River-God: He was angry too with *Achilles* on another account, because he had choak'd up his current with the bodies of his countreymen, the *Trojans.*

171. *From rich* Pæonia's – &c.] In the catalogue *Pyræchmes* is said to be commander of the *Pæonians*, where they are describ'd as bow-men; but here they are said to be arm'd with spears, and to have *Asteropæus* for their general. *Eustathius* tells us, some cricks asserted that this line in the *Cat.* v. 355.

Πηλέγονός θ' υἱὸς περιδέξιος Ἀστεροπαῖος.

[Pelegon and his son, the very dextrous Asteropaios.]

followed

Αὐτὰρ Πυραίχμης ἄγε Παίονας ἀγκυλοτόξους.

[Pyraichmes led the Paionians, who were armed with bent
    bows.]

but I see no reason for such an assertion. *Homer* has expressly told us in this speech that it was but ten days since he came to the aid of *Troy*; he might be made general of the *Pæonians* upon the death of *Pyræchmes*, who was kill'd in the sixteenth book. Why also might not the *Pæonians*, as well as *Teucer*, excel in the management both of the bow and the spear?

187. *Deep in the swelling bank was driv'n the spear,*
    Ev'n to the middle earth'd –]

It was impossible for the poet to give us a greater idea of the strength of *Achilles* than he has by this circumstance: His spear peirc'd so deep into the ground, that another hero of great strength could not disengage it by repeated efforts; but immediately after, *Achilles* draws it with the utmost ease: How prodigious was the force of that arm that could drive at one throw a spear half way into the earth, and then with a touch release it?

263. *Now bursting on his head,* &c.] There is a great beauty in the versification of this whole passage in *Homer*: Some of the verses run hoarse, full, and sonorous, like the torrent they describe; others by their broken cadences, and sudden stops, image the difficulty, labour, and interruption of the hero's march against it. The fall of the elm, the tearing up of the bank, the rushing of the branches in the water, are all put into such words, that almost every letter corresponds in its sound, and echoes to the sense of each particular.

274. *Bridg'd the rough flood across* –] If we had no other account of the river *Xanthus* but this, it were alone sufficient to shew that the current could not be very wide; for the poet here says that the elm stretch'd from bank to bank, and as it were made a bridge over it: The suddenness of this inundation perfectly well agrees with a narrow river.

276. *Leap'd from the chanel.*] *Eustathius* recites a criticism on this verse, in the original the word Λίμνη signifies *stagnum, palus,* a standing-water; now this is certainly contrary to the idea of a river, which always implies a *current*: To solve this, says that author, some have supposed that the tree which lay across the river stopp'd the flow of the waters, and forced them to spread as it were into a pool. Others, dissatisfy'd with this solution, think that a mistake is crept into the text, and that instead of ἐκ Λίμνης [from the standing water], should be inserted ἐκ δίνης [from the eddy]. But I do not see the necessity of having recourse to either of these solutions; for why may not the word Λίμνη signify here the *chanel* of the river, as it evidently does in the 317th verse? And nothing being more common than to substitute a part for the whole, why may not the chanel be suppos'd to imply the whole river?

289. *So when a peasant to his garden brings,* &c.] This changing of the character is very beautiful: No poet ever knew, like *Homer*, to pass from the vehement and the nervous, to the gentle and the agreeable; such transitions, when properly made, give a singular pleasure, as when in musick a master passes from the rough to the tender. *Demetrius Phalereus*, who only praises this comparison for its clearness, has not sufficiently recommended its beauty and value. *Virgil* has transfer'd it into his first book of the *Georgicks.* v. 106.

> *Deinde satis fluvium inducit, rivosque sequentes:*
> *Et cum exustus ager morientibus æstuat herbis,*
> *Ecce supercilio clivosi tramitis undam*
> *Elicit: Illa cadens raucum per levia murmur*
> *Saxa ciet, scatebrisque arentia temperat arva.*   *Dacier.*

> [And calls the floods from high, to rush amain
> With pregnant streams, to swell the teeming grain.
> Then, when the fiery suns too fiercely play,
> And shrivelled herbs on withering stems decay,
> The wary ploughman, on the mountain's brow,
> Undams his watery stores – huge torrents flow,
> And, rattling down the rocks, large moisture yield,
> Tempering the thirsty fever of the field.]

321. *Oh had I dy'd in fields of battel warm!* &c.] Nothing is more agreeable than this wish to the heroick character of *Achilles*: Glory is his prevailing passion; he grieves not that he must die, but that he should die unlike a man of honour. *Virgil* has made use of the same thought in the same circumstance, where *Æneas* is in danger of being drowned, *Æn.* 1. v. 98.

>   *– O terque quaterque beati,*
> *Queis ante ora patrum* Trojæ *sub mœnibus altis*
> *Contigit oppetere! O Danaum fortissime gentis*
> *Tydide, mene Iliacis occumbere campis*
> *Non potuisse? tuaque animam hanc effundere dextra!*

> [And thrice, and four times happy those, he cry'd,
> That under *Ilian* walls before their parents dy'd.
> *Tydides*, bravest of the *Grecian* train,
> Why cou'd not I by that strong arm be slain.]

Lucan, in the fifth book of his *Pharsalia*, representing *Cæsar* in the same circumstance, has (I think) carry'd yet farther the character of ambition, and a boundless thirst of glory, in his hero; when, after he has repin'd in the same manner with *Achilles*, he acquiesces at last in the reflection of the glory he had already acquired,

> — *Licet ingentes abruperit actus*
> *Festinata dies fatis, sat magna peregi.*
> *Arctoas domui gentes: inimica subegi*
> *Arma manu: vidit Magnum mihi* Roma *secundum.*

[Though fate may advance my day of departure,
　　Stopping my great career, I have done enough of
　　　　importance and sufficient.
　　I have tamed the tribes of the North; by the threat of my
　　　　presence,
　　Nothing more, I have routed the forces gathered against
　　　　me;
　　Rome has seen Pompey in second place, supplanted by
　　　　Cæsar.]

And only wishes that his obscure fate might be conceal'd, in the view that all the world might still fear and expect him.

> — *Lacerum retinete cadaver*
> *Fluctibus in mediis; desint mihi busta, rogusque,*
> *Dum metuar semper, terraque expecter ab omni.*

[Let my mangled body, unburied,
　　Unconsumed by a pyre, be borne on the waves in mid-
　　　　ocean:
　　So will my disappearance leave all the nations uneasy,
　　Every land awaiting with dread my sudden arrival.]

405. *While* Vulcan *breath'd the fiery blast around.*] It is in the original, v. 355.

> Πνοιῇ τειρόμενοι πολυμήτιος Ἡφαίστοιο.

[Worn down by the blasts of cunning Hephaistos.]

The epithet given to *Vulcan* in this verse (as well as in the 367th) Ἡφαίστοιο πολύφρονος [most wise Hephaistos], has no sort of allusion to the action describ'd: For what has his *wisdom* or *knowledge* to do with burning up the river *Xanthus*? This is usual in our author, and much exclaimed against by his modern antagonists, whom Mr. *Boileau* very well answers. 'It is not so strange in *Homer* to give these epithets to persons upon occasions which can have no reference to them; the same is frequent in modern languages, in which we call a man by the name of *Saint*, when we speak of any action of his that has not the least regard to his *sanctity*: As when we say, for example, that St. *Paul* held the garments of those who stoned St. *Stephen*.'

424. *As when the flames beneath a caldron rise.*] It is impossible to render literally such passages with any tolerable beauty. These ideas can never be made to shine in *English*, some particularities cannot be preserved; but the *Greek* language gives them lustre, the words are noble and musical.

Ὡς δὲ λέβης ζεῖ ἔνδον ἐπειγόμενος πυρὶ πολλῷ,
Κνίσην μελδόμενος ἁπαλοτρεφέος σιάλοιο,
Πάντοθεν ἀμβολάδην, ὑπὸ δὲ ξύλα κάγκανα κεῖται.

[Just so does a kitchen cauldron burn, brought to a boil by
   a great fire,
Melting the fat of a plump hog –
It bubbles up in every direction, and dry wood lies
   beneath it.]

All therefore that can be expected from a translator is to preserve the meaning of the simile, and embellish it with some words of affinity that carry nothing low in the sense or sound.

447. *And soft re-murmur in their wonted bed.*] Here ends the *episode* of the *river-fight*; and I must here lay before the reader my thoughts upon the whole of it: Which appears to be in part an allegory, and in part a true history. Nothing can give a better idea of *Homer*'s manner of enlivening his inanimate machines, and of making the plainest and simplest incidents noble and poetical, than to consider the whole passage in the common historical sense, which I suppose to be no more than this. There happen'd a great overflow of the river *Xanthus* during the siege, which very much incommoded the assailants: This gave occasion for the fiction of an engagement between *Achilles* and the River-God: *Xanthus* calling *Simoïs* to assist him, implies that these two neighbouring rivers joined in the inundation: *Pallas* and *Neptune*

relieve *Achilles*; that is, *Pallas*, or the *wisdom* of *Achilles*, found some means to divert the waters, and turn them into the *Sea*; wherefore *Neptune*, the God of it, is feign'd to assist him. *Jupiter* and *Juno* (by which are understood the aerial regions) consent to aid *Achilles*; that may signify, that after this great flood their happened a warm, dry, windy season, which asswaged the waters, and dried the ground: And what makes this in a manner plain, is, that *Juno* (which signifies the *air*) promises to send the *north* and *west winds* to distress the river. *Xanthus* being consum'd by *Vulcan*, that is dried up with heat, prays to *Juno* to relieve him: What is this, but that the drought having drunk up his streams, he has recourse to the *air* for rains to resupply his current? Or perhaps the whole may signify no more, than that *Achilles* being on the farther side of the river, plung'd himself in to pursue the enemy; that in this adventure he run the risk of being drown'd; that to save himself he laid hold on a fallen tree, which serv'd to keep him afloat; that he was still carried down the stream to the place where was the confluence of the two rivers, which is expressed by the one calling the other to his aid, and that when he came nearer the sea (*Neptune*) he found means by his prudence (*Pallas*) to save himself from his danger.

If the reader still should think the fiction of rivers speaking and fighting is too bold, the objection will vanish by considering how much the heathen mythology authorizes the representation of rivers as persons: Nay even in old historians nothing is more common than stories of rapes committed by River-Gods: And the fiction was no way unpresidented, after one of the same nature so well known, as the engagement between *Hercules* and the river *Achelous.*

454.   Jove *as his sport, the dreadful scene descries,*
   And views contending Gods with careless eyes.]

I was at a loss for the reason why *Jupiter* is said to smile at the discord of the Gods, till I found it in *Eustathius*; *Jupiter*, says he, who is the lord of nature, is well pleased with the war of the Gods, that is of earth, sea, and air, *&c.* because the harmony of all beings arises from that discord: Thus earth is opposite to water, air to earth, and water to them all; and yet from this opposition arises that discordant concord by which all nature subsists. Thus heat and cold, moist and dry, are in a continual war, yet upon this depends the fertility of the earth, and the beauty of the creation. So that *Jupiter* who according to the *Greeks* is the soul of all, may well be said to smile at this contention.

456. *The power of battels*, &c.] The combat of *Mars* and *Pallas* is plainly allegorical: Justice and Wisdom demanded that an end should be put to this terrible war: the God of war opposes this, but is worsted. *Eustathius* says that this holds forth the opposition of rage and wisdom; and no sooner has our reason subdued one temptation, but another succeeds to reinforce it, as *Venus* succours *Mars*. The poet seems farther to insinuate, that reason when it resists a temptation vigorously, easily overcomes it: So it is with the utmost facility that *Pallas* conquers both *Mars* and *Venus*. He adds, that *Pallas* retreated from *Mars* in order to conquer him; this shews us that the best way to subdue a temptation is to retreat from it.

468.   *Then heav'd the Goddess in her mighty hand*
        A Stone, &c.]

The poet has describ'd many of his heroes in former parts of his poem, as throwing stones of enormous bulk and weight; but here he rises in his image: He is describing a Goddess, and has found a way to make that action excel all human strength, and be equal to a deity.

Virgil has imitated this passage in his twelfth book, and apply'd it to *Turnus*; but I can't help thinking that the action in a mortal is somewhat extravagantly imagined: What principally renders it so, is an addition of two lines to this simile which he borrows from another part of *Homer*, only with this difference, that whereas *Homer* says no two men could raise such a stone, *Virgil* extends it to twelve.

> — *Saxum circumspicit ingens,*
> *Saxum, antiquum, ingens, campo quod forte jacebat,*
> *Limes agro positus, litem ut discerneret arvis.*

> [An antique stone he saw: the common bound
> Of neighb'ring fields; and barrier of the ground.]

(There is a beauty in the repetition of *saxum ingens* [a huge rock], in the second line; it makes us dwell upon the image, and gives us leisure to consider the vastness of the stone:) The other two lines are as follow,

> *Vix illud, lecti bis sex cervice subirent,*
> *Qualia nunc hominum producit corpora tellus.*

> [So vast, that twelve strong men of modern days,
> Th'enormous weight from earth cou'd hardly raise.]

May I be allowed to think too, they are not so well introduced in *Virgil*? For it is just after *Turnus* is describ'd as weaken'd and oppress'd with fears and ill omens; it exceeds probability; and *Turnus*, methinks, looks more like a knight-errant in a romance, than an hero in an epick poem.

507. *The God of Ocean dares the God of Light.*] The interview between *Neptune* and *Apollo* is very judiciously in this place enlarged upon by our author. The poem now draws to a conclusion, the *Trojans* are to be punish'd for their perjury and violence: *Homer* accordingly with a poetical justice sums up the evidence against them, and represents the very founder of *Troy* as an injurious person. There have been several references to this story since the beginning of the poem, but he forbore to give it at large till near the end of it; that it might be fresh upon the memory, and shew, the *Trojans* deserve the punishment they are going to suffer.

Eustathius gives the reason why *Apollo* assists the *Trojans*, tho' he had been equally with *Neptune* affronted by *Laomedon*: This proceeded from the honours which *Apollo* received from the posterity of *Laomedon*; *Troy* paid him no less worship than *Cilla*, or *Tenedos*; and by these means won him over to a forgiveness: But *Neptune* still was slighted, and consequently continued an enemy to the whole race.

The same author gives us various opinions why *Neptune* is said to have built the *Trojan* wall, and to have been defrauded of his wages: Some say that *Laomedon* sacrilegiously took away the treasures out of the temples of *Apollo* and *Neptune*, to carry on the fortifications: From whence it was fabled that *Neptune* and *Apollo* built the walls. Others will have it, that two of the workmen dedicated their wages to *Apollo* and *Neptune*; and that *Laomedon* detained them: So that he might in some sense be said to defraud the deities themselves, by with-holding what was dedicated to their temples.

The reason why *Apollo* is said to have kept the herds of *Laomedon* is not so clear: *Eustathius* observes that all plagues first seize upon the four-footed creation, and are suppos'd to arise from this deity: Thus *Apollo* in the first book sends the plague into the *Grecian* army: The ancients therefore made him to preside over cattel, that by preserving them from the plague, mankind might be safe from infectious diseases. Others tell us, that this employment is ascrib'd to *Apollo*, because he signifies the sun: Now the sun cloaths the pastures with grass and herbs: So that *Apollo* may be said himself to feed the cattel, by supplying them with food. Upon either of these accounts *Laomedon* may be said to be ungrateful to that deity, for raising no temple to his honour.

It is observable that *Homer* in this story ascribes the building of the wall to *Neptune* only: I should conjecture the reason might be, that *Troy* being a sea-port town, the chief strength of it depended upon its situation, so that the sea was in a manner a wall to it: Upon this account *Neptune* may not improbably be said to have built the wall.

537. *For what is man?* &c.] The poet is very happy in interspersing his poem with moral sentences; in this place he steals away his reader from war and horrour, and gives him a beautiful admonition of his own frailty. 'Shall I (says *Apollo*) contend with thee for the sake of man? Man, who is no more than a leaf of a tree, now green and flourishing, but soon wither'd away and gone?' The son of *Sirach* has an expression which very much resembles this, *Ecclus.* xiv. 18. *As the green leaves upon a thick tree some fall, and some grow, so is the generation of flesh and blood, one cometh to an end, and one is born.*

544. *And from the Senior Pow'r submiss retires.*] Two things hinder *Homer* from making *Neptune* and *Apollo* fight. First, because having already describ'd the fight between *Vulcan* and *Xanthus*, he has nothing farther to say here, for it is the same conflict between humidity and dryness. Secondly, *Apollo* being the same with destiny, and the ruin of the *Trojans* being concluded upon and decided, that God can no longer defer it.   *Dacier.*

557.   *The female plague –*
        Fierce to the feeble race of womankind, &c.]

The words in the original are, *Tho'* Jupiter *has made you a Lion to Women.* The meaning of this is, that *Diana* was terrible to that sex, as being the same with the moon, and bringing on the pangs of child-birth: Or else, that the ancients attributed all sudden deaths of women to the darts of *Diana*, as of men to those of *Apollo*: Which opinion is frequently alluded to in *Homer.*   *Eustathius.*

566. *She said, and seiz'd her wrists,* &c.] I must confess I am at a loss how to justify *Homer* in every point of these combats with the Gods: When *Diana* and *Juno* are to fight, *Juno* calls her an *impudent bitch,*

κύον ἀδεές: When they fight, she boxes her soundly, and sends her crying and trembling to heaven: As soon as she comes thither *Jupiter* falls a laughing at her: Indeed the rest of the deities seem to be in a merry vein during all the action: *Pallas* beats *Mars*, and laughs at him, *Jupiter* sees them in the same merry mood: *Juno* when she had cuff'd *Diana* is not more serious: In short, unless there be some depths that I am not able to fathom, *Homer* never better deserv'd than in this place the censure past upon him by the ancients, that as he raised the characters of his men up to Gods, so he sunk those of Gods down to men.

Yet I think it but reasonable to conclude, from the very absurdity of all this, supposing it had no hidden meaning or allegory, that there must therefore certainly be some. Nor do I think it any inference to the contrary, that it is too obscure for us to find out: The remoteness of our times must necessarily darken yet more and more such things as were mysteries at first. Not that it is at all impossible, notwithstanding their present darkness, but they might then have been very obvious; as it is certain, allegories ought to be disguis'd, but not obscur'd: An Allegory should be like a veil over a beautiful face, so fine and transparent, as to shew the very charms it covers.

580. *Whom Hermes viewing, thus declines the war.*] It is impossible that *Mercury* should encounter *Latona*: Such a fiction would be unnatural, he being a planet, and she representing the night; for the planets owe all their lustre to the shades of the night, and then only become visible to the world.   *Eustathius.*

607.   *As when avenging Flames with Fury driv'n,*
          On guilty Towns exert the Wrath of Heaven.]

This Passage may be explain'd two ways, each very remarkable. First, by taking this Fire for a real Fire, sent from Heaven to punish a criminal City, of which we have Example in holy Writ. Hence we find that *Homer* had a Notion of this great Truth, that God sometimes exerts his Judgments on whole Cities in this signal and terrible manner. Or if we take it in the other sense, simply as a Fire thrown into a Town by the Enemies who assault it, (and only express'd thus by the Author in the same manner as *Jeremy* makes the City of *Jerusalem* say, when the *Chaldæns* burnt the Temple, *The Lord from above hath sent Fire into my Bones. Lament.* i. 13.) Yet still this much will appear understood by *Homer*, that the Fire which is cast into a City comes not properly speaking from Men, but from God who delivers it up to their Fury.   *Dacier.*

613. *High on a turret hoary* Priam, &c.] The poet still raises the idea of the courage and strength of his hero, by making *Priam* in a terrour that he should enter the Town after the routed troops: For if he had not surpassed all mortals, what could have been more desirable for an enemy, than to have let him in, and then destroy'd him?

Here again there was need of another *machine* to hinder him from entring the city; for *Achilles* being vastly speedier than those he pursued, he must necessarily overtake some of them, and the narrow gates could not let in a body of troops without his mingling with the hindmost. The story of *Agenor* is therefore admirably contriv'd, and *Apollo*, (who was to take care that the fatal decrees should be punctually executed) interposes both to save *Agenor* and *Troy*; for *Achilles* might have kill'd *Agenor*, and still entered with the troops, if *Apollo* had not diverted him by the pursuit of that phantom. *Agenor* opposed himself to *Achilles* only because he could not do better; for he sees himself reduced to a dilemma, either ingloriously to perish among the fugitives, or hide himself in the forest; both which were equally unsafe: Therefore he is purposely inspir'd with a generous resolution to try to save his countreymen, and as the reward of that service, is at last sav'd himself.

651. *What shall I fly?* &c.] This is a very beautiful soliloquy of *Agenor*, such a one as would naturally arise in the soul of a brave man, going upon a desperate enterprise: He weighs every thing in the balance of reason; he sets before himself the baseness of flight, and the courage of his enemy, till at last the thirst of glory preponderates all other considerations. From the conclusion of this speech it is evident, that the story of *Achilles* his being invulnerable except in the heel, is an invention of latter ages; for had he been so, there had been nothing wonderful in his character.   *Eustathius.*

709. *Meanwhile the God, to cover their escape,* &c.] The poet makes a double use of this fiction of *Apollo*'s deceiving *Achilles* in the Shape of *Agenor*; by these means he draws him from the pursuit, and gives the *Trojans* time to enter the city, and at the same time brings *Agenor* handsomely off from the combat. The moral of this fable is, that destiny would not yet suffer *Troy* to fall.

Eustathius fancies that the occasion of the fiction might be this: *Agenor* fled from *Achilles* to the banks of *Xanthus*, and might there conceal himself from the pursuer behind some covert that grew on the shores; this perhaps might be the whole of the story. So plain a narration would have pass'd in the mouth of an historian, but the poet dresses it in fiction, and tells us that *Apollo* (or Destiny) conceal'd him in a cloud from the sight of his enemy.

The same author farther observes, that *Achilles* by an unseasonable piece of vain-glory, in pursuing a single enemy gives time to a whole army to escape; he neither kills *Agenor*, nor overtakes the *Trojans*.

THE
ILIAD
OF
HOMER

VOLUME VI

THE
TWENTY–SECOND BOOK
OF THE
ILIAD

The ARGUMENT

The Death of *Hector*

The Trojans *being safe within the walls,* Hector *only stays to oppose* Achilles. Priam *is struck at his approach, and tries to persuade his son to re-enter the town.* Hecuba *joins her entreaties, but in vain.* Hector *consults within himself what measures to take; but at the advance of* Achilles, *his resolution fails him, and he flies;* Achilles *pursues him thrice round the walls of* Troy. *The Gods debate concerning the fate of* Hector; *at length* Minerva *descends to the aid of* Achilles. *She deludes* Hector *in the shape of* Deïphobus; *he stands the combate, and is slain.* Achilles *drags the dead body at his chariot, in the sight of* Priam *and* Hecuba. *Their lamentations, tears, and despair. Their cries reach the ears of* Andromache, *who, ignorant of this, was retired into the inner part of the palace: She mounts up to the walls, and beholds her dead husband. She swoons at the spectacle. Her excess of grief, and lamentation.*

The thirtieth day still continues. The scene lies under the walls, and on the battlements of Troy.

Thus to their bulwarks, smit with panick fear,
The herded *Ilians* rush like driven deer;
There safe, they wipe the briny drops away,
And drown in bowls the labours of the day.
5 Close to the walls advancing o'er the fields,
Beneath one roof of well-compacted shields
March, bending on, the *Greeks* embodied pow'rs,
Far-stretching in the shade of *Trojan* tow'rs.
Great *Hector* singly stay'd; chain'd down by fate,
10 There fixt he stood before the *Scæan* gate;
Still his bold arms determin'd to employ,
The guardian still of long-defended *Troy.*
    Apollo now to tir'd *Achilles* turns;
(The pow'r confest in all his glory burns)
15 And what (he cries) has *Peleus'* son in view,
With mortal speed a Godhead to pursue?
For not to thee to know the Gods is giv'n,
Unskill'd to trace the latent marks of heav'n.
What boots thee now, that *Troy* forsook the plain?
20 Vain thy past labour, and thy present vain:
Safe in their walls are now her troops bestow'd,
While here thy frantick rage attacks a God.
    The chief incens'd – Too partial God of day!
To check my conquests in the middle way:
25 How few in *Ilion* else had refuge found?
What gasping numbers now had bit the ground?
Thou robb'st me of a glory justly mine,
Pow'rful of Godhead, and of fraud divine:

Mean fame, alas! for one of heav'nly strain,
To cheat a mortal, who repines in vain. 30
   Then to the city, terrible and strong,
With high and haughty steps he tow'rd along.
So the proud courser, victor of the prize,
To the near goal with double ardour flies.
Him, as he blazing shot across the field, 35
The careful eyes of *Priam* first beheld.
Not half so dreadful rises to the sight
Thro' the thick gloom of some tempestuous night
Orion's dog (the year when autumn weighs)
And o'er the feebler stars exerts his rays; 40
Terrifick glory! for his burning breath
Taints the red air with fevers, plagues, and death.
So flam'd his fiery mail. Then wept the sage;
He strikes his rev'rend head now white with age:
He lifts his wither'd arms; obtests the skies; 45
He calls his much-lov'd son with feeble cries;
The Son, resolv'd *Achilles*' force to dare,
Full at the *Scæan* gates expects the war;
While the sad father on the rampart stands,
And thus adjures him with extended hands. 50
   Ah stay not, stay not! guardless and alone;
Hector! my lov'd, my dearest, bravest son!
Methinks already I behold thee slain,
And stretch'd beneath that fury of the plain.
Implacable *Achilles!* might'st thou be 55
To all the Gods no dearer than to me!
Thee, vultures wild should scatter round the shore,
And bloody dogs grow fiercer from thy gore.
How many valiant sons I late enjoy'd,
Valiant in vain! by thy curst arm destroy'd: 60
Or, worse than slaughter'd, sold in distant isles
To shameful bondage and unworthy toils.
Two, while I speak, my eyes in vain explore,
Two from one mother sprung, my *Polydore*,
And lov'd *Lycaon*; now perhaps no more! 65
Oh if in yonder hostile camp they live,
What heaps of gold, what treasures would I give?

(Their grandsire's wealth, by right of birth their own,
Consign'd his daughter with *Lelegia*'s throne)
70   But if (which heav'n forbid) already lost,
All pale they wander on the *Stygian* coast;
What sorrows then must their sad mother know,
What anguish I? unutterable woe!
Yet less that anguish, less to her, to me,
75   Less to all *Troy*, if not depriv'd of thee,
Yet shun *Achilles!* enter yet the wall;
And spare thyself, thy father, spare us all!
Save thy dear life; or if a soul so brave
Neglect that thought, thy dearer glory save.
80   Pity, while yet I live, these silver hairs;
While yet thy father feels the woes he bears,
Yet curst with sense! a wretch, whom in his rage
(All trembling on the verge of helpless age)
Great *Jove* has plac'd, sad spectacle of pain!
85   The bitter dregs of fortune's cup to drain:
To fill with scenes of death his closing eyes,
And number all his days by miseries!
My heroes slain, my bridal bed o'erturn'd,
My daughters ravish'd, and my city burn'd,
90   My bleeding infants dash'd against the floor;
These I have yet to see, perhaps yet more!
Perhaps ev'n I, reserv'd by angry Fate
The last sad relick of my ruin'd state,
(Dire pomp of sov'reign wretchedness!) must fall,
95   And stain the pavement of my regal hall;
Where famish'd dogs, late guardians of my door,
Shall lick their mangled master's spatter'd gore.
Yet for my sons I thank ye Gods! 'twas well;
Well have they perish'd, for in fight they fell.
100   Who dies in youth, and vigour, dies the best,
Struck thro' with wounds, all honest on the breast.
But when the Fates, in fulness of their rage,
Spurn the hoar head of unresisting age,
In dust the rev'rend lineaments deform,
105   And pour to dogs the life-blood scarcely warm;
This, this is misery! the last, the worst,
That man can feel; man, fated to be curst!

He said, and acting what no words could say,
Rent from his head the silver locks away.
With him the mournful mother bears a part;   110
Yet all their sorrows turn not *Hector*'s heart:
The zone unbrac'd, her bosom she display'd;
And thus, fast-falling the salt tears, she said.

Have mercy on me, O my son! Revere
The words of age; attend a parent's pray'r!   115
If ever thee in these fond arms I prest,
Or still'd thy infant clamours at this breast;
Ah do not thus our helpless years forego,
But by our walls secur'd, repel the foe.
Against his rage if singly thou proceed,   120
Should'st thou (but heav'n avert it!) should'st thou bleed,
Nor must thy corps lye honour'd on the bier,
Nor spouse, nor mother, grace thee with a tear;
Far from our pious rites, those dear remains
Must feast the vultures on the naked plains.   125

So they, while down their cheeks the torrents roll;
But fix'd remains the purpose of his soul:
Resolv'd he stands, and with a fiery glance
Expects the hero's terrible advance.
So roll'd up in his den, the swelling snake   130
Beholds the traveller approach the brake;
When fed with noxious herbs his turgid veins
Have gather'd half the poisons of the plains;
He burns, he stiffens with collected ire,
And his red eye-balls glare with living fire.   135
Beneath a turret, on his shield reclin'd,
He stood, and question'd thus his mighty mind.

Where lies my way? To enter in the wall?
Honour and shame th' ungen'rous thought recall:
Shall proud *Polydamas* before the gate   140
Proclaim, his counsels are obey'd too late,
Which timely follow'd but the former night,
What numbers had been sav'd by *Hector*'s flight?
That wise advice rejected with disdain,
I feel my folly in my people slain.   145
Methinks my suff'ring country's voice I hear,
But most, her worthless sons insult my ear,

On my rash courage charge the chance of war,
And blame those virtues which they cannot share.
150 No – If I e'er return, return I must
Glorious, my country's terrour laid in dust:
Or if I perish, let her see me fall
In field at least, and fighting for her wall.
And yet suppose these measures I forego,
155 Approach unarm'd, and parly with the foe,
The warriour-shield, the helm, and lance lay down,
And treat on terms of peace to save the town:
The wife with-held, the treasure ill detain'd,
(Cause of the war, and grievance of the land)
160 With honourable justice to restore;
And add half *Ilion*'s yet remaining store,
Which *Troy* shall, sworn, produce; that injur'd *Greece*
May share our wealth, and leave our walls in peace.
But why this thought? Unarm'd if I should go, ⎤
165 What hope of mercy from this vengeful foe, ⎬
But woman-like to fall, and fall without a blow. ⎦
We greet not here, as man conversing man,
Met at an oak, or journeying o'er a plain;
No season now for calm familiar talk,
170 Like youths and maidens in an evening walk:
War is our business, but to whom is giv'n
To die or triumph, that, determine heav'n!
     Thus pond'ring, like a God the *Greek* drew nigh;
His dreadful plumage nodded from on high;
175 The *Pelian* jav'lin, in his better hand,
Shot trembling rays that glitter'd o'er the land;
And on his breast the beamy splendors shone
Like *Jove*'s own lightning, or the rising sun.
As *Hector* sees, unusual terrours rise,
180 Struck by some God, he fears, recedes, and flies.
He leaves the gates, he leaves the walls behind;
Achilles follows like the winged wind.
Thus at the panting dove a falcon flies,
(The swiftest racer of the liquid skies)
185 Just when he holds or thinks he holds his prey,
Obliquely wheeling thro' th' aerial way;

With open beak and shrilling cries he springs,
And aims his claws, and shoots upon his wings:
No less fore-right the rapid chace they held,
One urg'd by fury, one by fear impell'd;   190
Now circling round the walls their course maintain,
Where the high watch-tow'r overlooks the plain;
Now where the fig-trees spread their umbrage broad,
(A wider compass) smoke along the road.
Next by *Scamander*'s double source they bound,   195
Where two fam'd fountains burst the parted ground;
This hot thro' scorching clefts is seen to rise,
With exhalations steaming to the skies;
That the green banks in summer's heat o'erflows,
Like crystal clear, and cold as winter-snows.   200
Each gushing fount a marble cistern fills,
Whose polish'd bed receives the falling rills;
Where *Trojan* dames, (e'er yet alarm'd by *Greece*)
Wash'd their fair garments in the days of peace.
By these they past, one chasing, one in Flight,   205
(The mighty fled, pursu'd by stronger might)
Swift was the course; no vulgar prize they play,
No vulgar victim must reward the day,
(Such as in races crown the speedy strife)
The prize contended was great *Hector*'s life.   210
As when some hero's fun'rals are decreed
In grateful honour of the mighty dead;
Where high rewards the vig'rous youth inflame,
(Some golden tripod, or some lovely dame)
The panting coursers swiftly turn the goal,   215
And with them turns the rais'd spectator's soul.
Thus three times round the *Trojan* wall they fly;
The gazing Gods lean forward from the sky:
To whom, while eager on the chace they look,
The Sire of mortals and immortals spoke.   220
    Unworthy sight! the man, belov'd of heav'n,
Behold, inglorious round yon' city driv'n!
My heart partakes the gen'rous *Hector*'s pain;
Hector, whose zeal whole hecatombs has slain,
Whose grateful fumes the Gods receiv'd with joy,   225
From *Ida*'s summits, and the tow'rs of *Troy*:

Now see him flying! to his fears resign'd,
And Fate, and fierce *Achilles*, close behind.
Consult, ye pow'rs! ('tis worthy your debate)
230   Whether to snatch him from impending fate,
Or let him bear, by stern *Pelides* slain,
(Good as he is) the lot impos'd on man?
    Then *Pallas* thus: Shall he whose vengeance forms
The forky bolt, and blackens heav'n with storms,
235   Shall he prolong one *Trojan*'s forfeit breath!
A man, a mortal, pre-ordain'd to death!
And will no murmurs fill the courts above,
No Gods indignant blame their partial *Jove*?
    Go then (return'd the Sire) without delay,
240   Exert thy will: I give the fates their way.
Swift at the mandate pleas'd *Tritonia* flies,
And stoops impetuous from the cleaving skies.
    As thro' the forest, o'er the vale and lawn,
The well-breath'd beagle drives the flying fawn;
245   In vain he tries the covert of the brakes,
Or deep beneath the trembling thicket shakes;
Sure of the vapour in the tainted dews,
The certain hound his various maze pursues.
Thus step by step, where'er the *Trojan* wheel'd,
250   There swift *Achilles* compass'd round the field.
Oft' as to reach the *Dardan* gates he bends,
And hopes th'assistance of his pitying friends,
(Whose show'ring arrows, as he cours'd below,
From the high turrets might oppress the foe.)
255   So oft' *Achilles* turns him to the plain:
He eyes the city, but he eyes in vain.
As men in slumbers seem with speedy pace,
One to pursue, and one to lead the chace,
Their sinking limbs the fancy'd course forsake,
260   Nor this can fly, nor that can overtake.
No less the lab'ring heroes pant and strain;
While that but flies, and this pursues in vain.
    What God, O Muse! assisted *Hector*'s force,
With Fate itself so long to hold the course?
265   *Phœbus* it was; who, in his latest hour,
Endu'd his knees with strength, his nerves with pow'r:

And great *Achilles*, lest some *Greek*'s advance
Should snatch the glory from his lifted lance,
Sign'd to the troops, to yield his foe the way,
And leave untouch'd the honours of the day.   270
 Jove lifts the golden balances, that show
The fates of mortal men, and things below:
Here each contending hero's lot he tries,
And weighs, with equal hand, their destinies.
Low sinks the scale surcharg'd with *Hector*'s fate;   275
Heavy with death it sinks, and hell receives the weight.
 Then *Phœbus* left him. Fierce *Minerva* flies
To stern *Pelides*, and triumphing, cries:
Oh lov'd of *Jove!* this day our labours cease,
And conquest blazes with full beams on *Greece.*   280
Great *Hector* falls; that *Hector* fam'd so far,
Drunk with renown, insatiable of war,
Falls by thy hand, and mine! nor force, nor flight
Shall more avail him, nor his God of Light.
See, where in vain he supplicates above,   285
Roll'd at the feet of unrelenting *Jove!*
Rest here: my self will lead the *Trojan* on,
And urge to meet the fate he cannot shun.
 Her voice divine the chief with joyful mind
Obey'd; and rested, on his lance reclin'd.   290
While like *Deïphobus* the martial dame
(Her face, her gesture, and her arms the same)
In show an aid, by hapless *Hector*'s side
Approach'd, and greets him thus with voice bely'd.
 Too long, O *Hector!* have I born the sight   295
Of this distress, and sorrow'd in thy flight:
It fits us now a noble stand to make,
And here, as brothers, equal fates partake.
 Then he. O Prince! ally'd in blood and fame,
Dearer than all that own a brother's name;   300
Of all that *Hecuba* to *Priam* bore,
Long try'd, long lov'd; much lov'd, but honour'd more!
Since you of all our num'rous race, alone
Defend my life, regardless of your own.
 Again the Goddess. Much my father's pray'r,   305
And much my mother's, prest me to forbear:

My friends embrac'd my knees, adjur'd my stay,
But stronger love impell'd, and I obey.
Come then, the glorious conflict let us try,
310 Let the steel sparkle, and the jav'lin fly;
Or let us stretch *Achilles* on the field,
Or to his arm our bloody trophies yield.

Fraudful she said; then swiftly march'd before;
The *Dardan* hero shuns his foe no more.

315 Sternly they met. The Silence *Hector* broke;
His dreadful plumage nodded as he spoke.

Enough, O son of *Peleus! Troy* has view'd
Her walls thrice circled, and her chief pursu'd.
But now some God within me bids me try
320 Thine, or my fate: I kill thee, or I die.
Yet on the verge of battel let us stay,
And for a moment's space, suspend the day;
Let heav'ns high pow'rs be call'd to arbitrate
The just conditions of this stern debate.
325 (Eternal witnesses of all below,
And faithful guardians of the treasur'd vow!)
To them I swear; if victor in the strife
Jove by these hands shall shed thy noble life;
No vile dishonour shall thy corse pursue;
330 Stript of its arms alone (the conqu'ror's due)
The rest to *Greece* uninjur'd I'll restore:
Now plight thy mutual oath, I ask no more.

Talk not of oaths (the dreadful chief replies,
While anger flash'd from his disdainful eyes)
335 Detested as thou art, and ought to be,
Nor oath nor pact *Achilles* plights with thee:
Such pacts, as lambs and rabid wolves combine,
Such leagues, as men and furious lions join,
To such I call the Gods! One constant state
340 Of lashing rancour and eternal hate:
No thought but rage, and never-ceasing strife,
Till death extinguish rage, and thought, and life.
Rouze then thy forces this important hour;
Collect thy soul, and call forth all thy pow'r.
345 No farther subterfuge, no farther chance;
'Tis *Pallas, Pallas* gives thee to my lance.

Each *Grecian* ghost by thee depriv'd of breath,
Now hovers round, and calls thee to thy death.

He spoke, and lanch'd his jav'lin at the foe;
But *Hector* shun'd the meditated blow: 350
He stoop'd, while o'er his head the flying spear
Sung innocent, and spent its force in air.
Minerva watch'd it falling on the land,
Then drew, and gave to great *Achilles'* hand,
Unseen of *Hector*, who, elate with joy,   355
Now shakes his lance, and braves the dread of *Troy.*

The life you boasted to that jav'lin giv'n,
Prince! you have mist. My fate depends on heav'n.
To thee (presumptuous as thou art) unknown,
Or what must prove my fortune, or thy own.   360
Boasting is but an art, our fears to blind,
And with false terrours sink another's mind.
But know, whatever fate I am to try,
By no dishonest wound shall *Hector* die;
I shall not fall a fugitive at least,   365
My soul shall bravely issue from my breast.
But first, try thou my arm; and may this dart
End all my country's woes, deep buried in thy heart!

The weapon flew, its course unerring held,
Unerring, but the heav'nly shield repell'd   370
The mortal dart; resulting with a bound
From off the ringing orb, it struck the ground.
Hector beheld his jav'lin fall in vain,
Nor other lance, nor other hope remain;
He calls *Deïphobus*, demands a spear,   375
In vain, for no *Deïphobus* was there.
All comfortless he stands: Then, with a sigh,
'Tis so – heav'n wills it, and my hour is nigh!
I deem'd *Deïphobus* had heard my call,
But he secure lies guarded in the wall.   380
A God deceiv'd me; *Pallas*, 'twas thy deed.
Death, and black fate approach! 'Tis I must bleed.
No refuge now, no succour from above;
Great *Jove* deserts me, and the son of *Jove,*
Propitious once, and kind! Then welcome fate!   385
'Tis true I perish, yet I perish great:

Yet in a mighty deed I shall expire,
Let future ages hear it, and admire!
    Fierce, at the word, his weighty sword he drew,
390   And, all collected, on *Achilles* flew.
So *Jove*'s bold bird, high-balanc'd in the air,
Stoops from the clouds to truss the quiv'ring hare.
Nor less *Achilles* his fierce soul prepares;
Before his breast the flaming shield he bears,
395   Refulgent orb! Above his four-fold cone
The gilded horse-hair sparkled in the sun,
Nodding at ev'ry step: (*Vulcanian* frame!)
And as he mov'd, his figure seem'd on flame.
As radiant *Hesper* shines with keener light,
400   Far-beaming o'er the silver host of night,
When all the starry train emblaze the sphere:
So shone the point of great *Achilles*' spear.
In his right hand he waves the weapon round,
Eyes the whole man, and meditates the wound;
405   But the rich mail *Patroclus* lately wore,
Securely cas'd the warriour's body o'er.
One place at length he spies, to let in fate,
Where 'twixt the neck and throat the jointed plate
Gave entrance: Thro' that penetrable part
410   Furious he drove the well-directed dart:
Nor pierc'd the windpipe yet, nor took the pow'r
Of speech, unhappy! from thy dying hour.
Prone on the field the bleeding warriour lies,
While thus triumphing, stern *Achilles* cries.
415   At last is *Hector* stretch'd upon the plain,
Who fear'd no vengeance for *Patroclus* slain:
Then Prince! you should have fear'd, what now you feel;
Achilles absent, was *Achilles* still.
Yet a short space the great avenger stay'd,
420   Then low in dust thy strength and glory lay'd.
Peaceful he sleeps, with all our rites adorn'd,
For ever honour'd, and for ever mourn'd:
While cast to all the rage of hostile pow'r,
Thee, birds shall mangle, and the dogs devour.
425   Then *Hector*, fainting at th'approach of death.
By thy own soul! by those who gave thee breath!

By all the sacred prevalence of pray'r;
Ah, leave me not for *Grecian* dogs to tear!
The common rites of sepulture bestow,
To sooth a father's and a mother's woe;　　　　　430
Let their large gifts procure an urn at least,
And *Hector*'s ashes in his country rest.

　　No, wretch accurst! Relentless he replies,
(Flames, as he spoke, shot flashing from his eyes)
Not those who gave me breath shou'd bid me spare,　　　435
Nor all the sacred prevalence of pray'r.
Could I my self the bloody banquet join!
No – to the dogs that carcase I resign.
Shou'd *Troy*, to bribe me, bring forth all her store,
And giving thousands, offer thousands more;　　　　440
Should *Dardan Priam*, and his weeping dame
Drain their whole realm to buy one fun'ral flame:
Their *Hector* on the pile they should not see,
Nor rob the vultures of one limb of thee.

　　Then thus the chief his dying accents drew;　　　445
Thy rage, implacable! too well I knew:
The Furies that relentless breast have steel'd,
And curs'd thee with a heart that cannot yield.
Yet think, a day will come, when Fate's decree
And angry Gods, shall wreak this wrong on thee;　　　450
Phœbus and *Paris* shall avenge my fate,
And stretch thee here, before this *Scæan* gate.

　　He ceas'd. The Fates supprest his lab'ring breath,
And his eyes stiffen'd at the hand of death;
To the dark realm the spirit wings its way,　　　　455
(The manly body left a load of clay)
And plaintive glides along the dreary coast,
A naked, wand'ring, melancholy ghost!

　　Achilles, musing as he roll'd his eyes
O'er the dead hero, thus (unheard) replies.　　　　460
Die thou the first! When *Jove* and heav'n ordain,
I follow thee – He said, and stripp'd the slain.
Then forcing backward from the gaping wound
The reeking jav'lin, cast it on the ground.
The thronging *Greeks* behold with wond'ring eyes　　465
His manly beauty and superiour size:

While some ignobler, the great dead deface
With wounds ungen'rous, or with taunts disgrace.
'How chang'd that *Hector!* who like *Jove* of late,
470   Sent lightning on our fleets, and scatter'd fate?'
    High o'er the slain the great *Achilles* stands,
Begirt with heroes, and surrounding bands;
And thus aloud, while all the host attends.
Princes and Leaders! Countrymen and friends!
475   Since now at length the pow'rful will of heav'n
The dire destroyer to our arm has giv'n,
Is not *Troy* fall'n already? Haste, ye pow'rs!
See, if already their deserted tow'rs
Are left unmann'd; or if they yet retain
480   The souls of heroes, their great *Hector* slain?
But what is *Troy*, or glory what to me?
Or why reflects my mind on ought but thee,
Divine *Patroclus!* Death has seal'd his eyes;
Unwept, unhonour'd, uninterr'd he lies!
485   Can his dear image from my soul depart,
Long as the vital spirit moves my heart?
If, in the melancholy shades below,
The flames of friends and lovers cease to glow,
Yet mine shall sacred last; mine, undecay'd,
490   Burn on thro' death, and animate my shade.
Meanwhile, ye sons of *Greece*, in triumph bring
The corps of *Hector*, and your *Pæans* sing.
Be this the song, slow-moving tow'rd the shore,
'*Hector* is dead, and *Ilion* is no more.'
495   Then his fell soul a thought of vengeance bred,
(Unworthy of himself, and of the dead)
The nervous ancles bor'd, his feet he bound
With thongs inserted thro' the double wound;
These fix'd up high behind the rolling wain,
500   His graceful head was trail'd along the plain.
Proud on his car th'insulting victor stood,
And bore aloft his arms, distilling blood.
He smites the steeds; the rapid chariot flies;
The sudden clouds of circling dust arise.
505   Now lost is all that formidable air;
The face divine, and long-descending hair

Purple the ground, and streak the sable sand;
Deform'd, dishonour'd, in his native land!
Giv'n to the rage of an insulting throng!
And, in his parents' sight, now dragg'd along!   510
  The mother first beheld with sad survey;
She rent her tresses, venerably grey,
And cast, far off, the regal veils away.
With piercing shrieks his bitter fate she moans,
While the sad father answers groans with groans,   515
Tears after tears his mournful cheeks o'erflow,
And the whole city wears one face of woe.
No less than if the rage of hostile fires
From her foundations curling to her spires,
O'er the proud citadel at length should rise,   520
And the last blaze send *Ilion* to the skies.
The wretched monarch of the falling state
Distracted, presses to the *Dardan* gate.
Scarce the whole people stop his desp'rate course,
While strong affliction gives the feeble force: 525
Grief tears his heart, and drives him to and fro,
In all the raging impotence of woe.
At length he roll'd in dust, and thus begun:
Imploring all, and naming one by one.
Ah! let me, let me go where sorrow calls;   530
I, only I, will issue from your walls,
(Guide or companion, friends! I ask ye none)
And bow before the murd'rer of my son.
My grief perhaps his pity may engage;
Perhaps at least he may respect my age.   535
He has a father too; a man like me,
One, not exempt from age and misery,
(Vig'rous no more, as when his young embrace
Begot this pest of me, and all my race.)
How many valiant sons, in early bloom,   540
Has that curst hand sent headlong to the tomb?
Thee, *Hector!* last: Thy loss (divinely brave)
Sinks my sad soul with sorrow to the grave.
Oh had thy gentle spirit past in peace,
The son expiring in the sire's embrace,   545

While both thy parents wept thy fatal hour,
And bending o'er thee, mix'd the tender show'r!
Some comfort that had been, some sad relief,
To melt in full satiety of grief!

550   Thus wail'd the father, grov'ling on the ground,
And all the eyes of *Ilion* stream'd around.
     Amidst her matrons *Hecuba* appears,
(A mourning Princess, and a train in tears)
Ah why has heav'n prolong'd this hated breath,

555   Patient of horrours, to behold thy death?
O *Hector*, late thy parents pride and joy,
The boast of nations! the defence of *Troy!*
To whom her safety and her fame she ow'd,
Her chief, her hero, and almost her God!

560   O fatal change! become in one sad day
A senseless corps! inanimated clay!
     But not as yet the fatal news had spread
To fair *Andromache*, of *Hector* dead;
As yet no messenger had told his fate,

565   Nor ev'n his stay without the *Scæan* gate.
Far in the close recesses of the dome,
Pensive she ply'd the melancholy loom;
A growing work employ'd her secret hours,
Confus'dly gay with intermingled flow'rs.

570   Her fair-hair'd handmaids heat the brazen urn,
The bath preparing for her Lord's return:
In vain: Alas! her Lord returns no more!
Unbath'd he lies, and bleeds along the shore!
Now from the walls the clamours reach her ear,

575   And all her members shake with sudden fear;
Forth from her iv'ry hand the shuttle falls,
As thus, astonish'd, to her maids she calls.
     Ah follow me! (she cry'd) what plaintive noise
Invades my ear? 'Tis sure my mother's voice.

580   My falt'ring knees their trembling frame desert,
A pulse unusual flutters at my heart.
Some strange disaster, some reverse of fate
(Ye Gods avert it) threats the *Trojan* state.
Far be the omen which my thoughts suggest!

585   But much I fear my *Hector*'s dauntless breast

Confronts *Achilles*; chas'd along the plain,
Shut from our walls! I fear, I fear him slain!
Safe in the crowd he ever scorn'd to wait,
And sought for glory in the jaws of fate:
Perhaps that noble heat has cost his breath,   590
Now quench'd for ever in the arms of death.

   She spoke; and furious, with distracted pace,
Fears in her heart, and anguish in her face,
Flies thro' the dome, (the maids her steps pursue)
And mounts the walls, and sends around her view.   595
Too soon her eyes the killing object found,
The god-like *Hector* dragg'd along the ground.
A sudden darkness shades her swimming eyes:
She faints, she falls; her breath, her colour flies.
Her hair's fair ornaments, the braids that bound,   600
The net that held them, and the wreath that crown'd,
The veil and diadem, flew far away;
(The gift of *Venus* on her bridal day)
Around, a train of weeping sisters stands,
To raise her sinking with assistant hands.   605
Scarce from the verge of death recall'd, again
She faints, or but recovers to complain.

   O wretched husband of a wretched wife!
Born with one fate, to one unhappy life!
For sure one star its baneful beam display'd   610
On *Priam*'s roof, and *Hippoplacia*'s shade.
From diff'rent parents, diff'rent climes we came,
At diff'rent periods, yet our fate the same!
Why was my birth to great *Aëtion* ow'd,
And why was all that tender care bestow'd?   615
Would I had never been! – O thou, the ghost
Of my dead husband! miserably lost!
Thou to the dismal realms for ever gone!
And I abandon'd, desolate, alone!
An only child, once comfort of my Pains,   620
Sad product now of hapless love, remains!
No more to smile upon his Sire! no friend
To help him now! No father to defend!
For should he 'scape the sword, the common doom!
What wrongs attend him, and what griefs to come?   625

Ev'n from his own paternal roof expell'd,
Some stranger plows his patrimonial field.
The day, that to the shades the father sends,
Robs the sad orphan of his father's friends:
630   He, wretched outcast of mankind! appears
For ever sad, for ever bath'd in tears;
Amongst the happy, unregarded he,
Hangs on the robe, or trembles at the knee,
While those his father's former bounty fed,
635   Nor reach the goblet, nor divide the bread:
The kindest but his present wants allay,
To leave him wretched the succeeding day.
Frugal compassion! Heedless they who boast
Both parents still, nor feel what he has lost,
640   Shall cry, 'Begone! Thy father feasts not here':
The wretch obeys, retiring with a tear.
Thus wretched, thus retiring all in tears,
To my sad soul *Astyanax* appears!
Forc'd by repeated insults to return,
645   And to his widow'd mother vainly mourn.
He, who with tender delicacy bred,
With princes sported, and on dainties fed,
And when still ev'ning gave him up to rest,
Sunk soft in down upon the nurse's breast,
650   Must – ah what must he not? Whom *Ilion* calls
Astyanax, from her well-guarded walls,
Is now that name no more, unhappy boy!
Since now no more the father guards his *Troy*.
But thou my *Hector* ly'st expos'd in air,
655   Far from thy parent's and thy consort's care,
Whose hand in vain, directed by her love,
The martial scarf and robe of triumph wove.
Now to devouring flames be these a prey,
Useless to thee, from this accursed day!
660   Yet let the sacrifice at least be paid,
An honour to the living, not the dead!
      So spake the mournful dame: Her Matrons hear,
Sigh back her sighs, and answer tear with tear.

OBSERVATIONS

ON THE

TWENTY-SECOND BOOK

The epigraph on the frontispiece of Volume VI (Books 22–24) consists of the following lines:

> *Qui cupit* [*sic*] *optatam cursu contingere metam,*
> *Multa tulit, fecitque puer* – HOR.

[Whoever wishes, in his race, to reach his desired goal must, as a youth, have struggled and sacrificed. (Horace, *Ars Poetica*, 412–13)]

It is impossible but the whole attention of the reader must be awaken'd in this book: The heroes of the two armies are now to encounter; all the foregoing battels have been but so many preludes and underactions, in order to this great event: Wherein the whole fate of *Greece* and *Troy* is to be decided by the sword of *Achilles* and *Hector*.

This is the book, which of the whole *Iliad* appears to me the most charming. It assembles in it all that can be imagined of great and important on the one hand, and of tender and melancholy on the other. *Terrour* and *Pity* are here wrought up in perfection, and if the reader is not sensible of both in a high degree, either he is utterly void of all taste, or the translator of all skill, in poetry.

37. *Not half so dreadful rises,* &c.] With how much dreadful pomp is *Achilles* here introduced! How noble, and in what bold colours hath he drawn the blazing of his arms, the rapidity of his advance, the terrour of his appearance, the desolation around him; but above all, the certain death attending all his motions and his very looks; what a crowd of terrible ideas in this one simile!

But immediately after this, follows the moving image of the two aged parents, trembling, weeping, and imploring their son: That is succeeded again by the dreadful gloomy picture of *Hector*, all on fire, obstinately bent on death, and expecting *Achilles*; admirably painted in the simile of the snake roll'd up in his den and collecting his poisons: And indeed thro' the whole book this wonderful contrast and opposition of the *Moving* and of the *Terrible*, is perpetually kept up, each heightening the other: I can't find words to express how so great beauties affect me.

51. *The speech of* Priam *to* Hector.] The poet has entertain'd us all along with various scenes of slaughter and horrour: He now changes to the pathetick, and fills the mind of the reader with tender sorrows. *Eustathius* observes that *Priam* preludes to his words by actions expressive of misery: The unhappy orator introduces his speech to *Hector* with groans and tears, and rending his hoary hair. The father and the King plead with *Hector* to preserve his life and his country. He represents his own age, and the loss of many of his children; and adds, that if *Hector* falls, he should then be inconsolable, and the empire of *Troy* at an end.

It is a piece of great judgment in *Homer* to make the fall of *Troy* to depend upon the death of *Hector*: The poet does not openly tell us that *Troy* was taken by the *Greeks*, but that the reader might not be unacquainted with what happened after the period of his poem, he gives us to understand in this speech, that the city was taken, and that *Priam*, his wives, his sons and daughters, were either killed or made slaves.

76. *Enter yet the wall; and spare*, &c.] The argument that *Priam* uses (says *Eustathius*) to induce *Hector* to secure himself in *Troy* is remarkable; he draws it not from *Hector*'s fears, nor does he tell him that he is to save his own life; but he insists upon stronger motives: He tells him he may preserve his fellow-citizens, his country, and his father; and farther, persuades him not to add glory to his mortal enemy by his fall.

90. *My bleeding infants dash'd against the floor.*] Cruelties which the *Barbarians* usually exercised in the sacking of towns. Thus *Isaiah* foretels to *Babylon* that her children shall be dashed in pieces before her eyes by the *Medes*. *Infantes eorum allidentur in oculis eorum*, xii. 16. And *David* says to the same city, *Happy shall he be that taketh and*

dasheth thy little ones against the stones. Psal. cxxxvii. 9. And in the
prophet *Hosea*, xiii. 16. *Their infants shall be dash'd in pieces.*

Dacier.

102. *But when the Fates,* &c.] Nothing can be more moving than the
image which *Homer* gives here, in comparing the different Effects
produced by the view of a young man, and that of an old one, both
bleeding, and extended on the dust. The old man, 'tis certain touches
us most, and several reasons may be given for it; the principal is, that
the young man defended himself, and his death is glorious; whereas an
old man has no defence but his weakness, prayers, and tears. They
must be very insensible of what is dreadful, and have no taste in
poetry, who omit this passage in a translation, and substitute things of
a trivial and insipid nature.

Dacier.

114. *The speech of* Hecuba.] The speech of *Hecuba* opens with as
much tenderness as that of *Priam*: The circumstance in particular of
her shewing that breast to her son which had sustained his Infancy, is
highly moving: It is a silent kind of oratory, and prepares the heart to
listen, by prepossessing the eye in favour of the speaker.

Eustathius takes notice of the difference between the speeches of
Priam and *Hecuba*: *Priam* dissuades him from the combat by enumerat-
ing not only the loss of his own family, but of his whole country: *Hecuba*
dwells entirely upon his single death; this is a great beauty in the poet,
to make *Priam* a father to his whole country; but to describe the
fondness of the mother as prevailing over all other considerations, and
to mention that only which chiefly affects her.

This puts me in mind of a judicious stroke in *Milton*, with regard to
the several characters of *Adam* and *Eve*. When the Angel is driving
them both out of Paradise, *Adam* grieves that he must leave a place
where he had conversed with God and his angels; but *Eve* laments that
she shall never more behold the flowers of *Eden*: Here *Adam* mourns
like a man, and *Eve* like a woman.

138. *The soliloquy of* Hector.] There is much greatness in the senti-
ments of this whole soliloquy. *Hector* prefers death to an ignominious
Life: He knows how to die with glory, but not how to live with
dishonour. The reproach of *Polydamas* affects him; the scandals of the
meanest people have an influence on his thoughts.

'Tis remarkable that he does not say, he fears the insults of the braver *Trojans,* but of the most worthless only. Men of merit are always the most candid; but others are ever for bringing all men to a level with themselves. They cannot bear that any one should be so bold as to excel, and are ready to pull him down to them, upon the least miscarriage. This sentiment is perfectly fine, and agreeable to the way of thinking natural to a great and sensible mind.

There is a very beautiful break in the middle of this speech. *Hector*'s mind fluctuates every way, he is calling a council in his own breast, and consulting what method to pursue: He doubts if he should not propose terms of peace to *Achilles,* and grants him very large concessions; but of a sudden he checks himself, and leaves the sentence unfinish'd. The paragraph runs thus, 'If,' says *Hector,* 'I should offer him the largest conditions, give all that *Troy* contains –' There he stops, and immediately subjoins, 'But why do I delude myself,' *&c.*

'Tis evident from this speech that the power of making peace was in *Hector*'s hands: For unless *Priam* had transferred it to him, he could not have made these propositions. So that it was *Hector* who broke the treaty in the third book; (where the very same conditions were proposed by *Agamemnon.*) 'Tis *Hector* therefore that is guilty, he is blameable in continuing the war, and involving the *Greeks* and *Trojans* in blood. This conduct in *Homer* was necessary; he observes a poetical justice, and shews us that *Hector* is a criminal, before he brings him to death.

Eustathius.

140. *Shall proud* Polydamas, &c.] *Hector* alludes to the counsel given him by *Polydamas* in the eighteenth book, which he then neglected to follow: It was, to withdraw to the city, and fortify themselves there, before *Achilles* returned to the battel.

167.   *We greet not here, as man conversing man,*
   Met at an oak, or journeying o'er a plain, &c.]

The Words literally are these, '*There is no talking with* Achilles, ἀπὸ δρυὸς οὐδ᾽ ἀπὸ πέτρης, *from an oak, or from a rock,* (or about an oak or a rock) *as a young man and a maiden talk together.* It is thought an obscure passage, tho' I confess I am either too fond of my own explication in the above-cited verses, or they make it a very clear one. 'There is no conversing with this implacable enemy in the rage of battel; as when sauntring people talk at leisure to one another on the road, or when young men and women meet in a field.' I think the exposition of *Eustathius* more far-fetch'd, tho' it be ingenious; and therefore I must do him the justice not to suppress it. It was a common practice, says he, with the heathens, to expose such children as they either could not, or would not educate: The places where they deposited them were usually in the cavities of *rocks*, or the hollow of *oaks*: These children being frequently found and preserved by strangers, were said to be the offspring of those oaks or rocks where they were found. This gave occasion to the poets to feign that men were born of *oaks*, and there was a famous fable too of *Deucalion* and *Pyrrha*'s repairing mankind by casting *stones* behind them: It grew at last into a proverb, to signify idle tales; so that in the present passage it imports, that *Achilles will not listen to such idle tales as may pass with silly maids and fond lovers.* For fables and stories (and particularly such stories as the preservation, strange fortune, and adventures of exposed children) are the usual conversation of young men and maidens. *Eustathius* his explanation may be corroborated by a parallel place in the Odyssey; where the poet says,

Οὐ γὰρ ἀπὸ δρυὸς ἔσσι παλαιφάτου οὐδ' ἀπὸ πέτρης.

The meaning of which passage is plainly this, *Tell me of what race you are, for undoubtedly you had a father and mother; you are not, according to the old story, descended from an* oak *or a* rock. Where the Word παλαιφάτου shews that this was become an ancient proverb even in *Homer*'s days.

180. *Struck by some God, he fears, recedes, and flies.*] I doubt not most readers are shock'd at the flight of *Hector*: It is indeed a high exaltation of *Achilles* (which was the poet's chief hero) that so brave a Man as *Hector* durst not stand him. While *Achilles* was at a distance he had fortified his heart with noble resolutions, but at his approach they all vanish, and he flies. This (as exceptionable as some may think it) may yet be allowed to be a true portrait of human nature; for distance, as it lessens all objects, so it does our fears: But where inevitable danger approaches, the stoutest hearts will feel some apprehensions at certain fate. It was the saying of one of the bravest men in this age, to one who told him he feared nothing, *Shew me but a certain danger, and I shall be as much afraid as any of you.* I don't absolutely pretend to justify this passage in every point, but only to have thus much granted me, that *Hector* was in this desperate circumstance.

First, It will not be found in the whole Iliad, that *Hector* ever thought himself a match for *Achilles. Homer* (to keep this in our minds) had just now made *Priam* tell him (as a thing known, for certainly *Priam* would not insult him at that time) that there was no comparison between his own strength, and that of his antagonist.

– ἐπεὶ ἦ πολὺ φέρτερός ἐστιν.

Secondly, We may observe with *Dacier*, the degrees by which *Homer* prepares this incident. In the 18th book the mere sight and voice of *Achilles* unarmed has terrified and put the whole *Trojan* army into disorder. In the 19th, the very sound of the cœlestial arms given him by *Vulcan*, has affrighted his own *Myrmidons* as they stand about him. In the 20th, he has been upon the point of killing *Æneas*, and *Hector* himself was not saved from him but by *Apollo*'s interposing. In that and the following book, he makes an incredible slaughter of all that oppose him; he overtakes most of those that fly from him, and *Priam* himself opens the gates of *Troy* to receive the rest.

Thirdly, *Hector* stays, not that he hopes to overcome *Achilles*, but because shame and the dread of reproach forbid him to re-enter the city; a shame (says *Eustathius*) which was a fault, that betray'd him out of his life, and ruined his Country. Nay, *Homer* adds farther, that he only stay'd by the immediate *will of heaven*, intoxicated and irresistibly bound down by *fate*.

Ἕκτορα δ᾽ αὐτοῦ μεῖναι ὀλοὴ μοῖρ᾽ ἐπέδησεν.

[Destructive fate bound Hector to remain.]

Fourthly, He had just been reflecting on the injustice of the war he maintained; his spirits are deprest by heaven, he expects certain death, he perceives himself abandon'd by the Gods; (as he directly says in v. 300, &c. of the *Greek*, and 385 of the translation) so that he might say to *Achilles* what *Turnus* does to *Æneas*,

Dii *me terrent*, & Jupiter *hostis.*

[Tis hostile heav'n I dread; and partial *Jove.*]

This indeed is the strongest reason that can be offered for the flight of *Hector*. He flies not from *Achilles* as a mortal hero, but from one whom he sees clad in impenetrable armour, seconded by *Minerva*, and one who had put to flight the inferior Gods themselves. This is not cowardice according to the constant principles of *Homer*, who thought it no part of a hero's character to be impious, or to fancy himself independent on the supreme being.

Indeed it had been a grievous fault, had our author suffer'd the courage of *Hector* entirely to forsake him even in this extremity: A brave man's soul is still capable of rouzing itself, and acting honourably in the last struggles. Accordingly *Hector*, tho' deliver'd over to his destiny, abandon'd by the Gods, and certain of death, yet stops and attacks *Achilles*; When he loses his spear, he draws his sword: It was impossible he should conquer, it was only in his power to fall gloriously; this he did, and it was all that man could do.

If the reader, after all, cannot bring himself to like this passage, for his own particular; yet to induce him to suspend his absolute censure, he may consider that *Virgil* had an uncommon esteem for it, as he has testify'd in transferring it almost entirely to the death of *Turnus*; where there was no necessity of making use of the like incidents: But doubtless he was touch'd with this Episode, as with one of those which interest us most of the whole Iliad, by a spectacle at once so terrible, and so deplorable. I must also add the suffrage of *Aristotle*, who was so far from looking upon this passage as ridiculous or blameable, that he esteem'd it marvellous and admirable. 'The *wonderful*,' says he, 'ought to have place in tragedy, but still more in epic poetry, which proceeds in this point even to the unreasonable: For as in epic poems one sees not the persons acting, so whatever passes the bounds of reason is proper to produce the admirable and the marvellous. For example, what *Homer* says of *Hector* pursued by *Achilles*, would appear ridiculous on the stage; for the spectators could not forbear laughing to see on one side the *Greeks* standing without any motion, and on the other *Achilles* pursuing *Hector*, and making signs to the troops not to dart at him. But all this does not appear when we read the poem: For what is wonderful is always agreeable, and as a proof of it, we find that they who relate any thing usually add something to the truth, that it may the better please those who hear it.'

The same great critick vindicates this passage in the chapter following. 'A poet, says he, is inexcusable if he introduces such things as are impossible according to the rules of poetry: but this ceases to be a fault, if by those means he attains to the End propos'd; for he has then brought about what he intended: For example, if he renders by it any part of his poem more astonishing or admirable. Such is the place in the Iliad, where *Achilles* pursues *Hector*.'

Arist. Poet. chap. 25, 26.

196. *Where two fam'd fountains.*] *Strabo* blames *Homer* for saying that one of the sources of *Scamander* was a warm fountain; whereas (says he) there is but one spring, and that cold, neither is this in the place where *Homer* fixes it, but in the mountain. It is observ'd by *Eustathius*, that tho' this was not true in *Strabo*'s days, yet it might in *Homer*'s, greater changes having happen'd in less time than that which pass'd between those two authors. *Sandys*, who was both a geographer and critick of great accuracy, as well as a traveller of great veracity, affirms as an eye witness, that there are yet some hot-water springs in that part of the country, opposite to *Tenedos.* I cannot but think that gentleman must have been particularly diligent and curious in his enquiries into the remains of a place so celebrated in poetry; as he was not only perhaps the most learned, but one of the best poets of his time: I am glad of this occasion to do his memory so much justice as to say, the *English* versification owes much of its improvement to his translations, and especially that admirable one of *Job.* What chiefly pleases me in this place, is to see the exact landskip of old *Troy*, we have a clear idea of the town itself, and of the roads and country about it; the river, the fig-trees, and every part is set before our eyes.

218. *The gazing Gods lean forward from the skies.*] We have here an instance of the great judgment of *Homer.* The death of *Hector* being the chief action of the poem; he assembles the Gods, and calls a council in heaven concerning it: It is for the same reason that he represents *Jupiter* with the greatest solemnity weighing in his scales the fates of the two heroes: I have before observ'd at large upon the last circumstance in a preceding note, so that there is no occasion to repeat it.

I wonder that none of the commentators have taken notice of this beauty; in my opinion it is a very necessary observation, and shews the art and judgment of the poet, that he has made the greatest and finishing action of the poem of such importance that it engages the Gods in debates.

226. *From* Ida's *Summits* –] It was the custom of the *Pagans* to sacrifice to the Gods upon the hills and mountains, in scripture language upon the *high places*, for they were persuaded that the Gods in a particular manner inhabited such eminences: Wherefore God order'd his people to destroy all those high places, which the nations had prophan'd by their idolatry. *You shall utterly destroy all the places wherein the nations which you shall possess served their Gods, upon the*

high mountains, and upon the hills, and under every green tree. Deut. xii.
2. 'Tis for this reason that so many kings are reproach'd in scripture
for not *taking away the high places.*   *Dacier.*

249. *Thus step by step,* &c.] There is some difficulty in this passage,
and it seems strange that *Achilles* could not overtake *Hector* whom he
excell'd so much in swiftness, especially when the poet describes him
as running in a narrower circle than *Hector*: *Eustathius* gives us many
solutions from the ancients: *Homer* has already told us that they run
for the life of *Hector*; and consequently *Hector* would exert his utmost
speed, whereas *Achilles* might only endeavour to keep him from entering
the city: Besides, *Achilles* could not directly pursue him, because he
frequently made efforts to shelter himself under the wall, and he being
oblig'd to turn him from it, he might be forced to take more steps than
Hector; but the poet, to take away all grounds of an objection, tells us
afterwards, that *Apollo* gave him a supernatural swiftness.

257. *As men in slumbers.*] This beautiful comparison has been con-
demn'd by some of the ancients, even so far as to judge it unworthy of
having a place in the Iliad: They say the diction is mean, and the
similitude itself absurd, because it compares the swiftness of the heroes
to men asleep, who are in a state of rest and inactivity. But there
cannot be a more groundless criticism: The poet is so far from drawing
his comparison from the repose of men asleep, that he alludes only to
their dreams: It is a race in fancy that he describes; and surely the
imagination is nimble enough to illustrate the greatest degree of
swiftness: Besides the verses themselves run with the utmost rapidity,
and imitate the swiftness they describe.   *Eustathius.*

What sufficiently proves these verses to be genuine, is, that *Virgil*
has imitated them, *Æn.* 12.

> *Ac veluti in somnis –*

[And as, when heavy sleep has clos'd the sight –]

269. *Sign'd to the troops,* &c.] The Difference which *Homer* here
makes between *Hector* and *Achilles* deserves to be taken notice of;
Hector is running away towards the walls, to the end that the *Trojans*
who are upon them may overwhelm *Achilles* with their darts; and
Achilles in turning *Hector* towards the plain, makes a sign to his
troops not to attack him. This shews the great courage of *Achilles.* Yet

this action which appears so generous has been very much condemned by the ancients; *Plutarch* in the life of *Pompey* gives us to understand, that it was look'd upon as the action of a fool too greedy of glory: Indeed this is not a single combat of *Achilles* against *Hector*, (for in that case *Achilles* would have done very ill not to hinder his troops from assaulting him) this was a rencounter in a battel, and so *Achilles* might, and ought to take all advantage to rid himself, the readiest and the surest way, of an enemy whose death would procure an entire victory to his party. Wherefore does he leave this victory to chance? Why expose himself to the hazard of losing it? Why does he prefer his private glory to the publick weal, and the safety of all the *Greeks*, which he puts to the venture by delaying to conquer, and endangering his own person? I grant it is a fault, but it must be own'd to be the fault of a hero.   *Eustathius. Dacier.*

277. *Then* Phœbus *left him –*] This is a very beautiful and poetical manner of describing a plain circumstance: The hour of *Hector*'s death was now come, and the poet expresses it by saying that *Apollo*, or *Destiny*, forsakes him: That is, the Fates no longer protect him.
                                                                                 Eustathius.

Id. – Fierce Minerva *flies To stern* Pelides, &c.] The poet may seem to diminish the glory of *Achilles*, by ascribing the victory over *Hector* to the assistance of *Pallas*; whereas in truth he fell by the hand only of *Achilles*: But poetry loves to raise every thing into a wonder; it steps out of the common road of narration, and aims to surprize; and the poet would farther insinuate that it is a greater glory to *Achilles* to be belov'd by the Gods, than to be only excellent in valour: For many men have valour, but few the favour of heaven.   *Eustathius.*

290. *Obey'd and rested.*] The whole passage where *Pallas* deceives *Hector* is evidently an allegory: *Achilles* perceiving that he cannot overtake *Hector*, pretends to be quite spent and wearied in the pursuit; the stratagem takes effect, and recalls his enemy: This the poet expresses by saying that *Pallas*, or *Wisdom*, came to assist *Achilles.* *Hector* observing his enemy stay to rest concludes that he is quite fatigued, and immediately takes courage and advances upon him; he thinks he has him at an advantage, but at last finds himself deceiv'd: Thus making a wrong judgment he is betray'd into his death; so that his own *false judgment* is the *treacherous Pallas* that deceives him.
                                                                                 Eustathius.

317. *The speeches of* Hector, *and of* Achilles.] There is an opposition
between these speeches excellently adapted to the characters of both
the heroes: That of *Hector* is full of courage, but mixt with Humanity:
That of *Achilles*, of resentment and arrogance: We see the great *Hector*
disposing of his own remains, and that thirst of glory which has
made him live with honour, now bids him provide, as *Eustathius*
observes, that what once was *Hector* may not be dishonour'd: Thus we
see a sedate, calm courage, with a contempt of death, in the speeches
of *Hector*. But in that of *Achilles* there is a *fierté*, and an insolent air of
superiority; his magnanimity makes him scorn to steal a victory, he
bids him prepare to defend himself with all his forces, and that valour
and resentment which made him desirous that he might revenge
himself upon *Hector* with his own hand, and forbade the *Greeks* to
interpose, now directs him not to take any advantage over a brave
enemy. I think both their characters are admirably sustain'd, and tho'
Achilles be drawn with a great violence of features, yet the picture is
undoubtedly like him; and it had been the utmost absurdity to have
soften'd one line upon this occasion, when the soul of *Achilles* was all
on fire to revenge the death of his friend *Patroclus*. I must desire the
reader to carry this observation in his memory, and particularly in that
place, where *Achilles* says he could eat the very flesh of *Hector*; (tho' I
have a little soften'd it in the translation) v. 438.

391. *So* Jove's *bold bird*, &c.] The poet takes up some time in describ-
ing the two great heroes before they close in fight: The verses are
pompous and magnificent, and he illustrates his description with two
beautiful similes: He makes a double use of this conduct, which not
only raises our imagination to attend to so momentous an action, but
by lengthening his narration keeps the mind in a pleasing suspense,
and divides it between hopes and fears for the fate of *Hector* or
Achilles.

409. *Thro' that penetrable part Furious he drove*, &c.] It was necessary
that the poet should be very particular in this point, because the arms
that *Hector* wore, were the arms of *Achilles*, taken from *Patroclus*; and
consequently, as they were the work of *Vulcan*, they would preserve
Hector from the possibility of a wound: The poet therefore to give an
air of probability to his story, tells us that they were *Patroclus* his
arms, and as they were not made for *Hector*, they might not exactly fit
his body: So that it is not improbable but there might be some place

about the neck of *Hector* so open as to admit the spear of *Achilles.*   *Eustathius.*

437. *Could I my self the bloody banquet join!*] I have before hinted that there is something very fierce and violent in this passage; but I fancy that what I there observ'd will justify *Homer* in his relation, tho' not *Achilles* in his savage sentiments: Yet the poet softens the expression by making *Achilles* only wish that his heart would permit him to devour him: This is much more tolerable than a passage in the *Thebais* of *Statius*, where *Tydeus* in the very pangs of death is represented as gnawing the head of his enemy.

439. *Should* Troy, *to bribe me,* &c.] Such resolutions as *Achilles* here makes, are very natural to men in anger; he tells *Hector* that no motives shall ever prevail with him to suffer his body to be ransom'd; yet when time had cool'd his heat, and he had somewhat satisfy'd his revenge by insulting his remains, he restores them to *Priam.* This perfectly agrees with his conduct in the ninth book, where at first he gives a rough denial, and afterwards softens into an easier temper. And this is very agreeable to the nature of *Achilles*; his anger abates very slowly; it is stubborn, yet still it remits: Had the poet drawn him as never to be pacify'd, he had out-rag'd nature, and not represented his hero as a man, but as a monster.   *Eustathius.*

449. *A day will come –*] *Hector* prophesies at his death that *Achilles* shall fall by the hand of *Paris.* This confirms an observation made in a former note, that the words of dying men were look'd upon as prophecies; but whether such conjectures are true or false, it appears from hence, that such opinions have prevail'd in the world above three thousand years.

467. *The great dead deface With wounds,* &c.] *Eustathius* tells us that *Homer* introduces the soldiers wounding the dead Body of *Hector*, in order to mitigate the cruelties which *Achilles* exercises upon it. For if every common soldier takes a pride in giving him a wound, what insults may we not expect from the inexorable, inflam'd *Achilles*? But I must confess myself unable to vindicate the poet in giving us such an idea of his countrymen. I think the former courage of their enemy should have been so far from moving them to revenge, that it should

have recommended him to their esteem: What *Achilles* afterwards acts is suitable to his character, and consequently the poet is justify'd; but surely all the *Greeks* are not of his temper? *Patroclus* was not so dear to them all, as he was to *Achilles*. 'Tis true the poet represents *Achilles* (as *Eustathius* observes) enumerating the many ills they had suffer'd from *Hector*; and he seems to endeavour to infect the whole army with his resentment. Had *Hector* been living, they had been acted by a generous indignation against him: But these men seem as if they only dared approach him dead; in short, what they say over his body is a mean insult, and the stabs they give it are cowardly and barbarous.

474. *The speech of* Achilles.] We have a very fine observation of *Eustathius* on this place, that the judgment and address of *Homer* here is extremely worthy of remark: He knew, and had often said, that the gods and fate had not granted *Achilles* the glory of taking *Troy*: There was then no reason to make him march against the town after the death of *Hector*, since all his efforts must have been ineffectual. What has the poet done in this conjuncture? It was but reasonable that the first thought of *Achilles* should be to march directly to *Troy*, and to profit himself of the general consternation into which the death of *Hector* had thrown the *Trojans*. We here see he knows the duty, and does not want the ability, of a great General; but after this on a sudden he changes his design, and derives a plausible pretence from the impatience he has to pay the last devoirs to his friend. The manners of *Achilles*, and what he has already done for *Patroclus*, make this very natural. At the same time, this turning off to the tender and pathetic has a fine effect; the reader in the very fury of the hero's vengeance, perceives, that *Achilles* is still a man, and capable of softer passions.

494. 'Hector *is dead, and* Ilion *is no more*'.] I have follow'd the opinion of *Eustathius*, who thought that what *Achilles* says here was the chorus or burden of a song of triumph, in which his troops bear a part with him, as he returns from this glorious combate. *Dacier* observes that this is very correspondent to the manners of those times; and instances in that passage of the book of *Kings*, when *David* returns from the conquest of *Goliah*: The women there go out to meet him from all the cities of *Israel*, and sing a triumphal song, the chorus whereof is, Saul *has kill'd his thousands, and* David *his ten thousands*.

496. *Unworthy of himself, and of the dead.*] This inhumanity of *Achilles* in dragging the dead body of *Hector*, has been severely (and I think indeed not without some justice) censur'd by several both ancients and moderns. *Plato* in his third book *de Republica*, speaks of it with detestation: But methinks it is a great injustice to *Homer* to reflect upon the morals of the author himself, for things which he only paints as the manners of a vicious hero.

It may justly be observ'd in general of all *Plato*'s objections against *Homer*, that they are still in a view to morality, constantly blaming him for representing ill and immoral things as the opinions or actions of his persons. To every one of these one general answer will serve, which is, that *Homer* as often describes ill things, in order to make us avoid them, as good, to induce us to follow them (which is the case with all writers whatever.) But what is extremely remarkable, and evidently shews the injustice of *Plato*'s censure is, that many of those very actions for which he blames him are expressly characterized and marked by *Homer* himself as evil and detestable, by previous expressions or cautions. Thus in the present place, before he describes this barbarity of *Achilles*, he tells us it was a most unworthy action.

— καὶ Ἕκτορα δῖον ἀεικέα μήδετο ἔργα.

[— and the treatment he was pondering for brilliant Hector
    was disgraceful.]

When *Achilles* sacrifices the twelve young *Trojans* in l. 23. he repeats the same words. When *Pandarus* broke the Truce in l. 4. he told us it was a mad, unjust deed;

— τῷ δὲ φρένας ἄφρονι πεῖθεν.

[— he persuaded him, fool that he was.]

And so of the rest.

506. *The face divine, and long-descending hair.*] It is impossible to read the actions of great men without having our curiosity rais'd to know the least circumstance that relates to them: *Homer* to satisfy it, has taken care in the process of his poem to give us the shape of his heroes, and the very colour of their hair; thus he has told us that *Achilles*'s locks were yellow, and here the epithet Κυάνεαι shews us that those of *Hector* were of a darker colour: As to his person, he told us a little above that it was so handsome that all the *Greeks* were surpriz'd to see it. *Plutarch* recites a remarkable story of the beauty of *Hector*: It was reported in

Lacedæmon, that a handsome youth who very much resembled *Hector*, was arrived there; immediately the whole city run in such numbers to behold him, that he was trampled to death by the crowd. *Eustathius.*

543. *Sinks my sad soul with sorrow to the grave.*] It is in the *Greek*

Οὖ μ᾿ ἄχος ὀξὺ κατοίσεται Ἄϊδος εἴσω

[My piercing grief for him will catapult me to Hades.]

It is needless to observe to the reader with what a beautiful pathos the wretched father laments his son *Hector*: It is impossible not to join with *Priam* in his sorrows. But what I would chiefly point out to my reader, is the beauty of this line, which is particularly tender, and almost word for word the same with that of the Patriarch *Jacob*; who upon a like occasion breaks out into the same complaint, and tells his children, that if they deprive him of his son *Benjamin*, they will *bring down his grey hairs with sorrow to the grave.*

562, &c.] The grief of *Andromache*, which is painted in the following part, is far beyond all the praises that can be given it; but I must take notice of one particular which shews the great art of the poet. In order to make the wife of *Hector* appear yet more afflicted than his parents, he has taken care to encrease her affliction by *surprize*: It is finely prepared by the circumstances of her being retired to her innermost apartment, of her employment in weaving a robe for her husband (as may be conjectured from what she says afterward, v. 657.) and of her maids preparing the bath for his return: All which (as the criticks have observ'd) augment the surprize, and render this reverse of fortune much more dreadful and afflicting.

600. *Her hair's fair ornaments.*] *Eustathius* remarks, that in speaking of *Andromache* and *Hecuba*, *Homer* expatiates upon the ornaments of dress in *Andromache*, because she was a beautiful young princess; but is very concise about that of *Hecuba*, because she was old, and wore a dress rather suitable to her age and gravity, than to her state, birth, and condition. I cannot pass over a matter of such importance as a Lady's dress, without endeavouring to explain what sort of heads were worn above three thousand years ago.

It is difficult to describe particularly every ornament mentioned by the poet, but I shall lay before my female readers the Bishop's

explanation. The Ἄμπυξ [head-band] was used, τὸ τὰς ἐμπροσθίας τρί-
χας ἀναδεῖν, that is, to tie backwards the hair that grew on the
forepart of the head: The Κεκρύφαλος was a veil of net-work that
covered the hair when it was so ty'd; Ἀναδέσμη was an ornament used
κύκλῳ περὶ τοὺς κροτάφους ἀναδεῖν, to tye backwards the hair that
grew on the temples; and the Κρήδεμνον was a fillet, perhaps embroi-
dered with gold, (from the expression of χρυσῆ Ἀφροδίτη [golden
Aphrodite]) that bound the whole, and compleated the dress.

The Ladies cannot but be pleased to see so much learning and
Greek upon this important subject.

Homer is in nothing more excellent than in that distinction of
characters which he maintains thro' his whole poem: What *Andromache*
here says, cannot be spoken properly by any but *Andromache*: There is
nothing general in her sorrows, nothing that can be transferred to
another character: The mother laments the son, and the wife weeps
over the husband.

628. *The day that to the shades,* &c.] The following verses, which so
finely describe the condition of an orphan, have been rejected by some
ancient cardcks: It is a proof there were always cridcks of no manner of
taste; it being impossible any where to meet with a more exquisite
passage. I will venture to say, there are not in all *Homer* any lines more
worthy of him: The beauty of this tender and compassionate image is
such, that it even makes amends for the many cruel ones, with which
the Iliad is too much stained. These censurers imagined this descrip-
tion to be of too abject and mean a nature for one of the quality of
Astyanax; but had they considered (says *Eustathius*) that these are the
words of a fond mother who feared every thing for her son, that
women are by nature timorous and think all misfortunes will happen,
because there is a possibility that they may; that *Andromache* is in the
very height of her sorrows, in the instant she is speaking; I fancy they
would have altered their opinion.

It is undoubtedly an aggravation to our misfortunes when they sink
us in a moment from the highest flow of prosperity to the lowest
adversity: The Poet judiciously makes use of this circumstance, the
more to excite our pity, and introduces the mother with the utmost
tenderness, lamenting this reverse of fortune in her son; chang'd all
at once into a slave, a beggar, an orphan! Have we not examples in
our own times of unhappy Princes, whose condition renders this of
Astyanax but too probable?

647. *On dainties fed.*] It is in the *Greek*, 'Who upon his father's knees used to eat marrow and the fat of sheep.' This would seem gross if it were literally translated, but it is a figurative expression; in the style of the orientals, marrow and fatness are taken for whatever is best, tenderest, and most delicious. Thus in *Job* xxi. 24. *Viscera ejus plena sunt adipe & medullis ossa ejus irrigantur* ['His breasts are full of milk, and his bones are moistened with marrow' (King James version)]. And xxxvi. 16. *Requies autem mensæ tuæ erit plena pinguedine* ['That which should be set on thy table *should be* full of fatness' (King James version)]. In *Jer.* xxxi. 14. God says, that he will satiate the soul of the priests with fatness. *Inebriabo animam sacerdotum pinguedine.*

Dacier.

657. *The martial scarf and robe of triumph wove.*] This idea very naturally offers itself to a woman, who represents to herself the body of her husband dashed to pieces, and all his limbs dragged upon the ground uncovered; and nothing is more proper to excite pity. 'Tis well known that it was anciently the custom among princesses and great ladies to have large quantities of stuffs and moveables. This provision was more necessary in those times than now, because of the great consumption made of them on those occasions of mourning.

Dacier.

I am of opinion that *Homer* had a farther view in expatiating thus largely upon the death of *Hector*. Every word that *Hecuba*, *Priam*, and *Andromache* speak, shews us the Importance of *Hector*: Every word adds a weight to the concluding action of the poem, and at the same time represents the sad effects of the anger of *Achilles*, which is the subject of it.

THE
TWENTY-THIRD BOOK
OF THE
ILIAD

The ARGUMENT

The Funeral of *Patroclus*

Achilles *and the* Myrmidons *do honours to the body of* Patroclus. *After the funeral feast he retires to the sea-shore, where falling asleep, the ghost of his friend appears to him, and demands the rites of burial; the next morning the soldiers are sent with mules and waggons to fetch wood for the pyre. The funeral procession, and the offering of their hair to the dead.* Achilles *sacrifices several animals, and lastly, twelve* Trojan *captives at the pile, then sets fire to it. He pays libations to the winds, which (at the instance of* Iris*) rise, and raise the flames. When the pile has burn'd all night, they gather the bones, place 'em in an urn of gold, and raise the tomb.* Achilles *institutes the funeral games: The chariot race, the fight of the* Cæstus, *the wrestling, the foot-race, the single combat, the* discus, *the shooting with arrows, the darting the javelin: The various descriptions of which, and the various success of the several antagonists, make the greatest part of the book.*

In this book ends the thirtieth day: The night following, the ghost of Patroclus *appears to* Achilles: *The one and thirtieth Day is employ'd in felling the timber for the pile; the two and thirtieth in burning it; and the three and thirtieth in the games. The scene is generally on the sea-shore.*

Thus humbled in the dust, the pensive train
Thro' the sad city mourn'd her hero slain.
The body soil'd with dust, and black with gore,
Lyes on broad *Hellespont*'s resounding shore:
5 The *Grecians* seek their ships, and clear the strand,
All, but the martial *Myrmidonian* band:
These yet assembled great *Achilles* holds,
And the stern purpose of his mind unfolds.

   Not yet (my brave companions of the war)
10 Release your smoking coursers from the car;
But, with his chariot each in order led,
Perform due honours to *Patroclus* dead.
E'er yet from rest or food we seek relief,
Some rites remain, to glut our rage of grief.

15   The troops obey'd; and thrice in order led
(*Achilles* first) their coursers round the dead;
And thrice their sorrows and laments renew;
Tears bathe their arms, and tears the sands bedew.
For such a warriour *Thetis* aids their woe,
20 Melts their strong hearts, and bids their eyes to flow.
But chief, *Pelides*: thick succeeding sighs
Burst from his heart, and torrents from his eyes:
His slaught'ring hands, yet red with blood, he laid
On his dead friend's cold breast, and thus he said.

25   All hail, *Patroclus!* let thy honour'd ghost
Hear, and rejoice on *Pluto*'s dreary coast;
Behold! *Achilles*' promise is compleat;
The bloody *Hector* stretch'd before thy feet.

Lo! to the dogs his carcass I resign;
And twelve sad victims of the *Trojan* line   30
Sacred to vengeance, instant shall expire,
Their lives effus'd around thy fun'ral pyre.
   Gloomy he said, and (horrible to view)
Before the bier the bleeding *Hector* threw,
Prone on the dust. The *Myrmidons* around   35
Unbrac'd their armour, and the steeds unbound.
All to *Achilles'* sable ship repair,
Frequent and full, the genial feast to share.
Now from the well-fed swine black Smoakes aspire,
The bristly victims hissing o'er the fire: 40
The huge ox bellowing falls; with feebler cries
Expires the goat; the sheep in silence dies.
Around the hero's prostrate body flow'd
In one promiscuous stream, the reeking blood.
And now a band of *Argive* monarchs brings   45
The glorious victor to the king of kings.
From his dead friend the pensive warriour went,
With steps unwilling, to the regal tent.
Th'attending heralds, as by office bound,
With kindled flames the tripod-vase surround;   50
To cleanse his conqu'ring hands from hostile gore,
They urg'd in vain; the chief refus'd, and swore.
   No drop shall touch me, by almighty *Jove!*
The first and greatest of the Gods above!
Till on the pyre I place thee; till I rear   55
The grassy mound, and clip thy sacred hair.
Some ease at least those pious rites may give,
And sooth my sorrows, while I bear to live.
Howe'er, reluctant as I am, I stay,
And share your feast; but, with the dawn of day,   60
(O King of men!) it claims thy royal care,
That *Greece* the warriour's fun'ral pile prepare,
And bid the forests fall: (Such rites are paid
To heroes slumb'ring in eternal shade)
Then, when his earthly part shall mount in fire,   65
Let the leagu'd squadrons to their posts retire.
   He spoke; they hear him, and the word obey;
The rage of hunger and of thirst allay,
Then ease in sleep the labours of the day.

70   But great *Pelides*, stretch'd along the shore
      Where dash'd on rocks the broken billows roar,
      Lies inly groaning; while on either hand
      The martial *Myrmidons* confus'dly stand:
      Along the grass his languid members fall,
75   Tir'd with his chase around the *Trojan* wall;
      Hush'd by the murmurs of the rolling deep,
      At length he sinks in the soft arms of sleep.
      When lo! the shade before his closing eyes
      Of sad *Patroclus* rose, or seem'd to rise;
80   In the same robe he living wore, he came,
      In stature, voice, and pleasing look, the same.
      The form familiar hover'd o'er his head,
      And sleeps *Achilles* (thus the phantom said)
      Sleeps my *Achilles*, his *Patroclus* dead?
85   Living, I seem'd his dearest, tend'rest care,
      But now forgot, I wander in the air;
      Let my pale corse the rites of burial know,
      And give me entrance in the realms below:
      Till then, the spirit finds no resting place,
90   But here and there th' unbody'd spectres chace
      The vagrant dead around the dark abode,
      Forbid to cross th' irremeable flood.
      Now give thy hand; for to the farther shore
      When once we pass, the soul returns no more.
95   When once the last funereal flames ascend,
      No more shall meet *Achilles* and his friend,
      No more our thoughts to those we lov'd make known,
      Or quit the dearest, to converse alone.
      Me fate has sever'd from the sons of earth,
100   The fate fore-doom'd that waited from my birth:
      There too it waits; before the *Trojan* wall
      Ev'n great and godlike thou art doom'd to fall.
      Hear then; and as in fate and love we join,
      Ah suffer that my bones may rest with thine!
105   Together have we liv'd, together bred,
      One house receiv'd us, and one table fed;
      That golden urn thy goddess mother gave
      May mix our ashes in one common grave.
           And is it thou? (he answers) to my sight
110   Once more return'st thou from the realms of night?

Oh more than brother! Think each office paid,
Whate'er can rest a discontented shade;
But grant one last embrace, unhappy boy!
Afford at least that melancholy joy.

He said, and with his longing arms essay'd   115
In vain to grasp the visionary shade;
Like a thin smoak he sees the spirit fly,
And hears a feeble, lamentable cry.
Confus'd he wakes; amazement breaks the bands
Of golden sleep, and starting from the sands,   120
Pensive he muses with uplifted hands.

'Tis true, 'tis certain; man, tho' dead, retains
Part of himself; th'immortal mind remains:
The form subsists, without the body's aid,
Aerial semblance, and an empty shade!   125
This night my friend, so late in battel lost,
Stood at my side, a pensive, plaintive ghost;
Ev'n now familiar, as in life, he came,
Alas! how diff'rent! yet how like the same!

Thus while he spoke, each eye grew big with tears: 130
And now the rosy-finger'd morn appears,
Shews every mournful face with tears o'erspread,
And glares on the pale visage of the dead.
But *Agamemnon*, as the rites demand,
With mules and waggons sends a chosen band;   135
To load the timber, and the pile to rear,
A charge consign'd to *Merion*'s faithful care.
With proper instruments they take the road,
Axes to cut, and ropes to sling the load.
First march the heavy mules, securely slow,   140
O'er hills, o'er dales, o'er crags, o'er rocks they go:
Jumping high o'er the shrubs of the rough ground,
Rattle the clatt'ring cars, and the shockt axles bound.
But when arriv'd at *Ida*'s spreading woods,   145
(Fair *Ida*, water'd with descending floods)
Loud sounds the axe, redoubling strokes on strokes;
On all sides round the forest hurles her oaks
Headlong. Deep-echoing groan the thickets brown;
Then rustling, crackling, crashing, thunder down.
The wood the *Grecians* cleave, prepar'd to burn;   150
And the slow mules the same rough road return.

The sturdy woodmen equal burthens bore
(Such charge was giv'n 'em) to the sandy shore;
There on the spot which great *Achilles* show'd,
155   They eas'd their shoulders, and dispos'd the load;
Circling around the place, where times to come
Shall view *Patroclus'* and *Achilles'* tomb.
The hero bids his martial troops appear
High in their cars in all the pomp of war;
160   Each in refulgent arms his limbs attires,
All mount their chariots, combatants and squires.
The chariots first proceed, a shining train;
Then clouds of foot that smoak along the plain;
Next these a melancholy band appear,
165   Amidst, lay dead *Patroclus* on the bier:
O'er all the corse their scatter'd locks they throw;
Achilles next, opprest with mighty woe,
Supporting with his hands the hero's head,
Bends o'er th' extended body of the dead.
170   *Patroclus* decent on th' appointed ground
They place and heap the sylvan pile around.
But great *Achilles* stands apart in pray'r,
And from his head divides the yellow hair;
Those curling locks which from his youth he vow'd,
175   And sacred grew to *Sperchius'* honour'd flood:
Then sighing, to the deep his looks he cast,
And roll'd his eyes around the wat'ry waste.
    Sperchius! whose waves in mazy errours lost
Delightful roll along my native coast!
180   To whom we vainly vow'd, at our return,
These locks to fall, and hecatombs to burn:
Full fifty rams to bleed in sacrifice,
Where to the day thy silver fountains rise,
And where in shade of consecrated bow'rs
185   Thy altars stand, perfum'd with native flow'rs!
So vow'd my father, but he vow'd in vain;
No more *Achilles* sees his native plain;
In that vain hope these hairs no longer grow,
Patroclus bears them to the shades below.
190   Thus o'er *Patroclus* while the hero pray'd,
On his cold hand the sacred lock he laid.

Once more afresh the *Grecian* sorrows flow:
And now the sun had set upon their woe;
But to the King of Men thus spoke the chief.
Enough, *Atrides!* give the troops relief: 195
Permit the mourning legions to retire,
And let the chiefs alone attend the pyre;
The pious care be ours, the dead to burn –
He said: The people to their ships return:
While those deputed to inter the slain   200
Heap with a rising pyramid the plain.
A hundred foot in length, a hundred wide,
The growing structure spreads on ev'ry side;
High on the top the manly corse they lay,
And well-fed sheep, and sable oxen slay: 205
Achilles cover'd with their fat the dead,
And the pil'd victims round the body spread.
Then jars of honey, and of fragrant oil
Suspends around, low-bending o'er the pile.
Four sprightly coursers, with a deadly groan   210
Pour forth their lives, and on the pyre are thrown.
Of nine large dogs, domestick at his board,
Fall two, selected to attend their lord.
Then last of all, and horrible to tell,
Sad sacrifice! twelve *Trojan* captives fell.   215
On these the rage of fire victorious preys,
Involves and joins them in one common blaze.
Smear'd with the bloody rites, he stands on high,
And calls the spirit with a dreadful cry.
    All hail, *Patroclus!* let thy vengeful ghost   220
Hear, and exult on *Pluto*'s dreary coast.
Behold, *Achilles'* promise fully paid,
Twelve *Trojan* heroes offer'd to thy shade;
But heavier fates on *Hector*'s corse attend,
Sav'd from the flames, for hungry dogs to rend.   225
    So spake he, threat'ning: But the Gods made vain
His threat, and guard inviolate the slain:
Celestial *Venus* hover'd o'er his head,
And roseate unguents, heav'nly fragrance! shed:
She watch'd him all the night, and all the day,   230
And drove the bloodhounds from their destin'd prey.

Nor sacred *Phœbus* less employ'd his care;
He pour'd around a veil of gather'd air,
And kept the nerves undry'd, the flesh entire,
235   Against the solar beam and *Sirian* fire.
    Nor yet the pile where dead *Patroclus* lies,
Smokes, nor as yet the sullen flames arise;
But fast beside *Achilles* stood in pray'r,
Invok'd the Gods whose spirit moves the air,
240   And victims promis'd, and libations cast,
To gentle *Zephyr* and the *Boreal* blast:
He call'd th' aerial pow'rs, along the skies
To breathe, and whisper to the fires to rise.
The winged *Iris* heard the hero's call,
245   And instant hasten'd to their airy hall,
Where, in old *Zephyr*'s open courts on high,
Sate all the blustring brethren of the sky.
She shone amidst them, on her painted bow;
The rocky pavement glitter'd with the show.
250   All from the banquet rise, and each invites
The various goddess to partake the rites.
Not so, (the dame reply'd) I haste to go
To sacred Ocean, and the floods below:
Ev'n now our solemn hecatombs attend,
255   And heav'n is feasting on the world's green end,
With righteous *Æthiops* (uncorrupted train!)
Far on th' extreamest limits of the main.
But *Peleus*' son intreats, with sacrifice,
The *Western Spirit*, and the *North* to rise;
260   Let on *Patroclus*' pile your blast be driv'n,
And bear the blazing honours high to heav'n.
    Swift as the word, she vanish'd from their view;
Swift as the word, the *Winds* tumultuous flew;
Forth burst the stormy band with thund'ring roar,
265   And heaps on heaps the clouds are tost before.
To the wide main then stooping from the skies,
The heaving deeps in watry mountains rise:
Troy feels the blast along her shaking walls,
Till on the pyle the gather'd tempest falls.
270   The structure crackles in the roaring fires,
And all the night the plenteous flame aspires.

All Night *Achilles* hails *Patroclus*' soul,
With large libation from the golden bowl.
As a poor father, helpless and undone,
Mourns o'er the ashes of an only son,   275
Takes a sad pleasure the last bones to burn,
And pour in tears, e'er yet they close the urn:
So stay'd *Achilles*, circling round the shore,
So watch'd the flames, till now they flame no more.
'Twas when, emerging thro' the shades of night,   280
The morning planet told th' approach of light;
And fast behind, *Aurora*'s warmer ray
O'er the broad ocean pour'd the golden day:
Then sunk the blaze, the pyle no longer burn'd,
And to their caves the whistling winds return'd: 285
Across the *Thracian* seas their course they bore;
The ruffled seas beneath their passage roar.
Then parting from the pyle he ceas'd to weep,
And sunk to quiet in th' embrace of sleep,
Exhausted with his grief: Meanwhile the crowd   290
Of thronging *Grecians* round *Achilles* stood;
The tumult wak'd him: From his eyes he shook
Unwilling slumber, and the chiefs bespoke.

    Ye Kings and Princes of th' *Achaian* name!
First let us quench the yet remaining flame   295
With sable wine; then, (as the rites direct,)
The hero's bones with careful view select:
(Apart, and easy to be known they lie,
Amidst the heap, and obvious to the eye:
The rest around the margins will be seen,   300
Promiscuous, steeds, and immolated men)
These wrapt in double cawls of fat, prepare;
And in the golden vase dispose with care;
There let them rest, with decent honour laid,
Till I shall follow to th' infernal shade.   305
Meantime erect the tomb with pious hands,
A common structure on the humble sands;
Hereafter *Greece* some nobler work may raise,
And late posterity record our praise.

    The *Greeks* obey; where yet the embers glow   310
Wide o'er the pile the sable wine they throw,
And deep subsides the ashy heap below.

Next the white bones his sad companions place
With tears collected, in the golden vase.
315 The sacred relicks to the tent they bore;
The urn a veil of linen cover'd o'er.
That done, they bid the sepulchre aspire,
And cast the deep foundations round the pyre;
High in the midst they heap the swelling bed
320 Of rising earth, memorial of the dead.

The swarming populace the Chief detains,
And leads amidst a wide extent of plains;
There plac'd 'em round: Then from the ships proceeds
A train of oxen, mules, and stately steeds,
325 Vases and tripods, for the fun'ral games,
Resplendent brass, and more resplendent dames.
First stood the prizes to reward the force
Of rapid racers in the dusty course.
A woman for the first, in beauty's bloom,
330 Skill'd in the needle, and the lab'ring loom;
And a large vase, where two bright handles rise,
Of twenty measures its capacious size.
The second victor claims a mare unbroke,
Big with a mule, unknowing of the yoke;
335 The third, a charger yet untouch'd by flame;
Four ample measures held the shining frame:
Two golden talents for the fourth were plac'd;
An ample double bowl contents the last.
These in fair order rang'd upon the plain,
340 The hero, rising, thus addrest the train.

Behold the prizes, valiant *Greeks!* decreed
To the brave rulers of the racing steed;
Prizes which none beside our self could gain,
Should our immortal coursers take the plain;
345 (A race unrival'd, which from Ocean's God
Peleus receiv'd, and on his son bestow'd.)
But this no time our vigour to display,
Nor suit, with them, the games of this sad day:
Lost is *Patroclus* now, that wont to deck
350 Their flowing manes, and sleek their glossy neck.
Sad, as they shar'd in human grief, they stand,
And trail those graceful honours on the sand!

Let others for the noble task prepare,
Who trust the courser, and the flying car.
    Fir'd at his word, the rival racers rise;   355
But far the first, *Eumelus* hopes the prize,
Fam'd thro' *Pieria* for the fleetest breed,
And skill'd to manage the high-bounding steed.
With equal ardour bold *Tydides* swell'd
The steeds of *Tros* beneath his Yoke compell'd,   360
(Which late obey'd the *Dardan* chief's command,
When scarce a God redeem'd him from his hand)
Then *Menelaüs* his *Podargus* brings,
And the fam'd courser of the King of Kings:
Whom rich *Echepolus*, (more rich than brave)   365
To 'scape the wars, to *Agamemnon* gave,
(*Æthe* her Name) at home to end his days,
Base wealth preferring to eternal praise.
Next him *Antilochus* demands the course,
With beating heart, and chears his *Pylian* horse.   370
Experienc'd *Nestor* gives his son the reins,
Directs his judgment, and his heat restrains;
Nor idly warns the hoary sire, nor hears
The prudent son with unattending ears.
    My son! tho' youthful ardour fire thy breast,   375
The Gods have lov'd thee, and with arts have blest.
Neptune and *Jove* on thee conferr'd the skill,
Swift round the goal to turn the flying wheel.
To guide thy conduct, little precept needs;
But slow, and past their vigour, are my steeds.   380
Fear not thy rivals, tho' for swiftness known,
Compare those rivals judgment, and thy own:
It is not strength, but art, obtains the prize,
And to be swift is less than to be wise:
'Tis more by art, than force of num'rous strokes,   385
The dext'rous woodman shapes the stubborn oaks;
By Art the Pilot, thro' the boiling deep
And howling tempest, stears the fearless ship;
And 'tis the artist wins the glorious course,
Not those, who trust in chariots and in horse.   390
In vain unskilfull to the goal they strive,
And short, or wide, th' ungovern'd courser drive:

While with sure skill, tho' with inferior steeds,
The knowing racer to his end proceeds;
395 Fix'd on the goal his eye fore-runs the course,
His hand unerring steers the steady horse,
And now contracts, or now extends the rein,
Observing still the foremost on the plain.
Mark then the goal, 'tis easy to be found;
400 Yon' aged trunk, a cubit from the ground;
Of some once stately oak the last remains,
Or hardy fir, unperish'd with the rains.
Inclos'd with stones conspicuous from afar,
And round, a circle for the wheeling car.
405 (Some tomb perhaps of old, the dead to grace;
Or then, as now, the limit of a race)
Bear close to this, and warily proceed,
A little bending to the left hand steed;
But urge the right, and give him all the reins;
410 While thy strict hand his fellow's head restrains,
And turns him short; till, doubling as they roll,
The wheel's round naves appear to brush the goal.
Yet (not to break the car, or lame the horse)
Clear of the stony heap direct the course;
415 Lest thro' incaution failing, thou may'st be
A joy to others, a reproach to me.
So shalt thou pass the goal, secure of mind,
And leave unskilful swiftness far behind.
Tho' thy fierce rival drove the matchless steed
420 Which bore *Adrastus*, of celestial breed;
Or the fam'd race thro' all the regions known,
That whirl'd the car of proud *Laomedon.*

    Thus, (nought unsaid) the much-advising sage
Concludes; then sate, stiff with unwieldy age.
425 Next bold *Meriones* was seen to rise,
The last, but not least ardent for the prize.
They mount their seats; the lots their place dispose;
(Roll'd in his helmet, these *Achilles* throws.)
Young *Nestor* leads the race: *Eumelus* then;
430 And next the brother of the King of men:
Thy lot, *Meriones*, the fourth was cast;
And far the bravest, *Diomed*, was last.

They stand in order, an impatient Train;
Pelides points the barrier on the plain,
And sends before old *Phœnix* to the place,   435
To mark the racers, and to judge the race.
At once the coursers from the barrier bound;
The lifted scourges all at once resound;
Their heart, their eyes, their voice, they send before;
And up the champain thunder from the shore: 440
Thick, where they drive, the dusty clouds arise,
And the lost courser in the whirlwind flies;
Loose on their shoulders the long manes reclin'd,
Float in their speed, and dance upon the wind:
The smoaking chariots, rapid as they bound,   445
Now seem to touch the sky, and now the ground.
While hot for fame, and conquest all their care,
(Each o'er his flying courser hung in air)
Erect with ardour, pois'd upon the rein,
They pant, they stretch, they shout along the plain.   450
Now, (the last compass fetch'd around the goal)
At the near prize each gathers all his soul,
Each burns with double hope, with double pain,
Tears up the shore, and thunders tow'rd the main.
First flew *Eumelus* on *Pheretian* steeds;   455
With those of *Tros*, bold *Diomed* succeeds:
Close on *Eumelus'* back they puff the wind,
And seem just mounting on his car behind;
Full on his neck he feels the sultry breeze,
And hov'ring o'er, their stretching shadows sees.   460
Then had he lost, or left a doubtful prize;
But angry *Phœbus* to *Tydides* flies,
Strikes from his hand the scourge, and renders vain
His matchless horses labour on the plain.
Rage fills his eye with anguish, to survey   465
Snatch'd from his hope, the glories of the day.
The fraud celestial *Pallas* sees with pain,
Springs to her Knight, and gives the scourge again,
And fills his steeds with vigour. At a stroke,
She breaks his rival's chariot from the yoke;   470
No more their way the startled horses held;
The car revers'd came rat'ling on the field;

Shot headlong from his seat, beside the wheel,
Prone on the dust th' unhappy master fell;
475 His batter'd face and elbows strike the ground;
Nose, mouth and front, one undistinguish'd wound:
Grief stops his voice, a torrent drowns his eyes;
Before him far the glad *Tydides* flies;
Minerva's spirit drives his matchless pace,
480 And crowns him victor of the labour'd race.

The next, tho' distant, *Menelaüs* succeeds;
While thus young *Nestor* animates his steeds.
Now, now, my gen'rous pair, exert your force;
Not that we hope to match *Tydides*' horse,
485 Since great *Minerva* wings their rapid way,
And gives their Lord the honours of the day.
But reach *Atrides!* Shall his mare out-go
Your swiftness? vanquish'd by a female foe?
Thro' your neglect, if lagging on the plain
490 The last ignoble gift be all we gain;
No more shall *Nestor*'s hand your food supply,
The old man's fury rises, and ye die.
Haste then; yon' narrow road before our sight
Presents th' occasion, could we use it right.

495 Thus he. The coursers at their master's threat
With quicker steps the sounding champain beat.
And now *Antilochus* with nice survey,
Observes the compass of the hollow way.
'Twas where by force of wintry torrents torn,
500 Fast by the road a precipice was worn:
Here, where but one could pass, to shun the throng
The *Spartan* hero's chariot smoak'd along.
Close up the vent'rous youth resolves to keep,
Still edging near, and bears him tow'rd the steep.
505 *Atrides*, trembling casts his eye below,
And wonders at the rashness of his foe.
Hold, stay your steeds – What madness thus to ride
This narrow way? Take larger field (he cry'd)
Or both must fall – *Atrides* cry'd in vain;
510 He flies more fast, and throws up all the rein.
Far as an able arm the disk can send,
When youthful rivals their full force extend,

So far *Antilochus!* thy chariot flew
Before the King: He, cautious, backward drew
His horse compell'd; foreboding in his fears   515
The rattling ruin of the clashing cars,
The flound'ring coursers rolling on the plain,
And conquest lost thro' frantick haste to gain.
But thus upbraids his rival as he flies;
Go, furious youth! ungen'rous and unwise!   520
Go, but expect not I'll the prize resign;
Add perjury to fraud, and make it thine. –
Then to his steeds with all his force he cries;
Be swift, be vig'rous, and regain the prize!
Your rivals, destitute of youthful force,   525
With fainting knees shall labour in the course,
And yield the glory yours – The steeds obey;
Already at their heels they wing their way,
And seem already to retrieve the day.

Meantime the *Grecians* in a ring beheld   530
The coursers bounding o'er the dusty field.
The first who mark'd them was the *Cretan* King;
High on a rising ground, above the ring,
The Monarch sate; from whence with sure survey
He well observ'd the chief who led the way,   535
And heard from far his animating cries,
And saw the foremost steed with sharpen'd eyes;
On whose broad front a blaze of shining white,
Like the full moon, stood obvious to the sight.
He saw; and rising, to the *Greeks* begun.   540
Are yonder horse discern'd by me alone?
Or can ye, all, another chief survey,
And other steeds, than lately led the way?
Those, tho' the swiftest, by some God with-held,
Lie sure disabled in the middle field: 545
For since the goal they doubled, round the plain
I search to find them, but I search in vain.
Perchance the reins forsook the driver's hand,
And, turn'd too short, he tumbled on the strand,
Shot from the chariot; while his coursers stray   550
With frantick fury from the destin'd way.

Rise then some other, and inform my sight,
(For these dim Eyes, perhaps, discern not right)
Yet sure he seems, (to judge by shape and air,)
555   The great *Ætolian* chief, renown'd in war.
         Old man! (*Oïleus* rashly thus replies)
Thy tongue too hastily confers the prize.
Of those who view the course, not sharpest ey'd,
Nor youngest, yet the readiest to decide.
560   *Eumelus'* steeds high-bounding in the chace,
Still, as at first, unrivall'd lead the race:
I well discern him, as he shakes the rein,
And hear his shouts victorious o'er the plain.
         Thus he. *Idomeneus* incens'd rejoin'd.
565   Barb'rous of words! and arrogant of mind!
Contentious Prince! of all the *Greeks* beside
The last in merit, as the first in pride.
To vile reproach what answer can we make?
A goblet or a tripod let us stake,
570   And be the King the Judge. The most unwise
Will learn their rashness, when they pay the price.
         He said: and *Ajax* by mad passion born,
Stern had reply'd; fierce scorn inhancing scorn
To fell extreams. But *Thetis'* god-like son
575   Awful amidst them rose; and thus begun.
         Forbear, ye chiefs! reproachful to contend;
Much would ye blame, should others thus offend:
And lo! th' approaching steeds your contest end.
No sooner had he spoke, but thund'ring near
580   Drives, thro' a stream of dust, the charioteer;
High o'er his head the circling lash he wields;
His bounding horses scarcely touch the fields:
His car amidst the dusty whirlwind roll'd,
Bright with the mingled blaze of tin and gold;
585   Refulgent thro' the cloud: no Eye could find
The track his flying wheels had left behind:
And the fierce coursers urg'd their rapid pace
So swift, it seem'd a flight, and not a race.
Now victor at the goal *Tydides* stands,
590   Quits his bright car, and springs upon the sands;

From the hot steeds the sweaty torrents stream;
The well-ply'd whip is hung athwart the beam:
With joy brave *Sthenelus* receives the prize,
The tripod-vase, and dame with radiant eyes:
These to the ships his train triumphant leads,   595
The chief himself unyokes the panting steeds.

 Young *Nestor* follows (who by art, not force,
O'er-past *Atrides*) second in the course.
Behind, *Atrides* urg'd the race, more near
Than to the courser in his swift career   600
The following car, just touching with his heel
And brushing with his tail the whirling wheel.
Such, and so narrow now the space between
The rivals, late so distant on the green;
So soon swift *Æthe* her lost ground regain'd,   605
One length, one moment had the race obtain'd.

 Merion pursu'd, at greater distance still,
With tardier coursers, and inferior skill.
Last came, *Admetus!* thy unhappy son;
Slow dragg'd the steeds his batter'd chariot on: 610
Achilles saw, and pitying thus begun.

 Behold! the man whose matchless art surpast
The sons of *Greece!* the ablest, yet the last!
Fortune denies, but justice bids us pay
(Since great *Tydides* bears the first away)   615
To him, the second honours of the day.

 The *Greeks* consent with loud applauding cries,
And then *Eumelus* had receiv'd the prize,
But youthful *Nestor*, jealous of his fame,
Th' award opposes, and asserts his claim.   620
Think not (he cries) I tamely will resign
O *Peleus* son! the mare so justly mine.
What if the Gods, the skilful to confound,
Have thrown the horse and horseman to the ground?
Perhaps he sought not heav'n by sacrifice,   625
And vows omitted forfeited the prize.
If yet, (distinction to thy friend to show,
And please a soul desirous to bestow,)
Some gift must grace *Eumelus*; view thy store
Of beauteous handmaids, steeds, and shining ore.   630

An ample present let him thence receive,
And *Greece* shall praise thy gen'rous thirst to give.
But this, my prize, I never shall forego;
This, who but touches, warriours! is my foe.
635   Thus spake the youth, nor did his words offend;
Pleas'd with the well-turn'd flattery of a friend,
Achilles smil'd: The gift propos'd (he cry'd)
Antilochus! we shall our self provide.
With plates of brass the corselet cover'd o'er,
640   (The same renown'd *Asteropæus* wore)
Whose glitt'ring margins rais'd with silver shine;
(No vulgar gift) *Eumelus*, shall be thine.
  He said: *Automedon* at his command
The corselet brought, and gave it to his hand.
645   Distinguish'd by his friend, his bosom glows
With gen'rous joy: Then *Menelaüs* rose;
The herald plac'd the sceptre in his hands,
And still'd the clamour of the shouting bands.
Not without cause incens'd at *Nestor*'s son,
650   And inly grieving, thus the King begun:
      The praise of wisdom, in thy youth obtain'd,
An act so rash (*Antilochus*) has stain'd.
Robb'd of my glory and my just reward,
To you O *Grecians!* be my wrong declar'd:
655   So not a leader shall our conduct blame,
Or judge me envious of a rival's fame.
But shall not we, ourselves, the truth maintain?
What needs appealing in a fact so plain?
What *Greek* shall blame me, if I bid thee rise,
660   And vindicate by oath th'ill-gotten prize.
Rise if thou dar'st, before thy chariot stand,
The driving scourge high-lifted in thy hand,
And touch thy steeds, and swear, thy whole intent
Was but to conquer, not to circumvent.
665   Swear by that God whose liquid arms surround
The globe, and whose dread earthquakes heave the
              ground.
      The prudent chief with calm attention heard;
Then mildly thus: Excuse, if youth have err'd;

Superiour as thou art, forgive th' offence,
Nor I thy equal, or in years, or sense.   670
Thou know'st the errours of unripen'd age,
Weak are its counsels, headlong is its rage.
The Prize I quit, if thou thy wrath resign;
The mare, or ought thou ask'st, be freely thine,
E'er I become (from thy dear friendship torn)   675
Hateful to thee, and to the Gods forsworn.

    So spoke *Antilochus*; and at the word
The mare contested to the King restor'd.
Joy swells his soul, as when the vernal grain
Lifts the green ear above the springing plain,   680
The fields their vegetable life renew,
And laugh and glitter with the morning dew;
Such joy the *Spartan*'s shining face o'erspread,
And lifted his gay heart, while thus he said.

    Still may our souls, O gen'rous Youth! agree,   685
'Tis now *Atrides*' turn to yield to thee.
Rash heat perhaps a moment might controul,
Not break, the settled temper of thy soul.
Not but (my friend) 'tis still the wiser way
To wave contention with superiour sway;   690
For ah! how few, who should like thee offend,
Like thee, have talents to regain the friend?
To plead indulgence and thy fault attone,
Suffice thy father's merits, and thy own:
Gen'rous alike, for me, the sire and son   695
Have greatly suffer'd, and have greatly done.
I yield; that all may know, my soul can bend,
Nor is my pride preferr'd before my friend.

    He said; and pleas'd his passion to command,
Resign'd the courser to *Noëmon*'s hand,   700
Friend of the youthful chief: Himself content,
The shining charger to his vessel sent.
The golden talents *Merion* next obtain'd;
The fifth reward, the double bowl, remain'd.
Achilles this to rev'rend *Nestor* bears,   705
And thus the purpose of his gift declares.

    Accept thou this, O sacred sire! (he said)
In dear memorial of *Patroclus* dead;

Dead, and for ever lost *Patroclus* lies,
710   For ever snatch'd from our desiring eyes!
Take thou this token of a grateful heart,
Tho' 'tis not thine to hurl the distant dart,
The quoit to toss, the pond'rous mace to wield,
Or urge the race, or wrestle on the field.
715   Thy present vigour age has overthrown,
But left the glory of the past thy own.
     He said, and plac'd the goblet at his side;
With joy, the venerable King reply'd.
     Wisely and well, my son, thy words have prov'd
720   A senior honour'd, and a friend belov'd!
Too true it is, deserted of my strength,
These wither'd arms and limbs have fail'd at length.
Oh! had I now that force I felt of yore,
Known thro' *Buprasium* and the *Pylian* shore!
725   Victorious then in ev'ry solemn game
Ordain'd to *Amarynces'* mighty name;
The brave *Epeians* gave my glory way,
Ætolians, *Pylians*, all resign'd the day.
I quell'd *Clytomedes* in fights of hand,
730   And backward hurl'd *Ancæus* on the sand,
Surpast *Iphyclus* in the swift career,
Phyleus and *Polydorus*, with the spear.
The sons of *Actor* won the prize of horse,
But won by numbers, not by art or force:
735   For the fam'd twins, impatient to survey,
Prize after prize by *Nestor* born away,
Sprung to their car; and with united pains
One lash'd the coursers, while one rul'd the reins.
Such once I was! Now to these tasks succeeds
740   A younger race, that emulate our deeds:
I yield alas! (to age who must not yield?)
Tho' once the foremost hero of the field.
Go thou, my son! by gen'rous friendship led,
With martial honours decorate the dead;
745   While pleas'd I take the gift thy hands present,
(Pledge of benevolence, and kind intent)
Rejoic'd, of all the num'rous *Greeks*, to see
Not one but honours sacred age and me:

Those due distinctions thou so well can'st pay,
May the just Gods return another day. 750
    Proud of the gift, thus spake the full of days:
Achilles heard him, prouder of the praise.

    The prizes next are order'd to the field
For the bold champions who the *Cæstus* wield.
A stately mule, as yet by toils unbroke, 755
Of six years age, unconscious of the yoke,
Is to the *Circus* led, and firmly bound;
Next stands a goblet, massy, large and round.
Achilles rising, thus: Let *Greece* excite
Two heroes equal to this hardy fight; 760
Who dares his foe with lifted arms provoke,
And rush beneath the long-descending stroke?
On whom *Apollo* shall the palm bestow,
And whom the *Greeks* supreme by conquest know,
This mule his dauntless labours shall repay; 765
The vanquish'd bear the massy bowl away.

    This dreadful combate great *Epæus* chose,
High o'er the crowd, enormous bulk! he rose,
And seiz'd the beast, and thus began to say:
Stand forth some man, to bear the bowl away! 770
(Price of his ruin:) For who dares deny
This mule my right? th' undoubted victor I.
Others, 'tis own'd, in fields of battle shine,
But the first honours of this fight are mine;
For who excells in all? Then let my foe 775
Draw near, but first his certain fortune know,
Secure, this hand shall his whole frame confound,
Mash all his bones, and all his body pound:
So let his friends be nigh, a needful train
To heave the batter'd carcase off the plain. 780

    The Giant spoke; and in a stupid gaze
The Host beheld him, silent with amaze!
'Twas thou, *Euryalus!* who durst aspire
To meet his might, and emulate thy sire,
The great *Mecistheus*; who in days of yore 785
In *Theban* games the noblest trophy bore,
(The games ordain'd dead *Oedipus* to grace)
And singly vanquish'd the *Cadmæan* race.

Him great *Tydides* urges to contend,
790 Warm with the hopes of conquest for his friend,
Officious with the cincture girds him round;
And to his wrists the gloves of death are bound.
Amid the circle now each champion stands,
And poises high in air his iron hands;
795 With clashing gantlets now they fiercely close,
Their crackling jaws re-echoe to the blows,
And painful sweat from all their members flows.
At length *Epëus* dealt a weighty blow,
Full on the cheek of his unwary foe;
800 Beneath that pond'rous arm's resistless sway
Down dropt he, nerveless, and extended lay.
As a large fish, when winds and Waters roar,
By some huge billow dash'd against the shore,
Lies panting: Not less batter'd with his wound,
805 The bleeding hero pants upon the ground.
To rear his fallen foe, the victor lends
Scornful, his hand; and gives him to his friends;
Whose arms support him, reeling thro' the throng,
And dragging his disabled legs along;
810 Nodding, his head hangs down his shoulder o'er;
His mouth and nostrils pour the clotted gore;
Wrapt round in mists he lies, and lost to thought;
His friends receive the bowl, too dearly bought.
    The third bold game *Achilles* next demands,
815 And calls the wrestlers to the level sands:
A massy tripod for the victor lies,
Of twice six oxen its reputed price;
And next, the losers spirits to restore,
A female captive, valu'd but at four.
820 Scarce did the chief the vig'rous strife propose,
When tow'r-like *Ajax* and *Ulysses* rose.
Amid the ring each nervous rival stands,
Embracing rigid with implicit hands:
Close lock'd above, their heads and arms are mixt;
825 Below, their planted feet at distance fixt:
Like two strong rafters which the builder forms
Proof to the wintry winds and howling storms,

Their tops connected, but at wider space
Fixt on the center stands their solid base.
Now to the grasp each manly body bends;   830
The humid sweat from ev'ry pore descends;
Their bones resound with blows: sides, shoulders, thighs
Swell to each gripe, and bloody tumours rise.
Nor could *Ulysses*, for his art renown'd,
O'erturn the strength of *Ajax* on the ground;   835
Nor could the strength of *Ajax* overthrow
The watchful caution of his artful foe.
While the long strife ev'n tir'd the lookers-on,
Thus to *Ulysses* spoke great *Telamon.*
Or let me lift thee, Chief, or lift thou me: 870
Prove we our force, and *Jove* the rest decree.
    He said; and straining, heav'd him off the ground
With matchless strength; that time *Ulysses* found
The strength t'evade, and where the nerves combine,
His ankle strook: The giant fell supine: 845
Ulysses following, on his bosom lies;
Shouts of applause run rattling thro the skies.
Ajax to lift, *Ulysses* next essays,
He barely stirr'd him, but he could not raise:
His knee lock'd fast, the foe's attempt deny'd;   850
And grappling close, they tumble side by side.
Defil'd with honourable dust, they roll,
Still breathing strife, and unsubdu'd of soul:
Again they rage, again to combat rise;
When great *Achilles* thus divides the prize.   855
    Your noble vigour, oh my friends, restrain;
Nor weary out your gen'rous strength in vain.
Ye both have won: Let others who excel
Now prove that prowess you have prov'd so well.
    The hero's words the willing chiefs obey,   860
From their tir'd bodies wipe the dust away,
And, cloth'd anew, the following games survey.
And now succeed the gifts, ordain'd to grace
The youths contending in the rapid race.
A silver urn that full six measures held,   865
By none in weight or workmanship excell'd:

    Sidonian artists taught the frame to shine,
    Elaborate, with artifice divine;
    Whence *Tyrian* sailors did the prize transport,
870 And gave to *Thoas* at the *Lemnian* port:
    From him descended good *Eunæus* heir'd
    The glorious gift; and, for *Lycaon* spar'd,
    To brave *Patroclus* gave the rich reward.
    Now, the same hero's funeral rites to grace,
875 It stands the prize of swiftness in the race.
    A well-fed ox was for the second plac'd;
    And half a talent must content the last.
    Achilles rising then bespoke the train:
    Who hopes the palm of swiftness to obtain,
880 Stand forth, and bear these prizes from the plain.
      The hero said, and starting from his place,
    Oïlean Ajax rises to the race;
    Ulysses next; and he whose speed surpast
    His youthful equals, *Nestor*'s son the last.
885 Rang'd in a line the ready racers stand;
    Pelides points the barrier with his hand;
    All start at once; *Oileus* led the race;
    The next *Ulysses*, meas'ring pace with pace;
    Behind him, diligently close, he sped,
890 As closely following as the running thread
    The spindle follows, and displays the charms
    Of the fair spinster's breast, and moving arms:
    Graceful in motion thus, his foe he plies,
    And treads each footstep e'er the dust can rise:
895 His glowing breath upon his shoulders plays;
    Th' admiring *Greeks* loud acclamations raise,
    To him they give their wishes, hearts, and eyes,
    And send their souls before him as he flies.
    Now three times turn'd in prospect of the goal,
900 The panting chief to *Pallas* lifts his soul:
    Assist, O Goddess! (thus in thought he pray'd)
    And present at his thought, descends the Maid.
    Buoy'd by her heav'nly force, he seems to swim,
    And feels a pinion lifting ev'ry limb.
905 All fierce, and ready now the prize to gain,
    Unhappy *Ajax* stumbles on the plain;

(O'erturn'd by *Pallas*) where the slipp'ry shore
Was clogg'd with slimy dung, and mingled gore.
(The self-same place beside *Patroclus'* pyre,
Where late the slaughter'd victims fed the fire)   910
Besmear'd with filth, and blotted o'er with clay,
Obscene to sight, the rueful racer lay;
The well-fed bull (the second prize) he shar'd,
And left the urn *Ulysses'* rich reward.
Then, grasping by the horn the mighty beast,   915
The baffled hero thus the *Greeks* addrest.

Accursed fate! the conquest I forego;
A Mortal I, a Goddess was my foe:
She urg'd her fav'rite on the rapid way,
And *Pallas*, not *Ulysses* won the day.   920

Thus sow'rly wail'd he, sputt'ring dirt and gore;
A burst of laughter echo'd thro' the shore.
Antilochus, more hum'rous than the rest,
Takes the last prize, and takes it with a jest.

Why with our wiser elders should we strive?   925
The Gods still love them, and they always thrive.
Ye see, to *Ajax* I must yield the prize:
He to *Ulysses*, still more ag'd and wise;
(A green old age unconscious of decays,
That proves the hero born in better days!)   930
Behold his vigour in this active race!
Achilles only boasts a swifter pace:
For who can match *Achilles*? He who can,
Must yet be more than hero, more than man.

Th' effect succeeds the speech. *Pelides* cries,   935
Thy artful praise deserves a better prize.
Nor *Greece* in vain shall hear thy friend extoll'd;
Receive a talent of the purest gold.
The youth departs content. The host admire
The son of *Nestor*, worthy of his sire.   940

Next these a buckler, spear and helm, he brings,
Cast on the plain the brazen burthen rings:
Arms, which of late divine *Sarpedon* wore,
And great *Patroclus* in short triumph bore.
Stand forth the bravest of our host! (he cries)   945
Whoever dares deserve so rich a prize!

Now grace the lists before our army's sight,
And sheath'd in steel, provoke his foe to fight.
Who first the jointed armour shall explore,
950   And stain his rival's mail with issuing gore;
The sword, *Asteropeus* possest of old,
(A *Thracian* blade, distinct with studs of gold)
Shall pay the stroke, and grace the striker's side:
These arms in common let the chief divide:
955   For each brave champion, when the combat ends,
A sumptuous banquet at our tent attends.
   Fierce at the word, uprose great *Tydeus'* son,
And the huge bulk of *Ajax Telamon.*
Clad in refulgent steel, on either hand,
960   The dreadful chiefs amid the circle stand:
Low'ring they meet, tremendous to the sight;
Each *Argive* bosom beats with fierce delight.
Oppos'd in arms not long they idly stood,
But thrice they clos'd, and thrice the charge renew'd.
965   A furious pass the spear of *Ajax* made
Thro' the broad shield, but at the corselet stay'd:
Not thus the foe: His jav'lin aim'd above
The buckler's margin, at the neck he drove.
But *Greece* now trembling for her hero's life,
970   Bade share the honours, and surcease the strife.
Yet still the victor's due *Tydides* gains,
With him the sword and studded belt remains.
   Then hurl'd the hero, thund'ring on the ground
A mass of iron, (an enormous round)
975   Whose weight and size the circling *Greeks* admire,
Rude from the furnace, and but shap'd by fire.
This mighty quoit *Aëtion* wont to rear,
And from his whirling arm dismiss in air:
The Giant by *Achilles* slain, he stow'd
980   Among his spoils this memorable load.
For this, he bids those nervous artists vie,
That teach the disk to sound along the sky.
Let him whose might can hurl this bowl, arise,
Who farthest hurls it, take it as his prize:
985   If he be one, enrich'd with large domain
Of downs for flocks, and arable for grain,

Small stock of iron needs that man provide;
His hinds and swains whole years shall be supply'd
From hence: Nor ask the neighb'ring city's aid,
For plowshares, wheels, and all the rural trade.   990
  Stern *Polyphætes* stept before the throng,
And great *Leonteus*, more than mortal strong;
Whose force with rival forces to oppose,
Uprose great *Ajax*; up *Epëus* rose.
Each stood in order: First *Epëus* threw;   995
High o'er the wond'ring crowds the whirling circle flew.
Leonteus next a little space surpast,
And third, the strength of god-like *Ajax* cast.
O'er both their marks it flew; till fiercely flung
From *Polyphætes'* arm, the *Discus* sung: 1000
Far, as a swain his whirling sheephook throws,
That distant falls among the grazing cows,
So past them all the rapid circle flies:
His friends (while loud applauses shake the skies)
With force conjoin'd heave off the weighty prize.   1005
  Those, who in skilful archery contend
He next invites the twanging bow to bend:
And twice ten axes casts amidst the round,
(Ten double-edg'd, and ten that singly wound.)
The mast, which late a first-rate galley bore,   1010
The hero fixes in the sandy shore:
To the tall top a milk-white dove they tie,
The trembling mark at which their arrows fly.
Whose weapon strikes yon' flutt'ring bird, shall bear
These two-edg'd axes, terrible in war;   1015
The single, he, whose shaft divides the cord.
He said: Experienc'd *Merion* took the word;
And skilful *Teucer*: In the helm they threw
Their lots inscrib'd, and forth the latter flew.
Swift from the string the sounding arrow flies;   1020
But flies unblest! No grateful sacrifice,
No firstling lambs, unheedful! didst thou vow,
To *Phœbus*, patron of the shaft and bow.
For this, thy well-aim'd arrow, turn'd aside,
Err'd from the dove, yet cut the cord that ty'd: 1025

A-down the main-mast fell the parted string,
And the free bird to heav'n displays her wing:
Seas, shores, and skies with loud applause resound,
And *Merion* eager meditates the wound:
1030 He takes the bow, directs the shaft above,
And following with his eye the soaring dove,
Implores the God to speed it thro' the skies,
With vows of firstling lambs, and grateful sacrifice.
The dove, in airy circles as she wheels,
1035 Amid the clouds the piercing arrow feels;
Quite thro' and thro' the point its passage found,
And at his feet fell bloody to the ground.
The wounded bird, e'er yet she breath'd her last,
With flagging wings alighted on the mast,
1040 A moment hung, and spread her pinions there,
Then sudden dropt, and left her life in air.
From the pleas'd crowd new peals of thunder rise,
And to the ships brave *Merion* bears the prize.

To close the fun'ral games, *Achilles* last
1045 A massy spear amid the circle plac'd,
And ample charger of unsullied frame,
With flow'rs high-wrought, not blacken'd yet by flame.
For these he bids the heroes prove their art,
Whose dext'rous skill directs the flying dart.
1050 Here too great *Merion* hopes the noble prize;
Nor here disdain'd the King of men to rise.
With joy *Pelides* saw the honour paid,
Rose to the Monarch and respectful said.
Thee first in virtue, as in pow'r supreme,
1055 O King of Nations! all thy *Greeks* proclaim;
In ev'ry martial game thy worth attest,
And know thee both their greatest, and their best.
Take then the prize, but let brave *Merion* bear
This beamy jav'lin in thy brother's war.
1060 Pleas'd from the hero's lips his praise to hear,
The King to *Merion* gives the brazen spear:
But, set apart for sacred use, commands
The glitt'ring charger to *Talthybius'* hands.

OBSERVATIONS

ON THE

TWENTY-THIRD BOOK

This, and the following book, which contain the description of the funeral of *Patroclus*, and other matters relating to *Hector*, are undoubtedly superadded to the grand catastrophe of the poem; for the story is compleatly finish'd with the death of that hero in the 22d Book. Many judicious criticks have been of opinion that *Homer* is blameable for protracting it. *Virgil* closes the whole scene of action with the death of *Turnus*, and leaves the rest to be imagined by the mind of the reader: He does not draw the picture at full length, but delineates it so far, that we cannot fail of imagining the whole draught. There is however one thing to be said in favour of *Homer* which may perhaps justify him in his method, that what he undertook to paint was the *anger* of *Achilles*: And as that anger does not die with *Hector*, but persecutes his very remains, so the poet still keeps up to his Subject; nay it seems to require that he should carry down the relation of that resentment, which is the foundation of his poem, till it is fully satisfy'd: And as this survives *Hector*, and gives the poet an opportunity of still shewing many sad effects of *Achilles*'s anger, the two following books may be thought not to be excrescencies, but essential to the poem.

Virgil had been inexcusable had he trod in *Homer*'s footsteps; for it is evident that the fall of *Turnus*, by giving *Æneas* a full power over *Italy*, answers the whole design and intention of the poem; had he gone farther he had overshot his mark: And tho' *Homer* proceeds after *Hector*'s death, yet the subject is still the anger of *Achilles*.

We are now past the war and violence of the *Ilias*, the scenes of blood are closed during the rest of the poem; we may look back with a pleasing kind of horrour upon the anger of *Achilles*, and see what dire effects it has wrought in the compass of nineteen days: *Troy* and *Greece* are both in mourning for it, heaven and earth, Gods and men, have suffer'd in the conflict. The reader seems landed upon the shore after a violent storm; and has leisure to survey the consequences of the tempest, and the wreck occasion'd by the former commotions, *Troy* weeping for *Hector*, and *Greece* for *Patroclus*. Our passions have been in an agitation since the opening of the poem; wherefore the poet, like some great master in musick, softens his notes, and melts his readers into tenderness and pity.

18.   *Tears bathe their arms, and tears the sands bedew, –*
      – Thetis aids their woe –]

It is not easy to give a reason why *Thetis* should be said to excite the grief of the *Myrmidons*, and of *Achilles*; it had seem'd more natural for the mother to have compos'd the sorrows of the son, and restored his troubled mind to tranquillity.

But such a procedure would have outrag'd the character of *Achilles*, who is all along describ'd to be of such a violence of temper, that he is not easy to be pacify'd at any time, much less upon so great an incident as the death of his friend *Patroclus*. Perhaps the poet made use of this fiction in honour of *Achilles*; he makes every passion of his hero considerable, his sorrow as well as anger is important, and he cannot grieve but a Goddess attends him, and a whole Army weeps.

Some commentators fancy that *Homer* animates the very sands of the seas, and the arms of the *Myrmidons*, and makes them sensible of the loss of *Patroclus*; the preceding words seem to strengthen that opinion, because the poet introduces a Goddess to raise the sorrow of the army. But *Eustathius* seems not to give into this conjecture, and I think very judiciously; for what relation is there between the sands of the shores, and the arms of the *Myrmidons*? It would have been more poetical to have said, the sands and the rocks, than the sands and the arms; but it is very natural to say, that the soldiers wept so bitterly, that their armour and the very sands were wet with their tears. I believe this remark will appear very just by reading the verse, with a comma after τεύχεα, thus,

Δεύοντο ψάμαθοι, δεύοντο δὲ τεύχεα, φωτῶν
Δάκρυσι.

Then the Construction will be natural and easy, period will answer period in the *Greek*, and the sense in *English* will be, the sands were wet, and the arms were wet, with the tears of the mourners.

But however this be, there is a very remarkable beauty in the run of the verse in *Homer*, every word has a melancholy cadence, and the poet has not only made the sands and the arms, but even his very verse, to lament with *Achilles*.

23.   *His slaught'ring hands yet red with blood, he laid*
      On his dead friend's cold breast –]

I could not pass by this passage without observing to my reader the great beauty of this epithet, ἀνδροφόνους. An ordinary poet would have contented himself with saying, he laid his hand upon the breast of *Patroclus*, but *Homer* knows how to raise the most trivial circumstance, and by adding this one word, he laid his *deadly* hands, or his *murderous* hands, he fills our minds with great ideas, and by a single epithet recalls to our thoughts all the noble atchievements of *Achilles* thro' the Iliad.

25. *All hail*, Patroclus, *&c.*] There is in this apostrophe of *Achilles* to the ghost of *Patroclus*, a sort of savageness, and a mixture of softness and atrocity, which are highly conformable to his character.

                                                    Dacier.

51.   *To cleanse his conqu'ring hands –*
      – The chief refus'd –]

This is conformable to the custom of the orientals: *Achilles* will not be induc'd to wash, and afterwards retires to the sea-shore, and sleeps on the ground. It is just thus that *David* mourns in the scriptures; he refuses to wash, or to take any repast, but retires from company, and lies upon the earth.

78. *The Ghost of* Patroclus.] *Homer* has introduc'd into the former parts of the poem the personages of Gods and Goddesses from heav'n, and of Furies from hell: He has embellish'd it with ornaments from earth, sea, and air; and he here opens a new scene, and brings to the view a ghost, the shade of the departed friend; By these methods he diversifies his poem with new and surprizing circumstances, and awakens the attention of the reader; at the same time he very poetically adapts his language to the circumstances of this imaginary *Patroclus*, and teaches us the opinions that prevail'd in his time, concerning the state of separate souls.

92. *Forbid to cross th'irremeable flood.*] It was the common opinion of the ancients, that the souls of the departed were not admitted into the number of the happy till their bodies had receiv'd the funeral rites; they suppos'd those that wanted them wander'd an hundred years before they were wafted over the infernal river: *Virgil* perhaps had this passage of *Homer* in his view in the sixth *Æneis*, at least he coincides with his sentiments concerning the state of the departed souls.

> *Hæc omnis, quam cernis inops inhumataque turba est:*
> *Nec ripas datur horrendas, nec rauca fluenta*
> *Transportare prius, quam sedibus ossa quierunt;*
> *Centum errant annos volitantque hæc littora circum*
> *Tum demum admissi stagna exoptata revisunt.*

> [The ghosts rejected, are th'unhappy crew
> Depriv'd of sepulchers, and fun'ral due;
> Nor dares his transport vessel cross the waves,
> With such whose bones are not compos'd in graves.
> A hundred years they wander on the shore,
> At length, their pennance done, are wafted o're.]

It was during this interval, between death and the rites of funeral, that they supposed the only time allowed for separate spirits to appear to men; therefore *Patroclus* here tells his friend,

> *– To the farther shore*
> *When once we pass, the soul returns no more.*

For the fuller understanding of *Homer*, it is necessary to be acquainted with his notion of the state of the soul after death: He followed the philosophy of the *Ægyptians*, who supposed man to be compounded of three parts, an intelligent mind, a vehicle for that mind, and a body; the mind they call'd φρήν, or ψυχή, the vehicle εἴδωλον, *image* or *soul*, and the gross body σῶμα. The soul, in which the mind was lodg'd, was supposed exactly to resemble the body in shape, magnitude, and features; for this being in the body as the statue in its mold, so soon as it goes forth is properly the image of that body in which it was enclosed: This it was that appeared to *Achilles*, with the full resemblance of his friend *Patroclus.*   *Vid. Dacier*'s life of *Pythagoras*, p. 71.

104. *Ah suffer that my bones may rest with thine!*] There is something very pathetical in this whole speech of *Patroclus*; he begins it with kind reproaches, and blames *Achilles* with a friendly tenderness; he recounts to him the inseparable affection that had been between them in their lives, and makes it his last request, that they may not be parted even in death, but that their bones may rest in the same urn. The speech itself is of a due length; it ought not to be very short, because this apparition is an incident entirely different from any other in the whole poem, and consequently the reader would not have been satisfied with a cursory mention of it; neither ought it to be long, because this would have been contrary to the nature of such apparitions, whose stay upon earth has ever been described as very short, and consequently they cannot be supposed to use many words.

The circumstance of being buried in the same urn, is entirely conformable to the eastern custom: There are innumerable instances in the scriptures of great personages being buried with their fathers: So *Joseph* would not suffer his bones to rest in *Ægypt*, but commands his brethren to carry them into *Canaan* to the burying-place of his father *Jacob*.

124. *The form subsists without the body's aid,*
      Aërial semblance, and an empty shade.]

The words of *Homer* are

Ἀτὰρ φρένες οὐκ ἔνι πάμπαν.

[But there is no understanding in it.]

In which there seems to be a great difficulty; it being not easy to explain how *Achilles* can say that the ghost of his friend had no understanding, when it had but just made such a rational and moving speech: Especially when the poet introduces the apparition with the very shape, air, and voice of *Patroclus*.

But this Passage will be clearly understood, by explaining the notion which the ancients entertained of the souls of the departed, according to the fore-cited triple division of *mind*, *image*, and *body*. They imagined that the soul was not only separated from the body at the hour of death, but that there was a farther separation of the φρήν, or understanding, from its εἴδωλον, or vehicle; so that while the εἴδωλον, or image of the body, was in hell, the φρήν, or understanding, might be in heaven; And that this is a true explication is evident from a passage in the *Odysseis*, book 11. v. 600.

Τὸν δὲ μετ᾽, εἰσενόησα βίην, Ἡρακληείην
Εἴδωλον· αὐτὸς δὲ μετ᾽ ἀθανάτοισι θεοῖσι
Τέρπεται ἐν θαλίῃς, καὶ ἔχει καλλίσφυρον Ἥβην.

Now I the strength of Hercules *behold,*
A tow'ring spectre of gigantick mold;
A shadowy form! for high in heav'ns abodes
Himself resides, a God among the Gods:
There in the bright assemblies of the skies
He Nectar *quaffs, and* Hebe *crowns with joys.*

By this it appears that *Homer* was of opinion that *Hercules* was in heaven, while his εἴδωλον, or image, was in hell: So that when this second separation is made, the image or vehicle becomes a mere thoughtless form.

We have this whole doctrine very distinctly delivered by *Plutarch* in these words. 'Man is a compound subject; but not of two parts, as is commonly believed, because the *understanding* is generally accounted a part of the *soul*; whereas indeed it as far exceeds the soul, as the soul is diviner than the body. Now the soul, when compounded with the understanding, makes reason, and when compounded with the body, passion: Whereof the one is the source or principle of pleasure or pain, the other of vice or virtue. Man therefore properly dies two deaths; the first death makes him two of three, and the second makes him one of two.' Plutarch *of the face in the moon.*

141. *O'er hills, o'er dales, o'er crags, o'er rocks they go –*
      On all sides round the forest hurls her oaks
      Headlong –]

The numbers in the original of this whole passage are admirably adapted to the images the verses convey to us. Every ear must have felt the propriety of sound in this Line,

Πολλὰ δ᾽ ἄναντα, κάταντα, πάραντά τε, δόχμιά τ᾽ ἦλθον.

[They went in all directions: uphill, downhill, sideways, obliquely.]

That other in its kind is no less exact,

Τάμνον ἐπειγόμενοι, ταὶ δὲ μεγάλα κτυπέουσαι
Πῖπτον –

> [Leaning their weight on the trees, they cut them down;
> and thundering loudly, the trees fell.]

Dionysius of *Halicarnassus* has collected many instances of these sorts of beauties in *Homer*. This description of felling the forests, so excellent as it is, is comprehended in a few lines, which has left room for a larger and more particular one in *Statius*, one of the best (I think) in that author.

>   – *Cadit ardua fagus,*
> *Chaoniumque nemus, brumæque illæsa cupressus;*
> *Procumbunt piceæ, flammis alimenta supremis,*
> *Ornique, iliceæque trabes, metuendaque sulco*
> *Taxus, & infandos belli potura cruores*
> *Fraxinus, atque situ non expugnabile robur:*
> *Hinc audax abies, & odoræ vulnere pinus*
> *Scinditur, acclinant intonsa cacumina terræ*
> *Alnus amica fretis, nec inhospita vitibus ulmus,* &c.

[The lofty beech falls, and the Chaonian grove, and the cypress, unharmed by winter; the spruce-firs are laid low, food for high flames, and the ash-tree, the trunks of holm-oak and the yew (that is feared for ploughing); and the mountain-ash that will drink the unspeakable bloodshed of war, and the oak, not to be moved from its place: then the bold fir is split, the pine with its aromatic wound; the alder (friend to the sea) inclines its unshorn tip to the earth, and the non inhospitable elm to the vines.]

I the rather cite this fine passage, because I find it copied by two of the greatest poets of our own nation, *Chaucer* and *Spencer*. The first in the *Assembly of Fowls*, the second in his *Fairy Queen.* lib. 1.

>   *The sailing pine, the cedar proud and tall,*
>   *The vine-prop elm, the poplar never dry,*
>   *The builder oak, sole king of forests all,*
> *The aspin good for staves, the cypress funeral.*
>   *The laurel, meed of mighty conquerors,*
>   *And poets sage: The fir that weepeth still,*
>   *The willow, worn of forlorn paramours,*
>   *The ewe obedient to the bender's will,*
>   *The birch for shafts, the sallow for the mill,*
>   *The myrrh, sweet bleeding in the bitter wound,*

> *The warlike beech, the ash for nothing ill,*
> *The fruitful olive, and the platane round,*
> *The carver holme, the maple seldom inward sound.*

160. *Each in refulgent arms*, &c. –] 'Tis not to be supposed that this was a general custom used at all funerals; but *Patroclus* being a warriour, he is buried like a soldier, with military honours.   *Eustathius.*

166. *O'er all the corse their scattered locks they throw.*] The ceremony of cutting off the hair in honour of the dead was practis'd not only among the *Greeks*, but also among other nations; thus *Statius Thebaid* VI.

> – *Tergoque & pectore fusam*
> Cæsariem *ferro minuit, sectisque jacentis*
> *Obnubit tenuia ora comis.*

[And he cut with his sword the hair that flowed over his back and breast; and he covered, with these locks, the tender face of the person who lay wounded.]

This custom is taken notice of in holy scripture: *Ezekiel* describing a great lamentation, says, *They shall make themselves utterly bald for thee*, ch. 27. v. 31. I believe it was done not only in token of sorrow, but perhaps had a concealed meaning, that as the hair was cut from the head, and was never more to be joined to it, so was the dead for ever cut off from the living, never more to return.

I must observe that this ceremony of cutting off the hair was not always in token of sorrow; *Lycophron* in his *Cassandra*, v. 976. describing a general lamentation, says

> Κρατὸς δ' ἄκουρος νῶτα καλλύνει φόβη.

> *A length of unshorn hair adorn'd their backs.*

And that the ancients sometimes had their hair cut off in token of *joy* is evident from *Juvenal*, *Sat.* 12. v. 82.

> – *Gaudent ibi vertice raso*
> *Garrula securi narrare pericula nautæ.*

[There the carefree sailors, with shaved head, Take joy in recounting their garrulous tales of danger.]

This seeming Contradiction will be solv'd by having respect to the different Practices of different Nations. If it was the general Custom of any Country to wear long Hair, then the cutting it off was a token of Sorrow; but if it was the Custom to wear short Hair, then the letting it grow long and neglecting it, shew'd that such People were Mourners.

168. *Supporting with his hands the hero's head.*] *Achilles* follows the corpse as chief mourner, and sustains the head of his friend: This last circumstance seems to be general; thus *Euripides* in the funeral of *Rhesus*, v. 886.

> Τίς ὑπὲρ κεφαλῆς θεός, ὦ Βασιλεῦ,
> Τὸν νεόδμητον ἐν χειροῖν
> φοράδην πέμπει;

What God, O king, with his hands supports the head of the deceased?

175. *And sacred grew to* Sperchius' *honour'd flood.*] It was the custom of the ancients not only to offer their own hair, but likewise to consecrate that of their children to the river-gods of their country. This is what *Pausanias* shews in his *Attics*: *Before you pass the* Cephisa (says he) *you find the tomb of* Theodorus, *who was the most excellent actor of his time for tragedy; and on the banks you see two statues, one of* Mnesimachus, *and the other of his son, who cut off his hair in honour of the rivers; for that this was in all ages the custom of the* Greeks, *may be inferred from* Homer's *poetry, where* Peleus *promises by a solemn vow to consecrate to the river* Sperchius *the hair of his son, if he returns safe from the* Trojan *war.* This custom was likewise in *Ægypt*, where *Philostratus* tells us, that *Memnon* consecrated his hair to the *Nile.* This practice of *Achilles* was imitated by *Alexander* at the funeral of *Hephæstion.*   *Spondanus.*

228. *Cælestial* Venus, *&c.*] *Homer* has here introduced a series of allegories in the compass of a few lines: The body of *Hector* may be supposed to have continued beautiful even after he was slain; and *Venus* being the president of beauty, the poet by a natural fiction tells us it was preserv'd by that Goddess.

Apollo's covering the body with a cloud is a very natural allegory: For the sun (says *Eustathius*) has a double quality which produces contrary effects; the heat of it causes a dryness, but at the same time it exhales the vapours of the earth, from whence the clouds of heaven are formed. This allegory may be founded upon truth; there might happen to be a cool season while *Hector* lay unburied, and *Apollo*, or the sun, raising clouds which intercept the heat of his beams, by a very easy fiction in poetry may be introduced in person to preserve the body of *Hector*.

263. *The allegory of the winds.*] A poet ought to express nothing vulgarly; and sure no poet ever trespassed less against this rule than *Homer*; the fruitfulness of his invention is continually raising incidents new and surprising. Take this passage out of its poetical dress, and it will be no more than this: A strong gale of wind blew, and so increased the flame that it soon consumed the Pile. But *Homer* introduces the Gods of the winds in person: And *Iris*, or the rainbow, being (as *Eustathius* observes) a sign not only of showers, but of winds, he makes them come at her summons.

Every circumstance is well adapted: As soon as the winds see *Iris*, they rise; that is, when the rainbow appears, the wind rises: She refuses to sit, and immediately returns; that is, the rainbow is never seen long at one time, but soon appears, and soon vanishes: She returns over the ocean; that is, the bow is composed of waters, and it would have been an unnatural fiction to have described her as passing by land.

The winds are all together in the cave of *Zephyrus*, which may imply that they were there as at their general rendezvous; or that the nature of all the winds is the same; or that the western wind is in that country the most constant, and consequently it may be said that at such seasons all the winds are assembled in one corner, or rendezvous with *Zephyrus*.

Iris will not enter the cave: It is the nature of the rainbow to be stretch'd entirely upon the surface, and therefore this fiction is agreeable to reason.

When *Iris* says that the Gods are partaking hecatombs in *Æthiopia*, it is to be remembered that the Gods are represented there in the first book, before the scenes of war were opened, and now they are closed, they return thither. *Eustathius* – Thus *Homer* makes the anger of his hero so important, that it roused heaven to arms, and now when it is almost appeased, *Achilles* as it were gives peace to the Gods.

308. *Hereafter* Greece *a nobler work shall raise.*] We see how *Achilles* consults his own glory; the desire of it prevails over his tenderness for

Patroclus, and he will not permit any man, not even his beloved *Patroclus*, to share an equality of honour with himself, even in the grave. *Eustathius.*

321. *The Games for* Patroclus.] The conduct of *Homer* in enlarging upon the games at the funeral of *Patroclus* is very judicious: There had undoubtedly been such honours paid to several heroes during this war, as appears from a passage in the ninth book, where *Agamemnon* to enhance the value of the horses which he offers *Achilles*, says, that any person would be rich that had treasures equal to the value of the prizes they had won; which races must have been run during the siege: for had they been before it, the horses would now have been too old to be of any value, this being the tenth year of the war. But the poet passes all those games over in silence, and reserves them for this season; not only in honour of *Patroclus*, but also of his hero *Achilles*; who exhibits games to a whole army; great generals are candidates for the prizes, and he himself sits the judge and arbitrator: Thus in peace as well as war the poet maintains the superiority of the character of *Achilles.*

But there is another reason why the poet deferr'd to relate any games that were exhibited at any preceding funerals: The death of *Patroclus* was the most eminent period; and consequently the most proper time for such games.

'Tis farther observable, that he chuses this peculiar time with great judgment. When the fury of the war rag'd, the army could not well have found leisure for the games, and they might have met with interruption from the enemy: But *Hector* being dead, all *Troy* is in confusion: They are in too great a consternation to make any attempts, and therefore the poet could not possibly have chosen a more happy opportunity. *Eustathius.*

349. *Lost is* Patroclus *now*, &c.] I am not ignorant that *Homer* has frequently been blamed for such little digressions as these; in this passage he gives us the genealogy of his horses, which he has frequently told us in the preceding part of the poem. But *Eustathius* justifies his conduct, and says that it was very proper to commend the virtue of these horses upon this occasion, when horses were to contend for victory: At the same time he takes an opportunity to make an honourable mention of his friend *Patroclus*, in whose honour these games were exhibited.

It may be added as a farther justification of *Homer*, that this last circumstance is very natural: *Achilles* while he commends his horses remembers how careful *Patroclus* had been of them; His love for his friend is so great, that the minutest circumstance recalls him to his mind; and such little digressions, such avocations of thought as these, very naturally proceed from the overflows of love and sorrow.

365. *Whom rich* Echepolus, &c.] One wou'd think that *Agamemnon* might be accus'd of avarice, in dispensing a man from going to the war for the sake of a horse; but *Aristotle* very well observes, that this prince is praiseworthy for having preferr'd a horse to a person so cowardly, and so uncapable of service. It may also be conjectur'd from this passage, that even in those elder times it was the custom, that those who were willing to be excus'd from the war, should give either a horse or a man and often both. Thus *Scipio* going to *Africa* order'd the *Sicilians* either to attend him, or to give him horses or men: And *Agesilaus* being at *Ephesus* and wanting cavalry, made a proclamation, that the rich men who would not serve in the war should be dispens'd with, provided they furnish'd a man and a horse in their stead: In which, says *Plutarch*, he wisely follow'd the example of King *Agamemnon*, who excus'd a very rich coward from serving in person, for a present of a good mare.   *Eustathius. Dacier.*

371. *Experienc'd* Nestor, &c.] The poet omits no opportunity of paying honour to his old favourite *Nestor*, and I think he is no where more particularly complemented than in this book. His age had disabled him from bearing any share in the games; and yet he artfully introduces him not as a mere spectator, but as an actor in the sports. Thus he as it were wins the prize for *Antilochus*, *Antilochus* wins not by the swiftness of his horses, but by the wisdom of *Nestor*.

This fatherly tenderness is wonderfully natural: We see him in all imaginable inquietude and concern for his son; He comes to the barrier, stands beside the chariot, animates his son by his praises, and directs him by his lessons: You think the old man's soul mounts on the chariot with his *Antilochus*, to partake the same dangers, and run the same career.

Nothing can be better adapted to the character than this speech; he expatiates upon the advantages of wisdom over strength, which is a tacit complement to himself: And had there been a prize for wisdom, undoubtedly the old man would have claim'd it as his right.

                                        Eustathius.

427. *The lots their place dispose.*] According to these lots the charioteers took their places; but to know whether they stood all in an equal Front, or one behind the other, is a difficulty: *Eustathius* says the ancients were of opinion that they did not stand in one front; because it is evident that he who had the first lot had a great advantage of the other charioteers: If he had not, why should *Achilles* cast lots? Madam *Dacier* is of opinion that they all stood a breast at the barrier, and that the first would still have a sufficient advantage, as he was nearer the bound, and stood within the rest, whereas the others must take a larger circle, and consequently were forc'd to run a greater compass of ground. *Phœnix* was plac'd as an inspector of the race, that is, says *Eustathius*, he was to make report whether they had observ'd the laws of the race in their several turnings.

Sophocles observes the same method with *Homer* in relation to the lots and inspectors, in his *Electra*.

> — Οἱ τεταγμένοι βραβεῖς
> Κλήροις ἔπηλαν καὶ κατέστησαν δίφρον.

The constituted judges assign'd the places according to the lots.

The ancients say that the charioteers started at the *Sigæum*, where the ships of *Achilles* lay, and ran towards the *Rhæteum*, from the ships towards the shores. But *Aristarchus* affirm'd that they run in the compass of ground of five *stadia*, which lay between the wall and the tents toward the shore. *Eustathius.*

458. *And seem just mounting on his car behind.*] A more natural image than this could not be thought of. The poet makes us spectators of the race, we see *Diomed* pressing upon *Eumelus* so closely, that his chariot seems to climb the chariot of *Eumelus.*

465. *Rage fills his eye with anguish, to survey,* &c.] We have seen *Diomed* surrounded with innumerable dangers, acting in the most perilous scenes of blood and death, yet never shed one tear: And now he weeps on a small occasion, for a mere trifle: This must be ascrib'd to the nature of mankind, who are often transported with trifles; and there are certain unguarded moments in every man's life; so that he who could meet the greatest dangers with intrepidity, may thro' Anger be betray'd into an indecency. *Eustathius.*

The reason why *Apollo* is angry at *Diomed*, according to *Eustathius*, is because he was interested for *Eumelus*, whose mares he had fed, when he serv'd *Admetus*; but I fancy he is under a mistake: This indeed is a reason why he should favour *Eumelus*, but not why he should be angry at *Diomed*. I rather think that the quarrel of *Apollo* with *Diomed* was personal; because he offer'd him a violence in the first book, and *Apollo* still resents it.

The fiction of *Minerva*'s assisting *Diomed* is grounded upon his being so wise as to take a couple of whips to prevent any mischance: So that *Wisdom*, or *Pallas*, may be said to lend him one.

Eustathius.

483. *The speech of* Antilochus *to his horses.*] I fear *Antilochus* his speech to his horses is blameable; *Eustathius* himself seems to think it a fault that he should speak so much in the very heat of the race. He commands and sooths, counsels and threatens his horses, as if they were reasonable creatures. The subsequent speech of *Menelaus* is more excusable as it is more short, but both of them are spoken in a passion, and anger we know makes us speak to every thing, and we discharge it upon the most senseless objects.

565. *The Dispute between* Idomeneus *and* Ajax.] Nothing could be more naturally imagined than this contention at a horse-race: The leaders were divided into parties, and each was interested for his friend: The poet had a two-fold design, not only to embellish and diversify his poem by such natural circumstances, but also to shew us, as *Eustathius* observes, from the conduct of *Ajax*, that passionate men betray themselves into follies, and are themselves guilty of the faults of which they accuse others.

It is with a particular decency that *Homer* makes *Achilles* the arbitrator between *Idomeneus* and *Ajax*: *Agamemnon* was his superiour in the army, but as *Achilles* exhibited the shows, he was the proper judge of any difference that should arise about them; had the contest been between *Ajax* and *Idomeneus*, considered as soldiers, the cause must have been brought before *Agamemnon*; but as they are to be considered as spectators of the games, they ought to be determined by *Achilles*.

It may not be unnecessary just to observe to the reader the judicious-ness of *Homer*'s conduct in making *Achilles* exhibit the games, and not *Agamemnon*: *Achilles* is the hero of the poem, and consequently must be the chief actor in all the great scenes of it: He had remained inactive during a great part of the poem, yet the poet makes his very inactivity contribute to the carrying on the design of his *Ilias*: And to supply his absence from many of the busy scenes of the preceding parts of it, he now in the conclusion makes him almost the sole agent: By these means he leaves a noble idea of his hero upon the mind of his Reader; as he raised our expectations when he brought him upon the stage of action, so he makes him go off with the utmost pomp and applause.

581. *High o'er his head the circling lash he wields.*] I am persuaded that the common translation of the word Κατωμαδόν, in the original of this verse, is faulty: It is rendered, *he lash'd the horses continually over the shoulders*; whereas I fancy it should be translated thus, *assidue* (equos) *agitabat scutica ab humero ducta* [He continually drove the horses with a lash whipped by his shoulder]. This naturally expresses the very action, and whirl of the whip over the driver's shoulder, in the act of lashing the horses, and agrees with the use of the same word in the 431st line of this book, where δίσκου ούρα κατωμαδίοιο must be translated *jactus disci ab humero vibrati* [a throw of a disk hurled by his shoulder].

614. *Fortune denies, but Justice,* &c.] *Achilles* here intends to shew, that it is not just fortune should rule over virtue, but that a brave man who had performed his duty, and who did not bring upon himself his misfortune, ought to have the recompence he has deserved: And this principle is just, provided we do not reward him at the expence of another's right: *Eumelus* is a *Thessalian*, and it is probable *Achilles* has a partiality to his countryman.   *Dacier.*

633. *But this, my prize, I never shall forego –*] There is an air of bravery in this discourse of *Antilochus*: He speaks with the generosity of a gallant soldier, and prefers his honour to his interest; he tells *Achilles* if he pleases he may make *Eumelus* a richer present than his prize; he is not concern'd for the value of it, but as it was the reward of victory, he would not resign it, because that would be an acknowledgment that *Eumelus* deserved it.

The character of *Antilochus* is admirably sustained thro' this whole episode; he is a very sensible man, but transported with youthful heat, and ambitious of glory: His rashness in driving so furiously against *Menelaus* must be imputed to this; but his passions being gratify'd by the conquest in the race, his reason again returns, he owns his error, and is full of resignation to *Menelaus*.

663. *And touch thy steeds, and swear –*] 'Tis evident, says *Eustathius*, from hence, that all fraud was forbid in the chariot race; but it is not very plain what unlawful deceit *Antilochus* used against *Menelaus*: Perhaps *Antilochus* in his haste had declin'd from the race-ground, and avoided some of the uneven places of it, and consequently took an unfair advantage of his adversary; or perhaps his driving so furiously against *Menelaus* as to endanger both their chariots and their lives, might be reckon'd foul play; and therefore *Antilochus* refuses to take the oath.

679. *Joy swells his soul, as when the vernal grain,* &c.] *Eustathius* is very large in the explication of this similitude, which at the first view seems obscure: His words are these,

As the dew raises the blades of corn, that are for want of it weak and depressed, and by pervading the pores of the corn animates and makes it flourish, so did the behaviour of *Antilochus* raise the dejected mind of *Menelaus*, exalt his spirits, and restore him to a full satisfaction.

I have given the reader his interpretation, and translated it with the liberty of poetry: It is very much in the language of Scripture, and in the spirit of the Orientals.

707. *Accept thou this, O sacred sire!*] The poet in my opinion preserves a great deal of decency towards this old hero, and venerable counsellour: He gives him an honorary reward for his superior wisdom, and therefore *Achilles* calls it ἄεθλον, and not δῶρον, a prize, and not a present. The moral of *Homer* is, that princes ought no less to honour and recompense those who excel in wisdom and counsel, than those who are capable of actual service.

Achilles, perhaps, had a double view in paying him this respect, not only out of deference to his age, and wisdom, but also because he had, in a manner, won the prize by the advice he gave his son: So that *Nestor* may be said to have conquer'd in the person of *Antilochus.* *Eustathius.*

719. Nestor's *Speech to* Achilles.] This speech is admirably well adapted to the character of *Nestor*: He aggrandizes, with an infirmity peculiar to age, his own exploits; and one would think *Horace* had him in his eye,

– *Laudator temporis acti*
Se puero –

[A praiser of the days when he was a boy.]

Neither is it any blemish to the Character of *Nestor* thus to be a little talkative about his own atchievements: To have described him otherwise would have been an outrage to human nature, in as much as the wisest man living is not free from the infirmities of man: and as every stage of life has some imperfection peculiar to it self.

–Ὁ μὲν ἔμπεδον ἡνιόχευεν,
– Ἔμπεδον ἡνιόχευ᾽.

[One firmly held the reins, held the reins firmly.]

The reader may observe that the old man takes abundance of pains to give reasons how his rivals came to be victors in the chariot-race: He is very solicitous to make it appear that it was not thro᾽ any want of skill or power in himself: And in my opinion *Nestor* is never more vainglorious than in this recital of his own disappointment.

It is for the same reason he repeats the words I have cited above: He obtrudes (by that repetition) the disadvantages under which he labour'd, upon the observation of the reader, for fear he should impute the loss of the victory to his want of skill.

Nestor says that these *Moliones* overpower'd him by their *number*. The criticks, as *Eustathius* remarks, have labour'd hard to explain this difficulty; they tell us a formal story, that when *Nestor* was ready to enter the lists against these brothers, he objected against them as unfair adversaries, (for it must be remembered that they were monsters that grew together, and consequently had four hands to *Nestor*'s two) but the judges would not allow his plea, but determined, that as they grew together so they ought to be considered as one man.

Others tell us that they brought several chariots into the lists, whose charioteers combined together in favour of *Eurytus* and *Cteatus*, these brother-monsters.

Others say, that the multitude of the spectators conspir'd to disappoint *Nestor*.

I thought it necessary to give my reader these several conjectures; that he might understand why *Nestor* says he was overpower'd by Πλήθει, or *numbers*; and also, because it confirms my former observation, that *Nestor* is very careful to draw his own picture in the strongest colours, and to shew it in the fairest light.

819. *A female captive valu'd but at four.*] I cannot in civility neglect a remark made upon this passage by Madam *Dacier*, who highly resents the affront put upon her sex by the ancients, who set (it seems) thrice the value upon a *tripod* as upon a beautiful female slave: Nay, she is afraid the value of women is not raised even in our days; for she says there are curious persons now living who had rather have a true antique kettle, than the finest woman alive: I confess I entirely agree with the lady, and must impute such opinions of the fair sex to want of taste in both ancients and moderns: The reader may remember that these tripods were of no use, but made entirely for show, and consequently the most satyrical critick could only say, the woman and tripod ought to have born an equal value.

826. *Like two strong rafters,* &c.] I will give the reader the words of *Eustathius* upon this similitude, which very happily represents the wrestlers in the posture of wrestling. Their heads lean'd one against the other, like the rafters that support the roof of a house; at the foot they are disjoined, and stand at a greater distance, which naturally paints the attitude of body in these two wrestlers, while they contend for victory.

849. *He barely stirr'd him, but he could not raise.*] The poet by this circumstance excellently maintains the character of *Ajax*, who has all along been described as a strong, unwieldy warriour: He is so heavy that *Ulysses* can scarce lift him. The Words that follow will bear a different meaning, either that *Ajax* lock'd his leg within that of *Ulysses*, or that *Ulysses* did it. *Eustathius* observes, that if *Ajax* gave *Ulysses* this shock, then he may be allowed to have some appearance of an equality in the contest, but if *Ulysses* gave it, then *Ajax* must be acknowledged to have been foil'd: But (continues he) it appeared to be otherwise to *Achilles*, who was the judge of the field, and therefore he gives them an equal prize, because they were equal in the contest.

Madam *Dacier* misrepresents *Eustathius* on this place, in saying he thinks it was *Ulysses* who gave the second stroke to *Ajax*, whereas it appears by the foregoing note that he rather determines otherwise in consent with the judgment given by *Achilles.*

901. *Assist, O Goddess! (thus in thought he pray'd)*] Nothing could be better adapted to the present circumstance of *Ulysses* than this prayer: It is short, and ought to be so, because the time would not allow him to make a longer; nay he prefers this petition mentally, ὃν κατὰ θυμόν [in his own heart]; all his faculties are so bent upon the race, that he does not call off his attention from it, even to speak so short a petition as seven words, which comprehend the whole of it: Such Passages as these are instances of great judgment in the poet.

924. *And takes it with a jest.*] *Antilochus* comes off very well, and wittily prevents raillery; by attributing the victory of his rivals to the protection which the Gods gave to age. By this he insinuates, that he has something to comfort himself with; (for youth is better than the prize) and that he may pretend hereafter to the same protection, since 'tis a privilege of seniority.   *Dacier.*

933. *For who can match Achilles?*] There is great art in these transient complements to *Achilles*: That hero could not possibly shew his own superiority in these games by contending for any of the prizes, because he was the exhibiter of the sports: But *Homer* has found out a way to give him the victory in two of them. In the chariot-race *Achilles* is represented as being able to conquer every opponent, and tho' he speaks it himself, the poet brings it in so happily, that he speaks it without any indecency: And in this place *Antilochus* with a very good grace tells *Achilles*, that in the foot-race no one can dispute the prize with him. Thus tho' *Diomed* and *Ulysses* conquer in the chariot and foot-race, it is only because *Achilles* is not their antagonist.

949. *Who first the jointed armour shall explore.*] Some of the ancients have been shock'd at this combat, thinking it a barbarity that men in sport should thus contend for their lives; and therefore *Aristophanes* the *Grammarian* made this alteration in the verses.

> Ὁππότερός κεν πρῶτος ἐπιγράψας χρόα καλὸν
> Φθήῃ ἐπευξάμενος διὰ τ' ἔντεα, &c.

[Whichever of the two might be the first to graze his fair skin
And boast that he had stripped him of his armor.]

But it is evident that they entirely mistook the meaning and intention of *Achilles*; for he that gave the first wound was to be accounted the victor. How could *Achilles* promise to entertain them both in his tent after the combat, if he intended that one of them should fall in it? This duel therefore was only a trial of skill, and as such single combats were frequent in the wars of those ages against adversaries, so this was proposed only to shew the dexterity of the combatants in that exercise. *Eustathius.*

971. *Yet still the victor's due Tydides gains.*] *Achilles* in this place acts the part of a very just arbitrator: Tho' the combat did not proceed to a full issue, yet *Diomed* had evidently the advantage, and consequently ought to be rewarded as victor, because he would have been victorious, had not the *Greeks* interpos'd.

I could have wish'd that the poet had given *Ajax* the prize in some of these contests. He undoubtedly was a very gallant soldier, and has been describ'd as repulsing a whole army; yet in all these sports he is foil'd. But perhaps the poet had a double view in this representation, not only to shew, that Strength without conduct is usually unsuccessful, but also his design might be to complement the *Greeks* his countrymen; by shewing that this *Ajax*, who had repell'd a whole army of *Trojans*, was not able to conquer any one of the *Grecian* worthies: For we find him overpower'd in three of these exercises.

985. *If he be one, enrich'd,* &c.] The poet in this place speaks in the simplicity of ancient times: The prodigious weight and size of the quoit is describ'd with a noble plainness, peculiar to the Oriental way, and agreeable to the manners of those heroick ages. He does not set down the quantity of this enormous piece of iron, neither as to its bigness nor weight, but as to the use it will be of to him who shall gain it. We see from hence, that the ancients in the prizes they propos'd, had in view not only the honourable, but the useful; a captive for work, a bull for tillage, a quoit for the provision of iron. Besides it must be remember'd, that in those times iron was very scarce; and a sure sign of this scarcity, is, that their arms were brass.

Eustath. Dacier.

1030. *He takes the bow.*] There having been many editions of *Homer*, that of *Marseilles* represents these two rivals in archery as using two bows in the contest; and reads the verses thus,

> Σπερχόμενος δ' ἄρα Μηριόνης ἐπέθη κατ' ὀϊστὸν
> Τόξῳ, ἐν γὰρ χερσὶν ἔχε πάλαι, ὡς ἴθυνεν.

[In eager haste, Meriones placed an arrow in his bow and held it just now in his hands, as he aimed it.]

Our common editions follow the better alteration of *Antimachus*, with this only difference, that he reads it

Ἐξείρυσε Τεύκρου τόξον.

[He drew Teucer's bow.]

And they,

Ἐξείρυσε χειρὸς τόξον.

[He drew the bow with his hand.]

It is evident that these archers had but one bow, as they that threw the quoit had but one quoit; by these means the one had no advantage over the other, because both of them shot with the same bow. So that the common reading is undoubtedly the best, where the lines stand thus,

Σπερχόμενος δ' ἄρα Μηριόνης ἐξείρυσε χειρὸς or Τεύκρου
Τόξον, ἀτὰρ δὴ ὀϊστὸν ἔχε πάλαι ὡς ἴθυνεν. *Eustath.*

[In eager haste, Meriones drew the bow with his hand (or Teucer's bow), but he had an arrow already prepared, as Teucer was taking aim.]

This *Teucer* is the most eminent man for archery of any thro' the whole Iliad, yet he is here excell'd by *Meriones*: And the poet ascribes his miscarriage to the neglect of invoking *Apollo*, the God of archery; whereas *Meriones*, who invokes him, is crown'd with success. There is an excellent moral in this passage, and the poet would teach us, that without addressing to heaven we cannot succeed: *Meriones* does not conquer because he is the better archer, but because he is the better man.

1051. *Nor here disdain'd the King of men to rise.*] There is an admirable conduct in this passage; *Agamemnon* never contended for any of the former prizes, tho' of much greater value; so that he is a candidate for this, only to honour *Patroclus* and *Achilles.* The decency which the poet uses both in the choice of the game, in which *Agamemnon* is about to contend, and the giving him the prize without a contest, is very remarkable: The game was a warlike exercise, fit for the general of an army; the giving him the prize without a contest is a decency judiciously observed, because no one ought to be suppos'd to excel the general in any military art: *Agamemnon* does justice to his own character, for whereas he had been represented by *Achilles* in the opening of the poem as a covetous person, he now puts in for the prize that is of the least value, and generously gives even that to *Talthybius.*   *Eustathius.*

As to this last particular, of *Agamemnon*'s presenting the charger to *Talthybius,* I can't but be of a different opinion. It had been an affront to *Achilles* not to have accepted of his present on this occasion, and I believe the words of *Homer,*

Ταλθυβίῳ κήρυκι δίδου περικαλλὲς ἄεθλον,

[He gave the beautiful prize to Talthybius the herald;]

mean no more, than that he put it into the hands of this herald to carry it to his ships; *Talthybius* being by his office an attendant upon *Agamemnon.*

It will be expected I should here say something tending to a comparison between the games of *Homer* and those of *Virgil.* If I may own my private opinion, there is in general more variety of natural Incidents, and a more lively picture of natural passions, in the games and persons of *Homer.* On the other hand, there seems to me more art, contrivance, gradation, and a greater pomp of verse in those of *Virgil.* The *chariot-race* is that which *Homer* has most labour'd, of which *Virgil* being sensible, he judiciously avoided the imitation of what he could not improve, and substituted in its place the *naval-course,* or *ship-race.* It is in this the *Roman* poet has employ'd all his force, as if on set purpose to rival his great master; but it is extremely observable how constantly he keeps *Homer* in his eye, and is afraid to depart from his very track, even when he had vary'd the subject itself. Accordingly the accidents of the naval course have a strange resemblance with those of *Homer*'s chariot-race. He could not forbear at the very beginning to draw a part of that Description into a simile. Do not we see he has *Homer*'s chariots in his head, by these lines;

> *Non tam præcipites bijugo certamine campum*
> *Corripuere, ruuntque effusi carcere currus.*
> *Nec sic immissis aurigæ undantia lora*
> *Concussere jugis, pronique in verbera pendent.*
>
> Æn. v. v.144.

[Not fiery coursers, in a chariot race,
Invade the field with half so swift a pace.

Not the fierce driver with more fury lends
The sounding lash; and, e're the stroke descends,
Low to the wheels his pliant body bends.]

What is the encounter of *Cloanthus* and *Gyas* in the strait between the rocks, but the same with that of *Menelaus* and *Antilochus* in the hollow way? Had the galley of *Sergestus* been broken, if the chariot of *Eumelus* had not been demolish'd? Or *Mnestheus* been cast from the helm, had not the other been thrown from his seat? Does not *Mnestheus* exhort his rowers in the very Words *Antilochus* had us'd to his horses?

> *Non jam prima peto* Mnestheus, *neque vincere certo*
> *Quamquam O! sed superent quibus hoc* Neptune *dedisti;*
> *Extremos pudeat rediisse! hoc vincite, cives,*
> *Et prohibete nefas –*

[I seek not now the foremost palm to gain;
Tho yet – But ah, that haughty wish is vain!
Let those enjoy it whom the Gods ordain.
But to be last, the lags of all the race,
Redeem your selves and me from that disgrace.]

> Ἔμβητον καὶ σφῶϊ, τιταίνετον ὅττι τάχιστα.
> Ἤ τοι μὲν κείνοισιν ἐριζέμεν οὔ τι κελεύω
> Τυδεΐδεω ἵπποισι δαΐφρονος, οἷσιν Ἀθήνη
> Νῦν ὤρεξε τάχος –
> Ἵππους δ' Ἀτρείδαο κιχάνετε, μηδὲ λίπησθον,
> Καρπαλίμως, μὴ σφῶϊν ἐλεγχείην καταχεύῃ
> Αἴθη θῆλυς ἐοῦσα –

[cf. Pope's translation, XXIII, 483–8]

Upon the whole, the description of the Sea-Race I think has the more poetry and majesty, that of the chariots more nature, and lively incidents. There is nothing in *Virgil* so picturesque, so animated, or which so much marks the characters, as the episodes of *Antilochus* and *Menelaus, Ajax* and *Idomeneus,* with that beautiful interposition of old *Nestor,* (so naturally introduc'd into an affair where one so little expects him.) On the other side, in *Virgil* the description itself is nobler; it has something more ostentatiously grand, and seems a spectacle more worthy the presence of Princes and great persons.

In three other games we find the *Roman* poet contending openly with the *Grecian.* That of the *Cæstus* is in great part a verbal translation:

But it must be own'd in favour of *Virgil*, that he has vary'd from *Homer* in the event of the combate with admirable judgment and with an improvement of the moral. *Epëus* and *Dares* are described by both poets as vain boasters; but *Virgil* with more poetical justice punishes *Dares* for his arrogance, whereas the presumption and pride of *Epëus* is rewarded by *Homer*.

On the contrary, in the *foot-race*, I am of opinion that *Homer* has shewn more judgment and morality than *Virgil*. *Nisus* in the latter is unjust to his adversary in favour of his friend *Euryalus*; so that *Euryalus* wins the race by palpable fraud, and yet the poet gives him the first prize; whereas *Homer* makes *Ulysses* victorious, purely thro' the mischance of *Ajax*, and his own piety in invoking *Minerva*.

The *shooting* is also a direct copy, but with the addition of two circumstances which make a beautiful gradation. In *Homer* the first archer cuts the string that held the bird, and the other shoots him as he is mounting. In *Virgil* the first only hits the mast which the bird was fix'd upon, the second cuts the string, the third shoots him, and the fourth to vaunt the strength of his arm directs his arrow up to heaven, where it kindles into a flame, and makes a prodigy. This last is certainly superior to *Homer* in what they call the *wonderful*: but what is the intent or effect of this prodigy, or whether a reader is not at least as much surprized at it, as at the most unreasonable parts in *Homer*, I leave to those criticks who are more inclin'd to find faults than I am: Nor shall I observe upon the many literal imitations in the *Roman* poet, to object against which were to derogate from the merit of those fine passages, which *Virgil* was so very sensible of, that he was resolv'd to take them, at any rate, to himself.

There remain in *Homer* three games untouch'd by *Virgil*; the *wrestling*, the *single combate*, and the *Discus*. In *Virgil* there is only the *Lusus Trojæ* added, which is purely his own, and must be confest to be inimitable: I don't know whether I may be allow'd to say, it is worth all those three of *Homer*?

I could not forgive my self if I omitted to mention in this place the funeral games in the sixth *Thebaïd* of *Statius*; it is by much the most beautiful book of that poem. It's very remarkable, that he has follow'd *Homer* thro' the whole course of his games: There is the *chariot-race*, the *foot-race*, the *Discus*, the *Cæstus*, the *wrestling*, the *single combate* (which is put off in the same manner as in *Homer*) and the *shooting*; which last ends (as in *Virgil*) with a prodigy: Yet in the particular descriptions of each of these games this poet has not borrow'd from either of his predecessors, and his poem is so much the worse for it.

THE
TWENTY-FOURTH BOOK
OF THE
ILIAD

The ARGUMENT

The redemption of the body of *Hector*

The Gods deliberate about the redemption of Hector. Jupiter *sends* Thetis *to* Achilles *to dispose him for the restoring it, and* Iris *to* Priam, *to encourage him to go in person, and treat for it. The old King, notwithstanding the remonstrances of his Queen, makes ready for the journey, to which he is encourag'd by an omen from* Jupiter. *He sets forth in his chariot, with a waggon loaded with presents under the charge of* Idæus *the herald.* Mercury *descends in the shape of a young man, and conducts him to the pavilion of* Achilles. *Their conversation on the way.* Priam *finds* Achilles *at his table, casts himself at his feet, and begs for the body of his son;* Achilles, *mov'd with compassion, grants his request, detains him one night in his tent, and the next morning sends him home with the body: The* Trojans *run out to meet him. The lamentations of* Andromache, Hecuba, *and* Helen, *with the solemnities of the funeral.*

The time of twelve days is employ'd in this book, while the body of Hector *lies in the tent of* Achilles. *And as many more are spent in the truce allow'd for his interment. The scene is partly in* Achilles's *camp, and partly in* Troy.

Now from the finish'd games the *Grecian* band
Seek their black ships, and clear the crowded strand:
All stretch'd at ease the genial banquet share,
And pleasing slumbers quiet all their care.
5   Not so *Achilles*: He, to grief resign'd,
His friend's dear image present to his mind,
Takes his sad couch, more unobserv'd to weep,
Nor tastes the gifts of all-composing sleep.
Restless he roll'd around his weary bed,
10   And all his soul on his *Patroclus* fed:
The form so pleasing, and the heart so kind,
That youthful vigour, and that manly mind,
What toils they shar'd, what martial works they wrought,
What seas they measur'd, and what fields they fought;
15   All past before him in remembrance dear,
Thought follows thought, and tear succeeds to tear.
And now supine, now prone, the hero lay,
Now shifts his side, impatient for the day:
Then starting up, disconsolate he goes
20   Wide on the lonely beach to vent his woes.
There as the solitary mourner raves,
The ruddy morning rises o'er the waves:
Soon as it rose, his furious steeds he join'd;
The chariot flies, and *Hector* trails behind.
25   And thrice *Patroclus!* round thy monument
Was *Hector* dragg'd, then hurry'd to the tent.
There sleep at last o'ercomes the hero's eyes;
While foul in dust th'unhonour'd carcase lies,
But not deserted by the pitying skies.

For *Phœbus* watch'd it with superior care, 30
Preserv'd from gaping wounds, and tainting air;
And ignominious as it swept the field,
Spread o'er the sacred corse his golden shield.
All heav'n was mov'd, and *Hermes* will'd to go
By stealth to snatch him from th'insulting foe: 35
But *Neptune* this, and *Pallas* this denies,
And th'unrelenting Empress of the skies:
E'er since that day implacable to *Troy*,
What time young *Paris*, simple shepherd boy,
Won by destructive lust (reward obscene) 40
Their charms rejected for the *Cyprian* Queen.
But when the tenth celestial morning broke,
To heav'n assembled, thus *Apollo* spoke.

   Unpitying pow'rs! how oft each holy fane
Has *Hector* ting'd with blood of victims slain? 45
And can ye still his cold remains pursue?
Still grudge his body to the *Trojans* view?
Deny to consort, mother, son, and sire,
The last sad honours of a fun'ral fire?
Is then the dire *Achilles* all your care? 50
That iron heart, inflexibly severe;
A lion, not a man, who slaughters wide
In strength of rage and impotence of pride,
Who hastes to murder with a savage joy,
Invades around, and breathes but to destroy. 55
Shame is not of his soul; nor understood,
The greatest evil and the greatest good.
Still for one loss he rages unresign'd,
Repugnant to the lot of all mankind;
To lose a friend, a brother, or a son, 60
Heav'n dooms each mortal, and its will is done:
A while they sorrow, then dismiss their care;
Fate gives the wound, and man is born to bear.
But this insatiate the commission giv'n
By fate, exceeds; and tempts the wrath of heav'n: 65
Lo how his rage dishonest drags along
Hector's dead earth insensible of wrong!
Brave tho' he be, yet by no reason aw'd,
He violates the laws of man and God.

70   If equal honours by the partial skies
         Are doom'd both heroes, (*Juno* thus replies)
         If *Thetis'* son must no distinction know,
         Then hear, ye Gods! the Patron of the Bow.
         But *Hector* only boasts a mortal claim,
75   His birth deriving from a mortal dame:
         Achilles of your own ætherial race
         Springs from a Goddess by a man's embrace;
         (A Goddess by our self to *Peleus* giv'n,
         A man divine, and chosen friend of heav'n.)
80   To grace those nuptials, from the bright abode
         Your selves were present; where this Minstrel-God
         (Well-pleas'd to share the feast,) amid the quire
         Stood proud to hymn, and tune his youthful lyre.
             Then thus the Thund'rer checks th' imperial
                 dame:
85   Let not thy wrath the court of heav'n inflame;
         Their merits, nor their honours, are the same.
         But mine, and ev'ry God's peculiar grace
         Hector deserves, of all the *Trojan* race:
         Still on our shrines his grateful off'rings lay,
90   (The only honours men to Gods can pay)
         Nor ever from our smoking altar ceast
         The pure libation, and the holy feast.
         Howe'er by stealth to snatch the corse away,
         We will not: *Thetis* guards it night and day.
95   But haste, and summon to our courts above
         The azure Queen; let her persuasion move
         Her furious son from *Priam* to receive
         The proffer'd ransom, and the corps to leave.
             He added not: And *Iris* from the skies,
100   Swift as a whirlwind, on the message flies,
         Meteorous the face of Ocean sweeps,
         Refulgent gliding o'er the sable deeps.
         Between where *Samos* wide his forests spreads,
         And rocky *Imbrus* lifts its pointed heads,
105   Down plung'd the maid; (the parted waves resound)
         She plung'd, and instant shot the dark profound.
         As bearing death in the fallacious bait
         From the bent angle sinks the loaden weight;

So past the Goddess thro' the closing wave,
Where *Thetis* sorrow'd in her secret cave: 110
There plac'd amidst her melancholy train
(The blue-hair'd sisters of the sacred main)
Pensive she sate, revolving fates to come,
And wept her god-like son's approaching doom.

    Then thus the Goddess of the painted bow. 115
Arise! O *Thetis*, from thy seats below.
'Tis *Jove* that calls. And why (the Dame replies)
Calls *Jove* his *Thetis* to the hated skies?
Sad object as I am for heav'nly sight!
Ah! may my sorrows ever shun the light! 120
Howe'er be heav'ns almighty Sire obey'd –
She spake, and veil'd her head in sable shade,
Which, flowing long, her graceful person clad;
And forth she pac'd, majestically sad.

    Then thro' the world of waters, they repair 125
(The way fair *Iris* led) to upper air.
The deeps dividing, o'er the coast they rise,
And touch with momentary flight the skies.
There in the light'ning's blaze the Sire they found,
And all the Gods in shining synod round. 130
Thetis approach'd with anguish in her face,
(*Minerva* rising, gave the mourner place)
Ev'n *Juno* sought her sorrows to console,
And offer'd from her hand the nectar bowl:
She tasted, and resign'd it: Then began 135
The sacred sire of Gods and mortal man:

    Thou com'st fair *Thetis*, but with grief o'ercast,
Maternal sorrows, long, ah long to last!
Suffice, we know and we partake thy cares:
But yield to Fate, and hear what *Jove* declares. 140
Nine days are past, since all the court above
In *Hector*'s cause have mov'd the ear of *Jove*;
'Twas voted, *Hermes* from his god-like foe
By stealth should bear him, but we will'd not so:
We will, thy son himself the corse restore, 145
And to his conquest add this glory more.
Then hye thee to him, and our mandate bear;
Tell him he tempts the wrath of heav'n too far:

Nor let him more (our anger if he dread)
150 Vent his mad vengeance on the sacred dead:
But yield to ransom and the father's pray'r.
The mournful father *Iris* shall prepare,
With gifts to sue; and offer to his hands
Whate'er his honour asks, or heart demands.
155   His word the silver-footed Queen attends,
And from *Olympus'* snowy tops descends.
Arriv'd, she heard the voice of loud lament,
And echoing groans that shook the lofty tent.
His friends prepare the victim, and dispose
160 Repast unheeded, while he vents his woes.
The Goddess seats her by her pensive son,
She prest his hand, and tender thus begun.
    How long, unhappy! shall thy sorrows flow,
And thy heart waste with life-consuming woe?
165 Mindless of food, or love whose pleasing reign
Sooths weary life, and softens human pain.
O snatch the moments yet within thy Pow'r,
Nor long to live, indulge the am'rous hour!
Lo! *Jove* himself (for *Jove's* command I bear)
170 Forbids to tempt the wrath of heav'n too far,
No longer then (his fury if thou dread)
Detain the relicks of great *Hector* dead;
Nor vent on senseless earth thy vengeance vain,
But yield to ransom, and restore the slain.
175   To whom *Achilles*: Be the ransom giv'n,
And we submit, since such the will of heav'n.
    While thus they commun'd, from th' *Olympian* bow'rs
Jove orders *Iris* to the *Trojan* tow'rs.
Haste, winged Goddess! to the sacred town,
180 And urge her Monarch to redeem his son;
Alone, the *Ilian* ramparts let him leave,
And bear what stern *Achilles* may receive:
Alone, for so we will: No *Trojan* near;
Except, to place the dead with decent care,
185 Some aged herald, who with gentle hand,
May the slow mules and fun'ral car command.
Nor let him death, nor let him danger dread,
Safe thro' the foe by our protection led:

Him *Hermes* to *Achilles* shall convey,
Guard of his life, and partner of his way.   190
Fierce as he is, *Achilles'* self shall spare
His age, nor touch one venerable hair;
Some thought there must be, in a soul so brave,
Some sense of duty, some desire to save.

    Then down her bow the winged *Iris* drives,   195
And swift at *Priam*'s mournful court arrives;
Where the sad sons beside their father's throne
Sate bath'd in tears, and answer'd groan with groan.
And all amidst them lay the hoary sire,
(Sad scene of woe!) His face his wrapt attire   200
Conceal'd from sight; With frantick hands he spread
A show'r of ashes o'er his neck and head.
From room to room his pensive daughters roam;
Whose shrieks and clamours fill the vaulted dome;
Mindful of those, who, late their pride and joy,   205
Lie pale and breathless round the fields of *Troy!*
Before the King *Jove*'s messenger appears,
And thus in whispers greets his trembling ears.

    Fear not, oh father! no ill news I bear,
From *Jove* I come, *Jove* makes thee still his care: 210
For *Hector*'s sake these walls he bids thee leave,
And bear what stern *Achilles* may receive;
Alone, for so he wills: No *Trojan* near,
Except to place the dead with decent care,
Some aged herald, who with gentle hand   215
May the slow mules and fun'ral car command.
Nor shalt thou death, nor shalt thou danger dread;
Safe thro' the foe by his protection led;
Thee *Hermes* to *Pelides* shall convey,
Guard of thy life, and partner of thy way.   220
Fierce as he is, *Achilles'* self shall spare
Thy age, nor touch one venerable hair;
Some thought there must be, in a soul so brave,
Some sense of duty, some desire to save.

    She spoke, and vanish'd. *Priam* bids prepare   225
His gentle mules, and harness to the car;
There, for the gifts, a polish'd casket lay:
His pious sons the King's command obey.

Then past the Monarch to his bridal-room,
230   Where cedar-beams the lofty roofs perfume,
And where the treasures of his empire lay;
Then call'd his Queen, and thus began to say.
        Unhappy consort of a King distrest!
Partake the troubles of thy husband's breast:
235   I saw descend the messenger of *Jove*,
Who bids me try *Achilles*' mind to move;
Forsake these ramparts, and with gifts obtain
The corps of *Hector*, at yon' navy slain.
Tell me thy thought: My heart impels to go
240   Thro' hostile camps, and bears me to the foe.
        The hoary Monarch thus. Her piercing cries
Sad *Hecuba* renews, and then replies.
Ah! whither wanders thy distemper'd mind?
And where the prudence now that aw'd mankind?
245   Thro' *Phrygia* once, and foreign regions known,
Now all confus'd, distracted, overthrown!
Singly to pass thro' hosts of foes! to face
(Oh heart of steel!) the murd'rer of thy race!
To view that deathful eye, and wander o'er
250   Those hands, yet red with *Hector*'s noble gore!
Alas! my Lord! he knows not how to spare,
And what his mercy, thy slain sons declare;
So brave! so many fall'n! To calm his rage
Vain were thy dignity, and vain thy age.
255   No – pent in this sad palace let us give
To grief the wretched days we have to live.
Still, still for *Hector* let our sorrows flow,
Born to his own, and to his parents woe!
Doom'd from the hour his luckless life begun,
260   To dogs, to vultures, and to *Peleus*' son!
Oh! in his dearest blood might I allay
My rage, and these barbarities repay!
For ah! could *Hector* merit thus? whose breath
Expir'd not meanly, in unactive death:
265   He pour'd his latest blood in manly fight,
And fell a hero in his country's right.
        Seek not to stay me, nor my soul affright
With words of omen like a bird of night;

(Reply'd unmov'd the venerable man)
'Tis heav'n commands me, and you urge in vain.   270
Had any mortal voice th'injunction laid,
Nor augur, priest, or seer had been obey'd.
A present Goddess brought the high command,
I saw, I heard her, and the word shall stand.
I go, ye Gods! obedient to your call: 275
If in yon' camp your pow'rs have doom'd my fall,
Content – By the same hand let me expire!
Add to the slaughter'd son the wretched sire!
One cold embrace at least may be allow'd,
And my last tears flow mingled with his blood!   280
    From forth his open'd stores, this said, he drew
Twelve costly carpets of refulgent hue,
As many vests, as many mantles told,
And twelve fair veils, and garments stiff with gold.
Two tripods next, and twice two chargers shine,   285
With ten pure talents from the richest mine;
And last a large well-labour'd bowl had place,
(The pledge of treaties once with friendly *Thrace*)
Seem'd all too mean the stores he could employ,
For one last look to buy him back to *Troy!*   290
    Lo! the sad father, frantick with his pain,
Around him furious drives his menial train:
In vain each slave with duteous care attends,
Each office hurts him, and each face offends.
What make ye here? Officious crowds! (he cries)   295
Hence! nor obtrude your anguish on my eyes.
Have ye no griefs at home, to fix ye there?
Am I the only object of despair?
Am I become my people's common show,
Set up by *Jove* your spectacle of woe?   300
No, you must feel him too; your selves must fall;
The same stern God to ruin gives you all:
Nor is great *Hector* lost by me alone;
Your sole defence, your guardian pow'r is gone!
I see your blood the fields of *Phrygia* drown,   305
I see the ruins of your smoking town!
Oh send me, Gods! e'er that sad day shall come,
A willing ghost to *Pluto*'s dreary dome!

He said, and feebly drives his friends away:
310   The sorrowing friends his frantick rage obey.
Next on his sons his erring fury falls,
Polites, *Paris*, *Agathon*, he calls,
His threats *Deïphobus* and *Dius* hear,
Hippothoüs, *Pammon*, *Helenus* the seer,
315   And gen'rous *Antiphon*: For yet these nine
Surviv'd, sad relicks of his num'rous line.
  Inglorious sons of an unhappy sire!
Why did not all in *Hector*'s cause expire?
Wretch that I am! my bravest offspring slain,
320   You, the disgrace of *Priam*'s house, remain!
Mestor the brave, renown'd in ranks of war,
With *Troilus*, dreadful on his rushing car,
And last great *Hector*, more than man divine,
For sure he seem'd not of terrestial line!
325   All those relentless *Mars* untimely slew,
And left me these, a soft and servile crew,
Whose days the feast and wanton dance employ,
Gluttons and flatt'rers, the contempt of *Troy!*
Why teach ye not my rapid wheels to run,
330   And speed my journey to redeem my son?
  The sons their father's wretched age revere,
Forgive his anger, and produce the car.
High on the seat the cabinet they bind:
The new-made car with solid beauty shin'd;
335   Box was the yoke, embost with costly pains,
And hung with ringlets to receive the reins;
Nine cubits long the traces swept the ground;
These to the chariot's polish'd pole they bound,
Then fix'd a ring the running reins to guide,
340   And close beneath the gather'd ends were ty'd.
Next with the gifts (the price of *Hector* slain)
The sad attendants load the groaning wain:
Last to the yoke the well-match'd mules they bring,
(The gift of *Mysia* to the *Trojan* King.)
345   But the fair horses, long his darling care,
Himself receiv'd, and harness'd to his car:
Griev'd as he was, he not this task deny'd;
The hoary herald help'd him at his side.

While careful these the gentle coursers join'd,
Sad *Hecuba* approach'd with anxious mind;   350
A golden bowl that foam'd with fragrant wine,
(Libation destin'd to the pow'r divine)
Held in her right, before the steeds she stands,
And thus consigns it to the monarch's hands.

Take this, and pour to *Jove*: that safe from harms,   355
His grace restore thee to our roof, and arms;
Since victor of thy fears, and slighting mine,
Heav'n, or thy soul, inspire this bold design:
Pray to that God, who high on *Ida*'s brow
Surveys thy desolated realms below,   360
His winged messenger to send from high,
And lead thy way with heav'nly augury:
Let the strong sov'reign of the plumy race
Tow'r on the right of yon' æthereal space.
That sign beheld, and strengthen'd from above,   365
Boldly pursue the journey mark'd by *Jove*;
But if the God his augury denies,
Suppress thy impulse, nor reject advice.

'Tis just (said *Priam*) to the sire above
To raise our hands, for who so good as *Jove*?   370
He spoke, and bad th' attendant handmaid bring
The purest water of the living spring:
(Her ready hands the ew'er and bason held)
Then took the golden cup his Queen had fill'd,
On the mid pavement pours the rosy wine,   375
Uplifts his eyes, and calls the pow'r divine.

Oh first, and greatest! heav'ns imperial Lord!
On lofty *Ida*'s holy hill ador'd!
To stern *Achilles* now direct my ways,
And teach him mercy when a father prays.   380
If such thy will, dispatch from yonder sky
Thy sacred bird, cœlestial augury!
Let the strong sov'reign of the plumy race
Tow'r on the right of yon' æthereal space:
So shall thy suppliant, strengthen'd from above,   385
Fearless pursue the journey mark'd by *Jove*.

Jove heard his pray'r, and from the throne on high
Dispatch'd his bird, cœlestial augury!

The swift-wing'd chaser of the feather'd game,
390 And known to Gods by *Percnos'* lofty name.
Wide, as appears some palace gate display'd,
So broad, his pinions stretch'd their ample shade,
As stooping dexter with resounding wings
Th'imperial bird descends in airy rings.
395 A dawn of joy in ev'ry face appears;
The mourning matron dries her tim'rous tears.
Swift on his car th'impatient monarch sprung;
The brazen portal in his passage rung.
The mules preceding draw the loaded wain,
400 Charg'd with the gifts; *Idæus* holds the rein:
The King himself his gentle steeds controuls,
And thro surrounding friends the chariot rolls.
On his slow wheels the following people wait,
Mourn at each step, and give him up to Fate;
405 With hands uplifted, eye him as he past,
And gaze upon him as they gaz'd their last.
Now forward fares the Father on his way,
Thro' the lone fields, and back to *Ilion* they.
Great *Jove* beheld him as he crost the plain,
410 And felt the woes of miserable man.
Then thus to *Hermes.* Thou whose constant cares
Still succour mortals, and attend their pray'rs;
Behold an object to thy charge consign'd,
If ever pity touch'd thee for mankind.
415 Go, guard the sire; th'observing foe prevent,
And safe conduct him to *Achilles'* tent.
  The God obeys, his golden pinions binds,
And mounts incumbent on the wings of winds,
That high thro' fields of air his flight sustain,
420 O'er the wide earth, and o'er the boundless main:
Then grasps the wand that causes sleep to fly,
Or in soft slumbers seals the wakeful eye;
Thus arm'd, swift *Hermes* steers his airy way,
And stoops on *Hellespont*'s resounding sea.
425 A beauteous youth, majestick and divine,
He seem'd; fair offspring of some princely line!
Now twilight veil'd the glaring face of day,
And clad the dusky fields in sober gray;

What time the herald and the hoary King
Their chariots stopping, at the silver spring   430
That circling *Ilus'* ancient marble flows,
Allow'd their mules and steeds a short repose.
Thro' the dim shade the herald first espies
A man's approach, and thus to *Priam* cries.
I mark some foe's advance: O King! beware;   435
This hard adventure claims thy utmost care:
For much I fear, destruction hovers nigh:
Our state asks counsel; is it best to fly?
Or, old and helpless, at his feet to fall,
(Two wretched suppliants) and for mercy call?   440
    Th' afflicted Monarch shiver'd with despair;
Pale grew his face, and upright stood his hair;
Sunk was his heart; his colour went and came;
A sudden trembling shook his aged frame:
When *Hermes* greeting, touch'd his royal hand,   445
And gentle, thus accosts with kind demand.
    Say whither, father! when each mortal sight
Is seal'd in sleep, thou wander'st thro' the night?
Why roam thy mules and steeds the plains along,
Thro' *Grecian* foes, so num'rous and so strong?   450
What couldst thou hope, should these thy treasures view,
These, who with endless hate thy race pursue?
For what defence, alas! couldst thou provide?
Thy self not young, a weak old man thy guide.
Yet suffer not thy soul to sink with dread;   455
From me no harm shall touch thy rev'rend head;
From *Greece* I'll guard thee too; for in those lines
The living image of my father shines.
    Thy words, that speak benevolence of mind
Are true, my son! (the godlike sire rejoin'd)   460
Great are my hazards; but the Gods survey
My steps, and send thee, guardian of my way.
Hail, and be blest! For scarce of mortal kind
Appear thy form, thy feature, and thy mind.
    Nor true are all thy words, nor erring wide;   465
(The sacred messenger of heav'n reply'd)
But say, convey'st thou thro' the lonely plains
What yet most precious of thy store remains,

  To lodge in safety with some friendly hand?
470 Prepar'd perchance to leave thy native land.
  Or fly'st thou now? What hopes can *Troy* retain?
  Thy matchless son, her guard and glory, slain!
   The King, alarm'd. Say what, and whence thou art,
  Who search the sorrows of a parent's heart,
475 And know so well how god-like *Hector* dy'd?
  Thus *Priam* spoke, and *Hermes* thus reply'd.
   You tempt me, father, and with pity touch:
  On this sad subject you enquire too much.
  Oft have these eyes that godlike *Hector* view'd
480 In glorious fight with *Grecian* blood embru'd:
  I saw him, when like *Jove*, his flames he tost
  On thousand ships, and wither'd half a host:
  I saw, but help'd not: Stern *Achilles'* ire
  Forbad assistance, and enjoy'd the fire.
485 For him I serve, of *Myrmidonian* race;
  One ship convey'd us from our native place;
  Polyctor is my sire, an honour'd name,
  Old like thy self, and not unknown to fame;
  Of sev'n his sons by whom the lot was cast
490 To serve our Prince, it fell on me, the last.
  To watch this quarter my adventure falls,
  For with the morn the *Greeks* attack your walls;
  Sleepless they sit, impatient to engage,
  And scarce their rulers check their martial rage.
495 If then thou art of stern *Pelides'* train,
  (The mournful Monarch thus rejoin'd again)
  Ah tell me truly, where, oh where are laid
  My son's dear relicks? what befalls him dead?
  Have dogs dismember'd on the naked plains,
500 Or yet unmangled rest his cold remains?
   O favor'd of the skies! (Thus answer'd then
  The pow'r that mediates between Gods and men)
  Nor dogs nor vultures have thy *Hector* rent,
  But whole he lies, neglected in the tent:
505 This the twelfth evening since he rested there,
  Untouch'd by worms, untainted by the air.
  Still as *Aurora*'s ruddy beam is spread,
  Round his friend's tomb *Achilles* drags the dead:

Yet undisfigur'd, or in limb or face,
All fresh he lies, with ev'ry living grace,   510
Majestical in death! No stains are found
O'er all the corse, and clos'd is ev'ry wound;
(Tho' many a wound they gave) some heav'nly care,
Some hand divine, preserves him ever fair:
Or all the host of heav'n, to whom he led   515
A life so grateful, still regard him dead.

    Thus spoke to *Priam* the cœlestial guide,
And joyful thus the royal sire reply'd.
Blest is the man who pays the Gods above
The constant tribute of respect and love!   520
Those who inhabit the *Olympian* bow'r
My son forgot not, in exalted pow'r;
And heav'n, that ev'ry virtue bears in mind,
Ev'n to the ashes of the just, is kind.
But thou, oh gen'rous youth! this goblet take,   525
A pledge of gratitude for *Hector*'s sake;
And while the fav'ring Gods our steps survey,
Safe to *Pelides*' tent conduct my way.

    To whom the latent God. O King forbear
To tempt my youth, for apt is youth to err: 530
But can I, absent from my Prince's sight,
Take gifts in secret, that must shun the light?
What from our master's int'rest thus we draw,
Is but a licens'd theft that 'scapes the law.
Respecting him, my soul abjures th' offence;   535
And as the crime, I dread the consequence.
Thee, far as *Argos*, pleas'd I could convey:
Guard of thy life, and partner of thy way.
On thee attend, thy safety to maintain,
O'er pathless forests, or the roaring main.   540

    He said, then took the chariot at a bound,
And snatch'd the reins, and whirl'd the lash around:
Before th' inspiring God that urg'd them on,
The coursers fly with spirit not their own.
And now they reach'd the naval walls, and found   545
The guards repasting, while the bowls go round;
On these the virtue of his wand he tries,
And pours deep slumber on their watchful eyes:

Then heav'd the massy gates, remov'd the bars,
550   And o'er the trenches led the rolling cars.
Unseen, thro' all the hostile camp they went,
And now approach'd *Pelides'* lofty tent.
Of fir the roof was rais'd, and cover'd o'er
With reeds collected from the marshy shore;
555   And, fenc'd with palisades, a hall of state,
(The work of soldiers) where the hero sate.
Large was the door, whose well-compacted strength
A solid pine-tree barr'd, of wond'rous length;
Scarce three strong *Greeks* could lift its mighty weight,
560   But great *Achilles* singly clos'd the gate.
This *Hermes* (such the pow'r of Gods) set wide;
Then swift alighted the cœlestial guide,
And thus, reveal'd – Hear Prince! and understand
Thou ow'st thy guidance to no mortal hand:
565   *Hermes* I am, descended from above,
The King of Arts, the messenger of *Jove*.
Farewell: To shun *Achilles'* sight I fly;
Uncommon are such favours of the sky,
Nor stand confest to frail mortality.
570   Now fearless enter, and prefer thy pray'rs;
Adjure him by his father's silver hairs,
His son, his mother! urge him to bestow
Whatever pity that stern heart can know.
      Thus having said, he vanish'd from his eyes,
575   And in a moment shot into the skies:
The King, confirm'd from heav'n, alighted there,
And left his aged herald on the car.
With solemn pace thro' various rooms he went,
And found *Achilles* in his inner tent:
580   There sate the Hero; *Alcimus* the brave,
And great *Automedon*, attendance gave:
These serv'd his person at the royal Feast;
Around, at awful distance, stood the rest.
      Unseen by these, the King his entry made;
585   And prostrate now before *Achilles* laid,
Sudden, (a venerable sight!) appears;
Embrac'd his knees, and bath'd his hands in tears;
Those direful hands his kisses press'd, embru'd

Ev'n with the best, the dearest of his blood!
    As when a wretch, (who conscious of his crime, 590
Pursu'd for murder, flies his native clime)
Just gains some frontier, breathless, pale! amaz'd!
All gaze, all wonder: Thus *Achilles* gaz'd:
Thus stood th'attendants stupid with surprize;
All mute, yet seem'd to question with their eyes: 595
Each look'd on other, none the silence broke,
Till thus at last the kingly suppliant spoke.
    Ah think, thou favour'd of the pow'rs divine!
Think of thy father's age, and pity mine!
In me, that father's rev'rend image trace, 600
Those silver hairs, that venerable face;
His trembling limbs, his helpless person, see!
In all my equal, but in misery!
Yet now, perhaps, some turn of human fate
Expels him helpless from his peaceful state; 605
Think from some pow'rful foe tho see'st him fly,
And beg protection with a feeble cry.
Yet still one comfort in his soul may rise;
He hears his son still lives to glad his eyes;
And hearing still may hope, a better day 610
May send him thee, to chase that Foe away.
No comfort to my griefs, no hopes remain,
The best, the bravest of my sons are slain!
Yet what a race; e'er *Greece* to *Ilion* came,
The pledge of many a lov'd, and loving dame: 615
Nineteen one mother bore – Dead, all are dead!
How oft, alas! has wretched *Priam* bled?
Still one was left, their loss to recompense;
His father's hope, his country's last defence.
Him too thy rage has slain! beneath thy steel 620
Unhappy in his country's cause he fell!
    For him, thro' hostile camps I bent my way,
For him thus prostrate at thy feet I lay;
Large gifts proportion'd to thy Wrath I bear;
Oh hear the wretched, and the Gods revere! 625
    Think of thy father, and this face behold!
See him in me, as helpless and as old!

Tho' not so wretched: There he yields to me,
The first of men in sov'reign misery.
630   Thus forc'd to kneel, thus grov'ling to embrace
The scourge and ruin of my realm and race;
Suppliant my children's murd'rer to implore,
And kiss those hands yet reeking with their gore!
    These words soft pity in the chief inspire,
635   Touch'd with the dear remembrance of his Sire.
Then with his hand (as prostrate still he lay)
The old man's cheek he gently turn'd away.
Now each by turns indulg'd the gush of woe;
And now the mingled tides together flow:
640   This low on earth, that gently bending o'er,
A father one, and one a son deplore:
But great *Achilles* diff'rent passions rend,
And now his Sire he mourns, and now his friend.
Th' infectious softness thro' the heroes ran;
645   One universal solemn show'r began;
They bore as heroes, but they felt as man.
    Satiate at length with unavailing woes,
From the high throne divine *Achilles* rose;
The rev'rend monarch by the hand he rais'd;
650   On his white beard and form majestick gaz'd,
Not unrelenting: Then serene began
With words to sooth the miserable man.
    Alas! what weight of anguish hast thou known?
Unhappy Prince! thus guardless and alone
655   To pass thro' foes, and thus undaunted face
The man whose fury has destroy'd thy race?
Heav'n sure has arm'd thee with a heart of steel,
A strength proportion'd to the woes you feel.
Rise then: Let reason mitigate our care:
660   To mourn, avails not: Man is born to bear.
Such is, alas! the Gods severe decree:
They, only they are blest, and only free.
Two urns by *Jove's* high throne have ever stood,
The source of Evil one, and one of Good;
665   From thence the cup of mortal man he fills,
Blessings to these, to those distributes ills;

To most, he mingles both: The wretch decreed
To taste the bad, unmix'd, is curst indeed;
Pursu'd by wrongs, by meagre famine driv'n,
He wanders, outcast both of earth and heav'n. 670
The happiest taste not happiness sincere,
But find the cordial draught is dash'd with care.
Who more than *Peleus* shone in wealth and pow'r?
What stars concurring blest his natal hour?
A realm, a Goddess, to his wishes giv'n, 675
Grac'd by the Gods with all the gifts of heav'n!
One evil yet o'ertakes his latest day,
No race succeeding to imperial sway:
An only son! and he (alas!) ordain'd
To fall untimely in a foreign land! 680
See him, in *Troy*, the pious care decline
Of his weak age, to live the curse of thine!
Thou too, old man, hast happier days beheld;
In riches once, in children once excell'd;
Extended *Phrygia* own'd thy ample reign, 685
And all fair *Lesbos'* blissful seats contain,
And all wide *Hellespont*'s unmeasur'd main.
But since the God his hand has pleas'd to turn,
And fill thy measure from his bitter urn,
What sees the sun, but hapless heroes falls? 690
War, and the blood of men, surround thy walls!
What must be, must be. Bear thy lot, nor shed
These unavailing sorrows o'er the dead;
Thou can'st not call him from the *Stygian* shore,
But thou alas! may'st live to suffer more! 695

   To whom the King. Oh favour'd of the skies!
Here let me grow to earth! since *Hector* lies
On the bare beach, depriv'd of obsequies.
Oh give me *Hector!* to my eyes restore
His corse, and take the gifts: I ask no more. 700
Thou, as thou may'st, these boundless stores enjoy;
Safe may'st thou sail, and turn thy wrath from *Troy*;
So shall thy pity and forbearance give
A weak old man to see the light and live!

   Move me no more (*Achilles* thus replies, 705
While kindling anger sparkled in his eyes)

Nor seek by tears my steady soul to bend;
To yield thy *Hector* I my self intend:
For know, from *Jove* my Goddess-mother came,
710 (Old Ocean's daughter, silver-footed dame)
Nor com'st thou but by heav'n; nor com'st alone,
Some God impels with courage not thy own:
No human hand the weighty gates unbarr'd,
Nor could the boldest of our youth have dar'd
715 To pass our out-works, or elude the guard.
Cease; lest neglectful of high *Jove's* command
I show thee, King! thou tread'st on hostile land;
Release my knees, thy suppliant arts give o'er,
And shake the purpose of my soul no more.
720   The Sire obey'd him, trembling and o'er-aw'd.
Achilles, like a lion, rush'd abroad:
Automedon and *Alcimus* attend,
(Whom most he honour'd, since he lost his friend;)
These to unyoke the mules and horses went,
725 And led the hoary herald to the tent;
Next heap'd on high the num'rous presents bear
(Great *Hector's* ransome) from the polish'd car.
Two splendid mantles, and a carpet spread,
They leave; to cover, and inwrap the dead.
730 Then call the handmaids with assistant toil
To wash the body and anoint with oil;
Apart from *Priam*, lest th' unhappy sire
Provok'd to passion, once more rouze to ire
The stern *Pelides*; and nor sacred age
735 Nor *Jove's* command, should check the rising rage.
This done, the garments o'er the corse they spread;
Achilles lifts it to the fun'ral bed:
Then, while the body on the car they laid,
He groans, and calls on lov'd *Patroclus'* shade.
740   If, in that gloom which never light must know,
The deeds of mortals touch the ghosts below:
O friend! forgive me, that I thus fulfill
(Restoring *Hector*) heav'ns unquestion'd will.
The gifts the father gave, be ever thine,
745 To grace thy *manes*, and adorn thy shrine.

He said, and entring, took his seat of state,
Where full before him rev'rend *Priam* sate:
To whom, compos'd, the God-like chief begun.
Lo! to thy pray'r restor'd, thy breathless son;
Extended on the fun'ral couch he lies;   750
And soon as morning paints the eastern skies,
The sight is granted to thy longing eyes.
But now the peaceful hours of sacred night
Demand refection, and to rest invite:
Nor thou, O father! thus consum'd with woe,   755
The common cares that nourish life, forego.
Not thus did *Niobe*, of form divine,
A parent once, whose sorrows equal'd thine:
Six youthful sons, as many blooming maids,
In one sad day beheld the *Stygian* shades;   760
These by *Apollo*'s silver bow were slain,
Those, *Cynthia*'s arrows stretch'd upon the plain.
So was her pride chastiz'd by wrath divine,
Who match'd her own with bright *Latona*'s line;
But two the Goddess, twelve the Queen enjoy'd;   765
Those boasted twelve th'avenging two destroy'd.
Steep'd in their blood, and in the dust outspread,
Nine days neglected lay expos'd the dead;
None by to weep them, to inhume them none;
(For *Jove* had turn'd the nation all to stone:)   770
The Gods themselves at length relenting, gave
Th'unhappy race the honours of a grave.
Her self a rock, (for such was heav'ns high will)
Thro' desarts wild now pours a weeping rill;
Where round the bed whence *Acheloüs* springs,   775
The wat'ry fairies dance in mazy rings,
There high on *Sipylus* his shaggy brow,
She stands her own sad monument of woe;
The rock for ever lasts, the tears for ever flow!
Such griefs, O King! have other parents known;   780
Remember theirs, and mitigate thy own.
The care of heav'n thy *Hector* has appear'd,
Nor shall he lie unwept, and uninterr'd;
Soon may thy aged cheeks in tears be drown'd,
And all the eyes of *Ilion* stream around.   785

He said, and rising, chose the victim ewe
With silver fleece, which his attendants slew.
The limbs they sever from the reeking hide,
With skill prepare them, and in parts divide:
790 Each on the coals the sep'rate morsels lays,
And hasty, snatches from the rising blaze.
With bread the glitt'ring canisters they load,
Which round the board *Automedon* bestow'd:
The chief himself to each his portion plac'd,
795 And each indulging shar'd in sweet repast.
When now the rage of hunger was represt,
The wond'ring hero eyes his royal guest;
No less the royal guest the hero eyes;
His god-like aspect and majestick size;
800 Here, youthful grace and noble fire engage,
And there, the mild benevolence of age.
Thus gazing long, the silence neither broke,
(A solemn scene!) at length the father spoke.
    Permit me now, belov'd of *Jove!* to steep
805 My careful temples in the dew of sleep:
For since the day that numbred with the dead
My hapless son, the dust has been my bed,
Soft sleep a stranger to my weeping eyes,
My only food my sorrows and my sighs!
810 Till now, encourag'd by the grace you give,
I share thy banquet, and consent to live.
    With that, *Achilles* bad prepare the bed,
With purple soft, and shaggy carpets spread;
Forth, by the flaming lights, they bend their way,
815 And place the couches, and the cov'rings lay.
Then he: Now father sleep, but sleep not here.
Consult thy safety, and forgive my fear,
Lest any *Argive* (at this hour awake,
To ask our counsel or our orders take,)
820 Approaching sudden to our open'd tent,
Perchance behold thee, and our grace prevent.
Should such report thy honour'd person here,
The King of men the ransom might defer.
But say with speed, if ought of thy desire
825 Remains unask'd; what time the rites require

T' inter thy *Hector*? For, so long we stay
Our slaught'ring arm, and bid the hosts obey.
    If then thy will permit (the Monarch said)
To finish all due honours to the dead,
This, of thy grace, accord: To thee are known   830
The fears of *Ilion*, clos'd within her town,
And at what distance from our walls aspire
The hills of *Ide*, and forests for the fire.
Nine days to vent our sorrows I request,
The tenth shall see the fun'ral and the feast;   835
The next, to raise his monument be giv'n;
The twelfth we war, if war be doom'd by heav'n!
    This thy request (reply'd the chief) enjoy:
Till then, our arms suspend the fall of *Troy*.
    Then gave his hand at parting, to prevent   840
The old man's fears, and turn'd within the tent;
Where fair *Briseïs* bright in blooming charms
Expects her Hero with desiring arms.
But in the porch the King and herald rest,
Sad dreams of care yet wand'ring in their breast.   845
Now Gods and men the gifts of sleep partake;
Industrious *Hermes* only was awake,
The King's return revolving in his mind,
To pass the ramparts, and the watch to blind.
The pow'r descending hover'd o'er his head: 850
And sleep'st thou, father! (thus the vision said)
Now dost thou sleep, when *Hector* is restor'd?
Nor fear the *Grecian* foes, or *Grecian* Lord?
Thy presence here shou'd stern *Atrides* see,
Thy still-surviving sons may sue for thee,   855
May offer all thy treasures yet contain,
To spare thy age; and offer all in vain.
    Wak'd with the word, the trembling Sire arose,
And rais'd his friend: The God before him goes,
He joins the mules, directs them with his hand,   860
And moves in silence thro' the hostile land.
When now to *Xanthus'* yellow stream they drove,
(*Xanthus*, immortal progeny of *Jove*)
The winged deity forsook their view,
And in a moment to *Olympus* flew.   865

Now shed *Aurora* round her saffron ray,
Sprung thro' the gates of light, and gave the day:
Charg'd with their mournful load, to *Ilion* go
The Sage and King, majestically slow.
870 *Cassandra* first beholds, from *Ilion*'s spire,
The sad procession of her hoary sire,
Then, as the pensive pomp advanc'd more near,
Her breathless brother stretch'd upon the bier:
A show'r of tears o'erflows her beauteous eyes,
875 Alarming thus all *Ilion* with her cries.
   Turn here your steps, and here your eyes employ,
Ye wretched daughters, and ye sons of *Troy!*
If e'er ye rush'd in crowds, with vast delight
To hail your hero glorious from the fight;
880 Now meet him dead, and let your sorrows flow!
Your common triumph, and your common woe.
   In thronging crowds they issue to the plains,
Nor man, nor woman, in the walls remains.
In ev'ry face the self-same grief is shown,
885 And *Troy* sends forth one universal groan.
At *Scæa*'s gates they meet the mourning wain,
Hang on the wheels, and grovel round the slain.
The wife and mother, frantic with despair,
Kiss his pale cheek, and rend their scatter'd hair:
890 Thus wildly wailing, at the gates they lay;
And there had sigh'd and sorrow'd out the day;
But god-like *Priam* from the chariot rose:
Forbear (he cry'd) this violence of woes,
First to the palace let the car proceed,
895 Then pour your boundless sorrows o'er the dead.
   The waves of people at his word divide,
Slow rolls the chariot thro' the following tide;
Ev'n to the palace the sad pomp they wait:
They weep, and place him on the bed of state.
900 A melancholy choir attend around,
With plaintive sighs, and musick's solemn sound:
Alternately they sing, alternate flow
Th'obedient tears, melodious in their woe.
While deeper sorrows groan from each full heart,
905 And Nature speaks at ev'ry pause of Art.

First to the corse the weeping consort flew;
Around his neck her milk-white arms she threw,
And oh my *Hector!* oh my Lord! she cries,
Snatch'd in thy bloom from these desiring eyes!
Thou to the dismal realms for ever gone!   910
And I abandon'd, desolate, alone!
An only son, once comfort of our pains,
Sad product now of hapless love, remains!
Never to manly age that son shall rise,
Or with increasing graces glad my eyes: 915
For *Ilion* now (her great defender slain)
Shall sink a smoking ruin on the plain.
Who now protects her wives with guardian care?
Who saves her infants from the rage of war?
Now hostile fleets must waft those infants o'er,   920
(Those wives must wait 'em) to a foreign shore!
Thou too my son! to barb'rous climes shalt go,
The sad companion of thy mother's woe;
Driv'n hence a slave before the victor's sword;
Condemn'd to toil for some inhuman lord.   925
Or else some *Greek* whose father prest the plain,
Or son, or brother, by great *Hector* slain;
In *Hector's* blood his vengeance shall enjoy,
And hurl thee headlong from the tow'rs of *Troy*.
For thy stern father never spar'd a foe: 930
Thence all these tears, and all this scene of woe!
Thence, many evils his sad parents bore,
His parents many, but his consort more.
Why gav'st thou not to me thy dying hand?
And why receiv'd not I thy last command?   935
Some word thou would'st have spoke, which sadly dear,
My soul might keep, or utter with a tear;
Which never, never could be lost in air,
Fix'd in my heart, and oft repeated there!
    Thus to her weeping maids she makes her moan;   940
Her weeping handmaids echo groan for groan.
    The mournful mother next sustains her part.
Oh thou, the best, the dearest to my heart!
Of all my race thou most by heav'n approv'd,
And by th'immortals ev'n in death belov'd!   945

While all my other sons in barb'rous bands
Achilles bound, and sold to foreign lands,
This felt no chains, but went a glorious ghost
Free, and a hero, to the *Stygian* coast.
950   Sentenc'd, 'tis true, by his inhuman doom,
Thy noble corse was dragg'd around the tomb,
(The tomb of him thy warlike arm had slain)
Ungen'rous insult, impotent and vain!
Yet glow'st thou fresh with ev'ry living grace,
955   No mark of pain, or violence of face;
Rosy and fair! as *Phœbus'* silver bow
Dismiss'd thee gently to the shades below.
    Thus spoke the dame, and melted into tears.
Sad *Helen* next in pomp of grief appears:
960   Fast from the shining sluices of her eyes
Fall the round crystal drops, while thus she cries.
    Ah dearest friend! in whom the Gods had join'd
The mildest manners with the bravest mind;
Now twice ten years (unhappy years) are o'er
965   Since *Paris* brought me to the *Trojan* shore;
(Oh had I perish'd, e'er that form divine
Seduc'd this soft, this easy heart of mine!)
Yet was it ne'er my fate, from thee to find
A deed ungentle, or a word unkind:
970   When others curst the auth'ress of their woe,
Thy pity check'd my sorrows in their flow:
If some proud brother ey'd me with disdain,
Or scornful sister with her sweeping train,
Thy gentle accents soften'd all my pain.
975   For thee I mourn; and mourn my self in thee,
The wretched source of all this misery!
The fate I caus'd, for ever I bemoan;
Sad *Helen* has no friend now thou art gone!
Thro' *Troy's* wide streets abandon'd shall I roam!
980   In *Troy* deserted, as abhorr'd at home!
    So spoke the fair, with sorrow-streaming eye:
Distressful beauty melts each stander-by;
On all around th' infectious sorrow grows;
But *Priam* check'd the torrent as it rose.

Perform, ye *Trojans!* what the rites require,   985
And fell the forests for a fun'ral pyre;
Twelve days, nor foes, nor secret ambush dread;
Achilles grants these honours to the dead.

   He spoke; and at his word, the *Trojan* train
Their mules and oxen harness to the wain,   990
Pour thro' the gates, and, fell'd from *Ida*'s crown,
Roll back the gather'd forests to the town.
These toils continue nine succeeding days,
And high in air a sylvan structure raise.
But when the tenth fair morn began to shine,   995
Forth to the pile was born the man divine,
And plac'd aloft: while all, with streaming eyes,
Beheld the flames and rolling smokes arise.
Soon as *Aurora*, daughter of the dawn,
With rosy lustre streak'd the dewy lawn;   1000
Again the mournful crowds surround the pyre,
And quench with wine the yet remaining fire.
The snowy bones his friends and brothers place
(With tears collected) in a golden vase;
The golden vase in purple palls they roll'd,   1005
Of softest texture, and inwrought with gold.
Last o'er the urn the sacred earth they spread,
And rais'd the tomb, memorial of the dead.
(Strong guards and spies, till all the rites were done,
Watch'd from the rising to the setting sun.)   1010
All *Troy* then moves to *Priam*'s court again,
A solemn, silent, melancholy train:
Assembled there, from pious toil they rest,
And sadly shar'd the last sepulchral feast.
Such honours *Ilion* to her Hero paid,   1015
And peaceful slept the mighty *Hector*'s shade.

The End of the I L I A D

14. *What Seas they measur'd,* &c.] There is something very noble in these sentiments of *Achilles*: He does not recollect any soft moments, any tendernesses that had pass'd between him and *Patroclus*, but he revolves the many difficulties, the toils by land, and the dangers by sea, in which they had been companions: Thus the poet on all occasions admirably sustains the character of *Achilles*; when he play'd upon the harp in the ninth book, he sung the atchievements of Kings; and in this place there is an air of greatness in his very sorrows: *Achilles* is as much a hero when he weeps, as when he fights.

This passage in *Homer* has not escap'd the censure of *Plato*, who thought it a diminution to his character to be thus transported with grief; but the objection will vanish if we remember that all the passions of *Achilles* are in the extreme; his nature is violent, and it would have been an outrage to his general character to have represented him as mourning moderately for his friend. *Plato* spoke more like a philosopher than a critick when he blamed the behaviour of *Achilles* as unmanly: These Tears would have ill become *Plato*, but they are graceful in *Achilles.*

Besides there is something very instructive in this whole representation, it shews us the power of a sincere friendship, and softens and recommends the character of *Achilles*; the violence he used towards his enemy is alleviated by the sincerity he expresses towards his friend; he is a terrible enemy, but an amiable friend.

30. *For* Phœbus *watch'd it,* &c.] *Eustathius* says, that by this shield of *Apollo* are meant the clouds that are drawn up by the beams of the sun, which cooling and qualifying the sultriness of the air, preserved the body from decay: But perhaps the poet had something farther in his eye when he introduc'd *Apollo* upon this occasion: *Apollo* is a physician and the God of medicaments; if therefore *Achilles* used any Arts to preserve *Hector* from decay that he might be able the longer to insult his remains, *Apollo* may properly be said to protect it with his *Ægis.*

36. *But* Neptune *this, and* Pallas *this denies.*] It is with excellent art that the poet carries on this part of his poem, he shews that he could have contriv'd another way to recover the body of *Hector*, but as a God is never to be introduc'd but when human means fail, he rejects the interposition of *Mercury*, makes use of ordinary methods, and *Priam* redeems his son: This gives an air of probability to the relation, at the same time that it advances the glory of *Achilles*; for the greatest of his enemies labours to purchase his favour, the Gods hold a consultation, and a King becomes his suppliant.   *Eustathius.*

Those seven lines, from Κλέψαι δ' ὠτρύνεσκον to Μαχλοσύνην ἀλεγεινήν, have been thought spurious by some of the ancients: They judg'd it as an indecency that the Goddess of wisdom and *Achilles* should be equally inexorable; and thought it was below the majesty of the Gods to be said to steal. Besides, say they, had *Homer* been acquainted with the judgment of *Paris*, he would undoubtedly have mention'd it before this time in his poem, and consequently that story was of a later invention: And *Aristarchus* affirms that Μαχλοσύνη [lust] is a more modern word, and never known before the time of *Hesiod*, who uses it when he speaks of the daughters of *Prætus*; and adds, that it is appropriated to signify the incontinence of women, and cannot be at all apply'd to men: Therefore others read the last verse,

῀Η οἱ κεχαρισμένα δῶρ' ὀνόμηνε.

[Pleased with him, she gave him gifts.]

These objections are entirely gather'd from *Eustathius*; to which we may add, that *Macrobius* seems to have been one of those who rejected these verses, since he affirms that our author never mentions the judgment of *Paris.* It may be answer'd, that the silence of *Homer* in the foregoing part of the poem, as to the judgment of *Paris*, is no argument that he was ignorant of that story: Perhaps he might think it most proper to unfold the cause of the destruction of *Troy* in the conclusion of the *Ilias*; that the reader seeing the wrong done, and the punishment of that wrong immediately following, might acknowledge the justice of it.

The same reason will be an answer to the objection relating to the anger of *Pallas*: Wisdom cannot be satisfy'd without justice, and consequently *Pallas* ought not to cease from resentment, till *Troy* has suffer'd the deserts of her crimes.

I cannot think that the objection about the word Μαχλοσύνη is of any weight; the date of words is utterly uncertain, and as no one has been able to determine the ages of *Homer*, and *Hesiod*, so neither can any person be assured that such words were not in use in *Homer*'s days.

52. *A Lion, not a Man,* &c.] This is a very formal condemnation of the morals of *Achilles*, which *Homer* puts into the mouth of a God. One may see from this alone that he was far from designing his hero a virtuous character, yet the poet artfully introduces *Apollo* in the midst of his reproaches, intermingling the hero's praises with his blemishes: *Brave tho' he be,* &c. Thus what is the real Merit of *Achilles* is distinguish'd from what is blameable in his character, and we see *Apollo*, or the God of wisdom, is no less impartial than just in his representation of *Achilles.*

114. *And wept her god-like son's approaching doom.*] These words are very artfully inserted by the poet. The poem could not proceed to the death of *Achilles* without breaking the Action; and therefore to satisfy the curiosity of the reader concerning the fate of this great man, he takes care to inform us that his life draws to a period, and as it were celebrates his funeral before his death.

Such circumstances as these greatly raise the character of *Achilles*; he is so truly valiant, that tho' he knows he must fall before *Troy*, yet he does not abstain from the war, but couragiously meets his death: And here I think it proper to insert an observation that ought to have been made before, which is, that *Achilles* did not know that *Hector* was to fall by his hand; if he had known it, where would have been the mighty courage in engaging him in a single combat, in which he was sure to conquer? The contrary of this is evident from the words of *Achilles* to *Hector* just before the combat,

> – Πρὶν γ᾽ ἢ ἕτερόν γε πεσόντα
> Αἵματος ἆσαι ἄρηα, &c. –

I will make no compacts with thee, says *Achilles, but one of us shall fall.*

141. *Nine days are past since all the court above,* &c.] It may be thought that so many interpositions of the Gods, such messages from heaven to earth, and down to the seas, are needless machines; and it may be imagin'd that it is an offence against probability that so many Deities should be employ'd to pacify *Achilles*: But I am of opinion that the poet conducts this whole affair with admirable judgment. The poem is now almost at the conclusion, and *Achilles* is to pass from a state of an almost inexorable resentment to a state of perfect tranquillity; such a change could not be brought about by human means; *Achilles* is too stubborn to obey any thing less than a God: This is evident from his rejecting the persuasion of the whole *Grecian* army to return to the battle: So that it appears that this machinery was necessary, and consequently a beauty to the poem.

It may be farther added, that these several incidents proceed from *Jupiter*: It is by his appointment that so many Gods are employ'd to attend *Achilles.* By these means *Jupiter* fulfills the promise mention'd in the first book, of honouring the son of *Thetis*, and *Homer* excellently sustains his character by representing the inexorable *Achilles* as not parting with the body of his mortal enemy, but by the immediate command of *Jupiter.*

If the poet had conducted these incidents merely by human means, or suppos'd *Achilles* to restore the body of *Hector* entirely out of compassion, the draught had been unnatural, because unlike *Achilles*: Such a violence of temper was not to be pacify'd by ordinary methods. Besides, he has made use of the properest personages to carry on the affair; for who could be suppos'd to have so great an influence upon *Achilles* as his own mother, who is a Goddess?

164. *And thy heart waste with life-consuming woe.*] This expression in the original is very particular. Were it to be translated literally it must be render'd, how long wilt thou eat, or prey upon thy own heart by these sorrows? And it seems that it was a common way of expressing a deep sorrow; and *Pythagoras* uses it in this sense, μὴ ἐσθίειν καρδίαν [don't consume your heart], that is, grieve not excessively, let not sorrow make too great an impression upon thy heart. *Eustathius.*

168. – *Indulge the am'rous hour!*] The ancients (says *Eustathius*) rejected these verses because of the indecent idea they convey: The Goddess in plain terms advises *Achilles* to go to bed to his mistress, and tells him a woman will be a comfort. The good bishop is of opinion, that they ought to be rejected, but the reason he gives is as extraordinary as that of *Thetis*: Soldiers, says he, have more occasion for something to strengthen themselves with, than for women: And this is the reason, continues he, why wrestlers are forbid all commerce with that sex during the whole time of their exercise.

Dionysius of *Halicarnassus* endeavours to justify *Homer* by observing, that this advice of *Thetis* was not given him to induce him to any wantonness, but was intended to indulge a nobler passion, his desire of glory: She advises him to go to that captive who was restor'd to him in a publick manner, to satisfy his honour: To that captive, the detention of whom had been so great a punishment to the whole *Grecian* army: And therefore *Thetis* uses a very proper motive to comfort her son, by advising him to gratify at once both his love and his glory.

Plutarch has likewise labour'd in *Homer*'s justification; he observes that the poet has set the picture of *Achilles* in this place in a very fair and strong point of light: Tho' *Achilles* had so lately receiv'd his belov'd *Briseïs* from the hands of *Agamemnon*; tho' he knew that his own life drew to a sudden period, yet the hero prevails over the lover, and he does not haste to indulge his love: He does not lament *Patroclus* like a common man by neglecting the duties of life, but he abstains from all pleasures by an excess of sorrow, and the love of his mistress is lost in that of his friend.

This observation excellently justifies *Achilles*, in not indulging himself with the company of his mistress: The hero indeed prevails so much over the lover, that *Thetis* thinks her self oblig'd to recall *Briseïs* to his memory. Yet still the indecency remains. All that can be said in favour of *Thetis* is, that she was mother to *Achilles*, and consequently might take the greater freedom with her son.

Madam *Dacier* disapproves of both the former observations: She has recourse to the lawfulness of such a practice between *Achilles* and *Briseïs*; and because such commerces in those times were reputed honest, there-fore she thinks the advice was decent: The married ladies are oblig'd to her for this observation, and I hope all tender mothers, when their sons are afflicted, will advise them to comfort themselves in this manner.

In short, I am of opinion that this passage outrages decency; and 'tis a sign of some weakness to have so much occasion of justification. Indeed the whole passage is capable of a serious construction, and of such a sense as a mother might express to a son with decency: And then it will run thus; 'Why art thou, my Son, thus afflicted? Why thus resign'd to sorrow? Can neither sleep nor love divert you? Short is thy date of life, spend it not all in weeping, but allow some part of it to love and pleasure!' But still the indecency lies in the manner of the expression, which must be allow'd to be almost obscene, (for such is the word μίσγεσθ' *minisceri* [engage in sexual relations]) all that can be said in defence of it is, that as we are not competent judges of what ideas words might carry in *Homer*'s time, so we ought not entirely to condemn him, because it is possible the expression might not sound so indecently in ancient as in modern ears.

189. *Him* Hermes *to* Achilles *shall convey.*] The intervention of *Mercury* was very necessary at this time, and by it the poet not only gives an air of probability to the relation, but also pays a complement to his countrymen the *Grecians*: They kept so strict a guard that nothing but a God could pass unobserv'd, and this highly recommends their military discipline; and *Priam* not being able to carry the ransom without a chariot, it would have been an offence against probability, to have suppos'd him able to have pass'd all the guards of the army in his chariot, without the assistance of some deity: *Horace* had this passage in his view, Ode the 10th of the first book.

> *Iniqua* Trojæ *castra fefellit.*

[He escaped the notice of the camp hostile to Troy.]

191. – Achilles' *self shall spare*
His age, nor touch one venerable hair, &c.]

It is observable that every word here is a Negative, ἄφρων, ἄσκοπος, ἀλιτήμων [without intelligence, without guidance, in a blasphemous manner]; *Achilles* is still so angry that *Jupiter* cannot say he is wise, judicious, and merciful; he only commends him negatively, and barely says he is not a madman, nor perversely wicked.

It is the observation of the ancients, says *Eustathius*, that all the causes of the sins of man are included in those three words: Man offends either out of ignorance, and then he is ἄφρων; or thro' inadvertency, then he is ἄσκοπος; or wilfully and maliciously, and then he is ἀλιτήμων. So that this description agrees very well with the present disposition of *Achilles*; he is not ἄφρων, because his resentment begins to abate; he is not ἄσκοπος, because his mother has given him instructions, nor ἀλιτήμων, because he will not offend against the injunctions of *Jupiter*.

195. *The winged* Iris *flies, &c.*] Mons. *Rapin* has been very free upon this passage, where so many machines are made use of to cause *Priam* to obtain the body of *Hector* from *Achilles.* 'This father (says he) who has so much tenderness for his son, who is so superstitious in observing the funeral ceremonies, and saving those precious remains from the dogs and vultures; ought not he to have thought of doing this himself, without being thus expressly commanded by the Gods? Was there need of a machine to make him remember that he was a father?' But this critick entirely forgets what render'd such a conduct of absolute necessity; namely, the extreme danger and (in all probability) imminent ruin both of the King and state, upon *Priam's* putting himself into the power of his most inveterate enemy. There was no other method of recovering *Hector*, and of discharging his funeral rites (which were look'd upon by the ancients of so high importance) and therefore the message from *Jupiter* to encourage *Priam*, with the assistance of *Mercury* to conduct him, and to prepare *Achilles* to receive him with favour, was far from impertinent: It was *dignus vindice nodus* [a knot worthy of such an avenger], as *Horace* expresses it.

200. *His face his wrapt attire Conceal'd from sight.*] The poet has observ'd a great decency in this place; he was not able to express the grief of his royal mourner, and so covers what he could not represent. From this passage *Semanthes* the *Sicyonian* painter borrow'd his design in the sacrifice of *Iphigenia*, and represents his *Agamemnon*, as *Homer* does his *Priam*: *Æschylus* has likewise imitated this place, and draws his *Niobe* exactly after the manner of *Homer*.   *Eustathius.*

265.   *He pour'd his latest blood in manly fight,*
        And fell a hero –

This whole discourse of *Hecuba* is exceedingly natural, she aggravates the features of *Achilles*, and softens those of *Hector*: Her anger blinds her so much that she can see nothing great in *Achilles*, and her fondness so much, that she can discern no defects in *Hector*: Thus she draws *Achilles* in the fiercest colours, like a barbarian, and calls him ὠμηστής [savage]; But at the same time forgets that *Hector* ever fled from *Achilles*, and in the original directly tells us that he *knew not how to fear, or how to fly.*   *Eustathius.*

291. *Lo! the sad father,* &c.] This behaviour of *Priam* is very natural to a person in his circumstances: The loss of his favourite son makes so deep an Impression upon his spirits, that he is incapable of consolation; he is displeased with every body; he is angry he knows not why; the disorder and hurry of his spirits make him break out into passionate expressions, and those expressions are contain'd in short periods, very natural to men in anger, who give not themselves leisure to express their sentiments at full length: It is from the same passion that *Priam*, in the second speech, treats all his sons with the utmost indignity, calls them gluttons, dancers, and flatterers. *Eustathius* very justly remarks, that he had *Paris* particularly in his eye; but his anger makes him transfer that character to the rest of his children, not being calm enough to make a distinction between the innocent and guilty.

That passage where he runs into the praises of *Hector*, is particularly natural: His concern and fondness make him as extravagant in the commendation of him, as in the disparagement of his other sons: They are less than mortals, he more than man. *Rapin* has censur'd this anger of *Priam* as a breach of the *Manners*, and says he might have shewn himself a father, otherwise than by this usage of his children. But whoever considers his circumstances will judge after another manner. *Priam*, after having been the most wealthy, most powerful and formidable monarch of *Asia*, becomes all at once the most miserable of men; he loses in less than eight days the best of his army, and a great number of virtuous sons; he loses the bravest of them all, his glory and his defence, the gallant *Hector*. This last blow sinks him quite, and changes him so much, that he is no longer the same: He becomes impatient, frantick, unreasonable! The terrible effect of ill fortune! Whoever has the least insight into nature, must admire so fine a picture of the force of adversity on an unhappy old man.

313. *Deïphobus* and *Dius.*] It has been a dispute whether Δῖος or Ἀγανός, in v. 251. was a proper name, but *Pherecydes* (says *Eustathius*) determines it, and assures us that *Dios* was a spurious son of *Priam.*

342. *The sad attendants load the groaning wain.*] It is necessary to observe to the reader, to avoid confusion, that two cars are here prepared; the one drawn by mules, to carry the presents, and to bring back the body of *Hector*; the other drawn by horses, in which the herald and *Priam* rode. *Eustathius.*

377. *Oh first, and greatest!* &c.] *Eustathius* observes, that there is not one instance in the whole *Ilias* of any prayer that was justly prefer'd, that fail'd of success. This proceeding of *Homer*'s is very judicious, and answers exactly to the true end of poetry, which is to please and instruct. Thus *Priam* prays that *Achilles* may cease his wrath, and compassionate his miseries; and *Jupiter* grants his request: The unfortunate king obtains compassion, and in his most inveterate enemy finds a friend.

417. *The Description of* Mercury.] A man must have no Taste for poetry that does not admire this sublime description: *Virgil* has translated it almost *verbatim* in the 4th book of the *Æneis*, v. 240.

> — *Ille patris magni parere parabat*
> *Imperio, & primum pedibus talaria nectit*
> *Aurea, quæ sublimem alis, sive æquora supra,*
> *Seu terram rapido pariter cum flamine portant.*
> *Tum virgam capit, hac animas ille evocat orco*
> *Pallentes, alias sub tristia tartara mittit;*
> *Dat somnos, adimitque, & lumina morte resignat.*

> [*Hermes* obeys; with golden pinions binds
> His flying feet, and mounts the western winds:
> And whether o'er the seas or earth he flies,
> With rapid force, they bear him down the skies.
> But first he grasps within his awful hand,
> The mark of sov'reign pow'r, his magick wand:
> With this, he draws the ghosts from hollow graves,
> With this he drives them down the *Stygian* waves;
> With this he seals in sleep, the wakeful sight;
> And eyes, though clos'd in death restores to light.]

It is hard to determine which is more excellent, the copy, or the original: *Merucry* appears in both pictures with equal majesty; and the *Roman* dress becomes him, as well as the *Grecian*. *Virgil* has added the latter part of the fifth, and the whole sixth line to *Homer*, which makes it still more full and majestical.

Give me leave to produce a passage out of *Milton*, of near affinity with the lines above, which is not inferior to *Homer* or *Virgil*: It is the description of the descent of an angel,

> *— Down thither, prone in flight*
> *He speeds, and thro' the vast æthereal sky*
> *Sails between worlds and worlds; with steady wing*
> *Now on the polar winds: Then with quick force*
> *Winnows the buxom air —*
> *Of beaming sunny rays a golden Tiar*
> *Circled his head; nor less his locks behind*
> *Illustrious, on his shoulders fledg'd with wings,*
> *Lay waving round. —* &c.

427. *Now twilight veil'd the glaring face of day.*] The poet by such intimations as these recalls to our minds the exact time which *Priam* takes up in this journey to *Achilles*: He set out in the evening; and by the time that he reach'd the tomb of *Ilus*, it was grown somewhat dark, which shews that this tomb stood at some distance from the city: Here *Mercury* meets him, and when it was quite dark, guides him into the presence of *Achilles*. By these methods we may discover how exactly the poet preserves the unities of time and place, that he allots space sufficient for the actions which he describes, and yet does not crowd more incidents into any interval of time than may be executed in as much as he allows: Thus it being improbable that so stubborn a man as *Achilles* should relent in a few moments, the poet allows a whole night for this affair, so that *Priam* has leisure enough to go and return, and time enough remaining to persuade *Achilles*.

447, *&c. The speech of* Mercury *to* Priam.] I shall not trouble the reader with the dreams of *Eustathius*, who tells us that this fiction of *Mercury* is partly true, and partly false: 'Tis true that his father is old; for *Jupiter* is King of the whole universe, was from eternity, and created both men and Gods: In like manner, when *Mercury* says he is the seventh child of his father, *Eustathius* affirms that he meant that there were six planets besides *Mercury*. Sure it requires great pains and thought to be so learnedly absurd: The supposition which he makes afterwards is far more natural; *Priam*, says he, might by chance meet with one of the *Myrmidons*, who might conduct him unobserv'd thro' the camp into the presence of *Achilles*, and as the execution of any wise design is ascrib'd to *Pallas*, so may this clandestine enterprize be said to be manag'd by the guidance of *Mercury*.

But perhaps this whole passage may be better explain'd by having recourse to the pagan theology: It was an opinion that obtain'd in those early days, that *Jupiter* frequently sent some friendly messengers to protect the innocent, so that *Homer* might intend to give his readers a lecture of morality, by telling us that this unhappy king was under the protection of the Gods.

Madam *Dacier* carries it farther. *Homer* (says she) instructed by tradition, knew that God sends his angels to the succour of the afflicted. The scripture is full of examples of this truth. The story of *Tobit* has a wonderful relation with this of *Homer*: *Tobit* sent his son to *Rages*, a city of *Media*, to receive a considerable sum; *Tobias* did not know the way; he found at his door a young man cloath'd with a majestick glory, which attracted admiration: It was an angel under the form of a man. This angel being ask'd who he was, answer'd (as *Mercury* does here) by a fiction: He said that he was of the children of *Israel*, that his name was *Azarias*, and that he was son of *Ananias.* This angel conducted *Tobias* in safety; he gave him instructions; and when he was to receive the recompence which the father and son offer'd him, he declar'd that he was the angel of the Lord; took his flight towards heaven, and disappear'd. Here is a great conformity in the ideas and in the style; and the example of our author so long before *Tobit*, proves, that this opinion of God's sending his angels to the aid of man was very common, and much spread amongst the pagans in those former times.   *Dacier.*

519. *Blest is the man,* &c.] *Homer* now begins after a beautiful and long fable, to give the moral of it, and display his poetical justice in rewards and punishments: Thus *Hector* fought in a bad cause, and therefore suffers in the defence of it; but because he was a good man, and obedient to the Gods in other respects, his very remains become the care of heaven.

I think it necessary to take notice to the reader, that nothing is more admirable than the conduct of *Homer* throughout his whole poem, in respect to morality. He justifies the character of *Horace*,

> – *Quid pulchrum, quid turpe, quid utile, quid non,*
> *Plenius & melius Chrysippo & Crantore dicit.*

[Homer states – more fully and better than (the philosophers) Chrysippus and Crantor – what is beautiful, what is base, what is useful and what is not.]

If the Reader does not observe the morality of the *Ilias*, he loses half, and the nobler part of its beauty: He reads it as a common romance, and mistakes the chief aim of it, which is to instruct.

531. *But can I, absent, &c.*] In the original of this place (which I have paraphras'd a little) the word Συλεύειν [to rob] is remarkable. *Priam* offers *Mercury* (whom he looks upon as a soldier of *Achilles*) a present, which he refuses, because his prince is ignorant of it: This present he calls a direct *theft* or *robbery*; which may shew us how strict the notions of justice were in the days of *Homer*, when if a prince's servant receiv'd any present without the knowledge of his master, he was esteem'd a thief and a robber.   *Eustathius.*

553. *Of fir the roof was rais'd.*] I have in the course of these observations describ'd the method of encamping used by the *Grecians*: The reader has here a full and exact description of the tent of *Achilles*: This royal pavilion was built with long palisadoes made of fir; the top of it cover'd with reeds, and the inside was divided into several apartments: Thus *Achilles* had his αὐλὴ μεγάλη, or large hall, and behind it were lodging rooms. So in the ninth book *Phœnix* has a bed prepared for him in one apartment, *Patroclus* has another for himself and his captive *Iphis*, and *Achilles* has a third for himself and his mistress *Diomeda.*

But we must not imagine that the other *Myrmidons* had tents of the like dimensions: they were, as *Eustathius* observes, inferior to this royal one of *Achilles*: Which indeed is no better than an hovel, yet agrees very well with the duties of a soldier, and the simplicity of those early times.

I am of opinion that such fixed tents were not used by the *Grecians* in their common marches, but only during the time of sieges, when their long stay in one place made it necessary to build such tents as are here describ'd; at other times they lay like *Diomed* in the tenth book, in the open air, their spears standing upright, to be ready upon any alarm; and with the hides of beasts spread on the ground instead of a bed.

It is worthy observation that *Homer* even upon so trivial an occasion as the describing the tent of *Achilles*, takes an opportunity to shew the superior strength of his hero; and tells us that three men could scarce open the door of his pavilion, but *Achilles* could open it alone.

569. *Nor stand confest to frail mortality.*] *Eustathius* thinks it was from this maxim, that the Princes of the east assum'd that air of majesty which separates them from the sight of their subjects; but I should rather believe that *Homer* copied this after the originals from some Kings of his time: it not being unlikely that this policy is very ancient.

Dacier.

571. *Adjure him by his father,* &c.] *Eustathius* observes that *Priam* does not entirely follow the instructions of *Mercury*, but only calls to his remembrance his aged father *Peleus*: And this was judiciously done by *Priam*: For what motive to compassion could arise from the mention of *Thetis*, who was a Goddess, and incapable of misfortune? Or how could *Neoptolemus* be any inducement to make *Achilles* pity *Priam*, when at the same time he flourish'd in the greatest prosperity? Therefore *Priam* only mentions his father *Peleus*, who like him, stood upon the very brink of the grave, and was liable to the same misfortunes he suffer'd. These are the remarks of *Eustathius*, but how then shall we justify *Mercury*, who gave him such improper instructions with relation to *Thetis*? All that can be said in defence of the poet is, that *Thetis*, tho' a Goddess, has thro' the whole course of the *Ilias* been describ'd as a partner in all the afflictions of *Achilles*, and consequently might be made use of as an inducement to raise the compassion of *Achilles*. *Priam* might have said, I conjure thee by the love thou bearest to thy mother, take pity on me! For if she who is a Goddess would grieve for the loss of her beloved son, how greatly must the loss of *Hector* afflict the unfortunate *Hecuba* and *Priam*?

586. *Sudden, (a venerable sight!) appears.*] I fancy this interview between *Priam* and *Achilles* would furnish an admirable subject for a painter, in the surprize of *Achilles*, and the other spectators, the attitude of *Priam*, and the sorrows in the countenance of this unfortunate King.

That circumstance of *Priam*'s kissing the hands of *Achilles* is inimitably fine; he kiss'd, says *Homer*, the hands of *Achilles*, those terrible, murderous hands that had robb'd him of so many sons: By these two words the poet recalls to our mind all the noble actions perform'd by *Achilles* in the whole *Ilias*; and at the same time strikes us with the utmost compassion for this unhappy King, who is reduc'd so low as to be oblig'd to kiss those hands that had slain his subjects, and ruin'd his kingdom and family.

598. *The Speech of* Priam *to* Achilles.] The curiosity of the reader must needs be awaken'd to know how *Achilles* would behave to this unfortunate King; it requires all the art of the poet to sustain the violent character of *Achilles*, and yet at the same time to soften him into compassion. To this end the poet uses no preamble, but breaks directly into that circumstance which is most likely to mollify him, and the two first words he utters are, μνῆσαι Πατρὸς, *see thy father, O* Achilles, *in me!* Nothing could be more happily imagin'd than this entrance into his speech; *Achilles* has every where been describ'd as bearing a great affection to his father, and by two words the poet recalls all the tenderness that love and duty can suggest to an affectionate son.

Priam tells *Achilles* that *Hector* fell in the defence of his country: I am far from thinking that this was inserted accidentally; it could not fail of having a very good effect upon *Achilles*, not only as one brave man naturally loves another, but as it implies that *Hector* had no particular enmity against *Achilles*, but that tho' he fought against him it was in defence of his country.

The reader will observe that *Priam* repeats the beginning of his speech, and recalls his father to his memory in the conclusion of it. This is done with great judgment; the poet takes care to enforce his petition with the strongest motive, and leaves it fresh upon his memory; and possibly *Priam* might perceive that the mention of his father had made a deeper impression upon *Achilles* than any other part of his petition, therefore while the mind of *Achilles* dwells upon it, he again sets him before his imagination by this repetition, and softens him into compassion.

634. *These words soft pity,* &c.] We are now come almost to the end of the poem, and consequently to the end of the anger of *Achilles*: And *Homer* has describ'd the abatement of it with excellent judgment. We may here observe how necessary the conduct of *Homer* was, in sending *Thetis* to prepare her son to use *Priam* with civility: It would have ill suited with the violent temper of *Achilles* to have used *Priam* with tenderness without such pre-admonition; nay, the unexpected sight of his enemy might probably have carried him into violence and rage: But *Homer* has avoided these absurdities; for *Achilles* being already prepared for a reconciliation, the misery of this venerable prince naturally melts him into compassion.

653. Achilles's *speech to* Priam.] There is not a more beautiful passage in the whole *Ilias* than this before us: *Homer* to shew that *Achilles* was not a mere soldier, here draws him as a person of excellent sense and sound reason: *Plato* himself (who condemns this passage) could not speak more like a true philosopher: And it was a piece of great judgment thus to describe him; for the reader would have retain'd but a very indifferent opinion of the hero of a poem, that had no qualification but mere strength: It also shews the art of the poet thus to defer this part of his character till the very conclusion of the poem: By these means he fixes an idea of his greatness upon our minds, and makes his hero go off the stage with applause.

Neither does he here ascribe more wisdom to *Achilles* than he might really be master of; for as *Eustathius* observes, he had *Chiron* and *Phœnix* for his tutors, and a Goddess for his mother.

663. *Two urns by* Jove's *high throne*, &c.] This is an admirable allegory, and very beautifully imagin'd by the poet. *Plato* has accus'd it as an impiety to say that God gives evil: But it seems borrow'd from the eastern way of speaking, and bears a great resemblance to several expressions in scripture: This in the *Psalms*, *In the hand of the Lord there is a cup, and he poureth out of the same; as for the dregs thereof, all the ungodly of the earth shall drink them.*

It was the custom of the *Jews* to give condemn'd persons just before execution, οἶνον ἐσμυρνισμένον, wine mix'd with Myrrh to make them less sensible of pain: Thus *Proverbs* xxxi. 6. *Give strong drink to him that is ready to perish.* This custom was so frequent among the *Jews*, that the cup which was given before execution, came to denote death itself, as in that passage, *Father let this cup pass from me.*

Some have suppos'd that there were three urns, one of good, and two of evil; thus *Pindar*,

> Ἐν γὰρ ἐσθλὸν, πήματα σύνδυο
> Δαίονται βροτοῖς ἀθάνατοι.

[For the immortals distribute two evils for every good to mortals.]

But, as *Eustathius* observes, the word ἕτερος [the one (of two)] shews that there were but two, for that word is never used when more than two are intended.

685. *Extended* Phrygia, *&c.*] *Homer* here gives us a piece of geography, and shews the full extent of *Priam*'s kingdom. *Lesbos* bounded it on the south, *Phrygia* on the east, and the *Hellespont* on the north. This kingdom, according to *Strabo* in the 13th book, was divided into nine dynasties, who all depended upon *Priam* as their king: So that what *Homer* here relates of *Priam*'s power is literally true, and confirmed by History.   *Eustathius.*

706. *While kindling anger sparkled in his eyes.*] I believe every reader must be surpriz'd, as I confess I was, to see *Achilles* fly out into so sudden a passion, without any apparent reason for it. It can scarce be imagin'd that the name of *Hector* (as *Eustathius* thinks) could throw him into so much violence, when he had heard it mention'd with patience and calmness by *Priam* in this very conference: especially if we remember that *Achilles* had actually determin'd to restore the body of *Hector* to *Priam.* I was therefore very well pleas'd to find that the words in the original would bear another interpretation, and such a one as naturally solves the difficulty. The meaning of the passage I fancy may be this: *Priam* perceiving that his address had mollify'd the heart of *Achilles*, takes this opportunity to persuade him to give over the war, and return home; especially since his anger was sufficiently satisfy'd by the fall of *Hector.* Immediately *Achilles* takes fire at this proposal, and answers, 'Is it not enough that I have determin'd to restore thy son? ask no more, lest I retract that resolution.' In this view we see a natural reason for the sudden passion of *Achilles.*

What may perhaps strengthen this conjecture is the word πρῶτον [first]; and then the sense will run thus; since I have found so much favour in thy sight, as first to permit me to live, O wouldst thou still enlarge my happiness, and return home to thy own country! *&c.*

This opinion may be farther establish'd from what follows in the latter end of this interview, where *Achilles* asks *Priam* how many days he would request for the interment of *Hector?* *Achilles* had refus'd to give over the war, but yet consents to intermit it a few days; and then the sense will be this, 'I will not consent to return home, but ask a time for a cessation, and it shall be granted.' And what most strongly speaks for this interpretation is the answer of *Priam*; I ask, says he, eleven days to bury my son, and then let the war commence again, since *it must be so*, εἴπερ ἀνάγκη; since you necessitate me to it; or since you will not be persuaded to leave these shores.

706. *While kindling anger sparkled in his eyes.*] The reader may be

pleas'd to observe that this is the last sally of the resentment of *Achilles*; and the poet judiciously describes him moderating it by his own reflection: So that his reason now prevails over his anger, and the design of the poem is fully executed.

709. *For know, from* Jove *my Goddess-mother came.*] The injustice of *La Motte*'s criticism, (who blames *Homer* for representing *Achilles* so mercenary, as to enquire into the price offer'd for *Hector*'s body before he would restore it) will appear plainly from this passage, where he makes *Achilles* expressly say, it is not for any other reason that he delivers the body, but that heaven had directly commanded it. The words are very full.

> — Διόθεν δέ μοι ἄγγελος ἦλθε
> Μήτηρ ἥ μ' ἔτεκεν, θυγάτηρ ἁλίοιο γέροντος,
> Καὶ δέ σε γινώσκω Πρίαμε φρεσίν, οὐδέ με λήθεις,
> Ὅττι Θεῶν τις ἦγε θοὰς ἐπὶ νῆας Ἀχαιῶν.

[cf. Pope's translation, ll. 709–15.]

757. *Not thus did* Niobe, *&c.*] *Achilles*, to comfort *Priam*, tells him a known history; which was very proper to work this effect. *Niobe* had lost all her children, *Priam* had some remaining. *Niobe*'s had been nine days extended on the earth, drown'd in their blood, in the sight of their people, without any one presenting himself to interr them: *Hector* has likewise been twelve days, but in the midst of his enemies; therefore 'tis no wonder that no one has paid him the last duties. The Gods at last interr'd *Niobe*'s children, and the Gods likewise are concern'd to procure honourable funerals for *Hector*.   *Eustathius.*

798. *The royal Guest the Hero eyes, &c.*] The poet omits no opportunity of praising his hero *Achilles*, and it is observable that he now commends him for his more amiable qualities: He softens the terrible idea we have conceiv'd of him, as a warriour, with several virtues of humanity; and the angry, vindictive soldier is become calm and compassionate. In this place he makes his very enemy admire his personage, and be astonish'd at his manly beauty. So that tho' courage be his most distinguishing character, yet *Achilles* is admirable both for the endowments of mind and body.

Ἐπικερτομέων. The sense of this word differs in this place from that it usually bears: It does not imply τραχύτητα ὑβριστικήν, any reproachful asperity of language, but εἰσήγησιν ψευδοῦς φόβου, the raising of a false fear in the old man, that he might not be concern'd at his being lodg'd in the outermost part of the tent; and by this method he gives *Priam* an opportunity of going away in the morning without observation.

Eustathius.

819. *To ask our counsel, or our orders take.*] The poet here shews the importance of *Achilles* in the army; tho' *Agamemnon* be the general, yet all the chief commanders apply to him for advice; and thus he promises *Priam* a cessation of arms for several days, purely by his own authority. The method that *Achilles* took to confirm the truth of the cessation, agrees with the custom which we use at this day, he gave him his hand upon it.

> — χεῖρα γέροντος
> Ἔλλαβε δεξιτερὴν —   *Eustathius.*

[He grabbed hold of the old man's right hand.]

900. *A melancholy choir, &c.*] This was a custom generally receiv'd, and which passed from the *Hebrews* to the *Greeks*, *Romans*, and *Asiaticks.* There were weepers by profession, of both sexes, who sung doleful tunes round the dead. *Ecclesiasticus* cap. 12. v. 5. *When a man shall go into the house of his eternity, there shall encompass him weepers.* It appears from St. *Matthew* xi. 17. that children were likewise employed in this office.   *Dacier.*

906, &c. *The lamentations over* Hector.] The poet judiciously makes *Priam* to be silent in this general lamentation; he has already born a sufficient share in these sorrows, in the tent of *Achilles*, and said what grief can dictate to a father and a King upon such a melancholy subject. But he introduces three women as chief mourners, and speaks only in general of the lamentation of the men of *Troy*, an excess of sorrow being unmanly: Whereas these women might with decency indulge themselves in all the lamentation that fondness and grief could suggest. The wife, the mother of *Hector*, and *Helen*, are the three persons introduced; and tho' they all mourn upon the same occasion, yet their lamentations are so different, that not a sentence that is spoken by the one, could be made use of by the other: *Andromache* speaks like a tender wife, *Hecuba* like a fond mother, and *Helen* mourns with a sorrow rising from self-accusation: *Andromache* commends-his bravery, *Hecuba* his manly beauty, and *Helen* his gentleness and humanity.

Homer is very concise in describing the funeral of *Hector*, which was but a necessary piece of conduct, after he had been so full in that of *Patroclus.*

934. *Why gav'st thou not to me thy dying hand,*
            And why receiv'd not I thy last command?]

I have taken these two lines from Mr. *Congreve*, whose translation of this part was one of his first essays in poetry. He has very justly render'd the sense of Πυκινὸν ἔπος, *dictum prudens* [prudent advice], which is meant of the words of a dying man, or one in some dangerous exigence; at which times what is spoken is usually something of the utmost importance, and deliver'd with the utmost care: Which is the true signification of the epithet Πυκινὸν [solid or prudent] in this place.

We have now past thro' the *Iliad*, and seen the Anger of *Achilles*, and the terrible effects of it, at an end: As that only was the subject of the poem, and the nature of epic poetry would not permit our author to proceed to the event of the war, it may perhaps be acceptable to the common reader to give a short Account of what happen'd to *Troy* and the chief actors in this poem, after the conclusion of it.

I need not mention that *Troy* was taken soon after the death of *Hector*, by the stratagem of the wooden horse, the particulars of which are described by *Virgil* in the second book of the *Æneis.*

Achilles fell before *Troy*, by the hand of *Paris*, by the shot of an arrow in his heel, as *Hector* had prophesied at his death, *lib.* 22.

The unfortunate *Priam* was kill'd by *Pyrrhus* the son of *Achilles.*

Ajax, after the death of *Achilles*, had a contest with *Ulysses* for the armour of *Vulcan*, but being defeated in his aim, he slew himself thro' indignation.

Helen, after the death of *Paris*, married *Deiphobus* his brother, and at the taking of *Troy* betray'd him, in order to reconcile herself to *Menelaus* her first husband, who receiv'd her again into favour.

Agamemnon at his return was barbarously murther'd by *Ægysthus* at the instigation of *Clytæmnestra* his wife, who in his absence had dishonour'd his bed with *Ægysthus.*

Diomed after the fall of *Troy* was expell'd his own country, and scarce escap'd with life from his adulterous wife *Ægiale*; but at last was receiv'd by *Daunus* in *Apulia*, and shar'd his kingdom: 'Tis uncertain how he died.

Nestor liv'd in peace, with his Children, in *Pylos* his native country.

Ulysses also after innumerable troubles by sea and land, at last return'd in safety to *Ithaca*, which is the subject of *Homer*'s *Odysses*.

I must end these notes by discharging my duty to two of my friends, which is the more an indispensable piece of justice, as the one of them is since dead: The merit of their kindness to me will appear infinitely the greater, as the task they undertook was in its own nature of much more labour, than either pleasure or reputation. The larger part of the extracts from *Eustathius*, together with several excellent observations were sent me by Mr. *Broome*: And the whole essay upon *Homer* was written upon such memoirs as I had collected, by the late Dr. *Parnell*, Archdeacon of *Clogher* in *Ireland*: How very much that gentleman's friendship prevail'd over his genius, in detaining a writer of his spirit in the drudgery of removing the rubbish of past pedants, will soon appear to the world, when they shall see those beautiful pieces of poetry the publication of which he left to my charge, almost with his dying breath.

For what remains, I beg to be excused from the ceremonies of taking leave at the end of my work; and from embarassing myself, or others, with any defences or apologies about it. But instead of endeavouring to raise a vain monument to my self, of the merits or difficulties of it (which must be left to the world, to truth, and to posterity) let me leave behind me a memorial of my friendship, with one of the most valuable men as well as finest writers, of my age and country: One who has try'd, and knows by his own experience, how hard an undertaking it is to do justice to *Homer*: And one, who (I am sure) sincerely rejoices with me at the period of my labours. To him therefore, having brought this long work to a conclusion, I desire to *dedicate* it; and to have the honour and satisfaction of placing together, in this manner, the names of Mr. *C O N G R E V E,* and of

March 25.   *A. P O P E.*
1720.

Τῶν θεῶν δὲ εὐποΐα, τὸ μὴ ἐπὶ πλέον με προκόψαι ἐν Ποιητικοῖς ἐπιτηδεύμασι, ἐν οἷς ἴσως ἂν κατεσχέθην, εἰ ἠσθόμην ἐμαυτὸν εὐόδως προϊόντα. M. AUREL. ANTON. *de seipso*, L. 1. § 17.

[It was through the beneficence of the gods that I made no more progress in my poetic pursuits, in which I would perhaps have been detained had I perceived that my efforts were successful.]

FINIS

AN INDEX OF
PERSONS AND THINGS

A POETICAL INDEX
TO HOMER'S *ILIAD*

The first number marks the book, the second the verse.

FABLE

The great *Moral* of the Iliad, that *Concord, among Governours, is the preservation of States, and Discord the ruin of them*: pursued thro' the whole *Fable*.

The Anger of Achilles breaks this union in the opening of the poem, *l.* 1. He withdraws from the body of the *Greeks*, which first interrupts the success of the common cause, *ibid.* The Army mutiny, *l.* 2. The *Trojans* break the Truce, *l.* 4. A great number of the *Greeks* slain, 7. 392. Forc'd to build Fortifications to guard their Fleet, *ibid.* In great distress from the enemy, whose victory is only stopt by the night, 8. Ready to quit their design, and return with infamy, 9. Send to *Achilles* to persuade him to a re-union, in vain, *ibid.* The distress continues; the General and all the best warriours are wounded, 11. The fortification overthrown, and the fleet set on fire, 15. *Achilles* himself shares in the misfortunes he brought upon the allies, by the loss of his friend *Patroclus*, 16. Hereupon the hero is reconciled to the General, the victory over *Troy* is compleat, and *Hector* slain by *Achilles*, 19, 20, 21, 22, *&c.*

EPISODES *or* FABLES *which are interwoven into the Poem, but foreign to its design*

The Fable of the conspiracy of the Gods against *Jupiter*, 1. 516. Of *Vulcan*'s fall from heav'n on the Island of *Lemnos*, 1. 761. The imprisonment of *Mars* by *Otus* and *Ephialtes*, 5. 475. The story of *Thamyris*, 2. 721. The embassy of *Tydeus* to *Thebes*, 4. 430. The tale of *Bellerophon*, 6. 195. Of *Lycurgus* and the *Bacchanals*, 6. 161. The war of the *Pylians* and *Arcadians*, 6. 165. The story of *Phoenix*, 9. 572. Of *Meleager* and the Wars of the *Curetes* and *Ætolians*, 9. 653. The wars of *Pyle* and *Elis*, 11. 818. The birth of *Hercules* and labour of *Alcmena*, 19. 103. The expulsion of *Ate* from heaven, 19. 93. *Vulcan*'s abode with *Thetis*, and his employment there, 18. 463. The family and history of *Troy*, 20. 255. The transformation of *Niobe*, 24. 757. Building of the walls of *Troy* by *Neptune*, 21. 518.

ALLEGORICAL FABLES

Moral.] *Prudence* restraining *Passion*, represented in the machine of *Min-*

erva descending to calm *Achilles*, 1. 261. Love alluring, and extinguishing *Honour*, in *Venus* bringing *Paris* from the combate to the arms of *Helen*, 3. 460, &c. True *Courage* overcoming *Passion* in *Diomed*'s conquest of *Mars* and *Venus*, by the assistance of *Pallas*, 5. 407, &c. *through that whole book.* Prayers the daughters of *Jupiter*, following *Injustice* and persecuting her at the throne of heaven, 9. 625. The *Cestus*, or girdle of *Venus*, 14. 247. The allegory of *Sleep*, 14. 265. The allegory of *Discord* cast out of heaven, to earth, 19. 93. The allegory of the two *Urns* of *Pleasure* and *Pain*, 24. 663.

Physical or Philosophical.] The combate of the *elements* till the *water* subsided, in the fable of the wars of *Juno* or the *Air*, and *Neptune* or the *Sea*, with *Jupiter* or the *Æther*, till *Thetis* put an end to 'em, 1. 516. *Fire* deriv'd from heaven to earth, imag'd by the fall of *Vulcan* on *Lemnos*, 1. 761. The gravitation of the *Planets* upon the *Sun*, in the Allegory of the *golden chain* of *Jupiter*, 8. 25. The influence of the *Æther* upon the *Air*, in the allegory of the congress of *Jupiter* and *Juno*, 14. 395. The *Air* supply'd by the vapours of the *Ocean* and *Earth*, in the story of *Juno* nourish'd by *Oceanus* and *Tethys*, 14. 231. The allegory of the *Winds*, 23. 242. The quality of *Salt* preserving dead bodies from corruption, in *Thetis* or the *Sea* preserving the body of *Patroclus*, 19. 40.

For the rest of the Allegories, *see the* System of the Gods *as acting in their allegorical characters, under the article* CHARACTERS.

ALLEGORICAL *or* FICTITIOUS PERSONS *in* HOMER

The *lying dream* sent to *Agamemnon* by *Jupiter*, 2. 7. *Fame* the messenger of *Jove*, 2. 121. *Furies*, punishers of the wicked, 3. 351. *Hebe*, or *Youth*, attending the banquets of the Gods, 4. 3. *Flight* and *Terror* attendants upon *Mars*, 4. 500. *Discord* describ'd, 4. 502. *Bellona* Goddess of war, 5. 726. The *Hours*, keepers of the gates of heaven, 5. 929. Nymphs of the mountains, 6. 532. *Night*, a Goddess, 6. 342. *Iris*, or the *Rainbow*, 8. 486. *Prayers* the daughters of *Jupiter*, 9. 625. *Eris*, or *Discord*, 11. 5. *Ilythiæ*, Goddesses presiding in women's labour, 11. 349. *Terror* the son of *Mars*, 13. 386. *Sleep*, 14. 265. *Night*, 14. 293. *Death* and *Sleep*, two twins, 16. 831. *Nereids*, or nymphs of the sea, a catalogue of them, 18. 45. *Ate*, or the Goddess of *Discord*, 19. 93. *Scamander* the River-God, 21. 231. *Fire* and *Water* made Persons in the battel of *Scamander* and *Vulcan*, 21. 387. The *East* and *West-Winds*, ibid. *Iris*, or the *Rainbow*, and the *Winds*, 23. 242.

The MARVELLOUS, *or* supernatural FICTIONS *in* HOMER

Omen of the birds and serpent representing the event of the *Trojan* war, 2. 370. The miraculous rivers *Titaresius* and *Styx*, 2. 910. The giant *Typhon* under the burning mountain *Typhœus*, 2. 952. Battel of the cranes and pygmies, 3. 6. Prodigy of a comet, 4. 101. *Diomed*'s helmet ejecting fire, 5. 6. Horses of cœlestial breed, 5. 327. Vast stone heav'd by *Diomed*, 5. 370. And *Hector*, 12. 537. And *Minerva*, 20. 470. The miraculous chariot and arms of *Pallas*, 5. 885, 907, &c. The *Gorgon*; helmet, and *Ægis* of *Jupiter*, *ibid.* The gates of heaven, *ibid.* The leap of immortal horses, 5. 960. Shout of *Stentor*, 5. 978. Roaring of *Mars*, 5. 1054. Helmet of *Oreus*, which render'd the wearer invisible, 5. 1036. The *blood* of the Gods, 5. 422. The immediate healing of their wounds, 5. 1116. The *chimæra*, 6. 220. Destruction by *Neptune* of the *Grecian* rampart, 12. 15. Wall push'd down by *Apollo*, 15. 415. The golden chain of *Jupiter*, 8. 25. Horses and chariot of *Jupiter*, 8. 50. His balances, weighing the fates of men, 8. 88. 22. 271. *Jupiter's* assisting the *Trojans* by thunders and lightnings, and visible declarations of his favour, 8. 93, 165, &c. 17. 670. Prodigy of an eagle and fawn, 8. 297. Horses of the Gods, stables and chariots, pompously describ'd, 8. 535, &c. *Hector's* lance of ten cubits, 8. 615. Omen of an heron, 10. 320. The descent of *Eris*, 11. 5. A shower of blood, 11. 70 – 16. 560. Omen of an eagle and serpent, 12. 230. The progress of *Neptune* thro' the seas, 13. 42. The *War* and *Discord* stretch'd over the armies, 13. 451. The loud voice of *Neptune*, 14. 173. Solemn oath of the Gods, 14. 307 – 15. 41. *Minerva* spreads a light over the army, 15. 808. *Jupiter* involves the combatants in thick darkness, 16. 695, 422. Horses begot by the wind on a harpye, 16. 183. A shower of blood, 16. 560. Miraculous transportation and interment of *Sarpedon* by *Apollo*, *Sleep* and

Death, 16. 810, &c. Prophecy at the hour of death, 16. 1026 – 22. 450. *Achilles* unarmed puts the whole *Trojan* army to flight on his appearance, 18. 240, &c. Moving tripods and living statues of *Vulcan*, 18. 440, 488. The horse of *Achilles* speaks by a prodigy, 19. 450. The battel of the Gods, 20. 63, &c. Horses of a miraculous extraction, the transformation of *Boreas*, 20. 264. The wonderful battel of the *Xanthus*, 21. 230, &c. *Hector's* body preserv'd by *Apollo* and *Venus*, 23. 226. The ghost of *Patroclus*, 23. 77. The two urns of *Jupiter*, 24. 663. The vast quoit of *Aëtion*, 23. 975. The transformation of *Niobe* and her people into stones, 24. 757.

Under this head of the Marvellous *may also be included all the immediate* machines *and* appearances of the Gods *in the Poem, and their* transformations; *the* miraculous birth *of* heroes; *the* passions in human and visible forms, *and the rest.*

CHARACTERS, OR MANNERS

Characters of the GODS *of* HOMER, *as acting in the* PHYSICAL *or* MORAL *capacities of those deities*

JUPITER

Acting and governing all, as the supreme Being.] See the article *Theology* in the next *Index.*

JUNO

As the element of Air.] Her congress with *Jupiter*, or the *Æther*, and production of vegetables, 14. 390, &c. Her loud shout, the air being the cause of sound, 5. 978. Nourish'd by *Oceanus* and *Tethys*, 14. 231.

As Goddess of Empire and Honour.] Stops the *Greeks* from flying ignominiously, 2. 191. *and in many other places.* Incites and commands *Achilles* to revenge the death of his friend, 18. 203, &c. Inspires into *Helen* a contempt of *Paris*, and sends *Iris* to call her to behold the combate with *Menelaus*, 3. 185.

APOLLO

As the Sun.] Causes the plague in the heat of summer, 1. 61. Raises a phantom of clouds and vapours, 5. 545. Discovers in the morning the slaughter made the night before, 10. 606. Recovers *Hector* from fainting, and opens his eyes, 15. 280. Dazzles the eyes of the *Greeks*, and shakes his *Ægis* in their faces, 15. 362. Restores vigour to *Glaucus*, 16. 647. Preserves the body of *Sarpedon* from corruption, 16. 830. And that of *Hector*, 23. 230. Raises a cloud to conceal *Æneas*, 20. 515.

As Destiny.] Saves *Æneas* from death, 5. 441. And *Hector*, 20. 513. Saves *Agenor*, 21. 706. Deserts *Hector* when his hour is come, 22. 277.

As Wisdom.] He and *Minerva* inspire *Helenus* to keep off the general engagement by a single combate, 7.

25. Advises *Hector* to shun encountering *Achilles*, 20. 431.

MARS

As mere martial courage without conduct.] Goes to the fight against the orders of *Jupiter*, 5. 726. Again provoked to rebel against *Jupiter* by his passion, 15. 126. Is vanquish'd by *Minerva*, or *Conduct*, 21. 480.

MINERVA

As martial courage with Wisdom.] Joins with *Juno* in restraining the *Greeks* from flight, and inspires *Ulysses* to do it, 2. 210. Animates the army, 2. 525. Describ'd as leading a hero safe thro' a battel, 4. 632. Assists *Diomed* to overcome *Mars* and *Venus*, 5. 407, 1042. Overcomes them her self, 21. 480. Restrains *Mars* from rebellion against *Jupiter*, 5. 45 − 15. 140. Submits to *Jupiter*, 8. 40. Advises *Ulysses* to retire in time from the night expedition, 10. 593. Assists him throughout that expedition, 10. 350, &c. Discovers the ambush laid against the *Pylians* by night, and causes them to sally, 11. 851. Assists *Achilles* to conquer *Hector*, 22. 277, &c.

As Wisdom separately consider'd.] Suppresses *Achilles's* passion, 1. 261. Suppresses her own anger against *Jupiter*, 4. 31. Brings to pass *Jupiter's* Will in contriving the breach of the truce, 4. 95. Teaches *Diomed* to discern Gods from men, and to conquer *Venus*, 5. 155, &c. Call'd the best belov'd of *Jupiter*, 8. 48. Obtains leave of *Jupiter*, that while the other Gods do not assist the *Greeks*, she may direct 'em with her counsels, 8. 45. Is again check'd by the command of *Jupiter* and submits, 8. 506, 580. Is said to assist, or save any hero, in general thro' the Poem, when any act of prudence preserves him.

VENUS

As the passion of love.] Brings *Paris* from the fight to the embraces of *Helen*, and inflames the lovers, 3. 460, 530, &c. Is overcome by *Minerva*, or Wisdom, 5. 407. And again, 21. 500. Her *Cestos* or girdle, and the effects of it, 14. 247.

NEPTUNE

As the sea.] Overturns the *Grecian* wall with his waves, 12. 15. Assists the *Greeks* at their fleet, which was drawn up at the sea-side, 13. 67, &c. Retreats at the order of *Jupiter*, 15. 245. Shakes the whole field of battel and sea-shore with earthquakes, 20. 77.

VULCAN

Or the Element of Fire.] Falls from heaven to earth, 1. 761. Receiv'd in *Lemnos*, a place of subterraneous fires, *ibid.* His operations of various kinds, 18. 440, 468, 540. Dries up the river *Xanthus*, 21. 460. Assisted by the winds, 21. 390.

Characters of the
HEROES

N.B. *The* Speeches *which depend upon, and flow from these several characters, are distinguished by an* S.

ACHILLES

Furious, passionate, disdainful, and reproachful, *lib.* 1. 155. S. 195. S. 295. S – 9. 405. S. 746. S – 24. 705.
Revengeful and implacable in the highest degree, 9. 765. 755. – 16. 68. S. 121. S. – 19. 211. S – 22. 333. S. 437. S. 18. 120. 125. S. –
Cruel, 16. 122 – 19. 395 – 21. 112 – 22. 437. S. 495. S – 23. 30 – 24. 51 –
Superiour to all men in valour, 20. 60. 437, &c. – *l.* 21. 22. throughout.
Constant and violent in friendship, 9. 730. 18. 30 – 371 – 23. 54. 272 – 24. 5 – 16. 9. S. 208. S. 18. 100. S. 380. S – 19. 335. S – 22. 482. S. – *Achilles* scarce ever speaks without mention of his friend *Patroclus.*

ÆNEAS

Pious to the Gods, 5. 226. S – 20. 132. 290. 345 –
Sensible, and moral, 20. 242. 293, &c. S.
Valiant, not rash, 20. 130. 240 – S.
Tender to his friend, 13. 590.

See this character in the notes on l. 5. v. 212. *and on* l. 13. v. 578.

AGAMEMNON

Imperious and passionate, 1. 34. 729 S –
Sometimes cruel, 6. 80 – 2. 140 S –
Artful and designing, 2. 68. 95 –
Valiant and an excellent General, 4. 256.
    265, &c. 11. throughout.
Eminent for brotherly affection, 4. 183,
    &c. S. 7. 120 –

    See his character in the notes on l. 11.
v. 1.

AJAX

Of superiour strength and size, and fear-
    less on that account, 13. 410 – 7.
    227. S. 274. S – 15. 666.
Indefatigable and patient, 11. 683, &c.
    13. 877 – 15. throughout – 14. 535 –
    short in his speeches, 7. 227 – 9. 742
    – 15. 666, &c.

    See his character in the notes on l. 7. v.
226.

DIOMED

Daring and intrepid, 5. throughout, and
    8. 163. 180 S – 9. 65. 820 – 10. 260 –
Proud and boasting, 6. 152 – 11. 500.
Vain of his birth, 14. 125.
Generous, 6. 265 –
Is guided by Pallas or Wisdom, and
    chuses Ulysses to direct him, 5.
    throughout. 10. 287. 335.

    See his character in the notes on l. 5. v. 1.

HECTOR

A true lover of his country, 8. 621. S –
    12. 284 – 15. 582. S.

Valiant in the highest degree, 3. 89 – 7.
    80. 12. 270. S – 18. 333. S – &c.
Excellent in conduct, 8. 610. S. – 11.
    663 –
Pious, 6. 140. 335. 605 –
Tender to his parents, 6. 315.
    – to his wife, 6. 456.
    – to his child, 6. 606.
    – to his friends, 20. 485 – 24. 962 –

    See his character in the notes on l. 3. v. 53.

IDOMENEUS

An old soldier, 13. 455. 648 –
A lover of his soldiers, 13. 280 –
Talkative upon subjects of war, 13. 340
    – 355, &c. 4. 305. S –
Vain of his family, 13. 565, &c.
Stately and insulting, 13. 472 – &c.

    See his character in the notes on l. 13.
v. 279.

MENELAUS

Valiant, 3. 35 – 13. 733 – 17.
    throughout.
Tender of the people, 10. 32 –
Gentle in his nature, 10. 138 – 23. 685 –
But fir'd by a sense of his wrongs, 2.
    711 – 3. 45 – 7. 109. S – 13. 780. S
    – 17. 640.

    See his character in the notes on l. 3. v.
278.

NESTOR

Wise and experienced in council, 1. 331.
    340 – 2. 441 –
Skilful in the art of war, 2. 432. 670 – 4.
    338, &c. S. 7. 392. S –
Brave, 7. 165 – 11. 817 – 15. 796. S.

Eloquent, 1. 332. *&c.*
Vigilant, 10. 88. 186. 624 –
Pious, 15. 427.
Talkative thro' old age, 4. 370 – 7. 145
– 11. 800 – 23. 373. 718 – and in
general thro' the book.

See his character in the notes on l. 1. v.
339. *on* 2. 402, *&c.*

PARIS

Effeminate in dress and person, 3. 27.
55. 80. 409.
Amorous, 3. 550.
Ingenious in arts, musick, 3. 80. Build-
ing, 6. 390.
Patient of reproof, 3. 86.
Naturally valiant, 6. 669 – 13. 985.

See his characters in the notes on l. 3.
v. 26. 37. 86.

PATROCLUS

Compassionate of the sufferings of his
countrymen, 11. 947 – 16. 5. 31. S.
Rash, but valiant, 16. 709.
Of a gentle nature, 19. 320 – 17. 755 –

PRIAM

A tender father to *Hector*, 22. 51. S –
24. 275 – to *Paris*, 3. 381 – to *Helen*,
3. 212. S.
An easy Prince, of too yielding a temper,
7. 443.
Gentle and compassionate, 3. 211. 382.
Pious, 4. 70 – 24. 520. S.

See his character in the notes on l. 3. v.
211.

SARPEDON

Valiant, out of principle and honour, 5.
575. S – 12. 371. S.
Eloquent, *ibid.*
Careful only of the common cause in his
death, 16. 605. S.

See his character in the notes on l. 16.
v. 512.

ULYSSES

Prudent, 3. 261 – 10. 287 – 19. 218 –
Eloquent, 3. 283 – 9. 295. S. *&c.*
Valiant in the field with caution, 4. 566
– 11. 515, *&c.*
Bold in the council with prudence, 14.
90 –

See his character in the notes on l. 2. v.
402. *& sparsim.*

Characters of other
HEROES

Agenor, valiant and considerate, 21. 648.
Antenor, a prudent Counsellor, 7. 418.
Ajax Oïleus, famous for swiftness, 2.
631 – 14. 618.
Antilochus, bold-spirited, but reason-
able; and artful, 4. 522 – 23. 505.
618. 666. S – 23. 910, 930.
Euphorbus, beautiful and valiant, 16. 973
– 17. 11. 57 –
Glaucus, pious to his Friend, 16. 660 –
17. 165. 180.
Helenus, a Prophet and Hero, 6. 92.
Meriones, dauntless and faithful, 13. 325,
&c.
Machaon, an excellent physician, 2. 890
– 11. 630.

Phœnix, his friendship and tenderness for *Achilles*, 9. 605.

Polydamas, Prudent and eloquent. *See his speeches*, 12. 70. 245 – 13. 907 – 18. 300 –

Teucer, famous for archery, 8. 320 – 15. 510, &c.

Thoas, famous for eloquence, 15. 322.

For other less distinguished characters, see the article, Descriptions of the Passions.

SPEECHES, OR ORATIONS

A table of the most considerable in the
ILIAD

In the exhortatory or deliberative Kind

The oration of *Nestor* to *Agamemnon* and *Achilles*, persuading a reconciliation, 1. 340. The orations of *Nestor*, *Ulysses*, and *Agamemnon*, to persuade the army to stay, 2. 350. 402. 452. Of *Sarpedon* to *Hector* 5. 575. Of *Nestor* to encourage the *Greeks* to accept the challenge of *Hector*, 7. 145. Of *Hector* to the *Trojans*, 8. 621. Of *Nestor* to send to *Achilles*, 9. 127. Of *Ulysses*, *Phœnix* and *Ajax*, to move *Achilles* to a reconciliation, 9. 295. 562. 742. *Achilles*'s reply to each, *ibid*. Sarpedon to *Glaucus*, 12. 371. Of *Neptune* to the *Greeks*, to defend the fleet, 13. 131. Of *Ajax* to the *Greeks*, 15. 666. *Nestor* to the same, 15. 796. Of *Ajax* again, 15. 890. *Scamander* to the river *Simoïs*, 21. 360. *Juno* to *Vulcan*, 21. 387. *Achilles* to *Patroclus*, 16. 70, &c.

In the vituperative kind

The speech of *Thersites*, 2. 275. That of *Ulysses* answering him, 2. 306. Of *Hector* to *Paris*, 3. 55. Of *Agamemnon* to *Diomed*, 4. 422. Of *Hector* to *Paris*, 6. 406. Of *Diomed* to *Agamemnon*, 9. 43. Of *Ulysses* to the same, 14. 90. *Sarpedon* to *Hector*, 5. 575. *Glaucus* to *Hector*, 17. 153.

In the narrative

Achilles to *Thetis*, 1. 476. *Pandarus* to *Æneas*, 5. 230. *Glaucus* to *Diomed*, 6. 190. *Phœnix* to *Achilles*, 9. 562, 652. – *Agamemnon* to the *Greeks*, 19. 90. *Æneas* to *Achilles*, 20. 240. Of *Nestor*, 7. 163 – 11. 800 – and the speeches of *Nestor* in general.

In the pathetic

Agamemnon on *Menelaus* wounded, 4. 186.

Andromache to *Hector*, and his answer, 6. 510. 570.

Patroclus and *Achilles*, 16. 10, &c.

Jupiter on sight of *Hector*, 17. 231.

Lamentation of *Briseïs* for *Patroclus*, 19. 303.

Lamentation of *Achilles* for *Patroclus*, 19. 335.

— of *Priam* to *Hector*, 22. 51. 530.

— of *Hecuba* to the same, 22. 115. and again, 24. 243. 942.

— of *Andromache* at *Hector*'s death, 22. 608.

— of *Andromache* at his funeral, 24. 908.

— of *Helena*, 24. 962.

Lycaon to *Achilles*, 21. 85.

Thetis to the *Nereïds*, 17. 70.

The ghost of *Patroclus* to *Achilles*, 23. 83.

Priam to *Achilles*, 24. 600.

In the irony, or sarcasm

The speech of *Pallas* on *Venus* being wounded, 5. 509.

DESCRIPTIONS
OR IMAGES

*A collection of the
most remarkable
throughout the Poem*

Descriptions of PLACES

Descriptions of PERSONS

8. 417 – 12. 553 – 13. 1010 – 15. 730 – *Hector*'s dead body dragg'd at the chariot of *Achilles*, 22. 500.

Jupiter in his glory, 1. 15. 172. – 8. 550. in his chariot, 8. 50. 542, *&c.* in his terrors, 17. 670.

Juno, drest, 14. 200.

Lycaon, his youth and unhappy death, 21. 40, *&c.*

Mars and *Bellona* before *Hector* in battel, 5. 726. *Mars* in arms, 7. 252 – 13. 385 – 15. 726 – his monstrous size, 21. 473.

Mercury describ'd, 24. 417.

Neptune, his chariot and progress, 13. 28, *&c.*

Niobe, turn'd into a rock, 24. 773.

Old man, a venerable one, 1. 330. Old counsellors of *Troy* conversing, 3. 197, *&c.* A miserable old man, in *Priam*, 22. 80, *&c.*

Priam passing thro' his people, in
• sorrow, to go to redeem *Hector*, 24. 402. *Priam* weeping at the feet of *Achilles*, 24. 636.

Pallas, her descent from heaven, 4. 99. her armour, spear, and veil, 5. 905 – 8. 466.

Teucer, behind *Ajax*'s shield, 8. 321.

Youth, a beautiful one, kill'd, 4. 542 – 17. 55, *&c.* 20. 537. interceding for Mercy in vain, 21. 75.

A young, and old man slain in war, their picture, 22. 100 –

Descriptions of THINGS

Of an Assembly gathering together, 2. 110 –

Battel. [*See the Article Military Descriptions.*]

Burning up of a field, 21. 400. A bow, 4. 137 –

Blood trickling from a wound, 4. 170, *&c.*

Brightness of a helmet, 5. 5.

Burial of the dead, 7. 494.

A breach made in an attack, 12. 485 –

Boiling water in a cauldron, 18. 405 – 21. 425.

Beacon, 19. 405 –

Beasts sacrific'd, 23. 41.

A Bird shot thro', 23. 1033.

Chariot of *Jupiter*, 8. 50. 542. Of *Neptune*, 13. 41 – Chariot describ'd at large, 24. 335 – 5. 889, *&c.* A chariot race, 23. 353, *&c.* Chariot's over-turn'd, 16. 445. Chariots crushing the bodies, 20. 577.

A Child frighted at a helmet, 6. 595.

Golden chain of *Jupiter*, 8. 25.

A conflagration, 21. 387. 400.

Cookery describ'd, 9. 277 –

Cestus, the game describ'd, 23. 766, *&c.*

Deformity, 2. 263 –

Dancing, 18. 681, *&c.*

Discus, the game describ'd, 23. 927, *&c.*

Diving, 24. 105.

Driving a chariot, 11. 363. 655 –

Dreadful appearance of the Myrmidons, 16. 192 – of *Achilles*, 18. 254.

Darkness, 17. 422.

Death, 16. 1033. 22. 455 – *The Descriptions of different sorts of deaths in Homer, are innumerable, and scatter'd throughout the battels.*

Ægis, or shield of *Jupiter*, 2. 526 – 5. 909 – 15. 350 – 21. 465.

An entrenchment, 7. 520 –

Eagle stung by a serpent, 12. 233 – Eagle soaring, 24. 390.

Furnace and forge describ'd, 18. 540.

Fishes, scorch'd, 21. 413.

Flowers of various kinds, 14. 396 –

Famine, 19. 160, *&c.*

Fall of a warriour headlong into the deep sands, 5. 715.

Fatigue in the day of battel, 2. 58 – 16. 132 – 17. 445.

Fainting, 5. 856 – 11. 460 – 14. 487. 509 –

Fires by night describ'd, 8. 685, *&c.*

Recovery from fainting, 15. 271.

War, its miseries, 9. 709.

Watch by night, 10. 208.

Wrestling describ'd, 23. 821 –

Wound of *Venus* describ'd, 5. 417. *Diomed* wounded, 5. 988. A wound healing, 5. 1111.

Water, Troops plunging in, 21. 9. A fight in the water, 21. A Tree falling in the water, 21. 269. Water rolling down a hill in a current, 21. 290. Arms floating upon the water, 21. 351.

Winds rising, 23. 261.

Descriptions of TIMES *and* SEASONS

Day-break, 10. 295 –

Morning, 2. 60 – 7. 515 – 8. 183 – 9. 833 – 11. 1 – 11. 115 – 19. 1 –

Sun-rising, 11. 871 –

Noon, 16. 938 –

Sun-setting, 1. 716 – 7. 556 – 8. 605.

Evening, 16. 942 –

Night, 2. *init.* 10th book *throughout.* A starry night, 8. 687.

Spring, 14. 395 –

Summer, 18. 637.

Autumn, 18. 651. 5. 1060 – 22. 40.

Winter, 12. 175. 331.

MILITARY *Descriptions*

An Army descending on the shore, 2. 117. An army marching, 2. 181. 940. The day of battle, 2. 458. A vast army on the plain, 535, *&c.* to 563. An army going forth to battel, 2. 976 – 13. 59 – 16. 255 – 19. 377.

A Chariot of war, 5. 890, *&c.*

Confusion and noise of battel, 16. 921 –

A single combate, with all the ceremonial, 3. 123, *&c.*

The combate between *Paris* and *Menelaus,* 3. 423.

– of *Hector* and *Ajax*, 7. 250, to 335.

– of *Hector* and *Achilles*, 22.

Squadrons embattled, 4. 322 – 5. 637 – 8. 260 –

First onset of battel, 4. 498, to 515.

A circle inclosing the foe, 5. 772.

Stand of an army, 7. 75. Joining in battel, 8. 75, *&c.* 13. 422 – A rout, 11. 193 – 14. 166 – 16. 440, *&c.* 21. 720 – A fortification attack'd, 12. 170. 201. 304. A breach made, 12. 485. An obstinate close fight, 12. 510 – 15. 860. An army in close order, 13. 177, to 185 – 17. 406. An attack on the sea-side, 14. 452 – Levelling and passing a trench, 15. 408. Attack of the fleet, 15. 677, *&c.* 786. 855, *&c.* A hero arming at all points, *Agamemnon,* 11. 21. *Patroclus,* 16. 162. *Achilles,* 19. 390. Siege of a town, 18. 591, *&c.* Surprize of a convoy, *ibid.* Skirmish, *ibid.* Battle of the Gods, 20. 63, to 90. Two heroes meeting in battel, 20. 192. The rage, destruction and carnage of battel, 20. 574, *&c.*

Descriptions of the INTERNAL PASSIONS, *or of their visible* EFFECTS

Anxiety, in *Agamemnon,* 10. 13, *&c.* 100, *&c.*

Activity, in *Achilles,* 19. 416.

Admiration, 21. 62 – 24. 800 –

Affright, 16. 968 –

Amazement, 24. 590.

Ambition, 13. 458.

Anger, 1. 252.

Awe, 1. 430.

Buffoonry in *Thersites,* 2. 255, *&c.*

Contentment, 9. 520.

Conjugal love, in *Hector* and *Androm.* 6. 510, *&c.*

Courage, 13. 109. 366 – 17. 250.

SIMILES

From BEASTS

The stateliness of a bull, to the port of Agamemnon, 2. 566. – Or a ram stalking before the flock, to Ulysses, 3. 259. A wanton stallion breaking from the pastures and mares, to

Paris issuing from his apartment, 6. 652. A hound following a lion, to *Hector* following the *Grecians*, 8. 407. Dogs watching the folds, to the guards by night, 10. 211. Hounds chasing a hare thro' thick woods, to *Diomed* and *Ulysses* pursuing an enemy by night, 10. 427. A hind flying from a lion, to the *Trojans* flying from *Agamemnon*, 11. 153. Beasts flying from a lion to the same, 10. 227. Hounds chear'd by the hunter, to troops encourag'd by the General, 11. 378. A hunted boar to *Ajax*, 11. 526. A wounded deer encompass'd with wolves, to *Ulysses* surrounded by enemies, 11. 595. An ass surrounded by boys to *Ajax*, 11. 683. A fawn carry'd off by two lions, to the body of *Imbrius* carry'd by the *Ajaxes*, 13. 265. A boar enrag'd, to *Idomeneus* meeting his enemy, 13. 595. An ox rolling in the pangs of death, to a dying warriour, 13. 721. Beasts retreating from hunters, to the *Greeks* retiring, 15. 303. Oxen flying from lions, to the *Greeks* flying from *Apollo* and *Hector*, 15. 366. A hound fastening on a roe, to a hero flying on an enemy, 15. 697. A wild beast wounded and retiring from a multitude, to *Antilochus* his retreat, 15. 702. A hideous assembly of wolves, to the fierce figure of the Myrmidons, 16. 194. Wolves invading the flocks, to the *Greeks*, 16. 420. A bull torn by a lion, to *Sarpedon* kill'd by *Patroclus*, 16. 600. A bull sacrificed, to *Aretus*, 17. 588. Hounds following a boar, to the *Trojans* following *Ajax*, 17. 811. Mules dragging a beam, to heroes carrying a dead body, 17. 832. A panther hunted, to *Agenor*, 21. 978. A hound pursuing a fawn, to *Achilles* pursuing *Hector*, 22. 243.

From LIONS

A Lion rouzing at his prey, to *Menelaus* at sight of *Paris*, 3. 37. A lion falling on the flocks, and wounded by a shepherd, to *Diomed* wounded, 5. 174. A lion among heifers, to the same, 5. 206. Two young lions kill'd by hunters, to two young warriours, 5. 681. A lion destroying the sheep in their folds, to *Ulysses* slaughtering the *Thracians* asleep, 10. 564. The sowr retreat of a lion, to that of *Ajax*, 11. 675. Lion, or boar hunted, to a hero distress'd, 12. 47. A Lion rushing on the flocks, to *Sarpedon's* march, 12. 357. A lion killing a bull, to *Hector* killing *Periphas*, 15. 760. A lion slain, after he has made a great slaughter, apply'd to *Patroclus*, 16. 909. Two lions fighting, to *Hector* and *Patroclus*, 16. 915. A lion and boar at a spring, to the same, 16. 993. A lion putting a whole village to flight, to *Menelaus*, 17. 70. Retreat of a lion, to that of *Menelaus*, 17. 117. A lioness defending her young, to his defence of *Patroclus*, 17. 145. Another retreat of a lion, to that of *Menelaus*, 17. 741. The rage and grief of a lion for his young, to that of *Achilles* for *Patroclus*, 18. 371. A lion rushing on his foe, to *Achilles*, 20. 200.

From BIRDS

A Flight of cranes or swans, to a numerous army, 2. 540. The noise of cranes, to the shouts of an army, 3. 5. An eagle preserving and fighting for her young, to *Achilles* protecting the *Grecians*, 9. 424. A falcon flying at the quarry, to *Neptune's* flight, 13. 91. An eagle stooping at a swan, to *Hector*'s attacking a ship, 15. 836. Two vultures fighting, to *Sarpedon* and *Patroclus*, 16. 522. A vulture driving geese, to *Automedon* scattering the *Trojans*, 17. 527. An eagle casting his eyes on the quarry, to *Menelaus* looking thro' the ranks for *Antilochus*, 17. 761. Cranes afraid of falcons, to the *Greeks* afraid of *Hector* and *Æneas*, 17. 845. A dove afraid of a falcon, to *Diana* afraid of *Juno*, 21. 576. A falcon following a dove, to *Achilles* pursuing *Hector*, 22. 183. An eagle at an hare, to *Achilles* at *Hector*, 22. 391. The broad wings of an eagle extended, to palace-gates set open, 24. 391.

From SERPENTS

A traveller retreating from a serpent, to *Paris* afraid of *Menelaus*, 3. 47. A snake roll'd up in his den, and collecting his anger, to *Hector* expecting *Achilles*, 22. 130.

From INSECTS

Bees swarming, to a numerous army issuing out, 2. 111. Swarms of flies, to the same, 2. 552. Grasshoppers chirping in the sun, to old men talking, 3. 201. Wasps defending their nest, to the multitude and violence of soldiers defending a battlement, 12. 190. Wasps provok'd by children flying at the traveller, to troops violent in an attack, 16. 314. A hornet angry, to *Menelaus* incens'd, 17. 642. Locusts driv'n into a river, to the *Trojans* in *Scamander*, 21. 14.

From FIRES

A forest in flames, to the lustre of armour, 2. 534. The spreading of a conflagration, to the march of an army, 2. 948. Trees sinking in a conflagration, to squadrons falling in battel, 11. 201. The noise of fire in a wood, to that of an army in confusion, 14. 461. A conflagration, to *Hector*, 15. 728. The rumbling and rage of a fire, to the confusion and roar of a routed army, 17. 825. Fires on the hills, and beacons to give signals of distress, to the blaze of *Achilles*'s helmet, 18. 245. A fire running over fields and woods, to the progress and devastations made by *Achilles*, 20. 569. Fire boiling the waters, to *Vulcan* operating on *Scamander*, 21. 425. A fire raging in a town, to *Achilles* in the battel, 21. 608. A town on fire, 22. 518.

From ARTS

The staining of ivory, to the blood running down the thigh of *Menelaus*, 4. 170. An architect observing the rule and line, to leaders preserving the line of battel, 4. 474. An artist managing four horses, and leaping from one to another, compar'd to *Ajax* striding from ship to ship, 15. 822. A builder cementing a wall, to a leader embodying his men, 16. 256. Curriers straining to hide, to soldiers tugging for a dead body, 17. 450. Bringing a current to water a garden, to the pursuit of *Scamander* after *Achilles*, 21. 290. The placing of rafters in a building, to the posture of two wrestlers, 23. 825. The motions of a spinster, the spindle and thread, to the swiftness of a racer, 23. 889. The sinking of a plummet, to the passage of *Iris* thro' the sea, 24. 107.

From TREES

The Fall of a poplar, to that of *Simoisius*, 4. 552. Of a beautiful olive, to that of *Euphorbus*, 17. 57. Two tall oakes on the mountains, to two heroes, 12. 145. The fall of an ash, to that of *Imbrius*, 13. 241. Of a pine or oak stretch'd on the ground, to *Asius* dead, 13. 493. An oak overturn'd by a thunderbolt, to *Hector* fell'd by a stone, 14. 408. An oak, pine or poplar falling, to *Sarpedon*, 16. 591.

From the SEA

Rolling billows, to an army in motion, 2. 175. The murmurs of waves, to the noise of a multitude, 2. 249. Succession of waves, to the moving of troops, 4. 478. A fresh gale to weary mariners, like the coming of *Hector* to his troops, 7. 5. The seas settling themselves, to thick troops compos'd in order and silence, 7. 71. The sea agitated by different winds, to the army in doubt and confusion, 9. 5. The waves rolling neither way, till one wind sways 'em, to *Nestor*'s doubt and sudden resolution, 14. 21. A rock breaking the billows, to the body of *Greeks* resisting the *Trojans*, 15. 746. The sea roaring at its reception of a river into it, to the meeting of armies at a charge, 17. 310. A beacon to mariners at sea, to the light of *Achilles*'s shield, 19. 405. A dolphin pursuing the lesser fish, to *Achilles* in *Scamander*, 21. 30.

From the SUN, MOON, STARS

The moon and stars in glory, to the brightness and number of the *Trojan* fires, 8. 687. A star sometimes shewing and sometimes hiding itself in clouds, to *Hector* seen by fits thro' the battalions, 11. 83. The sun in glory, to *Achilles*, 19. 436. The evening star, to the point of his spear, 22. 399. The dog-star rising, to *Diomed*'s dreadful appearance, 5. 8. – to *Achilles*, 22. 37. The red rays of the dog star, to *Achilles*'s helmet, 19. 412. The morning star, its beauty, to young *Astyanax*, 6. 499.

From TORRENTS, STORMS, WINDS

Torrents rushing to the vallies, to armies meeting in an engagement, 4. 516. Torrents drowning the field, to the rage of a hero, 5. 116. A Torrent stopping a shepherd, to *Hector* stopping *Diomed*, 5. 734. The violence of a torrent, to *Ajax*, 11. 615. A storm overwhelming a ship at sea, to the *Trojans* mounting a breach, 15. 440. An autumnal storm and a deluge, to the ruin of a routed army, 16. 467. A storm roaring in a wood, to armies shouting, 16. 923. The wind tossing the clouds, to *Hector* driving the *Greeks*, 11. 396. Different winds driving the dust, to different passions urging the combatants, 13. 425. A whirlwind on the waters, to a hurry of an army in motion, 13. 1000. Winds roaring thro' woods, or on the seas, to the noise of an army,

14. 457. A tempest and shipwreck, compar'd to the rage of *Hector* and terrors of the *Greeks*, 15. 752. The north wind drying a garden, to *Vulcan* drying the field after an inundation, 21. 403.

From heavenly appearances, THUNDER and LIGHTNING, COMETS, CLOUDS, &c.

A mountain shaken by thunder, to the trampling of an army, 2. 950. The blaze of a comet, to the descent of *Pallas*, 4. 101. The darkness of troops, to the gathering of clouds, 4. 314. The regular appearance of clouds on the mountain tops, to a line of battel, 5. 641. Pestilential vapors ascending, to *Mars* flying to heaven, 5. 1058. The quick flashes of lightning, to the thick sighs of *Agamemnon*, 10. 5. Thick flakes of snow, to showers of arrows, 12. 175. Snow covering the earth, to heaps of stones hiding the fields, 12. 331. The blaze of lightning, to the arms of *Idomeneus*, 13. 318. Clouds dispers'd and the prospect appearing, to the smokes being clear'd from the ships, and the navy appearing, 16. 354. A cloud shading the fields as it rises, to the rout of *Trojans* flying over the plain, 16. 434. The figure of a rainbow, to the appearance of *Pallas*, 17. 616. The lustre of snow, to that of armour, 19. 380.

From RURAL AFFAIRS

Waving of corn in the field, to the motion of plumes and spears, 2. 179.

A shepherd gathering his flocks, to a general ranging his army, 2. 562. A thick mist on the mountains, to the dust rais'd by an army, 3. 15. The bleating of flocks, to the noise of men, 4. 492. Chaff flying from the barn-floor, to the dust, 5. 611. Corn falling in ranks, to men slain in battle, 10. 90. The joy of a shepherd seeing his flock, to the joy of a General surveying his army, 13. 620. The corn bounding from the threshing-floor, to an arrow bounding from armour, 13. 739. Two bulls plowing, to two heroes labouring in a battel side by side, 13. 879. Felling of timber, to the fall of heroes in battel, 16. 767. Oxen trampling out the corn, to horses trampling on the slain, 20. 580. The morning dew reviving the corn, to the exaltation of joy in a man's mind, 23. 678.

From LOW LIFE

A Mother defending her child from a wasp, to *Minerva*'s sheltering *Menelaus* from an arrow, 4. 162. A heifer standing over her young one, to *Menelaus* guarding the body of *Patroclus*, 17. 5. Two countrymen disputing about the limits of their land, to two armies disputing a post, 12. 511. A poor woman weighing wool, the scales hanging uncertain, to the doubtful fates of two armies, 12. 521. Boys building and destroying houses of sand, to *Apollo*'s overturning the *Grecian* wall, 15. 416. A child weeping to his mother, to *Patroclus*'s supplications to *Achilles*, 16. 11.

SIMILES *exalting the*
characters of men by
comparing them to
GODS

Agamemnon compar'd to *Jupiter*, *Mars*,
and *Neptune*, 2. 564. *Ajax* to *Mars*,
7. 252. *Meriones*, to *Mars* rushing to
the battel, 13. 384. *Hector*, to *Mars*
destroying armies, 15. 726.

SIMILES
disadvantagious to the
CHARACTERS

Paris running from *Menelaus*, to a travel-
ler frighted by a snake, 3. 47. A
gawdy, foppish soldier, to a woman
dress'd out, 2. 1063. *Teucer* skulking
behind *Ajax*'s shield, to a child, 8.
325. *Thestor* pull'd from his chariot,
to a fish drawn by an angler, 16.
495. *Ajax* to an ass, patient and
stubborn, 11. 683. *Patroclus* weep-
ing, to an infant, 16. 11. *Cebriones*
tumbling, to a diver, 16. 904.

MISCELLANEOUS
SIMILES

Soft piercing words, to snow, 3. 285.
The closing of a wound, to milk
turning to curd, 5. 1114. The fall of
a hero, to a tower, 4. 528. Indefatig-
able courage, to an axe, 3. 90. *Aga-
memnon* weeping, to a fountain, 9.
19. *Juno* flying, to the mind passing
over distant places, 15. 86. Dancers,
to a wheel turning round, 18. 695. A
warriour breaking the squadrons, to
a mound dividing the course of a
river, 17. 839. Men seeming to run
in a dream, to the course of *Hector*
and *Achilles*, 22. 257. A father

mourning at the funeral of his son,
to *Achilles* for *Patroclus*, 23. 272. A
fragment of a rock falling, to the
furious descent of *Hector*, 13. 191. A
poppy bending the head, to *Gor-
gythion* dying, 8. 371. The swift
motion of the Gods, to the eye pass-
ing over a prospect, 5. 960. The
smoothness of their motion, to the
flight of doves, 5. 971.

VERSIFICATION

Expressing in the sound
the thing describ'd

Made *abrupt* (and without conjunctions)
in expressing haste, 7. 282. 15. 402.
Short, in earnest and vehement entreat-
ies, 21. 420 – 23. 506.
Full of breaks, where disappointment is
imag'd. 18. 101, 144 – 22. 378.
— where rage and fury is express'd, 18.
137.
— where grief is scarce able to go on,
18. 101. 22. 616, 650.
Broken and disorder'd in describing a
stormy sea, 13. 1005.
Straining, imag'd in the sound, 15. 544.
Trembling, imag'd in the sound, 10.
446.
Panting, 13. 721.
Relaxation of all the limbs in death, 7.
18, 22.
A confused noise, 12. 410.
A hard-fought spot of ground, 12. 513,
&c.
Tumbling of a wall, 7. 552.
Bounding of a stone from a rock, 13.
198.
A sudden stop, 13. 199.
Stiffness and slowness of old age, 13.
649, 653 – 23. 423.
A sudden fall, 23. 146.
The rustling and crashing of trees fall-
ing, 23. 147.

The rattling and jumping of carts over rough and rocky way, 23. 139, 140.

A sudden shock of chariots stopp'd, 16. 445.

Leaping over a ditch, 16. 460.

The quivering of feathers in the sun, 19. 415.

Supplanted by a stream, 21. 268, 269.

The flashing of waters, 21. 273.

Bounding and heaving on the waters, 21. 350.

Out of breath, 21. 419, &c.

Voice of different animals expiring, 23. 41, 42, &c.

INDEX OF ARTS AND SCIENCES

The first number marks the book, the second the verse.

ART MILITARY

Praise of art military, 4. 631.

Ambush esteem'd a venturous manner of fighting, *l.* 1. v. 299. *l.* 13. v. 355.

Ambuscade describ'd, 18. 605.

Attack, 12. 95. *&c. ibid.* 171. *&c. ibid.* 305. *&c.*

Arming, the policy of giving the best arms to the strongest, 14. 438.

Besieging, 11. 61 − 12. 170. 303. 534 − 8. 262 − 22. 5.

Single combat, 3. 123, *&c.* − 7. 80, *&c.*

Courts of justice in the camp, 11. 938.

Councils of war, 7. 415 − 8. 610 − 9. 130, *&c.* 10. 146 − 232 − 357 − 18. 290.

Military exercise, 7. 289, *&c.*

Encamping. The manner of encampment of the *Trojans*, 10. 496. Of the *Thracians*, in three lines, their weapons on the ground before them, the chariots as a fence, outward, 10. 544.

Fortification. Walls with battlements, in a line, towers upon those walls, gates at proper distances, and trenches, inclos'd with palisades, 7. 406, and 523. The strong gates to a fortification, how compos'd, 12. 545.

Marshalling of armies, 2. 667, *&c.* Cantoning the troops of each nation under their own leaders, 2. 433. Embodying in an orb, 4. 312. Disposing in order of battle, 4. 342, *&c.* Lines of battle in exact order, 5. 641, *&c.* Where to place the worst soldiers, 4. 344.

Another order of battle, 11. 62.

— In an *orb*, 17. 411. Close fight, 15. 860.

— In the *Phalanx*, 13. 177, *&c.* 15. 744. In the *Testudo*, 22. 6.

Armies drawn up in *two wings*, with a *centre*, 13. 396.

The strength of the army placed in the centre, 13. 401.

Marching an army in silence and discipline, *l.* 3. v. 11 − *l.* 4. 487.

Method of passing a trench and palisades, 12. 65, *&c.*

Plunder and pillage forbidden till the conquest is compleat, 6. 85.

Retreat. The manner of retreat prescrib'd, 5. 746. That of *Ajax*, 11. 675 − 17. 837.

Soldiers taught to row in the gallies, serving both as soldiers and sailors, 2. 876.

Scouts, 10. 43 − 245. and at large in the story of *Diomed*, *Ulysses* and *Dolon*, in that book.

Spies, 18. 605.

Watch-towers, to observe the motions of the foe, 2. 261 – 22. 192.

Watch, at set stations, 7. 455 – Nightly watch by fires, 8. 632. at the fortifications in regular bodies under distinct captains, 9. 110, *&c.* Management of the army by night under fears of surprize, 10. 63, to 226. The manner of the warriors sleeping, 10. 170. The posture of the guards, 10. 210. Better to trust the guard to native troops than to foreigners, 10. 490, *&c.*

AGRICULTURE *and* RURAL ARTS

Tillage. The manner of plowing, 10. 420. 18. 627. Plowing with oxen, 13. 880. with mules, 10. 420. Usual to plow the field three times over, 18. 628. Reaping, 11. 89 – 18. 637. Treading out the corn by oxen instead of threshing, 20. 580. Fanning the chaff, 5. 611. 13. 740.

Pasturage, 18. 667. Meadow grounds with running water, *ibid.* Vintage, 18. 651. Bringing currents to water gardens, 21. 290.

Fishing, by angling, 24. 107. – By diving, 16. 905.

Hunting, the boar, 17. 814. – 11. 526. Lion, 11. 378 – 17. 743. The deer, 11. 595 – 15. 697. The panther, 21. 680. The hare, 10. 427.

Shooting flying, 23. 1030.

ARCHITECTURE

Architecture, the gift of *Minerva*, 5. 80.

Architecture of a palace upon arches, with apartments round a court, built entirely of marble, 6. 304.

— *Paris* skilful in architecture, brings together architects to erect his palace, 6. 391.

Rafters, how placed, 23. 827.

Building walls, 16. 256.

The rule and line, 15. 477.

Architecture of a tent, with a suite of apartments within one another, 24. 555, *&c.*

ASTRONOMY

In general, 18. 560.

Orion and the bear, 18. 563.

The rising of the *dog-star*, 5. 10.

A comet describ'd, 4. 101.

The rainbow, 11. 36.

Power of the stars in nativities, 22. 610.

DIVINATION

Divination *by Augury*, 2. 375, *&c.* 8. 297. 10. 320 – 12. 230 – 13. 1039 – 24. 361, *&c.*

Hector's opinion of augury, 12. 277.

By omens, thunder and lightnings, 7. 571 – 9. 310 – 11. 58 – 13. 319.

The rainbow, 11. 38 – 17. 616.

Comets, 4. 101.

Showers of blood, 11. 70 – 16. 560.

By lots, 7. 215.

By dreams, 1. 81 – 5. 191.

By oracles, 16. 54 – 16. 290, that of *Dodona*, and the manner of it, *&c.*

GYMNASTICKS

Dancing, 16. 217. The different kinds for men and women, 18. 687 – The circular, 18. 573 – mixed, 18. 690.

Dancing practised by warriors, 16. 746 — With swords, 18. 688.

Diving, 16. 905. 495.

Tumblers, 18. 698.

Mæeander, the river, 2. 1056.

Mæonia, under the mountains of *Tmolus*, 2. 1052.

Messe, a town of *Sparta*, abounding in doves, 2. 705.

Mycalessus, its plain famous for pine-trees, 2. 593.

Mycenæ, and its maritime towns, 2. 686.

Onchestus, the grove of *Neptune*, 2. 600.

Orchomenos, one of the principal cities for wealth in *Homer*'s time, 9. 498.

Parthenius, the river, and places adjacent, 2. 1038.

Pedasus, seated on the River *Satnio*, 6. 41.

Peneus, the river running thro' *Tempe*, and Mount *Pelion*, describ'd, 2. 918.

Phthia, its situation, 1. 204. Famous for horses, 203.

Phylace and *Pyrrhasus*, a beautiful country with groves and flow'ry meadows, describ'd, 2. 850.

Rhodes, its wealth, its plantation by *Tlepolemus*, and division into three dynasties, 2. 808, &c.

Samothracia, the view from its mountains, 13. 19.

Scamander, its two springs, 22. Its confluence with *Simoïs*, 5. 965.

Scyros, the island, 19. 353.

Sidon, famous for works of sculpture, 23. 866. and embroidery, 6. 360.

Sipylus, its mountains, rocks, and desarts, 24. 775.

Sperchius, a river of *Thessaly*, 23. 176.

Styx, the river describ'd, 2. 915.

Thebæ, in *Ægypt*, anciently the richest city in the world with a hundred gates, described, 9. 506.

Thessaly, its ancient division, and inhabitants, 2. 833.

Thisbe, famous for doves, 2. 601.

Thrace, its hills and promontories, 14. 260, &c.

Titaresius, the river, 2. 910.

Troy, its situation and remarkable places about it, 2. 982 – 11. 217.

Typhæus, the burning mountain, 2. 953.

Xanthus, the river of *Troy* describ'd, its banks and plants produc'd there, 21. 507, &c.

Xanthus, the river of *Lycia*, 2. v. *ult.*

Zelia, situate at the foot of mount *Ida*, 2. 998.

HISTORY

History preserv'd by Homer.] Of the heroes before the siege of *Troy*, *Centaurs*, &c. 1. 347. to 358. Of *Tlepolemus* planting a colony in *Rhodes*, 2. 808. Of the expulsion of the *Centaurs* from *Greece*, 2. 902. Of the wars of the *Phrygians* and *Amazons*, 3. 245. Of the war with *Thebes*, and embassy of *Tydeus*, 4. 430. Of *Bellerophon*, 6. 194. Of *Eruthalion* and *Lycurgus*, 7. 164. Of the *Curetes* and *Ætolians*, 9. 653. Of the wars of the *Pylians* and *Ætolians*, 11. 818. Of the race of *Troy*, 20. 255, &c. To this head may be referred the numerous Genealogies in our Author.

MUSICK

Musick practis'd by Princes, the use of the harp, in *Achilles*, 9. 247. in *Paris*, 3. 80.

The use of the pipe, 10. 15 – 18. 609.

Vocal musick accompanying the instruments, 1. 775.

Chorus's at intervals, 24. 902.

Musick used in the army, 10. 15.

– at funerals, 24. 900.

– in the vintage, 18. 661.

Trumpets in war, 18. 260.

MECHANICKS

Archery, Making a bow, and all its parts described, 4. 136, &c.

Chariot-making, A chariot described in all its parts, 5. 889, &c. 24. 335.

Poplar proper for wheels, 4. 554.

Sycamore fit for wheels, 21. 44.

Clockwork, 18. 441.

Enamelling, 18. 635.

Shipbuilding, 5. 80 – 15. 475.

Pine, a proper wood for the mast of a ship, 16. 592.

Smithery, iron-work, &c. The forge describ'd, 18. 435, 540. Bellows, 435, 482, 540. Hammer, tongs, anvil, 547.

Mixing of metals, *ibid.*

Spinning, 23. 890.

Weaving, 3. 580. 6. 580.

Embroidery, 6. 361.

Armory, and instruments of war.]

A compleat suit, that of *Paris*, 3. 410, &c. of *Agamemnon*, 11. 22 – &c.

Scale-armour, 15. 629.

Helmets, with four plumes, 5. 919 –

— without any crests, 10. 303 –

— lin'd with wool, and ornamented with boars teeth, of a particular make, 10. 311.

— lin'd with furr, 10. 397.

Bows, how made, 4. 137.

Battel-Ax, describ'd, 13. 766.

Belts, crossing each other, to hang the sword and the shield, 14. 468.

Corselets, ornamented with sculpture, 11. 33.

— how lin'd, 4. 165.

Mace, or club, 7. 170 – 15. 816.

Shields, so large as to cover from the neck to the ankles, 6. 145 – How made and cover'd, 7. 267. describ'd in every particular, 11. 43, &c.

Slings, 13. 899.

Spears, with brass points, 8. 617.

Ash fit to make them, 16. 143 – 19. 422.

How the wood was join'd to the point, 18. 618.

Swords, how ornamented, with ivory, gems, 19. 400.

ORATORY

See the Article Speeches *in the poetical index.*

POLICY

Kings.] Derive their honour from God, 2. 233 – 1. 315. Their names to be honour'd, 2. 313. One sole monarch, 2. 243. Hereditary right of kings represented by the sceptre of *Agamemnon* given by *Jove*, 2. 129. Kings not to be disobey'd on the one hand, nor to stretch too far their prerogative on the other, 1. 365, &c. Kings not absolute in council, 9. 133. Kings made so, only for their excelling others in virtue and valour, 12. 377. Vigilance continually necessary in princes, 2. 27 – 10. 102. Against monarchs delighting in war, 9. 82, &c. – 24. 55. The true valour, that which preserves, not destroys mankind, 6. 196. Kings may do wrong, and are oblig'd to reparation, 9. 144. Character of a great prince in war and peace, 3. 236.

Councils.] The danger of a subject's too bold advice, 1. 103. The advantage of wise counsels seconded by a wise prince, 9. 101. The use of advice, 9. 137. The singular blessing to a nation and prince, in a good and wise counsellor, 13. 918. The deliberations of the council to be free, the prince only to give a sanction to the best, 9. 133.

Laws.] deriv'd from God, and legislators his delegates, 1. 315. Committed to

Characters of Beauty.] *Alluring* beauty in the Goddess *Venus*, 14. 250. *Majestic* beauty in *Juno*, 14. 216. Beauty of a *woman* in *Helen*, 3. 205. Beauty of a *young man*, in *Paris*, 3. 26. *Euphorbus* 17. 53, *&c.* Beauty of a *fine infant*, in *Astyanax*, 6. 497.

Beauties of the parts of the body.] Largeness and majesty of the eyes, in *Juno's*. Blackness, in those of *Cryseïs.* Blue, in *Minerva's*, *&c.* Eye-brows, black, graceful, 1. 683. The beauty of the cheeks, and the fairness of hair, in the epithets of *Helen.* Whiteness of the arms in those of *Juno*. Fingers rather red than pale, in the epithet of *Rosie-finger'd* to *Aurora.* Whiteness of the feet in that of *Silver-footed* to *Thetis*, &c. Colour of the skin to be painted differently according to the condition of the personages, applied to the whiteness of the thigh of *Menelaus*, 4. 175.

Character of deformity, the opposites to beauty in the several parts, consider'd in the figure of *Thersites*, 2. 263, *&c.*

For pictures of particular things, see the article Images *in the* POETICAL INDEX.

History, landscape-painting, animals, &c. In the buckler of *Achilles*, 18. at large.

The design of a goblet in *sculpture*, 11. 775.

Sculpture of a corslet, 11. 33, *&c.* Of a bowl, 23. Horses carv'd on monuments, 17. 495.

Enameling, and *in-laying*, in the buckler of *Achilles*, 18. 635. 655, and breast-plate of *Agamemnon*, 11. 35.

Tapestry, or weaving histories, flowers, *&c.* 3. 171 – 6. 580 – 22. 569.

Embroidery of garments, 6. 360.

POETRY

See the entire INDEX.

THEOLOGY

A view of HOMER's THEOLOGY

JUPITER, or the SUPREME BEING

Superior to all powers of heaven, 7. 244. 8. 10, *&c.* Enjoying himself in the contemplation of his glory and power, 11. 107. Self-sufficient, and above all second causes, or inferior deities, 1. 647. The other deities resort to him as their sovereign appeal, 5. 1065 – 21. 590. His will his fate, 8. 10. His sole will the cause of all humane events, 1. 8. His will takes certain and instant effect, 1. 685. His will immutable and always just, 1. 730. All-seeing, 8. 65 – 2. 4 – Supreme above all, and sole sufficient, 11. 107. The sole governor and fate of all things, 2. 147 – 16. 845. Disposer of all the glories and success of men, 17. 198. Forseeing all things, 71. 228. The giver of victory, 7. 118. Disposer of all human affairs, 9. 32. His least regard, or thought restores mankind, 15. 274. or turns the fate of armies, 17. 675. Dispenser of all the good and evil that befalls mankind, 24. 663. His favour superiour to all human means, 9. 152. His counsels unsearchable, 1. 705. *Themis* or *Justice* is his messenger, 20. 5. God prospers those who worship him, 1. 290. Constantly punishes the wicked, tho' late, 4. 194. The avenger of injustice, 4. 202. Nothing so terrible as his wrath, 5. 227. His divine justice sometimes punishes whole nations by general calamities, 16. 468. Children punished for the sins of their parents, 11. 166 and 16. 393.

The inferiour DEITIES

Have different offices under God: Some preside over elements, 18. 46 – 23. 240.

Some over cities and countries, 4. 75.

Some over words, springs, &c. 20. 12.

They have subordinate power over one another. Inferiour Deities or Angels subject to pain, imprisonment, 5. 475. 1090. Threatened by *Jupiter* to be cast into *Tartarus*, 8. 15. Are supposed to converse in a language different from that of mortals, 2. 985 – Subsist not by material food, 5. 425. Compassionate mankind, 8. 42 – 24. 412. Able to assist mortals at any distance, 16. 633. Regard and take care of those who serve them, even to their remains after death, 24. 520. No resisting heavenly powers, 5. 495. The meanness and vileness of all earthly creatures in comparison of the divine natures, 5. 535.

Prayer recommended on all enterprizes, *throughout the poem.*

Prayers intercede at the throne of heaven, 9. 624.

Opinions of the ancients concerning *hell*, the place of punishment for the wicked after death, 8. 15 – 19. 271.

Opinions of the ancients concerning the state of separate *spirits*, 23. 89, &c. 120, &c.

Variant Readings in the Poetic Text

After the first edition (quarto and folio) of 1715–20, later editions of Pope's *Iliad* published during Pope's lifetime are the following:

1720a 6 vols., duodecimo. By Bowyer for Bernard Lintot.

1720b 6 vols., duodecimo. 'The Second Edition'. 1720–21, Vols. I–III; 1721, Vols. I–VI. Some of the six volumes printed by Bettenham.

1732 6 vols., duodecimo. 'The Third Edition'. Vol. III is dated 1731.

1736 6 vols., duodecimo. 'The Fourth Edition'. Woodfall for Lintot.

1743 6 vols., duodecimo. For Henry Lintot.

NOTE: I am indebted to the Twickenham text for recording a large number of these variant readings. Where I have not followed the readings of the 1743 edition, I have listed these readings here; the Twickenham text did not list all of the variant readings from the 1743 edition. The editors of the Twickenham text did not distinguish, in their apparatus, between the folio and quarto versions of 1715–20; references to the first edition in this list of variant readings refer to the folio, which was the more polished of the two first editions. While I have depended upon the Twickenham text for identifying most of the alternative readings, I have in each instance consulted the editions listed above in order to check the veracity of the variant readings recorded by the editors of the Twickenham text.

In general, when I have departed from the 1743 duodecimo edition, it has been in deference to the readings of the first-edition folio which, as discussed in the introduction, is the last edition that Pope carefully and systematically proofread.

The variants listed here refer to substantive alternative readings rather than to accidentals.

I have generally not listed as variant readings those readings that were corrected in the *errata* sheet included in the final volume of the first edition in 1720.

Book 1

1 Achilles' . . . Greece] The Wrath of *Peleus'* Son *1715–32*
The manuscript of the opening lines of Pope's translation read as follows:

>   wrath
> The stern Pelides Rage, O Goddess! sing,
> Of all the Grecian Woes the fatal Spring,
>   Heroes
> That strowd with Warriors dead the Phrygian Plain,
> Whose limbs unburyd on the hostile Shore
> Devouring Dogs and greedy Vultures tore.
>   (Add. MSS. 4807)

2 Of . . . heav'nly] Of all the *Grecian* Woes, O *1715–32*.

72 *Pyres*] Fires *1715*. Is Pope perhaps responding to Thomas Tickell's 'Fun'ral Piles' in his rival version? Pope's MS. reading is 'The fun'ral flames reflect a dreadful blase'.

102 truths, . . . Great,] Truths . . . Great *1715*.

117 man] Priest *1715*.

267 sees] saw *1715*.

268 sparkle] sparkled *1715*.

274 forsake] forsook *1715*.

296 *Atrides*] the Monarch *1715*.

331 Experienc'd] Th'experienc'd *1715*.

343 ye] you *1715*, *1732*.

360 me wise] we wise *1743* (an obvious misprint).

362 *Atrides*, seize not] *Atrides* seize not *1743*.

452–3]   Supported by the Chiefs on either Hand,
          In Silence past along the winding Strand. *1715*.

541 trickle] trickled *1715*.

557 feasts] Feasts *1743*.

607 off'ring] Victims *1715*.

608 flames] flame *1732, 1743.*

644 the] a *1715.*

667 fear?] fear; *1743.*

Book 2

50 numbers] Mountains *1715.*

110 by thousands] in Millions *1715.*

157 tens] ten *1736, 1743.*

490 hast] has *1720a–43.*

563 thousands] Millions *1715.*

587 *Peneleus*] *Peneleius 1743.*

646 *Carystos*] *Caristos 1743.*

947 sweep] swept *1715–32.*

1008 fates] Fate *1715–20b.*

Book 3

39–40]   In vain the Youths oppose, the Mastives bay,
            The Lordly Savage rends the panting Prey. *1715–36.*

251 martial] manly *1715.*

253 warriour-train] martial Train *1715.*

294 a] an *1715.*

340 draws] drew *1715.*

361 ev'ry] age to *1732.*

405 weighty] mighty *1732.*

412 with silver] and silver *1715.*

416 Sustained . . . glittered] Sustains . . . glitters *1715.*

476 borrow'd] *Groea*'s *1715*.

477 She seem'd an ancient] *Groea*, her Fav'rite *1715*.

Book 4

4 goblet] Goblets *1715*.

161 from its] from the *1715*.

297 warriours] Warrior's *1715*.

349 nor] or *1715*.

487 the] their *1715–32*.

579 Pond'rous he falls;] Down sinks the Chief: *1715*.

Book 5

40 bathe . . . shake] bath'st . . . shak'st *1716*.

110 diff'ring] diff'rent *1716–32*.

201 father] father's *1743* (most probably a misprint).

229 entreat] intreat *1743*.

278 Now haste, ascend my Seat, and from the Car *1716*.

279 fight] War *1716*.

291 hear the rein] bear the rein *1743* (probably a misprint).

314–15]   I loath in lazy Fights to press the Car,
            At distance wound, or wage a flying War; *1716*.

316 strong] strung *1716*.

390 match] match'd *1716*.

851 with] in *1716*.

930 they] to *1716*.

982 the] their *1716*.

1076 reveres] revere *1715*.

Book 6

10 And] That *1716*.

71 not sex] nor Sex *1732–43*.

97 aid's] Aid's *1716–43*. (I am speculating that 'aids'' was the intended meaning, although spelt as if it was the singular possessive.)

249 consum'd] oppress'd *1716*.

Book 7

67 like] of *1743*.

176 aught] ought *1716*.

189 he] I *1716*.

248 it] 'em *1716*.

305 their jav'lins] the Javelins *1716*.

336 And first] When thus *1716*.

376 man] Chief *1716*.

416 Order] Union *1716*.

Book 8

97 hosts] Host *1716*.

276 your] our *1716*.

277 Your] Our *1716*.

318 pass'd] pass *1716*.

384 All pale and] And ey'd him *1716*.

393 note This note is missing in the edition of *1743*.

395 bowstring] Tendon *1716–20b*.

398 a] the *1716*.

464 her] the *1716*.

519 dare to combate] dare combate *1743* (an obvious misprint).

523 King] Sire *1716*.

589 Those] These *1716*.

617 brass] Steel *1716*.

638 or] and *1716*.

646 our] the *1716*.

Book 9

232 take] took *1717*.

261 you] ye *1717*.

274 porket] Porker *1717*.

561 accent] Accents *1717*.

640 fierce, and] fierce and *1743*.

781 *Diomedè*] *Diomede* *1720a, 1743*.

Book 10

53 pray'r] Vows *1717*.

206 th'entrenchments] the entrenchments *1743*.

241 said he] he said *1717*.

Book 11

8 fleet] Fleets *1717.*

45 brims] brim *1743.*

64 rush] rush'd *1717–20b.*

216 death] Deaths *1717.*

270 Springs] Vaults *1717.*

333 sanguine] smoaking *1717.*

534 Falls . . . earth] Supinely falls *1717.*

588 host] Hosts *1717–32.*

589 loss not] loss, not *1720a, 1743.*

701 Marks] Drinks *1717* (corrected to Prints in *Errata*).

838 at] in *1717.*

Book 12

41 and] with *1717–32.*

69 bold] brave *1717, 1720b.*

103 glorious] glories *1717–20b.*

288 t' escape] to 'scape *1717, 1720a.*

303 his] their *1736, 1743.*

309 rampart] Ramparts *1717–32.*

497 hope] Hopes *1717.*

Book 13

109 my force] the Man *1718.*

117 meanwhile] mean while *1743.*

152 yours] your's *1743.*

249 forceful] boasted *1718–1720b.*

267 high-lifting] high-lifted *1718.*

268 drops of] dropping *1718.*

409 blazing] brazen *1736, 1743.*

451 infold] inclose *1718–36.*

454 close-compell'd] Heaps on Heaps *1718–36.*

485 valu'd coursers] crowded coursers *1743.*

497 dreadful] deathful *1718–20b.*

514 and] with *1718–20b.*

889–90 His Brave Associate had no following Band,
His Troops unpractis'd in the Fights of Stand:
1718–36.

891 For not the Spear the *Locrian* Squadrons wield, *1718–36.*

930 whose] thick *1718, 1720a.*

946 prepares] prepar'd *1718.*

985 inspires;] inspires: *1743.*

Book 14

135 past] fled *1718.*

156 warriour] Hero *1718.*

158 hero] Warrior *1718.*

162 unutterable] inutterable *1718.*

171 warriour] warring *1718–32.*

309 Titans . . . *Chronos*] Gods that round *Saturnus 1718–36.*

418 dew] drew *1743* (obvious misprint).

Book 15

44 drear] dear *1720a–43.*

48 rages] ranges *1720a–43.*

253 the] his *1718–32.*

310–11   They gain th'impervious Rock and safe retreat
(For *Fate* preserves them) from the Hunter's
Threat. *1718.*

420 vanish'd] vanish *1718.*

775 the] his *1718.*

Book 16

200 eye] Eyes *1718.*

226 those loves] her Love *1718.*

290 thy] their *1718.*

383 godlike] godly *1736, 1743.*

614 body,] Corpse, and *1718.*

673 view] view'd *1718.*

859 battlements] Battlement *1718.*

1010 Thy own] The fierce [*Errata 1720*]; The great *1718.*

Book 17

8 re–turns] returns *1720.*

34 Go,] To *1720.*

35 Or while] While yet *1720.*

343 thro'] from *1720.*

499 arching] arched *1732–43.*

745 an] a *1720.*

750 weary] weary'd *1720–20b.*

Book 18

205 show'ry] painted *1720.*

229 can] should *1720.*

242 shoulder] Shoulders *1720–32.*

353 purple Orient] rosie *Welkin 1720* (*Errata 1720* corrects *Welkin* with Orient)

364 worst] worse *1720.*

395 Sacred . . . hand] Slain by this Hand, sad Sacrifice! *1720.*

477 the labours] my Labours *1720.*

482 chests] Chest *1720–32.*

566 bathes . . . in] bends . . . to *1720.*

635 Behind, the rising earth in] The new-ear'd Earth in blacker *1720.*

636 And sable] Sable it *1720.*

Book 19

336 Once] Hast *1720–32.*

338 Once] Oft' *1720–32.*

Book 20

18 Pow'rs] Gods *1720.*

540 an] and *1720–32.*

550 the front] his Front *1720.*

Book 21

3 flying] scatt'ring (*Errata 1720*).

25 groan'd] groan *1720*.

44 from a sycamore] on a Fig-tree Top *1720*.

85 trembles] trembling *1720*.

258 deep] Deeps *1720*.

294 the] their *1720*.

403 gardens] Garden *1720*.

589 her blest] the blest *1720*.

660 dirt] Dust *1720*.

Book 22

34 double] doubled *1720–20b*.

56 the Gods no dearer than] th'Immortals hateful as *1720*.

394 the flaming] his flaming *1720*.

441 his] the *1720*.

487 melancholy shades] silent Shades of Hell *1720*.

534 grief] Griefs *1720*.

Book 23

18 bathe their arms, ... the sands] drop the Sands, ... their Arms *1720*.

80 he living] the Living *1720*.

146 redoubling] rebounding *1720*.

164 a] the *1736, 1743*.

170 *Patroclus*] The Body *1720*.

174 Those] The *1720*.

279 flame] flam'd *1720–36*.

371 his son] the Son *1720*.

827 winds] Wind *1736, 1743*.

934 hero, more] Hero, or *1720–32*.

939 host] Hosts *1720–32*.

Book 24

2 Seek . . . clear] Sought . . . clear'd *1720*.

49 a fun'ral] the fun'ral *1720*.

392 stretch'd] stretch *1720*.

397 his] the *1743*.

464 Appear] Appears *1720*.

482 a host] an Host *1720*.

494 their martial] the martial *1720–32*.

679 An only] One only *1720*.

853 or *Grecian*] nor *Grecian* *1720*.

Glossary

The following definitions are cued to the specific contexts in which the words that are here defined appear in Pope's *Iliad*. These definitions are not always the primary or most obvious meanings, even in Pope's time, but they are rather meant to elucidate the meaning of words when they are used in ways that may not be familiar to the modern reader. Examples of the listed definitions are recorded, by book and line number, in parentheses; these are not intended to be exhaustive.

SJ refers to Samuel Johnson's *Dictionary of the English Language* (London, 1755); OED to the *Oxford English Dictionary*, Second Edition (Oxford, 1989).

ABLUTION 'The act of cleansing, or washing clean.' SJ

ACCORD *v.* 'To assent or consent to. *Obs.*' OED

ADJURE 'To impose an oath upon another, prescribing the form in which he shall swear.' SJ

ADVENTURE *n.* 'An accident, a chance' (24:491) and 'a hazard' (24: 436). SJ

AEGIS The shield of Jove (Zeus).

ALARMS A call to arms.

AMAZE *n.* 'Astonishment; confusion, either of fear or wonder.' SJ

AMBIENT 'Surrounding; encompassing.' SJ

APPALL 'To depress; to discourage.' SJ

APPLY 'To have recourse to, as a solicitor or petitioner; with *to*' (9:234). SJ

APPROVE 'To prove; to show; to justify.' SJ

ARMIPOTENT 'Powerful in arms; mighty in war.' SJ

ARREARS 'That which remains behind unpaid, though due.' SJ

ART 'A science, a trade; cunning.' SJ

ARTFUL 'Cunning, skilful, dexterous.' SJ

ARTIST Artisan.

ASPERSE 'To bespatter with censure or calumny.' SJ

ASPIRE 'To rise higher' (1:608, 2:508). SJ

ATTAINT Taint.

ATTEND 'To await' SJ; 'to regard; to fix the mind upon' (13:922). SJ

ATTEST 'To bear witness of; to witness; to call to witness.' SJ

AWFUL 'That which strikes with awe; invested with dignity; that which fills with reverence.' SJ

BALDRICK An ornamented belt worn to support a sword.

BAND *v.* 'To unite together into one body or troop.' SJ

BEEVES 'Oxen.' SJ

BOARD 'Table.' SJ

BOREAS The north wind.

BOSSY Embossed, studded.

BRAKE *n.* 'A thicket of brambles, or of thorns.' SJ

BRAND 'To mark or stamp with infamy; stigmatize.' OED

BRAVE 'Courageous'; 'gallant; lofty; graceful.' SJ

BRINDLED 'Streaked; tabby.' SJ

BRUISE 'To crush; to beat into coarse powder' (11:982). SJ

BUCKLER Shield.

BUNCH 'A protuberance; a hump on the back.' OED

CAESTUS 'A contrivance consisting of thongs of bullhide, loaded with strips of iron and lead, and wound round the hands. Used by Roman boxers as a protection and to give greater weight to the blows.' OED

CANISTER Bread basket.

CARE *n.* 'The object of care, or caution, or of love.' SJ

CASQUE Helmet.

CATARACT Waterfall (12:27).

CAWL Caul, 'the omentum; the integument in which the guts are inclosed.' SJ

CENTINEL Sentinel.

CESTUS 'The girdle of Venus.' SJ

CHAMPAIN 'The field of military operations.' OED

CHANNEL BONE Neck or throat.

CHARGE *n.* 'Care; trust; custody; office.' SJ

CHARGER 'A large dish.' SJ

CHINE 'The part of the back in which the spine is found.' SJ

CINCTURE 'Something worn round the body' SJ. More specifically, a belt worn around the waist.

CIRCUS 'An open space or area for sports, with seats round for the spectators.' SJ

CISTERN 'A receptacle of water for domestick uses' (22:201). SJ

CLIFT Cliff.

CLOSE *adj.* 'Secret; private; hidden; not revealed' (1:677). SJ

COERULEAN 'Blue; sky coloured.' SJ

COFFER 'A box or chest, *esp.* a strong box in which money or valuables are kept.' OED

COMMUTUAL 'Reciprocal.' SJ

COMPACTED Joined tightly together.

COMPOSE 'To calm; to quiet' (7:81, 123, 440; 14:240). SJ

CONCLUSIVE 'Decisive.' SJ

CONDUCT *n.* 'The act of convoying or guarding'; 'behaviour' (23:379). SJ

CONE 'The conical top of a helmet.' OED

CONFESS 'To declare or acknowledge.' SJ

CONFEST 'Open; known; acknowledged; not concealed.' SJ

CONFIRM To make firm, strengthen, encourage (2:228, 16:299), as in the Latin *confirmo.*

CONFOUND To destroy.

CONGLOBE 'To gather into a round mass.' SJ

CONSISTORY 'Any solemn assembly' (10:232). SJ

CONSPIRE 'To agree together.' SJ; but used in the more common sense of 'to plot' in 6:408.

CORPS = CORSE = CORPSE

CORSLET 'A light armour for the forepart of the body.' SJ

COUCH *v.* 'To lie down on a place of repose.' SJ

COUNSEL *n.* 'Deliberation; scheme; purpose; design.' SJ

COURSER 'A swift horse; a war horse: a word not used in prose.' SJ

COVERT *n.* 'A shelter; a thicket or hiding place.' SJ

CUIRASS Breast-plate.

CUISH 'The armour that covers the thighs.' SJ

CYMARR 'A slight covering; a scarf.' SJ

DARDAN Trojan.

DASTARD *n.* and *adj.* Coward(ly).

DECENT 'Becoming, fit, suitable.' SJ

DEGEN'RATE *adj.* 'Fallen from the virtue and merit of his ancestors.' SJ

DENOUNCE 'To threaten by proclamation.' SJ

DEPEND 'To hang from'; 'to rely on' (18:323). SJ

DEPLORE To grieve over.

DEPRECATE 'To implore mercy of' (9:236). SJ

DEPUTE 'To send with a special commission; to empower one to transact instead of another.' SJ

DEVIOUS 'Out of the common track' (10:540). SJ

DEVOLVE 'To fall in succession into new hands.' SJ

DEVOTED Cursed, doomed to destruction.

DEXTER 'The right [which, for oracles, is auspicious; 13:1039, 24:393]; not the left.' SJ

DISCOV'RY 'Exploration, investigation, reconnoitring, reconaissance. *Obs.*' OED

DISDAIN *v. intrans.* 'To be moved with indignation, be indignant, take offence. *Obs.*' (18:317). OED

DISEMBOGUE 'To pour out at the mouth of a river; to vent' (17:311). SJ, who cites Skinner's derivation from the Old French *disem' oucher.*

DISHONEST 'Disgraceful; ignominious. These two senses are scarcely English, being borrowed from the Latin.' SJ; cf. *Windsor-Forest* 326, *Dunciad* (1743) 3:198.

DISTAIN To discolour or to dye.

DISTASTE *v. trans.* 'To excite the dislike or aversion of; to be distasteful to; to displease, offend.' OED

DISTEMPER *v. trans.* 'To disease; to disorder.' SJ

DISTRACT 'To pull different ways at once; to separate, divide; to fill the mind with contrary considerations; to make mad.' SJ

DOME House, home.

DOOM *n.* Judgement; *v.* to judge.

DOUBTFUL 'Uncertain; to be feared.' OED

DUCTILE 'Easy to be drawn out into length, or expanded.' SJ

EMBATTL'D Furnished with battlements; a battlement is 'an indented parapet [i.e. barrier] at the top of a wall.' OED

EMBODY'D United into a single body.

EMBRUE = IMBRUE 'To steep, to soak.' SJ

ENAMEL *v.* 'Variegate with colours.' SJ

ENCHASE Engrave.

ENGINE 'A military machine; any instrument.' SJ

ENGROSS *v. trans.* 'To gain or keep exclusive possession of.' OED

ENSANGUINE 'To smear with gore, suffuse with blood.' SJ

ENSIGN 'Badge or symbol of office or dignity.' SJ

ENVY 'Rivalry; competition; malice; malignity.' SJ

EUGH Yew tree.

EVENT Outcome.

EXPLORE To search for.

EXTANT 'Standing out to view.' SJ

FAINT 'To grow feeble; to sink into dejection' (12:323). SJ

FAN 'An instrument for winnowing grain. A basket of special form . . . used for separating the corn from the chaff by throwing it into the air. *Obs.*' OED

FANCY *n.* 'Imagination; the power by which the mind forms to itself images and representations of things, persons, or scenes of being.' SJ

FANE 'A temple; a place consecrated to religion. A poetical word.' SJ

FATAL 'Deadly' and 'proceeding by destiny, appointed by destiny.' SJ

FAULCHION Sword.

FETLOCK 'A tuft of hair as big as the hair of the mane that grows behind the pastern-joint of many horses: horses of a low size have scarce any such tuft' (13:55). SJ, quoting from *Farrier's Dictionary.*

FILE *n.* 'A line of soldiers ranged one behind another.' SJ

FLAGGY 'Weak; lax; limber; not stiff; not tense.' SJ

FLAGITIOUS 'Wicked; villainous; atrocious.' SJ

FLOUNCE 'To move with violence in the water or mire; to struggle or dash in the water.' SJ

FLOURET 'A small imperfect flower.' SJ

FOND 'Foolish; silly; indiscreet; imprudent; injudicious'; but also 'pleased in too great a degree; foolishly delighted' (1:156). SJ

FOOT 'Infantry.' SJ

FORBID *adj.* Forbidden, prohibited from (19:41).

FORE-RIGHT 'Directly forward, in or towards the front, straight ahead.' OED

FOSSE 'A ditch; a moat.' SJ

FULGID 'Shining; glittering; dazzling.' SJ

GANTLET Boxing glove. Cf. CAESTUS

GENIAL Festive.

GEN'ROUS 'Not of mean birth; noble of mind; liberal; strong; vigorous.' SJ

GENTLE 'Well born; well descended.' SJ

GLAD 'Wearing a gay appearance; fertile; bright, showy.' SJ

GLORIOUS 'Boastful; proud; haughty'; 'Noble, illustrious.' SJ

GLOW 'To burn with vehement heat' (11:986). SJ

GORGET 'The piece of armour that defends the throat.' SJ

GRATEFUL 'Pleasing; acceptable'; also 'having a due sense of benefits' (23:711). SJ

GREAVES Metal plates protecting the shin-bone.

GRIPE v. To grip. 'To hold with the fingers closed; to grasp.' SJ

GRIZLY Ghastly, horrific.

HANGER 'A short broad sword' (11:42).

HAST Haste.

HAUNCH 'The thigh; the hind hip.' SJ

HEADSTALL 'Part of the bridle [or halter] that covers the head.' SJ

HECATOMB A sacrifice of a hundred oxen, or any large and costly sacrifice.

HEIR v. 'To inherit.' SJ

HINDE or HIND A 'female of red deer' (16:915); a 'peasant' (18:628). SJ

HOLLOW adj. 'Noisy, like sound reverberated from a cavity'; 'having a void space within' (2:401).

HOMICIDE 'A murderer; a manslayer.' SJ

HONEST Honourable.

HONOUR 'Ornament; decoration'; 'Honours of the Head' (17:229) means 'hair'.

HUMOURS 'The different kind of moisture in man's body, reckoned by the old physicians to be phlegm, blood, choler, and melancholy, which, as they predominated, were supposed to determine the temper of mind; general turn or temper of mind.' SJ

HYMENAEAL 'Pertaining to marriage.' SJ

IGNIPOTENT 'Presiding over fire.' SJ

IMPEND 'To hang over.' SJ

IMPETUOUS 'Violent; fierce; vehement.' SJ

IMPLICIT 'Entangled; infolded; complicated.' SJ

IMPOTENT 'Without power of restraint'; 'weak, feeble' (20:556). SJ

INDULGENT 'Kind; gentle.' SJ

INFRANGIBLE 'Not to be broken.' SJ

INNOCENT adj. 'Pure from mischief; unhurtful; harmless in effects.' SJ

INNOXIOUS 'Free from mischievous effects'; 'pure from crimes.' SJ

INSULT *v. trans.* 'To treat with insolence or contempt. It is sometimes used with *over*' (13:558). SJ

INVEST 'To dress; to clothe; to adorn; to grace.' SJ

INVOLVE 'To inwrap, to cover with any thing circumfluent.' SJ

IRREMEABLE 'Admitting no return.' SJ

KIND *n.* 'Race; generical class.' SJ

LATENT 'Hidden; concealed; secret.' SJ

LAY *v.* 'To impose; enjoin' (11:740). SJ

LEAGUER'D Besieged.

LEAVE 'Grant of liberty; permission; allowance.' SJ

LEGAT = LEGATE 'A deputy; an ambassador.' SJ

LEV'RET 'A young hare.' SJ

LIBATION 'The act of pouring wine on the ground in honour of some god; the wine so poured.' SJ

LIGATURE Bandage.

LIST *v.* 'To enclose for combat.' SJ

LIST *n.* 'Inclosed ground in which tilts [military games at which the combatants run against each other with lances on horseback] are run and combats fought.' SJ

LIVID 'Discoloured, as with a blow; black and blue.' SJ

LOWER *v.* (rhymes with 'scour') 'To frown; to pout; to look sullen.' SJ

LOW'RING See LOWER

LUCID 'Shining; bright; glittering.' SJ

LUMBER 'Any thing useless or cumbersome.' SJ

LUSTRATION 'Purification by water.' SJ

MAGAZINE 'A storehouse, commonly an arsenal or armoury, or repository of provisions.' SJ

MAISTIFF (*maistives*, plural) 'A dog of the largest size; dogs kept to watch the house.' SJ

MANES (disyllabic) 'Ghost; shade.' SJ

MART 'A place of public traffick.' SJ

MATE *v. trans.* 'To be equal to' (13:414). SJ

MEAN *adj.* 'Wanting dignity; low-minded; base.' SJ

MISSILE *adj.* 'Thrown by the hand; striking at distance.' SJ

MISSIVE *adj.* 'Such as may be sent; used at distance.' SJ

MITRE Used by Pope (and Chapman before him) to translate the Homeric μίτρη, a belt or girdle.

MOLE Structure serving as a breakwater.

MOULDER 'To turn to dust; to crumble.' SJ

NARRATIVE *adj.* Garrulous or talkative.

NAVE 'The middle part of the wheel in which the axle moves.' SJ

NERVOUS 'Well strung; strong; vigorous.' SJ

NICE 'Accurate in judgement to minute exactness.' SJ

NOTUS The south wind.

OBLOQUY 'Censorious speech; blame; slander; reproach.' SJ

OBSCENE 'Immodest; offensive; inauspicious; ill-omened.' SJ

OBSEQUIES 'Funeral rites; funeral solemnities.' SJ

OBTEST 'To beseech, to supplicate.' SJ

OFFICIOUS 'Kind; doing good offices; importunely forward.' SJ

ORIENT *adj.* 'Rising as the sun; eastern.' SJ

ORTHIAN See Pope's note on 11:14.

PAEAN 'A song of triumph.' SJ

PALISADE 'Pales [a pale is a 'narow piece of wood joined above and below to a rail, to inclose grounds'] set by way of inclosure or defence.' SJ

PALL 'A cloak or mantle of state; the covering thrown over the dead.' SJ

PAP Nipple.

PENSIVE 'Sorrowfully thoughtful; sorrowful; melancholy.' SJ

PERIOD 'The end or conclusion' (4:206; 11:955); also 'a stated number of years; a round of time' (11:95, 12:9). SJ

PHALANX 'A troop of men closely embodied.' SJ

PINNACE 'A boat belonging to a ship of war. It seems formerly to have signified rather a small sloop [a small vessel furnished with a mast] or bark attending a larger ship.' SJ

PLIGHT *v.* To pledge, promise.

PLY *v.* 'To go in haste' (10:623); 'to solicit importunately' (11:82); 'to employ with diligence; to keep busy; to set on work; to practise diligently.' SJ

POMP 'A procession of splendour and ostentation'; 'splendour' (23:159). SJ

POMPOUS 'Splendid; magnificent; grand.' SJ

PORKET Pig.

PREFER v. To put forward.

PRESS n. 'Crowd, tumult, throng' SJ; 'a throng or crush in battle; the thick of the fight.' OED

PREVENT 'To hinder; to obviate; to obstruct'; 'to go before.' SJ

PROFFER n. Offer, proposal.

PROFOUND n. 'The deep; the main; the sea.' SJ

PROMISCUOUS 'Mingled; confused; undistinguished.' SJ

PRORE Prow of a ship.

PROTEND 'To hold out; to stretch forth.' SJ

PROVE 'To experience; make trial.' SJ

QUOIT Discus. 'The discus of the ancients is sometimes called in English quoit, but improperly; the game of quoits is a game of skill; the discus was only a trial of strength, as among us to throw the hammer.' SJ

RAMPIRES 'Ramparts.' SJ

RANGE v. trans. 'To place in order; to put in ranks.' SJ

RANK v. To arrange or draw up soldiers into rank.

REBATE v. 'To blunt; to beat to obtuseness; to deprive of keenness' (11:304). SJ

RECREANT 'Cowardly.' SJ

RED STAR Mars.

REFECTION 'Refreshment after hunger or fatigue.' SJ

REFLUENT adj. 'Running back; flowing back.' SJ

REFULGENT Shining.

REIGN n. 'Kingdom; dominions.' SJ

REMAIN v. trans. 'To await.' SJ

REMEMBRANCE 'Reminder.' SJ

REMISSIVE adj. 'Producing or allowing decrease of something.' SJ

REMIT v. trans. Forgive (9:744).

REMOVE v. Depart.

REPAIR v. 'To go to; to betake himself.' SJ

RESOLVE v. 'To melt; to be dissolved' (7:113); also 'to decree within oneself' (13:534). SJ

RESTIVE adj. 'Unwilling to stir; resolute against going forward; obstinate; stubborn.' SJ

RESULT v. intrans. 'To rebound; to spring up' OED; 'to fly back.' SJ

RESUME v. To take back to oneself something previously given or granted.

RETORTED adj. 'Thrown or cast back; returned.' OED

SACRED 'Inviolable' (cf. 19:42; 22:489); 'holy'; 'consecrated.' SJ

SALUBRIOUS 'Wholesome; healthful; promoting health.' SJ

SANCTION 'Binding force given to an oath; something which makes an oath or engagement binding; a solemn oath.' OED

SANGUINE Bloody.

SCIENCE 'Knowledge.' SJ

SCUD v. 'To run away with precipitation' (11:597). SJ

SEPULTURE n. Burial.

SERENE n. 'A calm damp evening.' SJ

SERENE v. 'To calm; to quiet; to brighten' (15:178).

SHELVING adj. 'Sloping; inclining; having declivity.' SJ

SHOCKING Assailing with a sudden and fierce attack; charging (with troops).

SIMPLE 'A single ingredient in a medicine; a drug.' SJ

SINISTER 'Left; not right; not dexter; inauspicious.' SJ

SLIDDER 'To slide with interruption.' SJ

SLOATH = SLOTH

SLOPE adj. 'Oblique; not perpendicular' (13:512). SJ

SMOAK 'To move with such swiftness as to kindle; to move very fast so as to raise dust like smoke.' SJ

SNUFF v. 'To scent.'

SOCIAL 'Easy to mix in friendly gaiety; companionable' (11:911). SJ

SOW'R = SOUR adj. 'Harsh of temper; severe.' SJ

SOWSE = SOUSE 'To fall as a bird on its prey.' SJ

SPOIL Booty. Can also mean 'the cast or stripped-off skin of any animal'. OED

STAND v. trans. 'To endure; to resist without flying or yielding.' SJ

STILL adv. 'Ever, always.' SJ

STOOP Swoop down (24:393).

STRICT 'Close; tight.' SJ

STRING v. trans. 'To make tense.' SJ

STROW 'To spread by being scattered; to besprinkle; to scatter.' SJ

STUDIOUS Zealous (19:49); 'intent on a purpose.' OED

STYGIAN 'Hellish; infernal; pertaining to Styx, one of the poetical rivers of hell.' SJ

STYLE (or STILE) v. 'To name.' SJ

STYPTICK 'Having the power to staunch [i.e. stop the flow of] blood; astringent.' SJ

SUBMISS adj. Submissive.

SUBTARTAREAN 'Being or living under Tartarus [the infernal region].' OED

SUCCEED 'To follow' SJ; also to confer success upon, to further.

SUE 'To petition.' SJ

SUPPLE *v. trans.* 'To make pliant; to make soft; to make flexible' (10:676). SJ

SUSTAIN 'To bear without yielding; to suffer; to bear as afflicted.' SJ

SWARTH = SWATH 'A line of grass cut down by the mower.' SJ

SWAY *n.* 'Power; rule; dominion; anything moving with bulk and power.' SJ

SWOLN = SWOLLEN.

SYLVAN 'One who (or something that) inhabits the woods.' OED

SYNOD 'An assembly called for consultation'; 'a conjunction of the heavenly bodies.' SJ

TALENT 'So much weight, or a sum of money, the value differing according to the different ages and countries.' SJ, citing Arbuthnot.

TAMARISK See Pope's note on 10:677.

TAPER *adj.* 'Regularly narrowed from the bottom to the top; pyramidical; conical' (10:350). SJ

TARGE 'A kind of buckler or shield borne on the left arm.' SJ

TERRIFIC 'Dreadful; causing terror.' SJ

THRILLING Piercing.

TRACE 'Harness for beasts of draught' SJ; rope connecting collar of a horse to the reins.

TRAIN *n.* 'A retinue; a number of followers or attendants.' SJ

TRIPLE DOG Cerberus, the three-headed dog guarding the entrance to Hades.

TROPHY 'Something taken from an enemy, and shewn or treasured up in proof of victory.' OED

TRUSS *v.* 'Of a bird of prey: to seize or clutch (the prey) in its talons.' OED

UNCONSCIOUS 'Having no mental perception' SJ; unknowing.

UNGRATEFUL 'Unpleasing; unacceptable' (8:253, 681). SJ

UNNERV'D 'Weak, feeble.' SJ

UNREPROV'D *adj.* 'Not censured; not liable to censure.' SJ

URGE *v.* 'To labour vehemently'; 'to incite; to push' (2:185).

VAGRANT *adj.* 'Wandering; unsettled.' SJ
VAN = VANGUARD The front of an army.
VARIOUS 'Variegated; diversified' SJ; of many colours (2:956).
VERGE Margin or border.
VEST *n.* 'A robe or gown.' OED
VIZOR Part of a helmet that covers the face.
VOLUME 'Something rolled or convolved [rolled together].' SJ
VULGAR Ordinary, common.

WAIN 'A carriage' SJ; in the *Iliad*, 'a chariot'.
WAIT *v. trans.* To escort or attend (17:34).
WARD *v. trans.* To parry or fend off (now always used with 'off').
WINDE = WIND *v.* 'To nose; to follow by scent' (10:427). SJ
WITHOUT *adv.* 'Not on the inside.' SJ

YARDS 'The supports of the sails.' SJ

ZONE 'A girdle' SJ; but also 'area', as in play on this word at 16:167.